PEARSON

ALWAYS LEARNING

Caitlin Newcomer • Scott Ortolano

Perspectives on the Short Story

Fifth Edition
Revised by Shonda Stevens

D1509696

Pearson Learning Solutions, 330 Hudson Street, New York, New York 10013
A Pearson Education Company
www.pearsoned.com

Printed in the United States of America

000200010272010958

RD

ISBN 10: 1-323-29470-8
ISBN 13: 978-1-323-29470-3

For Christopher, always
C.N.

For Michelle, who has always believed
S.O.

Acknowledgments

The editors would like to thank everyone who contributed to the creation of this anthology. First and foremost, Dr. Robin Goodman, whose generosity, unfailing support, and invaluable guidance made this work possible and to whom the editors are inexpressibly grateful. Thanks are also due to the English Department faculty at Florida State University for their advice and support, especially Dr. Ralph Berry, Dr. Barry Faulk, Dr. Elizabeth Spiller, Dr. Alisha Gaines, Dr. John Mac Kilgore, Dr. James O'Rourke, Dr. Lisa Wakimaya, Dr. Christina Parker, and Dr. Daniel Vitkus. Without the hard work of the English Department's office staff, especially Carolyn Moore, Jamekia Anderson, Lauryn Peterson, and Stephanie Prinz, this anthology may never have made it into print. The graduate students in the English Department deserve our thanks as well for the constant advice and encouragement they have provided throughout the development of this project, especially Paul Ardoin, Michael Barach, Thomas Bevilacqua, Eric Matthew Bledsoe, Robert Bowman, Katie Cortese, Jaclyn Dwyer, Brandi George, Micah Dean Hicks, Christopher Higgs, Laci Mattison, Fiona McWilliam, Kendall Parris, Amber Pearson, Rebecca Furlow Skinner, Kimberly Anderson, Jonathon Bellot, Matthew Dauphin, Heather Kelleher, Elizabeth Liebman, Natalie Perfetti-Oates, Patrick Osborne, Alexandra Oxner, Lindsay Sproul, Raymond Stricklin, Michael Wang, Emily Faison, Chris Jensen, Jessica Pitts, Kelsey Satalino, Esther Spencer, Sarah Stewart, David Thacker, and Cocoa Williams. We are also indebted to our friends at Pearson for their unflagging work on this anthology, especially Mary Jo Southern, Christina Ewen, Virginia Greer, Erin Chomat, Theresa Festa, and Kevin Clarke. Last but certainly not least, we would like to thank Mona, who has served as a constant source of energy and inspiration.

Table of Contents

Readings in black font appear only in the print book.
Readings in blue font appear only in the eBook.

Moving Fields and Shifting Focus: Perspectives on the Short Story

In 1842, Edgar Allen Poe famously defined the short story as a narrative that could be read in one sitting. He maintained that the short story offers "the fairest field for the exercise of the loftiest talent" because readers are not distracted by "external or extrinsic" influences produced by "weariness or interruption." For Poe, the form provides a balanced venue in which poetry's intensity of affect is blended with the novel's narrative complexity. Since then, the short story has undergone innumerable transformations, but Poe's defining characteristic of the short story—its ability to convey experiential truths to the reader without interruption—remains a constitutive feature of the form. This anthology is designed to explore the myriad paths the short story has taken as it has branched out from its crystallization in the nineteenth century. The anthology also reveals that the roots of the short story have historical depth, extending alongside folklore, oral literatures, and the very origins of the novel.

To promote an understanding of the vast range of the short story, this anthology incorporates a diversity of national and transnational genres that recognize the short story's rich history and contemporary scope. Like the short story itself, this anthology roams beyond formal binaries like "conventional" or "experimental," over the borders of geography, nation, ethnicity, race, class, region, and gender, and across lines of urban, suburban, and rural life as well as political and social affiliations. However, the stories that make up this great plurality do not exist in a vacuum but emerge from specific historical and social contexts and operate within and beyond enduring aesthetic traditions. While the short story can "express identities" or open up experiences defined through difference, it also has the ability to produce new ways of thinking about and conceptualizing human experience.

The short story can not only be said to define categories and exemplify genres but also to transgress them. This tension should be understood as an opportunity to create conversations that bridge superficial divides. This anthology pays careful attention to the ways in which individual stories and authors mix, match, and surpass multiple traditions and affiliations. For example, "The Last One," even as Robert Coover is an author usually identified with postmodernism, his story in this collection could be read as fitting within a tradition of fairy tales and folklore since his story refigures Charles Perrault's seventeenth century tale "Blue Beard." This prompts a dual reconceptualization of Coover as an author, on the one hand, as well as, on the other, of the genre of fairy tales and folklore, which are traditionally understood as oral and authorless literature. Similarly, the anthology allows for a critical reconsideration of canonical authors by placing them alongside underexplored writers. For example, within our inclusions of feminist literature, canonical feminist authors like Charlotte Perkins Gilman and Margaret Atwood appear alongside the rediscovered early twentieth century writer Edna

Ferber. Where possible, we have also used non-canonical stories by canonical authors in order to promote a fuller understanding of sometimes oversimplified figures. *Perspectives on the Short Story* recognizes that the short story is best conceived as a fluid mix of themes, encounters, viewpoints, and mediations—a plurality that enables the short story to provide illuminating perspectives on a dynamic world.

This anthology includes stories from a range of nations and historical periods. United States literature is progressively being seen through an increasing self-awareness that the United States is not an "America" so much as overlapping, reinforcing, and often contradictory "Americas." We hope that our exploration of United States literature continues this movement towards ever-more inclusive visions of multiplicitous American identities. Stories here representing the African-American literary tradition span over a hundred years, from Charles Chestnutt's post-bellum South, to Zora Neale Hurston's Harlem Renaissance, concluding with Toni Morrison's explorations of African-American identity in the post-Civil Rights era. Readers are also introduced to other African-American writers located throughout this anthology, such as the Naturalist writing of Richard Wright, the other-worldly visions of Octavia E. Butler's science fiction, and the postmodern comedy of Percival Everett. Given that the United States is a site of convergence for multiple cultures and peoples, we also include narratives from Chicano/Chicana, Native American, and Asian-American writers, from Sherman Alexie's heavenly fistfight to Sandra Cisneros' gender-inflected border crossing, to Gish Jen's world of pancakes and country clubs. The United States is a place in which region and community play significant roles in identity formation; we incorporate, for example, selections of Southern literature, focusing on the peculiar identity politics and narrative tropes of the American South, while also presenting examples of the literature of suburbia which explore a diffuse and spatially open "region" that became paradigmatic for middle class America in the post-World War II era. As the contemporary United States is a product of its history, we devote considerable attention, as well, to pre-1900 United States literature, a period when the nation and the short story genre were officially both just starting to define themselves.

Our section of world literature provides a survey of diverse authors that emphasize both European and non-Western sources, metropolitan and peripheral, noting literature's investments both in global processes and local belonging. We offer short stories from English, Scottish, and Irish writers of both the nineteenth and twentieth centuries, recognizing that the British Isles encompass a diversity of places and peoples. Works range from Irish writer Frank O'Connor's recollections of his first confession, to Graham Greene's critique of English morality in crisis, to the Scottish Robert Louis Stevenson's eerie nineteenth century grave-robbing tale. Chronologically, we begin considering the long trajectory of continental Europe's literary tradition with a tale by a seventeenth century Spanish writer, Miguel de Cervantes, the individual who many identify as the originator of "modern" literature. Our samplings from Europe bring together an array of writers who each investigate their worldly experiences through a cultural lens that undermines singular conceptions of "a" European literature.

Similarly, the selections of Caribbean literature provide a purview of stories and authors who defy simplistic narratives of subjectivity and national affiliation, like Edwidge Danticat's "Children of the Sea." Danticat combines a character's geographic mobility with narrative innovation. Our Latin American selections include authors who employ magical realist and other innovative techniques. In our selections of Middle Eastern, African, and South Asian literatures, we recognize both postcolonial narratives and stories derived from local tradition. For example, readers see R.K. Narayan's depiction of the struggle to deal with an economy increasingly enthralled to the ethics of corporate efficiency and Chinua Achebe's negotiation of the clash between Westernized cultural ideals and traditional cultural beliefs. Uneasy in their relationships to the status quo, these literary treatments are cosmopolitan and contain ideologies that speak to very different social-cultural realities often at odds with each other. Israeli Amos Oz's story tells of an intensely devout Jewish father and his disappointing son, for example, while Ghassan Kanafani's story relates a heart-wrenching experience of stateless Palestinian refugees. These stories approach life from divergent perspectives, but are linked by their conviction that the politically and religiously charged nature of life in the Middle East is ultimately unsustainable. We hope these selections will provide readers with an introductory knowledge of the short story's aesthetic, historical, and philosophical complexity as a global genre.

This anthology also emphasizes transnational genres and links thematic approaches, like comedy and detective fiction, with groupings premised on aesthetics and form, such as Realism and Modernism. We are committed to exploring the diversity of the short story from its earliest form to its twenty-first century manifestations. With comedy, for example, we begin with the work of Mark Twain, the father of American humor, and move through various iterations of the genre, including black humor in the work of Donald Barthelme and the dystopian satire of George Saunders. Similarly, for mystery and detective fiction, we have chosen a foundational text: Edgar Allen Poe's nineteenth century "The Murders in the Rue Morgue," which inaugurated the genre in the United States. We also trace the development of the genre from the 1920s hardboiled detective fiction of Dashiell Hammett to the psychological thrillers of Patricia Highsmith. Like mystery and detective fiction, fairy tales and folklore, at their core, are concerned with humanity's curiosity and its sometimes unsettling results. As such, while we include traditional stories, we also highlight twentieth and twenty-first century revisions of older tales. Similarly, graphic literature reconceptualizes what constitutes a work of literature by pushing the boundaries of the written page and emphasizing visuality as a means of conveying narrative. We offer a microcosm of how genres of the short story continue to find new fields of growth.

Additionally, the short story is a form that lends itself to imagining new directions for culture and society. Through environmental literature, we can consider humanity's varying relationships with and perspectives on the "natural" world. Stories move from Sarah Orne Jewett's traditionalist vision of "nature" as a removed sanctuary that must be protected from human exploitation to Terry Bisson's speciest undermining of the very notion of a division between humans and an "othered" nature. While environmental literature focuses on humanity's place in the natural world, science fiction explores the connections and negotiations of humanity and science. For example, H.G. Wells, who is commonly credited with originating the genre at the turn of the 20th century story, considers the possible repercussions of moving freely through time. This critical consideration of the paradoxical potentiality of scientific innovation is a defining aspect of the field, as is a focus on other worlds and alternate futures. Otherworldly imaginings also define the genre of Gothic literature. However, unlike science fiction, this genre depends on the macabre and the supernatural, often featuring the uncanny, ghostly tropes characteristic of the genre. We include stories written while the genre was still emerging and later works that appeared when the development of the genre had reached its apex. Importantly, works by writers from Germany, the United States, France, and Britain emphasize the genre's range as well as the short story's inexhaustible ability to rethink our place in past, current, and potential worlds.

The short story also provides means of negotiating the continually changing realities of our world, allowing us to make sense of the various social and cultural spaces we inhabit. Our selections of feminist literature provide a transhistorical narrative of feminism as a multi-generational, cross-regional, and multifaceted struggle by women to draw attention to political, social, cultural, and economic inequalities. Stories range from Charlotte Perkins Gilman's narrative of late nineteenth century women's confinement, to Dorothy Parker's discussion of women's objectification in an exploitative consumer culture, to Margaret Atwood's examination of the inequalities still present in contemporary heterosexual relationships. Our selections of Jewish literature consider the struggles and triumphs of the Jewish people both before and after the Holocaust and also consider the anxiety surrounding issues of identity in the Jewish-American community during the latter half of the twentieth century. Additionally, individuals have defined themselves through (and been defined by) the types of work they perform. Thus, our selections of working class literature deal with the quotidian realities of working class people, a subject that has occupied a central place in the industrial and postindustrial world. These stories do not simply focus on traditional workplaces like the factory or office, but also on often invisible workers like the housewife. Taken together, these stories provide varying narratives that both challenge and help to create or reinforce collective identities.

The changes that the short story has undergone over the centuries are tied to both material cultural changes and larger shifts in aesthetics. The emergence of Realism in the nineteenth century split literature away from its romantic and sentimental foundations as it moved towards a more "realistic" depiction of life and the individual's struggle in an often indifferent world. This shift was occasioned by the rising force of industrialization, the compelling "truth effects" of the empirical sciences, and the changes these new realities brought to bear on individual lives across social classes and geographic spaces. Naturalism further modified this form by viewing literature and life through the theories of Charles Darwin, Herbert Spencer, and other scientific and social theorists. In stories influenced by these trends, for example, Anton Chekhov's Realist "The Lady with the Dog," Jack London's Naturalist "In a Far Country," and Richard Wright's Social Realist "Down by the Riverside" the Realist objective of capturing an accurate picture of a uniform reality became increasingly untenable in a world fragmenting under the pressures of new scientific discoveries, shifts in formerly stable social identities, cultural cataclysms (best embodied by World War I), urbanization, psychoanalytic discoveries of an irrational core lurking beneath our consciousness, and drastic reconceptions of art's role in society. Given this hopelessly tangled landscape, modernist fiction is marked by paradox and ambiguity as it simultaneously reconsiders, rejects, and longs for older and more stable models of knowing and being. We emphasize canonical voices within the movement, such as Virginia Woolf and James Joyce, as well as figures who tend to be marginalized within modernism proper, for example, Jean Toomer, who has traditionally been left out of discussions of modernism. Postmodernist fiction arose as both a response to the increasingly stagnant nature of modernism and also as a continuation of modernism's innovative textual strategies. Postmodernism questions traditional narrative, form, and notions of coherent subjectivity in a fully commodified world governed by the sometimes liberating, sometimes oppressive and often absurd (il)logics of late capitalist society. We present a broad range of postmodern stories in an attempt to represent the uncountable forms and politics of the genre, from the radical post-punk politics of Kathy Acker to Kim Addonizio's playful life-history of condoms. These sections reveal the integral connections between aesthetics, content, and socio-historical context.

This is a field in a constant state of flux, and we encourage you to read across boundaries and time-lines, through genres and aesthetic practices, against established conventions, open to differences in identities, politics, and ideological convictions. Like the authors and stories they tell, we, as readers, simultaneously occupy multiple spaces and places. This anthology argues that such diversity is a site of endless possibilities from which we all can draw.

The Sacrificial Egg
(1959)

CHINUA ACHEBE

Julius Obi sat gazing at his typewriter. The fat Chief Clerk, his boss, was snoring at his table. Outside, the gatekeeper in his green uniform was sleeping at his post. You couldn't blame him; no customer had passed through the gate for nearly a week. There was an empty basket on the giant weighing machine. A few palm-kernels lay desolately in the dust around the machine. Only the flies remained in strength.

Julius went to the window that overlooked the great market on the bank of the River Niger. This market, though still called Nkwo, had long spilled over into Eke, Oye, and Af<u>o</u> with the coming of civilization and the growth of the town into the big palm-oil port. In spite of this encroachment, however, it was still busiest on its original Nkwo day, because the deity who had presided over it from antiquity still cast her spell only on her own day—let men in their greed spill over themselves. It was said that she appeared in the form of an old woman in the centre of the market just before cock-crow and waved her magic fan in the four directions of the earth—in front of her, behind her, to the right and to the left—to draw to the market men and women from distant places. And they came bringing the produce of their lands—palm-oil and kernels, cola nuts, cassava, mats, baskets and earthenware pots; and took home many-coloured cloths, smoked fish, iron pots and plates. These were the forest peoples. The other half of the world who lived by the great rivers came down also—by canoe, bringing yams and fish. Sometimes it was a big canoe with a dozen or more people in it; sometimes it was a lone fisherman and his wife in a small vessel from the swiftflowing Anambara. They moored their canoe on the bank and sold their fish, after much haggling. The woman then walked up the steep banks of the river to the heart of the market to buy salt and oil and, if the sales had been very good, even a length of cloth. And for her children at home she bought bean cakes and mai-mai which the Igara women cooked. As evening approached, they took up their paddles again and paddled away, the water shimmering in the sunset and their canoe becoming smaller and smaller in the distance until it was just a dark crescent on the water's face and two dark bodies swaying forwards and backwards in it. Umuru then was the meeting place of the forest people who were called Igbo and the alien river folk whom the Igbo called Olu and beyond whom the world stretched in indefiniteness.

Julius Obi was not a native of Umuru. He had come like countless others from some bush village inland. Having passed his Standard Six in a mission school he had come to Umuru to work as a clerk in the offices of the all-powerful European trading company which bought palm-kernels at its own price and cloth and metalware, also at its own price.

1

The offices were situated beside the famous market so that in his first two or three weeks Julius had to learn to work within its huge enveloping hum. Sometimes when the Chief Clerk was away he walked to the window and looked down on the vast anthill activity. Most of these people were not here yesterday, he thought, and yet the market had been just as full. There must be many, many people in the world to be able to fill the market day after day like this. Of course they say not all who came to the great market were real people. Janet's mother, Ma, had said so.

"Some of the beautiful young women you see squeezing through the crowds are not people like you or me but mammy-wota who have their town in the depths of the river," she said. "You can always tell them, because they are beautiful with a beauty that is too perfect and too cold. You catch a glimpse of her with the tail of your eye, then you blink and look properly, but she has already vanished in the crowd."

Julius thought about these things as he now stood at the window looking down on the silent, empty market. Who would have believed that the great boisterous market could ever be quenched like this? But such was the strength of Kitikpa, the incarnate power of smallpox. Only he could drive away all those people and leave the market to the flies.

When Umuru was a little village, there was an agegrade who swept its market-square every Nkwo day. But progress had turned it into a busy, sprawling, crowded and dirty river port, a no-man's-land where strangers outnumbered by far the sons of the soil, who could do nothing about it except shake their heads at this gross perversion of their prayer. For indeed they had prayed—who will blame them—for their town to grow and prosper. And it had grown. But there is good growth and there is bad growth. The belly does not bulge out only with food and drink; it might be the abominable disease which would end by sending its sufferer out of the house even before he was fully dead.

The strangers who came to Umuru came for trade and money, not in search of duties to perform, for they had those in plenty back home in their village which was real home.

And as if this did not suffice, the young sons and daughters of Umuru soil, encouraged by schools and churches were behaving no better than the strangers. They neglected all their old tasks and kept only the revelries.

Such was the state of the town when Kitikpa came to see it and to demand the sacrifice the inhabitants owed the gods of the soil. He came in confident knowledge of the terror he held over the people. He was an evil deity, and boasted it. Lest he be offended those he killed were not killed but decorated, and no one dared weep for them. He put an end to the coming and going between neighbours and between villages. They said, "Kitikpa is in that village," and immediately it was cut off by its neighbours.

Julius was sad and worried because it was almost a week since he had seen Janet, the girl he was going to marry. Ma had explained to him very gently that he should no longer go to see them "until this thing is over, by the power of Jehovah." (Ma was a very devout Christian convert and one reason why she approved of Julius for her only daughter was that he sang in the choir of the CMS church.)

"You must keep to your rooms," she had said in hushed tones, for Kitikpa strictly forbade any noise or boisterousness. "You never know whom you might meet on the streets. That family has got it." She lowered her voice even more and pointed surreptitiously at the house across the road whose doorway was barred with a yellow palm-frond. "He has decorated one of them already and the rest were moved away today in a big government lorry."

2

Janet walked a short way with Julius and stopped; so he stopped too. They seemed to have nothing to say to each other yet they lingered on. Then she said goodnight. and he said goodnight. And they shook hands, which was very odd, as though parting for the night were something new and grave.

He did not go straight home, because he wanted desperately to cling, even alone, to this strange parting. Being educated he was not afraid of whom he might meet, so he went to the bank of the river and just walked up and down it. He must have been there a long time because he was still there when the wooden gong of the night-mask sounded. He immediately set out for home, half-walking and half-running, for night-masks were not a matter of superstition; they were real. They chose the night for their revelry because like the bat's their ugliness was great.

In his hurry he stepped on something that broke with a slight liquid explosion. He stopped and peeped down at the footpath. The moon was not up yet but there was a faint light in the sky which showed that it would not be long delayed. In this half-light he saw that he had stepped on an egg offered in sacrifice. Someone oppressed by misfortune had brought the offering to the crossroads in the dusk. And he had stepped on it. There were the usual young palmfronds around it. But Julius saw it differently as a house where the terrible artist was at work. He wiped the sole of his foot on the sandy path and hurried away, carrying another vague worry in his mind. But hurrying was no use now; the fleet-footed mask was already abroad. Perhaps it was impelled to hurry by the threatening imminence of the moon. Its voice rose high and clear in the still night air like a flaming sword. It was yet a long way away, but Julius knew that distances vanished before it. So he made straight for the cocoyam farm beside the road and threw himself on his belly, in the shelter of the broad leaves. He had hardly done this when he heard the rattling staff of the spirit and a thundering stream of esoteric speech. He shook all over. The sounds came bearing down on him, almost pressing his face into the moist earth. And now he could hear the footsteps. It was as if twenty evil men were running together. Panic sweat broke all over him and he was nearly impelled to get up and run. Fortunately he kept a firm hold on himself . . . In no time at all the commotion in the air and on the earth—the thunder and torrential rain, the earthquake and flood—passed and disappeared in the distance on the other side of the road.

The next morning at the office, the Chief Clerk, a son of the soil spoke bitterly about last night's provocation of Kitikpa by the headstrong youngsters who had launched the noisy fleet-footed mask in defiance of their elders, who knew that Kitikpa would be enraged, and then . . .

The trouble was that the disobedient youths had never yet experienced the power of Kitikpa themselves; they had only heard of it. But soon they would learn.

As Julius stood at the window looking out on the emptied market he lived through the terror of that night again. It was barely a week ago but already it seemed like another life, separated from the present by a vast emptiness. This emptiness deepened with every passing day. On this side of it stood Julius, and on the other Ma and Janet whom the dread artist decorated.

Florida
(1978)

KATHY ACKER

Maybe you're dying and you don't care anymore.

In the nothingness, the gray, islands almost disappear into the water. Black ovals the shape of leaves hide the crumbling of the universe. Key West Islands disappearing into the ocean.

You don't have anything more to say. You don't know what to do. Your whole life has been a mess. Grabbing on to whatever romance came along and holding on to it for dear life until it went so sour you had to vomit and leave. Then you'd recover, just like you recover from a hangover, by grabbing the next piece of tail who came along and wasn't so helpless or so demanding she'd force you to perceive reality.

One cunt's like every other cunt. One ideal's like every other ideal. When one dream goes, another takes its place. You're sick of standing in this shit and so you step out.

At the end of the world. Almost no one living in this perpetual Florida grayness. It may not be paradise, but it doesn't stink of the shit of your dreams. Not much to set you dreaming in this grayness.

There's an old dilapidated hotel on the island. Some old croaker who wheezes instead of talking runs the spa. As far as you know, the croaker won't bother you, no one else's staying at the hotel, and room-and-board are cheap. You decide to stay for a night.

There's nothing else to say. You're a piece of meat among other pieces of meat. It's like when you were at the hospital. The doctor couldn't get the needle in your vein to extract blood. Every time he stuck the needle in your arm, the vein rolled away. You felt like a piece of meat and you didn't care. You saw that the doctor saw living and dying and screaming people and the doctor didn't care if you were dying or screaming. So you didn't care if you were dying or screaming.

You can't tell what matters anymore. Every day you look out at the ocean and you see a tiny boat going down that grayness. One dark tiny boat going down the turbulent waters.

You're gonna stick with him, not cause you love him, but you've gone this far. You've opened yourself to trusting him so deeply if you turn back now, you'll be throwing everything you've got away. The only thing you can call your life. You'll be left with a rotting carcass. Besides, he's not so bad even if he is a gangster. The dimple in his double chin.

He knows how to handle you. He's cruel to you just up to a certain point. He knows that point and he knows if he was one bit crueler to you, you'd leave him. He knows when to press you, when to be a little bit crueler, and when to leave you alone. He really cares about you because he bothers to know you so well. Other people he doesn't bother about, he just kills them. He's gotten into you and he knows how to manipulate your limbs with his big naked hands.

He's a killer. O my God, he kills people. You know you've got to get away from him.

You look up in the car, and there he is. Driving the car, as usual. Never looking at you.

Johnny's running away from trouble again. He's always more trouble than the trouble from which he's running away.

You're the big one. The big dingbat. The winner. You're in this little hick town, this island, and you're gonna take it over until the boat comes. As usual you've got everything arranged and under control. You know how to move the little people around so you can get everything you want.

It's quiet here, and gray. Layers of gray and layers of gray. Like a numbness you can slice with your hand. When the numbness separates, there's nothing. This's what you want.

The ocean waves're moving regularly up and down the beach. They leave lines of shells on the beach and sometimes large jellyfish. You can see the shells and the jellyfish only when the light manages to squeeze through the gray layers. Otherwise the shells and jellyfish look like darker gray blobs, then rows, on the gray.

The day gets darker. You see that the beach isn't the sea. The crummy wood boards that lead to the sea look wet. The whole joint's crumbling apart. How many more years does this hotel have? Three? One? One more hurricane? Maybe tomorrow. You can see the bones of the world.

Somewhere behind you, you hear a car stop and voices. You don't believe that you're hearing anything.

So now shitface is gonna take out his little gun. Order everyone around with his little gun, the old fuddy-duddy who doesn't keep up this palsied outhouse, probably pisses in his pants, and the doddering old man who's been the only hotel guest for the last twenty years. Phooey. Isn't Johnny tough? Johnny and his gun. You hope the hotel's got a bar cause you're gonna have to stick with Johnny until you can get out of this grayness.

You need another man. In this grayness it's easier to find a bottle of booze.

What man's gonna want you now? Once upon a time you were really hot stuff. With your blonde hair and big child's eyes, eyes so big and wide they denied the way your nipples got hard under your sweater, men were drooling after you. You could get anyone you wanted. For nothing. Now you get beaten up and shoved around. Every now and then you get a gun shoved in your mouth.

"OK. Everyone get your hands up. I'm taking over here."

You walk into the dark inner space of the hotel. You're gonna show them who's boss. A trembling white-haired guy appears with his hands held up.

You're dreaming that you're wearing your white Givenchy dress and your white and brown shoes. You're wading through about two feet of mud and water. Your dress is getting filthy, but you don't mind. You're trying to reach an old deserted house. Your fiancé's waiting for you there. You lift your eyes and see a large dark structure.

"We're almost there, dear." Your red fingernails carefully flick a cake-crumb off your summer dress.

You're still alone and with the grace of God you'll die alone.

Maybe you'll die soon and it'll all be over. No more fakes.

The ocean's calm. It's almost evening and it looks like dawn with that strange yellow sun, under the dark gray sky, making the lower third of the sky white-yellow-gray. Sending a triangle of yellow-white light out over the ocean.

The air's still and stinks of fish. You realize a storm's coming. One storm more or less don't make any difference to you. You walk into the dark interior of the hotel and see a gun pointed at your face.

"Back against the wall."

I moved back against the wall. I didn't feel frightened, yet.

"All of you, back against the wall."

The geezer who ran the hotel was already rubbing his back so hard against the wall, the wallpaper was crumbling. A dame with booze in her hand who was standing against the hotel register didn't move.

The guy with the gun walked over and slashed her face open with the point of his gun. She looked at him and walked over to the wall.

Lightning.

The hotel door flies open.

"OK Johnny. Men are for fucking and women for friendship. When I'm not fucking you, I'm your enemy."

I ignored what she said. The storm was coming up hard and fast and there was nothing I could do about that. The boat wouldn't come and I'd be stuck with these pawns for days.

"I want you to understand I'm boss here. This storm"

"It's a hurricane."

I gave the old guy a dirty look. "Hurricane. It's gonna be a while and I don't want trouble. As far as I'm concerned, you're pieces on a checkerboard that I'm moving around so everything's easiest for me. You're either on the board or you're off the board." I moved my gun.

The hotel door swung open and shut. When the door swung open again, an old guy in a wheelchair and a tall woman dressed in a lightish dress were standing in the doorway.

I thought I was hallucinating.

"Excuse me. I need help for my grandfather, Senator . . ."

"We're . . ."

You'd think this was Palm Springs at Christmas. "Both of you. Get over here. No, you," I pointed my gun at the hotel clerk. He should be doing his job. "Shove the wheelchair against the wall. No funny business."

I looked at the girl. "You can use your own legs, I presume?"

The girl was a looker. Legs and class. I wouldn't go near her if she was coated with hundred dollar bills. I didn't have to go near her. Johnny, as his drunk girlfriend called him, would be doing all our movements for us.

Hotel lights go out. Old geezer takes advantage of blackness to try to shove wheelchair with guy in it at me. I laugh and shoot geezer in arm.

"Looks like someone else is going to have to be hotel clerk for a while."

There're no lights and there's this storm, a hurricane I think, and there's this gangster and I'm totally confused. This isn't the way things are back home. Mummy and poppa always kept a quiet home, and now that they're dead,—they must not have loved me as much as I thought cause they died,—grandpa, the senator, takes care of me. I wish we were back home.

Grandpa said that politics was getting so crooked, he had to get away for awhile. He's not running from anyone; he's just trying to figure out how he can fight the crookedness more successfully. I want to be like grandpa: I want to fight for a better world.

I wonder if there are any more men in the world like grandpa.

"All of you. Get to your rooms. Remember that people die when they go out in hurricanes. The phone lines are dead. There's no way you can escape.

"Don't get any funny ideas. Brave pigeons become dead pigeons. Remember: to me you're just pieces of meat."

We were pieces of meat who were still bleeding. The worst was: we might stop bleeding soon.

"In two hours you'll all come down here for dinner. If we can't find any food, we'll live on the booze. I like giving parties. I'll wheel the senator to his room."

"Get upstairs like he says." She looked like an outraged mother hen, only her baby was an old man in a wheelchair and she was probably a virgin. I put my hand on her arm. I didn't want her making more trouble for all of us.

"Wait a second."

"Uh-huh."

"You look like . . . a reasonable man. Is that monster going to hurt my grandfather?"

"I doubt it. Your grandfather's probably too important a person."

"I didn't ask you to be smart. We're in a terrible situation and we have to help each other."

"The kind of help I could give you honey you wouldn't want."

"How do you know what I want?"

"I can tell by looking at your fingers. Your left hand pinky's shorter than the finger next to it. Now will you be a good girl and get upstairs?"

"You're a man! You could overpower this gangster. You wouldn't have to kill him. Just knock him cold."

"A woman friend once told me the only thing men are good for is fucking. I'm afraid that's true."

"You're not a man. A man would realize that his and other people's lives are in danger. Even if he didn't care about the other people, he'd try to save himself. You're a flea, or some kind of . . . amoeba who just accepts things."

"Listen. I'm not going to do anything. I don't care how I die, honey." I started walking up the stairs.

I began remembering her long legs and regretting I was walking away from her.

I wanted to kill him. The only thought in my mind was that I wanted to kill him.

I must have fallen asleep, for the next thing I know, I'm hearing these screamings and sounds of beating that make the old hotel seem like a flea-studded whorehouse:

". . . keep your mouth shut."

"Why don't cha beat me up again? Hurting me takes the place of sex these days."

"I'm a businessman. I want you to remember. I'm a quiet businessman and I like my friends to be quiet about me."

"The only friends you have are dead men.

"You're just a cheap dice man, Johnny. A cheap dice man who's running from the real crooks, the big crooks, and you think you can be a big guy to these crummy people in this crummy hotel."

"I suppose the takeover of The Flamingo and Virginia Hill's 'suicide' are small-time bits to you?

"I shouldn't ever talk to you. I weaken myself when I talk to you."

"Johnny, straighten out. You're nothing Johnny, like me."

"You stinkin' whore. I'm gonna kill you one of these days."

"You're nothing like me.
  "Get me another drink, please Johnny"

I wanted to find my grandfather. I left the little room at the end of the hall against which the wild wind was beating and the trees and the telephone poles, the only bit of safety I had left, and I started down the hall. I knew my grandfather was somewhere downstairs.

The hotel was dark, almost black. Walls seemed to drift into more and more corners and walls. Finally I reached the stairs.

Large dark shapes moved in and out of the corners of my eyes. As I walked down the stairs, I saw the walls move, bend and almost crack, as if they were bowing to me. I was walking down the endless stairs in my long white dress. The train of my dress was slowly draped upward behind me. I felt so tall and proud my head was almost touching the ceiling. Soon I would be a new woman.

All the people I had ever known were waiting for me at the bottom of the stairs. My mother was crying and even my father had tears in his eyes. I was so happy I was almost crying. Somewhere in that mass of people, my fiancé, soon: my husband, was waiting for me.

What was I thinking? I had to find my grandfather. I was in a hotel which was being, for some reason, run by a gangster and I had to find my grandfather before the gangster killed him.

I was standing at the bottom of that endless flight of stairs. I could see the hotel door flying open and closed, almost flying off its hinges but not quite, and I could see the winds wiping the panes of glass out of the windows and I could hear the palm trees break and fall against the old hotel. I wanted to run, but I didn't know where I could go.

I realized that I've always wanted to run and never have anywhere to run to. I had to find my grandfather quickly. There were rooms and rooms and most of the rooms were empty and my grandfather was in one room and the gangster was in another room. I could hardly tell the rooms from the doors cause the large dark shapes were moving in front of and away from my eyes.

I couldn't see but I had to keep going. I stuck my hands out in front of me.

I kept on moving. Something clattered to the floor, and I almost tumbled.

A hand grabbed my wrist.

I didn't want to, but I couldn't get those legs out of my mind. I looked outside my room and saw those legs again. I didn't want to, I must have stopped thinking, but I began to follow them.

Long white legs.

They led me through the hall, down the stairs, and into some large room.

I found myself looking into that man's eyes. The one who wouldn't help me. "What do you want with me?"

"I want to talk to you."

"We've done all our talking. I don't want anything to do with men who are cowards.
    "Excuse me, I have to find my grandfather."

"You've done all your talking. I still want to talk to you."
    She tried to brush by me. I put my two arms around the sides of her body.

"What d'you want?"

"I want to find out who you are."

"I'm in trouble. Or do you want the irrelevant details?"

"Let's say I want the irrelevant details."

"When I was two years old, I refused to drink milk. My parents, they were still alive then, were scared I was going to die. My father started to take a camera apart. Only when he started to break the camera, would I drink the milk."

"That's certainly irrelevant."
    "Is it? I want to stay alive, Mr. Coward. I'm only interested in people who are going to help me stay alive."

"Aren't you being self-centered? Tell me about mom and pops. When did they die on you?"

"When I was eight. Just old enough to start feeling insecure and not old enough to know how to ask someone for help. My grandfather took me into his house and gave me what attention he could."

"Could? You mean you were a lonely child who spent lonely days making up fantasies and living in them?"

"My personal history concerns only those people who love me. Excuse me please."

"Tell me more about your parents. Did they love you a lot when you were a child?"

"I want to find my grandfather." I was begging him to help me. "If you care at all about me, you'll help me find him."

"I didn't know I cared about you."

"Help me."

For some reason I wanted to hear the rest of her words, but I couldn't. I kept hearing that stupid popular song, bits of it, that everyone was singing back where everyone was still living and burning each other out.

Baby don't give, baby don't get.
When it's cold, baby gets wet.
When baby gets wet, baby gets weak.
Baby don't find, baby don't seek.

You want to know the story of this song
It's about a woman who loves to go wrong.
She gets contented like a big fat cat
Only when she's lying flat on her back.

Well, this woman fell in love with a man
Just like some women unfortunately can.
This man had nuts but was nuts in the head
He refused to take this hot babe to bed.

Baby don't give, baby don't get.
When it's cold, baby gets wet.
When baby gets wet, baby gets weak.
Baby don't find, baby don't seek.

He told her he loved her; he told her he'd give
Anything to her so she'd continue to live.
He'd buy her minks and he'd buy her pearls
He just wouldn't give her cunt a swirl.
Too many women were pursuing him
And he was fucking too many girls.

So she sang him this sad sad song
About how the world was always wrong:
DIE IF I DO, DIE IF I DON'T.
DIE IF I WRITE, DIE IF I DON'T
DIE IF I FALL IN LOVE AND DIE IF I WON'T

He didn't give a shit, he didn't care.
She shouted to the cold winter air;
She slashed her wrists; she shaved her head;
She refused to eat so she'd almost drop dead.

He didn't run to her, he told her he
Was sick of people and their needs.
All he wanted to do was sit alone
In his country house by his telephone.

Baby don't give, baby don't get.
When it's cold, baby gets wet.
When baby gets wet, baby gets weak.
Baby don't find, baby don't seek.

So listen girls, do what you can
To find a horny loving man.
Give him all you've got to give,
Give him more so you can live.

A Brief History of Condoms
(1999)

KIM ADDONIZIO

1. *Origins of the American Condom*

The so-called American Condom *(Prophylacticus Americanus)* began behind the counters of druggists, springing to life in the dust and dark among prescription bottles.[1] In the diaspora which followed, some migrated into the air-conditioned light of Walgreens and Thriftys, others to the flickering fluorescent haze of convenience stores. Still others settled behind glass cabinets in large grocery chains. The most colorful varieties live crowded in baskets on the counters of medical clinics. Condoms thrive in great numbers throughout the continent of North America, and tend to be concentrated in large cities. Fundamentalist Christians and the occasional zealous Catholic have decreased their numbers slightly, but the overall impact of such predation has been insignificant on the population as a whole.

2. *Life Cycle of the Condom*

A condom is a simple one-celled organism which appears, at first look, to be round and flat. When released from its foil "nest" and massaged, it changes its shape into a sock-like, membraneous creature which clings to human flesh—specifically, the male sexual organ. Condoms have a symbiotic relationship with humans; sperm released during human sexual activity is caught and eaten by the condom, allowing the condom to reproduce itself. Having fulfilled its evolutionary purpose, the condom then shrivels and dies. The fetus, or "conda," microscopic in size at this point, becomes airborne until it finds a suitable "nest," slips inside it and gestates in the warmth and protection the foil offers. A condom may lie dormant in its nest for years, but life outside the nest last from only a few minutes to half an hour or so.[2]

---

[1]The largely discredited "Big O Theory," first developed by Holstein, posits a divine origin, to wit: that the universe was originally the size and shape of a gigantic, cosmically conscious condom, which masturbated itself and exploded into particles which ripped it apart and sent particles streaming outward into space. There are still some elements of the scientific community who claim that there is an inner condom in each of us, remnant of the Great Rubber, and that we are reabsorbed into it at the end of earthly life. It's interesting to note that numerous mythologies of so-called primitive peoples offer variants of this proposition.

[2]The briefest known lifespan is .078 seconds; the longest, evidenced by a videotape of pornographic artist Jackoff Holmes, was well over an hour. Research has indicated that short-lived condoms tend to exhibit a high level of anxiety, whereas the longest-living emit alpha waves—an indication that, in human terms, these latter condoms tend to "stop and smell the roses," i.e. the odors of anal or vaginal secretions.

It is fair to say that these brief moments, however, are by far the most gratifying; condoms have been observed to burst from sheer pleasure, and occasionally to squirm off of the male penis and travel excitedly upwards into the interior regions of the partner's body.[3]

3. *Common Uses of the Condom*

There are many valuable uses of the condom beyond the aforementioned use in sexual activity. Condoms may be filled with water and dropped from high windows to terrify old people, or loaded with jello and thrown at parties. They may be blown up like balloons. The flavored variety, once the lubricant is wiped away, is favored for eating by adolescent girls. Condoms may be used in delaying sexual activity, as in, "I won't fuck you if I have to wear that thing on my dick."[4] Such a statement may have unfortunate results if the condom is then discarded, as it will simply dry up and die without reproducing itself. Condoms are dependent on human males, some of whom have an ambivalent relationship with them, and see them at best as a necessary evil.

4. *Inner Life of the Condom*

It is hard to ascertain whether a condom is capable of the emotions you and I regard as a part of sentient life. Does a condom experience depression, or fear death? Does it have a soul? If so, then we must examine carefully our treatment of this useful creature. Should it, for example, be so quickly relegated to the floor beside the bed, or the trash in the bathroom, or the weeds of the vacant lot? Perhaps our responsibility should extend to a decent burial, a few words said to mark the passing of our pleasure-seeking, short-lived friend. Perhaps it loves the woman whose vaginal walls drench it for a few minutes, or the man whose anus contracts around it. Perhaps it realizes that such bliss must soon, too soon, turn into pain and diminishment, into the awful isolation of the separate self. If the condom could speak, what truths might it tell us, privy as it is to some of our most intimate moments?

5. *One Condom's Story*

She carries me in her purse. She intends to be faithful, but just in case, she wants to be prepared. She is on a long trip, away from her lover. She meets a man who delights her, who is clever and interesting. He puts his hand on her hip as they are walking. They find a bar and drink until they can hardly stand up, then stagger to a hotel room. I hear them laughing and giggling, hear the rustle of clothes and good intentions being rapidly discarded. There is a blinding light as I am freed, feeling the cool air wash deliciously over me, and then I am lost in sensation, nothing matters but this, it is glorious, I am stretched taut, headed for that beautiful deadly opening; I go in and in. My head floods with sperm and I gorge myself, losing

---

[3]Emergency Room records indicate that a small percentage of patients seek treatment, but the incidence is undoubtedly more frequent, according to anecdotal sources.

[4]In the late twentieth century, this statement is an indication of gross stupidity on the part of the speaker. The best response to such an attitude is probably, "Go fuck yourself."

consciousness, and when I wake I find myself flushed down the pipes, along the sewers and out into the great river of the unborn, riding the currents down to the mothering sea.[5]

6. *Social Organization of Condom Communities*

There are many classes—one might even say castes—in the condom community. Brightly colored and flavored condoms are usually ostracized by those with a more uniform look and packaging. These second-class citizens are more likely to attempt to form what we can only call personal attachments with other condoms. Through a process known as "nest-ripping," two separate condoms may leak their lubricants and form a sort of gluey mass which causes the nests to bind to each other. They then become unfit for human use and hence unable to reproduce, so why this occurs remains an evolutionary mystery.[6]

7. *In Conclusion: A Personal Note*

There is much still to learn about this deceptively simple creature. I have here attempted the briefest outline of serious study and research. My own fascination began, perhaps, when as I boy I unrolled my first condom and jerked off into it, finding it a much neater method than rutting into the sheets my mother would have to wash. I have, frankly, never encountered a human body which gave me as much pleasure as the simple, unassuming condom, always eager to please, ready to take my jism and lap it up deliriously, then lie peacefully hanging from my penis while I relaxed with a cigarette. Several times during these jottings I have stopped to "denest" and massage one of the little creatures, to slip it over me and caress it, to squeeze and pull until we were both deliciously sated.[7] I confess to you now that I love them, that I think of nothing but their moist dripping bodies, that at night they come to me in my dreams, they hover over me and smile, and at last begin to speak.

---

[5]The account is fictional; see Christopher Peckerwood's *I Am A Condom*. There are no authenticated stories of condoms speaking or writing their views, though apocryphal ones abound. Various people have claimed to be kidnapped by condoms from outer space, or to hear the voices of dead condoms speaking to them.

[6]For further readings see "Nest-ripping: Nature or Nurture?" in *Scientific American*; "Nest-Rippers, Menace to Society," ibid.; and the San Francisco journal *Honey, Let It Rip*.

[7]I can't get enough. Desire is endless. Sometimes I want to fuck everything in sight. I want to fuck the sheets, the trees outside my window, the men and women passing on the streets below; I want that ecstasy that only sex provides, the loss of self and finding of it, the *petit-morte* that tells me there is no true death, there is only connection and ceaseless change, there is only love against the darkness surrounding us, we are all ripped from the nest, helpless and exposed together; oh friends and colleagues, it all comes down to this: So many condoms. So little time.

The Lone Ranger and Tonto Fistfight in Heaven (1993)

SHERMAN ALEXIE

Too hot to sleep so I walked down to the Third Avenue 7-11 for a Creamsicle and the company of a graveyard-shift cashier. I know that game. I worked graveyard for a Seattle 7-11 and got robbed once too often. The last time the bastard locked me in the cooler. He even took my money and basketball shoes.

The graveyard-shift worker in the Third Avenue 7-11 looked like they all do. Acne scars and a bad haircut, work pants that showed off his white socks, and those cheap black shoes that have no support. My arches still ache from my year at the Seattle 7-11.

"Hello," he asked when I walked into his store. "How you doing?"

I gave him a half wave as I headed back to the freezer. He looked me over so he could describe me to the police later. I knew the look. One of my old girlfriends said I started to look at her that way, too. She left me not long after that. No, I left her and don't blame her for anything. That's how it happened. When one person starts to look at another like a criminal, then the love is over. It's logical.

"I don't trust you," she said to me. "You get too angry."

She was white and I lived with her in Seattle. Some nights we fought so bad that I would just get in my car and drive all night, only stop to fill up on gas. In fact, I worked the graveyard shift to spend as much time away from her as possible. But I learned all about Seattle that way, driving its back ways and dirty alleys.

Sometimes, though, I would forget where I was and get lost. I'd drive for hours, searching for something familiar. Seems like I'd spent my whole life that way, looking for anything I recognized. Once, I ended up in a nice residential neighborhood and somebody must have been worried because the police showed up and pulled me over.

"What are you doing out here?" the police officer asked me as he looked over my license and registration.

"I'm lost."

"Well, where are you supposed to be?" he asked me, and I knew there were plenty of places I wanted to be, but none where I was supposed to be.

"I got in a fight with my girlfriend," I said. "I was just driving around, blowing off steam, you know?"

"Well, you should be more careful where you drive," the officer said. "You're making people nervous. You don't fit the profile of the neighborhood."

I wanted to tell him that I didn't really fit the profile of the country but I knew it would just get me into trouble.

"Can I help you?" the 7-11 clerk asked me loudly, searching for some response that would reassure him that I wasn't an armed robber. He knew this dark skin and long, black hair of mine was dangerous. I had potential.

"Just getting a Creamsicle," I said after a long interval. It was a sick twist to pull on the guy, but it was late and I was bored. I grabbed my Creamsicle and walked back to the counter slowly, scanned the aisles for effect. I wanted to whistle low and menacingly but I never learned to whistle.

"Pretty hot out tonight?" he asked, that old rhetorical weather bullshit question designed to put us both at ease.

"Hot enough to make you go crazy," I said and smiled. He swallowed hard like a white man does in those situations. I looked him over. Same old green, red, and white 7-11 jacket and thick glasses. But he wasn't ugly, just misplaced and marked by loneliness. If he wasn't working there that night, he'd be at home alone, flipping through channels and wishing he could afford HBO or Showtime.

"Will this be all?" he asked me, in that company effort to make me do some impulse shopping. Like adding a clause onto a treaty. *We'll take Washington and Oregon and you get six pine trees and a brand-new Chrysler Cordoba.* I knew how to make and break promises.

"No," I said and paused. "Give me a Cherry Slushie, too."

"What size?" he asked, relieved.

"Large," I said, and he turned his back to me to make the drink. He realized his mistake but it was too late. He stiffened, ready for the gunshot or the blow behind the ear. When it didn't come, he turned back to me.

"I'm sorry," he said, "What size did you say?"

"Small," I said and changed the story.

"But I thought you said large."

"If you knew I wanted a large, then why did you ask me again?" I asked him and laughed. He looked at me, couldn't decide if I was giving him serious shit or just goofing. There was something about him I liked, even if it was three in the morning and he was white.

"Hey," I said. "Forget the Slushie. What I want to know is if you know all the words to the theme from 'The Brady Bunch'?"

He looked at me, confused at first, then laughed.

"Shit," he said. "I was hoping you weren't crazy. You were scaring me."

"Well, I'm going to get crazy if you don't know the words."

He laughed loudly then, told me to take the Creamsicle for free. He was the graveyard-shift manager and those little demonstrations of power tickled him. All seventy-five cents of it. I knew how much everything cost.

"Thanks," I said to him and walked out the door. I took my time walking home, let the heat of the night melt the Creamsicle all over my hand. At three in the morning I could act just as young as I wanted to act. There was no one around to ask me to grow up.

In Seattle, I broke lamps. She and I would argue and I'd break a lamp, just pick it up and throw it down. At first she'd buy replacement lamps, expensive and beautiful. But after a while she'd buy lamps from Goodwill or garage sales. Then she just gave up the idea entirely and we'd argue in the dark.

"You're just like your brother," she'd yell. "Drunk all the time and stupid."

"My brother don't drink that much."

She and I never tried to hurt each other physically. I did love her, after all, and she loved me. But those arguments were just as damaging as a fist. Words can be like that, you know? Whenever I get into arguments now, I remember her and I also remember Muhammad Ali. He knew the power of his fists but, more importantly, he knew the power of his words, too. Even though he only had an IQ of 80 or so, Ali was a genius. And she was a genius, too. She knew exactly what to say to cause me the most pain.

But don't get me wrong. I walked through that relationship with an executioner's hood. Or more appropriately, with war paint and sharp arrows. She was a kindergarten teacher and I continually insulted her for that.

"Hey, schoolmarm," I asked. "Did your kids teach you anything new today?"

And I always had crazy dreams. I always have had them, but it seemed they became nightmares more often in Seattle.

In one dream, she was a missionary's wife and I was a minor war chief. We fell in love and tried to keep it secret. But the missionary caught us fucking in the barn and shot me. As I lay dying, my tribe learned of the shooting and attacked the whites all across the reservation. I died and my soul drifted above the reservation.

Disembodied, I could see everything that was happening. Whites killing Indians and Indians killing whites. At first it was small, just my tribe and the few whites who lived there. But my dream grew, intensified. Other tribes arrived on horseback to continue the slaughter of whites, and the United States Cavalry rode into battle.

The most vivid image of that dream stays with me. Three mounted soldiers played polo with a dead Indian woman's head. When I first dreamed it, I thought it was just a product of my anger and imagination. But since then, I've read similar accounts of that kind of evil in the old West. Even more terrifying, though, is the fact that those kinds of brutal things are happening today in places like El Salvador.

All I know for sure, though, is that I woke from that dream in terror, packed up all my possessions, and left Seattle in the middle of the night.

"I love you," she said as I left her. "And don't ever come back."

I drove through the night, over the Cascades, down into the plains of central Washington, and back home to the Spokane Indian Reservation.

When I finished the Creamsicle that the 7-11 clerk gave me, I held the wooden stick up into the air and shouted out very loudly. A couple lights flashed on in windows and a police car cruised by me a few minutes later. I waved to the men in blue and they waved back accidentally. When I got home it was still too hot to sleep so I picked up a week-old newspaper from the floor and read.

There was another civil war, another terrorist bomb exploded, and one more plane crashed and all aboard were presumed dead. The crime rate was rising in every city with populations larger than 100,000, and a farmer in Iowa shot his banker after foreclosure on his 1,000 acres.

A kid from Spokane won the local spelling bee by spelling the word *rhinoceros.*

When I got back to the reservation, my family wasn't surprised to see me. They'd been expecting me back since the day I left for Seattle. There's an old Indian poet who said that Indians can reside in the city, but they can never live there. That's as close to truth as any of us can get.

Mostly I watched television. For weeks I flipped through channels, searched for answers in the game shows and soap operas. My mother would circle the want ads in red and hand the paper to me.

"What are you going to do with the rest of your life?" she asked.

"Don't know," I said, and normally, for almost any other Indian in the country, that would have been a perfectly fine answer. But I was special, a former college student, a smart kid. I was one of those Indians who was supposed to make it, to rise above the rest of the reservation like a fucking eagle or something. I was the new kind of warrior.

For a few months I didn't even look at the want ads my mother circled, just left the newspaper where she had set it down. After a while, though, I got tired of television and started to play basketball again. I'd been a good player in high school, nearly great, and almost played at the college I attended for a couple years. But I'd been too out of shape from drinking and sadness to ever be good again. Still, I liked the way the ball felt in my hands and the way my feet felt inside my shoes.

At first I just shot baskets by myself. It was selfish, and I also wanted to learn the game again before I played against anybody else. Since I had been good before and embarrassed fellow tribal members, I knew they would want to take revenge on me. Forget about the cowboys versus Indians business. The most intense competition on any reservation is Indians versus Indians.

But on the night I was ready to play for real, there was this white guy at the gym, playing with all the Indians.

"Who is that?" I asked Jimmy Seyler.

"He's the new BIA chief's kid."

"Can he play?"

"Oh, yeah."

And he could play. He played Indian ball, fast and loose, better than all the Indians there.

"How long's he been playing here?" I asked.

"Long enough."

I stretched my muscles, and everybody watched me. All these Indians watched one of their old and dusty heroes. Even though I had played most of my ball at the white high school I went to, I was still all Indian, you know? I was Indian when it counted, and this BIA kid needed to be beaten by an Indian, any Indian.

I jumped into the game and played well for a little while. It felt good. I hit a few shots, grabbed a rebound or two, played enough defense to keep the other team honest. Then that white kid took over the game. He was too good. Later, he'd play college ball back East and would nearly make the Knicks team a couple years on. But we didn't know any of that would happen. We just knew he was better that day and every other day.

The next morning I woke up tired and hungry, so I grabbed the want ads, found a job I wanted, and drove to Spokane to get it. I've been working at the high school exchange program ever since, typing and answering phones. Sometimes I wonder if the people on the other end of the line know that I'm Indian and if their voices would change if they did know.

One day I picked up the phone and it was her, calling from Seattle.

"I got your number from your mom," she said. "I'm glad you're working."

"Yeah, nothing like a regular paycheck."

"Are you drinking?"

"No, I've been on the wagon for almost a year."

"Good."

The connection was good. I could hear her breathing in the spaces between our words. How do you talk to the real person whose ghost has haunted you? How do you tell the difference between the two?

"Listen," I said. "I'm sorry for everything."

"Me, too."

"What's going to happen to us?" I asked her and wished I had the answer for myself.

"I don't know," she said. "I want to change the world."

These days, living alone in Spokane, I wish I lived closer to the river, to the falls where ghosts of salmon jump. I wish I could sleep. I put down my paper or book and turn off all the lights, lie quietly in the dark. It may take hours, even years, for me to sleep again. There's nothing surprising or disappointing in that.

I know how all my dreams end anyway.

Nightfall
(1941)

ISAAC ASIMOV

"If the stars should appear one night in a thousand years, how would men believe and adore, and preserve for many generations the remembrance of the city of God?"

EMERSON

Aton 77, director of Saro University, thrust out a belligerent lower lip and glared at the young newspaperman in a hot fury.

Theremon 762 took that fury in his stride. In his earlier days, when his now widely syndicated column was only a mad idea in a cub reporter's mind, he had specialized in "impossible" interviews. It had cost him bruises, black eyes, and broken bones; but it had given him an ample supply of coolness and self-confidence.

So he lowered the outthrust hand that had been so pointedly ignored and calmly waited for the aged director to get over the worst. Astronomers were queer ducks, anyway, and if Aton's actions of the last two months meant anything, this same Aton was the queer-duckiest of the lot.

Aton 77 found his voice, and though it trembled with restrained emotion, the careful, somewhat pedantic phraseology, for which the famous astronomer was noted, did not abandon him.

"Sir," he said, "you display an infernal gall in coming to me with that impudent proposition of yours."

The husky telephotographer of the Observatory, Beenay 25, thrust a tongue's tip across dry lips and interposed nervously, "Now, sir, after all—"

The director turned to him and lifted a white eyebrow. "Do not interfere, Beenay. I will credit you with good intentions in bringing this man here; but I will tolerate no insubordination now."

Theremon decided it was time to take a part. "Director Aton, if you'll let me finish what I started saying, I think—"

"I don't believe, young man," retorted Aton, "that anything you could say now would count much as compared with your daily columns of these last two months. You have led a vast newspaper campaign against the efforts of myself and my colleagues to organize the world against the menace which it is now too late to avert. You have done your best with your highly personal attacks to make the staff of this Observatory objects of ridicule."

The director lifted a copy of the Saro City *Chronicle* from the table and shook it at Theremon furiously. "Even a person of your well-known impudence should have hesitated before coming to me with a request that he be allowed to cover today's events for his paper. Of all newsmen, you!"

Aton dashed the newspaper to the floor, strode to the window, and clasped his arms behind his back.

"You may leave," he snapped over his shoulder. He stared moodily out at the skyline where Gamma, the brightest of the planet's six suns, was setting. It had already faded and yellowed into the horizon mists, and Aton knew he would never see it again as a sane man.

He whirled. "No, wait, come here!" He gestured peremptorily. "I'll give you your story,"

The newsman had made no motion to leave, and now he approached the old man slowly. Aton gestured outward. "Of the six suns, only Beta is left in the sky. Do you see it?"

The question was rather unnecessary. Beta was almost at zenith, its ruddy light flooding the landscape to an unusual orange as the brilliant rays of setting Gamma died. Beta was at aphelion. It was small; smaller than Theremon had ever seen it before, and for the moment it was undisputed ruler of Lagash's sky.

Lagash's own sun, Alpha, the one about which it revolved, was at the antipodes, as were the two distant companion pairs. The red dwarf Beta—Alpha's immediate companion—was alone, grimly alone.

Aton's upturned face flushed redly in the sunlight. "In just under four hours," he said, "civilization, as we know it, comes to an end. It will do so because, as you see, Beta is the only sun in the sky." He smiled grimly. "Print that! There'll be no one to read it."

"But if it turns out that four hours pass—and another four—and nothing happens?" asked Theremon softly.

"Don't let that worry you. Enough will happen."

"Granted! And *still*—if nothing happens?"

For a second time, Beenay 25 spoke. "Sir, I think you ought to listen to him."

Theremon said, "Put it to a vote, Director Aton."

There was a stir among the remaining five members of the Observatory staff, who till now had maintained an attitude of wary neutrality.

"That," stated Aton flatly, "is not necessary." He drew out his pocket watch. "Since your good friend, Beenay, insists so urgently, I will give you five minutes. Talk away."

"Good! Now, just what difference would it make if you allowed me to take down an eyewitness account of what's to come? If your prediction comes true, my presence won't hurt; for in that case my column would never be written. On the other hand, if nothing comes of it, you will just have to expect ridicule or worse. It would be wise to leave that ridicule to friendly hands."

Aton snorted. "Do you mean yours when you speak of friendly hands?"

"Certainly!" Theremon sat down and crossed his legs. "My columns may have been a little rough, but I gave you people the benefit of the doubt every time. After all, this is not the century to preach 'The end of the world is at hand' to Lagash. Yon have to understand that people don't believe the *Book of Revelations* anymore, and it annoys them to have scientists turn about-face and tell us the Cultists are right after all—"

"No such thing, young man," interrupted Aton. "While a great deal of our data has been supplied us by the Cult, our results contain none of the Cult's mysticism. Facts are facts, and the Cult's so-called mythology *has* certain facts behind it. We've exposed them and ripped away their mystery. I assure you that the Cult hates us now worse than you do."

"I don't hate you. I'm just trying to tell you that the public is in an ugly humor. They're angry."

Aton twisted his mouth in derision. "Let them be angry."

"Yes, but what about tomorrow?"

"There'll be no tomorrow!"

"But if there is. Say that there is—just to see what happens. That anger might take shape into something serious. After all, you know, business has taken a nosedive these last two months. Investors don't really believe the world is coming to an end, but just the same they're being cagy with their money until it's all over. Johnny Public doesn't believe you, either, but the new spring furniture might just as well wait a few months—just to make sure.

"You see the point. Just as soon as this is all over, the business interests will be after your hide. They'll say that if crackpots—begging your pardon—can upset the country's prosperity any time they want, simply by making some cockeyed prediction—it's up to the planet to prevent them. The sparks will fly, sir."

The director regarded the columnist sternly. "And just what were you proposing to do to help the situation?"

"Well"— Theremon grinned— "I was proposing to take charge of the publicity. I can handle things so that only the ridiculous side will show. It would be hard to stand, I admit, because I'd have to make you all out to be a bunch of gibbering idiots, but if I can get people laughing at you, they might forget to be angry. In return for that, all my publisher asks is an exclusive story."

Beenay nodded and burst out, "Sir, the rest of us think he's right. These last two months we've considered everything but the million-to-one chance that there is an error somewhere in our theory or in our calculations. We ought to take care of that, too."

There was a murmur of agreement from the men grouped about the table, and Aton's expression became that of one who found his mouth full of something bitter and couldn't get rid of it.

"You may stay if you wish, then. You will kindly refrain, however, from hampering us in our duties in any way. You will also remember that I am in charge of all activities here, and in spite of your opinions as expressed in your columns, I will expect full cooperation and full respect—"

His hands were behind his back, and his wrinkled face thrust forward determinedly as he spoke. He might have continued indefinitely but for the intrusion of a new voice.

"Hello, hello, hello!" It came in a high tenor, and the plump cheeks of the newcomer expanded in a pleased smile. "What's this morgue-like atmosphere about here? No one's losing his nerve, I hope."

Aton started in consternation and said peevishly, "Now what the devil are you doing here, Sheerin? I thought you were going to stay behind in the Hideout."

Sheerin laughed and dropped his tubby figure into a chair. "Hideout be blowed! The place bored me. I wanted to be here, where things are getting hot. Don't you suppose I have my share of curiosity? I want to see these Stars the Cultists are forever speaking about." He rubbed his hands and added in a soberer tone, "It's freezing outside. The wind's enough to hang icicles on your nose. Beta doesn't seem to give any heat at all, at the distance it is."

The white-haired director ground his teeth in sudden exasperation. "Why do you go out of your way to do crazy things, Sheerin? What kind of good are you around here?"

"What kind of good am I around there?" Sheerin spread his palms in comical resignation. "A psychologist isn't worth his salt in the Hideout. They need men of action and strong, healthy women that can breed children. Me? I'm a hundred pounds too heavy for a man of action, and I wouldn't be a success at breeding children. So why bother them with an extra mouth to feed? I feel better over here."

Theremon spoke briskly. "Just what is the Hideout, sir?"

Sheerin seemed to see the columnist for the first time. He frowned and blew his ample cheeks out. "And just who in Lagash are you, redhead?"

Aton compressed his lips and then muttered sullenly, "That's Theremon 762, the newspaper fellow. I suppose you've heard of him."

The columnist offered his hand. "And, of course, you're Sheerin 501 of Saro University. I've heard of you." Then he repeated, "What is this Hideout, sir?"

"Well," said Sheerin, "we have managed to convince a few people of the validity of our prophecy of—er—doom, to be spectacular about it, and those few have taken proper measures. They consist mainly of the immediate members of the families of the Observatory staff, certain of the faculty of Saro University, and a few outsiders. Altogether, they number about three hundred, but three quarters are women and children."

"I see! They're supposed to hide where the Darkness and the—er—Stars can't get at them, and then hold out when the rest of the world goes poof."

"If they can. It won't be easy. With all of mankind insane, with the great cities going up in flames—environment will not be conducive to survival. But they have food, water, shelter, and weapons—"

"They've got more," said Aton. "They've got all our records, except for what we will collect today. Those records will mean everything to the next cycle, and *that's* what must survive. The rest can go hang."

Theremon uttered a long, low whistle and sat brooding for several minutes. The men about the table had brought out a multichess board and started a six-member game. Moves were made rapidly and in silence. All eyes bent in furious concentration on the board. Theremon watched them intently and then rose and approached Aton, who sat apart in whispered conversation with Sheerin.

"Listen," he said, "let's go somewhere where we won't bother the rest of the fellows. I want to ask some questions."

The aged astronomer frowned sourly at him, but Sheerin chirped up, "Certainly. It will do me good to talk. It always does. Aton was telling me about your ideas concerning world reaction to a failure of the prediction—and I agree with you. I read your column pretty regularly, by the way, and as a general thing I like your views."

"Please, Sheerin," growled Aton.

"Eh? Oh, all right. We'll go into the next room. It has softer chairs, anyway."

There were softer chairs in the next room. There were also thick red curtains on the windows and a maroon carpet on the floor. With the bricky light of Beta pouring in, the general effect was one of dried blood.

Theremon shuddered. "Say, I'd give ten credits for a decent dose of white light for just a second. I wish Gamma or Delta were in the sky."

"What are your questions?" asked Aton. "Please remember that our time is limited. In a little over an hour and a quarter we're going upstairs, and after that there will be no time for talk."

"Well, here it is." Theremon leaned back and folded his hands on his chest. "You people seem so all-fired serious about this that I'm beginning to believe you. Would you mind explaining what it's all about?"

Aton exploded, "Do you mean to sit there and tell me that you've been bombarding us with ridicule without even finding out what we've been trying to say?"

The columnist grinned sheepishly. "It's not that bad, sir. I've got the general idea. You say there is going to be a world-wide Darkness in a few hours and that all mankind will go violently insane. What I want now is the science behind it."

"No, you don't. No, you don't," broke in Sheerin. "If you ask Aton for that—supposing him to be in the mood to answer at all—he'll trot out pages of figures and volumes of graphs. You won't make head or tail of it. Now if you were to ask me, I could give you the layman's standpoint."

"All right; I ask you."

"Then first I'd like a drink." He rubbed his hands and looked at Aton.

"Water?" grunted Aton.

"Don't be silly!"

"Don't you be silly. No alcohol today. It would be too easy to get my men drunk. I can't afford to tempt them."

The psychologist grumbled wordlessly. He turned to Theremon, impaled him with his sharp eyes, and began.

"You realize, of course, that the history of civilization on Lagash displays a cyclic character—but I mean, *cyclic!*"

"I know," replied Theremon cautiously, "that that is the current archaeological theory. Has it been accepted as a fact?"

"Just about. In this last century it's been generally agreed upon. This cyclic character is—or rather, was—one of the great mysteries. We've located series of civilizations, nine of them definitely, and indications of others as well, all of which have reached heights comparable to our own, and all of which, without exception, were destroyed by fire at the very height of their culture.

"And no one could tell why. All centers of culture were thoroughly gutted by fire, with nothing left behind to give a hint as to the cause."

Theremon was following closely. "Wasn't there a Stone Age, too?"

"Probably, but as yet practically nothing is known of it, except that men of that age were little more than rather intelligent apes. We can forget about that."

"I see. Go on!"

"There have been explanations of these recurrent catastrophes, all of a more or less fantastic nature. Some say that there are periodic rains of fire; some that Lagash passes through a sun every so often; some even wilder things. But there is one theory, quite different from all of these, that has been handed down over a period of centuries."

"I know. You mean this myth of the 'Stars' that the Cultists have in their *Book of Revelations*."

"Exactly," rejoined Sheerin with satisfaction. "The Cultists said that every two thousand and fifty years Lagash entered a huge cave, so that all the suns disappeared, and there came *total darkness all over the world!* And then, they say, things called Stars appeared, which robbed men of their souls and left them unreasoning brutes, so that they destroyed the civilization they themselves had built up. Of course they mix all this up with a lot of religio-mystic notions, but that's the central idea."

There was a short pause in which Sheerin drew a long breath. "And now we come to the Theory of Universal Gravitation." He pronounced the phrase so that the capital letters sounded—and at that point Aton turned from the window, snorted loudly, and stalked out of the room.

The two stared after him, and Theremon said, "What's wrong?"

29

"Nothing in particular," replied Sheerin. "Two of the men were due several hours ago and haven't shown up yet. He's terrifically short-handed, of course, because all but the really essential men have gone to the Hideout."

"You don't think the two deserted, do you?"

"Who? Faro and Yimot? Of course not. Still, if they're not back within the hour, things would be a little sticky." He got to his feet suddenly, and his eyes twinkled. "Anyway, as long as Aton is gone—"

Tiptoeing to the nearest window, he squatted, and from the low window box beneath withdrew a bottle of red liquid that gurgled suggestively when he shook it.

"I *thought* Aton didn't know about this," he remarked as he trotted back to the table. "Here! We've only got one glass so, as the guest, you can have it. I'll keep the bottle." And he filled the tiny cup with judicious care.

Theremon rose to protest, but Sheerin eyed him sternly. "Respect your elders, young man."

The newsman seated himself with a look of anguish on his face. "Go ahead, then, you old villain."

The psychologist's Adam's apple wobbled as the bottle upended, and then, with a satisfied grunt and a smack of the lips, he began again. "But what do you know about gravitation?"

"Nothing, except that it is a very recent development, not too well established, and that the math is so hard that only twelve men in Lagash are supposed to understand it."

"*Tcha!* Nonsense! Baloney! I can give you all the essential math in a sentence. The Law of Universal Gravitation states that there exists a cohesive force among all bodies of the universe, such that the amount of this force between any two given bodies is proportional to the product of their masses divided by the square of the distance between them."

"Is that all?"

"That's enough! It took four hundred years to develop it."

"Why that long? It sounded simple enough, the way you said it."

"Because great laws are not divined by flashes of inspiration, whatever you may think. It usually takes the combined work of a world full of scientists over a period of centuries. After Genovi 41 discovered that Lagash rotated about the sun Alpha rather than vice versa—and that was four hundred years ago—astronomers have been working. The complex motions of the six suns were recorded and analyzed and unwoven. Theory after theory was advanced and checked and counterchecked and modified and abandoned and revived and converted to something else. It was a devil of a job."

Theremon nodded thoughtfully and held out his glass for more liquor. Sheerin grudgingly allowed a few ruby drops to leave the bottle.

"It was twenty years ago," he continued after remoistening his own throat, "that it was finally demonstrated that the Law of Universal Gravitation accounted exactly for the orbital motions of the six suns. It was a great triumph."

Sheerin stood up and walked to the window, still clutching his bottle. "And now we're getting to the point. In the last decade, the motions of Lagash about Alpha were computed according to gravity, and *it did not account for the orbit observed;* not even when all perturbations due to the other suns were included. Either the law was invalid, or there was another, as yet unknown, factor involved."

Theremon joined Sheerin at the window and gazed out past the wooded slopes to where the spires of Saro City gleamed bloodily on the horizon. The newsman felt the tension of uncertainty grow within him as he cast a short glance at Beta. It glowered redly at zenith, dwarfed and evil.

"Go ahead, sir," he said softly.

Sheerin replied, "Astronomers stumbled about for years, each proposed theory more untenable than the one before—until Aton had the inspiration of calling in the Cult. The head of the Cult, Sor 5, had access to certain data that simplified the problem considerably. Aton set to work on a new track.

"What if there were another nonluminous planetary body such as Lagash? If there were, you know, it would shine only by reflected light, and if it were composed of bluish rock, as Lagash itself largely is, then, in the redness of the sky, the eternal blaze of the suns would make it invisible—drown it out completely."

Theremon whistled. "What a screwy idea!"

"You think *that's* screwy? Listen to this: Suppose this body rotated about Lagash at such a distance and in such an orbit and had such a mass that its attraction would exactly account for the deviations of Lagash's orbit from theory—do you know what would happen?"

The columnist shook his head.

"Well, sometimes this body would get in the way of a sun." And Sheerin emptied what remained in the bottle at a draft.

"And it does, I suppose," said Theremon flatly.

"Yes! But only one sun lies in its plane of revolution." He jerked a thumb at the shrunken sun above. "Beta! And it has been shown that the eclipse will occur only when the arrangement of the suns is such that Beta is alone in its hemisphere and at maximum distance, at which time the moon is invariably at minimum distance. The eclipse that results, with the moon seven times the apparent diameter of Beta, covers all of Lagash and lasts well over half a day, so that no spot on the planet escapes the effects. *That eclipse comes once every two thousand and forty-nine years.*"

Theremon's face was drawn into an expressionless mask. "And that's my story?"

The psychologist nodded. "That's all of it. First the eclipse—which will start in three quarters of an hour—then universal Darkness and, maybe, these mysterious Stars—then madness, and end of the cycle."

He brooded. "We had two months' leeway—we at the Observatory—and that wasn't enough time to persuade Lagash of the danger. Two centuries might not have been enough. But our records are at the Hideout, and today we photograph the eclipse. The next cycle will *start off* with the truth, and when the *next* eclipse comes, mankind will at last be ready for it. Come to think of it, that's part of your story too."

A thin wind ruffled the curtains at the window as Theremon opened it and leaned out. It played coldly with his hair as he stared at the crimson sunlight on his hand. Then he turned in sudden rebellion.

"What is there in Darkness to drive *me* mad?"

Sheerin smiled to himself as he spun the empty liquor bottle with abstracted motions of his hand. "Have you ever experienced Darkness, young man?"

The newsman leaned against the wall and considered. "No. Can't say I have. But I know what it is. Just—uh—" He made vague motions with his fingers and then brightened. "Just no light. Like in caves."

"Have you ever been in a cave?"

"In a *cave!* Of course not!"

"I thought not. I tried last week—just to see—but I got out in a hurry. I went in until the mouth of the cave was just visible as a blur of light, with black everywhere else. I never thought a person my weight could run that fast."

Theremon's lip curled. "Well, if it comes to that, I guess I wouldn't have run if I had been there."

The psychologist studied the young man with an annoyed frown.

"My, don't you talk big! I dare you to draw the curtain."

Theremon looked his surprise and said, "What for? If we had four or five suns out there, we might want to cut the light down a bit for comfort, but now we haven't enough light as it is."

"That's the point. Just draw the curtain; then come here and sit down."

"All right." Theremon reached for the tasseled string and jerked. The red curtain slid across the wide window, the brass rings hissing their way along the crossbar, and a dusk-red shadow clamped down on the room.

Theremon's footsteps sounded hollowly in the silence as he made his way to the table, and then they stopped halfway. "I can't see you, sir," he whispered.

"Feel your way," ordered Sheerin in a strained voice.

"But I can't see you, sir." The newsman was breathing harshly. "I can't see anything."

"What did you expect?" came the grim reply. "Come here and sit down!"

The footsteps sounded again, waveringly, approaching slowly. There was the sound of someone fumbling with a chair. Theremon's voice came thinly, "Here I am. I feel . . . ulp . . . all right."

"You like it, do you?"

"N—no. It's pretty awful. The walls seem to be—" He paused. "They seem to be closing in on me. I keep wanting to push them away. But I'm not going *mad!* In fact, the feeling isn't as bad as it was."

"All right. Draw the curtain back again."

There were cautious footsteps through the dark, the rustle of Theremon's body against the curtain as he felt for the tassel, and then the triumphant *ro-o-osh* of the curtain slithering back. Red light flooded the room, and with a cry of joy Theremon looked up at the sun.

Sheerin wiped the moistness off his forehead with the back of a hand and said shakily, "And that was just a dark room."

"It can be stood," said Theremon lightly.

"Yes, a dark room can. But were you at the Jonglor Centennial Exposition two years ago?"

"No, it so happens I never got around to it. Six thousand miles was just a bit too much to travel, even for the exposition."

"Well, I was there. You remember hearing about the 'Tunnel of Mystery' that broke all records in the amusement area—for the first month or so, anyway?"

"Yes. Wasn't there some fuss about it?"

"Very little. It was hushed up. You see, that Tunnel of Mystery was just a mile-long tunnel—with no lights. You got into a little open car and jolted along through Darkness for fifteen minutes. It was very popular—while it lasted."

"Popular?

"Certainly. There's a fascination in being frightened *when it's part of a game.* A baby is born with three instinctive fears: of loud noises, of falling, and of the absence of light. That's why it's considered so funny to jump at someone and shout 'Boo!' That's why it's such fun to ride a roller coaster. And that's why that Tunnel of Mystery started cleaning up. People came out of that Darkness shaking, breathless, half dead with fear, but they kept on paying to get in."

"Wait a while, I remember now. Some people came out dead, didn't they? There were rumors of that after it shut down."

The psychologist snorted. "Bah! Two or three died. That was nothing! They paid off the families of the dead ones and argued the Jonglor City Council into forgetting it. After all, they said, if people with weak hearts want to go through the tunnel, it was at their own risk—and besides, it wouldn't happen again. So they put a doctor in the front office and had every customer go through a physical examination before getting into the car. That actually *boosted* ticket sales."

"Well, then?"

"But you see, there was something else. People sometimes came out in perfect order, except that they refused to go into buildings—any buildings; including palaces, mansions, apartment houses, tenements, cottages, huts, shacks, lean-tos, and tents."

Theremon looked shocked. "You mean they refused to come in out of the open? Where'd they sleep?"

"In the open."

"They should have *forced* them inside."

"Oh, they did, they did. Whereupon these people went into violent hysterics and did their best to bat their brains out against the nearest wall. Once you got them inside, you couldn't keep them there without a strait jacket or a heavy dose of tranquilizer."

"They must have been crazy."

"Which is exactly what they were. One person out of every ten who went into that tunnel came out that way. They called in the psychologists, and we did the only thing possible. We closed down the exhibit." He spread his hands.

"What was the matter with these people?" asked Theremon finally.

"Essentially the same thing that was the matter with you when you thought the walls of the room were crushing in on you in the dark. There is a psychological term for mankind's instinctive fear of the absence of light. We call it 'claustrophobia,' because the lack of light is always tied up with enclosed places, so that fear of one is fear of the other. You see?"

"And those people of the tunnel?"

"Those people of the tunnel consisted of those unfortunates whose mentality did not quite possess the resiliency to overcome the claustrophobia that overtook them in the Darkness. Fifteen minutes without light is a long time; you only had two or three minutes, and I believe you were fairly upset.

"The people of the tunnel had what is called a 'claustrophobic fixation.' Their latent fear of Darkness and enclosed places had crystallized and become active, and, as far as we can tell, permanent. That's what fifteen minutes in the dark will do."

There was a long silence, and Theremon's forehead wrinkled slowly into a frown. "I don't believe it's that bad."

"You mean you don't want to believe," snapped Sheerin. "You're afraid to believe. Look out the window!"

Theremon did so, and the psychologist continued without pausing. "Imagine Darkness—everywhere. No light, as far as you can see. The houses, the trees, the fields, the earth, the sky—black! And Stars thrown in, for all I know—whatever *they* are. Can you conceive it?"

"Yes, I can," declared Theremon truculently.

And Sheerin slammed his fist down upon the table in sudden passion. "You lie! You can't conceive that. Your brain wasn't built for the conception any more than it was built for the conception of infinity or of eternity. You can only talk about it. A fraction of the reality upsets you, and when the real thing comes, your brain is going to be presented with the phenomenon outside its limits of comprehension. You will go mad, completely and permanently! There is no question of it!"

He added sadly, "And another couple of millennia of painful struggle comes to nothing. Tomorrow there won't be a city standing unharmed in all Lagash."

Theremon recovered part of his mental equilibrium. "That doesn't follow. I still don't see that I can go loony just because there isn't a sun in the sky—but even if I did, and everyone else did, how does that harm the cities? Are we going to blow them down?"

But Sheerin was angry, too. "If you were in Darkness, what would you want more than anything else; what would it be that every instinct would call for? Light, damn you, *light!*"

"Well?"

"And how would you get light?"

"I don't know," said Theremon flatly.

"What's the *only* way to get light, short of a sun?"

"How should I know?"

They were standing face to face and nose to nose.

Sheerin said, "You burn something, mister. Ever see a forest fire? Ever go camping and cook a stew over a wood fire? Heat isn't the only thing burning wood gives off, you know. It gives off light, and people know that. And when it's dark they want light, and they're going to *get* it."

"So they burn wood?"

"So they burn whatever they can get. They've got to have light. They've got to burn something, and wood isn't handy—so they'll burn whatever is nearest. They'll have their light—and every center of habitation goes up in flames!"

Eyes held each other as though the whole matter were a personal affair of respective will powers, and then Theremon broke away wordlessly. His breathing was harsh and ragged, and he scarcely noted the sudden hubbub that came from the adjoining room behind the closed door.

Sheerin spoke, and it was with an effort that he made it sound matter-of-fact. "I think I heard Yimot's voice. He and Faro are probably back. Let's go in and see what kept them."

"Might as well!" muttered Theremon. He drew a long breath and seemed to shake himself. The tension was broken.

The room was in an uproar, with members of the staff clustering about two young men who were removing outer garments even as they parried the miscellany of questions being thrown at them.

Aton bustled through the crowd and faced the newcomers angrily. "Do you realize that it's less than half an hour before deadline? Where have you two been?"

Faro 24 seated himself and rubbed his hands. His cheeks were red with the outdoor chill. "Yimot and I have just finished carrying through a little crazy experiment of our own. We've been trying to see if we couldn't construct an arrangement by which we could simulate the appearance of Darkness and Stars so as to get an advance notion as to how it looked."

There was a confused murmur from the listeners, and a sudden look of interest entered Aton's eyes. "There wasn't anything said of this before. How did you go about it?"

"Well," said Faro, "the idea came to Yimot and myself long ago, and we've been working it out in our spare time. Yimot knew of a low one-story house down in the city with a domed roof—it had once been used as a museum, I think. Anyway, we bought it—"

"Where did you get the money?" interrupted Aton peremptorily.

"Our bank accounts," grunted Yimot 70. "It cost two thousand credits." Then, defensively, "Well, what of it? Tomorrow, two thousand credits will be two thousand pieces of paper. That's all."

"Sure," agreed Faro. "We bought the place and rigged it up with black velvet from top to bottom so as to get as perfect a Darkness as possible. Then we punched tiny holes in the ceiling and through the roof and covered them with little metal caps, all of which could be shoved aside simultaneously at the close of a switch. At least we didn't do that part ourselves; we got a carpenter and an electrician and some others—money didn't count. The point was that we could get the light to shine through those holes in the roof, so that we could get a starlike effect."

Not a breath was drawn during the pause that followed. Aton said stiffly, "You had no right to make a private—"

Faro seemed abashed. "I know, sir—but frankly, Yimot and I thought the experiment was a little dangerous. If the effect really worked, we half expected to go mad—from what Sheerin says about all this, we thought that would be rather likely. We wanted to take the risk ourselves. Of course if we found we could retain sanity, it occurred to us that we might develop immunity to the real thing, and then expose the rest of you the same way. But things didn't work out at all—"

"Why, what happened?"

It was Yimot who answered. "We shut ourselves in and allowed our eyes to get accustomed to the dark. It's an extremely creepy feeling because the total Darkness makes you feel as if the walls and ceiling are crushing in on you. But we got over that and pulled the switch. The caps fell away and the roof glittered all over with little dots of light—"

"Well?"

"Well—nothing. That was the whacky part of it. Nothing happened. It was just a roof with holes in it, and that's just what it looked like. We tried it over and over again—that's what kept us so late—but there just isn't any effect at all."

There followed a shocked silence, and all eyes turned to Sheerin, who sat motionless, mouth open.

Theremon was the first to speak. "You know what this does to this whole theory you've built up, Sheerin, don't you?" He was grinning with relief.

But Sheerin raised his hand. "Now wait a while. Just let me think this through." And then he snapped his fingers, and when he lifted his head there was neither surprise nor uncertainty in his eyes. "Of course—"

He never finished. From somewhere up above there sounded a sharp clang, and Beenay, starting to his feet, dashed up the stairs with a "What the devil!"

The rest followed after.

Things happened quickly. Once up in the dome, Beenay cast one horrified glance at the shattered photographic plates and at the man bending over them; and then hurled himself fiercely at the intruder, getting a death grip on his throat. There was a wild threshing, and as others of the staff joined in, the stranger was swallowed up and smothered under the weight of half a dozen angry men.

Aton came up last, breathing heavily. "Let him up!"

There was a reluctant unscrambling and the stranger, panting harshly, with his clothes torn and his forehead bruised, was hauled to his feet. He had a short yellow beard curled elaborately in the style affected by the Cultists.

Beenay shifted his hold to a collar grip and shook the man savagely. "All right, rat, what's the idea? These plates—"

"I wasn't after *them*," retorted the Cultist coldly. "That was an accident."

Beenay followed his glowering stare and snarled, "I see. You were after the cameras themselves. The accident with the plates was a stroke of luck for you, then. If you had touched Snapping Bertha or any of the others, you would have died by slow torture. As it is—" He drew his fist back.

Aton grabbed his sleeve. "Stop that! Let him go!"

The young technician wavered, and his arm dropped reluctantly. Aton pushed him aside and confronted the Cultist. "You're Latimer, aren't you?"

The Cultist bowed stiffly and indicated the symbol upon his hip. "I am Latimer 25, adjutant of the third class to his serenity, Sor 5."

"And"—Aton's white eyebrows lifted—"you were with his serenity when he visited me last week, weren't you?"

Latimer bowed a second time.

"Now, then, what do you want?"

"Nothing that you would give me of your own free will."

"Sor 5 sent you, I suppose—or is this your own idea?"

"I won't answer that question."

"Will there be any further visitors?"

"I won't answer that, either."

Aton glanced at his timepiece and scowled. "Now, man, what is it your master wants of me? I have fulfilled my end of the bargain."

Latimer smiled faintly, but said nothing.

"I asked him," continued Aton angrily, "for data only the Cult could supply, and it was given to me. For that, thank you. In return I promised to prove the essential truth of the creed of the Cult."

"There was no need to prove that," came the proud retort. "It stands proven by the *Book of Revelations.*"

"For the handful that constitute the Cult, yes. Don't pretend to mistake my meaning. I offered to present scientific backing for your beliefs. And I did!"

The Cultist's eyes narrowed bitterly. "Yes, you did—with a fox's subtlety, for your pretended explanation backed our beliefs, and at the same time removed all necessity for them. You made of the Darkness and of the Stars a natural phenomenon and removed all its real significance. That was blasphemy."

"If so, the fault isn't mine. The facts exist. What can I do but state them?"

"Your 'facts' are a fraud and a delusion."

Aton stamped angrily. "How do you know?"

And the answer came with the certainty of absolute faith. "I know!"

The director purpled and Beenay whispered urgently. Aton waved him silent. "And what does Sor 5 want us to do? He still thinks, I suppose, that in trying to warn the world to take measures against the menace of madness, we are placing innumerable souls in jeopardy. We aren't succeeding, if that means anything to him."

"The attempt itself has done harm enough, and your vicious effort to gain information by means of your devilish instruments must be stopped. We obey the will of the Stars, and I only regret that my clumsiness prevented me from wrecking your infernal devices."

"It wouldn't have done you too much good," returned Aton. "All our data, except for the direct evidence we intend collecting right now, is already safely cached and well beyond possibility of harm." He smiled grimly. "But that does not affect your present status as an attempted burglar and criminal."

He turned to the men behind him. "Someone call the police at Saro City."

There was a cry of distaste from Sheerin. "Damn it, Aton, what's wrong with you? There's no time for that. Here"—he bustled his way forward—"let me handle this."

Aton stared down his nose at the psychologist. "This is not the time for your monkeyshines, Sheerin. Will you please let me handle this my own way? Right now you are a complete outsider here, and don't forget it."

Sheerin's mouth twisted eloquently. "Now why should we go to the impossible trouble of calling the police—with Beta's eclipse a matter of minutes from now—when this young man here is perfectly willing to pledge his word of honor to remain and cause no trouble whatsoever?"

The Cultist answered promptly, "I will do no such thing. You're free to do what you want, but it's only fair to warn you that just as soon as I get my chance I'm going to finish what I came out here to do. If it's my word of honor you're relying on, you'd better call the police."

Sheerin smiled in a friendly fashion. "You're a determined cuss, aren't you? Well, I'll explain something. Do you see that young man at the window? He's a strong, husky fellow, quite handy with his fists, and he's an outsider besides. Once the eclipse starts there will be nothing for him to do except keep an eye on you. Besides him, there will be myself—a little too stout for active fisticuffs, but still able to help."

"Well, what of it?" demanded Latimer frozenly.

"Listen and I'll tell you," was the reply. "Just as soon as the eclipse starts, we're going to take you, Theremon and I, and deposit you in a little closet with one door, to which is attached one giant lock and no windows. You will remain there for the duration."

"And afterward," breathed Latimer fiercely, "there'll be no one to let me out. I know as well as you do what the coming of the Stars mean—I know it far better than you. With all your minds gone, you are not likely to free me. Suffocation or slow starvation, is it? About what I might have expected from a group of scientists. But I don't give my word. It's a matter of principle, and I won't discuss it further."

Aton seemed perturbed. His faded eyes were troubled. "Really, Sheerin, locking him—"

"Please!" Sheerin motioned him impatiently to silence. "I don't think for a moment things will go that far. Latimer has just tried a clever little bluff, but I'm not a psychologist just because I like the sound of the word." He grinned at the Cultist. "Come now, you don't really think I'm trying anything as crude as slow starvation. My dear Latimer, if I lock you in the closet, you are not going to see the Darkness, and you are not going to see the Stars. It does not take much knowledge of the fundamental creed of the Cult to realize that for you to be hidden from the Stars when they appear means the loss of your immortal soul. Now, I believe you to be an honorable man. I'll accept your word of honor to make no further effort to disrupt proceedings, if you'll offer it."

A vein throbbed in Latimer's temple, and he seemed to shrink within himself as he said thickly, "You have it!" And then he added with swift fury, "But it is my consolation that you will all be damned for your deeds of today." He turned on his heel and stalked to the high three-legged stool by the door.

Sheerin nodded to the columnist. "Take a seat next to him, Theremon—just as a formality. Hey, Theremon!"

But the newspaperman didn't move. He had gone pale to the lips. "Look at that!" The finger he pointed toward the sky shook, and his voice was dry and cracked.

There was one simultaneous gasp as every eye followed the pointing finger and, for one breathless moment, stared frozenly.

Beta was chipped on one side!

The tiny bit of encroaching blackness was perhaps the width of a fingernail, but to the staring watchers it magnified itself into the crack of doom.

Only for a moment they watched, and after that there was a shrieking confusion that was even shorter of duration and which gave way to an orderly scurry of activity—each man at his prescribed job. At the crucial moment there was no time for emotion. The men were merely scientists with work to do. Even Aton had melted away.

Sheerin said prosaically, "First contact must have been made fifteen minutes ago. A little early, but pretty good considering the uncertainties involved in the calculation." He looked about him and then tiptoed to Theremon, who still remained staring out the window, and dragged him away gently.

"Aton is furious," he whispered, "so stay away. He missed first contact on account of this fuss with Latimer, and if you get in his way he'll have you thrown out the window."

Theremon nodded shortly and sat down. Sheerin stared in surprise at him.

"The devil, man," he exclaimed, "you're shaking."

"Eh?" Theremon licked dry lips and then tried to smile. "I don't feel very well, and that's a fact."

The psychologist's eyes hardened. "You're not losing your nerve?"

"No!" cried Theremon in a flash of indignation. "Give me a chance, will you? I haven't really believed this rigmarole—not way down beneath, anyway—till just this minute. Give me a chance to get used to the idea. You've been preparing yourself for two months or more."

"You're right, at that," replied Sheerin thoughtfully. "Listen! Have you got a family—parents, wife, children?"

Theremon shook his head. "You mean the Hideout, I suppose. No, you don't have to worry about that. I have a sister, but she's two thousand miles away. I don't even know her exact address."

"Well, then, what about yourself? You've got time to get there, and they're one short anyway, since I left. After all, you're not needed here, and you'd make a darned fine addition—"

Theremon looked at the other wearily. "You think I'm scared stiff, don't you? Well, get this, mister, I'm a newspaperman and I've been assigned to cover a story. I intend covering it."

There was a faint smile on the psychologist's face. "I see. Professional honor, is that it?"

"You might call it that. But, man, I'd give my right arm for another bottle of that sockeroo juice even half the size of the one you hogged. If ever a fellow needed a drink, I do."

He broke off. Sheerin was nudging him violently. "Do you hear that? Listen!"

Therermon followed the motion of the other's chin and stared at the Cultist, who, oblivious to all about him, faced the window, a look of wild elation on his face, droning to himself the while in singsong fashion.

"What's he saying?" whispered the columnist.

"He's quoting *Book of Revelations*, fifth chapter," replied Sheerin. Then, urgently, "Keep quiet and listen, I tell you."

The Cultist's voice had risen in a sudden increase of fervor: "'And it came to pass that in those days the Sun, Beta, held lone vigil in the sky for ever longer periods as the revolutions passed; until such time as for full half a revolution, it alone, shrunken and cold, shone down upon Lagash.

"'And men did assemble in the public squares and in the highways, there to debate and to marvel at the sight, for a strange depression had seized them. Their minds were troubled and their speech confused, for the souls of men awaited the coming of the Stars.

"'And in the city of Trigon, at high noon, Vendret 2 came forth and said unto the men of Trigon, "Lo, ye sinners! Though ye scorn the ways of righteousness, yet will the time of reckoning come. Even now the Cave approaches to swallow Lagash; yea, and all it contains."

"'And even as he spoke the lip of the Cave of Darkness passed the edge of Beta so that to all Lagash it was hidden from sight. Loud were the cries of men as it vanished, and great the fear of soul that fell upon them.

"'It came to pass that the Darkness of the Cave fell upon Lagash, and there was no light on all the surface of Lagash. Men were even as blinded, nor could one man see his neighbor, though he felt his breath upon his face.

"'And in this blackness there appeared the Stars, in countless numbers, and to the strains of music of such beauty that the very leaves of the trees cried out in wonder.

"'And in that moment the souls of men departed from them, and their abandoned bodies became even as beasts; yea, even as brutes of the wild; so that through the blackened streets of the cities of Lagash they prowled with wild cries.

"'From the Stars there then reached down the Heavenly Flame, and where it touched, the cities of Lagash flamed to utter destruction, so that of man and of the works of man nought remained.

"'Even then—'"

There was a subtle change in Latimer's tone. His eyes had not shifted, but somehow he had become aware of the absorbed attention of the other two. Easily, without pausing for breath, the timbre of his voice shifted and the syllables became more liquid.

Theremon, caught by surprise, stared. The words seemed on the border of familiarity. There was an elusive shift in the accent, a tiny change in the vowel stress; nothing more—yet Latimer had become thoroughly unintelligible.

Sheerin smiled slyly. "He shifted to some old-cycle tongue, probably their traditional second cycle. That was the language in which the *Book of Revelations* was originally written, you know."

"It doesn't matter; I've heard enough." Theremon shoved his chair back and brushed his hair back with hands that no longer shook. "I feel much better now."

"You do?" Sheerin seemed mildly surprised.

"I'll say I do. I had a bad case of jitters just a while back. Listening to you and your gravitation and seeing that eclipse start almost finished me. But this"—he jerked a contemptuous thumb at the yellow-bearded Cultist—"*this* is the sort of thing my nurse used to tell me. I've been laughing at that sort of thing all my life. I'm not going to let it scare me *now*."

He drew a deep breath and said with a hectic gaiety, "But if I expect to keep on the good side of myself, I'm going to turn my chair away from the window."

Sheerin said, "Yes, but you'd better talk lower. Aton just lifted his head out of that box he's got it stuck into and gave you a look that should have killed you."

Theremon made a mouth. "I forgot about the old fellow." With elaborate care he turned the chair from the window, cast one distasteful look over his shoulder, and said, "It has occurred to me that there must be considerable immunity against this Star madness."

The psychologist did not answer immediately. Beta was past its zenith now, and the square of bloody sunlight that outlined the window upon the floor had lifted into Sheerin's lap. He stared at its dusky color thoughtfully and then bent and squinted into the sun itself.

The chip in its side had grown to a black encroachment that covered a third of Beta. He shuddered, and when he straightened once more his florid cheeks did not contain quite as much color as they had had previously.

With a smile that was almost apologetic, he reversed his chair also. "There are probably two million people in Saro City that are all trying to join the Cult at once in one gigantic revival." Then, ironically, "The Cult is in for an hour of unexampled prosperity. I trust they'll make the most of it. Now, what was it you said?"

"Just this. How did the Cultists manage to keep the *Book of Revelations* going from cycle to cycle, and how on Lagash did it get written in the first place? There must have been some sort of immunity, for if everyone had gone mad, who would be left to write the book?"

Sheerin stared at his questioner ruefully. "Well, now, young man, there isn't any eyewitness answer to that, but we've got a few damned good notions as to what happened. You see, there are three kinds of people who might remain relatively unaffected. First, the very few who don't see the Stars at all: the seriously retarded or those who drink themselves into a stupor at the beginning of the eclipse and remain so to the end. We leave them out—because they aren't really witnesses.

"Then there are children below six, to whom the world as a whole is too new and strange for them to be too frightened at Stars and Darkness. They would be just another item in an already surprising world. You see that, don't you?"

The other nodded doubtfully. "I suppose so."

"Lastly, there are those whose minds are too coarsely grained to be entirely toppled. The very insensitive would be scarcely affected—oh, such people as some of our older, work-broken peasants. Well, the children would have fugitive memories, and that, combined with the confused, incoherent babblings of the half-mad morons, formed the basis for the *Book of Revelations.*

"Naturally, the book was based, in the first place, on the testimony of those least qualified to serve as historians; that is, children and morons; and was probably edited and re-edited through the cycles."

"Do you suppose," broke in Theremon, "that they carried the book through the cycles the way we're planning on handing on the secret of gravitation?"

Sheerin shrugged. "Perhaps, but their exact method is unimportant. They do it, somehow. The point I was getting at was that the book can't help but be a mass of distortion, even if it is based on fact. For instance, do you remember the experiment with the holes in the roof that Faro and Yimot tried—the one that didn't work?"

"Yes."

"You know why it didn't w—" He stopped and rose in alarm, for Aton was approaching, his face a twisted mask of consternation. *"What's happened?"*

Aton drew him aside and Sheerin could feel the fingers on his elbow twitching.

"Not so loud!" Aton's voice was low and tortured. "I've just gotten word from the Hideout on the private line."

Sheerin broke in anxiously. "They are in trouble?"

"Not *they.*" Aton stressed the pronoun significantly. "They sealed themselves off just a while ago, and they're going to stay buried till day after tomorrow. They're safe. But the *city,* Sheerin—it's a shambles. You have no idea—" He was having difficulty in speaking.

"Well?" snapped Sheerin impatiently. "What of it? It will get worse. What are you shaking about?" Then, suspiciously, "How do you feel?"

Aton's eyes sparked angrily at the insinuation, and then faded to anxiety once more. "You don't understand. The Cultists are active. They're rousing the people to storm the Observatory—promising them immediate entrance into grace, promising them salvation, promising them anything. What are we to do, Sheerin?"

Sheerin's head bent, and he stared in long abstraction at his toes. He tapped his chin with one knuckle, then looked up and said crisply, "Do? What is there to do? Nothing at all. Do the men know of this?"

"No, of course not!"

"Good! Keep it that way. How long till totality?"

"Not quite an hour."

"There's nothing to do but gamble. It will take time to organize any really formidable mob, and it will take more time to get them out here. We're a good five miles from the city—"

He glared out the window, down the slopes to where the farmed patches gave way to clumps of white houses in the suburbs; down to where the metropolis itself was a blur on the horizon—a mist in the waning blaze of Beta.

He repeated without turning, "It will take time. Keep on working and pray that totality comes first."

Beta was cut in half, the line of division pushing a slight concavity into the still-bright portion of the Sun. It was like a gigantic eyelid shutting slantwise over the light of a world.

The faint clatter of the room in which he stood faded into oblivion, and he sensed only the thick silence of the fields outside. The very insects seemed frightened mute. And things were dim.

He jumped at the voice in his ear. Theremon said, "Is something wrong?"

"Eh? Er—no. Get back to the chair. We're in the way." They slipped back to their corner, but the psychologist did not speak for a time. He lifted a finger and loosened his collar. He twisted his neck back and forth but found no relief. He looked up suddenly.

"Are you having any difficulty in breathing?"

The newspaperman opened his eyes wide and drew two or three long breaths. "No. Why?"

"I looked out the window too long, I suppose. The dimness got me. Difficulty in breathing is one of the first symptoms of a claustrophobic attack."

Theremon drew another long breath. "Well, it hasn't got me yet. Say, here's another of the fellows."

Beenay had interposed his bulk between the light and the pair in the corner, and Sheerin squinted up at him anxiously. "Hello, Beenay."

The astronomer shifted his weight to the other foot and smiled feebly. "You won't mind if I sit down awhile and join in the talk? My cameras are set, and there's nothing to do till totality." He paused and eyed the Cultist, who fifteen minutes earlier had drawn a small, skin-bound book from his sleeve and had been poring intently over it ever since. "That rat hasn't been making trouble, has he?"

Sheerin shook his head. His shoulders were thrown back and he frowned his concentration as he forced himself to breathe regularly. He said, "Have you had any trouble breathing, Beenay?"

Beenay sniffed the air in his turn. "It doesn't seem stuffy to me."

"A touch of claustrophobia," explained Sheerin apologetically.

"Ohhh! It worked itself differently with me. I get the impression that my eyes are going back on me. Things seem to blur and—well, nothing is clear. And it's cold, too."

"Oh, it's cold, all right. That's no illusion." Theremon grimaced. "My toes feel as if I've been shipping them cross-country in a refrigerating car."

"What we need," put in Sheerin, "is to keep our minds busy with extraneous affairs. I was telling you a while ago, Theremon, why Faro's experiments with the holes in the roof came to nothing."

"You were just beginning," replied Theremon. He encircled a knee with both arms and nuzzled his chin against it.

"Well, as I started to say, they were misled by taking the *Book of Revelations* literally. There probably wasn't any sense in attaching any physical significance to the Stars. It might be, you know, that in the presence of total Darkness, the mind finds it absolutely necessary to create light. This illusion of light might be all the Stars there really are."

"In other words," interposed Theremon, "you mean the Stars are the results of the madness and not one of the causes. Then, what good will Beenay's photographs be?"

"To prove that it is an illusion, maybe; or to prove the opposite; for all I know. Then again—"

But Beenay had drawn his chair closer, and there was an expression of sudden enthusiasm on his face. "Say, I'm glad you two got onto this subject." His eyes narrowed and he lifted one finger. "I've been thinking about these Stars and I've got a really cute notion. Of course it's strictly ocean foam, and I'm not trying to advance it seriously, but I think it's interesting. Do you want to hear it?"

He seemed half reluctant, but Sheerin leaned back and said, "Go ahead! I'm listening."

"Well, then, supposing there were other suns in the universe." He broke off a little bashfully. "I mean suns that are so far away that they're too dim to see. It sounds as if I've been reading some of that fantastic fiction, I suppose."

"Not necessarily. Still, isn't that possibility eliminated by the fact that, according to the Law of Gravitation, they would make themselves evident by their attractive forces?"

"Not if they were far enough off," rejoined Beenay, "really far off—maybe as much as four light years, or even more. We'd never be able to detect perturbations then, because they'd be too small. Say that there were a lot of suns that far off; a dozen or two, maybe."

Theremon whistled melodiously. "What an idea for a good Sunday supplement article. Two dozen suns in a universe eight light years across. Wow! That would shrink our world into insignificance. The readers would eat it up."

"Only an idea," said Beenay with a grin, "but you see the point. During an eclipse, these dozen suns would become visible because there'd be no *real* sunlight to drown them out. Since they're so far off, they'd appear small, like so many little marbles. Of course the Cultists talk of millions of Stars, but that's probably exaggeration. There just isn't any place in the universe you could put a million Suns—unless they touch one another."

Sheerin had listened with gradually increasing interest. "You've hit something there, Beenay. And exaggeration is just exactly what would happen. Our minds, as you probably know, can't grasp directly any number higher than five; above that there is only the concept of 'many.' A dozen would become a million just like that. A damn good idea!"

"And I've got another cute little notion," Beenay said. "Have you ever thought what a simple problem gravitation would be if only you had a sufficiently simple system? Supposing you had a universe in which there was a planet with only one sun. The planet would travel in a perfect ellipse and the exact nature of the gravitational force would be so evident it could be accepted as an axiom. Astronomers on such a world would start off with gravity probably before they even invented the telescope. Naked-eye observation would be enough."

"But would such a system be dynamically stable?" questioned Sheerin doubtfully.

"Sure! They call it the 'one-and-one' case. It's been worked out mathematically, but it's the philosophical implications that interest me."

"It's nice to think about," admitted Sheerin, "as a pretty abstraction— like a perfect gas, or absolute zero."

"Of course," continued Beenay, "there's the catch that life would be impossible on such a planet. It wouldn't get enough heat and light, and if it rotated there would be total Darkness half of each day. You couldn't expect life—which is fundamentally dependent upon light— to develop under those conditions. Besides—"

Sheerin's chair went over backward as he sprang to his feet in a rude interruption. "Aton's brought out the lights."

Beenay said, "Huh," turned to stare, and then grinned halfway around his head in open relief.

There were half a dozen foot-long, inch-thick rods cradled in Aton's arms. He glared over them at the assembled staff members.

"Get back to work, all of you. Sheerin, come here and help me!"

Sheerin trotted to the older man's side and, one by one, in utter silence, the two adjusted the rods in makeshift metal holders suspended from the walls.

With the air of one carrying through the most sacred item of a religious ritual, Sheerin scraped a large, clumsy match into spluttering life and passed it to Aton, who carried the flame to the upper end of one of the rods.

It hesitated there awhile, playing futilely about the tip, until a sudden, crackling flare cast Aton's lined face into yellow highlights. He withdrew the match and a spontaneous cheer rattled the window.

The rod was topped by six inches of wavering flame! Methodically, the other rods were lighted, until six independent fires turned the rear of the room yellow.

The light was dim, dimmer even than the tenuous sunlight. The flames reeled crazily, giving birth to drunken, swaying shadows. The torches smoked devilishly and smelled like a bad day in the kitchen. But they emitted yellow light.

43

There was something about yellow light, after four hours of somber, dimming Beta. Even Latimer had lifted his eyes from his book and stared in wonder.

Sheerin warmed his hands at the nearest, regardless of the soot that gathered upon them in a fine, gray powder, and muttered ecstatically to himself. "Beautiful! Beautiful! I never realized before what a wonderful color yellow is."

But Theremon regarded the torches suspiciously. He wrinkled his nose at the rancid odor and said, "What are those things?"

"Wood," said Sheerin shortly.

"Oh, no, they're not. They aren't burning. The top inch is charred and the flame just keeps shooting up out of nothing."

"That's the beauty of it. This is a really efficient artificial-light mechanism. We made a few hundred of them, but most went to the Hideout, of course. You see" —he turned and wiped his blackened hands upon his handkerchief—"you take the pithy core of coarse water reeds, dry them thoroughly, and soak them in animal grease. Then you set fire to it and the grease burns, little by little. These torches will burn for almost half an hour without stopping. Ingenious, isn't it? It was developed by one of our own young men at Saro University."

After the momentary sensation, the dome had quieted. Latimer had carried his chair directly beneath a torch and continued reading, lips moving in the monotonous recital of invocations to the Stars. Beenay had drifted away to his cameras once more, and Theremon seized the opportunity to add to his notes on the article he was going to write for the Saro City *Chronicle* the next day—a procedure he had been following for the last two hours in a perfectly methodical, perfectly conscientious and, as he was well aware, perfectly meaningless fashion.

But, as the gleam of amusement in Sheerin's eyes indicated, careful note-taking occupied his mind with something other than the fact that the sky was gradually turning a horrible deep purple-red, as if it were one gigantic, freshly peeled beet; and so it fulfilled its purpose.

The air grew, somehow, denser. Dusk, like a palpable entity, entered the room, and the dancing circle of yellow light about the torches etched itself into ever-sharper distinction against the gathering grayness beyond. There was the odor of smoke and the presence of little chuckling sounds that the torches made as they burned; the soft pad of one of the men circling the table at which he worked, on hesitant tiptoes; the occasional indrawn breath of someone trying to retain composure in a world that was retreating into the shadow.

It was Theremon who first heard the extraneous noise. It was a vague, unorganized *impression* of sound that would have gone unnoticed but for the dead silence that prevailed within the dome.

The newsman sat upright and replaced his notebook. He held his breath and listened; then, with considerable reluctance, threaded his way between the solarscope and one of Beenay's cameras and stood before the window.

The silence ripped to fragments at his startled shout: *"Sheerin!"*

Work stopped! The psychologist was at his side in a moment. Aton joined him. Even Yimot 70, high in his little lean-back seat at the eyepiece of the gigantic solarscope, paused and looked downward.

Outside, Beta was a mere smoldering splinter, taking one last desperate look at Lagash. The eastern horizon, in the direction of the city, was lost in Darkness, and the road from Saro to the Observatory was a dull-red line bordered on both sides by wooded tracts, the trees of which had somehow lost individuality and merged into a continuous shadowy mass.

But it was the highway itself that held attention, for along it there surged another, and infinitely menacing, shadowy mass.

Aton cried in a cracked voice, "The madmen from the city! They've come!"

"How long to totality?" demanded Sheerin.

"Fifteen minutes, but . . . but they'll be here in five."

"Never mind, keep the men working. We'll hold them off. This place is built like a fortress. Aton, keep an eye on our young Cultist just for luck. Theremon, come with me."

Sheerin was out the door, and Theremon was at his heels. The stairs stretched below them in tight, circular sweeps about the central shaft, fading into a dank and dreary grayness.

The first momentum of their rush had carried them fifty feet down, so that the dim, flickering yellow from the open door of the dome had disappeared and both above and below the same dusky shadow crushed in upon them.

Sheerin paused, and his pudgy hand clutched at his chest. His eyes bulged and his voice was a dry cough. "I can't . . . breathe . . . Go down . . . yourself. Close all doors—"

Theremon took a few downward steps, then turned. "Wait! Can you hold out a minute?" He was panting himself. The air passed in and out his lungs like so much molasses, and there was a little germ of screeching panic in his mind at the thought of making his way into the mysterious Darkness below by himself.

Theremon, after all, was afraid of the dark!

"Stay here," he said. "I'll be back in a second." He dashed upward two steps at a time, heart pounding—not altogether from the exertion—tumbled into the dome and snatched a torch from its holder. It was foul-smelling, and the smoke smarted his eyes almost blind, but he clutched that torch as if he wanted to kiss it for joy, and its flame streamed backward as he hurtled down the stairs again.

Sheerin opened his eyes and moaned as Theremon bent over him. Theremon shook him roughly. "All right, get a hold on yourself. We've got light."

He held the torch at tiptoe height and, propping the tottering psychologist by an elbow, made his way downward in the middle of the protecting circle of illumination.

The offices on the ground floor still possessed what light there was, and Theremon felt the horror about him relax.

"Here," he said brusquely, and passed the torch to Sheerin. "You can hear *them* outside."

And they could. Little scraps of hoarse, wordless shouts.

But Sheerin was right; the Observatory was built like a fortress. Erected in the last century, when the neo-Gavottian style of architecture was at its ugly height, it had been designed for stability and durability rather than for beauty.

The windows were protected by the grillwork of inch-thick iron bars sunk deep into the concrete sills. The walls were solid masonry that an earthquake couldn't have touched, and the main door was a huge oaken slab reinforced with iron. Theremon shot the bolts and they slid shut with a dull clang.

At the other end of the corridor, Sheerin cursed weakly. He pointed to the lock of the back door which had been neatly jimmied into uselessness.

"That must be how Latimer got in," he said.

"Well, don't stand there," cried Theremon impatiently. "Help drag up the furniture—and keep that torch out of my eyes. The smoke's killing me."

He slammed the heavy table up against the door as he spoke, and in two minutes had built a barricade which made up for what it lacked in beauty and symmetry by the sheer inertia of its massiveness.

Somewhere, dimly, far off, they could hear the battering of naked fists upon the door; and the screams and yells from outside had a sort of half reality.

That mob had set off from Saro City with only two things in mind: the attainment of Cultist salvation by the destruction of the Observatory, and a maddening fear that all but paralyzed them. There was no time to think of ground cars, or of weapons, or of leadership, or even of organization. They made for the Observatory on foot and assaulted it with bare hands.

And now that they were there, the last flash of Beta, the last ruby–red drop of flame, flickered feebly over a humanity that had left only stark, universal fear!

Theremon groaned, "Let's get back to the dome!"

In the dome, only Yimot, at the solarscope, had kept his place. The rest were clustered about the cameras, and Beenay was giving his instructions in a hoarse, strained voice.

"Get it straight, all of you. I'm snapping Beta just before totality and changing the plate. That will leave one of you to each camera. You all know about . . . about times of exposure—"

There was a breathless murmur of agreement.

Beenay passed a hand over his eyes. "Are the torches still burning? Never mind, I see them!" He was leaning hard against the back of a chair. "Now remember, don't . . . don't try to look for good shots. Don't waste time trying to get t-two stars at a time in the scope field. One is enough. And . . . and if you feel yourself going, *get away from the camera.*"

At the door, Sheerin whispered to Theremon, "Take me to Aton. I don't see him."

The newsman did not answer immediately. The vague forms of the astronomers wavered and blurred, and the torches overhead had become only yellow splotches.

"It's dark," he whimpered.

Sheerin held out his hand. "Aton." He stumbled forward. "Aton!"

Theremon stepped after and seized his arm. "Wait, I'll take you." Somehow he made his way across the room. He closed his eyes against the Darkness and his mind against the chaos within it.

No one heard them or paid attention to them. Sheerin stumbled against the wall. "Aton!"

The psychologist felt shaking hands touching him, then withdrawing, and a voice muttering, "Is that you, Sheerin?"

"Aton!" He strove to breathe normally. "Don't worry about the mob. The place will hold them off."

Latimer, the Cultist, rose to his feet, and his face twisted in desperation. His word was pledged, and to break it would mean placing his soul in mortal peril. Yet that word had been forced from him and had not been given freely. The Stars would come soon! He could not stand by and allow— And yet his word was pledged.

Beenay's face was dimly flushed as it looked upward at Beta's last ray, and Latimer, seeing him bend over his camera, made his decision. His nails cut the flesh of his palms as he tensed himself.

He staggered crazily as he started his rush. There was nothing before him but shadows; the very floor beneath his feet lacked substance. And then someone was upon him and he went down with clutching fingers at his throat.

He doubled his knee and drove it hard into his assailant. "Let me up or I'll kill you."

Theremon cried out sharply and muttered through a blinding haze of pain. "You double-crossing rat!"

The newsman seemed conscious of everything at once. He heard Beenay croak, "I've got it. At your cameras, men!" and then there was the strange awareness that the last thread of sunlight had thinned out and snapped.

Simultaneously he heard one last choking gasp from Beenay, and a queer little cry from Sheerin, a hysterical giggle that cut off in a rasp—and a sudden silence, a strange, deadly silence from outside.

And Latimer had gone limp in his loosening grasp. Theremon peered into the Cultist's eyes and saw the blankness of them, staring upward, mirroring the feeble yellow of the torches. He saw the bubble of froth upon Latimer's lips and heard the low animal whimper in Latimer's throat.

With the slow fascination of fear, he lifted himself on one arm and turned his eyes toward the blood-curdling blackness of the window.

Through it shone the Stars!

Not Earth's feeble thirty-six hundred Stars visible to the eye; Lagash was in the center of a giant cluster. Thirty thousand mighty suns shone down in a soul-searing splendor that was more frighteningly cold in its awful indifference than the bitter wind that shivered across the cold, horribly bleak world.

Theremon staggered to his feet, his throat constricting him to breathlessness, all the muscles of his body writhing in an intensity of terror and sheer fear beyond bearing. He was going mad and knew it, and somewhere deep inside a bit of sanity was screaming, struggling to fight off the hopeless flood of black terror. It was very horrible to go mad and know that you were going mad—to know that in a little minute you would be here physically and yet all the real essence would be dead and drowned in the black madness. For this was the Dark—the Dark and the Cold and the Doom. The bright walls of the universe were shattered and their awful black fragments were falling down to crush and squeeze and obliterate him.

He jostled someone crawling on hands and knees, but stumbled somehow over him. Hands groping at his tortured throat, he limped toward the flame of the torches that filled all his mad vision.

"Light!" he screamed.

Aton, somewhere, was crying, whimpering horribly like a terribly frightened child. "Stars—all the Stars—we didn't know at all. We didn't know anything. We thought six stars in a universe is something the Stars didn't notice is Darkness forever and ever and ever and the walls are breaking in and we didn't know we couldn't know and anything—"

Someone clawed at the torch, and it fell and snuffed out. In the instant, the awful splendor of the indifferent Stars leaped nearer to them.

On the horizon outside the window, in the direction of Saro City, a crimson glow began growing, strengthening in brightness, that was not the glow of a sun.

The long night had come again.

Loulou; or, the Domestic Life of the Language
(1983)

MARGARET ATWOOD

Loulou is in the coach-house, wedging clay. She's wearing a pair of running shoes, once white, now grey, over men's wool work socks, a purple Indian-print cotton skirt, and a rust-coloured smock, so heavy with clay dust it hangs on her like brocade, the sleeves rolled up past the elbow. This is her favourite working outfit. To the music of *The Magic Flute,* brought to her by CBC stereo, she lifts the slab of clay and slams it down, gives a half-turn, lifts and slams. This is to get the air bubbles out, so nothing will explode in the kiln. Some potters would hire an apprentice to do this, but not Loulou.

It's true she has apprentices, two of them; she gets them through the government as free trainees. But they make plates and mugs from her designs, about all they're fit for. She doesn't consider them suitable for wedging clay, with their puny little biceps and match-stick wrists, so poorly developed compared with her own solid, smoothly muscled arms and broad, capable but shapely hands, so often admired by the poets. *Marmoreal,* one of them said—wrote, actually—causing Loulou to make one of her frequent sorties into the dictionary, to find out whether or not she'd been insulted.

Once she had done this openly, whenever they'd used a word about her she didn't understand, but when they'd discovered she was doing it they'd found it amusing and had started using words like that on purpose. "Loulou is so geomorphic," one of them would say, and when she would blush and scowl, another would take it up. "Not only that, she's fundamentally chthonic." "Telluric," a third would pipe up. Then they would laugh. She's decided that the only thing to do is to ignore them. But she's not so dumb as they think, she remembers the words, and when they aren't watching she sneaks a look at the Shorter Oxford (kept in the study which really belongs to only one of them but which she thinks of as *theirs*), washing her hands first so she won't leave any tell-tale signs of clay on the page.

She reads their journals, too, taking the same precautions. She suspects they know she does this. It's her way of keeping up with what they are really thinking about her, or maybe only with what they want her to think they're thinking. The journals are supposed to be secret, but Loulou considers it her right and also a kind of duty to read them. She views it in the same light as her mother viewed going through the family's sock and underwear drawers, to sort out the clean things from the ones they'd already worn and stuffed back in. This is what the poets' journals are like. Socks, mostly, but you never know what you will find.

"Loulou is becoming more metonymous," she's read recently. This has been bothering her for days. Sometimes she longs to say to them, "Now just what in hell did you mean by that?" But she knows she would get nowhere.

"Loulou is the foe of abstract order," one would say. This is a favourite belief of theirs.

"Loulou is the foe of abstract ordure."

"Loulou is the Great Goddess."

"Loulou is the great mattress."

It would end up with Loulou telling them to piss off. When that didn't stop them, she would tell them they couldn't have any more baked chicken if they went on like that. Threatening to deprive them of food usually works.

Overtly, Loulou takes care to express scorn for the poets; though not for them, exactly–they have their points–but for their pickiness about words. Her mother would have said they were finicky eaters. "Who cares what a thing's called?" she says to them. "A piece of bread is a piece of bread. You want some or not?" And she bends over to slide three of her famous loaves, high and nicely browned, out of the oven, and the poets admire her ass and haunches. Sometimes they do this openly, like other men, growling and smacking their lips, pretending to be construction workers. They like pretending to be other things; in the summers they play baseball games together and make a big fuss about having the right hats. Sometimes, though, they do it silently, and Loulou only knows about it from the poems they write afterwards. Loulou can tell these poems are about her, even though the nouns change: "my lady," "my friend's lady," "my woman," "my friend's woman" "my wife," "my friend's wife," and, when necessary for the length of the line, "the wife of my friend." Never "girl" though, and never her name. *Ass* and *haunches* aren't Loulou's words either; she would say *butt*.

Loulou doesn't know anything about music but she likes listening to it. Right now, the Queen of the Night runs up her trill, and Loulou pauses to see if she'll make it to the top. She does, just barely, and Loulou, feeling vicarious triumph, rams her fist into the mound of clay. Then she covers it with a sheet of plastic and goes to the sink to wash her hands. Soon the oven timer will go off and one of the poets, maybe her husband but you never know, will call her on the intercom to come and see about the bread. It isn't that they wouldn't take it out themselves, if she asked them to. Among the four or five of them they'd likely manage. It's just that Loulou doesn't trust them. She decided long ago that none of them knows his left tit from a hole in the ground when it comes to the real world. If she wants the bread taken out when it's done but not overdone, and she does, she'll have to do it herself.

She wonders who will be in the kitchen at the main house by now: her first husband for sure, and the man she lived with after that for three years without being married, and her second husband, the one she has now, and two ex-lovers. Half a dozen of them maybe, sitting around the kitchen table, drinking her coffee and eating her hermit cookies and talking about whatever they talk about when she isn't there. In the past there have been periods of strain among them, especially during the times when Loulou has been switching over, but they're all getting along well enough now. They run a collective poetry magazine, which keeps them out of trouble mostly. The name of this magazine is *Comma*, but among themselves the poets refer to it as *Coma*. At parties they enjoy going up to young female would-be poets ("proupies," they call them behind their backs, which means "poetry groupies"), and saying, "I'd like to put you in a *Coma*." A while ago *Comma* published mostly poems without commas, but this is going out now, just as beards are going out in favour of moustaches and even shaving. The more daring poets have gone so far as to cut off their sideburns. Loulou is not quite sure whether or not she approves of this.

She doesn't know whether the poets are good poets, whether the poems they write in such profusion are any good. Loulou has no opinion on this subject: all that matters is what they are writing about her. Their poems get published in books, but what does that mean? Not money, that's for sure. You don't make any money with poetry, the poets tell her, unless you sing and play the guitar too. Sometimes they give readings and make a couple of hundred bucks. For Loulou that's three medium-sized casseroles with lids. On the other hand, they don't have her expenses. Part of her expenses is them.

Loulou can't remember exactly how she got mixed up with the poets. It wasn't that she had any special thing for poets as such: it just happened that way. After the first one, the others seemed to follow along naturally, almost as if they were tied onto each other in a long line with a piece of string. They were always around, and she was so busy most of the time that she didn't go out much to look for other kinds of men. Now that her business is doing so well you'd think she would have more leisure time, but this isn't the case. And any leisure time she does have, she spends with the poets. They're always nagging her about working too hard.

Bob was the first one, and also her first husband. He was in art school at the same time she was, until he decided he wasn't suited for it. He wasn't practical enough, he let things dry out: paint, clay, even the left-overs in his tiny refrigerator, as Loulou discovered the first night she'd slept with him. She devoted the next morning to cleaning up his kitchen, getting rid of the saucers of mummified cooked peas and the shrivelled, half-gnawed chicken legs and the warped, cracked quarter-packages of two-month-old sliced bacon, and the bits of cheese, oily on the outside and hard as tiles. Loulou has always hated clutter, which she defines, though not in so many words, as matter out of its proper place. Bob looked on, sullen but appreciative, as she hurled and scoured. Possibly this was why he decided to love her: because she would do this sort of thing. What he said though was, "You complete me."

What he also said was that he'd fallen in love with her name. All the poets have done this, one after the other. The first symptom is that they ask her whether Loulou is short for something–Louise, maybe? When she says no, they look at her in that slightly glazed way she recognizes instantly, as if they've never paid proper attention to her or even seen her before. This look is her favourite part of any new relationship with a man. It's even better than the sex, though Loulou likes sex well enough and all the poets have been good in bed. But then, Loulou has never slept with a man she did not consider good in bed. She's beginning to think this is because she has low standards.

At first Loulou was intrigued by this obsession with her name, mistaking it for an obsession with her, but it turned out to be no such thing. It was the gap that interested them, one of them had explained (not Bob though; maybe Phil, the second and most linguistic of them all).

"What gap?" Loulou asked suspiciously. She knew her upper front teeth were a little wide apart and had been self-conscious about it when she was younger.

"The gap between the word and the thing signified," Phil said. His hand was on her breast and he'd given an absent-minded squeeze, as if to illustrate what he meant. They were in bed at the time. Mostly Loulou doesn't like talking in bed. But she's not that fond of talking at other times, either.

Phil went on to say that Loulou, as a name, conjured up images of French girls in can-can outfits, with corseted wasp-waists and blonde curls and bubbly laughs. But then there was the real Loulou–dark, straight-haired, firmly built, marmoreal, and well, not exactly bubbly. More earthy, you might say. (Loulou hadn't known then what he meant by "earthy," though by now she's learned that for him, for all of them, it means "functionally illiterate.") The thing was, Phil said, what existed in the space between Loulou and her name?

Loulou didn't know what he was talking about. What space? Once she'd resented her mother for having saddled her with this name; she would rather have been called Mary or Ann. Maybe she suspected that her mother would really have preferred a child more like the name–blonde, thin, curly-headed–but had disappointingly got Loulou instead, short, thick, stubborn-jawed, not much interested in the frilly dolls' clothes her mother had painstakingly crocheted for her. Instead, Loulou was fond of making mud pies on the back porch, placing them carefully along the railing where people wouldn't step on them and ruin them. Her mother's response to these pies was to say, "Oh, Loulou!" as if *Loulou* in itself meant mud, meant trouble and dismay.

"It's just a name," she said. "Phil is kind of a dumb name too if you ask me."

Phil said that wasn't the point, he wasn't *criticizing* her, but Loulou had stopped the conversation by climbing on top of him, letting her long hair fall down over his face.

That was early on; he'd liked her hair then. "Rank," he'd called it in a poem, quite a lot later. Loulou hadn't thought much of that when she looked it up. It could mean *too luxuriant* or *offensive and foul-smelling*. The effect of this poem on Loulou was to cause her to wash her hair more often. Sooner or later all the poets got into her hair, and she was tired of having it compared to horses' tails, Newfoundland dog fur, black holes in space and the insides of caves. When Loulou was feeling particularly enraged by the poets she would threaten to get a brush-cut, though she knew it would be pushing her luck.

When she has dried her hands, Loulou takes off her smock. Underneath it she's wearing a mauve sweatshirt with RAVING OPTIMIST stencilled across the front. The poets gave it to her, collectively, one Christmas, because a few weeks before one of them had said, "Why are you so grumpy, Loulou?" and Loulou had said, "I'm only grumpy when you pick on me," and then, after a pause, "Compared to you guys I'm a raving optimist." This was true, though they made fun of her for it. In a group they can laugh, but it's only Loulou who has seen them one at a time, sitting in chairs for hours on end with their heads down on their arms, almost unable to move. It's Loulou who's held their hands when they couldn't make it in bed and told them that other things are just as important, though she's never been able to specify what. It's Loulou who has gone out and got drunk with them and listened to them talking about the void and about the terrifying blankness of the page and about how any art form is just a way of evading suicide. Loulou thinks this is a load of b.s.: she herself does not consider the making of casseroles with lids or the throwing of porcelain fruit bowls as an evasion of suicide, but then, as they have often pointed out, what she's doing isn't an art form, it's only a craft. Bob once asked her when she was going to branch out into macramé, for which she emptied the dust-pan on him. But she matches them beer for beer; she's even gone so far as to throw up right along with them, if that seemed required. One of them once told her she was a soft touch.

The intercom buzzes as Loulou is hanging up her smock. She buzzes back to show she has heard, takes her hair out of the elastic band and smooths it down, looking in the round tin-framed Mexican mirror that hangs over the sink, and checks up on little Marilyn, her new apprentice, before heading out the door.

Marilyn is still having trouble with cup handles. Loulou will have to spend some time with her later and explain them to her. If the cup handles aren't on straight, she will say, the cup will be crooked when you pick it up and then the people drinking out of it will spill things and burn themselves. That's the way you have to put it for trainees: in terms of physical damage. It's important to Loulou that the production pieces should be done right. They're her bread and butter, though what she most likes to work on are the bigger things, the amphora-like vases, the tureens a size larger than anyone ought to be able to throw. Another potter once said that you'd need a derrick to give a dinner party with Loulou's stuff, but that was jealousy. What they say about her mostly is that she doesn't fool around.

Loulou flings her pink sweater-coat across her shoulders, bangs the coach-house door behind her to make it shut, and walks towards the house, whistling between her teeth and stomping her feet to get the clay dust off. The kitchen is filled with the yeasty smell of baking bread. Loulou breathes it in, revelling in it: a smell of her own creation.

The poets are sitting around the kitchen table, drinking coffee. Maybe they're having a meeting, it's hard to tell. Some nod at her, some grin. Two of the female poets are here today and Loulou isn't too pleased about that. As far as she's concerned they don't have a lot to offer: they're almost as bad as the male poets, but without the saving grace of being men. They wear black a lot and have cheek-bones.

Piss on their cheek-bones, thinks Loulou. She knows what cheek-bones mean. The poets, *her* poets, consider these female poets high-strung and interesting. Sometimes they praise their work, a little too extravagantly, but sometimes they talk about their bodies, though not when they are there of course, and about whether or not they would be any good in bed. Either of these approaches drives Loulou wild. She doesn't like the female poets–they eat her muffins and condescend to her, and Loulou suspects them of having designs on the poets, some of which may already have been carried out, judging from their snotty manner–but she doesn't like hearing them put down, either. What really gets her back up is that, during these discussions, the poets act as if she isn't there.

Really, though, the female poets don't count. They aren't even on the editorial board of *Comma;* they are only on the edges, like mascots, and today Loulou all but ignores them.

"You could've put on more coffee," she says in her grumpiest voice.

"What's the matter, Loulou?" says Phil, who has always been the quickest on the uptake when it comes to Loulou and her bad moods. Not that Loulou goes in for fine tuning.

"Nothing *you* can fix," says Loulou rudely. She takes off her sweater-coat and sticks out her chest. *Marmoreal,* she thinks. So much for the female poets, who are flat-chested as well as everything else.

"Hey Loulou, how about a little nictitation?" says one of the poets.

"Up your nose," says Loulou.

"She thinks it's something dirty," says a second one. "She's confusing it with micturition."

"All it means is winking, Loulou," says the first one.

"He got it out of Trivial Pursuit," says a third.

Loulou takes one loaf out of the oven, turns it out, taps the bottom, puts it back into the pan and into the oven. They can go on like that for hours. It's enough to drive you right out of your tree, if you pay any attention to them at all.

"Why do you put up with us, Loulou?" Phil asked her once. Loulou sometimes wonders, but she doesn't know. She knows why they put up with her though, apart from the fact that she pays the mortgage: she's solid, she's predictable, she's always there, she makes them feel safe. But lately she's been wondering: who is there to make her feel safe?

❧

It's another day, and Loulou is on her way to seduce her accountant. She's wearing purple boots, several years old and with watermarks on them from the slush, a cherry-coloured dirndl she made out of curtain material when she was at art school, and a Peruvian wedding shirt dyed mauve; this is the closest she ever comes to getting dressed up. Because of the section of the city she's going to, which is mostly middle-European shops, bakeries and clothing stores with yellowing embroidered blouses in the windows and places where you can buy hand-painted wooden Easter eggs and chess sets with the pawns as Cossacks, she's draped a black wool shawl over her head. This, she thinks, will make her look more ethnic and therefore more inconspicuous: she's feeling a little furtive. One of the poets has said that Loulou is to *subdued* as Las Vegas at night is to a sixty-watt light bulb, but in fact, with her long off-black hair and her large dark eyes and the strong planes of her face, she does have a kind of peasant look. This is enhanced by the two plastic shopping bags she carries, one in either hand. These do not contain groceries, however, but her receipts and cheque stubs for the two previous years. Loulou is behind on her income tax, which is why she got the accountant in the first place. She doesn't see why she shouldn't kill two birds with one stone.

Loulou is behind on her income tax because of her fear of money. When she was married to Bob, neither of them had any money anyway, so the income tax wasn't a problem. Phil, the man she lived with after that, was good with numbers, and although he had no income and therefore no income tax, he treated hers as a game, a kind of superior Scrabble. But her present husband, Calvin, considers money boring. It's all right to have some—as Loulou does, increasingly—but talking about it is sordid and a waste of time. Calvin claims that those who can actually read income-tax forms, let alone understand them, have already done severe and permanent damage to their brains. Loulou has taken to sending out her invoices and toting up her earnings in the coach-house, instead of at the kitchen table as she used to, and adding and subtracting are acquiring overtones of forbidden sex. Perhaps this is what has led her to the step she is now about to take. You may as well be hung, thinks Loulou, for a sheep as a lamb.

In addition, Loulou has recently been feeling a wistful desire to be taken care of. It comes and goes, especially on cloudy days, and mostly Loulou pays scant attention to it. Nevertheless it's there. Everyone depends on her, but when she needs help, with her income tax for instance, nobody's within call. She could ask Phil to do it again, but Calvin might make a fuss about it. She wants to be able to turn her two plastic shopping bags over to some man, some quiet methodical man with inner strength, and not too ugly, who could make sense of their contents and tell her she has nothing to worry about and, hopefully, nothing to pay.

Before Loulou found this particular accountant, she spent several afternoons window-shopping for one down at King and Bay. When it came right down to it, however, she was so intimidated by the hermetically sealed glass towers and the thought of receptionists with hair-dos and nail polish that she didn't even go in through the doors at any of the addresses she'd looked up in the Yellow Pages. Instead, she stood at street corners as if waiting for the light to change, watching the businessmen hurry past, sometimes in overcoats of the kind the poets never wear, solid-looking and beige or navy blue but slit provocatively up the back, or in three-piece suits, challengingly done up with hundreds of buttons and zippers, their tight tennis-playing butts concealed under layers of expensive wool blend, their ties waving enticingly under their chins like the loose ends of macramé wall hangings: one pull and the whole thing would unravel. The poets, in their track suits or jeans, seem easier of access, but they are hedged with paradox and often moody. The businessmen would be simple and unspoiled, primary reds and blues rather than puce and lilac, potatoes rather than, like the poets, slightly over-ripe avocadoes.

The sight of them filled Loulou with unspecific lust, though she found them touching also. She was like a middle-aged banker surrounded by sixteen-year-old virgins: she longed to be the first, though the first of what she wasn't sure. But she knew she knew lots of things they were unlikely to know: the poets, on their good days, have been nothing if not inventive.

Loulou doesn't think of the accountant she has now as a real one, by which she means a frightening one. He is not in a glass tower, he has no polished receptionist, though he does have a certificate on the wall and even a three-piece suit (though, Loulou suspects, only one). She discovered him by accident when she was down on Queen Street buying fresh chicken from A. Stork, the best place for it in her opinion, especially when you need a lot, as she did that day because all of the poets were coming for dinner. Heading for the streetcar stop with her sackful of tender flesh, Loulou saw a hand-lettered sign in the window of a dry-goods store: INCOME TAX, and underneath it some foreign language. It was the hand-lettered sign that did it for Loulou: badly lettered at that, she could do much better. On impulse she'd pushed open the door and gone in.

There was a tiny bald-headed man behind the counter, barricaded in with bolts of maroon cloth, a rack of cheesy-looking buttons on the wall behind him, but he turned out not to be the accountant. The accountant was in a separate room at the back, with nothing in it except a wooden desk of the sort Loulou associated with her grade-school teachers, and one other chair and a filing cabinet. He stood up when Loulou came in and offered to take her sack of chicken and put it somewhere for her. "No thanks," said Loulou, because she could see there was nowhere for him to put it—there was a fern on the filing cabinet, obviously on its last legs—and that he would merely get more flustered than he already was if she said yes; so she went through their first interview with a bag of still-warm cut-up chicken in her lap.

She's seen him twice since then. He takes more time with her than he really needs to, maybe because he's not what you would call all that busy. He also talks to her more than he needs to. By now, Loulou knows quite a lot about him. Getting started is harder than it used to be, he's told her. The dry-goods store belongs to his father, who gives him the office rent-free, in return for doing the accounts. The father is first-generation Czech, and he himself knows two other languages besides English. In this district—he spread his hands in a kind of resigned shrug while saying this—it helps. He does a couple of local bakeries and a hardware store and a second-hand jeweller's and a few of his father's old friends. Maybe when the recession is over things will pick up. He has volunteered, too, that his hobby is weight-lifting. Loulou has not asked whether or not he's married; she suspects not. If he were married, his fern would be in better shape.

While he talks, Loulou nods and smiles. She isn't sure how old he is. Young, she thinks, though he tries to make himself look older by wearing silver-rimmed glasses. She thinks he has nice hands, not like an accountant's at all, not spindly. The second time, he went out into the main store and came back with cups of tea, which Loulou found thoughtful. Then he asked her advice about a carpet. Already she felt sorry for him. He hardly ever goes out for lunch, she's discovered; mostly he just gets take-out from the deli across the street. She's considered bringing him some muffins.

These topics–carpets, weight-lifting, food–are easy for Loulou. What is more difficult is that he's decided she's not just a potter but an artist, and his idea of an artist does not at all accord with Loulou's view of herself. He wants her to be wispy and fey, impractical, unearthly almost; he talks, embarrassingly, about "the creative impulse." This is far too close to the poets for Loulou. She's tried to explain that she works with clay, which is hardly ethereal. "It's like mud pies," she said, but he didn't want to hear that. Nor could she find the words to make him understand what she meant: that when she's throwing a pot she feels exhilaration, exactly the same kind she felt as a child while making a terrible mess of her mother's back porch. If he could see her the way she really is when she's working, guck all over her hands, he'd know she's not exactly essence of roses.

The second time she saw him, the accountant said he envied her freedom. He would like to do something more creative himself, he said, but you have to make a living. Loulou refrained from pointing out that she seems to be doing a sight better at it than he is. She's much more tactful with him than she's ever been with the poets. The fact is that she's starting to enjoy his version of her. Sometimes she even believes it, and thinks she might be on the verge of learning something new about herself. She's beginning to find herself mysterious. It's partly for this reason she wants to sleep with the accountant; she thinks it will change her.

The poets would laugh if they knew, but then she's not about to tell them. She did announce his advent though, that first night, while the poets were all sitting around the table eating chicken and discussing something they called "the language." They do this frequently these days and Loulou is getting bored with it. "The language" is different from just words: it has this mystical aura around it, like religion, she can tell by the way their voices drop reverently whenever they mention it. That night they had all just finished reading a new book. "I'm really getting into the language," one said, and the others chewed in silent communion.

"I've got myself an accountant," Loulou said loudly, to break the spell.

"You've *got* him, but have you *had* him yet?" Bob said. The others laughed, all except Calvin, and began discussing the accountant's chances of escape from Loulou, which they rated at nil. They went on to detail the positions and locations in which Loulou could be expected to finally entrap him–under the desk, on top of the filing cabinet–and the injuries he would sustain. They pictured him fending her off with pens.

Loulou gnawed grimly at a chicken leg. They didn't believe any of this would happen, of course. They were too conceited: having known them, how could she stoop so low? Little did they know.

Loulou approaches the door of the dry-goods store, whistling Mozart between her teeth. Partly she's thinking about the accountant and what his body might be like under his suit, but partly she's thinking about tomorrow, when she has to start work on an order of twelve slab planters for one of her good customers. Either way, it's a question of the right placement of the feet. Like a Judo expert, which she is not, Loulou is always conscious of the position of her feet in relation to the rest of her.

The accountant is waiting for her, shadowy behind the dust-filmed glass of the door. It's after six and the store is closed. Loulou said, slyly, that she couldn't make it any earlier. She didn't want the little bald-headed man lurking around.

The accountant unlocks the door and lets her in. They go back through the smell of wool and freshly torn cotton into his office, and Loulou dumps out her bag of receipts (done up in bundles, with elastic bands: she's not without a sense of decency), all over his desk. He looks pleased, and says they certainly do have a lot of things to catch up on.

He brings in some cups of tea, sits down, picks up a newly sharpened pencil, and asks her how much of her living space can be written off as working space. Loulou explains about the coach-house. She doesn't use any of the actual house herself, she says, not for working, because the poets are always using it. Sometimes they live there too, though it depends.

"On what?" says the accountant, frowning a little.

"On whether they're living anywhere else," says Loulou.

When he hears that they don't pay rent, the accountant makes a tut-tutting sound and tells Loulou that she should not let things go on like this. Loulou says that the poets never have any money, except sometimes from grants. The accountant gets out of his chair and paces around the room, which is difficult for him because Loulou is taking up a lot of space in it. He says that Loulou is allowing herself to be imposed upon and she should get herself out of this situation, which is doing her no good all.

Loulou may have felt this herself from time to time, but hearing the accountant say it right out in the open air disturbs her. Where would the poets go? Who would take care of them? She doesn't wish to dwell on this right now, it's far too complicated, and perhaps even painful. Instead she stands up, plants her feet firmly apart, intercepts the accountant as he strides past, and, with a tug here and a little pressure there, ends up with his arms more or less around her. She backs herself up against the desk for balance, puts one hand behind her, and upsets his cup of tea into the wastepaper basket. He doesn't notice a thing; luckily it isn't hot.

After a short time the accountant takes off his silver-rimmed glasses, and after another short time he says, in a voice half an octave lower than his normal one, "I wasn't expecting this." Loulou says nothing—she lies only when absolutely necessary—and starts undoing his vest buttons. When she's down to the shirt he lifts his head, glances around the room, and murmurs, "Not here." Which is just as well, because he hasn't got his carpet yet and the floor is painted concrete.

He leads her into the darkened dry-goods store and begins sorting through the bolts of cloth. Loulou can't figure out what he's doing until he selects a roll of dark-pink velvet, unfurls it, and lays it out on the floor behind the counter, with a little flourish, like a cloak over a mud puddle. Loulou admires the way he does this; he's too deft not to have done it before. She lies down on the pink velvet, reaches up for him, and after a few minutes of shaky-fingered fumbling with the clothes they make love, somewhat rapidly. This floor is concrete too and the pink velvet isn't very thick. Loulou worries about his knees.

"Well," says the accountant. Then he sits up and starts putting on his clothes. He does this very skilfully. Loulou wishes he would wait a few minutes—it would be friendlier—but already he's doing up his buttons. Maybe he's afraid someone will come in. He rolls up the pink velvet and inserts the bolt back into its proper slot on the shelf. They go back to his office and he locates his glasses and puts them on, and tells her he'll have some figures for her in maybe two weeks. He doesn't say anything about seeing her in the meantime: perhaps his image of her as a delicate artistic flower has been shaken. He kisses her good-bye, though. The last thing he says to her is, "You shouldn't let people take advantage of you." Loulou knows he thinks he's just done this very thing himself. He's like the poets: he thinks she can't see through him.

Loulou decides to walk back to her house, which is at least a mile away, instead of taking the streetcar. She needs time to calm down. On the one hand she's elated, as she always is when she accomplishes something she's set out to do, but on the other hand she's disoriented. Is she different now, or not? Apart from the actual sex, which Loulou would never knock, and it was fine though a little on the swift side, what has it all boiled down to? She doesn't feel more known, more understood. Instead she feels less understood. She feels nameless. It's as if all those words which the poets have attached to her over the years have come undone and floated off into the sky, like balloons. If she were one of the poets, she would get something out of this: this is exactly the sort of thing they like to write about. A non-event, says Phil, is better to write about than an event, because with a non-event you can make up the meaning yourself, it means whatever you say it means. For the poets nothing is wasted, because even if it is, they can write about the waste. What she ought to do is throw them all out on their ears.

Loulou reaches her three-storey red-brick house and notes, as she always does, the mangy state of the lawn. The poets are divided on the subject of the lawn: some of them think lawns are bourgeois, others think that to say lawns are bourgeois is outdated. Loulou says she'll be damned if she'll cut it herself. The lawn is a stand-off. She goes up the front walk, not whistling, and unlocks her front door. In the hallway the familiar smell of the house envelops her, but it's like a smell from childhood. It's the smell of something left behind.

The poets are in the kitchen, sitting around the table, which is littered with papers and coffee cups and plates with crumbs and smears of butter on them. Loulou looks from one poet to another as if they are figures in a painting, as if she's never seen them before. She could walk out of this room, right this minute, and never come back, and fifty years later they would all still be in there, with the same plates, the same cups, the same crumby butter. Only she doesn't know where she would go.

"We're out of muffins," says Bob.

Loulou stares at him. "Piss on the muffins," she says at last, but without conviction. He looks tired, she thinks. He is showing signs of age, they all are. This is the first time she's noticed it. They won't go on forever.

"Where've you been?" says Calvin. "It's past seven-thirty." This is his way of saying they want their dinner.

"My God, you're helpless," says Loulou. "Why didn't you just phone out for some pizza?" To her knowledge they have never phoned out for pizza. They've never had to.

She sits down heavily at the table. The life she's led up to now seems to her entirely crazed. How did she end up in this madhouse? By putting one foot in front of the other and never taking her eyes off her feet. You could end up anywhere that way. It isn't that the accountant is normal, any more than the poets are; nor is he a possible alternative. She won't even sleep with him again, not on purpose anyway. But he is other, he is another. She too could be other. But which other? What, underneath it all, is Loulou really like? How can she tell? Maybe she is what the poets say she is, after all; maybe she has only their word, their words, for herself.

"*Pizza,*" Bob is beginning, in an injured tone. "Pig of a dog. . . ." But the others shut him up. They can see that something is wrong, and they very much don't want to know what.

"Reify the pizza," says Calvin to Phil. "You use phone. Is modern western invention of technology." Now they're pretending to be foreigners of some kind. This is a game they play more frequently when there is tension in the air than when there isn't.

"Insert finger in possible small hole," says Calvin. "Twist wrist."

"With anchovies then," says Bob, not joining in. Loulou hears their voices coming to her across space, as if they're in another room. What she sees is the grain of the wood in the table right by her hand.

"Loulou thinks to *reify* means to *make real*," says Phil to everyone, when he's hung up the phone. They're always talking about her in the third person like that, telling each other what she thinks. The truth is that she's never heard the word before in her life.

"So what is it, smartass?" says Loulou with an effort, squeezing out a little belligerence to set them at ease.

"If Loulou didn't exist, God would have to invent her," says Bob.

"God, hell," says Phil. "*We* would. We did it the first time, right?"

This is going too far for Loulou. Nobody invented her, thank you very much. They make things up about her, but that's a whole other story. "Up your nose," says Loulou.

"To reify is to make into a thing," says Phil, "which, as I'm sure most of us will agree, is hardly the same."

Loulou looks around the room. They are all in place, they're all watching her, to see what she will say next. She sticks out her chin at them. "Why not?" she says. "What's the big difference?" and they relax, they laugh, they give each other little punches on the shoulder as if they're part of a team and they've just scored a point. That, they tell each other, is just like Loulou, and suddenly she sees that this is what they require of her, possibly all they require: that she should be *just like Loulou*. No more, but certainly no less. Maybe it's not so bad.

Sonny's Blues
(1957)

JAMES BALDWIN

I read about it in the paper, in the subway, on my way to work. I read it, and I couldn't believe it, and I read it again. Then perhaps I just stared at it, at the newsprint spelling out his name, spelling out the story. I stared at it in the swinging lights of the subway car, and in the faces and bodies of the people, and in my own face, trapped in the darkness which roared outside.

It was not to be believed and I kept telling myself that, as I walked from the subway station to the high school. And at the same time I couldn't doubt it. I was scared, scared for Sonny. He became real to me again. A great block of ice got settled in my belly and kept melting there slowly all day long, while I taught my classes algebra. It was a special kind of ice. It kept melting, sending trickles of ice water all up and down my veins, but it never got less. Sometimes it hardened and seemed to expand until I felt my guts were going to come spilling out or that I was going to choke or scream. This would always be at a moment when I was remembering some specific thing Sonny had once said or done.

When he was about as old as the boys in my classes his face had been bright and open, there was a lot of copper in it; and he'd had wonderfully direct brown eyes, and great gentleness and privacy. I wondered what he looked like now. He had been picked up, the evening before, in a raid on an apartment downtown, for peddling and using heroin.

I couldn't believe it: but what I mean by that is that I couldn't find any room for it anywhere inside me. I had kept it outside me for a long time. I hadn't wanted to know. I had had suspicions, but I didn't name them, I kept putting them away. I told myself that Sonny was wild, but he wasn't crazy. And he'd always been a good boy, he hadn't ever turned hard or evil or disrespectful, the way kids can, so quick, so quick, especially in Harlem. I didn't want to believe that I'd ever see my brother going down, coming to nothing, all that light in his face gone out, in the condition I'd already seen so many others. Yet it had happened and here I was, talking about algebra to a lot of boys who might, every one of them for all I knew, be popping off needles every time they went to the head. Maybe it did more for them than algebra could.

I was sure that the first time Sonny had ever had horse, he couldn't have been much older than these boys were now. These boys, now, were living as we'd been living then, they were growing up with a rush and their heads bumped abruptly against the low ceiling of their actual possibilities. They were filled with rage. All they really knew were two darknesses, the darkness of their lives, which was now closing in on them, and the darkness of the movies, which had blinded them to that other darkness, and in which they now, vindictively, dreamed, at once more together than they were at any other time, and more alone.

When the last bell rang, the last class ended, I let out my breath. It seemed I'd been holding it for all that time. My clothes were wet—I may have looked as though I'd been sitting in a steam bath, all dressed up, all afternoon. I sat alone in the classroom a long time. I listened to the boys outside, downstairs, shouting and cursing and laughing. Their laughter struck me for perhaps the first time. It was not the joyous laughter which—God knows why—one associates with children. It was mocking and insular, its intent was to denigrate. It was disenchanted, and in this, also, lay the authority of their curses. Perhaps I was listening to them because I was thinking about my brother and in them I heard my brother. And myself.

One boy was whistling a tune, at once very complicated and very simple, it seemed to be pouring out of him as though he were a bird, and it sounded very cool and moving through all that harsh, bright air, only just holding its own through all those other sounds.

I stood up and walked over to the window and looked down into the courtyard. It was the beginning of the spring and the sap was rising in the boys. A teacher passed through them every now and again, quickly, as though he or she couldn't wait to get out of that courtyard, to get those boys out of their sight and off their minds. I started collecting my stuff. I thought I'd better get home and talk to Isabel.

The courtyard was almost deserted by the time I got down stairs. I saw this boy standing in the shadow of a doorway, looking just like Sonny. I almost called his name. Then I saw that it wasn't Sonny, but somebody we used to know, a boy from around our block. He'd been Sonny's friend. He'd never been mine, having been too young for me, and, anyway, I'd never liked him. And now, even though he was a grown-up man, he still hung around that block, still spent hours on the street corners, was always high and raggy. I used to run into him from time to time and he'd often work around to asking me for a quarter or fifty cents. He always had some real good excuse, too, and I always gave it to him, I don't know why.

But now, abruptly, I hated him. I couldn't stand the way he looked at me, partly like a dog, partly like a cunning child. I wanted to ask him what the hell he was doing in the school courtyard.

He sort of shuffled over to me, and he said, "I see you got the papers. So you already know about it."

"You mean about Sonny? Yes, I already know about it. How come they didn't get you?"

He grinned. It made him repulsive and it also brought to mind what he'd looked like as a kid. "I wasn't there. I stay away from them people."

"Good for you." I offered him a cigarette and I watched him through the smoke. "You come all the way down here just to tell me about Sonny?"

"That's right." He was sort of shaking his head and his eyes looked strange, as though they were about to cross. The bright sun deadened his damp dark brown skin and it made his eyes look yellow and showed up the dirt in his kinked hair. He smelled funky. I moved a little away from him and I said, "Well, thanks. But I already know about it and I got to get home."

"I'll walk you a little ways," he said. We started walking. There were a couple of kids still loitering in the courtyard and one of them said goodnight to me and looked strangely at the boy beside me.

"What're you going to do?" he asked me. "I mean, about Sonny?"

"Look. I haven't seen Sonny for over a year, I'm not sure I'm going to do anything. Anyway, what the hell *can* I do?"

"That's right," he said quickly, "ain't nothing you can do. Can't much help old Sonny no more, I guess."

It was what I was thinking and so it seemed to me he had no right to say it.

"I'm surprised at Sonny, though," he went on—he had a funny way of talking, he looked straight ahead as though he were talking to himself—"I thought Sonny was a smart boy, I thought he was too smart to get hung."

"I guess he thought so too," I said sharply, "and that's how he got hung. And how about you? You're pretty goddamn smart, I bet."

Then he looked directly at me, just for a minute. "I ain't smart," he said. "If I was smart, I'd have reached for a pistol a long time ago."

"Look. Don't tell *me* your sad story, if it was up to me, I'd give you one." Then I felt guilty— guilty, probably, for never having supposed that the poor bastard *had* a story of his own, much less a sad one, and I asked, quickly, "What's going to happen to him now?"

He didn't answer this. He was off by himself some place. "Funny thing," he said, and from his tone we might have been discussing the quickest way to get to Brooklyn, "when I saw the papers this morning, the first thing I asked myself was if I had anything to do with it. I felt sort of responsible."

I began to listen more carefully. The subway station was on the corner, just before us, and I stopped. He stopped, too. We were in front of a bar and he ducked slightly, peering in, but who-ever he was looking for didn't seem to be there. The juke box was blasting away with something black and bouncy and I half watched the barmaid as she danced her way from the juke box to her place behind the bar. And I watched her face as she laughingly responded to something someone said to her, still keeping time to the music. When she smiled one saw the little girl, one sensed the doomed, still-struggling woman beneath the battered face of the semi-whore.

"I never *give* Sonny nothing," the boy said finally, "but a long time ago I come to school high and Sonny asked me how it felt." He paused, I couldn't bear to watch him, I watched the barmaid, and I listened to the music which seemed to be causing the pavement to shake. "I told him it felt great." The music stopped, the barmaid paused and watched the juke box until the music began again. "It did."

All this was carrying me some place I didn't want to go. I certainly didn't want to know how it felt. It filled everything, the people, the houses, the music, the dark, quicksilver barmaid, with menace; and this menace was their reality.

"What's going to happen to him now?" I asked again.

"They'll send him away some place and they'll try to cure him." He shook his head. "Maybe he'll even think he's kicked the habit. Then they'll let him loose"—he gestured, throwing his cigarette into the gutter. "That's all."

"What do you mean, that's *all*?"

But I knew what he meant.

"I *mean*, that's *all*." He turned his head and looked at me, pulling down the corners of his mouth. "Don't you know what I mean?" he asked, softly.

"How the hell *would* I know what you mean?" I almost whispered it, I don't know why.

"That's right," he said to the air, "how would *he* know what I mean?" He turned toward me again, patient and calm, and yet I somehow felt him shaking, shaking as though he were going to fall apart. I felt that ice in my guts again, the dread I'd felt all afternoon; and again I watched the barmaid, moving about the bar, washing glasses, and singing. "Listen. They'll let him out and then it'll just start all over again. That's what I mean."

"You mean—they'll let him out. And then he'll just start working his way back in again. You mean he'll never kick the habit. Is that what you mean?"

"That's right," he said, cheerfully. "*You* see what I mean."

"Tell me," I said at last, "why does he want to die? He must want to die, he's killing himself, why does he want to die?"

He looked at me in surprise. He licked his lips. "He don't want to die. He wants to live. Don't nobody want to die, ever."

Then I wanted to ask him—too many things. He could not have answered, or if he had, I could not have borne the answers. I started walking. "Well, I guess it's none of my business."

"It's going to be rough on old Sonny," he said. We reached the subway station. "This is your station?" he asked. I nodded. I took one step down. "Damn!" he said, suddenly. I looked up at him. He grinned again. "Damn it if I didn't leave all my money home. You ain't got a dollar on you, have you? Just for a couple of days, is all."

All at once something inside gave and threatened to come pouring out of me. I didn't hate him any more. I felt that in another moment I'd start crying like a child.

"Sure," I said. "Don't sweat." I looked in my wallet and didn't have a dollar, I only had a five. "Here," I said. "That hold you?"

He didn't look at it—he didn't want to look at it. A terrible, closed look came over his face, as though he were keeping the number on the bill a secret from him and me. "Thanks," he said, and now he was dying to see me go. "Don't worry about Sonny. Maybe I'll write him or something."

"Sure," I said. "You do that. So long."

"Be seeing you," he said. I went on down the steps.

And I didn't write Sonny or send him anything for a long time. When I finally did, it was just after my little girl died, he wrote me back a letter which made me feel like a bastard.

Here's what he said:

> Dear brother,
>
> You don't know how much I needed to hear from you. I wanted to write you many a time but I dug how much I must have hurt you and so I didn't write. But now I feel like a man who's been trying to climb up out of some deep, real deep and funky hole and just saw the sun up there, outside. I got to get outside.
>
> I can't tell you much about how I got here. I mean I don't know how to tell you. I guess I was afraid of something or I was trying to escape from something and you know I have never been very strong in the head (smile). I'm glad Mama and Daddy are dead and can't see what's happened to their son and I swear if I'd known what I was doing I would never have hurt you so, you and a lot of other fine people who were nice to me and who believed in me.
>
> I don't want you to think it had anything to do with me being a musician. It's more than that. Or maybe less than that. I can't get anything straight in my head down here and I try not to think about what's going to happen to me when I get outside again. Sometime I think I'm going to flip and *never* get outside and sometime I think I'll come straight back. I tell you one thing, though, I'd rather blow my brains out than go through this again. But that's what they all say, so they tell me. If I tell you when I'm coming to New York and if you could meet me, I sure would appreciate it. Give my love to Isabel and the kids and I was sure sorry to hear about little Gracie. I wish

I could be like Mama and say the Lord's will be done, but I don't know it seems to me that trouble is the one thing that never does get stopped and I don't know what good it does to blame it on the Lord. But maybe it does some good if you believe it.

Your brother,
Sonny

Then I kept in constant touch with him and I sent him whatever I could and I went to meet him when he came back to New York. When I saw him many things I thought I had forgotten came flooding back to me. This was because I had begun, finally, to wonder about Sonny, about the life that Sonny lived inside. This life, whatever it was, had made him older and thinner and it had deepened the distant stillness in which he had always moved. He looked very unlike my baby brother. Yet, when he smiled, when we shook hands, the baby brother I'd never known looked out from the depths of his private life, like an animal waiting to be coaxed into the light.

"How you been keeping?" he asked me.

"All right. And you?"

"Just fine." He was smiling all over his face. "It's good to see you again."

"It's good to see you."

The seven years' difference in our ages lay between us like a chasm: I wondered if these years would ever operate between us as a bridge. I was remembering, and it made it hard to catch my breath, that I had been there when he was born; and I had heard the first words he had ever spoken. When he started to walk, he walked from our mother straight to me. I caught him just before he fell when he took the first steps he ever took in this world.

"How's Isabel?"

"Just fine. She's dying to see you."

"And the boys?"

"They're fine, too. They're anxious to see their uncle."

"Oh, come on. You know they don't remember me."

"Are you kidding? Of course they remember you."

He grinned again. We got into a taxi. We had a lot to say to each other, far too much to know how to begin.

As the taxi began to move, I asked, "You still want to go to India?"

He laughed. "You still remember that. Hell, no. This place is Indian enough for me."

"It used to belong to them," I said.

And he laughed again. "They damn sure knew what they were doing when they got rid of it."

Years ago, when he was around fourteen, he'd been all hipped on the idea of going to India. He read books about people sitting on rocks, naked, in all kinds of weather, but mostly bad, naturally, and walking barefoot through hot coals and arriving at wisdom. I used to say that it sounded to me as though they were getting away from wisdom as fast as they could. I think he sort of looked down on me for that.

"Do you mind," he asked, "if we have the driver drive alongside the park? On the west side—I haven't seen the city in so long."

"Of course not," I said. I was afraid that I might sound as though I were humoring him, but I hoped he wouldn't take it that way.

So we drove along, between the green of the park and the stony, lifeless elegance of hotels and apartment buildings, toward the vivid, killing streets of our childhood. These streets hadn't changed, though housing projects jutted up out of them now like rocks in the middle of a boiling sea. Most of the houses in which we had grown up had vanished, as had the stores from which we had stolen, the basements in which we had first tried sex, the rooftops from which we had hurled tin cans and bricks. But houses exactly like the houses of our past yet dominated the landscape, boys exactly like the boys we once had been found themselves smothering in these houses, came down into the streets for light and air and found themselves encircled by disaster. Some escaped the trap, most didn't. Those who got out always left something of themselves behind, as some animals amputate a leg and leave it in the trap. It might be said, perhaps, that I had escaped, after all, I was a school teacher; or that Sonny had, he hadn't lived in Harlem for years. Yet, as the cab moved uptown through streets which seemed, with a rush, to darken with dark people, and as I covertly studied Sonny's face, it came to me that what we both were seeking through our separate cab windows was that part of ourselves which had been left behind. It's always at the hour of trouble and confrontation that the missing member aches.

We hit 110th Street and started rolling up Lenox Avenue. And I'd known this avenue all my life, but it seemed to me again, as it had seemed on the day I'd first heard about Sonny's trouble, filled with a hidden menace which was its very breath of life.

"We almost there," said Sonny.

"Almost." We were both too nervous to say anything more.

We live in a housing project. It hasn't been up long. A few days after it was up it seemed uninhabitably new, now, of course, it's already rundown. It looks like a parody of the good, clean, faceless life—God knows the people who live in it do their best to make it a parody. The beat-looking grass lying around isn't enough to make their lives green, the hedges will never hold out the streets, and they know it. The big windows fool no one, they aren't big enough to make space out of no space. They don't bother with the windows, they watch the TV screen instead. The playground is most popular with the children who don't play at jacks, or skip rope, or roller skate, or swing, and they can be found in it after dark. We moved in partly because it's not too far from where I teach, and partly for the kids; but it's really just like the houses in which Sonny and I grew up. The same things happen, they'll have the same things to remember. The moment Sonny and I started into the house I had the feeling that I was simply bringing him back into the danger he had almost died trying to escape.

Sonny has never been talkative. So I don't know why I was sure he'd be dying to talk to me when supper was over the first night. Everything went fine, the oldest boy remembered him, and the youngest boy liked him, and Sonny had remembered to bring something for each of them; and Isabel, who is really much nicer than I am, more open and giving, had gone to a lot of trouble about dinner and was genuinely glad to see him. And she's always been able to tease Sonny in a way that I haven't. It was nice to see her face so vivid again and to hear her laugh and watch her make Sonny laugh. She wasn't, or, anyway, she didn't seem to be, at all uneasy or embarrassed. She chatted as though there were no subject which had to be avoided and she got Sonny past his first, faint stiffness. And thank God she was there, for I was filled with that icy dread again. Everything I did seemed awkward to me, and everything I said sounded freighted with hidden meaning. I was trying to remember everything I'd heard about dope addiction and I couldn't help watching Sonny for signs. I wasn't doing it out of malice.

I was trying to find out something about my brother. I was dying to hear him tell me he was safe.

"Safe!" my father grunted, whenever Mama suggested trying to move to a neighborhood which might be safer for children. "Safe, hell! Ain't no place safe for kids, nor nobody."

He always went on like this, but he wasn't, ever, really as bad as he sounded, not even on weekends, when he got drunk. As a matter of fact, he was always on the lookout for "something a little better," but he died before he found it. He died suddenly, during a drunken weekend in the middle of the war, when Sonny was fifteen. He and Sonny hadn't ever got on too well. And this was partly because Sonny was the apple of his father's eye. It was because he loved Sonny so much and was frightened for him, that he was always fighting with him. It doesn't do any good to fight with Sonny. Sonny just moves back, inside himself, where he can't be reached. But the principal reason that they never hit it off is that they were so much alike. Daddy was big and rough and loud-talking, just the opposite of Sonny, but they both had—that same privacy.

Mama tried to tell me something about this, just after Daddy died. I was home on leave from the army.

This was the last time I ever saw my mother alive. Just the same, this picture gets all mixed up in my mind with pictures I had of her when she was younger. The way I always see her is the way she used to be on a Sunday afternoon, say, when the old folks were talking after the big Sunday dinner. I always see her wearing pale blue. She'd be sitting on the sofa. And my father would be sitting in the easy chair, not far from her. And the living room would be full of church folks and relatives. There they sit, in chairs all around the living room, and the night is creeping up outside, but nobody knows it yet. You can see the darkness growing against the windowpanes and you hear the street noises every now and again, or maybe the jangling beat of a tambourine from one of the churches close by, but it's real quiet in the room. For a moment nobody's talking, but every face looks darkening, like the sky outside. And my mother rocks a little from the waist, and my father's eyes are closed. Everyone is looking at something a child can't see. For a minute they've forgotten the children. Maybe a kid is lying on the rug, half asleep. Maybe somebody's got a kid in his lap and is absent-mindedly stroking the kid's head. Maybe there's a kid, quiet and big-eyed, curled up in a big chair in the corner. The silence, the darkness coming, and the darkness in the faces frightens the child obscurely. He hopes that the hand which strokes his forehead will never stop—will never die. He hopes that there will never come a time when the old folks won't be sitting around the living room, talking about where they've come from, and what they've seen, and what's happened to them and their kinfolk.

But something deep and watchful in the child knows that this is bound to end, is already ending. In a moment someone will get up and turn on the light. Then the old folks will remember the children and they won't talk any more that day. And when light fills the room, the child is filled with darkness. He knows that every time this happens he's moved just a little closer to that darkness outside. The darkness outside is what the old folks have been talking about. It's what they've come from. It's what they endure. The child knows that they won't talk any more because if he knows too much about what's happened to *them*, he'll know too much too soon, about what's going to happen to *him*.

The last time I talked to my mother, I remember I was restless. I wanted to get out and see Isabel. We weren't married then and we had a lot to straighten out between us.

There Mama sat, in black, by the window. She was humming an old church song, *Lord, you brought me from a long ways off.* Sonny was out somewhere. Mama kept watching the streets.

"I don't know," she said, "if I'll ever see you again, after you go off from here. But I hope you'll remember the things I tried to teach you."

"Don't talk like that," I said, and smiled. "You'll be here a long time yet."

She smiled, too, but she said nothing. She was quiet for a long time. And I said, "Mama, don't you worry about nothing. I'll be writing all the time, and you be getting the checks. . . ."

"I want to talk to you about your brother," she said, suddenly. "If anything happens to me he ain't going to have nobody to look out for him."

"Mama," I said, "ain't nothing going to happen to you *or* Sonny. Sonny's all right. He's a good boy and he's got good sense."

"It ain't a question of his being a good boy," Mama said, "nor of his having good sense. It ain't only the bad ones, nor yet the dumb ones that gets sucked under." She stopped, looking at me. "Your Daddy once had a brother," she said, and she smiled in a way that made me feel she was in pain. "You didn't never know that, did you?"

"No," I said, "I never knew that," and I watched her face.

"Oh, yes," she said, "your Daddy had a brother." She looked out of the window again. "I know you never saw your Daddy cry. But *I* did—many a time, through all these years."

I asked her, "What happened to his brother? How come nobody's ever talked about him?"

This was the first time I ever saw my mother look old.

"His brother got killed," she said, "when he was just a little younger than you are now. I knew him. He was a fine boy. He was maybe a little full of the devil, but he didn't mean nobody no harm."

Then she stopped and the room was silent, exactly as it had sometimes been on those Sunday afternoons. Mama kept looking out into the streets.

"He used to have a job in the mill," she said, "and, like all young folks, he just liked to perform on Saturday nights. Saturday nights, him and your father would drift around to different place, go to dances and things like that, or just sit around with people they knew, and your father's brother would sing, he had a fine voice, and play along with himself on his guitar. Well, this particular Saturday night, him and your father was coming home from some place, and they were both a little drunk and there was a moon that night, it was bright like day. Your father's brother was feeling kind of good, and he was whistling to himself, and he had his guitar slung over his shoulder. They was coming down a hill and beneath them was a road that turned off from the highway. Well, your father's brother, being always kind of frisky, decided to run down this hill, and he did, with that guitar banging and clanging behind him, and he ran across the road, and he was making water behind a tree. And your father was sort of amused at him and he was still coming down the hill, kind of slow. Then he heard a car motor and that same minute his brother stepped from behind the tree, into the road, in the moonlight. And he started to cross the road. And your father started to run down the hill, he says he don't know why. This car was full of white men. They was all drunk, and when they seen your father's brother they let out a great whoop and holler and they aimed the car straight at him. They was having fun, they just wanted to scare him, the way they do sometimes, you know. But they was drunk. And I guess the boy, being drunk, too, and scared, kind of lost his head. By the time he jumped it was too late. Your father says he heard his brother scream when the car rolled over him, and he heard the wood of that guitar when it give, and he heard them strings go flying, and he heard them white men shouting, and the car kept on a-going and it ain't stopped till this day. And, time your father got down the hill, his brother weren't nothing but blood and pulp."

Tears were gleaming on my mother's face. There wasn't anything I could say.

"He never mentioned it," she said, "because I never let him mention it before you children. Your Daddy was like a crazy man that night and for many a night thereafter. He says he never in his life seen anything as dark as that road after the lights of that car had gone away. Weren't nothing, weren't nobody on that road, just your Daddy and his brother and that busted guitar. Oh, yes. Your Daddy never did really get right again. Till the day he died he weren't sure but that every white man he saw was the man that killed his brother."

She stopped and took out her handkerchief and dried her eyes and looked at me.

"I ain't telling you all this," she said, "to make you scared or bitter or to make you hate nobody. I'm telling you this because you got a brother. And the world ain't changed."

I guess I didn't want to believe this. I guess she saw this in my face. She turned away from me, toward the window again, searching those streets.

"But I praise my Redeemer," she said at last, "that He called your Daddy home before me. I ain't saying it to throw no flowers at myself, but, I declare, it keeps me from feeling too cast down to know I helped your father get safely through this world. Your father always acted like he was the roughest, strongest man on earth. And everybody took him to be like that. But if he hadn't had *me* there—to see his tears!"

She was crying again. Still, I couldn't move. I said, "Lord, Lord, Mama, I didn't know it was like that."

"Oh, honey," she said, "there's a lot that you don't know. But you are going to find it out." She stood up from the window and came over to me. "You got to hold on to your brother," she said, "and don't let him fall, no matter what it looks like is happening to him and no matter how evil you gets with him. You going to be evil with him many a time. But don't you forget what I told you, you hear?"

"I won't forget," I said. "Don't you worry, I won't forget. I won't let nothing happen to Sonny."

My mother smiled as though she were amused at something she saw in my face. Then, "You may not be able to stop nothing from happening. But you got to let him know you's *there*."

Two days later I was married, and then I was gone. And I had a lot of things on my mind and I pretty well forgot my promise to Mama until I got shipped home on a special furlough for her funeral.

And, after the funeral, with just Sonny and me alone in the empty kitchen, I tried to find out something about him.

"What do you want to do?" I asked him.

"I'm going to be a musician," he said.

For he had graduated, in the time I had been away, from dancing to the juke box to finding out who was playing what, and what they were doing with it, and he had bought himself a set of drums.

"You mean, you want to be a drummer?" I somehow had the feeling that being a drummer might be all right for other people but not for my brother Sonny.

"I don't think," he said, looking at me very gravely, "that I'll ever be a good drummer. But I think I can play a piano."

I frowned. I'd never played the role of the older brother quite so seriously before, had scarcely ever, in fact, *asked* Sonny a damn thing. I sensed myself in the presence of something I didn't really know how to handle, didn't understand. So I made my frown a little deeper as I asked: "What kind of musician do you want to be?"

He grinned. "How many kinds do you think there are?"

"Be *serious*," I said.

He laughed, throwing his head back, and then looked at me. "I *am* serious."

"Well, then, for Christ's sake, stop kidding around and answer a serious question. I mean, do you want to be a concert pianist, you want to play classical music and all that, or—or what?" Long before I finished he was laughing again. "For Christ's *sake*, Sonny!"

He sobered, but with difficulty. "I'm sorry. But you sound so—*scared!*" and he was off again.

"Well, you may think it's funny now, baby, but it's not going to be so funny when you have to make your living at it, let me tell you *that*." I was furious because I knew he was laughing at me and I didn't know why.

"No," he said, very sober now, and afraid, perhaps, that he'd hurt me, "I don't want to be a classical pianist. That isn't what interests me. I mean"—he paused, looking hard at me, as though his eyes would help me to understand, and then gestured helplessly, as though perhaps his hand would help—"I mean, I'll have a lot of studying to do, and I'll have to study *everything*, but, I mean, I want to play *with*—jazz musicians." He stopped. "I want to play jazz," he said.

Well, the word had never before sounded as heavy, as real, as it sounded that afternoon in Sonny's mouth. I just looked at him and I was probably frowning a real frown by this time. I simply couldn't see why on earth he'd want to spend his time hanging around nightclubs, clowning around on bandstands, while people pushed each other around a dance floor. It seemed—beneath him, somehow. I had never thought about it before, had never been forced to, but I suppose I had always put jazz musicians in a class with what Daddy called "good-time people."

"Are you *serious*?"

"Hell, *yes*, I'm serious."

He looked more helpless than ever, and annoyed, and deeply hurt.

I suggested, helpfully: "You mean—like Louis Armstrong?"

His face closed as though I'd struck him. "No. I'm not talking about none of that old-time, down home crap."

"Well, look, Sonny, I'm sorry, don't get mad. I just don't altogether get it, that's all. Name somebody—you know, a jazz musician you admire."

"Bird."

"Who?"

"Bird! Charlie Parker! Don't they teach you nothing in the goddamn army?"

I lit a cigarette. I was surprised and then a little amused to discover that I was trembling. "I've been out of touch," I said. "You'll have to be patient with me. Now. Who's this Parker character?"

"He's just one of the greatest jazz musicians alive," said Sonny, sullenly, his hands in his pockets, his back to me. "Maybe *the* greatest," he added, bitterly, "that's probably why *you* never heard of him."

"All right," I said, "I'm ignorant. I'm sorry. I'll go out and buy all the cat's records right away, all right?"

"It don't," said Sonny, with dignity, "make any difference to me. I don't care what you listen to. Don't do me no favors."

I was beginning to realize that I'd never seen him so upset before. With another part of my mind I was thinking that this would probably turn out to be one of those things kids go through and that I shouldn't make it seem important by pushing it too hard. Still, I didn't think it would do any harm to ask: "Doesn't all this take a lot of time? Can you make a living at it?"

He turned back to me and half leaned, half sat, on the kitchen table. "Everything takes time," he said, "and—well, yes, sure, I can make a living at it. But what I don't seem to be able to make you understand is that it's the only thing I want to do."

"Well, Sonny," I said, gently, "you know people can't always do exactly what they *want* to do—"

"*No*, I don't know that," said Sonny, surprising me. "I think people *ought* to do what they want to do, what else are they alive for?"

"You getting to be a big boy," I said desperately, "it's time you started thinking about your future."

"I'm thinking about my future," said Sonny, grimly. "I think about it all the time."

I gave up. I decided, if he didn't change his mind, that we could always talk about it later. "In the meantime," I said, "you got to finish school." We had already decided that he'd have to move in with Isabel and her folks. I knew this wasn't the ideal arrangement because Isabel's folks are inclined to be dicty and they hadn't especially wanted Isabel to marry me. But I didn't know what else to do. "And we have to get you fixed up at Isabel's."

There was a long silence. He moved from the kitchen table to the window. "That's a terrible idea. You know it yourself."

"Do you have a *better* idea?"

He just walked up and down the kitchen for a minute. He was as tall as I was. He had started to shave. I suddenly had the feeling that I didn't know him at all.

He stopped at the kitchen table and picked up my cigarettes. Looking at me with a kind of mocking, amused defiance, he put one between his lips. "You mind?"

"You smoking already?"

He lit the cigarette and nodded, watching me through the smoke. "I just wanted to see if I'd have the courage to smoke in front of you." He grinned and blew a great cloud of smoke to the ceiling. "It was easy." He looked at my face. "Come on, now. I bet you was smoking at my age, tell the truth."

I didn't say anything but the truth was on my face, and he laughed. But now there was something very strained in his laugh. "Sure. And I bet that ain't all you was doing."

He was frightening me a little. "Cut the crap," I said. "We already decided that you was going to go and live at Isabel's. Now what's got into you all of a sudden?"

"*You* decided it," he pointed out. "I didn't decide nothing." He stopped in front of me, leaning against the stove, arms loosely folded. "Look, brother. I don't want to stay in Harlem no more, I really don't." He was very earnest. He looked at me, then over toward the kitchen window. There was something in his eyes I'd never seen before, some thoughtfulness, some worry all his own. He rubbed the muscle of one arm. "It's time I was getting out of here."

"Where do you want to *go*, Sonny?"

"I want to join the army. Or the navy, I don't care. If I say I'm old enough, they'll believe me."

Then I got mad. It was because I was so scared. "You must be crazy. You goddamn fool, what the hell do you want to go and join the *army* for?"

"I just told you. To get out of Harlem."

"Sonny, you haven't even finished *school*. And if you really want to be a musician, how do you expect to study if you're in the *army*?"

He looked at me, trapped, and in anguish. "There's ways. I might be able to work out some kind of deal. Anyway, I'll have the G.I. Bill when I come out."

"*If* you come out." We stared at each other. "Sonny, please. Be reasonable. I know the setup is far from perfect. But we got to do the best we can."

"I ain't learning nothing in school," he said. "Even when I go." He turned away from me and opened the window and threw his cigarette out into the narrow alley. I watched his back. "At least, I ain't learning nothing you'd want me to learn." He slammed the window so hard I thought the glass would fly out, and turned back to me. "And I'm sick of the stink of these garbage cans!"

"Sonny," I said, "I know how you feel. But if you don't finish school now, you're going to be sorry later that you didn't." I grabbed him by the shoulders. "And you only got another year. It ain't so bad. And I'll come back and I swear I'll help you do *whatever* you want to do. Just try to put up with it till I come back. Will you please do that? For me?"

He didn't answer and he wouldn't look at me.

"Sonny. You hear me?"

He pulled away. "I hear you. But you never hear anything *I* say."

I didn't know what to say to that. He looked out of the window and then back at me. "OK," he said, and sighed. "I'll try."

Then I said, trying to cheer him up a little, "They got a piano at Isabel's. You can practice on it."

And as a matter of fact, it did cheer him up for a minute. "That's right," he said to himself. "I forgot that." His face relaxed a little. But the worry, the thoughtfulness, played on it still, the way shadows play on a face which is staring into the fire.

But I thought I'd never hear the end of that piano. At first, Isabel would write me, saying how nice it was that Sonny was so serious about his music and how, as soon as he came in from school, or wherever he had been when he was supposed to be at school, he went straight to that piano and stayed there until suppertime. And, after supper, he went back to that piano and stayed there until everybody went to bed. He was at the piano all day Saturday and all day Sunday. Then he bought a record player and started playing records. He'd play one record over and over again, all day long sometimes, and he'd improvise along with it on the piano. Or he'd play one section of the record, one chord, one change, one progression, then he'd do it on the piano. Then back to the record. Then back to the piano.

Well, I really don't know how they stood it. Isabel finally confessed that it wasn't like living with a person at all, it was like living with sound. And the sound didn't make any sense to her, didn't make any sense to any of them—naturally. They began, in a way, to be afflicted by this presence that was living in their home. It was as though Sonny were some sort of god, or monster. He moved in an atmosphere which wasn't like theirs at all. They fed him and he ate, he washed himself, he walked in and out of their door; he certainly wasn't nasty or unpleasant or rude, Sonny isn't any of those things; but it was as though he were all wrapped up in some cloud, some fire, some vision all his own; and there wasn't any way to reach him.

At the same time, he wasn't really a man yet, he was still a child, and they had to watch out for him in all kinds of ways. They certainly couldn't throw him out. Neither did they dare to make a great scene about that piano because even they dimly sensed, as I sensed, from so many thousands of miles away, that Sonny was at that piano playing for his life.

But he hadn't been going to school. One day a letter came from the school board and Isabel's mother got it—there had, apparently, been other letters but Sonny had torn them up. This day, when Sonny came in, Isabel's mother showed him the letter and asked where he'd been spending his time. And she finally got it out of him that he'd been down in Greenwich Village, with musicians and other characters, in a white girl's apartment. And this scared her and she started to scream at him and what came up, once she began—though she denies it to this day—was what sacrifices they were making to give Sonny a decent home and how little he appreciated it.

Sonny didn't play the piano that day. By evening, Isabel's mother had calmed down but then there was the old man to deal with, and Isabel herself. Isabel says she did her best to be calm but she broke down and started crying. She says she just watched Sonny's face. She could tell, by watching him, what was happening with him. And what was happening was that they penetrated his cloud, they had reached him. Even if their fingers had been a thousand times more gentle than human fingers ever are, he could hardly help feeling that they had stripped him naked and were spitting on that nakedness. For he also had to see that his presence, that music, which was life or death to him, had been torture for them and that they had endured it, not at all for his sake, but only for mine. And Sonny couldn't take that. He can take it a little better today than he could then but he's still not very good at it and, frankly, I don't know anybody who is.

The silence of the next few days must have been louder than the sound of all the music ever played since time began. One morning, before she went to work, Isabel was in his room for something and she suddenly realized that all of his records were gone. And she knew for certain that he was gone. And he was. He went as far as the navy would carry him. He finally sent me a postcard from some place in Greece and that was the first I knew that Sonny was still alive. I didn't see him any more until we were both back in New York and the war had long been over.

He was a man by then, of course, but I wasn't willing to see it. He came by the house from time to time, but we fought almost every time we met. I didn't like the way he carried himself, loose and dreamlike all the time, and I didn't like his friends, and his music seemed to be merely an excuse for the life he led. It sounded just that weird and disordered.

Then we had a fight, a pretty awful fight, and I didn't see him for months. By and by I looked him up, where he was living, in a furnished room in the Village, and I tried to make it up. But there were lots of other people in the room and Sonny just lay on his bed, and he wouldn't come downstairs with me, and he treated these other people as though they were his family and I weren't. So I got mad and then he got mad, and then I told him that he might just as well be dead as live the way he was living. Then he stood up and he told me not to worry about him any more in life, that he *was* dead as far as I was concerned. Then he pushed me to the door and the other people looked on as though nothing were happening, and he slammed the door behind me. I stood in the hallway, staring at the door. I heard somebody laugh in the room and then the tears came to my eyes. I started down the steps, whistling to keep from crying, I kept whistling to myself, *You going to need me, baby, one of these cold, rainy days.*

I read about Sonny's trouble in the spring. Little Grace died in the fall. She was a beautiful little girl. But she only lived a little over two years. She died of polio and she suffered. She had a slight fever for a couple of days, but it didn't seem like anything and we just kept her in bed. And we would certainly have called the doctor, but the fever dropped, she seemed to be all right. So we thought it had just been a cold. Then, one day, she was up, playing, Isabel was in the kitchen fixing lunch for the two boys when they'd come in from school, and she heard Grace fall down in the living room. When you have a lot of children you don't always start running when one of them falls, unless they start screaming or something. And, this time, Grace was quiet. Yet, Isabel says that when she heard that *thump* and then that silence, something happened in her to make her afraid. And she ran to the living room and there was little Grace on the floor, all twisted up, and the reason she hadn't screamed was that she couldn't get her breath. And when she did scream, it was the worst sound, Isabel says, that she'd ever heard in all her life, and she still hears it sometimes in her dreams. Isabel will sometimes wake me up with a low, moaning, strangled sound and I have to be quick to awaken her and hold her to me and where Isabel is weeping against me seems a mortal wound.

I think I may have written Sonny the very day that little Grace was buried. I was sitting in the living room in the dark, by myself, and I suddenly thought of Sonny. My trouble made his real.

One Saturday afternoon, when Sonny had been living with us, or, anyway, been in our house, for nearly two weeks, I found myself wandering aimlessly about the living room, drinking from a can of beer, and trying to work up the courage to search Sonny's room. He was out, he was usually out whenever I was home, and Isabel had taken the children to see their grandparents. Suddenly I was standing still in front of the living room window, watching Seventh Avenue. The idea of searching Sonny's room made me still. I scarcely dared to admit to myself what I'd be searching for. I didn't know what I'd do if I found it. Or if I didn't.

On the sidewalk across from me, near the entrance to a barbecue joint, some people were holding an old-fashioned revival meeting. The barbecue cook, wearing a dirty white apron, his conked hair reddish and metallic in the pale sun, and a cigarette between his lips, stood in the doorway, watching them. Kids and older people paused in their errands and stood there, along with some older men and a couple of very tough-looking women who watched everything that happened on the avenue, as though they owned it, or were maybe owned by it. Well, they were watching this, too. The revival was being carried on by three sisters in black, and a brother. All they had were their voices and their Bibles and a tambourine. The brother was testifying and while he testified two of the sisters stood together, seeming to say, amen, and the third sister walked around with the tambourine outstretched and a couple of people dropped coins into it. Then the brother's testimony ended and the sister who had been taking up the collection dumped the coins into her palm and transferred them to the pocket of her long black robe. Then she raised both hands, striking the tambourine against the air, and then against one hand, and she started to sing. And the two other sisters and the brother joined in.

It was strange, suddenly, to watch, though I had been seeing these street meetings all my life. So, of course, had everybody else down there. Yet, they paused and watched and listened and I stood still at the window. *"Tis the old ship of Zion,"* they sang, and the sister with the tambourine kept a steady, jangling beat, *"it has rescued many a thousand!"* Not a soul under the sound of their voices was hearing this song for the first time, not one of them had been rescued. Nor had they seen much in the way of rescue work being done around them. Neither did they especially believe in the holiness of the three sisters and the brother, they knew too much about them, knew where they lived, and how. The woman with the tambourine, whose voice dominated the air, whose face was bright with joy, was divided by very little from the woman who stood watching her, a cigarette between her heavy, chapped lips, her hair a cuckoo's nest, her face scarred and swollen from many beatings, and her black eyes glittering like coal. Perhaps they both knew this, which was why, when, as rarely, they addressed each other, they addressed each other as Sister. As the singing filled the air the watching, listening faces underwent a change, the eyes focusing on something within; the music seemed to soothe a poison out of them; and time seemed, nearly, to fall away from the sullen, belligerent, battered faces, as though they were fleeing back to their first condition, while dreaming of their last. The barbecue cook half shook his head and smiled, and dropped his cigarette and disappeared into his joint. A man fumbled in his pockets for change and stood holding it in his hand impatiently, as though he had just remembered a pressing appointment further up the avenue. He looked furious. Then I saw Sonny, standing on the edge of the crowd. He was carrying a wide, flat notebook with a green cover, and it made him look, from where I was standing, almost like a schoolboy. The coppery sun brought out the copper in his skin, he was very faintly smiling, standing very still. Then the singing stopped, the tambourine turned into a collection plate again. The furious man dropped in his coins and vanished, so did a couple of the women, and Sonny dropped some change in the plate, looking directly at the woman with a little smile. He started across the avenue, toward the house. He has a slow, loping walk, something like the way Harlem hipsters walk, only he's imposed on this his own half-beat, I had never really noticed it before.

I stayed at the window, both relieved and apprehensive. As Sonny disappeared from my sight, they began singing again. And they were still singing when his key turned in the lock.

"Hey," he said.

"Hey, yourself. You want some beer?"

"No. Well, maybe." But he came up to the window and stood beside me, looking out. "What a warm voice," he said.

They were singing *If I could only hear my mother pray again!*

"Yes," I said, "and she can sure beat that tambourine."

"But what a terrible song," he said, and laughed. He dropped his notebook on the sofa and disappeared into the kitchen. "Where's Isabel and the kids?"

"I think they went to see their grandparents. You hungry?"

"No." He came back into the living room with his can of beer. "You want to come some place with me tonight?"

I sensed, I don't know how, that I couldn't possibly say no. "Sure. Where?"

He sat down on the sofa and picked up his notebook and started leafing through it. "I'm going to sit in with some fellows in a joint in the Village."

"You mean, you're going to play, tonight?"

"That's right." He took a swallow of his beer and moved back to the window. He gave me a sidelong look. "If you can stand it."

"I'll try," I said.

He smiled to himself and we both watched as the meeting across the way broke up. The three sisters and the brother, heads bowed, were singing *God be with you till we meet again.* The faces around them were very quiet. Then the song ended. The small crowd dispersed. We watched the three women and the lone man walk slowly up the avenue.

"When she was singing before," said Sonny, abruptly, "her voice reminded me for a minute of what heroin feels like sometimes—when it's in your veins. It makes you feel sort of warm and cool at the same time. And distant. And—and sure." He sipped his beer, very deliberately not looking at me. I watched his face. "It makes you feel—in control. Sometimes you've got to have that feeling."

"Do you?" I sat down slowly in the easy chair.

"Sometimes." He went to the sofa and picked up his notebook again. "Some people do."

"In order," I asked, "to play?" And my voice was very ugly, full of contempt and anger.

"Well"—he looked at me with great, troubled eyes, as though, in fact, he hoped his eyes would tell me things he could never otherwise say—"they *think* so. And *if* they think so—!"

"And what do *you* think?" I asked.

He sat on the sofa and put his can of beer on the floor. "I don't know," he said, and I couldn't be sure if he were answering my question or pursuing his thoughts. His face didn't tell me. "It's not so much to *play.* It's to *stand* it, to be able to make it at all. On any level." He frowned and smiled: "In order to keep from shaking to pieces."

"But these friends of yours," I said, "they seem to shake themselves to pieces pretty goddamn fast."

"Maybe." He played with the notebook. And something told me that I should curb my tongue, that Sonny was doing his best to talk, that I should listen. "But of course you only know the ones that've gone to pieces. Some don't—or at least they haven't *yet* and that's just about all *any* of us can say." He paused. "And then there are some who just live, really, in hell, and they know it and they see what's happening and they go right on. I don't know." He sighed, dropped the notebook, folded his arms. "Some guys, you can tell from the way they play, they on something *all* the time. And you can see that, well, it makes something real for them. But of course," he picked up his beer from the floor and sipped it and put the can down again, "they *want* to, too, you've got to see that. Even some of them that say they don't—*some,* not all."

"And what about you?" I asked—I couldn't help it. "What about you? Do *you* want to?"

He stood up and walked to the window and remained silent for a long time. Then he sighed. "Me," he said. Then: "While I was downstairs before, on my way here, listening to that woman sing, it struck me all of a sudden how much suffering she must have had to go through—to sing like that. It's *repulsive* to think you have to suffer that much."

I said: "But there's no way not to suffer—is there, Sonny?"

"I believe not," he said and smiled, "but that's never stopped anyone from trying." He looked at me. "Has it?" I realized, with this mocking look, that there stood between us, forever, beyond the power of time or forgiveness, the fact that I had held silence—so long! —when he had needed human speech to help him. He turned back to the window. "No, there's no way not to suffer. But you try all kinds of ways to keep from drowning in it, to keep on top of it, and to make it seem—well, like *you*. Like you did something, all right, and now you're suffering for it. You know?" I said nothing. "Well you know," he said, impatiently, "why *do* people suffer? Maybe it's better to do something to give it a reason, *any* reason."

"But we just agreed," I said, "that there's no way not to suffer. Isn't it better, then, just to—take it?"

"But nobody just takes it," Sonny cried, "that's what I'm telling you! *Everybody* tries not to. You're just hung up on the *way* some people try—it's not *your way!*"

The hair on my face began to itch, my face felt wet. "That's not true," I said, "that's not true. I don't give a damn what other people do, I don't even care how they suffer. I just care how *you* suffer." And he looked at me. "Please believe me," I said, "I don't want to see you—die—trying not to suffer."

"I won't," he said, flatly, "die trying not to suffer. At least, not any faster than anybody else."

"But there's no need," I said, trying to laugh, "is there? in killing yourself."

I wanted to say more, but I couldn't. I wanted to talk about will power and how life could be—well, beautiful. I wanted to say that it was all within; but was it? or, rather, wasn't that exactly the trouble? And I wanted to promise that I would never fail him again. But it would all have sounded—empty words and lies.

So I made the promise to myself and prayed that I would keep it.

"It's terrible sometimes, inside," he said, "that's what's the trouble. You walk these streets, black and funky and cold, and there's not really a living ass to talk to, and there's nothing shaking, and there's no way of getting it out—that storm inside. You can't talk it and you can't make love with it, and when you finally try to get with it and play it, you realize *nobody's* listening. So *you've* got to listen. You got to find a way to listen."

And then he walked away from the window and sat on the sofa again, as though all the wind had suddenly been knocked out of him. "Sometimes you'll do *anything* to play, even cut your mother's throat." He laughed and looked at me. "Or your brother's." Then he sobered. "Or your own." Then: "Don't worry. I'm all right now and I think I'll *be* all right. But I can't forget—where I've been. I don't mean just the physical place I've been, I mean where I've *been*. And *what* I've been."

"What have you been, Sonny?" I asked.

He smiled—but sat sideways on the sofa, his elbow resting on the back, his fingers playing with his mouth and chin, not looking at me. "I've been something I didn't recognize, didn't know I could be. Didn't know anybody could be." He stopped, looking inward, looking helplessly young, looking old. "I'm not talking about it now because I feel *guilty* or anything like that—maybe it would be better if I did, I don't know. Anyway, I can't really talk about it. Not to you, not to anybody," and now he turned and faced me. "Sometimes, you know, and it was actually when I was most *out* of the world, I felt that I was in it, that I was *with* it, really, and I could play or I didn't really have to *play*, it just came out of me, it was there. And I don't know how I played, thinking about it now, but I know I did awful things, those times, sometimes, to people. Or it wasn't that I *did* anything to them—it was that they weren't real." He picked up the beer can; it was empty; he rolled it between his palms: "And other times—well, I needed a fix, I needed to find a place to lean, I needed to clear a space to *listen*—and I couldn't find it, and I—went crazy, I did terrible things to *me*, I was terrible *for* me." He began pressing the beer can between his hands, I watched the metal begin to give. It glittered, as he played with it, like a knife, and I was afraid he would cut himself, but I said nothing. "Oh well. I can never tell you. I was all by myself at the bottom of something, stinking and sweating and crying and shaking, and I smelled it, you know? *my* stink, and I thought I'd die if I couldn't get away from it and yet, all the same, I knew that everything I was doing was just locking me in with it. And I didn't know," he paused, still flattening the beer can, "I didn't know, I still *don't* know, something kept telling me that maybe it was good to smell your own stink, but I didn't think that *that* was what I'd been trying to do—and—who can stand it?" and he abruptly dropped the ruined beer can, looking at me with a small, still smile, and then rose, walking to the window as though it were the lodestone rock. I watched his face, he watched the avenue. "I couldn't tell you, when Mama died—but the reason I wanted to leave Harlem so bad was to get away from drugs. And then, when I ran away, that's what I was running from—really. When I came back, nothing had changed, *I* hadn't changed, I was just—older." And he stopped, drumming with his fingers on the windowpane. The sun had vanished, soon darkness would fall. I watched his face. "It can come again," he said, almost as though speaking to himself. Then he turned to me. "It can come again," he repeated. "I just want you to know that."

"All right," I said, at last. "So it can come again. All right."

He smiled, but the smile was sorrowful. "I had to try to tell you," he said.

"Yes," I said. "I understand that."

"You're my brother," he said, looking straight at me, and not smiling at all.

"Yes," I repeated, "yes. I understand that."

He turned back to the window, looking out. "All that hatred down there," he said, "all that hatred and misery and love. It's a wonder it doesn't blow the avenue apart."

We went to the only nightclub on a short, dark street, downtown. We squeezed through the narrow, chattering, jam-packed bar to the entrance of the big room, where the bandstand was. And we stood there for a moment, for the lights were very dim in this room and we couldn't see. Then, "Hello, boy," said a voice and an enormous black man, much older than Sonny or myself, erupted out of all that atmospheric lighting and put an arm around Sonny's shoulder. "I been sitting right here," he said, "waiting for you."

He had a big voice, too, and heads in the darkness turned toward us.

Sonny grinned and pulled a little away, and said, "Creole, this is my brother. I told you about him."

Creole shook my hand. "I'm glad to meet you, son," he said, and it was clear that he was glad to meet me *there*, for Sonny's sake. And he smiled, "You got a real musician in *your* family," and he took his arm from Sonny's shoulder and slapped him, lightly, affectionately, with the back of his hand.

"Well. Now I've heard it all," said a voice behind us. This was another musician, and a friend of Sonny's, a coal-black, cheerful-looking man, built close to the ground. He immediately began confiding to me, at the top of his lungs, the most terrible things about Sonny, his teeth gleaming like a lighthouse and his laugh coming up out of him like the beginning of an earthquake. And it turned out that everyone at the bar knew Sonny, or almost everyone; some were musicians, working there, or nearby, or not working, some were simply hangers-on, and some were there to hear Sonny play. I was introduced to all of them and they were all very polite to me. Yet, it was clear that, for them, I was only Sonny's brother. Here, I was in Sonny's world. Or, rather: his kingdom. Here, it was not even a question that his veins bore royal blood.

They were going to play soon and Creole installed me, by myself, at a table in a dark corner. Then I watched them, Creole, and the little black man, and Sonny, and the others, while they horsed around, standing just below the bandstand. The light from the bandstand spilled just a little short of them and, watching them laughing and gesturing and moving about, I had the feeling that they, nevertheless, were being most careful not to step into that circle of light too suddenly: that if they moved into the light too suddenly, without thinking, they would perish in flame. Then, while I watched, one of them, the small, black man, moved into the light and crossed the bandstand and started fooling around with his drums. Then—being funny and being, also, extremely ceremonious—Creole took Sonny by the arm and led him to the piano. A woman's voice called Sonny's name and a few hands started clapping. And Sonny, also being funny and being ceremonious, and so touched, I think, that he could have cried, but neither hiding it nor showing it, riding it like a man, grinned, and put both hands to his heart and bowed from the waist.

Creole then went to the bass fiddle and a lean, very bright-skinned brown man jumped up on the bandstand and picked up his horn. So there they were, and the atmosphere on the bandstand and in the room began to change and tighten. Someone stepped up to the microphone and announced them. Then there were all kinds of murmurs. Some people at the bar shushed others. The waitress ran around, frantically getting in the last orders, guys and chicks got closer to each other, and the lights on the bandstand, on the quartet, turned to a kind of indigo. Then they all looked different there. Creole looked about him for the last time, as though he were making certain that all his chickens were in the coop, and then he—jumped and struck the fiddle. And there they were.

All I know about music is that not many people ever really hear it. And even then, on the rare occasions when something opens within, and the music enters, what we mainly hear, or hear corroborated, are personal, private, vanishing evocations. But the man who creates the music is hearing something else, is dealing with the roar rising from the void and imposing order on it as it hits the air. What is evoked in him, then, is of another order, more terrible because it has no words, and triumphant, too, for that same reason. And his triumph, when he triumphs, is ours. I just watched Sonny's face. His face was troubled, he was working hard, but he wasn't with it. And I had the feeling that, in a way, everyone on the bandstand was waiting for him, both waiting for him and pushing him along. But as I began to watch Creole, I realized that it was Creole who held them all back. He had them on a short rein. Up there, keeping the beat with his whole body, wailing on the fiddle, with his eyes half closed, he was listening to everything, but he was listening to Sonny. He was having a dialogue with Sonny. He wanted Sonny to leave the shoreline and strike out for the deep water. He was Sonny's witness that deep water and drowning were not the same thing—he had been there, and he knew. And he wanted Sonny to know. He was waiting for Sonny to do the things on the keys which would let Creole know that Sonny was in the water.

And, while Creole listened, Sonny moved, deep within, exactly like someone in torment. I had never before thought of how awful the relationship must be between the musician and his instrument. He has to fill it, this instrument, with the breath of life, his own. He has to make it do what he wants it to do. And a piano is just a piano. It's made out of so much wood and wires and little hammers and big ones, and ivory. While there's only so much you can do with it, the only way to find this out is to try; to try and make it do everything.

And Sonny hadn't been near a piano for over a year. And he wasn't on much better terms with his life, not the life that stretched before him now. He and the piano stammered, started one way, got scared, stopped; started another way, panicked, marked time, started again; then seemed to have found a direction, panicked again, got stuck. And the face I saw on Sonny I'd never seen before. Everything had been burned out of it, and, at the same time, things usually hidden were being burned in, by the fire and fury of the battle which was occurring in him up there.

Yet, watching Creole's face as they neared the end of the first set, I had the feeling that something had happened, something I hadn't heard. Then they finished, there was scattered applause, and then, without an instant's warning, Creole started into something else, it was almost sardonic, it was *Am I Blue*. And, as though he conmmanded, Sonny began to play. Something began to happen. And Creole let out the reins. The dry, low, black man said something awful on the drums, Creole answered, and the drums talked back. Then the horn insisted, sweet and high, slightly detached perhaps, and Creole listened, commenting now and then, dry, and driving, beautiful and calm and old. Then they all came together again, and Sonny was part of the family again. I could tell this from his face. He seemed to have found, right there beneath his fingers, a damn brand-new piano. It seemed that he couldn't get over it. Then, for awhile, just being happy with Sonny, they seemed to be agreeing with him that brand-new pianos certainly were a gas.

Then Creole stepped forward to remind them that what they were playing was the blues. He hit something in all of them, he hit something in me, myself, and the music tightened and deepened, apprehension began to beat the air. Creole began to tell us what the blues were all about. They were not about anything very new. He and his boys up there were keeping it new, at the risk of ruin, destruction, madness, and death, in order to find new ways to make us listen. For, while the tale of how we suffer, and how we are delighted, and how we may triumph is never new, it always must be heard. There isn't any other tale to tell, it's the only light we've got in all this darkness.

And this tale, according to that face, that body, those strong hands on those strings, has another aspect in every country, and a new depth in every generation. Listen, Creole seemed to be saying, listen. Now these are Sonny's blues. He made the little black man on the drums know it, and the bright, brown man on the horn. Creole wasn't trying any longer to get Sonny in the water. He was wishing him Godspeed. Then he stepped back, very slowly, filling the air with the immense suggestion that Sonny speak for himself.

Then they all gathered around Sonny and Sonny played. Every now and again one of them seemed to say, amen. Sonny's fingers filled the air with life, his life. But that life contained so many others. And Sonny went all the way back, he really began with the spare, flat statement of the opening phrase of the song. Then he began to make it his. It was very beautiful because it wasn't hurried and it was no longer a lament. I seemed to hear with what burning he had made it his, with what burning we had yet to make it ours, how we could cease lamenting. Freedom lurked around us and I understood, at last, that he could help us to be free if we would listen, that he would never be free until we did. Yet, there was no battle in his face now. I heard what he had gone through, and would continue to go through until he came to rest in earth. He had made it his: that long line, of which we knew only Mama and Daddy. And he was giving it back, as everything must be given back, so that, passing through death, it can live forever. I saw my mother's face again, and felt, for the first time, how the stones of the road she had walked on must have bruised her feet. I saw the moonlit road where my father's brother died. And it brought something else back to me, and carried me past it, I saw my little girl again and felt Isabel's tears again, and I felt my own tears begin to rise. And I was yet aware that this was only a moment, that the world waited outside, as hungry as a tiger, and that trouble stretched above us, longer than the sky.

Then it was over. Creole and Sonny let out their breath, both soaking wet, and grinning. There was a lot of applause and some of it was real. In the dark, the girl came by and I asked her to take drinks to the bandstand. There was a long pause, while they talked up there in the indigo light and after awhile I saw the girl put a Scotch and milk on top of the piano for Sonny. He didn't seem to notice it, but just before they started playing again, he sipped from it and looked toward me, and nodded. Then he put it back on top of the piano. For me, then, as they began to play again, it glowed and shook above my brother's head like the very cup of trembling.

The Lesson
(1972)

TONI CADE BAMBARA

Back in the days when everyone was old and stupid or young and foolish and me and Sugar were the only ones just right, this lady moved on our block with nappy hair and proper speech and no makeup. And quite naturally we laughed at her, laughed the way we did at the junk man who went about his business like he was some big-time president and his sorry-ass horse his secretary. And we kinda hated her too, hated the way we did the winos who cluttered up our parks and pissed on our handball walls and stank up our hallways and stairs so you couldn't halfway play hide-and-seek without a goddamn gas mask. Miss Moore was her name. The only woman on the block with no first name. And she was black as hell, cept for her feet, which were fish-white and spooky. And she was always planning these boring-ass things for us to do, us being my cousin, mostly, who lived on the block cause we all moved North the same time and to the same apartment then spread out gradual to breathe. And our parents would yank our heads into some kinda shape and crisp up our clothes so we'd be presentable for travel with Miss Moore, who always looked like she was going to church, though she never did. Which is just one of the things the grownups talked about when they talked behind her back like a dog. But when she came calling with some sachet she'd sewed up or some gingerbread she'd made or some book, why then they'd all be too embarrassed to turn her down and we'd get handed over all spruced up. She'd been to college and said it was only right that she should take responsibility for the young ones' education, and she not even related by marriage or blood. So they'd go for it. Specially Aunt Gretchen. She was the main gofer in the family. You got some ole dumb shit foolishness you want somebody to go for, you send for Aunt Gretchen. She been screwed into the go-along for so long, it's a blood-deep natural thing with her. Which is how she got saddled with me and Sugar and Junior in the first place while our mothers were in a la-de-da apartment up the block having a good ole time.

So this one day Miss Moore rounds us all up at the mailbox and it's puredee hot and she's knockin herself out about arithmetic. And school suppose to let up in summer I heard, but she don't never let up. And the starch in my pinafore scratching the shit outta me and I'm really hating this nappy-head bitch and her goddamn college degree. I'd much rather go to the pool or to the show where it's cool. So me and Sugar leaning on the mailbox being surly, which is a Miss Moore word. And Flyboy checking out what everybody brought for lunch. And Fat Butt already wasting his peanut-butter-and-jelly sandwich like the pig he is. And Junebug punchin on Q.T.'s arm for potato chips. And Rosie Giraffe shifting from one hip to the other waiting for somebody to step on her foot or ask her if she from Georgia so she can kick ass, preferably Mercedes'. And Miss Moore asking us do we know what money is, like we a bunch of retards. I mean real money, she say, like it's only poker chips or monopoly papers we lay on the grocer. So right away I'm tired of this and say so. And would much rather snatch Sugar and go to the Sunset and terrorize the West Indian kids and take their hair ribbons and their money too. And Miss Moore files that remark away for next week's lesson on brotherhood, I can tell. And finally I say we oughta get to the subway cause it's cooler and besides we might meet some cute boys. Sugar done swiped her mama's lipstick, so we ready.

So we heading down the street and she's boring us silly about what things cost and what our parents make and how much goes for rent and how money ain't divided up right in this country. And then she gets to the part about we all poor and live in the slums, which I don't feature. And I'm ready to speak on that, but she steps out in the street and hails two cabs just like that. Then she hustles half the crew in with her and hands me a five-dollar bill and tells me to calculate 10 percent tip for the driver. And we're off. Me and Sugar and Junebug and Flyboy hangin out the window and hollering to everybody, putting lipstick on each other cause Flyboy a faggot anyway, and making farts with our sweaty armpits. But I'm mostly trying to figure how to spend this money. But they all fascinated with the meter ticking and Junebug starts laying bets as to how much it'll read when Flyboy can't hold his breath no more. Then Sugar lays bets as to how much it'll be when we get there. So I'm stuck. Don't nobody want to go for my plan, which is to jump out at the next light and run off to the first bar-b-que we can find. Then the driver tells us to get the hell out cause we there already. And the meter reads eighty-five cents. And I'm stalling to figure out the tip and Sugar say give him a dime. And I decide he don't need it bad as I do, so later for him. But then he tries to take off with Junebug foot still in the door so we talk about his mama something ferocious. Then we check out that we on Fifth Avenue and everybody dressed up in stockings. One lady in a fur coat, hot as it is. White folks crazy.

"This is the place," Miss Moore say, presenting it to us in the voice she uses at the museum. "Let's look in the windows before we go in."

"Can we steal?" Sugar asks very serious like she's getting the ground rules squared away before she plays. "I beg your pardon," say Miss Moore, and we fall out. So she leads us around the windows of the toy store and me and Sugar screamin, "This is mine, that's mine, I gotta have that, that was made for me, I was born for that," till Big Butt drowns us out.

"Hey, I'm goin to buy that there."

"That there? You don't even know what it is, stupid."

"I do so," he say punchin on Rosie Giraffe. "It's a microscope."

"Whatcha gonna do with a microscope, fool?"

"Look at things."

"Like what, Ronald?" ask Miss Moore. And Big Butt ain't got the first notion. So here go Miss Moore gabbing about the thousands of bacteria in a drop of water and the somethinorother in a speck of blood and the million and one living things in the air around us is invisible to the naked eye. And what she say that for? Junebug go to town on that "naked" and we rolling. Then Miss Moore ask what it cost. So we all jam into the window smudgin it up and the price tag say $300. So then she ask how long'd take for Big Butt and Junebug to save up their allowances. "Too long," I say. "Yeh," adds Sugar, "outgrown it by that time." And Miss Moore say no, you never outgrow learning instruments. "Why, even medical students and interns and," blah, blah, blah. And we ready to choke Big Butt for bringing it up in the first damn place.

"This here costs four hundred eighty dollars," say Rosie Giraffe. So we pile up all over her to see what she pointin out. My eyes tell me it's a chunk of glass cracked with something heavy, and different-color inks dripped into the splits, then the whole thing put into a oven or something. But for $480 it don't make sense.

"That's a paperweight made of semi-precious stones fused together under tremendous pressure," she explains slowly, with her hands doing the mining and all the factory work.

"So what's a paperweight?" asks Rosie Giraffe.

"To weigh paper with, dumbbell," say Flyboy, the wise man from the East.

"Not exactly," say Miss Moore, which is what she say when you warm or way off too. "It's to weigh paper down so it won't scatter and make your desk untidy." So right away me and Sugar curtsy to each other and then to Mercedes who is more the tidy type.

"We don't keep paper on top of the desk in my class," say Junebug, figuring Miss Moore crazy or lyin one.

"At home, then," she say. "Don't you have a calendar and a pencil case and a blotter and a letter-opener on your desk at home where you do your homework?" And she know damn well what our homes look like cause she nosys around in them every chance she gets.

"I don't even have a desk," say Junebug. "Do we?"

"No. And I don't get no homework neither," say Big Butt.

"And I don't even have a home," say Flyboy like he do at school to keep the white folks off his back and sorry for him. Send this poor kid to camp posters, is his specialty.

"I do," says Mercedes. "I have a box of stationery on my desk and a picture of my cat. My godmother bought the stationery and the desk. There's a big rose on each sheet and the envelopes smell like roses."

"Who wants to know about your smelly-ass stationery," say Rosie Giraffe fore I can get my two cents in.

"It's important to have a work area all your own so that . . ."

"Will you look at this sailboat, please," say Flyboy, cutting her off and pointin to the thing like it was his. So once again we tumble all over each other to gaze at this magnificent thing in the toy store which is just big enough to maybe sail two kittens across the pond if you strap them to the posts tight. We all start reciting the price tag like we in assembly. "Handcrafted sailboat of fiberglass at one thousand one hundred ninety-five dollars."

"Unbelievable," I hear myself say and am really stunned. I read it again for myself just in case the group recitation put me in a trance. Same thing. For some reason this pisses me off. We look at Miss Moore and she lookin at us, waiting for I dunno what.

"Who'd pay all that when you can buy a sailboat set for a quarter at Pop's, a tube of glue for a dime, and a ball of string for eight cents? "It must have a motor and a whole lot else besides," I say. "My sailboat cost me about fifty cents."

"But will it take water?" say Mercedes with her smart ass.

"Took mine to Alley Pond Park once," say Flyboy. "String broke, Lost it. Pity."

"Sailed mine in Central Park and it keeled over and sank. Had to ask my father for another dollar."

"And you got the strap," laugh Big Butt. "The jerk didn't even have a string on it. My old man wailed on his behind."

Little Q.T. was staring hard at the sailboat and you could see he wanted it bad. But he too little and somebody'd just take it from him. So what the hell. "This boat for kids, Miss Moore?"

"Parents silly to buy something like that just to get all broke up," say Rosie Giraffe.

"That much money it should last forever," I figure.

"My father'd buy it for me if I wanted it."

"Your father, my ass," say Rosie Giraffe getting a chance to finally push Mercedes.

"Must be rich people shop here," say Q.T.

"You are a very bright boy," say Flyboy. "What was your first clue?" And he rap him on the head with the back of his knuckles, since Q.T. the only one he could get away with. Though Q.T. liable to come up behind you years later and get his licks in when you half expect it.

"What I want to know is," I says to Miss Moore though I never talk to her, I wouldn't give the bitch that satisfaction, "is how much a real boat costs? I figure a thousand'd get you a yacht any day."

"Why don't you check that out," she says, "and report back to the group?" Which really pains my ass. If you gonna mess up a perfectly good swim day least you could do is have some answers. "Let's go in, " she say like she got something up her sleeve. Only she don't lead the way. So me and Sugar turn the corner to where the entrance is, but when we get there I kinda hang back. Not that I'm scared, what's there to be afraid of, just a toy store. But I feel funny, shame. But what I got to be shamed about? Got as much right to go in as anybody. But somehow I can't seem to get hold of the door, so I step away for Sugar to lead. But she hangs back too. And I look at her and she looks at me and this is ridiculous. I mean, damn, I have never ever been shy about doing nothing or going nowhere. But then Mercedes steps up and then Rosie Giraffe and Big Butt crowd in behind and shove, and next thing we all stuffed into the doorway with only Mercedes squeezing past us, smoothing out her jumper and walking right down the aisle. Then the rest of us tumble in like a glued-together jigsaw done all wrong. And people lookin at us. And it's like the time me and Sugar crashed into the Catholic church on a dare. But once we got in there and everything so hushed and holy and the candles and the bow-in and the handkerchiefs on all the drooping heads, I just couldn't go through with the plan. Which was for me to run up to the altar and do a tap dance while Sugar played the nose flute and messed around in the holy water. And Sugar kept givin me the elbow. Then later teased me so bad I tied her up in the shower and turned it on and locked her in. And she'd be there till this day if Aunt Gretchen hadn't finally figured I was lyin about the boarder takin a shower.

Same thing in the store. We all walkin on tiptoe and hardly touchin the games and puzzles and things. And I watched Miss Moore who is steady watchin us like she waitin for a sign. Like Mama Drewery watches the sky and sniffs the air and takes note of just how much slant is in the bird formation. Then me and Sugar bump smack into each other, so busy gazing at the toys, 'specially the sailboat. But we don't laugh and go into our fat-lady bump-stomach routine. We just stare at that price tag. Then Sugar run a finger over the whole boat. And I'm jealous and want to hit her. Maybe not her, but I sure want to punch somebody in the mouth.

"Watcha bring us here for, Miss Moore?"

"You sound angry, Sylvia. Are you mad about something?" Givin me one of them grins like she tellin a grown-up joke that never turns out to be funny. And she's lookin very closely at me like maybe she plannin to do my portrait from memory. I'm mad, but I won't give her that satisfaction. So I slouch around the store bein very bored and say, "Let's go."

Me and Sugar at the back of the train watchin the tracks whizzin by large then small then gettin gobbled up in the dark. I'm thinkin about this tricky toy I saw in the store. A clown that somersaults on a bar then does chin-ups just cause you yank lightly at his leg. Cost $35. I could see me askin my mother for a $35 birthday clown. "You wanna who that costs what?"

she'd say, cocking her head to the side to get a better view of the hole in my head. Thirty-five dollars could buy new bunk beds for Junior and Gretchen's boy. Thirty-five dollars and the whole household could go visit Granddaddy Nelson in the country. Thirty-five dollars would pay for the rent and the piano bill too. Who are these people that spend that much for performing clowns and $1,000 for toy sailboats? What kinda work they do and how they live and how come we ain't in on it? Where we are is who we are, Miss Moore always pointin out. But it don't necessarily have to be that way, she always adds then waits for somebody to say that poor people have to wake up and demand their share of the pie and don't none of us know what kind of pie she talkin about in the first damn place. But she ain't so smart cause I still got her four dollars from the taxi and she sure ain't getting it. Messin up my day with this shit. Sugar nudges me in my pocket and winks.

Miss Moore lines us up in front of the mailbox where we started from, seem like years ago, and I got a headache for thinkin so hard. And we lean all over each other so we can hold up under the draggy-ass lecture she always finishes us off with at the end before we thank her for borin us to tears. But she just looks at us like she readin tea leaves. Finally she say, "Well, what did you think of F.A.O. Schwarz?"

Rosie Giraffe mumbles, "White folks crazy."

"I'd like to go there again when I get my birthday money," says Mercedes, and we shove her out the pack so she has to lean on the mailbox by herself.

"I'd like a shower. Tiring day," say Flyboy.

Then Sugar surprises me by sayin, "You know, Miss Moore, I don't think all of us here put together eat in a year what that sailboat costs." And Miss Moore lights up like somebody goosed her. "And?" she say, urging Sugar on. Only I'm standin on her foot so she don't continue.

"Imagine for a minute what kind of society it is in which some people can spend on a toy what it would cost to feed a family of six or seven. What do you think?"

"I think," say Sugar pushing me off her feet like she never done before, cause I whip her ass in a minute, "that this is not much of a democracy if you ask me. Equal chance to pursue happiness means an equal crack at the dough, don't it?" Miss Moore is besides herself and I am disgusted with Sugar's treachery. So I stand on her foot one more time to see if she'll shove me. She shuts up, and Miss Moore looks at me, sorrowfully I'm thinkin. And somethin weird is goin on, I can feel it in my chest.

"Anybody else learn anything today?" lookin dead at me. I walk away and Sugar has to run to catch up and don't even seem to notice when I shrug her arm off my shoulder.

"Well, we got four dollars anyway," she says.

"Uh hunh."

"We could go to Hascombs and get half a chocolate layer and then go to the Sunset and still have plenty money for potato chips and ice-cream sodas."

"Uh hunh."

"Race you to Hascombs," she say.

We start down the block and she gets ahead which is O.K. by me cause I'm goin to the West End and then over to the Drive to think this day through. She can run if she want to and even run faster. But ain't nobody gonna beat me at nuthin.

A Shower of Gold
(1963)

DONALD BARTHELME

$\mathbb{B}$ecause he needed the money Peterson answered an ad that said *"We'll pay you* to be on TV if your opinions are strong enough or your personal experiences have a flavor of the unusual." He called the number and was told to come to Room 1551 in the Graybar Building on Lexington. This he did and after spending twenty minutes with a Miss Arbor who asked him if he had ever been in analysis was okayed for a program called *Who Am I?* "What do you have strong opinions about?" Miss Arbor asked. "Art," Peterson said, "life, money." "For instance?" "I believe," Peterson said, "that the learning ability of mice can be lowered or increased by regulating the amount of serotonin in the brain. I believe that schizophrenics have a high incidence of unusual fingerprints, including lines that make almost complete circles. I believe that the dreamer watches his dream in sleep, by moving his eyes" *"That's very interesting!"* Miss Arbor cried. "It's all in the *World Almanac,"* Peterson replied.

"I see you're a sculptor," Miss Arbor said, "that's wonderful." "What is the nature of the program?" Peterson asked. "I've never seen it." "Let me answer your question with another question," Miss Arbor said. "Mr. Peterson, are you absurd?" Her enormous lips were smeared with a glowing white cream. "I beg your pardon?" "I mean," Miss Arbor said earnestly, "do you encounter your own existence as gratuitous? Do you feel *de trop?* Is there nausea?" "I have an enlarged liver," Peterson offered. "That's *excellent!"* Miss Arbor exclaimed. "That's a *very* good beginning. *Who Am I?* tries, Mr. Peterson, to discover what people *really are.* People today, we feel, are hidden away inside themselves, alienated, desperate, living in anguish, despair and bad faith. Why have we been thrown here, and abandoned? That's the question we try to answer, Mr. Peterson. Man stands alone in a featureless, anonymous landscape, in fear and trembling and sickness unto death. God is dead. Nothingness everywhere. Dread. Estrangement. Finitude. *Who Am I?* approaches these problems in a root radical way." "On television?" "We're interested in basics, Mr. Peterson. We don't play around." "I see," Peterson said, wondering about the amount of the fee. "What I want to know now, Mr. Peterson, is this: are you *interested* in absurdity?" "Miss Arbor," he said, "to tell you the truth, I don't know. I'm not sure I believe in it." "Oh, Mr. Peterson!" Miss Arbor said, shocked. "Don't *say* that! You'll be . . ." "Punished?" Peterson suggested. *"You* may not be interested in absurdity," she said firmly, "but absurdity is interested in *you."* "I have a lot of problems, if that helps,"

89

Peterson said. "Existence is problematic for you," Miss Arbor said, relieved. "The fee is two hundred dollars."

"I'm going to be on television," Peterson said to his dealer. "A terrible shame," Jean-Claude responded. "Is it unavoidable?" "It's unavoidable," Peterson said, "if I want to eat." "How much?" Jean-Claude asked and Peterson said: "Two hundred." He looked around the gallery to see if any of his works were on display. "A ridiculous compensation considering the infamy. Are you using your own name?" "You haven't by any chance . . ." "No one is buying," Jean-Claude said. "Undoubtedly it is the weather. People are thinking in terms of—what do you call those things?— Chris-Crafts. To boat with. You would not consider again what I spoke to you about before?" "No," Peterson said, "I wouldn't consider it." "Two little ones would move much, much faster than a single huge big one," Jean-Claude said, looking away. "To saw it across the middle would be a very simple matter." "It's supposed to be a work of art," Peterson said, as calmly as possible. "You don't go around sawing works of art across the middle, remember?" "That place where it saws," Jean-Claude said, "is not very difficult. I can put my two hands around it." He made a circle with his two hands to demonstrate. "Invariably when I look at that piece I see two pieces. Are you absolutely sure you didn't conceive it wrongly in the first instance?" "Absolutely," Peterson said. Not a single piece of his was on view, and his liver expanded in rage and hatred. "You have a very romantic impulse," Jean-Claude said. "I admire, dimly, the posture. You read too much in the history of art. It estranges you from those possibilities for authentic selfhood that inhere in the present century." "I know," Peterson said, "could you let me have twenty until the first?"

Peterson sat in his loft on lower Broadway drinking Rheingold and thinking about the President. He had always felt close to the President but felt now that he had, in agreeing to appear on the television program, done something slightly disgraceful, of which the President would not approve. But I needed the money, he told himself, the telephone is turned off and the kitten is crying for milk. And I'm running out of beer. The President feels that the arts should be encouraged, Peterson reflected, surely he doesn't want me to go without beer? He wondered if what he was feeling was simple guilt at having sold himself to television or something more elegant: nausea? His liver groaned within him and he considered a situation in which his new relationship with the President was announced. He was working in the loft. The piece in hand was to be called *Season's Greetings* and combined three auto radiators, one from a Chevrolet Tudor, one from a Ford pickup, one from a 1932 Essex, with part of a former telephone switchboard and other items. The arrangement seemed right and he began welding. After a time the mass was freestanding. A couple of hours had passed. He put down the torch, lifted off the mask. He walked over to the refrigerator and found a sandwich left by a friendly junk dealer. It was a sandwich made hastily and without inspiration: a thin slice of ham between two pieces of bread. He ate it gratefully nevertheless. He stood looking at the work, moving from time to time so as to view it from a new angle. Then the door to the loft burst open and the President ran in, trailing a sixteen-pound sledge. His first blow cracked the principal weld in *Season's Greetings,* the two halves parting like lovers, clinging for a moment and then rushing off in opposite directions. Twelve Secret Service men held Peterson in a paralyzing combination of secret grips. He's looking good, Peterson thought, very good, healthy, mature, fit, trustworthy. I like his suit. The President's second and third blows smashed the Essex radiator and the Chevrolet radiator. Then he attacked the welding torch, the plaster sketches on the workbench, the Rodin cast and the Giacometti stickman Peterson had bought in Paris. *"But Mr. President!"* Peterson shouted. *"I thought we were friends!"* A Secret Service man bit him in the back of the neck. Then the President lifted the sledge high in the air, turned toward Peterson, and said, "Your liver is diseased? That's a good sign. You're making progress. You're thinking."

"I happen to think that guy in the White House is doing a pretty darn good job." Peterson's barber, a man named Kitchen who was also a lay analyst and the author of four books titled *The Decision to Be,* was the only person in the world to whom he had confided his former sense of community with the President. "As far as his relationship with you personally goes," the barber continued, "it's essentially a kind of I-Thou relationship, if you know what I mean. You got to handle it with full awareness of the implications. In the end one experiences only oneself, Nietzsche said. When you're angry with the President, what you experience is self-as-angry-with-the-President. When things are okay between you and him, what you experience is self-as-swinging-with-the-President. Well and good. *But,"* Kitchen said, lathering up, "you want the relationship to be such that what you experience is the-President-as-swinging-with-you. You want *his* reality, get it? So that you can break out of the hell of solipsism. How about a little more off the sides?" "Everybody knows the language but me," Peterson said irritably. "Look," Kitchen said, "when you talk about me to somebody else, you say 'my barber,' don't you? Sure you do. In the same way, I look on you as being 'my customer,' get it? But you don't regard yourself as being 'my' customer and I don't regard myself as 'your' barber. Oh, it's hell all right." The razor moved like a switchblade across the back of Peterson's neck. "Like Pascal said: 'The natural misfortune of our mortal and feeble condition is so wretched that when we consider it closely, nothing can console us.'" The razor rocketed around an ear. "Listen," Peterson said, "what do you think of this television program called *Who Am I?* Ever seen it?" "Frankly," the barber said, "it smells of the library. But they do a job on those people, I'll tell you that." "What do you mean?" Peterson said excitedly. "What kind of a job?" The cloth was whisked away and shaken with a sharp popping sound. "It's too horrible even to talk about," Kitchen said. "But it's what they deserve, those crumbs." "Which crumbs?" Peterson asked.

That night a tall foreign-looking man with a switchblade big as a butcherknife open in his hand walked into the loft without knocking and said "Good evening, Mr. Peterson, I am the cat-piano player, is there anything you'd particularly like to hear?" "Cat-piano?" Peterson said, gasping, shrinking from the knife. "What are you talking about? What do you want?" A biography of Nolde slid from his lap to the floor. "The cat-piano," said the visitor, "is an instrument of the devil, a diabolical instrument. You needn't sweat quite so much," he added, sounding aggrieved. Peterson tried to be brave. "I don't understand," he said. "Let me explain," the tall foreign-looking man said graciously. "The keyboard consists of eight cats—the octave—encased in the body of the instrument in such a way that only their heads and forepaws protrude. The player presses upon the appropriate paws, and the appropriate cats respond—with a kind of shriek. There is also provision made for pulling their tails. A tail-puller, or perhaps I should say tail *player"* (he smiled a disingenuous smile) "is stationed at the rear of the instrument, where the tails are. At the correct moment the tail-puller pulls the correct tail. The tail-note is of course quite different from the paw-note and produces sounds in the upper registers. Have you ever seen such an instrument, Mr. Peterson?" "No, and I don't believe it exists," Peterson said heroically.

"There is an excellent early seventeenth century engraving by Franz van der Wyngaert, Mr. Peterson, in which a cat-piano appears. Played, as it happens, by a man with a wooden leg. You will observe my own leg." The cat-piano player hoisted his trousers and a leglike contraption of wood, metal and plastic appeared. "And now, would you like to make a request? 'The Martyrdom of St. Sebastian'? The 'Romeo and Juliet' overture? 'Holiday for Strings'?" "But why—" Peterson began. "The kitten is crying for milk, Mr. Peterson. And whenever a kitten cries, the cat-piano plays." "But it's not my kitten," Peterson said reasonably "It's just a kitten that wished itself on me. I've been trying to give it away. I'm not sure it's still around. I haven't seen it since the day before yesterday." The kitten appeared, looked at Peterson reproachfully, and then rubbed itself against the cat-piano player's mechanical leg. "Wait a minute! " Peterson exclaimed. "This thing is rigged! That cat hasn't been here in two days. What do you want from me? What am I supposed to do?" "Choices, Mr. Peterson, choices. You *chose* that kitten as a way of encountering that which you are not, that is to say, kitten. An effort on the part of the *pour-soi* to—" "But it chose me!" Peterson cried, "the door was open and the first thing I knew it was lying in my bed, under the Army blanket. I didn't have anything to do with it!" The cat-piano player repeated his disingenuous smile. "Yes, Mr. Peterson, I know, I know. Things are done to you, it is all a gigantic conspiracy. I've heard the story a hundred times. But the kitten is here, is it not? The kitten is weeping, is it not?" Peterson looked at the kitten, which was crying huge tigerish tears into its empty dish. *"Listen,* Mr. Peterson," the cat-piano player said, *"listen!"* The blade of his immense knife jumped back into the handle with a thwack! and the hideous music began.

The day after the hideous music began the three girls from California arrived. Peterson opened his door, hesitantly, in response to an insistent ringing, and found himself being stared at by three girls in blue jeans and heavy sweaters, carrying suitcases. "I'm Sherry," the first girl said, "and this is Ann and this is Louise. We're from California and we need a place to stay." They were homely and extremely purposeful. "I'm sorry," Peterson said, "I can't—" "We sleep anywhere," Sherry said, looking past him into the vastness of his loft, "on the floor if we have to. We've done it before." Ann and Louise stood on their toes to get a good look. "What's that funny music?" Sherry asked, "it sounds pretty far-out. We really won't be any trouble at all and it'll just be a little while until we make a connection." "Yes," Peterson said, "but why me?" "You're an artist," Sherry said sternly, "we saw the AIR sign downstairs." Peterson cursed the fire laws which made posting of the signs obligatory. "Listen," he said, "I can't even feed the cat. I can't even keep myself in beer. This is not the place. You won't be happy here. My work isn't authentic. I'm a minor artist." "The natural misfortune of our mortal and feeble condition is so wretched that when we consider it closely, nothing can console us," Sherry said. "That's Pascal." "I know," Peterson said, weakly. "Where is the john?" Louise asked. Ann marched into the kitchen and began to prepare, from supplies removed from her rucksack, something called *veal engagé.* "Kiss me," Sherry said, "I need love." Peterson flew to his friendly neighborhood bar, ordered a double brandy, and thrust himself into a telephone booth. "Miss Arbor? This is Hank Peterson. Listen, Miss Arbor, I can't do it. No, I mean really. I'm being punished horribly for even thinking about it. No, I mean it. You can't imagine what's going on around here. Please, get somebody else? I'd regard it as a great personal favor. Miss Arbor? Please?"

The other contestants were a young man in white pajamas named Arthur Pick, a karate expert, and an airline pilot in full uniform, Wallace E. Rice. "Just be natural," Miss Arbor said, "and of course be frank. We score on the basis of the validity of your answers, and of course that's measured by the polygraph." "What's this about a polygraph?" the airline pilot said. "The polygraph measures the validity of your answers," Miss Arbor said, her lips glowing whitely. "How else are we going to know if you're ... " "Lying?" Wallace E. Rice supplied. The contestants were connected to the machine and the machine to a large illuminated tote board hanging over their heads. The master of ceremonies, Peterson noted without pleasure, resembled the President and did not look at all friendly.

The program began with Arthur Pick. Arthur Pick got up in his white pajamas and gave a karate demonstration in which he broke three half-inch pine boards with a single kick of his naked left foot. Then he told how he had disarmed a bandit, late at night at the A&P where he was an assistant manager, with a maneuver called a "rip-choong" which he demonstrated on the announcer. "How about that?" the announcer caroled. "Isn't that something? Audience?" The audience responded enthusiastically and Arthur Pick stood modestly with his hands behind his back. "Now," the announcer said, "let's play *Who Am I?* And here's your host, *Bill Lemmon!*" No, he doesn't look like the President, Peterson decided. "Arthur," Bill Lemmon said, "for twenty dollars—do you love your mother?" "Yes," Arthur Pick said. "Yes, of course." A bell rang, the tote board flashed, and the audience screamed. "He's lying!" the announcer shouted, "lying! lying! lying!" "Arthur," Bill Lemmon said, looking at his index cards, "the polygraph shows that the validity of your answer is . . . questionable Would you like to try it again? Take another crack at it?" "You're crazy," Arthur Pick said. "Of course I love my mother." He was fishing around inside his pajamas for a handkerchief. "Is your mother watching the show tonight, Arthur?" "Yes, Bill, she is." "How long have you been studying karate?" "Two years, Bill." "And who paid for the lessons?" Arthur Pick hesitated. Then he said: "My mother, Bill." "They were pretty expensive, weren't they, Arthur?" "Yes, Bill, they were." "How expensive?" "Twelve dollars an hour." "Your mother doesn't make very much. money, does she, Arthur?" "No, Bill, she doesn't." "Arthur, what does your mother do for a living?" "She's a garment worker, Bill. In the garment district." "And how long has she worked down there?" "All her life, I guess. Since my old man died." "And she doesn't make very much money, you said." "No. But she *wanted* to pay for the lessons. She *insisted* on it." Bill Lemmon said; "She wanted a son who could break boards with his feet?" Peterson's liver leaped and the tote board spelled out, in huge, glowing white letters, the words BAD FAITH. The airline pilot, Wallace E. Rice, was led to reveal that he had been caught, on a flight from Omaha to Miami, with a stewardess sitting on his lap and wearing his captain's cap, that the flight engineer had taken a Polaroid picture, and that he had been given involuntary retirement after nineteen years of faithful service. "It was perfectly safe, " Wallace E. Rice said, "you don't understand, the automatic pilot can fly that plane better than I can." He further confessed to a lifelong and intolerable itch after stewardesses which had much to do, he said, with the way their jackets fell just on top of their hips, and his own jacket with the three gold stripes on the sleeve darkened with sweat until it was black.

I was wrong, Peterson thought, the world is absurd. The absurdity is punishing me for not believing in it. I affirm the absurdity. On the other hand, absurdity is itself absurd Before the emcee could ask the first question, Peterson began to talk. "Yesterday," Peterson said to the television audience, "in the typewriter in front of the Olivetti showroom on Fifth Avenue, I found a recipe for Ten Ingredient Soup that included a stone from a toad's head. And while I stood there marveling a nice old lady pasted on the elbow of my best Haspel suit a little blue sticker reading THIS INDIVIDUAL IS A PART OF THE COMMUNIST CONSPIRACY FOR GLOBAL DOMINATION OF THE ENTIRE GLOBE. Coming home I passed a sign that said in ten-foot letters COWARD SHOES and heard a man singing "Golden Earrings" in a horrible voice, and last night I dreamed there was a shoot-out at our house on Meat Street and my mother shoved me in a closet to get me out of the line of fire." The emcee waved at the floor manager to turn Peterson off, but Peterson kept talking "In this kind of a world," Peterson said, "absurd if you will, possibilities nevertheless proliferate and escalate all around us and there are opportunities for beginning again. I am a minor artist and my dealer won't even display my work if he can help it but minor is as minor does and lightning may strike even yet. Don't be reconciled. Turn off your television sets," Peterson said, "cash in your life insurance, indulge in a mindless optimism Visit girls at dusk. Play the guitar. How can you be alienated without first having been connected? Think back and remember how it was." A man on the floor in front of Peterson was waving a piece of cardboard on which something threatening was written but Peterson ignored him and concentrated on the camera with the little red light. The little red light jumped from camera to camera in an attempt to throw him off balance but Peterson was too smart for it and followed wherever it went "My mother was a royal virgin," Peterson said, "and my father a shower of gold. My childhood was pastoral and energetic and rich in experiences which developed my character. As a young man I was noble in reason, infinite in faculty, in form express and admirable, and in apprehension . . ." Peterson went on and on and although he was, in a sense, lying, in a sense he was not.

First Love
(1973)

SAMUEL BECKETT

I ASSOCIATE, rightly or wrongly, my marriage with the death of my father, in time. That other links exist, on other levels, between these two affairs, is not impossible. I have enough trouble as it is in trying to say what I think I know.

I visited, not so long ago, my father's grave, that I do know, and noted the date of his death, of his death alone, for that of his birth had no interest for me, on that particular day. I set out in the morning and was back by night, having lunched lightly in the graveyard. But some days later, wishing to know his age at death, I had to return to the grave, to note the date of his birth. These two limiting dates I then jotted down on a piece of paper, which I now carry about with me. I am thus in a position to affirm that I must have been about twenty-five at the time of my marriage. For the date of my own birth, I repeat, my own birth, I have never forgotten, I never had to note it down, it remains graven in my memory, the year at least, in figures that life will not easily erase. The day itself comes back to me, when I put my mind to it, and I often celebrate it, after my fashion, I don't say each time it comes back, for it comes back too often, but often.

Personally I have no bone to pick with graveyards, I take the air there willingly, perhaps more willingly than elsewhere, when take the air I must. The smell of corpses, distinctly perceptible under those of grass and humus mingled, I do not find unpleasant, a trifle on the sweet side perhaps, a trifle heady, but how infinitely preferable to what the living emit, their feet, teeth, armpits, arses, sticky foreskins and frustrated ovules. And when my father's remains join in, however modestly, I can almost shed a tear. The living wash in vain, in vain perfume themselves, they stink. Yes, as a place for an outing, when out I must, leave me my graveyards and keep—you—to your public parks and beauty-spots. My sandwich, my banana, taste sweeter when I'm sitting on a tomb, and when the time comes to piss again, as it so often does, I have my pick. Or I wander, hands clasped behind my back, among the slabs, the flat, the leaning and the upright, culling the inscriptions. Of these I never weary, there are always three or four of such drollery that I have to hold on to the cross, or the stele, or the angel, so as not to fall. Mine I composed long since and am still pleased with it, tolerably pleased. My other writings are no sooner dry than they revolt me, but my epitaph still meets with my approval. There is little chance unfortunately of its ever being reared above the skull that conceived it, unless the State takes up the matter. But to be unearthed I must first be found, and I greatly fear those gentlemen will have as much trouble finding me dead as alive. So I hasten to record it here and now, while there is yet time:

Hereunder lies the above who up below
So hourly died that be lived on till now.

The second and last or rather latter line limps a little perhaps, but that is no great matter, I'll be forgiven more than that when I'm forgotten. Then with a little luck you hit on a genuine interment, with real live mourners and the odd relict trying to throw herself into the pit. And nearly always that charming business with the dust, though in my experience there is nothing less dusty than holes of this type, verging on muck for the most part, nor anything particularly powdery about the deceased, unless he happened to have died, or she, by fire. No matter, their little gimmick with the dust is charming. But my father's yard was not amongst my favourites. To begin with it was too remote, way out in the wilds of the country on the side of a hill, and too small, far too small, to go on with. Indeed it was almost full, a few more widows and they'd be turning them away. I infinitely preferred Ohlsdorf, particularly the Linne section, on Prussian soil, with its nine hundred acres of corpses packed tight, though I knew no one there, except by reputation the wild animal collector Hagenbeck. A lion, if I remember right, is carved on his monument, death must have had for Hagenbeck the countenance of a lion. Coaches ply to and fro, crammed with widows, widowers, orphans and the like. Groves, grottoes, artificial lakes with swans, offer consolation to the inconsolable. It was December, I had never felt so cold, the eel soup lay heavy on my stomach, I was afraid I'd die, I turned aside to vomit, I envied them.

But to pass on to less melancholy matters, on my father's death I had to leave the house. It was he who wanted me in the house. He was a strange man. One day he said, Leave him alone, he's not disturbing anyone. He didn't know I was listening. This was a view he must have often voiced, but the other times I wasn't by. They would never let me see his will, they simply said he had left me such a sum. I believed then and still believe he had stipulated in his will that I be left the room I had occupied in his lifetime and for food to be brought me there, as hitherto. He may even have given this the force of condition precedent. Presumably he liked to feel me under his roof, otherwise he would not have opposed my eviction. Perhaps he merely pitied me. But somehow I think not. He should have left me the entire house, then I'd have been all right, the others too for that matter, I'd have summoned them and said, Stay, stay by all means, your home is here. Yes, he was properly had, my poor father, if his purpose was really to go on protecting me from beyond the tomb. With regard to the money it is only fair to say they gave it to me without delay, on the very day following the inhumation. Perhaps they were legally bound to. I said to them, Keep this money and let me live on here, in my room, as in Papa's lifetime. I added, God rest his soul, in the hope of melting them. But they refused. I offered to place myself at their disposal, a few hours every day, for the little odd maintenance jobs every dwelling requires, if it is not to crumble away. Pottering is still just possible, I don't know why. I proposed in particular to look after the hothouse. There I would have gladly whiled away the hours, in the heat, tending the tomatoes, hyacinths, pinks and seedlings. My father and I alone, in that household, understood tomatoes. But they refused. One day, on my return from stool, I found my room locked and my belongings in a heap before the door. This will give you some idea how constipated I was, at this juncture. It was, I am now convinced, anxiety constipation. But was I genuinely constipated? Somehow I think not. Softly, softly. And yet I must have been, for how otherwise account for those long, those cruel sessions in the necessary house? At such times I never read, any more than at other times, never gave way to revery or meditation, just gazed dully at the almanac hanging from a nail before my eyes, with its chromo of a bearded stripling in the midst of sheep, Jesus no doubt, parted the cheeks with both hands and strained, heave! ho! heave! ho!, with the motions of one tugging at the oar, and only one thought in my mind, to be back in my room and flat on my back again. What can that have been but constipation? Or am I confusing it with diarrhoea? It's all a muddle in my head, graves and nuptials and the different varieties of motion. Of my scanty belongings they had made a little heap, on the floor, against the door. I can still see that little heap, in the kind of recess full of shadow between the landing and my room. It was in this narrow space, guarded on three sides only, that I had to change, I mean exchange my dressing-gown and nightgown for my travelling costume, I mean shoes, socks, trousers, shirt, coat, greatcoat and hat, I can think of nothing else. I tried other doors, turning the knobs and pushing, or pulling, before I left the house, but none yielded. I think if I'd found one open I'd have barricaded myself in the room, nothing less than gas would have dislodged me. I felt the house crammed as usual, the usual pack, but saw no one. I imagined them in their various rooms, all bolts drawn, every sense on the alert. Then the rush to the window, each holding back a little, hidden by the curtain, at the sound of the street door closing behind me, I should have left it open. Then the doors fly open and out they pour, men, women and children, and the voices, the sighs, the smiles, the hands, the keys in the hands, the blessed relief, the precautions rehearsed, if this then that, but if that then this, all clear and joy in every heart, come let's eat, the fumigation can wait. All imagination to be sure, I was already on my way, things may have passed quite differently, but who cares how things pass, provided they pass. All those lips that had kissed me, those hearts that had loved me (it is with the heart one loves, is it not, or am I confusing it with something else?), those hands that had played with mine and those minds that had almost made their own of me! Humans are truly strange. Poor Papa, a nice mug he must have felt that day if he could see me, see us, a nice mug on my account I mean. Unless in his great disembodied wisdom he saw further than his son whose corpse was not yet quite up to scratch.

But to pass on to less melancholy matters, the name of the woman with whom I was soon to be united was Lulu. So at least she assured me and I can't see what interest she could have had in lying to me, on this score. Of course one can never tell. She also disclosed her family name, but I've forgotten it. I should have made a note of it, on a piece of paper, I hate to forget a proper name. I met her on a bench, on the bank of the canal, one of the canals, for our town boasts two, though I never knew which was which. It was a well situated bench, backed by a mound of solid earth and garbage, so that my rear was covered. My flanks too, partially, thanks to a pair of venerable trees, more than venerable, dead, at either end of the bench. It was no doubt these trees one fine day, aripple with all their foliage, that had sown the idea of a bench, in someone's fancy. To the fore, a few yards away, flowed the canal, if canals flow, don't ask me, so that from that quarter too the risk of surprise was small. And yet she surprised me. I lay stretched out, the night being warm, gazing up through the bare boughs interlocking high above me, where the trees clung together for support, and through the drifting cloud, at a patch of starry sky as it came and went. Shove up, she said. My first movement was to go, but my fatigue, and my having nowhere to go, dissuaded me from acting on it. So I drew back my feet a little way and she sat. Nothing more passed between us that evening and she soon took herself off, without another word. All she had done was sing, beneath her breath as to herself, and without the words fortunately, some old folk songs, and so disjointedly, skipping from one to another and finishing none, that even I found it strange.

The voice, though out of tune, was not unpleasant. It breathed of a soul too soon wearied ever to conclude, that perhaps least arse-aching soul of all. The bench itself was soon more than she could bear and as for me, one look had been enough for her. Whereas in reality she was a most tenacious woman. She came back next day and the day after and all went off more or less as before. Perhaps a few words were exchanged. The next day it was raining and I felt in security. Wrong again. I asked her if she was resolved to disturb me every evening. I disturb you? she said. I felt her eyes on me. They can't have seen much, two eyelids at the most, with a hint of nose and brow, darkly, because of the dark. I thought we were easy, she said. You disturb me, I said, I can't stretch out with you there. The collar of my greatcoat was over my mouth and yet she heard me. Must you stretch out? she said. The mistake one makes is to speak to people. You have only to put your feet on my knees, she said. I didn't wait to be asked twice, under my miserable calves I felt her fat thighs. She began stroking my ankles. I considered kicking her in the cunt. You speak to people about stretching out and they immediately see a body at full length. What mattered to me in my dispeopled kingdom, that in regard to which the disposition of my carcass was the merest and most futile of accidents, was supineness in the mind, the dulling of the self and of that residue of execrable frippery known as the non-self and even the world, for short. But man is still today, at the age of twenty-five, at the mercy of an erection, physically too, from time to time, it's the common lot, even I was not immune, if that may be called an erection. It did not escape her naturally, women smell a rigid phallus ten miles away and wonder, How on earth did he spot me from there? One is no longer oneself, on such occasions, and it is painful to be no longer oneself, even more painful if possible than when one is. For when one is one knows what to do to be less so, whereas when one is not one is any old one irredeemably. What goes by the name of love is banishment, with now and then a postcard from the homeland, such is my considered opinion, this evening. When she had finished and my self been resumed, mine own, the mitigable, with the help of a brief torpor, it was alone. I sometimes wonder if that is not all invention, if in reality things did not take quite a different course, one I had no choice but to forget. And yet her image remains bound, for me, to that of the bench, not the bench by day, nor yet the bench by night, but the bench at evening, in such sort that to speak of the bench, as it appeared to me at evening, is to speak of her, for me. That proves nothing, but there is nothing I wish to prove. On the subject of the bench by day no words need be wasted, it never knew me, gone before morning and never back till dusk. Yes, in the daytime I foraged for food and marked down likely cover. Were you to inquire, as undoubtedly you itch, what I had done with the money my father had left me, the answer would be I had done nothing with it but leave it lie in my pocket. For I knew I would not be always young, and that summer does not last for ever either, nor even autumn, my mean soul told me so. In the end I told her I'd had enough. She disturbed me exceedingly, even absent. Indeed she still disturbs me, but no worse now than the rest. And it matters nothing to me now, to be disturbed, or so little, what does it mean, disturbed, and what would I do with myself if I wasn't? Yes, I've changed my system, it's the winning one at last, for the ninth or tenth time, not to mention not long now, not long till curtain down, on disturbers and disturbed, no more tattle about that, all that, her and the others, the shitball and heaven's high halls. So you don't want me to come any more, she said. It's incredible the way they repeat what you've just said to them, as if they risked faggot and fire in believing their ears. I told her to come just the odd time. I didn't understand women at that period. I still don't for that matter. Nor men either. Nor animals either. What I understand best, which is not saying much, are my pains. I think them through daily, it doesn't take long, thought moves so fast, but they are not only in my thought, not all. Yes, there are moments, particularly in the afternoon, when I go all syncretist, à la Reinhold. What equilibrium! But even them, my pains, I understand ill. That must come from my not being all pain and nothing else. There's the rub. Then they recede, or I, till they fill me with amaze and wonder, seen from a better planet. Not often, but I ask no more. Catch-cony life! To be nothing but pain, how that would simplify matters! Omnidolent! Impious dream. I'll tell them to you some day none the less, if I think of it, if I can, my strange pains, in detail, distinguishing between the different kinds, for the sake of clarity, those of the mind, those of the heart or emotional conative, those of the soul (none prettier than these) and finally those of the frame proper, first the inner or latent, then those affecting the surface, beginning with the hair and scalp and moving methodically down, without haste, all the way down to the feet beloved of the corn, the cramp, the kibe, the bunion, the hammer toe, the nail ingrown, the fallen arch, the common blain, the club foot, duck foot, goose foot, pigeon foot, flat foot, trench foot and other curiosities. And I'll tell by the same token, for those kind enough to listen, in accordance with a system whose inventor I forget, of those instants when, neither drugged, nor drunk, nor in ecstasy, one feels nothing. Next of course she desired to know what I meant by the odd time, that's what you get for opening your mouth. Once a week? Once in ten days? Once a fortnight? I replied less often, far less often, less often to the point of no more if she could, and if she could not the least often possible. And the next day (what is more) I abandoned the bench, less I must confess on her account than on its, for the site no longer answered my requirements, modest though they were, now that the air was beginning to strike chill, and for other reasons better not wasted on cunts like you, and took refuge in a deserted cowshed marked on one of my forays. It stood in the corner of a field richer on the surface in nettles than in grass and in mud than in nettles, but whose subsoil was perhaps possessed of exceptional qualities. It was in this byre, littered with dry and hollow cowclaps subsiding with a sigh at the poke of my finger, that for the first time in my life, and I would not hesitate to say the last if I had not to husband my cyanide, I had to contend with a feeling which gradually assumed, to my dismay, the dread name of love. What constitutes the charm of our country, apart of course from its scant population, and this without help of the meanest contraceptive, is that all is derelict, with the sole exception of history's ancient faeces. These are ardently sought after, stuffed and carried in procession. Wherever nauseated time has dropped a nice fat turd you will find our patriots, sniffing it up on all fours, their faces on fire. Elysium of the roofless. Hence my happiness at last. Lie down, all seems to say, lie down and stay down. I see no connexion between these remarks. But that one exists, and even more than one, I have little doubt, for my part. But what? Which? Yes, I loved her, it's the name I gave, still give alas, to what I was doing then. I had nothing to go by, having never loved before, but of course had heard of the thing, at home, in school, in brothel and at church, and read romances, in prose and verse, under the guidance of my tutor, in six or seven languages, both dead and living, in which it was handled at length. I was therefore in a position, in spite of all, to put a label on what I was about when I found myself inscribing the letters of Lulu in an old heifer pat or flat on my face in the mud under the moon trying to tear up the nettles by the roots. They were giant nettles some full three foot high, to tear them up assuaged my pain, and yet it's not like me to do that to weeds, on the contrary, I'd smother them in manure if I had any. Flowers are a different matter. Love brings out the worst in man and no error. But what kind of love was this, exactly? Love-passion? Somehow I think not. That's the priapic one, is it not? Or is this a different variety? There are so many, are there not? All equally if not more delicious, are they not? Platonic love, for example, there's another just occurs to me. It's disinterested. Perhaps I loved her with a platonic love? But somehow I think not. Would I have been tracing her name in old cowshit if my love had been pure and disinterested? And with my devil's finger into the bargain, which I then sucked. Come now! My thoughts were all of Lulu, if that doesn't give you some idea nothing will. Anyhow I'm sick and tired of this name Lulu, I'll give her another, more like her, Anna for example, it's not more like her but no matter. I thought of Anna then, I who had learnt to think of nothing, nothing except my pains, a quick think through, and of what steps to take not to perish off-hand of hunger, or cold, or shame, but never on any account of living beings as such (I wonder what that means) whatever I may have said, or may still say, to the contrary or otherwise, on this subject. But I have always spoken, no doubt always shall, of things that never existed, or that existed if you insist, no doubt always will, but not with the existence I ascribe to them. Kepis, for example, exist beyond a doubt, indeed there is little hope of their ever disappearing, but personally I never wore a kepi. I wrote somewhere, They gave me . . . a hat. Now the truth is they never gave me a hat, I have always had my own hat, the one my father gave me, and I have never had any other hat than that hat. I may add it has followed me to the grave. I thought of Anna then, long long sessions, twenty minutes, twenty-five minutes and even as long as half an hour daily. I obtain these figures by the addition of other, lesser figures. That must have been my way of loving. Are we to infer from this I loved her with that intellectual love which drew from me such drivel, in another place? Somehow I think not. For had my love been of this kind would I have stooped to inscribe the letters of Anna in time's forgotten cowpats? To divellicate urtica *plenis manibus*? And felt, under my tossing head, her thighs to bounce like so many demon bolsters? Come now! In order to put an end, to try and put an end, to this plight, I returned one evening to the bench, at the hour she had used to join me there. There was no sign of her and I waited in vain. It was December already, if not January, and the cold was seasonable, that is to say reasonable, like all that is seasonable. But one is the hour of the dial, and another that of changing air and sky, and another yet again the heart's. To this thought, once back in the straw, I owed an excellent night. The next day I was earlier to the bench, much earlier, night having barely fallen, winter night, and yet too late, for she was there already, on the bench, under the boughs tinkling with rime, her back to the frosted mound, facing the icy water. I told you she was a highly tenacious woman. I felt nothing. What interest could she have in pursuing me thus? I asked her, without sitting down, stumping to and fro. The cold had embossed the path. She replied she didn't know. What could she see in me, would she kindly tell me that at least, if she could. She replied she couldn't. She seemed warmly clad, her hands buried in a muff. As I looked at this muff, I remember, tears came to my eyes. And yet I forget what colour it was. The state I was in then! I have always wept freely, without the least benefit to myself, till recently. If I had to weep this minute I could squeeze till I was blue, I'm convinced not a drop would fall. The state I am in now! It was things made me weep. And yet I felt no sorrow. When I found myself in tears for no apparent reason it meant I had caught sight of something unbeknownst. So I wonder if it was really the muff that evening, if it was not rather the path, so iron hard and bossy as perhaps to feel like cobbles to my tread, or some other thing, some chance thing glimpsed below the threshold, that so unmanned me. As for her, I might as well never have laid eyes on her before. She sat all huddled and muffled up, her head sunk, the muff with her hands in her lap, her legs pressed tight together, her heels clear of the ground. Shapeless, ageless, almost lifeless, it might have been anything or anyone, an old woman or a little girl. And the way she kept on saying, I don't know, I can't. I alone did not know and could not. Is it on my account you came? I said. She managed yes to that. Well here I am, I said. And I? Had I not come on hers? Here we are, I said. I sat down beside her but sprang up again immediately as though scalded. I longed to be gone, to know if it was over. But before going, to be on the safe side, I asked her to sing me a song. I thought at first she was going to refuse, I mean simply not sing, but no, after a moment she began to sing and sang for some time, all the time the same song it seemed to me, without change of attitude. I did not know the song, I had never heard it before and shall never hear it again. It had something to do with lemon trees, or orange trees, I forget, that is all I remember, and for me that is no mean feat, to remember it had something to do with lemon trees, or orange trees, I forget, for of all the other songs I have ever heard in my life, and I have heard plenty, it being apparently impossible, physically impossible short of being deaf, to get through this world, even my way, without hearing singing, I have retained nothing, not a word, not a note, or so few words, so few notes, that, that what, that nothing, this sentence has gone on long enough. Then I started to go and as I went I heard her singing another song, or perhaps more verses of the same, fainter and fainter the further I went, then no more, either because she had come to an end or because I was gone too far to hear her. To have to harbour such a doubt was something I preferred to avoid, at that period. I lived of course in doubt, on doubt, but such trivial doubts as this, purely somatic as some say, were best cleared up without delay, they could nag at me like gnats for weeks on end. So I retraced my steps a little way and stopped. At first I heard nothing, then the voice again, but only just, so faintly did it carry. First I didn't hear it, then I did, I must therefore have begun hearing it, at a certain point, but no, there was no beginning, the sound emerged so softly from the silence and so resembled it. When the voice ceased at last I approached a little nearer, to make sure it had really ceased and not merely been lowered. Then in despair, saying, No knowing, no knowing, short of being beside her, bent over her, I turned on my heel and went, for good, full of doubt. But some weeks later, even more dead than alive than usual, I returned to the bench, for the fourth or fifth time since I had abandoned it, at roughly the same hour, I mean roughly the same sky, no, I don't mean that either, for it's always the same sky and never the same sky, what words are there for that, none I know, period. She wasn't there, then suddenly she was, I don't know how, I didn't see her come, nor hear her, all ears and eyes though I was. Let us say it was raining, nothing like a change, if only of weather. She had her umbrella up, naturally, what an outfit. I asked if she came every evening. No, she said, just the odd time. The bench was soaking wet, we paced up and down, not daring to sit. I took her arm, out of curiosity, to see if it would give me pleasure, it gave me none, I let it go. But why these particulars. To put off the evil hour. I saw her face a little clearer, it seemed normal to me, a face like millions of others. The eyes were crooked, but I didn't know that till later. It looked neither young nor old, the face, as though stranded between the vernal and the sere. Such ambiguity I found difficult to bear, at that period. As to whether it was beautiful, the face, or had once been beautiful, or could conceivably become beautiful, I confess I could form no opinion. I had seen faces in photographs I might have found beautiful had I known even vaguely in what beauty was supposed to consist. And my father's face, on his death-bolster, had seemed to hint at some form of aesthetics relevant to man. But the faces of the living, all grimace and flush, can they be described as objects? I admired in spite of the dark, in spite of my fluster, the way still or scarcely flowing water reaches up, as though athirst, to that falling from the sky. She asked if I would like her to sing something. I replied no, I would like her to say something. I thought she would say she had nothing to say, it would have been like her, and so was agreeably surprised when she said she had a room, most agreeably surprised, though I suspected as much. Who has not a room? Ah I hear the clamour. I have two rooms, she said. Just how many rooms do you have? I said. She said she had two rooms and a kitchen. The premises were expanding steadily, given time she would remember a bathroom. Is it two rooms I heard you say? I said. Yes, she said. Adjacent? I said. At last conversation worthy of the name. Separated by the kitchen, she said. I asked her why she had not told me before. I must have been beside myself, at this period. I did not feel easy when I was with her, but at least free to think of something else than her, of the old trusty things, and so little by little, as down steps towards a deep, of nothing. And I knew that away from her I would forfeit this freedom.

There were in fact two rooms, separated by a kitchen, she had not lied to me. She said I should have fetched my things. I explained I had no things. It was at the top of an old house, with a view of the mountains for those who cared. She lit an oil-lamp. You have no current? I said. No, she said, but I have running water and gas. Ha, I said, you have gas. She began to undress. When at their wit's end they undress, no doubt the wisest course. She took off everything, with a slowness fit to enflame an elephant, except her stockings, calculated presumably to bring my concupiscence to the boil. It was then I noticed the squint. Fortunately she was not the first naked woman to have crossed my path, so I could stay, I knew she would not explode. I asked to see the other room which I had not yet seen. If I had seen it already I would have asked to see it again. Will you not undress? she said. Oh you know, I said, I seldom undress. It was the truth, I was never one to undress indiscriminately. I often took off my boots when I went to bed, I mean when I composed myself (composed!) to sleep, not to mention this or that outer garment according to the outer temperature. She was therefore obliged, out of common savoir faire, to throw on a wrap and light me the way. We went via the kitchen. We could just as well have gone via the corridor, as I realized later, but we went via the kitchen, I don't know why, perhaps it was the shortest way. I surveyed the room with horror. Such density of furniture defeats imagination. Not a doubt, I must have seen that room somewhere. What's this? I cried. The parlour, she said. The parlour! I began putting out the furniture through the door to the corridor. She watched, in sorrow I suppose, but not necessarily. She asked me what I was doing. She can't have expected an answer. I put it out piece by piece, and even two at a time, and stacked it all up in the corridor, against the outer wall. There were hundreds of pieces, large and small, in the end they blocked the door, making egress impossible, and a *fortiori* ingress, to and from the corridor. The door could be opened and closed, since it opened inwards, but had become impassable. To put it mildly. At least take off your hat, she said. I'll treat of my hat some other time perhaps. Finally the room was empty but for a sofa and some shelves fixed to the wall. The former I dragged to the back of the room, near the door, and next day took down the latter and put them out, in the corridor, with the rest. As I was taking them down, strange memory, I heard the word fibrome, or brone, I don't know which, never knew, never knew what it meant and never had the curiosity to find out. The things one recalls! and records! When all was in order at last I dropped on the sofa. She had not raised her little finger to help me. I'll get sheets and blankets, she said. But I wouldn't hear of sheets. You couldn't draw the curtain? I said. The window was frosted over. The effect was not white, because of the night, but faintly luminous none the less. This faint cold sheen, though I lay with my feet towards the door, was more than I could bear. I suddenly rose and changed the position of the sofa, that is to say turned it round so that the back, hitherto against the wall, was now on the outside and consequently the front, or way in, on the inside. Then I climbed back, like a dog into its basket. I'll leave you the lamp, she said, but I begged her to take it with her. And suppose you need something in the night, she said. She was going to start quibbling again, I could feel it. Do you know where the convenience is? she said. She was right, I was forgetting. To relieve oneself in bed is enjoyable at the time, but soon a source of discomfort. Give me a chamberpot, I said. But she did not possess one. I have a close-stool of sorts, she said. I saw the grandmother on it, sitting up very stiff and grand, having just purchased it, pardon, picked it up, at a charity sale, or perhaps won it in a raffle, a period piece, and now trying it out, doing her best rather, almost wishing someone could see her. That's the idea, procrastinate. Any old recipient, I said, I don't have the flux. She came back with a kind of saucepan, not a true saucepan for it had no handle, it was oval in shape with two lugs and a lid. My stewpan, she said. I don't need the lid, I said. You don't need the lid? she said. If I had needed the lid she would have said, You need the lid? I drew this utensil down under the blanket, I like something in my hand when sleeping, it reassures me, and my hat was still wringing. I turned to the wall. She caught up the lamp off the mantelpiece where she had set it down, that's the idea, every particular, it flung her waving shadow over me, I thought she was off, but no, she came stooping down towards me over the sofa back. All family possessions, she said. I in her shoes would have tiptoed away, but not she, not a stir. Already my love was waning, that was all that mattered. Yes, already I felt better, soon I'd be up to the slow descents again, the long submersions, so long denied me through her fault. And I had only just moved in! Try and put me out now, I said. I seemed not to grasp the meaning of these words, nor even hear the brief sound they made, till some seconds after having uttered them. I was so unused to speech that my mouth would sometimes open, of its own accord, and vent some phrase or phrase, grammatically unexceptionable but entirely devoid if not of meaning, for on close inspection they would reveal one, and even several, at least of foundation. But I heard each word no sooner spoken. Never had my voice taken so long to reach me as on this occasion. I turned over on my back to see what was going on. She was smiling. A little later she went away, taking the lamp with her. I heard her steps in the kitchen and then the door of her room close behind her. Why behind her? I was alone at last, in the dark at last. Enough about that. I thought I was all set for a good night, in spite of the strange surroundings, but no, my night was most agitated. I woke next morning quite worn out, my clothes in disorder, the blanket likewise, and Anna beside me, naked naturally. One shudders to think of her exertions. I still had the stewpan in my grasp. It had not served. I looked at my member. If only it could have spoken! Enough about that. It was my night of love.

Gradually I settled down, in this house. She brought my meals at the appointed hours, looked in now and then to see if all was well and make sure I needed nothing, emptied the stewpan once a day and did out the room once a month. She could not always resist the temptation to speak to me, but on the whole gave me no cause to complain. Sometimes I heard her singing in her room, the song traversed her door, then the kitchen, then my door, and in this way won to me, faint but indisputable. Unless it travelled by the corridor. This did not greatly incommode me, this occasional sound of singing. One day I asked her to bring me a hyacinth, live, in a pot. She brought it and put it on the mantelpiece, now the only place in my room to put things, unless you put them on the floor. Not a day passed without my looking at it. At first all went well, it even put forth a bloom or two, then it gave up and was soon no more than a limp stem hung with limp leaves. The bulb, half clear of the clay as though in search of oxygen, smelt foul. She wanted to remove it, but I told her to leave it. She wanted to get me another, but I told her I didn't want another. I was more seriously disturbed by other sounds, stifled giggles and groans, which filled the dwelling at certain hours of the night, and even of the day. I had given up thinking of her, quite given up, but still I needed silence, to live my life. In vain I tried to listen to such reasonings as that air is made to carry the clamours of the world, including inevitably much groan and giggle, I obtained no relief. I couldn't make out if it was always the same gent or more than one. Lovers' groans are so alike, and lovers' giggles. I had such horror then of these paltry perplexities that I always fell into the same error, that of seeking to clear them up. It took me a long time, my lifetime so to speak, to realize that the colour of an eye half seen, or the source of some distant sound, are closer to Giudecca in the hell of unknowing than the existence of God, or the origins of protoplasm, or the existence of self, and even less worthy than these to occupy the wise. It's a bit much, a lifetime, to achieve this consoling conclusion, it doesn't leave you much time to profit by it. So a fat lot of help it was when, having put the question to her, I was told they were clients she received in rotation. I could obviously have got up and gone to look through the keyhole. But what can you see, I ask you, through holes the likes of those? So you live by prostitution, I said. We live by prostitution, she said. You couldn't ask them to make less noise? I said, as if I believed her. I added, Or a different kind of noise. They can't help but yap and yelp, she said. I'll have to leave, I said. She found some old hangings in the family junk and hung them before our doors, hers and mine. I asked her if it would not be possible, now and then, to have a parsnip. A parsnip! she cried, as if I had asked for a dish of sucking Jew. I reminded her that the parsnip season was fast drawing to a close and that if, before it finally got there, she could feed me nothing but parsnips I'd be grateful. I like parsnips because they taste like violets and violets because they smell like parsnips. Were there no parsnips on earth violets would leave me cold and if violets did not exist I would care as little for parsnips as I do for turnips, or radishes. And even in the present state of their flora, I mean on this planet where parsnips and violets contrive to coexist, I could do without both with the utmost ease, the uttermost ease. One day she had the impudence to announce she was with child, and four or five months gone into the bargain, by me of all people! She offered me a side view of her belly. She even undressed, no doubt to prove she wasn't hiding a cushion under her skirt, and then of course for the pure pleasure of undressing. Perhaps it's just wind, I said, by way of consolation. She gazed at me with her big eyes whose colour I forget, with one big eye rather, for the other seemed riveted on the remains of the hyacinth. The more naked she was the more cross-eyed. Look, she said, stooping over her breasts, the haloes are darkening already. I summoned up my remaining strength and said, Abort, abort, and they'll blush like new. She had drawn back the curtain for a clear view of all her rotundities. I saw the mountain, impassible, cavernous, secret, where from morning to night I'd hear nothing but the wind, the curlews, the clink like distant silver of the stone-cutters' hammers. I'd come out in the daytime to the heather and gorse, all warmth and scent, and watch at night the distant city lights, if I chose, and the other lights, the lighthouses and lightships my father had named for me, when I was small, and whose names I could find again, in my memory, if I chose, that I knew. From that day forth things went from bad to worse, to worse and worse. Not that she neglected me, she could never have neglected me enough, but the way she kept plaguing me with our child, exhibiting her belly and breasts and saying it was due any moment, she could feel it lepping already. If it's lepping, I said, it's not mine. I might have been worse off than I was, in that house, that was certain, it fell short of my ideal naturally, but I wasn't blind to its advantages. I hesitated to leave, the leaves were falling already, I dreaded the winter. One should not dread the winter, it too has its bounties, the snow gives warmth and deadens the tumult and its pale days are soon over. But I did not yet know, at that time, how tender the earth can be for those who have only her and how many graves in her giving, for the living. What finished me was the birth. It woke me up. What that infant must have been going through! I fancy she had a woman with her, I seemed to hear steps in the kitchen, on and off. It went to my heart to leave a house without being put out. I crawled out over the back of the sofa, put on my coat, greatcoat and hat, I can think of nothing else, laced up my boots and opened the door to the corridor. A mass of junk barred my way, but I scrabbled and barged my way through it in the end, regardless of the clatter. I used the word marriage, it was a kind of union in spite of all. Precautions would have been superfluous, there was no competing with those cries. It must have been her first. They pursued me down the stairs and out into the street. I stopped before the house door and listened. I could still hear them. If I had not known there was crying in the house I might not have heard them. But knowing it I did. I was not sure where I was. I looked among the stars and constellations for the Wains, but could not find them. And yet they must have been there. My father was the first to show them to me. He had shown me others, but alone, without him beside me, I could never find any but the Wains. I began playing with the cries, a little in the same way as I had played with the song, on, back, on, back, if that may be called playing. As long as I kept walking I didn't hear them, because of the footsteps. But as soon as I halted I heard them again, a little fainter each time, admittedly, but what does it matter, faint or loud, cry is cry, all that matters is that it should cease. For years I thought they would cease. Now I don't think so any more. I could have done with other loves perhaps. But there it is, either you love or you don't.

Translated by the author

An Occurrence at Owl Creek Bridge (1890)

AMBROSE BIERCE

A man stood upon a railroad bridge in northern Alabama, looking down into the swift water twenty feet below. The man's hands were behind his back, the wrists bound with a cord. A rope closely encircled his neck. It was attached to a stout cross-timber above his head and the slack fell to the level of his knees. Some loose boards laid upon the ties supporting the rails of the railway supplied a footing for him and his executioners—two private soldiers of the Federal army, directed by a sergeant who in civil life may have been a deputy sheriff. At a short remove upon the same temporary platform was an officer in the uniform of his rank, armed. He was a captain. A sentinel at each end of the bridge stood with his rifle in the position known as "support," that is to say, vertical in front of the left shoulder, the hammer resting on the forearm thrown straight across the chest—a formal and unnatural position, enforcing an erect carriage of the body. It did not appear to be the duty of these two men to know what was occurring at the center of the bridge; they merely blockaded the two ends of the foot planking that traversed it.

Beyond one of the sentinels nobody was in sight; the railroad ran straight away into a forest for a hundred yards, then, curving, was lost to view. Doubtless there was an outpost farther along. The other bank of the stream was open ground—a gentle slope topped with a stockade of vertical tree trunks, loopholed for rifles, with a single embrasure through which protruded the muzzle of a brass cannon commanding the bridge. Midway up the slope between the bridge and fort were the spectators—a single company of infantry in line, at "parade rest," the butts of their rifles on the ground, the barrels inclining slightly backward against the right shoulder, the hands crossed upon the stock. A lieutenant stood at the right of the line, the point of his sword upon the ground, his left hand resting upon his right. Excepting the group of four at the center of the bridge, not a man moved. The company faced the bridge, staring stonily, motionless. The sentinels, facing the banks of the stream, might have been statues to adorn the bridge. The captain stood with folded arms, silent, observing the work of his subordinates, but making no sign. Death is a dignitary who when he comes announced is to be received with formal manifestations of respect, even by those most familiar with him. In the code of military etiquette silence and fixity are forms of deference.

The man who was engaged in being hanged was apparently about thirty-five years of age. He was a civilian, if one might judge from his habit, which was that of a planter. His features were good—a straight nose, firm mouth, broad forehead, from which his long, dark hair was combed straight back, falling behind his ears to the collar of his well fitting frock coat. He wore a moustache and pointed beard, but no whiskers; his eyes were large and dark gray, and had a kindly expression which one would hardly have expected in one whose neck was in the hemp. Evidently this was no vulgar assassin. The liberal military code makes provision for hanging many kinds of persons, and gentlemen are not excluded.

The preparations being complete, the two private soldiers stepped aside and each drew away the plank upon which he had been standing. The sergeant turned to the captain, saluted and placed himself immediately behind that officer, who in turn moved apart one pace. These movements left the condemned man and the sergeant standing on the two ends of the same plank, which spanned three of the cross-ties of the bridge. The end upon which the civilian stood almost, but not quite, reached a fourth. This plank had been held in place by the weight of the captain; it was now held by that of the sergeant. At a signal from the former the latter would step aside, the plank would tilt and the condemned man go down between two ties. The arrangement commended itself to his judgement as simple and effective. His face had not been covered nor his eyes bandaged. He looked a moment at his "unsteadfast footing," then let his gaze wander to the swirling water of the stream racing madly beneath his feet. A piece of dancing driftwood caught his attention and his eyes followed it down the current. How slowly it appeared to move! What a sluggish stream!

He closed his eyes in order to fix his last thoughts upon his wife and children. The water, touched to gold by the early sun, the brooding mists under the banks at some distance down the stream, the fort, the soldiers, the piece of drift—all had distracted him. And now he became conscious of a new disturbance. Striking through the thought of his dear ones was sound which he could neither ignore nor understand, a sharp, distinct, metallic percussion like the stroke of a blacksmith's hammer upon the anvil; it had the same ringing quality. He wondered what it was, and whether immeasurably distant or near by—it seemed both. Its recurrence was regular, but as slow as the tolling of a death knell. He awaited each new stroke with impatience and—he knew not why—apprehension. The intervals of silence grew progressively longer; the delays became maddening. With their greater infrequency the sounds increased in strength and sharpness. They hurt his ear like the trust of a knife; he feared he would shriek. What he heard was the ticking of his watch.

He unclosed his eyes and saw again the water below him. "If I could free my hands," he thought, "I might throw off the noose and spring into the stream. By diving I could evade the bullets and, swimming vigorously, reach the bank, take to the woods and get away home. My home, thank God, is as yet outside their lines; my wife and little ones are still beyond the invader's farthest advance."

As these thoughts, which have here to be set down in words, were flashed into the doomed man's brain rather than evolved from it the captain nodded to the sergeant. The sergeant stepped aside.

II

Peyton Farquhar was a well-to-do planter, of an old and highly respected Alabama family. Being a slave owner and like other slave owners a politician, he was naturally an original secessionist and ardently devoted to the Southern cause. Circumstances of an imperious nature, which it is unnecessary to relate here, had prevented him from taking service with that gallant army which had fought the disastrous campaigns ending with the fall of Corinth, and he chafed under the inglorious restraint, longing for the release of his energies, the larger life of the soldier, the opportunity for distinction. That opportunity, he felt, would come, as it comes to all in wartime. Meanwhile he did what he could. No service was too humble for him to perform in the aid of the South, no adventure too perilous for him to undertake if consistent with the character of a civilian who was at heart a soldier, and who in good faith and without too much qualification assented to at least a part of the frankly villainous dictum that all is fair in love and war.

One evening while Farquhar and his wife were sitting on a rustic bench near the entrance to his grounds, a gray-clad soldier rode up to the gate and asked for a drink of water. Mrs. Farquhar was only too happy to serve him with her own white hands. While she was fetching the water her husband approached the dusty horseman and inquired eagerly for news from the front.

"The Yanks are repairing the railroads," said the man, "and are getting ready for another advance. They have reached the Owl Creek bridge, put it in order and built a stockade on the north bank. The commandant has issued an order, which is posted everywhere, declaring that any civilian caught interfering with the railroad, its bridges, tunnels, or trains will be summarily hanged. I saw the order."

"How far is it to the Owl Creek bridge?" Farquhar asked.

"About thirty miles."

"Is there no force on this side of the creek?"

"Only a picket post half a mile out, on the railroad, and a single sentinel at this end of the bridge."

"Suppose a man—a civilian and student of hanging—should elude the picket post and perhaps get the better of the sentinel," said Farquhar, smiling, "what could he accomplish?"

The soldier reflected. "I was there a month ago," he replied. "I observed that the flood of last winter had lodged a great quantity of driftwood against the wooden pier at this end of the bridge. It is now dry and would burn like tinder."

The lady had now brought the water, which the soldier drank. He thanked her ceremoniously, bowed to her husband and rode away. An hour later, after nightfall, he repassed the plantation, going northward in the direction from which he had come. He was a Federal scout.

III

As Peyton Farquhar fell straight downward through the bridge he lost consciousness and was as one already dead. From this state he was awakened—ages later, it seemed to him—by the pain of a sharp pressure upon his throat, followed by a sense of suffocation. Keen, poignant agonies seemed to shoot from his neck downward through every fiber of his body and limbs. These pains appeared to flash along well defined lines of ramification and to beat with an inconceivably rapid periodicity. They seemed like streams of pulsating fire heating him to an intolerable temperature. As to his head, he was conscious of nothing but a feeling of fullness—of congestion. These sensations were unaccompanied by thought. The intellectual part of his nature was already effaced; he had power only to feel, and feeling was torment. He was conscious of motion. Encompassed in a luminous cloud, of which he was now merely the fiery heart, without material substance, he swung through unthinkable arcs of oscillation, like a vast pendulum. Then all at once, with terrible suddenness, the light about him shot upward with the noise of a loud splash; a frightful roaring was in his ears, and all was cold and dark. The power of thought was restored; he knew that the rope had broken and he had fallen into the stream. There was no additional strangulation; the noose about his neck was already suffocating him and kept the water from his lungs. To die of hanging at the bottom of a river!—the idea seemed to him ludicrous. He opened his eyes in the darkness and saw above him a gleam of light, but how distant, how inaccessible! He was still sinking, for the light became fainter and fainter until it was a mere glimmer. Then it began to grow and brighten, and he knew that he was rising toward the surface—knew it with reluctance, for he was now very comfortable. "To be hanged and drowned," he thought, "that is not so bad; but I do not wish to be shot. No; I will not be shot; that is not fair."

He was not conscious of an effort, but a sharp pain in his wrist apprised him that he was trying to free his hands. He gave the struggle his attention, as an idler might observe the feat of a juggler, without interest in the outcome. What splendid effort!—what magnificent, what superhuman strength! Ah, that was a fine endeavor! Bravo! The cord fell away; his arms parted and floated upward, the hands dimly seen on each side in the growing light. He watched them with a new interest as first one and then the other pounced upon the noose at his neck. They tore it away and thrust it fiercely aside, its undulations resembling those of a water snake. "Put it back, put it back!" He thought he shouted these words to his hands, for the undoing of the noose had been succeeded by the direst pang that he had yet experienced. His neck ached horribly; his brain was on fire, his heart, which had been fluttering faintly, gave a great leap, trying to force itself out at his mouth. His whole body was racked and wrenched with an insupportable anguish! But his disobedient hands gave no heed to the command. They beat the water vigorously with quick, downward strokes, forcing him to the surface. He felt his head emerge; his eyes were blinded by the sunlight; his chest expanded convulsively, and with a supreme and crowning agony his lungs engulfed a great draught of air, which instantly he expelled in a shriek!

He was now in full possession of his physical senses. They were, indeed, preternaturally keen and alert. Something in the awful disturbance of his organic system had so exalted and refined them that they made record of things never before perceived. He felt the ripples upon his face and heard their separate sounds as they struck. He looked at the forest on the bank of the stream, saw the individual trees, the leaves and the veining of each leaf—he saw the very insects upon them: the locusts, the brilliant bodied flies, the gray spiders stretching their webs from twig to twig. He noted the prismatic colors in all the dewdrops upon a million blades of grass. The humming of the gnats that danced above the eddies of the stream, the beating of the dragon-flies' wings, the strokes of the water-spiders' legs, like oars which had lifted their boat—all these made audible music. A fish slid along beneath his eyes and he heard the rush of its body parting the water.

He had come to the surface facing down the stream; in a moment the visible world seemed to wheel slowly round, himself the pivotal point, and he saw the bridge, the fort, the soldiers upon the bridge, the captain, the sergeant, the two privates, his executioners. They were in silhouette against the blue sky. They shouted and gesticulated, pointing at him. The captain had drawn his pistol, but did not fire; the others were unarmed. Their movements were grotesque and horrible, their forms gigantic.

Suddenly he heard a sharp report and something struck the water smartly within a few inches of his head, spattering his face with spray. He heard a second report, and saw one of the sentinels with his rifle at his shoulder, a light cloud of blue smoke rising from the muzzle. The man in the water saw the eye of the man on the bridge gazing into his own through the sights of the rifle. He observed that it was a gray eye and remembered having read that gray eyes were keenest, and that all famous marksmen had them. Nevertheless, this one had missed.

A counter-swirl had caught Farquhar and turned him half round; he was again looking at the forest on the bank opposite the fort. The sound of a clear, high voice in a monotonous singsong now rang out behind him and came across the water with a distinctness that pierced and subdued all other sounds, even the beating of the ripples in his ears. Although no soldier, he had frequented camps enough to know the dread significance of that deliberate, drawling, aspirated chant; the lieutenant on shore was taking a part in the morning's work. How coldly and pitilessly—with what an even, calm intonation, presaging, and enforcing tranquility in the men—with what accurately measured interval fell those cruel words:

"Company! . . . Attention! . . . Shoulder arms! . . . Ready! . . . Aim! . . . Fire!"

Farquhar dived—dived as deeply as he could. The water roared in his ears like the voice of Niagara, yet he heard the dull thunder of the volley and, rising again toward the surface, met shining bits of metal, singularly flattened, oscillating slowly downward. Some of them touched him on the face and hands, then fell away, continuing their descent. One lodged between his collar and neck; it was uncomfortably warm and he snatched it out.

As he rose to the surface, gasping for breath, he saw that he had been a long time under water; he was perceptibly farther downstream—nearer to safety. The soldiers had almost finished reloading; the metal ramrods flashed all at once in the sunshine as they were drawn from the barrels, turned in the air, and thrust into their sockets. The two sentinels fired again, independently and ineffectually.

The hunted man saw all this over his shoulder; he was now swimming vigorously with the current. His brain was as energetic as his arms and legs; he thought with the rapidity of lightning:

"The officer," he reasoned, "will not make that martinet's error a second time. It is as easy to dodge a volley as a single shot. He has probably already given the command to fire at will. God help me, I cannot dodge them all!"

An appalling splash within two yards of him was followed by a loud, rushing sound, *diminuendo*, which seemed to travel back through the air to the fort and died in an explosion which stirred the very river to its deeps! A rising sheet of water curved over him, fell down upon him, blinded him, strangled him! The cannon had taken an hand in the game. As he shook his head free from the commotion of the smitten water he heard the deflected shot humming through the air ahead, and in an instant it was cracking and smashing the branches in the forest beyond.

"They will not do that again," he thought; "the next time they will use a charge of grape. I must keep my eye upon the gun; the smoke will apprise me—the report arrives too late; it lags behind the missile. That is a good gun."

Suddenly he felt himself whirled round and round—spinning like a top. The water, the banks, the forests, the now distant bridge, fort and men, all were commingled and blurred. Objects were represented by their colors only; circular horizontal streaks of color—that was all he saw. He had been caught in a vortex and was being whirled on with a velocity of advance and gyration that made him giddy and sick. In a few moments he was flung upon the gravel at the foot of the left bank of the stream—the southern bank—and behind a projecting point which concealed him from his enemies. The sudden arrest of his motion, the abrasion of one of his hands on the gravel, restored him, and he wept with delight. He dug his fingers into the sand, threw it over himself in handfuls and audibly blessed it. It looked like diamonds, rubies, emeralds; he could think of nothing beautiful which it did not resemble. The trees upon the bank were giant garden plants; he noted a definite order in their arrangement, inhaled the fragrance of their blooms. A strange roseate light shone through the spaces among their trunks and the wind made in their branches the music of Æolian harps. He had not wish to perfect his escape—he was content to remain in that enchanting spot until retaken.

A whiz and a rattle of grapeshot among the branches high above his head roused him from his dream. The baffled cannoneer had fired him a random farewell. He sprang to his feet, rushed up the sloping bank, and plunged into the forest.

All that day he traveled, laying his course by the rounding sun. The forest seemed interminable; nowhere did he discover a break in it, not even a woodman's road. He had not known that he lived in so wild a region. There was something uncanny in the revelation.

By nightfall he was fatigued, footsore, famished. The thought of his wife and children urged him on. At last he found a road which led him in what he knew to be the right direction. It was as wide and straight as a city street, yet it seemed untraveled. No fields bordered it, no dwelling anywhere. Not so much as the barking of a dog suggested human habitation. The black bodies of the trees formed a straight wall on both sides, terminating on the horizon in a point, like a diagram in a lesson in perspective. Overhead, as he looked up through this rift in the wood, shone great golden stars looking unfamiliar and grouped in strange constellations. He was sure they were arranged in some order which had a secret and malign significance. The wood on either side was full of singular noises, among which—once, twice, and again—he distinctly heard whispers in an unknown tongue.

His neck was in pain and lifting his hand to it found it horribly swollen. He knew that it had a circle of black where the rope had bruised it. His eyes felt congested; he could no longer close them. His tongue was swollen with thirst; he relieved its fever by thrusting it forward from between his teeth into the cold air. How softly the turf had carpeted the untraveled avenue—he could no longer feel the roadway beneath his feet!

Doubtless, despite his suffering, he had fallen asleep while walking, for now he sees another scene—perhaps he has merely recovered from a delirium. He stands at the gate of his own home. All is as he left it, and all bright and beautiful in the morning sunshine. He must have traveled the entire night. As he pushes open the gate and passes up the wide white walk, he sees a flutter of female garments; his wife, looking fresh and cool and sweet, steps down from the veranda to meet him. At the bottom of the steps she stands waiting, with a smile of ineffable joy, an attitude of matchless grace and dignity. Ah, how beautiful she is! He springs forwards with extended arms. As he is about to clasp her he feels a stunning blow upon the back of the neck; a blinding white light blazes all about him with a sound like the shock of a cannon—then all is darkness and silence!

Peyton Farquhar was dead; his body, with a broken neck, swung gently from side to side beneath the timbers of the Owl Creek bridge.

They're Made Out of Meat
(1991)

TERRY BISSON

"They're made out of meat."

"Meat?"

"Meat. They're made out of meat."

"Meat?"

"There's no doubt about it. We picked up several from different parts of the planet, took them aboard our recon vessels, and probed them all the way through. They're completely meat."

"That's impossible. What about the radio signals? The messages to the stars?"

"They use the radio waves to talk, but the signals don't come from them. The signals come from machines."

"So who made the machines? That's who we want to contact."

"*They* made the machines. That's what I'm trying to tell you. Meat made the machines."

"That's ridiculous. How can meat make a machine? You're asking me to believe in sentient meat."

"I'm not asking you, I'm telling you. These creatures are the only sentient race in that sector and they're made out of meat."

"Maybe they're like the orfolei. You know, a carbon based intelligence that goes through a meat stage."

"Nope. They're born meat and they die meat. We studied them for several of their life spans, which didn't take long. Do you have any idea what's the life span of meat?"

"Spare me. Okay, maybe they're only part meat. You know, like the weddilei. A meat head with an electron plasma brain inside."

"Nope. We thought of that, since they do have meat heads, like the weddilei. But I told you, we probed them. They're meat all the way through."

"No brain?"

"Oh, there's a brain all right. It's just that the brain is *made out of meat!* That's what I've been trying to tell you."

"So . . . what does the thinking?"

"You're not understanding, are you? You're refusing to deal with what I'm telling you. The brain does the thinking. The meat."

"Thinking meat! You're asking me to believe in thinking meat!"

"Yes, thinking meat! Conscious meat! Loving meat. Dreaming meat. The meat is the whole deal! Are you beginning to get the picture or do I have to start all over?"

"Omigod. You're serious, then. They're made out of meat."

"Thank you. Finally. Yes. They are indeed made out of meat. And they've been trying to get in touch with us for almost a hundred of their years."

"Omigod. So what does this meat have in mind?"

"First it wants to talk to us. Then I imagine it wants to explore the Universe, contact other sentiences, swap ideas and information. The usual."

"We're supposed to talk to meat."

"That's the idea. That's the message they're sending out by radio. 'Hello. Anyone out there. Anybody home.' That sort of thing."

"They actually do talk, then. They use words, ideas, concepts?"

"Oh, yes. Except they do it with meat."

"I thought you just told me they used radio."

"They do, but what do you think is *on* the radio? Meat sounds. You know how when you slap or flap meat, it makes a noise? They talk by flapping their meat at each other. They can even sing by squirting air through their meat."

"Omigod. Singing meat. This is altogether too much. So what do you advise?"

"Officially or unofficially?"

"Both."

"Officially, we are required to contact, welcome, and log in any and all sentient races or multibeings in this quadrant of the Universe, without prejudice, fear, or favor. Unofficially, I advise that we erase the records and forget the whole thing."

"I was hoping you would say that."

"It seems harsh, but there is a limit. Do we really want to make contact with meat?"

"I agree one hundred percent. What's there to say? 'Hello, meat. How's it going?' But will this work? How many planets are we dealing with here?"

"Just one. They can travel to other planets in special meat containers, but they can't live on them. And being meat, they can only travel through C space. Which limits them to the speed of light and makes the possibility of their ever making contact pretty slim. Infinitesimal, in fact."

"So we just pretend there's no one home in the Universe."

"That's it."

"Cruel. But you said it yourself, who wants to meet meat? And the ones who have been aboard our vessels, the ones you probed? You're sure they won't remember?"

"They'll be considered crackpots if they do. We went into their heads and smoothed out their meat so that we're just a dream to them."

"A dream to meat! How strangely appropriate, that we should be meat's dream."

"And we marked the entire sector *unoccupied*."

"Good. Agreed, officially and unofficially. Case closed. Any others? Anyone interesting on that side of the galaxy?"

"Yes, a rather shy but sweet hydrogen-core cluster intelligence in a class-nine star in G445 zone. Was in contact two galactic rotations ago, wants to be friendly again."

"They always come around."

"And why not? Imagine how unbearably, how unutterably cold the Universe would be if one were all alone . . ."

Pierre Menard, Author of the *Quixote* (1939)

JORGE LUIS BORGES

For Silvina Ocampo

The visible *œuvre* left by this novelist can be easily and briefly enumerated; unpardonable, therefore, are the omissions and additions perpetrated by Mme. Henri Bachelier in a deceitful catalog that a certain newspaper, whose Protestant leanings are surely no secret, has been so inconsiderate as to inflict upon that newspaper's deplorable readers—few and Calvinist (if not Masonic and circumcised) though they be. Menard's true friends have greeted that catalog with alarm, and even with a degree of sadness. One might note that only yesterday were we gathered before his marmoreal place of rest, among the dreary cypresses, and already Error is attempting to tarnish his bright Memory. . . . Most decidedly, a brief rectification is imperative.

I am aware that it is easy enough to call my own scant authority into question. I hope, nonetheless, that I shall not be prohibited from mentioning two high testimonials. The baroness de Bacourt (at whose unforgettable *vendredis* I had the honor to meet the mourned-for poet) has been so kind as to approve the lines that follow. Likewise, the countess de Bagnoregio, one of the rarest and most cultured spirits of the principality of Monaco (now of Pittsburgh, Pennsylvania, following her recent marriage to the international philanthropist Simon Kautzsch—a man, it grieves me to say, vilified and slandered by the victims of his disinterested operations), has sacrificed "to truth and to death" (as she herself has phrased it) the noble reserve that is the mark of her distinction, and in an open letter, published in the magazine *Luxe*, bestows upon me her blessing. Those commendations are sufficient, I should think.

I have said that the *visible* product of Menard's pen is easily enumerated. Having examined his personal files with the greatest care, I have established that his body of work consists of the following pieces:

a) a symbolist sonnet that appeared twice (with variants) in the review *La Conque* (in the numbers for March and October, 1899);

b) a monograph on the possibility of constructing a poetic vocabulary from concepts that are neither synonyms nor periphrastic locutions for the concepts that inform common speech, "but are, rather, ideal objects created by convention essentially for the needs of poetry" (Nîmes, 1901);

c) a monograph on "certain connections or affinities" between the philosophies of Descartes, Leibniz, and John Wilkins (Nîmes, 1903);

d) a monograph on Leibniz' *Characteristica universalis* (Nîmes, 1904);

e) a technical article on the possibility of enriching the game of chess by eliminating one of the rook's pawns (Menard proposes, recommends, debates, and finally rejects this innovation);

f) a monograph on Ramon Lull's *Ars magna generalis* (Nîmes, 1906);

g) a translation, with introduction and notes, of Ruy López de Segura's *Libro de la invención liberal y arte del juego del axedrez* (Paris, 1907);

h) drafts of a monograph on George Boole's symbolic logic;

i) a study of the essential metrical rules of French prose, illustrated with examples taken from Saint-Simon *(Revue des langues romanes,* Montpellier, October 1909);

j) a reply to Luc Durtain (who had countered that no such rules existed), illustrated with examples taken from Luc Durtain *(Revue des langues romanes,* Montpellier, December 1909);

k) a manuscript translation of Quevedo's *Aguja de navegar cultos,* tided *La boussole des précieux;*

l) a foreword to the catalog of an exhibit of lithographs by Carolus Hourcade (Nîmes, 1914);

m) a work entitled *Les problèmes d'un problème* (Paris, 1917), which discusses in chronological order the solutions to the famous problem of Achilles and the tortoise (two editions of this work have so far appeared; the second bears an epigraph consisting of Leibniz' advice *"Ne craignez point, monsieur, la tortue,"* and brings up to date the chapters devoted to Russell and Descartes);

n) a dogged analysis of the "syntactical habits" of Toulet (*N.R.F.,* March 1921) (Menard, I recall, affirmed that censure and praise were sentimental operations that bore not the slightest resemblance to criticism);

o) a transposition into alexandrines of Paul Valéry's *Cimetière marin* (*N.R.F.,* January 1928);

p) a diatribe against Paul Valéry, in Jacques Reboul's *Feuilles pour la suppression de la realité* (which diatribe, I might add parenthetically, states the exact reverse of Menard's true opinion of Valéry; Valéry understood this, and the two men's friendship was never imperiled);

q) a "definition" of the countess de Bagnoregio, in the "triumphant volume" (the phrase is that of another contributor, Gabriele d'Annunzio) published each year by that lady to rectify the inevitable biases of the popular press and to present "to the world and all of Italy" a true picture of her person, which was so exposed (by reason of her beauty and her bearing) to erroneous and/or hasty interpretations;

r) a cycle of admirable sonnets dedicated to the baroness de Bacourt (1934);

s) a handwritten list of lines of poetry that owe their excellence to punctuation.[1]

This is the full extent (save for a few vague sonnets of occasion destined for Mme. Henri Bachelier's hospitable, or greedy, *album des souvenirs)* of the *visible* lifework of Pierre Menard, in proper chronological order. I shall turn now to the other, the subterranean, the interminably heroic production—the *œuvre nonpareil,* the *œuvre* that must remain—for such are

---

[1]Mme. Henri Bachelier also lists a literal translation of Quevedo's literal translation of St. Francis de Sales's *Introduction à la vie dévote.* In Pierre Menard's library there is no trace of such a work. This must be an instance of one of our friend's droll jokes, misheard or misunderstood.

our human limitations!—unfinished. This work, perhaps the most significant writing of our time, consists of the ninth and thirty-eighth chapters of Part I of *Don Quixote* and a fragment of Chapter XXII. I know that such a claim is on the face of it absurd; justifying that "absurdity" shall be the primary object of this note.[2]

Two texts, of distinctly unequal value, inspired the undertaking. One was that philological fragment by Novalis—number 2005 in the Dresden edition, to be precise—which outlines the notion of *total identification* with a given author. The other was one of those parasitic books that set Christ on a boulevard, Hamlet on La Cannabière, or don Quixote on Wall Street. Like every man of taste, Menard abominated those pointless travesties, which, Menard would say, were good for nothing but occasioning a plebeian delight in anachronism or (worse yet) captivating us with the elementary notion that all times and places are the same, or are different. It might be more interesting, he thought, though of contradictory and superficial execution, to attempt what Daudet had so famously suggested: conjoin in a single figure (Tartarin, say) both the Ingenious Gentleman don Quixote and his squire. . . .

Those who have insinuated that Menard devoted his life to writing a contemporary *Quixote* besmirch his illustrious memory. Pierre Menard did not want to compose *another* Quixote, which surely is easy enough—he wanted to compose *the* Quixote. Nor, surely, need one have to say that his goal was never a mechanical transcription of the original; he had no intention of *copying* it. His admirable ambition was to produce a number of pages which coincided—word for word and line for line—with those of Miguel de Cervantes.

"My purpose is merely astonishing," he wrote me on September 30, 1934, from Bayonne. "The final term of a theological or metaphysical proof—the world around us, or God, or chance, or universal Forms—is no more final, no more uncommon, than my revealed novel. The sole difference is that philosophers publish pleasant volumes containing the intermediate stages of their work, while I am resolved to suppress those stages of my own." And indeed there is not a single draft to bear witness to that years-long labor.

Initially, Menard's method was to be relatively simple: Learn Spanish, return to Catholicism, fight against the Moor or Turk, forget the history of Europe from 1602 to 1918—*be* Miguel de Cervantes. Pierre Menard weighed that course (I know he pretty thoroughly mastered seventeenth-century Castilian) but he discarded it as too easy. Too *impossible*, rather!, the reader will say. Quite so, but the undertaking was impossible from the outset, and of all the impossible ways of bringing it about, this was the least interesting. To be a popular novelist of the seventeenth century in the twentieth seemed to Menard to be a diminution. Being, somehow, Cervantes, and arriving thereby at the Quixote—that looked to Menard less challenging (and therefore less interesting) than continuing to be Pierre Menard and coming to the Quixote *through the experiences of Pierre Menard*. (It was that conviction, by the way, that obliged him to leave out the autobiographical foreword to Part II of the novel. Including the prologue would have meant creating another character—"Cervantes"—and also presenting Quixote through that character's eyes, not Pierre Menard's. Menard, of course, spurned that easy solution.) "The task I have undertaken is not *in essence* difficult," I read at another place in that letter. "If I could just be immortal, I could do it." Shall I confess that I often imagine

---

[2] I did, I might say, have the secondary purpose of drawing a small sketch of the figure of Pierre Menard—but how dare I compete with the gilded pages I am told the baroness de Bacourt is even now preparing, or with the delicate sharp *crayon* of Carolus Hourcade?

that he did complete it, and that I read the Quixote—the *entire* Quixote—as if Menard had conceived it? A few nights ago, as I was leafing through Chapter XXVI (never attempted by Menard), I recognized our friend's style, could almost hear his voice in this marvelous phrase: "the nymphs of the rivers, the moist and grieving Echo." That wonderfully effective linking of one adjective of emotion with another of physical description brought to my mind a line from Shakespeare, which I recall we discussed one afternoon:

Where a malignant and a turban'd Turk . . .

Why the Quixote? my reader may ask. That choice, made by a Spaniard, would not have been incomprehensible, but it no doubt is so when made by a *Symboliste* from Nîmes, a devotee essentially of Poe—who begat Baudelaire, who begat Mallarmé, who begat Valéry, who begat M. Edmond Teste. The letter mentioned above throws some light on this point. "The *Quixote,*" explains Menard,

> deeply interests me, but does not seem to me—*comment dirai-je?*—inevitable. I cannot imagine the universe without Poe's ejaculation "Ah, bear in mind this garden was enchanted!" or the *Bateau ivre* or the *Ancient Mariner,* but I know myself able to imagine it without the *Quixote.* (I am speaking, of course, of my personal ability, not of the historical resonance of those works.) The *Quixote* is a contingent work; the *Quixote* is not necessary. I can premeditate committing it to writing, as it were—I can write it—without falling into a tautology. At the age of twelve or thirteen I read it—perhaps read it cover to cover, I cannot recall. Since then, I have carefully reread certain chapters, those which, at least for the moment, I shall not attempt. I have also glanced at the interludes, the comedies, the *Galatea,* the Exemplary Novels, the no doubt laborious *Travails of Persiles and Sigismunda,* and the poetic *Voyage to Parnassus.* . . . My general recollection of the *Quixote,* simplified by forgetfulness and indifference, might well be the equivalent of the vague foreshadowing of a yet unwritten book. Given that image (which no one can in good conscience deny me), my problem is, without the shadow of a doubt, much more difficult than Cervantes'. My obliging predecessor did not spurn the collaboration of chance; his method of composition for the immortal book was a bit *à la diable,* and he was often swept along by the inertiæ of the language and the imagination. I have assumed the mysterious obligation to reconstruct, word for word, the novel that for him was spontaneous. This game of solitaire I play is governed by two polar rules: the first allows me to try out formal or psychological variants; the second forces me to sacrifice them to the "original" text and to come, by irrefutable arguments, to those eradications. . . . In addition to these first two artificial constraints there is another, inherent to the project. Composing the *Quixote* in the early seventeenth century was a reasonable, necessary, perhaps even inevitable undertaking; in the early twentieth, it is virtually impossible. Not for nothing have three hundred years elapsed, freighted with the most complex events. Among those events, to mention but one, is the *Quixote* itself.

In spite of those three obstacles, Menard's fragmentary Quixote is more subtle than Cervantes'. Cervantes crudely juxtaposes the humble provincial reality of his country against the fantasies of the romance, while Menard chooses as his "reality" the land of Carmen during the century that saw the Battle of Lepanto and the plays of Lope de Vega. What burlesque brushstrokes of local color that choice would have inspired in a Maurice Barrès or a Rodríguez Larreta*! Yet Menard, with perfect naturalness, avoids them. In his work, there are no gypsy goings-on or conquistadors or mystics or Philip IIs or *autos da fé*. He ignores, overlooks—or banishes—local color. That disdain posits a new meaning for the "historical novel." That disdain condemns *Salammbô,* with no possibility of appeal.

No less amazement visits one when the chapters are considered in isolation. As an example, let us look at Part I, Chapter XXXVIII, "which treats of the curious discourse that Don Quixote made on the subject of arms and letters." It is a matter of common knowledge that in that chapter, don Quixote (like Quevedo in the analogous, and later, passage in *La hora de todos)* comes down against letters and in favor of arms. Cervantes was an old soldier; from him, the verdict is understandable. But that *Pierre Menard*'s don Quixote—a contemporary of *La trahison des clercs* and Bertrand Russell—should repeat those cloudy sophistries! Mme. Bachelier sees in them an admirable (typical) subordination of the author to the psychology of the hero; others (lacking all perspicacity) see them as a *transcription* of the Quixote; the baroness de Bacourt, as influenced by Nietzsche. To that third interpretation (which I consider irrefutable), I am not certain I dare to add a fourth, though it agrees very well with the almost divine modesty of Pierre Menard: his resigned or ironic habit of putting forth ideas that were the exact opposite of those he actually held. (We should recall that diatribe against Paul Valéry in the ephemeral Surrealist journal edited by Jacques Reboul.) The Cervantes text and the Menard text are verbally identical, but the second is almost infinitely richer. (More *ambiguous,* his detractors will say—but ambiguity is richness.)

It is a revelation to compare the *Don Quixote* of Pierre Menard with that of Miguel de Cervantes. Cervantes, for example, wrote the following (Part I, Chapter IX):

> . . . truth, whose mother is history, rival of time, depository of deeds, witness of the past, exemplar and adviser to the present, and the future's counselor.

This catalog of attributes, written in the seventeenth century, and written by the "ingenious layman" Miguel de Cervantes, is mere rhetorical praise of history. Menard, on the other hand, writes:

> . . . truth, whose mother is history, rival of time, depository of deeds, witness of the past, exemplar and adviser to the present, and the future's counselor.

History, the *mother* of truth!—the idea is staggering. Menard, a contemporary of William James, defines history not as a *delving into* reality but as the very *fount* of reality. Historical truth, for Menard, is not "what happened"; it is what we *believe* happened. The final phrases—*exemplar and adviser to the present, and the future's counselor*—are brazenly pragmatic.

The contrast in styles is equally striking. The archaic style of Menard—who is, in addition, not a native speaker of the language in which he writes—is somewhat affected. Not so the style of his precursor, who employs the Spanish of his time with complete naturalness.

There is no intellectual exercise that is not ultimately pointless. A philosophical doctrine is, at first, a plausible description of the universe; the years go by, and it is a mere chapter—if not a paragraph or proper noun—in the history of philosophy. In literature, that "falling by the wayside," that loss of "relevance," is even better known. The Quixote, Menard remarked, was first and foremost a pleasant book; it is now an occasion for patriotic toasts, grammatical arrogance, obscene *de luxe* editions. Fame is a form—perhaps the worst form—of incomprehension.

Those nihilistic observations were not new; what was remarkable was the decision that Pierre Menard derived from them. He resolved to anticipate the vanity that awaits all the labors of mankind; he undertook a task of infinite complexity, a task futile from the outset. He dedicated his scruples and his nights "lit by midnight oil" to repeating in a foreign tongue a book that already existed. His drafts were endless; he stubbornly corrected, and he ripped up thousands of handwritten pages. He would allow no one to see them, and took care that they not survive him.[3] In vain have I attempted to reconstruct them.

I have reflected that it is legitimate to see the "final" Quixote as a kind of palimpsest, in which the traces—faint but not undecipherable—of our friend's "previous" text must shine through. Unfortunately, only a second Pierre Menard, reversing the labors of the first, would be able to exhume and revive those Troys. . . .

"Thinking, meditating, imagining," he also wrote me, "are not anomalous acts—they are the normal respiration of the intelligence. To glorify the occasional exercise of that function, to treasure beyond price ancient and foreign thoughts, to recall with incredulous awe what some *doctor universalis* thought, is to confess our own languor, or our own *barbarie*. Every man should be capable of all ideas, and I believe that in the future he shall be."

Menard has (perhaps unwittingly) enriched the slow and rudimentary art of reading by means of a new technique—the technique of deliberate anachronism and fallacious attribution. That technique, requiring infinite patience and concentration, encourages us to read the *Odyssey* as though it came after the *Æneid,* to read Mme. Henri Bachelier's *Le jardin du Centaure* as though it were written by Mme. Henri Bachelier. This technique fills the calmest books with adventure. Attributing the *Imitatio Christi* to Louis Ferdinand Céline or James Joyce—is that not sufficient renovation of those faint spiritual admonitions?

Nîmes, 1939

[3]I recall his square-ruled notebooks, his black crossings-out, his peculiar typographical symbols, and his insect-like handwriting. In the evening, he liked to go out for walks on the outskirts of Nîmes; he would often carry along a notebook and make a cheery bonfire.

Bloodchild
(1984)

OCTAVIA E. BUTLER

My last night of childhood began with a visit home. T'Gatoi's sister had given us two sterile eggs. T'Gatoi gave one to my mother, brother, and sisters. She insisted that I eat the other one alone. It didn't matter. There was still enough to leave everyone feeling good. Almost everyone. My mother wouldn't take any. She sat, watching everyone drifting and dreaming without her. Most of the time she watched me.

I lay against T'Gatoi's long, velvet underside, sipping from my egg now and then, wondering why my mother denied herself such a harmless pleasure. Less of her hair would be gray if she indulged now and then. The eggs prolonged life, prolonged vigor. My father, who had never refused one in his life, had lived more than twice as long as he should have. And toward the end of his life, when he should have been slowing down, he had married my mother and fathered four children.

But my mother seemed content to age before she had to. I saw her turn away as several of T'Gatoi's limbs secured me closer. T'Gatoi liked our body heat and took advantage of it whenever she could. When I was little and at home more, my mother used to try to tell me how to behave with T'Gatoi—how to be respectful and always obedient because T'Gatoi was the Tlic government official in charge of the Preserve, and thus the most important of her kind to deal directly with Terrans. It was an honor, my mother said, that such a person had chosen to come into the family. My mother was at her most formal and severe when she was lying.

I had no idea why she was lying, or even what she was lying about. It *was* an honor to have T'Gatoi in the family, but it was hardly a novelty. T'Gatoi and my mother had been friends all my mother's life, and T'Gatoi was not interested in being honored in the house she considered her second home. She simply came in, climbed onto one of her special couches, and called me over to keep her warm. It was impossible to be formal with her while lying against her and hearing her complain as usual that I was too skinny.

"You're better," she said this time, probing me with six or seven of her limbs. "You're gaining weight finally. Thinness is dangerous." The probing changed subtly, became a series of caresses.

"He's still too thin," my mother said sharply.

T'Gatoi lifted her head and perhaps a meter of her body off the couch as though she were sitting up. She looked at my mother, and my mother, her face lined and old looking, turned away.

"Lien, I would like you to have what's left of Gan's egg."

"The eggs are for the children," my mother said.

"They are for the family. Please take it."

Unwillingly obedient, my mother took it from me and put it to her mouth. There were only a few drops left in the now-shrunken, elastic shell, but she squeezed them out, swallowed them, and after a few moments some of the lines of tension began to smooth from her face.

"It's good," she whispered. "Sometimes I forget how good it is."

"You should take more," T'Gatoi said. "Why are you in such a hurry to be old?"

My mother said nothing.

"I like being able to come here," T'Gatoi said. "This place is a refuge because of you, yet you won't take care of yourself."

T'Gatoi was hounded on the outside. Her people wanted more of us made available. Only she and her political faction stood between us and the hordes who did not understand why there was a Preserve—why any Terran could not be courted, paid, drafted, in some way made available to them. Or they did understand, but in their desperation, they did not care. She parceled us out to the desperate and sold us to the rich and powerful for their political support. Thus, we were necessities, status symbols, and an independent people. She oversaw the joining of families, putting an end to the final remnants of the earlier system of breaking up Terran families to suit impatient Tlic. I had lived outside with her. I had seen the desperate eagerness in the way some people looked at me. It was a little frightening to know that only she stood between us and that desperation that could so easily swallow us. My mother would look at her sometimes and say to me, "Take care of her." And I would remember that she too had been outside, had seen.

Now T'Gatoi used four of her limbs to push me away from her onto the floor. "Go on, Gan," she said. "Sit down there with your sisters and enjoy not being sober. You had most of the egg. Lien, come warm me."

My mother hesitated for no reason that I could see. One of my earliest memories is of my mother stretched alongside T'Gatoi, talking about things I could not understand, picking me up from the floor and laughing as she sat me on one of T'Gatoi's segments. She ate her share of eggs then. I wondered when she had stopped, and why.

She lay down now against T'Gatoi, and the whole left row of T'Gatoi's limbs closed around her, holding her loosely, but securely. I had always found it comfortable to lie that way, but except for my older sister, no one else in the family liked it. They said it made them feel caged.

T'Gatoi meant to cage my mother. Once she had, she moved her tail slightly, then spoke. "Not enough egg, Lien. You should have taken it when it was passed to you. You need it badly now."

T'Gatoi's tail moved once more, its whip motion so swift I wouldn't have seen it if hadn't been watching for it. Her sting drew only a single drop of blood from my mother's bare leg.

My mother cried out—probably in surprise. Being stung doesn't hurt. Then she sighed and I could see her body relax. She moved languidly into a more comfortable position within the cage of T'Gatoi's limbs. "Why did you do that?" she asked, sounding half asleep.

"I could not watch you sitting and suffering any longer."

My mother managed to move her shoulders in a small shrug. "Tomorrow," she said.

"Yes. Tomorrow you will resume your suffering—if you must. But just now, just for now, lie here and warm me and let me ease your way a little."

"He's still mine, you know," my mother said suddenly.

"Nothing can buy him from me." Sober, she would not have permitted herself to refer to such things.

"Nothing," T'Gatoi agreed, humoring her.

"Did you think I would sell him for eggs? For long life? My son?"

"Not for anything," T'Gatoi said, stroking my mother's shoulders, toying with her long, graying hair.

I would like to have touched my mother, shared that moment with her. She would take my hand if I touched her now. Freed by the egg and the sting, she would smile and perhaps say things long held in. But tomorrow, she would remember all this as a humiliation. I did not want to be part of a remembered humiliation. Best just be still and know she loved me under all the duty and pride and pain.

"Xuan Hoa, take off her shoes," T'Gatoi said. "In a little while I'll sting her again and she can sleep."

My older sister obeyed, swaying drunkenly as she stood up. When she had finished, she sat down beside me and took my hand. We had always been a unit, she and I.

My mother put the back of her head against T'Gatoi's underside and tried from that impossible angle to look up into the broad, round face. "You're going to sting me again?"

"Yes, Lien."

"I'll sleep until tomorrow noon."

"Good. You need it. When did you sleep last?"

My mother made a wordless sound of annoyance. "I should have stepped on you when you were small enough," she muttered.

It was an old joke between them. They had grown up together, sort of, though T'Gatoi had not, in my mother's life-time, been small enough for any Terran to step on. She was nearly three times my mother's present age, yet would still be young when my mother died of age. But T'Gatoi and my mother had met as T'Gatoi was coming into a period of rapid development—a kind of Tlic adolescence. My mother was only a child, but for a while they developed at the same rate and had no better friends than each other.

T'Gatoi had even introduced my mother to the man who became my father. My parents, pleased with each other in spite of their different ages, married as T'Gatoi was going into her family's business—politics. She and my mother saw each other less. But sometime before my older sister was born, my mother promised T'Gatoi one of her children. She would have to give one of us to someone, and she preferred T'Gatoi to some stranger.

Years passed. T'Gatoi traveled and increased her influence. The Preserve was hers by the time she came back to my mother to collect what she probably saw as her just reward for her hard work. My older sister took an instant liking to her and wanted to be chosen, but my mother was just coming to term with me and T'Gatoi liked the idea of choosing an infant and watching and taking part in all the phases of development. I'm told I was first caged within T'Gatoi's many limbs only three minutes after my birth. A few days later, I was given my first taste of egg. I tell Terrans that when they ask whether I was ever afraid of her. And I tell it to Tlic when T'Gatoi suggests a young Terran child for them and they, anxious and ignorant, demand an adolescent. Even my brother who had somehow grown up to fear and distrust the Tlic could probably have gone smoothly into one of their families if he had been adopted early enough. Sometimes, I think for his sake he should have been. I looked at him, stretched out on the floor across the room, his eyes open, but glazed as he dreamed his egg dream. No matter what he felt toward the Tlic, he always demanded his share of egg.

"Lien, can you stand up?" T'Gatoi asked suddenly.

"Stand?" my mother said. "I thought I was going to sleep."

"Later. Something sounds wrong outside." The cage was abruptly gone.

"What?"

"Up, Lien!"

My mother recognized her tone and got up just in time to avoid being dumped on the floor. T'Gatoi whipped her three meters of body off her couch, toward the door, and out at full speed. She had bones—ribs, a long spine, a skull, four sets of limb bones per segment. But when she moved that way, twisting, hurling herself into controlled falls, landing running, she seemed not only boneless, but aquatic—something swimming through the air as though it were water. I loved watching her move.

I left my sister and started to follow her out the door, though I wasn't very steady on my own feet. It would have been better to sit and dream, better yet to find a girl and share a waking dream with her. Back when the Tlic saw us as not much more than convenient, big, warm-blooded animals, they would pen several of us together, male and female, and feed us only eggs. That way they could be sure of getting another generation of us no matter how we tried to hold out. We were lucky that didn't go on long. A few generations of it and we would have *been* little more than convenient, big animals.

"Hold the door open, Gan," T'Gatoi said. "And tell the family to stay back."

"What is it?" I asked.

"N'Tlic."

I shrank back against the door. "Here? Alone?"

"He was trying to reach a call box, I suppose." She carried the man past me, unconscious, folded like a coat over some of her limbs. He looked young—my brother's age perhaps—and he was thinner than he should have been. What T'Gatoi would have called dangerously thin.

"Gan, go to the call box," she said. She put the man on the floor and began stripping off his clothing.

I did not move.

After a moment, she looked up at me, her sudden stillness a sign of deep impatience.

"Send Qui," I told her. "I'll stay here. Maybe I can help."

She let her limbs begin to move again, lifting the man and pulling his shirt over his head. "You don't want to see this," she said. "It will be hard. I can't help this man the way his Tlic could."

"I know. But send Qui. He won't want to be of any help here. I'm at least willing to try."

She looked at my brother—older, bigger, stronger, certainly more able to help her here. He was sitting up now, braced against the wall, staring at the man on the floor with undisguised fear and revulsion. Even she could see that he would be useless.

"Qui, go!" she said.

He didn't argue. He stood up, swayed briefly, then steadied, frightened sober.

"This man's name is Bram Lomas," she told him, reading from the man's armband. I fingered my own armband in sympathy. "He needs T'Khotgif Teh. Do you hear?"

"Bram Lomas, T'Khotgif Teh," my brother said. "I'm going." He edged around Lomas and ran out the door.

Lomas began to regain consciousness. He only moaned at first and clutched spasmodically at a pair of T'Gatoi's limbs. My younger sister, finally awake from her egg dream, came close to look at him, until my mother pulled her back.

T'Gatoi removed the man's shoes, then his pants, all the while leaving him two of her limbs to grip. Except for the final few, all her limbs were equally dexterous. "I want no argument from you this time, Gan," she said.

I straightened. "What shall I do?"

"Go out and slaughter an animal that is at least half your size."

"Slaughter? But I've never—"

She knocked me across the room. Her tail was an efficient weapon whether she exposed the sting or not.

I got up, feeling stupid for having ignored her warning, and went into the kitchen. Maybe I could kill something with a knife or an ax. My mother raised a few Terran animals for the table and several thousand local ones for their fur. T'Gatoi would probably prefer something local. An achti, perhaps. Some of those were the right size, though they had about three times as many teeth as I did and a real love of using them. My mother, Hoa, and Qui could kill them with knives. I had never killed one at all, had never slaughtered any animal. I had spent most of my time with T'Gatoi while my brother and sisters were learning the family business. T'Gatoi had been right. I should have been the one to go to the call box. At least I could do that.

I went to the corner cabinet where my mother kept her large house and garden tools. At the back of the cabinet there was a pipe that carried off waste water from the kitchen—except that it didn't anymore. My father had rerouted the waste water below before I was born. Now the pipe could be turned so that one half slid around the other and a rifle could be stored inside. This wasn't our only gun, but it was our most easily accessible one. I would have to use it to shoot one of the biggest of the achti. Then T'Gatoi would probably confiscate it. Firearms were illegal in the Preserve. There had been incidents right after the Preserve was established—Terrans shooting Tlic, shooting N'Tlic. This was before the joining of families began, before everyone had a personal stake in keeping the peace. No one had shot a Tlic in my lifetime or my mother's, but the law still stood—for our protection, we were told. There were stories of whole Terran families wiped out in reprisal back during the assassinations.

I went out to the cages and shot the biggest achti I could find. It was a handsome breeding male, and my mother would not be pleased to see me bring it in. But it was the right size, and I was in a hurry.

I put the achti's long, warm body over my shoulder—glad that some of the weight I'd gained was muscle—and took it to the kitchen. There, I put the gun back in its hiding place. If T'Gatoi noticed the achti's wounds and demanded the gun, I would give it to her. Otherwise, let it stay where my father wanted it.

I turned to take the achti to her, then hesitated. For several seconds, I stood in front of the closed door wondering why I was suddenly afraid. I knew what was going to happen. I hadn't seen it before but T'Gatoi had shown me diagrams and drawings. She had made sure I knew the truth as soon as I was old enough to understand it.

Yet I did not want to go into that room. I wasted a little time choosing a knife from the carved, wooden box in which my mother kept them. T'Gatoi might want one, I told myself, for the tough, heavily furred hide of the achti.

"Gan!" T'Gatoi called, her voice harsh with urgency.

I swallowed. I had not imagined a single moving of the feet could be so difficult. I realized I was trembling and that shamed me. Shame impelled me through the door.

I put the achti down near T'Gatoi and saw that Lomas was unconscious again. She, Lomas, and I were alone in the room—my mother and sisters probably sent out so they would not have to watch. I envied them.

But my mother came back into the room as T'Gatoi seized the achti. Ignoring the knife I offered her, she extended claws from several of her limbs and slit the achti from throat to anus. She looked at me, her yellow eyes intent. "Hold this man's shoulders, Gan."

I stared at Lomas in panic, realizing that I did not want to touch him, let alone hold him. This would not be like shooting an animal. Not as quick, not as merciful, and, I hoped, not as final, but there was nothing I wanted less than to be part of it.

My mother came forward. "Gan, you hold his right side," she said. "I'll hold his left." And if he came to, he would throw her off without realizing he had done it. She was a tiny woman. She often wondered aloud how she had produced, as she said, such "huge" children.

"Never mind," I told her, taking the man's shoulders. "I'll do it." She hovered nearby.

"Don't worry," I said. "I won't shame you. You don't have to stay and watch."

She looked at me uncertainly, then touched my face in a rare caress. Finally, she went back to her bedroom.

T'Gatoi lowered her head in relief. "Thank you, Gan," she said with courtesy more Terran than Tlic. "That one . . . she is always finding new ways for me to make her suffer."

Lomas began to groan and make choked sounds. I had hoped he would stay unconscious. T'Gatoi put her face near his so that he focused on her.

"I've stung you as much as I dare for now," she told him. "When this is over, I'll sting you to sleep and you won't hurt anymore."

"Please," the man begged. "Wait . . ."

"There's no more time, Bram. I'll sting you as soon as it's over. When T'Khotgif arrives she'll give you eggs to help you heal. It will be over soon."

"T'Khotgif!" the man shouted, straining against my hands.

"Soon, Bram." T'Gatoi glanced at me, then placed a claw against his abdomen slightly to the right of the middle, just below the left rib. There was movement on the right side—tiny, seemingly random pulsations moving his brown flesh, creating a concavity here, a convexity there, over and over until I could see the rhythm of it and knew where the next pulse would be.

Lomas's entire body stiffened under T'Gatoi's claw, though she merely rested it against him as she wound the rear section of her body around his legs. He might break my grip, but he would not break hers. He wept helplessly as she used his pants to tie his hands, then pushed his hands above his head so that I could kneel on the cloth between them and pin them in place. She rolled up his shirt and gave it to him to bite down on.

And she opened him.

His body convulsed with the first cut. He almost tore himself away from me. The sound he made . . . I had never heard such sounds come from anything human. T'Gatoi seemed to pay no attention as she lengthened and deepened the cut, now and then pausing to lick away blood. His blood vessels contracted, reacting to the chemistry of her saliva, and the bleeding slowed.

I felt as though I were helping her torture him, helping her consume him. I knew I would vomit soon, didn't know why I hadn't already. I couldn't possibly last until she was finished.

She found the first grub. It was fat and deep red with his blood—both inside and out. It had already eaten its own egg case but apparently had not yet begun to eat its host. At this stage, it would eat any flesh except its mother's. Let alone, it would have gone on excreting the poisons that had both sickened and alerted Lomas. Eventually it would have begun to eat. By the time it ate its way out of Lomas's flesh, Lomas would be dead or dying—and unable to take revenge on the thing that was killing him. There was always a grace period between the time the host sickened and the time the grubs began to eat him.

T'Gatoi picked up the writhing grub carefully and looked at it, somehow ignoring the terrible groans of the man.

Abruptly, the man lost consciousness.

"Good," T'Gatoi looked down at him. "I wish you Terrans could do that at will." She felt nothing. And the thing she held . . .

It was limbless and boneless at this stage, perhaps fifteen centimeters long and two thick, blind and slimy with blood. It was like a large worm. T'Gatoi put it into the belly of the achti, and it began at once to burrow. It would stay there and eat as long as there was anything to eat.

Probing through Lomas's flesh, she found two more, one of them smaller and more vigorous. "A male!" she said happily. He would be dead before I would. He would be through his metamorphosis and screwing everything that would hold still before his sisters even had limbs. He was the only one to make a serious effort to bite T'Gatoi as she placed him in the achti.

Paler worms oozed to visibility in Lomas's flesh. I closed my eyes. It was worse than finding something dead, rotting, and filled with tiny animal grubs. And it was far worse than any drawing or diagram.

"Ah, there are more," T'Gatoi said, plucking out two long, thick grubs. "You may have to kill another animal, Gan. Everything lives inside you Terrans."

I had been told all my life that this was a good and necessary thing Tlic and Terran did together—a kind of birth. I had believed it until now. I knew birth was painful and bloody, no matter what. But this was something else, something, worse. And I wasn't ready to see it. Maybe I never would be. Yet I couldn't not see it. Closing my eyes didn't help.

T'Gatoi found a grub still eating its egg case. The remains of the case were still wired into a blood vessel by their own little tube or hook or whatever. That was the way the grubs were anchored and the way they fed. They took only blood until they were ready to emerge. Then they ate their stretched, elastic egg cases. Then they ate their hosts.

T'Garoi bit away the egg case, licked away the blood. Did she like the taste? Did childhood habits die hard—or not die at all?

The whole procedure was wrong, alien. I wouldn't have thought anything about her could seem alien to me.

"One more, I think," she said. "Perhaps two. A good family. In a host animal these days, we would be happy to find one or two alive." She glanced at me. "Go outside, Gan, and empty your stomach. Go now while the man is unconscious."

I staggered out, barely made it. Beneath the tree just beyond the front door, I vomited until there was nothing left to bring up. Finally, I stood shaking, tears streaming down my face. I did not know why I was crying, but I could not stop. I went further from the house to avoid being seen. Every time I closed my eyes I saw red worms crawling over redder human flesh.

There was a car coming toward the house. Since Terrans were forbidden motorized vehicles except for certain farm equipment, I knew this must be Lomas's Tlic with Qui and perhaps a Terran doctor. I wiped my face on my shirt, struggled for control.

"Gan," Qui called as the car stopped. "What happened?" He crawled out of the low, round, Tlic-convenient car door. Another Terran crawled out the other side and went into the house without speaking to me. The doctor. With his help and a few eggs, Lomas might make it.

"T'Khotgif Teh?" I said.

The Tlic driver surged out of her car, reared up half her length before me. She was paler and smaller than T'Gatoi—probably born from the body of an animal. Tlic from Terran bodies were always larger as well as more numerous.

"Six young," I told her. "Maybe seven, all alive. At least one male."

"Lomas?" she said harshly. I liked her for the question and the concern in her voice when she asked it. The last coherent thing he had said was her name.

"He's alive," I said.

She surged away to the house without another word.

"She's been sick," my brother said, watching her go. "When I called, I could hear people telling her she wasn't well enough to go out even for this."

I said nothing. I had extended courtesy to the Tlic. Now I didn't want to talk to anyone. I hoped he would go in—out of curiosity if nothing else.

"Finally found out more than you wanted to know, eh?"

I looked at him.

"Don't give me one of *her* looks," he said. "You're not her. You're just her property."

One of her looks. Had I picked up even an ability to imitate her expressions?

"What'd you do, puke?" He sniffed the air. "So now you know what you're in for."

I walked away from him. He and I had been close when we were kids. He would let me follow him around when I was home, and sometimes T'Gatoi would let me bring him along when she took me into the city. But something had happened when he reached adolescence. I never knew what. He began keeping out of T'Gatoi's way. Then he began running away—until he realized there was no "away." Not in the Preserve. Certainly not outside. After that he concentrated on getting his share of every egg that came into the house and on looking out for me in a way that made me all but hate him—a way that clearly said, as long as I was all right, he was safe from the Tlic.

"How was it, really?" he demanded, following me.

"I killed an achti. The young ate it."

"You didn't run out of the house and puke because they ate an achti."

"I had . . . never seen a person cut open before." That was true, and enough for him to know. I couldn't talk about the other. Not with him.

"Oh," he said. He glanced at me as though he wanted to say more, but he kept quiet.

We walked, not really headed anywhere. Toward the back, toward the cages, toward the fields.

"Did he say anything?" Qui asked. "Lomas, I mean."

Who else would he mean? "He said 'T'Khotgif.'"

Qui shuddered. "If she had done that to me, she'd be the last person I'd call for."

"You'd call for her. Her sting would ease your pain without killing the grubs in you."

"You think I'd care if they died?"

No. Of course he wouldn't. Would I?

"Shit!" He drew a deep breath. "I've seen what they do. You think this thing with Lomas was bad? It was nothing."

I didn't argue. He didn't know what he was talking about.

"I saw them eat a man," he said.

I turned to face him. "You're lying!"

"*I saw them eat a man.*" He paused. "It was when I was little. I had been to the Hartmund house and I was on my way home. Halfway here, I saw a man and a Tlic and the man was N'Tlic. The ground was hilly. I was able to hide from them and watch. The Tlic wouldn't open the man because she had nothing to feed the grubs. The man couldn't go any further and there were no houses around. He was in so much pain, he told her to kill him. He begged her to kill him. Finally, she did. She cut his throat. One swipe of one claw. I saw the grubs eat their way out, then burrow in again, still eating."

His words made me see Lomas's flesh again, parasitized, crawling. "Why didn't you tell me that?" I whispered.

He looked startled as though he'd forgotten I was listening. "I don't know."

"You started to run away not long after that, didn't you?"

"Yeah. Stupid. Running inside the Preserve. Running in a cage."

I shook my head, said what I should have said to him long ago. "She wouldn't take you, Qui. You don't have to worry."

"She would . . . if anything happened to you."

"No. She'd take Xuan Hoa. Hoa . . . wants it." She wouldn't if she had stayed to watch Lomas.

"They don't take women," he said with contempt.

"They do sometimes." I glanced at him. "Actually, they prefer women. You should be around them when they talk among themselves. They say women have more body fat to protect the grubs. But they usually take men to leave the women free to bear their own young."

"To provide the next generation of host animals," he said, switching from contempt to bitterness.

"It's more than that!" I countered. Was it?

"If it were going to happen to me, I'd want to believe it was more, too."

"It *is* more!" I felt like a kid. Stupid argument.

"Did you think so while T'Gatoi was picking worms out of that guy's guts?"

"It's not supposed to happen that way."

"Sure it is. You weren't supposed to see it, that's all. And his Tlic was supposed to do it. She could sting him unconscious and the operation wouldn't have been as painful. But she'd still open him, pick out the grubs, and if she missed even one, it would poison him and eat him from the inside out."

There was actually a time when my mother told me to show respect for Qui because he was my older brother. I walked away, hating him. In his way, he was gloating. He was safe and I wasn't. I could have hit him, but I didn't think I would be able to stand it wben he refused to hit back, when he looked at me with contempt and pity.

He wouldn't let me get away. Longer legged, he swung ahead of me and made me feel as though I were following him.

"I'm sorry," he said.

I strode on, sick and furious.

"Look, it probably won't be that bad with you. T'Gatoi likes you. She'll be careful."

I turned back toward the house, almost running from him.

"Has she done it to you yet?" he asked, keeping up easily. "I mean, you're about the right age for implantation. Has she—"

I hit him. I didn't know I was going to do it, but I think I meant to kill him. If he hadn't been bigger and stronger, I think I would have.

He tried to hold me off, but in the end, had to defend himself. He only hit me a couple of times. That was plenty. I don't remember going down, but when I came to, he was gone. It was worth the pain to be rid of him.

I got up and walked slowly toward the house. The back was dark. No one was in the kitchen. My mother and sisters were sleeping in their bedrooms—or pretending to.

Once I was in the kitchen, I could hear voices—Tlic and Terran from the next room. I couldn't make out what they were saying—didn't want to make it out.

I sat down at my mother's table, waiting for quiet. The table was smooth and worn, heavy and well crafted. My father had made it for her just before he died. I remembered hanging around underfoot when he built it. He didn't mind. Now I sat leaning on it, missing him. I could have talked to him. He had done it three times in his long life. Three clutches of eggs, three times being opened up and sewed up. How had he done it? How did anyone do it?

I got up, took the rifle from its hiding place, and sat again with it. It needed cleaning, oiling. All I did was load it.

"Gan?"

She made a lot of little clicking sounds when she walked on bare floor, each limb clicking in succession as it touched down. Waves of little clicks.

She came to the table, raised the front half of her body above it, and surged onto it. Sometimes she moved so smoothly she seemed to flow like water itself. She coiled herself into a small hill in the middle of the table and looked at me.

"That was bad," she said softly. "You should not have seen it. It need not be that way."

"I know."

"T'Khotgif—Ch'Khotgif now—she will die of her disease. She will not live to raise her children. But her sister will provide for them, and for Bram Lomas." Sterile sister. One fertile female in every lot. One to keep the family going. That sister owed Lomas more than she could ever repay.

"He'll live then?"

"Yes."

"I wonder if he would do it again."

"No one would ask him to do that again."

I looked into the yellow eyes, wondering how much I saw and understood there, and how much I only imagined. "No one ever asks us," I said. "You never asked me."

She moved her head slightly. "What's the matter with your face?"

"Nothing. Nothing important." Human eyes probably wouldn't have noticed the swelling in the darkness. The only light was from one of the moons, shining through a window across the room.

"Did you use the rifle to shoot the achti?"

"Yes."

"And do you mean to use it to shoot me?"

I stared at her, outlined in the moonlight—coiled, graceful body. "What does Terran blood taste like to you?"

She said nothing.

"What are you?" I whispered. "What are we to you?"

She lay still, rested her head on her topmost coil. "You know me as no other does," she said softly. "You must decide."

"That's what happened to my face," I told her.

"What?"

"Qui goaded me into deciding to do something. It didn't turn out very well." I moved the gun slightly, brought the barrel up diagonally under my own chin. "At least it was a decision I made."

"As this will be."

"Ask me, Gatoi."

"For my children's lives?"

She would say something like that. She knew how to manipulate people, Terran and Tlic. But not this time.

"I don't want to be a host animal," I said. "Not even yours."

It took her a long time to answer. "We use almost no host animals these days," she said. "You know that."

"You use us."

"We do. We wait long years for you and teach you and join our families to yours." She moved restlessly. "You know you aren't animals to us."

I stared at her, saying nothing.

"The animals we once used began killing most of our eggs after implantation long before your ancestors arrived," she said softly. "You know these things, Gan. Because your people arrived, we are relearning what it means to be a healthy, thriving people. And your ancestors, fleeing from their homeworld, from their own kind who would have killed or enslaved them—they survived because of us. We saw them as people and gave them the Preserve when they still tried to kill us as worms."

At the word "worms," I jumped. I couldn't help it, and she couldn't help noticing it.

"I see," she said quietly. "Would you really rather die than bear my young, Gan?"

I didn't answer.

"Shall I go to Xuan Hoa?"

"Yes!" Hoa wanted it. Let her have it. She hadn't had to watch Lomas. She'd be proud . . . . Not terrified.

T'Gatoi flowed off the table onto the floor, startling me almost too much.

"I'll sleep in Hoa's room tonight," she said. "And sometime tonight or in the morning, I'll tell her."

This was going too fast. My sister Hoa had had almost as much to do with raising me as my mother. I was still close to her—not like Qui. She could want T'Gatoi and still love me.

"Wait! Gatoi!"

She looked back, then raised nearly half her length off the floor and turned to face me. "These are adult things, Gan. This is my life, my family!"

"But she's . . . my sister."

"I have done what you demanded. I have asked you!"

"But—"

133

"It will be easier for Hoa. She has always expected to carry other lives inside her."

Human lives. Human young who should someday drink at her breasts, not at her veins.

I shook my head. "Don't do it to her, Gatoi." I was not Qui. It seemed I could become him, though, with no effort at all. I could make Xuan Hoa my shield. Would it be easier to know that red worms were growing in her flesh instead of mine?

"Don't do it to Hoa," I repeated.

She stared at me, utterly still.

I looked away, then back at her. "Do it to me."

I lowered the gun from my throat and she leaned forward to take it.

"No," I told her.

"It's the law," she said.

"Leave it for the family. One of them might use it to save my life someday."

She grasped the rifle barrel, but I wouldn't let go. I was pulled into a standing position over her.

"Leave it here!" I repeated. "If we're not your animals, if these are adult things, accept the risk. There is risk, Gatoi, in dealing with a partner."

It was clearly hard for her to let go of the rifle. A shudder went through her and she made a hissing sound of distress. It occurred to me that she was afraid. She was old enough to have seen what guns could do to people. Now her young and this gun would be together in the same house. She did not know about the other guns. In this dispute, they did not matter.

"I will implant the first egg tonight," she said as I put the gun away. "Do you hear, Gan?"

Why else had I been given a whole egg to eat while the rest of the family was left to share one? Why else had my mother kept looking at me as though I were going away from her, going where she could not follow? Did T'Gatoi imagine I hadn't known?

"I hear."

"Now!" I let her push me out of the kitchen, then walked ahead of her toward my bedroom. The sudden urgency in her voice sounded real. "You would have done it to Hoa tonight!" I accused.

"I must do it to someone tonight."

I stopped in spite of her urgency and stood in her way. "Don't you care who?"

She flowed around me and into my bedroom. I found her waiting on the couch we shared. There was nothing in Hoa's room that she could have used. She would have done it to Hoa on the floor. The thought of her doing it to Hoa at all disturbed me in a different way now, and I was suddenly angry.

Yet I undressed and lay down beside her. I knew what to do, what to expect. I had been told all my life. I felt the familiar sting, narcotic, mildly pleasant. Then the blind probing of her ovipositor. The puncture was painless, easy. So easy going in. She undulated slowly against me, her muscles forcing the egg from her body into mine. I held on to a pair of her limbs until I remembered Lomas holding her that way. Then I let go, moved inadvertently, and hurt her. She gave a low cry of pain and I expected to be caged at once within her limbs. When I wasn't, I held on to her again, feeling oddly ashamed.

134

"I'm sorry," I whispered.

She rubbed my shoulders with four of her limbs.

"Do you care?" I asked. "Do you care that it's me?"

She did not answer for some time. Finally, "You were the one making the choices tonight, Gan. I made mine long ago."

"Would you have gone to Hoa?"

"Yes. How could I put my children into the care of one who hates them?"

"It wasn't . . . hate."

"I know what it was."

"I was afraid."

Silence.

"I still am." I could admit it to her here, now.

"But you came to me . . . to save Hoa."

"Yes." I leaned my forehead against her. She was cool velvet, deceptively soft. "And to keep you for myself," I said. It was so. I didn't understand it, but it was so.

She made a soft hum of contentment. "I couldn't believe I had made such a mistake with you," she said. "I chose you. I believed you had grown to choose me."

"I had, but . . ."

"Lomas."

"Yes."

"I had never known a Terran to see a birth and take it well. Qui has seen one, hasn't he?"

"Yes."

"Terrans should be protected from seeing."

I didn't like the sound of that—and I doubted that it was possible. "Not protected," I said. "Shown. Shown when we're young kids, and shown more than once. Gatroi, no Terran ever sees a birth that goes right. All we see is N'Tlic—pain and terror and maybe death."

She looked down at me. "It is a private thing. It has always been a private thing."

Her tone kept me from insisting—that and the knowledge that if she changed her mind, I might be the first public example. But I had planted the thought in her mind. Chances were it would grow, and eventually she would experiment.

"You won't see it again," she said. "I don't want you thinking any more about shooting me."

The small amount of fluid that came into me with her egg relaxed me as completely as a sterile egg would have, so that I could remember the rifle in my hands and my feelings of fear and revulsion, anger and despair. I could remember the feelings without reviving them. I could talk about them.

"I wouldn't have shot you," I said. "Not you." She had been taken from my father's flesh when he was my age.

"You could have," she insisted.

"Not you." She stood between us and her own people, protecting, interweaving.

"Would you have destroyed yourself?"

I moved carefully, uncomfortable. "I could have done that. I nearly did. That's Qui's 'away.' I wonder if he knows."

"What?"

I did not answer.

"You will live now."

"Yes." *Take care of her,* my mother used to say. Yes.

"I'm healthy and young," she said. "I won't leave you as Lomas was left—alone, N'Tlic. I'll take care of you."

The Bloody Chamber
(1979)

ANGELA CARTER

I remember how, that night, I lay awake in the wagon-lit in a tender, delicious ecstasy of excitement, my burning cheek pressed against the impeccable linen of the pillow and the pounding of my heart mimicking that of the great pistons ceaselessly thrusting the train that bore me through the night; away from Paris, away from girlhood, away from the white, enclosed quietude of my mother's apartment, into the unguessable country of marriage.

And I remember I tenderly imagined how, at this very moment, my mother would be moving slowly about the narrow bedroom I had left behind for ever, folding up and putting away all my little relics, the tumbled garments I would not need any more, the scores for which there had been no room in my trunks, the concert programmes I'd abandoned; she would linger over this torn ribbon and that faded photograph with all the half-joyous, half-sorrowful emotions of a woman on her daughter's wedding day. And, in the midst of my bridal triumph, I felt a pang of loss as if, when he put the gold band on my finger, I had, in some way, ceased to be her child in becoming his wife.

Are you sure, she'd said when they delivered the gigantic box that held the wedding dress he'd bought me, wrapped up in tissue paper and red ribbon like a Christmas gift of crystallized fruit. Are you sure you love him? There was a dress for her, too; black silk, with the dull, prismatic sheen of oil on water, finer than anything she'd worn since that adventurous girlhood in Indo-China, daughter of a rich tea planter. My eagle-featured, indomitable mother; what other student at the Conservatoire could boast that her mother had outfaced a junkful of Chinese pirates, nursed a village through a visitation of the plague, shot a man-eating tiger with her own hand and all before she was as old as I?

'Are you sure you love him?'

'I'm sure I want to marry him,' I said.

And would say no more. She sighed, as if it was with reluctance that she might at last banish the spectre of poverty from its habitual place at our meagre table. For my mother herself had gladly, scandalously, defiantly beggared herself for love; and, one fine day, her gallant soldier never returned from the wars, leaving his wife and child a legacy of tears that never quite dried, a cigar box full of medals and the antique service revolver that my mother, grown magnificently eccentric in hardship, kept always in her reticule, in case — how I teased her — she was surprised by footpads on her way home from the grocer's shop.

Now and then a starburst of lights spattered the drawn blinds as if the railway company had lit up all the stations through which we passed in celebration of the bride. My satin nightdress had just been shaken from its wrappings; it had slipped over my young girl's pointed breasts and shoulders, supple as a garment of heavy water, and now teasingly caressed me, egregious, insinuating, nudging between my thighs as I shifted restlessly in my narrow berth. His kiss, his kiss with tongue and teeth in it and a rasp of beard, had hinted to me, though with the same exquisite tact as this nightdress he'd given me, of the wedding night, which would be voluptuously deferred until we lay in his great ancestral bed in the sea-girt, pinnacled domain that lay, still, beyond the grasp of my imagination ... that magic place, the fairy castle whose walls were made of foam, that legendary habitation in which he had been born. To which, one day, I might bear an heir. Our destination, my destiny.

Above the syncopated roar of the train, I could hear his even, steady breathing. Only the communicating door kept me from my husband and it stood open. If I rose up on my elbow, I could see the dark, leonine shape of his head and my nostrils caught a whiff of the opulent male scent of leather and spices that always accompanied him and sometimes, during his courtship, had been the only hint he gave me that he had come into my mother's sitting room, for, though he was a big man, he moved as softly as if all his shoes had soles of velvet, as if his footfall turned the carpet into snow.

He had loved to surprise me in my abstracted solitude at the piano. He would tell them not to announce him, then soundlessly open the door and softly creep up behind me with his bouquet of hot-house flowers or his box of marrons glacés, lay his offering upon the keys and clasp his hands over my eyes as I was lost in a Debussy prelude. But that perfume of spiced leather always betrayed him; after my first shock, I was forced always to mimic surprise, so that he would not be disappointed.

He was older than I. He was much older than I; there were streaks of pure silver in his dark mane. But his strange, heavy, almost waxen face was not lined by experience. Rather, experience seemed to have washed it perfectly smooth, like a stone on a beach whose fissures have been eroded by successive tides. And sometimes that face, in stillness when he listened to me playing, with the heavy eyelids folded over eyes that always disturbed me by their absolute absence of light, seemed to me like a mask, as if his real face, the face that truly reflected all the life he had led in the world before he met me, before, even, I was born, as though that face lay underneath this mask. Or else, elsewhere. As though he had laid by the face in which he had lived for so long in order to offer my youth a face unsigned by the years.

And, elsewhere, I might see him plain. Elsewhere. But, where?

In, perhaps, that castle to which the train now took us, that marvelous castle in which he had been born.

Even when he asked me to marry him, and I said: 'Yes,' still he did not lose that heavy, fleshy composure of his. I know it must seem a curious analogy, a man with a flower, but sometimes he seemed to me like a lily. Yes. A lily. Possessed of that strange, ominous calm of a sentient vegetable, like one of those cobra-headed, funereal lilies whose white sheaths are curled out of a flesh as thick and tensely yielding to the touch as vellum. When I said that I would marry him, not one muscle in his face stirred, but he let out a long, extinguished sigh. I thought: Oh! how he must want me! And it was as though the imponderable weight of his desire was a force I might not withstand, not by virtue of its violence but because of its very gravity.

He had the ring ready in a leather box lined with crimson velvet, a fire opal the size of a pigeon's egg set in a complicated circle of dark antique gold. My old nurse, who still lived with my mother and me, squinted at the ring askance: opals are bad luck, she said. But this opal had been his own mother's ring, and his grandmother's, and her mother's before that, given to an ancestor by Catherine de Medici … every bride that came to the castle wore it, time out of mind. And did he give it to his other wives and have it back from them? asked the old woman rudely; yet she was a snob. She hid her incredulous joy at my marital coup — her little Marquise — behind a façade of fault-finding. But, here, she touched me. I shrugged and turned my back pettishly on her. I did not want to remember how he had loved other women before me, but the knowledge often teased me in the threadbare self-confidence of the small hours.

I was seventeen and knew nothing of the world; my Marquis had been married before, more than once, and I remained a little bemused that, after those others, he should now have chosen me. Indeed, was he not still in mourning for his last wife? Tsk, tsk, went my old nurse. And even my mother had been reluctant to see her girl whisked off by a man so recently bereaved. A Romanian countess, a lady of high fashion. Dead just three short months before I met him, a boating accident, at his home, in Brittany. They never found her body but I rummaged through the back copies of the society magazines my old nanny kept in a trunk under her bed and tracked down her photograph. The sharp muzzle of a pretty, witty, naughty monkey; such potent and bizarre charm, of a dark, bright, wild yet worldly thing whose natural habitat must have been some luxurious interior decorator's jungle filled with potted palms and tame, squawking parakeets.

Before that? *Her* face is common property; everyone painted her but the Redon engraving I liked best, *The Evening Star Walking on the Rim of Night*. To see her skeletal, enigmatic grace, you would never think she had been a barmaid in a café in Montmartre until Puvis de Chavannes saw her and had her expose her flat breasts and elongated thighs to his brush. And yet it was the absinthe doomed her, or so they said.

The first of all his ladies? That sumptuous diva; I had heard her sing Isolde, precociously musical child that I was, taken to the opera for a birthday treat. My first opera; I had heard her sing Isolde. With what white-hot passion had she burned from the stage! So that you could tell she would die young. We sat high up, halfway to heaven in the gods, yet she half-blinded me. And my father, still alive (oh, so long ago), took hold of my sticky little hand, to comfort me, in the last act, yet all I heard was the glory of her voice.

Married three times within my own brief lifetime to three different graces, now, as if to demonstrate the eclecticism of his taste, he had invited me to join this gallery of beautiful women, I, the poor widow's child with my mouse-coloured hair that still bore the kinks of the plaits from which it had so recently been freed, my bony hips, my nervous, pianist's fingers.

He was rich as Croesus. The night before our wedding — a simple affair, at the Mairie, because his countess was so recently gone — he took my mother and me, curious coincidence, to see *Tristan*. And, do you know, my heart swelled and ached so during the Liebestod that I thought I must truly love him. Yes. I did. On his arm, all eyes were upon me. The whispering crowd in the foyer parted like the Red Sea to let us through. My skin crisped at his touch.

How my circumstances had changed since the first time I heard those voluptuous chords that carry such a charge of deathly passion in them! Now, we sat in a loge, in red velvet armchairs, and a braided, bewigged flunkey brought us a silver bucket of iced champagne in the interval. The froth spilled over the rim of my glass and drenched my hands, I thought: My cup runneth over. And I had on a Poiret dress. He had prevailed upon my reluctant mother to let him buy my trousseau; what would I have gone to him in, otherwise? Twice-darned underwear, faded gingham, serge skirts, hand-me-downs. So, for the opera, I wore a sinuous shift of white muslin tied with a silk string under the breasts. And everyone stared at me. And at his wedding gift.

His wedding gift, clasped round my throat. A choker of rubies, two inches wide, like an extraordinarily precious slit throat.

After the Terror, in the early days of the Directory, the aristos who'd escaped the guillotine had an ironic fad of tying a red ribbon round their necks at just the point where the blade would have sliced it through, a red ribbon like the memory of a wound. And his grandmother, taken with the notion, had her ribbon made up in rubies; such a gesture of luxurious defiance! That night at the opera comes back to me even now ... the white dress; the frail child within it; and the flashing crimson jewels round her throat, bright as arterial blood.

I saw him watching me in the gilded mirrors with the assessing eye of a connoisseur inspecting horseflesh, or even of a housewife in the market, inspecting cuts on the slab. I'd never seen, or else had never acknowledged, that regard of his before, the sheer carnal avarice of it; and it was strangely magnified by the monocle lodged in his left eye. When I saw him look at me with lust, I dropped my eyes but, in glancing away from him, I caught sight of myself in the mirror. And I saw myself, suddenly, as he saw me, my pale face, the way the muscles in my neck stuck out like thin wire. I saw how much that cruel necklace became me. And, for the first time in my innocent and confined life, I sensed in myself a potentiality for corruption that took my breath away.

The next day, we were married.

The train slowed, shuddered to a halt. Lights; clank of metal; a voice declaring the name of an unknown, never-to-be visited station; silence of the night; the rhythm of his breathing, that I should sleep with, now, for the rest of my life. And I could not sleep. I stealthily sat up, raised the blind a little and huddled against the cold window that misted over with the warmth of my breathing, gazing out at the dark platform towards those rectangles of domestic lamplight that promised warmth, company, a supper of sausages hissing in a pan on the stove for the station master, his children tucked up in bed asleep in the brick house with the painted shutters ... all the paraphernalia of the everyday world from which I, with my stunning marriage, had exiled myself.

Into marriage, into exile; I sensed it, I knew it — that, henceforth, I would always be lonely. Yet that was part of the already familiar weight of the fire opal that glimmered like a gypsy's magic ball, so that I could not take my eyes off it when I played the piano. This ring, the bloody bandage of rubies, the wardrobe of clothes from Poiret and Worth, his scent of Russian leather — all had conspired to seduce me so utterly that I could not say I felt one single twinge of regret for the world of tartines and maman that now receded from me as if drawn away on a string, like a child's toy, as the train began to throb again as if in delighted anticipation of the distance it would take me.

The first grey streamers of the dawn now flew in the sky and an eldritch half-light seeped into the railway carriage. I heard no change in his breathing but my heightened, excited senses told me he was awake and gazing at me. A huge man, an enormous man, and his eyes, dark and motionless as those eyes the ancient Egyptians painted upon their sarcophagi, fixed upon me. I felt a certain tension in the pit of my stomach, to be so watched, in such silence. A match struck. He was igniting a Romeo y Julieta fat as a baby's arm.

'Soon,' he said in his resonant voice that was like the tolling of a bell and I felt, all at once, a sharp premonition of dread that lasted only as long as the match flared and I could see his white, broad face as if it were hovering, disembodied, above the sheets, illuminated from below like a grotesque carnival head. Then the flame died, the cigar glowed and filled the compartment with a remembered fragrance that made me think of my father, how he would hug me in a warm fug of Havana, when I was a little girl, before he kissed me and left me and died.

As soon as my husband handed me down from the high step of the train, I smelled the amniotic salinity of the ocean. It was November; the trees, stunted by the Atlantic gales, were bare and the lonely halt was deserted but for his leather-gaitered chauffeur waiting meekly beside the sleek black motor car. It was cold; I drew my furs about me, a wrap of white and black, broad stripes of ermine and sable, with a collar from which my head rose like the calyx of a wildflower. (I swear to you, I had never been vain until I met him.) The bell clanged; the straining train leapt its leash and left us at that lonely wayside halt where only he and I had descended. Oh, the wonder of it; how all that might of iron and steam had paused only to suit his convenience. The richest man in France.

'Madame.'

The chauffeur eyed me; was he comparing me, invidiously, to the countess, the artist's model, the opera singer? I hid behind my furs as if they were a system of soft shields. My husband liked me to wear my opal over my kid glove, a showy, theatrical trick — but the moment the ironic chauffeur glimpsed its simmering flash he smiled, as though it was proof positive I was his master's wife. And we drove towards the widening dawn, that now streaked half the sky with a wintry bouquet of pink of roses, orange of tiger-lilies, as if my husband had ordered me a sky from a florist. The day broke around me like a cool dream.

Sea; sand; a sky that melts into the sea — a landscape of misty pastels with a look about it of being continuously on the point of melting. A landscape with all the deliquescent harmonies of Debussy, of the études I played for him, the reverie I'd been playing that afternoon in the salon of the princess where I'd first met him, among the teacups and the little cakes, I, the orphan, hired out of charity to give them their digestive of music.

And, ah! his castle. The faery solitude of the place; with its turrets of misty blue, its courtyard, its spiked gate, his castle that lay on the very bosom of the sea with seabirds mewing about its attics, the casements opening on to the green and purple, evanescent departures of the ocean, cut off by the tide from land for half a day … that castle, at home neither on the land nor on the water, a mysterious, amphibious place, contravening the materiality of both earth and the waves, with the melancholy of a mermaiden who perches on her rock and waits, endlessly, for a lover who had drowned far away, long ago. That lovely, sad, sea-siren of a place!

The tide was low; at this hour, so early in the morning, the causeway rose up out of the sea. As the car turned on to the wet cobbles between the slow margins of water, he reached out for my hand that had his sultry, witchy ring on it, pressed my fingers, kissed my palm with extraordinary tenderness. His face was as still as ever I'd seen it, still as a pond iced thickly over, yet his lips, that always looked so strangely red and naked between the black fringes of his beard, now curved a little. He smiled; he welcomed his bride home.

No room, no corridor that did not rustle with the sound of the sea and all the ceilings, the walls on which his ancestors in the stern regalia of rank lined up with their dark eyes and white faces, were stippled with refracted light from the waves which were always in motion; that luminous, murmurous castle of which I was the châtelaine, I, the little music student whose mother had sold all her jewellery, even her wedding ring, to pay the fees at the Conservatoire.

First of all, there was the small ordeal of my initial interview with the housekeeper, who kept this extraordinary machine, this anchored, castellated ocean liner, in smooth running order no matter who stood on the bridge; how tenuous, I thought, might be my authority here! She had a bland, pale, impassive, dislikeable face beneath the impeccably starched white linen head-dress of the region. Her greeting, correct but lifeless, chilled me; daydreaming, I dared presume too much on my status ... briefly wondered how I might install my old nurse, so much loved, however cosily incompetent, in her place. Ill-considered schemings! He told me this one had been his foster mother; was bound to his family in the utmost feudal complicity, 'as much part of the house as I am, my dear.' Now her thin lips offered me a proud little smile. She would be my ally as long as I was his. And with that, I must be content.

But, here, it would be easy to be content. In the turret suite he had given me for my very own, I could gaze out over the tumultuous Atlantic and imagine myself the Queen of the Sea. There was a Bechstein for me in the music room and, on the wall, another wedding present — an early Flemish primitive of Saint Cecilia at her celestial organ. In the prim charm of this saint, with her plump, sallow cheeks and crinkled brown hair, I saw myself as I could have wished to be. I warmed to a loving sensitivity I had not hitherto suspected in him. Then he led me up a delicate spiral staircase to my bedroom; before she discreetly vanished, the housekeeper set him chuckling with some, I dare say, lewd blessing for newlyweds in her native Breton. That I did not understand. That he, smiling, refused to interpret.

And there lay the grand, hereditary matrimonial bed, itself the size, almost, of my little room at home, with the gargoyles carved on its surfaces of ebony, vermilion lacquer, gold leaf; and its white gauze curtains, billowing in the sea breeze. Our bed. And surrounded by so many mirrors! Mirrors on all the walls, in stately frames of contorted gold, that reflected more white lilies than I'd ever seen in my life before. He'd filled the room with them, to greet the bride, the young bride. The young bride, who had become that multitude of girls I saw in the mirrors, identical in their chic navy blue tailor-mades, for travelling, madame, or walking. A maid had dealt with the furs. Henceforth, a maid would deal with everything.

'See,' he said, gesturing towards those elegant girls. 'I have acquired a whole harem for myself!'

I found that I was trembling. My breath came thickly. I could not meet his eye and turned my head away, out of pride, out of shyness, and watched a dozen husbands approach me in a dozen mirrors and slowly, methodically, teasingly, unfasten the buttons of my jacket and slip it from my shoulders. Enough! No; more! Off comes the skirt; and, next, the blouse of apricot linen that cost more than the dress I had for first communion. The play of the waves outside in the cold sun glittered on his monocle; his movements seemed to me deliberately coarse, vulgar. The blood rushed to my face again, and stayed there.

And yet, you see, I guessed it might be so — that we should have a formal disrobing of the bride, a ritual from the brothel. Sheltered as my life had been, how could I have failed, even in the world of prim bohemia in which I lived, to have heard hints of *his* world?

He stripped me, gourmand that he was, as if he were stripping the leaves off an artichoke — but do not imagine much finesse about it; this artichoke was no particular treat for the diner nor was he yet in any greedy haste. He approached his familiar treat with a weary appetite. And when nothing but my scarlet, palpitating core remained, I saw, in the mirror, the living image of an etching by Rops from the collection he had shown me when our engagement permitted us to be alone together ... the child with her sticklike limbs, naked but for her button boots, her gloves, shielding her face with her hand as though her face were the last repository of her modesty; and the old, monocled lecher who examined her, limb by limb. He in his London tailoring; she, bare as a lamb chop. Most pornographic of all confrontations. And so my purchaser unwrapped his bargain. And, as at the opera, when I had first seen my flesh in his eyes, I was aghast to feel myself stirring.

At once he closed my legs like a book and I saw again the rare movement of his lips that meant he smiled.

Not yet. Later. Anticipation is the greater part of pleasure, my little love.

And I began to shudder, like a racehorse before a race, yet also with a kind of fear, for I felt both a strange, impersonal arousal at the thought of love and at the same time a repugnance I could not stifle for his white, heavy flesh that had too much in common with the armfuls of arum lilies that filled my bedroom in great glass jars, those undertakers' lilies with the heavy pollen that powders your fingers as if you had dipped them in turmeric. The lilies I always associate with him; that are white. And stain you.

This scene from a voluptuary's life was now abruptly terminated. It turns out he has business to attend to; his estates, his companies — even on your honeymoon? Even then, said the red lips that kissed me before he left me alone with my bewildered senses — a wet, silken brush from his beard; a hint of the pointed tip of the tongue. Disgruntled, I wrapped a négligé of antique lace around me to sip the little breakfast of hot chocolate the maid brought me; after that, since it was second nature to me, there was nowhere to go but the music room and soon I settled down at my piano.

Yet only a series of subtle discords flowed from beneath my fingers: out of tune ... only a little out of tune; but I'd been blessed with perfect pitch and could not bear to play any more. Sea breezes are bad for pianos; we shall need a resident piano-tuner on the premises if I'm to continue with my studies! I flung down the lid in a little fury of disappointment; what should I do now, how shall I pass the long, sea-lit hours until my husband beds me?

I shivered to think of *that*.

His library seemed the source of his habitual odour of Russian leather. Row upon row of calf-bound volumes, brown and olive, with gilt lettering on their spines, the octavo in brilliant scarlet morocco. A deep-buttoned leather sofa to recline on. A lectern, carved like a spread eagle, that held open upon it an edition of Huysmans's *Là-bas*, from some over-exquisite private press; it had been bound like a missal, in brass, with gems of coloured glass. The rugs on the floor, deep, pulsing blues of heaven and red of the heart's dearest blood, came from Isfahan and Bokhara; the dark panelling gleamed; there was the lulling music of the sea and a fire of apple logs. The flames flickered along the spines inside a glass-fronted case that held books still crisp and new. Eliphas Levy; the name meant nothing to me. I squinted at a title or two: *The Initiation, The Key of Mysteries, The Secret of Pandora's Box*, and yawned. Nothing, here, to detain a seventeen-year-old girl waiting for her first embrace. I should have liked, best of all, a novel in yellow paper; I wanted to curl up on the rug before the blazing fire, lose myself in a cheap novel, munch sticky liqueur chocolates. If I rang for them, a maid would bring me chocolates.

143

Nevertheless, I opened the doors of that bookcase idly to browse. And I think I knew, I knew by some tingling of the fingertips, even before I opened that slim volume with no title at all on the spine, what I should find inside it. When he showed me the Rops, newly bought, dearly prized, had he not hinted that he was a connoisseur of such things? Yet I had not bargained for this, the girl with tears hanging on her cheeks like stuck pearls, her cunt a split fig below the great globes of her buttocks on which the knotted tails of the cat were about to descend, while a man in a black mask fingered with his free hand his prick, that curved upwards like the scimitar he held. The picture had a caption: 'Reproof of curiosity.' My mother, with all the precision of her eccentricity, had told me what it was that lovers did; I was innocent but not naïve. *The Adventures of Eulalie at the Harem of the Grand Turk* had been printed, according to the flyleaf, in Amsterdam in 1748, a rare collector's piece. Had some ancestor brought it back himself from that northern city? Or had my husband bought it for himself, from one of those dusty little bookshops on the Left Bank where an old man peers at you through spectacles an inch thick, daring you to inspect his wares … I turned the pages in the anticipation of fear; the print was rusty. Here was another steel engraving: 'Immolation of the wives of the Sultan.' I knew enough for what I saw in that book to make me gasp.

There was a pungent intensification of the odour of leather that suffused his library; his shadow fell across the massacre.

'My little nun has found the prayerbooks, has she?' he demanded, with a curious mixture of mockery and relish; then, seeing my painful, furious bewilderment, he laughed at me aloud, snatched the book from my hands and put it down on the sofa.

'Have the nasty pictures scared Baby? Baby mustn't play with grownups' toys until she's learned how to handle them, must she?'

Then he kissed me. And with, this time, no reticence. He kissed me and laid his hand imperatively upon my breast, beneath the sheath of ancient lace. I stumbled on the winding stair that led to the bedroom, to the carved, gilded bed on which he had been conceived. I stammered foolishly: We've not taken luncheon yet; and, besides, it is broad daylight …

All the better to see you.

He made me put on my choker, the family heirloom of one woman who had escaped the blade. With trembling fingers, I fastened the thing about my neck. It was cold as ice and chilled me. He twined my hair into a rope and lifted it off my shoulders so that he could the better kiss the downy furrows below my ears; that made me shudder. And he kissed those blazing rubies, too. He kissed them before he kissed my mouth. Rapt, he intoned: 'Of her apparel she retains/Only her sonorous jewellery.'

A dozen husbands impaled a dozen brides while the mewing gulls swung on invisible trapezes in the empty air outside.

I was brought to my senses by the insistent shrilling of the telephone. He lay beside me, felled like an oak, breathing stertorously, as if he had been fighting with me. In the course of that one-sided struggle, I had seen his deathly composure shatter like a porcelain vase flung against a wall; I had heard him shriek and blaspheme at the orgasm; I had bled. And perhaps I had seen his face without its mask; and perhaps I had not. Yet I had been infinitely dishevelled by the loss of my virginity.

I gathered myself together, reached into the cloisonné cupboard beside the bed that concealed the telephone and addressed the mouthpiece. His agent in New York. Urgent.

144

I shook him awake and rolled over on my side, cradling my spent body in my arms. His voice buzzed like a hive of distant bees. My husband. My husband, who, with so much love, filled my bedroom with lilies until it looked like an embalming parlour. Those somnolent lilies, that wave their heavy heads, distributing their lush, insolent incense reminiscent of pampered flesh.

When he'd finished with the agent, he turned to me and stroked the ruby necklace that bit into my neck, but with such tenderness now, that I ceased flinching and he caressed my breasts. My dear one, my little love, my child, did it hurt her? He's so sorry for it, such impetuousness, he could not help himself; you see, he loves her so ... and this lover's recitative of his brought my tears in a flood. I clung to him as though only the one who had inflicted the pain could comfort me for suffering it. For a while, he murmured to me in a voice I'd never heard before, a voice like the soft consolations of the sea. But then he unwound the tendrils of my hair from the buttons of his smoking jacket, kissed my cheek briskly and told me the agent from New York had called with such urgent business that he must leave as soon as the tide was low enough. Leave the castle? Leave France! And would be away for at least six weeks.

'But it is our honeymoon!'

A deal, an enterprise of hazard and chance involving several millions, lay in the balance, he said. He drew away from me into that waxworks stillness of his; I was only a little girl, I did not understand. And, he said unspoken to my wounded vanity, I have had too many honeymoons to find them in the least pressing commitments. I know quite well that this child I've bought with a handful of coloured stones and the pelts of dead beasts won't run away. But, after he'd called his Paris agent to book a passage for the States next day — just one tiny call, my little one — we should have time for dinner together.

And I had to be content with that.

A Mexican dish of pheasant with hazelnuts and chocolate; salad; white, voluptuous cheese; a sorbet of muscat grapes and Asti spumante. A celebration of Krug exploded festively. And then acrid black coffee in precious little cups so fine it shadowed the birds with which they were painted. I had cointreau, he had cognac in the library, with the purple velvet curtains drawn against the night, where he took me to perch on his knee in a leather armchair beside the flickering log fire. He had made me change into that chaste little Poiret shift of white muslin; he seemed especially fond of it, my breasts showed through the flimsy stuff, he said, like little soft white doves that sleep, each one, with a pink eye open. But he would not let me take off my ruby choker, although it was growing very uncomfortable, nor fasten up my descending hair, the sign of a virginity so recently ruptured that still remained a wounded presence between us. He twined his fingers in my hair until I winced; I said, I remember, very little.

'The maid will have changed our sheets already,' he said. 'We do not hang the bloody sheets out of the window to prove to the whole of Brittany you are a virgin, not in these civilized times. But I should tell you it would have been the first time in all my married lives I could have shown my interested tenants such a flag.'

Then I realized, with a shock of surprise, how it must have been my innocence that captivated him — the silent music, he said, of my unknowingness, like *La Terrasse des audiences au clair de lune* played upon a piano with keys of ether. You must remember how ill at ease I was in that luxurious place, how unease had been my constant companion during the whole length of my courtship by this grave satyr who now gently martyrized my hair. To know that my naïvety gave him some pleasure made me take heart. Courage! I shall act the fine lady to the manner born one day, if only by virtue of default.

Then, slowly yet teasingly, as if he were giving a child a great, mysterious treat, he took out a bunch of keys from some interior hidey-hole in his jacket — key after key, a key, he said, for every lock in the house. Keys of all kinds — huge, ancient things of black iron; others slender, delicate, almost baroque; wafer-thin Yale keys for safes and boxes. And, during his absence, it was I who must take care of them all.

I eyed the heavy bunch with circumspection. Until that moment, I had not given a single thought to the practical aspects of marriage with a great house, great wealth, a great man, whose key ring was as crowded as that of a prison warder. Here were the clumsy and archaic keys for the dungeons, for dungeons we had in plenty although they had been converted to cellars for his wines; the dusty bottles inhabited in racks all those deep holes of pain in the rock on which the castle was built. These are the keys to the kitchens, this is the key to the picture gallery, a treasure house filled by five centuries of avid collectors — ah! he foresaw I would spend hours there.

He had amply indulged his taste for the Symbolists, he told me with a glint of greed. There was Moreau's great portrait of his first wife, the famous *Sacrificial Victim* with the imprint of the lacelike chains on her pellucid skin. Did I know the story of the painting of that picture? How, when she took off her clothes for him for the first time, she fresh from her bar in Montmartre, she had robed herself involuntarily in a blush that reddened her breasts, her shoulders, her arms, her whole body? He had thought of that story, of that dear girl, when first he had undressed me ... Ensor, the great Ensor, his monolithic canvas: *The Foolish Virgins*. Two or three late Gauguins, his special favourite the one of the tranced brown girl in the deserted house which was called: *Out of the Night We Come, Into the Night We Go.* And, besides the additions he had made himself, his marvellous inheritance of Watteaus, Poussins and a pair of very special Fragonards, commissioned for a licentious ancestor who, it was said, had posed for the master's brush himself with his own two daughters ... He broke off his catalogue of treasures abruptly.

Your thin white face, chérie; he said, as if he saw it for the first time. Your thin white face, with its promise of debauchery only a connoisseur could detect.

A log fell in the fire, instigating a shower of sparks; the opal on my finger spurted green flame. I felt as giddy as if I were on the edge of a precipice; I was afraid, not so much of him, of his monstrous presence, heavy as if he had been gifted at birth with more specific *gravity* than the rest of us, the presence that, even when I thought myself most in love with him, always subtly oppressed me ... No. I was not afraid of him; but of myself. I seemed reborn in his unreflective eyes, reborn in unfamiliar shapes. I hardly recognized myself from his descriptions of me and yet, and yet — might there not be a grain of beastly truth in them? And, in the red firelight, I blushed again, unnoticed, to think he might have chosen me because, in my innocence, he sensed a rare talent for corruption.

Here is the key to the china cabinet — don't laugh, my darling; there's a king's ransom in Sèvres in that closet, and a queen's ransom in Limoges. And a key to the locked, barred room where five generations of plate were kept.

Keys, keys, keys. He would trust me with the keys to his office, although I was only a baby; and the keys to his safes, where he kept the jewels I should wear, he promised me, when we returned to Paris. Such jewels! Why, I would be able to change my earrings and necklaces three times a day, just as the Empress Josephine used to change her underwear. He doubted, he said, with that hollow, knocking sound that served him for a chuckle, I would be quite so interested in his share certificate although they, of course, were worth infinitely more.

Outside our firelit privacy, I could hear the sound of the tide drawing back from the pebbles of the foreshore; it was nearly time for him to leave me. One single key remained unaccounted for on the ring and he hesitated over it; for a moment, I thought he was going to unfasten it from its brothers, slip it back into his pocket and take it away with him.

'What is *that* key?' I demanded, for his chaffing had made me bold. 'The key to your heart? Give it me!'

He dangled the key tantalizingly above my head, out of reach of my straining fingers; those bare red lips of his cracked sidelong in a smile.

'Ah, no,' he said. 'Not the key to my heart. Rather, the key to my enfer.'

He left it on the ring, fastened the ring together, shook it musically, like a carillon. Then threw the keys in a jingling heap in my lap. I could feel the cold metal chilling my thighs through my thin muslin frock. He bent over me to drop a beard-masked kiss on my forehead.

'Every man must have one secret, even if only one, from his wife,' he said. 'Promise me this, my whey-faced piano-player; promise me you'll use all the keys on the ring except that last little one I showed you. Play with anything you find, jewels, silver plate; make toy boats of my share certificates, if it pleases you, and send them sailing off to America after me. All is yours, everywhere is open to you — except the lock that this single key fits. Yet all it is is the key to a little room at the foot of the west tower, behind the still-room, at the end of a dark little corridor full of horrid cobwebs that would get into your hair and frighten you if you ventured there. Oh, and you'd find it such a dull little room! But you must promise me, if you love me, to leave it well alone. It is only a private study, a hideaway, a "den," as the English say, where I can go, sometimes, on those infrequent yet inevitable occasions when the yoke of marriage seems to weigh too heavily on my shoulders. There I can go, you understand, to savour the rare pleasure of imagining myself wifeless.'

There was a little thin starlight in the courtyard as, wrapped in my furs, I saw him to his car. His last words were, that he had telephoned the mainland and taken a piano-tuner on to the staff; this man would arrive to take up his duties the next day. He pressed me to his vicuña breast, once, and then drove away.

I had drowsed away that afternoon and now I could not sleep. I lay tossing and turning in his ancestral bed until another daybreak discoloured the dozen mirrors that were iridescent with the reflections of the sea. The perfume of the lilies weighed on my senses; when I thought that, henceforth, I would always share these sheets with a man whose skin, as theirs did, contained that toad-like, clammy hint of moisture, I felt a vague desolation that within me, now my female wound had healed, there had awoken a certain queasy craving like the cravings of pregnant women for the taste of coal or chalk or tainted food, for the renewal of his caresses. Had he not hinted to me, in his flesh as in his speech and looks, of the thousand, thousand baroque intersections of flesh upon flesh? I lay in our wide bed accompanied by, a sleepless companion, my dark newborn curiosity.

I lay in bed alone. And I longed for him. And he disgusted me.

Were there jewels enough in all his safes to recompense me for this predicament? Did all that castle hold enough riches to recompense me for the company of the libertine with whom I must share it? And what, precisely, was the nature of my desirous dread for this mysterious being who, to show his mastery over me, had abandoned me on my wedding night?

Then I sat straight up in bed, under the sardonic masks of the gargoyles carved above me, riven by a wild surmise. Might he have left me, not for Wall Street but for an importunate mistress tucked away God knows where who knew how to pleasure him far better than a girl whose fingers had been exercised, hitherto, only by the practice of scales and arpeggios? And, slowly, soothed, I sank back on to the heaping pillows; I acknowledged that the jealous scare I'd just given myself was not unmixed with a little tincture of relief.

At last I drifted into slumber, as daylight filled the room and chased bad dreams away. But the last thing I remembered, before I slept, was the tall jar of lilies beside the bed, how the thick glass distorted their fat stems so they looked like arms, dismembered arms, drifting drowned in greenish water.

Coffee and croissants to console this bridal, solitary waking. Delicious. Honey, too, in a section of comb on a glass saucer. The maid squeezed the aromatic juice from an orange into a chilled goblet while I watched her as I lay in the lazy, midday bed of the rich. Yet nothing, this morning, gave me more than a fleeting pleasure except to hear that the piano-tuner had been at work already. When the maid told me that, I sprang out of bed and pulled on my old serge skirt and flannel blouse, costume of a student, in which I felt far more at ease with myself than in any of my fine new clothes.

After my three hours of practice, I called the piano-tuner in, to thank him. He was blind, of course; but young, with a gentle mouth and grey eyes that fixed upon me although they could not see me. He was a blacksmith's son from the village across the causeway; a chorister in the church whom the good priest had taught a trade so that he could make a living. All most satisfactory. Yes. He thought he would be happy here. And if, he added shyly, he might sometimes be allowed to hear me play … for, you see, he loved music. Yes. Of course, I said. Certainly. He seemed to know that I had smiled.

After I dismissed him, even though I'd woken so late, it was still barely time for my 'five o'clock.' The housekeeper, who, thoughtfully forewarned by my husband, had restrained herself from interrupting my music, now made me a solemn visitation with a lengthy menu for a late luncheon. When I told her I did not need it, she looked at me obliquely, along her nose. I understood at once that one of my principal functions as châtelaine was to provide work for the staff. But, all the same, I asserted myself and said I would wait until dinner-time, although I looked forward nervously to the solitary meal. Then I found I had to tell her what I would like to have prepared for me; my imagination, still that of a schoolgirl, ran riot. A fowl in cream — or should I anticipate Christmas with a varnished turkey? No; I have decided. Avocado and shrimp, lots of it, followed by no entrée at all. But surprise me for dessert with every ice-cream in the ice box. She noted all down but sniffed; I'd shocked her. Such tastes! Child that I was, I giggled when she left me.

But, now ... what shall I do, now?

I could have spent a happy hour unpacking the trunks that contained my trousseau but the maid had done that already, the dresses, the tailor-mades hung in the wardrobe in my dressing room, the hats on wooden heads to keep their shape, the shoes on wooden feet as if all these inanimate objects were imitating the appearance of life, to mock me. I did not like to linger in my overcrowded dressing room, nor in my lugubriously lily-scented bedroom. How shall I pass the time?

I shall take a bath in my own bathroom! And found the taps were little dolphins made of gold, with chips of turquoise for eyes. And there was a tank of goldfish, who swam in and out of moving fronds of weeds, as bored, I thought, as I was. How I wished he had not left me. How I wished it were possible to chat with, say, a maid; or, the piano-tuner ... but I knew already my new rank forbade overtures of friendship to the staff.

I had been hoping to defer the call as long as I could, so that I should have something to look forward to in the dead waste of time I foresaw before me, after my dinner was done with, but, at a quarter before seven, when darkness already surrounded the castle, I could contain myself no longer. I telephoned my mother. And astonished myself by bursting into tears when I heard her voice.

No, nothing was the matter. Mother, I have gold bath taps.

I said, gold bath taps!

No; I suppose that's nothing to cry about, Mother.

The line was bad, I could hardly make out her congratulations, her questions, her concern, but I was a little comforted when I put the receiver down.

Yet there still remained one whole hour to dinner and the whole unimaginable desert of the rest of the evening.

The bunch of keys lay, where he had left them, on the rug before the library fire which had warmed their metal so that they no longer felt cold to the touch but warm, almost, as my own skin. How careless I was; a maid, tending the logs, eyed me reproachfully as if I'd set a trap for her as I picked up the clinking bundle of keys, the keys to the interior doors of this lovely prison of which I was both the inmate and the mistress and had scarcely seen. When I remembered that, I felt the exhilaration of the explorer.

Lights! More lights!

At the touch of a switch, the dreaming library was brilliantly illuminated. I ran crazily about the castle, switching on every light I could find — I ordered the servants to light up all their quarters, too, so the castle would shine like a seaborne birthday cake lit with a thousand candles, one for every year of its life, and everybody on shore would wonder at it. When everything was lit as brightly as the cafe in the Gare du Nord, the significance of the possessions implied by that bunch of keys no longer intimidated me, for I was determined, now, to search through them all for evidence of my husband's true nature.

His office first, evidently.

A mahogany desk half a mile wide, with an impeccable blotter and a bank of telephones. I allowed myself the luxury of opening the safe that contained the jewellery and delved sufficiently among the leather boxes to find out how my marriage had given me access to a jinn's treasury — parures, bracelets, rings ... While I was thus surrounded by diamonds, a maid knocked on the door and entered before I spoke; a subtle discourtesy. I would speak to my husband about it. She eyed my serge skirt superciliously; did madame plan to dress for dinner?

She made a moue of disdain when I laughed to hear that, she was far more the lady than I. But, imagine — to dress up in one of my Poiret extravaganzas, with the jewelled turban and aigrette on my head, roped with pearl to the navel, to sit down all alone in the baronial dining hall at the head of that massive board at which King Mark was reputed to have fed his knights ... I grew calmer under the cold eye of her disapproval. I adopted the crisp inflections of an officer's daughter. No, I would not dress for dinner. Furthermore, I was not hungry enough for dinner itself. She must tell the housekeeper to cancel the dormitory feast I'd ordered. Could they leave me sandwiches and a flask of coffee in my music room? And would they all dismiss for the night?

Mais oui, madame.

I knew by her bereft intonation I had let them down again but I did not care; I was armed against them by the brilliance of his hoard. But I would not find his heart amongst the glittering stones; as soon as she had gone, I began a systematic search of the drawers of his desk.

All was in order, so I found nothing. Not a random doodle on an old envelope, nor the faded photograph of a woman. Only the files of business correspondence, the bills from the home farms, the invoices from tailors, the billets-doux from international financiers. Nothing. And this absence of the evidence of his real life began to impress me strangely; there must, I thought, be a great deal to conceal if he takes such pains to hide it.

His office was a singularly impersonal room, facing inwards, on to the courtyard, as though he wanted to turn his back on the siren sea in order to keep a clear head while he bankrupted a small businessman in Amsterdam or — I noticed with a thrill of distaste — engaged in some business in Laos that must, from certain cryptic references to his amateur botanist's enthusiasm for rare poppies, be to do with opium. Was he not rich enough to do without crime? Or was the crime itself his profit? And yet I saw enough to appreciate his zeal for secrecy.

Now I had ransacked his desk, I must spend a cool-headed quarter of an hour putting every last letter back where I had found it, and, as I covered the traces of my visit, by some chance, as I reached inside a little drawer that had stuck fast, I must have touched a hidden spring, for a secret drawer flew open within that drawer itself; and this secret drawer contained — at last! — a file marked: *Personal.*

I was alone, but for my reflection in the uncurtained window.

I had the brief notion that his heart, pressed flat as a flower, crimson and thin as tissue paper, lay in this file. It was a very thin one.

I could have wished, perhaps, I had not found that touching, ill-spelt note, on a paper napkin marked *La Coupole,* that began: 'My darling, I cannot wait for the moment when you may make me yours completely.' The diva had sent him a page of the score of *Tristan,* the Liebestod, with the single, cryptic word: 'Until ...' scrawled across it. But the strangest of all these love letters was a postcard with a view of a village graveyard, among mountains, where some black-coated ghoul enthusiastically dug at a grave; this little scene, executed with the lurid exuberance of Grand Guignol, was captioned: 'Typical Transylvanian Scene — Midnight, All Hallows.' And, on the other side, the message: 'On the occasion of this marriage to the descendant of Dracula — always remember, "the supreme and unique pleasure of love is the certainty that one is doing evil." Toutes amitiés, C.'

A joke. A joke in the worst possible taste; for had he not been married to a Romanian countess? And then I remembered her pretty, witty face, and her name — Carmilla. My most recent predecessor in this castle had been, it would seem, the most sophisticated.

I put away the file, sobered. Nothing in my life of family love and music had prepared me for these grown-up games and yet these were clues to his self that showed me, at least, how much he had been loved, even if they did not reveal any good reason for it. But I wanted to know still more; and, as I closed the office door and locked it, the means to discover more fell in my way.

Fell, indeed; and with the clatter of a dropped canteen of cutlery, for, as I turned the slick Yale lock, I contrived, somehow, to open up the key ring itself, so that all the keys tumbled loose on the floor. And the very first key I picked out of that pile was, as luck or ill fortune had it, the key to the room he had forbidden me, the room he would keep for his own so that he could go there when he wished to feel himself once more a bachelor.

I made my decision to explore it before I felt a faint resurgence of my ill-defined fear of his waxen stillness. Perhaps I half-imagined, then, that I might find his real self in his den, waiting there to see if indeed I had obeyed him; that he had sent a moving figure of himself to New York, the enigmatic, self-sustaining carapace of his public person, while the real man, whose face I had glimpsed in the storm of orgasm, occupied himself with pressing private business in the study at the foot of the west tower, behind the still-room. Yet, if that were so, it was imperative that I should find him, should know him; and I was too deluded by his apparent taste for me to think my disobedience might truly offend him.

I took the forbidden key from the heap and left the others lying there.

It was now very late and the castle was adrift, as far as it could go from the land, in the middle of the silent ocean where, at my orders, it floated, like a garland of light. And all silent, all still, but for the murmuring of the waves.

I felt no fear, no intimation of dread. Now I walked as firmly as I had done in my mother's house.

Not a narrow, dusty little passage at all; why had he lied to me? But an ill-lit one, certainly; the electricity, for some reason, did not extend here, so I retreated to the still-room and found a bundle of waxed tapers in a cupboard, stored there with matches to light the oak board at grand dinners. I put a match to my little taper and advanced with it in my hand, like a penitent, along the corridor hung with heavy, I think Venetian, tapestries. The flame picked out, here, the head of a man, there, the rich breast of a woman spilling through a rent in her dress — the Rape of the Sabines, perhaps? The naked swords and immolated horses suggested some grisly mythological subject. The corridor wound downwards; there was an almost imperceptible ramp to the thickly carpeted floor. The heavy hangings on the wall muffled my footsteps, even my breathing. For some reason, it grew very warm; the sweat sprang out in beads on my brow. I could no longer hear the sound of the sea.

A long, a winding corridor, as if I were in the viscera of the castle; and this corridor led to a door of worm-eaten oak, low, round-topped, barred with black iron.

And still I felt no fear, no raising of the hairs on the back of the neck, no prickling of the thumbs.

The key slid into the new lock as easily as a hot knife into butter.

No fear; but a hesitation, a holding of the spiritual breath.

If I had found some traces of his heart in a file marked: *Personal*, perhaps, here, in his subterranean privacy, I might find a little of his soul. It was the consciousness of the possibility of such a discovery, of its possible strangeness, that kept me for a moment motionless, before, in the foolhardiness of my already subtly tainted innocence, I turned the key and the door creaked slowly back.

'There is a striking resemblance between the act of love and the ministrations of a torturer,' opined my husband's favourite poet; I had learned something of the nature of that similarity on my marriage bed. And now my taper showed me the outlines of a rack. There was also a great wheel, like the ones I had seen in woodcuts of the martyrdoms of the saints, in my old nurse's little store of holy books. And — just one glimpse of it before my little flame caved in and I was left in absolute darkness — a metal figure, hinged at the side, which I knew to be spiked on the inside and to have the name: the Iron Maiden.

Absolute darkness. And, about me, the instruments of mutilation.

Until that moment, this spoiled child did not know she had inherited nerves and a will from the mother who had defied the yellow outlaws of Indo-China. My mother's spirit drove me on, into that dreadful place, in a cold ecstasy to know the very worst. I fumbled for the matches in my pocket; what a dim, lugubrious light they gave! And yet, enough, oh, more than enough, to see a room designed for desecration and some dark night of unimaginable lovers whose embraces were annihilation.

The walls of this stark torture chamber were the naked rock; they gleamed as if they were sweating with fright. At the four corners of the room were funerary urns, of great antiquity, Etruscan, perhaps, and, on three-legged ebony stands, the bowls of incense he had left burning which filled the room with a sacerdotal reek. Wheel, rack and Iron Maiden were, I saw, displayed as grandly as if they were items of statuary and I was almost consoled, then, and almost persuaded myself that I might have stumbled only upon a little museum of his perversity, that he had installed these monstrous items here only for contemplation.

Yet at the centre of the room lay a catafalque, a doomed, ominous bier of Renaissance workmanship, surrounded by long white candles and, at its foot, an armful of the same lilies with which he had filled my bedroom, stowed in a four-foot-high jar glazed with a sombre Chinese red. I scarcely dared examine this catafalque and its occupant more closely; yet I knew I must.

Each time I struck a match to light those candles round her bed, it seemed a garment of that innocence of mine for which he had lusted fell away from me.

The opera singer lay, quite naked, under a thin sheet of very rare and precious linen, such as the princes of Italy used to shroud those whom they had poisoned. I touched her, very gently, on the white breast; she was cool, he had embalmed her. On her throat I could see the blue imprint of his strangler's fingers. The cool, sad flame of the candles flickered on her white, closed eyelids. The worst thing was, the dead lips smiled.

Beyond the catafalque, in the middle of the shadows, a white, nacreous glimmer; as my eyes accustomed themselves to the gathering darkness, I at last — oh, horrors! — made out a skull; yes, a skull, so utterly denuded, now, of flesh, that it scarcely seemed possible the stark bone had once been richly upholstered with life. And this skull was strung up by a system of unseen cords, so that it appeared to hang, disembodied, in the still, heavy air, and it had been crowned with a wreath of white roses, and a veil of lace, the final image of his bride.

Yet the skull was still so beautiful, had shaped with its sheer planes so imperiously the face that had once existed above it, that I recognized her the moment I saw her; face of the evening star walking on the rim of night. One false step, oh, my poor, dear girl, next in the fated sisterhood of his wives; one false step and into the abyss of the dark you stumbled.

And where was she, the latest dead, the Romanian countess who might have thought her blood would survive his depredations? I knew she must be here, in the place that had wound me through the castle towards it on a spool of inexorability. But, at first, I could see no sign of her. Then, for some reason — perhaps some change of atmosphere wrought by my presence — the metal shell of the Iron Maiden emitted a ghostly twang; my feverish imagination might have guessed its occupant was trying to clamber out, though, even in the midst of my rising hysteria, I knew she must be dead to find a home there.

With trembling fingers, I prised open the front of the upright coffin, with its sculpted face caught in a rictus of pain. Then, overcome, I dropped the key I still held in my other hand. It dropped into the forming pool of her blood.

She was pierced, not by one but by a hundred spikes, this child of the land of the vampires who seemed so newly dead, so full of blood ... oh God! how recently had he become a widower? How long had he kept her in this obscene cell? Had it been all the time he had courted me, in the clear light of Paris?

I closed the lid of her coffin very gently and burst into a tumult of sobbing that contained both pity for his other victims and also a dreadful anguish to know I, too, was one of them.

The candles flared, as if in a draught from a door to elsewhere. The light caught the fire opal on my hand so that it flashed, once, with a baleful light, as if to tell me the eye of God — his eye — was upon me. My first thought, when I saw the ring for which I had sold myself to this fate, was, how to escape it.

I retained sufficient presence of mind to snuff out the candles round the bier with my fingers, to gather up my taper, to look around, although shuddering, to ensure I had left behind me no traces of my visit.

I retrieved the key from the pool of blood, wrapped it in my handkerchief to keep my hands clean, and fled the room, slamming the door behind me.

It crashed to with a juddering reverberation, like the door of hell.

I could not take refuge in my bedroom, for that retained the memory of his presence trapped in the fathomless silvering of his mirrors. My music room seemed the safest place, although I looked at the picture of Saint Cecilia with a faint dread; what had been the nature of her martyrdom? My mind was in a tumult; schemes for flight jostled with one another ... as soon as the tide receded from the causeway, I would make for the mainland — on foot, running, stumbling; I did not trust that leather-clad chauffeur, nor the well-behaved housekeeper, and I dared not take any of the pale, ghostly maids into my confidence, either, since they were his creatures, all. Once at the village, I would fling myself directly on the mercy of the gendarmerie.

But — could I trust them, either? His forefathers had ruled this coast for eight centuries, from this castle whose moat was the Atlantic. Might not the police, the advocates, even the judge, all be in his service, turning a common blind eye to his vices since he was milord whose word must be obeyed? Who, on this distant coast, would believe the white-faced girl from Paris who came running to them with a shuddering tale of blood, of fear, of the ogre murmuring in the shadows? Or, rather, they would immediately know it to be true. But were all honour-bound to let me carry it no further.

Assistance. My mother. I ran to the telephone; and the line, of course, was dead.

Dead as his wives.

A thick darkness, unlit by any star, still glazed the windows. Every lamp in my room burned, to keep the dark outside, yet it seemed still to encroach on me, to be present beside me but as if masked by my lights, the night like a permeable substance that could seep into my skin. I looked at the precious little clock made from hypocritically innocent flowers long ago, in Dresden; the hands had scarcely moved one single hour forward from when I first descended to that private slaughterhouse of his. Time was his servant, too; it would trap me, here, in a night that would last until he came back to me, like a black sun on a hopeless morning.

And yet the time might still be my friend; at that hour, that very hour, he set sail for New York.

To know that, in a few moments, my husband would have left France calmed my agitation a little. My reason told me I had nothing to fear; the tide that would take him away to the New World would let me out of the imprisonment of the castle. Surely I could easily evade the servants. Anybody can buy a ticket at a railway station. Yet I was still filled with unease. I opened the lid of the piano; perhaps I thought my own particular magic might help me, now, that I could create a pentacle out of music that would keep me from harm for, if my music had first ensnared him, then might it not also give me the power to free myself from him?

Mechanically, I began to play but my fingers were stiff and shaking. At first, I could manage nothing better than the exercises of Czerny but simply the act of playing soothed me and, for solace, for the sake of the harmonious rationality of its sublime mathematics I searched among his scores until I found *The Well-Tempered Clavier*. I set myself the therapeutic task of playing all Bach's equations, every one, and, I told myself, if I played them all through without a single mistake — then the morning would find me once more a virgin.

Crash of a dropped stick.

His silver-headed cane! What else? Sly, cunning, he had returned; he was waiting for me outside the door!

I rose to my feet; fear gave me strength. I flung back my head defiantly.

'Come in!' My voice astonished me by its firmness, its clarity.

The door slowly, nervously opened and I saw not the massive irredeemable bulk of my husband but the slight, stooping figure of the piano-tuner, and he looked far more terrified of me than my mother's daughter would have been of the Devil himself. In the torture chamber, it seemed to me that I would never laugh again; now, helplessly, laugh I did, with relief, and, after a moment's hesitation, the boy's face softened and he smiled a little, almost in shame. Though they were blind, his eyes were singularly sweet.

'Forgive me,' said Jean-Yves. 'I know I've given you grounds for dismissing me, that I should be crouching outside your door at midnight ... but I heard you walking about, up and down — I sleep in a room at the foot of the west tower — and some intuition told me you could not sleep and might, perhaps, pass the insomniac hours at your piano. And I could not resist that. Besides, I stumbled over these — '

And he displayed the ring of keys I'd dropped outside my husband's office door, the ring from which one key was missing. I took them from him, looked round for a place to stow them, fixed on the piano stool as if to hide them would protect me. Still he stood smiling at me. How hard it was to make everyday conversation.

'It's perfect,' I said. 'The piano. Perfectly in tune.'

But he was full of the loquacity of embarrassment, as though I would only forgive him for his impudence if he explained the cause of it thoroughly.

'When I heard you play this afternoon, I thought I'd never heard such a touch. Such technique. A treat for me, to hear a virtuoso! So I crept up to your door now, humbly as a little dog might, madame, and put my ear to the keyhole and listened, and listened — until my stick fell to the floor through a momentary clumsiness of mine, and I was discovered.'

He had the most touchingly ingenuous smile.

'Perfectly in tune,' I repeated. To my surprise, now I had said it, I found I could not say anything else. I could only repeat: 'In tune ... perfect ... in tune,' over and over again. I saw a dawning surprise in his face. My head throbbed. To see him, in his lovely, blind humanity, seemed to hurt me very piercingly, somewhere inside my breast; his figure blurred, the room swayed about me. After the dreadful revelation of that bloody chamber, it was his tender look that made me faint.

When I recovered consciousness, I found I was lying in the piano-tuner's arms and he was tucking the satin cushion from the piano-stool under my head.

'You are in some great distress,' he said. 'No bride should suffer so much, so early in her marriage.'

His speech had the rhythms of the countryside, the rhythms of the tides.

'Any bride brought to this castle should come ready dressed in mourning, should bring a priest and a coffin with her,' I said.

'What's this?'

It was too late to keep silent; and if he, too, were one of my husband's creatures, then at least he had been kind to me. So I told him everything, the keys, the interdiction, my disobedience, the room, the rack, the skull, the corpses, the blood.

'I can scarcely believe it,' he said, wondering. 'That man ... so rich; so well-born.'

'Here's proof,' I said and tumbled the fatal key out of my handkerchief on to the silken rug.

'Oh God,' he said. 'I can smell the blood.'

He took my hand; he pressed his arms about me. Although he was scarcely more than a boy, I felt a great strength flow into me from his touch.

'We whisper all manner of strange tales up and down the coast,' he said. 'There was a Marquis, once, who used to hunt young girls on the mainland; he hunted them with dogs, as though they were foxes. My grandfather had it from his grandfather, how the Marquis pulled a head out of his saddle bag and showed it to the blacksmith while the man was shoeing his horse. "A fine specimen of the genus, brunette, eh, Guillaume?" And it was the head of the blacksmith's wife.'

But, in these more democratic times, my husband must travel as far as Paris to do his hunting in the salons. Jean-Yves knew the moment I shuddered.

'Oh, madame! I thought all these were old wives' tales, chattering of fools, spooks to scare bad children into good behaviour! Yet how could you know, a stranger, that the old name for this place is the Castle of Murder?'

How could I know, indeed? Except that, in my heart, I'd always known its lord would be the death of me.

'Hark!' said my friend suddenly. 'The sea has changed key; it must be near morning, the tide is going down.'

He helped me up. I looked from the window, towards the mainland, along the causeway where the stones gleamed wetly in the thin light of the end of the night and, with an almost unimaginable horror, a horror the intensity of which I cannot transmit to you, I saw, in the distance, still far away yet drawing moment by moment inexorably nearer, the twin headlamps of his great black car, gouging tunnels through the shifting mist.

My husband had indeed returned; this time, it was no fancy.

'The key!' said Jean-Yves. 'It must go back on the ring, with the others. As though nothing had happened.'

But the key was still caked with wet blood and I ran to my bathroom and held it under the hot tap. Crimson water swirled down the basin but, as if the key itself were hurt, the bloody token stuck. The turquoise eyes of the dolphin taps winked at me derisively; they knew my husband had been too clever for me! I scrubbed the stain with my nail brush but still it would not budge. I thought how the car would be rolling silently towards the closed courtyard gate; the more I scrubbed the key, the more vivid grew the stain.

The bell in the gatehouse would jangle. The porter's drowsy son would push back the patchwork quilt, yawning, pull the shirt over his head, thrust his feet into his sabots … slowly, slowly; open the door for your master as slowly as you can …

And still the bloodstain mocked the fresh water that spilled from the mouth of the leering dolphin.

'You have no more time,' said Jean-Yves. 'He is here. I know it. I must stay with you.'

'You shall not!' I said. 'Go back to your room, now. Please.'

He hesitated. I put an edge of steel in my voice, for I knew I must meet my lord alone.

'Leave me!'

As soon as he had gone, I dealt with the keys and went to my bedroom. The causeway was empty; Jean-Yves was correct, my husband had already entered the castle. I pulled the curtains close, stripped off my clothes and pulled the bedcurtains round me as a pungent aroma of Russian leather assured me my husband was once again beside me.

'Dearest!'

With the most treacherous, lascivious tenderness, he kissed my eyes, and, mimicking the new bride newly wakened, I flung my arms around him, for on my seeming acquiescence depended my salvation.

'Da Silva of Rio outwitted me,' he said wryly. 'My New York agent telegraphed Le Havre and saved me a wasted journey. So we may resume our interrupted pleasures, my love.'

I did not believe one word of it. I knew I had behaved exactly according to his desires; had he not bought me so that I should do so? I had been tricked into my own betrayal to that illimitable darkness whose source I had been compelled to seek in his absence and, now that I had met that shadowed reality of his that came to life only in the presence of its own atrocities, I must pay the price of my new knowledge. The secret of Pandora's box; but he had given me the box, himself, knowing I must learn the secret. I had played a game in which every move was governed by a destiny as oppressive and omnipotent as himself, since that destiny was himself; and I had lost. Lost at that charade of innocence and vice in which he had engaged me. Lost, as the victim loses to the executioner.

His hand brushed my breast, beneath the sheet. I strained my nerves yet could not help but flinch from the intimate touch, for it made me think of the piercing embrace of the Iron Maiden and of his lost lovers in the vault. When he saw my reluctance, his eyes veiled over and yet his appetite did not diminish. His tongue ran over red lips already wet. Silent, mysterious, he moved away from me to draw off his jacket. He took the gold watch from his waistcoat and laid it on the dressing table like a good bourgeois; scooped out his rattling loose change and now — oh God! — makes a great play of patting his pockets officiously, puzzled lips pursed, searching for something that has been mislaid. Then turns to me with a ghastly, a triumphant smile.

'But of course! I gave the keys to you!'

'Your keys? Why, of course. Here, they're under the pillow; wait a moment — what — Ah! No ... now, where can I have left them? I was whiling away the evening without you at the piano, I remember. Of course! The music room!'

Brusquely he flung my négligé of antique lace on the bed.

'Go and get them.'

'Now? This moment? Can't it wait until morning, my darling?'

I forced myself to be seductive. I saw myself, pale, pliant as a plant that begs to be trampled underfoot, a dozen vulnerable, appealing girls reflected in as many mirrors, and I saw how he almost failed to resist me. If he had come to me in bed, I would have strangled him, then.

But he half-snarled: 'No. It won't wait. Now.'

The unearthly light of dawn filled the room; had only one previous dawn broken upon me in that vile place? And there was nothing for it but to go and fetch the keys from the music stool and pray he would not examine them too closely, pray to God his eyes would fail him, that he might be struck blind.

When I came back into the bedroom carrying the bunch of keys that jangled at every step like a curious musical instrument, he was sitting on the bed in his immaculate shirtsleeves, his head sunk in his hands.

And it seemed to me he was in despair.

Strange. In spite of my fear of him, that made me whiter than my wrap, I felt there emanate from him, at that moment, a stench of absolute despair, rank and ghastly, as if the lilies that surrounded him had all at once begun to fester, or the Russian leather of his scent were reverting to the elements of flayed hide and excrement of which it was composed. The chthonic gravity of his presence exerted a tremendous pressure on the room, so that the blood pounded in my ears as if we had been precipitated to the bottom of the sea, beneath the waves that pounded against the shore.

I held my life in my hands amongst those keys and, in a moment, would place it between his well-manicured fingers. The evidence of that bloody chamber had showed me I could expect no mercy. Yet, when he raised his head and stared at me with his blind, shuttered eyes as though he did not recognize me, I felt a terrified pity for him, for this man who lived in such strange, secret places that, if I loved him enough to follow him, I should have to die.

The atrocious loneliness of that monster!

The monocle had fallen from his face. His curling mane was disordered, as if he had run his hands through it in his distraction. I saw how he had lost his impassivity and was now filled with suppressed excitement. The hand he stretched out for those counters in his game of love and death shook a little; the face that turned towards me contained a sombre delirium that seemed to me compounded of a ghastly, yes, shame but also of a terrible, guilty joy as he slowly ascertained how I had sinned.

That tell-tale stain had resolved itself into a mark the shape and brilliance of the heart on a playing card. He disengaged the key from the ring and looked at it for a while, solitary, brooding.

'It is the key that leads to the kingdom of the unimaginable,' he said. His voice was low and had in it the timbre of certain great cathedral organs that seem, when they are played, to be conversing with God.

I could not restrain a sob.

'Oh, my love, my little love who brought me a white gift of music,' he said, almost as if grieving. 'My little love, you'll never know how much I hate daylight!'

Then he sharply ordered: 'Kneel!'

I knelt before him and he pressed the key lightly to my forehead, held it there for a moment, I felt a faint tingling of the skin and, when I involuntarily glanced at myself in the mirror, I saw the heart-shaped stain had transferred itself to my forehead, to the space between the eyebrows, like the caste mark of a brahmin woman. Or the mark of Cain. And now the key gleamed as freshly as if it had just been cut. He clipped it back on the ring, emitting that same, heavy sigh as he had done when I said that I would marry him.

'My virgin of the arpeggios, prepare yourself for martyrdom.'

'What form shall it take?' I said.

'Decapitation,' he whispered, almost voluptuously. 'Go and bathe yourself; put on that white dress you wore to hear *Tristan* and the necklace that prefigures your end. And I shall take myself off to the armoury, my dear, to sharpen my great-grandfather's ceremonial sword.'

'The servants?'

'We shall have absolute privacy for our last rites; I have already dismissed them. If you look out of the window you can see them going to the mainland.'

It was now the full, pale light of morning; the weather was grey, indeterminate the sea had an oily, sinister look, a gloomy day on which to die. Along the causeway I could see trouping every maid and scullion, every pot-boy and pan-scourer, valet, laundress and vassal who worked in that great house, most on foot, a few on bicycles. The faceless housekeeper trudged along with a great basket in which, I guessed, she'd stowed as much as she could ransack from the larder. The Marquis must have given the chauffeur leave to borrow the motor for the day, for it went last of all, at a stately pace, as though the procession were a cortège and the car already bore my coffin to the mainland for burial.

But I knew no good Breton earth would cover me, like a last, faithful lover; I had another fate.

'I have given them all a day's holiday, to celebrate our wedding,' he said. And smiled.

However hard I stared at the receding company, I could see no sign of Jean-Yves, our latest servant, hired but the preceding morning.

'Go, now. Bathe yourself; dress yourself. The lustratory ritual and the ceremonial robing; after that, the sacrifice. Wait in the music room until I telephone for you. No, my dear!' And he smiled, as I started, recalling the line was dead. 'One may call inside the castle just as much as one pleases; but, outside — never.'

I scrubbed my forehead with the nail brush as I had scrubbed the key but this red mark would not go away, either, no matter what I did, and I knew I should wear it until I died, though that would not be long. Then I went to my dressing room and put on that white muslin shift, costume of a victim of an auto-da-fé, he had bought me to listen to the Liebestod in. Twelve young women combed out twelve listless sheaves of brown hair in the mirrors; soon, there would be none. The mass of lilies that surrounded me exhaled, now, the odour of their withering. They looked like the trumpets of the angels of death.

On the dressing table, coiled like a snake about to strike, lay the ruby choker.

Already almost lifeless, cold at heart, I descended the spiral staircase to the music room but there I found I had not been abandoned.

'I can be of some comfort to you,' the boy said. 'Though not much use.'

We pushed the piano stool in front of the open window so that, for as long as I could, I would be able to smell the ancient, reconciling smell of the sea that, in time, will cleanse everything, scour the old bones white, wash away all the stains. The last little chambermaid had trotted along the causeway long ago and now the tide, fated as I, came tumbling in, the crisp wavelets splashing on the old stones.

'You do not deserve this,' he said.

'Who can say what I deserve or no?' I said. 'I've done nothing; but that may be sufficient reason for condemning me.'

'You disobeyed him,' he said. 'That is sufficient reason for him to punish you.'

'I only did what he knew I would.'

'Like Eve,' he said.

The telephone rang a shrill imperative. Let it ring. But my lover lifted me up and set me on my feet; I knew I must answer it. The receiver felt heavy as earth.

'The courtyard. Immediately.'

My lover kissed me, he took my hand. He would come with me if I would lead him. Courage. When I thought of courage, I thought of my mother. Then I saw a muscle in my lover's face quiver.

'Hoofbeats!' he said.

I cast one last, desperate glance from the window and, like a miracle, I saw a horse and rider galloping at a vertiginous speed along the causeway, though the waves crashed, now, high as the horse's fetlocks. A rider her black skirts tucked up around her waist so she could ride hard and fast, a crazy, magnificent horsewoman in widow's weeds.

As the telephone rang again.

'Am I to wait all morning?'

Every moment, my mother drew nearer.

'She will be too late,' Jean-Yves said and yet he could not restrain a note of hope that, though it must be so, yet it might not be so.

The third, intransigent call.

'Shall I come up to heaven to fetch you down, Saint Cecilia? You wicked woman, do you wish me to compound my crimes by desecrating the marriage bed?'

So I must go to the courtyard where my husband waited in his London-tailored trousers and the shirt from Turnbull and Asser, beside the mounting block, with, in his hand, the sword which his great-grandfather had presented to the little corporal, in token of surrender to the Republic, before he shot himself. The heavy sword, unsheathed, grey as that November morning, sharp as childbirth, mortal.

When my husband saw my companion, he observed: 'Let the blind lead the blind, eh? But does even a youth as besotted as you are think she was truly blind to her own desires when she took my ring? Give it me back, whore.'

The fires in the opal had all died down. I gladly slipped it from my finger and, even in that dolorous place, my heart was lighter for the lack of it. My husband took it lovingly and lodged it on the tip of his little finger; it would go no further.

'It will serve me for a dozen more fiancées,' he said. 'To the block, woman. No — leave the boy; I shall deal with him later, utilizing a less exalted instrument than the one with which I do my wife the honour of her immolation, for do not fear that in death you will be divided.'

Slowly, slowly, one foot before the other, I crossed the cobbles. The longer I dawdled over my execution, the more time it gave the avenging angel to descend …

'Don't loiter, girl! Do you think I shall lose appetite for the meal if you are so long about serving it? No; I shall grow hungrier, more ravenous with each moment, more cruel … Run to me, run! I have a place prepared for your exquisite corpse in my display of flesh!'

He raised the sword and cut bright segments from the air with it, but still I lingered although my hopes, so recently raised, now began to flag. If she is not here by now, her horse must have stumbled on the causeway, have plunged into the sea … One thing only made me glad; that my lover would not see me die.

My husband laid my branded forehead on the stone and, as he had done once before, twisted my hair into a rope and drew it away from my neck.

'Such a pretty neck,' he said with what seemed to be a genuine, retrospective tenderness. 'A neck like the stem of a young plant.'

I felt the silken bristle of his beard and the wet touch of his lips as he kissed my nape. And, once again, of my apparel I must retain only my gems; the sharp blade ripped my dress in two and it fell from me. A little green moss, growing in the crevices of the mounting block, would be the last thing I should see in all the world.

The whizz of that heavy sword.

And — a great battering and pounding at the gate, the jangling of the bell, the frenzied neighing of a horse! The unholy silence of the place shattered in an instant. The blade did *not* descend, the necklace did *not* sever, my head did *not* roll. For, for an instant, the beast wavered in his stroke, a sufficient split second of astonished indecision to let me spring upright and dart to the assistance of my lover as he struggled sightlessly with the great bolts that kept her out.

The Marquis stood transfixed, utterly dazed, at a loss. It must have been as if he had been watching his beloved *Tristan* for the twelfth, the thirteenth time and Tristan stirred, then leapt from his bier in the last act, announced in a jaunty aria interposed from Verdi that bygones were bygones, crying over spilt milk did nobody any good and, as for himself, he proposed to live happily ever after. The puppet master, open-mouthed, wide-eyed, impotent at the last, saw his dolls break free of their strings, abandon the rituals he had ordained for them since time began and start to live for themselves; the king, aghast, witnesses the revolt of his pawns.

You never saw such a wild thing as my mother, her hat seized by the winds and blown out to sea so that her hair was her white mane, her black lisle legs exposed to the thigh, her skirts tucked round her waist, one hand on the reins of the rearing horse while the other clasped my father's service revolver and, behind her, the breakers of the savage, indifferent sea, like the witnesses of a furious justice. And my husband stood stock-still, as if she had been Medusa, the sword still raised over his head as in those clockwork tableaux of Bluebeard that you see in glass cases at fairs.

And then it was as though a curious child pushed his centime into the slot and set all in motion. The heavy, bearded figure roared out aloud, braying with fury, and, wielding the honourable sword as if it were a matter of death or glory, charged us, all three.

On her eighteenth birthday, my mother had disposed of a man-eating tiger that had ravaged the villages in the hills north of Hanoi. Now without a moment's hesitation, she raised my father's gun, took aim and put a single, irreproachable bullet through my husband's head.

We lead a quiet life, the three of us. I inherited, of course, enormous wealth but we have given most of it away to various charities. The castle is now a school for the blind, though I pray that the children who live there are not haunted by any sad ghosts looking for, crying for, the husband who will never return to the bloody chamber, the contents of which are buried or burned, the door sealed.

I felt I had a right to retain sufficient funds to start a little music school here, on the outskirts of Paris, and we do well enough. Sometimes we can even afford to go to the Opéra, though never to sit in a box, of course. We know we are the source of many whisperings and much gossip but the three of us know the truth of it and mere chatter can never harm us. I can only bless the — what shall I call it? — the *maternal telepathy* that sent my mother running headlong from the telephone to the station after I had called her, that night. I never heard you cry before, she said, by way of explanation. Not when you were happy. And who ever cried because of gold bath taps?

The night train, the one I had taken; she lay in her berth, sleepless as I had been. When she could not find a taxi at that lonely halt, she borrowed old Dobbin from a bemused farmer, for some internal urgency told her that she must reach me before the incoming tide sealed me away from her for ever. My poor old nurse, left scandalized at home — what? interrupt milord on his honeymoon? — she died soon after. She had taken so much secret pleasure in the fact that her little girl had become a marquise; and now here I was, scarcely a penny the richer, widowed at seventeen in the most dubious circumstances and busily engaged in setting up house with a piano-tuner. Poor thing, she passed away in a sorry state of disillusion! But I do believe my mother loves him as much as I do.

No paint nor powder, no matter how thick or white, can mask that red mark on my forehead; I am glad he cannot see it — not for fear of his revulsion, since I know he sees me clearly with his heart — but, because it spares my shame.

The Glass Graduate
(1613)

MIGUEL DE CERVANTES

Two students were one day passing along the banks of the Tormes, when they found a boy, about eleven years old, dressed as a labourer, and sleeping under a tree. They sent a servant to wake him, and when he had well opened his eyes, they asked him whence he came, and what he was doing, to be lying asleep and defenceless in that lonely place. The boy replied, that he had forgotten the name of his birthplace, but was going to Salamanca, there to seek a master whom he might serve, on condition of being permitted and aided to pursue his studies.

The gentlemen then asked if he could read, and he replied that he could, and write also.

"It is not from want of memory, then, that you have forgotten the name of your country," remarked the students.

"Let the cause be what it may," replied the boy, "neither that nor the name of my parents shall be known to any one until I can do honour to them both."

"But in what manner do you propose to do them honour?" inquired the gentlemen.

"By the results of my studies," said the boy, "and when I have rendered myself famous by the learning I mean to acquire; for I have heard that some men have made themselves bishops by their studies."

This reply moved the two gentlemen to receive the lad into their service, and take him with them to Salamanca, giving him such facilities for studying as it is not unusual for masters to afford in that university to those who serve them.

The youth subsequently informed his masters, that they might call him Thomas Rodaja; whence the students judged him to be the son of some poor labourer. A day or two after their meeting, they caused him to be clothed in a suit of black; and, in the course of a few weeks, he gave proof of extraordinary talent. He was, besides, very grateful, and laboured so earnestly in the service of his masters, that although in fact exceedingly attentive to his studies, it might well have been thought that he did nothing but wait upon those he served.

Now the good service of the valet led the masters to treat him well; Thomas soon became their companion rather than servant, and, during eight years, all of which he passed with them, he acquired for himself so high a reputation in the university, by his great ability and excellent conduct, that he was beloved and esteemed by those of every rank.

The principal object of Rodaja's study was the law, but he was almost equally distinguished in polite learning, and his memory was matter of marvel to all; and the correctness of his views on all subjects was not less remarkable.

The time had now arrived when the studies of his masters were completed, and they returned to their birthplace, which was one of the most important cities of Andalusia. They took Rodaja with them, and he remained in their company for some time; but, assailed by a perpetual longing to return to his studies at Salamanca,—a city that enchains the will of all who have tasted the amenities of life in that fair seat of learning—he entreated permission of his masters to depart for that purpose. With their usual kindness, they accorded him the favour he desired, and took such measures in his behalf that by their bounty he was supplied with a sufficiency to support him in the university for three years.

Rodaja took his leave with manifest proofs of gratitude, and departed from Malaga, for that was the native city of his masters, without further delay. Descending the declivity of the Zambra on the road to Antequera, he chanced to encounter a gentleman on horseback, gaily accoutred in a rich travelling dress, and attended by two servants, also on horseback, whose company he joined; their journey thenceforward lay in the same direction, and the gentleman accepted Thomas as his comrade.[1] They discoursed of various matters, and, in a short time, Rodaja gave such proof of his quality as much delighted his fellow-traveller; while the latter, on his part, soon proved himself to be a kind and courteous man. He told Rodaja that he was a captain of infantry in the service of the king, and that his ensign was then completing their company at Salamanca. He praised the life of a soldier in the highest terms, describing, with much encomium, the many cities and other places visited by those who lead that life. Among other themes of which he spoke were the beauty of Naples, the feasting and pleasures of Palermo, the rich abundance of Milan, and the frequent festivals held in other parts of Lombardy—not omitting the good cheer of the numerous hostelries—in the description of which he broke forth rapturously in the Tuscan language, discoursing of *Macarela, Macarroni,* and *Polastri*, with the most cordial goodwill. He expatiated largely on the free enjoyment of life in Italy, and on the pleasures of the soldier's life in general, which he exalted to the skies; but he did not say a word of the chilling night-watch, the perils of the assault, the terrors of battle, the hunger and privation endured in blockades and sieges, or the ruin caused by mines, with other matters of similar kind whereof he might have spoken, but which he passed over in silence—although there are those who would consider such things as having something to do with the life of the soldier, not to call them its principal features. In a word, he said so much on the subject, that the resolution of our Thomas Rodaja began to waver, and his inclination went near to fix itself on that life, which is so near a neighbour to death.

The captain, whose name was Don Diego de Valdivia, charmed, on his part, with the handsome looks, cheerful manners, and admirable abilities of Rodaja, entreated him to accompany the march into Italy, were it only for the purpose of seeing the country. He offered him his table, and even, if he would adopt the military life, he proposed to procure him a pair of colours; nay, he assured him that those of his own regiment would soon be vacant, and should be at his service.

But little persuasion was required to induce Rodaja's acceptance of a part of this offer. Weighing it in his mind, he considered that it would be well to see Italy and Flanders, to say nothing of other countries, since travel contributes to increase knowledge and discretion. He thought, too, that although he should spend three, or even four years in that occupation, yet these, added to the few he then counted, would not make him so old but that he might afterwards return to his studies. These and other considerations had their weight, and the opportunity being so much to his taste, Rodaja finally told the captain that he would go with him into Italy; but it must be on condition of being left at perfect liberty. He would not consent to enlist under his banner, nor to have his name enrolled in the books of the regiment, that he might not be subjected to the restraints of service. The captain represented that his being inscribed on the lists was a matter which involved no duty, and that he would thereby obtain all the appointments, with the regular pay accorded to his rank; while he, Don Diego, would take care that he should have leave of absence whenever he might demand it. Yet Rodaja was not to be moved from his determination. "For this," said he, "would be to act against the dictates of my conscience and of yours, señor captain; I would, besides, much rather go free than be attached to military service in any manner."

"A conscience so scrupulous is more suitable to the cowl of a monk than the helmet of a soldier," said Don Diego, laughing; "but let it be as you will, so we but remain comrades."

The first night of their journey they had passed at Antequera, and making long stages each day, they speedily arrived at the place where the captain was to join his company. All arrangements being completed, the company began its march with four others to Carthagena, quartering at such places as fell in their way.

And now Rodaja could not fail to remark the authority assumed by the commissaries; the intractable character of many among the captains; the rapacity of the quartermasters, and the unreasonable nature of their demands; the fashion in which the paymasters managed their accounts; the complaints of the people; the traffic in and exchange of billets; the insolence of the undisciplined troops; their quarrels with the other guests at the inns; the requisition of more rations and other stores than were rightful or necessary; and, finally, the almost inevitable consequences of all this. Much besides came under his observation, which he could not but see to be in every way wrong and injurious.

For Rodaja himself, he had now abandoned the garb of a student, and dressed himself parrot-fashion (as we say), conforming to such things as the life around him presented. The many books he had possessed were now reduced to the "Orisons of Our Lady," and a "Garcilaso without Comments," which he carried in two of his pockets.

The party with which he travelled arrived at Carthagena much earlier than he desired, for the varied life he led was very pleasant, and each day brought something new and agreeable. At Carthagena the troops embarked in four galleys for Naples; and in his cabin, also, Kodaja made many observations on the strange life passed in those maritime houses, where, for the most part, a man is devoured by vermin and destroyed by rats, vexed by the sailors, robbed by the galley-slaves, and tormented by the swell of the waters. He endured terrible fear from violent storms and tempests, more especially in the Gulf of Lyons, where they had two, by one of which they were cast on the Island of Corsica, while the other drove them back upon Toulon, in France. At last, weary and half-drowned, they reached land in the darkness of the night, and with great difficulty arrived at the most peaceful and beautiful city of Genoa.

Having disembarked, and hastily visited a church to return thanks for their safety, the captain with all his comrades adjourned to a tavern, where they quickly forgot past storms and tempests in present rejoicing and feasting.

Here they learned to appreciate the respective merits of the different wines presented to them by their active and voluble host; the delicacy of Trebbiano, the fine body of Montefiascone, the purity of Asperino, the generous spirit of the wines from Candia and Soma, and the strength of those from the Cincovinas, or Five Vineyards. Neither did they disregard the sweetness and amenity of the Señora Guarnacha, or the rustic bloom of the

Centola, not forgetting even in this bright array the humble Romanesco, which likewise came in for its meed of praise.

The host having passed in review all these and other wines, of many various qualities, offered besides to place before his guests, without having any recourse to magic, and not as one marks down places on a map, but in all their vivid reality, Madriga, Coca, Alacjos, and the imperial, rather than royal city—that favourite abode of the god of smiles—Ciudad Real. He furthermore offered Esquibias, Alanis, Cazalla, Guadalcanal, and Membrilla, without forgetting the wines of Ribadavia or of Descargamaria. At a word, the host offered and even gave them more wines than Bacchus himself could have stored in all his cellars.

Nor was the good Thomas unmindful of the admiration due to the radiant locks of the Genoese maidens, renowned for those fair tresses, while he likewise appreciated the obliging and cheerful disposition of the male inhabitants, and was never weary of expatiating on the beauty of the city itself, which, as you look at it from the sea, appears to hold the houses enchased amidst the rocks, as diamonds are set in gold.

The day after their arrival, such of the companies as were destined for Piedmont were disembarked; Rodaja, however, had no wish to proceed thither, but determined to go from Genoa by land to Rome and Naples, and return by the way of Our Lady of Loretto to the great and magnificent Venice, and thence to Milan and Piedmont, where it was agreed that he should rejoin Don Diego, if the latter had not previously been compelled to set off for Flanders, as was expected.

Two days after these arrangements were made, Rodaja took leave of the captain, and in five days from that time he reached Florence, having first seen Lucca, a city which is small but very well built, and one where Spaniards are more kindly received and better treated than in any other part of Italy.

With Florence Rodaja was infinitely delighted, as well for the pleasantness of its position as for its sumptuous buildings, its fine river, agreeable streets, and cleanliness of aspect. He remained there but four days, and then departed for Rome, the queen of cities and mistress of the world, whose temples he visited, whose relics he adored, and whose grandeur he admired: and as from the claws of the lion you may judge of its mass and force, so did Rodaja infer the greatness of Rome from the fragments of her marbles—her statues, broken or entire—her arches, fallen or fractured—her baths, crumbled to ruin—her magnificent porticos and vast amphitheatres—her renowned and holy river, which ever fills the banks with water to the brim, while it blesses them with innumerable remains of the martyrs whose bodies have found a burial beneath its waves. Nor did our traveller fail to estimate the beauty of the bridges, which one might fancy to be admiring each other, or the streets, which, by their very names alone, claim authority and pre-eminence over those of all other cities in the world: the Via Flaminia, for example, the Via Julia, the Appia, and others of the same character.

No less was Rodaja satisfied with the division of those hills which exist within the city itself, the Cælian, the Quirinal, the Vatican, and the other four, whose very names bear evidence to the Roman greatness and majesty. He took careful note, moreover, of that authority which attaches to the College of Cardinals, and of the dignity represented in the person of the Supreme Pontiff; nor did he suffer to pass unnoticed that great concourse and variety of men from all nations ever congregated within the walls of the city.

All these things Rodaja admired, reflected on, and arranged in the order of their importance; and having made the station of the Seven Churches, confessed to a Penitentiary, and kissed the feet of his Holiness, he departed, well loaded with *Agnus Deis* and legends, determining thence to proceed to Naples.

But the time was one of important changes and much disorder; this rendered the roads dangerous for all desiring to enter or travel out of Rome; and as he had come to the city by land, so he now resolved to depart by sea, wherefore, proceeding to the port of Ostia, he there embarked, and having reached Naples, added to the satisfaction which he had previously felt at seeing Rome, that of finding himself in a city, in his estimation, and in the opinion of all who have seen it, the finest in Europe, or even in the whole world.

From Naples, Rodaja proceeded to Sicily, where he visited Palermo and Messina; the first of these cities he admired for the advantages of its position and its beauty, and the second for the convenience of its port; while to the whole island he could not but offer the tribute of his praise for that abundance which causes it to be justly denominated the granary of all Italy.

Returning from Sicily to Naples and Rome, Rodaja thence proceeded to Our Lady of Loretto, in whose Holy Temple he could see neither walls nor partitions, since every part was covered with crutches, biers, shrouds, chains, padlocks, fetters, and locks of hair; with arms, hands, legs, or busts in wax, to say nothing of pictures and prints, all giving manifest indication of the mercies and favours innumerable which hundreds of men have received in that place from the hand of God, by the intercession of his Divine Mother, whose sacred Image (there preserved) He has been pleased to exalt and sanction by a vast number of miracles, which have been performed in recompense of the devotion of her votaries; for by them it is that the walls of her house have been adorned in the manner described.[2]

Here Rodaja beheld that very chamber of the Virgin, wherein was delivered the most stupendous embassy ever heard or witnessed by all the heavens, all the angels, and all the archangels, or other inhabitants of the everlasting abodes.

From this place our traveller proceeded to Ancona, where he embarked and repaired to Venice, a city which, had Columbus never appeared in the world, would certainly be still supposed to have no equal; but, by the favour of heaven, and thanks to the great Fernando Cortez who conquered Mexico, the magnificent Venice has now found a city that may be compared to herself. The streets of these two renowned capitals, which are almost wholly of water, make them the admiration and terror of all mankind—that of Europe dominating the old world, and that of America the new. For of the former it would appear that her riches are infinite, her position impregnable, her government most wise, the abundance of her products inexhaustible; in a word, she is herself, as a whole, and in all her parts, entirely worthy of that fame for greatness and majesty which has penetrated to all the regions of the world: the justice of the praise bestowed on Venice is, besides, accredited by her renowned arsenal, wherein are constructed her potent galleys, with other vessels of which the number is not to be told.

To our curious traveller the delights and pastimes found in Venice had almost proved fatal as those of Calypso, since they had nearly caused him to forget his first intentions. Yet when he had passed a month in that enchanting place, he found resolution to continue his journey, passing by Ferrara, Parma, and Placentia, to Milan, that workshop of Vulcan—that grudge and despair of France—that superb city of which more wonders are reported than words can tell, her own grandeur being increased by that of her famous Temple, and by the marvellous abundance of all things necessary to human life that are to be found therein.

From Milan, Rodaja journeyed to Asti, where he arrived in very good time, since the regiment of Don Diego was to depart for Flanders on the following day. He was received very kindly by his friend the captain, with whom he passed into Flanders, and arrived at Antwerp, a city no less worthy of admiration than those which he had seen in Italy. He visited Ghent and Brussels likewise, finding the whole country preparing to take arms, and well disposed to enter on the campaign of the following year.

Rodaja having now seen all that he had desired to behold, resolved to return to his native Spain, and to the city of Salamanca, there to complete his studies. He had no sooner determined than he instantly put his purpose into execution, to the great regret of his friend, who, finding him resolved to depart, entreated him at least to write him word of his safe arrival, and likewise of his future success. This Rodaja promised to do, and then returned to Spain through France, but he did not see Paris, which was at that time in arms. At length he arrived at Salamanca, where he was well received by his friends, and with the facilities which they procured him, he continued his studies until he finally attained to the degree of doctor of laws.

Now it chanced that, about this time, there arrived in Salamanca one of those ladies who belong to all the points of the compass; she was besides well furnished with devices of every colour. To the whistle and bird-call of this fowler there instantly came flocking all the birds of the place; nor was there a *vade mecum*[3] who refrained from paying a visit to that gay decoy. Among the rest our Thomas was informed that the Señora said she had been in Italy and Flanders when he, to ascertain if he were acquainted with the dame, likewise paid her a visit. She, on her part, immediately fell in love with Rodaja, but he rejected her advances, and never approached her house but when led thither by others, and almost by force. Attending much more zealously to his studies than his amusements, he did not in any manner return her affection, even when she had made it known to him by the offer of her hand and all her possessions.

Seeing herself thus scorned, and perceiving that she could not bend the will of Rodaja by ordinary means, the woman determined to seek others, which in her opinion would be more efficacious, and must, as she thought, ensure the desired effect. So, by the advice of a Morisca woman, she took a Toledan quince, and in that fruit she gave him one of those contrivances called charms, thinking that she was thereby forcing him to love her; as if there were, in this world, herbs, enchantments, or words of power, sufficient to enchain the free-will of any creature. These things are called charms, but they are in fact poisons: and those who administer them are actual poisoners, as has been proved by sundry experiences.

In an unhappy moment Rodaja ate the quince, but had scarcely done so when he began to tremble from head to foot as if struck by apoplexy, remaining many hours before he could be brought to himself. At the end of that time he partially recovered, but appeared to have become almost an idiot. He complained, with a stammering tongue and feeble voice, that a quince which he had eaten had poisoned him, and also found means to intimate by whom it had been given, when justice at once began to move in quest of the criminal; but she, perceiving the failure of her attempt, took care to hide herself, and never appeared again.

Six months did Thomas remain confined to his bed; and during that time he not only became reduced to a skeleton, but seemed also to have lost the use of his faculties. Every remedy that could be thought of was tried in his behalf; but although the physicians succeeded in curing the physical malady, they could not remove that of the mind; so that when he was at last pronounced cured, he was still afflicted with the strangest madness that was ever heard of among the many kinds by which humanity has been assailed. The unhappy man imagined that he was entirely made of glass; and, possessed with this idea, when any one approached him he would utter the most terrible outcries, begging and beseeching them not to come near him, or they would assuredly break him to pieces, as he was not like other men but entirely of glass from head to foot.

In the hope of rousing him from this strange hallucination, many persons, without regard to his prayers and cries, threw themselves upon him and embraced him, bidding him observe that he was not broken for all that. But all they gained by this was to see the poor creature sink to the earth, uttering lamentable moans, and instantly fall into a fainting fit, from which he could not be recovered for several hours; nay, when he did recover, it was but to renew his complaints, from which he never desisted but to implore that such a misfortune might not be suffered to happen again.

He exhorted every one to speak to him from a great distance; declaring that on this condition they might ask him what they pleased, and that he could reply with all the more effect, now he was a man of glass and not of flesh and bones, since glass, being a substance of more delicate subtlety, permits the soul to act with more promptitude and efficacy than it can be expected to do in the heavier body formed of mere earth.

Certain persons then desiring to ascertain if what he had said were true, asked him many questions of great difficulty respecting various circumstances; to all these he replied with the utmost acuteness, insomuch that his answers awakened astonishment in the most learned professors of medicine and philosophy whom that university could boast. And well they might be amazed at seeing a man who was subject to so strange an hallucination as that of believing himself to be made of glass, still retain such extraordinary judgment on other points as to be capable of answering difficult questions with the marvellous propriety and truth which distinguished the replies of Rodaja.

The poor man had often entreated that some case might be given to him wherein he might enclose the brittle vase of his body, so that he might not break it in putting on the ordinary clothing. He was consequently furnished with a surplice of ample width, and a cloth wrapper, which he folded around him with much care, confining it to his waist with a girdle of soft cotton, but he would not wear any kind of shoes. The method he adopted to prevent any one from approaching him when they brought him food, was to fix an earthen pot into the cleft of a stick prepared for that purpose, and in this vessel he would receive such fruits as the season presented. He would not eat flesh or fish; nor would he drink anything but the water of the river, which he lapped from his hands.

In passing through the streets, Rodaja was in the habit of walking carefully in the middle of them, lest a tile should fall from the houses upon his head and break it. In the summer he slept in the open air, and in the winter he lodged at one of the inns, where he buried himself in straw to his throat, remarking that this was the most proper and secure bed for men of glass. When it thundered, Rodaja trembled like an aspen leaf, and would rush out into the fields, not returning to the city until the storm had passed.

His friends kept him shut up for some time, but perceiving that his malady increased, they at last complied with his earnest request that they would let him go about freely; and he might be seen walking through the streets of the city, dressed as we have described, to the astonishment and regret of all who knew him.

The boys soon got about him, but he kept them off with his staff, requesting them to speak to him from a distance, lest they should break him, seeing that he, being a man of glass, was exceedingly tender and brittle. But far from listening to his request, the boys, who are the most perverse generation in the world, soon began to throw various missiles and even stones at him, notwithstanding all his prayers and exclamations. They declared that they wished to see if he were in truth of glass, as he affirmed; but the lamentations and outcries of the poor maniac induced the grown persons who were near to reprove and even beat the boys, whom they drove away for the moment, but who did not fail to return at the next opportunity.

One day, that a horde of these tormentors had pursued him with more than their usual pertinacity, and had worn out his patience, he turned to them, saying—"What do you want with me you varlets? more obstinate than flies, more disgusting than *Chinches*,[4] and bolder than the boldest fleas. Am I, perchance, the Monte Testacio[5] of Rome, that you cast upon me so many potsherds and tiles?" But Rodaja was followed by many who kept about him for the purpose of hearing him reply to the questions asked, or reprove the questioner, as the case might be. And after a time, even the boys found it more amusing to listen to his words than to throw tiles at him; when they gave him, for the most part, somewhat less annoyance.

The maniac Rodaja was one day passing through the Ropery at Salamanca, when a woman who was working there accosted him, and said, "By my soul, Señor Doctor, I am sorry for your misfortune, but what shall I do for you, since, try as I may, I cannot weep?" To which Rodaja, fixedly regarding her, gravely replied, "*Filiæ Jerusalem, plorate super vos et super filios vestros.*" The husband of the ropeworker was standing by, and comprehending the reply, he said to Rodaja, "Brother Glasscase, for so they tell me you are to be called, you have more of the rogue than the fool in you!" "You are not called on to give me an obolus," rejoined Rodaja, "for I have not a grain of the fool about me!" One day that he was passing near a house well known as the resort of thieves and other disorderly persons, he saw several of the inhabitants assembled round the door, and called out, "See, here you have baggage belonging to the army of Satan, and it is lodged in the house of hell accordingly."

A man once asked him what advice he should give to a friend whose wife had left him for another, and who was in great sorrow for her loss. "You shall bid him thank God," replied Rodaja, "for the favour he has obtained, in that his enemy is removed from his house."

"Then you would not have him go seek her?" inquired the other.

"Let him not even think of doing so," returned Rodaja, "for if he find her, what will he have gained but the perpetual evidence of his dishonour?"

"And what shall I do to keep peace with my own wife?" inquired the same person.

"Give her all that she can need or rightfully claim," said the maniac, "and let her be mistress of every person and thing thy house contains, but take care that she be not mistress of thyself."

A boy one day said to him, "Señor Glasscase, I have a mind to run away from my father, and leave my home for ever, because he beats me." "I would have thee beware, boy," replied Rodaja; "the stripes given by a father are no dishonour to the son, and may save him from those of the hangman, which are indeed a disgrace."

Intelligence of his peculiar state, with a description of the replies he gave, and the remarks he uttered, was much spread abroad, more especially among those who had known him in different parts, and great sorrow was expressed for the loss of a man who had given so fair a promise of distinction. A person of high rank then at Court wrote to a friend of his at Salamanca, begging that Rodaja might be sent to him at Valladolid, and charging his friend to make all needful arrangements for that purpose. The gentleman consequently accosted Vidriera the next time he met him, and said, "Señor Glasscase, you are to know that a great noble of the Court is anxious to have you go to Valladolid;" whereupon Rodaja replied, "Your worship will excuse me to that nobleman, and say that I am not fit to dwell at Court, nor in the Palace, because I have some sense of shame left, and do not know how to flatter." He was nevertheless persuaded to go, and the mode in which he travelled was as follows: a large pannier of that kind in which glass is transported was prepared, and in this Rodaja was placed, well defended by straw, which was brought up to his neck, the opposite pannier being carefully balanced by means of stones, among which appeared the necks of bottles, since Rodaja desired it to be understood that he was sent as a vessel of glass. In this fashion he journeyed to Valladolid, which city he entered by night, and was not unpacked until he had first been carefully deposited in the house of the noble who had requested his presence.

By this gentleman he was received with much kindness, and the latter said to him, "You are extremely welcome, Doctor Glasscase; I hope you have had a pleasant journey." Rodaja replied, that no journey could be called a bad one if it took you safe to your end, unless indeed it were that which led to the gallows.

Being one day shown the Falconry, wherein were numerous falcons and other birds of similar kind, he remarked that the sport pursued by means of those birds was entirely suitable to great nobles, since the cost was as two thousand to one of the profit.

When it pleased Rodaja to go forth into the city, the nobleman caused him to be attended by a servant, whose office it was to protect him from intrusion, and see that he was not molested by the boys of the place, by whom he was at once remarked; indeed but few days had elapsed before he became known to the whole city, since he never failed to find a reply for all who questioned or consulted him.

Among those of the former class, there once came a student, who inquired if he were a poet, to which Rodaja replied, that up to the moment they had then arrived at, he had neither been so stupid nor so bold as to become a poet. "I do not understand what you mean by so stupid or so bold, Señor Glasscase," rejoined the student; to which Rodaja made answer, "I am not so stupid as to be a bad poet, nor so bold as to think myself capable of being a good one." The student then inquired in what estimation he held poets, to which he answered that he held the poets themselves in but little esteem; but as to their art, that he esteemed greatly. His hearer inquiring further what he meant by that, Rodaja said that among the innumerable poets, by courtesy so called, the number of good ones was so small as scarcely to count at all, and that as the bad were not true poets, he could not admire them: but that he admired and even reverenced greatly the art of poetry, which does in fact comprise every other in itself, since it avails itself of all things, and purifies and beautifies all things, bringing its own marvellous productions to light for the advantage, the delectation, and the wonder of the world, which it fills with its benefits. He added further, "I know thoroughly to what extent, and for what qualities, we ought to estimate the good poet, since I perfectly well remember those verses of Ovid, wherein he says:—

"'Cura ducum fuerunt olim regumque poetæ, Præmiaque antiqui magna tulere chori.
Sanctaque majestas, et erat venerabile nomen Vatibus; et largæ sæpe dabantur opes.'[6]

And still less do I forget the high quality of the poets whom Plato calls the interpreters of the Gods, while Ovid says of them—

"'Est deus in nobis; agitante calescimus illo.'[7]

171

And again—

"'At sacri vates et divum cura vocamur.'[8]

"These things are said of good poets; but, as respects the bad ones—the gabbling pretenders—what can we say, save only that they are the idiocy and the arrogance of the world.

"Who is there that has not seen one of this sort when he is longing to bring forth some sonnet to the ears of his neighbours? How he goes round and round them with—'Will your worships excuse me if I read you a little sonnet, which I made one night on a certain occasion; for it appears to me, although indeed it be worth nothing, to have yet a certain something—a *je ne sais quoi* of pretty, and pleasing.' Then shall he twist his lips, and arch his eyebrows, and make a thousand antics, diving into his pockets meanwhile and bringing out half a hundred scraps of paper, greasy and torn, as if he had made a good million of sonnets; he then recites that which he proffered to the company, reading it in a chanting and affected voice.

"If, perchance, those who hear him, whether because of their knowledge or their ignorance, should fail to commend him, he says, 'Either your worships have not listened to the verses, or I have not been able to read them properly, for indeed and in truth they deserve to be heard;' and he begins, as before, to recite his poem, with new gestures and varied pauses.

"Then to hear these poetasters censure and tear one another to pieces! And what shall I say of the thefts committed by these cubs and whelps of modern pretence on the grave and ancient masters of the art, or of their malevolent carpings at those excellent persons of their own day in whom shines the true light of poetry; who, making a solace and recreation of their arduous labours, prove the divinity of their genius and the elevation of their thoughts to the despite and vexation of these ignorant pretenders, who presume to judge that of which they know nothing, and abhor the beauties which they are not able to comprehend? What will you have me esteem in the nullity which seeks to find place for itself under the canopy spread for others—in the ignorance which is ever leaning for support on another man's chair?"

Rodaja was once asked how it happened that poets are always poor; to which he replied, "That if they were poor, it was because they chose to be so, since it was always in their power to be rich if they would only take advantage of the opportunities in their hands. For see how rich are their ladies," he added; "have they not all a very profusion of wealth in their possession? Is not their hair of gold, their brows of burnished silver, their eyes of the most precious jewels, their lips of coral, their throats of ivory and transparent crystal? Are not their tears liquid pearls, and where they plant the soles of their feet do not jasmine and roses spring up at the moment, however rebellious and sterile the earth may previously have been? Then what is their breath but pure amber, musk, and frankincense? Yet to whom do all these things belong, if not to the poets? They are, therefore, manifest signs and proofs of their great riches."

In this manner he always spoke of bad poets; as to the good ones, he was loud in their praise, and exalted them above the horns of the moon.

Being at San Francisco, he one day saw some very indifferent pictures, by an incapable hand; whereupon he remarked that the good painters imitate nature, while the bad ones have the impertinence to daub her face.

Having planted himself one day in front of a bookseller's shop with great care, to avoid being broken, he began to talk to the owner, and said, "This trade would please me greatly, were it not for one fault that it has." The bookseller inquiring what that might be, Rodaja replied, "It is the tricks you play on the writers when you purchase the copyright of a book, and the sport you make of the author if, perchance, he desire to print at his own cost. For what is your method of proceeding? Instead of the one thousand five hundred copies which you agree to print for him, you print three thousand; and when the author supposes that you are selling his books, you are but disposing of your own."

One of those men who carry sedan-chairs, once standing by while Rodaja was enumerating the faults committed by various trades and occupations, remarked to the latter, "Of us, Señor Doctor, you can find nothing amiss to say." "Nothing," replied Rodaja, "except that you are made acquainted with more sins than are known to the confessor; but with this difference, that the confessor learns them to keep all secret, but you to make them the public talk of the taverns."

A muleteer who heard this, for all kinds of people were continually listening to him, said aloud, "There is little or nothing that you can say of us, Señor Phial, for we are people of great worth, and very useful servants to the commonwealth." To which the man of glass replied, "The honour of the master exalts the honour of the servant. You, therefore, who call those who hire your mules your masters, see whom you serve, and what honour you may borrow from them; for your employers are some of the dirtiest rubbish that this earth endures.

"Once, when I was not a man of glass, I was travelling on a mule which I had hired, and I counted in her master one hundred and twenty-one defects, all capital ones, and all enemies to the human kind. All muleteers have a touch of the ruffian, a spice of the thief, and a dash of the mountebank. If their masters, as they call those they take on their mules, be of the butter-mouthed kind, they play more pranks with them than all the rogues of this city could perform in a year. If they be strangers, the muleteers rob them; if students, they malign them; if monks, they blaspheme them; but if soldiers, they tremble before them. These men, with the sailors, the carters, and the arrieros or pack carriers, lead a sort of life which is truly singular, and belongs to themselves alone.

"The carter passes the greater part of his days in a space not more than a yard and a half long, for there cannot be much more between the yoke of his mules and the mouth of his cart. He is singing for one half of his time, and blaspheming the other; and if he have to drag one of his wheels out of a hole in the mire, he is more aided, as it might seem, by two great oaths than by three strong mules.

"The mariners are a pleasant people, but little like those of the towns, and they can speak no other language than that used in ships. When the weather is fine they are very diligent, but very idle, when it is stormy. During the tempest they order much and obey little. Their ship, which is their mess-room, is also their god, and their pastime is the torment endured by sea-sick passengers.

"As to the mule-carriers, they are a race which has taken out a divorce from all sheets, and has married the pack-saddle. So diligent and careful are these excellent men, that to save themselves from losing a day, they will lose their souls. Their music is the tramp of a hoof; their sauce is hunger; their matins are an exchange of abuse and bad words; their mass is—to hear none at all."

While speaking thus, Rodaja stood at an apothecary's door, and turning to the master of the shop, he said, "Your worship's occupation would be a most salutary one if it were not so great an enemy to your lamps."

"Wherein is my trade an enemy to my lamps?" asked the apothecary.

"In this way," replied Rodaja; "whenever other oils fail you, immediately you take that of the lamp, as being the one which most readily comes to hand. But there is, indeed, another fault in your trade, and one that would suffice to ruin the most accredited physician in the world." Being asked what that was, he replied that an apothecary never ventured to confess, or would admit, that any drug was absent from his stock; and so, if he have not the medicine prescribed, he makes use of some other which, in his opinion, has the same virtues and qualities; but as that is very seldom the case, the medicine, being badly compounded, produces an effect contrary to that expected by the physician.

Rodaja was then asked what he thought of the physicians themselves, and he replied as follows: "*Honora medicum propter necessitatem, etenim creavit cum altissimus: à Deo enim est omnis medela, et a rege accipiet donationem: disciplina medici exaltavit caput illius, et in conspectu magnatum collaudabitur. Altissimus de terra creavit medicinam, et vir prudens non abhorrebit illam.*[9] Thus," he added, "speaketh the Book of Ecclesiasticus, of Medicine, and good Physicians; but of the bad ones we may safely affirm the very contrary, since there are no people more injurious to the commonwealth than they are. The judge may distort or delay the justice which he should render us; the lawyer may support an unjust demand; the merchant may help us to squander our estate, and, in a word, all those with whom we have to deal in common life may do us more or less injury; but to kill us without fear and standing quietly at his ease; unsheathing no other sword than that wrapped in the folds of a recipe, and without being subject to any danger of punishment, that can be done only by the physician; he alone can escape all fear of the discovery of his crimes, because at the moment of committing them he puts them under the earth. When I was a man of flesh, and not of glass, as I now am, I saw many things that might be adduced in support of what I have now said, but the relation of these I refer to some other time."

A certain person asked him what he should do to avoid envying another, and Rodaja bade him go to sleep, for, said he, "While you sleep you will be the equal of him whom you envy."

It happened on a certain occasion that the Criminal Judge passed before the place where Rodaja stood. There was a great crowd of people, and two alguazils attended the magistrate, who was proceeding to his court, when Rodaja inquired his name. Being told, he replied, "Now, I would lay a wager that this judge has vipers in his bosom, pistols in his inkhorn, and flashes of lightning in his hands, to destroy all that shall come within his commission. I once had a friend who inflicted so exorbitant a sentence in respect to a criminal commission which he held, that it exceeded by many carats the amount of guilt incurred by the crime of the delinquents. I inquired of him wherefore he had uttered so cruel a sentence, and committed so manifest an injustice? To which he replied that he intended to grant permission of appeal, and that in this way he left the field open for the Lords of the Council to show their mercy by moderating and reducing that too rigorous punishment to its due proportions. But I told him it would have been still better for him to have given such a sentence as would have rendered their labour unnecessary, by which means he would also have merited and obtained the reputation of being a wise and exact judge."

Among the number of those by whom Rodaja, as I have said, was constantly surrounded, was an acquaintance of his own, who permitted himself to be saluted as the Señor Doctor, although Thomas knew well that he had not taken even the degree of bachelor. To him, therefore, he one day said, "Take care, gossip mine, that you and your title do not meet with the Fathers of the Redemption, for they will certainly take possession of your doctorship as being a creature unrighteously detained captive."

"Let us behave well to each other, Señor Glasscase," said the other, "since you know that I am a man of high and profound learning."

"I know you rather to be a Tantalus in the same," replied Rodaja; "for if learning reach high to you, you are never able to plunge into its depths."

He was one day leaning against the stall of a tailor, who was seated with his hands before him, and to whom he said—

"Without doubt, Señor Maeso,[10] you are in the way to salvation."

"From what symptom do you judge me to be so, Señor Doctor?" inquired the tailor.

"From the fact that, as you have nothing to do, so you have nothing to lie about, and may cease lying, which is a great step."

Of the shoemakers he said, that not one of that trade ever performed his office badly; seeing that if the shoe be too narrow, and pinches the foot, the shoemaker says, "In two hours it will be as wide as an alpargate;" or he declares it right that it should be narrow, since the shoe of a gentleman must needs fit closely; and if it be too wide, he maintains that it still ought to be so, for the ease of the foot, and lest a man should have the gout.

Seeing the waiting-maid of an actress attending her mistress, he said she was much to be pitied who had to serve so many women, to say nothing of the men whom she also had to wait on; and the bystanders requiring to know how the damsel, who had but to serve one, could be said to wait on so many, he replied, "Is she not the waiting-maid of a queen, a nymph, a goddess, a scullery-maid, and a shepherdess? besides that she is also the servant of a page and a lackey? for all these, and many more, are in the person of an actress."

Some one asked Rodaja, who had been the happiest man in the world? To which he answered—"*Nemo*, seeing that *Nemo novit patrem—Nemo sine crimine vivit—Nemo sua sorte contentus—Nemo ascendit in coelum*," &c. &c.

Of the fencing masters he said, that they were professors of an art which was never to be known when it was most wanted, since they pretended to reduce to mathematical demonstrations, which are infallible, the angry thoughts and movements of a man's adversaries.

To such men as dyed their beards, Rodaja always exhibited a particular enmity; and one day observing a Portuguese, whose beard he knew to be dyed, in dispute with a Spaniard, to whom he said, "I swear by the beard that I wear on my face," Rodaja called out to him, "Halt there, friend; you should not say that you *wear* on your face, but that you dye on your face."[11] To another, whose beard had been streaked by an imperfect dye, Doctor Glasscase said, "Your beard is of the true dust-coloured pieball." He related, on another occasion, that a certain damsel, discreetly conforming to the will of her parents, had agreed to marry an old man with a white beard, who, on the evening before his marriage was to take place, thought fit to have his beard dyed, and whereas he had taken it from the sight of his betrothed as white as snow, he presented it at the altar with a colour blacker than that of pitch.

Seeing this, the damsel turned to her parents and requested them to give her the spouse they had promised, saying that she would have him, and no other.

They assured her, that he whom she there saw was the person they had before shewn her, and given her for her spouse: but she refused to believe it, maintaining, that he whom her parents had given her was a grave person, with a white beard: nor was she, by any means, to be persuaded that the dyed man before her was her betrothed, and the marriage was broken off.

Towards Duennas he entertained as great a dislike as towards those who dyed their beards—uttering wonderful things respecting their falsehood and affectation, their tricks and pretences, their simulated scruples and their real wickedness,—reproaching them with their fancied maladies of stomach, and the frequent giddiness with which they were afflicted in the head; nay, even their mode of speaking, was made the subject of his censure; and he declared that there were more turns in their speech than folds in their great togas and wide gowns; finally, he declared them altogether useless, if not much worse.

Being one day much tormented by a hornet which settled on his neck, he nevertheless refused to take it off, lest in seeking to catch the insect he should break himself; but he still complained woefully of the sting. Some one then remarked to him, that it was scarcely to be supposed he would feel it much, since his whole person was of glass. But Rodaja replied, that the hornet in question must needs be a slanderer, seeing that slanderers were of a race whose tongues were capable of penetrating bodies of bronze, to say nothing of glass.

A monk, who was enormously fat, one day passed near where Rodaja was sitting, when one who stood by ironically remarked, that the father was so reduced and consumptive, as scarcely to be capable of walking. Offended by this, Rodaja exclaimed, "Let none forget the words of Holy Scripture, '*Nolite tangere Christos meos*;' and, becoming still more heated, he bade those around him reflect a little," when they would see, that of the many saints canonised, and placed among the number of the blessed by the Church within a few years in those parts, none had been called the Captain Don Such a one, or the Lawyer Don So and So, or the Count Marquis, or Duke of Such a Place; but all were brother Diego, brother Jacinto, or brother Raimundo: all monks and friars, proceeding, that is to say, from the monastic orders." "These," he added, "are the orange-trees of heaven, whose fruits are placed on the table of God." Of evil-speakers Rodaja said, that they were like the feathers of the eagle which gnaw, wear away, and reduce to nothing, whatever feathers of other birds are mingled with them in beds or cushions, how good soever those feathers may be.

Concerning the keepers of gaming-houses he uttered wonders, and many more than can here be repeated—commending highly the patience of a certain gamester, who would remain all night playing and losing; yea, though of choleric disposition by nature, he would never open his mouth to complain, although he was suffering the martyrdom of Barabbas, provided only his adversary did not cut the cards. At a word, Rodaja uttered so many sage remarks, that, had it not been for the cries he sent forth when any one approached near enough to touch him, for his peculiar dress, slight food, strange manner of eating, and sleeping in the air, or buried in straw, as we have related, no one could have supposed but that he was one of the most acute persons in the world.

He remained more than two years in this condition; but, at the end of that time, a monk of the order of St. Jerome, who had extraordinary powers in the cure of lunacy, nay, who even made deaf and dumb people hear and speak in a certain manner; this monk, I say, undertook the care and cure of Rodaja, being moved thereto by the charity of his disposition. Nor was it long before the lunatic was restored to his original state of judgment and understanding. When the cure was effected, the monk presented his patient with his previous dress of a doctor of laws, exhorting him to return to his earlier mode of life, and assuring him that he might now render himself as remarkable for the force of his intellect, as he had before done for his singular folly.

Thomas returned accordingly to his past pursuits; but, instead of calling himself Rodaja, as before, he assumed the name of Rueda. He had scarcely appeared in the street, before he was recognised by the boys; but seeing him in a dress so different from that he had before worn and been known by, they dared not cry after him or ask him questions, but contented themselves with saying, one to another, "Is not this the madman, Doctor Glasscase? It is certainly he; and though he now looks so discreet, he may be just as mad in this handsome dress as he was in that other. Let us ask him some questions, and get rid of our doubts."

All this was heard by Thomas, who maintained silence, but felt much confused, and hurried along more hastily than he had been wont to do before he regained his senses. The men at length made the same remarks as the boys and before he had arrived at the courts he had a train of more than two hundred persons of all classes following him, being more amply attended than the most popular professor of the university.

Having gained the first court, which is that of the entrance, these people ended by surrounding him completely; when, perceiving that he was so crowded on as no longer to have the power of proceeding, he finally raised his voice, and said—

"Señores, it is true that I am Doctor Glasscase, but not he whom you formerly knew. I am now Doctor Rueda. Misfortunes such as not unfrequently happen in this world, by the permission of heaven, had deprived me of my senses, but the mercy of God has restored them; and by those things which you have heard me say when I was mad, you may judge of what I shall say now that I am become sane. I am a doctor in laws of the university of Salamanca, where I studied in much poverty, but raised myself through all the degrees to that I now hold; but my poverty may serve to assure you that I owe my rank to industry and not to favour. I have come to this great sea of the Court, hoping to swim and get forward and gain the bread of my life; but if you do not leave me I shall be more likely to sink and find my death. For the love of God, I entreat that you follow me no further, since, in doing so, you persecute and injure me. What you formerly enquired of me in the streets, I beg you now to come and ask me at my house, when you shall see that the questions to which I before replied, impromptu, shall be more perfectly answered now that I shall take time to consider."

All listened to him, many left him as he desired, and he returned to his abode with a much smaller train. But it was every day the same: his exhortations availed nothing; and Thomas finally resolved to repair to Flanders, there to support himself by the strength of his arm, since he could no longer profit by that of his intellect.

This resolution he executed accordingly, exclaiming as he departed—"Oh, city and court! you by whom the expectations of the bold pretender are fulfilled, while the hopes of the modest labourer are destroyed; you who abundantly sustain the shameless Buffoon, while the worthy sage is left to die of hunger; I bid you farewell." That said, he proceeded to Flanders, where he finished in arms the life which he might have rendered immortal by letters, and died in the company of his friend the Captain Don Diego, leaving behind him the reputation of a most valiant soldier and upright man.

Notes

[1] Don Augustin de Arrieta, a Spanish commentator of our author, informs us that the *camarada* not only journeyed and lived with his companion of the way, but even slept in the same chamber, and not unfrequently in the same bed.

[2] The *ex-votos*, or pictures and figures here described, are too familiar to the visitor of Catholic churches to need any explanation.

[3] Student: they are so called from the name given to the portfolio in which they carry their books and papers to the university, and which they always have with them.

[4] The reader will be pleased to guess the name of that insufferable insect which the Spaniards denominate *Chinche*, and with the English equivalent of which I am unwilling to offend his eyes. Happy, indeed, if he cannot guess; but then he cannot have seen either Seville or Granada, and one might almost encounter an acquaintance with the animal called *Chinche* rather than renounce *them*.

[5] Such of our readers as have visited Rome, will remember that enormous mound which is seen rising on the right hand as you leave the city, by the Porta Salaria, and is said to have been formed by the numberless fragments of pottery cast on the spot from time immemorial.

[6] "Poets once were the care of chieftains and of kings, and choirs of old won great rewards. Sacred was the majesty and venerable the name of the poet; and oft times lavish wealth was given them."

[7] "There is a god within us. It is when he stirs that our bosom warms."

[8] "Yes, we bards are called sacred and the care of the gods."

[9] "Honour the doctor for his services, for the Lord created him. His skill comes from the Most High, and he is rewarded by kings. The doctor's knowledge gives him high standing and wins him the admiration of the great. The Lord has created medicines from the earth, and a sensible man will not disparage them."

[10] Master.

[11] Here Rodaja spoke mockingly, an impure Portuguese, and not Spanish (*olhay, homen, naon, digais, teno, sino tino*). The spirit of the remark (as in some other passages omitted for that reason) consists in a play on words resembling each other in sound, though not in sense, and is necessarily lost in translation.

The Death of Justina
(1960)

JOHN CHEEVER

So help me God it gets more and more preposterous, it corresponds less and less to what I remember and what I expect as if the force of life were centrifugal and threw one further and further away from one's purest memories and ambitions; and I can barely recall the old house where I was raised, where in midwinter Parma violets bloomed in a cold frame near the kitchen door, and down the long corridor, past the seven views of Rome—up two steps and down three—one entered the library where all the books were in order, the lamps were bright, where there was a fire and a dozen bottles of good bourbon locked in a cabinet with a veneer like tortoise shell whose silver key my father wore on his watch chain. Fiction is art and art is the triumph over chaos (no less) and we can accomplish this only by the most vigilant exercise of choice, but in a world that changes more swiftly than we can perceive there is always the danger that our powers of selection will be mistaken and that the vision we serve will come to nothing. We admire decency and we despise death but even the mountains seem to shift in the space of a night and perhaps the exhibitionist at the corner of Chestnut and Elm streets is more significant than the lovely woman with a bar of sunlight in her hair, putting a fresh piece of cuttlebone in the nightingale's cage. Just let me give you one example of chaos and if you disbelieve me look honestly into your own past and see if you can't find a comparable experience. . . .

On Saturday the doctor told me to stop smoking and drinking and I did. I won't go into the commonplace symptoms of withdrawal but I would like to point out that, standing at my window in the evening, watching the brilliant afterlight and the spread of darkness, I felt, through the lack of these humble stimulants, the force of some primitive memory in which the coming of night with its stars and its moon was apocalyptic. I thought suddenly of the neglected graves of my three brothers on the mountainside and that death is a loneliness much crueler than any loneliness hinted at in life. The soul (I thought) does not leave the body but lingers with it through every degrading stage of decomposition and neglect, through heat, through cold, through the long winter nights when no one comes with a wreath or a plant and no one says a prayer. This unpleasant premonition was followed by anxiety. We were going out for dinner and I thought that the oil burner would explode in our absence and burn the house. The cook would get drunk and attack my daughter with a carving knife or my wife and I would be killed in a collision on the main highway, leaving our children bewildered orphans with nothing in life to look forward to but sadness. I was able to observe, along with these foolish and terrifying anxieties, a definite impairment of my discretionary poles. I felt as if I were being lowered by ropes into the atmosphere of my childhood. I told my wife—when she passed through the living room—that I had stopped smoking and drinking but she didn't seem to care and who would reward me for my privations? Who cared about the bitter taste in my mouth and that my head seemed to be leaving my shoulders? It seemed to me that men had honored one another with medals, statuary, and cups for much less and that abstinence is a social matter. When I abstain from sin it is more often a fear of scandal than a private resolve to improve on the purity of my heart, but here was a call for abstinence without the worldly enforcement of society, and death is not the threat that scandal is. When it was time for us to go out I was so lightheaded that I had to ask my wife to drive the car. On Sunday I sneaked seven cigarettes in various hiding places and drank two Martinis in the downstairs coat closet. At breakfast on Monday my English muffin stared up at me from the plate. I mean I *saw* a face there in the rough, toasted surface. The moment of recognition was fleeting, but it was deep, and I wondered who it had been. Was it a friend, an aunt, a sailor, a ski instructor, a bartender, or a conductor on a train? The smile faded off the muffin but it had been there for a second—the sense of a person, a life, a pure force of gentleness and censure—and I am convinced that the muffin had contained the presence of some spirit. As you can see, I was nervous.

On Monday my wife's old cousin, Justina, came to visit her. Justina was a lively guest although she must have been crowding eighty. On Tuesday my wife gave her a lunch party. The last guest left at three and a few minutes later Cousin Justina, sitting on the living-room sofa with a glass of good brandy, breathed her last. My wife called me at the office and I said that I would be right out. I was clearing my desk when my boss, MacPherson, came in.

"Spare me a minute," he asked. "I've been bird dogging all over the place, trying to track you down. Pierce had to leave early and I want you to write the last Elixircol commercial."

"Oh, I can't, Mac," I said. "My wife just called. Cousin Justina is dead."

"You write that commercial," he said. His smile was satanic. "Pierce had to leave early because his grandmother fell off a stepladder."

Now I don't like fictional accounts of office life. It seems to me that if you're going to write fiction you should write about mountain climbing and tempests at sea, and I will go over my predicament with MacPherson briefly, aggravated as it was by his refusal to respect and honor the death of dear old Justina. It was like MacPherson. It was a good example of the way I've been treated. He is, I might say, a tall, splendidly groomed man of about sixty who changes his shirt three times a day, romances his secretary every afternoon between two and two-thirty and makes the habit of continuously chewing gum seem hygienic and elegant. I write his speeches for him and it has not been a happy arrangement for me. If the speeches are successful MacPherson takes all the credit. I can see that his presence, his tailor and his fine voice are all a part of the performance but it makes me angry never to be given credit for what was said. On the other hand if the speeches are unsuccessful—if his presence and his voice can't carry the hour—his threatening and sarcastic manner is surgical and I am obliged to contain myself in the role of a man who can do no good in spite of the piles of congratulatory mail that my eloquence sometimes brings in. I must pretend—I must, like an actor, study and improve on my pretension—to have nothing to do with his triumphs, and I must bow my head gracefully in shame when we have both failed. I am forced to appear grateful for injuries, to lie, to smile falsely and to play out a role as inane and as unrelated to the facts as a minor prince in an operetta, but if I speak the truth it will be my wife and my children who will pay in hardships for my outspokenness. Now he refused to respect or even to admit the solemn fact of a death in our family and if I couldn't rebel it seemed as if I could at least hint at it.

The commercial he wanted me to write was for a tonic called Elixircol and was to be spoken on television by an actress who was neither young nor beautiful but who had an appearance of ready abandon and who was anyhow the mistress of one of the sponsor's uncles. *Are you growing old? I wrote. Are you falling out of love with your image in the looking glass? Does your face in the morning seem rucked and seamed with alcoholic and sexual excesses and does the rest of you appear to be a grayish-pink lump, covered all over with brindle hair? Walking in the autumn woods do you feel that a subtle distance has come between you and the smell of wood smoke? Have you drafted your obituary? Are you easily winded? Do you wear a girdle? Is your sense of smell fading, is your interest in gardening waning, is your fear of heights increasing, and are your sexual drives as ravening and intense as ever and does your wife look more and more to you like a stranger with sunken cheeks who has wandered into your bedroom by mistake? If this or any of this is true you need Elixircol, the true juice of youth. The small economy size (business with the bottle) costs seventy-five dollars and the giant family bottle comes at two hundred and fifty. It's a lot of scratch, God knows, but these are inflationary times and who can put a price on youth? If you don't have the cash borrow it from your neighborhood loan shark or hold up the local bank. The odds are three to one that with a ten-cent water pistol and a slip of paper you can shake ten thousand out of any fainthearted teller. Everybody's doing it. (Music up and out.)* I sent this in to MacPherson via Ralphie, the messenger boy, and took the 4:16 home, traveling through a landscape of utter desolation.

Now my journey is a digression and has no real connection to Justina's death but what followed could only have happened in my country and in my time and since I was an American traveling across an American landscape the trip may be part of the sum. There are some Americans who, although their fathers emigrated from the Old World three centuries ago, never seem to have quite completed the voyage and I am one of these. I stand, figuratively, with one wet foot on Plymouth Rock, looking with some delicacy, not into a formidable and challenging wilderness but onto a half-finished civilization embracing glass towers, oil derricks, suburban continents and abandoned movie houses and wondering why, in this most prosperous, equitable, and accomplished world—where even the cleaning women practice the Chopin preludes in their spare time—everyone should seem to be so disappointed.

At Proxmire Manor I was the only passenger to get off the random, meandering and profitless local that carried its shabby lights off into the dusk like some game-legged watchman or beadle making his appointed rounds. I went around to the front of the station to wait for my wife and to enjoy the traveler's fine sense of crisis. Above me on the hill were my home and the homes of my friends, all lighted and smelling of fragrant wood smoke like the temples in a sacred grove, dedicated to monogamy, feckless childhood, and domestic bliss but so like a dream that I felt the lack of viscera with much more than poignance—the absence of that inner dynamism we respond to in some European landscapes. In short, I was disappointed. It was my country, my beloved country, and there have been mornings when I could have kissed the earth that covers its many provinces and states. There was a hint of bliss; romantic and domestic bliss. I seemed to hear the jinglebells of the sleigh that would carry me to grandmother's house although in fact grandmother spent the last years of her life working as a hostess on an ocean liner and was lost in the tragic sinking of the S.S. *Lorelei* and I was responding to a memory that I had not experienced. But the hill of light rose like an answer to some primitive dream of homecoming. On one of the highest lawns I saw the remains of a snowman who still smoked a pipe and wore a scarf and a cap but whose form was wasting away and whose anthracite eyes stared out at the view with terrifying bitterness. I sensed some disappointing greenness of spirit in the scene although I knew in my bones, no less, how like yesterday it was that my father left the Old World to found a new; and I thought of the forces that had brought stamina to the image: the cruel towns of Calabria with their cruel princes, the badlands northwest of Dublin, ghettos, despots, whorehouses, bread lines, the graves of children, intolerable hunger, corruption, persecution, and despair had generated these faint and mellow lights and wasn't it all a part of the great migration that is the life of man?

My wife's cheeks were wet with tears when I kissed her. She was distressed, of course, and really quite sad. She had been attached to Justina. She drove me home, where Justina was still sitting on the sofa. I would like to spare you the unpleasant details but I will say that both her mouth and her eyes were wide open. I went into the pantry to telephone Dr. Hunter. His line was busy. I poured myself a drink—the first since Sunday—and lighted a cigarette. When I called the doctor again he answered and I told him what had happened. "Well, I'm awfully sorry to hear about it, Moses," he said. "I can't get over until after six and there isn't much that I can do. This sort of thing has come up before and I'll tell you all I know. You see, you live in Zone B—two-acre lots, no commercial enterprises and so forth. A couple of years ago some stranger bought the old Plewett Mansion and it turned out that he was planning to operate it as a funeral home. We didn't have any zoning provision at the time that would protect us and one was rushed through the village council at midnight and they overdid it. It seems that you not only can't have a funeral home in Zone B—you can't bury anything there and you can't die there. Of course it's absurd, but we all make mistakes, don't we? Now there are two things you can do. I've had to deal with this before. You can take the old lady and put her into the car and drive her over to Chestnut Street, where Zone C begins. The boundary is just beyond the traffic light by the high school. As soon as you get her over to Zone C, it's all right. You can just say she died in the car. You can do that or if this seems distasteful you can call the mayor and ask him to make an exception to the zoning laws. But I can't write you out a death certificate until you get her out of that neighborhood and of course no undertaker will touch her until you get a death certificate."

"I don't understand," I said, and I didn't, but then the possibility that there was some truth in what he had just told me broke against me or over me like a wave, exciting mostly indignation. "I've never heard such a lot of damned foolishness in my life," I said. "Do you mean to tell me that I can't die in one neighborhood and that I can't fall in love in another and that I can't eat . . ."

"Listen. Calm down, Moses. I'm not telling you anything but the facts and I have a lot of patients waiting. I don't have the time to listen to you fulminate. If you want to move her, call me as soon as you get her over to the traffic light. Otherwise, I'd advise you to get in touch with the mayor or someone on the village council." He cut the connection. I was outraged but this did not change the fact that Justina was still sitting on the sofa. I poured a fresh drink and lit another cigarette.

Justina seemed to be waiting for me and to be changing from an inert into a demanding figure. I tried to imagine carrying her out to the station wagon but I couldn't complete the task in my imagination and I was sure that I couldn't complete it in fact. I then called the mayor but this position in our village is mostly honorary and as I might have known he was in his New York law office and was not expected home until seven. I could cover her, I thought, that would be a decent thing to do, and I went up the back stairs to the linen closet and got a sheet. It was getting dark when I came back into the living room but this was no merciful twilight. Dusk seemed to be playing directly into her hands and she gained power and stature with the dark. I covered her with a sheet and turned on a lamp at the other end of the room but the rectitude of the place with its old furniture, flowers, paintings, etc., was demolished by her monumental shape. The next thing to worry about was the children, who would be home in a few minutes. Their knowledge of death, excepting their dreams and intuitions of which I know nothing, is zero and the bold figure in the parlor was bound to be traumatic. When I heard them coming up the walk I went out and told them what had happened and sent them up to their rooms. At seven I drove over to the mayor's.

He had not come home but he was expected at any minute and I talked with his wife. She gave me a drink. By this time I was chain-smoking. When the mayor came in we went into a little office or library, where he took up a position behind a desk, putting me in the low chair of a supplicant. "Of course I sympathize with you, Moses," he said, "it's an awful thing to have happened, but the trouble is that we can't give you a zoning exception without a majority vote of the village council and all the members of the council happen to be out of town. Pete's in California and Jack's in Paris and Larry won't be back from Stowe until the end of the week."

I was sarcastic. "Then I suppose Cousin Justina will have to gracefully decompose in my parlor until Jack comes back from Paris."

"Oh no," he said, "oh *no*. Jack won't be back from Paris for another month but I think you might wait until Larry comes from Stowe. Then we'd have a majority, assuming of course that they would agree to your appeal."

"For Christ's sake," I snarled.

"Yes, yes," he said, "it is difficult, but after all you must realize that this is the world you live in and the importance of zoning can't be overestimated. Why, if a single member of the council could give out zoning exceptions, I could give you permission right now to open a saloon in your garage, put up neon lights, hire an orchestra and destroy the neighborhood and all the human and commercial values we've worked so hard to protect."

"I don't want to open a saloon in my garage," I howled. "I don't want to hire an orchestra. I just want to bury Justina."

"I know, Moses, I know," he said. "I understand that. But it's just that it happened in the wrong zone and if I make an exception for you I'll have to make an exception for everyone and this kind of morbidity, when it gets out of hand, can be very depressing. People don't like to live in a neighborhood where this sort of thing goes on all the time."

"Listen to me," I said. "You give me an exception and you give it to me now or I'm going home and dig a hole in my garden and bury Justina myself."

"But you can't do that, Moses. You can't bury anything in Zone B. You can't even bury a cat."

"You're mistaken," I said. "I can and I will. I can't function as a doctor and I can't function as an undertaker, but I can dig a hole in the ground and if you don't give me my exception, that's what I'm going to do."

"Come back, Moses, come back," he said. "Please come back. Look, I'll give you an exception if you'll promise not to tell anyone. It's breaking the law, it's a forgery but I'll do it if you promise to keep it a secret."

I promised to keep it a secret, he gave me the documents and I used his telephone to make the arrangements. Justina was removed a few minutes after I got home but that night I had the strangest dream. I dreamed that I was in a crowded supermarket. It must have been night because the windows were dark. The ceiling was paved with fluorescent light—brilliant, cheerful but, considering our prehistoric memories, a harsh link in the chain of light that binds us to the past. Music was playing and there must have been at least a thousand shoppers pushing their wagons among the long corridors of comestibles and victuals. Now is there—or isn't there—something about the posture we assume when we push a wagon that unsexes us? Can it be done with gallantry? I bring this up because the multitude of shoppers seemed that evening, as they pushed their wagons, penitential and unsexed. There were all kinds, this being my beloved country. There were Italians, Finns, Jews, Negroes, Shropshiremen, Cubans—anyone who had heeded the voice of liberty—and they were dressed with that sumptuary abandon that European caricaturists record with such bitter disgust. Yes, there were grandmothers in shorts, big-butted women in knitted pants and men wearing such an assortment of clothing that it looked as if they had dressed hurriedly in a burning building. But this, as I say, is my own country and in my opinion the caricaturist who vilifies the old lady in shorts vilifies himself. I am a native and I was wearing buckskin jump boots, chino pants cut so tight that my sexual organs were discernible and a rayon-acetate pajama top printed with representations of the *Pinta*, the *Niña* and the *Santa María* in full sail. The scene was strange—the strangeness of a dream where we see familiar objects in an unfamiliar light—but as I looked more closely I saw that there were some irregularities. Nothing was labeled. Nothing was identified or known. The cans and boxes were all bare. The frozenfood bins were full of brown parcels but they were such odd shapes that you couldn't tell if they contained a frozen turkey or a Chinese dinner. All the goods at the vegetable and the bakery counters were concealed in brown bags and even the books for sale had no titles. In spite of the fact that the contents of nothing was known, my companions of the dream—my thousands of bizarrely dressed compatriots—were deliberating gravely over these mysterious containers as if the choices they made were critical. Like any dreamer, I was omniscient, I was with them and I was withdrawn, and stepping above the scene for a minute I noticed the men at the check-out counters. They were brutes. Now sometimes in a crowd, in a bar or a street, you will see a face so full-blown in its obdurate resistance to the appeals of love, reason and decency, so lewd, so brutish and unregenerate, that you turn away. Men like these were stationed at the only way out and as the shoppers approached them they tore their packages open—I still couldn't see what they contained—but in every case the customer, at the sight of what he had chosen, showed all the symptoms of the deepest guilt; that force that brings us to our knees. Once their choice had been opened to their shame they were pushed—in some cases kicked—toward the door and beyond the door I saw dark water and heard a terrible noise of moaning and crying in the air. They waited at the door in groups to be taken away in some conveyance that I couldn't see. As I watched, thousands and thousands pushed their wagons through the market, made their careful and mysterious choices and were reviled and taken away. What could be the meaning of this?

We buried Justina in the rain the next afternoon. The dead are not, God knows, a minority, but in Proxmire Manor their unexalted kingdom is on the outskirts, rather like a dump, where they are transported furtively as knaves and scoundrels and where they lie in an atmosphere of perfect neglect. Justina's life had been exemplary, but by ending it she seemed to have disgraced us all. The priest was a friend and a cheerful sight, but the undertaker and his helpers, hiding behind their limousines, were not; and aren't they at the root of most of our troubles, with their claim that death is a violet-flavored kiss? How can a people who do not mean to understand death hope to understand love, and who will sound the alarm?

I went from the cemetery back to my office. The commercial was on my desk and MacPherson had written across it in grease pencil: *Very funny, you broken-down bore. Do again.* I was tired but unrepentant and didn't seem able to force myself into a practical posture of usefulness and obedience. I did another commercial. *Don't lose your loved ones,* I wrote, *because of excessive radioactivity. Don't be a wallflower at the dance because of strontium 90 in your bones. Don't be a victim of fallout. When the tart on Thirty-sixth Street gives you the big eye does your body stride off in one direction and your imagination in another? Does your mind follow her up the stairs and taste her wares in revolting detail while your flesh goes off to Brooks Brothers or the foreign exchange desk of the Chase Manhattan Bank? Haven't you noticed the size of the ferns, the lushness of the grass, the bitterness of the string beans and the brilliant markings on the new breeds of butterflies? You have been inhaling lethal atomic waste for the last twenty-five years and only Elixircol can save you.* I gave this to Ralphie and waited perhaps ten minutes when it was returned, marked again with grease pencil. *Do,* he wrote, *or you'll be dead.* I felt very tired. I put another piece of paper into the machine and wrote: *The Lord is my shepherd; therefore can I lack nothing. He shall feed me in a green pasture and lead me forth beside the waters of comfort. He shall convert my soul and bring me forth in the paths of righteousness for his Name's sake. Yea, though I walk through the valley of the shadow of death I will fear no evil for thou art with me; thy rod and thy staff comfort me. Thou shalt prepare a table before me in the presence of them that trouble me; thou hast anointed my head with oil and my cup shall be full. Surely thy loving-kindness and mercy shall follow me all the days of my life and I will dwell in the house of the Lord for ever.* I gave this to Ralphie and went home.

The Lady with the Dog
(1899)

ANTON CHEKHOV

I

It was said that a new person had appeared on the sea-front: a lady with a little dog. Dmitri Dmitritch Gurov, who had by then been a fortnight at Yalta, and so was fairly at home there, had begun to take an interest in new arrivals. Sitting in Verney's pavilion, he saw, walking on the sea-front, a fair-haired young lady of medium height, wearing a *béret*; a white Pomeranian dog was running behind her.

And afterwards he met her in the public gardens and in the square several times a day. She was walking alone, always wearing the same *béret*, and always with the same white dog; no one knew who she was, and every one called her simply "the lady with the dog."

"If she is here alone without a husband or friends, it wouldn't be amiss to make her acquaintance," Gurov reflected.

He was under forty, but he had a daughter already twelve years old, and two sons at school. He had been married young, when he was a student in his second year, and by now his wife seemed half as old again as he. She was a tall, erect woman with dark eyebrows, staid and dignified, and, as she said of herself, intellectual. She read a great deal, used phonetic spelling, called her husband, not Dmitri, but Dimitri, and he secretly considered her unintelligent, narrow, inelegant, was afraid of her, and did not like to be at home. He had begun being unfaithful to her long ago—had been unfaithful to her often, and, probably on that account, almost always spoke ill of women, and when they were talked about in his presence, used to call them "the lower race."

It seemed to him that he had been so schooled by bitter experience that he might call them what he liked, and yet he could not get on for two days together without "the lower race." In the society of men he was bored and not himself, with them he was cold and uncommunicative; but when he was in the company of women he felt free, and knew what to say to them and how to behave; and he was at ease with them even when he was silent. In his appearance, in his character, in his whole nature, there was something attractive and elusive which allured women and disposed them in his favour; he knew that, and some force seemed to draw him, too, to them.

Experience often repeated, truly bitter experience, had taught him long ago that with decent people, especially Moscow people—always slow to move and irresolute—every

187

intimacy, which at first so agreeably diversifies life and appears a light and charming adventure, inevitably grows into a regular problem of extreme intricacy, and in the long run the situation becomes unbearable. But at every fresh meeting with an interesting woman this experience seemed to slip out of his memory, and he was eager for life, and everything seemed simple and amusing.

One evening he was dining in the gardens, and the lady in the *béret* came up slowly to take the next table. Her expression, her gait, her dress, and the way she did her hair told him that she was a lady, that she was married, that she was in Yalta for the first time and alone, and that she was dull there. . . . The stories told of the immorality in such places as Yalta are to a great extent untrue; he despised them, and knew that such stories were for the most part made up by persons who would themselves have been glad to sin if they had been able; but when the lady sat down at the next table three paces from him, he remembered these tales of easy conquests, of trips to the mountains, and the tempting thought of a swift, fleeting love affair, a romance with an unknown woman, whose name he did not know, suddenly took possession of him.

He beckoned coaxingly to the Pomeranian, and when the dog came up to him he shook his finger at it. The Pomeranian growled: Gurov shook his finger at it again.

The lady looked at him and at once dropped her eyes.

"He doesn't bite," she said, and blushed.

"May I give him a bone?" he asked; and when she nodded he asked courteously, "Have you been long in Yalta?"

"Five days."

"And I have already dragged out a fortnight here."

There was a brief silence.

"Time goes fast, and yet it is so dull here!" she said, not looking at him.

"That's only the fashion to say it is dull here. A provincial will live in Belyov or Zhidra and not be dull, and when he comes here it's 'Oh, the dulness! Oh, the dust!' One would think he came from Grenada."

She laughed. Then both continued eating in silence, like strangers, but after dinner they walked side by side; and there sprang up between them the light jesting conversation of people who are free and satisfied, to whom it does not matter where they go or what they talk about. They walked and talked of the strange light on the sea: the water was of a soft warm lilac hue, and there was a golden streak from the moon upon it. They talked of how sultry it was after a hot day. Gurov told her that he came from Moscow, that he had taken his degree in Arts, but had a post in a bank; that he had trained as an opera-singer, but had given it up, that he owned two houses in Moscow. . . . And from her he learnt that she had grown up in Petersburg, but had lived in S—— since her marriage two years before, that she was staying another month in Yalta, and that her husband, who needed a holiday too, might perhaps come and fetch her. She was not sure whether her husband had a post in a Crown Department or under the Provincial Council—and was amused by her own ignorance. And Gurov learnt, too, that she was called Anna Sergeyevna.

Afterwards he thought about her in his room at the hotel—thought she would certainly meet him next day; it would be sure to happen. As he got into bed he thought how lately she had been a girl at school, doing lessons like his own daughter; he recalled the diffidence, the angularity, that was still manifest in her laugh and her manner of talking with a stranger. This must have been the first time in her life she had been alone in surroundings in which she was followed, looked at, and spoken to merely from a secret motive which she could hardly fail to guess. He recalled her slender, delicate neck, her lovely grey eyes.

"There's something pathetic about her, anyway," he thought, and fell asleep.

II

A week had passed since they had made acquaintance. It was a holiday. It was sultry indoors, while in the street the wind whirled the dust round and round, and blew people's hats off. It was a thirsty day, and Gurov often went into the pavilion, and pressed Anna Sergeyevna to have syrup and water or an ice. One did not know what to do with oneself.

In the evening when the wind had dropped a little, they went out on the groyne to see the steamer come in. There were a great many people walking about the harbour; they had gathered to welcome some one, bringing bouquets. And two peculiarities of a well-dressed Yalta crowd were very conspicuous: the elderly ladies were dressed like young ones, and there were great numbers of generals.

Owing to the roughness of the sea, the steamer arrived late, after the sun had set, and it was a long time turning about before it reached the groyne. Anna Sergeyevna looked through her lorgnette at the steamer and the passengers as though looking for acquaintances, and when she turned to Gurov her eyes were shining. She talked a great deal and asked disconnected questions, forgetting next moment what she had asked; then she dropped her lorgnette in the crush.

The festive crowd began to disperse; it was too dark to see people's faces. The wind had completely dropped, but Gurov and Anna Sergeyevna still stood as though waiting to see some one else come from the steamer. Anna Sergeyevna was silent now, and sniffed the flowers without looking at Gurov.

"The weather is better this evening," he said. "Where shall we go now? Shall we drive somewhere?"

She made no answer.

Then he looked at her intently, and all at once put his arm round her and kissed her on the lips, and breathed in the moisture and the fragrance of the flowers; and he immediately looked round him, anxiously wondering whether any one had seen them.

"Let us go to your hotel," he said softly. And both walked quickly.

The room was close and smelt of the scent she had bought at the Japanese shop. Gurov looked at her and thought: "What different people one meets in the world!" From the past he preserved memories of careless, good-natured women, who loved cheerfully and were grateful to him for the happiness he gave them, however brief it might be; and of women like his wife who loved without any genuine feeling, with superfluous phrases, affectedly, hysterically, with an expression that suggested that it was not love nor passion, but something more significant; and of two or three others, very beautiful, cold women, on whose faces he had caught a glimpse of a rapacious expression—an obstinate desire to snatch from life more than it could give, and these were capricious, unreflecting, domineering, unintelligent women not in their first youth, and when Gurov grew cold to them their beauty excited his hatred, and the lace on their linen seemed to him like scales.

But in this case there was still the diffidence, the angularity of inexperienced youth, an awkward feeling; and there was a sense of consternation as though some one had suddenly knocked at the door. The attitude of Anna Sergeyevna—"the lady with the dog"—to what had happened was somehow peculiar, very grave, as though it were her fall—so it seemed, and it was strange and inappropriate. Her face dropped and faded, and on both sides of it her long hair hung down mournfully; she mused in a dejected attitude like "the woman who was a sinner" in an old-fashioned picture.

"It's wrong," she said. "You will be the first to despise me now."

There was a water-melon on the table. Gurov cut himself a slice and began eating it without haste. There followed at least half an hour of silence.

Anna Sergeyevna was touching; there was about her the purity of a good, simple woman who had seen little of life. The solitary candle burning on the table threw a faint light on her face, yet it was clear that she was very unhappy.

"How could I despise you?" asked Gurov. "You don't know what you are saying."

"God forgive me," she said, and her eyes filled with tears. "It's awful."

"You seem to feel you need to be forgiven."

"Forgiven? No. I am a bad, low woman; I despise myself and don't attempt to justify myself. It's not my husband but myself I have deceived. And not only just now; I have been deceiving myself for a long time. My husband may be a good, honest man, but he is a flunkey! I don't know what he does there, what his work is, but I know he is a flunkey! I was twenty when I was married to him. I have been tormented by curiosity; I wanted something better. 'There must be a different sort of life,' I said to myself. I wanted to live! To live, to live! . . . I was fired by curiosity . . . you don't understand it, but, I swear to God, I could not control myself; something happened to me: I could not be restrained. I told my husband I was ill, and came here. . . . And here I have been walking about as though I were dazed, like a mad creature; . . . and now I have become a vulgar, contemptible woman whom any one may despise."

Gurov felt bored already, listening to her. He was irritated by the naïve tone, by this remorse, so unexpected and inopportune; but for the tears in her eyes, he might have thought she was jesting or playing a part.

"I don't understand," he said softly. "What is it you want?"

She hid her face on his breast and pressed close to him.

"Believe me, believe me, I beseech you . . ." she said. "I love a pure, honest life, and sin is loathsome to me. I don't know what I am doing. Simple people say: 'The Evil One has beguiled me.' And I may say of myself now that the Evil One has beguiled me."

"Hush, hush! . . ." he muttered.

He looked at her fixed, scared eyes, kissed her, talked softly and affectionately, and by degrees she was comforted, and her gaiety returned; they both began laughing.

Afterwards when they went out there was not a soul on the sea-front. The town with its cypresses had quite a deathlike air, but the sea still broke noisily on the shore; a single barge was rocking on the waves, and a lantern was blinking sleepily on it.

They found a cab and drove to Oreanda.

"I found out your surname in the hall just now: it was written on the board—Von Diderits," said Gurov. "Is your husband a German?"

"No; I believe his grandfather was a German, but he is an Orthodox Russian himself."

At Oreanda they sat on a seat not far from the church, looked down at the sea, and were silent. Yalta was hardly visible through the morning mist; white clouds stood motionless on the mountain-tops. The leaves did not stir on the trees, grasshoppers chirruped, and the monotonous hollow sound of the sea rising up from below, spoke of the peace, of the eternal sleep awaiting us. So it must have sounded when there was no Yalta, no Oreanda here; so it sounds now, and it will sound as indifferently and monotonously when we are all no more. And in this constancy, in this complete indifference to the life and death of each of us, there lies hid, perhaps, a pledge of our eternal salvation, of the unceasing movement of life upon earth, of unceasing progress towards perfection. Sitting beside a young woman who in the dawn seemed so lovely, soothed and spellbound in these magical surroundings—the sea, mountains, clouds, the open sky—Gurov thought how in reality everything is beautiful in this world when one reflects: everything except what we think or do ourselves when we forget our human dignity and the higher aims of our existence.

A man walked up to them—probably a keeper—looked at them and walked away. And this detail seemed mysterious and beautiful, too. They saw a steamer come from Theodosia, with its lights out in the glow of dawn.

"There is dew on the grass," said Anna Sergeyevna, after a silence.

"Yes. It's time to go home."

They went back to the town.

Then they met every day at twelve o'clock on the sea-front, lunched and dined together, went for walks, admired the sea. She complained that she slept badly, that her heart throbbed violently; asked the same questions, troubled now by jealousy and now by the fear that he did not respect her sufficiently. And often in the square or gardens, when there was no one near them, he suddenly drew her to him and kissed her passionately. Complete idleness, these kisses in broad daylight while he looked round in dread of some one's seeing them, the heat, the smell of the sea, and the continual passing to and fro before him of idle, well-dressed, well-fed people, made a new man of him; he told Anna Sergeyevna how beautiful she was, how fascinating. He was impatiently passionate, he would not move a step away from her, while she was often pensive and continually urged him to confess that he did not respect her, did not love her in the least, and thought of her as nothing but a common woman. Rather late almost every evening they drove somewhere out of town, to Oreanda or to the waterfall; and the expedition was always a success, the scenery invariably impressed them as grand and beautiful.

They were expecting her husband to come, but a letter came from him, saying that there was something wrong with his eyes, and he entreated his wife to come home as quickly as possible. Anna Sergeyevna made haste to go.

"It's a good thing I am going away," she said to Gurov. "It's the finger of destiny!"

She went by coach and he went with her. They were driving the whole day. When she had got into a compartment of the express, and when the second bell had rung, she said:

"Let me look at you once more . . . look at you once again. That's right."

She did not shed tears, but was so sad that she seemed ill, and her face was quivering.

"I shall remember you . . . think of you," she said. "God be with you; be happy. Don't remember evil against me. We are parting forever —it must be so, for we ought never to have met. Well, God be with you."

The train moved off rapidly, its lights soon vanished from sight, and a minute later there was no sound of it, as though everything had conspired together to end as quickly as possible that sweet delirium, that madness. Left alone on the platform, and gazing into the dark distance, Gurov listened to the chirrup of the grasshoppers and the hum of the telegraph wires, feeling as though he had only just waked up. And he thought, musing, that there had been another episode or adventure in his life, and it, too, was at an end, and nothing was left of it but a memory. . . . He was moved, sad, and conscious of a slight remorse. This young woman whom he would never meet again had not been happy with him; he was genuinely warm and affectionate with her, but yet in his manner, his tone, and his caresses there had been a shade of light irony, the coarse condescension of a happy man who was, besides, almost twice her age. All the time she had called him kind, exceptional, lofty; obviously he had seemed to her different from what he really was, so he had unintentionally deceived her. . . .

Here at the station was already a scent of autumn; it was a cold evening.

"It's time for me to go north," thought Gurov as he left the platform. "High time!"

III

At home in Moscow everything was in its winter routine; the stoves were heated, and in the morning it was still dark when the children were having breakfast and getting ready for school, and the nurse would light the lamp for a short time. The frosts had begun already. When the first snow has fallen, on the first day of sledge-driving it is pleasant to see the white earth, the white roofs, to draw soft, delicious breath, and the season brings back the days of one's youth. The old limes and birches, white with hoar-frost, have a good-natured expression; they are nearer to one's heart than cypresses and palms, and near them one doesn't want to be thinking of the sea and the mountains.

Gurov was Moscow born; he arrived in Moscow on a fine frosty day, and when he put on his fur coat and warm gloves, and walked along Petrovka, and when on Saturday evening he heard the ringing of the bells, his recent trip and the places he had seen lost all charm for him. Little by little he became absorbed in Moscow life, greedily read three newspapers a day, and declared he did not read the Moscow papers on principle! He already felt a longing to go to restaurants, clubs, dinner-parties, anniversary celebrations, and he felt flattered at entertaining distinguished lawyers and artists, and at playing cards with a professor at the doctors' club. He could already eat a whole plateful of salt fish and cabbage.

In another month, he fancied, the image of Anna Sergeyevna would be shrouded in a mist in his memory, and only from time to time would visit him in his dreams with a touching smile as others did. But more than a month passed, real winter had come, and everything was still clear in his memory as though he had parted with Anna Sergeyevna only the day before. And his memories glowed more and more vividly.

When in the evening stillness he heard from his study the voices of his children, preparing their lessons, or when he listened to a song or the organ at the restaurant, or the storm howled in the chimney, suddenly everything would rise up in his memory: what had happened on the groyne, and the early morning with the mist on the mountains, and the steamer coming from Theodosia, and the kisses. He would pace a long time about his room, remembering it all and smiling; then his memories passed into dreams, and in his fancy the past was mingled with what was to come. Anna Sergeyevna did not visit him in dreams, but followed him about everywhere like a shadow and haunted him. When he shut his eyes he saw her as though she were living before him, and she seemed to him lovelier, younger, tenderer than she was; and he imagined himself finer than he had been in Yalta. In the evenings she peeped out at him from the bookcase, from the fireplace, from the corner—he heard her breathing, the caressing rustle of her dress. In the street he watched the women, looking for some one like her.

He was tormented by an intense desire to confide his memories to some one. But in his home it was impossible to talk of his love, and he had no one outside; he could not talk to his tenants nor to any one at the bank. And what had he to talk of? Had he been in love, then? Had there been anything beautiful, poetical, or edifying or simply interesting in his relations with Anna Sergeyevna? And there was nothing for him but to talk vaguely of love, of woman, and no one guessed what it meant; only his wife twitched her black eyebrows, and said:

"The part of a lady-killer does not suit you at all, Dimitri."

One evening, coming out of the doctors' club with an official with whom he had been playing cards, he could not resist saying:

"If only you knew what a fascinating woman I made the acquaintance of in Yalta!"

The official got into his sledge and was driving away, but turned suddenly and shouted:

"Dmitri Dmitritch!"

"What?"

"You were right this evening: the sturgeon was a bit too strong!"

These words, so ordinary, for some reason moved Gurov to indignation, and struck him as degrading and unclean. What savage manners, what people! What senseless nights, what uninteresting, uneventful days! The rage for card-playing, the gluttony, the drunkenness, the continual talk always about the same thing. Useless pursuits and conversations always about the same things absorb the better part of one's time, the better part of one's strength, and in the end there is left a life grovelling and curtailed, worthless and trivial, and there is no escaping or getting away from it—just as though one were in a madhouse or a prison.

Gurov did not sleep all night, and was filled with indignation. And he had a headache all next day. And the next night he slept badly; he sat up in bed, thinking, or paced up and down his room. He was sick of his children, sick of the bank; he had no desire to go anywhere or to talk of anything.

In the holidays in December he prepared for a journey, and told his wife he was going to Petersburg to do something in the interests of a young friend—and he set off for S——. What for? He did not very well know himself. He wanted to see Anna Sergeyevna and to talk with her—to arrange a meeting, if possible.

He reached S—— in the morning, and took the best room at the hotel, in which the floor was covered with grey army cloth, and on the table was an inkstand, grey with dust and adorned with a figure on horseback, with its hat in its hand and its head broken off. The hotel porter gave him the necessary information; Von Diderits lived in a house of his own in Old Gontcharny Street—it was not far from the hotel: he was rich and lived in good style, and had his own horses; every one in the town knew him. The porter pronounced the name "Dridirits."

Gurov went without haste to Old Gontcharny Street and found the house. Just opposite the house stretched a long grey fence adorned with nails.

"One would run away from a fence like that," thought Gurov, looking from the fence to the windows of the house and back again.

He considered: to-day was a holiday, and the husband would probably be at home. And in any case it would be tactless to go into the house and upset her. If he were to send her a note it might fall into her husband's hands, and then it might ruin everything. The best thing was to trust to chance. And he kept walking up and down the street by the fence, waiting for the chance. He saw a beggar go in at the gate and dogs fly at him; then an hour later he heard a piano, and the sounds were faint and indistinct. Probably it was Anna Sergeyevna playing. The front door suddenly opened, and an old woman came out, followed by the familiar white Pomeranian. Gurov was on the point of calling to the dog, but his heart began beating violently, and in his excitement he could not remember the dog's name.

He walked up and down, and loathed the grey fence more and more, and by now he thought irritably that Anna Sergeyevna had forgotten him, and was perhaps already amusing herself with some one else, and that that was very natural in a young woman who had nothing to look at from morning till night but that confounded fence. He went back to his hotel room and sat for a long while on the sofa, not knowing what to do, then he had dinner and a long nap.

"How stupid and worrying it is!" he thought when he woke and looked at the dark windows: it was already evening. "Here I've had a good sleep for some reason. What shall I do in the night?"

He sat on the bed, which was covered by a cheap grey blanket, such as one sees in hospitals, and he taunted himself in his vexation:

"So much for the lady with the dog . . . so much for the adventure . . . . You're in a nice fix. . . ."

That morning at the station a poster in large letters had caught his eye. "The Geisha" was to be performed for the first time. He thought of this and went to the theatre.

"It's quite possible she may go to the first performance," he thought.

The theatre was full. As in all provincial theatres, there was a fog above the chandelier, the gallery was noisy and restless; in the front row the local dandies were standing up before the beginning of the performance, with their hands behind them; in the Governor's box the Governor's daughter, wearing a boa, was sitting in the front seat, while the Governor himself lurked modestly behind the curtain with only his hands visible; the orchestra was a long time tuning up; the stage curtain swayed. All the time the audience were coming in and taking their seats Gurov looked at them eagerly.

Anna Sergeyevna, too, came in. She sat down in the third row, and when Gurov looked at her his heart contracted, and he understood clearly that for him there was in the whole world no creature so near, so precious, and so important to him; she, this little woman, in no way remarkable, lost in a provincial crowd, with a vulgar lorgnette in her hand, filled his whole life now, was his sorrow and his joy, the one happiness that he now desired for himself, and to the sounds of the inferior orchestra, of the wretched provincial violins, he thought how lovely she was. He thought and dreamed.

A young man with small side-whiskers, tall and stooping, came in with Anna Sergeyevna and sat down beside her; he bent his head at every step and seemed to be continually bowing. Most likely this was the husband whom at Yalta, in a rush of bitter feeling, she had called a flunkey. And there really was in his long figure, his side-whiskers, and the small bald patch on his head, something of the flunkey's obsequiousness; his smile was sugary, and in his buttonhole there was some badge of distinction like the number on a waiter.

During the first interval the husband went away to smoke; she remained alone in her stall. Gurov, who was sitting in the stalls, too, went up to her and said in a trembling voice, with a forced smile:

"Good-evening."

She glanced at him and turned pale, then glanced again with horror, unable to believe her eyes, and tightly gripped the fan and the lorgnette in her hands, evidently struggling with herself not to faint. Both were silent. She was sitting, he was standing, frightened by her confusion and not venturing to sit down beside her. The violins and the flute began tuning up. He felt suddenly frightened; it seemed as though all the people in the boxes were looking at them. She got up and went quickly to the door; he followed her, and both walked senselessly along passages, and up and down stairs, and figures in legal, scholastic, and civil service uniforms, all wearing badges, flitted before their eyes. They caught glimpses of ladies, of fur coats hanging on pegs; the draughts blew on them, bringing a smell of stale tobacco. And Gurov, whose heart was beating violently, thought:

"Oh, heavens! Why are these people here and this orchestra! . . ."

And at that instant he recalled how when he had seen Anna Sergeyevna off at the station he had thought that everything was over and they would never meet again. But how far they were still from the end!

On the narrow, gloomy staircase over which was written "To the Amphitheatre," she stopped.

"How you have frightened me!" she said, breathing hard, still pale and overwhelmed. "Oh, how you have frightened me! I am half dead. Why have you come? Why?"

"But do understand, Anna, do understand . . ." he said hastily in a low voice. "I entreat you to understand. . . ."

She looked at him with dread, with entreaty, with love; she looked at him intently, to keep his features more distinctly in her memory.

"I am so unhappy," she went on, not heeding him. "I have thought of nothing but you all the time; I live only in the thought of you. And I wanted to forget, to forget you; but why, oh, why, have you come?"

On the landing above them two schoolboys were smoking and looking down, but that was nothing to Gurov; he drew Anna Sergeyevna to him, and began kissing her face, her cheeks, and her hands.

"What are you doing, what are you doing!" she cried in horror, pushing him away. "We are mad. Go away to-day; go away at once. . . . I beseech you by all that is sacred, I implore you. . . . There are people coming this way!"

Some one was coming up the stairs.

"You must go away," Anna Sergeyevna went on in a whisper. "Do you hear, Dmitri Dmitritch? I will come and see you in Moscow. I have never been happy; I am miserable now, and I never, never shall be happy, never! Don't make me suffer still more! I swear I'll come to Moscow. But now let us part. My precious, good, dear one, we must part!"

She pressed his hand and began rapidly going downstairs, looking round at him, and from her eyes he could see that she really was unhappy. Gurov stood for a little while, listened, then, when all sound had died away, he found his coat and left the theatre.

IV

And Anna Sergeyevna began coming to see him in Moscow. Once in two or three months she left S——, telling her husband that she was going to consult a doctor about an internal complaint—and her husband believed her, and did not believe her. In Moscow she stayed at the Slaviansky Bazaar hotel, and at once sent a man in a red cap to Gurov. Gurov went to see her, and no one in Moscow knew of it.

Once he was going to see her in this way on a winter morning (the messenger had come the evening before when he was out). With him walked his daughter, whom he wanted to take to school: it was on the way. Snow was falling in big wet flakes.

"It's three degrees above freezing-point, and yet it is snowing," said Gurov to his daughter. "The thaw is only on the surface of the earth; there is quite a different temperature at a greater height in the atmosphere."

"And why are there no thunderstorms in the winter, father?"

He explained that, too. He talked, thinking all the while that he was going to see her, and no living soul knew of it, and probably never would know. He had two lives: one, open, seen and known by all who cared to know, full of relative truth and of relative falsehood, exactly like the lives of his friends and acquaintances; and another life running its course in secret. And through some strange, perhaps accidental, conjunction of circumstances, everything that was essential, of interest and of value to him, everything in which he was sincere and did not deceive himself, everything that made the kernel of his life, was hidden from other people; and all that was false in him, the sheath in which he hid himself to conceal the truth—such, for instance, as his work in the bank, his discussions at the club, his "lower race," his presence with his wife at anniversary festivities—all that was open. And he judged of others by himself, not believing in what he saw, and always believing that every man had his real, most interesting life under the cover of secrecy and under the cover of night. All personal life rested on secrecy, and possibly it was partly on that account that civilised man was so nervously anxious that personal privacy should be respected.

After leaving his daughter at school, Gurov went on to the Slaviansky Bazaar. He took off his fur coat below, went upstairs, and softly knocked at the door. Anna Sergeyevna, wearing his favourite grey dress, exhausted by the journey and the suspense, had been expecting him since the evening before. She was pale; she looked at him, and did not smile, and he had hardly come in when she fell on his breast. Their kiss was slow and prolonged, as though they had not met for two years.

"Well, how are you getting on there?" he asked. "What news?"

"Wait; I'll tell you directly. . . . I can't talk."

She could not speak; she was crying. She turned away from him, and pressed her handkerchief to her eyes.

"Let her have her cry out. I'll sit down and wait," he thought, and he sat down in an arm-chair.

Then he rang and asked for tea to be brought him, and while he drank his tea she remained standing at the window with her back to him. She was crying from emotion, from the miserable consciousness that their life was so hard for them; they could only meet in secret, hiding themselves from people, like thieves! Was not their life shattered?

"Come, do stop!" he said.

It was evident to him that this love of theirs would not soon be over, that he could not see the end of it. Anna Sergeyevna grew more and more attached to him. She adored him, and it was unthinkable to say to her that it was bound to have an end some day; besides, she would not have believed it!

He went up to her and took her by the shoulders to say something affectionate and cheering, and at that moment he saw himself in the looking-glass.

His hair was already beginning to turn grey. And it seemed strange to him that he had grown so much older, so much plainer during the last few years. The shoulders on which his hands rested were warm and quivering. He felt compassion for this life, still so warm and lovely, but probably already not far from beginning to fade and wither like his own. Why did she love him so much? He always seemed to women different from what he was, and they loved in him not himself, but the man created by their imagination, whom they had been eagerly seeking all their lives; and afterwards, when they noticed their mistake, they loved him all the same. And not one of them had been happy with him. Time passed, he had made their acquaintance, got on with them, parted, but he had never once loved; it was anything you like, but not love.

And only now when his head was grey he had fallen properly, really in love—for the first time in his life.

Anna Sergeyevna and he loved each other like people very close and akin, like husband and wife, like tender friends; it seemed to them that fate itself had meant them for one another, and they could not understand why he had a wife and she a husband; and it was as though they were a pair of birds of passage, caught and forced to live in different cages. They forgave each other for what they were ashamed of in their past, they forgave everything in the present, and felt that this love of theirs had changed them both.

In moments of depression in the past he had comforted himself with any arguments that came into his mind, but now he no longer cared for arguments; he felt profound compassion, he wanted to be sincere and tender. . . .

"Don't cry, my darling," he said. "You've had your cry; that's enough. . . . Let us talk now, let us think of some plan."

Then they spent a long while taking counsel together, talked of how to avoid the necessity for secrecy, for deception, for living in different towns and not seeing each other for long at a time. How could they be free from this intolerable bondage?

"How? How?" he asked, clutching his head. "How?"

And it seemed as though in a little while the solution would be found, and then a new and splendid life would begin; and it was clear to both of them that they had still a long, long road before them, and that the most complicated and difficult part of it was only just beginning.

The Sheriff's Children
(1889)

CHARLES CHESNUTT

Branson County, North Carolina, is in a sequestered district of one of the staidest and most conservative States of the Union. Society in Branson County is almost primitive in its simplicity. Most of the white people own the farms they till, and even before the war there were no very wealthy families to force their neighbors, by comparison, into the category of "poor whites."

To Branson County, as to most rural communities in the South, the war is the one historical event that overshadows all others. It is the era from which all local chronicles are dated,—births, deaths, marriages, storms, freshets. No description of the life of any Southern community would be perfect that failed to emphasize the all pervading influence of the great conflict.

Yet the fierce tide of war that had rushed through the cities and along the great highways of the country had comparatively speaking but slightly disturbed the sluggish current of life in this region, remote from railroads and navigable streams. To the north in Virginia, to the west in Tennessee, and all along the seaboard the war had raged; but the thunder of its cannon had not disturbed the echoes of Branson County, where the loudest sounds heard were the crack of some hunter's rifle, the baying of some deep-mouthed hound, or the yodel of some tuneful negro on his way through the pine forest. To the east, Sherman's army had passed on its march to the sea; but no straggling band of "bummers" had penetrated the confines of Branson County. The war, it is true, had robbed the county of the flower of its young manhood; but the burden of taxation, the doubt and uncertainty of the conflict, and the sting of ultimate defeat, had been borne by the people with an apathy that robbed misfortune of half its sharpness.

The nearest approach to town life afforded by Branson County is found in the little village of Troy, the county seat, a hamlet with a population of four or five hundred.

Ten years make little difference in the appearance of these remote Southern towns. If a railroad is built through one of them, it infuses some enterprise; the social corpse is galvanized by the fresh blood of civilization that pulses along the farthest ramifications of our great system of commercial highways. At the period of which I write, no railroad had come to Troy. If a traveler, accustomed to the bustling life of cities, could have ridden through Troy on a summer day, he might easily have fancied himself in a deserted village. Around him he would have seen weather-beaten houses, innocent of paint, the shingled roofs in many instances covered with a rich growth of moss. Here and there he would have met a razor-backed

199

hog lazily rooting his way along the principal thoroughfare; and more than once he would probably have had to disturb the slumbers of some yellow dog, dozing away the hours in the ardent sunshine, and reluctantly yielding up his place in the middle of the dusty road.

On Saturdays the village presented a somewhat livelier appearance, and the shade trees around the court house square and along Front Street served as hitching-posts for a goodly number of horses and mules and stunted oxen, belonging to the farmer-folk who had come in to trade at the two or three local stores.

A murder was a rare event in Branson County. Every well-informed citizen could tell the number of homicides committed in the county for fifty years back, and whether the slayer, in any given instance, had escaped, either by flight or acquittal, or had suffered the penalty of the law. So, when it became known in Troy early one Friday morning in summer, about ten years after the war, that old Captain Walker, who had served in Mexico under Scott, and had left an arm on the field of Gettysburg, had been foully murdered during the night, there was intense excitement in the village. Business was practically suspended, and the citizens gathered in little groups to discuss the murder, and speculate upon the identity of the murderer. It transpired from testimony at the coroner's inquest, held during the morning, that a strange mulatto had been seen going in the direction of Captain Walker's house the night before, and had been met going away from Troy early Friday morning, by a farmer on his way to town. Other circumstances seemed to connect the stranger with the crime. The sheriff organized a posse to search for him, and early in the evening, when most of the citizens of Troy were at supper, the suspected man was brought in and lodged in the county jail.

By the following morning the news of the capture had spread to the farthest limits of the county. A much larger number of people than usual came to town that Saturday,— bearded men in straw hats and blue homespun shirts, and butternut trousers of great amplitude of material and vagueness of outline; women in homespun frocks and slatbonnets, with faces as expressionless as the dreary sandhills which gave them a meagre sustenance.

The murder was almost the sole topic of conversation. A steady stream of curious observers visited the house of mourning, and gazed upon the rugged face of the old veteran, now stiff and cold in death; and more than one eye dropped a tear at the remembrance of the cheery smile, and the joke—sometimes superannuated, generally feeble, but always good-natured—with which the captain had been wont to greet his acquaintances. There was a growing sentiment of anger among these stern men, toward the murderer who had thus cut down their friend, and a strong feeling that ordinary justice was too slight a punishment for such a crime.

Toward noon there was an informal gathering of citizens in Dan Tyson's store.

"I hear it 'lowed that Square Kyahtah's too sick ter hol' co'te this evenin'," said one, "an' that the purlim'nary hearin' 'll haf ter go over 'tel nex' week."

A look of disappointment went round the crowd.

"Hit 's the durndes', meanes' murder ever committed in this caounty," said another, with moody emphasis.

"I s'pose the nigger 'lowed the Cap'n had some green-backs," observed a third speaker.

"The Cap'n," said another, with an air of superior information, "has left two bairls of Confedrit money, which he 'spected 'ud be good some day er nuther."

This statement gave rise to a discussion of the speculative value of Confederate money; but in a little while the conversation returned to the murder.

"Hangin' air too good fer the murderer," said one; "he oughter be burnt, stidier bein' hung."

There was an impressive pause at this point, during which a jug of moonlight whiskey went the round of the crowd.

"Well," said a round-shouldered farmer, who, in spite of his peaceable expression and faded gray eye, was known to have been one of the most daring followers of a rebel guerrilla chieftain, "what air yer gwine ter do about it? Ef you fellers air gwine ter set down an' let a wuthless nigger kill the bes' white man in Branson, an' not say nuthin' ner do nuthin', *I'll* move outen the caounty."

This speech gave tone and direction to the rest of the conversation. Whether the fear of losing the round-shouldered farmer operated to bring about the result or not is immaterial to this narrative; but, at all events, the crowd decided to lynch the negro. They agreed that this was the least that could be done to avenge the death of their murdered friend, and that it was a becoming way in which to honor his memory. They had some vague notions of the majesty of the law and the rights of the citizen, but in the passion of the moment these sunk into oblivion; a white man had been killed by a negro.

"The Cap'n was an ole sodger," said one of his friends solemnly. "He'll sleep better when he knows that a co'te-martial has be'n hilt an' jestice done."

By agreement the lynchers were to meet at Tyson's store at five o'clock in the afternoon, and proceed thence to the jail, which was situated down the Lumberton Dirt Road (as the old turnpike antedating the plank-road was called), about half a mile south of the court-house. When the preliminaries of the lynching had been arranged, and a committee appointed to manage the affair, the crowd dispersed, some to go to their dinners, and some to secure recruits for the lynching party.

It was twenty minutes to five o'clock, when an excited negro, panting and perspiring, rushed up to the back door of Sheriff Campbell's dwelling, which stood at a little distance from the jail and somewhat farther than the latter building from the courthouse. A turbaned colored woman came to the door in response to the negro's knock.

"Hoddy, Sis' Nance."

"Hoddy, Brer Sam."

"Is de shurff in," inquired the negro.

"Yas, Brer Sam, he's eatin' his dinner," was the answer.

"Will yer ax 'im ter step ter de do' a minute, Sis' Nance?"

The woman went into the dining-room, and a moment later the sheriff came to the door. He was a tall, muscular man, of a ruddier complexion than is usual among Southerners. A pair of keen, deep-set gray eyes looked out from under bushy eyebrows, and about his mouth was a masterful expression, which a full beard, once sandy in color, but now profusely sprinkled with gray, could not entirely conceal. The day was hot; the sheriff had discarded his coat and vest, and had his white shirt open at the throat.

"What do you want, Sam?" he inquired of the negro, who stood hat in hand, wiping the moisture from his face with a ragged shirt-sleeve.

"Shurff, dey gwine ter hang de pris'ner w'at's lock' up in de jail. Dey're comin' dis away now. I wuz layin' down on a sack er corn down at de sto', behine a pile er flourbairls, w'en I hearn Doc' Cain en Kunnel Wright talkin' erbout it. I slip' outen de back do', en run here as fas' as I could. I hearn you say down ter de sto' once't dat you would n't let nobody take a pris'ner 'way fum you widout walkin' over yo' dead body, en I thought I'd let you know 'fo' dey come, so yer could pertec' de pris'ner."

The sheriff listened calmly, but his face grew firmer, and a determined gleam lit up his gray eyes. His frame grew more erect, and he unconsciously assumed the attitude of a soldier who momentarily expects to meet the enemy face to face.

"Much obliged, Sam," he answered. "I'll protect the prisoner. Who's coming?"

"I dunno who-all *is* comin'," replied the negro. "Dere's Mistah McSwayne, en Doc' Cain, en Maje' McDonal', en Kunnel Wright, en a heap er yuthers. I wuz so skeered I done furgot mo' d'n half un em. I spec' dey mus' be mos' here by dis time, so I'll git outen de way, fer I don' want nobody fer ter think I wuz mix' up in dis business." The negro glanced nervously down the road toward the town, and made a movement as if to go away.

"Won't you have some dinner first?" asked the sheriff.

The negro looked longingly in at the open door, and sniffed the appetizing odor of boiled pork and collards.

"I ain't got no time fer ter tarry, Shurff," he said, "but Sis' Nance mought gin me sump'n I could kyar in my han' en eat on de way."

A moment later Nancy brought him a huge sandwich of split corn-pone, with a thick slice of fat bacon inserted between the halves, and a couple of baked yams. The negro hastily replaced his ragged hat on his head, dropped the yams in the pocket of his capacious trousers, and, taking the sandwich in his hand, hurried across the road and disappeared in the woods beyond.

The sheriff reentered the house, and put on his coat and hat. He then took down a double-barreled shotgun and loaded it with buckshot. Filling the chambers of a revolver with fresh cartridges, he slipped it into the pocket of the sack-coat which he wore.

A comely young woman in a calico dress watched these proceedings with anxious surprise.

"Where are you going, father?" she asked. She had not heard the conversation with the negro.

"I am goin' over to the jail," responded the sheriff. "There's a mob comin' this way to lynch the nigger we've got locked up. But they won't do it," he added, with emphasis.

"Oh, father! don't go!" pleaded the girl, clinging to his arm; "they'll shoot you if you don't give him up."

"You never mind me, Polly," said her father reassuringly, as he gently unclasped her hands from his arm. "I'll take care of myself and the prisoner, too. There ain't a man in Branson County that would shoot me. Besides, I have faced fire too often to be scared away from my duty. You keep close in the house," he continued, "and if any one disturbs you just use the old horse-pistol in the top bureau drawer. It's a little old-fashioned, but it did good work a few years ago."

The young girl shuddered at this sanguinary allusion, but made no further objection to her father's departure.

The sheriff of Branson was a man far above the average of the community in wealth, education, and social position. His had been one of the few families in the county that before the war had owned large estates and numerous slaves. He had graduated at the State University at Chapel Hill, and had kept up some acquaintance with current literature and advanced thought. He had traveled some in his youth, and was looked up to in the county as an authority on all subjects connected with the outer world. At first an ardent supporter of the Union, he had opposed the secession movement in his native State as long as opposition availed to stem the tide of public opinion. Yielding at last to the force of circumstances, he had entered the Confederate service rather late in the war, and served with distinction through several campaigns, rising in time to the rank of colonel. After the war he had taken the oath of allegiance, and had been chosen by the people as the most available candidate for the office of sheriff, to which he had been elected without opposition. He had filled the office for several terms, and was universally popular with his constituents.

Colonel or Sheriff Campbell, as he was indifferently called, as the military or civil title happened to be most important in the opinion of the person addressing him, had a high sense of the responsibility attaching to his office. He had sworn to do his duty faithfully, and he knew what his duty was, as sheriff, perhaps more clearly than he had apprehended it in other passages of his life. It was, therefore, with no uncertainty in regard to his course that he prepared his weapons and went over to the jail. He had no fears for Polly's safety.

The sheriff had just locked the heavy front door of the jail behind him when a half dozen horsemen, followed by a crowd of men on foot, came round a bend in the road and drew near the jail. They halted in front of the picket fence that surrounded the building, while several of the committee of arrangements rode on a few rods farther to the sheriff's house. One of them dismounted and rapped on the door with his riding-whip.

"Is the sheriff at home?" he inquired.

"No, he has just gone out," replied Polly, who had come to the door.

"We want the jail keys," he continued.

"They are not here," said Polly. "The sheriff has them himself." Then she added, with assumed indifference, "He is at the jail now."

The man turned away, and Polly went into the front room, from which she peered anxiously between the slats of the green blinds of a window that looked toward the jail. Meanwhile the messenger returned to his companions and announced his discovery. It looked as though the sheriff had learned of their design and was preparing to resist it.

One of them stepped forward and rapped on the jail door.

"Well, what is it?" said the sheriff, from within.

"We want to talk to you, Sheriff," replied the spokesman.

There was a little wicket in the door; this the sheriff opened, and answered through it.

"All right, boys, talk away. You are all strangers to me, and I don't know what business you can have." The sheriff did not think it necessary to recognize anybody in particular on such an occasion; the question of identity sometimes comes up in the investigation of these extra-judicial executions.

"We're a committee of citizens and we want to get into the jail."

"What for? It ain't much trouble to get into jail. Most people want to keep out."

The mob was in no humor to appreciate a joke, and the sheriff's witticism fell dead upon an unresponsive audience.

"We want to have a talk with the nigger that killed Cap'n Walker."

"You can talk to that nigger in the court-house, when he's brought out for trial. Court will be in session here next week. I know what you fellows want, but you can't get my prisoner to-day. Do you want to take the bread out of a poor man's mouth? I get seventy-five cents a day for keeping this prisoner, and he's the only one in jail. I can't have my family suffer just to please you fellows."

One or two young men in the crowd laughed at the idea of Sheriff Campbell's suffering for want of seventy-five cents a day; but they were frowned into silence by those who stood near them.

"Ef yer don't let us in," cried a voice, "we'll bu's' the do' open."

"Bust away," answered the sheriff, raising his voice so that all could hear. "But I give you fair warning. The first man that tries it will be filled with buckshot. I'm sheriff of this county; I know my duty, and I mean to do it."

"What's the use of kicking, Sheriff," argued one of the leaders of the mob. "The nigger is sure to hang anyhow; he richly deserves it; and we've got to do something to teach the niggers their places, or white people won't be able to live in the county."

"There's no use talking, boys," responded the sheriff. "I'm a white man outside, but in this jail I'm sheriff; and if this nigger's to be hung in this county, I propose to do the hanging. So you fellows might as well right-about-face, and march back to Troy. You've had a pleasant trip, and the exercise will be good for you. You know *me*. I've got powder and ball, and I've faced fire before now, with nothing between me and the enemy, and I don't mean to surrender this jail while I'm able to shoot." Having thus announced his determination, the sheriff closed and fastened the wicket, and looked around for the best position from which to defend the building.

The crowd drew off a little, and the leaders conversed together in low tones.

The Branson County jail was a small, two-story brick building, strongly constructed, with no attempt at architectural ornamentation. Each story was divided into two large cells by a passage running from front to rear. A grated iron door gave entrance from the passage to each of the four cells. The jail seldom had many prisoners in it, and the lower windows had been boarded up. When the sheriff had closed the wicket, he ascended the steep wooden stairs to the upper floor. There was no window at the front of the upper passage, and the most available position from which to watch the movements of the crowd below was the front window of the cell occupied by the solitary prisoner.

The sheriff unlocked the door and entered the cell. The prisoner was crouched in a corner, his yellow face, blanched with terror, looking ghastly in the semi-darkness of the room. A cold perspiration had gathered on his forehead, and his teeth were chattering with affright.

"For God's sake, Sheriff," he murmured hoarsely, "don't let 'em lynch me; I did n't kill the old man."

The sheriff glanced at the cowering wretch with a look of mingled contempt and loathing.

"Get up," he said sharply. "You will probably be hung sooner or later, but it shall not be to-day, if I can help it. I'll unlock your fetters, and if I can't hold the jail, you'll have to make the best fight you can. If I'm shot, I'll consider my responsibility at an end."

There were iron fetters on the prisoner's ankles, and handcuffs on his wrists. These the sheriff unlocked, and they fell clanking to the floor.

"Keep back from the window," said the sheriff. "They might shoot if they saw you."

The sheriff drew toward the window a pine bench which formed a part of the scanty furniture of the cell, and laid his revolver upon it. Then he took his gun in hand, and took his stand at the side of the window where he could with least exposure of himself watch the movements of the crowd below.

The lynchers had not anticipated any determined resistance. Of course they had looked for a formal protest, and perhaps a sufficient show of opposition to excuse the sheriff in the eye of any stickler for legal formalities. They had not however come prepared to fight a battle, and no one of them seemed willing to lead an attack upon the jail. The leaders of the party conferred together with a good deal of animated gesticulation, which was visible to the sheriff from his outlook, though the distance was too great for him to hear what was said. At length one of them broke away from the group, and rode back to the main body of the lynchers, who were restlessly awaiting orders.

"Well, boys," said the messenger, "we'll have to let it go for the present. The sheriff says he'll shoot, and he's got the drop on us this time. There ain't any of us that want to follow Cap'n Walker jest yet. Besides, the sheriff is a good fellow, and we don't want to hurt 'im. But," he added, as if to reassure the crowd, which began to show signs of disappointment, "the nigger might as well say his prayers, for he ain't got long to live."

There was a murmur of dissent from the mob, and several voices insisted that an attack be made on the jail. But pacific counsels finally prevailed, and the mob sullenly withdrew.

The sheriff stood at the window until they had disappeared around the bend in the road. He did not relax his watchfulness when the last one was out of sight. Their withdrawal might be a mere feint, to be followed by a further attempt. So closely, indeed, was his attention drawn to the outside, that he neither saw nor heard the prisoner creep stealthily across the floor, reach out his hand and secure the revolver which lay on the bench behind the sheriff, and creep as noiselessly back to his place in the corner of the room.

A moment after the last of the lynching party had disappeared there was a shot fired from the woods across the road; a bullet whistled by the window and buried itself in the wooden casing a few inches from where the sheriff was standing. Quick as thought, with the instinct born of a semi-guerrilla army experience, he raised his gun and fired twice at the point from which a faint puff of smoke showed the hostile bullet to have been sent. He stood a moment watching, and then rested his gun against the window, and reached behind him mechanically for the other weapon. It was not on the bench. As the sheriff realized this fact, he turned his head and looked into the muzzle of the revolver.

"Stay where you are, Sheriff," said the prisoner, his eyes glistening, his face almost ruddy with excitement.

The sheriff mentally cursed his own carelessness for allowing him to be caught in such a predicament. He had not expected anything of the kind. He had relied on the negro's cowardice and subordination in the presence of an armed white man as a matter of course. The sheriff was a brave man, but realized that the prisoner had him at an immense disadvantage. The two men stood thus for a moment, fighting a harmless duel with their eyes.

"Well, what do you mean to do?" asked the sheriff with apparent calmness.

"To get away, of course," said the prisoner, in a tone which caused the sheriff to look at him more closely, and with an involuntary feeling of apprehension; if the man was not mad, he was in a state of mind akin to madness, and quite as dangerous. The sheriff felt that he must speak the prisoner fair, and watch for a chance to turn the tables on him. The keen-eyed, desperate man before him was a different being altogether from the groveling wretch who had begged so piteously for life a few minutes before.

At length the sheriff spoke:——

"Is this your gratitude to me for saving your life at the risk of my own? If I had not done so, you would now be swinging from the limb of some neighboring tree."

"True," said the prisoner, "you saved my life, but for how long? When you came in, you said court would sit next week. When the crowd went away they said I had not long to live. It is merely a choice of two ropes."

"While there's life there's hope," replied the sheriff. He uttered this commonplace mechanically, while his brain was busy in trying to think out some way of escape. "If you are innocent you can prove it."

The mulatto kept his eye upon the sheriff. "I did n't kill the old man," he replied; "but I shall never be able to clear myself. I was at his house at nine o'clock. I stole from it the coat that was on my back when I was taken. I would be convicted, even with a fair trial, unless the real murderer were discovered beforehand."

The sheriff knew this only too well. While he was thinking what argument next to use, the prisoner continued:——

"Throw me the keys—no, unlock the door."

The sheriff stood a moment irresolute. The mulatto's eye glittered ominously. The sheriff crossed the room and unlocked the door leading into the passage.

"Now go down and unlock the outside door."

The heart of the sheriff leaped within him. Perhaps he might make a dash for liberty, and gain the outside. He descended the narrow stairs, the prisoner keeping close behind him.

The sheriff inserted the huge iron key into the lock. The rusty bolt yielded slowly. It still remained for him to pull the door open.

"Stop!" thundered the mulatto, who seemed to divine the sheriff's purpose. "Move a muscle, and I'll blow your brains out."

The sheriff obeyed; he realized that his chance had not yet come.

"Now keep on that side of the passage, and go back upstairs."

Keeping the sheriff under cover of the revolver, the mulatto followed him up the stairs. The sheriff expected the prisoner to lock him into the cell and make his own escape. He had about come to the conclusion that the best thing he could do under the circumstances was to submit quietly, and take his chances of recapturing the prisoner after the alarm had been given. The sheriff had faced death more than once upon the battlefield. A few minutes before, well armed, and with a brick wall between him and them he had dared a hundred men to fight; but he felt instinctively that the desperate man confronting him was not to be trifled with, and he was too prudent a man to risk his life against such heavy odds. He had Polly to look after, and there was a limit beyond which devotion to duty would be quixotic and even foolish.

"I want to get away," said the prisoner, "and I don't want to be captured; for if I am I know I will be hung on the spot. I am afraid," he added somewhat reflectively, "that in order to save myself I shall have to kill you."

"Good God!" exclaimed the sheriff in involuntary terror; "you would not kill the man to whom you owe your own life."

"You speak more truly than you know," replied the mulatto. "I indeed owe my life to you."

The sheriff started, he was capable of surprise, even in that moment of extreme peril. "Who are you?" he asked in amazement.

"Tom, Cicely's son," returned the other. He had closed the door and stood talking to the sheriff through the grated opening. "Don't you remember Cicely—Cicely whom you sold, with her child, to the speculator on his way to Alabama?"

The sheriff did remember. He had been sorry for it many a time since. It had been the old story of debts, mortgages, and bad crops. He had quarreled with the mother. The price offered for her and her child had been unusually large, and he had yielded to the combination of anger and pecuniary stress.

"Good God!" he gasped, "you would not murder your own father?"

"My father?" replied the mulatto. "It were well enough for me to claim the relationship, but it comes with poor grace from you to ask anything by reason of it. What father's duty have you ever performed for me? Did you give me your name, or even your protection? Other white men gave their colored sons freedom and money, and sent them to the free States. *You* sold *me* to the rice swamps."

"I at least gave you the life you cling to," murmured the sheriff.

"Life?" said the prisoner, with a sarcastic laugh. "What kind of a life? You gave me your own blood, your own features,—no man need look at us together twice to see that,—and you gave me a black mother. Poor wretch! She died under the lash, because she had enough womanhood to call her soul her own. You gave me a white man's spirit, and you made me a slave, and crushed it out."

"But you are free now," said the sheriff. He had not doubted, could not doubt, the mulatto's word. He knew whose passions coursed beneath that swarthy skin and burned in the black eyes opposite his own. He saw in this mulatto what he himself might have become had not the safeguards of parental restraint and public opinion been thrown around him.

"Free to do what?" replied the mulatto. "Free in name, but despised and scorned and set aside by the people to whose race I belong far more than to my mother's."

"There are schools," said the sheriff. "You have been to school." He had noticed that the mulatto spoke more eloquently and used better language than most Branson County people.

"I have been to school, and dreamed when I went that it would work some marvelous change in my condition. But what did I learn? I learned to feel that no degree of learning or wisdom will change the color of my skin and that I shall always wear what in my own country is a badge of degradation. When I think about it seriously I do not care particularly for such a life. It is the animal in me, not the man, that flees the gallows. I owe you nothing," he went on, "and expect nothing of you; and it would be no more than justice if I should avenge upon you my mother's wrongs and my own. But still I hate to shoot you; I have never yet taken human life—for I did *not* kill the old captain. Will you promise to give no alarm and make no attempt to capture me until morning, if I do not shoot?"

So absorbed were the two men in their colloquy and their own tumultuous thoughts that neither of them had heard the door below move upon its hinges. Neither of them had heard a light step come stealthily up the stairs, nor seen a slender form creep along the darkening passage toward the mulatto.

The sheriff hesitated. The struggle between his love of life and his sense of duty was a terrific one. It may seem strange that a man who could sell his own child into slavery should hesitate at such a moment, when his life was trembling in the balance. But the baleful influence of human slavery poisoned the very fountains of life, and created new standards of right. The sheriff was conscientious; his conscience had merely been warped by his environment. Let no one ask what his answer would have been; he was spared the necessity of a decision.

"Stop," said the mulatto, "you need not promise. I could not trust you if you did. It is your life for mine; there is but one safe way for me; you must die."

He raised his arm to fire, when there was a flash—a report from the passage behind him. His arm fell heavily at his side, and the pistol dropped at his feet.

The sheriff recovered first from his surprise, and throwing open the door secured the fallen weapon. Then seizing the prisoner he thrust him into the cell and locked the door upon him;

after which he turned to Polly, who leaned half-fainting against the wall, her hands clasped over her heart.

"Oh, father, I was just in time!" she cried hysterically, and, wildly sobbing, threw herself into her father's arms.

"I watched until they all went away," she said. "I heard the shot from the woods and I saw you shoot. Then when you did not come out I feared something had happened, that perhaps you had been wounded. I got out the other pistol and ran over here. When I found the door open, I knew something was wrong, and when I heard voices I crept upstairs, and reached the top just in time to hear him say he would kill you. Oh, it was a narrow escape!"

When she had grown somewhat calmer, the sheriff left her standing there and went back into the cell. The prisoner's arm was bleeding from a flesh wound. His bravado had given place to a stony apathy. There was no sign in his face of fear or disappointment or feeling of any kind. The sheriff sent Polly to the house for cloth, and bound up the prisoner's wound with a rude skill acquired during his army life.

"I'll have a doctor come and dress the wound in the morning," he said to the prisoner. "It will do very well until then, if you will keep quiet. If the doctor asks you how the wound was caused, you can say that you were struck by the bullet fired from the woods. It would do you no good to have it known that you were shot while attempting to escape."

The prisoner uttered no word of thanks or apology, but sat in sullen silence. When the wounded arm had been bandaged, Polly and her father returned to the house.

The sheriff was in an unusually thoughtful mood that evening. He put salt in his coffee at supper, and poured vinegar over his pancakes. To many of Polly's questions he returned random answers. When he had gone to bed he lay awake for several hours.

In the silent watches of the night, when he was alone with God, there came into his mind a flood of unaccustomed thoughts. An hour or two before, standing face to face with death, he had experienced a sensation similar to that which drowning men are said to feel—a kind of clarifying of the moral faculty, in which the veil of the flesh, with its obscuring passions and prejudices, is pushed aside for a moment, and all the acts of one's life stand out, in the clear light of truth, in their correct proportions and relations,—a state of mind in which one sees himself as God may be supposed to see him. In the reaction following his rescue, this feeling had given place for a time to far different emotions. But now, in the silence of midnight, something of this clearness of spirit returned to the sheriff. He saw that he had owed some duty to this son of his,—that neither law nor custom could destroy a responsibility inherent in the nature of mankind. He could not thus, in the eyes of God at least, shake off the consequences of his sin. Had he never sinned, this wayward spirit would never have come back from the vanished past to haunt him. As these thoughts came, his anger against the mulatto died away, and in its place there sprang up a great pity. The hand of parental authority might have restrained the passions he had seen burning in the prisoner's eyes when the desperate man spoke the words which had seemed to doom his father to death. The sheriff felt that he might have saved this fiery spirit from the slough of slavery; that he might have sent him to the free North, and given him there, or in some other land, an opportunity to turn to usefulness and honorable pursuits the talents that had run to crime, perhaps to madness; he might, still less, have given this son of his the poor simulacrum of liberty which men of his caste could possess in a slave-holding community; or least of all, but still something, he might have kept the boy on the plantation, where the burdens of slavery would have fallen lightly upon him.

The sheriff recalled his own youth. He had inherited an honored name to keep untarnished; he had had a future to make; the picture of a fair young bride had beckoned him on to happiness. The poor wretch now stretched upon a pallet of straw between the brick walls of the jail had had none of these things,—no name, no father, no mother—in the true meaning of motherhood,—and until the past few years no possible future, and then one vague and shadowy in its outline, and dependent for form and substance upon the slow solution of a problem in which there were many unknown quantities.

From what he might have done to what he might yet do was an easy transition for the awakened conscience of the sheriff. It occurred to him, purely as a hypothesis, that he might permit his prisoner to escape; but his oath of office, his duty as sheriff, stood in the way of such a course, and the sheriff dismissed the idea from his mind. He could, however, investigate the circumstances of the murder, and move Heaven and earth to discover the real criminal, for he no longer doubted the prisoner's innocence; he could employ counsel for the accused, and perhaps influence public opinion in his favor. An acquittal once secured, some plan could be devised by which the sheriff might in some degree atone for his crime against this son of his—against society—against God.

When the sheriff had reached this conclusion he fell into an unquiet slumber, from which he awoke late the next morning.

He went over to the jail before breakfast and found the prisoner lying on his pallet, his face turned to the wall; he did not move when the sheriff rattled the door.

"Good-morning," said the latter, in a tone intended to waken the prisoner.

There was no response. The sheriff looked more keenly at the recumbent figure; there was an unnatural rigidity about its attitude.

He hastily unlocked the door and, entering the cell, bent over the prostrate form. There was no sound of breathing; he turned the body over—it was cold and stiff. The prisoner had torn the bandage from his wound and bled to death during the night. He had evidently been dead several hours.

The Storm
A Sequel to "The 'Cadian Ball"
(1969)

KATE CHOPIN

I

The leaves were so still that even Bibi thought it was going to rain. Bobinôt, who was accustomed to converse on terms of perfect equality with his little son, called the child's attention to certain sombre clouds that were rolling with sinister intention from the west, accompanied by a sullen, threatening roar. They were at Friedheimer's store and decided to remain there till the storm had passed. They sat within the door on two empty kegs. Bibi was four years old and looked very wise.

"Mama'll be 'fraid, yes," he suggested with blinking eyes.

"She'll shut the house. Maybe she got Sylvie helpin' her this evenin'," Bobinôt responded reassuringly.

"No; she ent got Sylvie. Sylvie was helpin' her yistiday," piped Bibi.

Bobinôt arose and going across to the counter purchased a can of shrimps, of which Calixta was very fond. Then he returned to his perch on the keg and sat stolidly holding the can of shrimps while the storm burst. It shook the wooden store and seemed to be ripping great furrows in the distant field. Bibi laid his little hand on his father's knee and was not afraid.

II

Calixta, at home, felt no uneasiness for their safety. She sat at a side window sewing furiously on a sewing machine. She was greatly occupied and did not notice the approaching storm. But she felt very warm and often stopped to mop her face on which the perspiration gathered in beads. She unfastened her white sacque at the throat. It began to grow dark, and suddenly realizing the situation she got up hurriedly and went about closing windows and doors.

Out on the small front gallery she had hung Bobinôt's Sunday clothes to air and she hastened out to gather them before the rain fell. As she stepped outside, Alcée Laballière rode in at the gate. She had not seen him very often since her marriage, and never alone. She stood there with Bobinôt's coat in her hands, and the big rain drops began to fall. Alcée rode his

211

horse under the shelter of a side projection where the chickens had huddled and there were plows and a harrow piled up in the corner.

"May I come and wait on your gallery till the storm is over, Calixta?" he asked.

"Come 'long in, M'sieur Alcée."

His voice and her own startled her as if from a trance, and she seized Bobinôt's vest. Alcée, mounting to the porch, grabbed the trousers and snatched Bibi's braided jacket that was about to be carried away by a sudden gust of wind. He expressed an intention to remain outside, but it was soon apparent that he might as well have been out in the open: the water beat in upon the boards in driving sheets, and he went inside, closing the door after him. It was even necessary to put something beneath the door to keep the water out.

"My! what a rain! It's good two years sence it rain' like that," exclaimed Calixta as she rolled up a piece of bagging and Alcée helped her to thrust it beneath the crack.

She was a little fuller of figure than five years before when she married; but she had lost nothing of her vivacity. Her blue eyes still retained their melting quality; and her yellow hair, dishevelled by the wind and rain, kinked more stubbornly than ever about her ears and temples.

The rain beat upon the low, shingled roof with a force and clatter that threatened to break an entrance and deluge them there. They were in the dining room—the sitting room—the general utility room. Adjoining was her bed room, with Bibi's couch along side her own. The door stood open, and the room with its white, monumental bed, its closed shutters, looked dim and mysterious.

Alcée flung himself into a rocker and Calixta nervously began to gather up from the floor the lengths of a cotton sheet which she had been sewing.

"If this keeps up, *Dieu sait* if the levees goin' to stan' it!" she exclaimed.

"What have you got to do with the levees?"

"I got enough to do! An' there's Bobinôt with Bibi out in that storm—if he only didn' left Friedheimer's!"

"Let us hope, Calixta, that Bobinôt's got sense enough to come in out of a cyclone."

She went and stood at the window with a greatly disturbed look on her face. She wiped the frame that was clouded with moisture. It was stiflingly hot. Alcée got up and joined her at the window, looking over her shoulder. The rain was coming down in sheets obscuring the view of far-off cabins and enveloping the distant wood in a gray mist. The playing of the lightning was incessant. A bolt struck a tall chinaberry tree at the edge of the field. It filled all visible space with a blinding glare and the crash seemed to invade the very boards they stood upon.

Calixta put her hands to her eyes, and with a cry, staggered backward. Alcée's arm encircled her, and for an instant he drew her close and spasmodically to him.

"*Bonté!*" she cried, releasing herself from his encircling arm and retreating from the window, "the house'll go next! If I only knew w'ere Bibi was!" She would not compose herself; she would not be seated. Alcée clasped her shoulders and looked into her face. The contact of her warm, palpitating body when he had unthinkingly drawn her into his arms, had aroused all the old-time infatuation and desire for her flesh.

"Calixta," he said, "don't be frightened. Nothing can happen. The house is too low to be struck, with so many tall trees standing about. There! aren't you going to be quiet? say, aren't you?" He pushed her hair back from her face that was warm and steaming. Her lips were as red and moist as pomegranate seed. Her white neck and a glimpse of her full, firm bosom disturbed him powerfully. As she glanced up at him the fear in her liquid blue eyes had given place to a drowsy gleam that unconsciously betrayed a sensuous desire. He looked down into her eyes and there was nothing for him to do but to gather her lips in a kiss. It reminded him of Assumption.

"Do you remember—in Assumption, Calixta?" he asked in a low voice broken by passion. Oh! she remembered; for in Assumption he had kissed her and kissed and kissed her; until his senses would well nigh fail, and to save her he would resort to a desperate flight. If she was not an immaculate dove in those days, she was still inviolate; a passionate creature whose very defenselessness had made her defense, against which his honor forbade him to prevail. Now—well, now—her lips seemed in a manner free to be tasted, as well as her round, white throat and her whiter breasts.

They did not heed the crashing torrents, and the roar of the elements made her laugh as she lay in his arms. She was a revelation in that dim, mysterious chamber; as white as the couch she lay upon. Her firm, elastic flesh that was knowing for the first time its birthright, was like a creamy lily that the sun invites to contribute its breath and perfume to the undying life of the world.

The generous abundance of her passion, without guile or trickery, was like a white flame which penetrated and found response in depths of his own sensuous nature that had never yet been reached.

When he touched her breasts they gave themselves up in quivering ecstasy, inviting his lips. Her mouth was a fountain of delight. And when he possessed her, they seemed to swoon together at the very borderland of life's mystery.

He stayed cushioned upon her, breathless, dazed, enervated, with his heart beating like a hammer upon her. With one hand she clasped his head, her lips lightly touching his forehead. The other hand stroked with a soothing rhythm his muscular shoulders.

The growl of the thunder was distant and passing away. The rain beat softly upon the shingles, inviting them to drowsiness and sleep. But they dared not yield.

The rain was over; and the sun was turning the glistening green world into a palace of gems. Calixta, on the gallery, watched Alcée ride away. He turned and smiled at her with a beaming face; and she lifted her pretty chin in the air and laughed aloud.

III

Bobinôt and Bibi, trudging home, stopped without at the cistern to make themselves presentable.

"My! Bibi, w'at will yo' mama say! You ought to be ashame'. You oughtn' put on those good pants. Look at 'em! An' that mud on yo' collar! How you got that mud on yo' collar, Bibi? I never saw such a boy!" Bibi was the picture of pathetic resignation. Bobinôt was the embodiment of serious solicitude as he strove to remove from his own person and his son's the signs of their tramp over heavy roads and through wet fields. He scraped the mud off Bibi's bare legs and feet with a stick and carefully removed all traces from his heavy brogans. Then, prepared for the worst—the meeting with an over-scrupulous housewife, they entered cautiously at the back door.

Calixta was preparing supper. She had set the table and was dripping coffee at the hearth. She sprang up as they came in.

"Oh, Bobinôt! You back! My! but I was uneasy. W'ere you been during the rain? An' Bibi? he ain't wet? he ain't hurt?" She had clasped Bibi and was kissing him effusively. Bobinôt's explanations and apologies which he had been composing all along the way, died on his lips as Calixta felt him to see if he were dry, and seemed to express nothing but satisfaction at their safe return.

"I brought you some shrimps, Calixta," offered Bobinôt, hauling the can from his ample side pocket and laying it on the table.

"Shrimps! Oh, Bobinôt! you too good fo' anything! and she gave him a smacking kiss on the cheek that resounded. "*J'vous réponds*, we'll have a feas' to night! umph-umph!"

Bobinôt and Bibi began to relax and enjoy themselves, and when the three seated themselves at table they laughed much and so loud that anyone might have heard them as far away as Laballière's.

IV

Alcée Laballière wrote to his wife, Clarisse, that night. It was a loving letter, full of tender solicitude. He told her not to hurry back, but if she and the babies liked it at Biloxi, to stay a month longer. He was getting on nicely; and though he missed them, he was willing to bear the separation a while longer—realizing that their health and pleasure were the first things to be considered.

V

As for Clarisse, she was charmed upon receiving her husband's letter. She and the babies were doing well. The society was agreeable; many of her old friends and acquaintances were at the bay. And the first free breath since her marriage seemed to restore the pleasant liberty of her maiden days. Devoted as she was to her husband, their intimate conjugal life was something which she was more than willing to forego for a while.

So the storm passed and every one was happy.

Never Marry a Mexican
(1991)

SANDRA CISNEROS

Never marry a Mexican, my ma said once and always. She said this because of my father. She said this though she was Mexican too. But she was born here in the U.S., and he was born there, and it's *not* the same, you know.

I'll *never* marry. Not any man. I've known men too intimately, I've witnessed their infidelities, and I've helped them to it. Unzipped and unhooked and agreed to clandestine maneuvers. I've been accomplice, committed premeditated crimes. I'm guilty of having caused deliberate pain to other women. I'm vindictive and cruel, and I'm capable of anything.

I admit, there was a time when all I wanted was to belong to a man. To wear that gold band on my left hand and be worn on his arm like an expensive jewel brilliant in the light of day. Not the sneaking around I did in different bars that all looked the same, red carpets with a black grillwork design, flocked wallpaper, wooden wagon-wheel light fixtures with hurricane lampshades a sick amber color like the drinking glasses you get for free at gas stations.

Dark bars, dark restaurants then. And if not—my apartment, with his toothbrush firmly planted in the toothbrush holder like a flag on the North Pole. The bed so big because he never stayed the whole night. Of course not.

Borrowed. That's how I've had my men. Just the cream skimmed off the top. Just the sweetest part of the fruit, without the bitter skin that daily living with a spouse can rend. They've come to me when they wanted the sweet meat then.

So, no. I've never married and never will. Not because I couldn't, but because I'm too romantic for marriage. Marriage has failed me, you could say. Not a man exists who hasn't disappointed me, whom I could trust to love the way I've loved. It's because I believe too much in marriage that I don't. Better to not marry than live a lie.

Mexican men, forget it. For a long time the men clearing off the tables or chopping meat behind the butcher counter or driving the bus I rode to school every day, those weren't men. Not men I considered as potential lovers. Mexican, Puerto Rican, Cuban, Chilean, Colombian, Panamanian, Salvadorean, Bolivian, Honduran, Argentine, Dominican, Venezuelan, Guatemalan, Ecuadorean, Nicaraguan, Peruvian, Costa Rican, Paraguayan, Uruguayan, I don't care. I never saw them. My mother did this to me.

I guess she did it to spare me and Ximena the pain she went through. Having married a Mexican man at seventeen. Having had to put up with all the grief a Mexican family can put on a girl because she was from *el otro lado*, the other side, and my father had married down by marrying her. If he had married a white woman from *el otro lado*, that would've been different. That would've been marrying up, even if the white girl was poor. But what could be more ridiculous than a Mexican girl who couldn't even speak Spanish, who didn't know enough to set a separate plate for each course at dinner, nor how to fold cloth napkins, nor how to set the silverware.

In my ma's house the plates were always stacked in the center of the table, the knives and forks and spoons standing in a jar, help yourself. All the dishes chipped or cracked and nothing matched. And no tablecloth, ever. And newspapers set on the table whenever my grandpa sliced watermelons, and how embarrassed she would be when her boyfriend, my father, would come over and there were newspapers all over the kitchen floor and table. And my grandpa, big hardworking Mexican man, saying Come, come and eat, and slicing a big wedge of those dark green watermelons, a big slice, he wasn't stingy with food. Never, even during the Depression. Come, come and eat, to whoever came knocking on the back door. Hobos sitting at the dinner table and the children staring and staring. Because my grandfather always made sure they never went without. Flour and rice, by the barrel and by the sack. Potatoes. Big bags of pinto beans. And watermelons, bought three or four at a time, rolled under his bed and brought out when you least expected. My grandpa had survived three wars, one Mexican, two American, and he knew what living without meant. He knew.

My father, on the other hand, did not. True, when he first came to this country he had worked shelling clams, washing dishes, planting hedges, sat on the back of the bus in Little Rock and had the bus driver shout, You—sit up here, and my father had shrugged sheepishly and said, No speak English.

But he was no economic refugee, no immigrant fleeing a war. My father ran away from home because he was afraid of facing his father after his first-year grades at the university proved he'd spent more time fooling around than studying. He left behind a house in Mexico City that was neither poor nor rich, but thought itself better than both. A boy who would get off a bus when he saw a girl he knew board if he didn't have the money to pay her fare. That was the world my father left behind.

I imagine my father in his *fanfarrón* clothes, because that's what he was, a *fanfarrón*. That's what my mother thought the moment she turned around to the voice that was asking her to dance. A big show-off, she'd say years later. Nothing but a big show-off. But she never said why she married him. My father in his shark-blue suits with the starched handkerchief in the breast pocket, his felt fedora, his tweed topcoat with the big shoulders, and heavy British wing tips with the pin-hole design on the heel and toe. Clothes that cost a lot. Expensive. That's what my father's things said. *Calidad.* Quality.

My father must've found the U.S. Mexicans very strange, so foreign from what he knew at home in Mexico City where the servant served watermelon on a plate with silverware and a cloth napkin, or mangos with their own special prongs. Not like this, eating with your legs wide open in the yard, or in the kitchen hunkered over newspapers. *Come, come and eat.* No, never like this.

❀

How I make my living depends. Sometimes I work as a translator. Sometimes I get paid by the word and sometimes by the hour, depending on the job. I do this in the day, and at night I paint. I'd do anything in the day just so I can keep on painting.

I work as a substitute teacher, too, for the San Antonio Independent School District. And that's worse than translating those travel brochures with their tiny print, believe me. I can't stand kids. Not any age. But it pays the rent.

Any way you look at it, what I do to make a living is a form of prostitution. People say, "A painter? How nice," and want to invite me to their parties, have me decorate the lawn like an exotic orchid for hire. But do they buy art?

I'm amphibious. I'm a person who doesn't belong to any class. The rich like to have me around because they envy my creativity; they know they can't buy *that*. The poor don't mind if I live in their neighborhood because they know I'm poor like they are, even if my education and the way I dress keeps us worlds apart. I don't belong to any class. Not to the poor, whose neighborhood I share. Not to the rich, who come to my exhibitions and buy my work. Not to the middle class from which my sister Ximena and I fled.

When I was young, when I first left home and rented that apartment with my sister and her kids right after her husband left, I thought it would be glamorous to be an artist. I wanted to be like Frida or Tina. I was ready to suffer with my camera and my paint brushes in that awful apartment we rented for $150 each because it had high ceilings and those wonderful glass skylights that convinced us we had to have it. Never mind there was no sink in the bathroom, and a tub that looked like a sarcophagus, and floorboards that didn't meet, and a hallway to scare away the dead. But fourteen-foot ceilings was enough for us to write a check for the deposit right then and there. We thought it all romantic. You know the place, the one on Zarzamora on top of the barber shop with the Casasola prints of the Mexican Revolution. Neon BIRRIA TEPATITLÁN sign round the corner, two goats knocking their heads together, and all those Mexican bakeries, Las Brisas for *huevos rancheros* and *carnitas* and *barbacoa* on Sundays, and fresh fruit milk shakes, and mango *paletas,* and more signs in Spanish than in English. We thought it was great, great. The barrio looked cute in the daytime, like Sesame Street. Kids hopscotching on the sidewalk, blessed little boogers. And hardware stores that still sold ostrich-feather dusters, and whole families marching out of Our Lady of Guadalupe Church on Sundays, girls in their swirly-whirly dresses and patent-leather shoes, boys in their dress Stacys and shiny shirts.

But nights, that was nothing like what we knew up on the north side. Pistols going off like the wild, wild West, and me and Ximena and the kids huddled in one bed with the lights off listening to it all, saying, Go to sleep, babies, it's just firecrackers. But we knew better. Ximena would say, Clemencia, maybe we should go home. And I'd say, Shit! Because she knew as well as I did there was no home to go home to. Not with our mother. Not with that man she married. After Daddy died, it was like we didn't matter. Like Ma was so busy feeling sorry for herself, I don't know. I'm not like Ximena. I still haven't worked it out after all this time, even though our mother's dead now. My half brothers living in that house that should've been ours, me and Ximena's. But that's—how do you say it?—water under the damn? I can't ever get the sayings right even though I was born in this country. We didn't say shit like that in our house.

Once Daddy was gone, it was like my ma didn't exist, like if she died, too. I used to have a little finch, twisted one of its tiny red legs between the bars of the cage once, who knows how. The leg just dried up and fell off. My bird lived a long time without it, just a little red stump of a leg. He was fine, really. My mother's memory is like that, like if something already dead dried up and fell off, and I stopped missing where she used to be. Like if I never had a mother. And I'm not ashamed to say it either. When she married that white man, and he and his boys moved into my father's house, it was as if she stopped being my mother. Like I never even had one.

Ma always sick and too busy worrying about her own life, she would've sold us to the Devil if she could. "Because I married so young, *mi'ja*," she'd say. "Because your father, he was so much older than me, and I never had a chance to be young. Honey, try to understand . . ." Then I'd stop listening.

That man she met at work, Owen Lambert, the foreman at the photo-finishing plant, who she was seeing even while my father was sick. Even then. That's what I can't forgive.

When my father was coughing up blood and phlegm in the hospital, half his face frozen, and his tongue so fat he couldn't talk, he looked so small with all those tubes and plastic sacks dangling around him. But what I remember most is the smell, like death was already sitting on his chest. And I remember the doctor scraping the phlegm out of my father's mouth with a white washcloth, and my daddy gagging and I wanted to yell, Stop, you stop that, he's my daddy. Goddamn you. Make him live. Daddy, don't. Not yet, not yet, not yet. And how I couldn't hold myself up, I couldn't hold myself up. Like if they'd beaten me, or pulled my insides out through my nostrils, like if they'd stuffed me with cinnamon and cloves, and I just stood there dry-eyed next to Ximena and my mother, Ximena between us because I wouldn't let her stand next to me. Everyone repeating over and over the Ave Marías and Padre Nuestros. The priest sprinkling holy water, *mundo sin fin, amén.*

❁

Drew, remember when you used to call me your Malinalli? It was a joke, a private game between us, because you looked like a Cortez with that beard of yours. My skin dark against yours. Beautiful, you said. You said I was beautiful, and when you said it, Drew, I was.

My Malinalli, Malinche, my courtesan, you said, and yanked my head back by the braid. Calling me that name in between little gulps of breath and the raw kisses you gave, laughing from that black beard of yours.

Before daybreak, you'd be gone, same as always, before I even knew it. And it was as if I'd imagined you, only the teeth marks on my belly and nipples proving me wrong.

Your skin pale, but your hair blacker than a pirate's. Malinalli, you called me, remember? *Mi doradita.* I liked when you spoke to me in my language. I could love myself and think myself worth loving.

Your son. Does he know how much I had to do with his birth? I was the one who convinced you to let him be born. Did you tell him, while his mother lay on her back laboring his birth, I lay in his mother's bed making love to you.

You're nothing without me. I created you from spit and red dust. And I can snuff you between my finger and thumb if I want to. Blow you to kingdom come. You're just a smudge of paint I chose to birth on canvas. And when I made you over, you were no longer a part of her, you were all mine. The landscape of your body taut as a drum. The heart beneath that hide thrumming and thrumming. Not an inch did I give back.

I paint and repaint you the way I see fit, even now. After all these years. Did you know that? Little fool. You think I went hobbling along with my life, whimpering and whining like some twangy country-and-western when you went back to her. But I've been waiting. Making the world look at you from my eyes. And if that's not power, what is?

218

Nights I light all the candles in the house, the ones to La Virgen de Guadalupe, the ones to El Niño Fidencio, Don Pedrito Jaramillo, Santo Niño de Atocha, Nuestra Señora de San Juan de los Lagos, and especially, Santa Lucía, with her beautiful eyes on a plate.

Your eyes are beautiful, you said. You said they were the darkest eyes you'd ever seen and kissed each one as if they were capable of miracles. And after you left, I wanted to scoop them out with a spoon, place them on a plate under these blue blue skies, food for the blackbirds.

The boy, your son. The one with the face of that redheaded woman who is your wife. The boy red-freckled like fish food floating on the skin of water. That boy.

I've been waiting patient as a spider all these years, since I was nineteen and he was just an idea hovering in his mother's head, and I'm the one that gave him permission and made it happen, see.

Because your father wanted to leave your mother and live with me. Your mother whining for a child, at least *that*. And he kept saying, Later, we'll see, later. But all along it was me he wanted to be with, it was me, he said.

I want to tell you this evenings when you come to see me. When you're full of talk about what kind of clothes you're going to buy, and what you used to be like when you started high school and what you're like now that you're almost finished. And how everyone knows you as a rocker, and your band, and your new red guitar that you just got because your mother gave you a choice, a guitar or a car, but you don't need a car, do you, because I drive you everywhere. You could be my son if you weren't so light-skinned.

This happened. A long time ago. Before you were born. When you were a moth inside your mother's heart, I was your father's student, yes, just like you're mine now. And your father painted and painted me, because he said, I was his *doradita*, all golden and sun-baked, and that's the kind of woman he likes best, the ones brown as river sand, yes. And he took me under his wing and in his bed, this man, this teacher, your father. I was honored that he'd done me the favor. I was that young.

All I know is I was sleeping with your father the night you were born. In the same bed where you were conceived. I was sleeping with your father and didn't give a damn about that woman, your mother. If she was a brown woman like me, I might've had a harder time living with myself, but since she's not, I don't care. I was there first, always. I've always been there, in the mirror, under his skin, in the blood, before you were born. And he's been here in my heart before I even knew him. Understand? He's always been here. Always. Dissolving like a hibiscus flower, exploding like a rope into dust. I don't care what's right anymore. I don't care about his wife. She's not *my* sister.

And it's not the last time I've slept with a man the night his wife is birthing a baby. Why do I do that, I wonder? Sleep with a man when his wife is giving life, being suckled by a thing with its eyes still shut. Why do that? It's always given me a bit of crazy joy to be able to kill those women like that, without their knowing it. To know I've had their husbands when they were anchored in blue hospital rooms, their guts yanked inside out, the baby sucking their breasts while their husband sucked mine. All this while their ass stitches were still hurting.

❀

Once, drunk on margaritas, I telephoned your father at four in the morning, woke the bitch up. Hello, she chirped. I want to talk to Drew. Just a moment, she said in her most polite drawing-room English. Just a moment. I laughed about that for weeks. What a stupid ass to pass the phone over to the lug asleep beside her. Excuse me, honey, it's for you. When Drew mumbled hello I was laughing so hard I could hardly talk. Drew? That dumb bitch of a wife of yours, I said, and that's all I could manage. That stupid stupid stupid. No Mexican woman would react like that. Excuse me, honey. It cracked me up.

※

He's got the same kind of skin, the boy. All the blue veins pale and clear just like his mama. Skin like roses in December. Pretty boy. Little clone. Little cells split into you and you and you. Tell me, baby, which part of you is your mother. I try to imagine her lips, her jaw, her long long legs that wrapped themselves around this father who took me to his bed.

※

This happened. I'm asleep. Or pretend to be. You're watching me, Drew. I feel your weight when you sit on the corner of the bed, dressed and ready to go, but now you're just watching me sleep. Nothing. Not a word. Not a kiss. Just sitting. You're taking me in, under inspection. What do you think already?

I haven't stopped dreaming you. Did you know that? Do you think it's strange? I never tell, though. I keep it to myself like I do all the thoughts I think of you.

After all these years.

I don't want you looking at me. I don't want you taking me in while I'm asleep. I'll open my eyes and frighten you away.

There. What did I tell you? *Drew? What is it?* Nothing. I'd knew you'd say that.

Let's not talk. We're no good at it. With you I'm useless with words. As if somehow I had to learn to speak all over again, as if the words I needed haven't been invented yet. We're cowards. Come back to bed. At least there I feel I have you for a little. For a moment. For a catch of the breath. You let go. You ache and tug. You rip my skin.

You're almost not a man without your clothes. How do I explain it? You're so much a child in my bed. Nothing but a big boy who needs to be held. I won't let anyone hurt you. My pirate. My slender boy of a man.

After all these years.

I didn't imagine it, did I? A Ganges, an eye of the storm. For a little. When we forgot ourselves, you tugged me, I leapt inside you and split you like an apple. Opened for the other to look and not give back. Something wrenched itself loose. Your body doesn't lie. It's not silent like you.

You're nude as a pearl. You've lost your train of smoke. You're tender as rain. If I'd put you in my mouth you'd dissolve like snow.

You were ashamed to be so naked. Pulled back. But I saw you for what you are, when you opened yourself for me. When you were careless and let yourself through. I caught that catch of the breath. I'm not crazy.

When you slept, you tugged me toward you. You sought me in the dark. I didn't sleep. Every cell, every follicle, every nerve, alert. Watching you sigh and roll and turn and hug me closer to you. I didn't sleep. I was taking *you* in that time.

※

Your mother? Only once. Years after your father and I stopped seeing each other. At an art exhibition. A show on the photographs of Eugéne Atget. Those images, I could look at them for hours. I'd taken a group of students with me.

It was your father I saw first. And in that instant I felt as if everyone in the room, all the sepia-toned photographs, my students, the men in business suits, the high-heeled women, the security guards, everyone, could see me for what I was. I had to scurry out, lead my kids to another gallery, but some things destiny has cut out for you.

He caught up with us in the coat-check area, arm in arm with a redheaded Barbie doll in a fur coat. One of those scary Dallas types, hair yanked into a ponytail, big shiny face like the women behind the cosmetic counters at Neiman's. That's what I remember. She must've been with him all along, only I swear I never saw her until that second.

You could tell from a slight hesitancy, only slight because he's too suave to hesitate, that he was nervous. Then he's walking toward me, and I didn't know what to do, just stood there dazed like those animals crossing the road at night when the headlights stun them.

And I don't know why, but all of a sudden I looked at my shoes and felt ashamed at how old they looked. And he comes up to me, my love, your father, in that way of his with that grin that makes me want to beat him, makes me want to make love to him, and he says in the most sincere voice you ever heard, "Ah, Clemencia! *This* is Megan." No introduction could've been meaner. *This* is Megan. Just like that.

I grinned like an idiot and held out my paw—"Hello, Megan"—and smiled too much the way you do when you can't stand someone. Then I got the hell out of there, chattering like a monkey all the ride back with my kids. When I got home I had to lie down with a cold washcloth on my forehead and the TV on. All I could hear throbbing under the washcloth in that deep part behind my eyes: *This* is Megan.

And that's how I fell asleep, with the TV on and every light in the house burning. When I woke up it was something like three in the morning. I shut the lights and TV and went to get some aspirin, and the cats, who'd been asleep with me on the couch, got up too and followed me into the bathroom as if they knew what's what. And then they followed me into bed, where they aren't allowed, but this time I just let them, fleas and all.

❀

This happened, too. I swear I'm not making this up. It's all true. It was the last time I was going to be with your father. We had agreed. All for the best. Surely I could see that, couldn't I? My own good. A good sport. A young girl like me. Hadn't I understood . . . responsibilities. Besides, he could *never* marry *me*. You didn't think. . .? *Never marry a Mexican. Never marry a Mexican.* . . No, of course not. I see. I see.

We had the house to ourselves for a few days, who knows how. You and your mother had gone somewhere. Was it Christmas? I don't remember.

I remember the leaded-glass lamp with the milk glass above the dining-room table. I made a mental inventory of everything. The Egyptian lotus design on the hinges of the doors. The narrow, dark hall where your father and I had made love once. The four-clawed tub where he had washed my hair and rinsed it with a tin bowl. This window. That counter. The bedroom with its light in the morning, incredibly soft, like the light from a polished dime.

The house was immaculate, as always, not a stray hair anywhere, not a flake of dandruff or a crumpled towel. Even the roses on the dining-room table held their breath. A kind of airless cleanliness that always made me want to sneeze.

Why was I so curious about this woman he lived with? Every time I went to the bathroom, I found myself opening the medicine cabinet, looking at all the things that were hers. Her Estée Lauder lipsticks. Corals and pinks, of course. Her nail polishes—mauve was as brave as she could wear. Her cotton balls and blond hairpins. A pair of bone-colored sheepskin slippers, as clean as the day she'd bought them. On the door hook—a white robe with a MADE IN ITALY label, and a silky nightshirt with pearl buttons. I touched the fabrics. *Calidad.* Quality.

I don't know how to explain what I did next. While your father was busy in the kitchen, I went over to where I'd left my backpack, and took out a bag of gummy bears I'd bought. And while he was banging pots, I went around the house and left a trail of them in places I was sure *she* would find them. One in her lucite makeup organizer. One stuffed inside each bottle of nail polish. I untwisted the expensive lipsticks to their full length and smushed a bear on the top before recapping them. I even put a gummy bear in her diaphragm case in the very center of that luminescent rubber moon.

Why bother? Drew could take the blame. Or he could say it was the cleaning woman's Mexican voodoo. I knew that, too. It didn't matter. I got a strange satisfaction wandering about the house leaving them in places only she would look.

And just as Drew was shouting, "Dinner!" I saw it on the desk. One of those wooden babushka dolls Drew had brought her from his trip to Russia. I know. He'd bought one just like it for me.

I just did what I did, uncapped the doll inside a doll inside a doll, until I got to the very center, the tiniest baby inside all the others, and this I replaced with a gummy bear. And then I put the dolls back, just like I'd found them, one inside the other, inside the other. Except for the baby, which I put inside my pocket. All through dinner I kept reaching in the pocket of my jean jacket. When I touched it, it made me feel good.

On the way home, on the bridge over the *arroyo* on Guadalupe Street, I stopped the car, switched on the emergency blinkers, got out, and dropped the wooden toy into that muddy creek where winos piss and rats swim. The Barbie doll's toy stewing there in that muck. It gave me a feeling like nothing before and since.

Then I drove home and slept like the dead.

These mornings, I fix coffee for me, milk for the boy. I think of that woman, and I can't see a trace of my lover in this boy, as if she conceived him by immaculate conception.

I sleep with this boy, their son. To make the boy love me the way I love his father. To make him want me, hunger, twist in his sleep, as if he'd swallowed glass. I put him in my mouth. Here, little piece of my *corazòn.* Boy with hard thighs and just a bit of down and a small hard downy ass like his father's, and that back like a valentine. Come here, *mi cariñito.* Come to *mamita.* Here's a bit of toast.

222

I can tell from the way he looks at me, I have him in my power. Come, sparrow. I have the patience of eternity. Come to *mamita*. My stupid little bird. I don't move. I don't startle him. I let him nibble. All, all for you. Rub his belly. Stroke him. Before I snap my teeth.

🌸

What is it inside me that makes me so crazy at 2 A.M.? I can't blame it on alcohol in my blood when there isn't any. It's something worse. Something that poisons the blood and tips me when the night swells and I feel as if the whole sky were leaning against my brain.

And if I killed someone on a night like this? And if it was *me* I killed instead, I'd be guilty of getting in the line of crossfire, innocent bystander, isn't it a shame. I'd be walking with my head full of images and my back to the guilty. Suicide? I couldn't say. I didn't see it.

Except it's not me who I want to kill. When the gravity of the planets is just right, it all tilts and upsets the visible balance. And that's when it wants to out from my eyes. That's when I get on the telephone, dangerous as a terrorist. There's nothing to do but let it come.

So. What do you think? Are you convinced now I'm as crazy as a tulip or a taxi? As vagrant as a cloud?

Sometimes the sky is so big and I feel so little at night. That's the problem with being cloud. The sky is so terribly big. Why is it worse at night, when I have such an urge to communicate and no language with which to form the words? Only colors. Pictures. And you know what I have to say isn't always pleasant.

Oh, love, there. I've gone and done it. What good is it? Good or bad, I've done what I had to do and needed to. And you've answered the phone, and startled me away like a bird. And now you're probably swearing under your breath and going back to sleep, with that wife beside you, warm, radiating her own heat, alive under the flannel and down and smelling a bit like milk and hand cream, and that smell familiar and dear to you, oh.

Human beings pass me on the street, and I want to reach out and strum them as if they were guitars. Sometimes all humanity strikes me as lovely. I just want to reach out and stroke someone, and say There, there, it's all right, honey. There, there, there.

An Outpost of Progress
(1897)

JOSEPH CONRAD

I

There were two white men in charge of the trading station. Kayerts, the chief, was short and fat; Carlier, the assistant, was tall, with a large head and a very broad trunk perched upon a long pair of thin legs. The third man on the staff was a Sierra Leone nigger, who maintained that his name was Henry Price. However, for some reason or other, the natives down the river had given him the name of Makola, and it stuck to him through all his wanderings about the country. He spoke English and French with a warbling accent, wrote a beautiful hand, understood bookkeeping, and cherished in his innermost heart the worship of evil spirits. His wife was a negress from Loanda, very large and very noisy. Three children rolled about in sunshine before the door of his low, shed-like dwelling. Makola, taciturn and impenetrable, despised the two white men. He had charge of a small clay storehouse with a dried-grass roof, and pretended to keep a correct account of beads, cotton cloth, red kerchiefs, brass wire, and other trade goods it contained. Besides the storehouse and Makola's hut, there was only one large building in the cleared ground of the station. It was built neatly of reeds, with a verandah on all the four sides. There were three rooms in it. The one in the middle was the living-room, and had two rough tables and a few stools in it. The other two were the bedrooms for the white men. Each had a bedstead and a mosquito net for all furniture. The plank floor was littered with the belongings of the white men; open half-empty boxes, torn wearing apparel, old boots; all the things dirty, and all the things broken, that accumulate mysteriously round untidy men. There was also another dwelling-place some distance away from the buildings. In it, under a tall cross much out of the perpendicular, slept the man who had seen the beginning of all this; who had planned and had watched the construction of this outpost of progress. He had been, at home, an unsuccessful painter who, weary of pursuing fame on an empty stomach, had gone out there through high protections. He had been the first chief of that station. Makola had watched the energetic artist die of fever in the just finished house with his usual kind of "I told you so" indifference. Then, for a time, he dwelt alone with his family, his account books, and the Evil Spirit that rules the lands under the equator. He got on very well with his god. Perhaps he had propitiated him by a promise of more white men to play with, by and by. At any rate the director of the Great Trading Company, coming up in a steamer that resembled an enormous sardine box with a flat-roofed shed erected on it, found the station in good order, and Makola as usual quietly diligent. The director had the cross put up over the first agent's grave, and appointed Kayerts to the post. Carlier was told off as second in charge. The director was a man ruthless and efficient, who at times, but very imperceptibly, indulged in grim humour. He made a speech to Kayerts and Carlier, pointing out to them the promising aspect of their station. The nearest trading-post was about three hundred miles away. It was an exceptional opportunity for them to distinguish themselves and to earn percentages on the trade. This appointment was a favour done to beginners. Kayerts was moved almost to tears by his director's kindness. He would, he said, by doing his best, try to justify the flattering confidence, & c., & c. Kayerts had been in the Administration of the Telegraphs, and knew how to express himself correctly. Carlier, an ex-non-commissioned officer of cavalry in an army guaranteed from harm by several European Powers, was less impressed. If there were commissions to get, so much the better; and, trailing a sulky glance over the river, the forests, the impenetrable bush that seemed to cut off the station from the rest of the world, he muttered between his teeth, "We shall see, very soon."

Next day, some bales of cotton goods and a few cases of provisions having been thrown on shore, the sardine-box steamer went off, not to return for another six months. On the deck the director touched his cap to the two agents, who stood on the bank waving their hats, and turning to an old servant of the Company on his passage to headquarters, said, "Look at those two imbeciles. They must be mad at home to send me such specimens. I told those fellows to plant a vegetable garden, build new storehouses and fences, and construct a landing-stage. I bet nothing will be done! They won't know how to begin. I always thought the station on this river useless, and they just fit the station!"

"They will form themselves there," said the old stager with a quiet smile.

"At any rate, I am rid of them for six months," retorted the director.

The two men watched the steamer round the bend, then, ascending arm in arm the slope of the bank, returned to the station. They had been in this vast and dark country only a very short time, and as yet always in the midst of other white men, under the eye and guidance of their superiors. And now, dull as they were to the subtle influences of surroundings, they felt themselves very much alone, when suddenly left unassisted to face the wilderness; a wilderness rendered more strange, more incomprehensible by the mysterious glimpses of the vigorous life it contained. They were two perfectly insignificant and incapable individuals, whose existence is only rendered possible through the high organization of civilized crowds. Few men realize that their life, the very essence of their character, their capabilities and their audacities, are only the expression of their belief in the safety of their surroundings. The courage, the composure, the confidence; the emotions and principles; every great and every insignificant thought belongs not to the individual but to the crowd: to the crowd that believes blindly in the irresistible force of its institutions and of its morals, in the power of its police and of its opinion. But the contact with pure unmitigated savagery, with primitive nature and primitive man, brings sudden and profound trouble into the heart. To the sentiment of being alone of one's kind, to the clear perception of the loneliness of one's thoughts, of one's sensations—to the negation of the habitual, which is safe, there is added the affirmation of the unusual, which is dangerous; a suggestion of things vague, uncontrollable, and repulsive, whose discomposing intrusion excites the imagination and tries the civilized nerves of the foolish and the wise alike.

Kayerts and Carlier walked arm in arm, drawing close to one another as children do in the dark; and they had the same, not altogether unpleasant, sense of danger which one half suspects to be imaginary. They chatted persistently in familiar tones. "Our station is prettily situated," said one. The other assented with enthusiasm, enlarging volubly on the beauties of the situation. Then they passed near the grave. "Poor devil!" said Kayerts. "He died of fever, didn't he?" muttered Carlier, stopping short. "Why," retorted Kayerts, with indignation, "I've been told that the fellow exposed himself recklessly to the sun. The climate here, everybody says, is not at all worse than at home, as long as you keep out of the sun. Do you hear that, Carlier? I am chief here, and my orders are that you should not expose yourself to the sun!" He assumed his superiority jocularly, but his meaning was serious. The idea that he would, perhaps, have to bury Carlier and remain alone, gave him an inward shiver. He felt suddenly that this Carlier was more precious to him here, in the centre of Africa, than a brother could be anywhere else. Carlier, entering into the spirit of the thing, made a military salute and answered in a brisk tone, "Your orders shall be attended to, chief!" Then he burst out laughing, slapped Kayerts on the back and shouted, "We shall let life run easily here! Just sit still and gather in the ivory those savages will bring. This country has its good points, after all!" They both laughed loudly while Carlier thought: "That poor Kayerts; he is so fat and unhealthy. It would be awful if I had to bury him here. He is a man I respect." . . . Before they reached the verandah of their house they called one another "my dear fellow."

The first day they were very active, pottering about with hammers and nails and red calico, to put up curtains, make their house habitable and pretty; resolved to settle down comfortably to their new life. For them an impossible task. To grapple effectually with even purely material problems requires more serenity of mind and more lofty courage than people generally imagine. No two beings could have been more unfitted for such a struggle. Society, not from any tenderness, but because of its strange needs, had taken care of those two men, forbidding them all independent thought, all initiative, all departure from routine; and forbidding it under pain of death. They could only live on condition of being machines. And now, released from the fostering care of men with pens behind the ears, or of men with gold lace on the sleeves, they were like those lifelong prisoners who, liberated after many years, do not know what use to make of their freedom. They did not know what use to make of their faculties, being both, through want of practice, incapable of independent thought.

At the end of two months Kayerts often would say, "If it was not for my Melie, you wouldn't catch me here." Melie was his daughter. He had thrown up his post in the Administration of the Telegraphs, though he had been for seventeen years perfectly happy there, to earn a dowry for his girl. His wife was dead, and the child was being brought up by his sisters. He regretted the streets, the pavements, the cafes, his friends of many years; all the things he used to see, day after day; all the thoughts suggested by familiar things—the thoughts effortless, monotonous, and soothing of a Government clerk; he regretted all the gossip, the small enmities, the mild venom, and the little jokes of Government offices. "If I had had a decent brother-in-law," Carlier would remark, "a fellow with a heart, I would not be here." He had left the army and had made himself so obnoxious to his family by his laziness and impudence, that an exasperated brother-in-law had made superhuman efforts to procure him an appointment in the Company as a second-class agent. Having not a penny in the world he was compelled to accept this means of livelihood as soon as it became quite clear to him that there was nothing more to squeeze out of his relations. He, like Kayerts, regretted his old life. He regretted the clink of sabre and spurs on a fine afternoon, the barrack-room witticisms, the girls of garrison towns; but, besides, he had also a sense of grievance. He was evidently a much ill-used man. This made him moody, at times. But the two men got on well together in the fellowship of their stupidity and laziness. Together they did nothing, absolutely nothing, and enjoyed the sense of the idleness for which they were paid. And in time they came to feel something resembling affection for one another.

They lived like blind men in a large room, aware only of what came in contact with them (and of that only imperfectly), but unable to see the general aspect of things. The river, the forest, all the great land throbbing with life, were like a great emptiness. Even the brilliant sunshine disclosed nothing intelligible. Things appeared and disappeared before their eyes in an unconnected and aimless kind of way. The river seemed to come from nowhere and flow nowhither. It flowed through a void. Out of that void, at times, came canoes, and men with spears in their hands would suddenly crowd the yard of the station. They were naked, glossy black, ornamented with snowy shells and glistening brass wire, perfect of limb. They made an uncouth babbling noise when they spoke, moved in a stately manner, and sent quick, wild glances out of their startled, never-resting eyes. Those warriors would squat in long rows, four or more deep, before the verandah, while their chiefs bargained for hours with Makola over an elephant tusk. Kayerts sat on his chair and looked down on the proceedings, understanding nothing. He stared at them with his round blue eyes, called out to Carlier, "Here, look! look at that fellow there—and that other one, to the left. Did you ever such a face? Oh, the funny brute!"

Carlier, smoking native tobacco in a short wooden pipe, would swagger up twirling his moustaches, and surveying the warriors with haughty indulgence, would say—

"Fine animals. Brought any bone? Yes? It's not any too soon. Look at the muscles of that fellow third from the end. I wouldn't care to get a punch on the nose from him. Fine arms, but legs no good below the knee. Couldn't make cavalry men of them." And after glancing down complacently at his own shanks, he always concluded: "Pah! Don't they stink! You, Makola! Take that herd over to the fetish" (the storehouse was in every station called the fetish, perhaps because of the spirit of civilization it contained) "and give them up some of the rubbish you keep there. I'd rather see it full of bone than full of rags."

Kayerts approved.

"Yes, yes! Go and finish that palaver over there, Mr. Makola. I will come round when you are ready, to weigh the tusk. We must be careful." Then turning to his companion: "This is the tribe that lives down the river; they are rather aromatic. I remember, they had been once before here. D'ye hear that row? What a fellow has got to put up with in this dog of a country! My head is split."

Such profitable visits were rare. For days the two pioneers of trade and progress would look on their empty courtyard in the vibrating brilliance of vertical sunshine. Below the high bank, the silent river flowed on glittering and steady. On the sands in the middle of the stream, hippos and alligators sunned themselves side by side. And stretching away in all directions, surrounding the insignificant cleared spot of the trading post, immense forests, hiding fateful complications of fantastic life, lay in the eloquent silence of mute greatness. The two men understood nothing, cared for nothing but for the passage of days that separated them from the steamer's return. Their predecessor had left some torn books. They took up these wrecks of novels, and, as they had never read anything of the kind before, they were surprised and amused. Then during long days there were interminable and silly discussions about plots and personages. In the centre of Africa they made acquaintance of Richelieu and of d'Artagnan, of Hawk's Eye and of Father Goriot, and of many other people. All these imaginary personages became subjects for gossip as if they had been living friends. They discounted their virtues, suspected their motives, decried their successes; were scandalized at their duplicity or were doubtful about their courage. The accounts of crimes filled them with indignation, while tender or pathetic passages moved them deeply. Carlier cleared his throat and said in a soldierly voice, "What nonsense!" Kayerts, his round eyes suffused with tears, his fat cheeks quivering, rubbed his bald head, and declared. "This is a splendid book. I had no idea there were such clever fellows in the world." They also found some old copies of a home paper. That print discussed what it was pleased to call "Our Colonial Expansion" in high-flown language. It spoke much of the rights and duties of civilization, of the sacredness of the civilizing work, and extolled the merits of those who went about bringing light, and faith and commerce to the dark places of the earth. Carlier and Kayerts read, wondered, and began to think better of themselves. Carlier said one evening, waving his hand about, "In a hundred years, there will be perhaps a town here. Quays, and warehouses, and barracks, and— and—billiard-rooms. Civilization, my boy, and virtue—and all. And then, chaps will read that two good fellows, Kayerts and Carlier, were the first civilized men to live in this very spot!" Kayerts nodded, "Yes, it is a consolation to think of that." They seemed to forget their dead predecessor; but, early one day, Carlier went out and replanted the cross firmly. "It used to make me squint whenever I walked that way," he explained to Kayerts over the morning coffee. "It made me squint, leaning over so much. So I just planted it upright. And solid, I promise you! I suspended myself with both hands to the cross-piece. Not a move. Oh, I did that properly."

At times Gobila came to see them. Gobila was the chief of the neighbouring villages. He was a gray-headed savage, thin and black, with a white cloth round his loins and a mangy panther skin hanging over his back. He came up with long strides of his skeleton legs, swinging a staff as tall as himself, and, entering the common room of the station, would squat on his heels to the left of the door. There he sat, watching Kayerts, and now and then making a speech which the other did not understand. Kayerts, without interrupting his occupation, would from time to time say in a friendly manner: "How goes it, you old image?" and they would smile at one another. The two whites had a liking for that old and incomprehensible creature, and called him Father Gobila. Gobila's manner was paternal, and he seemed really to love all white men. They all appeared to him very young, indistinguishably alike (except for stature), and he knew that they were all brothers, and also immortal. The death of the artist, who was the first white man whom he knew intimately, did not disturb this belief, because he was firmly convinced that the white stranger had pretended to die and got himself buried for some mysterious purpose of his own, into which it was useless to inquire. Perhaps it was his way of going home to his own country? At any rate, these were his brothers, and he transferred his absurd affection to them. They returned it in a way. Carlier slapped him on the back, and recklessly struck off matches for his amusement. Kayerts was always ready to let him have a sniff at the ammonia bottle. In short, they behaved just like that other white creature that had hidden itself in a hole in the ground. Gobila considered them attentively. Perhaps they were the same being with the other—or one of them was. He couldn't decide—clear up that mystery; but he remained always very friendly. In consequence of that friendship the women of Gobila's village walked in single file through the reedy grass, bringing every morning to the station, fowls, and sweet potatoes, and palm wine, and sometimes a goat. The Company never provisions the stations fully, and the agents required those local supplies to live. They had them through the good-will of Gobila, and lived well. Now and then one of them had a bout of fever, and the other nursed him with gentle devotion. They did not think much of it. It left them weaker, and their appearance changed for the worse. Carlier was hollow-eyed and irritable. Kayerts showed a drawn, flabby face above the rotundity of his stomach, which gave him a weird aspect. But being constantly together, they did not notice the change that took place gradually in their appearance, and also in their dispositions.

Five months passed in that way.

Then, one morning, as Kayerts and Carlier, lounging in their chairs under the verandah, talked about the approaching visit of the steamer, a knot of armed men came out of the forest and advanced towards the station. They were strangers to that part of the country. They were tall, slight, draped classically from neck to heel in blue fringed cloths, and carried percussion muskets over their bare right shoulders. Makola showed signs of excitement, and ran out of the storehouse (where he spent all his days) to meet these visitors. They came into the courtyard and looked about them with steady, scornful glances. Their leader, a powerful and determined-looking negro with bloodshot eyes, stood in front of the verandah and made a long speech. He gesticulated much, and ceased very suddenly.

There was something in his intonation, in the sounds of the long sentences he used, that startled the two whites. It was like a reminiscence of something not exactly familiar, and yet resembling the speech of civilized men. It sounded like one of those impossible languages which sometimes we hear in our dreams.

"What lingo is that?" said the amazed Carlier. "In the first moment I fancied the fellow was going to speak French. Anyway, it is a different kind of gibberish to what we ever heard."

"Yes," replied Kayerts. "Hey, Makola, what does he say? Where do they come from? Who are they?"

But Makola, who seemed to be standing on hot bricks, answered hurriedly, "I don't know. They come from very far. Perhaps Mrs. Price will understand. They are perhaps bad men."

The leader, after waiting for a while, said something sharply to Makola, who shook his head. Then the man, after looking round, noticed Makola's hut and walked over there. The next moment Mrs. Makola was heard speaking with great volubility. The other strangers—they were six in all—strolled about with an air of ease, put their heads through the door of the storeroom, congregated round the grave, pointed understandingly at the cross, and generally made themselves at home.

"I don't like those chaps—and, I say, Kayerts, they must be from the coast; they've got firearms," observed the sagacious Carlier.

Kayerts also did not like those chaps. They both, for the first time, became aware that they lived in conditions where the unusual may be dangerous, and that there was no power on earth outside of themselves to stand between them and the unusual. They became uneasy, went in and loaded their revolvers. Kayerts said, "We must order Makola to tell them to go away before dark."

The strangers left in the afternoon, after eating a meal prepared for them by Mrs. Makola. The immense woman was excited, and talked much with the visitors. She rattled away shrilly, pointing here and there at the forests and at the river. Makola sat apart and watched. At times he got up and whispered to his wife. He accompanied the strangers across the ravine at the back of the station-ground, and returned slowly looking very thoughtful. When questioned by the white men he was very strange, seemed not to understand, seemed to have forgotten French—seemed to have forgotten how to speak altogether. Kayerts and Carlier agreed that the nigger had had too much palm wine.

There was some talk about keeping a watch in turn, but in the evening everything seemed so quiet and peaceful that they retired as usual. All night they were disturbed by a lot of drumming in the villages. A deep, rapid roll near by would be followed by another far off—then all ceased. Soon short appeals would rattle out here and there, then all mingle together, increase, become vigorous and sustained, would spread out over the forest, roll through the night, unbroken and ceaseless, near and far, as if the whole land had been one immense drum booming out steadily an appeal to heaven. And through the deep and tremendous noise sudden yells that resembled snatches of songs from a madhouse darted shrill and high in discordant jets of sound which seemed to rush far above the earth and drive all peace from under the stars.

Carlier and Kayerts slept badly. They both thought they had heard shots fired during the night—but they could not agree as to the direction. In the morning Makola was gone somewhere. He returned about noon with one of yesterday's strangers, and eluded all Kayerts' attempts to close with him: had become deaf apparently. Kayerts wondered. Carlier, who had been fishing off the bank, came back and remarked while he showed his catch, "The niggers seem to be in a deuce of a stir; I wonder what's up. I saw about fifteen canoes cross the river during the two hours I was there fishing." Kayerts, worried, said, "Isn't this Makola very queer to-day?" Carlier advised, "Keep all our men together in case of some trouble."

II

There were ten station men who had been left by the Director. Those fellows, having engaged themselves to the Company for six months (without having any idea of a month in particular and only a very faint notion of time in general), had been serving the cause of progress for upwards of two years. Belonging to a tribe from a very distant part of the land of darkness and sorrow, they did not run away, naturally supposing that as wandering strangers they would be killed by the inhabitants of the country; in which they were right. They lived in straw huts on the slope of a ravine overgrown with reedy grass, just behind the station buildings. They were not happy, regretting the festive incantations, the sorceries, the human sacrifices of their own land; where they also had parents, brothers, sisters, admired chiefs, respected magicians, loved friends, and other ties supposed generally to be human. Besides, the rice rations served out by the Company did not agree with them, being a food unknown to their land, and to which they could not get used. Consequently they were unhealthy and miserable. Had they been of any other tribe they would have made up their minds to die—for nothing is easier to certain savages than suicide—and so have escaped from the puzzling difficulties of existence. But belonging, as they did, to a warlike tribe with filed teeth, they had more grit, and went on stupidly living through disease and sorrow. They did very little work, and had lost their splendid physique. Carlier and Kayerts doctored them assiduously without being able to bring them back into condition again. They were mustered every morning and told off to different tasks—grass-cutting, fence-building, tree-felling, &c., &c., which no power on earth could induce them to execute efficiently. The two whites had practically very little control over them.

In the afternoon Makola came over to the big house and found Kayerts watching three heavy columns of smoke rising above the forests. "What is that?" asked Kayerts. "Some villages burn," answered Makola, who seemed to have regained his wits. Then he said abruptly: "We have got very little ivory; bad six months' trading. Do you like get a little more ivory?"

"Yes," said Kayerts, eagerly. He thought of percentages which were low.

"Those men who came yesterday are traders from Loanda who have got more ivory than they can carry home. Shall I buy? I know their camp."

"Certainly," said Kayerts. "What are those traders?"

"Bad fellows," said Makola, indifferently. "They fight with people, and catch women and children. They are bad men, and got guns. There is a great disturbance in the country. Do you want ivory?"

"Yes," said Kayerts. Makola said nothing for a while. Then: "Those workmen of ours are no good at all," he muttered, looking round. "Station in very bad order, sir. Director will growl. Better get a fine lot of ivory, then he say nothing."

"I can't help it; the men won't work," said Kayerts. "When will you get that ivory?"

"Very soon," said Makola. "Perhaps to-night. You leave it to me, and keep indoors, sir. I think you had better give some palm wine to our men to make a dance this evening. Enjoy themselves. Work better to-morrow. There's plenty palm wine—gone a little sour."

Kayerts said "yes," and Makola, with his own hands carried big calabashes to the door of his hut. They stood there till the evening, and Mrs. Makola looked into every one. The men got them at sunset. When Kayerts and Carlier retired, a big bonfire was flaring before the men's huts. They could hear their shouts and drumming. Some men from Gobila's village had joined the station hands, and the entertainment was a great success.

In the middle of the night, Carlier waking suddenly, heard a man shout loudly; then a shot was fired. Only one. Carlier ran out and met Kayerts on the verandah. They were both startled. As they went across the yard to call Makola, they saw shadows moving in the night. One of them cried, "Don't shoot! It's me, Price." Then Makola appeared close to them. "Go back, go back, please," he urged, "you spoil all." "There are strange men about," said Carlier. "Never mind; I know," said Makola. Then he whispered, "All right. Bring ivory. Say nothing! I know my business." The two white men reluctantly went back to the house, but did not sleep. They heard footsteps, whispers, some groans. It seemed as if a lot of men came in, dumped heavy things on the ground, squabbled a long time, then went away. They lay on their hard beds and thought: "This Makola is invaluable." In the morning Carlier came out, very sleepy, and pulled at the cord of the big bell. The station hands mustered every morning to the sound of the bell. That morning nobody came. Kayerts turned out also, yawning. Across the yard they saw Makola come out of his hut, a tin basin of soapy water in his hand. Makola, a civilized nigger, was very neat in his person. He threw the soapsuds skilfully over a wretched little yellow cur he had, then turning his face to the agent's house, he shouted from the distance, "All the men gone last night!"

They heard him plainly, but in their surprise they both yelled out together: "What!" Then they stared at one another. "We are in a proper fix now," growled Carlier. "It's incredible!"

muttered Kayerts. "I will go to the huts and see," said Carlier, striding off. Makola coming up found Kayerts standing alone.

"I can hardly believe it," said Kayerts, tearfully. "We took care of them as if they had been our children."

"They went with the coast people," said Makola after a moment of hesitation.

"What do I care with whom they went—the ungrateful brutes!" exclaimed the other. Then with sudden suspicion, and looking hard at Makola, he added: "What do you know about it?"

Makola moved his shoulders, looking down on the ground. "What do I know? I think only. Will you come and look at the ivory I've got there? It is a fine lot. You never saw such."

He moved towards the store. Kayerts followed him mechanically, thinking about the incredible desertion of the men. On the ground before the door of the fetish lay six splendid tusks.

"What did you give for it?" asked Kayerts, after surveying the lot with satisfaction.

"No regular trade," said Makola. "They brought the ivory and gave it to me. I told them to take what they most wanted in the station. It is a beautiful lot. No station can show such tusks. Those traders wanted carriers badly, and our men were no good here. No trade, no entry in books: all correct."

Kayerts nearly burst with indignation. "Why!" he shouted, "I believe you have sold our men for these tusks!" Makola stood impassive and silent. "I—I—will—I," stuttered Kayerts. "You fiend!" he yelled out.

"I did the best for you and the Company," said Makola, imperturbably. "Why you shout so much? Look at this tusk."

"I dismiss you! I will report you—I won't look at the tusk. I forbid you to touch them. I order you to throw them into the river. You—you!"

"You very red, Mr. Kayerts. If you are so irritable in the sun, you will get fever and die—like the first chief!" pronounced Makola impressively.

They stood still, contemplating one another with intense eyes, as if they had been looking with effort across immense distances. Kayerts shivered. Makola had meant no more than he said, but his words seemed to Kayerts full of ominous menace! He turned sharply and went away to the house. Makola retired into the bosom of his family; and the tusks, left lying before the store, looked very large and valuable in the sunshine.

Carlier came back on the verandah. "They're all gone, hey?" asked Kayerts from the far end of the common room in a muffled voice. "You did not find anybody?"

"Oh, yes," said Carlier, "I found one of Gobila's people lying dead before the huts—shot through the body. We heard that shot last night."

Kayerts came out quickly. He found his companion staring grimly over the yard at the tusks, away by the store. They both sat in silence for a while. Then Kayerts related his conversation with Makola. Carlier said nothing. At the midday meal they ate very little. They hardly exchanged a word that day. A great silence seemed to lie heavily over the station and press on their lips. Makola did not open the store; he spent the day playing with his children. He lay full-length on a mat outside his door, and the youngsters sat on his chest and clambered all over him. It was a touching picture. Mrs. Makola was busy cooking all day, as usual. The white men made a somewhat better meal in the evening. Afterwards, Carlier smoking his pipe strolled over to the store; he stood for a long time over the tusks, touched one or two with his foot, even tried to lift the largest one by its small end. He came back to his chief, who had not stirred from the verandah, threw himself in the chair and said—

"I can see it! They were pounced upon while they slept heavily after drinking all that palm wine you've allowed Makola to give them. A put-up job! See? The worst is, some of Gobila's people were there, and got carried off too, no doubt. The least drunk woke up, and got shot for his sobriety. This is a funny country. What will you do now?"

"We can't touch it, of course," said Kayerts.

"Of course not," assented Carlier.

"Slavery is an awful thing," stammered out Kayerts in an unsteady voice.

"Frightful—the sufferings," grunted Carlier with conviction.

They believed their words. Everybody shows a respectful deference to certain sounds that he and his fellows can make. But about feelings people really know nothing. We talk with indignation or enthusiasm; we talk about oppression, cruelty, crime, devotion, self-sacrifice, virtue, and we know nothing real beyond the words. Nobody knows what suffering or sacrifice mean—except, perhaps the victims of the mysterious purpose of these illusions.

Next morning they saw Makola very busy setting up in the yard the big scales used for weighing ivory. By and by Carlier said: "What's that filthy scoundrel up to?" and lounged out into the yard. Kayerts followed. They stood watching. Makola took no notice. When the balance was swung true, he tried to lift a tusk into the scale. It was too heavy. He looked up helplessly without a word, and for a minute they stood round that balance as mute and still as three statues. Suddenly Carlier said: "Catch hold of the other end, Makola—you beast!" and together they swung the tusk up. Kayerts trembled in every limb. He muttered, "I say! O! I say!" and putting his hand in his pocket found there a dirty bit of paper and the stump of a pencil. He turned his back on the others, as if about to do something tricky, and noted stealthily the weights which Carlier shouted out to him with unnecessary loudness. When all was over Makola whispered to himself: "The sun's very strong here for the tusks." Carlier said to Kayerts in a careless tone: "I say, chief, I might just as well give him a lift with this lot into the store."

As they were going back to the house Kayerts observed with a sigh: "It had to be done." And Carlier said: "It's deplorable, but, the men being Company's men the ivory is Company's ivory. We must look after it." "I will report to the Director, of course," said Kayerts. "Of course; let him decide," approved Carlier.

At midday they made a hearty meal. Kayerts sighed from time to time. Whenever they mentioned Makola's name they always added to it an opprobrious epithet. It eased their conscience. Makola gave himself a half-holiday, and bathed his children in the river. No one from Gobila's villages came near the station that day. No one came the next day, and the next, nor for a whole week. Gobila's people might have been dead and buried for any sign of life they gave. But they were only mourning for those they had lost by the witchcraft of white men, who had brought wicked people into their country. The wicked people were gone, but fear remained. Fear always remains. A man may destroy everything within himself, love and hate and belief, and even doubt; but as long as he clings to life he cannot destroy fear: the fear, subtle, indestructible, and terrible, that pervades his being; that tinges his thoughts; that lurks in his heart; that watches on his lips the struggle of his last breath. In his fear, the mild old Gobila offered extra human sacrifices to all the Evil Spirits that had taken possession of his white friends. His heart was heavy. Some warriors spoke about burning and killing, but the cautious old savage dissuaded them. Who could foresee the woe those mysterious creatures, if irritated, might bring? They should be left alone. Perhaps in time they would disappear into the earth as the first one had disappeared. His people must keep away from them, and hope for the best.

Kayerts and Carlier did not disappear, but remained above on this earth, that, somehow, they fancied had become bigger and very empty. It was not the absolute and dumb solitude of the post that impressed them so much as an inarticulate feeling that something from within them was gone, something that worked for their safety, and had kept the wilderness from interfering with their hearts. The images of home; the memory of people like them, of men that thought and felt as they used to think and feel, receded into distances made indistinct by the glare of unclouded sunshine. And out of the great silence of the surrounding wilderness, its very hopelessness and savagery seemed to approach them nearer, to draw them gently, to look upon them, to envelop them with a solicitude irresistible, familiar, and disgusting.

Days lengthened into weeks, then into months. Gobila's people drummed and yelled to every new moon, as of yore, but kept away from the station. Makola and Carlier tried once in a canoe to open communications, but were received with a shower of arrows, and had to fly back to the station for dear life. That attempt set the country up and down the river into an uproar that could be very distinctly heard for days. The steamer was late. At first they spoke of delay jauntily, then anxiously, then gloomily. The matter was becoming serious. Stores were running short. Carlier cast his lines off the bank, but the river was low, and the fish kept out in the stream. They dared not stroll far away from the station to shoot. Moreover, there was no game in the impenetrable forest. Once Carlier shot a hippo in the river. They had no boat to secure it, and it sank. When it floated up it drifted away, and Gobila's people secured the carcase. It was the occasion for a national holiday, but Carlier had a fit of rage over it and talked about the necessity of exterminating all the niggers before the country could be made habitable. Kayerts mooned about silently; spent hours looking at the portrait of his Melie. It represented a little girl with long bleached tresses and a rather sour face. His legs were much swollen, and he could hardly walk. Carlier, undermined by fever, could not swagger any more, but kept tottering about, still with a devil-may-care air, as became a man who remembered his crack regiment. He had become hoarse, sarcastic, and inclined to say unpleasant things. He called it "being frank with you." They had long ago reckoned their percentages on trade, including in them that last deal of "this infamous Makola." They had also concluded not to say anything about it. Kayerts hesitated at first—was afraid of the Director.

"He has seen worse things done on the quiet," maintained Carlier, with a hoarse laugh. "Trust him! He won't thank you if you blab. He is no better than you or me. Who will talk if we hold our tongues? There is nobody here."

That was the root of the trouble! There was nobody there; and being left there alone with their weakness, they became daily more like a pair of accomplices than like a couple of devoted friends. They had heard nothing from home for eight months. Every evening they said, "To-morrow we shall see the steamer." But one of the Company's steamers had been wrecked, and the Director was busy with the other, relieving very distant and important stations on the main river. He thought that the useless station, and the useless men, could wait. Meantime Kayerts and Carlier lived on rice boiled without salt, and cursed the Company, all Africa, and the day they were born. One must have lived on such diet to discover what ghastly trouble the necessity of swallowing one's food may become. There was literally nothing else in the station but rice and coffee; they drank the coffee without sugar. The last fifteen lumps Kayerts had solemnly locked away in his box, together with a half-bottle of Cognac, "in case of sickness," he explained. Carlier approved. "When one is sick," he said, "any little extra like that is cheering."

They waited. Rank grass began to sprout over the courtyard. The bell never rang now. Days passed, silent, exasperating, and slow. When the two men spoke, they snarled; and their silences were bitter, as if tinged by the bitterness of their thoughts.

One day after a lunch of boiled rice, Carlier put down his cup untasted, and said: "Hang it all! Let's have a decent cup of coffee for once. Bring out that sugar, Kayerts!"

"For the sick," muttered Kayerts, without looking up.

"For the sick," mocked Carlier. "Bosh! . . . Well! I am sick."

"You are no more sick than I am, and I go without," said Kayerts in a peaceful tone.

"Come! out with that sugar, you stingy old slave-dealer."

Kayerts looked up quickly. Carlier was smiling with marked insolence. And suddenly it seemed to Kayerts that he had never seen that man before. Who was he? He knew nothing about him. What was he capable of? There was a surprising flash of violent emotion within him, as if in the presence of something undreamt-of, dangerous, and final. But he managed to pronounce with composure—

"That joke is in very bad taste. Don't repeat it."

"Joke!" said Carlier, hitching himself forward on his seat. "I am hungry—I am sick—I don't joke! I hate hypocrites. You are a hypocrite. You are a slave-dealer. I am a slave-dealer. There's nothing but slave-dealers in this cursed country. I mean to have sugar in my coffee to-day, anyhow!"

"I forbid you to speak to me in that way," said Kayerts with a fair show of resolution.

"You!—What?" shouted Carlier, jumping up.

Kayerts stood up also. "I am your chief," he began, trying to master the shakiness of his voice.

"What?" yelled the other. "Who's chief? There's no chief here. There's nothing here: there's nothing but you and I. Fetch the sugar—you pot-bellied ass."

"Hold your tongue. Go out of this room," screamed Kayerts. "I dismiss you—you scoundrel!"

Carlier swung a stool. All at once he looked dangerously in earnest. "You flabby, good-for-nothing civilian—take that!" he howled.

Kayerts dropped under the table, and the stool struck the grass inner wall of the room. Then, as Carlier was trying to upset the table, Kayerts in desperation made a blind rush, head low, like a cornered pig would do, and over-turning his friend, bolted along the verandah, and into his room. He locked the door, snatched his revolver, and stood panting. In less than a minute Carlier was kicking at the door furiously, howling, "If you don't bring out that sugar, I will shoot you at sight, like a dog. Now then—one—two—three. You won't? I will show you who's the master."

Kayerts thought the door would fall in, and scrambled through the square hole that served for a window in his room. There was then the whole breadth of the house between them. But the other was apparently not strong enough to break in the door, and Kayerts heard him running round. Then he also began to run laboriously on his swollen legs. He ran as quickly as he could, grasping the revolver, and unable yet to understand what was happening to him. He saw in succession Makola's house, the store, the river, the ravine, and the low bushes; and he saw all those things again as he ran for the second time round the house. Then again they flashed past him. That morning he could not have walked a yard without a groan.

And now he ran. He ran fast enough to keep out of sight of the other man.

Then as, weak and desperate, he thought, "Before I finish the next round I shall die," he heard the other man stumble heavily, then stop. He stopped also. He had the back and Carlier the front of the house, as before. He heard him drop into a chair cursing, and suddenly his own legs gave way, and he slid down into a sitting posture with his back to the wall. His mouth was as dry as a cinder, and his face was wet with perspiration—and tears. What was it all about? He thought it must be a horrible illusion; he thought he was dreaming; he thought he was going mad! After a while he collected his senses. What did they quarrel about? That sugar! How absurd! He would give it to him—didn't want it himself. And he began scrambling to his feet with a sudden feeling of security. But before he had fairly stood upright, a commonsense reflection occurred to him and drove him back into despair. He thought: "If I give way now to that brute of a soldier, he will begin this horror again to-morrow—and the day after—every day—raise other pretensions, trample on me, torture me, make me his slave—and I will be lost! Lost! The steamer may not come for days—may never come." He shook so that he had to sit down on the floor again. He shivered forlornly. He felt he could not, would not move any more. He was completely distracted by the sudden perception that the position was without issue—that death and life had in a moment become equally difficult and terrible.

All at once he heard the other push his chair back; and he leaped to his feet with extreme facility. He listened and got confused. Must run again! Right or left? He heard footsteps. He darted to the left, grasping his revolver, and at the very same instant, as it seemed to him, they came into violent collision. Both shouted with surprise. A loud explosion took place between them; a roar of red fire, thick smoke; and Kayerts, deafened and blinded, rushed back thinking: "I am hit—it's all over." He expected the other to come round—to gloat over his agony. He caught hold of an upright of the roof—"All over!" Then he heard a crashing fall on the other side of the house, as if somebody had tumbled headlong over a chair—then silence. Nothing more happened. He did not die. Only his shoulder felt as if it had been badly wrenched, and he had lost his revolver. He was disarmed and helpless! He waited for his fate. The other man made no sound. It was a stratagem. He was stalking him now! Along what side? Perhaps he was taking aim this very minute!

After a few moments of an agony frightful and absurd, he decided to go and meet his doom. He was prepared for every surrender. He turned the corner, steadying himself with one hand on the wall; made a few paces, and nearly swooned. He had seen on the floor, protruding past the other corner, a pair of turned-up feet. A pair of white naked feet in red slippers. He felt deadly sick, and stood for a time in profound darkness. Then Makola appeared before him, saying quietly: "Come along, Mr. Kayerts. He is dead." He burst into tears of gratitude; a loud, sobbing fit of crying. After a time he found himself sitting in a chair and looking at Carlier, who lay stretched on his back. Makola was kneeling over the body.

"Is this your revolver?" asked Makola, getting up.

"Yes," said Kayerts; then he added very quickly, "He ran after me to shoot me—you saw!"

"Yes, I saw," said Makola. "There is only one revolver; where's his?"

"Don't know," whispered Kayerts in a voice that had become suddenly very faint.

"I will go and look for it," said the other, gently. He made the round along the verandah, while Kayerts sat still and looked at the corpse. Makola came back empty-handed, stood in deep thought, then stepped quietly into the dead man's room, and came out directly with a revolver, which he held up before Kayerts. Kayerts shut his eyes. Everything was going round. He found life more terrible and difficult than death. He had shot an unarmed man.

After meditating for a while, Makola said softly, pointing at the dead man who lay there with his right eye blown out—

"He died of fever." Kayerts looked at him with a stony stare. "Yes," repeated Makola, thoughtfully, stepping over the corpse, "I think he died of fever. Bury him to-morrow."

And he went away slowly to his expectant wife, leaving the two white men alone on the verandah.

Night came, and Kayerts sat unmoving on his chair. He sat quiet as if he had taken a dose of opium. The violence of the emotions he had passed through produced a feeling of exhausted serenity. He had plumbed in one short afternoon the depths of horror and despair, and now found repose in the conviction that life had no more secrets for him: neither had death! He sat by the corpse thinking; thinking very actively, thinking very new thoughts. He seemed to have broken loose from himself altogether. His old thoughts, convictions, likes and dislikes, things he respected and things he abhorred, appeared in their true light at last! Appeared contemptible and childish, false and ridiculous. He revelled in his new wisdom while he sat by the man he had killed. He argued with himself about all things under heaven with that kind of wrong-headed lucidity which may be observed in some lunatics. Incidentally he reflected that the fellow dead there had been a noxious beast anyway; that men died every day in thousands; perhaps in hundreds of thousands—who could tell?—and that in the number, that one death could not possibly make any difference; couldn't have any importance, at least to a thinking creature. He, Kayerts, was a thinking creature. He had been all his life, till that moment, a believer in a lot of nonsense like the rest of mankind—who are fools; but now he thought! He knew! He was at peace; he was familiar with the highest wisdom! Then he tried to imagine himself dead, and Carlier sitting in his chair watching him; and his attempt met with such unexpected success, that in a very few moments he became not at all sure who was dead and who was alive. This extraordinary achievement of his fancy startled him, however, and by a clever and timely effort of mind he saved himself just in time from becoming Carlier. His heart thumped, and he felt hot all over at the thought of that danger. Carlier! What a beastly thing! To compose his now disturbed nerves—and no wonder!—he tried to whistle a little. Then, suddenly, he fell asleep, or thought he had slept; but at any rate there was a fog, and somebody had whistled in the fog.

He stood up. The day had come, and a heavy mist had descended upon the land: the mist penetrating, enveloping, and silent; the morning mist of tropical lands; the mist that clings and kills; the mist white and deadly, immaculate and poisonous. He stood up, saw the body, and threw his arms above his head with a cry like that of a man who, waking from a trance, finds himself immured forever in a tomb. "Help! . . . . My God!"

A shriek inhuman, vibrating and sudden, pierced like a sharp dart the white shroud of that land of sorrow. Three short, impatient screeches followed, and then, for a time, the fog-wreaths rolled on, undisturbed, through a formidable silence. Then many more shrieks, rapid and piercing, like the yells of some exasperated and ruthless creature, rent the air.

Progress was calling to Kayerts from the river. Progress and civilization and all the virtues. Society was calling to its accomplished child to come, to be taken care of, to be instructed, to be judged, to be condemned; it called him to return to that rubbish heap from which he had wandered away, so that justice could be done.

Kayerts heard and understood. He stumbled out of the verandah, leaving the other man quite alone for the first time since they had been thrown there together. He groped his way through the fog, calling in his ignorance upon the invisible heaven to undo its work. Makola flitted by in the mist, shouting as he ran—

"Steamer! Steamer! They can't see. They whistle for the station. I go ring the bell. Go down to the landing, sir. I ring."

He disappeared. Kayerts stood still. He looked upwards; the fog rolled low over his head. He looked round like a man who has lost his way; and he saw a dark smudge, a cross-shaped stain, upon the shifting purity of the mist. As he began to stumble towards it, the station bell rang in a tumultuous peal its answer to the impatient clamour of the steamer.

The Managing Director of the Great Civilizing Company (since we know that civilization follows trade) landed first, and incontinently lost sight of the steamer. The fog down by the river was exceedingly dense; above, at the station, the bell rang unceasing and brazen.

The Director shouted loudly to the steamer:

"There is nobody down to meet us; there may be something wrong, though they are ringing. You had better come, too!"

And he began to toil up the steep bank. The captain and the engine-driver of the boat followed behind. As they scrambled up the fog thinned, and they could see their Director a good way ahead. Suddenly they saw him start forward, calling to them over his shoulder:—"Run! Run to the house! I've found one of them. Run, look for the other!"

He had found one of them! And even he, the man of varied and startling experience, was somewhat discomposed by the manner of this finding. He stood and fumbled in his pockets (for a knife) while he faced Kayerts, who was hanging by a leather strap from the cross. He had evidently climbed the grave, which was high and narrow, and after tying the end of the strap to the arm, had swung himself off. His toes were only a couple of inches above the ground; his arms hung stiffly down; he seemed to be standing rigidly at attention, but with one purple cheek playfully posed on the shoulder. And, irreverently, he was putting out a swollen tongue at his Managing Director.

The Last One
(2005)

ROBERT COOVER

This one asks at breakfast about the first one. My impertinent bride. Impertinent and imprudent (I tell her so and a gentle blush colors her cheeks and her lashes blink away a dewy mist, though her adoring gaze does not waver). Of course she will go the way of all the others. Perhaps before the day is over. Such a pity. But she is young and beautiful, not yet seventeen, and I indulge her. She was young and beautiful, I say, no older than you, and I indulged her in everything. But she did not respect my wishes.

Are your wishes so terrible then? she asks. There is a hint of a smile on her soft unrouged lips. Is she flirting with me?

Not at all, I say with an answering halfsmile. You will find me a devoted, attentive, and considerate husband, demanding almost nothing of you and desiring only to enrich your young life with all the means at my disposal.

Then I shall have to invent your demands that I might please you, she says, putting down her golden fork and fondly covering my hand with hers, for I am like that, too, and truly love you with all my heart. Her touch seems to find its way directly to my loins as if her sweet hand held me there and I am deliciously aroused, but I am also overswept by a sudden sorrow, for, though I have loved and miss them all, I know I shall miss this one more than any other. Indeed, I am already missing her. I shall begin by learning prudence and discretion, she adds, and her lips seem to draw together as though to form a kiss. She lets go my hand and reaches out to touch my blue beard with her fingertips. You are so beautiful! she sighs.

I know that I am not, I reply with a melancholic smile, recalling her ingenuous endearments of the night before, but I love your innocent love and wish that it might last forever.

And so it shall, she says. Why should it not? I am here to serve you in all ways that you might wish until death do us part, exactly as I promised and as is my one desire.

Alas, that's just short of forever, my dear, but I understand your loving intent. So now, to serve me well, please state your other, more intimate desires, that I might have the pleasure of fulfilling them. My entire wealth is at your disposal.

Oh, as your wife, of course, I can and do demand nothing, for that would be an impertinence worse than any other.

You have not a single favor to ask?

No. Well . . . No . . .

Please. Name it. It's yours.

I hope it's not impertinent, too. She lowers her head, peering modestly down into her lap where one hand now enfolds the other. As she does so, she exposes her alluring young nape with its delicate spinal knuckles and skin like silk. It is unutterably precious to me and begs a kiss, not of my ruthless blade (which regretfully I must sharpen before I leave), but of my worshipful lips, and it receives one. But . . . well . . . the nursery . . .

Yes? Inwardly, I am delighted—and flattered—that the thoughts of this playful and sensuous child have been so quickly drawn to aspirations of such maturity, however unlikely it is they can ever be realized. You wish it to be redecorated perhaps? A more cheerful color, a bit more light—?

No, no, it's lovely! It's only . . . well . . . She lifts her head to gaze wistfully up at me, and her soft bosom into which I am peering heaves with a tremulous sigh, and I think: Though I shall leave her today and test her as I always do—and must—we shall perhaps first taste the fruits of love once more . . . It's just that I sometimes feel so lost and inadequate in this grand world of yours, I need a quiet little place all my own to which I might retire to gather my poor child-ish wits about me and recover my composure. A place where I can be just by myself to reflect upon my love for you and upon ways that I might better please you. The nursery next to our bed chamber is as yet unoccupied—and here she blushes becomingly, and casts her eyes down once again, then timorously looks back up at me—and I feel at home in it, perhaps because I've not been long away from one. Might it just be mine, until . . . until we . . . you know. . .?

This is not the request that I have anticipated, but it befits her modesty and I recall that when she first arrived she brought with her all her childhood toys—as familiar company for her in this strange place, as she said, begging my pardon for her inability as yet to leave her past behind entirely. I've only brought the little things, she said. Granted, I say now, roguishly arching my brow and taking her hands to draw her up from her chair, provided I might now occupy for a short time that lovely place where I have so come to feel at home.

It is yours to possess without provision, she responds with a shy but welcoming smile.

She is of course vastly disappointed and not a little alarmed when later, clasped still in her arms, I inform her that I must undertake a sudden journey and leave her here to tend the castle while I am gone. We dress and I show her through those parts she has not yet visited, keeping my instructions to a minimum, assuring her that the staff is well-trained and accustomed to my frequent absences, providing her with keys to all my strongboxes and personal wealth and all the castle's rooms, including the blue room with the blue door, which I tell her, as I have told them all, she is not on any condition to enter. I add that she is not even to put the key in the lock, for if she does so she might expect the most dread-ful of punishments, but though I tell her this with my sword at the whetstone, she seems hardly to be listening, fascinated instead by a pair of songbirds in a gilded cage. When they stroke each other with their bills, she laughs and claps her hands and says: I'm not afraid! I know you will come back to me! Of course I will, I say. You can count on it. And which one of these unlocks the nursery door? she asks.

My invented travels take me, as they always do, to a small inn on a lake nearby, known for the quality of its food and wine, and for its privacy and discretion. I order a platter of succulent plump partridges with wild mushrooms, braised onions, and roasted aubergines and peppers, together with an opulent red wine, perfectly aged, from the north, but I find my appetite has failed me. I have known brief moments of the most intense pleasure and beauty, but my life has not on the whole been a happy one, and on this day I am as unhappy as I have ever been. I am utterly smitten by this pretty child, and I do not want to lose her, although no doubt I shall. I will return and find the bloodstained key and she will lose her head, as have the countless others, and I will lose a wife I dearly love, as I have loved them all. I am reminded in particular on this gray day of a lovely auburn-haired bride, a few years older than the present one, wilier perhaps, and wittier, yet delightfully fresh and childlike in her ways, who tried to stay my hand with story. Her tale, as she knelt there at the chopping block, was of a room with many doors, the rooms beyond them inhabited more by ghostly concepts than by persons and enmazed into a pretty riddle, whose solution, I supposed (we never got that far), was wisdom, or what passes for it in tales like these. Just for a moment I was enthralled and paused, her conjured room or rooms more real to me than my own, and had she not smiled to see me so and so unmasked my passing weakness, she might still wear her comely head. Alas. And it is not obedience I seek, but mere respect. I am a reasonable man, generous to a fault, demanding only this one small thing: that there be no intrusions upon my private quarters. Which, once upon a time, was what the blue room was for me, though now I dread to enter it myself, such a reeking charnel house it has become. So what am I defending? A principle, I suppose, as dead as the heap of headless corpses it has produced and now contains. And yet I can do no other. It is who I am, it is the bleak lot cast for me and for those I love; to do otherwise than as I must would be an act of the most abject cowardice and self-betrayal. I know that (I accept a truffled chocolate from a proffered tray, my appetite somewhat, if only faintly, revived by my recovered resolution). But oh how I long for a wife I might keep with her head on for more than a day or two! I think that I deserve as much.

I return by surprise and am surprised. My bride emerges from the nursery with tears of happiness in her eyes to see me, the blue room has not been entered, the golden key is immaculate, she has not even remembered that I asked her not to go there. She chatters on about her day, the games she's played and how she's missed me, and we enjoy another night together more delightful than the night before, if that is possible. Perhaps at last! I think, and fall asleep with my loved one securely in my arms, her sweet breath (she is alive! alive!) upon my breast.

I am tempted on the morrow to let the matter of the blue room rest. Has she not already proven that she is different from all the others? No, not yet, for she would not be the first to pass the first day's test, only to fall upon the second, and I know that I must do as I have always done. To honor the dead, if for no other reason. So once again I announce my abrupt departure, once again we walk the premises, opening and closing doors, visiting all the treasures of the castle, and once again I show her the key to the blue room and admonish her never to go there. Be not too curious, I say, and she replies, with barely a glance at the forbidden door, Do you know that, when you are being stern, a tiny furrow appears between your brows, exactly like the one that appears there when we are making love? And she pulls my head down with both her hands and kisses it. I love you so! she sighs.

My appetite this second day is much improved, and at the inn I order a handsome fish plucked fresh from the lake, beheaded, gutted, stuffed, and baked, with saffron rice on the side and tender wild asparagus. I am feeling elated. I am convinced I have found a love at last that I may keep. I sip the rich straw-colored wine that I have chosen, served precisely at the temperature of the lake itself, and allow myself to contemplate a future quite unlike my ensanguined past. I often use these mock journeys to seek out and woo a possible future bride, knowing that I must soon lose the one I have, but on this day my thoughts are wholly upon the castle I have left behind and the beautiful and obedient child who awaits me there, more mine than I am mine. Today I have even forgotten, I realize with a pained smile, to hone my monstrous blade. Well, perhaps it will join the mounted antlers, portraits, historic tapestries, and the other useless relics upon the walls. I replay the events of the day before, satisfied that she has satisfied me in all particulars. Excepting perhaps that when she returned the keys the one to the nursery was not among them. But, then, I told her the room was solely hers, did I not, she committed no infraction, broke no command, and I feel certain she will not again today, and so order up a bowl of tiny wild strawberries in a delicate liqueur, brushed with mint, to complete in festive manner my lakeside repast.

I am right. My surprise return does not even wholly surprise her. The blue room has not been invaded, the key's unstained. My bride has spent the day in the nursery, playing with her toys, she explains when she emerges from the room and locks it, and then she throws her arms around me and hugs me with such warm passion, my whole body feels like love's erected organ. Don't go away again! she whispers. Stay here with me always! We spend the rest of the dying day in bed and servants later bring us cheese and wine and fresh fruit, peeled and quartered. She tells me about the serving girl she had to scold for failing to remove the night-cloth from the songbirds' cage (You see, I can be useful to you when you're gone, she exclaims with a teasing smile and plucks a fishbone from my beard) and I provide her a fictitious account of my luncheon visit to a neighboring castellan to discuss proposed changes in the game laws. He is widowed yet again, I say, and is looking for a new young bride, both virtuous and beautiful. I told him to resign himself to cease his search. There was only one such left in the whole world and she is mine.

That night my dreams are free for once of severed heads, fountaining blood, eyes popping with terror from their sockets, and I am returned instead to the happier days of my all-but-forgotten childhood. My dream companion, though also a mere infant, is not unlike my present wife and we play games alone in some wild place that end in shy caresses. I awake in a state of profound joy and gratitude, as though some terrible burden has been lifted, receiving in reality the tender caresses of which I have been dreaming. But then later, after breakfast, when my bride has withdrawn to dress herself for the out of doors (It's a beautiful day! Let's walk the castle grounds! she exclaimed happily, and how could I refuse her, recalling, as I was, a certain sunny wild-flowered meadow where we might at midday lie?), my waking joy fades to despair, for I know that I must test her one more time, a third time, I can do no other, and I fear this day will be the one to break my heart.

Of course she is tearfully disappointed and clings to me, pleading with me not to go, and for a moment my resolution wavers—why must I torture myself this way?—but in the end I do, as I always do, what I must do. I explain: an urgent message, a friend in need, I must leave immediately and am not sure when I might return. We tour the castle and its wealth as before, I warn her about the blue room, I give her the keys. She accepts them without so much as a glance, throws herself into my arms, then tears herself away and runs weeping into the nursery. What have I done? I am weeping, too, unable to stay, unable to leave, wringing my hands, pulling at my beard, pacing the castle corridors. No, I shall not go! And yet I must! I do remember this time to sharpen my sword, not because I wish to use it—oh no, please no!—but because, if I must use it, I wish it to be mercifully swift in its barbarous labors. And perhaps because it gives me something more to do, to delay a departure I am so loathe to make. As the whetstone sings its shrieking song, I think: Of course I must go, this trial is not over and must as always be concluded, but need it be today? Another message might arrive: Stay, my friend. Come tomorrow if you can. Why not? Even should she fail me this third time, we would at least have this last day and night together.

I sheathe my sword and hurry to the nursery to tell her so. It is locked. I lift my hand to knock but am stopped by the sound of voices within, her voice at least. Are you lonely? she is asking. Are you in need of company? Probably she is talking to herself in the mirror. Or to her toys. Yet I am troubled by it, and quietly withdraw. I go outside to peer in through the window, but the drapes are drawn. Now, why would she do that on such a lovely day as this? I ask myself, feeling my suspicions rise, and then as quickly ask: And what am I doing prowling around here outside her window like a common thief, a lowly peeper? I reject my behavior as improper and ungallant—as for the darkened room, she is mourning my departure, after all—and I decide to continue on my way as first announced. It is time to bring this sorry business to an end.

Before I reach the inn, however, I turn back. Was hers the only voice I heard? Almost certainly, and yet . . . I approach the castle from a stand of trees and watch awhile from there. What do I expect to see? I do not know, though disturbing thoughts race through my head and my perspiring hand is on my sword. Of course, nothing happens. Why should it? I begin to feel a fool, all the more so for having passed up that innocent frolic on the meadow, in exchange for such base misery as this, unworthy of my age and of my station. I decide to return immediately: My friend is well, his problem solved, a messenger met me on the way.

My bride greets me as before, throwing herself tearfully into my arms with abject delight as if I've been absent for many days. I try to peek past her shoulder into the nursery, but the door is closed. Locked, no doubt. She strips my shirt away to nuzzle my bare chest as she is wont to do when making love, then tugs me toward our bed chamber, whispering her maidenly endearments. I long for the pleasure that she offers, but am too agitated to perform my part or even to think of doing so. I suggest instead the stroll through the castle grounds we had originally planned and gaily—Oh yes! she cries—she hurries off to the kitchen to arrange a basket lunch. The nursery door is indeed locked, I discover, and I recall now that she has left my side from time to time at night to visit there. A restless sleeper lonely for her lost past? Or . . .? I put my ear to the door. Nothing. Of course, nothing. What's the matter with me? Standing there, leaning against the locked nursery door with my shirttails dangling like drooping pennants, I suddenly feel desperately old and world-weary, and I know that our walk will not revive my spirits.

It does not. The meadow is there, just as I have remembered it, with its downy bed of soft grasses and silken petals, and naked upon it in the sunlight under the blue breezeless sky, my young bride is a most voluptuous sight, but I am as unaroused as before, and turn quite irritable when she tries to be of help to me. Where has she learned such things? I do not ask her that of course, but complain instead that I feel unwell and fear I may have caught a fever. She could not be more solicitous, insisting that we return to the castle immediately where I shall spend the rest of the day in bed, and she will care for me, and bring me tea and read to me and with her own gentle hands rub all the aches away, but that too, inexplicably, causes my choler to rise and I must bite my beard to refrain from bellowing something at her I would afterwards regret.

Only much later, after she has left me, presumably sleeping peacefully following her wifely ministrations, to return to her precious nursery, do I realize I have forgotten to check the blue room key (I do: no stains), that's not the point any longer. Stealthily, I creep once more to that door between us and press my ear against it: She is singing to herself in there, or humming, a kind of marching tune—Step lively now! she says—and now and then a happy little laugh escapes her, a girlish giggle. That she can enjoy such carefree play all by herself, if she is by herself, when I am ill, or presumably ill—I might be dying for all she knows—also stirs my fury and resentment, and to calm myself (I fully intend now to visit the nursery, with or without her invitation, and regardless of any promises to the contrary, but only when in full control of my emotions, now in such turmoil) I take the keys and pace the castle corridors in my nightshirt, counting by candlelight, it would seem to anyone who saw me, my possessions, one madness thus (my possessions are uncountable) concealing another.

At some point in my midnight wanderings, I find myself in front of the infamous blue door, the room beyond it once the very locus of my honor and my integrity, and I wonder at the life that I have made. A man of my wealth and power has certain obligations, of course, but I never meant to be cruel, my intentions always noble and instructive, no matter how my actions may appear. I enter it (the nursery key is missing) but am immediately driven out by the stench within: there are rotting heads and bodies and mutilated limbs everywhere and the floor is covered with clotted blood, the horrid proofs of my severe and lonely existence. I have lived, without remorse, a principled life, and I must be resolutely who I am, else I am no one at all—and yet . . . Well . . . Such a sickening mess here at the center! Even I am excluded from what might be called the very heart of my own being!

This encounter with the ghastly carnage of my past has a sobering and calmative effect, and I return much subdued to our room wherein my bride lies sleeping now, determined that on the morrow I shall seal that fatal chamber up forever and throw away the key, not so much for her sake, or any who might follow, as for my own. My beloved sleeps there peacefully upon her back, herself toylike in her pretty stillness, the faintest traces of a smile upon her lips, as though her dreams were sweet and pleasing her. That I somewhat shape those dreams I know and know that I must treat her always with tolerance and loving kindness, and beware my volcanic temper. I have heard her, alone, secluded, give vent to the loneliness she suffers in my absence and as well to her more playful whims, which in my preceptive solemnity beyond the nursery I have perhaps unwittingly suppressed, and maybe she meant for me to overhear these things that I might learn to remain always by her side and to join her games, however lightsome, with an open and willing heart. To do so is anyway now my firm resolve, and I slip into the bed beside her full of affection and tenderness and easefully enter her and, at peace with myself at last, fall asleep in our locked embrace.

I wake at dawn to an empty bed and think I hear her in the nursery again. I smile sleepily, imagining her there in all her loveliness, surrounded by her little things, and I close my eyes again and think: Let her be. But even as this thought drifts benignly through my mind, I find myself at the door once more, my ear pressed against it, my hand testing the handle. Did I hear a sound within? No, it's someone coming down the corridor! I leap back into bed and pull the covers up just as she enters cheerfully with a breakfast tray. Good morning, my sweet love! I've brought you all your favorite things! I want to make you well again!

I'm much improved, I say, and I rub my eyes and scratch my beard, which I know amuses her. Your kisses have quite revived me, though I think I may require yet another dosage or two.

I am not well trained in the healing arts, she replies with a twinkling smile, setting the breakfast tray aside and crawling in beside me, but you will find me a quick and eager pupil.

I decide to pass the day in bed, close to the nursery door, and I ask my chamberlain to bring me my accounts that I might go over them there, suggesting to my bride that she is free to do as she pleases while I am working. I assume that she will return to the nursery, but she chooses instead to acquaint herself more thoroughly with the running of the castle that she might, as she says, better serve it as its new mistress. Sometimes I hear noises in there, or think I do, and I hurry over to hear what I can hear, but these excursions are often as not interrupted by her sudden arrival from the hallway, and I must make clumsy excuses about a fallen pen or a troublesome insect or a cramp in my leg: Oh let me squeeze the hurt away! she exclaims, and I must feign an appetite, quite vanished suddenly, for her amorous attentions.

Finally there is nothing for it but to arrange her longer absence somehow that I might, leisurely and unobserved, examine her retreat. And so my illness worsens. She must take the carriage and go visit the doctor, some miles hence, and deliver to him the sealed letter which I place into her hands, then bring back to me the potion I request therein. She protests, she cannot bear to leave me alone in my suffering, let a manservant go, she will stay and care for me. Servants are a meddlesome and unreliable lot, I say. A sealed letter is like an open invitation. I trust only you.

She kisses me passionately, almost tearfully. Don't even move till I return! she cries and, hastily tossing a silken shawl over her shoulders for the journey, she dashes away.

I watch the gilded carriage careen at full gallop out of the yard, then try the nursery door. It is locked, as I have supposed, and its key is missing from the ring, also as I have supposed. What surprises me is that my old master key does not work either. I have a drawerful of ancient keys and think to try them, though it means another visit to the stomach-turning horrors of the blue room. They are equally useless, that hellish errand in vain, and I heave the lot across the room, my frustration mounting. Outside, the window is also locked, or stuck. What's worse, there are fresh boot tracks out there, both coming and going, and my mind is suddenly awhirl with the most abominable imaginings. Of course I myself was standing there only yesterday, those tracks are no doubt mine: I try to calm myself. I drop the brick I might in my madness have heaved through the window, without regard for the stories I would have had to invent thereafter, and I return to my bed chamber, now truly ill.

I prepare to retire once more, perhaps this time with a glass of wine, something noble, complex, engaging, that I might free my thoughts from the intolerable virulence that has invaded them, but just as I am about to ring for a servant, I hear whispering inside the nursery. A man! Or men! My worst fears are justified! I try to force the door without success, my fever raging now, but it will not give way. I rush out to get my sword and as I'm hurriedly sharpening its blade, I hear the carriage returning to the yard. There is no time to lose! I am back at the nursery door, hacking wildly at it, when I hear her enter the castle, breathlessly calling out my name: I am here, dear love! I have returned! And, as I break through at last, she appears behind me. Oh my, she says. Whatever are you doing?

Inside the room, her toys are neatly spread about: a miniature roofless castle, richly appointed, set upon parklike grounds made of a green blanket and pebbles from the garden for the drives on which tiny horsedrawn carriages are placed, a mirror for a pond, twisted yarn for trees and shrubs, porcelain figurines standing as statues on wooden blocks, and pillows heaped about to represent the surrounding hills. The rooms inside the toy castle are elegantly carpeted and hung with tapestries and damask, the chairs and sofas are covered with silks and velvet and fringed with gold, the tiny carved dining table set with branched candlesticks and a golden dinner service, and full-length looking-glasses with gilded frames have been mounted in the corridors and private chambers. In one of the these there is a small sign which reads: THE REWARD OF DISOBEDIENCE AND IMPRUDENT CURIOSITY, and the dolls that populate it, all little bearded men, are alive, even the ones whose heads have been taken off and mounted on the walls. Do you like them, my little toys? my bride asks from behind my shoulder. She is smiling tenderly but somewhat wistfully down upon me, and I am touched for a moment by the mystery of her and of all the brides before her. You promised, she says without reproach, though not without a trace of regret, and I feel the withering power of her affectionate disappointment. You were so lovely, she sighs. I so much wished you might at last be the one that I could keep. And she picks me up by my head and sets me inside the castle with the others.

Continuity of Parks
(1956)

JULIO CORTÁZAR

He had begun to read the novel a few days before. He had put it down because of some urgent business conferences, opened it again on his way back to the estate by train; he permitted himself a slowly growing interest in the plot, in the characterizations. That afternoon, after writing a letter giving his power of attorney and discussing a matter of joint ownership with the manager of his estate, he returned to the book in the tranquillity of his study which looked out upon the park with its oaks. Sprawled in his favorite armchair, its back toward the door—even the possibility of an intrusion would have irritated him, had he thought of it— he let his left hand caress repeatedly the green velvet upholstery and set to reading the final chapters. He remembered effortlessly the names and his mental image of the characters; the novel spread its glamour over him almost at once. He tasted the almost perverse pleasure of disengaging himself line by line from the things around him, and at the same time feeling his head rest comfortably on the green velvet of the chair with its high back, sensing that the cigarettes rested within reach of his hand, that beyond the great windows the air of afternoon danced under the oak trees in the park. Word by word, licked up by the sordid dilemma of the hero and heroine, letting himself be absorbed to the point where the images settled down and took on color and movement, he was witness to the final encounter in the mountain cabin. The woman arrived first, apprehensive; now the lover came in, his face cut by the backlash of a branch. Admirably, she stanched the blood with her kisses, but he rebuffed her caresses, he had not come to perform again the ceremonies of a secret passion, protected by a world of dry leaves and furtive paths through the forest. The dagger warmed itself against his chest, and underneath liberty pounded, hidden close. A lustful, panting dialogue raced down the pages like a rivulet of snakes, and one felt it had all been decided from eternity. Even to those caresses which writhed about the lover's body, as though wishing to keep him there, to dissuade him from it; they sketched abominably the frame of that other body it was necessary to destroy. Nothing had been forgotten: alibis, unforeseen hazards, possible mistakes. From this hour on, each instant had its use minutely assigned. The cold-blooded, twice-gone-over reexamination of the details was barely broken off so that a hand could caress a cheek. It was beginning to get dark.

Not looking at one another now, rigidly fixed upon the task which awaited them, they separated at the cabin door. She was to follow the trail that led north. On the path leading in the opposite direction, he turned for a moment to watch her running, her hair loosened and flying. He ran in turn, crouching among the trees and hedges until, in the yellowish fog of dusk, he could distinguish the avenue of trees which led up to the house. The dogs were not supposed to bark, they did not bark. The estate manager would not be there at this hour, and he was not there. He went up the three porch steps and entered. The woman's words reached him over the thudding of blood in his ears: first a blue chamber, then a hall, then a carpeted stairway. At the top, two doors. No one in the first room, no one in the second. The door of the salon, and then, the knife in hand, the light from the great windows, the high back of an armchair covered in green velvet, the head of the man in the chair reading a novel.

Children of the Sea
(1993)

EDWIDGE DANTICAT

They say behind the mountains are more mountains. Now I know it's true. I also know there are timeless waters, endless seas, and lots of people in this world whose names don't matter to anyone but themselves. I look up at the sky and I see you there. I see you crying like a crushed snail, the way you cried when I helped you pull out your first loose tooth. Yes, I did love you then. Somehow when I looked at you, I thought of fiery red ants. I wanted you to dig your fingernails into my skin and drain out all my blood.

I don't know how long we'll be at sea. There are thirty-six other deserting souls on this little boat with me. White sheets with bright red spots float as our sail.

When I got on board I thought I could still smell the semen and the innocence lost to those sheets. I look up there and I think of you and all those times you resisted. Sometimes I felt like you wanted to, but I knew you wanted me to respect you. You thought I was testing your will, but all I wanted was to be near you. Maybe it's like you've always said. I imagine too much. I am afraid I am going to start having nightmares once we get deep at sea. I really hate having the sun in my face all day long. If you see me again, I'll be so dark.

Your father will probably marry you off now, since I am gone. Whatever you do, please don't marry a soldier. They're almost not human.

❀

haiti est comme tu l'as laissé. yes, just the way you left it. bullets day and night. same hole. same everything. i'm tired of the whole mess. i get so cross and irritable. i pass the time by chasing roaches around the house. i pound my heel on their heads. they make me so mad. everything makes me mad. i am cramped inside all day. they've closed the schools since the army took over. no one is mentioning the old president's name. papa burnt all his campaign posters and old buttons. manman buried her buttons in a hole behind the house. she thinks he might come back. she says she will unearth them when he does. no one comes out of their house. not a single person. papa wants me to throw out those tapes of your radio shows. i destroyed some music tapes, but i still have your voice. i thank god you got out when you did. all the other youth federation members have disappeared. no one has heard from them. i think they might all be in prison. maybe they're all dead. papa worries a little about you. he doesn't hate you as much as you think. the other day i heard him asking manman, do you think the boy is dead? manman said she didn't know. i think

251

he regrets being so mean to you. i don't sketch my butterflies anymore because i don't even like seeing the sun. besides, manman says that butterflies can bring news. the bright ones bring happy news and the black ones warn us of deaths. we have our whole lives ahead of us. you used to say that, remember? but then again things were so very different then.

There is a pregnant girl on board. She looks like she might be our age. Nineteen or twenty. Her face is covered with scars that look like razor marks. She is short and speaks in a singsong that reminds me of the villagers in the north. Most of the other people on the boat are much older than I am. I have heard that a lot of these boats have young children on board. I am glad this one does not. I think it would break my heart watching some little boy or girl every single day on this sea, looking into their empty faces to remind me of the hopelessness of the future in our country. It's hard enough with the adults. It's hard enough with me.

I used to read a lot about America before I had to study so much for the university exams. I am trying to think, to see if I read anything more about Miami. It is sunny. It doesn't snow there like it does in other parts of America. I can't tell exactly how far we are from there. We might be barely out of our own shores. There are no borderlines on the sea. The whole thing looks like one. I cannot even tell if we are about to drop off the face of the earth. Maybe the world is flat and we are going to find out, like the navigators of old. As you know, I am not very religious. Still I pray every night that we won't hit a storm. When I do manage to sleep, I dream that we are caught in one hurricane after another. I dream that the winds come of the sky and claim us for the sea. We go under and no one hears from us again.

I am more comfortable now with the idea of dying. Not that I have completely accepted it, but I know that it might happen. Don't be mistaken. I really do not want to be a martyr. I know I am no good to anybody dead, but if that is what's coming, I know I cannot just scream at it and tell it to go away.

I hope another group of young people can do the radio show. For a long time that radio show was my whole life. It was nice to have radio like that for a while, where we could talk about what we wanted from government, what we wanted for the future of our country. There are a lot of Protestants on this boat. A lot of them see themselves as Job or the Children of Israel. I think some of them are hoping something will plunge down from the sky and part the sea for us. They say the Lord gives and the Lord takes away. I have never been given very much. What was there to take away?

if only i could kill. if i knew some good *wanga* magic, i would wipe them off the face of the earth. a group of students got shot in front of fort dimanche prison today. they were demonstrating for the bodies of the radio six. that is what they are calling you all. the radio six. you have a name. you have a reputation. a lot of people think you are dead like the others. they want the bodies turned over to the families. this afternoon, the army finally did give some bodies back. they told the families to go collect them at the rooms for indigents at the morgue. our neighbor madan roger came home with her son's head and not much else. honest to god, it was just his head. at the morgue, they say a car ran over him and took the head off his body. when madan roger went to the morgue, they gave her the head. by the time we saw her, she had been carrying the head all over port-au-prince. just to show what's been done to her son. the macoutes by the house were laughing at her. they asked her if that was her dinner. it took ten people to hold her back from jumping on them. they would have killed her, the dogs. i will never go outside again. not even in the yard to breathe the air. they are always watching you, like vultures. at night i can't sleep. i count the bullets in the dark. i keep wondering if it is true. did you really get out? i wish there was some way i could be sure that you really went away. yes, i will. i will keep writing like we promised to do. i hate it, but i will keep writing. you keep writing too, okay? and when we see each other again, it will seem like we lost no time.

Today was our first real day at sea. Everyone was vomiting with each small rocking of the boat. The faces around me are showing their first charcoal layer of sunburn. "Now we will never be mistaken for Cubans," one man said. Even though some of the Cubans are black too. The man said he was once on a boat with a group of Cubans. His boat had stopped to pick up the Cubans on an island off the Bahamas. When the Coast Guard came for them, they took the Cubans to Miami and sent him back to Haiti. Now he was back on the boat with some papers and documents to show that the police in Haiti were after him. He had a broken leg too, in case there was any doubt.

One old lady fainted from sunstroke. I helped revive her by rubbing some of the salt water on her lips. During the day it can be so hot. At night, it is so cold. Since there are no mirrors, we look at each others faces to see just how frail and sick we are starting to look.

Some of the women sing and tell stories to each other to appease the vomiting. Still, I watch the sea. At night, the sky and the sea are one. The stars look so huge and so close. They make for very bright reflections in the sea. At times I feel like I can just reach out and pull a star down from the sky as though it is a breadfruit or a calabash or something that could be of use to us on this journey.

When we sing, *Beloved Haiti, there is no place like you. I had to leave you before I could understand you,* some of the women start crying. At times, I just want to stop in the middle of the song and cry myself. To hide my tears, I pretend like I am getting another attack of nausea, from the sea smell. I no longer join in the singing.

You probably do not know much about this, because you have always been so closely watched by your father in that well-guarded house with your genteel mother. No, I am not making fun of you for this. If anything, I am jealous. If I was a girl, maybe I would have been at home and not out politicking and getting myself into something like this. Once you have been at sea for a couple of days, it smells like every fish you have ever eaten, every crab you have ever caught, every jellyfish that has ever bitten your leg. I am so tired of the smell. I am also tired of the way the people on this boat are starting to stink. The pregnant girl, Célianne, I don't know how she takes it. She stares into space all the time and rubs her stomach.

I have never seen her eat. Sometimes the other women offer her a piece of bread and she takes it, but she has no food of her own. I cannot help feeling like she will have this child as soon as she gets hungry enough.

She woke up screaming the other night. I thought she had a stomach ache. Some water started coming into the boat in the spot where she was sleeping. There is a crack at the bottom of the boat that looks as though, if it gets any bigger, it will split the boat in two. The captain cleared us aside and used some tar to clog up the hole. Everyone started asking him if it was okay, if they were going to be okay. He said he hoped the Coast Guard would find us soon.

You can't really go to sleep after that. So we all stared at the tar by the moonlight. We did this until dawn. I cannot help but wonder how long this tar will hold out.

※

papa found your tapes. he started yelling at me, asking if I was crazy keeping them. he is just waiting for the gasoline ban to be lifted so we can get out of the city. he is always pestering me these days because he cannot go out driving his van. all the american factories are closed. he kept yelling at me about the tapes. he called me selfish, and he asked if i hadn't seen or heard what was happening to man-crazy whores like me. i shouted that i wasn't a whore. he had no business calling me that. he pushed me against the wall for disrespecting him. he spat in my face. i wish those macoutes would kill him. i wish he would catch a bullet so we could see how scared he really is. he said to me, i didn't send your stupid trouble maker away. i started yelling at him. yes, you did. yes, you did. yes, you did, you pig peasant. i don't know why i said that. he slapped me and kept slapping me really hard until manman came and grabbed me away from him. i wish one of those bullets would hit me.

※

The tar is holding up so far. Two days and no more leaks. Yes, I am finally an African. I am even darker than your father. I wanted to buy a straw hat from one of the ladies, but she would not sell it to me for the last two gourdes I have left in change. Do you think your money is worth anything to me here? she asked me. Sometimes, I forget where I am. If I keep daydreaming like I have been doing, I will walk off the boat to go for a stroll.

The other night I dreamt that I died and went to heaven. This heaven was nothing like I expected. It was at the bottom of the sea. There were starfishes and mermaids all around me. The mermaids were dancing and singing in Latin like the priests do at the cathedral during Mass. You were there with me too, at the bottom of the sea. You were with your family, off to the side. Your father was acting like he was better than everyone else and he was standing in front of a sea cave blocking you from my view. I tried to talk to you, but every time I opened my mouth, water bubbles came out. No sounds.

※

they have this thing now that they do. if they come into a house and there is a son and mother there, they hold a gun to their heads. they make the son sleep with his mother. if it is a daughter and father, they do the same thing. some nights papa sleeps at his brother's, uncle pressoir's house. uncle pressoir sleeps at our house, just in case they come. that way papa will never be forced to lie down in bed with me. instead, uncle pressoir would be forced to, but that would not be so bad. we know a girl who had a child by her father that way. that is what papa does not want to happen, even if he is killed. there is still no gasoline to buy. otherwise we would be in ville rose already. papa has a friend who is going to get him some gasoline from a soldier. as soon as we get the gasoline, we are going to drive quick and fast until we

find civilization. that's how papa puts it, civilization. he says things are not as bad in the provinces. i am still not talking to him. i don't think i ever will. manman says it is not his fault. he is trying to protect us. he cannot protect us. only god can protect us. the soldiers can come and do with us what they want. that makes papa feel weak, she says. he gets angry when he feels weak. why should he be angry with me? i am not one of the pigs with the machine guns. she asked me what really happened to you. she said she saw your parents before they left for the provinces. they did not want to tell her anything. i told her you took a boat after they raided the radio station. you escaped and took a boat to heaven knows where. she said, he was going to make a good man, that boy. sharp, like a needle point, that boy, he took the university exams a year before everyone else in this area. manman has respect for people with ambitions. she said papa did not want you for me because it did not seem as though you were going to do any better for me than he and manman could. he wants me to find a man who will do me some good. someone who will make sure that i have more than i have now. it is not enough for a girl to be just pretty anymore. we are not that well connected in society. the kind of man that papa wants for me would never have anything to do with me. all anyone can hope for is just a tiny bit of love, manman says, like a drop in a cup if you can get it, or a waterfall, a flood, if you can get that too. we do not have all that many high-up connections, she says, but you are an educated girl. what she counts for educated is not much to anyone but us anyway. they should be announcing the university exams on the radio next week. then i will know if you passed. i will listen for your name.

※

We spent most of yesterday telling stories. Someone says, Krik? You answer, Krak! And they say, I have many stories I could tell you, and then they go on and tell these stories to you, but mostly to themselves. Sometimes it feels like we have been at sea longer than the many years that I have been on this earth. The sun comes up and goes down. That is how you know it has been a whole day. I feel like we are sailing for Africa. Maybe we will go to Guinin, to live with the spirits, to be with everyone who has come and has died before us. They would probably turn us away from there too. Someone has a transistor and sometimes we listen to radio from the Bahamas. They treat Haitians like dogs in the Bahamas, a woman says. To them, we are not human. Even though their music sounds like ours. Their people look like ours. Even though we had the same African fathers who probably crossed these same seas together.

Do you want to know how people go to the bathroom on the boat? Probably the same way they did on those slaves ships years ago. They set aside a little corner for that. When I have to pee, I just pull it, lean over the rail, and do it very quickly. When I have to do the other thing, I rip a piece of something, squat down and do it, and throw the waste in the sea. I am always embarrassed by the smell. It is so demeaning having to squat in front of so many people. People turn away, but not always. At times I wonder if there is really land on the other side of the sea. Maybe the sea is endless. Like my love for you.

※

last night they came to madan roger's house. papa hurried inside as soon as madan roger's screaming started. the soldiers were looking for her son. madan roger was screaming, you killed him already. we buried his head. you can't kill him twice. they were shouting at her, do you belong to the youth federation with those vagabonds who were on the radio? she was yelling, do i look like a youth to you? can you identify your son's other associates? they asked her. papa had us tiptoe from the house into the latrine out back. we could hear it all from there. i thought i was going to choke on the smell of rotting poupou. they kept shouting at madan roger, did your son belong to the youth federation? wasn't he on the radio talking about the police? did he say, down with tonton macoutes? did he say, down with the army? he said that the military had to go; didn't he write slogans? he had meetings, didn't he? he demonstrated on the streets. you should have advised him better. she cursed on their mothers' graves. she just came out and shouted it, i hope your mothers will never rest in their cursed graves! she was just shouting it out, you killed him once already! you want to kill me too? go ahead. i don't care anymore. I'm dead already. you have already done the worst to me that you can do. you have killed my soul. they kept at it, asking her questions at the top of their voices: was your son a traitor? tell me all the names of his friends who were traitors just like him. madan roger finally shouts, yes, he was one! he belonged to that group. he was on the radio. he was on the streets at these demonstrations. he hated you like i hate you criminals. you killed him. they start to pound at her. you can hear it. you can hear the guns coming down on her head. it sounds like they are cracking all the bones in her body. manman whispers to papa, you can't just let them kill her. go and give them some money like you gave them for your daughter. papa says, the only money i have left is to get us out of here tomorrow. manman whispers, we cannot just stay here and let them kill her. manman starts moving like she is going out the door. papa grabs her neck and pins her to the latrine wall. tomorrow we are going to ville rose, he says. you will not spoil that for the family. you will not put us in that situation. you will not get us killed. going out there will be like trying to raise the dead. she is not dead yet, manman says, maybe we can help her. i will make you stay if i have to, he says to her. my mother buries her face in the latrine wall. she starts to cry. you can hear madan roger screaming. they are beating her, pounding on her until you don't hear anything else. manman tells papa, you cannot let them kill somebody just because you are afraid. papa says, oh yes, you *can* let them kill somebody because you are afraid. they are the law. it is their right. we are just being good citizens, following the law of the land. it has happened before all over this country and tonight it will happen again and there is nothing we can do.

Célianne spent the night groaning. She looks like she has been ready for a while, but maybe the child is being stubborn. She just screamed that she is bleeding. There is an older woman here who looks like she has had a lot of children herself. She says Célianne is not bleeding at all. Her water sack has broken.

The only babies I have ever seen right after birth are baby mice. Their skin looks veil thin. You can see all the blood vessels and all their organs. I have always wanted to poke them to see if my finger would go all the way through the skin.

I have moved to the other side of the boat so I will not have to look *inside* Célianne. People are just watching. The captain asks the midwife to keep Célianne steady so she will not rock any more holes into the boat. Now we have three cracks covered with tar. I am scared to think of what would happen if we had to choose among ourselves who would stay on the boat and who should die. Given the choice to make a decision like that, we would all act like vultures, including me.

The sun will set soon. Someone says that this child will be just another pair of hungry lips. At least it will have its mother's breasts, says an old man. Everyone will eat their last scraps of food today.

※

there is a rumor that the old president is coming back. there is a whole bunch of people going to the airport to meet him. papa says we are not going to stay in port-au-prince to find out if this is true or if it is a lie. they are selling gasoline at the market again. the carnival groups have taken to the streets. we are heading the other way, to ville rose. maybe there i will be able to sleep at night. it is not going to turn out well with the old president coming back, manman now says. people are just too hopeful, and sometimes hope is the biggest weapon of all to use against us. people will believe anything. they will claim to see the christ return and march on the cross backwards if there is enough hope. manman told papa that you took the boat. papa told me before we left this morning that he thought himself a bad father for everything that happened. he says a father should be able to speak to his children like a civilized man. all the craziness here has made him feel like he cannot do that anymore. all he wants to do is live. he and manman have not said a word to one another since we left the latrine. i know that papa does not hate us, not in the way that i hate those soldiers, those macoutes, and all those people here who shoot guns. on our way to ville rose, we saw dogs licking two dead faces. one of them was a little boy who was lying on the side of the road with the sun in his dead open eyes. we saw a soldier shoving a woman out of a hut, calling her a witch. he was shaving the woman's head, but of course we never stopped. papa didn't want to go in madan roger's house and check on her before we left. he thought the soldiers might still be there. papa was driving the van real fast. i thought he was going to kill us. we stopped at an open market on the way. manman got some black cloth for herself and for me. she cut the cloth in two pieces and we wrapped them around our heads to mourn madan roger. when i am used to ville rose, maybe i will sketch you some butterflies, depending on the news that they bring me.

※

Célianne had a girl baby. The woman acting as a midwife is holding the baby to the moon and whispering prayers. . . . *God, this child You bring into the world, please guide her as You please through all her days on this earth.* The baby has not cried.

We had to throw our extra things in the sea because the water is beginning to creep in slowly. The boat needs to be lighter. My two gourdes in change had to be thrown overboard as an offering to Agwé, the spirit of the water. I heard the captain whisper to someone yesterday that they might have to *do something* with some of the people who never recovered from seasickness. I am afraid that soon they may ask me to throw out this notebook. We might all have to strip down to the way we were born, to keep ourselves from drowning.

Célianne's child is a beautiful child. They are calling her Swiss, because the word *Swiss* was written on the small knife they used to cut her umbilical cord. If she was my daughter, I would call her soleil, sun, moon, or star, after the elements. She still hasn't cried. There is gossip circulating about how Célianne became pregnant. Some people are saying that she had an affair with a married man and her parents threw her out. Gossip spreads here like everywhere else.

Do you remember our silly dreams? Passing the university exams and then studying hard to go until the end, the farthest of all that we can go in school. I know your father might never approve of me. I was going to try to win him over. He would have to cut out my heart to keep me from loving you. I hope you are writing like you promised. Jésus, Marie, Joseph! Everyone smells so bad. They get into arguments and they say to one another, "It is only my misfortune that would lump me together with an indigent like you." Think of it. They are fighting about being superior when we all might drown like straw.

There is an old toothless man leaning over to see what I am writing. He is sucking on the end of an old wooden pipe that has not seen any fire for a very long time now. He looks like a painting. Seeing things simply, you could fill a museum with the sights you have here. I still feel like such a coward for running away. Have you heard anything about my parents? Last time I saw them on the beach, my mother had a *kriz*. She just fainted on the sand. I saw her coming to as we started sailing away. But of course I don't know if she is doing all right.

The water is really piling into the boat. We take turns pouring bowls of it out. I don't know what is keeping the boat from splitting in two. Swiss isn't crying. They keep slapping her behind, but she is not crying.

of course the old president didn't come. they arrested a lot of people at the airport, shot a whole bunch of them down. i heard it on the radio. while we were eating tonight, i told papa that i love you. i don't know if it will make a difference. i just want him to know that i have loved somebody in my life. in case something happens to one of us, i think he should know this about me, that i have loved someone besides only my mother and father in my life. i know you would understand. you are the one for large noble gestures. i just wanted him to know that i was capable of loving somebody. he looked me straight in the eye and said nothing to me. i love you until my hair shivers at the thought of anything happening to you. papa just turned his face away like he was rejecting my very birth. i am writing you from under the banyan tree in the yard in our new house. there are only two rooms and a tin roof that makes music when it rains, especially when there is hail, which falls like angry tears from heaven. there is a stream down the hill from the house, a stream that is too shallow for me to drown myself. manman and i spend a lot of time talking under the banyan tree. she told me today that sometimes you have to choose between your father and the man you love. her whole family did not want her to marry papa because he was a gardener from ville rose and her family was from the city and some of them had even gone to university. she whispered everything under the banyan tree in the yard so as not to hurt his feelings. i saw him looking at us hard from the house. i heard him clearing his throat like he heard us anyway, like we hurt him very deeply somehow just by being together.

Célianne is lying with her head against the side of the boat. The baby still will not cry. They both look very peaceful in all this chaos. Célianne is holding her baby tight against her chest.

She just cannot seem to let herself throw it in the ocean. I asked her about the baby's father. She keeps repeating the story now with her eyes closed, her lips barely moving.

She was home one night with her mother and brother Lionel when some ten or twelve soldiers burst into the house. The soldiers held a gun to Lionel's head and ordered him to lie down and become intimate with his mother. Lionel refused. Their mother told him to go ahead and obey the soldiers because she was afraid that they would kill Lionel on the spot if he put up more of a fight. Lionel did as his mother told him, crying as the soldiers laughed at him, pressing the gun barrels farther and farther into his neck.

Afterwards, the soldiers tied up Lionel and their mother, then they each took turns raping Célianne. When they were done, they arrested Lionel, accusing him of moral crimes. After that night, Célianne never heard from Lionel again.

The same night, Célianne cut her face with a razor so that no one would know who she was. Then as facial scars were healing, she started throwing up and getting rashes. Next thing she knew, she was getting big. She found out about the boat and got on. She is fifteen.

❀

manman told me the whole story today under the banyan tree. the bastards were coming to get me. they were going to arrest me. they were going to peg me as a member of the youth federation and then take me away. papa heard about it. he went to the post and paid them money, all the money he had. our house in port-an-prince and all the land his father had left him, he gave it all away to save my life. this is why he was so mad. tonight manman told me this under the banyan tree. i have no words to thank him for this. i don't know how. you must love him for this, manman says, you must. it is something you can never forget, the sacrifice he has made. i cannot bring my self to say thank you. now he is more than my father. he is a man who gave everything he had to save my life. on the radio tonight, they read the list of names of people who passed the university exams. you passed.

❀

We got some relief from the seawater coming in. The captain used the last of his tar, and most of the water is staying out for a while. Many people have volunteered to throw Célianne's baby overboard for her. She will not let them. They are waiting for her to go to sleep so they can do it, but she will not sleep. I never knew before that dead children looked purple. The lips are the most purple because the baby is so dark. Purple like the sea after the sun has set.

Célianne is slowly drifting off to sleep. She is very tired from the labor. I do not want to touch the child. If anybody is going to throw it in the ocean, I think it should be her. I keep thinking, they have thrown every piece of flesh that followed the child out of her body into the water. They are going to throw the dead baby in the water. Won't these things attract sharks?

Célianne's fingernails are buried deep in the child's naked back. The old man with the pipe just asked, "Kampè, what are you Writing?" I told him, "My will."

❀

i am getting used to ville rose. there are butterflies here, tons of butterflies. so far none has landed on my hand, which means they have no news for me. i cannot always bathe in the

259

stream near the house because the water is freezing cold. the only time it feels just right is at noon, and then there are a dozen eyes who might see me bathing. i solved that by getting a bucket of water in the morning and leaving it in the sun and then bathing myself once it is night under the banyan tree. the banyan now is my most trusted friend. they say banyans can last hundreds of years. even the branches that lean down from them become like trees themselves. a banyan could become a forest, manman says, if it were given a chance. from the spot where i stand under the banyan, i see the mountains, and behind those are more mountains still. so many mountains that are bare like rocks. i feel like all those mountains are pushing me farther and farther away from you.

⁂

She threw it overboard. I watched her face knot up like a thread, and then she let go. It fell in a splash, floated for a while, and then sank. And quickly after that she jumped in too. And just as the baby's head sank, so did hers. They went together like two bottles beneath a water-fall. The shock lasts only so long. There was no time to even try and save her. There was no question of it. The sea in that spot is like the sharks that live there. It has no mercy.

They say I have to throw my notebook out. The old man has to throw out his hat and his pipe. The water is rising again and they are scooping it out. I asked for a few seconds to write this last page and then promised that I would let it go. I know you will probably never see this, but it was nice imagining that I had you here to talk to.

I hope my parents are alive. I asked the old man to tell them what happened to me, if he makes it anywhere. He asked me to write his name in "my book." I asked him for his full name. It is Justin Moïse André Nozius Joseph Frank Osnac Maximilien. He says it all with such an air that you would think him a king. The old man says, "I know a Coast Guard ship is coming. It came to me in my dream." He points to a spot far into the distance. I look where he is pointing. I see nothing. From here, ships must be like a mirage in the desert.

I must throw my book out now. It goes down to them, Célianne and her daughter and all those children of the sea who might soon be claiming me.

I go to them now as though it was always meant to be, as though the very day that my mother birthed me, she had chosen me to live life eternal, among the children of the deep blue sea, those who have escaped the chains of slavery to form a world beneath the heavens and the blood-drenched earth where you live.

Perhaps I was chosen from the beginning of time to live there with Agwé at the bottom of the sea. Maybe this is why I dreamed of the starfish and the mermaids having the Catholic Mass under the sea. Maybe this was my invitation to go. In any case, I know that my memory of you will live even there as I too become a child of the sea.

⁂

today i said thank you. i said thank you, papa, because you saved my life. he groaned and just touched my shoulder, moving his hand quickly away like a butterfly. and then there it was, the black butterfly floating around us. i began to run and run so it wouldn't land on me, but it had already carried its news. i know what must have happened. tonight i listened to manman's transistor under the banyan tree. all i hear from the radio is more killing in port-au-prince. the pigs are refusing to let up. i don't know what's going to happen, but i cannot see staying here forever. i am writing to you from the bottom of the banyan tree. manman says that banyan trees are holy and sometimes if we call the gods from beneath them, they will hear our voices dearer. now there are always butterflies around me, black ones that i refuse to let find my hand. i throw big rocks at them, but they are always too fast. last night on the radio, i heard that another boat sank off the coast of the bahamas. i can't think about you being in there in the waves. my hair shivers. from here, i cannot even see the sea. Behind these mountains are more mountains and more black butterflies still and a sea that is endless like my love for you.

The Hunt
(1995)

MAHASWETA DEVI

I

The place is on the Gomo-Daltonganj line. *Trains* stopped at this *station* once upon a time. The expense of having *trains* stop was perhaps too much. Now one sees a stray cow or a goat in the *station* room, in the residential *quarters* and the porters' shanties. The *billboard* says "Kuruda *Outstation, Abandoned.*" Arrived here, the *train* slows. It gasps as it climbs. It climbs Kuruda Hill bit by bit right from here. It is a low hill. After a while the *train* enters a ravine. On both sides of the half-mile ravine there are *blasted* stones. There's a bamboo thicket on the hill, and occasionally the bamboo bends in the wind and hits the *train*. Then the *train* descends and it gathers speed. Now the *station* is Tohri. The busiest *station* in this area. The *junction* of many *bus* routes. Tohri is also a *coal halt*. The *train* picks up coal. There are *surface collieries* all around. In these parts low-grade coal is to be found almost above ground. But Tohri's real benefactors are the timber brokers. It is a Sal growing area. Sal logs arrive night and day by *truck*. They are split in sawmills and sent in every direction. Tohri's bustle is an experience after the silence of Kuruda.

It is an experience to watch the *train* move on the hilltop from distant villages. The villagers see this every day, yet their amazement never ends. The *train* goes on, the *engine* gasps; now the ravine swallows the *train*. If you run you can see where it will spit it out. There were some elephants seen one day at the top of the hill. The elephants stopped as they ate the bamboo. From a distance they looked like toy elephants. After the *train* passed on they ran off trumpeting, trunks raised.

The village of Kuruda is a good way behind the *station*. There are two hills, one beyond the wide meadow. If it had been a bit closer the villagers might have started living in the abandoned brick built house.

For people who live in villages like Kuruda, life holds few breaks other than annual festivals. So their eyes are charmed by the scenes on top of Kuruda Hill.

When Mary Oraon comes up, she looks at the *train*, as the passengers look at her if they see her. Eighteen years old, tall, flat-featured, light copper skin. Usually she wears a print sari. At a distance she looks most seductive, but close up you see a strong message of rejection in her glance.

You wouldn't call her a tribal at first sight. Yet she is a tribal. Once upon a time whites had *timber plantations* in Kuruda. They left gradually after Independence. Mary's mother looked after the Dixons' bungalow and household. Dixon's son came back in 1959 and sold the house, the forest, everything else. He put Mary in Bhikni's womb before he left. He went to Australia. The padre at the local church christened her Mary. Bhikni was still a *Christian*. But when Prasadji from Ranchi came to live in the Dixon bungalow and refused to employ Bhikni, she gave up *Christianity*. Mary pastures the Prasads' cattle. She is a most capable cowherd. She also sells custard apple and guava from the Prasads' orchards, driving terrifically hard bargains with the Kunjaras, the wholesale fruit buyers. She takes the *train* to Tohri with vegetables from the field.

Everyone says Prasadji is most fortunate. He pays Bhikni a wage. With Mary the agreement is for board and lodging, clothing and sundries. The Dixon bungalow was built as a residence for whites. Bhikni says the whites kept twelve ayahs—servants—sweepers. Under Prasadji Mary alone keeps the huge bungalow clean.

Mary has countless admirers at Tohri market. She gets down at the *station* like a queen. She sits in her own rightful place at the market. She gets smokes from the other marketeers, drinks tea and chews betel leaf at their expense, but encourages no one. Jalim, the leader of the marketeers and a sharp lad, is her chosen mate. They will marry when either's savings reach a hundred rupees.

She has let Jalim approach her on the promise of marriage. Daughter of an Oraon mother, she looks different, and she is also exceptionally tall. So she couldn't find a boy of her own kind. The color of Mary's skin is a resistant barrier to young Oraon men. Mrs. Prasad had looked for a match. Their gardener's son. She had said, You can stay on the compound.

Bhikni was ecstatic. Mary said, "No. Mistress Mother has said it to keep her worker captive."

— She will give shelter.

— A shack.

— He's a good boy.

— No. Living in a shack, eating mush, the man drinking, no soap or oil, no clean clothes. I don't want such a life.

Mary was unwilling. She is accepted in the village society. The women are her friends, she is the best dancer at the feasts. But that doesn't mean she wants to live their life.

Many men had wanted to be her lover. Mary had lifted her machete. They are outsiders. Who can tell that they wouldn't leave her, like Bhikni was left with a baby in her belly?

There was a fight over her once in Tohri market. Ratan Singh, the *driver* of a *timber truck*, had got drunk and tried to carry her off. It was then that Jalim had cut in and hit Ratan Singh. After that Mary was seen selling vegetables or peanuts or corn sitting beside Jalim. She has never been to his room. No, marriage first. Jalim respects this greatly. Yes, there is something true in Mary, the power of Australian blood.

There is distrust in Mary somewhere. She doesn't trust even Jalim fully. Even the marketeers of Tohri know that they'll marry as soon as there is a hundred rupees. Jalim's version is that he himself will save those hundred rupees. It will be good if Mary brings something herself. So she has left to Jalim the responsibility of saving money. It's not easy for Jaiim. He has his parents, brothers, and sisters in the village. Here he'll have to rent a place, buy pots and pans. He won't be able to carry all the expenses. And he wants to give Mary clothes, the odd cake of soap.

Mary gave him the first present. A colored cotton vest.

— Your gift? Jalim is delighted.

— No. Your brother's wife sent it, Mary says sarcastically.

After that Jalim gave her presents now and then. Mary doesn't wear those clothes. She'll wear them after the wedding.

Mary understands that Jalim is taking many pains to save money. Even so she says nothing, for she has saved ninety-two if not a hundred rupees.

She has earned that money. At the Prasad establishment. By government regulation, if there are mahua trees on anyone's land in the forest areas, the right to the fruit goes to the picker. Mahua is a *cash* fruit. You get liquor from mahua, you cook with the oil of the black seed of the mahua fruit, the skin goes to make washing soap. It is Mary who picks the fruit of the four mahua trees on the Prasad property. No villager has been able to touch the fruit even in jest. Mary has instantly raised her machete. This is hers by right. This is why she works so hard for no wages at the Prasad house.

Mrs. Prasad doesn't like it much, but Lachhman Prasad says, "Take no notice. Who will clean so well, pasture the cows so well? Sell fruit and vegetables and nuts at a profit in Tohri?"

Mary works like a dog but does not tolerate familiarity from Prasadji.

— So Mary, how much did you make on your sale of mahua?

— What's it to you?

— Open a moneylending business.

— Yes, I will.

— It's good of me to let you pick the mahua. It is government property. I could hire people and have the fruit picked and I don't do it.

— Let the hired people come and see. I have my machete. Mary's voice is harsh and grim. Prasadji says, It figures. White blood.

Mrs. Prasad has Mary give her an oil rubdown. Out of her lardy body she looks at Mary's hard perfect frame. She says, "So, what about your marriage? What does Jalim say?"

— What do you want with poor folks' talk? Will you organize my marriage?

— God be praised! With a Muslim? I run such a marriage?

— Why not? The Muslim says he'll marry. Your brother wanted only to keep me.

The mistress swallows the slap and says nothing. You have to take words from a girl who works like an animal, carries a forty-pound bag on her back and boards the *train*, cleans the whole house in half an hour.

Everyone is afraid of Mary. Mary cleans house and pastures cattle with her inviolate constitution, her infinite energy, and her razor-sharp mind. On the field she *lunches* on fried corn. She stands and picks fruit and oversees picking. She weighs the stuff herself for the buyers. She puts the fruit bitten by bats and birds into a sack, and feeds it to her mother's chickens. When the rains come she replants the seedlings carefully. She watches out for everything. She buys rice, oil, butter, and spices for the Prasads at Tohri market. She says herself, "The money I save you, and the money I make for you, how much do you put together out of it yearly, Mistress Mother? Why should I take a cheap sari? I'll dress well, use soap and oil, give me everything."

Mrs. Prasad is obliged to dress her well.

Sometimes Mary goes to the village to gossip. When she can. Then she puts her sari around her belly and becomes Mrs. Prasad, limps and becomes Prasadji, makes everyone laugh. There she is easy. When the young men say, "Hey Mussulman's chick, why here?"

— Would any of you marry me?

— Would you?

— Why aren't you tall and white like me?

— You are a white man's daughter.

— Big white chief! Puts a child in a woman's belly and runs like a rat. My mother is bad news. When you see a white daughter, you kill her right away. Then there are no problems!

— What about you if she'd killed?

— I wouldn't have been.

— Stop that talk. Be a Mussulman if you like. Before that, for us . . .

— What?

— Rice-chicken-mutton and booze?

— Sure, I'll throw a fan-tas-tic feast. When have I not fed you? Tell me?

— Yes, true, you do give.

The same Mary who pulls hundreds of pounds, fights the Kunjaras over fruit, doesn't hand out a single peanut to keep Prasadji's profits intact, also steals peanut oil, flour, molasses from the house. Salt and spices.

She sits at any Oraon house in the village, fries wheatcakes on a clay stove, eats with everyone. Just as she knows she'll marry Jalim, she also knows that if she had resembled any Oraon girl—if her father had been Somra or Budhna or Mangla Oraon—the Oraons would not have let this marriage happen.

Because she is the illegitimate daughter of a white father the Oraons don't think of her as their blood and do not place the harsh injunctions of their own society upon her.

She would have rebelled if they had. She is unhappy that they don't. In her inmost heart there is somewhere a longing to be part of the Oraons. She would have been very glad if, when she was thirteen or fourteen, some brave Oraon lad had pulled her into marriage. Mary has seen two or three Hindi films in Tohri. At harvest time itinerant *film* people come to Tohri. They show *moving pictures* in the open field. Not only the girls, but even the boys of Kuruda village have hardly ever been to the *movies*. They haven't been to the *movies*, haven't worn good clothes, haven't eaten a full meal. Mary has a certain sympathy for them as well.

So goes Mary's life. Suddenly one day, stopping the *train*, Tehsildar Singh descends with Prasadji's son, and Mary's life is troubled. A storm gathers in Kuruda's quiet and impoverished existence.

II

Seventy-five acres or two hundred and twenty-five bighas of land are attached to Prasadji's bungalow. Nobody around here obeys the land *ceiling* laws. All the far-flung bungalows of the old *timber planters* have large tracts of attached land. Mr. Dixon had planted Sal on fifty acres. Not the dwarf Sal of the area but *giant* Sal. In time they've grown immense and ready for *felling*. Prasadji used to lament about all that he could have done with this land if there had been no Sal. Now that he knows the price of Sal, his one goal is to sell the trees at the highest price. Lalchand and Mulniji, the two other forest proprietors of the area, are also happy at this news. Prasad's son Banwari takes the initiative and starts looking around in Daltonganj and Chhipador. The fruit of his labors is Tehsildar Singh.

The first thing Tehsildar Singh looks at is trees to be felled. Then they start negotiating prices. Prasad says, "Such Sal wood! How can I sell at such a price?"

— Why sell? You'll sell where you can make a profit.

— Name a proper price.

— Prasadji! Banwari is a real friend. He does *service* in Chhipador, and I'm a broker. Why tell a lie, the trees are *mature*, and the wood solid.

— The whites planted the stuff.

— Yes. But here I'll have them cut, in pieces! *Trucks* won't come here. This is not the white man's rule when I could have brought elephants from the *Forest Department* and pulled the timber to Tohri. I'll have to take it to Murhai. Flat *tires* on the dirt roads. I'll have to cut the trees before that, think of the expense!

— But you'll make a profit!

— Sure. Who works without profit? Still your profit is higher. Bought the bungalow dirt cheap, got a ready-made Sal forest! Whatever you get is your profit. Because you had no *investment* for it. No corn that buffaloes pulled the plow, and fieldhands reaped. No custard apple or guava that you chased birds and bats. *Forest area*, Sal *area*, have trees, sell straight off.

Lalchand and Mulni also said, "Don't make so much trouble, brother. What do we do if he leaves? When the wind's in the Sal and you hear the sea, will he hear? Do you want to watch the flowers of a tree that bears no fruit? He wants to buy, we'll sell."

The broker wants the same thing. What trees the whites had planted. The tops break the sky, the trunks are as big as *railway engines*. Why buy only Prasadji's trees? He'll buy all the trees of the area.

— Every five years or so some trees will be ready and I'll buy. One two three. This is still a *virgin area*, and I'll take the tree *felling monopoly*.

That was the decision. Prasadji realized later that the argument about the expense of carrying the trees was not altogether correct. For the *trucks* came past Murhai, close to Kuruda. That side is flat and stony. No problem with the arrival of *trucks*. The broker pitched his tent there. Two experts came to fell trees.

The broker started planning the deployment of *manpower*. Oraon and Munda men and women came from six villages—Kuruda, Murhai, Seeho, Thapari, Dhuma, Chinadoha. Unbelievable. Money at home. Others will fell the trees, twelve annas daily for men, eight annas for women for trimming branches and carrying the *pieced* timber to the *trucks*. And a *tiffin* of cornmeal in the afternoon. Unbelievable! Salt and cayenne with the meal. The village priest and elders will bring the men and women. A sack of salt weekly for each village. The elders said, How about the women's honor if they work?

The contractor said, They are everybody's mothers and sisters! Whoever forgets will be sacked.

The elders' heads turned with the *trucks'* speed and the efficiency of fast work. So they couldn't think that the contractor's words were untrue. Everyone can't be brothers and sisters. After the final agreement the contractor gave six bottles of *number* one country liquor to the six elders. The elders of Kuruda told the others, "Go to the village, tell the chief, and offer prayers at the shrine. Good times are coming."

The contractor had a word with the driver of the *train* as well. The *train* stops at Murhai. There could be a deal so that the *train* would stop at Kuruda if needed. They'll get a container car. The contractor gave the *driver* a bottle. He's offering fifteen rupees for a full-grown Sal. No expense will block his tremendous profits. He'll sell by the *cubic foot*. He gave Banwari a *transistor*. If Banwari hadn't told him, he wouldn't have known that one could get Sal of this *quality* in this area of dwarf Sals. The entire venture is highly profitable. The contractor praised the uninstructed ignorance of his caste-brothers Prasad, Mulni, and Lalchand. The idiots don't even know what goods they are abandoning. He has given Banwari a rupee per tree in secret. This too leaves him a wide margin of profit. Countless trees will be ready for felling in a few years. Prasad must be kept happy. Soon these parts will be joined to Tohri at that end and Nirlaghat at this. Roads are under construction. Once there are roads, future *transportation* expenses will be saved.

In a little while, the contractor comes to Prasad's house with a box of sweets and a pot of clarified butter. Prasad says, "Mary! Here's our guest. Bring a bit of tea."

Mary has had a bath today. So her body is clean and smooth, her hair oiled and braided. A printed sari worn with the end spread in front of her breasts, brass ornaments on wrist and ear. Mary enters with tea and snacks on a *tray*, Tehsildar Singh sits up. Wow! what a dish! In these woods?

Prasadji saw it happening. As soon as Mary left he said, My maidservant's daughter. When her mother was as young as she, then . . .

He explained the secret of Mary's beauty and said in conclusion, My wife thinks of her as daughter, she respects us as her parents.

"Of course." Tehsildar Singh says, "Otherwise why do people call you a big man? A big man has a big heart." He thought, the business of felling trees in this forest is most profitable. Mary can make his stay profitable in the other sense as well. Mary is the regular contact and bridge between the outside world of Tohri and Kuruda. At night when she brought Prasadji warm water for his medicine she said, "The bastard tricked you. He took all the profit. Everyone from Tohri to Chhipador is laughing."

Prasadji took off his false teeth and put them in a bowl of water. Then he took his medicine. In a while he said, "What to do, Mary? With no *road*, have I the power to sell at profit to anyone? This happens if you live in the forest. Banwari brought him. Banwari is pigheaded and takes after his mother. I first said 'no,' then Lalchand and Mulni got angry. There were many objections at home."

— Banwari's taken his cut.

— You know this?

— I am aware of it.

— What a shame.

Prasadji sighed and gave her a rupee. He gives her like this from time to time. "You take such trouble so I don't get tricked over a piece of fruit, a grain of corn," he said. "My own son understands nothing. What shall I do? Don't I know that he'll sell everything and take off when I die?"

— When you sell trees later, there will be a *road*, don't give it to him. Go yourself to Chhipador. Talk to the big *companies* and do your business. Don't be soft then.

— You're right.

Mary told the Kuruda elders as well, "Twelve annas and eight annas! No porter carries gentlemen's *cases* for this price."

The elders said, "What to do, Mary? If I said 'no' the villagers would go wild. They would say, Who gives us this kind of money?"

Mary said, "He's greedy now. He'll come again in five years. Then we'll bargain for three or two rupees. And he'll have to give. Otherwise how will he get an outsider here?"

— No *road*, no jobs, you know how it is.

Mary thought, in return for the broker's glance she had shrewdly revealed the man's true nature to everyone.

But Tehsildar Singh didn't forget her. A few days later, when Mary was returning on a water-buffalo's back herding other cattle, the contractor came up to her. How pretty, he said. You look like Hema Malini.

— What?

— You look like Hema Malini.

— You look like a monkey.

Tehsildar Singh felt much encouraged by such a remark and came up close. Mary didn't stop her water-buffalo. As she moved on she took out a sharp machete and said in a lazy voice, "Brokers like you, with tight *pants* and dark glasses, are ten a rupee on the streets of Tohri, and to them I show this machete. Go ask if you don't believe me."

Tehsildar found her way of speaking most beguiling.

Banwari said at the evening meal, "Mary has insulted my friend."

He was speaking to his father, but it was Mary who replied, "How did I insult your friend?"

— You spoke to him rudely.

— This time I let him go with words. If he comes to fuck with me again I'll cut off his nose.

Banwari was scared as well. He said, "What, did he do something crazy?"

— It's crazy talk to me. It may be good talk to you.

Prasadji said, "Ask him not to. These problems don't go with buying trees."

— And Mary shouldn't talk about selling Sal trees at Tohri market. It is illegal to sell Sal trees if they are on your own land. The Sal belongs to the Government.

— Ah, keep your laws. Who keeps land legally here, who doesn't sell Sal in these parts?

Mary said straight to Banwari, "Have I spoken about your tree sale in Tohri market?"

— Have I said you've said? I just asked you not to.

— Don't try to set me straight.

Mary left. Prasadji said, "This is not correct. Tell your friend. Lives in the house, like a daughter, I am insulted if she's accosted."

Banwari said to Tehsildar, "She's a real bitch, a rude girl, doesn't give a damn for anyone."

— Who wants a damn?

— Besides, her marriage is fixed.

— Where?

— A Muslim's house.

— Dear God! Isn't there a man in her tribe?

— Her choice,

Tehsildar didn't believe that a Mary Oraon from a wild village like Kuruda could blow him away. He stuck to Mary through marking and felling the trees, cutting and transporting them. That Mary wouldn't look at him and would rather marry a Muslim increased his anger.

Then he brings a *nylon* sari for Mary from Daltonganj, sweets for Prasadji. He says to Prasadji, "I come and go, she feeds me tea, I give her a sari." Prasadji didn't accept it, but Tehsildar insisted. Mary had gone to Tohri. She heard about the sari when she got back. First she gave Prasadji the accounts for Tohri market. Then she had tea and toast in the kitchen. Then she went out with the sari.

Tehsildar was sitting in the tent paying the men and women. Lots of people. Mary enters and throws the sari at him. She says, "You think I'm a city whore? You want to grab me with a sari? If you bother me again I'll cut off your nose." She goes off proudly swinging her arms.

Tehsildar loses face in everyone's eyes. He wants to say, I gave something in good faith ...
The elders say, "Don't give again."

— What?

— Don't give again.

— Is she a good character? Would a good one marry a Muslim?

— Don't say that again.

Suddenly Tehsildar understands, he and his men are in a minority, the others are greater in number. Everyone has a spear or a machete. He shuts up.

At night the *driver* tells him as well, "Don't make trouble with all this. These tribals are a bloodyminded lot. Be problems if they tell the police."

The *driver* knows Tehsildar has a wife and children. He knows that Tehsildar still lusts after women. Mary is indeed an eyeful, but it would be stupid to provoke the tribals and create a *police* case on her account. If Mary was willing, there would have been no problem. Mary is unwilling. Tehsildar must accept that.

Now Prasadji gets serious as well. It is Bhikni who brings tea these days. Tehsildar stops going to the house. But he doesn't give up chasing Mary.

When Mary returns from pasturing cattle, returns from Tohri, or goes the three miles to Murhai *station to* go to Tohri, or goes marketing to Dhuma, Tehsildar keeps his distance and follows her.

The girls say, "Mary, that broker loves you."

— Because he can't catch me. If he does his love will vanish. The white man also loved my mother.

— He'll marry you.

— He has a wife.

— So what?

— Let it go.

The felling goes on. Slowly the weather warms. There are *miles* and *miles* of the flamboyant plant in bloom all around here. New buds appear. Then the gong sounds one day in the priest's house. It is revealed that the ritual of the hunt that the tribes celebrate at the spring festival is for the women to perform this year. For twelve years men run the hunt. Then comes the women's turn. It's Jani Parab. Like the men they too go out with bow and arrow. They run in forest and hill. They kill hedgehogs, rabbits, birds, whatever they can get. Then they picnic together, drink liquor, sing, and return home at evening. They do exactly what the men do. Once in twelve years. Then they light the fire of the spring festival and start talking. Budhni tells stories. That time we killed a leopard. I was young then.

The old women listen, the aging women cook, the young women sing.

They don't know why they hunt. The men know. They have been playing the hunt for a thousand million moons on this day.

Once there were animals in the forest, life was wild, the hunt game had meaning. Now the forest is empty, life wasted and drained, the hunt game meaningless. Only the day's joy is real.

Mary was getting tired of Tehsildar's tireless single-minded pursuit. Jalim might get to know. He'd be wild if she let him know. He might go to Tohri market to kill Tehsildar if he got the chance. Tehsildar has a lot of money, a lot of men. A city bastard. He can destroy Jalim by setting up a larceny case against him.

Tehsildar too was losing patience. The felling would soon be over, they would have to pull up stakes and then what?

Tehsildar caught Mary's hand one day.

The timing was good. No hunt for the men this year. The men will drink and make up new songs for the Spring festival, dress up as clowns and go out to sing for money. Tehsildar has promised them liquor for the festival.

Returning from the felling there is singing every day. In a droning monotone. Mary was listening. On the way back from market. Dusk fell as she listened. She started home.

Tehsildar knew she would come. Tehsildar caught her hand. He said, "I won't let you go today."

At first Mary was scared. Struggling she lost her machete. With great effort, after a good deal of struggling, Mary was able to spring out of his grasp. Both of them stood up. Tehsildar did not have his dark glasses on. Long sideburns, long hair, *polyester trousers,* pointed shoes, a dark red shirt on his back. Against the background of the spring songs Mary thought he was an animal. A-ni-mal. The syllables beat on her mind. Suddenly Mary smiled.

— Mary!

— Stop, stop right there. Don't move up.

— What are you looking at?

— You.

— I, you—

— You want me a lot, no?

— A lot.

— Good.

— What's good?

— I see that you really want me.

— Really want. I've never seen a woman like you. You are worth a million. How will that marketeer know your worth? That Muslim?

— Will you?

— Sure. I'll give you clothes, jewels—

— Really?

— Everything.

Mary took a deep breath. Then said, "Not today. Today I'm unclean."

— When Mary, when?

Mary's eye and face softened. She said, "On the day of the feast. Stay near that rock. The women will go far to play the hunt. I will come to you. You know which rock! You look for me from behind that stone."

— All right.

— Then that's our pact?

— Yes, Mary.

— But don't tell anyone! A man can do no wrong, but a woman is soiled. As it is I am illegitimate, and then I was going to marry a Muslim.

— Tell me you won't.

— Why anymore? Have a bit of patience. Don't follow me around like that.

— I took so much trouble over you . . .

— I'll make up for everything. On the day of the spring festival.

Mary patted his cheek. She said, "You are nice, dear! I didn't see at first." She took off sinuously. She knew Tehsildar wouldn't clasp her from behind a second time.

III

The fire burned last night and tonight as well. Last night the spring festival fire burned very high and reddened the sky for quite some time. Today from first light the men are wild with drink and songs and color. The very old women are looking after the children.

The women are all in the forest. Each woman has stood excited in front of her own door armed with machetes and the men's bows and arrows. As soon as the priest struck the gong they burst the sky with sharp halloos and ran forward. Bhikni is running in Prasadji's *shirt* and Mrs. Prasad's petticoat.

Budhni, Mungri, Somari, Sanichari—their running days are over. They have gone to the abandoned Bomfield bungalow with bottles of liquor, food for cooking, pots, snacks, fried corn, onion-chili. There is water in the well there. The men too cook and eat there after the hunt. Budhni had said to the women, "In our time we never returned without something, a hedgehog, a hare, a partridge. Let's see what you do. How you hunt."

Mary is wearing a new sari today. Jalim's gift. There are beads around her neck. Dancing she clasps Budhni and says, "I'll marry you after I play the hunt. Then I am the husband, you the wife."

— Good.

— I'll make you dance.

— I'll dance.

Mary is running over with joy today. She has put ten rupees into her mother's hands and bought four of her mother's chickens. The chickens are now in Sanichari's hands. Mary has also contributed two bottles of liquor. This is over and above. The women have already asked and received liquor from Tehsildar. Tehsildar has given the men a goat plus the liquor. He has promised to demonstrate the *twist* dance of the city in the evening. He will drink bottle after bottle. His tree-felling is done, just small pieces are left. Many bits. With great generosity he has given them to the people of Kuruda as firewood. He has said, I'll come again, I'll hire only you to fell trees. I'll keep you pickled in liquor then.

Joking with Budhni's group Mary also ran along. Sanichari said, "Look how Mary is looking today. As if she's Mulniji's daughter-in-law."

Budhni said, "When she leaves after marriage Kuruda will lose an eye."

Mungri said, "She has never come to the village empty-handed. You see her now, you've forgotten how pretty Bhikni was as a young woman?"

Somri was half-asleep as she walked. Suddenly she sang out with eyes almost closed:

Fire in the Spring   Fire at the feast
Look and come home   Not to forget—

The others took up the refrain. Four elderly decrepit women long past their youth singing songs of love, the sun warming, the mood thickening, and the sound of gong and horn in the distance.

Mary ran on. The women are all going up Kuruda Hill, entering the forest, going to the side of the cut. Mary is laughing. They won't find a kill. Like all games the hunt game has its rules. Why kill hedgehogs or hares or partridges? You get the big beast with bait.

In her colored sari and red blouse Mary is now like the flamboyant tree in motion. As if a bunch of flowers from that flamboyant tree is running in the wind. Red flowers on all sides. Everything is red. A hare ran past. Mary laughed. She knows where the hare lives. Go back! No fear! Mary said laughing. In her drunken abandon. A great thirst dances in her blood. Tehsildar, Tehsildar, I'm almost there. Tehsildar wants her a lot. Now Jalim is nothing to her. With how much violence can Tehsildar want her? How many *degrees Fahrenheit?* Is his blood as wild as Mary's? As daring?

A hedgehog. Go, go away! If it hadn't been today Mary would have killed it, eaten the flesh. Today a small thing cannot please her. She wants to hunt the big beast! A man, Tehsildar. She sees the rock from a distance. Straight, steep stone. Stone jutting out from the top like a *ledge.* Gitginda vines have come down in a dense mat. On it the yellow flower of the gitginda. Behind the creeper is concealment. Mary's blood burst up at the thought. Forward behind the creeper is the ravine, loose stones on its sides. No one knows how deep the ravine is. No one has gone all the way down. If one could go down into that bottomless cold darkness? She and Tehsildar! She noticed Tehsildar's red *shirt.*

Imported liquor, *cigarettes,* Tehsildar.

— Come inside, dear.

— Where is inside? Inside you?

— Yes dear, yes.

— By the ravine. Behind the creeper.

— First have a drink?

— Why just a drink? Give me a *cigarette.*

— How does it taste?

— Great.

— Not so fast.

— I want to get drunk.

— How drunk?

— I want to get very very drunk.

More booze. She's getting drunk. Stars are strobing in her head. Ah, the stuff is putting spangles in front of her eyes. Shining spangles. Behind them is Tehsildar's face. More liquor. The bottle rolls off. Into the depths of the ravine. Not even a sound. How deep is the ravine? Yes, the face is beginning to look like the hunted animal's.

Mary caresses Tehsildar's face, gives him love bites on the lips. There's fire in Tehsildar's eyes, his mouth is open, his lips wet with spittle, his teeth glistening. Mary is watching, watching, the face changes and changes into? Now? Yes, becomes an animal.

— Now take me?

Mary laughed and held him, laid him on the ground. Tehsildar is laughing, Mary lifts the machete, lowers it, lifts, lowers.

A few million moons pass. Mary stands up. Blood? On her clothes? She'll wash in the cut. With great deftness she takes the *wallet* from Tehsildar's *pocket.* A lot of money. A lot of money. She undoes the fold in the cloth at her waist and puts the money with her own savings.

Then first she throws Tehsildar in the ravine, his *wallet, cigarettes,* his handkerchief. Stone after stone. Hyenas and leopards will come at night, smelling blood. Or they won't.

Mary comes out. Walks naked to the cut. Bathing naked in the cut her face fills with deep satisfaction. As if she has been infinitely satisfied in a sexual embrace.

273

In the women's gathering Mary drank the most wine, sang, danced, ate the meat and rice with the greatest relish. At first everyone mocked her for not having made a kill. Then Budhni said, "Look how she's eating? As if she has made the biggest kill."

Mary kissed Budhni with her unwashed mouth. Then she started dancing, beating two empty bottles together. The night air is cool. Sanichari lights the fire.

Drink and song, drink and dance. When everyone is dancing around the fire and singing,
Ooh Haramdeo our god
Let there be a Spring feast like this every year—
Let us hunt this way every year—
We'll give you wine
We'll give you wine—

Then Mary moves back as she dances. Backing in the dark. They are dancing, dancing hard. Mary runs fast in the dark. She knows the way by heart. She will walk seven *miles* tonight by way of Kuruda Hill and reach Tohri. She will awaken Jalim. From Tohri there are *buses, trucks*. They will go away somewhere. Ranchi, Hazaribagh, Gomo, Patna. Now, after the big kill, she wants Jalim.

The spring festival fires are scattered in the distance. Mary is not afraid, she fears no animal as she walks, watching the *railway line* in the dark, by starlight. Today all the mundane blood-conditioned fears of the wild quadruped are gone because she has killed the biggest beast.

The Sun, the Moon,
the Stars
(1998)

JUNOT DÍAZ

If she's all that, what can go wrong?

I'm not a bad guy. I know how that sounds—defensive, unscrupulous—but it's true. I'm like everybody else: weak, full of mistakes, but basically good. Magdalena disagrees. She considers me a typical Dominican man: a *sucio,* an asshole. See, many months ago, when Magda was still my girl, when I didn't have to be careful about almost everything, I cheated on her with this chick who had tons of eighties freestyle hair. Didn't tell Magda about it, either. You know how it is. A smelly bone like that, better off buried in the back yard of your life. Magda only found out because home girl wrote her a fucking *letter.* And the letter had *details.* Shit you wouldn't even tell your boys drunk.

The thing is, that particular bit of stupidity had been over for months. Me and Magda were on an upswing. We weren't as distant as we'd been the winter I was cheating. The freeze was over. She was coming over to my place and instead of us hanging with my knucklehead boys—me smoking, her bored out of her skull—we were seeing movies. Driving out to different places to eat. Even caught a play at the Crossroads and I took her picture with some bigwig black playwrights, pictures where she's smiling so much you'd think her wide-ass mouth was going to unhinge. We were a couple again. Visiting each other's family on the weekends. Eating breakfast at diners hours before anybody else was up, rummaging through the New Brunswick library together, the one Carnegie built with his guilt money. A nice rhythm we had going. But then the Letter hits like a *Star Trek* grenade and detonates everything, past, present, future. Suddenly her folks want to kill me. It don't matter that I helped them with their taxes two years running or that I mow their lawn. Her father, who used to treat me like his *hijo,* calls me an asshole on the phone, sounds like he's strangling himself with the cord. "You no deserve I speak to you in Spanish," he says. I see one of Magda's girlfriends at the Woodbridge Mall—Claribel, the *ecuatoriana* with the biology degree and the *chinita* eyes—and she treats me like I ate somebody's kid.

You don't even want to hear how it went down with Magda. Like a five-train collision. She threw Cassandra's letter at me—it missed and landed under a Volvo—and then she sat down on the curb and started hyperventilating. "Oh, God," she wailed. "Oh, my God."

275

This is when my boys claim they would have pulled a Total Fucking Denial. Cassandra who? I was too sick to my stomach even to try. I sat down next to her, grabbed her flailing arms, and said some dumb shit like "You have to listen to me, Magda. Or you won't understand."

Let me tell you something about Magda. She's a Bergenline original: short with big eyes and big hips and dark curly hair you could lose a hand in. Her father's a baker, her mother sells kids' clothes door to door. She's a forgiving soul. A Catholic. Dragged me into church every Sunday for Spanish Mass, and when one of her relatives is sick, especially the ones in Cuba, she writes letters to some nuns in Pennsylvania, asks the sisters to pray for her family. She's the nerd every librarian in town knows, a teacher whose students fall in love with her. Always cutting shit out for me from the newspapers, Dominican shit. I see her like, what, every week, and she still sends me corny little notes in the mail: "So you won't forget me." You couldn't think of anybody worse to screw than Magda.

I won't bore you with the details. The begging, the crawling over glass, the crying. Let's just say that after two weeks of this, of my driving out to her house, sending her letters, and calling her at all hours of the night, we put it back together. Didn't mean I ever ate with her family again or that her girlfriends were celebrating. Those *cabronas*, they were like, *No, jamás*, never. Even Magda wasn't too hot on the rapprochement at first, but I had the momentum of the past on my I side. When she asked me "Why don't you leave me alone?" I told her the truth: "It's because I love you, *mami*." I know this sounds like a load of doo-doo, but it's true: Magda's my heart. I didn't want her to leave me; I wasn't about to start looking for a girlfriend because I'd fucked up one lousy time.

Don't think it was a cakewalk, because it wasn't. Magda's stubborn; back when we first started dating, she said she wouldn't sleep with me until we'd been together at least a month, and homegirl stuck to it, no matter how hard I tried to get into her knickknacks. She's sensitive, too. Takes to hurt the way water takes to paper. You can't imagine how many times she asked (especially after we finished fucking), "Were you ever going to tell me?" This and "Why?" were her favorite questions. My favorite answers were "Yes" and "It was a stupid mistake."

We even had some conversation about Cassandra-usually in the dark, when we couldn't see each other. Magda asked me if I'd loved Cassandra and I told her no, I didn't. "Do you still think about her?" "Nope." "Did you like fucking her?" "To be honest, baby, it was lousy." And for a while after we got back together everything was as fine as it could be.

But what was strange was that instead of shit improving between us, things got worse and worse. My Magda was turning into another Magda. Who didn't want to sleep over as much or scratch my back when I asked her to. Amazing how you notice the little things. Like how she never used to ask me to call back when she was on the line with somebody else. I always had priority. Not anymore. So of course I blamed all that shit on her girls, who I knew for a fact were still feeding her a bad line about me.

She wasn't the only one with counsel. My boys were like, "Fuck her, don't sweat that bitch," but every time I tried I couldn't pull it off. I was into Magda for real. I started working overtime on her, but nothing seemed to pan out. Every movie we went to, every night drive we took, every time she did sleep over seemed to confirm something negative about me. I felt like I was dying by degrees, but when I brought it up she told me that I was being paranoid.

About a month later, she started making the sort of changes that would have alarmed a paranoid nigger. Cuts her hair, buys better makeup, rocks new clothes, goes out dancing on Friday nights with her friends. When I ask her if we can chill, I'm no longer sure it's a done deal. A lot of the time she Bartlebys me, says, "No, I'd rather not." I ask her what the hell she thinks this is and she says, "That's what I'm trying to figure out."

I know what she's doing. Making me aware of my precarious position in her life. Like I'm not aware.

Then it was June. Hot white clouds stranded in the sky, cars being washed down with hoses, music allowed outside. Everybody getting ready for summer, even us. We'd planned a trip to Santo Domingo early in the year, an anniversary present, and had to decide whether we were still going or not. It had been on the horizon awhile, but I figured it was something that would resolve itself. When it didn't, I brought the tickets out and asked her, "How do you feel about it?"

"Like it's too much of a commitment."

"Could be worse. It's a vacation, for Christ's sake."

"I see it as pressure."

"Doesn't have to be pressure."

I don't know why I get stuck on it the way I do. Bringing it up every day, trying to get her to commit. Maybe I was getting tired of the situation we were in. Wanted to flex, wanted something to change. Or maybe I'd gotten this idea in my head that if she said, "Yes, we're going," then shit would be fine between us. If she said, "No, it's not for me," then at least I'd know that it was over.

Her girls, the sorest losers on the planet, advised her to take the trip and then never speak to me again. She, of course, told me this shit, because she couldn't stop herself from telling me everything she's thinking. "How do you feel about that suggestion?" I asked her.

She shrugged. "It's an idea."

Even my boys were like, "Nigger, sounds like you're wasting a whole lot of loot on some bullshit," but I really thought it would be good for us. Deep down, where my boys don't know me, I'm an optimist. I thought, Me and her on the Island. What couldn't this cure?

Let me confess: I love Santo Domingo. I love coming home to the guys in blazers trying to push little cups of Brugal into my hands. Love the plane landing, everybody clapping when the wheels kiss the runway. Love the fact that I'm the only nigger on board without a Cuban link or a flapjack of makeup on my face. Love the redhead woman on her way to meet the daughter she hasn't seen in eleven years. The gifts she holds on her lap, like the bones of a saint. *"M'ija* has *tetas* now," the woman whispers to her neighbor. "Last time I saw her, she could barely speak in sentences. Now she's a woman. *Imagínate."* I love the bags my mother packs, shit for relatives and something for Magda, a gift. "You give this to her no matter what happens."

If this was another kind of story, I'd tell you about the sea. What it looks like after it's been forced into the sky through a blowhole. How when I'm driving in from the airport and see it like this, like shredded silver, I know I'm back for real. I'd tell you how many poor mother-fuckers there are. More albinos, more cross-eyed niggers, more *tígueres* than you'll ever see. And the *mujeres*—*olvídate*. How you can't go five feet without running into one you wouldn't mind kicking it with. I'd tell you about the traffic: the entire history of late-twentieth-century automobiles swarming across every flat stretch of ground, a cosmology of battered cars, battered motorcycles, battered trucks, and battered buses, and an equal number of repair shops, run by any fool with a wrench. I'd tell you about the shanties and our no-running-water faucets and the sambos on the billboards and the fact that my family house comes equipped with an ever-reliable latrine. I'd tell you about my *abuelo* and his *campo* hands, how unhappy he is that I'm not sticking around, and I'd tell you about the street where I was born, Calle XXI, how it hasn't decided yet if it wants to be a slum or not and how it's been in this state of indecision for years.

But that would make it another kind of story, and I'm having enough trouble as it is with this one. You'll have to take my word for it. Santo Domingo is Santo Domingo. Let's pretend we all know what goes on there.

I must have been smoking dust, because I thought we were fine those first couple of days. Sure, staying locked up at my *abuelo's* house bored Magda to tears, she even said so—"I'm bored, Yunior"—but I'd warned her about the obligatory Visit with Abuelo. I thought she wouldn't mind; she's normally mad cool with the *viejitos*. But she didn't say much to him. Just fidgeted in the heat and drank fifteen bottles of water. Point is, we were out of the capital and on a *guagua* to the interior before the second day had even begun. The landscapes were superfly—even though there was a drought on and the whole *campo*, even the houses, was covered in that red dust. There I was. Pointing out all the shit that had changed since the year before. The new Pizza Huts and Dunkin' Donuts and the little plastic bags of water the *tigueritos* were selling. Even kicked the historicals. This is where Trujillo and his Marine pals slaughtered the *gavilleros*, here's where the Jefe used to take his girls, here's where Balaguer sold his soul to the Devil. And Magda seemed to be enjoying herself. Nodded her head. Talked back a little. What can I tell you? I thought we were on a positive vibe.

I guess when I look back there were signs. First off, Magda's not quiet. She's a talker, a fucking *boca*, and we used to have this thing where I would lift my hand and say, "Time out," and she would have to be quiet for at least two minutes, just so I could process some of the information she'd been spouting. She'd be embarrassed and chastened, but not so embarrassed and chastened that when I said, "O.K., time's up," she didn't launch right into it again.

Maybe it was my good mood. It was like the first time in weeks that I felt relaxed, that I wasn't acting like something was about to give at any moment. It bothered me that she insisted on reporting to her girls every night—like they were expecting me to kill her or something—but, fuck it, I still thought we were doing better than anytime before.

We were in this crazy budget hotel near the university. I was standing outside staring out at the Septentrionales and the blacked-out city when I heard her crying. I thought it was something serious, found the flashlight, and fanned the light over her heat-swollen face. "Are you O.K., *mami?*"

She shook her head. "I don't want to be here."

"What do you mean?"

"What don't you understand? I. Don't. Want. To. Be. Here."

This was not the Magda I knew. The Magda I knew was super courteous. Knocked on a door before she opened it.

I almost shouted, "What is your fucking problem!" But I didn't. I ended up hugging and babying her and asking her what was wrong. She cried for a long time and then after a silence started talking. By then the lights had flickered back on. Turned out she didn't want to travel around like a hobo. "I thought we'd be on a beach," she said.

"We're going to be on a beach. The day after tomorrow."

"Can't we go now?"

What could I do? She was in her underwear, waiting for me to say something. So what jumped out of my mouth? "Baby, we'll do whatever you want." I called the hotel in La Romana, asked if we could come early, and the next morning I put us on an express *guagua* to the capital and then a second one to La Romana. I didn't say a fucking word to her and she didn't say nothing to me. She seemed tired and watched the world outside like maybe she was expecting it to speak to her.

By the middle of Day 3 of our All-Quisqueya Redemption Tour we were in an air-conditioned bungalow watching HBO. Exactly where I want to be when I'm in Santo Domingo. In a fucking resort. Magda was reading a book by a Trappist, in a better mood, I guess, and I was sitting on the edge of the bed, fingering my useless map.

I was thinking, For this I deserve something nice. Something physical. Me and Magda were pretty damn casual about sex, but since the breakup shit has gotten weird. First of all, it ain't regular like before. I'm lucky to score some once a week. I have to nudge her, start things up, or we won't fuck at all. And she plays like she doesn't want it, and sometimes she doesn't and then I have to cool it, but other times she does want it and I have to touch her pussy, which is my way of initiating things, of saying, "So, how about we kick it, *mami?*" And she'll turn her head, which is her way of saying, "I'm too proud to acquiesce openly to your animal desires, but if you continue to put your finger in me I won't stop you."

Today we started no problem, but then halfway through she said, "Wait, we shouldn't."

I wanted to know why.

She closed her eyes like she was embarrassed at herself. "Forget about it," she said, moving her hips under me. "Just forget about it."

I don't even want to tell you where we're at. We're in Casa de Campo. The Resort That Shame Forgot. The average asshole would love this place. It's the largest, wealthiest resort on the Island, which means it's a goddam fortress, walled away from everybody else. *Guachimanes* and peacocks and ambitious topiaries everywhere. Advertises itself in the States as its own country, and it might as well be. Has its own airport, thirty-six holes of golf, beaches so white they ache to be trampled, and the only Island Dominicans you're guaranteed to see are either caked up or changing your sheets. Let's just say my *abuelo* has never been here, and neither has yours. This is where the Garcias and the Colóns come to relax after a long month of oppressing the masses, where the *tutumpotes* can trade tips with their colleagues from abroad. Chill here too long and you'll be sure to have your ghetto pass revoked, no questions asked.

We wake up bright and early for the buffet, get served by cheerful women in Aunt Jemima costumes. I shit you not: these sisters even have to wear hankies on their heads. Magda is scratching out a couple of cards to her family. I want to talk about the day before, but when I bring it up she puts down her pen. Jams on her shades.

"I feel like you're pressuring me."

"How am I pressuring you?" I ask.

We get into one of those no-fun twenty-minute arguments, which the waiters keep interrupting by bringing over more orange juice and café, the two things this island has plenty of.

"I just want some space to myself every now and then. Every time I'm with you I have this sense that you want something from me."

"Time to yourself," I say. "What does that mean?"

"Like maybe once a day, you do one thing, I do another."

"Like when? Now?"

"It doesn't have to be now." She looks exasperated. "Why don't we just go down to the beach?"

As we walk over to the courtesy golf cart, I say, "I feel like you rejected my whole country, Magda."

"Don't be ridiculous." She drops one hand in my lap. "I just wanted to relax. What's wrong with that?"

The sun is blazing and the blue of the ocean is an overload on the brain. Casa de Campo has got beaches the way the rest of the island has got problems. These, though, have no merengue, no little kids, nobody trying to sell you *chicharrones,* and there's a massive melanin deficit in evidence. Every fifty feet there's at least one Eurofuck beached out on a towel like some scary pale monster that the sea's vomited up. They look like philosophy professors, like budget Foucaults, and too many of them are in the company of a dark-assed Dominican girl. I mean it, these girls can't be no more than sixteen, look *puro ingenio* to me. You can tell by their inability to communicate that these two didn't meet back in their Left Bank days.

Magda's rocking a dope Ochun-colored bikini that her girls helped her pick out so she could torture me, and I'm in these old ruined trunks that say "Sandy Hook Forever!" I'll admit it, with Magda half naked in public I'm feeling vulnerable and uneasy. I put my hand on her knee. "I just wish you'd say you love me."

"Yunior, please."

"Can you say you like me a lot?"

"Can you leave me alone? You're such a pestilence."

I let the sun stake me out to the sand. It's disheartening, me and Magda together. We don't look like a couple. When she smiles niggers ask her for her hand in marriage; when I smile folks check their wallets. Magda's been a star the whole time we've been here. You know how it is when you're on the Island and your girl's an octoroon. Brothers go apeshit. On buses, the machos were like, *"Tu sí eres bella, muchacha."* Every time I dip into the water for a swim, some Mediterranean Messenger of Love starts rapping to her. Of course, I'm not polite. "Why don't you beat it, *pancho?* We're on our honeymoon here." There's this one squid who's mad persistent, even sits down near us so he can impress her with the hair around his nipples, and instead of ignoring him she starts a conversation and it turns out he's Dominican, too, from Quisqueya Heights, an Assistant D.A. who loves his people. "Better I'm their prosecutor," he says. "At least I understand them." I'm thinking he sounds like the sort of nigger who in the old days used to lead bwana to the rest of us. After three minutes of him, I can't take it no more, and say, "Magda, stop talking to that asshole."

The Assistant D.A. startles. "I know you ain't talking to me," he says.

"Actually," I say, "I am."

"This is unbelievable." Magda gets to her feet and walks stiff-legged toward the water. She's got a half-moon of sand stuck to her butt. A total fucking heartbreak.

Homeboy's saying something else to me, but I'm not listening. I already know what she'll say when she sits back down. "Time for you to do your thing and me to do mine."

That night I loiter around the pool and the local bar, Club Cacique, Magda nowhere to be found. I meet a Dominicana from West New York. Fly, of course. *Triguña*, with the most outrageous perm this side of Dyckman. Lucy is her name. She's hanging out with three of her teen-age girl cousins. When she removes her robe to dive into the pool, I see a spiderweb of scars across her stomach. Tells me in Spanish, "I have family in La Romana, but I refuse to stay with them. No way. My uncle won't let any of us out of the house after dark. So I'd rather go broke and stay here than be locked in the prison."

I meet these two rich older dudes drinking cognac at the bar. Introduce themselves as the Vice-President and Bárbaro, his bodyguard. I must have the footprint of fresh disaster on my face. They listen to my troubles like they're a couple of capos and I'm talking murder. They commiserate. It's a thousand degrees out and the mosquitoes hum like they're about to inherit the earth, but both these cats are wearing expensive suits, and Bárbaro is even sporting a purple ascot. Once a soldier tried to saw open his neck and now he covers the scar. "I'm a modest man," he says.

I go off to phone the room. No Magda. I check with reception. No messages. I return to the bar and smile.

The Vice-President is a young brother, in his late thirties, and pretty cool for a *chupabarrio*. He advises me to find another woman. Make her *bella* and *negra*. I think, Cassandra.

The Vice-President waves his hand and shots of Barceló appear so fast you'd think it's science fiction.

"Jealousy is the best way to jumpstart a relationship," the Vice-President says. "I learned that when I was a student at Syracuse. Dance with another woman, dance merengue with her, and see if your *jeva's* not roused to action."

"You mean roused to violence."

"She hit you?"

"When I first told her. She smacked me right across the chops."

"*Pero, hermano*, why'd you tell her?" Bárbaro wants to know. "Why didn't you just deny it?"

"*Compadre*, she received a letter. It had evidence."

The Vice-President smiles fantastically and I can see why he's a vice-president. Later, when I get home, I'll tell my mother about this whole mess, and she'll tell me what this brother was the vice-president of.

"They only hit you," he says, "when they care."

"Amen," Bárbaro murmurs. "Amen."

All of Magda's friends say I cheated because I was Dominican, that all us Dominican men are dogs and can't be trusted. But it wasn't genetics; there were reasons. Causalities.

The truth is there ain't no relationship in the world that doesn't hit turbulence. Ours certainly did.

I was living in Brooklyn and she was with her folks in Jersey. We talked every day on the phone and on weekends we saw each other. Usually I went in. We were real Jersey, too: malls, the parents, movies, a lot of TV. After a year of us together, this was where we were at. Our relationship wasn't the sun, the moon, and the stars, but it wasn't bullshit, either. Especially not on Saturday mornings, over at my apartment, when she made us coffee *campo* style, straining it through the sock thing. Told her parents the night before she was staying over at Claribel's; they must have known where she was, but they never said shit. I'd sleep late and she'd read, scratching my back in slow arcs, and when I was ready to get up I would start kissing her until she would say, "God, Yunior, you're making me wet."

I wasn't unhappy and wasn't actively pursuing ass like some niggers. Sure, I checked out other females, even danced with them when I went out, but I wasn't keeping numbers or nothing. Still, it's not like seeing somebody once a week doesn't cool shit out, because it does. Nothing you'd really notice until some new chick arrives at your job with a big chest and a smart mouth and she's like on you almost immediately, touching your pectorals, moaning about some *moreno* she's dating who's always treating her like shit, saying, "Black guys don't understand Spanish girls."

Cassandra. She organized the football pool and did crossword puzzles while she talked on the phone, and had a thing for denim skirts. We got into a habit of going to lunch and having the same conversation. I advised her to drop the *moreno*, she advised me to find a girlfriend who could fuck. First week of knowing her, I made the mistake of telling her that sex with Magda had never been topnotch.

"God, I feel sorry for you," Cassandra laughed. "At least Rupert gives me some Grade A dick."

The first night we did it—and it was good, too, she wasn't false advertising—I felt so lousy that I couldn't sleep, even though she was one of those sisters whose body fits next to you perfect. I was like, She knows, so I called Magda right from the bed and asked her if she was O.K.

"You sound strange," she said.

I remember Cassandra pressing the hot cleft of her pussy against my leg and me saying, "I just miss you."

Another day, and the only thing Magda has said is "Give me the lotion." Tonight the resort is throwing a party. All guests are invited. Attire's formal, but I don't have the clothes or the energy to dress up. Magda, though, has both. She pulls on these supertight gold lame pants and a matching halter that shows off her belly ring. Her hair is shiny and as dark as night and I can remember the first time I kissed those curls, asking her, "Where are the stars?" And she said, "They're a little lower, *papi*."

We both end up in front of the mirror. I'm in slacks and a wrinkled guayabera. She's applying her lipstick; I've always believed that the universe invented the color red solely for Latinas.

"We look good," she says.

It's true. My optimism is starting to come back. I'm thinking, This is the night for reconciliation. I put my arms around her, but she drops her bomb without blinking a fucking eye: tonight, she says, she needs space.

My arms drop.

"I knew you'd be pissed," she says.

"You're a real bitch, you know that."

"I didn't want to come here. You made me."

"If you didn't want to come, why didn't you have the fucking guts to say so?"

And on and on and on, until finally I just say, "Fuck this," and head out. I feel unmoored and don't have a clue of what comes next. This is the endgame, and instead of pulling out all the stops, instead of *pongándome más chivo que un chivo*, I'm feeling sorry for myself, *como un parigüayo sin suerte*. I'm thinking, I'm not a bad guy.

Club Cacique is jammed. I'm looking for Lucy. I find the Vice-President and Bárbaro instead. At the quiet end of the bar, they're drinking cognac and arguing about whether there are fifty-six Dominicans in the major leagues or fifty-seven. They clear out a space for me and clap me on the shoulder.

"This place is killing me," I say.

"How dramatic." The Vice-President reaches into his suit for his keys. He's wearing those Italian leather shoes that look like braided slippers. "Are you inclined to ride with us?"

"Sure," I say. "Why the fuck not?"

"I wish to show you the birthplace of our nation."

Before we leave I check out the crowd. Lucy has arrived. She's alone at the edge of the bar in a fly black dress. Smiles excitedly, lifts her arm, and I can see the dark stubbled spot in her armpit. She's got sweat patches over her outfit, and mosquito bites on her beautiful arms. I think, I should stay, but my legs carry me right out of the club.

We pile in a diplomat's black BMW. I'm in the back seat with Bárbaro; the Vice-President's up front driving. We leave Casa de Campo behind and the frenzy of La Romana, and soon everything starts smelling of processed cane. The roads are dark—I'm talking no fucking lights—and in our beams the bugs swarm like a Biblical plague. We're passing the cognac around. I'm with a vice-president, I figure what the fuck.

He's talking—about his time in upstate New York—but so is Bárbaro. The bodyguard's suit's rumpled and his hand shakes as he smokes his cigarettes. Some fucking bodyguard. He's telling me about his childhood in San Juan, near the border of Haiti. Liborio's country. "I wanted to be an engineer," he tells me. "I wanted to build schools and hospitals for the pueblo." I'm not really listening to him; I'm thinking about Magda, how I'll probably never taste her *chocha* again.

And then we're out of the car, stumbling up a slope, through bushes and *guineo* and bamboo, and the mosquitoes are chewing us up like we're the special of the day. Bárbaro's got a huge flashlight, a darkness obliterator. The Vice-President's cursing, trampling through the underbrush, saying, "It's around here somewhere. This is what I get for being in office so long." It's only then I notice that Bárbaro's holding a huge fucking machine gun and his hand ain't shaking no more. He isn't watching me or the Vice-President—he's listening. I'm not scared, but this is getting a little too freaky for me.

"What kind of gun is that?" I ask, by way of conversation.

"A P-90."

"What the fuck is that?"

"Something old made new."

Great, I'm thinking, a philosopher.

"It's here," the Vice-President says.

I creep over and see that he's standing over a hole in the ground. The earth is red. Bauxite. And the hole is blacker than any of us.

"This is the Cave of the Jagua," the Vice-President announces in a deep, respectful voice. "The birthplace of the Tainos."

I raise my eyebrow. "I thought they were South America."

"We're speaking mythically here."

Bárbaro points the light down the hole, but that doesn't improve anything.

"Would you like to see inside?" the Vice-President asks me.

I must have said yes, because Bárbaro gives me the flashlight and the two of them grab me by my ankles and lower me into the hole. All my coins fly out of my pockets. *Bendiciones.* I don't see much, just some odd colors on the eroded walls, and the Vice-President's calling down, "Isn't it beautiful?"

This is the perfect place for insight, for a person to become somebody better. The Vice-President probably saw his future self hanging in this darkness, bulldozing the poor out of their shanties, and Bárbaro, too—buying a concrete house for his mother, showing her how to work the air-conditioner—but, me, all I can manage is a memory of the first time me and Magda talked. Back at Rutgers. We were waiting for an E bus together on George Street and she was wearing purple. All sorts of purple.

And that's when I know it's over. As soon as you start thinking about the beginning, it's the end.

I cry, and when they pull me up the Vice-President says, indignantly, "God, you don't have to be a pussy about it."

That must have been some serious Island voodoo: the ending I saw in the cave came true. The next day we went back to the United States. Five months later I got a letter from my ex-baby. I was dating someone new, but Magda's handwriting still blasted every molecule of air out of my lungs.

It turned out she was also going out with somebody else. A very nice guy she'd met. Dominican, like me.

But I'm getting ahead of myself. I need to finish by showing you what kind of fool I am.

When I returned to the bungalow that night, Magda was waiting up for me. Was packed, looked like she'd been bawling. "I'm going home tomorrow," she said. I sat down next to her. Took her hand. "This can work," I said. "All we have to do is try."

There Is No Exile
(1959)

ASSIA DJEBAR

That particular morning, I'd finished the housework a little earlier, by nine o'clock. Mother had put on her veil, taken her basket; in the opening of the door, she repeated as she had been repeating every day for three years: "Not until we had been chased out of our own country did I find myself forced to go out to market like a man."

"Our men have other things to do," I answered, as I'd been answering every day for three years. "May God protect us!"

I saw Mother to the staircase, then watched her go down heavily because of her legs: "May God protect us," I said again to myself as I went back in.

The cries began around ten o'clock, more or less. They were coming from the apartment next door and soon changed into shrieks. All three of us, my two sisters—Aïcha, Anissa, and I—recognized it by the way in which the women received it: it was death.

Aïcha, the eldest, ran to the door, opened it in order to hear more clearly: "May misfortune stay away from us," she mumbled. "Death has paid the Smaïn family a visit."

At that moment, Mother came in. She put the basket on the floor, stopped where she stood, her face distraught, and began to beat her chest spasmodically with her hands. She was uttering little stifled cries, as when she was about to get sick.

Anissa, although she was the youngest of us, never lost her calm. She ran to close the door, lifted Mother's veil, took her by the shoulders and made her sit down on a mattress.

"Now don't get yourself in that state on account of someone else's misfortune," she said. "Don't forget you have a bad heart. May God shelter and keep us always."

While she repeated the phrase several more times, she went to get some water and sprinkled it on Mother, who now, stretched out full length on the mattress, was moaning. Then Anissa washed her entire face, took a bottle of cologne from the wardrobe, opened it, and put it under her nostrils.

"No!" Mother said. "Bring me some lemon."

And she started to moan again.

Anissa continued to bustle about. I was just watching her. I've always been slow to react. I'd begun to listen to the sobs outside that hadn't ceased, would surely not cease before nightfall. There were five or six women in the Smaïn family, and they were all lamenting in chorus, each one settling, forever it seemed, into the muddled outbreak of their grief. Later, of course, they'd have to prepare the meal, busy themselves with the poor, wash the body. . . . There are so many things to do the day of a burial.

285

For now, the voices of the hired mourners, all alike without anyone of them distinguishable from the other if only by a more anguished tone, were making one long, gasping chant, and I knew that it would hang over the entire day like a fog in winter.

"Who actually died over there?" I asked Mother, who had almost quieted down.

"Their young son," she said, inhaling the lemon deeply. "A car drove over him in front of the door. I was coming home when my eyes saw him twisting one last time, like a worm. The ambulance took him to the hospital, but he was already dead."

Then she began to sigh again.

"Those poor people," she was saying, "they saw him go out jumping with life and now they're going to bring him back in a bloodstained sheet."

She raised herself halfway, repeated: "jumping with life."

Then she fell back down on the mattress and said nothing other than the ritual formulas to keep misfortune away. But the low voice she always used to address God had a touch of hardness, vehemence.

"This day has an evil smell," I said, still standing in front of Mother, motionlessly. "I've sensed it since this morning, but I didn't know then that it was the smell of death."

"You have to add: May God protect us!" Mother said sharply. Then she raised her eyes to me. We were alone in the room, Anissa and Aïcha had gone back to the kitchen.

"What's the matter with you?" she said. "You look pale. Are you feeling sick, too?"

"May God protect us!" I said and left the room.

✻

At noon, Omar was the first one home. The weeping continued. I'd attended to the meal while listening to the threnody and its modulations. I was growing used to them. I thought Omar would start asking questions. But no. He must have heard about it in the street.

He pulled Aïcha into a room. Then I heard them whispering. When some important event occurred, Omar spoke first to Aïcha in this way, because she was the eldest and the most serious one. Previously, Father used to do the same thing, but outside, with Omar, for he was the only son.

So there was something new; and it had nothing to do with death visiting the Smaïn family. I wasn't curious at all. Today is the day of death, all the rest becomes immaterial.

"Isn't that so?" I said to Anissa, who jumped.

"What's the matter now?"

"Nothing," I said without belaboring the point, for I was familiar with her always disconcerted answers whenever I'd start thinking out loud. Even this morning. . . .

But why this sudden, blatant desire to stare at myself in a mirror, to confront my own image at some length, and to say, while letting my hair fall down my back so that Anissa would gaze upon it: "Look. At twenty-five, after having been married, after having lost my two children one after the other, having been divorced, after this exile and after this war, here I am busy admiring myself, smiling at myself like a young girl, like you. . . ."

"Like me!" Anissa said, and she shrugged her shoulders.

Father came home a little late because it was Friday and he'd gone to say the prayer of *dhor* at the mosque. He immediately asked why they were in mourning.

"Death has visited the Smaïns," I said, running toward him to kiss his hand. "It has taken their young son away."

"Those poor people," he said after a silence.

I helped him get settled in his usual place, on the same mattress. Then, as I put his meal in front of him and made sure he didn't have to wait for anything, I forgot about the neighbors for a while. I liked to serve Father; it was, I think, the only household task I enjoyed. Especially now. Since our departure, Father had aged a great deal. He gave too much thought to those who weren't with us, even though he never spoke of them, unless a letter arrived from Algeria and he asked Omar to read it.

In the middle of the meal I heard Mother murmur: "They can't possibly feel like eating today."

"The body is still at the hospital," someone said.

Father said nothing. He rarely spoke during meals.

"I'm not really hungry," I said, getting up, to excuse myself.

The sobs outside seemed more muffled, but I could still distinguish their singsong. Their gentle singsong. This is the moment, I said to myself, when grief becomes familiar, and pleasurable, and nostalgic. This is the moment when you weep almost voluptuously, for this gift of tears is a gift without end. This was the moment when the bodies of my children would turn cold fast, so fast, and when I knew it. . . .

At the end of the meal, Aïcha came into the kitchen, where I was by myself. First she went to close the windows that looked out over the neighboring terraces, through which the weeping reached me. But I could still hear it. And, oddly, it was that which made me so tranquil today, a little gloomy.

"There are some women coming this afternoon to see you and to propose marriage," she began. "Father says the candidate is suitable in every way."

Without answering, I turned my back to her and went to the window.

"Now what's your problem?" she said a little sharply.

"I need some air," I said and opened the window all the way, so that the song could come in. It had already been a while since the breathing of death had become, for me, "the song."

Aïcha remained a moment without answering. "When Father goes out, you'll attend to yourself a little," she said at last. "These women know very well that we're refugees like so many others, and that they're not going to find you dressed like a queen. But you should look your best, nevertheless."

"They've stopped weeping," I remarked, "or perhaps they're already tired," I said, thinking of that strange fatigue that grasps us at the depth of our sorrow.

"Why don't you keep your mind on the women who're coming?" Aïcha replied in a slightly louder voice.

Father had left. Omar too, when Hafsa arrived. Like us, she was Algerian and we'd known her there, a young girl of twenty with an education. She was a teacher but had been working only since her mother and she had been exiled, as had so many others. "An honorable woman doesn't work outside her home," her mother used to say. She still said it, but with a sigh of helplessness. One had to live, and there was no man in their household now.

Hafsa found Mother and Anissa in the process of preparing pastries, as if these were a must for refugees like us. But her sense of protocol was instinctive in Mother; an inheritance from her past life that she could not readily abandon.

"These women you're waiting for," I asked, "who are they?" "Refugees like us," Aïcha exclaimed. "You don't really think we'd give you away in marriage to strangers?" Then with heart and soul: "Remember," she said, "the day we return to our own country, we shall all go back home, all of us, without exception."

"The day that we return," Hafsa, standing in the middle of the room, suddenly cried out, her eyes wide with dreams. "The day that we return to our country!" she repeated. "How I'd like to go back there on foot, the better to feel the Algerian soil under my feet, the better to see all our women, one after the other, all the widows, and all the orphans, and finally all the men, exhausted, sad perhaps, but free—free! And then I'll take a bit of soil in my hands, oh, just a tiny handful of soil, and I'll say to them: 'See, my brothers, see these drops of blood in these grains of soil in this hand, that's how much Algeria has bled throughout her body, all over her vast body, that's how much Algeria has paid for our freedom and for this, our return, with her own soil. But her martyrdom now speaks in terms of grace. So you see, my brothers. . . .'"

"The day that we return," Mother repeated softly in the silence that followed . . . "if God wills it."

It was then that the cries began again through the open window. Like an orchestra that brusquely starts a piece of music. Then, in a different tone, Hafsa reminded us: "I'm here for the lesson."

Aïcha pulled her into the next room.

During their meeting, I didn't know what to do. The windows of the kitchen and of the other two rooms looked out over the terraces. I went from one to the other, opening them, closing them, opening them again. All of this without hurrying, as if I weren't listening to the song.

Anissa caught me in my rounds.

"You can tell they're not Algerian," she said. "They're not even accustomed to being in mourning."

"At home, in the mountains," Mother answered, "the dead have nobody to weep over them before they grow cold."

"Weeping serves no purpose," Anissa was stoic, "whether you die in your bed or on the bare ground for your country."

"What do you know about it?" I suddenly said to her. "You're too young to know."

"Soon they're going to bury him," Mother whispered.

Then she raised her head and looked at me. I had once again closed the window behind me. I couldn't hear anything anymore.

"They're going to bury him this very day," Mother said again a little louder, "that's our custom."

"They shouldn't," I said. "It's a hateful custom to deliver a body to the earth when beauty still shines on it. Really quite hateful. . . . It seems to me they're burying him while he's still shivering, still . . ." (but I couldn't control my voice any longer).

"Stop thinking about your children!" Mother said. "The earth that was thrown on them is a blanket of gold. My poor daughter, stop thinking about your children!" Mother said again.

"I'm not thinking about anything," I said. "No, really. I don't want to think about anything. About anything at all."

※

It was already four o'clock in the afternoon when they came in. From the kitchen where I was hiding, I heard them exclaim, once the normal phrases of courtesy had been uttered: "What is that weeping?"

"May misfortune stay far away from us! May God protect us!"

"It gives me goose bumps," the third one was saying. "I've almost forgotten death and tears, these days. I've forgotten them, even though our hearts are always heavy."

"That is the will of God," the second one would respond.

In a placid voice, Mother explained the reason for the mourning next door as she invited them into the only room we had been able to furnish decently. Anissa, close by me, was already making the first comments on the way the women looked. She was questioning Aïcha, who had been with Mother to welcome them. I had opened the window again and watched them exchange their first impressions.

"What are you thinking?" Anissa said, her eye still on me.

"Nothing," I said feebly; then, after a pause: "I was thinking of the different faces of fate. I was thinking of God's will. Behind that wall, there is a dead person and women going mad with grief. Here, in our house, other women are talking of marriage . . . I was thinking of that difference."

"Just stop 'thinking'," Aïcha cut in sharply. Then to Hafsa, who was coming in: "You ought to be teaching *her*, not me. She spends all her time thinking. You'd almost believe she's read as many books as you have."

"And why not?" Hafsa asked.

"I don't need to learn French," I answered. "What purpose would it serve? Father has taught us all our language. 'That's all you need,' he always says."

"It's useful to know languages other than your own," Hafsa said slowly. "It's like knowing other people, other countries."

I didn't answer. Perhaps she was right. Perhaps you ought to learn and not waste your time letting your mind wander, like mine, through the deserted corridors of the past. Perhaps I should take lessons and study French, or anything else. But I, I never felt the need to jostle my body or my mind. . . . Aïcha was different. Like a man: hard and hardworking. She was thirty. She hadn't seen her husband in three years, who was still incarcerated in Barberousse prison, where he had been since the first days of the war. Yet, she was getting an education and didn't settle for household work. Now, after just a few months of Hafsa's lessons, Omar no longer read her husband's infrequent letters, the few that might reach her. She managed to decipher them by herself. Sometimes I caught myself being envious of her.

"Hafsa," she said, "it's time for my sister to go in and greet these ladies. Please go with her."

But Hafsa didn't want to. Aïcha insisted, and I was watching them play their little game of politeness.

"Does anyone know if they've come for the body yet?" I asked.

"What? Didn't you hear the chanters just now?" Anissa said.

"So that's why the weeping stopped for a moment," I said.

"It's strange, as soon as some parts of the Koranic verses are chanted, the women immediately stop weeping. And yet, that's the most painful moment, I know it all too well myself. As long as the body is there in front of you, it seems the child isn't quite dead yet, can't be dead, you see? . . . Then comes the moment when the men get up, and that is to take him, wrapped in a sheet, on their shoulders. That's how he leaves, quickly, as on the day that he came. . . . For me, may God forgive me, they can chant Koranic verses all they want, the house is still empty after they've gone, completely empty. . . ."

Hafsa was listening, her head leaning toward the window. With a shiver, she turned toward me. She seemed younger even than Anissa, then.

"My God," she said, emotion in her voice, "I've just turned twenty and yet I've never encountered death. Never in my whole life!"

"Haven't you lost anyone in your family in this war?" Anissa asked.

"Oh yes," she said, "but the news always comes by mail. And death by mail, you see, I can't believe it. A first cousin of mine died under the guillotine as one of the first in Barberousse. Well, I've never shed a tear over him because I cannot believe that he's dead. And yet he was like a brother to me, I swear. But I just can't believe he's dead, you understand?" she said in a voice already wrapped in tears.

"Those who've died for the Cause aren't really dead," Anissa answered with a touch of pride.

"So, let's think of the present. Let's think about today," Aïcha said in a dry voice. "The rest is in God's hand."

꙳

There were three of them: an old woman who had to be the suitor's mother and who hastily put on her glasses as soon as I arrived; two other women, seated side by side, resembled each other. Hafsa, who'd come in behind me, sat down next to me. I lowered my eyes.

I knew my part, it was one I'd played before; stay mute like this, eyes lowered, and patiently let myself be examined until the very end: it was simple. Everything is simple, beforehand, for a girl who's being married off.

Mother was talking. I was barely listening. I knew the themes to be developed all too well: Mother was talking about our sad state as refugees; then they'd be exchanging opinions on when the end might be announced: ". . . another Ramadan to be spent away from home . . . perhaps this was the last one . . . perhaps, if God wills it! Of course, we were saying the same thing last year, and the year before that. . . . Let's not complain too much. . . . In any event, victory is certain, all our men say the same thing. And we, we know the day of our return will come. . . . We should be thinking of those who stayed behind. . . . We should be thinking of those who are suffering. . . . The Algerian people are a people whom God loves. . . . And our fighters are made of steel. . . ." Then they'd come back to the tale of the flight, to the different means by which each one had left her soil where the fires were burning. . . . Then they'd evoke the sadness of exile, the heart yearning for its country. . . . And the fear of dying far from the land of one's birth. . . . Then. . . . But may God be praised and may he grant our prayers!"

This time it lasted a bit longer; an hour perhaps, or more. Until the time came to serve coffee. By then, I was hardly listening at all. I too was thinking in my own way of this exile, of these somber days.

I was thinking how everything had changed, how on the day of my first engagement we had been in the long, bright living room of our house in the hills of Algiers; how we'd been prosperous then, we had prosperity and peace; how Father used to laugh, how he used to give thanks to God for the abundance of his home. . . . And I, I wasn't as I was today, my soul grey, gloomy and with this idea of death beating faintly inside me since the morning. . . . Yes, I was thinking how everything had changed and that, still, in some way everything remained the same. They were still concerned with marrying me off. And why exactly? I suddenly wondered. And why exactly? I repeated to myself, feeling something like fury inside me, or its echo. Just so I could have worries that never change whether it's peace or wartime, so I could wake up in the middle of the night and question myself on what it is that sleeps in the depths of the heart of the man sharing my bed. . . . Just so I could give birth and weep, for life never comes unaccompanied to a woman, death is always right behind, furtive, quick, and smiling at the mothers. . . . Yes, why indeed? I said to myself.

Coffee had now been served. Mother was inviting them to drink.

"We won't take even one sip," the old woman began, "before you've given us your word about your daughter."

"Yes," the other one said, "my brother impressed upon us that we weren't to come back without your promising to give her to him as his wife."

I was listening to Mother avoid answering, have herself be begged hypocritically, and then again invite them to drink. Aïcha joined in with her. The women were repeating their request. . . . It was all as it should be.

The game went on a few minutes longer. Mother invoked the father's authority: "I, of course, would give her to you. . . . I know you are people of means. . . . But there is her father."

"Her father has already said yes to my brother," one of the two women who resembled each other replied. "The question remains only to be discussed between us."

"Yes," said the second one, "it's up to us now. Let's settle the question."

I raised my head; it was then, I think, that I met Hafsa's gaze. There was, deep in her eyes, a strange light, surely of interest or of irony, I don't know, but you could feel Hafsa as an outsider, attentive and curious at the same time, but an outsider. I met that look.

"I don't want to marry," I said. "I don't want to marry," I repeated, barely shouting.

There was much commotion in the room: Mother got up with a deep sigh; Aïcha was blushing, I saw. And the two women who turned to me, with the same slow movement of shock: "And why not?" one of them asked.

"My son," the old woman exclaimed with some arrogance, "my son is a man of science. In a few days he is leaving for the Orient."

"Of course," Mother said with touching haste. "We know he's a scholar. We know him to have a righteous heart. . . . Of course. . . ."

"It's not because of your son," I said. "But I don't want to get married. I see the future before my eyes, it's totally black. I don't know how to explain it, surely it must come from God. . . . But I see the future totally black before my eyes!" I said again, sobbing, as Aïcha led me out of the room in silence.

✺

Later, but why even tell the rest, except that I was consumed with shame and I didn't understand. Only Hafsa stayed close to me after the women had left.

"You're engaged," she said sadly. "Your mother said she'd give you away. Will you accept?" and she stared at me with imploring eyes.

"What difference does it make?" I said and really thought inside myself: What difference does it make? "I don't know what came over me before. But they were all talking about the present and its changes and its misfortunes. And I was saying to myself: of what possible use is it to be suffering like this, far away from home, if I have to continue here as before in Algiers, to stay home and sit and pretend. . . . Perhaps when life changes, everything should change with it, absolutely everything. I was thinking of all that," I said, "but I don't even know if that's bad or good. . . . You, you're smart, and you know these things, perhaps you'll understand. . . ."

"I do understand," she said, hesitating as if she were going to start talking and then preferred to remain silent.

"Open the window," I said. "It's almost dark."

She went to open it and then came back to my bed where I'd been lying down to cry, without reason, crying for shame and fatigue all at the same time. In the silence that followed, I was feeling distant, pondering the night that little by little engulfed the room. The sounds from the kitchen, where my sisters were, seemed to be coming from somewhere else.

Then Hafsa began to speak: "Your father," she said, "once spoke of exile, of our present exile, and he said—oh, I remember it well, for nobody speaks like your father—he said: 'There is no exile for any man loved by God. There is no exile for the one who is on God's path. There are only trials.'"

She went on a while, but I've forgotten the rest, except that she repeated *we* very often with a note of passion. She said that word with a peculiar vehemence, so much so that I began to wonder toward the end whether that word really meant the two of us alone, or rather other women, all the women of our country.

To tell the truth, even if I'd known, what could I have answered? Hafsa was too knowledgeable for me. And that's what I would have liked to have told her when she stopped talking, perhaps in the expectation that I would speak.

But it was another voice that answered, a woman's voice that rose, through the open window, rose straight as an arrow toward the sky, that rounded itself out, spread out in its flight, a flight ample as a bird's after the storm, then came falling back down in sudden torrents.

"The other women have grown silent," I said. "The only one left to weep now is the mother. . . . Such is life," I added a moment later. "There are those who forget or who simply sleep. And then there are those who keep bumping into the walls of the past. May God take pity on them!"

"Those are the true exiles," said Hafsa.

Battle Royal
(1947)

RALPH ELLISON

It goes a long way back, some twenty years. All my life I had been looking for something, and everywhere I turned someone tried to tell me what it was. I accepted their answers too, though they were often in contradiction and even self-contradictory. I was naïve. I was looking for myself and asking everyone except myself questions which I, and only I, could answer. It took me a long time and much painful boomeranging of my expectations to achieve a realization everyone else appears to have been born with: That I am nobody but myself. But first I had to discover that I am an invisible man!

And yet I am no freak of nature, nor of history. I was in the cards, other things having been equal (or unequal) eighty-five years ago. I am not ashamed of my grandparents for having been slaves. I am only ashamed of myself for having at one time been ashamed. About eighty-five years ago they were told that they were free, united with others of our country in everything pertaining to the common good, and, in everything social, separate like the fingers of the hand. And they believed it. They exulted in it. They stayed in their place, worked hard, and brought up my father to do the same. But my grandfather is the one. He was an odd old guy, my grandfather, and I am told I take after him. It was he who caused the trouble. On his death-bed he called my father to him and said, "Son, after I'm gone I want you to keep up the good fight. I never told you, but our life is a war and I have been a traitor all my born days, a spy in the enemy's country ever since I give up my gun back in the Reconstruction. Live with your head in the lion's mouth. I want you to overcome 'em with yeses, undermine 'em with grins, agree 'em to death and destruction, let 'em swoller you till they vomit or bust wide open." They thought the old man had gone out of his mind. He had been the meekest of men. The younger children were rushed from the room, the shades drawn and the flame of the lamp turned so low that it sputtered on the wick like the old man's breathing. "Learn it to the younguns," he whispered fiercely; then he died.

But my folks were more alarmed over his last words than over his dying. It was as though he had not died at all, his words caused so much anxiety. I was warned emphatically to forget what he had said and, indeed, this is the first time it has been mentioned outside the family circle. It had a tremendous effect upon me, however. I could never be sure of what he meant. Grandfather had been a quiet old man who never made any trouble, yet on his death-bed he had called himself a traitor and a spy, and he had spoken of his meekness as a dangerous activity. It became a constant puzzle which lay unanswered in the back of my mind. And whenever things went well for me I remembered my grandfather and felt guilty and uncomfortable. It was as though I was carrying out his advice in spite of myself. And to make it worse, everyone loved me for it. I was praised by the most lily-white men of the town. I was considered an example of desirable conduct—just as my grandfather had been. And what puzzled me was that the old man had defined it as *treachery*. When I was praised for my conduct I felt a guilt that in some way I was doing something that was really against the wishes of the white folks, that if they had understood they would have desired me to act just the opposite, that I should have been sulky and mean, and that that really would have been what they wanted, even though they were fooled and thought they wanted me to act as I did. It made me afraid that some day they would look upon me as a traitor and I would be lost. Still I was more afraid to act any other way because they didn't like that at all. The old man's words were like a curse. On my graduation day I delivered an oration in which I showed that humility was the secret, indeed, the very essence of progress. (Not that I believed this—how could I, remembering my grandfather?—I only believed that it worked.) It was a great success. Everyone praised me and I was invited to give the speech at a gathering of the town's leading white citizens. It was a triumph for our whole community.

It was in the main ballroom of the leading hotel. When I got there I discovered that it was on the occasion of a smoker, and I was told that since I was to be there anyway I might as well take part in the battle royal to be fought by some of my schoolmates as part of the entertainment. The battle royal came first.

All of the town's big shots were there in their tuxedoes, wolfing down the buffet foods, drinking beer and whiskey and smoking black cigars. It was a large room with a high ceiling. Chairs were arranged in neat rows around three sides of a portable boxing ring. The fourth side was clear, revealing a gleaming space of polished floor. I had some misgivings over the battle royal, by the way. Not from a distaste for fighting, but because I didn't care too much for the other fellows who were to take part. They were tough guys who seemed to have no grandfather's curse worrying their minds. No one could mistake their toughness. And besides, I suspected that fighting a battle royal might detract from the dignity of my speech. In those pre-invisible days I visualized myself as a potential Booker T. Washington. But the other fellows didn't care too much for me either, and there were nine of them. I felt superior to them in my way, and I didn't like the manner in which we were all crowded together into the servants' elevator. Nor did they like my being there. In fact, as the warmly lighted floors flashed past the elevator we had words over the fact that I, by taking part in the fight, had knocked one of their friends out of a night's work.

We were led out of the elevator through a rococo hall into an anteroom and told to get into our fighting togs. Each of us was issued a pair of boxing gloves and ushered out into the big mirrored hall, which we entered looking cautiously about us and whispering, lest we might accidentally be heard above the noise of the room. It was foggy with cigar smoke. And already the whiskey was taking effect. I was shocked to see some of the most important men of the town quite tipsy. They were all there—bankers, lawyers, judges, doctors, fire chiefs, teachers, merchants. Even one of the more fashionable pastors. Something we could not see was going on up front. A clarinet was vibrating sensuously and the men were standing up and moving eagerly forward. We were a small tight group, clustered together, our bare upper bodies touching and shining with anticipatory sweat; while up front the big shots were becoming increasingly excited over something we still could not see. Suddenly I heard the school superintendent, who had told me to come, yell, "Bring up the shines, gentlemen! Bring up the little shines!"

We were rushed up to the front of the ballroom, where it smelled even more strongly of tobacco and whiskey. Then we were pushed into place. I almost wet my pants. A sea of faces, some hostile, some amused, ringed around us, and in the center, facing us, stood a magnificent blonde—stark naked. There was dead silence. I felt a blast of cold air chill me. I tried to back away, but they were behind me and around me. Some of the boys stood with lowered heads, trembling. I felt a wave of irrational guilt and fear. My teeth chattered, my skin turned to goose flesh, my knees knocked. Yet I was strongly attracted and looked in spite of myself. Had the price of looking been blindness, I would have looked. The hair was yellow like that of a circus kewpie doll, the face heavily powdered and rouged, as though to form an abstract mask, the eyes hollow and smeared a cool blue, the color of a baboon's butt. I felt a desire to spit upon her as my eyes brushed slowly over her body. Her breasts were firm and round as the domes of East Indian temples, and I stood so close as to see the fine skin texture and beads of pearly perspiration glistening like dew around the pink and erected buds of her nipples. I wanted at one and the same time to run from the room, to sink through the floor, or go to her and cover her from my eyes and the eyes of the others with my body; to feel the soft thighs, to caress her and destroy her, to love her and murder her, to hide from her, and yet to stroke where below the small American flag tattooed upon her belly her thighs formed a capital V. I had a notion that of all in the room she saw only me with her impersonal eyes.

And then she began to dance, a slow sensuous movement; the smoke of a hundred cigars clinging to her like the thinnest of veils. She seemed like a fair bird-girl girdled in veils calling to me from the angry surface of some gray and threatening sea. I was transported. Then I became aware of the clarinet playing and the big shots yelling at us. Some threatened us if we looked and others if we did not. On my right I saw one boy faint. And now a man grabbed a silver pitcher from a table and stepped close as he dashed ice water upon him and stood him up and forced two of us to support him as his head hung and moans issued from his thick bluish lips. Another boy began to plead to go home. He was the largest of the group, wearing dark red fighting trunks much too small to conceal the erection which projected from him as though in answer to the insinuating low-registered moaning of the clarinet. He tried to hide himself with his boxing gloves.

And all the while the blonde continued dancing, smiling faintly at the big shots who watched her with fascination, and faintly smiling at our fear. I noticed a certain merchant who followed her hungrily, his lips loose and drooling. He was a large man who wore diamond studs in a shirtfront which swelled with the ample paunch underneath, and each time the blonde swayed her undulating hips he ran his hand through the thin hair of his bald head and, with his arms upheld, his posture clumsy like that of an intoxicated panda, wound his belly in a slow and obscene grind. This creature was completely hypnotized. The music had quickened. As the dancer flung herself about with a detached expression on her face, the men began reaching out to touch her. I could see their beefy fingers sink into the soft flesh. Some of the others tried to stop them and she began to move around the floor in graceful circles, as they gave chase, slipping and sliding over the polished floor. It was mad. Chairs went crashing, drinks were spilt, as they ran laughing and howling after her. They caught her just as she reached a door, raised her from the floor, and tossed her as college boys are tossed at a hazing, and above her red, fixed-smiling lips I saw the terror and disgust in her eyes, almost like my own terror and that which I saw in some of the other boys. As I watched, they tossed her twice and her soft breasts seemed to flatten against the air and her legs flung wildly as she spun. Some of the more sober ones helped her to escape. And I started off the floor, heading for the anteroom with the rest of the boys.

Some were still crying and in hysteria. But as we tried to leave we were stopped and ordered to get into the ring. There was nothing to do but what we were told. All ten of us climbed under the ropes and allowed ourselves to be blind folded with broad bands of white cloth. One of the men seemed to feel a bit sympathetic and tried to cheer us up as we stood with our backs against the ropes. Some of us tried to grin. "See that boy over there?" one of the men said. "I want you to run across at the bell and give it to him right in the belly. If you don't get him, I'm going to get you. I don't like his looks." Each of us was told the same. The blindfolds were put on. Yet even then I had been going over my speech. In my mind each word was as bright as flame. I felt the cloth pressed into place, and frowned so that it would be loosened when I relaxed.

But now I felt a sudden fit of blind terror. I was unused to darkness. It was as though I had suddenly found myself in a dark room filled with poisonous cottonmouths. I could hear the bleary voices yelling insistently for the battle royal to begin.

"Get going in there!"

"Let me at that big nigger!"

I strained to pick up the school superintendent's voice, as though to squeeze some security out of that slightly more familiar sound.

"Let me at those black sonsabitches!" someone yelled.

"No, Jackson, no!" another voice yelled. "Here, somebody, help me hold Jack."

"I want to get at that ginger-colored nigger. Tear him limb from limb," the first voice yelled.

I stood against the ropes trembling. For in those days I was what they called ginger-colored, and he sounded as though he might crunch me between his teeth like a crisp ginger cookie.

Quite a struggle was going on. Chairs were being kicked about and I could hear voices grunting as with a terrific effort. I wanted to see, to see more desperately than ever before. But the blindfold was tight as a thick skin-puckering scab and when I raised my gloved hands to push the layers of white aside a voice yelled, "Oh, no you don't, black bastard! Leave that alone!"

"Ring the bell before Jackson kills him a coon!" someone boomed in the sudden silence. And I heard the bell clang and the sound of the feet scuffing forward.

A glove smacked against my head. I pivoted, striking out stiffly as someone went past, and felt the jar ripple along the length of my arm to my shoulder. Then it seemed as though all nine of the boys had turned upon me at once. Blows pounded me from all sides while I struck out as best I could. So many blows landed upon me that I wondered if I were not the only blindfolded fighter in the ring, or if the man called Jackson hadn't succeeded in getting me after all.

Blindfolded, I could no longer control my motions. I had no dignity. I stumbled about like a baby or a drunken man. The smoke had become thicker and with each new blow it seemed to sear and further restrict my lungs. My saliva became like hot bitter glue. A glove connected with my head, filling my mouth with warm blood. It was everywhere. I could not tell if the moisture I felt upon my body was sweat or blood. A blow landed hard against the nape of my neck. I felt myself going over, my head hitting the floor. Streaks of blue light filled the black world behind the blindfold. I lay prone, pretending that I was knocked out, but felt myself seized by hands and yanked to my feet. "Get going, black boy! Mix it up!" My arms were like lead, my head smarting from blows. I managed to feel my way to the ropes and held on, trying to catch my breath. A glove landed in my mid-section and I went over again, feeling as though the smoke had become a knife jabbed into my guts. Pushed this way and that by the legs milling around me, I finally pulled erect and discovered that I could see the black, sweat-washed forms weaving in the smoky-blue atmosphere like drunken dancers weaving to the rapid drum-like thuds of blows.

Everyone fought hysterically. It was complete anarchy. Everybody fought everybody else. No group fought together for long. Two, three, four, fought one, then turned to fight each other, were themselves attacked. Blows landed below the belt and in the kidney, with the gloves open as well as closed, and with my eye partly opened now there was not so much terror. I moved carefully, avoiding blows, although not too many to attract attention, fighting from group to group. The boys groped about like blind, cautious crabs crouching to protect their mid-sections, their heads pulled in short against their shoulders, their arms stretched nervously before them, with their fists testing the smoke-filled air like the knobbed feelers of hypersensitive snails. In one corner I glimpsed a boy violently punching the air and heard him scream in pain as he smashed his hand against a ring post. For a second I saw him bent over holding his hand, then going down as a blow caught his unprotected head. I played one group against the other, slipping in and throwing a punch then stepping out of range while pushing the others into the melee to take the blows blindly aimed at me. The smoke was agonizing and there were no rounds, no bells at three-minute intervals to relieve our exhaustion. The room spun round me, a swirl of lights, smoke, sweating bodies surrounded by tense white faces. I bled from both nose and mouth, the blood spattering upon my chest.

The men kept yelling, "Slug him, black boy! Knock his guts out!"

"Uppercut him! Kill him! Kill that big boy!"

Taking a fake fall, I saw a boy going down heavily beside me as though we were felled by a single blow, saw a sneaker-clad foot shoot into his groin as the two who had knocked him down stumbled upon him. I rolled out of range, feeling a twinge of nausea.

The harder we fought the more threatening the men became. And yet, I had begun to worry about my speech again. How would it go? Would they recognize my ability? What would they give me?

I was fighting automatically when suddenly I noticed that one after another of the boys was leaving the ring. I was surprised, filled with panic, as though I had been left alone with an unknown danger. Then I understood. The boys had arranged it among themselves. It was the custom for the two men left in the ring to slug it out for the winner's prize. I discovered this too late. When the bell sounded two men in tuxedoes leaped into the ring and removed the blindfold. I found myself facing Tatlock, the biggest of the gang. I felt sick at my stomach. Hardly had the bell stopped ringing in my ears than it clanged again and I saw him moving swiftly toward me. Thinking of nothing else to do I hit him smash on the nose. He kept coming, bringing the rank sharp violence of stale sweat. His face was a black blank of a face, only his eyes alive—with hate of me and aglow with a feverish terror from what had happened to us all. I became anxious. I wanted to deliver my speech and he came at me as though he meant to beat it out of me. I smashed him again and again, taking his blows as they came. Then on a sudden impulse I struck him lightly and as we clinched, I whispered, "Fake like I knocked you out, you can have the prize."

"I'll break your behind," he whispered hoarsely.

"For *them?*"

"For *me*, sonofabitch!"

They were yelling for us to break it up and Tatlock spun me half around with a blow, and as a joggled camera sweeps in a reeling scene, I saw the howling red faces crouching tense beneath the cloud of blue-gray smoke. For a moment the world wavered, unraveled, flowed, then my head cleared and Tatlock bounced before me. That fluttering shadow before my eyes was his jabbing left hand. Then falling forward, my head against his damp shoulder, I whispered,

"I'll make it five dollars more."

"Go to hell!"

But his muscles relaxed a trifle beneath my pressure and I breathed, "Seven?"

"Give it to your ma," he said, ripping me beneath the heart.

And while I still held him I butted him and moved away. I felt myself bombarded with punches. I fought back with hopeless desperation. I wanted to deliver my speech more than anything else in the world, because I felt that only these men could judge truly my ability, and now this stupid clown was ruining my chances. I began fighting carefully now, moving in to punch him and out again with my greater speed. A lucky blow to his chin and I had him going too—until I heard a loud voice yell, "I got my money on the big boy."

Hearing this, I almost dropped my guard. I was confused: Should I try to win against the voice out there? Would not this go against my speech, and was not this a moment for humility, for nonresistance? A blow to my head as I danced about sent my right eye popping like a jack-in-the-box and settled my dilemma. The room went red as I fell. It was a dream fall, my body languid and fastidious as to where to land, until the floor became impatient and smashed up to meet me. A moment later I came to. An hypnotic voice said FIVE emphatically. And I lay there, hazily watching a dark red spot of my own blood shaping itself into a butterfly, glistening and soaking into the soiled gray world of the canvas.

When the voice drawled TEN I was lifted up and dragged to a chair. I sat dazed. My eye pained and swelled with each throb of my pounding heart and I wondered if now I would be allowed to speak. I was wringing wet, my mouth still bleeding. We were grouped along the wall now. The other boys ignored me as they congratulated Tatlock and speculated as to how much they would be paid. One boy whimpered over his smashed hand. Looking up front, I saw attendants in white jackets rolling the portable ring away and placing a small square rug in the vacant space surrounded by chairs. Perhaps, I thought, I will stand on the rug to deliver my speech.

Then the M.C. called to us, "Come on up here boys and get your money."

We ran forward to where the men laughed and talked in their chairs, waiting. Everyone seemed friendly now.

"There it is on the rug," the man said. I saw the rug covered with coins of all dimensions and a few crumpled bills. But what excited me, scattered here and there, were the gold pieces.

"Boys, it's all yours," the man said. "You get all you grab."

"That's right, Sambo," a blond man said, winking at me confidentially.

I trembled with excitement, forgetting my pain. I would get the gold and the bills, I thought. I would use both hands. I would throw my body against the boys nearest me to block them from the gold.

"Get down around the rug now," the man commanded, "and don't anyone touch it until I give the signal."

"This ought to be good," I heard.

As told, we got around the square rug on our knees. Slowly the man raised his freckled hand as we followed it upward with our eyes.

I heard, "These niggers look like they're about to pray!"

Then, "Ready," the man said. "Go!"

I lunged for a yellow coin lying on the blue design of the carpet, touching it and sending a surprised shriek to join those rising around me. I tried frantically to remove my hand but could not let go. A hot, violent force tore through my body, shaking me like a wet rat. The rug was electrified. The hair bristled up on my head as I shook myself free. My muscles jumped, my nerves jangled, writhed. But I saw that this was not stopping the other boys. Laughing in fear and embarrassment, some were holding back and scooping up the coins knocked off by the painful contortions of the others. The men roared above us as we struggled.

"Pick it up, goddamnit, pick it up!" someone called like a bass-voiced parrot. "Go on, get it!"

I crawled rapidly around the floor, picking up the coins, trying to avoid the coppers and to get greenbacks and the gold. Ignoring the shock by laughing, as I brushed the coins off quickly, I discovered that I could contain the electricity—a contradiction, but it works. Then the men began to push us onto the rug. Laughing embarrassedly, we struggled out of their hands and kept after the coins. We were all wet and slippery and hard to hold. Suddenly I saw a boy lifted into the air, glistening with sweat like a circus seal, and dropped, his wet back landing flush upon the charged rug, heard him yell and saw him literally dance upon his back, his elbows beating a frenzied tattoo upon the floor, his muscles twitching like the flesh of a horse stung by many flies. When he finally rolled off, his face was gray and no one stopped him when he ran from the floor amid booming laughter.

"Get the money," the M.C. called. "That's good hard American cash!"

And we snatched and grabbed, snatched and grabbed. I was careful not to come too close to the rug now, and when I felt the hot whiskey breath descend upon me like a cloud of foul air I reached out and grabbed the leg of a chair. It was occupied and I held on desperately.

"Leggo, nigger! Leggo!"

The huge face wavered down to mine as he tried to push me free. But my body was slippery and he was too drunk. It was Mr. Colcord, who owned a chain of movie houses and "entertainment palaces." Each time he grabbed me I slipped out of his hands. It became a real struggle. I feared the rug more than I did the drunk, so I held on, surprising myself for a moment by trying to topple *him* upon the rug. It was such an enormous idea that I found myself actually carrying it out. I tried not to be obvious, yet when I grabbed his leg, trying to tumble him out of the chair, he raised up roaring with laughter, and, looking at me with soberness dead in the eye, kicked me viciously in the chest. The chair leg flew out of my hand and I felt myself going and rolled. It was as though I had rolled through a bed of hot coals. It seemed a whole century would pass before I would roll free, a century in which I was seared through the deepest levels of my body to the fearful breath within me and the breath seared and heated to the point of explosion. It'll all be over in a flash, I thought as I rolled clear. It'll all be over in a flash.

But not yet, the men on the other side were waiting, red faces swollen as though from apoplexy as they bent forward in their chairs. Seeing their fingers coming toward me I rolled away as a fumbled football rolls off the receiver's fingertips, back into the coals. That time I luckily sent the rug sliding out of place and heard the coins ringing against the floor and the boys scuffling to pick them up and the M.C. calling, "All right, boys, that's all. Go get dressed and get your money."

I was limp as a dish rag. My back felt as though it had been beaten with wires.

When we had dressed the M.C. came in and gave us each five dollars, except Tatlock, who got ten for being last in the ring. Then he told us to leave. I was not to get a chance to deliver my speech, I thought. I was going out into the dim alley in despair when I was stopped and told to go back. I returned to the ballroom, where the men were pushing back their chairs and gathering in groups to talk.

The M.C. knocked on a table for quiet. "Gentlemen," he said, "we almost forgot an important part of the program. A most serious part, gentlemen. This boy was brought here to deliver a speech which he made at his graduation yesterday. . . "

"Bravo!"

"I'm told that he is the smartest boy we've got out there in Greenwood. I'm told that he knows more big words than a pocket-sized dictionary."

Much applause and laughter.

"So now, gentlemen, I want you to give him your attention."

There was still laughter as I faced them, my mouth dry, my eye throbbing. I began slowly, but evidently my throat was tense, because they began shouting, "Louder! Louder!"

"We of the younger generation extol the wisdom of that great leader and educator," I shouted, "who first spoke these flaming words of wisdom: 'A ship lost at sea for many days suddenly sighted a friendly vessel. From the mast of the unfortunate vessel was seen a signal: "Water, water; we die of thirst!" The answer from the friendly vessel came back: "Cast down your bucket where you are." The captain of the distressed vessel, at last heeding the injunction, cast down his bucket, and it came up full of fresh sparkling water from the mouth of the Amazon River.' And like him I say, and in his words, 'To those of my race who depend upon bettering their condition in a foreign land, or who underestimate the importance of cultivating friendly relations with the southern white man, who is his next-door neighbor, I would say: "Cast down your bucket where you are"—cast it down in making friends in every manly way of the people of all races by whom we are surrounded . . .'"

I spoke automatically and with such fervor that I did not realize that the men were still talking and laughing until my dry mouth, filling up with blood from the cut, almost strangled me. I coughed, wanting to stop and go to one of the tall brass, sand-filled spittoons to relieve myself, but a few of the men, especially the superintendent, were listening and I was afraid. So I gulped it down, blood, saliva and all, and continued. (What powers of endurance I had during those days! What enthusiasm! What a belief in the rightness of things!) I spoke even louder in spite of the pain. But still they talked and still they laughed, as though deaf with cotton in dirty ears. So I spoke with greater emotional emphasis. I closed my ears and swallowed blood until I was nauseated. The speech seemed a hundred times as long as before, but I could not leave out a single word. All had to be said, each memorized nuance considered, rendered. Nor was that all. Whenever I uttered a word of three or more syllables a group of voices would yell for me to repeat it. I used the phrase "social responsibility" and they yelled:

"What's that word you say, boy?"

"Social responsibility," I said.

"What?"

"Social . . ."

"Louder."

". . . responsibility."

"More!"

"Respon—"

"Repeat!"

"—sibility."

The room filled with the uproar of laughter until, no doubt distracted by having to gulp down my blood, I made a mistake and yelled a phrase I had often seen denounced in newspaper editorials, heard debated in private.

"Social . . ."

"What?" they yelled.

". . . equality—"

The laughter hung smokelike in the sudden stillness. I opened my eyes, puzzled. Sounds of displeasure filled the room. The M.C. rushed forward. They shouted hostile phrases at me. But I did not understand.

A small dry mustached man in the front row blared out, "Say that slowly, son!"

"What, sir?"

"What you just said!"

"Social responsibility, sir," I said.

"You weren't being smart, were you, boy?" he said, not unkindly.

"No, sir!"

"You sure that about 'equality' was a mistake?"

"Oh, yes, sir," I said. "I was swallowing blood."

"Well, you had better speak more slowly so we can understand. We mean to do right by you, but you've got to know your place at all times. All right, now, go on with your speech."

I was afraid. I wanted to leave but I wanted also to speak and I was afraid they'd snatch me down.

"Thank you, sir," I said, beginning where I had left off, and having them ignore me as before.

Yet when I finished there was a thunderous applause. I was surprised to see the superintendent come forth with a package wrapped in white tissue paper, and, gesturing for quiet, address the men.

"Gentlemen, you see that I did not overpraise this boy. He makes a good speech and some day he'll lead his people in the proper paths. And I don't have to tell you that that is important in these days and times. This is a good, smart boy, and so to encourage him in the right direction, in the name of the Board of Education I wish to present him a prize in the form of this . . ."

He paused, removing the tissue paper and revealing a gleaming calfskin brief case.

". . . in the form of this first-class article from Shad Whitmore's shop."

"Boy," he said, addressing me, "take this prize and keep it well. Consider it a badge of office. Prize it. Keep developing as you are and some day it will be filled with important papers that will help shape the destiny of your people."

I was so moved that I could hardly express my thanks. A rope of bloody saliva forming a shape like an undiscovered continent drooled upon the leather and I wiped it quickly away. I felt an importance that I had never dreamed.

"Open it and see what's inside," I was told.

My fingers a-tremble, I complied, smelling the fresh leather and finding an official-looking document inside. It was a scholarship to the state college for Negroes. My eyes filled with tears and I ran awkwardly off the floor.

I was overjoyed; I did not even mind when I discovered that the gold pieces I had scrambled for were brass pocket tokens advertising a certain make of automobile.

When I reached home everyone was excited. Next day the neighbors came to congratulate me. I even felt safe from grandfather, whose deathbed curse usually spoiled my triumphs. I stood beneath his photograph with my brief case in hand and smiled triumphantly into his stolid black peasant's face. It was a face that fascinated me. The eyes seemed to follow everywhere I went.

That night I dreamed I was at a circus with him and that he refused to laugh at the clowns no matter what they did. Then later he told me to open my brief case and read what was inside and I did, finding an official envelope stamped with the state seal; and inside the envelope I found another and another, endlessly, and I thought I would fall of weariness. "Them's years," he said, "Now open that one," And I did and in it I found an engraved document containing a short message in letters of gold. "Read it," my grandfather said. "Out loud!"

"To Whom It May Concern," I intoned, "Keep This Nigger-Boy Running."

I awoke with the old man's laughter ringing in my ears.

(It was a dream I was to remember and dream again for many years after. But at that time I had no insight into its meaning. First I had to attend college.)

American Horse
(1983)

LOUISE ERDRICH

The woman sleeping on the cot in the woodshed was Albertine American Horse. The name was left over from her mother's short marriage. The boy was the son of the man she had loved and let go. Buddy was on the cot too, sitting on the edge because he'd been awake three hours watching out for his mother and besides, she took up the whole cot. Her feet hung over the edge, limp and brown as two trout. Her long arms reached out and slapped at things she saw in her dreams.

Buddy had been knocked awake out of hiding in a washing machine while herds of policemen with dogs searched through a large building with many tiny rooms. When the arm came down, Buddy screamed because it had a blue cuff and sharp silver buttons. "Tss," his mother mumbled, half awake, "wasn't nothing." But Buddy sat up after her breathing went deep again, and he watched.

There was something coming and he knew it.

It was coming from very far off but he had a picture of it in his mind. It was a large thing made of metal with many barbed hooks, points, and drag chains on it, something like a giant potato peeler that rolled out of the sky, scraping clouds down with it and jabbing or crushing everything that lay in its path on the ground.

Buddy watched his mother. If he woke her up, she would know what to do about the thing, but he thought he'd wait until he saw it for sure before he shook her. She was pretty, sleeping, and he liked knowing he could look at her as long and close up as he wanted. He took a strand of her hair and held it in his hands as if it was the rein to a delicate beast. She was strong enough and could pull him along like the horse their name was.

Buddy had his mother's and his grandmother's name because his father had been a big mistake.

"They're all mistakes, even your father. But *you* are the best thing that ever happened to me."

That was what she said when he asked.

Even Kadie, the boyfriend crippled from being in a car wreck, was not as good a thing that had happened to his mother as Buddy was. "He was a medium-size mistake," she said. "He's hurt and I shouldn't even say that, but it's the truth." At the moment, Buddy knew that being the best thing in his mother's life, he was also the reason they were hiding from the cops.

He wanted to touch the satin roses sewed on her pink tee-shirt, but he knew he shouldn't do that even in her sleep. If she woke up and found him touching the roses, she would say, "Quit that, Buddy." Sometimes she told him to stop hugging her like a gorilla. She never said that in the mean voice she used when he oppressed her, but when she said that he loosened up anyway.

There were times he felt like hugging her so hard and in such a special way that she would say to him, "Let's get married." There were also times he closed his eyes and wished that she would die, only a few times, but still it haunted him that his wish might come true. He and Uncle Lawrence would be left alone. Buddy wasn't worried, though, about his mother getting married to somebody else. She had said to her friend, Madonna, "All men suck," when she thought Buddy wasn't listening. He had made an uncertain sound, and when they heard him they took him in their arms.

"Except for you, Buddy," his mother said. "All except for you and maybe Uncle Lawrence, although he's pushing it."

"The cops suck the worst though," Buddy whispered to his mother's sleeping face, "because they're after us." He felt tired again, slumped down, and put his legs beneath the blanket. He closed his eyes and got the feeling that the cot was lifting up beneath him, that it was arching its canvas back and then traveling, traveling very fast and in the wrong direction for when he looked up he saw the three of them were advancing to meet the great metal thing with hooks and barbs and all sorts of sharp equipment to catch their bodies and draw their blood. He heard its insides as it rushed toward them, purring softly like a powerful motor and then they were right in its shadow. He pulled the reins as hard as he could and the beast reared, lifting him. His mother clapped her hand across his mouth.

"Okay," she said. "Lay low. They're outside and they're gonna hunt."

She touched his shoulder and Buddy leaned over with her to look through a crack in the boards.

They were out there all right, Albertine saw them. Two officers and that social worker woman. Vicki Koob. There had been no whistle, no dream, no voice to warn her that they were coming. There was only the crunching sound of cinders in the yard, the engine purring, the dust sifting off their car in a fine light brownish cloud and settling around them.

The three people came to a halt in their husk of metal—the car emblazoned with the North Dakota State Highway Patrol emblem which is the glowing profile of the Sioux policeman, Red Tomahawk, the one who killed Sitting Bull. Albertine gave Buddy the blanket and told him that he might have to wrap it around him and hide underneath the cot.

"We're gonna wait and see what they do." She took him in her lap and hunched her arms around him. "Don't you worry," she whispered against his ear. "Lawrence knows how to fool them."

Buddy didn't want to look at the car and the people. He felt his mother's heart beating beneath his ear so fast it seemed to push the satin roses in and out. He put his face to them carefully and breathed the deep, soft powdery woman smell of her. That smell was also in her little face cream bottles, in her brushes, and around the washbowl after she used it. The satin felt so unbearably smooth against his cheek that he had to press closer. She didn't push him away, like he expected, but hugged him still tighter until he felt as close as he had ever been to back inside her again where she said he came from. Within the smells of her things, her soft skin and the satin of her roses, he closed his eyes then, and took his breaths softly and quickly with her heart.

They were out there, but they didn't dare get out of the car yet because of Lawrence's big, ragged dogs. Three of these dogs had loped up the dirt driveway with the car. They were rangy, alert, and bounced up and down on their cushioned paws like wolves. They didn't waste their energy barking, but positioned themselves quietly, one at either car door and the third in front of the bellied-out screen door to Uncle Lawrence's house. It was six in the morning but the wind was up already, blowing dust, ruffling their short moth-eaten coats. The big brown one on Vicki Koob's side had unusual black and white markings, stripes almost, like a hyena and he grinned at her, tongue out and teeth showing.

"Shoo!" Miss Koob opened her door with a quick jerk.

The brown dog sidestepped the door and jumped before her, tiptoeing. Its dirty white muzzle curled and its eyes crossed suddenly as if it was zeroing its cross-hair sights in on the exact place it would bite her. She ducked back and slammed the door.

"It's mean," she told officer Brackett. He was printing out some type of form. The other officer, Harmony, a slow man, had not yet reacted to the car's halt. He had been sitting quietly in the back seat, but now he rolled down his window and with no change in expression unsnapped his holster and drew his pistol out and pointed it at the dog on his side. The dog smacked down on its belly, wiggled under the car and was out and around the back of the house before Harmony drew his gun back. The other dogs vanished with him. From wherever they had disappeared to they began to yap and howl, and the door to the low shoebox style house fell open.

"Heya, what's going on?"

Uncle Lawrence put his head out the door and opened wide the one eye he had in working order. The eye bulged impossibly wider in outrage when he saw the police car. But the eyes of the two officers and Miss Vicki Koob were wide open too because they had never seen Uncle Lawrence in his sleeping get up or, indeed, witnessed anything like it. For his ribs, which were cracked from a bad fall and still mending, Uncle Lawrence wore a thick white corset laced up the front with a striped sneakers lace. His glass eye and his set of dentures were still out for the night so his face puckered here and there, around its absences and scars, like a damaged but fierce little cake. Although he had a few gray streaks now, Uncle Lawrence's hair was still thick, and because he wore a special contraption of elastic straps around his head every night, two oiled waves always crested on either side of his middle part. All of this would have been sufficient to astonish, even without the most striking part of his outfit—the smoking jacket. It was made of black satin and hung open around his corset, dragging a tasseled belt. Gold thread dragons struggled up the lapels and blasted their furry red breath around his neck. As Lawrence walked down the steps, he put his arms up in surrender and the gold tassels in the inner seams of his sleeves dropped into view.

"My heavens, what a sight." Vicki Koob was impressed.

"A character," apologized Officer Harmony.

As a tribal police officer who could be counted on to help out the State Patrol, Harmony thought he always had to explain about Indians or get twice as tough to show he did not favor them. He was slow-moving and shy but two jumps ahead of other people all the same, and now, as he watched Uncle Lawrence's splendid approach, he gazed speculatively at the torn and bulging pocket of the smoking jacket. Harmony had been inside Uncle Lawrence's house before and knew that above his draped orange-crate shelf of war medals a blue-black German luger was hung carefully in a net of flat-headed nails and fishing line. Thinking of this deadly exhibition, he got out of the car and shambled toward Lawrence with a dreamy little smile of welcome on his face. But when he searched Lawrence, he found that the bulging pocket held only the lonesome looking dentures from Lawrence's empty jaw. They were still dripping denture polish.

"I had been cleaning them when you arrived," Uncle Lawrence explained with acid dignity.

He took the toothbrush from his other pocket and aimed it like a rifle.

"Quit that, you old idiot." Harmony tossed the toothbrush away. "For once you ain't done nothing. We came for your nephew."

Lawrence looked at Harmony with a faint air of puzzlement.

"Ma Frere, listen," threatened Harmony amiably, "those two white people in the car came to get him for the welfare. They got papers on your nephew that give them the right to take him."

"Papers?" Uncle Lawrence puffed out his deeply pitted cheeks. "Let me see them papers."

The two of them walked over to Vicki's side of the car and she pulled a copy of the court order from her purse. Lawrence put his teeth back in and adjusted them with busy workings of his jaw.

"Just a minute," he reached into his breast pocket as he bent close to Miss Vicki Koob. "I can't read these without I have in my eye."

He took the eye from his breast pocket delicately, and as he popped it into his face the social worker's mouth fell open in a consternated O.

"What is this," she cried in a little voice.

Uncle Lawrence looked at her mildly. The white glass of the eye was cold as lard. The black iris was strangely charged and menacing.

"He's nuts," Brackett huffed along the side of Vicki's neck. "Never mind him."

Vicki's hair had sweated down her nape in tiny corkscrews and some of the hairs were so long and dangly now that they disappeared into the zippered back of her dress. Brackett noticed this as he spoke into her ear. His face grew red and the backs of his hands prickled. He slid under the steering wheel and got out of the car. He walked around the hood to stand with Leo Harmony.

"We could take you in too," said Brackett roughly. Lawrence eyed the officers in what was taken as defiance. "If you don't cooperate, we'll get out the handcuffs," they warned.

One of Lawrence's arms was stiff and would not move until he'd rubbed it with witch hazel in the morning. His other arm worked fine though, and he stuck it out in front of Brackett.

"Get them handcuffs," he urged them. "Put me in a welfare home."

Brackett snapped one side of the handcuffs on Lawrence's good arm and the other to the handle of the police car.

"That's to hold you," he said. "We're wasting our time. Harmony, you search that little shed over by the tall grass and Miss Koob and myself will search the house."

"My rights is violated!" Lawrence shrieked suddenly. They ignored him. He tugged at the handcuff and thought of the good heavy file he kept in his tool box and the German luger oiled and ready but never loaded, because of Buddy, over his shelf. He should have used it on these bad ones, even Harmony in his big-time white man job. He wouldn't last long in that job anyway before somebody gave him what for.

"It's a damn scheme," said Uncle Lawrence, rattling his chains against the car. He looked over at the shed and thought maybe Albertine and Buddy had sneaked away before the car pulled into the yard. But he sagged, seeing Albertine move like a shadow within the boards. "Oh, it's all a damn scheme," he muttered again.

"I want to find that boy and salvage him," Vicki Koob explained to Officer Brackett as they walked into the house. "Look at his family life—the old man crazy as a bedbug, the mother intoxicated somewhere."

Brackett nodded, energetic, eager. He was a short hopeful redhead who failed consistently to win the hearts of women. Vicki Koob intrigued him. Now, as he watched, she pulled a tiny pen out of an ornamental clip on her blouse. It was attached to a retractable line that would suck the pen back, like a child eating one strand of spaghetti. Something about the pen on its line excited Brackett to the point of discomfort. His hand shook as he opened the screendoor and stepped in, beckoning Miss Koob to follow.

They could see the house was empty at first glance. It was only one rectangular room with whitewashed walls and a little gas stove in the middle. They had already come through the cooking lean-to with the other stove and washstand and rusty old refrigerator. That refrigerator had nothing in it but some wrinkled potatos and a package of turkey necks. Vicki Koob noted that in her perfect-bound notebook. The beds along the walls of the big room were covered with quilts that Albertine's mother, Sophie, had made from bits of old wool coats and pants that the Sisters sold in bundles at the mission. There was no one hiding beneath the beds. No one was under the little aluminum dinette table covered with a green oilcloth, or the soft brown wood chairs tucked up to it. One wall of the big room was filled with neatly stacked crates of things—old tools and springs and small half-dismantled appliances. Five or six television sets were stacked against the wall. Their control panels spewed colored wires and at least one was cracked all the way across. Only the topmost set, with coathanger antenna angled sensitively to catch the bounding signals around Little Shell, looked like it could possibly work.

Not one thing escaped Vicki Koob's trained and cataloguing gaze. She made note of the cupboard that held only commodity flour and coffee. The unsanitary tin oil drum beneath the kitchen window, full of empty surplus pork cans and beer bottles, caught her eye as did Uncle Lawrence's physical and mental deteriorations. She quickly described these "benchmarks of alcoholic dependency within the extended family of Woodrow (Buddy) American Horse" as she walked around the room with the little notebook open, pushed against her belly to steady it. Although Vicki had been there before, Albertine's presence had always made it difficult for her to take notes.

"Twice the maximum allowable space between door and threshold," she wrote now. "Probably no insulation. 2-3 inch cracks in walls inadequately sealed with whitewashed mud." She made a mental note but could see no point in describing Lawrence's stuffed reclining chair that only reclined, the shadeless lamp with its plastic orchid in the bubble glass base, or the three dimensional picture of Jesus that Lawrence had once demonstrated to her. When plugged in, lights rolled behind the water the Lord stood on so that he seemed to be strolling although he never actually went forward, of course, but only pushed the glowing waves behind him forever like a poor tame rat in a treadmill.

Brackett cleared his throat with a nervous rasp and touched Vicki's shoulder.

"What are you writing?"

She moved away and continued to scribble as if thoroughly absorbed in her work. "Officer Brackett displays an undue amount of interest in my person," she wrote. "Perhaps?"

He snatched playfully at the book, but she hugged it to her chest and moved off smiling. More curls had fallen, wetted to the base of her neck. Looking out the window, she sighed long and loud.

"All night on brush rollers for this. What a joke."

Brackett shoved his hands in his pockets. His mouth opened slightly, then shut with a small throttled cluck.

When Albertine saw Harmony ambling across the yard with his big brown thumbs in his belt, his placid smile, and his tiny black eyes moving back and forth, she put Buddy under the cot. Harmony stopped at the shed and stood quietly. He spread his arms wide to show her he hadn't drawn his big police gun.

"Ma Cousin," he said in the Michif dialect that people used if they were relatives or sometimes if they needed gas or a couple of dollars, "why don't you come out here and stop this foolishness?"

"I ain't your cousin," Albertine said. Anger boiled up in her suddenly. "I ain't related to no pigs."

She bit her lip and watched him through the cracks, circling, a big tan punching dummy with his boots full of sand so he never stayed down once he fell. He was empty inside, all stale air. But he knew how to get to her so much better than a white cop could. And now he was circling because he wasn't sure she didn't have a weapon, maybe a knife or the German luger that was the only thing that her father, Albert American Horse, had left his wife and daughter besides his name. Harmony knew that Albertine was a tall strong woman who took two big men to subdue when she didn't want to go in the drunk tank. She had hard hips, broad shoulders, and stood tall like her Sioux father, the American Horse who was killed threshing in Belle Prairie.

"I feel bad to have to do this," Harmony said to Albertine. "But for godsakes, let's nobody get hurt. Come on out with the boy why don't you. I know you got him in there."

Albertine did not give herself away this time. She let him wonder. Slowly and quietly she pulled her belt through its loops and wrapped it around and around her hand until only the big oval buckle with turquoise chunks shaped into a butterfly stuck out over her knuckles. Harmony was talking but she wasn't listening to what he said. She was listening to the pitch of his voice, the tone of it that would tighten or tremble at a certain moment when he decided to rush the shed. He kept talking slowly and reasonably, flexing the dialect from time to time, even mentioning her father.

"He was a damn good man. I don't care what they say, Albertine, I knew him."

Albertine looked at the stone butterfly that spread its wings across her fist. The wings looked light and cool, not heavy. It almost looked like it was ready to fly. Harmony wanted to get to Albertine through her father but she would not think about American Horse. She concentrated on the sky-blue stone.

Yet the shape of the stone, the color, betrayed her.

She saw her father suddenly, bending at the grill of their old grey car. She was small then. The memory came from so long ago it seemed like a dream—narrowly focused, snapshot clear. He was bending by the grill in the sun. It was hot summer. Wings of sweat, dark blue, spread across the back of his work shirt. He always wore soft blue shirts, the color of shade cloudier than this stone. His stiff hair had grown out of its short haircut and flopped over his forehead. When he stood up and turned away from the car, Albertine saw that he had a butterfly.

"It's dead," he told her, "Broke its wings and died on the grill."

She must have been five, maybe six, wearing one of the boy's tee-shirts Mama bleached in hilex-water. American Horse took the butterfly, a black and yellow one, and rubbed it on

Albertine's collarbone and chest and arms until the color and the powder of it were blended into her skin.

"For grace," he said.

And Albertine had felt a strange lightening in her arms, in her chest, when he did this and said, "For grace." The way he said it, grace meant everything the butterfly was. The sharp delicate wings. The way it floated over grass. The way its wings seemed to breathe fanning in the sun. The wisdom of the way it blended into flowers or changed into a leaf. In herself she felt the same kind of possibilities and closed her eyes almost in shock or pain she felt so light and powerful at that moment.

Then her father had caught her and thrown her high into the air. She could not remember landing in his arms or landing at all. She only remembered the sun filling her eyes and the world tipping crazily behind her, out of sight.

"He was a damn good man," Harmony said again.

Albertine heard his starched uniform gathering before his boots hit the ground. Once, twice, three times. It took him four solid jumps to get right where she wanted him. She kicked the plank door open when he reached for the handle and the corner caught him on the jaw. He faltered, and Albertine hit him flat on the chin with the butterfly. She hit him so hard the shock of it went up her arm like a string pulled taut. Her fist opened, numb, and she let the belt unloop before she closed her hand on the tip end of it and sent the stone butterfly swooping out in a wide circle around her as if it was on the end of a leash. Harmony reeled backward as she walked toward him swinging the belt. She expected him to fall but he just stumbled. And then he took the gun from his hip.

Albertine let the belt go limp. She and Harmony stood within feet of each other, breathing. Each heard the human sound of air going in and out of the other person's lungs. Each read the face of the other as if deciphering letters carved into softly eroding veins of stone. Albertine saw the pattern of tiny arteries that age, drink, and hard living had blown to the surface of the man's face. She saw the spoked wheels of his iris and the arteries like tangled threads that sewed him up. She saw the living net of springs and tissue that held him together, and trapped him. She saw the random, intimate plan of his person.

She took a quick shallow breath and her face went strange and tight. She saw the black veins in the wings of the butterfly, roads burnt into a map, and then she was located somewhere in the net of veins and sinew that was the tragic complexity of the world so she did not see Officer Brackett and Vicki Koob rushing toward her, but felt them instead like flies caught in the same web, rocking it.

"Albertine!" Vicki Koob had stopped in the grass. Her voice was shrill and tight. "It's better this way, Albertine. We're going to help you."

Albertine straightened, threw her shoulders back. Her father's hand was on her chest and shoulders lightening her wonderfully. Then on wings of her father's hands, on dead butterfly wings, Albertine lifted into the air and flew toward the others. The light powerful feeling swept her up the way she had floated higher, seeing the grass below. It was her father throwing her up into the air and out of danger. Her arms opened for bullets but no bullets came. Harmony did not shoot. Instead, he raised his fist and brought it down hard on her head.

Albertine did not fall immediately, but stood in his arms a moment. Perhaps she gazed still farther back behind the covering of his face. Perhaps she was completely stunned and did not think as she sagged and fell. Her face rolled forward and hair covered her features, so it was impossible for Harmony to see with just what particular expression she gazed into the headsplitting wheel of light, or blackness, that overcame her.

Harmony turned the vehicle onto the gravel road that led back to town. He had convinced the other two that Albertine was more trouble than she was worth, and so they left her behind, and Lawrence too. He stood swearing in his cinder driveway as the car rolled out of sight. Buddy sat between the social worker and Officer Brackett. Vicki tried to hold Buddy fast and keep her arm down at the same time, for the words she'd screamed at Albertine had broken the seal of antiperspirant beneath her arms. She was sweating now as though she'd stored an ocean up inside of her. Sweat rolled down her back in a shallow river and pooled at her waist and between her breasts. A thin sheen of water came out on her forearms, her face. Vicki gave an irritated moan but Brackett seemed not to take notice, or take offense at least. Air-conditioned breezes were sweeping over the seat anyway, and very soon they would be comfortable. She smiled at Brackett over Buddy's head. The man grinned back. Buddy stirred. Vicki remembered the emergency chocolate bar she kept in her purse, fished it out, and offered it to Buddy. He did not react, so she closed his fingers over the package and peeled the paper off one end.

The car accelerated. Buddy felt the road and wheels pummeling each other and the rush of the heavy motor purring in high gear. Buddy knew that what he'd seen in his mind that morning, the thing coming out of the sky with barbs and chains, had hooked him. Somehow he was caught and held in the sour tin smell of the pale woman's armpit. Somehow he was pinned between their pounds of breathless flesh. He looked at the chocolate in his hand. He was squeezing the bar so hard that a thin brown trickle had melted down his arm. Automatically, he put the bar in his mouth.

As he bit down he saw his mother very clearly, just as she had been when she carried him from the shed. She was stretched flat on the ground, on her stomach, and her arms were curled around her head as if in sleep. One leg was drawn up and it looked for all the world like she was running full tilt into the ground, as though she had been trying to pass into the earth, to bury herself, but at the last moment something had stopped her.

There was no blood on Albertine, but Buddy tasted blood now at the sight of her, for he bit down hard and cut his own lip. He ate the chocolate, every bit of it, tasting his mother's blood. And when he had the chocolate down inside him and all licked off his hands, he opened his mouth to say thank you to the woman, as his mother had taught him. But instead of a thank you coming out he was astonished to hear a great rattling scream, and then another, rip out of him like pieces of his own body and whirl onto the sharp things all around him.

The Appropriation of Cultures
(1996)

PERCIVAL EVERETT

Daniel Barkley had money left to him by his mother. He had a house that had been left to him by his mother. He had a degree in American Studies from Brown University that he had in some way earned, but that had not yet earned anything for him. He played a 1940 Martin guitar with a Barkus-Berry pickup and drove a 1976 Jensen Interceptor, which he had purchased after his mother's sister had died and left him her money because she had no children of her own. Daniel Barkley didn't work and didn't pretend to need to, spending most of his time reading. Some nights he went to a joint near the campus of the University of South Carolina and played jazz with some old guys who all worked very hard during the day, but didn't hold Daniel's condition against him.

Daniel played standards with the old guys, but what he loved to play were old-time slide tunes. One night, some white boys from a fraternity yelled forward to the stage at the black man holding the acoustic guitar and began to shout, "Play 'Dixie' for us! Play 'Dixie' for us!"

Daniel gave them a long look, studied their big-toothed grins and the beer-shiny eyes stuck into puffy, pale faces, hovering over golf shirts and chinos. He looked from them to the uncomfortable expressions on the faces of the old guys with whom he was playing and then to the embarrassed faces of the other college kids in the club.

And then he started to play. He felt his way slowly through the chords of the song once and listened to the deadened hush as it fell over the room. He used the slide to squeeze out the melody of the song he had grown up hating, the song the whites had always pulled out to remind themselves and those other people just where they were. Daniel sang the song. He sang it slowly. He sang it, feeling the lyrics, deciding that the lyrics were his, deciding that the song was his. *Old times there are not forgotten* . . . He sang the song and listened to the silence around him. He resisted the urge to let satire ring through his voice. He meant what he sang. *Look away, look away, look away, Dixieland.*

When he was finished, he looked up to see the roomful of eyes on him. One person clapped. Then another. And soon the tavern was filled with applause and hoots. He found the frat boys in the back and watched as they stormed out, a couple of people near the door chuckling at them as they passed.

Roger, the old guy who played tenor sax, slapped Daniel on the back and said something like, "Right on" or "Cool." Roger then played the first few notes of "Take the A Train" and they were off. When the set was done, all the college kids slapped Daniel on the back as he walked toward the bar where he found a beer waiting.

311

Daniel didn't much care for the slaps on the back, but he didn't focus too much energy on that. He was busy trying to sort out his feelings about what he had just played. The irony of his playing the song straight and from the heart was made more ironic by the fact that as he played it, it came straight and from his heart, as he was claiming Southern soil, or at least recognizing his blood in it. His was the land of cotton and hell no, it was not forgotten. At twenty-three, his anger was fresh and typical, and so was his ease with it, the way it could be forgotten for chunks of time, until something like that night with the white frat boys or simply a flashing blue light in the rearview mirror brought it all back. He liked the song, wanted to play it again, knew that he would.

He drove home from the bar on Green Street and back to his house where he made tea and read about Pickett's charge at Gettysburg while he sat in the big leather chair that had been his father's. He fell asleep and had a dream in which he stopped Pickett's men on the Emmitsburg Road on their way to the field and said, "Give me back my flag."

Daniel's friend Sarah was a very large woman with a very large Afro hairdo. They were sitting on the porch of Daniel's house having tea. The late fall afternoon was mild and slightly overcast. Daniel sat in the wicker rocker while Sarah curled her feet under her on the glider.

"I wish I could have heard it." Sarah said.

"Yeah, me too."

"Personally, I can't even stand to go in that place. All that drinking. Those white kids love to drink." Sarah studied her fingernails.

"I guess. The place is harmless. They seem to like the music."

"Do you think I should paint my nails?"

Daniel frowned at her. "If you want to."

"I mean really paint them. You know, black, or with red, white, and blue stripes. Something like that." She held her hand out, appearing to imagine the colors. "I'd have to grow them long."

"What are you talking about?"

"Just bullshitting."

Daniel and Sarah went to a grocery market to buy food for lunch and Daniel's dinner. Daniel pushed the cart through the Piggly Wiggly while Sarah walked ahead of him. He watched her large movements and her confident stride. At the checkout, he added a bulletin full of pictures of local cars and trucks for sale to his items on the conveyer.

"What's that for?" Sarah asked.

"I think I want to buy a truck."

"Buy a truck?"

"So I can drive you around when you paint your nails."

Later, after lunch and after Sarah had left him alone, Daniel sat in his living room and picked up the car-sale magazine. As he suspected, there were several trucks he liked and one in particular, a 1968 Ford three-quarter ton with the one thing it shared with the other possibilities, a full rear cab window decal of the Confederate flag. He called the number the following morning and arranged with Barb, Travis's wife, to stop by and see the truck.

Travis and Barb lived across the river in the town of Irmo, a name that Daniel had always thought suited a disease for cattle. He drove around the maze of tract homes until he found the right street and number. A woman in a housecoat across the street watched from her porch, safe inside the chain-link fence around her yard. From down the street a man and a teenager, who were covered with grease and apparently engaged in work on a torn-apart Dodge Charger, mindlessly wiped their hands and studied him.

Daniel walked across the front yard, through a maze of plastic toys, and knocked on the front door. Travis opened the door and asked in a surly voice, "What is it?"

"I called about the truck," Daniel said.

"Oh, you're Dan?"

Daniel nodded.

"The truck's in the backyard. Let me get the keys." He pushed the door to, but it didn't catch. Daniel heard the quality of the exchange between Travis and Barb, but not the words. He did hear Barb say, as Travis pulled open the door, "I couldn't tell over the phone."

"Got 'em," Travis said. "Come on with me." He looked at Daniel's Jensen as they walked through the yard. "What kind of car is that?"

"It's a Jensen."

"Nice looking. Is it fast?"

"I guess."

The truck looked a little rough, a pale blue with a bleached-out hood and a crack across the top of the windshield. Travis opened the driver's side door and pushed the key into the ignition. "It's a strong runner," he said. Daniel put his hand on the faded hood and felt the warmth, knew that Travis had already warmed up the motor. Travis turned the key and the engine kicked over. He nodded to Daniel. Daniel nodded back. He looked up to see a blond woman looking on from behind the screen door of the back porch.

"The clutch and the alternator are new this year." Travis stepped backward to the wall of the bed and looked in. "There's some rust back here, but the bottom's pretty solid."

Daniel attended to the sound of the engine. "Misses just a little," he said.

"A tune-up will fix that."

Daniel regarded the rebel-flag decal covering the rear window of the cab, touched it with his finger.

"That thing will peel right off," Travis said.

"No, I like it." Daniel sat down in the truck behind the steering wheel. "Mind if I take it for a spin?"

"Sure thing." Travis looked toward the house, then back to Daniel. "The brakes are good, but you got to press hard."

Daniel nodded.

Travis shut the door, his long fingers wrapped over the edge of the half-lowered glass. Daniel noticed that one of the man's fingernails was blackened.

"I'll just take it around a block or two."

The blond woman was now standing outside the door on the concrete steps. Daniel put the truck in gear and drove out of the yard, past his car and down the street by the man and teenager who were still at work on the Charger. They stared at him, were still watching him as he turned right at the corner. The truck handled decently, but that really wasn't important.

Back at Travis's house Daniel left the keys in the truck and got out to observe the bald tires while Travis looked on. "The ad in the magazine said two thousand."

"Yeah, but I'm willing to work with you."

"Tell you what, I'll give you twenty-two hundred if you deliver it to my house."

Travis was lost, scratching his head and looking back at the house for his wife, who was no longer standing there. "Whereabouts do you live?"

"I live over near the university. Near Five Points."

"Twenty-two hundred?" Travis said more to himself than to Daniel. "Sure I can get it to your house."

"Here's two hundred." Daniel counted out the money and handed it to the man. "I'll have the rest for you in cash when you deliver the truck." He watched Travis feel the bills with his skinny fingers. "Can you have it there at about four?"

"I can do that."

⚘

"What in the world do you need a truck for?" Sarah asked. She stepped over to the counter and poured herself another cup of coffee, then sat back down at the table with Daniel.

"I'm not buying the truck. Well, I am buying a truck, but only because I need the truck for the decal. I'm buying the decal."

"Decal?"

"Yes. This truck has a Confederate flag in the back window."

"What?"

"I've decided that the rebel flag is my flag. My blood is Southern blood, right? Well, it's my flag."

Sarah put down her cup and saucer and picked up a cookie from the plate in the middle of the table. "You've flipped. I knew this would happen to you if you didn't work. A person needs to work."

"I don't need money."

"That's not the point. You don't have to work for money." She stood and walked to the edge of the porch and looked up and down the street.

"I've got my books and my music."

"You need a job so you can be around people you don't care about, doing stuff you don't care about. You need a job to occupy that part of your brain. I suppose it's too late now, though."

"Nonetheless," Daniel said. "You should have seen those redneck boys when I took 'Dixie' from them. They didn't know what to do. So, the goddamn flag is flying over the State Capitol. Don't take it down, just take it. That's what I say."

"That's all you have to do? That's all there is to it?"

"Yep." Daniel leaned back in his rocker. "You watch ol' Travis when he gets here."

⚘

Travis arrived with the pickup a little before four, his wife pulling up behind him in a yellow TransAm. Barb got out of the car and walked up to the porch with Travis. She gave the house a careful look.

314

"Hey, Travis," Daniel said. "This is my friend, Sarah."

Travis nodded hello.

"You must be Barb," Daniel said.

Barb smiled weakly.

Travis looked at Sarah, then back at the truck, and then to Daniel. "You sure you don't want me to peel that thing off the window?"

"I'm positive."

"Okay."

Daniel gave Sarah a glance, to be sure she was watching Travis's face. "Here's the balance," he said, handing over the money. He took the truck keys from the skinny fingers.

Barb sighed and asked, as if the question were burning right through her, "Why do you want that flag on the truck?"

"Why shouldn't I want it?" Daniel asked.

Barb didn't know what to say. She studied her feet for a second, then regarded the house again. "I mean, you live in a nice house and drive that sports car. What do you need a truck like that for?"

"You don't want the money?"

"Yes, we want the money," Travis said, trying to silence Barb with a look.

"I need the truck for hauling stuff," Daniel said. "You know like groceries and—" he looked to Sarah for help.

"Books," Sarah said.

"Books. Things like that." Daniel held Barb's eyes until she looked away. He watched Travis sign his name to the back of the title and hand it to him and as he took it, he said, "I was just lucky enough to find a truck with the black-power flag already on it."

"What?" Travis screwed up his face, trying to understand.

"The black-power flag on the window. You mean, you didn't know?"

Travis and Barb looked at each other.

"Well, anyway," Daniel said, "I'm glad we could do business." He turned to Sarah. "Let me take you for a ride in my new truck." He and Sarah walked across the yard, got into the pickup, and waved to Travis and Barb who were still standing in Daniel's yard as they drove away.

Sarah was on the verge of hysterics by the time they were out of sight. "That was beautiful," she said.

"No," Daniel said, softly. "That was true."

Over the next weeks, sightings of Daniel and his truck proved problematic for some. He was accosted by two big white men in a '72 Monte Carlo in the parking lot of a 7-Eleven on Two Notch Road.

"What are you doing with that on your truck, boy?" the bigger of the two asked.

"Flying it proudly," Daniel said, noticing the rebel front plate on the Chevrolet. "Just like you, brothers."

The confused second man took a step toward Daniel. "What did you call us?"

"Brothers."

The second man pushed Daniel in the chest with two extended fists, but not terribly hard.

"I don't want any trouble," Daniel told them.

Then a Volkswagen with four black teenagers parked in the slot beside Daniel's truck and they jumped out, staring and looking serious. "What's going on?" the driver and largest of the teenagers asked.

"They were admiring our flag," Daniel said, pointing to his truck.

The teenagers were confused.

"We fly the flag proudly, don't we, young brothers?" Daniel gave a bent-arm, black-power, closed-fist salute. "Don't we?" he repeated. "Don't we?"

"Yeah," the young men said.

The white men had backed away to their car. They slipped into it and drove away.

Daniel looked at the teenagers and, with as serious a face as he could manage, he said, "Get a flag and fly it proudly."

✿

At a gas station, a lawyer named Ahmad Wilson stood filling the tank of his BMW and staring at the back window of Daniel's truck. He then looked at Daniel. "Your truck?" he asked.

Daniel stopped cleaning the windshield and nodded.

Wilson didn't ask a question, just pointed at the rear window of Daniel's pickup.

"Power to the people," Daniel said and laughed.

✿

Daniel played "Dixie" in another bar in town, this time with a R&B dance band at a banquet of the black medical association. The strange looks and expressions of outrage changed to bemused laughter and finally to open joking and acceptance as the song was played fast enough for dancing. Then the song was sung, slowly, to the profound surprise of those singing the song. *I wish I was in the land of cotton, old times there are not forgotten . . . Look away, look away, look away . . .*

✿

Soon, there were several, then many cars and trucks in Columbia, South Carolina, sporting Confederate flags and being driven by black people. Black businessmen and ministers wore rebel-flag buttons on their lapels and clips on their ties. The marching band of South Carolina State College, a predominantly black land-grant institution in Orangeburg, paraded with the flag during homecoming. Black people all over the state flew the Confederate flag. The symbol began to disappear from the fronts of big rigs and the back windows of jacked-up four-wheelers. And after the emblem was used to dress the yards and mark picnic sites of black family reunions the following Fourth of July, the piece of cloth was quietly dismissed from its station with the U.S. and State flags atop the State Capitol. There was no ceremony, no notice. One day, it was not there.

Look away, look away, look away . . .

That Evening Sun
(1931)

WILLIAM FAULKNER

I

Monday is no different from any other weekday in Jefferson now. The streets are paved now, and the telephone and electric companies are cutting down more and more of the shade trees—the water oaks, the maples and locusts and elms—to make room for iron poles bearing clusters of bloated and ghostly and bloodless grapes, and we have a city laundry which makes the rounds on Monday morning, gathering the bundles of clothes into bright-colored, specially-made motor cars: the soiled wearing of a whole week now flees apparition-like behind alert and irritable electric horns, with a long diminishing noise of rubber and asphalt like tearing silk, and even the Negro women who still take in white people's washing after the old custom, fetch and deliver it in automobiles.

But fifteen years ago, on Monday morning the quiet, dusty, shady streets would be full of Negro women with, balanced on their steady, turbaned heads, bundles of clothes tied up in sheets, almost as large as cotton bales, carried so without touch of hand between the kitchen door of the white house and the blackened washpot beside a cabin door in Negro Hollow.

Nancy would set her bundle on the top of her head, then upon the bundle in turn she would set the black straw sailor hat which she wore winter and summer. She was tall, with a high, sad face sunken a little where her teeth were missing. Sometimes we would go a part of the way down the lane and across the pasture with her, to watch the balanced bundle and the hat that never bobbed nor wavered, even when she walked down into the ditch and up the other side and stooped through the fence. She would go down on her hands and knees and crawl through the gap, her head rigid, uptilted, the bundle steady as a rock or a balloon, and rise to her feet again and go on.

Sometimes the husbands of the washing women would fetch and deliver the clothes, but Jesus never did that for Nancy, even before father told him to stay away from our house, even when Dilsey was sick and Nancy would come to cook for us.

And then about half the time we'd have to go down the lane to Nancy's cabin and tell her to come on and cook breakfast. We would stop at the ditch, because father told us to not have anything to do with Jesus—he was a short black man, with a razor scar down his face—and we would throw rocks at Nancy's house until she came to the door, leaning her head around it without any clothes on.

317

"What yawl mean, chunking my house?" Nancy said. "What you little devils mean?"

"Father says for you to come on and get breakfast," Caddy said. "Father says it's over a half an hour now, and you've got to come this minute."

"I aint studying no breakfast," Nancy said. "I going to get my sleep out."

"I bet you're drunk," Jason said. "Father says you're drunk. Are you drunk, Nancy?"

"Who says I is?" Nancy said. "I got to get my sleep out. I aint studying no breakfast."

So after a while we quit chunking the cabin and went back home. When she finally came, it was too late for me to go to school. So we thought it was whisky until that day they arrested her again and they were taking her to jail and they passed Mr Stovall. He was the cashier in the bank and a deacon in the Baptist church, and Nancy began to say:

"When you going to pay me, white man? When you going to pay me, white man? It's been three times now since you paid me a cent—" Mr Stovall knocked her down, but she kept on saying, "When you going to pay me, white man? It's been three times now since—" until Mr Stovall kicked her in the mouth with his heel and the marshal caught Mr Stovall back, and Nancy lying in the street, laughing. She turned her head and spat out some blood and teeth and said, "It's been three times now since he paid me a cent."

That was how she lost her teeth, and all that day they told about Nancy and Mr Stovall, and all that night the ones that passed the jail could hear Nancy singing and yelling. They could see her hands holding to the window bars, and a lot of them stopped along the fence, listening to her and to the jailer trying to make her stop. She didn't shut up until almost daylight, when the jailer began to hear a bumping and scraping upstairs and he went up there and found Nancy hanging from the window bar. He said that it was cocaine and not whisky, because no nigger would try to commit suicide unless he was full of cocaine, because a nigger full of cocaine wasn't a nigger any longer.

The jailer cut her down and revived her; then he beat her, whipped her. She had hung herself with her dress. She had fixed it all right, but when they arrested her she didn't have on anything except a dress and so she didn't have anything to tie her hands with and she couldn't make her hands let go of the window ledge. So the jailer heard the noise and ran up there and found Nancy hanging from the window, stark naked, her belly already swelling out a little, like a little balloon.

When Dilsey was sick in her cabin and Nancy was cooking for us, we could see her apron swelling out; that was before father told Jesus to stay away from the house. Jesus was in the kitchen, sitting behind the stove, with his razor scar on his black face like a piece of dirty string. He said it was a watermelon that Nancy had under her dress.

"It never come off of your vine, though," Nancy said.

"Off of what vine?" Caddy said.

"I can cut down the vine it did come off of," Jesus said.

"What makes you want to talk like that before these chillen?" Nancy said. "Whyn't you go on to work? You done et. You want Mr Jason to catch you hanging around his kitchen, talking that way before these chillen?"

"Talking what way?" Caddy said. "What vine?"

"I cant hang around white man's kitchen," Jesus said. "But white man can hang around mine. White man can come in my house, but I cant stop him. When white man want to come in my house, I aint got no house. I cant stop him, but he cant kick me outen it. He cant do that."

Dilsey was still sick in her cabin. Father told Jesus to stay off our place. Dilsey was still sick. It was a long time. We were in the library after supper.

"Isn't Nancy through in the kitchen yet?" mother said. "It seems to me that she has had plenty of time to have finished the dishes."

"Let Quentin go and see," father said. "Go and see if Nancy is through, Quentin. Tell her she can go on home."

I went to the kitchen. Nancy was through. The dishes were put away and the fire was out. Nancy was sitting in a chair, close to the cold stove. She looked at me.

"Mother wants to know if you are through," I said.

"Yes," Nancy said. She looked at me. "I done finished." She looked at me.

"What is it?" I said. "What is it?"

"I aint nothing but a nigger," Nancy said. "It aint none of my fault."

She looked at me, sitting in the chair before the cold stove, the sailor hat on her head. I went back to the library. It was the cold stove and all, when you think of a kitchen being warm and busy and cheerful. And with a cold stove and the dishes all put away, and nobody wanting to eat at that hour.

"Is she through?" mother said.

"Yessum," I said.

"What is she doing?" mother said.

"She's not doing anything. She's through."

"I'll go and see," father said.

"Maybe she's waiting for Jesus to come and take her home," Caddy said.

"Jesus is gone," I said. Nancy told us how one morning she woke up and Jesus was gone.

"He quit me," Nancy said. "Done gone to Memphis, I reckon. Dodging them city *po*-lice for a while, I reckon."

"And a good riddance," father said. "I hope he stays there."

"Nancy's scaired of the dark," Jason said.

"So are you," Caddy said.

"I'm not," Jason said.

"Scairy cat," Caddy said.

"I'm not," Jason said.

"You, Candace!" mother said. Father came back.

"I am going to walk down the lane with Nancy," he said. "She says that Jesus is back."

"Has she seen him?" mother said.

"No. Some Negro sent her word that he was back in town. I wont be long."

"You'll leave me alone, to take Nancy home?" mother said. "Is her safety more precious to you than mine?"

"I wont be long," father said.

"You'll leave these children unprotected, with that Negro about?"

"I'm going too," Caddy said. "Let me go, Father."

"What would he do with them, if he were unfortunate enough to have them?" father said.

"I want to go, too," Jason said.

"Jason!" mother said. She was speaking to father. You could tell that by the way she said the name. Like she believed that all day father had been trying to think of doing the thing she wouldn't like the most, and that she knew all the time that after a while he would think of it. I stayed quiet, because father and I both knew that mother would want him to make me

319

stay with her if she just thought of it in time. So father didn't look at me. I was the oldest. I was nine and Caddy was seven and Jason was five.

"Nonsense," father said. "We wont be long."

Nancy had her hat on. We came to the lane. "Jesus always been good to me," Nancy said. "Whenever he had two dollars, one of them was mine." We walked in the lane. "If I can just get through the lane," Nancy said, "I be all right then."

The lane was always dark. "This is where Jason got scared on Hallowe'en," Caddy said.

"I didn't," Jason said.

"Cant Aunt Rachel do anything with him?" father said. Aunt Rachel was old. She lived in a cabin beyond Nancy's, by herself. She had white hair and she smoked a pipe in the door, all day long; she didn't work any more. They said she was Jesus' mother. Sometimes she said she was and sometimes she said she wasn't any kin to Jesus.

"Yes, you did," Caddy said. "You were scairder than Frony. You were scairder than T.P. even. Scairder than niggers."

"Cant nobody do nothing with him," Nancy said. "He say I done woke up the devil in him and aint but one thing going to lay it down again."

"Well, he's gone now," father said. "There's nothing for you to be afraid of now. And if you'd just let white men alone."

"Let what white men alone?" Caddy said. "How let them alone?"

"He aint gone nowhere," Nancy said. "I can feel him. I can feel him now, in this lane. He hearing us talk, every word, hid somewhere, waiting. I aint seen him, and I aint going to see him again but once more, with that razor in his mouth. That razor on that string down his back, inside his shirt. And then I aint going to be even surprised."

"I wasn't scaired," Jason said.

"If you'd behave yourself, you'd have kept out of this," father said. "But it's all right now. He's probably in St. Louis now. Probably got another wife by now and forgot all about you."

"If he has, I better not find out about it," Nancy said. "I'd stand there right over them, and every time he wropped her, I'd cut that arm off. I'd cut his head off and I'd slit her belly and I'd shove—"

"Hush," father said.

"Slit whose belly, Nancy?" Caddy said.

"I wasn't scaired," Jason said. "I'd walk right down this lane by myself."

"Yah," Caddy said. "You wouldn't dare to put your foot down in it if we were not here too."

II

Dilsey was still sick, so we took Nancy home every night until mother said, "How much longer is this going on? I to be left alone in this big house while you take home a frightened Negro?"

We fixed a pallet in the kitchen for Nancy. One night we waked up, hearing the sound. It was not singing and it was not crying, coming up the dark stairs. There was a light in mother's room and we heard father going down the hall, down the back stairs, and Caddy and I went into the hall. The floor was cold. Our toes curled away from it while we listened to the sound. It was like singing and it wasn't like singing, like the sounds that Negroes make.

Then it stopped and we heard father going down the back stairs, and we went to the head of the stairs. Then the sound began again, in the stairway, not loud, and we could see Nancy's eyes halfway up the stairs, against the wall. They looked like cat's eyes do, like a big cat against the wall, watching us. When we came down the steps to where she was, she quit making the sound again, and we stood there until father came back up from the kitchen, with his pistol in his hand. He went back down with Nancy and they came back with Nancy's pallet.

We spread the pallet in our room. After the light in mother's room went off, we could see Nancy's eyes again. "Nancy," Caddy whispered, "are you asleep, Nancy?"

Nancy whispered something. It was oh or no, I dont know which. Like nobody had made it, like it came from nowhere and went nowhere, until it was like Nancy was not there at all; that I had looked so hard at her eyes on the stairs that they had got printed on my eyeballs, like the sun does when you have closed your eyes and there is no sun. "Jesus," Nancy whispered. "Jesus."

"Was it Jesus?" Caddy said. "Did he try to come into the kitchen?"

"Jesus," Nancy said. Like this: Jeeeeeeeeeeeeeeeesus, until the sound went out, like a match or a candle does.

"It's the other Jesus she means," I said.

"Can you see us, Nancy?" Caddy whispered. "Can you see our eyes too?"

"I aint nothing but a nigger," Nancy said. "God knows. God knows."

"What did you see down there in the kitchen?" Caddy whispered. "What tried to get in?"

"God knows," Nancy said. We could see her eyes. "God knows."

Dilsey got well. She cooked dinner. "You'd better stay in bed a day or two longer," father said.

"What for?" Dilsey said. "If I had been a day later, this place would be to rack and ruin. Get on out of here now, and let me get my kitchen straight again."

Dilsey cooked supper too. And that night, just before dark, Nancy came into the kitchen.

"How do you know he's back?" Dilsey said. "You aint seen him."

"Jesus is a nigger," Jason said.

"I can feel him," Nancy said. "I can feel him laying yonder in the ditch."

"Tonight?" Dilsey said. "Is he there tonight?"

"Dilsey's a nigger too," Jason said.

"You try to eat something," Dilsey said.

"I dont want nothing," Nancy said.

"I aint a nigger," Jason said.

"Drink some coffee," Dilsey said. She poured a cup of coffee for Nancy. "Do you know he's out there tonight? How come you know it's tonight?"

"I know," Nancy said. "He's there, waiting. I know. I done lived with him too long. I know what he is fixing to do fore he know it himself."

"Drink some coffee," Dilsey said. Nancy held the cup to her mouth and blew into the cup. Her mouth pursed out like a spreading adder's, like a rubber mouth, like she had blown all the color out of her lips with blowing the coffee.

"I aint a nigger," Jason said. "Are you a nigger, Nancy?"

"I hellborn, child," Nancy said. "I wont be nothing soon. I going back where I come from soon."

III

She began to drink the coffee. While she was drinking, holding the cup in both hands, she began to make the sound again. She made the sound into the cup and the coffee sploshed out onto her hands and her dress. Her eyes looked at us and she sat there, her elbows on her knees, holding the cup in both hands, looking at us across the wet cup, making the sound. "Look at Nancy," Jason said. "Nancy cant cook for us now. Dilsey's got well now."

"You hush up," Dilsey said. Nancy held the cup in both hands, looking at us, making the sound, like there were two of them: one looking at us and the other making the sound. "Whyn't you let Mr Jason telefoam the marshal?" Dilsey said. Nancy stopped then, holding the cup in her long brown hands. She tried to drink some coffee again, but it sploshed out of the cup, onto her hands and her dress, and she put the cup down. Jason watched her.

"I cant swallow it," Nancy said. "I swallows but it wont go down me."

"You go down to the cabin," Dilsey said. "Frony will fix you a pallet and I'll be there soon."

"Wont no nigger stop him," Nancy said.

"I aint a nigger," Jason said. "Am I, Dilsey?"

"I reckon not," Dilsey said. She looked at Nancy. "I dont reckon so. What you going to do, then?"

Nancy looked at us. Her eyes went fast, like she was afraid there wasn't time to look, without hardly moving at all. She looked at us, at all three of us at one time. "You member that night I stayed in yawls' room?" she said. She told about how we waked up early the next morning, and played. We had to play quiet, on her pallet, until father woke up and it was time to get breakfast. "Go and ask your maw to let me stay here tonight," Nancy said. "I wont need no pallet. We can play some more."

Caddy asked mother. Jason went too. "I cant have Negroes sleeping in the bedrooms," mother said. Jason cried. He cried until mother said he couldn't have any dessert for three days if he didn't stop. Then Jason said he would stop if Dilsey would make a chocolate cake. Father was there.

"Why dont you do something about it?" mother said. "What do we have officers for?"

"Why is Nancy afraid of Jesus?" Caddy said. "Are you afraid of father, mother?"

"What could the officers do?" father said. "If Nancy hasn't seen him, how could the officers find him?"

"Then why is she afraid?" mother said.

"She says he is there. She says she knows he is there tonight."

"Yet we pay taxes," mother said. "I must wait here alone in this big house while you take a Negro woman home."

"You know that I am not lying outside with a razor," father said.

"I'll stop if Dilsey will make a chocolate cake," Jason said. Mother told us to go out and father said he didn't know if Jason would get a chocolate cake or not, but he knew what Jason was going to get in about a minute. We went back to the kitchen and told Nancy.

"Father said for you to go home and lock the door, and you'll be all right," Caddy said. "All right from what, Nancy? Is Jesus mad at you?" Nancy was holding the coffee cup in her hands again, her elbows on her knees and her hands holding the cup between her knees. She was looking into the cup. "What have you done that made Jesus mad?" Caddy said. Nancy let the cup go. It didn't break on the floor, but the coffee spilled out, and Nancy sat there with her hands still making the shape of the cup. She began to make the sound again, not loud. Not singing and not unsinging. We watched her.

"Here," Dilsey said. "You quit that, now. You get aholt of yourself. You wait here. I going to get Versh to walk home with you." Dilsey went out.

We looked at Nancy. Her shoulders kept shaking, but she quit making the sound. We watched her. "What's Jesus going to do to you?" Caddy said. "He went away."

Nancy looked at us. "We had fun that night I stayed in yawls' room, didn't we?"

"I didn't," Jason said. "I didn't have any fun."

"You were asleep in mother's room," Caddy said. "You were not there."

"Let's go down to my house and have some more fun," Nancy said.

"Mother wont let us," I said. "It's too late now."

"Dont bother her," Nancy said. "We can tell her in the morning. She wont mind."

"She wouldn't let us," I said.

"Dont ask her now," Nancy said. "Dont bother her now."

"She didn't say we couldn't go," Caddy said.

"We didn't ask," I said.

"If you go, I'll tell," Jason said.

"We'll have fun," Nancy said. "They won't mind, just to my house. I been working for yawl a long time. They won't mind."

"I'm not afraid to go," Caddy said. "Jason is the one that's afraid. He'll tell."

"I'm not," Jason said.

"Yes, you are," Caddy said. "You'll tell."

"I won't tell," Jason said. "I'm not afraid."

"Jason ain't afraid to go with me," Nancy said. "Is you, Jason?"

"Jason is going to tell," Caddy said. The lane was dark. We passed the pasture gate. "I bet if something was to jump out from behind that gate, Jason would holler."

"I wouldn't," Jason said. We walked down the lane. Nancy was talking loud.

"What are you talking so loud for, Nancy?" Caddy said.

"Who; me?" Nancy said. "Listen at Quentin and Caddy and Jason saying I'm talking loud."

"You talk like there was five of us here," Caddy said. "You talk like father was here too."

"Who; me talking loud, Mr Jason?" Nancy said.

"Nancy called Jason 'Mister,'" Caddy said.

"Listen how Caddy and Quentin and Jason talk," Nancy said.

"We're not talking loud," Caddy said. "You're the one that's talking like father—"

"Hush," Nancy said; "hush, Mr Jason."

"Nancy called Jason 'Mister' aguh—"

"Hush," Nancy said. She was talking loud when we crossed the ditch and stooped through the fence where she used to stoop through with the clothes on her head. Then we came to her house. We were going fast then. She opened the door. The smell of the house was like the lamp and the smell of Nancy was like the wick, like they were waiting for one another to begin to smell. She lit the lamp and closed the door and put the bar up. Then she quit talking loud, looking at us.

"What're we going to do?" Caddy said.

"What do yawl want to do?" Nancy said.

"You said we would have some fun," Caddy said.

There was something about Nancy's house; something you could smell besides Nancy and the house. Jason smelled it, even. "I don't want to stay here," he said. "I want to go home."

"Go home, then," Caddy said.

"I don't want to go by myself," Jason said.

"We're going to have some fun," Nancy said.

"How?" Caddy said.

Nancy stood by the door. She was looking at us, only it was like she had emptied her eyes, like she had quit using them. "What do you want to do?" she said.

"Tell us a story," Caddy said. "Can you tell a story?"

"Yes," Nancy said.

"Tell it," Caddy said. We looked at Nancy. "You don't know any stories."

"Yes," Nancy said. "Yes, I do."

She came and sat in a chair before the hearth. There was a little fire there. Nancy built it up, when it was already hot inside. She built a good blaze. She told a story. She talked like her eyes looked, like her eyes watching us and her voice talking to us did not belong to her. Like she was living somewhere else, waiting somewhere else. She was outside the cabin. Her voice was inside and the shape of her, the Nancy that could stoop under a barbed wire fence with a bundle of clothes balanced on her head as though without weight, like a balloon, was there. But that was all. "And so this here queen come walking up to the ditch, where that bad man was hiding. She was walking up to the ditch, and she say, 'If I can just get past this here ditch,' was what she say ..."

"What ditch?" Caddy said. "A ditch like that one out there? Why did a queen want to go into a ditch?"

"To get to her house," Nancy said. She looked at us. "She had to cross the ditch to get into her house quick and bar the door."

"Why did she want to go home and bar the door?" Caddy said.

IV

Nancy looked at us. She quit talking. She looked at us. Jason's legs stuck straight out of his pants where he sat on Nancy's lap. "I don't think that's a good story," he said. "I want to go home."

"Maybe we had better," Caddy said. She got up from the floor. "I bet they are looking for us right now." She went toward the door.

"No," Nancy said. "Don't open it." She got up quick and passed Caddy. She didn't touch the door, the wooden bar.

"Why not?" Caddy said.

"Come back to the lamp," Nancy said. "We'll have fun. You don't have to go."

"We ought to go," Caddy said. "Unless we have a lot of fun." She and Nancy came back to the fire, the lamp.

"I want to go home," Jason said. "I'm going to tell."

"I know another story," Nancy said. She stood close to the lamp. She looked at Caddy, like when your eyes look up at a stick balanced on your nose. She had to look down to see Caddy, but her eyes looked like that, like when you are balancing a stick.

"I won't listen to it," Jason said. "I'll bang on the floor."

"It's a good one," Nancy said. "It's better than the other one."

"What's it about?" Caddy said. Nancy was standing by the lamp. Her hand was on the lamp, against the light, long and brown.

"Your hand is on that hot globe," Caddy said. "Don't it feel hot to your hand?"

Nancy looked at her hand on the lamp chimney. She took her hand away, slow. She stood there, looking at Caddy, wringing her long hand as though it were tied to her wrist with a string.

"Let's do something else," Caddy said.

"I want to go home," Jason said.

"I got some popcorn," Nancy said. She looked at Caddy and then at Jason and then at me and then at Caddy again. "I got some popcorn."

"I don't like popcorn," Jason said. "I'd rather have candy."

Nancy looked at Jason. "You can hold the popper." She was still wringing her hand; it was long and limp and brown.

"All right," Jason said. "I'll stay a while if I can do that. Caddy can't hold it. I'll want to go home again if Caddy holds the popper."

Nancy built up the fire. "Look at Nancy putting her hands in the fire," Caddy said. "What's the matter with you, Nancy?"

"I got popcorn," Nancy said. "I got some." She took the popper from under the bed. It was broken. Jason began to cry.

"Now we can't have any popcorn," he said.

"We ought to go home, anyway," Caddy said. "Come on, Quentin."

"Wait," Nancy said; "wait. I can fix it. Don't you want to help me fix it?"

"I don't think I want any," Caddy said. "It's too late now."

"You help me, Jason," Nancy said. "Don't you want to help me?"

"No," Jason said. "I want to go home."

"Hush," Nancy said; "hush. Watch. Watch me. I can fix it so Jason can hold it and pop the corn." She got a piece of wire and fixed the popper.

"It won't hold good," Caddy said.

"Yes, it will," Nancy said. "Yawl watch. Yawl help me shell some corn."

The popcorn was under the bed too. We shelled it into the popper and Nancy helped Jason hold the popper over the fire.

"It's not popping," Jason said. "I want to go home."

"You wait," Nancy said. "It'll begin to pop. We'll have fun then." She was sitting close to the fire. The lamp was turned up so high it was beginning to smoke.

"Why don't you turn it down some?" I said.

"It's all right," Nancy said. "I'll clean it. Yawl wait. The popcorn will start in a minute."

"I don't believe it's going to start," Caddy said. "We ought to start home, anyway. They'll be worried."

"No," Nancy said. "It's going to pop. Dilsey will tell um yawl with me. I been working for yawl long time. They won't mind if yawl at my house. You wait, now. It'll start popping any minute now."

Then Jason got some smoke in his eyes and he began to cry. He dropped the popper into the fire. Nancy got a wet rag and wiped Jason's face, but he didn't stop crying.

"Hush," she said. "Hush." But he didn't hush. Caddy took the popper out of the fire.

"It's burned up," she said. "You'll have to get some more popcorn, Nancy."

"Did you put all of it in?" Nancy said.

"Yes," Caddy said. Nancy looked at Caddy. Then she took the popper and opened it and poured the cinders into her apron and began to sort the grains, her hands long and brown, and we watching her.

"Haven't you got any more?" Caddy said.

"Yes," Nancy said; "yes. Look. This here ain't burnt. All we need to do is—"

"I want to go home," Jason said. "I'm going to tell."

"Hush," Caddy said. We all listened. Nancy's head was already turned toward the barred door, her eyes filled with red lamplight. "Somebody is coming," Caddy said.

Then Nancy began to make that sound again, not loud, sitting there above the fire, her long hands dangling between her knees; all of a sudden water began to come out on her face in big drops, running down her face, carrying in each one a little turning ball of firelight like a spark until it dropped off her chin. "She's not crying," I said.

"I ain't crying," Nancy said. Her eyes were closed. "I ain't crying. Who is it?"

"I don't know," Caddy said. She went to the door and looked out. "We've got to go now," she said. "Here comes father."

"I'm going to tell," Jason said. "Yawl made me come."

The water still ran down Nancy's face. She turned in her chair. "Listen. Tell him. Tell him we going to have fun. Tell him I take good care of yawl until in the morning. Tell him to let me come home with yawl and sleep on the floor. Tell him I won't need no pallet. We'll have fun. You member last time how we had so much fun?"

"I didn't have fun," Jason said. "You hurt me. You put smoke in my eyes. I'm going to tell."

V

Father came in. He looked at us. Nancy did not get up.

"Tell him," she said.

"Caddy made us come down here," Jason said. "I didn't want to."

Father came to the fire. Nancy looked up at him. "Can't you go to Aunt Rachel's and stay?" he said. Nancy looked up at father, her hands between her knees. "He's not here," father said. "I would have seen him. There's not a soul in sight."

"He in the ditch," Nancy said. "He waiting in the ditch yonder."

"Nonsense," father said. He looked at Nancy. "Do you know he's there?"

"I got the sign," Nancy said.

"What sign?"

"I got it. It was on the table when I come in. It was a hogbone, with blood meat still on it, laying by the lamp. He's out there. When yawl walk out that door, I gone."

"Gone where, Nancy?" Caddy said.

"I'm not a tattletale," Jason said.

"Nonsense," father said.

"He out there," Nancy said. "He looking through that window this minute, waiting for yawl to go. Then I gone."

"Nonsense," father said. "Lock up your house and we'll take you on to Aunt Rachel's."

"'Twont do no good," Nancy said. She didn't look at father now, but he looked down at her, at her long, limp, moving hands. "Putting it off wont do no good."

"Then what do you want to do?" father said.

"I don't know," Nancy said. "I can't do nothing. Just put it off. And that don't do no good. I reckon it belong to me. I reckon what I going to get ain't no more than mine."

"Get what?" Caddy said. "What's yours?"

"Nothing," father said. "You all must get to bed."

"Caddy made me come," Jason said.

"Go on to Aunt Rachel's," father said.

"It won't do no good," Nancy said. She sat before the fire, her elbows on her knees, her long hands between her knees. "When even your own kitchen wouldn't do no good. When even if I was sleeping on the floor in the room with your chillen, and the next morning there I am, and blood—"

"Hush," father said. "Lock the door and put out the lamp and go to bed."

"I scared of the dark," Nancy said. "I scared for it to happen in the dark."

"You mean you're going to sit right here with the lamp lighted?" father said. Then Nancy began to make the sound again, sitting before the fire, her long hands between her knees. "Ah, damnation," father said. "Come along, chillen. It's past bedtime."

"When yawl go home, I gone," Nancy said. She talked quieter now, and her face looked quiet, like her hands. "Anyway, I got my coffin money saved up with Mr. Lovelady." Mr. Lovelady was a short, dirty man who collected the Negro insurance, coming around to the cabins or the kitchens every Saturday morning, to collect fifteen cents. He and his wife lived at the hotel. One morning his wife committed suicide. They had a child, a little girl. He and the child went away. After a week or two he came back alone. We would see him going along the lanes and the back streets on Saturday mornings.

"Nonsense," father said. "You'll be the first thing I'll see in the kitchen tomorrow morning."

"You'll see what you'll see, I reckon," Nancy said. "But it will take the Lord to say what that will be."

VI

We left her sitting before the fire.

"Come and put the bar up," father said. But she didn't move. She didn't look at us again, sitting quietly there between the lamp and the fire. From some distance down the lane we could look back and see her through the open door.

"What, Father?" Caddy said. "What's going to happen?"

"Nothing," father said. Jason was on father's back, so Jason was the tallest of all of us. We went down into the ditch. I looked at it, quiet. I couldn't see much where the moonlight and the shadows tangled.

"If Jesus is hid here, he can see us, cant he?" Caddy said.

"He's not there," father said. "He went away a long time ago."

"You made me come," Jason said, high; against the sky it looked like father had two heads, a little one and a big one. "I didn't want to."

We went up out of the ditch. We could still see Nancy's house and the open door, but we couldn't see Nancy now, sitting before the fire with the door open, because she was tired. "I just done got tired," she said. "I just a nigger. It ain't no fault of mine."

But we could hear her, because she began just after we came up out of the ditch, the sound that was not singing and not unsinging. "Who will do our washing now, Father?" I said.

"I'm not a nigger," Jason said, high and close above father's head.

"You're worse," Caddy said, "you are a tattletale. If something was to jump out, you'd be scairder than a nigger."

"I wouldn't," Jason said.

"You'd cry," Caddy said.

"Caddy," father said.

"I wouldn't!" Jason said.

"Scairy cat," Caddy said.

"Candace!" father said.

One of the Old Girls
(1912)

EDNA FERBER

All of those ladies who end their conversation with you by wearily suggesting that you go down to the basement to find what you seek, do not receive a meager seven dollars a week as a reward for their efforts. Neither are they all obliged to climb five weary flights of stairs to reach the dismal little court room which is their home, and there are several who need not walk thirty-three blocks to save carfare, only to spend wretched evenings washing out hand-kerchiefs and stockings in the cracked little washbowl, while one ear is cocked for the stealthy tread of the Lady Who Objects.

The earnest compiler of working girls' budgets would pass Effie Bauer hurriedly by. Effie's budget bulged here and there with such pathetic items as hand-embroidered blouses, thick club steaks, and parquet tickets for Maude Adams. That you may visualize her at once I may say that Effie looked twenty-four—from the rear (all women do in these days of girlish simplicity in hats and tailor-mades); her skirts never sagged, her shirtwaists were marvels of plainness and fit, and her switch had cost her sixteen dollars, wholesale (a lady friend in the business). Oh, there was nothing tragic about Effie. She had a plump, assured style, a keen blue eye, a gift of repartee, and a way of doing her hair so that the gray at the sides scarcely showed at all. Also a knowledge of corsets that had placed her at the buying end of that important department at Spiegel's. Effie knew to the minute when coral beads went out and pearl beads came in, and just by looking at her blouses you could tell when Cluny died and Irish was born. Meeting Effie on the street, you would have put her down as one of the many well-dressed, prosperous-looking women shoppers—if you hadn't looked at her feet. Veteran clerks and policemen cannot disguise their feet.

Effie Bauer's reason for not marrying when a girl was the same as that of most of the capable, wise-eyed, good-looking women one finds at the head of departments. She had not had a chance. If Effie had been as attractive at twenty as she was at—there, we won't betray confidences. Still, it is certain that if Effie had been as attractive when a young girl as she was when an old girl, she never would have been an old girl and head of Spiegel's corset department at a salary of something very comfortably over one hundred and twenty-five a month (and commissions). Effie had improved with the years, and ripened with experience. She knew her value. At twenty she had been pale, anaemic and bony, with a startled-faun manner and bad teeth. Years of saleswomanship had broadened her, mentally and physically, until she possessed a wide and varied knowledge of that great and diversified subject known as human nature. She knew human nature all the way from the fifty-nine-cent girdles to the

329

twenty-five-dollar made-to-orders. And if the years had brought, among other things, a certain hardness about the jaw and a line or two at the corners of the eyes, it was not surprising. You can't rub up against the sharp edges of this world and expect to come out without a scratch or so.

So much for Effie. Enter the hero. Webster defines a hero in romance as the person who has the principal share in the transactions related. He says nothing which would debar a gentleman just because he may be a trifle bald and in the habit of combing his hair over the thin spot, and he raises no objections to a matter of thickness and color in the region of the back of the neck. Therefore Gabe I. Marks qualifies. Gabe was the gentleman about whom Effie permitted herself to be guyed. He came to Chicago on business four times a year, and he always took Effie to the theater, and to supper afterward. On those occasions, Effie's gown, wrap and hat were as correct in texture, lines, and paradise aigrettes as those of any of her non-working sisters about her. On the morning following these excursions into Lobsterdom, Effie would confide to her friend, Miss Weinstein, of the lingeries and negligees:

"I was out with my friend, Mr. Marks, last evening. We went to Rector's after the show. Oh, well, it takes a New Yorker to know how. Honestly, I feel like a queen when I go out with him. H'm? Oh, nothing like that, girlie. I never could see that marriage thing. Just good friends."

Gabe had been coming to Chicago four times a year for six years. Six times four are twenty-four. And one is twenty-five. Gabe's last visit made the twenty-fifth.

"Well, Effie," Gabe said when the evening's entertainment had reached the restaurant stage, "this is our twenty-fifth anniversary. It's our silver wedding, without the silver and the wedding. We'll have a bottle of champagne. That makes it almost legal. And then suppose we finish up by having the wedding. The silver can be omitted."

Effie had been humming with the orchestra, holding a lobster claw in one hand and wielding the little two-pronged fork with the other. She dropped claw, fork, and popular air to stare open-mouthed at Gabe. Then a slow, uncertain smile crept about her lips, although her eyes were still unsmiling.

"Stop your joking, Gabie," she said. "Some day you'll say those things to the wrong lady, and then you'll have a breach-of-promise suit on your hands."

"This ain't no joke, Effie," Gabe had replied. "Not with me it ain't. As long as my mother selig lived I wouldn't ever marry a Goy. It would have broken her heart. I was a good son to her, and good sons make good husbands, they say. Well, Effie, you want to try it out?"

There was something almost solemn in Effie's tone and expression. "Gabie," she said slowly, "you're the first man that's ever asked me to marry him."

"That goes double," answered Gabe.

"Thanks," said Effie. "That makes it all the nicer."

"Then——" Gabe's face was radiant. But Effie shook her head quickly.

"You're just twenty years late," she said.

"Late!" expostulated Gabe. "I ain't no dead one yet."

Effie pushed her plate away with a little air of decision, folded her plump arms on the table, and, leaning forward, looked Gabe I. Marks squarely in the eyes.

"Gabie," she said gently, "I'll bet you haven't got a hundred dollars in the bank——"

"But——" interrupted Gabe.

"Wait a minute. I know you boys on the road. Besides your diamond scarf pin and your ring and watch, have you got a cent over your salary? Nix. You carry just about enough insurance to bury you, don't you? You're fifty years old if you're a minute, Gabie, and if I ain't mistaken you'd have a pretty hard time of it getting ten thousand dollars' insurance after the doctors got through with you. Twenty-five years of pinochle and poker and the fat of the land haven't added up any bumps in the old stocking under the mattress."

"Say, looka here," objected Gabe, more red-faced than usual, "I didn't know I was proposing to no Senatorial investigating committee. Say, you talk about them foreign noblemen being mercenary! Why, they ain't in it with you girls to-day. A feller is got to propose to you with his bank book in one hand and a bunch of life-insurance policies in the other. You're right; I ain't saved much. But Ma selig always had everything she wanted. Say, when a man marries it's different. He begins to save."

"There!" said Effie quickly. "That's just it. Twenty years ago I'd have been glad and willing to start like that, saving and scrimping and loving a man, and looking forward to the time when four figures showed up in the bank account where but three bloomed before. I've got what they call the home instinct. Give me a yard or so of cretonne, and a photo of my married sister down in Iowa, and I can make even a boarding-house inside a bedroom look like a place where a human being could live. If I had been as wise at twenty as I am now, Gabie, I could have married any man I pleased. But I was what they call capable. And men aren't marrying capable girls. They pick little yellow-headed, blue-eyed idiots that don't know a lamb stew from a soup bone when they see it. Well, Mr. Man didn't show up, and I started in to clerk at six per. I'm earning as much as you are now. More. Now, don't misunderstand me, Gabe. I'm not throwing bouquets at myself. I'm not that kind of a girl. But I could sell a style 743 Slimshape to the Venus de Milo herself. The Lord knows she needed one, with those hips of hers. I worked my way up, alone. I'm used to it. I like the excitement down at the store. I'm used to luxuries. I guess if I was a man I'd be the kind they call a good provider—the kind that opens wine every time there's half an excuse for it, and when he dies his widow has to take in boarders. And, Gabe, after you've worn tailored suits every year for a dozen years, you can't go back to twenty-five-dollar ready-mades and be happy."

"You could if you loved a man," said Gabe stubbornly.

The hard lines around the jaw and the experienced lines about the eyes seemed suddenly to stand out on Effie's face.

"Love's young dream is all right. But you've reached the age when you let your cigar ash dribble down onto your vest. Now me, I've got a kimono nature but a straight-front job, and it's kept me young. Young! I've got to be. That's my stock in trade. You see, Gabie, we're just twenty years late, both of us. They're not going to boost your salary. These days they're looking for kids on the road—live wires, with a lot of nerve and a quick come-back. They don't want old-timers. Why, say, Gabie, if I was to tell you what I spend in face powder and toilette water and hairpins alone, you'd think I'd made a mistake and given you the butcher bill instead. And I'm no professional beauty, either. Only it takes money to look cleaned and pressed in this town."

In the seclusion of the cafe corner, Gabe laid one plump, highly manicured hand on Effie's smooth arm. "You wouldn't need to stay young for me, Effie. I like you just as you are, with out the powder, or the toilette water, or the hair-pins."

His red, good-natured face had an expression upon it that was touchingly near patient resignation as he looked up into Effie's sparkling countenance. "You never looked so good to me as you do this minute, old girl. And if the day comes when you get lonesome—or change your mind—or——"

Effie shook her head, and started to draw on her long white gloves. "I guess I haven't refused you the way the dames in the novels do it. Maybe it's because I've had so little practice. But I want to say this, Gabe. Thank God I don't have to die knowing that no man ever wanted me to be his wife. Honestly, I'm that grateful that I'd marry you in a minute if I didn't like you so well."

"I'll be back in three months, like always," was all that Gabe said. "I ain't going to write. When I get here we'll just take in a show, and the younger you look the better I'll like it."

But on the occasion of Gabe's spring trip he encountered a statuesque blonde person where Effie had been wont to reign.

"Miss—er Bauer out of town?"

The statue melted a trifle in the sunshine of Gabe's ingratiating smile.

"Miss Bauer's ill," the statue informed him, using a heavy Eastern accent. "Anything I can do for you? I'm taking her place."

"Why—ah—not exactly; no," said Gabe. "Just a temporary indisposition, I suppose?"

"Well, you wouldn't hardly call it that, seeing that she's been sick with typhoid for seven weeks."

"Typhoid!" shouted Gabe.

"While I'm not in the habit of asking gentlemen their names, I'd like to inquire if yours happens to be Marks—Gabe I. Marks?"

"Sure," said Gabe. "That's me."

"Miss Bauer's nurse telephones down last week that if a gentleman named Marks—Gabe I. Marks—drops in and inquires for Miss Bauer, I'm to tell him that she's changed her mind."

On the way from Spiegel's corset department to the car, Gabe stopped only for a bunch of violets. Effie's apartment house reached, he sent up his card, the violets, and a message that the gentleman was waiting. There came back a reply that sent Gabie up before the violets were relieved of their first layer of tissue paper.

Effie was sitting in a deep chair by the window, a flowered quilt bunched about her shoulders, her feet in gray knitted bedroom slippers. She looked every minute of her age, and she knew it, and didn't care. The hand that she held out to Gabe was a limp, white, fleshless thing that seemed to bear no relation to the plump, firm member that Gabe had pressed on so many previous occasions.

Gabe stared at this pale wraith in a moment of alarm and dismay. Then:

"You're looking—great!" he stammered. "Great! Nobody'd believe you'd been sick a minute. Guess you've just been stalling for a beauty rest, what?"

Effie smiled a tired little smile, and shook her head slowly.

"You're a good kid, Gabie, to lie like that just to make me feel good. But my nurse left yesterday and I had my first real squint at myself in the mirror. She wouldn't let me look while she was here. After what I saw staring back at me from that glass a whole ballroom full of French courtiers whispering sweet nothings in my ear couldn't make me believe that I look like anything but a hunk of Roquefort, green spots included. When I think of how my clothes won't fit it makes me shiver."

"Oh, you'll soon be back at the store as good as new. They fatten up something wonderful after typhoid. Why, I had a friend——"

"Did you get my message?" interrupted Effie.

"I was only talking to hide my nervousness," said Gabe, and started forward. But Effie waved him away.

"Sit down," she said. "I've got something to say." She looked thoughtfully down at one shining finger nail. Her lower lip was caught between her teeth. When she looked up again her eyes were swimming in tears. Gabe started forward again. Again Effie waved him away.

"It's all right, Gabie. I don't blubber as a rule. This fever leaves you as weak as a rag, and ready to cry if any one says 'Boo!' I've been doing some high-pressure thinking since nursie left. Had plenty of time to do it in, sitting here by this window all day. My land! I never knew there was so much time. There's been days when I haven't talked to a soul, except the nurse and the chambermaid. Lonesome! Say, the amount of petting I could stand would surprise you. Of course, my nurse was a perfectly good nurse—at twenty-five per. But I was just a case to her. You can't expect a nurse to ooze sympathy over an old maid with the fever. I tell you I was dying to have some one say 'Sh-sh-sh!' when there was a noise, just to show they were interested. Whenever I'd moan the nurse would come over and stick a thermometer in my mouth and write something down on a chart. The boys and girls at the store sent flowers. They'd have done the same if I'd died. When the fever broke I just used to lie there and dream, not feeling anything in particular, and not caring much whether it was day or night. Know what I mean?"

Gabie shook a sympathetic head.

There was a little silence. Then Effie went on. "I used to think I was pretty smart, earning my own good living, dressing as well as the next one, and able to spend my vacation in Atlantic City if I wanted to. I didn't know I was missing anything. But while I was sick I got to wishing that there was somebody that belonged to me. Somebody to worry about me, and to sit up nights—somebody that just naturally felt they had to come tiptoeing into my room every three or four minutes to see if I was sleeping, or had enough covers on, or wanted a drink, or something. I got to thinking what it would have been like if I had a husband and a—home. You'll think I'm daffy, maybe."

Gabie took Effie's limp white hand in his, and stroked it gently. Effie's face was turned away from him, toward the noisy street.

"I used to imagine how he'd come home at six, stamping his feet, maybe, and making a lot of noise the way men do. And then he'd remember, and come creaking up the steps, and he'd stick his head in at the door in the funny, awkward, pathetic way men have in a sick room. And he'd say, 'How's the old girl to-night? I'd better not come near you now, puss, because I'll bring the cold with me. Been lonesome for your old man?'"

"And I'd say, 'Oh, I don't care how cold you are, dear. The nurse is downstairs, getting my supper ready.'"

"And then he'd come tiptoeing over to my bed, and stoop down, and kiss me, and his face would be all cold, and rough, and his mustache would be wet, and he'd smell out-doorsy and smoky, the way husbands do when they come in. And I'd reach up and pat his cheek and say, 'You need a shave, old man.'"

"'I know it,' he'd say, rubbing his cheek up against mine."

"'Hurry up and wash, now. Supper'll be ready.'"

"'Where are the kids?' he'd ask. 'The house is as quiet as the grave. Hurry up and get well, kid. It's darn lonesome without you at the table, and the children's manners are getting something awful, and I never can find my shirts. Lordy, I guess we won't celebrate when you get up! Can't you eat a little something nourishing for supper—beefsteak, or a good plate of soup, or something?'"

"Men are like that, you know. So I'd say then: 'Run along, you old goose! You'll be suggesting sauerkraut and wieners next. Don't you let Millie have any marmalade to-night. She's got a spoiled stomach.'"

"And then he'd pound off down the hall to wash up, and I'd shut my eyes, and smile to myself, and everything would be all right, because he was home."

There was a long silence. Effie's eyes were closed. But two great tears stole out from beneath each lid and coursed their slow way down her thin cheeks. She did not raise her hand to wipe them away.

Gabie's other hand reached over and met the one that already clasped Effie's.

"Effie," he said, in a voice that was as hoarse as it was gentle.

"H'm?" said Effie.

"Will you marry me?"

"I shouldn't wonder," replied Effie, opening her eyes. "No, don't kiss me. You might catch something. But say, reach up and smooth my hair away from my forehead, will you, and call me a couple of fool names. I don't care how clumsy you are about it. I could stand an awful fuss being made over me, without being spoiled any."

Three weeks later Effie was back at the store. Her skirt didn't fit in the back, and the little hollow places in her cheeks did not take the customary dash of rouge as well as when they had been plumper. She held a little impromptu reception that extended down as far as the lingeries and up as far as the rugs. The old sparkle came back to Effie's eye. The old assurance and vigor seemed to return. By the time that Miss Weinstein, of the French lingeries, arrived, breathless, to greet her Effie was herself again.

"Well, if you're not a sight for sore eyes, dearie," exclaimed Miss Weinstein. "My goodness, how grand and thin you are! I'd be willing to take a course in typhoid myself, if I thought I could lose twenty-five pounds."

"I haven't a rag that fits me," Effie announced proudly.

Miss Weinstein lowered her voice discreetly. "Dearie, can you come down to my department for a minute? We're going to have a sale on imported lawnjerie blouses, slightly soiled, from nine to eleven to-morrow. There's one you positively must see. Hand-embroidered, Irish motifs, and eyeleted from soup to nuts, and only eight-fifty."

"I've got a fine chance of buying hand-made waists, no matter how slightly soiled," Effie made answer, "with a doctor and nurse's bill as long as your arm."

"Oh, run along!" scoffed Miss Weinstein. "A person would think you had a husband to get a grouch every time you get reckless to the extent of a new waist. You're your own boss. And you know your credit's good. Honestly, it would be a shame to let this chance slip. You're not getting tight in your old age, are you?"

"N-no," faltered Effie, "but——"

"Then come on," urged Miss Weinstein energetically. "And be thankful you haven't got a man to raise the dickens when the bill comes in."

"Do you mean that?" asked Effie slowly, fixing Miss Weinstein with a thoughtful eye.

"Surest thing you know. Say, girlie, let's go over to Klein's for lunch this noon. They have pot roast with potato pfannkuchen on Tuesdays, and we can split an order between us."

"Hold that waist till to-morrow, will you?" said Effie. "I've made an arrangement with a—friend that might make new clothes impossible just now. But I'm going to wire my party that the arrangement is all off. I've changed my mind. I ought to get an answer to-morrow. Did you say it was a thirty-six?"

Bernice Bobs Her Hair
(1920)

F. SCOTT FITZGERALD

After dark on Saturday night one could stand on the first tee of the golf-course and see the country-club windows as a yellow expanse over a very black and wavy ocean. The waves of this ocean, so to speak, were the heads of many curious caddies, a few of the more ingenious chauffeurs, the golf professional's deaf sister—and there were usually several stray, diffident waves who might have rolled inside had they so desired. This was the gallery.

The balcony was inside. It consisted of the circle of wicker chairs that lined the wall of the combination clubroom and ballroom. At these Saturday-night dances it was largely feminine; a great babel of middle-aged ladies with sharp eyes and icy hearts behind lorgnettes and large bosoms. The main function of the balcony was critical, it occasionally showed grudging admiration, but never approval, for it is well known among ladies over thirty-five that when the younger set dance in the summer-time it is with the very worst intentions in the world, and if they are not bombarded with stony eyes stray couples will dance weird barbaric interludes in the corners, and the more popular, more dangerous, girls will sometimes be kissed in the parked limousines of unsuspecting dowagers.

But, after all, this critical circle is not close enough to the stage to see the actors' faces and catch the subtler byplay. It can only frown and lean, ask questions and make satisfactory deductions from its set of postulates, such as the one which states that every young man with a large income leads the life of a hunted partridge. It never really appreciates the drama of the shifting, semicruel world of adolescence. No; boxes, orchestra-circle, principals, and chorus are represented by the medley of faces and voices that sway to the plaintive African rhythm of Dyer's dance orchestra.

From sixteen-year-old Otis Ormonde, who has two more years at Hill School, to G. Reece Stoddard, over whose bureau at home hangs a Harvard law diploma; from little Madeleine Hogue, whose hair still feels strange and uncomfortable on top of her head, to Bessie MacRae, who has been the life of the party a little too long—more than ten years—the medley is not only the centre of the stage but contains the only people capable of getting an unobstructed view of it.

With a flourish and a bang the music stops. The couples exchange artificial, effortless smiles, facetiously repeat "*la*-de-*da-da* dum-*dum*," and then the clatter of young feminine voices soars over the burst of clapping.

A few disappointed stags caught in midfloor as they had been about to cut in subsided listlessly back to the walls, because this was not like the riotous Christmas dances—these summer hops were considered just pleasantly warm and exciting, where even the younger marrieds rose and performed ancient waltzes and terrifying fox trots to the tolerant amusement of their younger brothers and sisters.

Warren McIntyre, who casually attended Yale, being one of the unfortunate stags, felt in his dinner-coat pocket for a cigarette and strolled out onto the wide, semidark veranda, where couples were scattered at tables, filling the lantern-hung night with vague words and hazy laughter. He nodded here and there at the less absorbed and as he passed each couple some half-forgotten fragment of a story played in his mind, for it was not a large city and every one was Who's Who to every one else's past. There, for example, were Jim Strain and Ethel Demorest, who had been privately engaged for three years. Every one knew that as soon as Jim managed to hold a job for more than two months she would marry him. Yet how bored they both looked, and how wearily Ethel regarded Jim sometimes, as if she wondered why she had trained the vines of her affection on such a wind-shaken poplar.

Warren was nineteen and rather pitying with those of his friends who hadn't gone East to college. But, like most boys, he bragged tremendously about the girls of his city when he was away from it. There was Genevieve Ormonde, who regularly made the rounds of dances, house-parties, and football games at Princeton, Yale, Williams, and Cornell; there was black-eyed Roberta Dillon, who was quite as famous to her own generation as Hiram Johnson or Ty Cobb; and, of course, there was Marjorie Harvey, who besides having a fairylike face and a dazzling, bewildering tongue was already justly celebrated for having turned five cart-wheels in succession during the last pump-and-slipper dance at New Haven.

Warren, who had grown up across the street from Marjorie, had long been "crazy about her." Sometimes she seemed to reciprocate his feeling with a faint gratitude, but she had tried him by her infallible test and informed him gravely that she did not love him. Her test was that when she was away from him she forgot him and had affairs with other boys. Warren found this discouraging, especially as Marjorie had been making little trips all summer, and for the first two or three days after each arrival home he saw great heaps of mail on the Harveys' hall table addressed to her in various masculine handwritings. To make matters worse, all during the month of August she had been visited by her cousin Bernice from Eau Claire, and it seemed impossible to see her alone. It was always necessary to hunt round and find some one to take care of Bernice. As August waned this was becoming more and more difficult.

Much as Warren worshipped Marjorie he had to admit that Cousin Bernice was sorta dopeless. She was pretty, with dark hair and high color, but she was no fun on a party. Every Saturday night he danced a long arduous duty dance with her to please Marjorie, but he had never been anything but bored in her company.

"Warren"——a soft voice at his elbow broke in upon his thoughts, and he turned to see Marjorie, flushed and radiant as usual. She laid a hand on his shoulder and a glow settled almost imperceptibly over him.

"Warren," she whispered "do something for me—dance with Bernice. She's been stuck with little Otis Ormonde for almost an hour."

Warren's glow faded.

"Why—sure," he answered half-heartedly.

"You don't mind, do you? I'll see that you don't get stuck."

" 'Sall right."

Marjorie smiled—that smile that was thanks enough.

"You're an angel, and I'm obliged loads."

With a sigh the angel glanced round the veranda, but Bernice and Otis were not in sight. He wandered back inside, and there in front of the women's dressing-room he found Otis in the centre of a group of young men who were convulsed with laughter. Otis was brandishing a piece of timber he had picked up, and discoursing volubly.

"She's gone in to fix her hair," he announced wildly. "I'm waiting to dance another hour with her."

Their laughter was renewed.

"Why don't some of you cut in?" cried Otis resentfully. "She likes more variety."

"Why, Otis," suggested a friend "you've just barely got used to her."

"Why the two-by-four, Otis?" inquired Warren, smiling.

"The two-by-four? Oh, this? This is a club. When she comes out I'll hit her on the head and knock her in again."

Warren collapsed on a settee and howled with glee.

"Never mind, Otis," he articulated finally. "I'm relieving you this time."

Otis simulated a sudden fainting attack and handed the stick to Warren.

"If you need it, old man," he said hoarsely.

No matter how beautiful or brilliant a girl may be, the reputation of not being frequently cut in on makes her position at a dance unfortunate. Perhaps boys prefer her company to that of the butterflies with whom they dance a dozen times an evening but, youth in this jazz-nourished generation is temperamentally restless, and the idea of fox-trotting more than one full fox trot with the same girl is distasteful, not to say odious. When it comes to several dances and the intermissions between she can be quite sure that a young man, once relieved, will never tread on her wayward toes again.

Warren danced the next full dance with Bernice, and finally, thankful for the intermission, he led her to a table on the veranda. There was a moment's silence while she did unimpressive things with her fan.

"It's hotter here than in Eau Claire," she said.

Warren stifled a sigh and nodded. It might be for all he knew or cared. He wondered idly whether she was a poor conversationalist because she got no attention or got no attention because she was a poor conversationalist.

"You going to be here much longer?" he asked and then turned rather red. She might suspect his reasons for asking.

"Another week," she answered, and stared at him as if to lunge at his next remark when it left his lips.

Warren fidgeted. Then with a sudden charitable impulse he decided to try part of his line on her. He turned and looked at her eyes.

"You've got an awfully kissable mouth," he began quietly.

This was a remark that he sometimes made to girls at college proms when they were talking in just such half dark as this. Bernice distinctly jumped. She turned an ungraceful red and became clumsy with her fan. No one had ever made such a remark to her before.

"Fresh!"——the word had slipped out before she realized it, and she bit her lip. Too late she decided to be amused, and offered him a flustered smile.

Warren was annoyed. Though not accustomed to have that remark taken seriously, still it usually provoked a laugh or a paragraph of sentimental banter. And he hated to be called fresh, except in a joking way. His charitable impulse died and he switched the topic.

"Jim Strain and Ethel Demorest sitting out as usual," he commented.

This was more in Bernice's line, but a faint regret mingled with her relief as the subject changed. Men did not talk to her about kissable mouths, but she knew that they talked in some such way to other girls.

"Oh, yes," she said, and laughed. "I hear they've been mooning around for years without a red penny. Isn't it silly?"

Warren's disgust increased. Jim Strain was a close friend of his brother's, and anyway he considered it bad form to sneer at people for not having money. But Bernice had had no intention of sneering. She was merely nervous.

II

When Marjorie and Bernice reached home at half after midnight they said good night at the top of the stairs. Though cousins, they were not intimates. As a matter of fact Marjorie had no female intimates—she considered girls stupid. Bernice on the contrary all through this parent-arranged visit had rather longed to exchange those confidences flavored with giggles and tears that she considered an indispensable factor in all feminine intercourse. But in this respect she found Marjorie rather cold; felt somehow the same difficulty in talking to her that she had in talking to men. Marjorie never giggled, was never frightened, seldom embarrassed, and in fact had very few of the qualities which Bernice considered appropriately and blessedly feminine.

As Bernice busied herself with tooth-brush and paste this night she wondered for the hundredth time why she never had any attention when she was away from home. That her family were the wealthiest in Eau Claire; that her mother entertained tremendously, gave little diners for her daughter before all dances and bought her a car of her own to drive round in, never occurred to her as factors in her home-town social success. Like most girls she had been brought up on the warm milk prepared by Annie Fellows Johnston and on novels in which the female was beloved because of certain mysterious womanly qualities, always mentioned but never displayed.

Bernice felt a vague pain that she was not at present engaged in being popular. She did not know that had it not been for Marjorie's campaigning she would have danced the entire evening with one man; but she knew that even in Eau Claire other girls with less position and less pulchritude were given a much bigger rush. She attributed this to something subtly unscrupulous in those girls. It had never worried her, and if it had her mother would have assured her that the other girls cheapened themselves and that men really respected girls like Bernice.

She turned out the light in her bathroom, and on an impulse decided to go in and chat for a moment with her aunt Josephine, whose light was still on. Her soft slippers bore her noiselessly down the carpeted hall, but hearing voices inside she stopped near the partly opened door. Then she caught her own name, and without any definite intention of eavesdropping lingered—and the thread of the conversation going on inside pierced her consciousness sharply as if it had been drawn through with a needle.

"She's absolutely hopeless!" It was Marjorie's voice. "Oh, I know what you're going to say! So many people have told you how pretty and sweet she is, and how she can cook! What of it? She has a bum time. Men don't like her."

"What's a little cheap popularity?"

Mrs. Harvey sounded annoyed.

"It's everything when you're eighteen," said Marjorie emphatically. "I've done my best. I've been polite and I've made men dance with her, but they just won't stand being bored. When I think of that gorgeous coloring wasted on such a ninny, and think what Martha Carey could do with it—oh!"

"There's no courtesy these days."

Mrs. Harvey's voice implied that modern situations were too much for her. When she was a girl all young ladies who belonged to nice families had glorious times.

"Well," said Marjorie, "no girl can permanently bolster up a lame-duck visitor, because these days it's every girl for herself. I've even tried to drop hints about clothes and things, and she's been furious—given me the funniest looks. She's sensitive enough to know she's not getting away with much, but I'll bet she consoles herself by thinking that she's very virtuous and that I'm too gay and fickle and will come to a bad end. All unpopular girls think that way. Sour grapes! Sarah Hopkins refers to Genevieve and Roberta and me as gardenia girls! I'll bet she'd give ten years of her life and her European education to be a gardenia girl and have three or four men in love with her and be cut in on every few feet at dances."

"It seems to me," interrupted Mrs. Harvey rather wearily, "that you ought to be able to do something for Bernice. I know she's not very vivacious."

Marjorie groaned.

"Vivacious! Good grief! I've never heard her say anything to a boy except that it's hot or the floor's crowded or that she's going to school in New York next year. Sometimes she asks them what kind of car they have and tells them the kind she has. Thrilling!"

There was a short silence and then Mrs. Harvey took up her refrain:

"All I know is that other girls not half so sweet and attractive get partners. Martha Carey, for instance, is stout and loud, and her mother is distinctly common. Roberta Dillon is so thin this year that she looks as though Arizona were the place for her. She's dancing herself to death."

"But, mother," objected Marjorie impatiently, "Martha is cheerful and awfully witty and an awfully slick girl, and Roberta's a marvellous dancer. She's been popular for ages!"

Mrs. Harvey yawned.

"I think it's that crazy Indian blood in Bernice," continued Marjorie. "Maybe she's a reversion to type. Indian women all just sat round and never said anything."

"Go to bed, you silly child," laughed Mrs. Harvey. "I wouldn't have told you that if I'd thought you were going to remember it. And I think most of your ideas are perfectly idiotic," she finished sleepily.

There was another silence, while Marjorie considered whether or not convincing her mother was worth the trouble. People over forty can seldom be permanently convinced of anything. At eighteen our convictions are hills from which we look; at forty-five they are caves in which we hide.

Having decided this, Marjorie said good night. When she came out into the hall it was quite empty.

III

While Marjorie was breakfasting late next day Bernice came into the room with a rather formal good morning, sat down opposite, stared intently over and slightly moistened her lips.

"What's on your mind?" inquired Marjorie, rather puzzled.

Bernice paused before she threw her hand-grenade.

"I heard what you said about me to your mother last night."

Marjorie was startled, but she showed only a faintly heightened color and her voice was quite even when she spoke.

"Where were you?"

"In the hall. I didn't mean to listen—at first."

After an involuntary look of contempt Marjorie dropped her eyes and became very interested in balancing a stray corn-flake on her finger.

"I guess I'd better go back to Eau Claire—if I'm such a nuisance." Bernice's lower lip was trembling violently and she continued on a wavering note: "I've tried to be nice, and—and I've been first neglected and then insulted. No one ever visited me and got such treatment."

Marjorie was silent.

"But I'm in the way, I see. I'm a drag on you. Your friends don't like me." She paused, and then remembered another one of her grievances. "Of course I was furious last week when you tried to hint to me that that dress was unbecoming. Don't you think I know how to dress myself?"

"No," murmured less than half-aloud.

"What?"

"I didn't hint anything," said Marjorie succinctly. "I said, as I remember, that it was better to wear a becoming dress three times straight than to alternate it with two frights."

"Do you think that was a very nice thing to say?"

"I wasn't trying to be nice." Then after a pause: "When do you want to go?"

Bernice drew in her breath sharply.

"Oh!" It was a little half-cry.

Marjorie looked up in surprise.

"Didn't you say you were going?"

"Yes, but——"

"Oh, you were only bluffing!"

They stared at each other across the breakfast-table for a moment. Misty waves were passing before Bernice's eyes, while Marjorie's face wore that rather hard expression that she used when slightly intoxicated undergraduates were making love to her.

"So you were bluffing," she repeated as if it were what she might have expected.

Bernice admitted it by bursting into tears. Marjorie's eyes showed boredom.

"You're my cousin," sobbed Bernice. "I'm v-v-visiting you. I was to stay a month, and if I go home my mother will know and she'll wah-wonder——"

Marjorie waited until the shower of broken words collapsed into little sniffles.

"I'll give you my month's allowance," she said coldly, "and you can spend this last week anywhere you want. There's a very nice hotel——"

Bernice's sobs rose to a flute note, and rising of a sudden she fled from the room.

An hour later, while Marjorie was in the library absorbed in composing one of those non-committal marvelously elusive letters that only a young girl can write, Bernice reappeared, very red-eyed, and consciously calm. She cast no glance at Marjorie but took a book at random from the shelf and sat down as if to read. Marjorie seemed absorbed in her letter and continued writing. When the clock showed noon Bernice closed her book with a snap.

"I suppose I'd better get my railroad ticket."

This was not the beginning of the speech she had rehearsed up-stairs, but as Marjorie was not getting her cues—wasn't urging her to be reasonable; it's all a mistake—it was the best opening she could muster.

"Just wait till I finish this letter," said Marjorie without looking round. "I want to get it off in the next mail."

After another minute, during which her pen scratched busily, she turned round and relaxed with an air of "at your service." Again Bernice had to speak.

"Do you want me to go home?"

"Well," said Marjorie, considering, "I suppose if you're not having a good time you'd better go. No use being miserable."

"Don't you think common kindness——"

"Oh, please don't quote 'Little Women'!" cried Marjorie impatiently. "That's out of style."

"You think so?"

"Heavens, yes! What modern girl could live like those inane females?"

"They were the models for our mothers."

Marjorie laughed.

"Yes, they were—not! Besides, our mothers were all very well in their way, but they know very little about their daughters' problems."

Bernice drew herself up.

"Please don't talk about my mother."

Marjorie laughed.

"I don't think I mentioned her."

Bernice felt that she was being led away from her subject.

"Do you think you've treated me very well?"

"I've done my best. You're rather hard material to work with."

The lids of Bernice's eyes reddened.

"I think you're hard and selfish, and you haven't a feminine quality in you."

"Oh, my Lord!" cried Marjorie in desperation. "You little nut! Girls like you are responsible for all the tiresome colorless marriages; all those ghastly inefficiencies that pass as feminine qualities. What a blow it must be when a man with imagination marries the beautiful bundle of clothes that he's been building ideals round, and finds that she's just a weak, whining, cowardly mass of affectations!"

Bernice's mouth had slipped half open.

"The womanly woman!" continued Marjorie. "Her whole early life is occupied in whining criticisms of girls like me who really do have a good time."

Bernice's jaw descended farther as Marjorie's voice rose.

"There's some excuse for an ugly girl whining. If I'd been irretrievably ugly I'd never have forgiven my parents for bringing me into the world. But you're starting life without any handicap—" Marjorie's little fist clinched, "If you expect me to weep with you you'll be disappointed. Go or stay, just as you like." And picking up her letters she left the room.

Bernice claimed a headache and failed to appear at luncheon. They had a matinée date for the afternoon, but the headache persisting, Marjorie made explanation to a not very downcast boy. But when she returned late in the afternoon she found Bernice with a strangely set face waiting for her in her bedroom.

"I've decided," began Bernice without preliminaries, "that maybe you're right about things—possibly not. But if you'll tell me why your friends aren't—aren't interested in me I'll see if I can do what you want me to."

Marjorie was at the mirror shaking down her hair.

"Do you mean it?"

"Yes."

"Without reservations? Will you do exactly what I say?"

"Well, I——"

"Well nothing! Will you do exactly as I say?"

"If they're sensible things."

"They're not! You're no case for sensible things."

"Are you going to make—to recommend——"

"Yes, everything. If I tell you to take boxing-lessons you'll have to do it. Write home and tell your mother you're going to stay another two weeks.

"If you'll tell me——"

"All right—I'll just give you a few examples now. First you have no ease of manner. Why? Because you're never sure about your personal appearance. When a girl feels that she's perfectly groomed and dressed she can forget that part of her. That's charm. The more parts of yourself you can afford to forget the more charm you have."

"Don't I look all right?"

"No; for instance you never take care of your eyebrows. They're black and lustrous, but by leaving them straggly they're a blemish. They'd be beautiful if you'd take care of them in one-tenth the time you take doing nothing. You're going to brush them so that they'll grow straight."

Bernice raised the brows in question.

"Do you mean to say that men notice eyebrows?"

"Yes—subconsciously. And when you go home you ought to have your teeth straightened a little. It's almost imperceptible, still——"

"But I thought," interrupted Bernice in bewilderment, "that you despised little dainty feminine things like that."

"I hate dainty minds," answered Marjorie. "But a girl has to be dainty in person. If she looks like a million dollars she can talk about Russia, ping-pong, or the League of Nations and get away with it."

"What else?"

"Oh, I'm just beginning! There's your dancing."

"Don't I dance all right?"

"No, you don't—you lean on a man; yes, you do—ever so slightly. I noticed it when we were dancing together yesterday. And you dance standing up straight instead of bending over a little. Probably some old lady on the side-line once told you that you looked so dignified that way. But except with a very small girl it's much harder on the man, and he's the one that counts."

"Go on." Bernice's brain was reeling.

"Well, you've got to learn to be nice to men who are sad birds. You look as if you'd been insulted whenever you're thrown with any except the most popular boys. Why, Bernice, I'm cut in on every few feet—and who does most of it? Why, those very sad birds. No girl can afford to neglect them. They're the big part of any crowd. Young boys too shy to talk are the very best conversational practice. Clumsy boys are the best dancing practice. If you can follow them and yet look graceful you can follow a baby tank across a barb-wire sky-scraper."

Bernice sighed profoundly, but Marjorie was not through.

"If you go to a dance and really amuse, say, three sad birds that dance with you; if you talk so well to them that they forget they're stuck with you, you've done something. They'll come back next time, and gradually so many sad birds will dance with you that the attractive boys will see there's no danger of being stuck—then they'll dance with you."

"Yes," agreed Bernice faintly. "I think I begin to see."

"And finally," concluded Marjorie, "poise and charm will just come. You'll wake up some morning knowing you've attained it and men will know it too."

Bernice rose.

"It's been awfully kind of you—but nobody's ever talked to me like this before, and I feel sort of startled."

Marjorie made no answer but gazed pensively at her own image in the mirror.

"You're a peach to help me," continued Bernice.

Still Marjorie did not answer, and Bernice thought she had seemed too grateful.

"I know you don't like sentiment," she said timidly.

Marjorie turned to her quickly.

"Oh, I wasn't thinking about that. I was considering whether we hadn't better bob your hair."

Bernice collapsed backward upon the bed.

IV

On the following Wednesday evening there was a dinner-dance at the country club. When the guests strolled in Bernice found her place-card with a slight feeling of irritation. Though at her right sat G. Reece Stoddard, a most desirable and distinguished young bachelor, the all-important left held only Charley Paulson. Charley lacked height, beauty, and social shrewdness, and in her new enlightenment Bernice decided that his only qualification to be her partner was that he had never been stuck with her. But this feeling of irritation left with the last of the soup-plates, and Marjorie's specific instruction came to her. Swallowing her pride she turned to Charley Paulson and plunged.

"Do you think I ought to bob my hair, Mr. Charley Paulson?"

Charley looked up in surprise.

"Why?"

"Because I'm considering it. It's such a sure and easy way of attracting attention."

Charley smiled pleasantly. He could not know this had been rehearsed. He replied that he didn't know much about bobbed hair. But Bernice was there to tell him.

"I want to be a society vampire, you see," she announced coolly, and went on to inform him that bobbed hair was the necessary prelude. She added that she wanted to ask his advice, because she had heard he was so critical about girls.

Charley, who knew as much about the psychology of women as he did of the mental states of Buddhist contemplatives, felt vaguely flattered.

"So I've decided," she continued, her voice rising slightly, "that early next week I'm going down to the Sevier Hotel barber-shop, sit in the first chair, and get my hair bobbed." She faltered, noticing that the people near her had paused in their conversation and were listening; but after a confused second Marjorie's coaching told, and she finished her paragraph to the vicinity at large. "Of course I'm charging admission, but if you'll all come down and encourage me I'll issue passes for the inside seats."

There was a ripple of appreciative laughter, and under cover of it G. Reece Stoddard leaned over quickly and said close to her ear: "I'll take a box right now."

She met his eyes and smiled as if he had said something surprisingly brilliant.

"Do you believe in bobbed hair?" asked G. Reece in the same undertone.

"I think it's unmoral," affirmed Bernice gravely. "But, of course, you've either got to amuse people or feed 'em or shock 'em." Marjorie had culled this from Oscar Wilde. It was greeted with a ripple of laughter from the men and a series of quick, intent looks from the girls. And then as though she had said nothing of wit or moment Bernice turned again to Charley and spoke confidentially in his ear.

"I want to ask you your opinion of several people. I imagine you're a wonderful judge of character."

Charley thrilled faintly—paid her a subtle compliment by overturning her water.

Two hours later, while Warren McIntyre was standing passively in the stag line abstractedly watching the dancers and wondering whither and with whom Marjorie had disappeared, an unrelated perception began to creep slowly upon him—a perception that Bernice, cousin to Marjorie, had been cut in on several times in the past five minutes. He closed his eyes, opened them and looked again. Several minutes back she had been dancing with a visiting boy, a matter easily accounted for; a visiting boy would know no better. But now she was dancing with some one else, and there was Charley Paulson headed for her with enthusiastic determination in his eye. Funny—Charley seldom danced with more than three girls an evening.

Warren was distinctly surprised when—the exchange having been effected—the man relieved proved to be none ether than G. Reece Stoddard himself. And G. Reece seemed not at all jubilant at being relieved. Next time Bernice danced near, Warren regarded her intently. Yes, she was pretty, distinctly pretty; and to-night her face seemed really vivacious. She had that look that no woman, however histrionically proficient, can successfully counterfeit—she looked as if she were having a good time. He liked the way she had her hair arranged, wondered if it was brilliantine that made it glisten so. And that dress was becoming—a dark red that set off her shadowy eyes and high coloring. He remembered that he had thought her pretty when she first came to town, before he had realized that she was dull. Too bad she was dull—dull girls unbearable—certainly pretty though.

His thoughts zigzagged back to Marjorie. This disappearance would be like other disappearances. When she reappeared he would demand where she had been—would be told emphatically that it was none of his business. What a pity she was so sure of him! She basked in the knowledge that no other girl in town interested him; she defied him to fall in love with Genevieve or Roberta.

Warren sighed. The way to Marjorie's affections was a labyrinth indeed. He looked up. Bernice was again dancing with the visiting boy. Half unconsciously he took a step out from the stag line in her direction, and hesitated. Then he said to himself that it was charity. He walked toward her—collided suddenly with G. Reece Stoddard.

"Pardon me," said Warren.

But G. Reece had not stopped to apologize. He had again cut in on Bernice.

That night at one o'clock Marjorie, with one hand on the electric-light switch in the hall, turned to take a last look at Bernice's sparkling eyes.

"So it worked?"

"Oh, Marjorie, yes!" cried Bernice.

"I saw you were having a gay time."

"I did! The only trouble was that about midnight I ran short of talk. I had to repeat myself—with different men of course. I hope they won't compare notes."

"Men don't," said Marjorie, yawning, "and it wouldn't matter if they did—they'd think you were even trickier."

She snapped out the light, and as they started up the stairs Bernice grasped the banister thankfully. For the first time in her life she had been danced tired.

"You see," said Marjorie at the top of the stairs, "one man sees another man cut in and he thinks there must be something there. Well, we'll fix up some new stuff to-morrow. Good night."

"Good night."

As Bernice took down her hair she passed the evening before her in review. She had followed instructions exactly. Even when Charley Paulson cut in for the eighth time she had simulated delight and had apparently been both interested and flattered. She had not talked about the weather or Eau Claire or automobiles or her school, but had confined her conversation to me, you, and us.

But a few minutes before she fell asleep a rebellious thought was churning drowsily in her brain—after all, it was she who had done it. Marjorie, to be sure, had given her her conversation, but then Marjorie got much of her conversation out of things she read. Bernice had bought the red dress, though she had never valued it highly before Marjorie dug it out of her trunk—and her own voice had said the words, her own lips had smiled, her own feet had danced. Marjorie nice girl—vain, though—nice evening—nice boys—like Warren—Warren—Warren—what's his name—Warren——

She fell asleep.

V

To Bernice the next week was a revelation. With the feeling that people really enjoyed looking at her and listening to her came the foundation of self-confidence. Of course there were numerous mistakes at first. She did not know, for instance, that Draycott Deyo was studying for the ministry; she was unaware that he had cut in on her because he thought she was a quiet, reserved girl. Had she known these things she would not have treated him to the line which began "Hello, Shell Shock!" and continued with the bathtub story—"It takes a frightful lot of energy to fix my hair in the summer—there's so much of it—so I always fix it first and powder my face and put on my hat; then I get into the bathtub, and dress afterward. Don't you think that's the best plan?"

Though Draycott Deyo was in the throes of difficulties concerning baptism by immersion and might possibly have seen a connection, it must be admitted that he did not. He considered feminine bathing an immoral subject, and gave her some of his ideas on the depravity of modern society.

But to offset that unfortunate occurrence Bernice had several signal successes to her credit. Little Otis Ormonde pleaded off from a trip East and elected instead to follow her with a puppylike devotion, to the amusement of his crowd and to the irritation of G. Reece Stoddard, several of whose afternoon calls Otis completely ruined by the disgusting tenderness of the glances he bent on Bernice. He even told her the story of the two-by-four and the dressing-room to show her how frightfully mistaken he and every one else had been in their first judgment of her. Bernice laughed off that incident with a slight sinking sensation.

Of all Bernice's conversation perhaps the best known and most universally approved was the line about the bobbing of her hair.

"Oh, Bernice, when you goin' to get the hair bobbed?"

"Day after to-morrow maybe," she would reply, laughing. "Will you come and see me? Because I'm counting on you, you know."

"Will we? You know! But you better hurry up."

Bernice, whose tonsorial intentions were strictly dishonorable, would laugh again.

"Pretty soon now. You'd be surprised."

But perhaps the most significant symbol of her success was the gray car of the hypercritical Warren McIntyre, parked daily in front of the Harvey house. At first the parlor-maid was distinctly startled when he asked for Bernice instead of Marjorie; after a week of it she told the cook that Miss Bernice had gotta holda Miss Marjorie's best fella.

And Miss Bernice had. Perhaps it began with Warren's desire to rouse jealousy in Marjorie; perhaps it was the familiar though unrecognized strain of Marjorie in Bernice's conversation; perhaps it was both of these and something of sincere attraction besides. But somehow the collective mind of the younger set knew within a week that Marjorie's most reliable beau had made an amazing face-about and was giving an indisputable rush to Marjorie's guest. The question of the moment was how Marjorie would take it. Warren called Bernice on the 'phone twice a day, sent her notes, and they were frequently seen together in his roadster, obviously engrossed in one of those tense, significant conversations as to whether or not he was sincere.

Marjorie on being twitted only laughed. She said she was mighty glad that Warren had at last found some one who appreciated him. So the younger set laughed, too, and guessed that Marjorie didn't care and let it go at that.

One afternoon when there were only three days left of her visit Bernice was waiting in the hall for Warren, with whom she was going to a bridge party. She was in rather a blissful mood, and when Marjorie—also bound for the party—appeared beside her and began casually to adjust her hat in the mirror, Bernice was utterly unprepared for anything in the nature of a clash. Marjorie did her work very coldly and succinctly in three sentences.

"You may as well get Warren out of your head," she said coldly.

"What?" Bernice was utterly astounded.

"You may as well stop making a fool of yourself over Warren McIntyre. He doesn't care a snap of his fingers about you."

For a tense moment they regarded each other—Marjorie scornful, aloof; Bernice astounded, half-angry, half-afraid. Then two cars drove up in front of the house and there was a riotous honking. Both of them gasped faintly, turned, and side by side hurried out.

All through the bridge party Bernice strove in vain to master a rising uneasiness. She had offended Marjorie, the sphinx of sphinxes. With the most wholesome and innocent intentions in the world she had stolen Marjorie's property. She felt suddenly and horribly guilty. After the bridge game, when they sat in an informal circle and the conversation became general, the storm gradually broke. Little Otis Ormonde inadvertently precipitated it.

"When you going back to kindergarten, Otis?" some one had asked.

"Me? Day Bernice gets her hair bobbed."

"Then your education's over," said Marjorie quickly. "That's only a bluff of hers. I should think you'd have realized."

"That a fact?" demanded Otis, giving Bernice a reproachful glance.

Bernice's ears burned as she tried to think up an effectual come-back. In the face of this direct attack her imagination was paralyzed.

"There's a lot of bluffs in the world," continued Marjorie quite pleasantly. "I should think you'd be young enough to know that, Otis."

"Well," said Otis, "maybe so. But gee! With a line like Bernice's——"

"Really?" yawned Marjorie. "What's her latest bon mot?"

No one seemed to know. In fact, Bernice, having trifled with her muse's beau, had said nothing memorable of late.

"Was that really all a line?" asked Roberta curiously.

Bernice hesitated. She felt that wit in some form was demanded of her, but under her cousin's suddenly frigid eyes she was completely incapacitated.

"I don't know," she stalled.

"Splush!" said Marjorie. "Admit it!"

Bernice saw that Warren's eyes had left a ukulele he had been tinkering with and were fixed on her questioningly.

"Oh, I don't know!" she repeated steadily. Her cheeks were glowing.

"Splush!" remarked Marjorie again.

"Come through, Bernice," urged Otis. "Tell her where to get off." Bernice looked round again—she seemed unable to get away from Warren's eyes.

"I like bobbed hair," she said hurriedly, as if he had asked her a question, "and I intend to bob mine."

"When?" demanded Marjorie.

"Any time."

"No time like the present," suggested Roberta.

Otis jumped to his feet.

"Good stuff!" he cried. "We'll have a summer bobbing party. Sevier Hotel barber-shop, I think you said."

In an instant all were on their feet. Bernice's heart throbbed violently.

"What?" she gasped.

Out of the group came Marjorie's voice, very clear and contemptuous.

"Don't worry—she'll back out!"

"Come on, Bernice!" cried Otis, starting toward the door.

Four eyes—Warren's and Marjorie's—stared at her, challenged her, defied her. For another second she wavered wildly.

"All right," she said swiftly. "I don't care if I do."

An eternity of minutes later, riding down-town through the late afternoon beside Warren, the others following in Roberta's car close behind, Bernice had all the sensations of Marie Antoinette bound for the guillotine in a tumbrel. Vaguely she wondered why she did not cry out that it was all a mistake. It was all she could do to keep from clutching her hair with both hands to protect it from the suddenly hostile world. Yet she did neither. Even the thought of her mother was no deterrent now. This was the test supreme of her sportsmanship; her right to walk unchallenged in the starry heaven of popular girls.

Warren was moodily silent, and when they came to the hotel he drew up at the curb and nodded to Bernice to precede him out. Roberta's car emptied a laughing crowd into the shop, which presented two bold plate-glass windows to the street.

Bernice stood on the curb and looked at the sign, Sevier Barber-Shop. It was a guillotine indeed, and the hangman was the first barber, who, attired in a white coat and smoking a cigarette, leaned nonchalantly against the first chair. He must have heard of her; he must have been waiting all week, smoking eternal cigarettes beside that portentous, too-often-mentioned first chair. Would they blindfold her? No, but they would tie a white cloth round her neck lest any of her blood—nonsense—hair—should get on her clothes.

"All right, Bernice," said Warren quickly.

With her chin in the air she crossed the sidewalk, pushed open the swinging screen-door, and giving not a glance to the uproarious, riotous row that occupied the waiting bench, went up to the fat barber.

"I want you to bob my hair."

The first barber's mouth slid somewhat open. His cigarette dropped to the floor.

"Huh?"

"My hair—bob it!"

Refusing further preliminaries, Bernice took her seat on high. A man in the chair next to her turned on his side and gave her a glance, half lather, half amazement. One barber started and spoiled little Willy Schuneman's monthly haircut. Mr. O'Reilly in the last chair grunted and swore musically in ancient Gaelic as a razor bit into his cheek. Two bootblacks became wide-eyed and rushed for her feet. No, Bernice didn't care for a shine.

Outside a passer-by stopped and stared; a couple joined him; half a dozen small boys' noses sprang into life, flattened against the glass; and snatches of conversation borne on the summer breeze drifted in through the screen-door.

"Lookada long hair on a kid!"

"Where'd yuh get 'at stuff? 'At's a bearded lady he just finished shavin'."

But Bernice saw nothing, heard nothing. Her only living sense told her that this man in the white coat had removed one tortoise-shell comb and then another; that his fingers were fumbling clumsily with unfamiliar hairpins; that this hair, this wonderful hair of hers, was going—she would never again feel its long voluptuous pull as it hung in a dark-brown glory down her back. For a second she was near breaking down, and then the picture before her swam mechanically into her vision—Marjorie's mouth curling in a faint ironic smile as if to say:

"Give up and get down! You tried to buck me and I called your bluff. You see you haven't got a prayer."

And some last energy rose up in Bernice, for she clinched her hands under the white cloth, and there was a curious narrowing of her eyes that Marjorie remarked on to some one long afterward.

Twenty minutes later the barber swung her round to face the mirror, and she flinched at the full extent of the damage that had been wrought. Her hair was not curls and now it lay in lank lifeless blocks on both sides of her suddenly pale face. It was ugly as sin—she had known it would be ugly as sin. Her face's chief charm had been a Madonna-like simplicity. Now that was gone and she was—well, frightfully mediocre—not stagy; only ridiculous, like a Greenwich Villager who had left her spectacles at home.

As she climbed down from the chair she tried to smile—failed miserably. She saw two of the girls exchange glances; noticed Marjorie's mouth curved in attenuated mockery—and that Warren's eyes were suddenly very cold.

"You see,"—her words fell into an awkward pause—"I've done it."

"Yes, you've—done it," admitted Warren.

"Do you like it?"

There was a half-hearted "Sure" from two or three voices, another awkward pause, and then Marjorie turned swiftly and with serpentlike intensity to Warren.

"Would you mind running me down to the cleaners?" she asked. "I've simply got to get a dress there before supper. Roberta's driving right home and she can take the others."

Warren stared abstractedly at some infinite speck out the window. Then for an instant his eyes rested coldly on Bernice before they turned to Marjorie.

"Be glad to," he said slowly.

VI

Bernice did not fully realize the outrageous trap that had been set for her until she met her aunt's amazed glance just before dinner.

"Why, Bernice!"

"I've bobbed it, Aunt Josephine."

"Why, child!"

"Do you like it?"

"Why, Bernice!"

"I suppose I've shocked you."

"No, but what'll Mrs. Deyo think tomorrow night? Bernice, you should have waited until after the Deyo's dance—you should have waited if you wanted to do that."

"It was sudden, Aunt Josephine. Anyway, why does it matter to Mrs. Deyo particularly?"

"Why child," cried Mrs. Harvey, "in her paper on 'The Foibles of the Younger Generation' that she read at the last meeting of the Thursday Club she devoted fifteen minutes to bobbed hair. It's her pet abomination. And the dance is for you and Marjorie!"

"I'm sorry."

"Oh, Bernice, what'll your mother say? She'll think I let you do it."

"I'm sorry."

Dinner was an agony. She had made a hasty attempt with a curling-iron, and burned her finger and much hair. She could see that her aunt was both worried and grieved, and her uncle kept saying, "Well, I'll be darned!" over and over in a hurt and faintly hostile tone. And Marjorie sat very quietly, intrenched behind a faint smile, a faintly mocking smile.

Somehow she got through the evening. Three boys called; Marjorie disappeared with one of them, and Bernice made a listless unsuccessful attempt to entertain the two others—sighed thankfully as she climbed the stairs to her room at half past ten. What a day!

When she had undressed for the night the door opened and Marjorie came in.

"Bernice," she said, "I'm awfully sorry about the Deyo dance. I'll give you my word of honor I'd forgotten all about it."

" 'Sall right," said Bernice shortly. Standing before the mirror she passed her comb slowly through her short hair.

"I'll take you down-town to-morrow," continued Marjorie, "and the hairdresser'll fix it so you'll look slick. I didn't imagine you'd go through with it. I'm really mighty sorry."

"Oh, 'sall right!"

"Still it's your last night, so I suppose it won't matter much."

Then Bernice winced as Marjorie tossed her own hair over her shoulders and began to twist it slowly into two long blond braids until in her cream-colored negligée she looked like a delicate painting of some Saxon princess. Fascinated, Bernice watched the braids grow. Heavy and luxurious they were moving under the supple fingers like restive snakes—and to Bernice remained this relic and the curling-iron and a to-morrow full of eyes. She could see G. Reece Stoddard, who liked her, assuming his Harvard manner and telling his dinner partner that Bernice shouldn't have been allowed to go to the movies so much; she could see Draycott Deyo exchanging glances with his mother and then being conscientiously charitable to her. But then perhaps by to-morrow Mrs. Deyo would have heard the news; would send round an icy little note requesting that she fail to appear—and behind her back they would all laugh and know that Marjorie had made a fool of her; that her chance at beauty had been sacrificed to the jealous whim of a selfish girl. She sat down suddenly before the mirror, biting the inside of her cheek.

"I like it," she said with an effort. "I think it'll be becoming."

Marjorie smiled.

"It looks all right. For heaven's sake, don't let it worry you!"

"I won't."

"Good night Bernice."

But as the door closed something snapped within Bernice. She sprang dynamically to her feet, clinching her hands, then swiftly and noiseless crossed over to her bed and from underneath it dragged out her suitcase. Into it she tossed toilet articles and a change of clothing, then she turned to her trunk and quickly dumped in two drawerfulls of lingerie and summer dresses. She moved quietly, but with deadly efficiency, and in three-quarters of an hour her trunk was locked and strapped and she was fully dressed in a becoming new travelling suit that Marjorie had helped her pick out.

Sitting down at her desk she wrote a short note to Mrs. Harvey, in which she briefly outlined her reasons for going. She sealed it, addressed it, and laid it on her pillow. She glanced at her watch. The train left at one, and she knew that if she walked down to the Marborough Hotel two blocks away she could easily get a taxicab.

Suddenly she drew in her breath sharply and an expression flashed into her eyes that a practiced character reader might have connected vaguely with the set look she had worn in the barber's chair—somehow a development of it. It was quite a new look for Bernice—and it carried consequences.

She went stealthily to the bureau, picked up an article that lay there, and turning out all the lights stood quietly until her eyes became accustomed to the darkness. Softly she pushed open the door to Marjorie's room. She heard the quiet, even breathing of an untroubled conscience asleep.

She was by the bedside now, very deliberate and calm. She acted swiftly. Bending over she found one of the braids of Marjorie's hair, followed it up with her hand to the point nearest the head, and then holding it a little slack so that the sleeper would feel no pull, she reached down with the shears and severed it. With the pigtail in her hand she held her breath. Marjorie had muttered something in her sleep. Bernice deftly amputated the other braid, paused for an instant, and then flitted swiftly and silently back to her own room.

Down-stairs she opened the big front door, closed it carefully behind her, and feeling oddly happy and exuberant stepped off the porch into the moonlight, swinging her heavy grip like a shopping-bag. After a minute's brisk walk she discovered that her left hand still held the two blond braids. She laughed unexpectedly—had to shut her mouth hard to keep from emitting an absolute peal. She was passing Warren's house now, and on the impulse she set down her baggage, and swinging the braids like pieces of rope flung them at the wooden porch, where they landed with a slight thud. She laughed again, no longer restraining herself.

"Huh," she giggled wildly. "Scalp the selfish thing!"

Then picking up her suitcase she set off at a half-run down the moonlit street.

The Handsomest Drowned Man in the World
A Tale for Children
(1968)

GABRIEL GARCÍA MÁRQUEZ

The first children who saw the dark and slinky bulge approaching through the sea let themselves think it was an enemy ship. Then they saw it had no flags or masts and they thought it was a whale. But when it was washed up on the beach, they removed the clumps of seaweed, the jellyfish tentacles, and the remains of fish and flotsam, and only then did they see that it was a drowned man.

They had been playing with him all afternoon, burying him in the sand and digging him up again, when someone chanced to see them and spread the alarm in the village. The men who carried him to the nearest house noticed that he weighed more than any dead man they had ever known, almost as much as a horse, and they said to each other that maybe he'd been floating too long and the water had got into his bones. When they laid him on the floor they said he'd been taller than all other men because there was barely enough room for him in the house, but they thought that maybe the ability to keep on growing after death was part of the nature of certain drowned men. He had the smell of the sea about him and only his shape gave one to suppose that it was the corpse of a human being, because the skin was covered with a crust of mud and scales.

They did not even have to clean off his face to know that the dead man was a stranger. The village was made up of only twenty-odd wooden houses that had stone courtyards with no flowers and which were spread about on the end of a desertlike cape. There was so little land that mothers always went about with the fear that the wind would carry off their children and the few dead that the years had caused among them had to be thrown off the cliffs. But the sea was calm and bountiful and all the men fit into seven boats. So when they found the drowned man they simply had to look at one another to see that they were all there.

That night they did not go out to work at sea. While the men went to find out if anyone was missing in neighboring villages, the women stayed behind to care for the drowned man. They took the mud off with grass swabs, they removed the underwater stones entangled in his hair, and they scraped the crust off with tools used for scaling fish. As they were doing that they noticed that the vegetation on him came from faraway oceans and deep water and that his clothes were in tatters, as if he had sailed through labyrinths of coral. They noticed too that he bore his death with pride, for he did not have the lonely look of other drowned men who came out of the sea or that haggard, needy look of men who drowned in rivers. But only when they finished cleaning him off did they become aware of the kind of man he was and it left them breathless. Not only was he the tallest, strongest, most virile, and best built man they had ever seen, but even though they were looking at him there was no room for him in their imagination.

They could not find a bed in the village large enough to lay him on nor was there a table solid enough to use for his wake. The tallest men's holiday pants would not fit him, not the fattest ones' Sunday shirts, nor the shoes of the one with the biggest feet. Fascinated by his huge size and his beauty, the women then decided to make him some pants from a large piece of sail and a shirt from some bridal brabant linen so that he could continue through his death with dignity. As they sewed, sitting in a circle and gazing at the corpse between stitches, it seemed to them that the wind had never been so steady nor the sea so restless as on that night and they supposed that the change had something to do with the dead man. They thought that if that magnificent man had lived in the village, his house would have had the widest doors, the highest ceiling, and the strongest floor, his bedstead would have been made from a midship frame held together by iron bolts, and his wife would have been the happiest woman. They thought that he would have had so much authority that he could have drawn fish out of the sea simply by calling their names and that he would have put so much work into his land that springs would have burst forth from among the rocks so that he would have been able to plant flowers on the cliffs. They secretly compared him to their own men, thinking that for all their lives theirs were incapable of doing what he could do in one night, and they ended up dismissing them deep in their hearts as the weakest, meanest, and most useless creatures on earth. They were wandering through that maze of fantasy when the oldest woman, who as the oldest had looked upon the drowned man with more compassion than passion, sighed:

"He has the face of someone called Esteban."

It was true. Most of them had only to take another look at him to see that he could not have any other name. The more stubborn among them, who were the youngest, still lived for a few hours with the illusion that when they put his clothes on and he lay among the flowers in patent leather shoes his name might be Lautaro. But it was a vain illusion. There had not been enough canvas, the poorly cut and worse sewn pants were too tight, and the hidden strength of his heart popped the buttons on his shirt. After midnight the whistling of the wind died down and the sea fell into its Wednesday drowsiness. The silence put an end to any last doubts: he was Esteban. The women who had dressed him, who had combed his hair, had cut his nails and shaved him were unable to hold back a shudder of pity when they had to resign themselves to his being dragged along the ground. It was then that they understood how unhappy he must have been with that huge body since it bothered him even after death. They could see him in life, condemned to going through doors sideways, cracking his head on crossbeams, remaining on his feet during visits, not knowing what to do with his soft, pink, sea lion hands while the lady of the house looked for her most resistant chair and begged him, frightened to death, sit here, Esteban, please, and he, leaning against the wall, smiling, don't bother, ma'am, I'm fine where I am, his heels raw and his back roasted from having done the same thing so many times whenever he paid a visit, don't bother, ma'am, I'm fine where I am, just to avoid the embarrassment of breaking up the chair, and never knowing perhaps that the ones who said don't go, Esteban, at least wait till the coffee's ready, were the ones who later on would whisper the big boob finally left, how nice, the handsome fool has gone. That was what the women were thinking beside the body a little before dawn. Later, when they covered his face with a handkerchief so that the light would not bother him, he looked so forever dead, so defenseless, so much like their men that the first furrows of tears opened in their hearts. It was one of the younger ones who began the weeping. The others, coming to, went from sighs to wails, and the more they sobbed the more they felt like weeping, because the drowned man was becoming all the more Esteban for them, and so they wept so much, for he was the most destitute, most peaceful, and most obliging man on earth, poor Esteban. So when the men returned with the news that the drowned man was not from the neighboring villages either, the women felt an opening of jubilation in the midst of their tears.

"Praise the Lord," they sighed, "he's ours!"

The men thought the fuss was only womanish frivolity. Fatigued because of the difficult nighttime inquiries, all they wanted was to get rid of the bother of the newcomer once and for all before the sun grew strong on that arid, windless day. They improvised a litter with the remains of foremasts and gaffs, tying it together with rigging so that it would bear the weight of the body until they reached the cliffs. They wanted to tie the anchor from a cargo ship to him so that he would sink easily into the deepest waves, where fish are blind and divers die of nostalgia, and bad currents would not bring him back to shore, as had happened with other bodies. But the more they hurried, the more the women thought of ways to waste time. They walked about like startled hens, pecking with the sea charms on their breasts, some interfering on one side to put a scapular of the good wind on the drowned man, some on the other side to put a wrist compass on him, and after a great deal of *get away from there, woman, stay out of the way, look, you almost made me fall on top of the dead man,* the men began to feel mistrust in their livers and started grumbling about why so many main-altar decorations for a stranger, because no matter how many nails and holy-water jars he had on him, the sharks would chew him all the same, but the women kept piling on their junk relics, running back and forth, stumbling, while they released in sighs what they did not in tears, so that the men finally exploded with *since when has there ever been such a fuss over a drifting corpse, a drowned nobody, a piece of cold Wednesday meat.* One of the women, mortified by so much lack of care, then removed the handkerchief from the dead man's face and the men were left breathless too.

He was Esteban. It was not necessary to repeat it for them to recognize him. If they had been told Sir Walter Raleigh, even they might have been impressed with his gringo accent, the macaw on his shoulder, his cannibal-killing blunderbuss, but there could be only one Esteban in the world and there he was, stretched out like a sperm whale, shoeless, wearing the pants of an undersized child, and with those stony nails that had to be cut with a knife. They only had to take the handkerchief off his face to see that he was ashamed, that it was not his fault that he was so big or so heavy or so handsome, and if he had known that this was going to happen, he would have looked for a more discreet place to drown in, seriously, I even would have tied the anchor off a galleon around my neck and staggered off a cliff like someone who doesn't like things in order not to be upsetting people now with this Wednesday dead body, as you people say, in order not to be bothering anyone with this filthy piece of cold meat that doesn't have anything to do with me. There was so much truth in his manner that even the most mistrustful men, the ones who felt the bitterness of endless nights at sea fearing that their women would tire of dreaming about them and begin to dream of drowned men, even they and others who were harder still shuddered in the marrow of their bones at Esteban's sincerity.

That was how they came to hold the most splendid funeral they could conceive of for an abandoned drowned man. Some women who had gone to get flowers in the neighboring villages returned with other women who could not believe what they had been told, and those women went back for more flowers when they saw the dead man, and they brought more and more until there were so many flowers and so many people that it was hard to walk about. At the final moment it pained them to return him to the waters as an orphan and they chose a father and mother from among the best people, and aunts and uncles and cousins, so that through him all the inhabitants of the village became kinsmen. Some sailors who heard the weeping from a distance went off course and people heard of one who had himself tied to the mainmast, remembering ancient fables about sirens. While they fought for the privilege of carrying him on their shoulders along the steep escarpment by the cliffs, men and women became aware for the first time of the desolation of their streets, the dryness of their courtyards, the narrowness of their dreams as they faced the splendor and beauty of their drowned man. They let him go without an anchor so that he could come back if he wished and whenever he wished, and they all held their breath for the fraction of centuries the body took to fall into the abyss. They did not need to look at one another to realize that they were no longer all present, that they would never be. But they also knew that everything would be different from then on, that their houses would have wider doors, higher ceilings, and stronger floors so that Esteban's memory could go everywhere without bumping into beams and so that no one in the future would dare whisper the big boob finally died, too bad, the handsome fool has finally died, because they were going to paint their house fronts gay colors to make Esteban's memory eternal and they were going to break their backs digging for springs among the stones and planting flowers on the cliffs so that in future years at dawn the passengers on great liners would awaken, suffocated by the smell of gardens on the high seas, and the captain would have to come down from the bridge in his dress uniform, with his astrolabe, his pole star, and his row of war medals and, pointing to the promontory of roses on the horizon, he would say in fourteen languages, look there, where the wind is so peaceful now that it's gone to sleep beneath the beds, over there, where the sun's so bright that the sunflowers don't know which way to turn, yes, over there, that's Esteban's village.

The Yellow Wallpaper
(1892)

CHARLOTTE PERKINS GILMAN

It is very seldom that mere ordinary people like John and myself secure ancestral halls for the summer.

A colonial mansion, a hereditary estate, I would say a haunted house, and reach the height of romantic felicity—but that would be asking too much of fate!

Still I will proudly declare that there is something queer about it.

Else, why should it be let so cheaply? And why have stood so long untenanted?

John laughs at me, of course, but one expects that in marriage.

John is practical in the extreme. He has no patience with faith, an intense horror of superstition, and he scoffs openly at any talk of things not to be felt and seen and put down in figures.

John is a physician, and *perhaps*—(I would not say it to a living soul, of course, but this is dead paper and a great relief to my mind)—*perhaps* that is one reason I do not get well faster.

You see he does not believe I am sick!

And what can one do?

If a physician of high standing, and one's own husband, assures friends and relatives that there is really nothing the matter with one but temporary nervous depression—a slight hysterical tendency—what is one to do?

My brother is also a physician, and also of high standing, and he says the same thing.

So I take phosphates or phosphites—whichever it is, and tonics, and journeys, and air, and exercise, and am absolutely forbidden to "work" until I am well again.

Personally, I disagree with their ideas.

Personally, I believe that congenial work, with excitement and change, would do me good. But what is one to do?

I did write for a while in spite of them; but it *does* exhaust me a good deal—having to be so sly about it, or else meet with heavy opposition.

I sometimes fancy that in my condition if I had less opposition and more society and stimulus—but John says the very worst thing I can do is to think about my condition, and I confess it always makes me feel bad.

So I will let it alone and talk about the house.

The most beautiful place! It is quite alone, standing well back from the road, quite three miles from the village. It makes me think of English places that you read about, for there are hedges and walls and gates that lock, and lots of separate little houses for the gardeners and people.

There is a *delicious* garden! I never saw such a garden—large and shady, full of box-bordered paths, and lined with long grape-covered arbors with seats under them.

There were greenhouses, too, but they are all broken now.

There was some legal trouble, I believe, something about the heirs and coheirs; anyhow, the place has been empty for years.

That spoils my ghostliness, I am afraid, but I don't care—there is something strange about the house—I can feel it.

I even said so to John one moonlight evening, but he said what I felt was a *draught*, and shut the window.

I get unreasonably angry with John sometimes. I'm sure I never used to be so sensitive. I think it is due to this nervous condition.

But John says if I feel so, I shall neglect proper self-control; so I take pains to control myself—before him, at least, and that makes me very tired.

I don't like our room a bit. I wanted one downstairs that opened on the piazza and had roses all over the window, and such pretty old-fashioned chintz hangings! but John would not hear of it.

He said there was only one window and not room for two beds, and no near room for him if he took another.

He is very careful and loving, and hardly lets me stir without special direction.

I have a schedule prescription for each hour in the day; he takes all care from me, and so I feel basely ungrateful not to value it more.

He said we came here solely on my account, that I was to have perfect rest and all the air I could get. "Your exercise depends on your strength, my dear," said he, "and your food somewhat on your appetite; but air you can absorb all the time." So we took the nursery at the top of the house.

It is a big, airy room, the whole floor nearly, with windows that look all ways, and air and sunshine galore. It was nursery first and then playroom and gymnasium, I should judge; for the windows are barred for little children, and there are rings and things in the walls.

The paint and paper look as if a boys' school had used it. It is stripped off—the paper—in great patches all around the head of my bed, about as far as I can reach, and in a great place on the other side of the room low down. I never saw a worse paper in my life.

One of those sprawling flamboyant patterns committing every artistic sin.

It is dull enough to confuse the eye in following, pronounced enough to constantly irritate and provoke study, and when you follow the lame uncertain curves for a little distance they suddenly commit suicide—plunge off at outrageous angles, destroy themselves in unheard of contradictions.

The color is repellent, almost revolting; a smouldering unclean yellow, strangely faded by the slow-turning sunlight.

It is a dull yet lurid orange in some places, a sickly sulphur tint in others.

No wonder the children hated it! I should hate it myself if I had to live in this room long.

There comes John, and I must put this away,—he hates to have me write a word.

We have been here two weeks, and I haven't felt like writing before, since that first day.

I am sitting by the window now, up in this atrocious nursery, and there is nothing to hinder my writing as much as I please, save lack of strength.

John is away all day, and even some nights when his cases are serious.

I am glad my case is not serious!

But these nervous troubles are dreadfully depressing.

John does not know how much I really suffer. He knows there is no *reason* to suffer, and that satisfies him.

Of course it is only nervousness. It does weigh on me so not to do my duty in any way!

I meant to be such a help to John, such a real rest and comfort, and here I am a comparative burden already!

Nobody would believe what an effort it is to do what little I am able,—to dress and entertain, and order things.

It is fortunate Mary is so good with the baby. Such a dear baby!

And yet I *cannot* be with him, it makes me so nervous.

I suppose John never was nervous in his life. He laughs at me so about this wall-paper!

At first he meant to repaper the room, but afterwards he said that I was letting it get the better of me, and that nothing was worse for a nervous patient than to give way to such fancies.

He said that after the wall-paper was changed it would be the heavy bedstead, and then the barred windows, and then that gate at the head of the stairs, and so on.

"You know the place is doing you good," he said, "and really, dear, I don't care to renovate the house just for a three months' rental."

"Then do let us go downstairs," I said, "there are such pretty rooms there."

Then he took me in his arms and called me a blessed little goose, and said he would go down to the cellar, if I wished, and have it whitewashed into the bargain.

But he is right enough about the beds and windows and things.

It is an airy and comfortable room as any one need wish, and, of course, I would not be so silly as to make him uncomfortable just for a whim.

I'm really getting quite fond of the big room, all but that horrid paper.

Out of one window I can see the garden, those mysterious deepshaded arbors, the riotous old-fashioned flowers, and bushes and gnarly trees.

Out of another I get a lovely view of the bay and a little private wharf belonging to the estate. There is a beautiful shaded lane that runs down there from the house. I always fancy I see people walking in these numerous paths and arbors, but John has cautioned me not to give way to fancy in the least. He says that with my imaginative power and habit of story-making, a nervous weakness like mine is sure to lead to all manner of excited fancies, and that I ought to use my will and good sense to check the tendency. So I try.

I think sometimes that if I were only well enough to write a little it would relieve the press of ideas and rest me.

But I find I get pretty tired when I try.

It is so discouraging not to have any advice and companionship about my work. When I get really well, John says we will ask Cousin Henry and Julia down for a long visit; but he says he would as soon put fireworks in my pillow-case as to let me have those stimulating people about now.

I wish I could get well faster.

But I must not think about that. This paper looks to me as if it *knew* what a vicious influence it had!

There is a recurrent spot where the pattern lolls like a broken neck and two bulbous eyes stare at you upside down.

I get positively angry with the impertinence of it and the everlastingness. Up and down and sideways they crawl, and those absurd, unblinking eyes are everywhere. There is one place where two breadths didn't match, and the eyes go all up and down the line, one a little higher than the other.

I never saw so much expression in an inanimate thing before, and we all know how much expression they have! I used to lie awake as a child and get more entertainment and terror out of blank walls and plain furniture than most children could find in a toy store.

I remember what a kindly wink the knobs of our big, old bureau used to have, and there was one chair that always seemed like a strong friend.

I used to feel that if any of the other things looked too fierce I could always hop into that chair and be safe.

The furniture in this room is no worse than inharmonious, however, for we had to bring it all from downstairs. I suppose when this was used as a playroom they had to take the nursery things out, and no wonder! I never saw such ravages as the children have made here.

The wall-paper, as I said before, is torn off in spots, and it sticketh closer than a brother—they must have had perseverance as well as hatred.

Then the floor is scratched and gouged and splintered, the plaster itself is dug out here and there, and this great heavy bed which is all we found in the room, looks as if it had been through the wars.

But I don't mind it a bit—only the paper.

There comes John's sister. Such a dear girl as she is, and so careful of me! I must not let her find me writing.

She is a perfect and enthusiastic housekeeper, and hopes for no better profession. I verily believe she thinks it is the writing which made me sick!

But I can write when she is out, and see her a long way off from these windows.

There is one that commands the road, a lovely shaded winding road, and one that just looks off over the country. A lovely country, too, full of great elms and velvet meadows.

This wall-paper has a kind of sub-pattern in a different shade, a particularly irritating one, for you can only see it in certain lights, and not clearly then.

But in the places where it isn't faded and where the sun is just so—I can see a strange, provoking, formless sort of figure, that seems to skulk about behind that silly and conspicuous front design.

There's sister on the stairs!

Well, the Fourth of July is over! The people are gone and I am tired out. John thought it might do me good to see a little company, so we just had mother and Nellie and the children down for a week.

Of course I didn't do a thing. Jennie sees to everything now.

But it tired me all the same.

John says if I don't pick up faster he shall send me to Weir Mitchell in the fall.

But I don't want to go there at all. I had a friend who was in his hands once, and she says he is just like John and my brother, only more so!

Besides, it is such an undertaking to go so far.

I don't feel as if it was worth while to turn my hand over for anything, and I'm getting dreadfully fretful and querulous.

I cry at nothing, and cry most of the time.

Of course I don't when John is here, or anybody else, but when I am alone.

And I am alone a good deal just now. John is kept in town very often by serious cases, and Jennie is good and lets me alone when I want her to.

So I walk a little in the garden or down that lovely lane, sit on the porch under the roses, and lie down up here a good deal.

I'm getting really fond of the room in spite of the wall-paper. Perhaps *because* of the wall-paper.

It dwells in my mind so!

I lie here on this great immovable bed—it is nailed down, I believe—and follow that pattern about by the hour. It is as good as gymnastics, I assure you. I start, we'll say, at the bottom, down in the corner over there where it has not been touched, and I determine for the thousandth time that I *will* follow that pointless pattern to some sort of a conclusion.

I know a little of the principle of design, and I know this thing was not arranged on any laws of radiation, or alternation, or repetition, or symmetry, or anything else that I ever heard of.

It is repeated, of course, by the breadths, but not otherwise.

Looked at in one way each breadth stands alone, the bloated curves and flourishes—a kind of "debased Romanesque" with delirium tremens—go waddling up and down in isolated columns of fatuity.

But, on the other hand, they connect diagonally, and the sprawling outlines run off in great slanting waves of optic horror, like a lot of wallowing seaweeds in full chase.

The whole thing goes horizontally, too, at least it seems so, and I exhaust myself in trying to distinguish the order of its going in that direction.

They have used a horizontal breadth for a frieze, and that adds wonderfully to the confusion.

There is one end of the room where it is almost intact, and there, when the crosslights fade and the low sun shines directly upon it, I can almost fancy radiation after all,—the interminable grotesques seem to form around a common centre and rush off in headlong plunges of equal distraction.

It makes me tired to follow it. I will take a nap I guess.

I don't know why I should write this.

I don't want to.

I don't feel able.

And I know John would think it absurd. But I *must* say what I feel and think in some way—it is such a relief!

But the effort is getting to be greater than the relief.

Half the time now I am awfully lazy, and lie down ever so much.

John says I musn't lose my strength, and has me take cod liver oil and lots of tonics and things, to say nothing of ale and wine and rare meat.

Dear John! He loves me very dearly, and hates to have me sick. I tried to have a real earnest reasonable talk with him the other day, and tell him how I wish he would let me go and make a visit to Cousin Henry and Julia.

But he said I wasn't able to go, nor able to stand it after I got there; and I did not make out a very good case for myself, for I was crying before I had finished.

It is getting to be a great effort for me to think straight. Just this nervous weakness I suppose.

And dear John gathered me up in his arms, and just carried me upstairs and laid me on the bed, and sat by me and read to me till it tired my head.

He said I was his darling and his comfort and all he had, and that I must take care of myself for his sake, and keep well.

He says no one but myself can help me out of it, that I must use my will and self-control and not let any silly fancies run away with me.

There's one comfort, the baby is well and happy, and does not have to occupy this nursery with the horrid wall-paper.

If we had not used it, that blessed child would have! What a fortunate escape! Why, I wouldn't have a child of mine, an impressionable little thing, live in such a room for worlds.

I never thought of it before, but it is lucky that John kept me here after all, I can stand it so much easier than a baby, you see.

Of course I never mention it to them any more—I am too wise,—but I keep watch of it all the same.

There are things in that paper that nobody knows but me, or ever will.

Behind that outside pattern the dim shapes get clearer every day.

It is always the same shape, only very numerous.

And it is like a woman stooping down and creeping about behind that pattern. I don't like it a bit. I wonder—I begin to think—I wish John would take me away from here!

It is so hard to talk with John about my case, because he is so wise, and because he loves me so.

But I tried it last night.

It was moonlight. The moon shines in all around just as the sun does.

I hate to see it sometimes, it creeps so slowly, and always comes in by one window or another.

John was asleep and I hated to waken him, so I kept still and watched the moonlight on that undulating wall-paper till I felt creepy.

The faint figure behind seemed to shake the pattern, just as if she wanted to get out.

I got up softly and went to feel and see if the paper *did* move, and when I came back John was awake.

"What is it, little girl?" he said. "Don't go walking about like that—you'll get cold."

I though it was a good time to talk, so I told him that I really was not gaining here, and that I wished he would take me away.

"Why darling!" said he, "our lease will be up in three weeks, and I can't see how to leave before."

"The repairs are not done at home, and I cannot possibly leave town just now. Of course if you were in any danger, I could and would, but you really are better, dear, whether you can see it or not. I am a doctor, dear, and I know. You are gaining flesh and color, your appetite is better, I feel really much easier about you."

"I don't weigh a bit more," said I, "nor as much; and my appetite may be better in the evening when you are here, but it is worse in the morning when you are away!"

"Bless her little heart!" said he with a big hug, "she shall be as sick as she pleases! But now let's improve the shining hours by going to sleep, and talk about it in the morning!"

"And you won't go away?" I asked gloomily.

"Why, how can I, dear? It is only three weeks more and then we will take a nice little trip of a few days while Jennie is getting the house ready. Really dear you are better!"

"Better in body perhaps—" I began, and stopped short, for he sat up straight and looked at me with such a stern, reproachful look that I could not say another word.

"My darling," said he, "I beg of you, for my sake and for our child's sake, as well as for your own, that you will never for one instant let that idea enter your mind! There is nothing so dangerous, so fascinating, to a temperament like yours. It is a false and foolish fancy. Can you not trust me as a physician when I tell you so?"

So of course I said no more on that score, and we went to sleep before long. He thought I was asleep first, but I wasn't, and lay there for hours trying to decide whether that front pattern and the back pattern really did move together or separately.

On a pattern like this, by daylight, there is a lack of sequence, a defiance of law, that is a constant irritant to a normal mind.

The color is hideous enough, and unreliable enough, and infuriating enough, but the pattern is torturing.

You think you have mastered it, but just as you get well underway in following, it turns a back-somersault and there you are. It slaps you in the face, knocks you down, and tramples upon you. It is like a bad dream.

The outside pattern is a florid arabesque, reminding one of a fungus. If you can imagine a toadstool in joints, an interminable string of toadstools, budding and sprouting in endless convolutions—why, that is something like it.

That is, sometimes!

There is one marked peculiarity about this paper, a thing nobody seems to notice but myself, and that is that it changes as the light changes.

When the sun shoots in through the east window—I always watch for that first long, straight ray—it changes so quickly that I never can quite believe it.

That is why I watch it always.

By moonlight—the moon shines in all night when there is a moon—I wouldn't know it was the same paper.

At night in any kind of light, in twilight, candle light, lamplight, and worst of all by moonlight, it becomes bars! The outside pattern I mean, and the woman behind it is as plain as can be.

I didn't realize for a long time what the thing was that showed behind, that dim sub-pattern, but now I am quite sure it is a woman.

By daylight she is subdued, quiet. I fancy it is the pattern that keeps her so still. It is so puzzling. It keeps me quiet by the hour.

I lie down ever so much now. John says it is good for me, and to sleep all I can.

Indeed he started the habit by making me lie down for an hour after each meal.

It is a very bad habit I am convinced, for you see I don't sleep.

And that cultivates deceit, for I don't tell them I'm awake—O no!

The fact is I am getting a little afraid of John.

He seems very queer sometimes, and even Jennie has an inexplicable look.

It strikes me occasionally, just as a scientific hypothesis,—that perhaps it is the paper!

I have watched John when he did not know I was looking, and come into the room suddenly on the most innocent excuses, and I've caught him several times *looking at the paper!* And Jennie too. I caught Jennie with her hand on it once.

She didn't know I was in the room, and when I asked her in a quiet, a very quiet voice, with the most restrained manner possible, what she was doing with the paper—she turned around as if she had been caught stealing, and looked quite angry—asked me why I should frighten her so!

Then she said that the paper stained everything it touched, that she had found yellow smooches on all my clothes and John's, and she wished we would be more careful!

Did not that sound innocent? But I know she was studying that pattern, and I am determined that nobody shall find it out but myself!

Life is very much more exciting now than it used to be. You see I have something more to expect, to look forward to, to watch. I really do eat better, and am more quiet than I was.

John is so pleased to see me improve! He laughed a little the other day, and said I seemed to be flourishing in spite of my wall-paper.

I turned it off with a laugh. I had no intention of telling him it was *because* of the wall-paper—he would make fun of me. He might even want to take me away.

I don't want to leave now until I have found it out. There is a week more, and I think that will be enough.

I'm feeling ever so much better! I don't sleep much at night, for it is so interesting to watch developments; but I sleep a good deal in the daytime.

In the daytime it is tiresome and perplexing.

There are always new shoots on the fungus, and new shades of yellow all over it. I cannot keep count of them, though I have tried conscientiously.

It is the strangest yellow, that wall-paper! It makes me think of all the yellow things I ever saw—not beautiful ones like buttercups, but old foul, bad yellow things.

But there is something else about that paper—the smell! I noticed it the moment we came into the room, but with so much air and sun it was not bad. Now we have had a week of fog and rain, and whether the windows are open or not, the smell is here.

It creeps all over the house.

I find it hovering in the dining-room, skulking in the parlor, hiding in the hall, lying in wait for me on the stairs.

It gets into my hair.

Even when I go to ride, if I turn my head suddenly and surprise it—there is that smell!

Such a peculiar odor, too! I have spent hours in trying to analyze it, to find what it smelled like.

It is not bad—at first, and very gentle, but quite the subtlest, most enduring odor I ever met.

In this damp weather it is awful, I wake up in the night and find it hanging over me.

It used to disturb me at first. I thought seriously of burning the house—to reach the smell.

But now I am used to it. The only thing I can think of that it is like is the *color* of the paper! A yellow smell.

There is a very funny mark on this wall, low down, near the mopboard. A streak that runs round the room. It goes behind every piece of furniture, except the bed, a long, straight, even *smooch*, as if it had been rubbed over and over.

I wonder how it was done and who did it, and what they did it for. Round and round and round—round and round and round—it makes me dizzy!

I really have discovered something at last.

Through watching so much at night, when it changes so, I have finally found out.

The front pattern *does* move—and no wonder! The woman behind shakes it!

Sometimes I think there are a great many women behind, and sometimes only one, and she crawls around fast, and her crawling shakes it all over.

Then in the very bright spots she keeps still, and in the very shady spots she just takes hold of the bars and shakes them hard.

And she is all the time trying to climb through. But nobody could climb through that pattern—it strangles so; I think that is why it has so many heads.

They get through, and then the pattern strangles them off and turns them upside down, and makes their eyes white!

If those heads were covered or taken off it would not be half so bad.

I think that woman gets out in the daytime!

And I'll tell you why—privately—I've seen her!

I can see her out of every one of my windows!

It is the same woman, I know, for she is always creeping, and most women do not creep by daylight.

I see her on that long road under the trees, creeping along, and when a carriage comes she hides under the blackberry vines.

I don't blame her a bit. It must be very humiliating to be caught creeping by daylight!

I always lock the door when I creep by daylight. I can't do it at night, for I know John would suspect something at once.

And John is so queer now, that I don't want to irritate him. I wish he would take another room! Besides, I don't want anybody to get that woman out at night but myself.

I often wonder if I could see her out of all the windows at once.

But, turn as fast as I can, I can only see out of one at one time.

And though I always see her, she *may* be able to creep faster than I can turn!

I have watched her sometimes away off in the open country, creeping as fast as a cloud shadow in a high wind.

If only that top pattern could be gotten off from the under one! I mean to try it, little by little.

I have found out another funny thing, but I shan't tell it this time! It does not do to trust people too much.

There are only two more days to get this paper off, and I believe John is beginning to notice. I don't like the look in his eyes.

And I heard him ask Jennie a lot of professional questions about me. She had a very good report to give.

She said I slept a good deal in the daytime.

John knows I don't sleep very well at night, for all I'm so quiet!

He asked me all sorts of questions, too, and pretended to be very loving and kind.

As if I couldn't see through him!

Still, I don't wonder he acts so, sleeping under this paper for three months.

It only interests me, but I feel sure John and Jennie are secretly affected by it.

Hurrah! This is the last day, but it is enough. John is to stay in town over night, and won't be out until this evening.

Jennie wanted to sleep with me—the sly thing! but I told her I should undoubtedly rest better for a night all alone.

That was clever, for really I wasn't alone a bit! As soon as it was moonlight and that poor thing began to crawl and shake the pattern, I got up and ran to help her.

I pulled and she shook, I shook and she pulled, and before morning we had peeled off yards of that paper.

A strip about as high as my head and half around the room.

And then when the sun came and that awful pattern began to laugh at me, I declared I would finish it to-day!

We go away to-morrow, and they are moving all my furniture down again to leave things as they were before.

Jennie looked at the wall in amazement, but I told her merrily that I did it out of pure spite at the vicious thing.

She laughed and said she wouldn't mind doing it herself, but I must not get tired.

How she betrayed herself that time!

But I am here, and no person touches this paper but me—not *alive!*

She tried to get me out of the room—it was too patent! But I said it was so quiet and empty and clean now that I believed I would lie down again and sleep all I could; and not to wake me even for dinner—I would call when I woke.

So now she is gone, and the servants are gone, and the things are gone, and there is nothing left but that great bedstead nailed down, with the canvas mattress we found on it.

We shall sleep downstairs to-night, and take the boat home to-morrow.

I quite enjoy the room, now it is bare again.

How those children did tear about here!

This bedstead is fairly gnawed!

But I must get to work.

I have locked the door and thrown the key down into the front path.

I don't want to go out, and I don't want to have anybody come in, till John comes.

I want to astonish him.

I've got a rope up here that even Jennie did not find. If that woman does get out, and tries to get away, I can tie her!

But I forgot I could not reach far without anything to stand on!

This bed will *not* move!

I tried to lift and push it until I was lame, and then I got so angry I bit off a little piece at one corner—but it hurt my teeth.

Then I peeled off all the paper I could reach standing on the floor. It sticks horribly and the pattern just enjoys it! All those strangled heads and bulbous eyes and waddling fungus growths just shriek with derision!

I am getting angry enough to do something desperate. To jump out of the window would be admirable exercise, but the bars are too strong even to try.

Besides I wouldn't do it. Of course not. I know well enough that a step like that is improper and might be misconstrued.

I don't like to *look* out of the windows even—there are so many of those creeping women, and they creep so fast.

I wonder if they all come out of that wall-paper as I did?

But I am securely fastened now by my well-hidden rope—you don't get *me* out in the road there!

I suppose I shall have to get back behind the pattern when it comes night, and that is hard!

It is so pleasant to be out in this great room and creep around as I please!

I don't want to go outside. I won't, even if Jennie asks me to.

For outside you have to creep on the ground, and everything is green instead of yellow.

But here I can creep smoothly on the floor, and my shoulder just fits in that long smooch around the wall, so I cannot lose my way.

Why there's John at the door!

It is no use, young man, you can't open it!

How he does call and pound!

Now he's crying for an axe.

It would be a shame to break down that beautiful door!

"John dear!" said I in the gentlest voice, "the key is down by the front steps, under a plantain leaf!"

That silenced him for a few moments.

Then he said—very quietly indeed, "Open the door, my darling!"

"I can't," said I. "The key is down by the front door under a plantain leaf!"

And then I said it again, several times, very gently and slowly, and said it so often that he had to go and see, and he got it of course, and came in. He stopped short by the door.

"What is the matter?" he cried. "For God's sake, what are you doing!"

I kept on creeping just the same, but I looked at him over my shoulder.

"I've got out at last," said I, "in spite of you and Jane. And I've pulled off most of the paper, so you can't put me back!"

Now why should that man have fainted? But he did, and right across my path by the wall, so that I had to creep over him every time!

A Jury of Her Peers
(1917)

SUSAN GLASPELL

When Martha Hale opened the storm-door and got a cut of the north wind, she ran back for her big woolen scarf. As she hurriedly wound that round her head her eye made a scandalized sweep of her kitchen. It was no ordinary thing that called her away—it was probably farther from ordinary than anything that had ever happened in Dickson County. But what her eye took in was that her kitchen was in no shape for leaving: her bread all ready for mixing, half the flour sifted and half unsifted.

She hated to see things half done; but she had been at that when the team from town stopped to get Mr. Hale, and then the sheriff came running in to say his wife wished Mrs. Hale would come too—adding, with a grin, that he guessed she was getting scarey and wanted another woman along. So she had dropped everything right where it was.

"Martha!" now came her husband's impatient voice. "Don't keep folks waiting out here in the cold."

She again opened the storm-door, and this time joined the three men and the one woman waiting for her in the big two-seated buggy.

After she had the robes tucked around her she took another look at the woman who sat beside her on the back seat. She had met Mrs. Peters the year before at the county fair, and the thing she remembered about her was that she didn't seem like a sheriff's wife. She was small and thin and didn't have a strong voice. Mrs. Gorman, sheriff's wife before Gorman went out and Peters came in, had a voice that somehow seemed to be backing up the law with every word. But if Mrs. Peters didn't look like a sheriff's wife, Peters made it up in looking like a sheriff. He was to a dot the kind of man who could get himself elected sheriff—a heavy man with a big voice, who was particularly genial with the law-abiding, as if to make it plain that he knew the difference between criminals and non-criminals. And right there it came into Mrs. Hale's mind, with a stab, that this man who was so pleasant and lively with all of them was going to the Wrights' now as a sheriff.

"The country's not very pleasant this time of year," Mrs. Peters at last ventured, as if she felt they ought to be talking as well as the men.

Mrs. Hale scarcely finished her reply, for they had gone up a little hill and could see the Wright place now, and seeing it did not make her feel like talking. It looked very lonesome this cold March morning. It had always been a lonesome-looking place. It was down in a hollow, and the poplar trees around it were lonesome-looking trees. The men were looking at it and talking about what had happened. The county attorney was bending to one side of the buggy, and kept looking steadily at the place as they drew up to it.

"I'm glad you came with me," Mrs. Peters said nervously, as the two women were about to follow the men in through the kitchen door.

Even after she had her foot on the door-step, her hand on the knob, Martha Hale had a moment of feeling she could not cross that threshold. And the reason it seemed she couldn't cross it now was simply because she hadn't crossed it before. Time and time again it had been in her mind, "I ought to go over and see Minnie Foster"—she still thought of her as Minnie Foster, though for twenty years she had been Mrs. Wright. And then there was always something to do and Minnie Foster would go from her mind. But *now* she could come.

The men went over to the stove. The women stood close together by the door. Young Henderson, the county attorney, turned around and said, "Come up to the fire, ladies."

Mrs. Peters took a step forward, then stopped. "I'm not—cold," she said.

And so the two women stood by the door, at first not even so much as looking around the kitchen.

The men talked for a minute about what a good thing it was the sheriff had sent his deputy out that morning to make a fire for them, and then Sheriff Peters stepped back from the stove, unbuttoned his outer coat, and leaned his hands on the kitchen table in a way that seemed to mark the beginning of official business. "Now, Mr. Hale," he said in a sort of semi-official voice, "before we move things about, you tell Mr. Henderson just what it was you saw when you came here yesterday morning."

The county attorney was looking around the kitchen.

"By the way," he said, "has anything been moved?" He turned to the sheriff. "Are things just as you left them yesterday?"

Peters looked from cupboard to sink; from that to a small worn rocker a little to one side of the kitchen table.

"It's just the same."

"Somebody should have been left here yesterday," said the county attorney.

"Oh—yesterday," returned the sheriff, with a little gesture as of yesterday having been more than he could bear to think of. "When I had to send Frank to Morris Center for that man who went crazy—let me tell you, I had my hands full *yesterday*. I knew you could get back from Omaha by to-day, George, and as long as I went over everything here myself—"

"Well, Mr. Hale," said the county attorney, in a way of letting what was past and gone go, "tell just what happened when you came here yesterday morning."

Mrs. Hale, still leaning against the door, had that sinking feeling of the mother whose child is about to speak a piece. Lewis often wandered along and got things mixed up in a story. She hoped he would tell this straight and plain, and not say unnecessary things that would just make things harder for Minnie Foster. He didn't begin at once, and she noticed that he looked queer—as if standing in that kitchen and having to tell what he had seen there yesterday morning made him almost sick.

"Yes, Mr. Hale?" the county attorney reminded.

"Harry and I had started to town with a load of potatoes," Mrs. Hale's husband began.

Harry was Mrs. Hale's oldest boy. He wasn't with them now, for the very good reason that those potatoes never got to town yesterday and he was taking them this morning, so he hadn't been home when the sheriff stopped to say he wanted Mr. Hale to come over to the Wright place and tell the county attorney his story there, where he could point it all out. With all Mrs. Hale's other emotions came the fear now that maybe Harry wasn't dressed warm enough—they hadn't any of them realized how that north wind did bite.

"We come along this road," Hale was going on, with a motion of his hand to the road over which they had just come, "and as we got in sight of the house I says to Harry, 'I'm goin'to see if I can't get John Wright to take a telephone.' You see," he explained to Henderson, "unless I can get somebody to go in with me they won't come out this branch road except for a price *I* can't pay. I'd spoke to Wright about it once before; but he put me off, saying folks talked too much anyway, and all he asked was peace and quiet—guess you know about how much he talked himself. But I thought maybe if I went to the house and talked about it before his wife, and said all the women-folks liked the telephones, and that in this lonesome stretch of road it would be a good thing—well, I said to Harry that that was what I was going to say—though I said at the same time that I didn't know as what his wife wanted made much difference to John—"

Now, there he was!—saying things he didn't need to say. Mrs. Hale tried to catch her husband's eye, but fortunately the county attorney interrupted with:

"Let's talk about that a little later, Mr. Hale. I do want to talk about that, but I'm anxious now to get along to just what happened when you got here."

When he began this time, it was very deliberately and carefully:

"I didn't see or hear anything. I knocked at the door. And still it was all quiet inside. I knew they must be up—it was past eight o'clock. So I knocked again, louder, and I thought I heard somebody say, 'Come in.' I wasn't sure—I'm not sure yet. But I opened the door—this door," jerking a hand toward the door by which the two women stood, "and there, in that rocker"—pointing to it—"sat Mrs. Wright."

Every one in the kitchen looked at the rocker. It came into Mrs. Hale's mind that that rocker didn't look in the least like Minnie Foster—the Minnie Foster of twenty years before. It was a dingy red, with wooden rungs up the back, and the middle rung was gone, and the chair sagged to one side.

"How did she—look?" the county attorney was inquiring.

"Well," said Hale, "she looked—queer."

"How do you mean—queer?"

As he asked it he took out a note-book and pencil. Mrs. Hale did not like the sight of that pencil. She kept her eye fixed on her husband, as if to keep him from saying unnecessary things that would go into that note-book and make trouble.

Hale did speak guardedly, as if the pencil had affected him too.

"Well, as if she didn't know what she was going to do next. And kind of—done up."

"How did she seem to feel about your coming?"

"Why, I don't think she minded—one way or other. She didn't pay much attention. I said, 'Ho' do, Mrs. Wright? It's cold, ain't it?' And she said, 'Is it?'—and went on pleatin' at her apron.

"Well, I was surprised. She didn't ask me to come up to the stove, or to sit down, but just set there, not even lookin' at me. And so I said: 'I want to see John.'

"And then she—laughed. I guess you would call it a laugh.

"I thought of Harry and the team outside, so I said, a little sharp, 'Can I see John?' 'No,' says she—kind of dull like. 'Ain't he home?' says I. Then she looked at me. 'Yes,' says she, 'he's home.' 'Then why can't I see him?' I asked her, out of patience with her now. ''Cause he's dead,' says she, just as quiet and dull—and fell to pleatin' her apron. 'Dead?' says I, like you do when you can't take in what you've heard.

"She just nodded her head, not getting a bit excited, but rockin' back and forth.

" 'Why—where is he?' says I, not knowing *what* to say.

"She just pointed upstairs—like this"—pointing to the room above.

"I got up, with the idea of going up there myself. By this time I—didn't know what to do. I walked from there to here; then I says: 'Why, what did he die of?'

" 'He died of a rope round his neck,' says she; and just went on pleatin' at her apron."

Hale stopped speaking, and stood staring at the rocker, as if he were still seeing the woman who had sat there the morning before. Nobody spoke; it was as if every one were seeing the woman who had sat there the morning before.

"And what did you do then?" the county attorney at last broke the silence.

"I went out and called Harry. I thought I might—need help. I got Harry in, and we went upstairs." His voice fell almost to a whisper. "There he was—lying over the—"

"I think I'd rather have you go into that upstairs," the county attorney interrupted, "where you can point it all out. Just go on now with the rest of the story."

"Well, my first thought was to get that rope off. It looked—"

He stopped, his face twitching.

"But Harry, he went up to him, and he said, 'No, he's dead all right, and we'd better not touch anything.' So we went downstairs.

"She was still sitting that same way. 'Has anybody been notified?' I asked. 'No,' says she, unconcerned.

" 'Who did this, Mrs. Wright?' said Harry. He said it businesslike, and she stopped pleatin' at her apron. 'I don't know,' she says. 'You don't *know?*' says Harry. 'Weren't you sleepin' in the bed with him?' 'Yes,' says she, 'but I was on the inside.' 'Somebody slipped a rope round his neck and strangled him, and you didn't wake up?' says Harry. 'I didn't wake up,' she said after him.

"We may have looked as if we didn't see how that could be, for after a minute she said, 'I sleep sound.'

"Harry was going to ask her more questions, but I said maybe that weren't our business; maybe we ought to let her tell her story first to the coroner or the sheriff. So Harry went fast as he could over to High Road—the Rivers' place, where there's a telephone."

"And what did she do when she knew you had gone for the coroner?" The attorney got his pencil in his hand all ready for writing.

"She moved from that chair to this one over here"—Hale pointed to a small chair in the corner—"and just sat there with her hands held together and looking down. I got a feeling that I ought to make some conversation, so I said I had come in to see if John wanted to put in a telephone; and at that she started to laugh, and then she stopped and looked at me—scared."

At sound of a moving pencil the man who was telling the story looked up.

"I dunno—maybe it wasn't scared," he hastened; "I wouldn't like to say it was. Soon Harry got back, and then Dr. Lloyd came, and you, Mr. Peters, and so I guess that's all I know that you don't."

He said that last with relief, and moved a little, as if relaxing. Every one moved a little. The county attorney walked toward the stair door.

"I guess we'll go upstairs first—then out to the barn and around there."

He paused and looked around the kitchen.

"You're convinced there was nothing important here?" he asked the sheriff. "Nothing that would—point to any motive?"

The sheriff too looked all around, as if to re-convince himself.

"Nothing here but kitchen things," he said, with a little laugh for the insignificance of kitchen things.

The county attorney was looking at the cupboard—a peculiar, ungainly structure, half closet and half cupboard, the upper part of it being built in the wall, and the lower part just the old-fashioned kitchen cupboard. As if its queerness attracted him, he got a chair and opened the upper part and looked in. After a moment he drew his hand away sticky.

"Here's a nice mess," he said resentfully.

The two women had drawn nearer, and now the sheriff's wife spoke.

"Oh—her fruit," she said, looking to Mrs. Hale for sympathetic understanding. She turned back to the county attorney and explained: "She worried about that when it turned so cold last night. She said the fire would go out and her jars might burst."

Mrs. Peters' husband broke into a laugh.

"Well, can you beat the women! Held for murder and worrying about her preserves!"

The young attorney set his lips.

"I guess before we're through with her she may have something more serious than preserves to worry about."

"Oh, well," said Mrs. Hale's husband, with good-natured superiority, "women are used to worrying over trifles."

The two women moved a little closer together. Neither of them spoke. The county attorney seemed suddenly to remember his manners—and think of his future.

"And yet," said he, with the gallantry of a young politician, "for all their worries, what would we do without the ladies?"

The women did not speak, did not unbend. He went to the sink and began washing his hands. He turned to wipe them on the roller towel—whirled it for a cleaner place.

"Dirty towels! Not much of a housekeeper, would you say, ladies?"

He kicked his foot against some dirty pans under the sink.

"There's a great deal of work to be done on a farm," said Mrs. Hale stiffly.

"To be sure. And yet"—with a little bow to her—"I know there are some Dickson County farm-houses that do not have such roller towels." He gave it a pull to expose its full length again.

"Those towels get dirty awful quick. Men's hands aren't always as clean as they might be."

"Ah, loyal to your sex, I see," he laughed. He stopped and gave her a keen look. "But you and Mrs. Wright were neighbors. I suppose you were friends, too."

Martha Hale shook her head.

"I've seen little enough of her of late years. I've not been in this house—it's more than a year."

"And why was that? You didn't like her?"

"I liked her well enough," she replied with spirit. "Farmers' wives have their hands full, Mr. Henderson. And then—" She looked around the kitchen.

"Yes?" he encouraged.

"It never seemed a very cheerful place," said she, more to herself than to him.

"No," he agreed; "I don't think any one would call it cheerful. I shouldn't say she had the home-making instinct."

"Well, I don't know as Wright had, either," she muttered.

"You mean they didn't get on very well?" he was quick to ask.

"No; I don't mean anything," she answered, with decision. As she turned a little away from him, she added: "But I don't think a place would be any the cheerfuler for John Wright's bein' in it."

"I'd like to talk to you about that a little later, Mrs. Hale," he said. "I'm anxious to get the lay of things upstairs now."

He moved toward the stair door, followed by the two men.

"I suppose anything Mrs. Peters does'll be all right?" the sheriff inquired. "She was to take in some clothes for her, you know—and a few little things. We left in such a hurry yesterday."

The county attorney looked at the two women whom they were leaving alone there among the kitchen things.

"Yes—Mrs. Peters," he said, his glance resting on the woman who was not Mrs. Peters, the big farmer woman who stood behind the sheriff's wife. "Of course Mrs. Peters is one of us," he said, in a manner of entrusting responsibility. "And keep your eye out, Mrs. Peters, for anything that might be of use. No telling; you women might come upon a clue to the motive—and that's the thing we need."

Mr. Hale rubbed his face after the fashion of a show man getting ready for a pleasantry.

"But would the women know a clue if they did come upon it?" he said; and, having delivered himself of this, he followed the others through the stair door.

The women stood motionless and silent, listening to the footsteps, first upon the stairs, then in the room above them.

Then, as if releasing herself from something strange, Mrs. Hale began to arrange the dirty pans under the sink, which the county attorney's disdainful push of the foot had deranged.

"I'd hate to have men comin' into my kitchen," she said testily—"snoopin' round and criticizin'."

"Of course it's no more than their duty," said the sheriff's wife, in her manner of timid acquiescence.

"Duty's all right," replied Mrs. Hale bluffly; "but I guess that deputy sheriff that come out to make the fire might have got a little of this on." She gave the roller towel a pull. "Wish I'd thought of that sooner! Seems mean to talk about her for not having things slicked up, when she had to come away in such a hurry."

She looked around the kitchen. Certainly it was not "slicked up." Her eye was held by a bucket of sugar on a low shelf. The cover was off the wooden bucket, and beside it was a paper bag—half full.

Mrs. Hale moved toward it.

"She was putting this in there," she said to herself—slowly.

She thought of the flour in her kitchen at home—half sifted, half not sifted. She had been interrupted, and had left things half done. What had interrupted Minnie Foster? Why had that work been left half done? She made a move as if to finish it,—unfinished things always bothered her,—and then she glanced around and saw that Mrs. Peters was watching her—and she didn't want Mrs. Peters to get that feeling she had got of work begun and then—for some reason—not finished.

"It's a shame about her fruit," she said, and walked toward the cupboard that the county attorney had opened, and got on the chair, murmuring: "I wonder if it's all gone."

It was a sorry enough looking sight, but "Here's one that's all right," she said at last. She held it toward the light. "This is cherries, too." She looked again. "I declare I believe that's the only one."

With a sigh, she got down from the chair, went to the sink, and wiped off the bottle.

"She'll feel awful bad, after all her hard work in the hot weather. I remember the afternoon I put up my cherries last summer."

She set the bottle on the table, and, with another sigh, started to sit down in the rocker. But she did not sit down. Something kept her from sitting down in that chair. She straightened—stepped back, and, half turned away, stood looking at it, seeing the woman who had sat there "pleatin' at her apron."

The thin voice of the sheriff's wife broke in upon her: "I must be getting those things from the front room closet." She opened the door into the other room, started in, stepped back. "You coming with me, Mrs. Hale?" she asked nervously. "You—you could help me get them."

They were soon back—the stark coldness of that shut-up room was not a thing to linger in.

"My!" said Mrs. Peters, dropping the things on the table and hurrying to the stove.

Mrs. Hale stood examining the clothes the woman who was being detained in town had said she wanted.

"Wright was close!" she exclaimed, holding up a shabby black skirt that bore the marks of much making over. "I think maybe that's why she kept so much to herself. I s'pose she felt she couldn't do her part; and then, you don't enjoy things when you feel shabby. She used to wear pretty clothes and be lively—when she was Minnie Foster, one of the town girls, singing in the choir. But that—oh, that was twenty years ago."

With a carefulness in which there was something tender, she folded the shabby clothes and piled them at one corner of the table. She looked up at Mrs. Peters and there was something in the other woman's look that irritated her.

"She don't care," she said to herself. "Much difference it makes to her whether Minnie Foster had pretty clothes when she was a girl."

Then she looked again, and she wasn't so sure; in fact, she hadn't at any time been perfectly sure about Mrs. Peters. She had that shrinking manner, and yet her eyes looked as if they could see a long way into things.

"This all you was to take in?" asked Mrs. Hale.

"No," said the sheriff's wife; "she said she wanted an apron. Funny thing to want," she ventured in her nervous little way, "for there's not much to get you dirty in jail, goodness knows. But I suppose just to make her feel more natural. If you're used to wearing an apron—. She said they were in the bottom drawer of this cupboard. Yes—here they are. And then her little shawl that always hung on the stair door."

She took the small gray shawl from behind the door leading upstairs, and stood a minute looking at it.

Suddenly Mrs. Hale took a quick step toward the other woman.

"Mrs. Peters!"

"Yes, Mrs. Hale?"

"Do you think she—did it?"

A frightened look blurred the other thing in Mrs. Peters' eyes.

"Oh, I don't know," she said, in a voice that seemed to shrink away from the subject.

"Well, I don't think she did," affirmed Mrs. Hale stoutly. "Asking for an apron, and her little shawl. Worryin' about her fruit."

"Mr. Peters says—." Footsteps were heard in the room above; she stopped, looked up, then went on in a lowered voice: "Mr. Peters says—it looks bad for her. Mr. Henderson is awful sarcastic in a speech, and he's going to make fun of her saying she didn't—wake up."

For a moment Mrs. Hale had no answer. Then, "Well, I guess John Wright didn't wake up—when they was slippin' that rope under his neck," she muttered.

"No, it's *strange*," breathed Mrs. Peters. "They think it was such a—funny way to kill a man." She began to laugh; at sound of the laugh, abruptly stopped.

"That's just what Mr. Hale said," said Mrs. Hale, in a resolutely natural voice. "There was a gun in the house. He says that's what he can't understand."

"Mr. Henderson said, coming out, that what was needed for the case was a motive. Something to show anger—or sudden feeling."

"Well, I don't see any signs of anger around here," said Mrs. Hale. "I don't—"

She stopped. It was as if her mind tripped on something. Her eye was caught by a dish-towel in the middle of the kitchen table. Slowly she moved toward the table. One half of it was wiped clean, the other half messy. Her eyes made a slow, almost unwilling turn to the bucket of sugar and the half empty bag beside it. Things begun—and not finished.

After a moment she stepped back, and said, in that manner of releasing herself:

"Wonder how they're finding things upstairs? I hope she had it a little more red up up there. You know,"—she paused, and feeling gathered,—"it seems kind of *sneaking*: locking her up in town and coming out here to get her own house to turn against her!"

"But, Mrs. Hale," said the sheriff's wife, "the law is the law."

"I s'pose 'tis," answered Mrs. Hale shortly.

She turned to the stove, saying something about that fire not being much to brag of. She worked with it a minute, and when she straightened up she said aggressively:

"The law is the law—and a bad stove is a bad stove. How'd you like to cook on this?"—pointing with the poker to the broken lining. She opened the oven door and started to express her opinion of the oven; but she was swept into her own thoughts, thinking of what it would mean, year after year, to have that stove to wrestle with. The thought of Minnie Foster trying to bake in that oven—and the thought of her never going over to see Minnie Foster—.

She was startled by hearing Mrs. Peters say: "A person gets discouraged—and loses heart."

The sheriff's wife had looked from the stove to the sink—to the pail of water which had been carried in from outside. The two women stood there silent, above them the footsteps of the men who were looking for evidence against the woman who had worked in that kitchen. That look of seeing into things, of seeing through a thing to something else, was in the eyes of the sheriff's wife now. When Mrs. Hale next spoke to her, it was gently:

"Better loosen up your things, Mrs. Peters. We'll not feel them when we go out."

Mrs. Peters went to the back of the room to hang up the fur tippet she was wearing. A moment later she exclaimed, "Why, she was piecing a quilt," and held up a large sewing basket piled high with quilt pieces.

Mrs. Hale spread some of the blocks out on the table.

"It's log-cabin pattern," she said, putting several of them together. "Pretty, isn't it?"

They were so engaged with the quilt that they did not hear the footsteps on the stairs. Just as the stair door opened Mrs. Hale was saying:

"Do you suppose she was going to quilt it or just knot it?"

The sheriff threw up his hands.

"They wonder whether she was going to quilt it or just knot it!"

There was a laugh for the ways of women, a warming of hands over the stove, and then the county attorney said briskly:

"Well, let's go right out to the barn and get that cleared up."

"I don't see as there's anything so strange," Mrs. Hale said resentfully, after the outside door had closed on the three men—"our taking up our time with little things while we're waiting for them to get the evidence. I don't see as it's anything to laugh about."

"Of course they've got awful important things on their minds," said the sheriff's wife apologetically.

They returned to an inspection of the block for the quilt. Mrs. Hale was looking at the fine, even sewing, and preoccupied with thoughts of the woman who had done that sewing, when she heard the sheriff's wife say, in a queer tone:

"Why, look at this one."

She turned to take the block held out to her.

"The sewing," said Mrs. Peters, in a troubled way. "All the rest of them have been so nice and even—but—this one. Why, it looks as if she didn't know what she was about!"

Their eyes met—something flashed to life, passed between them; then, as if with an effort, they seemed to pull away from each other. A moment Mrs. Hale sat there, her hands folded over that sewing which was so unlike all the rest of the sewing. Then she had pulled a knot and drawn the threads.

"Oh, what are you doing, Mrs. Hale?" asked the sheriff's wife, startled.

"Just pulling out a stitch or two that's not sewed very good," said Mrs. Hale mildly.

"I don't think we ought to touch things," Mrs. Peters said, a little helplessly.

"I'll just finish up this end," answered Mrs. Hale, still in that mild, matter-of-fact fashion.

She threaded a needle and started to replace bad sewing with good. For a little while she sewed in silence. Then, in that thin, timid voice, she heard:

"Mrs. Hale!"

"Yes, Mrs. Peters?"

"What do you suppose she was so—nervous about?"

"Oh, *I* don't know," said Mrs. Hale, as if dismissing a thing not important enough to spend much time on. "I don't know as she was—nervous. I sew awful queer sometimes when I'm just tired."

She cut a thread, and out of the corner of her eye looked up at Mrs. Peters. The small, lean face of the sheriff's wife seemed to have tightened up. Her eyes had that look of peering into something. But next moment she moved, and said in her thin, indecisive way:

"Well, I must get those clothes wrapped. They may be through sooner than we think. I wonder where I could find a piece of paper—and string."

"In that cupboard, maybe," suggested Mrs. Hale, after a glance around.

One piece of the crazy sewing remained unripped. Mrs. Peters' back turned, Martha Hale now scrutinized that piece, compared it with the dainty, accurate sewing of the other blocks. The difference was startling. Holding this block made her feel queer, as if the distracted thoughts of the woman who had perhaps turned to it to try and quiet herself were communicating themselves to her.

Mrs. Peters' voice roused her.

"Here's a bird-cage," she said. "Did she have a bird, Mrs. Hale?"

"Why, I don't know whether she did or not." She turned to look at the cage Mrs. Peters was holding up. "I've not been here in so long." She sighed. "There was a man round last year selling canaries cheap—but I don't know as she took one. Maybe she did. She used to sing real pretty herself."

Mrs. Peters looked around the kitchen.

"Seems kind of funny to think of a bird here." She half laughed—an attempt to put up a barrier. "But she must have had one—or why would she have a cage? I wonder what happened to it."

"I suppose maybe the cat got it," suggested Mrs. Hale, resuming her sewing.

"No; she didn't have a cat. She's got that feeling some people have about cats—being afraid of them. When they brought her to our house yesterday, my cat got in the room, and she was real upset and asked me to take it out."

"My sister Bessie was like that," laughed Mrs. Hale.

The sheriff's wife did not reply. The silence made Mrs. Hale turn round. Mrs. Peters was examining the bird-cage.

"Look at this door," she said slowly. "It's broke. One hinge has been pulled apart."

Mrs. Hale came nearer.

"Looks as if some one must have been—rough with it."

Again their eyes met—startled, questioning, apprehensive. For a moment neither spoke nor stirred. Then Mrs. Hale, turning away, said brusquely:

"If they're going to find any evidence, I wish they'd be about it. I don't like this place."

"But I'm awful glad you came with me, Mrs. Hale," Mrs. Peters put the bird-cage on the table and sat down. "It would be lonesome for me—sitting here alone."

"Yes, it would, wouldn't it?" agreed Mrs. Hale, a certain determined naturalness in her voice. She had picked up the sewing, but now it dropped in her lap, and she murmured in a different voice: "But I tell you what I *do* wish, Mrs. Peters. I wish I had come over sometimes when she was here. I wish—I had."

"But of course you were awful busy, Mrs. Hale. Your house—and your children."

"I could've come," retorted Mrs. Hale shortly. "I stayed away because it weren't cheerful—and that's why I ought to have come. I"—she looked around—"I've never liked this place. Maybe because it's down in a hollow and you don't see the road. I don't know what it is, but it's a lonesome place, and always was. I wish I had come over to see Minnie Foster sometimes. I can see now—" She did not put it into words.

"Well, you mustn't reproach yourself," counseled Mrs. Peters. "Somehow, we just don't see how it is with other folks till—something comes up."

"Not having children makes less work," mused Mrs. Hale, after a silence, "but it makes a quiet house—and Wright out to work all day—and no company when he did come in. Did you know John Wright, Mrs. Peters?"

"Not to know him. I've seen him in town. They say he was a good man."

"Yes—good," conceded John Wright's neighbor grimly. "He didn't drink, and kept his word as well as most, I guess, and paid his debts. But he was a hard man, Mrs. Peters. Just to pass the time of day with him—." She stopped, shivered a little. "Like a raw wind that gets to the bone." Her eye fell upon the cage on the table before her, and she added, almost bitterly: "I should think she would've wanted a bird!"

Suddenly she leaned forward, looking intently at the cage. "But what do you s'pose went wrong with it?"

"I don't know," returned Mrs. Peters; "unless it got sick and died."

But after she said it she reached over and swung the broken door. Both women watched it as if somehow held by it.

"You didn't know—her?" Mrs. Hale asked, a gentler note in her voice.

"Not till they brought her yesterday," said the sheriff's wife.

"She—come to think of it, she was kind of like a bird herself. Real sweet and pretty, but kind of timid and—fluttery. How—she—did—change."

That held her for a long time. Finally, as if struck with a happy thought and relieved to get back to every-day things, she exclaimed:

"Tell you what, Mrs. Peters, why don't you take the quilt in with you? It might take up her mind."

"Why, I think that's a real nice idea, Mrs. Hale," agreed the sheriff's wife, as if she too were glad to come into the atmosphere of a simple kindness. "There couldn't possibly be any objection to that, could there? Now, just what will I take? I wonder if her patches are in here—and her things."

They turned to the sewing basket.

"Here's some red," said Mrs. Hale, bringing out a roll of cloth. Underneath that was a box. "Here, maybe her scissors are in here—and her things." She held it up. "What a pretty box! I'll warrant that was something she had a long time ago—when she was a girl."

She held it in her hand a moment; then, with a little sigh, opened it.

Instantly her hand went to her nose.

"Why—!"

Mrs. Peters drew nearer—then turned away.

"There's something wrapped up in this piece of silk," faltered Mrs. Hale.

"This isn't her scissors," said Mrs. Peters, in a shrinking voice.

Her hand not steady, Mrs. Hale raised the piece of silk. "Oh, Mrs. Peters!" she cried. "It's—"

Mrs. Peters bent closer.

"It's the bird," she whispered.

"But, Mrs. Peters!" cried Mrs. Hale. "*Look* at it! Its *neck*—look at its neck! It's all—other side *to*."

She held the box away from her.

The sheriff's wife again bent closer.

"Somebody wrung its neck," said she, in a voice that was slow and deep.

And then again the eyes of the two women met—this time clung together in a look of dawning comprehension, of growing horror. Mrs. Peters looked from the dead bird to the broken door of the cage. Again their eyes met. And just then there was a sound at the outside door.

Mrs. Hale slipped the box under the quilt pieces in the basket, and sank into the chair before it. Mrs. Peters stood holding to the table. The county attorney and the sheriff came in from outside.

"Well, ladies," said the county attorney, as one turning from serious things to little pleasantries, "have you decided whether she was going to quilt it or knot it?"

"We think," began the sheriff's wife in a flurried voice, "that she was going to—knot it."

He was too preoccupied to notice the change that came in her voice on that last.

"Well, that's very interesting, I'm sure," he said tolerantly. He caught sight of the bird-cage. "Has the bird flown?"

"We think the cat got it," said Mrs. Hale in a voice curiously even.

He was walking up and down, as if thinking something out.

"Is there a cat?" he asked absently.

Mrs. Hale shot a look up at the sheriff's wife.

"Well, not *now*," said Mrs. Peters. "They're superstitious, you know; they leave."

She sank into her chair.

The county attorney did not heed her. "No sign at all of any one having come in from the outside," he said to Peters, in the manner of continuing an interrupted conversation. "Their own rope. Now let's go upstairs again and go over it, piece by piece. It would have to have been some one who knew just the—"

The stair door closed behind them and their voices were lost.

The two women sat motionless, not looking at each other, but as if peering into something and at the same time holding back. When they spoke now it was as if they were afraid of what they were saying, but as if they could not help saying it.

"She liked the bird," said Martha Hale, low and slowly. "She was going to bury it in that pretty box."

"When I was a girl," said Mrs. Peters, under her breath, "my kitten—there was a boy took a hatchet, and before my eyes—before I could get there—" She covered her face an instant. "If they hadn't held me back I would have"—she caught herself, looked upstairs where footsteps were heard, and finished weakly—"hurt him."

Then they sat without speaking or moving.

"I wonder how it would seem," Mrs. Hale at last began, as if feeling her way over strange ground—"never to have had any children around?" Her eyes made a slow sweep of the kitchen, as if seeing what that kitchen had meant through all the years. "No, Wright wouldn't like the bird," she said after that—"a thing that sang. She used to sing. He killed that too." Her voice tightened.

Mrs. Peters moved uneasily.

"Of course we don't know who killed the bird."

"I knew John Wright," was Mrs. Hale's answer.

"It was an awful thing was done in this house that night, Mrs. Hale," said the sheriff's wife. "Killing a man while he slept—slipping a thing round his neck that choked the life out of him."

Mrs. Hale's hand went out to the bird-cage.

"His neck. Choked the life out of him."

"We don't *know* who killed him," whispered Mrs. Peters wildly. "We don't *know*."

Mrs. Hale had not moved. "If there had been years and years of—nothing, then a bird to sing to you, it would be awful—still—after the bird was still."

It was as if something within her not herself had spoken, and it found in Mrs. Peters something she did not know as herself.

"I know what stillness is," she said, in a queer, monotonous voice. "When we homesteaded in Dakota, and my first baby died—after he was two years old—and me with no other then—"

Mrs. Hale stirred.

"How soon do you suppose they'll be through looking for the evidence?"

"I know what stillness is," repeated Mrs. Peters, in just that same way. Then she too pulled back. "The law has got to punish crime, Mrs. Hale," she said in her tight little way.

"I wish you'd seen Minnie Foster," was the answer, "when she wore a white dress with blue ribbons, and stood up there in the choir and sang."

The picture of that girl, the fact that she had lived neighbor to that girl for twenty years, and had let her die for lack of life, was suddenly more than she could bear.

"Oh, I *wish* I'd come over here once in a while!" she cried. "That was a crime! That was a crime! Who's going to punish that?"

"We mustn't take on," said Mrs. Peters, with a frightened look toward the stairs.

"I might 'a' *known* she needed help! I tell you, it's *queer*, Mrs. Peters. We live close together, and we live far apart. We all go through the same things—it's all just a different kind of the same thing! If it weren't—why do you and I *understand*? Why do we *know*—what we know this minute?"

She dashed her hand across her eyes. Then, seeing the jar of fruit on the table, she reached for it and choked out:

"If I was you I wouldn't *tell* her her fruit was gone! Tell her it *ain't*. Tell her it's all right—all of it. Here—take this in to prove it to her! She—she may never know whether it was broke or not."

She turned away.

Mrs. Peters reached out for the bottle of fruit as if she were glad to take it—as if touching a familiar thing, having something to do, could keep her from something else. She got up, looked about for something to wrap the fruit in, took a petticoat from the pile of clothes she had brought from the front room, and nervously started winding that round the bottle.

"My!" she began, in a high, false voice, "it's a good thing the men couldn't hear us! Getting all stirred up over a little thing like a—dead canary." She hurried over that. "As if that could have anything to do with—with—My, wouldn't they *laugh*?"

Footsteps were heard on the stairs.

"Maybe they would," muttered Mrs. Hale—"maybe they wouldn't."

"No, Peters," said the county attorney incisively; "it's all perfectly clear, except the reason for doing it. But you know juries when it comes to women. If there was some definite thing—something to show. Something to make a story about. A thing that would connect up with this clumsy way of doing it."

In a covert way Mrs. Hale looked at Mrs. Peters. Mrs. Peters was looking at her. Quickly they looked away from each other. The outer door opened and Mr. Hale came in.

"I've got the team round now," he said. "Pretty cold out there."

"I'm going to stay here awhile by myself," the county attorney suddenly announced. "You can send Frank out for me, can't you?" he asked the sheriff. "I want to go over everything. I'm not satisfied we can't do better."

Again, for one brief moment, the two women's eyes found one another.

The sheriff came up to the table.

"Did you want to see what Mrs. Peters was going to take in?"

The county attorney picked up the apron. He laughed.

"Oh, I guess they're not very dangerous things the ladies have picked out."

Mrs. Hale's hand was on the sewing basket in which the box was concealed. She felt that she ought to take her hand off the basket. She did not seem able to. He picked up one of the quilt blocks which she had piled on to cover the box. Her eyes felt like fire. She had a feeling that if he took up the basket she would snatch it from him.

But he did not take it up. With another little laugh, he turned away, saying:

"No; Mrs. Peters doesn't need supervising. For that matter, a sheriff's wife is married to the law. Ever think of it that way, Mrs. Peters?"

Mrs. Peters was standing beside the table. Mrs. Hale shot a look up at her; but she could not see her face. Mrs. Peters had turned away. When she spoke, her voice was muffled.

"Not—just that way," she said.

"Married to the law!" chuckled Mrs. Peters' husband. He moved toward the door into the front room, and said to the county attorney: "I just want you to come in here a minute, George. We ought to take a look at these windows."

"Oh—windows," said the county attorney scoffingly.

"We'll be right out, Mr. Hale," said the sheriff to the farmer, who was still waiting by the door.

Hale went to look after the horses. The sheriff followed the county attorney into the other room. Again—for one final moment—the two women were alone in that kitchen.

Martha Hale sprang up, her hands tight together, looking at that other woman, with whom it rested. At first she could not see her eyes, for the sheriff's wife had not turned back since she turned away at that suggestion of being married to the law. But now Mrs. Hale made her turn back. Her eyes made her turn back. Slowly, unwillingly, Mrs. Peters turned her head until her eyes met the eyes of the other woman. There was a moment when they held each other in a steady, burning look in which there was no evasion nor flinching. Then Martha Hale's eyes pointed the way to the basket in which was hidden the thing that would make certain the conviction of the other woman—that woman who was not there and yet who had been there with them all through that hour.

For a moment Mrs. Peters did not move. And then she did it. With a rush forward, she threw back the quilt pieces, got the box, tried to put it in her handbag. It was too big. Desperately she opened it, started to take the bird out. But there she broke—she could not touch the bird. She stood there helpless, foolish.

There was the sound of a knob turning in the inner door. Martha Hale snatched the box from the sheriff's wife, and got it in the pocket of her big coat just as the sheriff and the county attorney came back into the kitchen.

"Well, Henry," said the county attorney facetiously, "at least we found out that she was not going to quilt it. She was going to—what is it you call it, ladies?"

Mrs. Hale's hand was against the pocket of her coat.

"We call it—knot it, Mr. Henderson."

The Nose
(1836)

NIKOLAI GOGOL

I

On the 25th of March, 18—, a very strange occurrence took place in St Petersburg. On the Ascension Avenue there lived a barber of the name of Ivan Jakovlevitch. He had lost his family name, and on his sign-board, on which was depicted the head of a gentleman with one cheek soaped, the only inscription to be read was, "Blood-letting done here."

On this particular morning he awoke pretty early. Becoming aware of the smell of fresh-baked bread, he sat up a little in bed, and saw his wife, who had a special partiality for coffee, in the act of taking some fresh-baked bread out of the oven.

"To-day, Prasskovna Ossipovna," he said, "I do not want any coffee; I should like a fresh loaf with onions."

"The blockhead may eat bread only as far as I am concerned," said his wife to herself; "then I shall have a chance of getting some coffee." And she threw a loaf on the table.

For the sake of propriety, Ivan Jakovlevitch drew a coat over his shirt, sat down at the table, shook out some salt for himself, prepared two onions, assumed a serious expression, and began to cut the bread. After he had cut the loaf in two halves, he looked, and to his great astonishment saw something whitish sticking in it. He carefully poked round it with his knife, and felt it with his finger.

"Quite firmly fixed!" he murmured in his beard. "What can it be?"

He put in his finger, and drew out—a nose!

Ivan Jakovlevitch at first let his hands fall from sheer astonishment; then he rubbed his eyes and began to feel it. A nose, an actual nose; and, moreover, it seemed to be the nose of an acquaintance! Alarm and terror were depicted in Ivan's face; but these feelings were slight in comparison with the disgust which took possession of his wife.

"Whose nose have you cut off, you monster?" she screamed, her face red with anger. "You scoundrel! You tippler! I myself will report you to the police! Such a rascal! Many customers have told me that while you were shaving them, you held them so tight by the nose that they could hardly sit still."

But Ivan Jakovlevitch was more dead than alive; he saw at once that this nose could belong to no other than to Kovaloff, a member of the Municipal Committee whom he shaved every Sunday and Wednesday.

"Stop, Prasskovna Ossipovna! I will wrap it in a piece of cloth and place it in the corner. There it may remain for the present; later on I will take it away."

"No, not there! Shall I endure an amputated nose in my room? You understand nothing except how to strop a razor. You know nothing of the duties and obligations of a respectable man. You vagabond! You good-for-nothing! Am I to undertake all responsibility for you at the police-office? Ah, you soap-smearer! You blockhead! Take it away where you like, but don't let it stay under my eyes!"

Ivan Jakovlevitch stood there flabbergasted. He thought and thought, and knew not what he thought.

"The devil knows how that happened!" he said at last, scratching his head behind his ear. "Whether I came home drunk last night or not, I really don't know; but in all probability this is a quite extraordinary occurrence, for a loaf is something baked and a nose is something different. I don't understand the matter at all." And Ivan Jakovlevitch was silent. The thought that the police might find him in unlawful possession of a nose and arrest him, robbed him of all presence of mind. Already he began to have visions of a red collar with silver braid and of a sword—and he trembled all over.

At last he finished dressing himself, and to the accompaniment of the emphatic exhortations of his spouse, he wrapped up the nose in a cloth and issued into the street.

He intended to lose it somewhere—either at somebody's door, or in a public square, or in a narrow alley; but just then, in order to complete his bad luck, he was met by an acquaintance, who showered inquiries upon him. "Hullo, Ivan Jakovlevitch! Whom are you going to shave so early in the morning?" etc., so that he could find no suitable opportunity to do what he wanted. Later on he did let the nose drop, but a sentry bore down upon him with his halberd, and said, "Look out! You have let something drop!" and Ivan Jakovlevitch was obliged to pick it up and put it in his pocket.

A feeling of despair began to take possession of him; all the more as the streets became more thronged and the merchants began to open their shops. At last he resolved to go to the Isaac Bridge, where perhaps he might succeed in throwing it into the Neva.

But my conscience is a little uneasy that I have not yet given any detailed information about Ivan Jakovlevitch, an estimable man in many ways.

Like every honest Russian tradesman, Ivan Jakovlevitch was a terrible drunkard, and although he shaved other people's faces every day, his own was always unshaved. His coat (he never wore an overcoat) was quite mottled, i.e. it had been black, but become brownish-yellow; the collar was quite shiny, and instead of the three buttons, only the threads by which they had been fastened were to be seen.

Ivan Jakovlevitch was a great cynic, and when Kovaloff, the member of the Municipal Committee, said to him, as was his custom while being shaved, "Your hands always smell, Ivan Jakovlevitch!" the latter answered, "What do they smell of?" "I don't know, my friend, but they smell very strong." Ivan Jakovlevitch after taking a pinch of snuff would then, by way of reprisals, set to work to soap him on the cheek, the upper lip, behind the ears, on the chin, and everywhere.

This worthy man now stood on the Isaac Bridge. At first he looked round him, then he leant on the railings of the bridge, as though he wished to look down and see how many fish were swimming past, and secretly threw the nose, wrapped in a little piece of cloth, into the water. He felt as though a ton weight had been lifted off him, and laughed cheerfully. Instead, however, of going to shave any officials, he turned his steps to a building, the sign-board of which bore the legend "Teas served here," in order to have a glass of punch, when suddenly he perceived at the other end of the bridge a police inspector of imposing exterior, with long whiskers, three-cornered hat, and sword hanging at his side. He nearly fainted; but the police inspector beckoned to him with his hand and said, "Come here, my dear sir."

Ivan Jakovlevitch, knowing how a gentleman should behave, took his hat off quickly, went towards the police inspector and said, "I hope you are in the best of health."

"Never mind my health. Tell me, my friend, why you were standing on the bridge."

"By heaven, gracious sir, I was on the way to my customers, and only looked down to see if the river was flowing quickly."

"That is a lie! You won't get out of it like that. Confess the truth."

"I am willing to shave Your Grace two or even three times a week gratis," answered Ivan Jakovlevitch.

"No, my friend, don't put yourself out! Three barbers are busy with me already, and reckon it a high honour that I let them show me their skill. Now then, out with it! What were you doing there?"

Ivan Jakovlevitch grew pale. But here the strange episode vanishes in mist, and what further happened is not known.

II

Kovaloff, the member of the Municipal Committee, awoke fairly early that morning, and made a droning noise—"Brr! Brr!"—through his lips, as he always did, though he could not say why. He stretched himself, and told his valet to give him a little mirror which was on the table. He wished to look at the heat-boil which had appeared on his nose the previous evening; but to his great astonishment, he saw that instead of his nose he had a perfectly smooth vacancy in his face. Thoroughly alarmed, he ordered some water to be brought, and rubbed his eyes with a towel. Sure enough, he had no longer a nose! Then he sprang out of bed, and shook himself violently! No, no nose any more! He dressed himself and went at once to the police superintendent.

But before proceeding further, we must certainly give the reader some information about Kovaloff, so that he may know what sort of a man this member of the Municipal Committee really was. These committee-men, who obtain that title by means of certificates of learning, must not be compared with the committee-men appointed for the Caucasus district, who are of quite a different kind. The learned committee-man—but Russia is such a wonderful country that when one committeeman is spoken of all the others from Riga to Kamschatka refer it to themselves. The same is also true of all other titled officials. Kovaloff had been a Caucasian committee-man two years previously, and could not forget that he had occupied that position; but in order to enhance his own importance, he never called himself "committee-man" but "Major."

"Listen, my dear," he used to say when he met an old woman in the street who sold shirt-fronts; "go to my house in Sadovaia Street and ask 'Does Major Kovaloff live here?' Any child can tell you where it is."

Accordingly we will call him for the future Major Kovaloff. It was his custom to take a daily walk on the Neffsky Avenue. The collar of his shirt was always remarkably clean and stiff. He wore the same style of whiskers as those that are worn by governors of districts, architects, and regimental doctors; in short, all those who have full red cheeks and play a good game of whist. These whiskers grow straight across the cheek towards the nose.

Major Kovaloff wore a number of seals, on some of which were engraved armorial bearings, and others the names of the days of the week. He had come to St Petersburg with the view of obtaining some position corresponding to his rank, if possible that of vice-governor of a province; but he was prepared to be content with that of a bailiff in some department or other. He was, moreover, not disinclined to marry, but only such a lady who could bring with her a dowry of two hundred thousand roubles. Accordingly, the reader can judge for himself what his sensations were when he found in his face, instead of a fairly symmetrical nose, a broad, flat vacancy.

To increase his misfortune, not a single droshky was to be seen in the street, and so he was obliged to proceed on foot. He wrapped himself up in his cloak, and held his handkerchief to his face as though his nose bled. "But perhaps it is all only my imagination; it is impossible that a nose should drop off in such a silly way," he thought, and stepped into a confectioner's shop in order to look into the mirror.

Fortunately no customer was in the shop; only small shop-boys were cleaning it out, and putting chairs and tables straight. Others with sleepy faces were carrying fresh cakes on trays, and yesterday's newspapers stained with coffee were still lying about. "Thank God no one is here!" he said to himself. "Now I can look at myself leisurely."

He stepped gingerly up to a mirror and looked.

"What an infernal face!" he exclaimed, and spat with disgust. "If there were only something there instead of the nose, but there is absolutely nothing."

He bit his lips with vexation, left the confectioner's, and resolved, quite contrary to his habit, neither to look nor smile at anyone on the street. Suddenly he halted as if rooted to the spot before a door, where something extraordinary happened. A carriage drew up at the entrance; the carriage door was opened, and a gentleman in uniform came out and hurried up the steps. How great was Kovaloff's terror and astonishment when he saw that it was his own nose!

At this extraordinary sight, everything seemed to turn round with him. He felt as though he could hardly keep upright on his legs; but, though trembling all over as though with fever, he resolved to wait till the nose should return to the carriage. After about two minutes the nose actually came out again. It wore a gold-embroidered uniform with a stiff, high collar, trousers of chamois leather, and a sword hung at its side. The hat, adorned with a plume, showed that it held the rank of a state-councillor. It was obvious that it was paying "duty-calls." It looked round on both sides, called to the coachman "Drive on," and got into the carriage, which drove away.

Poor Kovaloff nearly lost his reason. He did not know what to think of this extraordinary procedure. And indeed how was it possible that the nose, which only yesterday he had on his face, and which could neither walk nor drive, should wear a uniform. He ran after the carriage, which fortunately had stopped a short way off before the Grand Bazar of Moscow. He hurried towards it and pressed through a crowd of beggar-women with their faces bound up, leaving only two openings for the eyes, over whom he had formerly so often made merry.

There were only a few people in front of the Bazar. Kovaloff was so agitated that he could decide on nothing, and looked for the nose everywhere. At last he saw it standing before a shop. It seemed half buried in its stiff collar, and was attentively inspecting the wares displayed.

"How can I get at it?" thought Kovaloff. "Everything—the uniform, the hat, and so on—show that it is a state-councillor. How the deuce has that happened?"

He began to cough discreetly near it, but the nose paid him not the least attention.

"Honourable sir," said Kovaloff at last, plucking up courage, "honourable sir."

"What do you want?" asked the nose, and turned round.

"It seems to me strange, most respected sir—you should know where you belong—and I find you all of a sudden—where? Judge yourself."

"Pardon me, I do not understand what you are talking about. Explain yourself more distinctly."

"How shall I make my meaning plainer to him?" Then plucking up fresh courage, he continued, "Naturally—besides I am a Major. You must admit it is not befitting that I should go about without a nose. An old apple-woman on the Ascension Bridge may carry on her business without one, but since I am on the look out for a post; besides in many houses I am acquainted with ladies of high position—Madame Tchektyriev, wife of a state-councillor, and many others. So you see—I do not know, honourable sir, what you——" (here the Major shrugged his shoulders). "Pardon me; if one regards the matter from the point of view of duty and honour—you will yourself understand——"

"I understand nothing," answered the nose. "I repeat, please explain yourself more distinctly."

"Honourable sir," said Kovaloff with dignity, "I do not know how I am to understand your words. It seems to me the matter is as clear as possible. Or do you wish—but you are after all my own nose!"

The nose looked at the Major and wrinkled its forehead. "There you are wrong, respected sir; I am myself. Besides, there can be no close relations between us. To judge by the buttons of your uniform, you must be in quite a different department to mine." So saying, the nose turned away.

Kovaloff was completely puzzled; he did not know what to do, and still less what to think. At this moment he heard the pleasant rustling of a lady's dress, and there approached an elderly lady wearing a quantity of lace, and by her side her graceful daughter in a white dress which set off her slender figure to advantage, and wearing a light straw hat. Behind the ladies marched a tall lackey with long whiskers.

Kovaloff advanced a few steps, adjusted his cambric collar, arranged his seals which hung by a little gold chain, and with smiling face fixed his eyes on the graceful lady, who bowed lightly like a spring flower, and raised to her brow her little white hand with transparent fingers. He smiled still more when he spied under the brim of her hat her little round chin, and part of her cheek faintly tinted with rose-colour. But suddenly he sprang back as though he had been scorched. He remembered that he had nothing but an absolute blank in place of a nose, and tears started to his eyes. He turned round in order to tell the gentleman in uniform that he was only a state-councillor in appearance, but really a scoundrel and a rascal, and nothing else but his own nose; but the nose was no longer there. He had had time to go, doubtless in order to continue his visits.

His disappearance plunged Kovaloff into despair. He went back and stood for a moment under a colonnade, looking round him on all sides in hope of perceiving the nose somewhere. He remembered very well that it wore a hat with a plume in it and a gold-embroidered uniform; but he had not noticed the shape of the cloak, nor the colour of the carriages and the horses, nor even whether a lackey stood behind it, and, if so, what sort of livery he wore. Moreover, so many carriages were passing that it would have been difficult to recognise one, and even if he had done so, there would have been no means of stopping it.

The day was fine and sunny. An immense crowd was passing to and fro in the Neffsky Avenue; a variegated stream of ladies flowed along the pavement. There was his acquaintance, the Privy Councillor, whom he was accustomed to style "General," especially when strangers were present. There was Iarygin, his intimate friend who always lost in the evenings at whist; and there another Major, who had obtained the rank of committee-man in the Caucasus, beckoned to him.

"Go to the deuce!" said Kovaloff *sotto voce*. "Hi! Coachman, drive me straight to the superintendent of police." So saying, he got into a droshky and continued to shout all the time to the coachman, "Drive hard!"

"Is the police superintendent at home?" he asked on entering the front hall.

"No, sir," answered the porter, "he has just gone out."

"Ah, just as I thought!"

"Yes," continued the porter, "he has only just gone out; if you had been a moment earlier you would perhaps have caught him."

Kovaloff, still holding his handkerchief to his face, re-entered the droshky and cried in a despairing voice, "Drive on!"

"Where?" asked the coachman.

"Straight on!"

"But how? There are cross-roads here. Shall I go to the right or the left?"

This question made Kovaloff reflect. In his situation it was necessary to have recourse to the police; not because the affair had anything to do with them directly but because they acted more promptly than other authorities. As for demanding any explanation from the department to which the nose claimed to belong, it would, he felt, be useless, for the answers of that gentleman showed that he regarded nothing as sacred, and he might just as likely have lied in this matter as in saying that he had never seen Kovaloff.

But just as he was about to order the coachman to drive to the police-station, the idea occurred to him that this rascally scoundrel who, at their first meeting, had behaved so disloyally towards him, might, profiting by the delay, quit the city secretly; and then all his searching would be in vain, or might last over a whole month. Finally, as though visited with a heavenly inspiration, he resolved to go directly to an advertisement office, and to advertise the loss of his nose, giving all its distinctive characteristics in detail, so that anyone who found it might bring it at once to him, or at any rate inform him where it lived. Having decided on this course, he ordered the coachman to drive to the advertisement office, and all the way he continued to punch him in the back—"Quick, scoundrel! Quick!"

"Yes, sir!" answered the coachman, lashing his shaggy horse with the reins.

At last they arrived, and Kovaloff, out of breath, rushed into a little room where a grey-haired official, in an old coat and with spectacles on his nose, sat at a table holding his pen between his teeth, counting a heap of copper coins.

"Who takes in the advertisements here?" exclaimed Kovaloff.

"At your service, sir," answered the grey-haired functionary, looking up and then fastening his eyes again on the heap of coins before him.

"I wish to place an advertisement in your paper——"

"Have the kindness to wait a minute," answered the official, putting down figures on paper with one hand, and with the other moving two balls on his calculating-frame.

A lackey, whose silver-laced coat showed that he served in one of the houses of the nobility, was standing by the table with a note in his hand, and speaking in a lively tone, by way of showing himself sociable. "Would you believe it, sir, this little dog is really not worth twenty-four kopecks, and for my own part I would not give a farthing for it; but the countess is quite gone upon it, and offers a hundred roubles' reward to anyone who finds it. To tell you the truth, the tastes of these people are very different from ours; they don't mind giving five hundred or a thousand roubles for a poodle or a pointer, provided it be a good one."

The official listened with a serious air while counting the number of letters contained in the note. At either side of the table stood a number of housekeepers, clerks and porters, carrying notes. The writer of one wished to sell a barouche, which had been brought from Paris in 1814 and had been very little used; others wanted to dispose of a strong droshky which wanted one spring, a spirited horse seventeen years old, and so on. The room where these people were collected was very small, and the air was very close; but Kovaloff was not affected by it, for he had covered his face with a handkerchief, and because his nose itself was heaven knew where.

"Sir, allow me to ask you—I am in a great hurry," he said at last impatiently.

"In a moment! In a moment! Two roubles, twenty-four kopecks—one minute! One rouble, sixty-four kopecks!" said the grey-haired official, throwing their notes back to the housekeepers and porters. "What do you wish?" he said, turning to Kovaloff.

"I wish—" answered the latter, "I have just been swindled and cheated, and I cannot get hold of the perpetrator. I only want you to insert an advertisement to say that whoever brings this scoundrel to me will be well rewarded."

"What is your name, please?"

"Why do you want my name? I have many lady friends—Madame Tchektyriev, wife of a state-councillor, Madame Podtotchina, wife of a Colonel. Heaven forbid that they should get to hear of it. You can simply write 'committee-man,' or, better, Major.'"

"And the man who has run away is your serf."

"Serf! If he was, it would not be such a great swindle! It is the nose which has absconded."

"H'm! What a strange name. And this Mr Nose has stolen from you a considerable sum?"

"Mr Nose! Ah, you don't understand me! It is my own nose which has gone, I don't know where. The devil has played a trick on me."

"How has it disappeared? I don't understand."

"I can't tell you how, but the important point is that now it walks about the city itself a state-councillor. That is why I want you to advertise that whoever gets hold of it should bring it as soon as possible to me. Consider; how can I live without such a prominent part of my body? It is not as if it were merely a little toe; I would only have to put my foot in my boot and no one would notice its absence. Every Thursday I call on the wife of M. Tchektyriev, the state-councillor; Madame Podtotchina, a Colonel's wife who has a very pretty daughter, is one of my acquaintances; and what am I to do now? I cannot appear before them like this."

The official compressed his lips and reflected. "No, I cannot insert an advertisement like that," he said after a long pause.

"What! Why not?"

"Because it might compromise the paper. Suppose everyone could advertise that his nose was lost. People already say that all sorts of nonsense and lies are inserted."

"But this is not nonsense! There is nothing of that sort in my case."

"You think so? Listen a minute. Last week there was a case very like it. An official came, just as you have done, bringing an advertisement for the insertion of which he paid two roubles, sixty-three kopecks; and this advertisement simply announced the loss of a black-haired poodle. There did not seem to be anything out of the way in it, but it was really a satire; by the poodle was meant the cashier of some establishment or other."

"But I am not talking of a poodle, but my own nose; i.e. almost myself."

"No, I cannot insert your advertisement."

"But my nose really has disappeared!"

"That is a matter for a doctor. There are said to be people who can provide you with any kind of nose you like. But I see that you are a witty man, and like to have your little joke."

"But I swear to you on my word of honour. Look at my face yourself."

"Why put yourself out?" continued the official, taking a pinch of snuff. "All the same, if you don't mind," he added with a touch of curiosity, "I should like to have a look at it."

The committee-man removed the handkerchief from before his face.

"It certainly does look odd," said the official. "It is perfectly flat like a freshly fried pancake. It is hardly credible."

"Very well. Are you going to hesitate any more? You see it is impossible to refuse to advertise my loss. I shall be particularly obliged to you, and I shall be glad that this incident has procured me the pleasure of making your acquaintance." The Major, we see, did not even shrink from a slight humiliation.

"It certainly is not difficult to advertise it," replied the official; "but I don't see what good it would do you. However, if you lay so much stress on it, you should apply to someone who has a skilful pen, so that he may describe it as a curious, natural freak, and publish the article in the *Northern Bee*" (here he took another pinch) "for the benefit of youthful readers" (he wiped his nose), "or simply as a matter worthy of arousing public curiosity."

The committee-man felt completely discouraged. He let his eyes fall absentmindedly on a daily paper in which theatrical performances were advertised. Reading there the name of an actress whom he knew to be pretty, he involuntarily smiled, and his hand sought his pocket to see if he had a blue ticket—for in Kovaloff's opinion superior officers like himself should not take a lesser-priced seat; but the thought of his lost nose suddenly spoilt everything.

The official himself seemed touched at his difficult position. Desiring to console him, he tried to express his sympathy by a few polite words. "I much regret," he said, "your extraordinary mishap. Will you not try a pinch of snuff? It clears the head, banishes depression, and is a good preventive against hæmorrhoids."

So saying, he reached his snuff-box out to Kovaloff, skilfully concealing at the same time the cover, which was adorned with the portrait of some lady or other.

This act, quite innocent in itself, exasperated Kovaloff. "I don't understand what you find to joke about in the matter," he exclaimed angrily. "Don't you see that I lack precisely the essential feature for taking snuff? The devil take your snuff-box. I don't want to look at snuff now, not even the best, certainly not your vile stuff!"

So saying, he left the advertisement office in a state of profound irritation, and went to the commissary of police. He arrived just as this dignitary was reclining on his couch, and saying to himself with a sigh of satisfaction, "Yes, I shall make a nice little sum out of that."

It might be expected, therefore, that the committee-man's visit would be quite inopportune.

This police commissary was a great patron of all the arts and industries; but what he liked above everything else was a cheque. "It is a thing," he used to say, "to which it is not easy to find an equivalent; it requires no food, it does not take up much room, it stays in one's pocket, and if it falls, it is not broken."

The commissary accorded Kovaloff a fairly frigid reception, saying that the afternoon was not the best time to come with a case, that nature required one to rest a little after eating (this showed the committee-man that the commissary was acquainted with the aphorisms of the ancient sages), and that respectable people did not have their noses stolen.

The last allusion was too direct. We must remember that Kovaloff was a very sensitive man. He did not mind anything said against him as an individual, but he could not endure any reflection on his rank or social position. He even believed that in comedies one might allow attacks on junior officers, but never on their seniors.

The commissary's reception of him hurt his feelings so much that he raised his head proudly, and said with dignity, "After such insulting expressions on your part, I have nothing more to say." And he left the place.

He reached his house quite wearied out. It was already growing dark. After all his fruitless search, his room seemed to him melancholy and even ugly. In the vestibule he saw his valet Ivan stretched on the leather couch and amusing himself by spitting at the ceiling, which he did very cleverly, hitting every time the same spot. His servant's equanimity enraged him; he struck him on the forehead with his hat, and said, "You good-for-nothing, you are always playing the fool!"

Ivan rose quickly and hastened to take off his master's cloak.

Once in his room, the Major, tired and depressed, threw himself in an armchair and, after sighing a while, began to soliloquise:

"In heaven's name, why should such a misfortune befall me? If I had lost an arm or a leg, it would be less insupportable; but a man without a nose! Devil take it!—what is he good for? He is only fit to be thrown out of the window. If it had been taken from me in war or in a duel, or if I had lost it by my own fault! But it has disappeared inexplicably. But no! it is impossible," he continued after reflecting a few moments, "it is incredible that a nose can disappear like that—quite incredible. I must be dreaming, or suffering from some hallucination; perhaps I swallowed, by mistake instead of water, the brandy with which I rub my chin after being shaved. That fool of an Ivan must have forgotten to take it away, and I must have swallowed it."

In order to find out whether he were really drunk, the Major pinched himself so hard that he unvoluntarily uttered a cry. The pain convinced him that he was quite wide awake. He walked slowly to the looking-glass and at first closed his eyes, hoping to see his nose suddenly in its proper place; but on opening them, he started back. "What a hideous sight!" he exclaimed.

It was really incomprehensible. One might easily lose a button, a silver spoon, a watch, or something similar; but a loss like this, and in one's own dwelling!

After considering all the circumstances, Major Kovaloff felt inclined to suppose that the cause of all his trouble should be laid at the door of Madame Podtotchina, the Colonel's wife, who wished him to marry her daughter. He himself paid her court readily, but always avoided coming to the point. And when the lady one day told him point-blank that she wished him to marry her daughter, he gently drew back, declaring that he was still too young, and that he had to serve five years more before he would be forty-two. This must be the reason why the lady, in revenge, had resolved to bring him into disgrace, and had hired two sorceresses for that object. One thing was certain—his nose had not been cut off; no one had entered his room, and as for Ivan Jakovlevitch—he had been shaved by him on Wednesday, and during that day and the whole of Thursday his nose had been there, as he knew and well remembered. Moreover, if his nose had been cut off he would naturally have felt pain, and doubtless the wound would not have healed so quickly, nor would the surface have been as flat as a pancake.

All kinds of plans passed through his head: should he bring a legal action against the wife of a superior officer, or should he go to her and charge her openly with her treachery?

His reflections were interrupted by a sudden light, which shone through all the chinks of the door, showing that Ivan had lit the wax-candles in the vestibule. Soon Ivan himself came in with the lights. Kovaloff quickly seized a handkerchief and covered the place where his nose had been the evening before, so that his blockhead of a servant might not gape with his mouth wide open when he saw his master's extraordinary appearance.

Scarcely had Ivan returned to the vestibule than a stranger's voice was heard there.

"Does Major Kovaloff live here?" it asked.

"Come in!" said the Major, rising rapidly and opening the door.

He saw a police official of pleasant appearance, with grey whiskers and fairly full cheeks—the same who at the commencement of this story was standing at the end of the Isaac Bridge. "You have lost your nose?" he asked.

"Exactly so."

"It has just been found."

"What—do you say?" stammered Major Kovaloff.

Joy had suddenly paralysed his tongue. He stared at the police commissary on whose cheeks and full lips fell the flickering light of the candle.

"How was it?" he asked at last.

"By a very singular chance. It has been arrested just as it was getting into a carriage for Riga. Its passport had been made out some time ago in the name of an official; and what is still more strange, I myself took it at first for a gentleman. Fortunately I had my glasses with me, and then I saw at once that it was a nose. I am shortsighted, you know, and as you stand before me I cannot distinguish your nose, your beard, or anything else. My mother-in-law can hardly see at all."

Kovaloff was beside himself with excitement. "Where is it? Where? I will hasten there at once."

"Don't put yourself out. Knowing that you need it, I have brought it with me. Another singular thing is that the principal culprit in the matter is a scoundrel of a barber living in the Ascension Avenue, who is now safely locked up. I had long suspected him of drunkenness and theft; only the day before yesterday he stole some buttons in a shop. Your nose is quite uninjured." So saying, the police commissary put his hand in his pocket and brought out the nose wrapped up in paper.

"Yes, yes, that is it!" exclaimed Kovaloff. "Will you not stay and drink a cup of tea with me?"

"I should like to very much, but I cannot. I must go at once to the House of Correction. The cost of living is very high nowadays. My mother-in-law lives with me, and there are several children; the eldest is very hopeful and intelligent, but I have no means for their education."

After the commissary's departure, Kovaloff remained for some time plunged in a kind of vague reverie, and did not recover full consciousness for several moments, so great was the effect of this unexpected good news. He placed the recovered nose carefully in the palm of his hand, and examined it again with the greatest attention.

"Yes, this is it!" he said to himself. "Here is the heat-boil on the left side, which came out yesterday." And he nearly laughed aloud with delight.

But nothing is permanent in this world. Joy in the second moment of its arrival is already less keen than in the first, is still fainter in the third, and finishes by coalescing with our normal mental state, just as the circles which the fall of a pebble forms on the surface of water, gradually die away. Kovaloff began to meditate, and saw that his difficulties were not yet over; his nose had been recovered, but it had to be joined on again in its proper place.

And suppose it could not? As he put this question to himself, Kovaloff grew pale. With a feeling of indescribable dread, he rushed towards his dressing-table, and stood before the mirror in order that he might not place his nose crookedly. His hands trembled.

Very carefully he placed it where it had been before. Horror! It did not remain there. He held it to his mouth and warmed it a little with his breath, and then placed it there again; but it would not hold.

"Hold on, you stupid!" he said.

But the nose seemed to be made of wood, and fell back on the table with a strange noise, as though it had been a cork. The Major's face began to twitch feverishly. "Is it possible that it won't stick?" he asked himself, full of alarm. But however often he tried, all his efforts were in vain.

He called Ivan, and sent him to fetch the doctor who occupied the finest flat in the mansion. This doctor was a man of imposing appearance, who had magnificent black whiskers and a healthy wife. He ate fresh apples every morning, and cleaned his teeth with extreme care, using five different tooth-brushes for three-quarters of an hour daily.

The doctor came immediately. After having asked the Major when this misfortune had happened, he raised his chin and gave him a fillip with his finger just where the nose had been, in such a way that the Major suddenly threw back his head and struck the wall with it. The doctor said that did not matter; then, making him turn his face to the right, he felt the vacant place and said "H'm!" then he made him turn it to the left and did the same; finally he again gave him a fillip with his finger, so that the Major started like a horse whose teeth are being examined. After this experiment, the doctor shook his head and said, "No, it cannot be done. Rather remain as you are, lest something worse happen. Certainly one could replace it at once, but I assure you the remedy would be worse than the disease."

"All very fine, but how am I to go on without a nose?" answered Kovaloff. "There is nothing worse than that. How can I show myself with such a villainous appearance? I go into good society, and this evening I am invited to two parties. I know several ladies, Madame Tchektyriev, the wife of a state-councillor, Madame Podtotchina—although after what she has done, I don't want to have anything to do with her except through the agency of the police. I beg you," continued Kovaloff in a supplicating tone, "find some way or other of replacing it; even if it is not quite firm, as long as it holds at all; I can keep it in place sometimes with my hand, whenever there is any risk. Besides, I do not even dance, so that it is not likely to be injured by any sudden movement. As to your fee, be in no anxiety about that; I can well afford it."

"Believe me," answered the doctor in a voice which was neither too high nor too low, but soft and almost magnetic, "I do not treat patients from love of gain. That would be contrary to my principles and to my art. It is true that I accept fees, but that is only not to hurt my patients' feelings by refusing them. I could certainly replace your nose, but I assure you on my word of honour, it would only make matters worse. Rather let Nature do her own work. Wash the place often with cold water, and I assure you that even without a nose, you will be just as well as if you had one. As to the nose itself, I advise you to have it preserved in a bottle of spirits, or, still better, of warm vinegar mixed with two spoonfuls of brandy, and then you can sell it at a good price. I would be willing to take it myself, provided you do not ask too much."

"No, no, I shall not sell it at any price. I would rather it were lost again."

"Excuse me," said the doctor, taking his leave. "I hoped to be useful to you, but I can do nothing more; you are at any rate convinced of my good-will." So saying, the doctor left the room with a dignified air.

Kovaloff did not even notice his departure. Absorbed in a profound reverie, he only saw the edge of his snow-white cuffs emerging from the sleeves of his black coat.

The next day he resolved, before bringing a formal action, to write to the Colonel's wife and see whether she would not return to him, without further dispute, that of which she had deprived him.

The letter ran as follows:

To MADAME ALEXANDRA PODTOTCHINA,

"I hardly understand your method of action. Be sure that by adopting such a course you will gain nothing, and will certainly not succeed in making me marry your daughter. Believe me, the story of my nose has become well known; it is you and no one else who have taken the principal part in it. Its unexpected separation from the place which it occupied, its flight and its appearances sometimes in the disguise of an official, sometimes in proper person, are nothing but the consequence of unholy spells employed by you or by persons who, like you, are addicted to such honourable pursuits. On my part, I wish to inform you, that if the above-mentioned nose is not restored to-day to its proper place, I shall be obliged to have recourse to legal procedure.

"For the rest, with all respect, I have the honour to be your humble servant,

PLATON KOVALOFF.

The reply was not long in coming, and was as follows:

Major PLATON KOVALOFF,—

"Your letter has profoundly astonished me. I must confess that I had not expected such unjust reproaches on your part. I assure you that the official of whom you speak has not been at my house, either disguised or in his proper person. It is true that Philippe Ivanovitch Potantchikoff has paid visits at my house, and though he has actually asked for my daughter's hand, and was a man of good breeding, respectable and intelligent, I never gave him any hope.

"Again, you say something about a nose. If you intend to imply by that that I wished to snub you, i.e. to meet you with a refusal, I am very astonished because, as you well know, I was quite of the opposite mind. If after this you wish to ask for my daughter's hand, I should be glad to gratify you, for such has also been the object of my most fervent desire, in the hope of the accomplishment of which, I remain, yours most sincerely,

ALEXANDRA PODTOTCHINA.

"No," said Kovaloff, after having reperused the letter, "she is certainly not guilty. It is impossible. Such a letter could not be written by a criminal." The committee-man was experienced in such matters, for he had been often officially deputed to conduct criminal investigations while in the Caucasus. "But then how and by what trick of fate has the thing happened?" he said to himself with a gesture of discouragement. "The devil must be at the bottom of it."

Meanwhile the rumour of this extraordinary event had spread all over the city, and, as is generally the case, not without numerous additions. At that period there was a general disposition to believe in the miraculous; the public had recently been impressed by experiments in magnetism. The story of the floating chairs in Koniouchennaia Street was still quite recent, and there was nothing astonishing in hearing soon afterwards that Major Kovaloff's nose was to be seen walking every day at three o'clock on the Neffsky Avenue. The crowd of curious spectators which gathered there daily was enormous. On one occasion someone spread a report that the nose was in Junker's stores and immediately the place was besieged by such a crowd that the police had to interfere and establish order. A certain speculator with a grave, whiskered face, who sold cakes at a theatre door, had some strong wooden benches made which he placed before the window of the stores, and obligingly invited the public to stand on them and look in, at the modest charge of twenty-four kopecks. A veteran colonel, leaving his house earlier than usual expressly for the purpose, had the greatest difficulty in elbowing his way through the crowd, but to his great indignation he saw nothing in the store window but an ordinary flannel waistcoat and a coloured lithograph representing a young girl darning a stocking, while an elegant youth in a waistcoat with large lappels watched her from behind a tree. The picture had hung in the same place for more than ten years. The colonel went off, growling savagely to himself, "How can the fools let themselves be excited by such idiotic stories?"

Then another rumour got abroad, to the effect that the nose of Major Kovaloff was in the habit of walking not on the Neffsky Avenue but in the Tauris Gardens. Some students of the Academy of Surgery went there on purpose to see it. A high-born lady wrote to the keeper of the gardens asking him to show her children this rare phenomenon, and to give them some suitable instruction on the occasion.

All these incidents were eagerly collected by the town wits, who just then were very short of anecdotes adapted to amuse ladies. On the other hand, the minority of solid, sober people were very much displeased. One gentleman asserted with great indignation that he could not understand how in our enlightened age such absurdities could spread abroad, and he was astonished that the Government did not direct their attention to the matter. This gentleman evidently belonged to the category of those people who wish the Government to interfere in everything, even in their daily quarrels with their wives.

But here the course of events is again obscured by a veil.

III

Strange events happen in this world, events which are sometimes entirely improbable. The same nose which had masqueraded as a state-councillor, and caused so much sensation in the town, was found one morning in its proper place, i.e. between the cheeks of Major Kovaloff, as if nothing had happened.

This occurred on 7th April. On awaking, the Major looked by chance into a mirror and perceived a nose. He quickly put his hand to it; it was there beyond a doubt!

"Oh!" exclaimed Kovaloff. For sheer joy he was on the point of performing a dance barefooted across his room, but the entrance of Ivan prevented him. He told him to bring water, and after washing himself, he looked again in the glass. The nose was there! Then he dried his face with a towel and looked again. Yes, there was no mistake about it!

"Look here, Ivan, it seems to me that I have a heat-boil on my nose," he said to his valet.

And he thought to himself at the same time, "That will be a nice business if Ivan says to me 'No, sir, not only is there no boil, but your nose itself is not there!'"

But Ivan answered, "There is nothing, sir; I can see no boil on your nose."

"Good! Good!" exclaimed the Major, and snapped his fingers with delight.

At this moment the barber, Ivan Jakovlevitch, put his head in at the door, but as timidly as a cat which has just been beaten for stealing lard.

"Tell me first, are your hands clean?" asked Kovaloff when he saw him.

"Yes, sir."

"You lie."

"I swear they are perfectly clean, sir."

"Very well; then come here."

Kovaloff seated himself. Jakovlevitch tied a napkin under his chin, and in the twinkling of an eye covered his beard and part of his cheeks with a copious creamy lather.

"There it is!" said the barber to himself, as he glanced at the nose. Then he bent his head a little and examined it from one side. "Yes, it actually is the nose—really, when one thinks——" he continued, pursuing his mental soliloquy and still looking at it. Then quite gently, with infinite precaution, he raised two fingers in the air in order to take hold of it by the extremity, as he was accustomed to do.

"Now then, take care!" Kovaloff exclaimed.

Ivan Jakovlevitch let his arm fall and felt more embarrassed than he had ever done in his life. At last he began to pass the razor very lightly over the Major's chin, and although it was very difficult to shave him without using the olfactory organ as a point of support, he succeeded, however, by placing his wrinkled thumb against the Major's lower jaw and cheek, thus overcoming all obstacles and bringing his task to a safe conclusion.

When the barber had finished, Kovaloff hastened to dress himself, took a droshky, and drove straight to the confectioner's. As he entered it, he ordered a cup of chocolate. He then stepped straight to the mirror; the nose was there!

He returned joyfully, and regarded with a satirical expression two officers who were in the shop, one of whom possessed a nose not much larger than a waistcoat button.

After that he went to the office of the department where he had applied for the post of vice-governor of a province or Government bailiff. As he passed through the hall of reception, he cast a glance at the mirror; the nose was there! Then he went to pay a visit to another committee-man, a very sarcastic personage, to whom he was accustomed to say in answer to his raillery, "Yes, I know, you are the funniest fellow in St Petersburg."

On the way he said to himself, "If the Major does not burst into laughter at the sight of me, that is a most certain sign that everything is in its accustomed place."

But the Major said nothing. "Very good!" thought Kovaloff.

As he returned, he met Madame Podtotchina with her daughter. He accosted them, and they responded very graciously. The conversation lasted a long time, during which he took more than one pinch of snuff, saying to himself, "No, you haven't caught me yet, coquettes that you are! And as to the daughter, I shan't marry her at all."

After that, the Major resumed his walks on the Neffsky Avenue and his visits to the theatre as if nothing had happened. His nose also remained in its place as if it had never quitted it. From that time he was always to be seen smiling, in a good humour, and paying attentions to pretty girls.

IV

Such was the occurrence which took place in the northern capital of our vast empire. On considering the account carefully we see that there is a good deal which looks improbable about it. Not to speak of the strange disappearance of the nose, and its appearance in different places under the disguise of a councillor of state, how was it that Kovaloff did not understand that one cannot decently advertise for a lost nose? I do not mean to say that he would have had to pay too much for the advertisement—that is a mere trifle, and I am not one of those who attach too much importance to money; but to advertise in such a case is not proper nor befitting.

Another difficulty is—how was the nose found in the baked loaf, and how did Ivan Jakovlevitch himself—no, I don't understand it at all!

But the most incomprehensible thing of all is, how authors can choose such subjects for their stories. That really surpasses my understanding. In the first place, no advantage results from it for the country; and in the second place, no harm results either.

All the same, when one reflects well, there really is something in the matter. Whatever may be said to the contrary, such cases do occur—rarely, it is true, but now and then actually.

The Legacy of Raizel Kaidish
(1989)

REBECCA GOLDSTEIN

In 1945 the following incident took place in the death camp of Buchenwald.

There were two young Jewish girls, each the last survivor of her family, and they had become very devoted to one another during the few months of their imprisonment. One morning one of them woke up too weak to work. Her name was put on the death list. The other, Raizel Kaidish, argued with her friend that she, Raizel, should go instead. She would tell the Germans there had been a mistake, and when they saw how strong and fit for work she was, it would be all right. Someone informed on the girls and they were both gassed. The informer was rewarded with Raizel's kitchen job.

I'm named after Raizel Kaidish. My mother knew her from the camp. It's noteworthy that, though the war took all her family from her, my mother chose to name her first child, her only child, after an outsider—the heroine of block eight, Buchenwald.

My mother's moral framework was formed in Buchenwald. Forged in the fires, it was strong and inflexible. One of her central concerns was that I should come to know, without myself suffering, all that she had learned there.

My moral education began at an early age. It consisted at first of tales from the camp.

People in my real life were nice or mean, usually a little of both. But in the tales there were only saints and sinners, heroes and villains. I remember questioning my mother about this, and her answer to me:

"When times are normal, then normal people are a little nice and a little mean together. But when there are hard times, when there's not enough to eat or drink, when there's war, then you don't find a little nice and a little mean mixed together. You find only greatness. Very great badness and very great goodness."

The people in my life didn't seem so real to me as the people in the tales. When I closed my eyes I couldn't picture the faces of my friends or family. All that I could make out of my father was a vaguely sad face around the glinting rimless glasses. Even my mother's features wouldn't come into focus, only the outline of her: tall and always erect, in the gray or dark-blue suit and the white blouse, her light-brown hair in a low bun at the nape of her neck.

But my images of the camp were vivid and detailed. The pink rosebuds on my wallpaper weren't so real to me as the grayness of the barracks, the brown of the mud. It seemed to me that I knew the feel through decaying shoes of the sharp stones in the main square, the sight, twice daily, of the terrifying roll call.

It seemed I, too, had quickly glanced up at the open sky, and wondered that others outside saw the same sky.

My father, like my mother a doctor, didn't approve of the tales:

"She's too young. You'll give her nightmares, traumas. A child this age shouldn't know."

"A child this age. You know you would never consider her old enough to know."

"And why should she know? Can't we forget already? Can't we live like others?"

"Would you really want it, Saul, to live like the others? To join the mass of sleepwalkers, with the glazed eyes and the smug smiles? Is that why we lived when all those others didn't? Is that what we want for Rose?"

And at this point I can hear my father's sigh, the deep drawn-out sigh so characteristic of him, which had always seemed to me, when I was young, to hold the slight tremor of a sob. My father's sadness was something I felt I could almost reach out and touch, like my mother's goodness.

The arguments between my parents continued throughout my childhood. And my father, so gentle, was a man who hated to fight. In the quiet of the night, awake in my bed, I would catch the cadences of their voices, my father's sad and low, so that I missed much of what he said, my mother's burning with the pure flame of her certainty.

And the lessons continued, the simple stark tales of cruelty and sacrifice, cowardice and courage, which always came back to the story of my namesake. My mother would tell me that she had honored both Raizel and me in choosing my name. She sometimes called me Raizel, or even Raizela, in rare moments of tenderness, stroking back my hair.

When I reached fourteen, my mother, deeming me to have arrived at long last at the age of reason (and also, perhaps not coincidentally, at the age at which Raizel had lost her life), began to instruct me in the moral theory she had worked out in Buchenwald.

The theory is elaborate and detailed, reminiscent of the German my parents spoke to one another: complications nesting within complications. The brief account I give here is necessarily inadequate, and perhaps not intrinsically interesting. But I feel that the picture of my mother is incomplete without a description of her moral outlook.

My mother believed that the ethical view is the impersonal view. One is morally obliged to look at a situation without regard for one's own identity in it, and to act in the way dictated by this impersonal view; to act in the way one believes will minimize the sum of suffering.

My mother's emphasis was always on minimizing pain and suffering, never maximizing happiness or well-being. She explained this to me once, when, much older, I asked her:

"I know what is evil. To know suffering is to know evil. None of the attempts to identify the good have this same certainty."

So far there's nothing, except for its pessimistic cast, to distinguish my mother's view from the great bulk of utilitarian theories. The special twist comes in the foundations she claimed, and it's a twist that mirrors her personality: her uncompromising rationality.

Ethics, she believed, is nothing "separate"; it's a branch of logic. The moral obligation is nothing over and above the obligation to be logically consistent, and virtue reduces to rationality.

Why is this so? Because, she explained, to deny the obligation of acting on the impersonal viewpoint, one would have to maintain that one's self has some special metaphysical significance, that it makes a difference that one is who one is. And how can this consistently be maintained once one has recognized the existence of other selves, each of whom is who he is? Only the solipsist can consistently be unethical.

To use one of my mother's favorite analogies: the person who acts only in his own interest is like a person who says there is always something special about his own location, because he can always say, "I'm *here*," whereas everyone else is merely *there*.

Once one has granted that there are other subjects of experience, other selves who suffer, then one can maintain that one's own pain matters—and who would deny *that?*—only if one grants that the pain of everyone else matters in exactly the same way.

Raizel Kaidish's behavior was therefore, by my mother's accounting, paradigmatically ethical. Viewing the situation impersonally, this fourteen-year-old had seen that the stronger child would have a better, although slim, chance to survive. She acted on this view, undeterred by the fact that it was she who was the stronger, she who was unnecessarily risking her life.

In fact, I have no doubt at all that my mother's ethical view was the straightforward consequence of taking Raizel Kaidish as her paradigm, and not the other way round. The heroic action of that child was the real foundation of her theory—which, like my name, honored the girl's memory.

After the liberation my mother returned to Berlin to continue her formal training in medicine. She also began her lifelong study of philosophy. She was curious to see who among the philosophically great had shared her discovery.

She considered Kant to be the most worthwhile ethicist. Socrates she loved for his devotion to the ethical questions, for his conviction that nothing ought to concern us more than the questions of how to live our lives. Hanging over my bed, the only piece of embroidery I've ever known her to do, was the Socratic quotation: "The unexamined life is not worth living."

But for the most part my mother found the great philosophers of the past a supreme disappointment. The truth, so simple, had eluded them, because they had assumed the separateness of the ethical realm. Some had grasped pieces of it, but few had seen the seamless whole.

It was contemporary philosophers, however, particularly the positivists and their "fellow travelers," who aroused her genuine wrath.

For here were theorists who dismissed the possibility of all ethical theory, who denied the very subject matter of the field. Instead of conducting inquiries into the nature of our moral obligations, they offered analyses of the grammar of ethical propositions.

She would look up from some contemporary philosophical book or journal, her eyes blazing their blue fury:

"Positivists." The intonation she gave the word was similar to that she gave "Nazi." "They don't see, because their eyes aren't turned outward but inward, into the tabulae rasae of their own minds. To forsake the important questions for this dribble! To spend your life examining endless quibbles!"

And I? How did I feel about my intensive moral upbringing?

The object of so much attention, of all the pedagogical theorizing, the fights in the night: I felt ignored, unloved, of no significance.

And, especially as I grew older, I felt angry: an unvoiced and unacknowledged outrage.

It wasn't just a matter of the rigidity of my upbringing, the lack of laughter in a home where one could reach out and touch one's father's sadness and mother's goodness.

It wasn't just the fact that I was always made to feel so different from my friends, so that I often, though always with an overwhelming sense of guilt, fantasized myself in another family, with parents who were frivolously pursuing happiness, and didn't have numbers burned into their arms.

It was something else, more elusive and more potent, that infuriated me.

Of course, there's nothing unusual in a daughter's resentment of a mother. My friends, from early adolescence onward, were always enraged with one or the other of their parents. But theirs was the pure clean indignation unashamed of itself.

Hadn't she suffered enough? Shouldn't I try to do everything to make it up to her? By hating her, I joined the ranks of her enemies. I allied myself with the murderers.

And so the resentment was folded back on itself, again and again, always thickening, always darkening.

I never spoke it, not even to myself. Its acknowledgment came only years later, after my mother had died, during the years I spent deliberating over whether to have a child of my own. The mental delivery of that decision was so much more agonizing than the physical birth.

In debating the reasons for having a child, I asked myself whether any reasons could ever be right, whether one was ever justified in bringing a person into being for some reason of one's own? But if not for one's own reason, then for whose? It seemed a moral inconsistency woven into the very fabric of human existence.

The solution really only came to me after I was a mother: It's possible—it's right—for the reasons one had for creating a child to recede into insignificance when faced with the fact of that child's existence. Whatever considerations went into the decision to have a child lose themselves in the knowledge of the child itself.

In my view, this is the essence of good parenting, and once I finally knew this I knew at last what I had felt all along to be wrong about my mother and myself. I had known what no child should ever know: that my mother had had me for some definite reason, and that she would always see me in terms of this reason. I sensed this in my mother, and I hated her for it.

I said that my anger never showed itself. Actually there was a brief rebellion, whose form was so typical of my family's peculiarity that now, years later, even I can see its comic aspect and smile.

My first semester of college, while my friends developed their own conventional modes of rebellion, I worked out mine. I became a positivist. I took Introduction to Philosophy with a self-intoxicated young professor, a new Ph.D. from Harvard, and, although this wouldn't be his own description, a neopositivist.

He told us during the first lecture that he was going to show us, over the course of the semester, why we were lucky, insofar as we were philosophy students, to have been born now; that it was now possible to see that previous generations had devoted themselves to pseudo-questions concerning the nature of Reality, Truth, and the Good; and that such questions were expressions of logical confusion. These fine big words don't name anything, and thus there is nothing there whose nature is to be explored.

I sat there, drinking in his words, thinking: "This is it. This is why I came to college."

All through that term, Monday, Wednesday, and Friday, from ten to eleven, while others dozed and doodled, I listened in a state of delirium, following the arguments with a concentration I've never attained since. My mind bubbled over with the excitement of this illicit doctrine, this forbidden philosophy.

And the most forbidden, and therefore enticing, view offered in the course was that devoted to ethics, or, rather, to the dismissal of ethics.

I memorized whole passages out of my favorite book, A. J. Ayer's *Language, Truth, and Logic:*

> We can now see why it is impossible to find a criterion for determining the validity of ethical judgements. It is not because they have an 'absolute' validity which is mysteriously independent of ordinary sense-experience, but because they have no objective validity whatsoever. If a sentence makes no statement at all, there is obviously no sense in asking whether what it says is true or false. And we have seen that sentences which simply express moral judgements do not say anything. They are pure expressions of feeling and as such do not come under the category of truth and falsehood.

I was inexpressibly moved by the sparse beauty of the arguments. How had I never seen it before, never seen that my mother's supposedly impermeable theory was nothing but an insubstantial confection fabricated of pseudo-statements?

My preparations for final exams were trivial compared with my cramming for the visit home during intersession. I arrived back about eleven at night, too late for philosophical debate. But my mind was so teeming with my professor's methods of query that when my mother wished me "good night" I almost challenged her: "What do you mean by that? What do you mean by 'good'?"

The next evening, after my mother and father arrived home from the hospital, we all sat in the living room, while Bertha, our housekeeper, finished dinner. I was waiting for the right moment for launching my attack, poised to pounce on any comment that was mildly speculative.

But my mother, with her practiced perversity, was being very concrete that night. She asked me about the food at school, about my roommate, even told a funny story about her own roommate, in Berlin, before the war. Then, finally:

"You were always so brief on the phone when I asked you about your classes. Tell me more about them. You seemed to have enjoyed them very much."

"They were wonderful. Especially philosophy. I'm going to major in it."

"Really? And are you thinking of this as a profession?"

"Absolutely. It's it. There's nothing else I'll even consider."

"Well, that's interesting. Very interesting."

"That's *all:* interesting? Are you pleased, horrified, what?"

"At the moment maybe a little baffled. To tell you the truth, I've always thought it a rather funny kind of profession. Every person should of course think about the big questions, but it seems an odd way to earn one's living."

"But what about teaching, Marta?" my father, the eternal peacemaker, asked. "Don't you think it's important to have people teaching philosophy?"

"Well, yes, that's true. Yet I suspect that most of them don't think of themselves primarily as teachers, but as thinkers, professional thinkers, however peculiar that sounds. Well, we can ask Rose here. What do you fancy yourself, a teacher or a philosopher?"

"A philosopher, of course. The need for professional training in philosophy is no different than anywhere else, no different than in medicine. People think they can just jump in and start philosophizing and that they'll make sense. They rarely do. It takes technical training. Years and years of it."

"Oh? I disagree very much, as you know, with this emphasis on technical training. Instead of humanizing the mathematical sciences, they try to mathematize the humanities. Translating into a lot of fancy symbols doesn't show the truth of what you're saying."

"But it does often show its meaninglessness."

I brought out this positivist buzzword with all the provocative emphasis I could muster.

"Do you think so?" responded my mother, not even lifting an eyebrow. "Yes, I can see how that might often be true."

Impossible woman! What was wrong with her? Her kindling point was usually so frighteningly low, but tonight she wouldn't burn. She wouldn't even flicker.

The explanation, of course, would have been obvious to anyone not occupying my vantage point. She was, quite simply, very happy to see me.

I had no more patience for her unwonted tolerance. I abandoned my hopes for a smooth transition.

"Mom, there's a question about ethics that's been bothering me."

There. I had opened the door. Now I had to walk through.

"Yes? Tell me. Perhaps I can be of some help."

"You've always said that the moral obligation is nothing but the obligation to be logically consistent. But why do we have to be logically consistent?"

My mother smiled.

"I must say, you surprise me. Such an antirationalist question. And after a whole semester of college! The answer is, of course, that the truth is important. And logical inconsistencies can't be true. If you ask me, as I can see you're about to, why the truth is important, I can't give you a noncircular answer. Anything I say is going to presuppose the importance of truth, as all rational discourse presupposes it. And this impossibility of a noncircular answer is itself the answer."

"I don't understand a word you're saying!" I exploded. "The Truth! The holy Truth! What's the Truth? Where's the Truth? Let me see you point to it! What can it possibly mean to say, 'The Truth is important'? What cognitive content can it possibly have? It's nonsense! Emotive nonsense! And the same with all the other so-called truths of your so-called theory! You claim to be so rational, so superior and so rational! But you're only emoting—eternally emoting—and I'm sick to death of it!"

My speech was not delivered in that calm voice of detached reason I had so obsessively rehearsed. Instead it tore out of me with a force that frightened me, sweeping me along.

The effect was immediate. My mother's face had the capacity for instantaneous transformation I've observed in my own young daughter. In fact, I often find myself wondering whether this is a trait characteristic of early childhood, or whether it's something my daughter has inherited from her grandmother, along with her name.

My mother had never raised her voice to me, and she didn't raise it now. As always, her eyes did all the screaming.

"Positivist!"

Her intonation wasn't the usual one. There was anger, but it was softened by sadness.

"After all that I have taught you, you lose everything in one semester of college? Do you have so little substance that at your first exposure to the jargon of these antithinkers you disintegrate?"

I had no answer for my mother. The brilliant arguments spilling over in my mind only the night before were all vanished. My head was so hollow it felt as if it were floating away from the rest of me. The deadening fog, of shame and guilt, was settling back over everything.

Dimly, I saw my father sitting there, staring out at us over the wall of his sadness. My mother's voice cut through the haze.

"You disappoint me. You disappoint us all. You aren't worthy to be named after Raizel Kaidish."

Soon after my wedding, when my mother was fifty-six, she learned that she had ovarian cacer and didn't have more than six month to live.

She reacted to the news of her impending death as if she had been preparing for it her whole life. She looked at it with her customary objectivity: Yes, she was relatively young, and there were still many things that she would have liked to experience, particularly being a grandmother. But that she, a Jew from Berlin, had been given these past thirty years was a fact to which the proper response was gratitude, not a greedy demand for yet more years.

She never complained. Her grief seemed entirely focused on the anguish her terrible illness was causing my father and me.

She died as I had always known her to live: with super-human discipline, courage, and rationality.

A week before she died, she told me that it had been she who had informed on Raizel Kaidish. She asked my forgiveness.

The Bridegroom
(1959)

NADINE GORDIMER

He came into his road camp that afternoon for the last time. It was neater than any house would ever be; the sand raked smooth in the clearing, the water drums under the tarpaulin, the flaps of his tent closed against the heat. Thirty yards away a black woman knelt, pounding mealies, and two or three children, grey with Kalahari dust, played with a skinny dog. Their shrillness was no more than a bird's piping in the great spaces in which the camp was lost.

Inside his tent, something of the chill of the night before always remained, stale but cool, like the air of a church. There was his iron bed, with its clean pillowcase and big kaross. There was his table, his folding chair with the red canvas seat, and the chest in which his clothes were put away. Standing on the chest was the alarm clock that woke him at five every morning and the photograph of the seventeen-year-old girl from Francistown whom he was going to marry. They had been there a long time, the girl and the alarm clock; in the morning when he opened his eyes, in the afternoon when he came off the job. But now this was the last time. He was leaving for Francistown in the Roads Department ten-tonner, in the morning; when he came back, the next week, he would be married and he would have with him the girl, and the caravan which the department provided for married men. He had his eye on her as he sat down on the bed and took off his boots; the smiling girl was like one of those faces cut out of a magazine. He began to shed his working overalls, a rind of khaki stiff with dust that held his shape as he discarded it, and he called, easily and softly, *'Ou Piet, ek wag.'* But the bony black man with his eyebrows raised like a clown's, in effort, and his bare feet shuffling under the weight, was already at the tent with a tin bath in which hot water made a twanging tune as it slopped from side to side.

When he had washed and put on a clean khaki shirt and a pair of worn grey trousers, and streaked back his hair with sweet-smelling pomade, he stepped out of his tent just as the lid of the horizon closed on the bloody eye of the sun. It was winter and the sun set shortly after five; the grey sand turned a fading pink, the low thorn scrub gave out spreading stains of lilac shadow that presently all ran together; then the surface of the desert showed pocked and pored, for a minute or two, like the surface of the moon through a telescope, while the sky remained light over the darkened earth and the clean crystal pebble of the evening star shone. The campfires—his own and the black men's, over there—changed from near-invisible flickers of liquid colour to brilliant focuses of leaping tongues of light; it was dark. Every evening he sat like this through the short ceremony of the closing of the day, slowly filling his pipe, slowly easing his back round to the fire, yawning off the stiff-ness of his labour. Suddenly he gave a smothered giggle, to himself, of excitement. Her existence became real to him; he saw the face of the photograph, posed against a caravan door. He got up and began to pace about the camp, alert to promise. He kicked a log far-ther into the fire, he called an order to Piet, he walked up towards the tent and then changed his mind and strolled away again. In their own encampment at the edge of his, the road gang had taken up the exchange of laughing, talking, yelling and arguing that never failed them when their work was done. Black arms gestured under a thick foam of white soap, there was a gasp and splutter as a head broke the cold force of a bucketful of water, the gleaming bellies of iron cooking-pots were carried here and there in the talkative prepa-ration of food. He did not understand much of what they were saying—he knew just enough Tswana to give them his orders, with help from Piet and one or two others who understood his own tongue, Afrikaans—but the sound of their voices belonged to this time of evening. One or other of the babies who always cried was keeping up a thin, ignored wail; the naked children were playing the chasing game that made the dog bark. He came back and sat down again at the fire, to finish his pipe.

After a certain interval (it was exact, though it was not timed by a watch but by long habit that had established the appropriate lapse of time between his bath, his pipe, and his food) he called out, in Afrikaans, 'Have you forgotten my dinner, man?'

From across the patch of distorted darkness where the light of the two fires did not meet, but flung wobbling shapes and opaque, overlapping radiances, came the hoarse, protesting laugh that was, better than the tribute to a new joke, the pleasure in constancy to an old one.

Then a few minutes later, 'Piet! I suppose you've burned everything, eh?'

'Baas?'

'Where's the food, man?'

In his own time the black man appeared with the folding table and an oil-lamp. He went back and forth between the dark and light, bringing pots and dishes and food, and nagging with deep satisfaction, in a mixture of English and Afrikaans. 'You want *koeksusters*, so I make *koeksusters*. You ask me this morning. So I got to make the oil nice and hot, I got to get every-thing ready… It's a little bit slow. Yes, I know. But I can't get everything quick, quick. You hurry tonight, you don't want wait, then it's better you have *koeksusters* on Saturday, then I'm got time in the afternoon, I do it nice … Yes, I think next time it's better…'

Piet was a good cook. 'I've taught my boy how to make everything,' the young man always told people, back in Francistown. 'He can even make *koeksusters*,' he had told the girl's mother, in one of those silences of the woman's disapproval it was so difficult to fill. He had had a hard time, trying to overcome the prejudice of the girl's parents against the sort of life he could offer her. He had managed to convince them that the life was not impossible, and they had given their consent to the marriage, but they still felt the life was unsuitable, and his desire to please and reassure them had made him anxious to see it with their eyes and forestall, by changes, their objections. The girl was a farm girl, and would not pine for town life, but at the same time he could not deny to her parents that living on a farm with her family around her, and neighbours only 30 or 40 miles away would be very different from living 220 miles from a town or village, alone with him in a road camp, 'sur-rounded by a gang of kaffirs all day,' as her mother had said. He himself simply did not think at all about what the girl would do while he was out on the road; and as for the girl, until it was over, nothing could exist for her but the wedding, with her two little sisters in pink walking behind her, and her dress that she didn't recognize herself in being made at the dressmaker's, and the cake that was going to have a tiny china bride and groom in evening dress on the top.

He looked at the scored table, and the rim of the open jam tin, and the salt-cellar with a piece of brown paper tied neatly over the broken top, and said to Piet, 'You must do everything nice when the missus comes.'

'Baas?'

They looked at each other and it was not really necessary to say anything.

'You must make the table properly and do everything clean.'

'Always I make everything clean. Why you say now I must make clean—'

The young man bent his head over his food, dismissing him.

While he ate, his mind went automatically over the changes that would have to be made for the girl. He was not used to visualizing situations, but to dealing with what existed. It was like a lesson learned by rote; he knew the totality of what was needed, but if he found himself confronted by one of the component details, he foundered: he did not recognize it or know how to deal with it. The boys must keep out of the way. That was the main thing. Piet would have to come to the caravan quite a lot, to cook and clean. The boys—specially the boys who were responsible for the maintenance of the lorries and road-making equipment—were always coming with questions, what to do about this and that. They'd mess things up, otherwise. He spat out a piece of gristle he could not swallow; his mind went to something else. The women over there—they could do the washing for the girl. They were such a raw bunch of kaffirs, would they ever be able to do anything right? Twenty boys and about five of their women—you couldn't hide them under a thorn bush. They just mustn't hang around, that's all. They must just understand that they mustn't hang around. He looked keenly through the shadow-puppets of the half-dark on the margin of his fire's light; the voices, companionably quieter, now, intermittent over food, the echoing chut! of wood being chopped, the thin film of a baby's wail through which all these sounded—they were on their own side. Yet he felt an odd, rankling suspicion.

His thoughts shuttled, as he ate, in a slow and painstaking way that he had never experienced before in his life—he was worrying. He sucked on a tooth; Piet, Piet, that kaffir talks such a hell of a lot. How's Piet going to stop talking, talking every time he comes near? If he talks to her... Man, it's sure he'll talk to her. He thought, in actual words, what he would say to Piet about this; the words were like those unsayable things people write on walls for others to see in private moments, but that are never spoken in their mouths.

Piet brought coffee and *koeksusters* and the young man did not look at him.

But the *koeksusters* were delicious, crisp, sticky, and sweet, and as he felt the familiar substance and taste on his tongue, alternating with the hot bite of the coffee, he at once became occupied with the pure happiness of eating, as a child is fully occupied with a bag of sweets. *Koeksusters* never failed to give him this innocent, total pleasure. When first he had taken the job of overseer to the road gang, he had had strange, restless hours at night and on Sundays. It seemed that he was hungry. He ate but never felt satisfied. He walked about all the time, like a hungry creature. One Sunday he actually set out to walk (the Roads Department was very strict about the use of the ten-tonner for private purposes) the fourteen miles across the sand to the cattle-dipping post where the government cattle officer and his wife, Afrikaners

411

like himself and the only other white people between the road camp and Francistown, lived in their corrugated-iron house. By a coincidence, they had decided to drive over and see him, that day, and they had met him a little less than half way, when he was already slowed and dazed by heat. But shortly after that Piet had taken over the cooking of his meals and the care of his person, and Piet had even learned to make *koeksusters*, according to instructions given to the young man by the cattle officer's wife. The *koeksusters*, a childhood treat that he could indulge in whenever he liked, seemed to mark his settling down; the solitary camp became a personal way of life, with its own special arrangements and indulgences.

'*Ou Piet! Kêrel!* What did you do to the *koeksusters*, hey?' he called out joyously.

A shout came that meant 'Right away.' The black man appeared, drying his hands on a rag, with the diffident, kidding manner of someone who knows he has excelled himself.

'Whatsa matter with the *koeksusters*, man?'

Piet shrugged. 'You must tell me. I don't know what's matter.'

'Here, bring me some more, man.' The young man shoved the empty plate at him, with a grin. And as the other went off, laughing, the young man called. 'You must always make them like that, see?'

He liked to drink at celebrations, at weddings or Christmas, but he wasn't a man who drank his brandy every day. He would have two brandies on a Saturday afternoon, when the week's work was over, and for the rest of the time the bottle that he brought from Francistown when he went to collect stores lay in the chest in his tent. But on this last night he got up from the fire on impulse and went over to the tent to fetch the bottle (one thing he didn't do, he didn't expect a kaffir to handle his drink for him; it was too much of a temptation to put in their way). He brought a glass with him, too, one of a set of six made of tinted, imitation cut-glass, and he poured himself a tot and stretched out his legs where he could feel the warmth of the fire through the soles of his boots. The nights were not cold, until the wind came up at two or three in the morning, but there was a clarifying chill to the air; now and then a figure came over from the black men's camp to put another log on the fire whose flames had dropped and become blue. The young man felt inside himself a similar low incandescence; he poured himself another brandy. The long yelping of the jackals prowled the sky without, like the wind about a house; there was no house, but the sounds beyond the light his fire tremblingly inflated into the dark—that jumble of meaningless voices, crying babies, coughs, and hawking—had built walls to enclose and a roof to shelter. He was exposed, turning naked to space on the sphere of the world, but he was not aware of it.

The lilt of various kinds of small music began and died in the dark; threads of notes, blown and plucked, that disappeared under the voices. Presently a huge man whose thick black body had strained apart every seam in his ragged pants and shirt loped silently into the light and dropped just within it, not too near the fire. His feet, intimately crossed, were cracked and weathered like driftwood. He held to his mouth a one-stringed instrument shaped like a lyre, made out of a half-moon of bent wood with a ribbon of dried palm leaf tied from tip to tip. His big lips rested gently on the strip, and while he blew, his one hand, by controlling the vibration of the palm leaf, made of his breath a small, faint, perfect music. It was caught by the very limits of the capacity of the human ear; it was almost out of range. The first music men ever heard, when they began to stand upright among the rushes at the river, might have been like it. When it died away it was difficult to notice at what point it really had gone.

'Play that other one,' said the young man, in Tswana. Only the smoke from his pipe moved.

The pink-palmed hands settled down round the instrument. The thick, tender lips were wet once. The faint desolate voice spoke again, so lonely a music that it came to the player and listener as if they heard it inside themselves. This time the player took a short stick in his other hand and, while he blew, scratched it back and forth inside the curve of the lyre, where the notches cut there produced a dry, shaking, slithering sound, like the far-off movement of dancers' feet. There were two or three figures with more substance than the shadows, where the firelight merged with the darkness. They came and squatted. One of them had half a paraffin tin, with a wooden neck and other attachments of gut and wire. When the lyre-player paused, lowering his piece of stick and leaf slowly, in ebb, from his mouth, and wiping his lips on the back of his hand, the other began to play. It was a thrumming, repetitive, banjo-tune. The young man's boot patted the sand in time to it, and he took it up with handclaps once or twice. A thin, yellowish man in an old hat pushed his way to the front past sarcastic remarks and twittings and sat on his haunches with a little clay bowl between his feet. Over its mouth there was a keyboard of metal tongues. After some exchange, he played it and the others sang low and nasally, bringing a few more strollers to the fire. The music came to an end, pleasantly, and started up again, like a breath drawn. In one of the intervals the young man said, 'Let's have a look at that contraption of yours, isn't it a new one?' and the man to whom he signalled did not understand what was being said to him but handed over his paraffin-tin mandolin with pride and also with amusement at his own handiwork.

The young man turned it over, twanged it once, grinning and shaking his head. Two bits of string and an old jam tin and they'll make a whole band, man. He'd heard them playing some crazy-looking things. The circle of faces watched him with pleasure; they laughed and lazily remarked to each other; it was a funny-looking thing, all right, but it worked. The owner took it back and played it, clowning a little. The audience laughed and joked appreciatively; they were sitting close in to the fire now, painted by it. 'Next week,' the young man raised his voice gaily, 'next week when I come back, I bring radio with me, plenty real music. All the big white bands play over it... Someone who had once worked in Johannesburg said 'Satchmo', and the others took it up, understanding that this was the word for what the white man was going to bring from town. Satchmo. Satch-mo. They tried it out, politely. 'Music, just like at a big white dance in town. Next week.' A friendly, appreciative silence fell, with them all resting back in the warmth of the fire and looking at him indulgently. A strange thing happened to him. He felt hot, over first his neck, then his ears and his face. It didn't matter, of course; by next week they would have forgotten. They wouldn't expect it. He shut down his mind on a picture of them, hanging round the caravan to listen, and him coming out on the steps to tell them...

He thought for a moment that he would give them the rest of the bottle of brandy. Hell, no, man, it was mad. If they got the taste for the stuff, they'd be pinching it all the time. He'd give Piet some sugar and yeast and things from the stores, for them to make beer with tomorrow when he was gone. He put his hands deep in his pockets and stretched out to the fire with his head sunk on his chest. The lyre-player picked up his flimsy piece of wood again, and slowly what the young man was feeling inside himself seemed to find a voice; up into the night beyond the fire it went, uncoiling from his breast and bringing ease. As if it had been made audible out of infinity and could be returned to infinity at any point, the lonely voice of the lyre went on and on. Nobody spoke, the barriers of tongues fell with silence. The whole dirty tide of worry and planning had gone out of the young man. The small, high moon, outshone by a spiky spread of cold stars, repeated the shape of the lyre. He sat for he was not aware how long, just as he had for so many other nights, with the stars at his head and the fire at his feet.

But at last the music stopped and time began again. There was tonight; there was tomorrow, when he was going to drive to Francistown. He stood up; the company fragmented. The lyre-player blew his nose into his fingers. Dusty feet took their accustomed weight. They went off to their tents and he went off to his. Faint plangencies followed them. The young man gave a loud, ugly, animal yawn, the sort of unashamed personal noise a man can make when he lives alone. He walked very slowly across the sand; it was dark but he knew the way more surely than with his eyes. 'Piet! Hey!' he bawled as he reached his tent. 'You get up early tomorrow, eh? And I don't want to hear the lorry won't start. You get it going and then you call me. D'you hear?'

He was lighting the oil-lamp that Piet had left ready on the chest and as it came up softly it brought the whole interior of the tent with it; the chest, the bed, the clock, and the coy smiling face of the seventeen-year-old girl. He sat down on the bed, sliding his palms through the silky fur of the kaross. He drew a breath and held it for a moment, looking round purposefully. And then he picked up the photograph, folded the cardboard support back flat to the frame, and put it in the chest with all his other things, ready for the journey.

The Gutting of Couffignal
(1925)

DASHIELL HAMMETT

Wedge-shaped Couffignal is not a large island, and not far from the mainland, to which it is linked by a wooden bridge. Its western shore is a high, straight cliff that jumps abruptly up out of San Pablo Bay. From the top of this cliff the island slopes eastward, down to a smooth pebble beach that runs into the water again, where there are piers and a clubhouse and moored pleasure boats.

Couffignal's main street, paralleling the beach, has the usual bank, hotel, moving-picture theater, and stores. But it differs from most main streets of its size in that it is more carefully arranged and preserved. There are trees and hedges and strips of lawn on it, and no glaring signs. The buildings seem to belong beside one another, as if they had been designed by the same architect, and in the stores you will find goods of a quality to match the best city stores.

The intersecting streets—running between rows of neat cottages near the foot of the slope— become winding hedged roads as they climb toward the cliff. The higher these roads get, the farther apart and larger are the houses they lead to. The occupants of these higher houses are the owners and rulers of the island. Most of them are well-fed old gentlemen who, the profits they took from the world with both hands in their younger days now stowed away at safe percentages, have bought into the island colony so they may spend what is left of their lives nursing their livers and improving their golf among their kind. They admit to the island only as many store-keepers, working people, and similar riffraff as are needed to keep them comfortably served.

That is Couffignal.

It was some time after midnight. I was sitting in a second-story room in Couffignal's largest house, surrounded by wedding presents whose value would add up to something between fifty and a hundred thousand dollars.

Of all the work that comes to a private detective (except divorce work, which the Continental Detective Agency doesn't handle) I like weddings as little as any. Usually I manage to avoid them, but this time I hadn't been able to. Dick Foley, who had been slated for the job, had been handed a black eye by an unfriendly pickpocket the day before. That let Dick out and me in. I had come up to Couffignal —a two-hour ride from San Francisco by ferry and auto stage—that morning, and would return the next.

This had been neither better nor worse than the usual wedding detail. The ceremony had been performed in a little stone church down the hill. Then the house had begun to fill with reception guests. They had kept it filled to overflowing until some time after the bride and groom had sneaked off to their eastern train.

415

The world had been well represented. There had been an admiral and an earl or two from England; an ex-president of a South American country; a Danish baron; a tall young Russian princess surrounded by lesser titles, including a fat, bald, jovial and black- bearded Russian general, who had talked to me for a solid hour about prize fights, in which he had a lot of interest, but not so much knowledge as was possible; an ambassador from one of the Central European countries; a justice of the Supreme Court; and a mob of people whose prominence and near-prominence didn't carry labels.

In theory, a detective guarding wedding presents is supposed to make himself indistinguishable from the other guests. In practice, it never works out that way. He has to spend most of his time within sight of the booty, so he's easily spotted. Besides that, eight or ten people I recognized among the guests were clients or former clients of the Agency, and so knew me. However, being known doesn't make so much difference as you might think, and everything had gone off smoothly.

A couple of the groom's friends, warmed by wine and the necessity of maintaining their reputations as cutups, had tried to smuggle some of the gifts out of the room where they were displayed and hide them in the piano. But I had been expecting that familiar trick, and blocked it before it had gone far enough to embarrass anybody.

Shortly after dark a wind smelling of rain began to pile storm clouds up over the bay. Those guests who lived at a distance, especially those who had water to cross, hurried off for their homes. Those who lived on the island stayed until the first raindrops began to patter down. Then they left.

The Hendrixson house quieted down. Musicians and extra servants left. The weary house servants began to disappear in the direction of their bedrooms. I found some sandwiches, a couple of books and a comfortable armchair, and took them up to the room where the presents were now hidden under gray-white sheeting.

Keith Hendrixson, the bride's grandfather—she was an orphan— put his head in at the door. "Have you everything you need for your comfort?" he asked.

"Yes, thanks."

He said good night and went off to bed—a tall old man, slim as a boy.

The wind and the rain were hard at it when I went downstairs to give the lower windows and doors the up-and-down. Everything on first floor was tight and secure, everything in the cellar. I went upstairs again.

Pulling my chair over by a floor lamp, I put sandwiches, books, ashtray, gun and flashlight on a small table beside it. Then I switched off the other lights, set fire to a Fatima, sat down, wriggled my spine comfortably into the chair's padding, picked up one of the books, and prepared to make a night of it.

The book was called *The Lord of the Sea*, and had to do with a strong, tough and violent fellow named Hogarth, whose modest plan was to hold the world in one hand. There were plots and counterplots, kidnapings, murders, prisonbreakings, forgeries and burglaries, diamonds large as hats and floating forts larger than Couffignal. It sounds dizzy here, but in the book it was as real as a dime.

Hogarth was still going strong when the lights went out.

In the dark, I got rid of the glowing end of my cigarette by grinding it in one of the sandwiches. Putting the book down, I picked up gun and flashlight, and moved away from the chair.

Listening for noises was no good. The storm was making hundreds of them. What I needed to know was why the lights had gone off. All the other lights in the house had been turned off some time ago. So the darkness of the hall told me nothing.

I waited. My job was to watch the presents. Nobody had touched them yet. There was nothing to get excited about.

Minutes went by, perhaps ten of them.

The floor swayed under my feet. The windows rattled with a violence beyond the strength of the storm. The dull boom of a heavy explosion blotted out the sounds of wind and falling water. The blast was not close at hand, but not far enough away to be off the island.

Crossing to the window, peering through the wet glass, I could see nothing. I should have seen a few misty lights far down the hill. Not being able to see them settled one point. The lights had gone out all over Couffignal, not only in the Hendrixson house.

That was better. The storm could have put the lighting system out of whack, could have been responsible for the explosion—maybe.

Staring through the black window, I had an impression of great excitement down the hill, of movement in the night. But all was too far away for me to have seen or heard even had there been lights, and all too vague to say what was moving. The impression was strong but worthless. It didn't lead anywhere. I told myself I was getting feeble minded, and turned away from the window.

Another blast spun me back to it. This explosion sounded nearer than the first, maybe because it was stronger. Peering through the glass again, I still saw nothing. And still had the impression of things that were big moving down there.

Bare feet pattered in the hall. A voice was anxiously calling my name. Turning from the window again, I pocketed my gun and snapped on the flashlight. Keith Hendrixson, in pajamas and bathrobe, looking thinner and older than anybody could be, came into room.

"Is it—"

"I don't think it's an earthquake," I said, since that is the first calamity your Californian thinks of. "The lights went off a little while ago. There have been a couple of explosions down the hill since the—"

I stopped. Three shots, close together, had sounded. Rifle-shots but of the sort that only the heaviest of rifles could make. Then, sharp and small in the storm, came the report of a far-away pistol.

"What is it?" Hendrixson demanded.

"Shooting."

More feet were pattering in the halls, some bare, some shod. Excited voices whispered questions and exclamations. The butler, a solemn, solid block of a man, partly dressed and carrying a lighted five-pronged candlestick, came in.

"Very good, Brophy," Hendrixson said as the butler put the candlestick on the table beside my sandwiches. "Will you try to learn what is the matter?"

"I have tried, sir. The telephone seems to be out of order, sir. Shall I send Oliver down to the village?"

"No-o. I don't suppose it's that serious. Do you think it is anything serious?" he asked me.

I said I didn't think so, but I was paying more attention to the outside than to him. I had heard a thin screaming that could have come from a distant woman, and a volley of small-arms shots. The rocket of the storm muffled these shots, but when the heavier firing we had heard before broke out again, it was clear enough.

To have opened the window would have been to let in gallons of water without helping us to hear much clearer. I stood with an ear titled to the pane, trying to arrive at some idea of what was happening outside.

Another sound took my attention from the window—the ringing of the bell-pull at the front door. It rang loudly and persistently.

Hendrixson looked at me. I nodded. "See who it is, Brophy," he said.

The butler went solemnly away, and came back even more solemnly. "Princess Zhukovski," he announced.

She came running into the room—the tall Russian girl I had seen at the reception. Her eyes were wide and dark with excitement. Her face was very white and wet. Water ran in streams down her blue waterproof cape, the hood of which covered her dark hair.

"Oh, Mr. Hendrixson!" She had caught one of his hands in both of hers. Her voice, with nothing foreign in its accents, was the voice of one who is excited over a delightful surprise. "The bank is being robbed, and the—what do you call him?—marshal of police has been killed!"

"What's that?" the old man exclaimed, jumping awkwardly because water from her cape had dripped down on one of his bare feet. "Weegan killed? And the bank robbed?"

"Yes! Isn't it terrible?" She said it as if she were saying wonderful. "When the first explosion woke us, the general sent Ignati down to find out what was the matter, and he got down there just in time to see the bank blown up. Listen!"

We listened, and heard a wild outbreak of mixed gunfire.

"That will be the general arriving!" she said. "He'll enjoy himself most wonderfully. As soon as Ignati returned with the news, the general armed every male in the household from Aleksandr Sergyeevich to Ivan the cook, and led them out happier than he's been since he took his division to East Prussia in 1914."

"And the duchess?" Hendrixson asked.

"He left her at home with me, of course, and I furtively crept out and away from her while she was trying for the first time in her life to put water in a samovar. This is not the night for one to stay at home!"

"H-m-m." Hendrixson said, his mind obviously not on her words. "And the bank!"

He looked at me. I said nothing. The racket of another volley came to us.

"Could you do anything down there?" he asked.

"Maybe, but—" I nodded at the presents under their covers.

"Oh, those!" the old man said. "I'm as much interested in the bank as in them; and besides, we will be here."

"All right!" I was willing enough to carry my curiosity down the hill. "I'll go down. You'd better have the butler stay in here, and plant the chauffeur inside the front door. Better give them guns if you have any. Is there a raincoat I can borrow? I brought only a light overcoat with me."

Brophy found a yellow slicker that fit me. I put it on, stowed gun and flashlight conveniently under it, and found my hat while Brophy was getting and loading an automatic pistol for himself and a rifle for Oliver, the mulatto chauffeur.

Hendrixson and the princess followed me downstairs. At the door I found she wasn't exactly following me—she was going with me.

"But, Sonya!" the old man protested.

418

"I'm not going to be foolish, though I'd like to," she promised him. "But I'm going back to my Irinia Androvna, who will perhaps have the samovar watered by now."

"That's a sensible girl!" Hendrixson said, and let us out into the rain and the wind.

It wasn't weather to talk in. In silence we turned downhill between two rows of hedging, with the storm driving at our backs. At the first break in the hedge I stopped, nodding toward the black blot a house made. "That is your—"

Her laugh cut me short. She caught my arm and began to urge me down the road again. "I only told Mr. Hendrixson that so he would not worry," she explained. "You do not think I am not going down to see the sights."

She was tall. I am short and thick. I had to look up to see her face—to see as much of it as the rain-gray night would let me see. "You'll be soaked to the hide, running around in this rain," I objected.

"What of that? I am dressed for it." She raised a foot to show me a heavy waterproof boot and a woolen-stockinged leg.

"There's no telling what we'll run into down there, and I've got work to do," I insisted. "I can't be looking out for you."

"I can look out for myself." She pushed her cape aside to show me a square automatic pistol in one hand.

"You'll be in my way."

"I will not," she retorted. "You'll probably find I can help you. I'm as strong as you, and quicker, and I can shoot."

The reports of scattered shooting had punctuated our argument, but now the sound of heavier firing silenced the dozen objections to her company that I could still think of. After all, I could slip away from her in the dark if she became too much of a nuisance.

"Have it your own way," I growled, "but don't expect anything from me."

"You're so kind," she murmured as we got under way again, hurrying now, with the wind at our backs speeding us along.

Occasionally dark figures moved on the road ahead of us, but too far away to be recognizable. Presently a man passed us, running uphill—a tall man whose nightshirt hung out of his trousers, down below his coat, identifying him as a resident.

"They've finished the bank and are at Medcraft's!" he yelled as he went by.

"Medcraft is the jeweler," the girl informed me.

The sloping under our feet grew less sharp. The houses—dark but with faces vaguely visible here and there at windows—came closer together. Below, the flash of a gun could be seen now and then—orange streaks in the rain.

Our road put us into the lower end of the main street just as a staccato rat-ta-tat broke out.

I pushed the girl into the nearest doorway, and jumped in after her.

Bullets ripped through walls with the sound of hail tapping on leaves.

That was the thing I had taken for an exceptionally heavy rifle—a machine gun.

The girl had fallen back in a corner, all tangled up with something. I helped her up. The something was a boy of seventeen or so, with one leg and a crutch.

"It's the boy who delivers papers," Princess Zhukovski said, "and you've hurt him with your clumsiness."

The boy shook his head, grinning as he got up. "No'm, I ain't hurt none, but you kind of scared me, jumping on me like that."

She had to stop and explain that she hadn't jumped on him, that she had been pushed into him by me, and that she was sorry and so was I.

"What's happening?" I asked the newsboy when I could get a word in.

"Everything," he boasted, as if some of the credit were his. "There must be a hundred of them, and they've blowed the bank wide open, and now some of 'em is in Medcraft's, and I guess they'll blow that up, too. And they killed Tom Weegan. They got a machine gun on a car in the middle of the street. That's it shooting now."

"Where's everybody—all the merry villagers?"

"Most of 'em are up behind the Hall. They can't do nothing, though, because the machine gun won't let 'em get near enough to see what they're shooting at, and that smart Bill Vincent told me to clear out, 'cause I've only got one leg, as if I couldn't shoot as good as the next one, if I only had something to shoot with!"

"That wasn't right of them," I sympathized. "But you can do something for me. You can stick here and keep your eye on this end of the street, so I'll know if they leave in this direction."

"You're not just saying that so I'll stay here out of the way, are you?"

"No," I lied. "I need somebody to watch. I was going to leave the princess here, but you'll do better."

"Yes," she backed me up, catching the idea. "This gentleman is a detective, and if you do what he asks you'll be helping more than if you were up with the others."

The machine gun was still firing, but not in our direction now.

"I'm going across the street," I told the girl. "If you—"

"Aren't you going to join the others?"

"No. If I can get around behind the bandits while they're busy with the others, maybe I can turn a trick."

"Watch sharp now!" I ordered the boy, and the princess and I made a dash for the opposite sidewalk.

We reached it without drawing lead, sidled along a building for a few yards, and turned into an alley. From the alley's other end came the smell and wash and the dull blackness of the bay.

While we moved down this alley I composed a scheme by which I hoped to get rid of my companion, sending her off on a safe wild goose chase. But I didn't get a chance to try it out.

The big figure of a man loomed ahead of us.

Stepping in front of the girl, I went on toward him. Under my slicker I held my gun on the middle of him.

He stood still. He was larger than he had looked at first. A big slope-shouldered, barrel-bodied husky. His hands were empty. I spotted the flashlight on his face for a split second. A flat-cheeked, thick-featured face, with high cheekbones and a lot of ruggedness in it.

"Ignati!" the girl exclaimed over my shoulder.

He began to talk what I suppose was Russian to the girl. She laughed and replied. He shook his big head stubbornly, insisting on something. She stamped her foot and spoke sharply. He shook his head again and addressed me. "General Pleshskev, he tell me bring Princess Sonya to home."

His English was almost as hard to understand as his Russian. His tone puzzled me. It was as if he was explaining some absolutely necessary thing that he didn't want to be blamed for, but that nevertheless he was going to do.

While the girl was speaking to him again, I guessed the answer. This big Ignati had been sent out by the general to bring the girl home, and he was going to obey his orders if he had to carry her. He was trying to avoid trouble with me by explaining the situation.

"Take her," I said, stepping aside.

The girl scowled at me, laughed. "Very well, Ignati," she said in English, "I shall go home," and she turned on her heel and went back up the alley, the big man close behind her.

Glad to be alone, I wasted no time in moving in the opposite direction until the pebbles of the beach were under my feet. The pebbles ground harshly under my heels. I moved back to more silent ground and began to work my way as swiftly as I could up the shore toward the center of action. The machine gun barked on. Smaller guns snapped. Three concussions, close together—bombs, hand grenades, my ears and my memory told me.

The stormy sky glared pink over a roof ahead of me and to the left. The boom of the blast beat my eardrums. Fragments I couldn't see fell around me. That, I thought, would be the jeweler's safe blowing apart.

I crept on up the shore line. The machine gun went silent. Lighter guns snapped, snapped. Another grenade went off. A man's voice shrieked pure terror.

Risking the crunch of pebbles, I turned down to the water's edge again. I had seen no dark shape on the water that could have been a boat. There had been boats moored along this beach in the afternoon. With my feet in the water of the bay I still saw no boat. The storm could have scattered them, but I didn't think it had. The island's western height shielded this shore. The wind was strong here, but not violent.

My feet sometimes on the edge of the pebbles, sometimes in the water, I went on up the shore line. Now I saw a boat. A gently bobbing black shape ahead. No light was on it. Nothing I could see moved on it. It was the only boat on that shore. That made it important.

Foot by foot, I approached.

A shadow moved between me and the dark rear of a building. I froze. The shadow, man-size, moved again, in the direction from which I was coming.

Waiting, I didn't know how nearly invisible, or how plain, I might be against my background. I couldn't risk giving myself away by trying to improve my position.

Twenty feet from me the shadow suddenly stopped.

I was seen. My gun was on the shadow.

"Come on," I called softly. "Keep coming. Let's see who you are."

The shadow hesitated, left the shelter of the building, drew nearer. I couldn't risk the flash-light. I made out dimly a handsome face boyishly reckless, one cheek dark-stained.

"Oh, how d'you do?" the face's owner said in a musical baritone voice. "You were at the reception this afternoon."

"Yes."

"Have you seen Princess Zhukovski? You know her?"

"She went home with Ignati ten minutes or so ago."

"Excellent!" He wiped his stained cheek with a stained handkerchief, and turned to look at the boat. "That's Hendrixson's boat," he whispered. "They've got it and they've cast the others off."

"That would mean they are going to leave by water."

"Yes," he agreed, "unless—Shall we have a try at it?"

"Yon mean jump it?"

"Why not?" he asked. "There can't be very many aboard. God knows there are enough of them ashore. You're armed. I've a pistol."

"We'll size it up first," I decided, "so we'll know what we're jumping."

"That is wisdom," he said, and led the way back to the shelter of the buildings.

Hugging the rear walls of the buildings, we stole toward the boat.

The boat grew clearer in the night. A craft perhaps forty-five feet long, its stern to the shore, rising and falling beside a small pier. Across the stern something protruded. Something I couldn't quite make out. Leather soles scuffled now and then on the wooden deck. Presently a dark head and shoulders showed over the puzzling thing in the stern.

The Russian lad's eyes were better than mine.

"Masked," he breathed in my ear. "Something like a stocking over his head and face."

The masked man was motionless where he stood. We were motionless where we stood.

"Could you hit him from here?" the lad asked.

"Maybe, but night and rain aren't a good combination for sharp shooting. Our best bet is to sneak as close as we can, and start shooting when he spots us."

"That is wisdom," he agreed.

Discovery came with our first step forward. The man in the boat grunted. The lad at my side jumped forward. I recognized the thing in the boat's stern just in time to throw out a leg and trip the young Russian. He tumbled down, all sprawled out on the pebbles. I dropped behind him.

The machine gun in the boat's stern poured metal over our heads.

"No good rushing that!" I said. "Roll out of it!"

I set the example by revolving toward the back of the building we had just left.

The man at the gun sprinkled the beach, but sprinkled it at random, his eyes no doubt spoiled for night-seeing by the flash of his gun.

Around the corner of the building, we sat up.

"You saved my life by tripping me," the lad said coolly.

"Yes. I wonder if they've moved the machine gun from the street, or if—"

The answer to that came immediately. The machine gun in the street mingled its vicious voice with the drumming of the one in the boat.

"A pair of them!" I complained. "Know anything about the lay-out?"

"I don't think there are more than ten or twelve of them," he said, "although it is not easy to count in the dark. The few I have seen are completely masked—like the man in the boat. They seem to have disconnected the telephone and light lines first and then to have destroyed the bridge. We attacked them while they were looting the bank, but in front they had a machine gun mounted in an automobile, and were not equipped to combat on equal terms."

"Where are the islanders now?"

"Scattered, and most of them in hiding, I fancy, unless General Pleshskev has succeeded in rallying them again."

I frowned and beat my brains together. You can't fight machine guns and hand grenades with peaceful villagers and retired capitalists. No matter how well led and armed they are, you

422

can't do anything with them. For that matter, how could anybody do much against a game of that toughness?

"Suppose you stick here and keep your eye on the boat," I suggested. "I'll scout around and see what's doing farther up, and if I can get a few good men together, I'll try to jump the boat again, probably from the other side. But we can't count on that. The getaway will be by boat. We can count on that, and try to block it. If you lie down you can watch the boat around the corner of the building without making much of a target of yourself. I wouldn't do anything to attract attention until the break for the boat comes. Then you can do all the shooting you want."

"Excellent!" he said. "You'll probably find most of the islanders up behind the church. You can get to it by going straight up the hill until you come to an iron fence, and then follow that to the right."

"Right."

I moved off in the direction he had indicated.

At the main street I stopped to look around before venturing across. Everything was quiet there. The only man I could see was spread out face-down on the sidewalk near me.

On hands and knees I crawled to his side. He was dead. I didn't stop to examine him further, but sprang up and streaked for the other side of the street.

Nothing tried to stop me. In a doorway, flat against a wall, I peeped out. The wind had stopped. The rain was no longer a driving deluge, but a steady down-pouring of small drops. Couffignal's main street, to my senses, was a deserted street.

I wondered if the retreat to the boat had already started. On the sidewalk, walking swiftly toward the bank, I heard the answer to that guess.

High up on the slope, almost up to the edge of the cliff, by the sound, a machine gun began to hurl out its stream of bullets.

Mixed with the racket of the machine gun were the sounds of smaller arms, and a grenade or two.

At the first crossing, I left the main street and began to run up the hill. Men were running toward me. Two of them passed, paying no attention to my shouted, "What's up now?"

The third man stopped because I grabbed him—a fat man whose breath bubbled, and whose face was fish-belly white.

"They've moved the car with the machine gun on it up behind us," he gasped when I had shouted my question into his ear again.

"What are you doing without a gun?" I asked.

"I—I dropped it."

"Where's General Pleshskev?"

"Back there somewhere. He's trying to capture the car, but he'll never do it. It's suicide! Why don't help come?"

Other men had passed us, running downhill, as we talked. I let the white-faced man go, and stopped four men who weren't running so fast as the others.

"What's happening now?" I questioned them.

"They's going through the houses up the hill," a sharp-featured man with a small mustache and a rifle said.

"Has anybody got word off the island yet?" I asked.

"Can't," another informed me. "They blew up the bridge first thing."

"Can't anybody swim?"

"Not in that wind. Young Catlan tried it and was lucky to get out again with a couple of broken ribs."

"The wind's gone down," I pointed out.

The sharp-featured man gave his rifle to one of the others and took off his coat. "I'll try it," he promised.

"Good! Wake up the whole country, and get word through to the San Francisco police boat and to the Mare Island Navy Yard. They'll lend a hand if you tell 'em the bandits have machine guns. Tell 'em the bandits have an armed boat waiting to leave in. It's Hendrixson's."

The volunteer swimmer left.

"A boat?" two of the men asked together.

"Yes. With a machine gun on it. If we're going to do anything, it'll have to be now, while we're between them and their get-away. Get every man and every gun you can find down there. Tackle the boat from the roofs if you can. When the bandits' car comes down there, pour it into it. You'll do better from the buildings than from the street."

The three men went on downhill. I went uphill, toward the crackling of firearms ahead. The machine gun was working irregularly. It would pour out its rat-tat-tat for a second or so, and then stop for a couple of seconds. The answering fire was thin, ragged.

I met more men, learned from them the general, with less than a dozen men, was still fighting the car. I repeated the advice I had given the other men. My informants went down to join them. I went on up.

A hundred yards farther along, what was left of the general's dozen broke out of the night, around and past me, flying downhill, with bullets hailing after them.

The road was no place for mortal man. I stumbled over two bodies, scratched myself in a dozen places getting over a hedge. On soft, wet sod I continued my uphill journey.

The machine gun on the hill stopped its clattering. The one in the boat was still at work.

The one ahead opened again, firing too high for anything near at hand to be its target. It was helping its fellow below, spraying the main street.

Before I could get closer it had stopped. I heard the car's motor racing. The car moved toward me.

Rolling into the hedge, I lay there, straining my eyes through the spaces between the stems. I had six bullets in a gun that hadn't yet been fired on this night that had seen tons of powder burned.

When I saw wheels on the lighter face of the road, I emptied my gun, holding it low.

The car went on.

I sprang out of my hiding-place.

The car was suddenly gone from the empty road.

There was a grinding sound. A crash. The noise of metal folding on itself. The tinkle of glass.

I raced toward those sounds.

Out of a black pile where an engine sputtered, a black figure leaped—to dash off across the soggy lawn. I cut after it, hoping that the others in the wreck were down for keeps.

I was less than fifteen feet behind the fleeing man when he cleared a hedge. I'm no sprinter, but neither was he. The wet grass made slippery going.

He stumbled while I was vaulting the hedge. When we straightened out again I was not more than ten feet behind him.

Once I clicked my gun at him, forgetting I had emptied it. Six cartridges were wrapped in a piece of paper in my vest pocket, but this was no time for loading.

I was tempted to chuck the empty gun at his head. But that was too chancy.

A building loomed ahead. My fugitive bore off to the right, to clear the corner.

To the left a heavy shotgun went off.

The running man disappeared around the house-corner.

"Sweet God!" General Pleshskev's mellow voice complained. "That with a shotgun I should miss all of a man at the distance!"

"Go round the other way!" I yelled, plunging around the corner after my quarry.

His feet thudded ahead. I could not see him. The general puffed around from the other side of the house.

"You have him?"

"No."

In front of us was a stone-faced bank, on top of which ran a path. On either side of us was a high and solid hedge.

"But, my friend," the general protested. "How could he have—?"

A pale triangle showed on the path above—a triangle that could have been a bit of shirt showing above the opening of a vest.

"Stay here and talk!" I whispered to the general, and crept forward.

"It must be that he has gone the other way," the general carried out my instructions, rambling on as if I were standing beside him, "because if he had come my way I should have seen him, and if he had raised himself over either of the hedges or the embankment, one of us would surely have seen him against . . ."

He talked on and on while I gained the shelter of the bank on which the path sat, while I found places for my toes in the rough stone facing.

The man on the road, trying to make himself small with his back in a bush, was looking at the talking general. He saw me when I had my feet on the path.

He jumped, and one hand went up.

I jumped, with both hands out.

A stone, turning under my foot, threw me sidewise, twisting my ankle, but saving my head from the bullet he sent at it.

My outflung left arm caught his legs as I spilled down. He came over on top of me. I kicked him once, caught his gun-arm, and had just decided to bite it when the general puffed up over the edge of the path and prodded the man off me with the muzzle of the shotgun.

When it came my turn to stand up, I found it not so good. My twisted ankle didn't like to support its share of my hundred-and-eighty-some pounds. Putting most of my weight on the other leg, I turned my flashlight on the prisoner.

"Hello, Flippo!" I exclaimed.

"Hello!" he said without joy in the recognition.

He was a roly-poly Italian youth of twenty-three or -four. I had helped send him to San Quentin four years ago for his part in a payroll stick-up. He had been out on parole for several months now.

"The prison board isn't going to like this," I told him.

425

"You got me wrong," he pleaded. "I ain't been doing a thing. I was up here to see some friends. And when this thing busted loose I had to hide, because I got a record, and if I'm picked up I'll be railroaded for it. And now you got me, and you think I'm in on it!"

"You're a mind reader," I assured him, and asked the general, "Where can we pack this bird away for a while, under lock and key?"

"In my house there is a lumber-room with a strong door and not a window."

"That'll do it. March, Flippo!"

General Pleshskev collared the youth, while I limped along behind them, examining Flippo's gun, which was loaded except for the one shot he had fired at me, and reloading my own.

We had caught our prisoner on the Russian's grounds, so we didn't have far to go.

The general knocked on the door and called out something in his language. Bolts clicked and grated, and the door was swung open by a heavily mustached Russian servant. Behind him the princess and a stalwart older woman stood.

We went in while the general was telling his household about the capture, and took the captive up to the lumber-room. I frisked him for his pocketknife and matches—he had nothing else that could help him get out—locked him in and braced the door solidly with a length of board. Then we went downstairs again.

"You are injured!" the princess cried, seeing me limp across the floor.

"Only a twisted ankle," I said. "But it does bother me some. Is there any adhesive tape around?"

"Yes," and she spoke to the mustached servant, who went out of the room and presently returned, carrying rolls of gauze and tape and a basin of steaming water.

"If you'll sit down," the princess said, taking these things from the servant.

But I shook my head and reached for the adhesive tape.

"I want cold water, because I've got to go out in the wet again. If you'll show me the bathroom, I can fix myself up in no time."

We had to argue about that, but I finally got to the bathroom, where I ran cold water on my foot and ankle, and strapped it with adhesive tape, as tight as I could without stopping the circulation altogether. Getting my wet shoe on again was a job, but when I was through I had two firm legs under me, even if one of them did hurt some.

When I rejoined the others I noticed that sounds of firing no longer came up the hill, and that the patter of rain was lighter, and a gray streak of coming daylight showed under a drawn blind.

I was buttoning my slicker when the knocker rang on the front door. Russian words came through, and the young Russian I had met on the beach came in.

"Aleksander, you're—" The stalwart older woman screamed, when she saw the blood on his cheek, and fainted.

He paid no attention to her at all, as if he was used to having her faint.

"They've gone in the boat," he told me while the girl and two men servants gathered up the woman and laid her on an ottoman.

"How many?" I asked.

"I counted ten, and I don't think I missed more than one or two, if any."

"The men I sent down there couldn't stop them?"

He shrugged. "What would you? It takes a strong stomach to face a machine gun. Your men had been cleared out of the buildings almost before they arrived."

The woman who had fainted had revived by now and was pouring anxious questions in Russian at the lad. The princess was getting into her blue cape. The woman stopped questioning the lad and asked her something.

"It's all over," the princess said. "I am going to view the ruins."

That suggestion appealed to everybody. Five minutes later all of us, including the servants, were on our way downhill. Behind us, around us, in front of us, were other people going downhill, hurrying along in the drizzle that was very gentle now, their faces tired and excited in the bleak morning light.

Halfway down, a woman ran out of a cross-path and began to tell me something. I recognized her as one of Hendrixson's maids.

I caught some of her words.

"Presents gone. . . . Mr. Brophy murdered . . . Oliver . . ."

"I'll be down later," I told the others, and set out after the maid.

She was running back to the Hendrixson house. I couldn't run, couldn't even walk fast. She and Hendrixson and more of his servants were standing on the front porch when I arrived.

"They killed Oliver and Brophy," the old man said.

"How?"

"We were in the back of the house, the rear second story, watching the flashes of the shooting down in the village. Oliver was down here, just inside the front door, and Brophy in the room with the presents. We heard a shot in there, and immediately a man appeared in the doorway of our room, threatening us with two pistols, making us stay there for perhaps ten minutes. Then he shut and locked the door and went away. We broke the door down—and found Brophy and Oliver dead."

"Let's look at them."

The chauffeur was just inside the front door. He lay on his back, with his brown throat cut straight across the front, almost back to the vertebrae. His rifle was under him. I pulled it out and examined it. It had not been fired.

Upstairs, the butler Brophy was huddled against a leg of one of the tables on which the presents had been spread. His gun was gone. I turned him over, straightened him out, and found a bullet-hole in his chest. Around the hole his coat was charred in a large area.

Most of the presents were still there. But the most valuable pieces were gone. The others were in disorder, lying around any which way, their covers pulled off.

"What did the one you saw look like?" I asked.

"I didn't see him very well," Hendrixson said. "There was no light in our room. He was simply a dark figure against the candle burning in the hall. A large man in a black rubber raincoat, with some sort of black mask that covered his whole head and face, with small eyeholes."

"No hat?"

"No, just the mask over his entire face and head."

As we went downstairs again I gave Hendrixson a brief account of what I had seen and heard and done since I had left him. There wasn't enough of it to make a long tale.

"Do you think you can get information about the others from the one you caught?" he asked, as I prepared to go out.

"No. But I expect to bag them just the same."

Couffignal's main street was jammed with people when I limped into it again. A detachment of Marines from Mare Island was there, and men from a San Francisco police boat. Excited citizens in all degrees of partial nakedness boiled around them. A hundred voices were talking at once, recounting their personal adventures and braveries and losses and what they had seen. Such words as machine gun, bomb, bandit, car, shot, dynamite, and killed sounded again and again, in every variety of voice and tone.

The bank had been completely wrecked by the charge that had blown the vault. The jewelry store was another ruin. A grocer's across the street was serving as a field hospital. Two doctors were toiling there, patching up damaged villagers.

I recognized a familiar face under a uniform cap—Sergeant Roche of the harbor police—and pushed through the crowd to him.

"Just get here?" he asked as we shook hands. "Or were you in on it?"

"In on it."

"What do you know?"

"Everything."

"Who ever heard of a private detective that didn't," he joshed as I led him out of the mob.

"Did you people run into an empty boat out in the bay?" I asked when we were away from audiences.

"Empty boats have been floating around the bay all night," he said.

I hadn't thought of that.

"Where's your boat now?" I asked him.

"Out trying to pick up the bandits. I stayed with a couple of men to lend a hand here."

"You're in luck," I told him. "Now sneak a look across the street. See the stout old boy with the black whiskers, standing in front of the druggist's?"

General Pleshskev stood there, with the woman who had fainted, the young Russian whose bloody cheek had made her faint, and a pale, plump man of forty-something who had been with them at the reception. A little to one side stood big Ignati, the two men-servants I had seen at the house, and another who was obviously one of them. They were chatting together and watching the excited antics of a red-faced property-owner who was telling a curt lieutenant of Marines that it was his own personal private automobile that the bandits had stolen to mount their machine gun on, and what he thought should be done about it.

"Yes," said Roche, "I see your fellow with the whiskers."

"Well, he's your meat. The woman and two men with him are also your meat. And those four Russians standing to the left are some more of it. There's another missing, but I'll take care of that one. Pass the word to the lieutenant, and you can round up those babies without giving them a chance to fight back. They think they're safe as angels."

"Sure, are you?" the sergeant asked.

"Don't be silly!" I growled, as if I had never made a mistake in my life.

I had been standing on my one good prop. When I put my weight on the other to turn away from the sergeant, it stung me all the way to the hip. I pushed my back teeth together and began to work painfully through the crowd to the other side of the street.

The princess didn't seem to be among those present. My idea was that, next to the general, she was the most important member of the push. If she was at their house, and not yet suspicious, I figured I could get close enough to yank her in without a riot.

Walking was hell. My temperature rose. Sweat rolled out on me.

"Mister, they didn't none of 'em come down that way."

428

The one-legged newsboy was standing at my elbow. I greeted him as if he were my pay-check.

"Come on with me," I said, taking his arm. "You did fine down there, and now I want you to do something else for me."

Half a block from the main street I led him up on the porch of a small yellow cottage. The front door stood open, left that way when the occupants ran down to welcome police and Marines, no doubt. Just inside the door, beside a hall rack, was a wicker porch chair. I commited unlawful entry to the extent of dragging that chair out on the porch.

"Sit down, son," I urged the boy.

He sat, looking up at me with puzzled freckled face, I took a firm grip on his crutch and pulled it out of his hand.

"Here's five bucks for rental," I said, "and if I lose it I'll buy you one of ivory and gold."

And I put the crutch under my arm and began to propel myself up the hill.

It was my first experience with a crutch. I didn't break any records. But it was a lot better than tottering along on an unassisted bum ankle.

The hill was longer and steeper than some mountains I've seen, but the gravel walk to the Russians' house was finally under my feet.

I was still some dozen feet from the porch when Princess Zhukovski opened the door.

"Oh!" she exclaimed, and then, recovering from her surprise, "your ankle is worse!" She ran down the steps to help me climb them. As she came I noticed that something heavy was sagging and swinging in the right-hand pocket of her gray flannel jacket.

With one hand under my elbow, the other arm across my back, she helped me up the steps and across the porch. That assured me she didn't think I had tumbled to the game. If she had, she wouldn't have trusted herself within reach of my hands. Why, I wondered, had she come back to the house after starting downhill with the others?

While I was wondering we went into the house, where she planted me in a large and soft leather chair.

"You must certainly be starving after your strenuous night," she said. "I will see if—"

"No, sit down," I nodded at a chair facing mine. "I want to talk to you."

She sat down, clasping her slender white hands in her lap. In neither face nor pose was there any sign of nervousness, not even of curiosity. And that was overdoing it.

"Where have you cached the plunder?" I asked.

The whiteness of her face was nothing to go by. It had been white as marble since I had first seen her. The darkness of her eyes was as natural. Nothing happened to her other features. Her voice was smoothly cool.

"I am sorry," she said. "The question doesn't convey anything to me."

"Here's the point," I explained. "I'm charging you with complicity in the gutting of Couffignal, and in the murders that went with it. And I'm asking you where the loot has been hidden."

Slowly she stood up, raised her chin, and looked at least a mile down at me.

"How dare you? How dare you speak so to me, a Zhukovski!"

"I don't care if you're one of the Smith Brothers!" Leaning forward, I had pushed my twisted ankle against a leg of the chair, and the resulting agony didn't improve my disposition. "For the purpose of this talk you are a thief and a murderer."

Her strong slender body became the body of a lean crouching animal. Her white face became the face of an enraged animal. One hand—claw now—swept to the heavy pocket of her jacket.

Then, before I could have batted an eye—though my life seemed to depend on my not batting it—the wild animal had vanished. Out of it—and now I know where the writers of the old fairy stories got their ideas—rose the princess again, cool and straight and tall.

She sat down, crossed her ankles, put an elbow on an arm of her chair, propped her chin on the back of that hand, and looked curiously in to my face.

"How ever," she murmured, "did you chance to arrive at so strange and fanciful a theory?"

"It wasn't chance, and it's neither strange nor fanciful," I said. "Maybe it'll save time and trouble if I show you part of the score against you. Then you'll know how you stand and won't waste your brains pleading innocence."

"I shall be grateful," she smiled, "very!"

I tucked my crutch in between one knee and the arm of my chair, so my hands would be free to check off my points on my fingers.

"First—whoever planned the job knew the island—not fairly well, but every inch of it. There's no need to argue about that. Second—the car on which the machine gun was mounted was local property, stolen from the owner here. So was the boat in which the bandits were supposed to have escaped. Bandits from the outside would have needed a car or a boat to bring their machine guns, explosives, and grenades here, and there doesn't seem to be any reason why they shouldn't have used that car or boat instead of stealing a fresh one. Third—there wasn't the least of hint of the professional bandit touch on this job. If you ask me, it was a military job from beginning to end. And the worst safe-burglar in the world could have got into both the bank vault and the jeweler's safe without wrecking the buildings. Fourth—bandits from the outside wouldn't have destroyed the bridge. They might have blocked it, but they wouldn't have destroyed it. They'd have saved it in case they had to make their get-away in that direction. Fifth—bandits figuring on a get-away by boat would have cut the job short, wouldn't have spread it over the whole night. Enough racket was made here to wake up California all the way from Sacramento to Los Angeles. What you people did was to send one man out in the boat, shooting, and he didn't go far. As soon as he was at a safe distance, he went overboard, and swam back to the island. Big Ignati could have done it without turning a hair."

That exhausted my right hand. I switched over, counting on my left.

"Sixth—I met one of your party, the lad, down on the beach, and he was coming from the boat. He suggested that we jump it. We were shot at, but the man behind the gun was playing with us. He could have wiped us out in a second if he had been in earnest, but he shot over our heads. Seventh—that same lad is the only man on the island, so far as I know, who saw the departing bandits. Eight—all of your people that I ran into were especially nice to me, the general even spending an hour talking to me at the reception this afternoon. That's a distinctive amateur crook trait. Ninth—after the machine gun car had been wrecked I chased its occupant. I lost him around this house. The Italian boy I picked up wasn't him. He couldn't have climbed up on the path without my seeing him. But he could have run around to the general's side of the house and vanished indoors there. The general liked him, and would have helped him. I know that, because the general performed a downright miracle by missing him at some six feet with a shotgun. Tenth—you called at Hendrixson's house for no other purpose than to get me away from there."

That finished the left hand. I went back to the right.

"Eleventh—Hendrixson's two servants were killed by someone they knew and trusted. Both were killed at close quarters and without firing a shot. I'd say you got Oliver to let you into the house, and were talking to him when one of your men cut his throat from behind. Then you went upstairs and probably shot the unsuspecting Brophy yourself. He wouldn't have been on his guard against you. Twelfth—but that ought to be enough, and I'm getting a sore throat from listing them."

She took her chin off her hand, took a fat white cigarette out of a thin black case, and held it in her mouth while I put a match to the end of it. She took a long pull at it—a draw that accounted for a third of its length—and blew the smoke down at her knees.

"That would be enough," she said when all these things had been done, "if it were not that you yourself know it was impossible for us to have been so engaged. Did you not see us—did not everyone see us—time and time again?"

"That's easy!" I argued. "With a couple of machine guns, a trunkful of grenades, knowing the island from top to bottom, in the darkness and in a storm, against bewildered civilians— it was duck soup. There are nine of you that I know of, including two women. Any five of you could have carried on the work, once it was started, while the others took turns appearing here and there, establishing alibis. And that is what you did. You took turns slipping out to alibi yourselves. Everywhere I went I ran into one of you. And the general! That whiskered old joker running around leading the simple citizens to battle! I'll bet he led 'em plenty! They're lucky there are any of 'em alive this morning!"

She finished her cigarette with another inhalation, dropped the stub on the rug, ground out the light with one foot, sighed wearily, put her hands on her hips, and asked, "And now what?"

"Now I want to know where you have stowed the plunder."

The readiness of her answer surprised me.

"Under the garage, in a cellar we secretly dug there some months ago."

I didn't believe that, of course, but it turned out to be the truth.

I didn't have anything else to say. When I fumbled with my borrowed crutch, preparing to get up, she raised a hand and spoke gently. "Wait a moment, please. I have something to suggest."

Half standing, I leaned toward her, stretching out one hand until it was close to her side.

I want the gun," I said.

She nodded, and sat still while I plucked it from her pocket, put it in one of my own, and sat down again.

"You said a little while ago that you didn't care who I was," she began immediately. "But I want you to know. There are so many of us Russians who once were somebodies and who now are nobodies that I won't bore you with the repetition of a tale the world has grown tired of hearing. But you must remember that this weary tale is real to us who are its subjects. However, we fled from Russia with what we could carry of our property, which fortunately was enough to keep us in bearable comfort for a few years.

"In London we opened a Russian restaurant, but London was suddenly full of Russian restaurants, and ours became, instead of a means of livelihood, a source of loss. We tried teaching music and languages, and so on. In short, we hit on all the means of earning our living that other Russian exiles hit upon, and so always found ourselves in overcrowded, and thus unprofitable, fields. But what else did we know—could we do?

"I promised not to bore you. Well, always our capital shrank, and always the day approached on which we should be shabby and hungry, the day when we should become familiar to readers of your Sunday papers—charwomen who had been princesses, dukes who now were butlers. There was no place for us in the world. Outcasts easily become outlaws. Why not? Could it be said that we owed the world any fealty? Had not the world sat idly by and seen us despoiled of place and property and country?

"We planned it before we had heard of Couffignal. We could find a small settlement of the wealthy, sufficiently isolated, and, after establishing ourselves there, we would plunder it. Couffignal, when we found it, seemed to be the ideal place. We leased this house for six months, having just enough capital remaining to do that and to live properly here while our plans matured. Here we spent four months establishing ourselves, collecting our arms and our explosives, mapping our offensive, waiting for a favorable night. Last night seemed be that night, and we had provided, we thought, against every eventuality. But we had not, of course, provided against your presence and your genius. They were simply others of the unforeseen misfortunes to which we seem eternally condemned."

She stopped, and fell to studying me with mournful large eyes that made me feel like fidgeting.

"It's no good calling me a genius," I objected. "The truth is you people botched your job from beginning to end. Your general would get a big laugh out of a man without military training who tried to lead an army. But here are you people with absolutely no criminal experience trying to swing a trick that needed the highest sort of criminal skill. Look at how you all played around with me! Amateur stuff! A professional crook with any intelligence would have either let me alone or knocked me off. No wonder you flopped! As for the rest of it—your troubles—I can't do anything about them."

"Why?" very softly. "Why can't you?"

"Why should I?" I made it blunt.

"No one else knows what you know." She bent forward to put a white hand on my knee. "There is wealth in that cellar beneath the garage. You may have whatever you ask."

I shook my head.

"You aren't a fool!" she protested. "You know————"

"Let me straighten this out for you," I interrupted. "We'll disregard whatever honesty I happen to have, sense of loyalty to employers, and so on. You might doubt them, so we'll throw them out. Now I'm a detective because I happen to like the work. It pays me a fair salary, but I could find other jobs that would pay more. Even a hundred dollars more a month would be twelve hundred a year. Say twenty-five or thirty thousand dollars in the years between now and my sixtieth birthday.

"Now I pass up about twenty-five or thirty thousand of honest gain because I like being a detective, like the work. And liking work makes you want to do it as well as you can. Otherwise there'd be no sense to it. That's the fix I am in. I don't know anything else, don't enjoy anything else, don't want to know or enjoy anything else. You can't weigh that against any sum of money. Money is good stuff. I haven't anything against it. But in the past eighteen years I've been getting my fun out of chasing crooks and tackling puzzles, my satisfaction out of catching crooks and solving riddles. It's the only kind of sport I know anything about, and I can't imagine a pleasanter future than twenty-some years more of it. I'm not going to blow that up!"

She shook her head slowly, lowering it, so that now her dark eyes looked up at me under the thin arcs of her brows.

"You speak only of money," she said. "I said you may have whatever you ask."

That was out. I don't know where these women get their ideas.

"You're still all twisted up," I said brusquely, standing now and adjusting my borrowed crutch. "You think I'm a man and you're a woman. That's wrong. I'm a manhunter and you're something that has been running in front of me. There's nothing human about it. You might just as well expect a hound to play tiddly-winks with the fox he's caught. We're wasting time anyway. I've been thinking the police or Marines might come up here and save me a walk. You've been waiting for your mob to come back and grab me. I could have told you they were being arrested when I left them."

That shook her. She had stood up. Now she fell back a step, putting a hand behind her for steadiness, on her chair. An exclamation I didn't understand popped out of her mouth. Russian, I thought, but the next moment I knew it had been Italian.

"Put your hands up." It was Flippo's husky voice. Flippo stood in doorway, holding an automatic.

I raised my hands as high as I could without dropping my supporting crutch, meanwhile cursing myself for having been too careless, or too vain, to keep a gun in my hand while I talked to the girl.

So this was why she had come back to the house. If she freed the Italian, she had thought, we would have no reason for supecting that he hadn't been in on the robbery, and so we would look for the bandits among his friends. A prisoner, of course, he might have persuaded us of his innocence. She had given him the gun so he could either shoot his way clear, or, what would help her as much, get himself killed trying.

While I was arranging these thoughts in my head, Flippo had come up behind me. His empty hand passed over my body, taking away my own gun, his, and the one I had taken from the girl.

"A bargain, Flippo," I said when he had moved away from me, a little to one side, where he made one corner of a triangle whose other corners were the girl and I. "You're out on parole, with some years still to be served. I picked you up with a gun on you. That's plenty to send you back to the big house. I know you weren't in on this job. My idea is that you were up here on a smaller one of your own, but I can't prove that and don't want to. Walk out of here, alone and neutral, and I'll forget I saw you."

Little thoughtful lines grooved the boy's round, dark face.

The princess took a step toward him.

"You heard the offer I just now made him?" she asked. "Well, I make that offer to you, if you will kill him."

The thoughtful lines in the boy's face deepened.

"There's your choice, Flippo," I summed up for him. "All I can give you is freedom from San Quentin. The princess can give you a fat cut of the profits in a busted caper, with a good chance to get yourself hanged."

The girl, remembering her advantage over me, went at him hot and heavy in Italian, a language in which I know only four words. Two of them are profane and the other two obscene. I said all four.

The boy was weakening. If he had been ten years older, he'd have taken my offer and thanked me for it. But he was young and she—now that I thought of it—was beautiful. The answer wasn't hard to guess.

"But not to bump him off," he said to her in English, for my benefit. "We'll lock him up in there where I was at."

I suspected Flippo hadn't any great prejudice against murder. It was just that he thought this one unnecessary, unless he was kidding me to make the killing easier.

The girl wasn't satisfied with his suggestion. She poured more hot Italian at him. Her game looked surefire, but it had a flaw. She couldn't persuade him that his chances of getting any of the loot away were good. She had to depend on her charms to swing him. And that meant she had to hold his eye.

He wasn't far from me.

She came close to him. She was singing, chanting, crooning Italian syllables into his round face.

She had him.

He shrugged. His whole face said yes. He turned—

I knocked him on the noodle with my borrowed crutch.

The crutch splintered apart. Flippo's knees bent. He stretched up to his full height. He fell on his face on the floor. He lay there, dead-still, except for a thin worm of blood that crawled out of his hair to the rug.

A step, a tumble, a foot or so of hand-and-knee scrambling put me within reach of Flippo's gun.

The girl, jumping out of my path, was halfway to the door when I sat up with the gun in my hand.

"Stop!" I ordered.

"I shan't," she said, but she did, for the time at least. "I am going out."

"You are going out when I take you."

She laughed, a pleasant laugh, low and confident.

"I'm going out before that," she insisted good-naturedly. I shook my head.

How do you purpose stopping me?" she asked.

"I don't think I'll have to," I told her. "You've got too much sense to try to run while I'm holding a gun on you."

She laughed again, an amused ripple.

"I've got too much sense to stay," she corrected me. "Your crutch is broken, and you're lame. You can't catch me by running after me, then. You pretend you'll shoot me, but I don't believe you. You'd shoot me if I attacked you, of course, but I shan't do that. I shall simply walk out, and you know you won't shoot me for that. You'll wish you could, but you won't. You'll see."

Her face turned over her shoulder, her dark eyes twinkling at me, she took a step toward the door.

"Better not count on that!" I threatened.

For answer to that she gave me a cooing laugh. And took another step.

"Stop, you idiot!" I bawled at her.

Her face laughed over her shoulder at me. She walked without haste to the door, her short skirt of gray flannel shaping itself to the calf of each gray wool-stockinged leg as its mate stepped forward.

Sweat greased the gun in my hand.

When her right foot was on the doorsill, a little chuckling sound came from her throat.

"Adieu!" she said softly.

And I put a bullet in the calf of her left leg.

She sat down—plump! Utter surprise stretched her white face. It was too soon for pain.

I had never shot a woman before. I felt queer about it.

"You ought to have known I'd do it!" My voice sounded harsh and savage and like a stranger's in my ears. "Didn't I steal a crutch from a cripple?"

The Minister's Black Veil
A Parable
(1836)

NATHANIEL HAWTHORNE

The sexton stood in the porch of Milford meeting-house pulling lustily at the bell-rope. The old people of the village came stooping along the street. Children with bright faces tripped merrily beside their parents or mimicked a graver gait in the conscious dignity of their Sunday clothes. Spruce bachelors looked sidelong at the pretty maidens, and fancied that the Sabbath sunshine made them prettier than on week-days. When the throng had mostly streamed into the porch, the sexton began to toll the bell, keeping his eye on the Reverend Mr. Hooper's door. The first glimpse of the clergyman's figure was the signal for the bell to cease its summons.

"But what has good Parson Hooper got upon his face?" cried the sexton, in astonishment.

All within hearing immediately turned about and beheld the semblance of Mr. Hooper pacing slowly his meditative way toward the meeting-house. With one accord they started, expressing more wonder than if some strange minister were coming to dust the cushions of Mr. Hooper's pulpit.

"Are you sure it is our parson?" inquired Goodman Gray of the sexton.

"Of a certainty it is good Mr. Hooper," replied the sexton. "He was to have exchanged pulpits with Parson Shute of Westbury, but Parson Shute sent to excuse himself yesterday, being to preach a funeral sermon."

The cause of so much amazement may appear sufficiently slight. Mr. Hooper, a gentlemanly person of about thirty, though still a bachelor, was dressed with due clerical neatness, as if a careful wife had starched his band and brushed the weekly dust from his Sunday's garb. There was but one thing remarkable in his appearance. Swathed about his forehead and hanging down over his face, so low as to be shaken by his breath, Mr. Hooper had on a black veil. On a nearer view it seemed to consist of two folds of crape, which entirely concealed his features except the mouth and chin, but probably did not intercept his sight further than to give a darkened aspect to all living and inanimate things. With this gloomy shade before him good Mr. Hooper walked onward at a slow and quiet pace, stooping somewhat and looking on the ground, as is customary with abstracted men, yet nodding kindly to those of his parishioners who still waited on the meeting-house steps. But so wonder-struck were they that his greeting hardly met with a return.

"I can't really feel as if good Mr. Hooper's face was behind that piece of crape," said the sexton.

"I don't like it," muttered an old woman as she hobbled into the meeting-house. "He has changed himself into something awful only by hiding his face."

"Our parson has gone mad!" cried Goodman Gray, following him across the threshold.

A rumor of some unaccountable phenomenon had preceded Mr. Hooper into the meeting-house and set all the congregation astir. Few could refrain from twisting their heads toward the door; many stood upright and turned directly about; while several little boys clambered upon the seats, and came down again with a terrible racket. There was a general bustle, a rustling of the women's gowns and shuffling of the men's feet, greatly at variance with that hushed repose which should attend the entrance of the minister. But Mr. Hooper appeared not to notice the perturbation of his people. He entered with an almost noiseless step, bent his head mildly to the pews on each side and bowed as he passed his oldest parishioner, a white-haired great-grandsire, who occupied an arm-chair in the centre of the aisle. It was strange to observe how slowly this venerable man became conscious of something singular in the appearance of his pastor. He seemed not fully to partake of the prevailing wonder till Mr. Hooper had ascended the stairs and showed himself in the pulpit, face to face with his congregation except for the black veil. That mysterious emblem was never once withdrawn. It shook with his measured breath as he gave out the psalm, it threw its obscurity between him and the holy page as he read the Scriptures, and while he prayed the veil lay heavily on his uplifted countenance. Did he seek to hide it from the dread Being whom he was addressing?

Such was the effect of this simple piece of crape that more than one woman of delicate nerves was forced to leave the meeting-house. Yet perhaps the pale-faced congregation was almost as fearful a sight to the minister as his black veil to them.

Mr. Hooper had the reputation of a good preacher, but not an energetic one: he strove to win his people heavenward by mild, persuasive influences rather than to drive them thither by the thunders of the word. The sermon which he now delivered was marked by the same characteristics of style and manner as the general series of his pulpit oratory, but there was something either in the sentiment of the discourse itself or in the imagination of the auditors which made it greatly the most powerful effort that they had ever heard from their pastor's lips. It was tinged rather more darkly than usual with the gentle gloom of Mr. Hooper's temperament. The subject had reference to secret sin and those sad mysteries which we hide from our nearest and dearest, and would fain conceal from our own consciousness, even forgetting that the Omniscient can detect them. A subtle power was breathed into his words. Each member of the congregation, the most innocent girl and the man of hardened breast, felt as if the preacher had crept upon them behind his awful veil and discovered their hoarded iniquity of deed or thought. Many spread their clasped hands on their bosoms. There was nothing terrible in what Mr. Hooper said—at least, no violence; and yet with every tremor of his melancholy voice the hearers quaked. An unsought pathos came hand in hand with awe. So sensible were the audience of some unwonted attribute in their minister that they longed for a breath of wind to blow aside the veil, almost believing that a stranger's visage would be discovered, though the form, gesture and voice were those of Mr. Hooper.

At the close of the services the people hurried out with indecorous confusion, eager to communicate their pent-up amazement, and conscious of lighter spirits the moment they lost sight of the black veil. Some gathered in little circles, huddled closely together, with their mouths all whispering in the centre; some went homeward alone, wrapped in silent meditation; some talked loudly and profaned the Sabbath-day with ostentatious laughter. A few shook their sagacious heads, intimating that they could penetrate the mystery, while one or two affirmed that there was no mystery at all, but only that Mr. Hooper's eyes were so weakened by the midnight lamp as to require a shade.

After a brief interval forth came good Mr. Hooper also, in the rear of his flock. Turning his veiled face from one group to another, he paid due reverence to the hoary heads, saluted the middle-aged with kind dignity as their friend and spiritual guide, greeted the young with mingled authority and love, and laid his hands on the little children's heads to bless them. Such was always his custom on the Sabbath-day. Strange and bewildered looks repaid him for his courtesy. None, as on former occasions, aspired to the honor of walking by their pastor's side. Old Squire Saunders—doubtless by an accidental lapse of memory—neglected to invite Mr. Hooper to his table, where the good clergyman had been wont to bless the food almost every Sunday since his settlement. He returned, therefore, to the parsonage, and at the moment of closing the door was observed to look back upon the people, all of whom had their eyes fixed upon the minister. A sad smile gleamed faintly from beneath the black veil and flickered about his mouth, glimmering as he disappeared.

"How strange," said a lady, "that a simple black veil, such as any woman might wear on her bonnet, should become such a terrible thing on Mr. Hooper's face!"

"Something must surely be amiss with Mr. Hooper's intellects," observed her husband, the physician of the village. "But the strangest part of the affair is the effect of this vagary even on a sober-minded man like myself. The black veil, though it covers only our pastor's face, throws its influence over his whole person and makes him ghost-like from head to foot. Do you not feel it so?"

"Truly do I," replied the lady; "and I would not be alone with him for the world. I wonder he is not afraid to be alone with himself."

"Men sometimes are so," said her husband.

The afternoon service was attended with similar circumstances. At its conclusion the bell tolled for the funeral of a young lady. The relatives and friends were assembled in the house and the more distant acquaintances stood about the door, speaking of the good qualities of the deceased, when their talk was interrupted by the appearance of Mr. Hooper, still covered with his black veil. It was now an appropriate emblem. The clergyman stepped into the room where the corpse was laid, and bent over the coffin to take a last farewell of his deceased parishioner. As he stooped the veil hung straight down from his forehead, so that, if her eye-lids had not been closed for ever, the dead maiden might have seen his face. Could Mr. Hooper be fearful of her glance, that he so hastily caught back the black veil? A person who watched the interview between the dead and living scrupled not to affirm that at the instant when the clergyman's features were disclosed the corpse had slightly shuddered, rustling the shroud and muslin cap, though the countenance retained the composure of death. A superstitious old woman was the only witness of this prodigy.

From the coffin Mr. Hooper passed into the chamber of the mourners, and thence to the head of the staircase, to make the funeral prayer. It was a tender and heart-dissolving prayer, full of sorrow, yet so imbued with celestial hopes that the music of a heavenly harp swept by the fingers of the dead seemed faintly to be heard among the saddest accents of the minister. The people trembled, though they but darkly understood him, when he prayed that they and himself, and all of mortal race, might be ready, as he trusted this young maiden had been, for the dreadful hour that should snatch the veil from their faces. The bearers went heavily forth and the mourners followed, saddening all the street, with the dead before them and Mr. Hooper in his black veil behind.

"Why do you look back?" said one in the procession to his partner.

"I had a fancy," replied she, "that the minister and the maiden's spirit were walking hand in hand."

"And so had I at the same moment," said the other.

That night the handsomest couple in Milford village were to be joined in wedlock. Though reckoned a melancholy man, Mr. Hooper had a placid cheerfulness for such occasions which often excited a sympathetic smile where livelier merriment would have been thrown away. There was no quality of his disposition which made him more beloved than this. The company at the wedding awaited his arrival with impatience, trusting that the strange awe which had gathered over him throughout the day would now be dispelled. But such was not the result. When Mr. Hooper came, the first thing that their eyes rested on was the same horrible black veil which had added deeper gloom to the funeral and could portend nothing but evil to the wedding. Such was its immediate effect on the guests that a cloud seemed to have rolled duskily from beneath the black crape and dimmed the light of the candles. The bridal pair stood up before the minister, but the bride's cold fingers quivered in the tremulous hand of the bridegroom, and her death-like paleness caused a whisper that the maiden who had been buried a few hours before was come from her grave to be married. If ever another wedding were so dismal, it was that famous one where they tolled the wedding-knell.

After performing the ceremony Mr. Hooper raised a glass of wine to his lips, wishing happiness to the new-married couple in a strain of mild pleasantry that ought to have brightened the features of the guests like a cheerful gleam from the hearth. At that instant, catching a glimpse of his figure in the looking-glass, the black veil involved his own spirit in the horror with which it overwhelmed all others. His frame shuddered, his lips grew white, he spilt the untasted wine upon the carpet and rushed forth into the darkness, for the Earth too had on her black veil.

The next day the whole village of Milford talked of little else than Parson Hooper's black veil. That, and the mystery concealed behind it, supplied a topic for discussion between acquaintances meeting in the street and good women gossiping at their open windows. It was the first item of news that the tavernkeeper told to his guests. The children babbled of it on their way to school. One imitative little imp covered his face with an old black hand-kerchief, thereby so affrighting his playmates that the panic seized himself and he wellnigh lost his wits by his own waggery.

It was remarkable that, of all the busybodies and impertinent people in the parish, not one ventured to put the plain question to Mr. Hooper wherefore he did this thing. Hitherto, when-ever there appeared the slightest call for such interference, he had never lacked advisers nor shown himself averse to be guided by their judgment. If he erred at all, it was by so painful a degree of self-distrust that even the mildest censure would lead him to consider an indifferent action as a crime. Yet, though so well acquainted with this amiable weakness, no individual among his parishioners chose to make the black veil a subject of friendly remonstrance. There was a feeling of dread, neither plainly confessed nor carefully concealed, which caused each to shift the responsibility upon another, till at length it was found expedient to send a deputation of the church, in order to deal with Mr. Hooper about the mystery before it should grow into a scandal. Never did an embassy so ill discharge its duties. The minister received them with friendly courtesy, but became silent after they were seated, leaving to his visitors the whole burden of introducing their important business. The topic, it might be supposed, was obvious enough. There was the black veil swathed round Mr. Hooper's forehead and concealing every feature above his placid mouth, on which, at times, they could perceive the glimmering of a melancholy smile. But that piece of crape, to their imagination, seemed to hang down before his heart, the symbol of a fearful secret between him and them. Were the veil but cast aside, they might speak freely of it, but not till then. Thus they sat a considerable time, speechless, confused and shrinking uneasily from Mr. Hooper's eye, which they felt to be fixed upon them with an invisible glance. Finally, the deputies returned abashed to their constituents, pronouncing the matter too weighty to be handled except by a council of the churches, if, indeed, it might not require a General Synod.

But there was one person in the village unappalled by the awe with which the black veil had impressed all besides herself. When the deputies returned without an explanation, or even venturing to demand one, she with the calm energy of her character determined to chase away the strange cloud that appeared to be settling round Mr. Hooper every moment more darkly than before. As his plighted wife it should be her privilege to know what the black veil concealed. At the minister's first visit, therefore, she entered upon the subject with a direct simplicity which made the task easier both for him and her. After he had seated himself she fixed her eyes steadfastly upon the veil, but could discern nothing of the dreadful gloom that had so overawed the multitude; it was but a double fold of crape hanging down from his forehead to his mouth and slightly stirring with his breath.

"No," said she, aloud, and smiling, "there is nothing terrible in this piece of crape, except that it hides a face which I am always glad to look upon. Come, good sir; let the sun shine from behind the cloud. First lay aside your black veil, then tell me why you put it on."

Mr. Hooper's smile glimmered faintly.

"There is an hour to come," said he, "when all of us shall cast aside our veils. Take it not amiss, beloved friend, if I wear this piece of crape till then."

"Your words are a mystery too," returned the young lady. "Take away the veil from them, at least."

"Elizabeth, I will," said he, "so far as my vow may suffer me. Know, then, this veil is a type and a symbol, and I am bound to wear it ever, both in light and darkness, in solitude and before the gaze of multitudes, and as with strangers, so with my familiar friends. No mortal eye will see it withdrawn. This dismal shade must separate me from the world; even you, Elizabeth, can never come behind it."

"What grievous affliction hath befallen you," she earnestly inquired, "that you should thus darken your eyes for ever?"

"If it be a sign of mourning," replied Mr. Hooper, "I, perhaps, like most other mortals, have sorrows dark enough to be typified by a black veil."

"But what if the world will not believe that it is the type of an innocent sorrow?" urged Elizabeth. "Beloved and respected as you are, there may be whispers that you hide your face under the consciousness of secret sin. For the sake of your holy office do away this scandal."

The color rose into her cheeks as she intimated the nature of the rumors that were already abroad in the village. But Mr. Hooper's mildness did not forsake him. He even smiled again—that same sad smile which always appeared like a faint glimmering of light proceeding from the obscurity beneath the veil.

"If I hide my face for sorrow, there is cause enough," he merely replied; "and if I cover it for secret sin, what mortal might not do the same?" And with this gentle but unconquerable obstinacy did he resist all her entreaties.

At length Elizabeth sat silent. For a few moments she appeared lost in thought, considering, probably, what new methods might be tried to withdraw her lover from so dark a fantasy, which, if it had no other meaning, was perhaps a symptom of mental disease. Though of a firmer character than his own, the tears rolled down her cheeks. But in an instant, as it were, a new feeling took the place of sorrow: her eyes were fixed insensibly on the black veil, when like a sudden twilight in the air its terrors fell around her. She arose and stood trembling before him.

"And do you feel it, then, at last?" said he, mournfully.

She made no reply, but covered her eyes with her hand and turned to leave the room. He rushed forward and caught her arm.

"Have patience with me, Elizabeth!" cried he, passionately. "Do not desert me though this veil must be between us here on earth. Be mine, and hereafter there shall be no veil over my face, no darkness between our souls. It is but a mortal veil; it is not for eternity. Oh, you know not how lonely I am, and how frightened to be alone behind my black veil! Do not leave me in this miserable obscurity for ever."

"Lift the veil but once and look me in the face," said she.

"Never! It cannot be!" replied Mr. Hooper.

"Then farewell!" said Elizabeth.

She withdrew her arm from his grasp and slowly departed, pausing at the door to give one long, shuddering gaze that seemed almost to penetrate the mystery of the black veil. But even amid his grief Mr. Hooper smiled to think that only a material emblem had separated him from happiness, though the horrors which it shadowed forth must be drawn darkly between the fondest of lovers.

From that time no attempts were made to remove Mr. Hooper's black veil or by a direct appeal to discover the secret which it was supposed to hide. By persons who claimed a superiority to popular prejudice it was reckoned merely an eccentric whim, such as often mingles with the sober actions of men otherwise rational and tinges them all with its own semblance of insanity. But with the multitude good Mr. Hooper was irreparably a bugbear. He could not walk the street with any peace of mind, so conscious was he that the gentle and timid would turn aside to avoid him, and that others would make it a point of hardihood to throw themselves in his way. The impertinence of the latter class compelled him to give up his customary walk at sunset to the burial-ground; for when he leaned pensively over the gate, there would always be faces behind the gravestones peeping at his black veil. A fable went the rounds that the stare of the dead people drove him thence. It grieved him to the very depth of his kind heart to observe how the children fled from his approach, breaking up their merriest sports while his melancholy figure was yet afar off. Their instinctive dread caused him to feel more strongly than aught else that a preternatural horror was interwoven with the threads of the black crape. In truth, his own antipathy to the veil was known to be so great that he never willingly passed before a mirror nor stooped to drink at a still fountain lest in its peaceful bosom he should be affrighted by himself. This was what gave plausibility to the whispers that Mr. Hooper's conscience tortured him for some great crime too horrible to be entirely concealed or otherwise than so obscurely intimated. Thus from beneath the black veil there rolled a cloud into the sunshine, an ambiguity of sin or sorrow, which enveloped the poor minister, so that love or sympathy could never reach him. It was said that ghost and fiend consorted with him there. With self-shudderings and outward terrors he walked continually in its shadow, groping darkly within his own soul or gazing through a medium that saddened the whole world. Even the lawless wind, it was believed, respected his dreadful secret and never blew aside the veil. But still good Mr. Hooper sadly smiled at the pale visages of the worldly throng as he passed by.

Among all its bad influences, the black veil had the one desirable effect of making its wearer a very efficient clergyman. By the aid of his mysterious emblem—for there was no other apparent cause—he became a man of awful power over souls that were in agony for sin. His converts always regarded him with a dread peculiar to themselves, affirming, though but figuratively, that before he brought them to celestial light they had been with him behind the black veil. Its gloom, indeed, enabled him to sympathize with all dark affections. Dying sinners cried aloud for Mr. Hooper and would not yield their breath till he appeared, though ever, as he stooped to whisper consolation, they shuddered at the veiled face so near their own. Such were the terrors of the black veil even when Death had bared his visage. Strangers came long distances to attend service at his church with the mere idle purpose of gazing at his figure because it was forbidden them to behold his face. But many were made to quake ere they departed. Once, during Governor Belcher's administration, Mr. Hooper was appointed to preach the election sermon. Covered with his black veil, he stood before the chief magistrate, the council and the representatives, and wrought so deep an impression that the legislative measures of that year were characterized by all the gloom and piety of our earliest ancestral sway.

In this manner Mr. Hooper spent a long life, irreproachable in outward act, yet shrouded in dismal suspicions; kind and loving, though unloved and dimly feared; a man apart from men, shunned in their health and joy, but ever summoned to their aid in mortal anguish. As years wore on, shedding their snows above his sable veil, he acquired a name throughout the New England churches, and they called him Father Hooper. Nearly all his parishioners who were of mature age when he was settled had been borne away by many a funeral: he had one congregation in the church and a more crowded one in the churchyard; and, having wrought so late into the evening and done his work so well, it was now good Father Hooper's turn to rest.

Several persons were visible by the shaded candlelight in the death-chamber of the old clergyman. Natural connections he had none. But there was the decorously grave though unmoved physician, seeking only to mitigate the last pangs of the patient whom he could not save. There were the deacons and other eminently pious members of his church. There, also, was the Reverend Mr. Clark of Westbury, a young and zealous divine who had ridden in haste to pray by the bedside of the expiring minister. There was the nurse—no hired handmaiden of Death, but one whose calm affection had endured thus long in secrecy, in solitude, amid the chill of age, and would not perish even at the dying-hour. Who but Elizabeth! And there lay the hoary head of good Father Hooper upon the death-pillow with the black veil still swathed about his brow and reaching down over his face, so that each more difficult gasp of his faint breath caused it to stir. All through life that piece of crape had hung between him and the world; it had separated him from cheerful brotherhood and woman's love and kept him in that saddest of all prisons his own heart; and still it lay upon his face, as if to deepen the gloom of his darksome chamber and shade him from the sunshine of eternity.

For some time previous his mind had been confused, wavering doubtfully between the past and the present, and hovering forward, as it were, at intervals, into the indistinctness of the world to come. There had been feverish turns which tossed him from side to side and wore away what little strength he had. But in his most convulsive struggles and in the wildest vagaries of his intellect, when no other thought retained its sober influence, he still showed an awful solicitude lest the black veil should slip aside. Even if his bewildered soul could have forgotten, there was a faithful woman at his pillow who with averted eyes would have covered that aged face which she had last beheld in the comeliness of manhood.

At length the death-stricken old man lay quietly in the torpor of mental and bodily exhaustion, with an imperceptible pulse and breath that grew fainter and fainter except when a long, deep and irregular inspiration seemed to prelude the flight of his spirit.

The minister of Westbury approached the bedside.

"Venerable Father Hooper," said he, "the moment of your release is at hand. Are you ready for the lifting of the veil that shuts in time from eternity?"

Father Hooper at first replied merely by a feeble motion of his head; then—apprehensive, perhaps, that his meaning might be doubtful—he exerted himself to speak.

"Yea," said he, in faint accents; "my soul hath a patient weariness until that veil be lifted."

"And is it fitting," resumed the Reverend Mr. Clark, "that a man so given to prayer, of such a blameless example, holy in deed and thought, so far as mortal judgment may pronounce,— is it fitting that a father in the Church should leave a shadow on his memory that may seem to blacken a life so pure? I pray you, my venerable brother, let not this thing be! Suffer us to be gladdened by your triumphant aspect as you go to your reward. Before the veil of eternity be lifted let me cast aside this black veil from your face;" and, thus speaking, the Reverend Mr. Clark bent forward to reveal the mystery of so many years.

But, exerting a sudden energy that made all the beholders stand aghast, Father Hooper snatched both his hands from beneath the bedclothes and pressed them strongly on the black veil, resolute to struggle if the minister of Westbury would contend with a dying man.

"Never!" cried the veiled clergyman. "On earth, never!"

"Dark old man," exclaimed the affrighted minister, "with what horrible crime upon your soul are you now passing to the judgment?"

Father Hooper's breath heaved: it rattled in his throat; but, with a mighty effort grasping forward with his hands, he caught hold of life and held it back till he should speak. He even raised himself in bed, and there he sat shivering with the arms of Death around him, while the black veil hung down, awful at that last moment in the gathered terrors of a lifetime. And yet the faint, sad smile so often there now seemed to glimmer from its obscurity and linger on Father Hooper's lips.

"Why do you tremble at me alone?" cried he, turning his veiled face round the circle of pale spectators. "Tremble also at each other. Have men avoided me and women shown no pity and children screamed and fled only for my black veil? What but the mystery which it obscurely typifies has made this piece of crape so awful? When the friend shows his inmost heart to his friend, the lover to his best-beloved; when man does not vainly shrink from the eye of his Creator, loathsomely treasuring up the secret of his sin,—then deem me a monster for the symbol beneath which I have lived and die. I look around me, and, lo! on every visage a black veil!"

While his auditors shrank from one another in mutual affright, Father Hooper fell back upon his pillow, a veiled corpse with a faint smile lingering on the lips. Still veiled, they laid him in his coffin, and a veiled corpse they bore him to the grave. The grass of many years has sprung up and withered on that grave, the burial-stone is moss-grown, and good Mr. Hooper's face is dust; but awful is still the thought that it mouldered beneath the black veil.

Blow It
(1981)

PATRICIA HIGHSMITH

The two other young and unmarried men in the office considered Harry Rowe lucky, very. Harry had two pretty girls in love with him. Sometimes one girl or the other picked him up at his midtown Manhattan office, because Harry often had to stay a half hour or more after the usual quitting time at five or five-thirty, and one girl, Connie, could leave her office rather easily at five. The other girl, Lesley, was a fashion model with irregular hours, but she had been to his office a few times. That was how the firm of five men knew about Harry's girls. Otherwise Harry would have kept his mouth shut, not introduced them to—well, everybody, because someone would have been bound to blabble to one girl about the other girl. Harry did not mind, however, that Dick Hanson knew the situation. Dick was a thirty-five-year-old married man who could be trusted to be discreet, because he must have had experiences along the same lines, and even now had a girlfriend, Harry knew. Dick was a senior partner in the accounting firm of Raymond and Hanson.

Harry really didn't know which girl he preferred, and wanted to give himself time to consider, to choose. These days, Harry thought, lots of girls didn't care about marriage, didn't believe in it, especially at the age of twenty-three, as these girls were. But both Lesley and Connie were quite interested in marriage. They had not proposed to him, but he could tell. This further boosted Harry's ego, because he saw himself as a good catch. What man wouldn't, under such circumstances? That meant, he was earning well (true), and would go on to bigger and better, and also he wasn't bad looking, if he did say so himself (and he did), and he took the trouble to dress in a way that girls liked, always a clean shirt, not always a tie if the occasion didn't demand it, good shoes informal or not, far-out shirts sometimes, safari trousers or shorts maybe on the weekends when he loafed around with Lesley on Saturday and Connie on Sunday, for instance. Harry was a lawyer as well as a Certified Public Accountant.

Lesley Marker, a photographers' model, made even better money than Harry. She had dark brown, straight hair, shining brown eyes, and the loveliest complexion Harry had ever seen, not to mention a divine body, not even too thin, as a lot of models were, or so Harry had always heard. Lesley had a standing date with her parents and grandmother for Sunday lunch, so this ruled out Lesley for Sundays, but there was Friday night and Saturdays. There were of course seven nights in the week, and Lesley could spend the night at his apartment, or he at hers, if she did not have to get up very early. Lesley was always cheerful, it wasn't even an act with her. It was marvelous and refreshing to Harry. She had a sense of humor in bed. She was a delight.

445

Connie Jaeger was different, more mysterious, less open, and certainly she had more moods than Lesley. Harry had to be careful with Connie, subtle, understanding of her moods, which she did not always explain in words. She was an editor in a publishing house. Sometimes she wrote short stories, and showed them to Harry. Two or three she had sold to little magazines. Connie often gave Harry the impression that she was brooding, thinking of things she would not disclose to him. Yet she loved him or was in love with him, of that Harry was sure. Connie was more interesting than Lesley, Harry would have had to admit, if anyone asked him.

Harry had a walk-up apartment on Jane Street, on the fourth floor. It was an old house, but the plumbing worked, the kitchen and bath were nicely painted, and he had a terrace with a roof garden of sorts: the garden was some three yards square, its earth contained within a wooden frame, and the watering drained into a corner hole on the terrace. Harry had acquired deck chairs, metal chairs and a round table. He and Lesley or Connie could lunch or dine out here, and the girls could take naked sunbaths, if they wished, as in a certain corner no one could see them. Lesley did that more often than Connie, who had done it only once, and then not naked entirely. He had met both girls around the same time, about four months ago. Which did he like better? Or love more? Harry could not tell as yet, but he had realized weeks ago that his other girlfriends, two or three, had simply faded away. Harry hadn't rung them up for dates, didn't care to see them. He was in love with two girls at the same time, he supposed. He had heard of it before, and somehow never believed it was possible. He supposed also that Lesley and Connie might think he had other girlfriends, and for all Harry knew, both the girls might be going to bed with other men now and then too. But considering the time they both gave Harry, they hadn't a lot of time, or many nights, for other fellows.

Meanwhile Harry was careful to keep the girls apart, very good about changing his bedsheets, which were drip-dry and which he could hang on a line on his terrace. He was also careful to keep out of sight Lesley's shampoo and Connie's cologne. Twice he had found one of Connie's little crescent-shaped yellow combs in the bed when he changed it, had stuck them in a pocket of one of his raincoats and returned them the next time he saw Connie. He was not going to be tripped up by the usual, the cliché of a hairpin or something like that on the night table.

"I'd love to live in the country," Connie said one night around eleven, lying in his bed naked and smoking a cigarette, with the sheet pulled up to her waist. "Not too far from New York, of course."

"I too," said Harry. He meant it. He was in pajama pants, barefoot, slumped in an armchair with his hands behind his head. A vision of a country house, maybe in Connecticut, maybe Westchester if he could afford it, came into his eyes: white maybe, a bit of lawn, old trees. And with Connie. Yes, Connie. She wanted it. Lesley would always have to spend her nights in New York, Harry thought, because of having to get up so often at six and seven in the morning for the photographers. On the other hand, how long did a model's career last? Harry was ashamed of his thoughts. He and Connie had just spent a wonderful hour in bed. How dare he think of Lesley now! But he did think of Lesley, and he was thinking of her. Would he have to give up those enchanting brown eyes, that smile, that straight brown hair (always with an excellent cut, of course) that looked freshly washed every time he saw it? Yes, he would have to give it up, if he married Connie and slept in Connecticut every night.

"What're you thinking about?" Connie smiled, sleepy looking. Her full lips were lovely without rouge, as they were now.

"Us," said Harry. It was a Sunday night. He had been in the same bed with Lesley last night, and she had left this morning for her Sunday parental lunch.

"Let's do something about it," Connie said in her soft but very definite voice, and put out her cigarette. She held the sheet against her breasts, but one breast was exposed.

Harry stared at the one breast, stupidly. What was he going to do? Stall both girls indefinitely? Enjoy them both and not get married? How long could that go on until one or the other got fed up? Two more months? One month? Some girls moved fast, others hung on. Connie was the patient type, but too intelligent to waste a lot of time. Lesley would fly even sooner, Harry believed, if she thought he was being evasive on the subject of marriage; Lesley would leave him with a smile and without a scene. In that way, the two girls were the same: neither was going to wait forever. Why couldn't a man have two wives?

Lesley, on the following Tuesday evening, brought him flowers, in a pot. "A Japanese something or other. Geranium, I think they said. Anyway the studio would just've thrown it away."

They both went out on the terrace and chose a spot for the new orange-colored plant. Harry had a climbing rose, a large pot of parsley from which he took sprigs when he needed them. He pinched off some now. Harry had bought halibut steaks for their dinner. Lesley was fond of fish. After dinner they watched a television program as they lay on Harry's bed, holding hands. The program became boring, lovemaking more interesting. *Lesley.* Lesley was the girl he wanted, Harry thought. Why should he doubt it? Why debate? She was every bit as pretty as Connie. And Lesley was more cheerful, better balanced. Wouldn't Connie's moods get in the way sometimes, make things difficult—because Harry didn't know how to pull Connie out of them, her silences sometimes, as if she were brooding on something far away, or maybe deep inside her, but she would never enlighten him, therefore he never knew what to say or do.

Around midnight Harry and Lesley went out to a disco three streets away, a modest place as discos went, where the music didn't break your eardrums. Harry had a beer, Lesley a tonic without the gin.

"It's almost as if we're married," Lesley said in a moment when the music was not so loud. She smiled her fresh smile, the corners of her lips went up like a child's. "You're the kind of man I could live with. There are very few."

"Easygoing, eh? No demands," Harry replied in a mocking tone, but his heart was thumping with pride. A couple of fellows at the table on their right were looking at Lesley with envy, even though they had their girls with them.

Harry put Lesley into a taxi a few minutes later. She had to be up by 7:30, and her make-up kit was at her apartment. As he walked back to Jane Street, Harry found himself thinking of Connie. Connie *was* as beautiful as Lesley, if one wanted to think about beauty. Connie didn't earn her living by it, as it happened, as Lesley did. Connie had admirers too, whom she brushed off like gnats, because she preferred him. Harry had seen this. Could he really abandon *Connie*? It was unthinkable! Was he drunk? On two gin-and-tonics before dinner and one beer? Two beers counting the one with dinner? Of course he wasn't drunk. He just couldn't come to a decision. Twenty past midnight now. He was tired. That was logical. People couldn't think after a sixteen-hour day. Could they? Think tomorrow, Harry told himself.

When he got home, the telephone was ringing. Harry ran for it. "Hello?"

"Hello, darling. I just wanted to say good night," Connie said in a quiet, sleepy voice. She always sounded young on the telephone, like a child of twelve sometimes.

"Thanks, my love. You all right?"

"Sure. Reading a manuscript—which is putting me to sleep." Here she sounded as if she were stretching in bed. "Where were you?"

"Out buying cigarettes and milk."

"When do we see each other? Friday? I forgot."

"Friday. Sure." Was she deliberately avoiding Saturday, Lesley's night? Had Connie done this before? Harry couldn't remember. "Come to my place Friday? I'll be home by six-thirty anyway."

The next day, Wednesday, Dick Hanson buzzed Harry's office around ten and said, "Got a little news that might interest you, Harry. Can I come in for a minute?"

"I would be honored," said Harry.

Dick came in smiling, with a couple of photographs in his hand, a manila envelope, a couple of typewritten pages. "House for sale in my neck of the woods," said Dick, after closing Harry's door. "We know the owners, their name is Buck. Anyway, look. See if it interests you."

Harry looked at the two photographs of a Westchester house—white, with a lawn, with grown-up trees, and it looked to him like his dream house, the one that came into his head when he was with Connie or Lesley. Dick explained that the Bucks didn't want to put it with an agent if they could avoid it, that they wanted to sell it quickly at a fair price, because Nelson Buck's company was transferring him to California on short notice, and they had to buy a house in California.

"Ninety thousand dollars," Dick said, "and I can tell you it'd go for a hundred and fifty thousand via an agent. It's five miles from where we live. Think about it, Harry, before it's too late—meaning in the next two or three days. I could see that you get good mortgage terms, because I know the town bank people . . . What do you think?"

Harry had been speechless for several seconds. Could he? Dare he?

Dick Hanson's reddish brown eyes looked down affectionately at Harry, eagerly. Harry had the feeling he stood on the edge of a swimming pool or a diving board, hesitating.

"Handsome, isn't it? Helen and I know the house well, because we're good friends with the Bucks. This is on the up and up. And . . . well, the general impression is that you're going to get married soon. I hope I'm not jumping the gun by saying that." Dick looked as if he were doing anything but talking out of turn, as if Harry were already due for congratulations. "Which girl is it going to be—you lucky swine," Dick drawled with good humor. "You look like the cat—who just swallowed the bird."

Harry was thinking, *I dunno which girl.* But he kept a smug silence, as if he did know.

"You're interested?" Dick asked.

"Sure I'm interested," Harry replied. He held a photograph in each hand.

"Think it over for a couple of days. Take the photos. I brought the envelope. Show them—you know." Dick meant to one of the girls, Harry knew. "It'd be great to be neighbors, Harry. I mean that. We could have fun up there—besides a little useful business on weekends, maybe."

Around three, Dick sent a memo in a sealed envelope to Harry with more information on mortgage terms, and Dick added that Harry couldn't go wrong on this house purchase, even if he didn't intend to get married in the immediate future. An 1850s house in superb condition, three bedrooms, two baths, and the value could only go up.

That afternoon Harry seized ten or fifteen minutes, did some figuring on his computer, and also in his own head with pencil and paper. He could swing the Westchester house, all right. But he wouldn't want to move there alone. Could Lesley live there with him and still commute? At very early hours sometimes? She might not consider a country house worth it. Could Connie? Yes, more easily. She didn't have to get to work till nine-thirty or even ten. But a man didn't choose a wife for her ease of commuting. That was absurd.

Harry's thoughts drifted back to a perfect weekend (Sunday noon till Monday morning), when he and Connie had painted his kitchen bright orange. Wonderful! Connie in already paint-spattered jeans, on the ladder, alternating with him on the ladder—drinking beer, laughing, making love. God! He could see Connie more easily in the Westchester house than Lesley.

By five o'clock, Harry had came to at least one decision, He would take a look at the house, and right away, if possible. He rang Dick's office, caught Dick in the middle of a talk with Raymond, but Harry was able to say, "I'd love to *see* the house. Can I maybe drive up with you this evening?"

"Absolutely! Stay overnight with us? See it in the morning too?—I'll give Helen a blast. She'll be pleased, Harry."

So at 6 P.M. Harry walked with Dick to his garage, and got into Dick's car. It was a pleasant drive of less than forty minutes, Dick in cheerful mood, and not trying to query Harry again about which girl it might be. Dick talked about the easy driving, the easy route he was taking. Harry was thinking that he would have to acquire a car too. But that would still be within his financial possibilities. His parents in Florida would give him a car as a wedding present, Harry was sure, if he dropped a hint. No problem there.

"You seem to have pre-marital tension," Dick remarked.

"No. Ha-ha." Harry supposed he had been silent for several minutes.

They went to the Bucks' house first, because it was on the way, and because Dick wanted Harry to see the place and sleep on it. Dick said he had not bothered telephoning Julie Buck, because he knew the Bucks so well, and Julie was quite informal.

Julie welcomed them with a smile on the white front porch.

Harry and Dick went into a large hall which had a polished wooden staircase, carpeted, three handsome rooms going off the hall, one being the library. Julie said she was packing up the books, and there were cartons of books on the floor, some of the shelves empty. The Bucks' ten-year-old son, in blue jeans with holes in the knees, followed them around, tossing his football in his hands and eyeing Harry with curiosity.

"Very good apple trees. You'll have to give the apples away to the neighbors, they're so many," Julie said as they gazed from a second-story window.

The lawn sloped beautifully downward from the back of the house. Julie said something about a brook in the hollow beyond, which marked property boundary. The upstairs bedrooms were square and generous, the two baths not the last word in modernity but somehow just right for the country. The upstairs hall had a window front and back of the house. Harry was sold, though he didn't at once say so.

"I like it. But I've got to think, you know," Harry said. "A couple of days, Dick said I had."

"Oh, of course. You ought to look at some other houses too," said Julie. "Of course we love this one. And we'd like to think of a friend of the Hansons taking it over."

Julie insisted on giving them a scotch before they left. Dick and Harry drank theirs standing up in the living room, which had a fireplace. The scotch was neat and tasted lovely. Wouldn't it be great to be master of such a house, Harry was thinking. And which girl would be mistress? He had a vision of Lesley walking through the door from the hall, bearing a tray of something, smiling her divine smile. And almost immediately he saw Connie strolling through, blonde, calm and gentle, lifting her blue eyes to meet his.

Good Christ!

That night, after roast beef, cheese and wine at the Hansons', Harry hoped he would have a dream that might enlighten him about Connie and Lesley. Connie or Lesley. He did not dream at all, or if he did, he did not remember any dream. He awakened to blue-flowered wallpaper, maple furniture, sunlight streaming into his room, and thought, *this* was the kind of life he wanted. Fresh air, no city grit.

Dick and Harry departed at 8:30 with well-wishes from Helen, who hoped as much as Dick that Harry would opt for the Bucks' house. In the early morning, Harry fell more deeply in love with the white house which could, with a word and a check, be his. One solution was, Harry thought, to speak to both girls and ask them straight out if they would like such a house, in such a location, and—either Lesley or Connie might say no. Maybe for different reasons. Lesley might find it impossible with her present work. Connie might prefer a house in Long Island. Harry hated feeling vague, but what else could he do? How else could he feel?

When Harry tried to get down to it, asking the question, in the next days, he found that he couldn't. He spent one night at Connie's manuscript-and-book-cluttered apartment, and couldn't get the question out. That was Thursday night. Was he really hanging onto Lesley, therefore, because he preferred Lesley? But the same thing happened with Lesley during a hasty Friday lunch. Harry was rather obliged to give an answer to Dick that day. The Bucks were leaving Tuesday, and Monday was the date for putting the house on the market, before their departure for California. Harry had considered looking at other houses in the area, but the low price of the Bucks' house made the effort appear absurd. From a glance at newspaper ads, Harry saw that the Bucks' property was a bargain, with its acreage. Harry pulled himself together at the end of the lunch with Lesley, and said:

"I've seen a house—"

Lesley looked at him over her coffee cup. "Yes? What house?"

"House for sale, Westchester. In the area where Dick Hanson lives. You know, Dick in my office. You've met him."

They went on from there. Harry told her about spending the night at Dick's, that the house was a bargain and about thirty-five minutes from Manhattan, a railway station two miles away, a bus also.

Lesley looked dubious, or hesitant. She was concerned about the commuting angle. They didn't even mention marriage, maybe because Lesley took that for granted, Harry thought.

"The problem is, it's such a bargain, they want an answer now, or it'll be put with an agent Monday at a higher price. The house."

Lesley said she'd love to see the place, anyway, since Harry seemed to like it so much, and maybe they could go up tomorrow? Saturday? Harry said he was sure he could arrange that, either through Dick or the Bucks who would probably not mind at all picking them up at the railway station or the bus stop. That afternoon, Harry spoke with Dick Hanson about a Saturday afternoon appointment with the Bucks. Dick said he would ring Norman Buck at his New York office and fix it. By 4:30 that afternoon, Harry had a date with Norman, who would meet the train that left from Grand Central and got in at Gresham, Westchester, at 3:30.

Harry had a date that evening with Connie, who was to come to his apartment. Harry did some shopping in his neighborhood, having decided to speak to Connie at home and not in a restaurant. He was so nervous, a bottle of red wine slipped from his hands and broke on the kitchen floor, before Connie arrived. Fortunately he had another bottle in his rack, and it was so warm Connie might prefer beer, but the wine had been a good one.

He had come to a desperate but at the same time not very clear conclusion that afternoon just before leaving the office: he would invite *both* girls to see the Westchester house. He could at least see which girl liked the house better. Maybe there would be a scene, maybe there wouldn't be. Maybe they'd both say no. At least it would clear the atmosphere. Harry had not been able to concentrate during the afternoon, and had scraped through the minimum of work that he should have done. He had reasoned: if he showed the house to the girls one at a time, what then? Suppose both Lesley and Connie liked the house equally? Would he have come to any decision about Connie or Lesley even then? No. He somehow had to confront both of them, and himself, with the Westchester house at the same time. Since the girls had never met, this presented a different problem: introduce them at Grand Central, and they would all ride up on the same train? This seemed unthinkable.

Harry poured himself a straight scotch, not a big one, and lifted it with a shaking hand. There were times when a person needed steadying, he thought, and this was one of them. Harry remembered that he had said after lunch with Lesley today that he would ring her back about a time to meet tomorrow to go up to Westchester. He hadn't rung Lesley, however. Why not? Well, for one thing, more than half the time he didn't know where to ring her, because of her hopping around at her work. Should he try her at her apartment now? As Harry frowned at his telephone, it rang.

It was Lesley.

Harry smiled, "I was just about to call *you*."

"Did you make any arrangement about tomorrow?"

Harry said he had, and stammered out something about the train from Grand Central at 3 P.M. or a couple of minutes before. Lesley asked him why he was so nervous.

"I dunno," Harry said, and Lesley laughed.

"If you've got it all arranged with the Bucks, don't change anything, but I can't make it by three, I know," Lesley said. "Werner—you know, Werner Ludwig, he needs me at two tomorrow, and I know he'll need an hour anyway, but the good thing is, he lives near that town you mentioned."

"Gresham?"

"That's it, and he said he'd be glad to take me up with him in his car. I think he even knows the Bucks' house. So I could be there by four, I should think."

Suddenly that problem was solved, for Harry. Or postponed, he thought, the girls' meeting. At least they wouldn't be meeting in Grand Central.

They hung up, and the doorbell rang. Connie had his key (so did Lesley), but Connie always buzzed when she knew he was home.

Harry's nerves did not improve during the evening. He was cheerful, even made Connie laugh once, but be felt that his hands were shaking. When he looked at his hands, they were not shaking.

"Jitters already, and you haven't even signed anything?" Connie asked. "You don't have to take *this* house. It's the first one you've looked at up there, isn't it? Nobody buys the first thing they see." Connie spoke in her serious, logical way.

He was no good in bed that night. Connie thought it funny, but not as funny as Lesley would have. Connie had brought two manuscripts. They slept late on Saturday morning (Harry had at last fallen asleep after hours of trying to, and trying to be motionless so as not to disturb Connie), and she read one of the manuscripts after their brunch, until it was time to leave for Grand Central. They took a taxi to the station. Connie read the second manuscript, absorbed and silent, during the short ride, and was not even half through the script when they got to Gresham, doing as usual her careful job, Harry was sure.

Dick Hanson met them, not Nelson Buck as Harry had expected.

"Welcome, Harry!" Dick said, all smiles. "So it's—" He looked at Connie.

"Connie Jaeger," Harry said. "You've met her, I think. I know."

Dick and Connie exchanged "Hellos" and they got into Dick's car, Harry in the back seat, and off they went into the countryside. Twenty to four. Would Lesley be there ahead of time? Would it be any worse than her coming five minutes *after* they got to the Bucks'? No. Should he mention now that he was expecting someone else? Harry tried rehearsing the first sentence, and realized that he couldn't have got the first words out. Maybe Lesley wouldn't be able to make it, after all. Maybe Werner had had a puncture, was going to be delayed? And what then?

"There's the house," said Dick as he made a turn in the road.

"Oh. Very lovely;" said Connie, quietly and politely.

Connie never went overboard about anything, Harry reminded himself, with a little comfort.

Harry saw a car in front of the Bucks' house on the curving graveled driveway. Then Harry saw Lesley come out the front door, onto the porch, with Julie Buck.

"Well, well, they've got visitors," said Dick, pulling his handbrake.

"My friend Lesley," Harry mumbled. Did he black out for the next seconds? He opened the car door for Connie.

Much chatter, introductions.

"Connie—this is Lesley—Marker. Connie Jaeger," Harry said.

"How do you do?" the girls said simultaneously, looking each other in the eyes, as if each was trying to memorize the other's face. Their smiles were polite and minimal.

Dick shuffled, brushed his hands together for no reason, and said, "Well, shall we all go in and look around? May we, Julie?"

"Su-ure! That's what we're here for!" said Julie cheerfully, not digging a whit of the situation, Harry realized.

Harry felt that he walked into purgatory, into hell, into another life, or maybe death. The girls were stiff as pokers, didn't even look at him as they all walked from room to room. Julie gave them a guided tour, mentioning defects and assets, and as on many a guided tour, Harry felt, some of the tourists were not listening. He caught the girls sizing each other up with lightning glances, which were followed by an ignoring of each other. Dick Hanson wore a puzzled frown, even when he looked at Harry.

"What's going on?" Dick whispered to Harry, when he could.

Harry shrugged. It was more like a twitch, though he tried for a desperate couple of seconds to say something intelligent or normal to Dick. He couldn't. The situation was bizarre, the rooms, the house suddenly meaningless, their parading back down the stairs as useless as some rehearsal in a play in which no one had any interest.

"*Thank* you, Mrs. Buck," Lesley was saying with careful politeness in the downstairs hall.

Lesley's friend, who had brought her, had evidently departed, because his car was gone, Harry saw. Connie looked at him with her quiet, knowing smile. Her smile was not friendly, but rather amused.

"Harry, if you—"

"I'm afraid it's off," Harry said, interrupting Dick. "Off, yes." Dick still looked puzzled. So did both the Bucks, maybe Julie Buck less so.

The end, Harry thought. *Ruin, finish.* He tried to stand up straighter but mentally he was on the floor, crawling along like a worm.

"Maybe you'd like to talk a little—by yourselves," said Nelson Buck to Harry and the girls, gesturing toward the library on his right, which now had more cartons on the floor and fewer books on the shelves. His gesture, his glance had included Harry and the two girls.

Did Nelson Buck think he maintained a harem, Harry wondered.

"No," said Lesley, coolly. "Not your fault, Mr. Buck. It's a lovely house. Really. Thank you too, Mrs. Buck. I think I must be on my way, because of an appointment in New York tonight. Maybe I can phone for a taxi?"

"Oh, I can take you to the station!" said Nelson.

"Or I can," said Dick. "No problem."

It was agreed that Dick would take Lesley, now. Harry walked out with them to Dick's car. Dick went ahead of them, and opened his car door.

Lesley said to Harry, "What was the idea, Harry? That we'd *both* commute?" She laughed aloud, and in it Harry heard a little bitterness but also a real amusement. "I knew you had a friend, but *this*—It's a bit much, isn't it? Bye-bye, Harry."

"*How* did you know?" Harry asked.

Lesley had got into the front seat. "Easy," she said in her easy voice.

"Not coming, Harry?" Dick asked.

"No. I'll stay here with Connie. Bye-bye, Lesley."

Harry turned back to the house as they drove off. Stay here with Connie? What was *she* going to say? Harry walked back into the hall.

Connie and Julie and Nelson Buck were conversing pleasantly in the big hall, Connie with her hand on the newel post, one trousered leg and sneakered foot extended. Her face was smiling, her eyes steady as she looked at Harry. The Bucks faded away, Julie to the rear of the house somewhere, Nelson into the living room on Harry's right.

"I'll be going too," said Connie, not changing her stance. "I hope you'll be happy with Lesley."

"*Lesley?*" said Harry in a tone of astonishment. It had simply come out of him. He had nothing to say afterward.

Connie gave a silent laugh, shrugged her shoulders. "Nice to meet her finally. I knew she existed."

Were Harry's cheeks warm because of shame? He was not sure. "How?"

"Lots of little things. The dishes were always stacked differently when I turned up on Sundays. Different from Wednesdays maybe. Little things." Slowly she got a cigarette from her canvas jacket pocket, having put her briefcase with her manuscripts in it on the floor between her feet.

Harry sprang to light the cigarette for her, but Connie swung herself slightly, out of his reach, and had the cigarette lit. He had lost her, Harry knew. "I'm sorry, Connie."

"Are you? I don't know. You couldn't have got your *dates* mixed," she said, not like a question, not quite like a statement either, something in between. Connie's serious, straight blue eyes, her shake of her head seemed to penetrate Harry's body from his head down to his feet. Connie was finished, had said good-bye to him, inside. "My taxi's there," Connie said, looking past Harry through the open front door. She went down the hall to find Julie.

Then Connie went out to the taxi, talked to the Bucks for an instant through the open taxi window, before the taxi moved off.

The Bucks came into the house, both looking puzzled, Julie barely managing a faint smile, absurd below her frown.

"Well," Nelson said, a little heavily.

The moment was relieved by Dick's car crunching up the driveway. Both the Bucks turned to it as if it were a lifesaver. How soon could he take off, Harry was thinking. Thank God for Dick! Dick could whisk him off. Unthinkable that Harry would have taken the same train as one of the girls, or both of them.

"Harry, old boy," Dick said, then added, as Nelson had and in the same tone, "Well!"

"Maybe you two would like a word by yourselves," said Nelson to Dick and Harry.

"I should be leaving," Harry said. "I thank you both—for your time."

A few more polite phrases, then Harry was in Dick's car, rolling away.

"Harry, what in the name of God," Dick began in the gruff tone of a senior brother, a man of the world who had made some mistakes in life but learned a little from them.

"I think I did it deliberately," Harry said. The words came out before his brain had formed them, or so he felt. "I couldn't make up my mind. I had to—get rid of them both. I love them *both*."

"Rubbish! Well, it isn't rubbish, I don't mean that. Something—could've been arranged . . . But my God, Harry, to bring them both like that! I had the feeling they hadn't met before."

"They hadn't."

"Come to our place and have a drink. Won't hurt you."

"No, thanks," Harry said. He knew they were heading for Dick's house. "I'd better get to the station, if you don't mind."

Harry insisted, over Dick's protests. Dick wanted to put him up for the night, have a talk with him. Dick knew the next train, and it would not be the train the girls would have taken. There were quite a few trains, Dick said, and probably the girls had taken different ones, and anyway there was plenty of room on the trains, so they needn't have ridden in the same car. On the way to the station, Dick began again his speech about there being a way to patch things up, to decide which girl he wanted, and then either drop the other girl or hang onto her in some way.

"They're both *lovely*," Dick said. "I can understand your problem! Believe me, Harry! But don't give up. You look like a guy who's just been through a war. Don't be silly. You can patch things up."

"Not with those girls. No," Harry said. "That's why I liked them so. They're different."

Dick shook his head in despair. They had arrived at the station. Harry bought his ticket. Then Harry and Dick shook hands with a hard grip that left Harry's hand tingling for a couple of minutes. Harry walked alone onto the platform and waited, then the train came and he rode back to Grand Central. Deliberately. He knew he had done it deliberately. He had somehow wanted to do this, break it all up, but what did he have now? People said the world was full of girls, pretty girls. True maybe. But not many as interesting as Lesley and Connie.

During the next week the girls came, separately, and picked up their few belongings from Harry's Jane Street apartment, each leaving her key under his doormat.

Sweat
(1926)

ZORA NEALE HURSTON

It was eleven o'clock of a Spring night in Florida. It was Sunday. Any other night, Delia Jones would have been in bed for two hours by this time. But she was a washwoman, and Monday morning meant a great deal to her. So she collected the soiled clothes on Saturday when she returned the clean things. Sunday night after church, she sorted them and put the white things to soak. It saved her almost a half day's start. A great hamper in the bedroom held the clothes that she brought home. It was so much neater than a number of bundles lying around.

She squatted in the kitchen floor beside the great pile of clothes, sorting them into small heaps according to color, and humming a song in a mournful key, but wondering through it all where Sykes, her husband, had gone with her horse and buckboard.

Just then something long, round, limp and black fell upon her shoulders and slithered to the floor beside her. A great terror took hold of her. It softened her knees and dried her mouth so that it was a full minute before she could cry out or move. Then she saw that it was the big bull whip her husband liked to carry when he drove.

She lifted her eyes to the door and saw him standing there bent over with laughter at her fright. She screamed at him.

"Sykes, what you throw dat whip on me like dat? You know it would skeer me—looks just like a snake, an' you knows how skeered Ah is of snakes."

"Course Ah knowed it! That's how come Ah done it." He slapped his leg with his hand and almost rolled on the ground in his mirth. "If you such a big fool dat you got to have a fit over a earth worm or a string, Ah don't keer how bad Ah skeer you."

"You aint got no business doing it. Gawd knows it's a sin. Some day Ah'm gointuh drop dead from some of yo' foolishness. 'Nother thing, where you been wid mah rig? Ah feeds dat pony. He aint fuh you to be drivin' wid no bull whip."

"You sho is one aggravatin' nigger woman!" he declared and stepped into the room. She resumed her work and did not answer him at once. "Ah done tole you time and again to keep them white folks' clothes outa dis house."

He picked up the whip and glared down at her. Delia went on with her work. She went out into the yard and returned with a galvanized tub and sat it on the washbench. She saw that Sykes had kicked all of the clothes together again, and now stood in her way truculently, his whole manner hoping, *praying*, for an argument. But she walked calmly around him and commenced to re-sort the things.

457

"Next time, Ah'm gointer kick' em outdoors," he threatened as he struck a match along the leg of his corduroy breeches.

Delia never looked up from her work, and her thin, stooped shoulders sagged further.

"Ah aint for no fuss t'night, Sykes. Ah just come from taking sacrament at the church house."

He snorted scornfully. "Yeah, you just come from de church house on a Sunday night, but heah you is gone to work on them clothes. You ain't nothing but a hypocrite. One of them amen-corner Christians—sing, whoop, and shout; then come home and wash white folks clothes on the Sabbath."

He stepped roughly upon the whitest pile of things, kicking them helter-skelter as he crossed the room. His wife gave a little scream of dismay, and quickly gathered them together again.

"Sykes, you quit grindin' dirt into these clothes! How can Ah git through by Sat'day if Ah don't start on Sunday?"

"Ah don't keer if you never git through. Anyhow, Ah done promised Gawd and a couple of other men, Ah aint gointer have it in mah house. Don't gimme no lip neither, else Ah'll throw 'em out and put mah fist up side yo' head to boot."

Delia's habitual meekness seemed to slip from her shoulders like a blown scarf. She was on her feet; her poor little body, her bare knuckly hands bravely defying the strapping hulk before her.

"Looka heah, Sykes, you done gone too fur. Ah been married to you fur fifteen years, and Ah been takin' in washin' fur fifteen years. Sweat, sweat, sweat! Work and sweat, cry and sweat, pray and sweat!"

"What's that got to do with me?" he asked brutally.

"What's it got to do with you, Sykes? Mah tub of suds is filled yo' belly with vittles more times than yo' hands is filled it. Mah sweat is done paid for this house and Ah reckon Ah kin keep on sweatin' in it."

She seized the iron skillet from the stove and struck a defensive pose, which act surprised him greatly, coming from her. It cowed him and he did not strike her as he usually did.

"Naw you won't," she panted, "that ole snaggle-toothed black woman you runnin' with aint comin' heah to pile up on *mah* sweat and blood. You aint paid for nothin' on this place, and Ah'm gointer stay right heah till Ah'm toted out foot foremost."

"Well, you better quit gittin' me riled up, else they'll be totin' you out sooner than you expect. Ah'm so tired of you Ah don't know whut to do. Gawd! how Ah hates skinny wimmen!"

A little awed by this new Delia, he sidled out of the door and slammed the back gate after him. He did not say where he had gone, but she knew too well. She knew very well that he would not return until nearly daybreak also. Her work over, she went on to bed but not to sleep at once. Things had come to a pretty pass!

She lay awake, gazing upon the debris that cluttered their matrimonial trail. Not an image left standing along the way. Anything like flowers had long ago been drowned in the salty stream that had been pressed from her heart. Her tears, her sweat, her blood. She had brought love to the union and he had brought a longing after the flesh. Two months after the wedding, he had given her the first brutal beating. She had the memory of his numerous trips to Orlando with all of his wages when he had returned to her penniless, even before the first year had passed. She was young and soft then, but now she thought of her knotty, muscled limbs, her harsh knuckly hands, and drew herself up into an unhappy little ball in the middle of the big feather bed. Too late now to hope for love, even if it were not Bertha it would be someone else. This case differed from the others only in that she was bolder than the others. Too late for everything except her little home. She had built it for her old days, and planted one by one the trees and flowers there. It was lovely to her, lovely.

Somehow, before sleep came, she found herself saying aloud: "Oh well, whatever goes over the Devil's back, is got to come under his belly. Sometime or ruther, Sykes, like everybody else, is gointer reap his sowing." After that she was able to build a spiritual earthworks against her husband. His shells could no longer reach her. *Amen.* She went to sleep and slept until he announced his presence in bed by kicking her feet and rudely snatching the covers away.

"Gimme some kivah heah, an' git yo' damn foots over on yo' own side! Ah oughter mash you in yo' mouf fuh drawing dat skillet on me."

Delia went clear to the rail without answering him. A triumphant indifference to all that he was or did.

The week was as full of work for Delia as all other weeks, and Saturday found her behind her little pony, collecting and delivering clothes.

It was a hot, hot day near the end of July. The village men on Joe Clarke's porch even chewed cane listlessly. They did not hurl the cane-knots as usual. They let them dribble over the edge of the porch. Even conversation had collapsed under the heat.

"Heah come Delia Jones," Jim Merchant said, as the shaggy pony came 'round the bend of the road toward them. The rusty buckboard was heaped with baskets of crisp, clean laundry.

"Yep," Joe Lindsay agreed. "Hot or col', rain or shine, jes ez reg'lar ez de weeks roll roun' Delia carries 'em an' fetches 'em on Sat'day."

"She better if she wanter eat," said Moss. "Sykes Jones aint wuth de shot an' powder hit would tek tuh kill 'em. Not to *huh* he aint."

"He sho' aint," Walter Thomas chimed in. "It's too bad, too, cause she wuz a right pritty lil trick when he got huh. Ah'd uh mah'ied huh mahseff if he hadnter beat me to it."

Delia nodded briefly at the men as she drove past.

"Too much knockin' will ruin *any* 'oman. He done beat huh 'nough tuh kill three women, let 'lone change they looks," said Elijah Moseley. "How Sykes kin stommuck dat big black greasy Mogul he's layin' roun' wid, gits me. Ah swear dat eight-rock couldn't kiss a sardine can Ah done thowed out de back do' 'way las' yeah."

"Aw, she's fat, thass how come. He's allus been crazy 'bout fat women," put in Merchant. "He'd a' been tied up wid one long time ago if he could a' found one tuh have him. Did Ah tell yuh 'bout him come sidlin' roun' *mah* wife—bringin' her a basket uh peecans outa his yard fuh a present? Yeah, mah wife! She tol' him tuh take 'em right straight back home, cause Delia works so hard ovah dat washtub she reckon everything on de place taste lak sweat an' soapsuds. Ah jus' wisht Ah'd a' caught 'im 'roun' dere! Ah'd a' made his hips ketch on fiah down dat shell road."

"Ah know he done it, too. Ah sees 'im grinnin' at every 'oman dat passes," Walter Thomas said. "But even so, he useter eat some mighty big hunks uh humble pie tuh git dat lil' 'oman he got. She wuz ez pritty ez a speckled pup! Dat wuz fifteen yeahs ago. He useter be so skeered uh losin' huh, she could make him do some parts of a husband's duty. Dey never wuz de same in de mind."

"There oughter be a law about him," said Lindsay. "He aint fit tuh carry guts tuh a bear."

Clarke spoke for the first time. "Taint no law on earth dat kin make a man be decent if it aint in 'im. There's plenty men dat takes a wife lak dey do a joint uh sugar-cane. It's round, juicy an' sweet when dey gits it. But dey squeeze an' grind, squeeze an' grind an' wring tell dey wring every drop uh pleasure dat's in 'em out. When dey's satisfied dat dey is wrung dry, dey treats 'em jes lak dey do a cane-chew. Dey thows 'em away. Dey knows whut dey is doin' while dey is at it, an' hates theirselves fuh it but they keeps on hangin' after huh tell she's empty. Den dey hates huh fuh bein' a cane-chew an' in de way."

"We oughter take Sykes an' dat stray 'oman uh his'n down in Lake Howell swamp an' lay on de rawhide till they cain't say Lawd a' mussy. He allus wuz uh ovahbearin' niggah, but since dat white 'oman from up north done teached 'im how to run a automobile, he done got too biggety to live—an' we oughter kill 'im," Old Man Anderson advised.

A grunt of approval went around the porch. But the heat was melting their civic virtue and Elijah Moseley began to bait Joe Clarke.

"Come on, Joe, git a melon outa dere an' slice it up for yo' customers. We'se all sufferin' wid de heat. De bear's done got *me!*"

"Thass right, Joe, a watermelon is jes' whut Ah needs tuh cure de eppizudicks." Walter Thomas joined forces with Moseley. "Come on dere, Joe. We all is steady customers an' you aint set us up in a long time. Ah chooses dat long, bowlegged Floridy favorite."

"A god, an' be dough. You all gimme twenty cents and slice away," Clarke retorted, "Ah needs a col' slice m'self. Heah, everybody chip in. Ah'll lend y'all mah meat knife."

The money was quickly subscribed and the huge melon brought forth. At that moment, Sykes and Bertha arrived. A determined silence fell on the porch and the melon was put away again.

Merchant snapped down the blade of his jack-knife and moved toward the store door.

"Come on in, Joe, an' gimme a slab uh sow belly an' uh pound uh coffee—almost fuhgot 'twas Sat'day. Got to git on home." Most of the men left also.

Just then Delia drove past on her way home, as Sykes was ordering magnificently for Bertha. It pleased him for Delia to see.

"Git whutsoever yo' heart desires, Honey. Wait a minute, Joe. Give huh two botles uh strawberry soda-water, uh quart uh parched ground-peas, an a block uh chewin' gum."

With all this they left the store, with Sykes reminding Bertha that this was his town and she could have it if she wanted it.

The men returned soon after they left, and held their watermelon feast.

"Where did Sykes Jones git dat 'oman from nohow?" Lindsay asked.

"Ovah Apopka. Guess dey musta been cleanin' out de town when she lef'. She don't look lak a thing but a hunk uh liver wid hair on it."

"Well, she sho' kin squall," Dave Carter contributed. "When she gits ready tuh laff, she jes' opens huh mouf an' latches it back tuh de las' notch. No ole grandpa alligator down in Lake Bell aint got nothin' on huh."

Bertha had been in town three months now. Sykes was still paying her room rent at Della Lewis'—the only house in town that would have taken her in. Sykes took her frequently to Winter Park to "stomps." He still assured her that he was the swellest man in the state.

"Sho' you kin have dat lil' ole house soon's Ah kin git dat 'oman outa dere. Everything b'longs tuh me an' you sho' kin have it. Ah sho' 'bominates uh skinny 'oman. Lawdy, you sho' is got one portly shape on you! You kin git *anything* you wants. Dis is *mah* town an' you sho' kin have it."

Delia's work-worn knees crawled over the earth in Gethsemane and up the rocks of Calvary many, many times during these months. She avoided the villagers and meeting places in her efforts to be blind and deaf. But Bertha nullified this to a degree, by coming to Delia's house to call Sykes out to her at the gate.

Delia and Sykes fought all the time now with no peaceful interludes. They slept and ate in silence. Two or three times Delia had attempted a timid friendliness, but she was repulsed each time. It was plain that the breaches must remain agape.

❀

The sun had burned July to August. The heat streamed down like a million hot arrows, smiting all things living upon the earth. Grass withered, leaves browned, snakes went blind in shedding and men and dogs went mad. Dog days!

Delia came home one day and found Sykes there before her. She wondered, but started to go on into the house without speaking, even though he was standing in the kitchen door and she must either stoop under his arm or ask him to move. He made no room for her. She noticed a soap box beside the steps, but paid no particular attention to it, knowing that he must have brought it there. As she was stooping to pass under his outstretched arm, he suddenly pushed her backward, laughingly.

"Look in de box dere Delia, Ah done brung yuh somethin'!"

She nearly fell upon the box in her stumbling, and when she saw what it held, she all but fainted outright.

"Sykes! Sykes, mah Gawd! You take dat rattlesnake 'way from heah! You *gottuh.* Oh, Jesus, have mussy!"

"Ah aint gut tuh do nuthin' uh de kin'—fact is Ah aint got tuh do nothin' but die. Taint no use uh you puttin' on airs makin' out lak you skeered uh dat snake—he's gointer stay right heah tell he die. He wouldn't bite me cause Ah knows how tuh handle 'im. Nohow he wouldn't risk breakin' out his fangs 'gin *yo'* skinny laigs. "

"Naw, now Sykes, don't keep dat thing 'roun' heah tuh skeer me tuh death. You knows Ah'm even feared uh earth worms. Thass de biggest snake Ah evah did see. Kill 'im Sykes, please."

"Doan ast me tuh do nothin' fuh yuh. Goin' 'roun' tryin' tuh be so damn asterperious. Naw, Ah aint gonna kill it. Ah think uh damn sight mo' uh him dan you! Dat's a nice snake an' anybody doan lak 'im kin jes' hit de grit."

The village soon heard that Sykes had the snake, and came to see and ask questions.

"How de hen-fire did you ketch dat six-foot rattler, Sykes?" Thomas asked.

"He's full uh frogs so he caint hardly move, thass how Ah eased up on 'm. But Ah'm a snake charmer an' knows how tuh handle 'em. Shux, dat aint nothin'. Ah could ketch one eve'y day if Ah so wanted tuh."

"Whut he needs is a heavy hick'ry club leaned real heavy on his head. Dat's de bes 'way tuh charm a rattlesnake."

"Naw, Walt, y'll jes' don't understand dese diamon' backs lak Ah do," said Sykes in a superior tone of voice.

The village agreed with Walter, but the snake stayed on. His box remained by the kitchen door with its screen wire covering. Two or three days later it had digested its meal of frogs and literally came to life. It rattled at every movement in the kitchen or the yard. One day as Delia came down the kitchen steps she saw his chalky-white fangs curved like scimitars hung in the wire meshes. This time she did not run away with averted eyes as usual. She stood for a long time in the doorway in a red fury that grew bloodier for every second that she regarded the creature that was her torment.

That night she broached the subject as soon as Sykes sat down to the table.

"Sykes, Ah wants you tuh take dat snake 'way fum heah. You done starved me an' Ah put up widcher, you done beat me an Ah took dat, but you done kilt all mah insides bringin' dat varmint heah."

Sykes poured out a saucer full of coffee and drank it deliberately before he answered her.

"A whole lot Ah keer 'bout how you feels inside uh out. Dat snake aint goin' no damn wheah till Ah gits ready fuh 'im tuh go. So fur as beatin' is concerned, yuh aint took near all dat you gointer take ef yuh stay 'roun' *me*."

Delia pushed back her plate and got up from the table. "Ah hates you, Sykes," she said calmly. "Ah hates you tuh de same degree dat Ah useter love yuh. Ah done took an' took till mah belly is full up tuh mah neck. Dat's de reason Ah got mah letter fum de church an' moved mah membership tuh Woodbridge—so Ah don't haftuh take no sacrament wid yuh. Ah don't wantuh see yuh 'roun' me a tall. Lay 'roun' wid dat 'oman all yuh wants tuh, but gwan 'way fum me an' mah house. Ah hates yuh lak uh suck-egg dog."

Sykes almost let the huge wad of corn bread and collard greens he was chewing fall out of his mouth in amazement. He had a hard time whipping himself up to the proper fury to try to answer Delia.

"Well, Ah'm glad you does hate me. Ah'm sho' tiahed uh you hangin' ontuh me. Ah don't want yuh. Look at yuh stringey ole neck! Yo' rawbony laigs an' arms is enough tuh cut uh man tuh death. You looks jes' lak de devvul's doll-baby tuh *me*. You cain't hate me no worse dan Ah hates you. Ah been hatin' *you* fuh years."

"Yo' ole black hide don't look lak nothin' tuh me, but uh passele uh wrinkled up rubber, wid yo' big ole yeahs flappin' on each side lak uh paih uh buzzard wings. Don't think Ah'm gointuh be run 'way fum mah house neither. Ah'm goin' tuh de white folks bout *you*, mah young man, de very nex' time you lay yo' han's on me. Mah cup is done run ovah." Delia said this with no signs of fear and Sykes departed from the house, threatening her, but made not the slightest move to carry out any of them.

That night he did not return at all, and the next day being Sunday, Delia was glad that she did not have to quarrel before she hitched up her pony and drove the four miles to Woodbridge.

She stayed to the night service—"love feast"—which was very warm and full of spirit. In the emotional winds her domestic trials were borne far and wide so that she sang as she drove homeward,

> *Jurden water, black an' col'*
> *Chills de body, not de soul*
> *An' Ah wantah cross Jurden in uh calm time.*

She came from the barn to the kitchen door and stopped.

"Whut's de mattah, ol' satan, you aint kickin' up yo' racket?" She addressed the snake's box. Complete silence. She went on into the house with a new hope in its birth struggles. Perhaps her threat to go to the white folks had frightened Sykes! Perhaps he was sorry! Fifteen years of misery and suppression had brought Delia to the place where she would hope *anything* that looked towards a way over or through her wall of inhibitions.

She felt in the match safe behind the stove at once for a match. There was only one there.

"Dat niggah wouldn't fetch nothin' heah tuh save his rotten neck, but he kin run thew whut Ah brings quick enough. Now he done toted off nigh on tuh haff uh box uh matches. He done had dat 'oman heah in mah house, too."

Nobody but a woman could tell how she knew this even before she struck the match. But she did and it put her into a new fury.

Presently she brought in the tubs to put the white things to soak. This time she decided she need not bring the hamper out of the bedroom; she would go in there and do the sorting. She picked up the pot-bellied lamp and went in. The room was small and the hamper stood hard by the foot of the white iron bed. She could sit and reach through the bedposts—resting as she worked.

"Ah wantah cross Jurden in uh calm time." She was singing again. The mood of the "love feast" had returned. She threw back the lid of the basket almost gaily. Then, moved by both horror and terror, she sprung back toward the door. *There lay the snake in the basket!* He moved sluggishly at first, but even as she turned round and round, jumped up and down in an insanity of fear, he began to stir vigorously. She saw him pouring his awful beauty from the basket upon the bed, then she seized the lamp and ran as fast as she could to the kitchen. The wind from the open door blew out the light and the darkness added to her terror. She sped to the darkness of the yard, slamming the door after her before she thought to set down the lamp. She did not feel safe even on the ground, so she climbed up in the hay barn.

There for an hour or more she lay sprawled upon the hay a gibbering wreck.

Finally she grew quiet, and after that, coherent thought. With this, stalked through her a cold, bloody rage. Hours of this. A period of introspection, a space of retrospection, then a mixture of both. Out of this an awful calm.

"Well, Ah done de bes' Ah could. If things aint right, Gawd knows taint mah fault."

She went to sleep—a twitch sleep—and woke up to a faint gray sky. There was a loud hollow sound below. She peered out. Sykes was at the wood-pile, demolishing a wire-covered box.

He hurried to the kitchen door, but hung outside there some minutes before he entered, and stood some minutes more inside before he closed it after him.

The gray in the sky was spreading. Delia descended without fear now, and crouched beneath the low bedroom window. The drawn shade shut out the dawn, shut in the night. But the thin walls held back no sound.

"Dat ol' scratch is woke up now!" She mused at the tremendous whirr inside, which every woodsman knows, is one of the sound illusions. The rattler is a ventriloquist. His whirr sounds to the right, to the left, straight ahead, behind, close under foot—everywhere but where it is. Woe to him who guesses wrong unless he is prepared to hold up his end of the argument! Sometimes he strikes without rattling at all.

Inside, Skyes heard nothing until he knocked a pot lid off the stove while trying to reach the match safe in the dark. He had emptied his pockets at Bertha's.

The snake seemed to wake up under the stove and Skyes made a quick leap into the bedroom. In spite of the gin he had had, his head was clearing now.

"Mah Gawd!" he chattered, "ef Ah could on'y strack uh light!"

The rattling ceased for a moment as he stood paralyzed. He waited. It seemed that the snake waited also.

"Oh fuh de light! Ah thought he'd be too sick"—Skyes was muttering to himself when the whirr began again, closer, right underfoot this time. Long before this, Skyes' ability to think had been flattened down to primitive instinct and he leaped—onto the bed.

Outside Delia heard a cry that might have come from a maddened chimpanzee, a stricken gorilla. All the terror, all the horror, all the rage that man possibly could express, without a recognizable human sound.

A tremendous stir inside there, another series of animal screams, the intermittent whirr of the reptile. The shade torn violently down from the window, letting in the red dawn, a huge brown hand seizing the window stick, great dull blows upon the wooden floor punctuating the gibberish of sound long after the rattle of the snake had abruptly subsided. All this Delia could see and hear from her place beneath the window, and it made her ill. She crept over to the four-o'clocks and stretched herself on the cool earth to recover.

She lay there. "Delia, Delia!" She could hear Skyes calling in a most despairing tone as one who expected no answer. The sun crept on up, and he called. Delia could not move—her legs were gone flabby. She never moved, he called, and the sun kept rising.

"Mah Gawd!" she heard him moan. "Mah Gawd fum Heben!" She heard him stumbling about and got up from her flower-bed. The sun was growing warm. As she approached the door she heard him call out hopefully, "Delia, is dat you Ah heah?"

She saw him on his hands and knees as soon as she reached the door. He crept an inch or two toward her—all that he was able, and she saw his horribly swollen neck and his one open eye shining with hope. A surge of pity too strong to support bore her away from that eye that must, could not, fail to see the tubs. He would see the lamp. Orlando with its doctors was too far. She could scarcely reach the Chinaberry tree, where she waited in the growing heat while inside she knew the cold river was creeping up and up to extinguish that eye which must know by now that she knew.

A House of Flesh
(1971)

YUSUF IDRIS

The ring is beside the lamp. Silence prevails, and ears grow blind. In silence fingers move stealthily, put on the ring and turn off the light, in silence. Darkness reigns, and in the darkness eyes grow blind too.

The widow and her three daughters.
Their house a mere room.
The beginning is silence.

The widow is tall, fair-skinned and willowy, about thirty-five. Her daughters are also tall and blooming; they always wear their long, black mourning dresses, whether in mourning or not. The youngest is sixteen, the eldest in her twenties. All three are unattractive, having inherited their father's dark, unproportioned body, corpulent and flabby, while retaining their mother's build. In spite of its size, the room holds them all during the daytime. It is neatly set up in spite of its starkness and has an intimate, homey atmosphere about it which reflects their feminine touch. When night falls, their bodies are scattered all over the room, huge piles of warm, throbbing flesh, some sprawled on the single bed or the couch, others around it, hot, sleepless, occasionally sighing deeply. . .

Silence has hovered over them ever since the man died; that was two years ago, after a long illness. The mourning period was over, but the habits of those in mourning remained, most predominantly the habit of silence. A long, endless silence, it was in fact a silence of waiting. The girls were growing old, and the period of waiting was weighing upon them. No suitors came knocking on their doors, for what man would be so crazy as to come knocking on the door of poor, unattractive girls, particularly when they happened to be fatherless? But hope was there, of course; after all, wine can remain in its barrels until the right buyer comes along. For each girl the right luck would come along too. Even if they were poor, there would always be someone even poorer; if ugly, there would always be someone uglier. And all dreams are answered, if only one has enough patience.

The silence was occasionally interrupted by the sound of a voice reciting the Qurān, a voice rising monotonously and without emotion. It belongs to a *muqri'* (Qurān reciter), and he is blind. The prayers are for the soul of the deceased father, always delivered at the same time, every Friday afternoon. He comes poking his stick at their door and abandons himself to the extended hand that leads him inside. There he sits cross-legged on the mat and recites. When it is over, he gropes for his sandals, pronounces a greeting which no one bothers to reciprocate and then leaves. Out of habit he comes, out of habit he recites, and out of habit he leaves, so much so that no one even notices him any more.

Always there is the silence, even when the Friday afternoon recitation interrupts it. It is as if silence is broken only by silence. Waiting is for ever, like hope, little hope but constant. Yet there still remains some hope; for every insignificant being, there is somewhere one who is yet more so. These women, they do not aspire to anything more, no indeed, they do not.

Silence persisted until something happened. A Friday afternoon came, and the reciter did not appear. Every agreement comes to an end, however long it has lasted; and it seemed that this agreement had come to its end. Only then did the widow and her daughters realize that not only was his the sole voice that broke their silence, but also that he was the only man who ever knocked at their door, even if it was just once a week. Other things began to dawn on them. He was as poor as they were, true, but his outfits were always clean, his sandals shining, his headdress meticulously wrapped (putting any seeing man to shame); above all, his voice was strong, deep and melodious. The proposition takes shape: why not renew the agreement, and why not summon him immediately? Could he be busy elsewhere? They can wait; waiting is an old game as far as they are concerned.

The evening was drawing to its end. He recited as if for the very first time. The proposition comes up: why shouldn't one of them marry a man whose voice will fill the house?

He is a bachelor with a sprouting moustache, a young man. Words generate other words, and he too, it seems, is looking for the right woman. The girls confer about the matter, and the mother peruses their faces, trying to figure who the lucky one will be. But their faces evade her searching looks. "Is this the way we'll be rewarded for our long wait?" they seem to say. "Shall we break our fast with a blind man?" They were, after all, still dreaming of suitors, and suitors usually imply men who can see.

Poor things, they had yet to learn about the world of men. How could they know that a man cannot be judged by his seeing capacity?

"You marry him, Mother, why don't you?"

"Me!! What a disgrace! What would people say?!"

"Let them say what they like! No matter what, it will be better than living in a house without a man, the resounding voice of a man."

"Do you want me to marry before you? Never. . ."

"Wouldn't it be better if you did? Then our house will again echo to the sound of men's footsteps, and we can marry after you."

"Yes, Mother, marry him, marry him!"

And she married him. One more breath was added, their income grew just a little bit more, and a much greater problem arose. True, the married couple spent their first night together, but they did not dare to come close to each other, even inadvertently. The girls were sleeping close by, or pretending to do so. The mother could feel pairs of searchlight beams aimed at the space in between them, searching lights of human eyes, ears and senses as probing antennae. The girls were old enough to know, to understand. Their watchful presence made the whole room seem to be in the glare of broad daylight.

One by one, each of them left the house when morning set in, only to return by sunset, hesitant, embarrassed, and dragging their feet. As they came closer to the house, something gave them a start and made them hurry: laughter, a man's guffawing, occasionally interrupted by the faint sounds of a woman. It must be their mother laughing, and the dignified, humble reciter they had come to know was now laughing too. Their mother greeted them with open arms, bareheaded, her hair wet and combed and still laughing. They looked at her face and realized that for all those years it had been like an unlit lamp in whose crevices spiders and cobwebs had made their homes. Now suddenly, that same face had burst into light; those eyes which had cowered in the bottom of their sockets now shone out and glistened with tears of laughter.

Silence dissipated and vanished altogether. Before, during and after suppertime, there was a bustle of loud voices and jokes, highlighted by the reciter's imitation of Umm Kulthum and ᶜAbd al-Wahhab in his beautiful, resounding voice made hoarse by his own happiness.

Well done, Mother! This gaiety and laughter will soon bring more men to the house, for the presence of men attracts other men.

Be confident, girls. Soon men will be coming and suitors will start making their calls. But, actually, what was preoccupying her mind was the young man, not suitors. True, he was blind, but then, how often are we blinded ourselves from seeing others, just because they happen to be blind. Yes, she was noticing this healthy young man whose overflowing vitality had made up for all those years of sickness, impotence and early old age.

Silence was gone, never to return. The throb of life was there to stay. The man was her legal husband; she had married him according to the law of God and the canon of the Prophet. So, what was there to be ashamed of? Everything she was doing was legitimate. She no longer made any effort to be discreet or keep things secret. When night came and they were all huddled together, when the power of the body and soul took over, the girls would be lying there, keeping their distance and yet fully aware and alert at their observation posts, stifling all movement and coughing. Suddenly sighs would be heard, only to be suppressed by others.

The mother spent her mornings washing clothes in rich people's houses, while his days were whiled away in recitation of the Qurān in poor people's homes. At first, he did not return home for a break during the day, but, as his nights grew longer, he started coming home at noon to rest his exhausted body, to regain his strength for the night to come.

Once, after they had had their fill of the night and the night had had its fill of them, he suddenly asked her what was the matter with her at noontime. Why was it, he asked, that she was so voluble and eager to talk now, whereas then she had been totally silent? Why was she wearing his cherished ring now, that being the only thing he had given her as a dowry, gift or wedding band? Why wasn't she wearing it then?

She could have torn herself away, distraught, screaming. She could have lost her senses. He could have gotten himself killed. After all, there could be but one meaning to what he was saying, and it was horrible and atrocious. However, a choking sob kept it all back; she held her breath and kept her peace. With her ears transformed into noses, eyes and senses all at once, she strained every fiber in her body to find out which of the girls was the culprit. For some reason, she was positive that it was the middle one. There was a certain daring in her look which not even a bullet could check. But she listened. The breathing of the three girls grew louder, deep and feverish, flaming hot, growling with youth, hesitating and intermittent, dreaming dreams which it would be sinful to interrupt; heavings that turn into the hiss of flames burning, lava vomited by thirsty lands. The knot in her throat is deeper, it chokes. Hungry breaths can be heard. For all her straining, she cannot differentiate between one vibrant, hot pile of flesh and another. They are all hungry, all groaning and screaming; the groans breathe, not breaths but pleas, supplications even, perhaps something more.

She had totally immersed herself in her second legitimate right, and forgotten all about her first legitimate duty, her girls. Patience became a bitter pill. Even the mirage of suitors was no more. Suddenly, she feels bitten, like someone awakened with a start by a secret call. The girls are hungry; the food is forbidden, it's true, and yet, hunger is still more sinful. There exists nothing more sinful than hunger. She has known hunger, and it has known her, drained her spirit and sapped her marrow. Yes, she knows it well and has had her fill of it. She can never forget its taste. Now, here they are hungry. Can she really have forgotten them, she who used to take bread out of her own mouth to feed them, whose only preoccupation was to keep them fed even if she had to go hungry, she, their mother?!

No matter how much he insisted, her torment was transformed into silence. The mother became silent, and from that moment on, the silence never left her. At breakfast, just as she had thought, the middle girl was silent. From that moment on, she remained silent too. At suppertime, the young man was happy and jovial, blind, singing cheerfully and laughing, but only the youngest and eldest daughters paid any attention.

Patience goes on and on. The bitterness of it becomes a sickness. No men came knocking at the door. One day, the eldest looked at her mother's ring and expressed her admiration. The mother's heart started pounding, and when the daughter begged to wear it just for the day, the pounding became more intense. In silence the mother took the ring off her finger, and in silence the girl slipped it on to her own.

That evening, the eldest girl remained silent and refused to utter a single word. The blind man sang and laughed boisterously, but only the youngest girl paid any attention.

With her patience unrewarded and luck and worry unrequited, the youngest grew older and asked for her turn at the ring game. In silence her turn came.

The ring is lying beside the lamp. Silence prevails, and ears grow blind. In silence the finger whose turn comes gropes stealthily for the ring and turns off the light. Darkness reigns, and in darkness eyes grow blind.

The blind man alone remains happy, joking and singing. Yet behind his boisterous happiness there lurked a desire which made him feel like lashing out at this silence and smashing it once and for all. The uncertainty was torturing him. At first, he would tell himself that it was part of a woman's nature to be changing all the time. One time, she will be as fresh as the morning dew; another time she is worn out and exhausted, just like swamp water; sometimes satiny like rose petals, prickly at other times like a cactus. True, the ring is always there, but each time the finger it encircles seems to be different. He was almost positive, and they all knew for sure. So, why doesn't the silence say something, why doesn't it speak?

But what if it did talk? The question gave him a shock, and the mere thought of it made him choke on his bread. From that moment on, he never uttered a word. He lived in fear of violating the silence. If one word were uttered, the whole edifice of silence would be brought crashing down; and woe to him if that happened. This time, the silence was different, strange, and they all respected it; it was a conscious silence, not caused by poverty, nor ugliness, nor patience, nor despair. No, this was the most profound kind of silence, the most binding of all, one which is implemented without any formal agreement.

The widow and her three daughters.
Their house a mere room.
The silence is new.

468

The blind reciter brought this silence with him, convincing himself thereby that his companion in bed was always his legitimate wife, the bearer of his ring, ever changing, unpredictable. Young and old, silky soft or callous and scaly, fat sometimes, thin at others. Whatever the case, it was her business. In fact, it was the business of the people who could see, part of their responsibility. They alone have the blessing of certainty, since they are able to make distinctions. All he could offer was doubt, something which could only become a certainty through the blessing of sight. As long as he was deprived of that blessing, the certainty was missing too. He was blind, after all, and you cannot reproach the blind.

Or can you?

In the American Society
(1986)

His Own Society

When my father took over the pancake house, it was to send my little sister, Mona, and me to college. We were only in junior high at the time, but my father believed in getting a jump on things. "Those Americans always saying it," he told us. "Smart guys thinking in advance." My mother elaborated, explaining that businesses took bringing up, like children. They could take years to get going, she said, years.

In this case, though, we got rich right away. At two months, we were breaking even, and at four, those same hotcakes that could barely withstand the weight of butter and syrup were supporting our family with ease. My mother bought a station wagon with air conditioning, my father an oversized red vinyl recliner for the back room; and as time went on and the business continued to thrive, my father started to talk about his grandfather, and the village he had reigned over in China—things my father had never talked about when he worked for other people. He told us about the bags of rice his family would give out to the poor at New Year's, and about the people who came to beg, on their hands and knees, for his grandfather to intercede for the more wayward of their relatives. "Like that Godfather in the movie," he would tell us as, feet up, he distributed paychecks. Sometimes an employee would get two green envelopes instead of one, which meant that Jimmy needed a tooth pulled, say, or that Tiffany's husband was in the clinker again. "It's nothing, nothing," he would insist, sinking back into his chair. "Who else is going to taking care of you people?"

My mother would mostly just sigh about it. "Your father thinks this is China," she would say, and then she would go back to her mending. Once in a while, though, when my father had given away a particularly large sum, she would exclaim, outraged, "But this here is the *U—S—of—A!*"—this apparently having been what she used to tell immigrant stock boys when they came in late.

She didn't work at the supermarket anymore; but she had made it to the rank of manager before she left, and this had given her not only new words and phrases but new ideas about herself, and about America, and about what was what in general. She had opinions about how downtown should be zoned; she could pump her own gas and check her own oil; and for all

471

that she used to chide Mona and me for being copycats, she herself was now interested in espadrilles, and wallpaper, and, most recently, the town country club.

"So join already," said Mona, flicking a fly off her knee.

My mother enumerated the problems as she sliced up a quarter round of watermelon. There was the cost. There was the waiting list. There was the fact that no one in our family played either tennis or golf.

"So what?" said Mona.

"It would be waste," said my mother.

"Me and Callie can swim in the pool."

"Anyway, you need that recommendation letter from a member."

"Come *on*," said Mona. "Annie's mom'd write you a letter in a *sec.*"

My mother's knife glinted in the early-summer sun. I spread some more newspaper on the picnic table.

"Plus, you have to eat there twice a month. You know what that means." My mother cut another, enormous slice of fruit.

"No, I *don't* know what that means," said Mona.

"It means Dad would have to wear a jacket, dummy," I said.

"Oh! Oh! Oh!" said Mona, clasping her hand to her breast. "Oh! Oh! Oh! Oh! Oh!"

We all laughed: My father had no use for nice clothes, and would wear only ten-year-old shirts, with grease-spotted pants, to show how little he cared what anyone thought.

"Your father doesn't believe in joining the American society," said my mother. "He wants to have his own society."

"So go to dinner without him." Mona shot her seeds out in long arcs over the lawn. "Who cares what he thinks?"

But of course, we all did care, and knew my mother could not simply up and do as she pleased. For to embrace what my father embraced was to love him; and to embrace something else was to betray him.

He demanded a similar sort of loyalty of his workers, whom he treated more like servants than employees. Not in the beginning, of course. In the beginning, all he wanted was for them to keep on doing what they used to do, to which end he concentrated mostly on leaving them alone. As the months passed, though, he expected more and more of them, with the result that, for all his largesse, he began to have trouble keeping help. The cooks and busboys complained that he asked them to fix radiators and trim hedges, not only at the restaurant but at our house; the waitresses, that he sent them on errands, and made them chauffeur him around. Our headwaitress, Gertrude, claimed that he once even asked her to scratch his back.

"It's not just the blacks don't believe in slavery," she said when she quit.

My father never quite registered her complaints, though, nor those of the others who left. Even after Eleanor quit, then Tiffany, and Gerald, and Jimmy, and even his best cook, Eureka Andy, for whom he had bought new glasses, he remained mostly convinced that the fault lay with them.

"All they understand is that assemble line," he lamented. "Robots, they are. They want to be robots."

There were occasions when the clear running truth seemed to eddy, when he would pinch the vinyl of his chair up into little peaks and wonder if he was doing things right. But with time he would always smooth the peaks back down; and when business started to slide in the spring, he kept on like a horse in his ways.

By the summer, our dish boy was overwhelmed with scraping. It was no longer just the hash browns that people were leaving for trash, and the service was as bad as the food. The waitresses served up French pancakes instead of German, apple juice instead of orange. They spilled things on laps, on coats. On the Fourth of July, some greenhorn sent an entire side of fries slaloming down a lady's *Massif Central*. Meanwhile, in the back room, my father labored through articles on the economy.

"What is housing starts?" he puzzled. "What is GNP?"

Mona and I did what we could, filling in as busgirls and dishwashers, and, one afternoon, stuffing the comments box by the cashier's desk. That was Mona's idea. We rustled up a variety of pens and pencils, checked boxes for an hour, smeared the cards with coffee and grease, and waited. It took a few days for my father to notice that the box was full, and he didn't say anything about it for a few days more. Finally, though, he started to complain of fatigue; and then he began to complain that the staff was not what it could be. We encouraged him in this—pointing out, for instance, how many dishes got chipped. But in the end all that happened was that, for the first time since we took over the restaurant, my father got it into his head to fire someone. Skip, a skinny busboy who was saving up for a sports car, said nothing as my father mumbled on about the price of dishes. My father's hands shook as he wrote out the severance check; and once it was over, he spent the rest of the day napping in his chair.

Since it was going on midsummer, Skip wasn't easy to replace. We hung a sign in the window and advertised in the paper, but no one called the first week, and the person who called the second didn't show up for his interview. The third week, my father phoned Skip to see if he would come back, but a friend of his had already sold him a Corvette for cheap.

Finally, a Chinese guy named Booker turned up. He couldn't have been more than thirty, and was wearing a lighthearted seersucker suit, but he looked as though life had him pinned. His eyes were bloodshot and his chest sunken, and the muscles of his neck seemed to strain with the effort of holding his head up. In a single dry breath he told us that he had never bused tables but was willing to learn, and that he was on the lam from the deportation authorities.

"I do not want to lie to you," he kept saying. He had come to the United States on a student visa but had run out of money and was now in a bind. He was loath to go back to Taiwan, as it happened—he looked up at this point, to be sure my father wasn't pro-KMT—but all he had was a phony Social Security card, and a willingness to absorb all blame, should anything untoward come to pass.

"I do not think, anyway, that it is against law to hire me, only to be me," he said, smiling faintly.

Anyone else would have examined him on this, but my father conceived of laws as speed bumps rather than curbs. He wiped the counter with his sleeve, and told Booker to report the next morning.

"I will be good worker," said Booker.

"Good," said my father.

"Anything you want me to do, I will do."

My father nodded.

Booker seemed to sink into himself for a moment. "Thank you," he said finally. "I am appreciate your help. I am very, very appreciate for everything."

My father looked at him. "Did you eat today?" he asked in Mandarin.

Booker pulled at the hem of his jacket.

"Sit down," said my father. "Please, have a seat."

My father didn't tell my mother about Booker, and my mother didn't tell my father about the country club. She would never have applied, except that Mona, while over at Annie's, had let it drop that our mother wanted to join. Mrs. Lardner came by the very next day.

"Why, I'd be honored and delighted to write you people a letter," she said. Her skirt billowed around her.

"Thank you so much," said my mother. "But it's too much trouble for you, and also my husband is . . ."

"Oh, it's no trouble at all, no trouble at all. I tell you." She leaned forward, so that her chest freckles showed. "I know just how it is. It's a secret of course, but, you know, my natural father was Jewish. Can you see it? Just look at my skin."

"My husband," said my mother.

"I'd be honored and delighted," said Mrs. Lardner, with a little wave of her hands. "Just honored and delighted."

Mona was triumphant. "See, Mom," she said, waltzing around the kitchen when Mrs. Lardner left. "What did I tell you? 'I'm honored and delighted, just honored and delighted.'" She waved her hands in the air.

"You know, the Chinese have a saying," said my mother. "To do nothing is better than to overdo. You mean well, but you tell me now what will happen."

"I'll talk Dad into it," said Mona, still waltzing. "Or I bet Callie can. He'll do anything Callie says."

"I can try, anyway," I said.

"Did you hear what I said?" said my mother. Mona bumped into the broom closet door. "You're not going to talk anything. You've already made enough trouble." She started on the dishes with a clatter.

Mona poked diffidently at a mop.

I sponged off the counter. "Anyway," I ventured. "I bet our name'll never even come up."

"That's if we're lucky," said my mother.

"There's all these people waiting," I said.

"Good." She started on a pot.

I looked over at Mona, who was still cowering in the broom closet. "In fact, there's some black family's been waiting so long, they're going to sue," I said.

My mother turned off the water. "Where'd you hear that?"

"Patty told me."

She turned the water back on, started to wash a dish, then put it down and shut the faucet. "I'm sorry," said Mona.

"Forget it," said my mother. "Just forget it."

Booker turned out to be a model worker, whose boundless gratitude translated into a willingness to do anything. As he also learned quickly, he soon knew not only how to bus but how to cook, and how to wait tables, and how to keep the books. He fixed the walk-in door so that it stayed shut, reupholstered the torn seats in the dining room, and devised a system for tracking inventory. The only stone in the rice was that he tended to be sickly; but, reliable even in illness, he would always send a friend to take his place. In this way, we got to know Ronald, Lynn, Dirk, and Cedric, all of whom, like Booker, had problems with their legal status, and were anxious to please. They weren't all as capable as Booker, though, with the exception of Cedric, whom my father often hired even when Booker was well. A round wag of a man who called Mona and me *shou hou*—skinny monkeys—he was a professed nonsmoker who was nevertheless always begging drags off other people's cigarettes. This last habit drove our head cook, Fernando, crazy, especially since, when refused a hit, Cedric would occasionally snitch one. Winking impishly at Mona and me, he would steal up to an ashtray, take a quick puff, and then break out laughing, so that the smoke came rolling out of his mouth in a great incriminatory cloud. Fernando accused him of stealing fresh cigarettes, too, even whole packs.

"Why else do you think he's weaseling around in the back of the store all the time?" he said. His face was blotchy with anger. "The man is a frigging thief."

Other members of the staff supported him in this contention, and joined in on an "Operation Identification," which involved numbering and initialing their cigarettes—even though what they seemed to fear for wasn't so much their cigarettes as their jobs. Then one of the cooks quit; and, rather than promote someone, my father hired Cedric for the position. Rumor had it that Cedric was taking only half the normal salary; that Alex had been pressured to resign; and that my father was looking for a position with which to placate Booker, who had been bypassed because of his health.

The result was that Fernando categorically refused to work with Cedric.

"The only way I'll cook with that piece of slime," he said, shaking his huge, tattooed fist, "is if it's his ass frying on the grill."

My father cajoled and cajoled, but in the end was simply forced to put them on different schedules.

The next week, Fernando got caught stealing a carton of minute steaks. My father would not tell even Mona and me how he knew to be standing by the back door when Fernando was on his way out, but everyone suspected Booker. Everyone but Fernando, that is, who was sure Cedric had been the tip-off. My father held a staff meeting, in which he tried to reassure everyone that Alex had left on his own, and that he had no intention of firing anyone. But though he was careful not to mention Fernando, everyone was so amazed that he was being allowed to stay that Fernando was incensed nonetheless.

"Don't you all be putting your bug eyes on me," he said. *"He's* the frigging crook." He grabbed Cedric by the collar.

Cedric raised an eyebrow. "Cook, you mean," he said.

At this, Fernando punched Cedric in the mouth; and, the words he had just uttered notwithstanding, my father fired Fernando on the spot.

With everything that was happening, Mona and I were ready to be finishing up at the restaurant. It was almost time: The days were still stuffy with summer, but our window shade had started flapping in the evening as if gearing up to go out. That year, the breezes were full of salt, as they sometimes were when they came in from the east, and they blew anchors and docks through my mind like so many tumbleweeds, filling my dreams with wherries and lobsters and grainy-faced men who squinted, day in and day out, at the sky.

It was time for a change—you could feel it—and yet the pancake house was the same as ever. The day before school started, my father came home with bad news.

"Fernando called police," he said, wiping his hand on his pant leg.

My mother naturally wanted to know what police; and so, with much coughing and hawing, the long story began, the latest installment of which had the police calling Immigration, and Immigration sending an investigator. My mother sat stiff as whalebone as my father described how the man had summarily refused lunch on the house, and how my father had admitted, under pressure, that he knew there were "things" about his workers.

"So now what happens?"

My father didn't know. "Booker and Cedric went with him to the jail," he said. "But me, here I am." He laughed uncomfortably.

The next day, my father posted bail for "his boys," and waited apprehensively for something to happen. The day after that, he waited again, and the day after that, he called our neighbor's law student son, who suggested my father call the Immigration Department under an alias. My father took his advice; and it was thus that he discovered that Booker was right. It was illegal for aliens to work, but it wasn't to hire them.

In the happy interval that ensued, my father apologized to my mother, who in turn confessed about the country club, for which my father had no choice but to forgive her. Then he turned his attention back to "his boys."

My mother didn't see that there was anything to do.

"I like to talking to the judge," said my father.

"This is not China," said my mother.

"I'm only talking to him. I'm not give him money unless he wants it."

"You're going to land up in jail."

"So what else I should do?" My father threw up his hands. "Those are my boys."

"Your boys!" exploded my mother. "What about your family? What about your wife?"

My father took a long sip of tea. "You know," he said finally, "in the war my father sent our cook to the soldiers to use. He always said it—the province comes before the town, the town comes before the family."

"A restaurant is not a town," said my mother.

My father sipped at his tea again. "You know, when I first come to the United States, I also had to hide-and-seek with those deportation guys. If people did not helping me, I am not here today."

My mother scrutinized her hem.

After a minute, I volunteered that before seeing a judge, he might try a lawyer.

He turned. "Since when did you become so afraid like your mother?"

I started to say that it wasn't a matter of fear, but he cut me off.

"What I need today," he said, "is a son."

My father and I spent the better part of the next day standing on lines at the Immigration office. He did not get to speak to a judge, but with much persistence he managed to speak to a special clerk, who tried to persuade him that it was not her place to extend him advice. My father, though, shamelessly plied her with compliments and offers of free pancakes, until she finally conceded that she personally doubted anything would happen to either Cedric or Booker.

"Especially if they're 'needed workers,'" she said, rubbing at the red marks her glasses left on her nose. She yawned. "Have you thought about sponsoring them to become permanent residents?"

Could he do that? My father was overjoyed. And what if he saw to it right away? Would she perhaps put in a good word with the judge?

She yawned again, her nostrils flaring. "Don't worry," she said. "They'll get a fair hearing."

My father returned jubilant. Booker and Cedric hailed him as their savior. He was like a father to them, they said; and, laughing and clapping, they made him tell the story over and over, sorting through the details like jewels. And how old was the assistant judge? And what did she say?

That evening, my father tipped the paperboy a dollar and bought a pot of mums for my mother, who suffered them to be placed on the dining room table. The next night, he took us all out to dinner. Then on Saturday, Mona found a letter and some money in an envelope on my father's chair at the restaurant.

Dear Mr. Chang,
You are the grat boss. But, we do not like to trial, so will runing away now. Plese to excus us.
People saying the law in America is fears like dragon. Here is only $140. We hope some day we
can pay back the rest bale. You will getting intrest, as you diserving, so grat a boss you are.
Thank you for every thing. In next life you will be burn in rich family, with no more pancaks.

Yours truley,
Booker + Cedric

In the weeks that followed, my father went to the pancake house for crises, but otherwise hung around our house, fiddling idly with the sump pump and boiler in an effort, he said, to get ready for winter. It was as though he had gone into retirement, except that instead of moving south, he had moved to the basement. He even took to showering my mother with little attentions, and to calling her "old girl," and when we finally heard that the club had entertained all the applications it could for the year, he was so sympathetic that he seemed more disappointed than my mother.

In the American Society

Mrs. Lardner tempered the bad news with an invitation to a bon voyage bash she was throwing for her friend Jeremy Brothers, who was going to Greece for six months.

"Do come," she urged. "You'll meet everyone, and then, you know, if things open up in the spring. . ." She waved her hands.

My mother wondered if it would be appropriate to show up at a party for someone they didn't know, but "the honest truth" was that this was an annual affair. "If it's not Greece, it's Italy," sighed Mrs. Lardner. "We really just do it because his wife left him and his daughter doesn't speak to him, and poor Jeremy just feels so *unloved*."

She also invited Mona and me to the goings-on, to keep Annie out of the champagne. I wasn't too keen on the idea, but before I could say anything, she had already thanked us for so generously agreeing to honor her with our presence.

"A pair of little princesses, you are!" she told us. "A pair of princesses!"

The party was that Sunday. On Saturday, my mother took my father out shopping for a suit. Since it was the end of September, she insisted that he buy a worsted rather than a seersucker, even though it was only 10, rather than 50, percent off. My father protested that the weather was as hot as ever, which was true—a thick Indian summer had cozied murderously up to us—but to no avail. Summer clothes, said my mother, were not properly worn after Labor Day.

The suit was unfortunately as extravagant in length as it was in price, which posed an additional quandary, since the tailor wouldn't be in until Monday. The salesgirl, though, found a way of tacking it up temporarily.

"Maybe this suit not fit me," fretted my father.

"Just don't take your jacket off," said the salesgirl.

He gave her a tip before they left, but when he got home, he refused to remove the price tag.

"I like to asking the tailor about the size," he insisted.

"You mean you're going to *wear* it and then *return* it?" Mona rolled her eyes.

"I didn't say I'm return it," said my father stiffly. "I like to asking the tailor, that's all."

The party started off swimmingly, except that most people were wearing Bermudas or wrap skirts. Still, my parents carried on, sharing with great feeling the complaints about the heat. Of course, my father tried to eat a cracker full of shallots, and burned himself in an attempt to help Mr. Lardner turn the coals of the barbecue; but on the whole, he seemed to be doing all right. Not nearly so well as my mother, though, who had accepted an entire cupful of Mrs. Lardner's magic punch and indeed seemed to be under some spell. As Mona and Annie skirmished over whether some boy in their class inhaled when he smoked, I watched my mother take off her shoes, laughing and laughing as a man with a beard regaled her with navy stories by the pool. Apparently he had been stationed in the Orient and remembered a few words of Chinese, which made my mother laugh still more. My father excused himself to go to the bathroom, then drifted back and weighed anchor at the hors d'oeuvres table, while my mother sailed on to a group of women, who tinkled at length over the clarity of her complexion. I dug out a book I had brought.

Just when I'd cracked the spine, though, Mrs. Lardner came by to bewail her shortage of servers. Her caterers were criminals, I agreed; and the next thing I knew, I was handing out bits of marine life as amiably as I could.

"Here you go, Dad," I said, when I got to the hors d'oeuvres table.

"Everything is fine," he said.

I hesitated to leave him alone; but then the man with the beard zeroed in on him, and though he talked of nothing but my mother, I thought it would be okay to get back to work. Just at that moment, though, Jeremy Brothers lurched our way, an empty, albeit corked, wine bottle in hand. He was a slim, well-proportioned man, with a Roman nose and small eyes and a nice manly jaw that he allowed to hang agape.

"Hello," he said drunkenly. "Pleased to meet you."

"Pleased to meeting you," said my father.

"Right," said Jeremy. "Right. Listen. I have this bottle here, this most recalcitrant bottle. You see that it refuses to do my bidding. I bid it open sesame, please, and it does nothing." He pulled the cork out with his teeth, then turned the bottle upside down.

My father nodded.

"Would you have a word with it, please?" said Jeremy. The man with the beard excused himself. "Would you please have a god-damned word with it?"

My father laughed uncomfortably.

"Ah!" Jeremy bowed a little. "Excuse me, excuse me, excuse me. You are not my man, not my man at all." He bowed again and started to leave, but then circled back. "Viticulture is not your forte. Yes, I can see that, see that plainly. But may I trouble you on another matter? Forget the damned bottle." He threw it into the pool, winking at the people he splashed. "I have another matter. Do you speak Chinese?"

My father said he did not, but Jeremy pulled out a handkerchief with some characters on it anyway, saying that his daughter had sent it from Hong Kong and that he thought the characters might be some secret message.

"Long life," said my father.

"But you haven't looked at it yet."

"I know what it says without looking." My father winked at me.

"You do?"

"Yes, I do."

"You're making fun of me, aren't you?"

"No, no, no," said my father, winking again.

"Who are you anyway?" said Jeremy.

His smile fading, my father shrugged.

"Who are you?"

My father shrugged again.

Jeremy began to roar. "This is my party, *my party*, and I've never seen you before in my life." My father backed up as Jeremy came toward him. *"Who are you? WHO ARE YOU?"*

Just as my father was going to step into the pool, Mrs. Lardner came running up. Jeremy informed her that there was a man crashing his party.

"Nonsense," said Mrs. Lardner. "This is Ralph Chang, whom I invited extra specially so he could meet you." She straightened the collar of Jeremy's peach-colored polo shirt for him.

"Yes, well we've had a chance to chat," said Jeremy.

She whispered in his ear; he mumbled something; she whispered something more.

"I do apologize," he said finally.

My father didn't say anything.

"I do." Jeremy seemed genuinely contrite. "Doubtless you've seen drunks before, haven't you? You must have them in China."

"Okay," said my father.

As Mrs. Lardner glided off, Jeremy clapped his arm over my father's shoulders. "You know, I really am quite sorry, quite sorry."

My father nodded.

"What can I do? How can I make it up to you?"

"No, thank you."

"No, tell me, tell me," wheedled Jeremy. "Tickets to casino night?" My father shook his head. "You don't gamble. Dinner at Bartholomew's?" My father shook his head again. "You don't eat." Jeremy scratched his chin. "You know, my wife was like you. Old Annabelle could never let me make things up—never, never, never, never, never."

My father wriggled out from under his arm.

"How about sport clothes? You are rather overdressed, you know. Excuse me for saying so. But here." He took off his polo shirt and folded it up. "You can have this with my most profound apologies." He ruffled his chest hairs with his free hand.

"No, thank you," said my father.

"No, take it, take it. Accept my apologies." He thrust the shirt into my father's arms. "I'm so very sorry, so very sorry. Please, try it on."

Helplessly holding the shirt, my father searched the crowd for my mother.

"Here, I'll help you with your coat."

My father froze.

Jeremy reached over and took the jacket off. "Milton's, one hundred twenty-five dollars reduced to one hundred twelve-fifty," he read. "What a bargain, what a bargain!"

"Please give it back," pleaded my father. "Please."

"Now for your shirt," ordered Jeremy.

Heads began to turn.

"Take off your shirt."

"I do not taking orders like a servant," announced my father stiffly.

"Take off your shirt, or I'm going to throw this jacket right into the pool, just right into this little pool here." Jeremy held it over the water.

"Go ahead."

"One hundred twelve-fifty," taunted Jeremy. "One hundred twelve . . ."

My father flung the polo shirt into the water with such force that part of it bounced back up into the air like a fluorescent fountain. Then it settled into a soft heap on top of the water. My mother hurried up.

"You're a sport!" said Jeremy, suddenly breaking into a smile, and slapping my father on the back. "You're a sport! I like that. A man with spirit, that's what you are. A man with panache. Allow me to return to you your jacket," He handed it back to my father. "Good value you got on that, good value."

My father hurled the coat into the pool, too. "We're leaving," he said grimly. "Leaving!"

"Now, Ralphie," said Mrs. Lardner, bustling up; but my father was already stomping off.

"Get your sister," he told me. To my mother: "Get your shoes."

"That was *great*, Dad," said Mona as we walked to the car. "You were *stupendous*."

"Way to show 'em," I said.

"What?" said my father offhandedly.

Although it was only just dusk, we were in a gulch, which made it hard to see anything except the gleam of his white shirt moving up the hill ahead of us.

"It was all my fault," began my mother.

"Forget it," said my father grandly. Then he said, "The only trouble is, I left those keys in my jacket pocket."

"Oh *no*," said Mona.

"Oh no is right," said my mother.

"So we'll walk home," I said.

"But how're we going to get into the *house?*" said Mona.

The noise of the party churned through the silence.

"Someone has to going back," said my father.

"Let's go to the pancake house first," suggested my mother. "We can wait there until the party is finished, and then call Mrs. Lardner."

Having all agreed that was a good plan, we started walking again.

"God, just think," said Mona. "We're going to have to *dive* for them."

My father stopped a moment. We waited.

"You girls are good swimmers," he said finally. "Not like me."

Then his shirt started moving again, and we trooped up the hill after it, into the dark.

A White Heron
(1886)

SARAH ORNE JEWETT

I.

The woods were already filled with shadows one June evening, just before eight o'clock, though a bright sunset still glimmered faintly among the trunks of the trees. A little girl was driving home her cow, a plodding, dilatory, provoking creature in her behavior, but a valued companion for all that. They were going away from the western light, and striking deep into the dark woods, but their feet were familiar with the path, and it was no matter whether their eyes could see it or not.

There was hardly a night the summer through when the old cow could be found waiting at the pasture bars; on the contrary, it was her greatest pleasure to hide herself away among the high huckleberry bushes, and though she wore a loud bell she had made the discovery that if one stood perfectly still it would not ring. So Sylvia had to hunt for her until she found her, and call Co'! Co'! with never an answering Moo, until her childish patience was quite spent. If the creature had not given good milk and plenty of it, the case would have seemed very different to her owners. Besides, Sylvia had all the time there was, and very little use to make of it. Sometimes in pleasant weather it was a consolation to look upon the cow's pranks as an intelligent attempt to play hide and seek, and as the child had no playmates she lent herself to this amusement with a good deal of zest. Though this chase had been so long that the wary animal herself had given an unusual signal of her whereabouts, Sylvia had only laughed when she came upon Mistress Moolly at the swamp-side, and urged her affectionately homeward with a twig of birch leaves. The old cow was not inclined to wander farther, she even turned in the right direction for once as they left the pasture, and stepped along the road at a good pace. She was quite ready to be milked now, and seldom stopped to browse. Sylvia wondered what her grandmother would say because they were so late. It was a great while since she had left home at half past five o'clock, but everybody knew the difficulty of making this errand a short one. Mrs. Tilley had chased the hornéd torment too many summer evenings herself to blame any one else for lingering, and was only thankful as she waited that she had Sylvia, nowadays, to give such valuable assistance. The good woman suspected that Sylvia loitered occasionally on her own account; there never was such a child for straying about out-of-doors since the world was made! Everybody said that it was a good change for a little maid who had tried to grow for eight years in a crowded manufacturing town, but, as for Sylvia herself, it seemed as if she never had been alive at all before she came to live at the farm. She thought often with wistful compassion of a wretched dry geranium that belonged to a town neighbor.

"'Afraid of folks,'" old Mrs. Tilley said to herself, with a smile, after she had made the unlikely choice of Sylvia from her daughter's houseful of children, and was returning to the farm. "'Afraid of folks,' they said! I guess she won't be troubled no great with 'em up to the old place!" When they reached the door of the lonely house and stopped to unlock it, and the cat came to purr loudly, and rub against them, a deserted pussy, indeed, but fat with young robins, Sylvia whispered that this was a beautiful place to live in, and she never should wish to go home.

The companions followed the shady wood-road, the cow taking slow steps, and the child very fast ones. The cow stopped long at the brook to drink, as if the pasture were not half a swamp, and Sylvia stood still and waited, letting her bare feet cool themselves in the shoal water, while the great twilight moths struck softly against her. She waded on through the brook as the cow moved away, and listened to the thrushes with a heart that beat fast with pleasure. There was a stirring in the great boughs overhead. They were full of little birds and beasts that seemed to be wide-awake, and going about their world, or else saying good-night to each other in sleepy twitters. Sylvia herself felt sleepy as she walked along. However, it was not much farther to the house, and the air was soft and sweet. She was not often in the woods so late as this, and it made her feel as if she were a part of the gray shadows and the moving leaves. She was just thinking how long it seemed since she first came to the farm a year ago, and wondering if everything went on in the noisy town just the same as when she was there; the thought of the great red-faced boy who used to chase and frighten her made her hurry along the path to escape from the shadow of the trees.

Suddenly this little woods-girl is horror-stricken to hear a clear whistle not very far away. Not a bird's whistle, which would have a sort of friendliness, but a boy's whistle, determined, and somewhat aggressive. Sylvia left the cow to whatever sad fate might await her, and stepped discreetly aside into the bushes, but she was just too late. The enemy had discovered her, and called out in a very cheerful and persuasive tone, "Halloa, little girl, how far is it to the road?" and trembling Sylvia answered almost inaudibly, "A good ways."

She did not dare to look boldly at the tall young man, who carried a gun over his shoulder, but she came out of her bush and again followed the cow, while he walked alongside.

"I have been hunting for some birds," the stranger said kindly, "and I have lost my way, and need a friend very much. Don't be afraid," he added gallantly. "Speak up and tell me what your name is, and whether you think I can spend the night at your house, and go out gunning early in the morning."

Sylvia was more alarmed than before. Would not her grandmother consider her much to blame? But who could have foreseen such an accident as this? It did not appear to be her fault, and she hung her head as if the stem of it were broken, but managed to answer "Sylvy," with much effort when her companion again asked her name.

Mrs. Tilley was standing in the doorway when the trio came into view. The cow gave a loud moo by way of explanation.

"Yes, you'd better speak up for yourself, you old trial! Where'd she tucked herself away this time, Sylvy?" Sylvia kept an awed silence; she knew by instinct that her grandmother did not comprehend the gravity of the situation. She must be mistaking the stranger for one of the farmer-lads of the region.

The young man stood his gun beside the door, and dropped a heavy game-bag beside it; then he bade Mrs. Tilley good-evening, and repeated his wayfarer's story, and asked if he could have a night's lodging.

"Put me anywhere you like," he said. "I must be off early in the morning, before day; but I am very hungry, indeed. You can give me some milk at any rate, that's plain."

"Dear sakes, yes," responded the hostess, whose long slumbering hospitality seemed to be easily awakened. "You might fare better if you went out on the main road a mile or so, but you're welcome to what we've got. I'll milk right off, and you make yourself at home. You can sleep on husks or feathers," she proffered graciously. "I raised them all myself. There's good pasturing for geese just below here towards the ma'sh. Now step round and set a plate for the gentleman, Sylvy!" And Sylvia promptly stepped. She was glad to have something to do, and she was hungry herself.

It was a surprise to find so clean and comfortable a little dwelling in this New England wilderness. The young man had known the horrors of its most primitive housekeeping, and the dreary squalor of that level of society which does not rebel at the companionship of hens. This was the best thrift of an old-fashioned farmstead, though on such a small scale that it seemed like a hermitage.

He listened eagerly to the old woman's quaint talk, he watched Sylvia's pale face and shining gray eyes with ever growing enthusiasm, and insisted that this was the best supper he had eaten for a month; then, afterward, the new-made friends sat down in the doorway together while the moon came up.

Soon it would be berry-time, and Sylvia was a great help at picking. The cow was a good milker, though a plaguy thing to keep track of, the hostess gossiped frankly, adding presently that she had buried four children, so that Sylvia's mother, and a son (who might be dead) in California were all the children she had left. "Dan, my boy, was a great hand to go gunning," she explained sadly. "I never wanted for pa'tridges or gray squer'ls while he was to home. He's been a great wand'rer, I expect, and he's no hand to write letters. There, I don't blame him, I'd ha' seen the world myself if it had been so I could.

"Sylvia takes after him," the grandmother continued affectionately, after a minute's pause. "There ain't a foot o' ground she don't know her way over, and the wild creatur's counts her one o' themselves. Squer'ls she'll tame to come an' feed right out o' her hands, and all sorts o' birds. Last winter she got the jay-birds to bangeing here, and I believe she'd 'a' scanted herself of her own meals to have plenty to throw out amongst 'em, if I had n't kep' watch. Anything but crows, I tell her, I'm willin' to help support, — though Dan he went an' tamed one o' them that did seem to have reason same as folks. It was round here a good spell after he went away. Dan an' his father they did n't hitch, — but he never held up his head ag'in after Dan had dared him an' gone off."

The guest did not notice this hint of family sorrows in his eager interest in something else.

"So Sylvy knows all about birds, does she?" he exclaimed, as he looked round at the little girl who sat, very demure but increasingly sleepy, in the moonlight. "I am making a collection of birds myself. I have been at it ever since I was a boy." (Mrs. Tilley smiled.) "There are two or three very rare ones I have been hunting for these five years. I mean to get them on my own ground if they can be found."

"Do you cage 'em up?" asked Mrs. Tilley doubtfully, in response to this enthusiastic announcement.

"Oh, no, they're stuffed and preserved, dozens and dozens of them," said the ornithologist, "and I have shot or snared every one myself. I caught a glimpse of a white heron three miles from here on Saturday, and I have followed it in this direction. They have never been found in this district at all. The little white heron, it is," and he turned again to look at Sylvia with the hope of discovering that the rare bird was one of her acquaintances.

But Sylvia was watching a hop-toad in the narrow footpath.

"You would know the heron if you saw it," the stranger continued eagerly. "A queer tall white bird with soft feathers and long thin legs. And it would have a nest perhaps in the top of a high tree, made of sticks, something like a hawk's nest."

Sylvia's heart gave a wild beat; she knew that strange white bird, and had once stolen softly near where it stood in some bright green swamp grass, away over at the other side of the woods. There was an open place where the sunshine always seemed strangely yellow and hot, where tall, nodding rushes grew, and her grandmother had warned her that she might sink in the soft black mud underneath and never be heard of more. Not far beyond were the salt marshes and beyond those was the sea, the sea which Sylvia wondered and dreamed about, but never had looked upon, though its great voice could often be heard above the noise of the woods on stormy nights.

"I can't think of anything I should like so much as to find that heron's nest," the handsome stranger was saying. "I would give ten dollars to anybody who could show it to me," he added desperately, "and I mean to spend my whole vacation hunting for it if need be. Perhaps it was only migrating, or had been chased out of its own region by some bird of prey."

Mrs. Tilley gave amazed attention to all this, but Sylvia still watched the toad, not divining, as she might have done at some calmer time, that the creature wished to get to its hole under the doorstep, and was much hindered by the unusual spectators at that hour of the evening. No amount of thought, that night, could decide how many wished-for treasures the ten dollars, so lightly spoken of, would buy.

The next day the young sportsman hovered about the woods, and Sylvia kept him company, having lost her first fear of the friendly lad, who proved to be most kind and sympathetic. He told her many things about the birds and what they knew and where they lived and what they did with themselves. And he gave her a jack-knife, which she thought as great a treasure as if she were a desert-islander. All day long he did not once make her troubled or afraid except when he brought down some unsuspecting singing creature from its bough. Sylvia would have liked him vastly better without his gun; she could not understand why he killed the very birds he seemed to like so much. But as the day waned, Sylvia still watched the young man with loving admiration. She had never seen anybody so charming and delightful; the woman's heart, asleep in the child, was vaguely thrilled by a dream of love. Some premonition of that great power stirred and swayed these young foresters who traversed the solemn woodlands with soft-footed silent care. They stopped to listen to a bird's song; they pressed forward again eagerly, parting the branches, — speaking to each other rarely and in whispers; the young man going first and Sylvia following, fascinated, a few steps behind, with her gray eyes dark with excitement.

She grieved because the longed-for white heron was elusive, but she did not lead the guest, she only followed, and there was no such thing as speaking first. The sound of her own unquestioned voice would have terrified her, — it was hard enough to answer yes or no when there was need of that. At last evening began to fall, and they drove the cow home together, and Sylvia smiled with pleasure when they came to the place where she heard the whistle and was afraid only the night before.

II.

Half a mile from home, at the farther edge of the woods, where the land was highest, a great pine-tree stood, the last of its generation. Whether it was left for a boundary mark, or for what reason, no one could say; the woodchoppers who had felled its mates were dead and gone long ago, and a whole forest of sturdy trees, pines and oaks and maples, had grown again. But the stately head of this old pine towered above them all and made a landmark for sea and shore miles and miles away. Sylvia knew it well. She had always believed that whoever climbed to the top of it could see the ocean; and the little girl had often laid her hand on the great rough trunk and looked up wistfully at those dark boughs that the wind always stirred, no matter how hot and still the air might be below. Now she thought of the tree with a new excitement, for why, if one climbed it at break of day, could not one see all the world, and easily discover whence the white heron flew, and mark the place, and find the hidden nest?

What a spirit of adventure, what wild ambition! What fancied triumph and delight and glory for the later morning when she could make known the secret! It was almost too real and too great for the childish heart to bear.

All night the door of the little house stood open, and the whippoorwills came and sang upon the very step. The young sportsman and his old hostess were sound asleep, but Sylvia's great design kept her broad awake and watching. She forgot to think of sleep. The short summer night seemed as long as the winter darkness, and at last when the whippoorwills ceased, and she was afraid the morning would after all come too soon, she stole out of the house and followed the pasture path through the woods, hastening toward the open ground beyond, listening with a sense of comfort and companionship to the drowsy twitter of a half-awakened bird, whose perch she had jarred in passing. Alas, if the great wave of human interest which flooded for the first time this dull little life should sweep away the satisfactions of an existence heart to heart with nature and the dumb life of the forest!

There was the huge tree asleep yet in the paling moonlight, and small and hopeful Sylvia began with utmost bravery to mount to the top of it, with tingling, eager blood coursing the channels of her whole frame, with her bare feet and fingers that pinched and held like bird's claws to the monstrous ladder reaching up, up, almost to the sky itself. First she must mount the white oak tree that grew alongside, where she was almost lost among the dark branches and the green leaves heavy and wet with dew; a bird fluttered off its nest, and a red squirrel ran to and fro and scolded pettishly at the harmless housebreaker. Sylvia felt her way easily. She had often climbed there, and knew that higher still one of the oak's upper branches chafed against the pine trunk, just where its lower boughs were set close together. There, when she made the dangerous pass from one tree to the other, the great enterprise would really begin.

She crept out along the swaying oak limb at last, and took the daring step across into the old pine-tree. The way was harder than she thought; she must reach far and hold fast, the sharp dry twigs caught and held her and scratched her like angry talons, the pitch made her thin little fingers clumsy and stiff as she went round and round the tree's great stem, higher and higher upward. The sparrows and robins in the woods below were beginning to wake and twitter to the dawn, yet it seemed much lighter there aloft in the pine-tree, and the child knew that she must hurry if her project were to be of any use.

The tree seemed to lengthen itself out as she went up, and to reach farther and farther upward. It was like a great main-mast to the voyaging earth; it must truly have been amazed that morning through all its ponderous frame as it felt this determined spark of human spirit creeping and climbing from higher branch to branch. Who knows how steadily the least twigs held themselves to advantage this light, weak creature on her way! The old pine must have loved his new dependent. More than all the hawks, and bats, and moths, and even the sweet-voiced thrushes, was the brave, beating heart of the solitary gray-eyed child. And the tree stood still and held away the winds that June morning while the dawn grew bright in the east.

Sylvia's face was like a pale star, if one had seen it from the ground, when the last thorny bough was past, and she stood trembling and tired but wholly triumphant, high in the tree-top. Yes, there was the sea with the dawning sun making a golden dazzle over it, and toward that glorious east flew two hawks with slow-moving pinions. How low they looked in the air from that height when before one had only seen them far up, and dark against the blue sky. Their gray feathers were as soft as moths; they seemed only a little way from the tree, and Sylvia felt as if she too could go flying away among the clouds. Westward, the woodlands and farms reached miles and miles into the distance; here and there were church steeples, and white villages; truly it was a vast and awesome world.

The birds sang louder and louder. At last the sun came up bewilderingly bright. Sylvia could see the white sails of ships out at sea, and the clouds that were purple and rose-colored and yellow at first began to fade away. Where was the white heron's nest in the sea of green branches, and was this wonderful sight and pageant of the world the only reward for having climbed to such a giddy height? Now look down again, Sylvia, where the green marsh is set among the shining birches and dark hemlocks; there where you saw the white heron once you will see him again; look, look! a white spot of him like a single floating feather comes up from the dead hemlock and grows larger, and rises, and comes close at last, and goes by the landmark pine with steady sweep of wing and outstretched slender neck and crested head. And wait! wait! do not move a foot or a finger, little girl, do not send an arrow of light and consciousness from your two eager eyes, for the heron has perched on a pine bough not far beyond yours, and cries back to his mate on the nest, and plumes his feathers for the new day!

The child gives a long sigh a minute later when a company of shouting cat-birds comes also to the tree, and vexed by their fluttering and lawlessness the solemn heron goes away. She knows his secret now, the wild, light, slender bird that floats and wavers, and goes back like an arrow presently to his home in the green world beneath. Then Sylvia, well satisfied, makes her perilous way down again, not daring to look far below the branch she stands on, ready to cry sometimes because her fingers ache and her lamed feet slip. Wondering over and over again what the stranger would say to her, and what he would think when she told him how to find his way straight to the heron's nest.

"Sylvy, Sylvy!" called the busy old grandmother again and again, but nobody answered, and the small husk bed was empty, and Sylvia had disappeared.

The guest waked from a dream, and remembering his day's pleasure hurried to dress himself that it might sooner begin. He was sure from the way the shy little girl looked once or twice yesterday that she had at least seen the white heron, and now she must really be persuaded to tell. Here she comes now, paler than ever, and her worn old frock is torn and tattered, and smeared with pine pitch. The grandmother and the sportsman stand in the door together and question her, and the splendid moment has come to speak of the dead hemlock-tree by the green marsh.

But Sylvia does not speak after all, though the old grandmother fretfully rebukes her, and the young man's kind appealing eyes are looking straight in her own. He can make them rich with money; he has promised it, and they are poor now. He is so well worth making happy, and he waits to hear the story she can tell.

No, she must keep silence! What is it that suddenly forbids her and makes her dumb? Has she been nine years growing, and now, when the great world for the first time puts out a hand to her, must she thrust it aside for a bird's sake? The murmur of the pine's green branches is in her ears, she remembers how the white heron came flying through the golden air and how they watched the sea and the morning together, and Sylvia cannot speak; she cannot tell the heron's secret and give its life away.

Dear loyalty, that suffered a sharp pang as the guest went away disappointed later in the day, that could have served and followed him and loved him as a dog loves! Many a night Sylvia heard the echo of his whistle haunting the pasture path as she came home with the loitering cow. She forgot even her sorrow at the sharp report of his gun and the piteous sight of thrushes and sparrows dropping silent to the ground, their songs hushed and their pretty feathers stained and wet with blood. Were the birds better friends than their hunter might have been, — who can tell? Whatever treasures were lost to her, woodlands and summer-time, remember! Bring your gifts and graces and tell your secrets to this lonely country child!

After the Race
(1914)

JAMES JOYCE

The cars came scudding in towards Dublin, running evenly like pellets in the groove of the Naas Road. At the crest of the hill at Inchicore sightseers had gathered in clumps to watch the cars careering homeward and through this channel of poverty and inaction the Continent sped its wealth and industry. Now and again the clumps of people raised the cheer of the gratefully oppressed. Their sympathy, however, was for the blue cars—the cars of their friends, the French.

The French, moreover, were virtual victors. Their team had finished solidly; they had been placed second and third and the driver of the winning German car was reported a Belgian. Each blue car, therefore, received a double measure of welcome as it topped the crest of the hill and each cheer of welcome was acknowledged with smiles and nods by those in the car. In one of these trimly built cars was a party of four young men whose spirits seemed to be at present well above the level of successful Gallicism: in fact, these four young men were almost hilarious. They were Charles Ségouin, the owner of the car; André Rivière, a young electrician of Canadian birth; a huge Hungarian named Villona and a neatly groomed young man named Doyle. Ségouin was in good humour because he had unexpectedly received some orders in advance (he was about to start a motor establishment in Paris) and Rivière was in good humour because he was to be appointed manager of the establishment; these two young men (who were cousins) were also in good humour because of the success of the French cars. Villona was in good humour because he had had a very satisfactory luncheon; and besides he was an optimist by nature. The fourth member of the party, however, was too excited to be genuinely happy.

He was about twenty-six years of age, with a soft, light brown moustache and rather innocent-looking grey eyes. His father, who had begun life as an advanced Nationalist, had modified his views early. He had made his money as a butcher in Kingstown and by opening shops in Dublin and in the suburbs he had made his money many times over. He had also been fortunate enough to secure some of the police contracts and in the end he had become rich enough to be alluded to in the Dublin newspapers as a merchant prince. He had sent his son to England to be educated in a big Catholic college and had afterwards sent him to Dublin University to study law. Jimmy did not study very earnestly and took to bad courses for a while. He had money and he was popular; and he divided his time curiously between musical and motoring circles. Then he had been sent for a term to Cambridge to see a little life. His father, remonstrative, but covertly proud of the excess, had paid his bills and brought him home. It was at Cambridge that he had met Ségouin. They were not much more than acquaintances as yet but Jimmy found great pleasure in the society of one who had seen so much of the world and was reputed to own some of the biggest hotels in France. Such a person (as his father agreed) was well worth knowing, even if he had not been the charming companion he was. Villona was entertaining also—a brilliant pianist—but, unfortunately, very poor.

The car ran on merrily with its cargo of hilarious youth. The two cousins sat on the front seat; Jimmy and his Hungarian friend sat behind. Decidedly Villona was in excellent spirits; he kept up a deep bass hum of melody for miles of the road. The Frenchmen flung their laughter and light words over their shoulders and often Jimmy had to strain forward to catch the quick phrase. This was not altogether pleasant for him, as he had nearly always to make a deft guess at the meaning and shout back a suitable answer in the face of a high wind. Besides Villona's humming would confuse anybody; the noise of the car, too.

Rapid motion through space elates one; so does notoriety; so does the possession of money. These were three good reasons for Jimmy's excitement. He had been seen by many of his friends that day in the company of these Continentals. At the control Ségouin had presented him to one of the French competitors and, in answer to his confused murmur of compliment, the swarthy face of the driver had disclosed a line of shining white teeth. It was pleasant after that honour to return to the profane world of spectators amid nudges and significant looks. Then as to money—he really had a great sum under his control. Ségouin, perhaps, would not think it a great sum but Jimmy who, in spite of temporary errors, was at heart the inheritor of solid instincts knew well with what difficulty it had been got together. This knowledge had previously kept his bills within the limits of reasonable recklessness and, if he had been so conscious of the labour latent in money when there had been question merely of some freak of the higher intelligence, how much more so now when he was about to stake the greater part of his substance! It was a serious thing for him.

Of course, the investment was a good one and Ségouin had managed to give the impression that it was by a favour of friendship the mite of Irish money was to be included in the capital of the concern. Jimmy had a respect for his father's shrewdness in business matters and in this case it had been his father who had first suggested the investment; money to be made in the motor business, pots of money. Moreover Ségouin had the unmistakable air of wealth. Jimmy set out to translate into days' work that lordly car in which he sat. How smoothly it ran. In what style they had come careering along the country roads! The journey laid a magical finger on the genuine pulse of life and gallantly the machinery of human nerves strove to answer the bounding courses of the swift blue animal.

They drove down Dame Street. The street was busy with unusual traffic, loud with the horns of motorists and the gongs of impatient tram-drivers. Near the Bank Ségouin drew up and Jimmy and his friend alighted. A little knot of people collected on the footpath to pay homage to the snorting motor. The party was to dine together that evening in Ségouin's hotel and, meanwhile, Jimmy and his friend, who was staying with him, were to go home to dress. The car steered out slowly for Grafton Street while the two young men pushed their way through the knot of gazers. They walked northward with a curious feeling of disappointment in the exercise, while the city hung its pale globes of light above them in a haze of summer evening.

In Jimmy's house this dinner had been pronounced an occasion. A certain pride mingled with his parents' trepidation, a certain eagerness, also, to play fast and loose for the names of great foreign cities have at least this virtue. Jimmy, too, looked very well when he was dressed and, as he stood in the hall giving a last equation to the bows of his dress tie, his father may have felt even commercially satisfied at having secured for his son qualities often unpurchaseable. His father, therefore, was unusually friendly with Villona and his manner expressed a real respect for foreign accomplishments; but this subtlety of his host was probably lost upon the Hungarian, who was beginning to have a sharp desire for his dinner.

The dinner was excellent, exquisite. Ségouin, Jimmy decided, had a very refined taste. The party was increased by a young Englishman named Routh whom Jimmy had seen with Ségouin at Cambridge. The young men supped in a snug room lit by electric candle lamps. They talked volubly and with little reserve. Jimmy, whose imagination was kindling, conceived the lively youth of the Frenchmen twined elegantly upon the firm framework of the Englishman's manner. A graceful image of his, he thought, and a just one. He admired the dexterity with which their host directed the conversation. The five young men had various tastes and their tongues had been loosened. Villona, with immense respect, began to discover to the mildly surprised Englishman the beauties of the English madrigal, deploring the loss of old instruments. Rivière, not wholly ingenuously, undertook to explain to Jimmy the triumph of the French mechanicians. The resonant voice of the Hungarian was about to prevail in ridicule of the spurious lutes of the romantic painters when Ségouin shepherded his party into politics. Here was congenial ground for all. Jimmy, under generous influences, felt the buried zeal of his father wake to life within him: he aroused the torpid Routh at last. The room grew doubly hot and Ségouin's task grew harder each moment: there was even danger of personal spite. The alert host at an opportunity lifted his glass to Humanity and, when the toast had been drunk, he threw open a window significantly.

That night the city wore the mask of a capital. The five young men strolled along Stephen's Green in a faint cloud of aromatic smoke. They talked loudly and gaily and their cloaks dangled from their shoulders. The people made way for them. At the corner of Grafton Street a short fat man was putting two handsome ladies on a car in charge of another fat man. The car drove off and the short fat man caught sight of the party.

"André."

"It's Farley!"

A torrent of talk followed. Farley was an American. No one knew very well what the talk was about. Villona and Rivière were the noisiest, but all the men were excited. They got up on a car, squeezing themselves together amid much laughter. They drove by the crowd, blended now into soft colours, to a music of merry bells. They took the train at Westland Row and in a few seconds, as it seemed to Jimmy, they were walking out of Kingstown Station. The ticket-collector saluted Jimmy; he was an old man:

"Fine night, sir!"

It was a serene summer night; the harbour lay like a darkened mirror at their feet. They proceeded towards it with linked arms, singing *Cadet Roussel* in chorus, stamping their feet at every:

"*Ho! Ho! Hohé, vraiment!*"

They got into a rowboat at the slip and made out for the American's yacht. There was to be supper, music, cards. Villona said with conviction:

"It is delightful!"

There was a yacht piano in the cabin. Villona played a waltz for Farley and Rivière, Farley acting as cavalier and Rivière as lady. Then an impromptu square dance, the men devising original figures. What merriment! Jimmy took his part with a will; this was seeing life, at least. Then Farley got out of breath and cried *"Stop!"* A man brought in a light supper, and the young men sat down to it for form's sake. They drank, however: it was Bohemian. They drank Ireland, England, France, Hungary, the United States of America. Jimmy made a speech, a long speech, Villona saying: *"Hear! Hear!"* whenever there was a pause. There was a great clapping of hands when he sat down. It must have been a good speech.

Farley clapped him on the back and laughed loudly. What jovial fellows! What good company they were!

Cards! cards! The table was cleared. Villona returned quietly to his piano and played voluntaries for them. The other men played game after game, flinging themselves boldly into the adventure. They drank the health of the Queen of Hearts and of the Queen of Diamonds. Jimmy felt obscurely the lack of an audience: the wit was flashing. Play ran very high and paper began to pass. Jimmy did not know exactly who was winning but he knew that he was losing. But it was his own fault for he frequently mistook his cards and the other men had to calculate his I.O.U.'s for him. They were devils of fellows but he wished they would stop: it was getting late. Someone gave the toast of the yacht *The Belle of Newport* and then someone proposed one great game for a finish.

The piano had stopped; Villona must have gone up on deck. It was a terrible game. They stopped just before the end of it to drink for luck. Jimmy understood that the game lay between Routh and Ségouin. What excitement! Jimmy was excited too; he would lose, of course. How much had he written away? The men rose to their feet to play the last tricks, talking and gesticulating. Routh won. The cabin shook with the young men's cheering and the cards were bundled together. They began then to gather in what they had won. Farley and Jimmy were the heaviest losers.

He knew that he would regret in the morning but at present he was glad of the rest, glad of the dark stupor that would cover up his folly. He leaned his elbows on the table and rested his head between his hands, counting the beats of his temples. The cabin door opened and he saw the Hungarian standing in a shaft of grey light:

"Daybreak, gentlemen!"

A Report to an Academy
(1917)

FRANZ KAFKA

Gentlemen of the Academy:

You have honored me with your invitation to submit a report to the Academy about my former life as an ape.

Taking this invitation in its literal sense, I am unfortunately unable to comply with it. Nearly five years stand between me and my apehood, a period that may be short in terms of the calendar but is an infinitely long one to gallop through as I have done, accompanied for certain stretches by excellent people, advice, applause and band music, but fundamentally on my own, because, to remain within the metaphor, all that accompaniment never got very close to the rail. This achievement would have been impossible if I had willfully clung to my origins, to the memories of my youth. In fact, avoidance of all willfulness was the supreme commandment I had imposed on myself; I, a free ape, accepted that yoke. Thereby, however, my memories were in turn increasingly lost to me. If at first a return to the past, should the humans have so wished, was as wide open to me as the universal archway the sky forms over the earth, at the same time my wildly accelerated development made this archway increasingly low and narrow; I felt more at ease and sheltered in the human world; the storm winds that blew out of my past grew calm; today there is only a breeze that cools my heels; and the hole in the distance through which it issues, and from which I once issued, has become so small that, if I ever had sufficient strength and desire to run all the way back there, I would have to scrape the hide off my body to squeeze through. Speaking frankly (although I enjoy using figures of speech for these matters), speaking frankly: your own apehood, gentlemen, to the extent that there is anything like that in your past, cannot be more remote from you than mine is from me. But every wanderer on earth feels a tickling in his heels: the little chimpanzee and great Achilles. In the most limited sense, however, I may be able to satisfy your demands, and, in fact, I do so with great pleasure. The first thing I learned was shaking hands; shaking hands indicates candidness; today, when I am at the pinnacle of my career, why not add my candid words to that first handshake? My report will not teach the Academy anything basically new and will fall far short of what has been asked of me, which, with the best will in the world, I am unable to tell you — nevertheless, it is meant to show the guidelines by which a former ape has burst into the human world and established himself there. But I certainly would not have the right to make even the insignificant statement that follows, if I were not completely sure of myself and had not secured a truly unassailable position on all the great vaudeville stages of the civilized world.

I come from the Gold Coast. For the story of how I was captured I must rely on the reports of others. A hunting expedition of the Hagenbeck firm — incidentally, since then I've drained many a fine bottle of red wine with its leader — was lying in wait in the brush by the shore when I ran down to the watering place one evening in the midst of a pack of apes. They fired; I was the only one hit; I was wounded in two places.

One wound was in the cheek; that was slight, but left behind a large, red, hairless scar, which won me the repulsive, totally unsuitable name of Red Peter, which must have been invented by an ape! — as if the red spot on my cheek were the only difference between me and the trained ape Peter, who had a local reputation here and there and who kicked the bucket recently. But that's by the by.

The second bullet hit me below the hip. It was a serious wound and the cause of my limping a little even today. Not long ago I read in an article by one of the ten thousand windbags who gab about me in the papers, saying my ape nature is not yet suppressed; the proof being that, when visitors come, I'm fond of taking off my trousers to show where the bullet hit me. That guy should have every last finger of the hand he writes with individually blasted off! *I, I* have the right to drop my pants in front of anyone I feel like; all they'll see there is a well-tended coat of fur and the scar left over from — here let us choose a specific word for a specific purpose, but a word I wouldn't want misunderstood — the scar left over from an infamous shot. Everything is open and aboveboard; there's nothing to hide; when it comes to the truth, every high-minded person rejects namby-pamby etiquette. On the other hand, if that writer were to take his trousers off when company came, you can be sure it would look quite different, and I'm ready to accept it as a token of his good sense that he refrains from doing so. But then he shouldn't bedevil me with his delicate sensibilities!

After those shots I woke up — and here my own recollections gradually begin — in a cage between decks on the Hagenbeck steamer. It wasn't a four-sided cage with bars all around; instead, there were only three barred sides attached to a crate, so that the crate formed the fourth wall. The whole thing was too low for standing erect in, and too narrow for sitting down in. And so I squatted with bent, constantly trembling knees, and, since at first I probably didn't want to see anyone and felt like being in the dark all the time, I faced the crate, while behind me the bars cut into my flesh. This way of keeping wild animals right after their capture is considered advantageous, and, with the experience I have today, I can't deny that, in a human sense, it is really the case.

But at that time I didn't think about it. For the first time in my life I had no way out, or at least not straight ahead of me; right in front of me was the crate, each board tightly joined to the next. True, between the boards there was a gap running right through, and when I first discovered it I greeted it with a joyful howl of ignorance, but this gap wasn't even nearly wide enough for me to push my tail through, and all my ape's strength couldn't widen it.

They told me later on that I made unusually little noise, from which they concluded that I would either go under, or else, if I managed to live through the first, critical period, I would be extremely trainable. I lived through that period. Muffled sobbing, painful searching for fleas, weary licking of a coconut, banging the side of the crate with my cranium, sticking out my tongue whenever someone approached — those were my first occupations in my new life. But, throughout it all, only that one feeling: no way out. Today, naturally, I can only sketch from hindsight, and in human words, what I then felt as an ape, and therefore I am sketching it incorrectly, but even if I can no longer attain the old apish truth, my description isn't basically off course, and no doubt about it.

And yet, up to then, I had had so many ways out and now no longer one. I had boxed myself in. If I had been nailed down that couldn't have subtracted from my freedom of action. Why so? Scratch the skin between your toes till it bleeds, and you still won't find the reason. Press yourself backwards against the bars until they nearly cut you in two, you won't find the reason. I had no way out, but had to create one for myself, because without it I couldn't live. Always up against the side of that crate — I would definitely have dropped dead. But, for Hagenbeck, apes belong at the side of the crate — so I stopped being an ape. A lucid, elegant train of thought, which I must have somehow hatched out with my belly, because apes think with their belly.

I'm afraid that it may not be clearly understood what I mean by "a way out." I am using the phrase in its most common and most comprehensive sense. I purposely do not say "freedom." I don't mean that expansive feeling of freedom on all sides. As an ape I might have known it, and I've met human beings who long for it. As for me, however, I didn't desire freedom then, and I don't now. Incidentally: human beings fool themselves all too often on the subject of freedom. And just as freedom counts among the loftiest feelings, so does the corresponding delusion count among the loftiest. Often in vaudeville houses, before my act came on, I've seen some pair of artists do their trapeze routine way up near the ceiling. They swung to and fro, they rocked back and forth, they made leaps, they floated into each other's arms, one held the other by the hair with his teeth. "That, too, is human freedom," I would muse, "movement achieved in sovereign self-confidence." You mockery of holy Nature! No building would remain unshaken by the laughter of the ape world at that sight.

No, it wasn't freedom I wanted. Only a way out; to the right, to the left, in any direction at all; I made no other demands; even if the way out were a delusion; the demand was a small one, the delusion wouldn't be any bigger. To move forward, to move forward! Anything but standing still with raised arms, flattened against the side of a crate.

Today I see it clearly: without the utmost inner calm I would never have been able to save myself. And, in reality, I may owe everything that I've achieved to the calm that came over me after the first few days there on the ship. But, in turn, I probably owe that calm to the people on the ship.

They're good sorts, despite everything. Even today I enjoy recalling the sound of their heavy steps, which at the time reechoed in my half-slumber. They had the habit of tackling everything as slowly as possible. If one of them wanted to rub his eyes, he would lift his hand as if it were a hanging weight. Their jokes were coarse but hearty. Their laughter was always mingled with a coughing sound that sounded dangerous but was insignificant. They always had something in their mouth they could spit out and they didn't care a bit where they spat it. They were always complaining that my fleas were jumping onto them; but they were never seriously mad at me for it; they were perfectly well aware that fleas thrive in my fur and that fleas jump; they reconciled themselves to it. When they had no duties, sometimes a few of them would sit down in a semicircle around me; they rarely spoke but just mumbled to one another like pigeons cooing; they would stretch out on crates and smoke their pipes; they would slap their knees the minute I made the slightest movement; and from time to time one of them would take a stick and tickle me where I liked it. If I were to be invited today to take part in a voyage on that ship, I would certainly decline the invitation, but it is equally certain

497

that the memories I could muse over from my days between the decks there are not all unpleasant.

The calm I acquired in the company of those people restrained me especially from any attempt to escape. From the vantage point of today, it seems to me I had at least a vague notion that I had to find a way out if I were to survive, but that the way out was not to be attained by escape. I no longer know for certain whether escape was possible, but I think so; an ape probably always has some means of escape. With my teeth as they are today, I have to be careful even when cracking an ordinary nut, but at the time I would probably certainly have managed to bite through the lock on the door in a matter of time. I didn't. What would I have gained if I had? They would have caught me again the minute I stuck my head out and locked me in a cage that was worse yet; or else I might have escaped unnoticed and run over to other animals, for instance the giant snakes opposite me and breathed my last in their embraces; or I might even have successfully stolen away onto the top deck and jumped overboard; in that case, I would have rocked on the ocean for a while and then drowned. Deeds of desperation. My calculations weren't that human, but under the influence of my environment I behaved as if I had calculated it all.

I didn't calculate, but I did observe things very calmly. I watched those human beings walk back and forth, always the same faces the same motions; it often seemed to me as if it was just a single person. Well, that person or those persons were walking around unmolested. A lofty goal hazily entered my mind. Nobody promised me that, if I became like them, the bars would be removed. Promises like that based on apparently impossible terms just aren't made. But if the terms are met, later on the promises turn up exactly where they were formerly sought in vain. Now, there was nothing about these humans in themselves that allured me all that much. If I were a devotee of that abovementioned freedom, I would certainly have chosen the ocean over the kind of way out that offered itself to me in the dull eyes of those people. At any rate, I had already been observing them long before I thought about such things; in fact, it was the accumulation of observations that first pushed me in the chosen direction.

It was so easy to imitate people. I could already spit within the first few days. Then we would mutually spit in each other's faces; the only difference being that I licked my face clean afterwards, and they didn't. I was soon smoking a pipe like an old hand; if, when doing so, I still stuck my thumb into the bowl, everyone between the decks whooped with joy; it was only the difference between the empty and filled pipe that I didn't understand for a long time.

It was the liquor bottle that gave me most trouble. The smell was torture to me; I forced myself with all my strength; but weeks went by before I overcame the resistance. Oddly, it was these inward struggles that the people took more seriously than anything else about me. Although in my recollections I can't tell the people apart, there was one of them who came again and again, alone or with comrades, by day and night, at the most varied hours; he would place himself in front of me with the bottle and give me instruction. He couldn't comprehend me, he wanted to solve the riddle of my being. Slowly he uncorked the bottle and then looked at me to see if I had understood; I confess, I always watched him with frantic, exaggerated attention; no human teacher will ever find such a human pupil anywhere on earth; after the bottle was uncorked, he lifted it to his mouth; my eyes followed him all the way into his gullet; he nodded, contented with me, and put the bottle to his lips; I, delighted by dawning knowledge, then squeal and scratch myself all over wherever I feel the need; he is happy, presses the bottle against his mouth and takes a swallow; I, impatient and desperate to emulate him, soil myself in my cage, and this, too, gives him great satisfaction; and now, holding the bottle far away from himself and lifting it toward himself again briskly, he bends backwards with pedagogical exaggeration and empties it in one draught. I, worn out by the excess of my desire, am unable to follow any longer and hang weakly on the bars while he concludes the theoretical instruction by rubbing his stomach and grinning.

Only now does the practical exercise begin. Am I not too exhausted already by the theoretical part? Far too exhausted, most likely. That's how my destiny goes. All the same, I do the best I can as I reach for the bottle he holds out to me; trembling, I uncork it; as I succeed, I gradually acquire new strength; I lift the bottle, by this time imitating my model so closely that there's hardly any difference; I put it to my mouth and — and with loathing, with loathing, even though it's empty and only the smell is left, with loathing I throw it on the ground. To my teacher's sorrow, to my own greater sorrow; I fail to make things right with either him or myself when, even after throwing away the bottle, I don't forget to do an excellent job of rubbing my stomach and grinning at the same time.

Things went that way all too often during my course of instruction. And to my teacher's credit: he wasn't angry with me; true, he sometimes held his lit pipe against my fur until it started to get singed in some spot that was very hard to reach, but then he would put it out again himself with his gigantic, kindly hand; he wasn't angry with me, he realized that we were both fighting as allies against ape nature, and the difficulty was more on my side.

What a victory it was, then, for him and for me, when one evening, before a large group of spectators — maybe it was a party, a gramophone was playing, an officer was walking about among the men — when on that evening, while no one was observing me, I grasped a liquor bottle that had been accidentally left in front of my cage, uncorked it according to all the rules as the people paid increasingly greater attention, put it to my mouth and, without hesitating, without twisting my lips, like a drinker from way back; with rolling eyes and gurgling throat, really and truly emptied the bottle; threw it away, no longer like someone in despair, but like an artiste; did actually forget to rub my stomach; but, instead, because I simply had to, because I had the urge to, because my senses were in an uproar — in a word, I called out "Hello," breaking into human speech, leaping into the human community by means of that outcry, and feeling its echo, "Listen, he's talking," like a kiss all over my sweat-soaked body.

I repeat: I didn't imitate human beings because they appealed to me; I imitated because I was looking for a way out, for no other reason. And that victory still didn't amount to much. My speaking voice failed me again immediately, and it took months for it to come back; my aversion to the liquor bottle returned and was even stronger than before. But, all the same, my course was set once and for all.

When I was handed over to the first trainer in Hamburg, I immediately recognized the two possibilities that were open to me: zoo or vaudeville. I didn't hesitate. I told myself: make every effort to get into vaudeville; that's the way out; the zoo is just another cage; once you land there, you're lost.

And I learned, gentlemen. Oh, you learn when you have to; you learn when you want a way out; you learn regardless of all else. You observe yourself, whip in hand; you lacerate yourself at the least sign of resistance. My ape nature, turning somersaults, raged out of me and away, so that my first teacher nearly became apelike himself, and soon had to give up the instruction and go to a sanatorium. Fortunately he came out again before long.

But I used up many teachers, sometimes a few teachers simultaneously. When I had become more sure of my abilities, when the public was following my progress and my future began to look bright, I took on teachers on my own, sat them down in five successive rooms and took lessons from all of them at once, uninterruptedly leaping from one room to another.

That progress! That penetration of rays of knowledge from all sides into my awakening brain! I won't deny it: it made me happy. But I also admit: I didn't overestimate it, not even then, let alone today. Through an effort that hasn't found its match on earth to the present day, I have attained the educational level of an average European. Perhaps that wouldn't be anything by itself, but it is really something when you consider that it helped me out of my cage and gave me this particular way out, this human way out. There's an excellent German expression: *sich in die Büsche schlagen,* to steal away secretly. That's what I did, I stole away secretly. I had no other way, always presupposing that I couldn't choose freedom.

When I survey my development and the goal it has had up to now, I am neither unhappy nor contented. My hands in my trousers pockets, the wine bottle on the table, I half recline, half sit, in my rocking chair and look out the window. When a visitor comes, I receive him in a proper manner. My impresario sits in the anteroom; when I ring, he comes and listens to what I have to say. There's a performance almost every evening, and my success probably can't get much greater. When I come home late at night from banquets, learned societies or friendly gatherings, a little half-trained female chimpanzee is waiting for me and I have a good time with her, ape fashion; in the daytime I don't want to see her, because her eyes have that deranged look which bewildered trained animals have; I'm the only one who recognizes it, and I can't stand it.

All in all, however, I have achieved what I wanted to achieve. Let nobody say that it wasn't worth the trouble. Anyway, I don't want any human being's opinion, I merely wish to disseminate information; I am merely making a report; even to you, gentlemen of the Academy, I have merely made a report.

Men in the Sun
(1963)

GHASSAN KANAFANI

Abu Qais

Abu Qais rested on the damp ground, and the earth began to throb under him with tired heartbeats, which trembled through the grains of sand and penetrated the cells of his body. Every time he threw himself down with his chest to the ground he sensed that throbbing, as though the heart of the earth had been pushing its difficult way towards the light from the utmost depths of hell, ever since the first time he had lain there. Once when he said that to his neighbor, with whom he shared the field in the land he left ten years ago, the man answered mockingly:

"It's the sound of your own heart. You can hear it when you lay your chest close to the ground."

What wicked nonsense! And the smell, then? The smell that, when he sniffed it, surged into his head and then poured down into his veins. Every time he breathed the scent of the earth, as he lay on it, he imagined that he was sniffing his wife's hair when she had just walked out of the bathroom, after washing with cold water. The very same smell, the smell of a woman who had washed with cold water and covered his face with her hair while it was still damp. The same throbbing, like carrying a small bird tenderly in your hands.

The damp earth, he thought, was no doubt the remains of yesterday's rain. No, yesterday it had not rained. The sky now could rain nothing but scorching heat and dust. Have you forgotten where you are? Have you forgotten?

He turned himself over and lay on his back, cradling his head in his hands. He started to stare at the sky. It was blazing white, and there was one black bird circling high up, alone and aimless. He did not know why, but he was suddenly filled with a bitter feeling of being a stranger, and for a moment he thought he was on the point of weeping. No, yesterday it didn't rain. We are in August now. Have you forgotten? Those miles of road speeding through a void, like black eternity. Have you forgotten it? The bird was still circling around alone like a black spot in that blaze spread out above him. We are in August. Then why this dampness in the ground? It's the Shatt. Can't you see it stretching out beside you as far as the eye can see?

"When the two great rivers, Tigris and Euphrates, meet, they form one river called the Shatt al-Arab, which extends from just above Basra to . . ."

Ustaz Selim, a thin, gray-haired old man, said it a dozen times in his loud voice to a small child standing beside the blackboard, when he was walking past the school in his village. So

501

he stood on a stone and began to eavesdrop through the window. Ustaz Selim was standing in front of the young pupil, shouting at the top of his voice as he shook his thin stick:

"When the two great rivers, Tigris and Euphrates, meet. . . ."

The child was trembling with anxiety, while the laughter of the other children in the class could be heard. Abu Qais stretched out his arm and tapped a child on the head. The child raised his eyes to him as he was eavesdropping by the window.

"What's going on?"

The child laughed and replied in a whisper:

"Idiot!"

He drew back, got down off the stone and went on his way, still followed by the voice of Ustaz Selim repeating: "When the two great rivers, Tigris and Euphrates, meet. . . ."

That night he saw Ustaz Selim sitting in the headman's reception room, smoking his gurgling water pipe. Ustaz Selim had been sent to their village from Jaffa to teach the boys, and he had spent so much of his life teaching that the title "Ustaz" had become an inseparable part of his name. That night in the reception room someone asked him:

". . . and you will lead the prayers on Friday, won't you?"

"No, I'm a teacher, not an imam. I can't lead the prayers."

The headman said to him:

"What's the difference? Our teacher was an imam."

"He was a teacher in a Quran school, but I teach in a secular school."

The headman repeated his question, insistently:

"What's the difference?"

Ustaz Selim did not answer, but behind his spectacles his eyes ran over the faces as though he was imploring the help of one of those sitting there. However, everyone was confused about this, like the headman.

After a long period of silence, Ustaz Selim cleared his throat and said quietly:

"Well, I don't know how to perform the prayers."

"You don't know?"

There were growls from everyone, but Ustaz Selim reaffirmed what he had said:

"I don't know."

The seated men exchanged looks of surprise, and then fixed their eyes on the face of the headman, who felt that it was for him to say something. He burst out without thinking:

"And what *do* you know, then?"

Ustaz Selim seemed to be expecting a question like that, for he answered quickly, as he was rising:

"Many things. I'm a good shot, for instance."

He reached the door and turned, and his thin face was trembling.

"If they attack you, wake me; I may be of some use."

This, then, was the Shatt that Ustaz Selim had spoken of ten years before. Here he was lying thousands of miles and days away from his village and Ustaz Selim's school. The mercy of God be upon you, Ustaz Selim, the mercy of God be upon you. God was certainly good to you when he made you die one night before the wretched village fell into the hands of the Jews, One night only. O God, is there any divine favor greater than that? It is true that the men were too busy to bury you and honor you in your death. But all the same you stayed there. You stayed there. You saved yourself humiliation and wretchedness, and you preserved

502

your old age from shame. The mercy of God be upon you, Ustaz Selim. If you had lived, if you had been drowned by poverty as I have, I wonder if you would have done what I am doing now. Would you have been willing to carry all your years on your shoulders and flee across the desert to Kuwait to find a crust of bread?

He sat up, leaned on the ground with his elbows, and began to look at the great river again as though he had not seen it before. . . . So this was the Shatt al-Arab, "a vast river that steamers sail along carrying dates and straw, like a street full of passing cars in the center of town."

That's what his son Qais had shouted, hurriedly, when he had asked him that night:

"What is the Shatt al-Arab?"

He meant to test him, but Qais quickly answered in a loud voice, adding:

"I saw you looking through the classroom window today. . . ."

Abu Qais turned to his wife, who grinned. He felt a little embarrassed, and slowly remarked:

"I knew it before."

"No, you didn't. You learned it today while you were peeping through the window."

"All right. And what does it matter whether I know it or not; is it the end of the world?"

His wife glanced at him out of the corner of her eye, and then said:

"Qais, go and play in the other room." When he slammed the door behind him, she turned to her husband:

"Don't speak like that in front of him. The boy is happy because he knows it. Why do you discourage him?"

He stood up, went over to her and put his hand on her stomach, whispering:

"When?"

"In seven months' time."

"Ah!"

"We want a girl this time."

"No, we want a boy. A boy."

But she gave birth to a girl he named Hosna, who died two months later. The doctor said distastefully:

"She was extremely emaciated."

It happened a month after he left his village, in an old house in another village far from the firing line.

"Abu Qais! I feel I'm going to give birth!"

"All right. All right. Keep calm."

He said to himself:

"I wish that women gave birth after a pregnancy of a hundred months. Is this the time for labour?"

"O God!"

"What?"

"I'm going to give birth."

"Shall I call anyone?"

"Umm Umar."

"Where can I find her now?"

"Hand me that cushion!"

"Where can I find Umm Umar?"

"O my God! Lift me up a little. Let me rest against the wall."

"Don't move much. Let me call Umm Umar."

"Hurry! Hurry! O Lord of creation!"

He hurried outside. But as he shut the door behind him he heard the cry of the newborn child, so he turned back and put his ear to the wood of the door. . . .

The roar of the Shatt, the sailors shouting to each other, the sky blazing, and the black bird still circling aimlessly.

He got up, brushed the earth from his clothes, and stood looking at the river.

More than at any time in the past he felt alien and insignificant. Rubbing his hand over his rough chin, he brushed from his head all the thoughts that had gathered like teeming hosts of ants.

On the other side of this Shatt, just the other side, were all the things he had been deprived of. Over there was Kuwait. What only lived in his mind as a dream and a fantasy existed there. It was certainly something real, of stones, earth, water, and sky, not as it slumbered in his troubled mind. There must be lanes and streets, men and women, and children running about between the trees.

No. No. There were no trees there. Saad, his friend who had emigrated there, worked as a driver, and come back with sacks of money, said there were no trees there. The trees exist in your head, Abu Qais, in your tired old head, Abu Qais. Ten trees with twisted trunks that brought down olives and goodness every spring. There are no trees in Kuwait, Saad said so. You must believe Saad because he knows more than you, although he is younger than you. All of them know more than you, all of them.

In the last ten years you have done nothing but wait. You have needed ten big hungry years to be convinced that you have lost your trees, your house, your youth, and your whole village. People have been making their own way during these long years, while you have been squatting like an old dog in a miserable hut. What do you think you were waiting for? Wealth to come through the roof of your house? Your house? It is not your house. A generous man said to you: "Live here!" That is all. And a year later he said to you: "Give me half the room," so you put up patched sacks between yourself and the new neighbors. You stayed squatting till Saad came and started to shake you as milk is churned to make butter.

"If you get to the Shatt, you can easily reach Kuwait. Basra is full of guides who will undertake to smuggle you there across the desert. Why don't you go?"

When his wife heard what Saad said, she glanced from one to the other and began to rock her baby again.

"It's a risk, and who knows what the outcome will be?"

"What will the outcome be? Ha, ha! Abu Qais, says: 'Who knows what the outcome will be?' Ha, ha!"

Then Saad looked at her and said:

"Have you heard what your husband says? Who knows what the outcome will be! As though life were like eating yogurt. Why doesn't he behave like us? Is he better?"

She did not raise her eyes to Abu Qais, who was hoping she would not.

"Do you like this life here? Ten years have passed and you live like a beggar. It's disgraceful. Your son, Qais, when will he go back to school? Soon the other one will grow up. How will you be able to look at him when you haven't . . . ?"

"All right. That's enough."

"No. It's not enough. It's terrible. You are responsible for a big family now. Why don't you go there? What's *your* opinion, Umm Qais?"

His wife was silent, while he thought: "Soon he too will grow up . . ." but he said:

"It's a long way. And I'm an old man; I can't walk as you did. I might die."

No one in the room spoke. His wife was still rocking her child. Saad gave up insisting, but the rough voice exploded inside his own head:

"Die! Who says that isn't preferable to your life at the moment? For ten years you have been hoping to return to the ten olive trees that you once owned in your village. Your village! Ha!?

He turned to his wife.

"What do you think, Umm Qais?"

She gazed at him, whispering:

"It's just as you think."

"We'll be able to send Qais to school."

"Yes."

"And perhaps buy one or two olive shoots."

"Of course."

"Maybe we'll be able to build a shack somewhere."

"Certainly."

"If I arrive. If I arrive."

He broke off, and looked at her. He had known that she would start weeping; her lower lip would tremble a little and then one tear would well up, gradually growing bigger and slipping down her brown, wrinkled cheek. He tried to say something, but he was unable to. A choking lump was tearing his throat. A lump just like the one he had felt when he arrived in Basra and went to the shop belonging to the fat man whose job was smuggling people from Basra to Kuwait. He stood before him, bearing on his shoulders all the humiliation and hope that an old man can carry. And there was a blanket of echoing silence after the fat proprietor of the office had repeated:

"It's a difficult journey, I tell you. It will cost you fifteen dinars."

"And can you guarantee that we shall arrive safely?"

"Of course you will arrive safely. But you will have to suffer a little discomfort. You know, we are in August now. The heat is intense and the desert has no shade. But you will arrive."

The lump was still in his throat. But he felt that if he put off saying what he had to say, he would not be able to pronounce the words later.

"I have traveled thousands of miles to reach you. Saad sent me. Do you remember him? But I have only got fifteen dinars. What do you say to taking ten and leaving me the rest?"

The man interrupted him:

"We are not playing games. Didn't your friend tell you that the price is fixed here? We are risking the guide's life for your sake."

"We too are risking our lives."

"I didn't force you to."

"Ten dinars?"

"Fifteen dinars, can't you hear?"

He could not go on any longer. The fat man, sitting behind his desk, dripping with sweat, was gazing at him, his eyes wide open. He wished the man would stop staring. Then he felt them, hot, filling his eyes, about to fall. He wanted to say something but could not. He felt that his whole head had filled with tears, welling up from inside, so he turned and went out into the street. There human beings began to swim behind a mist of tears, the horizon of the river and the sky came together, and everything around him became simply an endless white glow. He went back, and threw himself down with his chest on the damp earth, which began to beat beneath him again, while the scent of the earth rose to his nostrils and poured into his veins like a flood.

Assad

Assad stood in front of the fat man, the proprietor of the office that undertook to smuggle people from Basra to Kuwait, and burst out: "Fifteen dinars I'll pay you. Fine! But after I arrive, not before."

The man looked at him from under his heavy eyelids, asking stupidly: "Why?"

"Why? Ha! Because the guide you send with us will run away before we get halfway there. Fifteen dinars, fine, but not before we arrive."

Folding some yellow papers in front of him, the man said reproachfully: "I'm not forcing you to do anything, I'm not forcing you."

"What do you mean?"

"I mean that if you don't like our conditions, you can turn around, take three steps, and find yourself in the road."

The road! Were there still roads in this world? Hadn't he wiped them with his forehead and washed them with his sweat for days and days? They all say that: "You'll find yourself in the road." Abul-Abd, who smuggled him from Jordan to Iraq, had told him:

"You've only got to go round H4, it doesn't matter if you stray a little into the interior. You're still a boy and you can take a bit of heat. Then come back, and you will find me waiting for you in the road."

"But that wasn't one of the conditions. You told me, when we were in Amman, that you would take me to Baghdad, and I paid you twenty whole dinars. You didn't tell me I was to walk around H4."

Abul-Abd hit the dusty bonnet of his lorry, so that his five fingers made a mark and the vivid red of the lorry showed up under them. The big truck was standing by the house near Jebel Amman when he negotiated with him, and he remembered exactly the conditions that were mentioned.

"It's a difficult business. They'll take me to prison if they catch you with me. All the same I'll do you a very great service because I knew your father, may God have mercy on him. In fact we fought together in Ramleh ten years ago."

Abul-Abd said nothing for a while. His blue shirt was damp with sweat, and his hard face gave Assad the feeling that he was one of those men who do not expect the head of a family to accomplish miracles. "I'll take twenty dinars from you. And you will find yourself in Baghdad."

"Twenty dinars?"

"Yes, and you must help me the whole of the way, too. We'll set off the day after tomorrow. I must deliver a small car to a rich Baghdadi who spent part of the summer in Ramallah and then decided to return to Baghdad by plane."

"But . . . twenty dinars?"

Abul-Abd looked at him intently, and then exploded: "I'll save your life for twenty dinars. Do you think you'll spend your life here in hiding? Tomorrow they'll arrest you."

"But where from? Where can I get you the twenty dinars from?"

"Borrow them, borrow them. Any friend will give you twenty dinars if he knows you are traveling to Kuwait."

"Twenty dinars?"

"Twenty, twenty."

"To Baghdad?"

"Directly."

But he lied to him. He took advantage of his innocence and ignorance, tricking him, making him get out of the lorry after a journey on a burning hot day, telling him that he must walk round H4 so as not to fall into the hands of the frontier guards, and then promising to meet him on the road.

"But I don't know this area. Do you realize what it means for me to walk all this distance round H4, when the sun is at its height?"

Abul-Abd hit the dusty side of his lorry again. They were standing by themselves a mile before H4. He shouted out:

"What do you think will happen? Your name is registered at all the frontier posts. If they see you with me now, without a passport or an exit visa, a plotter against the state, what do you think will happen? Stop making difficulties. You are as strong as a bull, and you can move your legs. I'll meet you on the road beyond H4."

They all talked about roads. They said: "You will find yourself on the road!" And all they knew of the road was its blackness and its pavements. Here was the fat man, the Basran smuggler, repeating the very same tale. "Can't you hear? I am a very busy man. I told you: fifteen dinars and I will get you to Kuwait. Of course you will have to walk a little, but you're young and strong; it will not do you any harm."

"But why don't you listen to me? I told you that I will give you the money when we reach Kuwait."

"You will get there. You will get there"

"How?"

"I swear to you on my honor that you will get to Kuwait."

"You swear on your honor?"

"I swear to you on my honor that I will meet you beyond H4. You have only got to walk round that damned place and you will find me, waiting for you."

He had given H4 a wide berth. The sun was pouring flame down on his head, and as he climbed the yellow slopes, he felt he was alone in the whole world. He dragged his feet over the sand as though he were walking on the seashore after pulling up a heavy boat that had drained the firmness from his legs. He crossed hard patches of brown rocks like splinters, climbed low hills with flattened tops of soft yellow earth like flour. If they had taken me to the desert prison, Al-Jafr, at H4, I wonder if life would have been kinder than it is now. Pointless, pointless. The desert was everywhere. Abul-Abd had given him a headdress, and he had wrapped it round his head, but it was no use for keeping off the blaze. Indeed it seemed to him that it too was catching fire. The horizon was a collection of straight, orange lines, but he had taken a firm decision to go forward, doggedly. Even when the earth turned into shining sheets of yellow paper he did not slow down. Suddenly the yellow sheets began to fly about, and he stooped to gather them up.

"Thanks. Thanks. This damned fan makes the papers fly about in front of me, but I can't breathe without it. Ha! What have you decided?"

"Are you sure the guide you send with us won't run away?"

"How will he be able to run away, you fool? There will be more than ten of you. He won't be able to escape from you."

"Where will he take us to?"

"As far as the Jahra road, beyond Mutlaa. There you will be inside Kuwait."

"Will we have a lot of walking to do?"

"Six or seven hours, no more."

Four hours later he reached the road. He had left H4 behind him, and the sun had set behind the brown hills. But his head was still burning, and he had the feeling that his forehead was dripping blood. He sat down on a stone and gazed into the distance at the end of the straight black road. His head felt muddled, with thousands of confused voices throbbing in it, and it seemed to him that the appearance of a big red lorry at the end of the road was a stupid fantasy. He stood up, looking at the road again, but he could not see clearly yet. Was it twilight or sweat? His head was still humming like a beehive, and he cried with all his strength:

"Abul-Abd, damn your father, damn your forefathers!"

"What did you say?"

"Me? Nothing, nothing. When will the journey begin?"

"As soon as there are ten of you. You know, we cannot send a guide with each of you. So we wait till the number reaches ten and we send one guide with them. Will you give me the cash now?"

He tightened his hold on the money in his pocket, and reflected:

"I will be able to return the amount to my uncle in less than a month. A man can collect money in the twinkling of an eye there in Kuwait."

"Don't be too optimistic. Dozens of people have gone before you and come back without bringing a penny with them. All the same I'll give you the fifty dinars you have asked for. You must realize that they are the fruits of a lifetime."

"Then why do you give me the money, if you're sure that I won't return it to you?"

"You know why, don't you? I want you to make a start, even in hell, so that you'll be in a position to marry Nada. I can't imagine my poor daughter waiting any longer. Do you understand?"

He felt the unuttered insult wound his throat, and he had an urge to give the fifty dinars back to his uncle, to throw them in his face with all the strength in his arms and all the hatred in his heart. To marry him off to Nada! Who told him that he wanted to marry Nada? Just because his father had recited the Fatiha with his uncle when he and Nada were born on the same day? His uncle considered that was fate. Indeed he had refused a hundred suitors who had asked for his daughter's hand and told them she was engaged. O God of devils! Who told him that he, Assad, wanted to marry her? Who told him that he ever wanted to get married? Here he was now reminding him again. He wanted to buy him for his daughter as you buy a sack of manure for a field. He tightened his grasp on the money in his pocket and got ready to get up. But when he touched it there in his pocket, soft and warm, he felt he was holding the keys of his whole future. If he allowed his rage to get the better of him now and gave the money back to his uncle, he would never be offered the opportunity to obtain fifty dinars by any means. He calmed himself, firmly shutting his mouth and tightening his grasp on the bundle of money in his trouser pocket. Then he remarked:

"No. No. I will give you the money when all the preparations for the journey are made. I will see you once a day. I am staying in a nearby hotel."

The fat man smiled. He went on smiling, and then burst out, laughing loudly:

"It's better for you not to waste your time, my boy. All the smugglers ask the same price. We have come to an agreement among ourselves. Don't wear yourself out. All the same, keep your money till the preparations are made. It's up to you. What's the name of the hotel where you are staying?"

"The Shatt Hotel."

"Ah, the rats' hotel."

The wild rat ran across the road, its little eyes shining in the car's headlamps. The blonde woman said to her husband, who was concentrating on driving:

"It's a fox. Did you see it?"

The husband, a foreigner, laughed. "You women! You make a rat into a fox."

They had picked him up a little after sunset, after he had waved to them in their small car. When the husband stopped the car, he looked through the window. He was trembling from the extreme cold. The wife was frightened of him, but he gathered together in his mind all the English he had learned, and said:

"My friend had to go back to H4 with the car, and he left me—"

The man interrupted him:

"Don't lie. You're escaping from there. All right. Get in. I'll take you to Baaquba."

The back seat was comfortable, and the girl handed him a blanket, which he wrapped himself in; he could not tell exactly whether he was trembling because of the desert cold, or from fear, or exhaustion. The man asked:

"Have you walked a lot?"

"I don't know. Four hours perhaps."

"The guide abandoned you, didn't he? That's always happening."

The girl turned to him with a question:

"Why are you escaping from there?"

Her husband gave her the answer:

"It's a long story. Tell me, do you drive well?"

"Yes."

"You can take my place when you've had a little rest. I may be able to help you cross the Iraqi frontier. We will get there at two in the morning, and the officials will be asleep."

He could not get his mind to focus on one subject. He was confused and did not know where to start asking the host of questions that needed an answer, so he tried to get to sleep, even if it was just for half an hour.

"Where are you from?"

"Palestine. Ramleh."

"Oh. Ramleh is a very long way away. A couple of weeks ago I was in Zeita. Do you know Zeita? I stood in front of the barbed wire. A little child came up to me and said in English that his house was a few feet beyond the barbed wire."

"Do you work in an office?"

"Work in an office? Ha! The devil himself is too innocent to be employed in an office. No, my friend, I'm a tourist."

"Look! Look! There's another fox. Didn't you see how his eyes glitter?"

"He's a rat, my dear, a rat. Why do you insist that he's a fox? Have you heard what happened there recently, near Zeita?"

"No. What happened?"

"The devil himself doesn't know what happened. Will you stay in Baghdad?"

"No."

"Oh. This desert is full of rats. What on earth do they eat?"

He answered quietly:

"Rats smaller than them."

"Really?" said the girl. "It's frightening. Rats themselves are horrible, frightening animals."

The fat man who owned the office said:

"Rats are horrible animals. How can you sleep in that hotel?"

"It's cheap."

The fat owner of the office stood up and came towards him, putting his heavy arms on his shoulders:

"You look tired, my boy. What's happened? Are you ill?"

"Me? No."

"If you are ill, tell me. I may be able to help you. I have many friends who are doctors. Don't worry, you won't pay anything."

"You're very kind. But I'm a little tired, that's all there is to it. Will the preparations take long?"

"No. Thank heavens there are many of you. You'll find yourself on the road in two days."

He turned his back and went towards the door, but before he went through it he heard the fat man chuckling behind his back:

"But take care the rats don't eat you before you set out."

Marwan

Marwan came out of the shop belonging to the fat man who smuggled people from Basra to Kuwait, and found himself in the crowded covered street, which smelt of dates and big straw baskets. He had no definite idea where to make for now; there, inside the shop, the last threads of hope that had held together everything inside him for long years had been snapped. The last words the fat man had spoken were decisive and final; it seemed to him that they were forged from lead.

"Fifteen dinars, can't you hear?"

"But. . . ."

"I beg you, I beg you. Don't start wailing. You all come here and then start wailing like widows. My friend! My dear friend! No one's forcing you to stay here. Why don't you go and ask someone else? Basra is full of smugglers."

Yes, of course Marwan would go and ask someone else. Hasan, who had worked in Kuwait for four years, had told him that to smuggle one person from Basra to Kuwait cost five dinars and no more, and that when he came to stand in front of the smuggler he must be more than a man, and show more than courage, or they would laugh at him, cheat him, and take advantage of his sixteen years.

"They told me that the price for one person was five dinars."

"Five dinars? Ha, ha! That was before Adam married Eve. Turn around, my boy, take three steps, and you will find yourself in the road without being thrown out."

Marwan gathered all his courage and put it into his words. There were only seven dinars left in his pocket, and a moment before he had thought himself rich. But now . . . was he being treated like a child?

"You'll take five dinars from me and be satisfied, or else. . . ."

"Or else?"

"Or else I'll denounce you to the police."

Getting up, the fat man came round his desk, till he stood, panting and dripping with sweat, in front of Marwan. He stared at him for a second, looking him up and down, and then raised his heavy hand in the air. "You want to complain to the police about me, son of a . . ."

The heavy hand crashed down onto his cheek, and the word was lost in a fearful roar, which began reverberating between his ears. He almost lost his balance for a moment, and staggered a couple of steps back. The voice of the fat man, hoarse with anger, reached him:

"Go and tell the pimps that I've hit you. You'll complain to the police about me?"

Marwan stood his ground for a short while, which was enough for him to realize that any attempt to restore his honor was futile. In fact he felt, to the marrow of his bones, that he had committed an unforgivable sin. As the marks of the fingers on his left cheek burned, he began to digest his humiliation.

"What are you waiting here for?"

He turned on his heel and went out through the door. His nose was assailed by the smell of dates and big straw baskets. What should he do now? He had no wish to ask himself the question. Yet he didn't know why he felt some sort of relief; what could be the reason for it? He wanted to distract himself by searching for the reason. Part of his mind was taken up with feelings of happiness and relief, but they couldn't sidetrack him from all the sorrows that had filled his heart in the last half hour. When all his efforts failed, he leaned against the wall. Crowds of people walked past without paying him any attention. Perhaps it was the first time in his life that he had found himself alone and a stranger in a throng of people like this. He wanted to know the reason for that remote sensation that gave him contentment and rest; a sensation like the one he used to have when he had finished watching a film, and felt that life was grand and vast, and that in the future he would be one of those men who spend every hour and day of their lives in exciting fulfilment and variety. But what was the reason for his having such a feeling now, when he had not seen a film like that for a long time, and only a few minutes before the threads of hope that had woven fine dreams in his heart had been broken in the fat man's shop?

It was no use. It seemed he would not be able to penetrate the thick veil of disappointment that separated him from that distinct feeling which existed, unexpressed, somewhere in his mind. In the end he decided not to wear his brain out, but to occupy himself with walking. But as soon as he left the wall and began to walk through the crowd, he felt a hand grasp his shoulder.

"Don't be so desperate. Where are you going now?"

The tall man had begun to walk beside him familiarly, and when Marwan looked at him he thought he'd seen him somewhere before. All the same, he moved a step away from him and gave him a questioning look.

"He's a well-known thief," said the man. "What made you go to him?"

He answered after a short hesitation:

"Everyone goes to him."

The man came closer to Marwan and linked his arm through his, as though he had known him for ages.

"Do you want to go to Kuwait?"

"How did you know?"

"I was standing by the door of that shop, and I saw you go in and come out. What's your name?"

"Marwan. And you?"

"They call me Abul Khaizuran."

For the first time since Marwan had set eyes on the man, he noticed that he really did remind one of a cane. He was very tall, very thin, but his neck and hands had a suggestion of strength and firmness, and for some reason he looked as though he could bend down and put his head between his legs without its upsetting his spine or his other bones at all.

"Well, what do you want of me?"

Abul Khaizuran sidestepped the question with one of his own:

"Why do you want to go to Kuwait?"

"I want to work. You know how things are there. For months I. . . ." He suddenly fell silent and stood still.

Only now did he recognize the source of that feeling of rest and contentment which he had not been able to discover a few minutes before. It was suddenly revealed to him in its full depth and clarity; in fact, in some wonderful way it had broken down all the barriers of despondency that stood between him and the realization of it. Here was this feeling taking possession of him again with unparalleled force. The first thing he had done that morning, early, had been to write a long letter to his mother. Now he felt all the more relief because he had written that letter before seeing all his hopes dashed in the fat man's shop, and losing the pure joy that he had poured into the letter. It had been wonderful to spend some time with his mother.

He'd got up early that morning. The servant had taken the bed up to the roof of the hotel, because sleeping in the room when it was as hot and damp as that was impossible. When the sun rose he opened his eyes. The weather was beautiful and calm, and the sky was still blue, with black pigeons hovering low in it. He could hear their wings fluttering when they flew over the hotel in a wide circle. A thick blanket of silence covered everything, and the air had a clean, moist scent of early morning. He stretched out his hand to the small case under the bed, took out a notebook and pen, and proceeded to write to his mother as he lay there.

It was the best thing he'd done for months. He was not obliged to do it, but he did it quite willingly. He was in an excellent mood, and the letter reflected the tranquillity of the sky above him. He didn't know how he had allowed himself to describe his father as nothing but a depraved beast, but he was unwilling to cross the words out once he'd written them; he didn't want to cross out anything in the whole letter—not only because his mother would see the crossed-out words as a bad omen, but also, quite simply, because he didn't want to.

In any case, he didn't hate his father so much. His father had certainly done something horrible, but which of us doesn't from time to time? He could quite understand his father's circumstances and he could forgive him. But could his father forgive himself for such a crime?

"To leave four children, to divorce you for no reason, then to marry that deformed woman. It is something for which he won't forgive himself, when he wakes up one day and realizes what he's done.

"I don't want to hate anybody; it is beyond me to do so even if I wanted to. But why did he do that, to *you*? You don't like any of us to talk about him, I know. But why do you think he did that?

"It's all over and done with now, and there's no hope of us getting him back again. But why did he do it? At least let us ask why.

"I'll tell you why. When we stopped hearing news of my brother Zakaria the situation finally changed. Zakaria used to send us about two hundred rupees from Kuwait every month. That sum gave my father some of the stability he dreamed of. But when we stopped hearing news of Zakaria—let us hope he's all right—what do you suppose my father thought?

"He told himself, in fact he told us all, that life is an extraordinary business, and that a man wants to be able to settle down in his old age and not find himself obliged to feed half a dozen open mouths. Didn't he say that? Zakaria had gone . . . there had been no news of him. Who would feed the mouths? Who would pay for the rest of Marwan's education, and buy May's clothes, and bring back bread for Riyad, Salma, and Hasan? Who?

"He is penniless, you know that. His one and only ambition was to move from the mud house that he had occupied in the camp for ten years and live under a concrete roof as he used to say. Now, Zakaria had gone. All his hopes had collapsed, his dreams had been destroyed, his ambition had seeped away. So what would he do, do you think?

"His old friend, Shafiqa's father, suggested he should marry her. He told him she owned a three-roomed house on the edge of the town, which she had bought with the money collected for her by a charity. Shafiqa's father had one desire: to transfer to a husband's shoulders the burden of his daughter, who had lost her right leg during the bombardment of Jaffa. He already had one foot in the grave and wanted to go down into it reassured about the fate of his daughter, who had been turned down by everyone because of that leg, amputated at the top of the thigh. My father thought about the matter; if he let two rooms and lived with his lame wife in the third, he would live out the rest of his life in security, untroubled by anything. And more important than that, under a concrete roof."

"Do you want to stand here forever?"

He shook his head and walked on. Abul Khaizuran was looking at him out of the corner of his eye, and he imagined he was about to smile sarcastically.

"What's the matter with you, thinking like this? Thinking doesn't suit you, Marwan. You're still young, and life is long. . . ."

Marwan stopped again and jerked his head back slightly.

"And now, what do you want from me?"

Abul Khaizuran went on walking, so Marwan caught up with him again.

"I can smuggle you to Kuwait."

"How?"

"That's my affair. You want to go to Kuwait, don't you? Here is someone who can take you there. What more do you want?"

"How much do you want from me?"

"That's not really important."

"It is."

513

Abul Khaizuran smiled broadly, and his lips parted to show two rows of large teeth, gleaming white. Then he said:

"I'll be quite honest with you. I have got to go to Kuwait, and I said to myself: why not earn a little money and take someone with you who wants to go there? How much can you pay?"

"Five dinars."

"Is that all?"

"I haven't any more."

"Very well. I accept."

Abul Khaizuran put his hands in his pockets and strode forward, taking such big steps that Marwan almost lost him and had to hurry after him. Bur he stopped suddenly and shook his finger in front of his lips. "But . . . you mustn't tell anyone that. I mean, if I ask someone else for ten dinars, don't tell him I'm just getting five from you."

"But how do you expect me to trust you?"

Abul Khaizuran thought for a moment, then he smiled the same broad smile again, saying:

"You're right. You'll give me the money in Al-Safa Square in Kuwait—in the capital, in the middle of the capital. Satisfied?"

"All right."

"But we'll need some more people to make the journey. You must help me. That is a condition."

"I know someone staying in the same hotel with me who wants to go."

"That's splendid. I know someone else. He comes from the town where I lived in Palestine, in the old days, and I came across him here. But I haven't asked you: what do you want to do in Kuwait? Do you know anyone there?"

Marwan stopped again, but Abul Khaizuran pulled him by the arm and he trotted along by his side.

"My brother works there."

Abul Khaizuran shook his head as he hurried along. Then he raised his shoulders so that his neck sank between them and he seemed shorter than before.

"If your brother is working there, why do you want to take a job? People of your age are still at school."

"I was at school two months ago. But now I want to work to support my family."

Abul Khaizuran stopped and took his hands out of his pockets, putting them on his hips. He began to stare laughingly at Marwan.

"Ah! Now I understand. Your brother has stopped sending you money, hasn't he?"

Marwan nodded and tried to walk on, but Abul Khaizuran caught his arm and stopped him.

"Why? Has he got married?"

Amazed, Marwan looked at Abul Khaizuran, and whispered:

"How did you know?"

"Ah! One doesn't have to be a genius to understand. Everyone stops sending money to their families when they get married or fall in love."

Marwan felt a small disappointment growing in his heart, not because he had been surprised, but because he had discovered that it was something common and well known. He had thought that his heart held a great secret that no one else knew. He had guarded it from his mother and father for months and months, and here it was now, seeming on the tongue of Abul Khaizuran like a well-known, self-evident principle. "But . . . why do they do that? Why do they deny . . . ?"

He suddenly fell silent. Abul Khaizuran had begun to laugh.

"I'm glad you are going to Kuwait, because you will learn many things there. The first thing you will learn is: money comes first, and then morals."

When Abul Khaizuran left him, having arranged to meet him again in the afternoon, he had lost, yet again, those wonderful sensations which had purified him inside throughout the morning. In fact it surprised him that the letter he had written to his mother could give him that marvellous feeling which made his disappointment appear less important than it really was. A silly letter, which he had written under the influence of a feeling of loneliness and hope on the roof of a miserable hotel at the end of the world. What was so extraordinary about it? Did he think his mother didn't know the whole story? What did he want to say? Did he want to convince her that her husband's desertion of her and her children was a fine and natural thing? Then why all that talk? He loved his father with a great and unshakeable love. But that changed nothing of the terrible truth, the truth that proclaimed that his father had fled . . . fled . . . fled. Just as Zakaria had done, when he got married and sent him a short letter, telling him that his turn had come and he must leave that stupid school, which taught nothing, and plunge into the frying pan with everyone else.

All his life Marwan had found himself at odds with Zakaria. In fact, they hated each other. Zakaria had been quite unable to understand why he had to spend ten years providing for the family while Marwan went off to school every day like a baby. He, Marwan, wanted to become a doctor. He used to tell his mother that Zakaria would never understand what it meant for someone to get an education, because he had left school when he left Palestine, and since then he had plunged into the frying pan, as he liked to say.

And here he was now, having married without telling anyone except Marwan, as though he wanted to confront him with his conscience. But what choice had he left him? Nothing except to leave the school, to plunge into the frying pan and stay there from now until eternity.

All right! All right! In a few days he would reach Kuwait. It would be better if Zakaria helped him, but if he pretended not to know him, he would find out how to start off, as many others had done. He would send every penny he earned to his mother, and overwhelm her and his brothers and sisters with gifts till he made the mud hut into a paradise on earth and his father bit his nails with regret.

Yet he couldn't hate his father so much, for the simple reason that his father still loved them all. Marwan had been completely convinced of that when he went to say good-bye to his father before he left. He did not tell his mother that he was going to Shafiqa's house, or she would have been beside herself. His father said to him there:

"Marwan, you know that I have had no choice in the matter. It is something that has been decreed for us since the beginning of creation."

Shafiqa said:

"We suggested to your mother that she should come and live here but she didn't agree. What more do you want us to do?"

She was sitting on a carpet of goatskin. The stick was lying beside her, and he thought: "I wonder where her thigh ends?" Her face was beautiful, but hard-featured like the faces of all those who are incurably ill, and her lower lip was twisted as though she were about to cry.

His father said:

"Take this. It is ten dinars; you may need them. You will write to us, won't you?"

When he stood up, Shafiqa raised her arms in the air, praying for his success. Her voice was hoarse, and when he turned to her before going through the door, she broke down and sobbed. His father said to him:

"May God send you success, Marwan, you brave boy."

And he tried to laugh. He couldn't, so he began rubbing the boy's back with his large, hard hand, while Shafiqa picked up her stick and stood up with a quick movement. She had stopped crying.

Marwan shut the door behind him and walked away. He could still hear Shafiqa's stick tapping the tiles monotonously, but as he turned the corner the sound died away.

The Deal

Marwan brought his companion Assad to the meeting with Abul Khaizuran. They arrived a little late and found Abul Khaizuran waiting for them, sitting with Abu Qais on a big concrete seat on the pavement of the street, which ran parallel to the Shatt.

"The whole group's here together now, isn't it!" Abul Khaizuran laughed loudly, striking Marwan on the shoulder with one hand and stretching out the other to shake hands with Assad.

"So this is your friend. What's his name?"

Marwan answered curtly:

"Assad."

"Let me introduce you to my old friend, Abu Qais. Now the group's complete. It doesn't matter if one more comes too, but already we have enough, now."

Assad said:

"You seem to me to be a Palestinian. Are you the one who's undertaking to smuggle us?"

"Yes, I am."

"How?"

"That's my affair."

Assad laughed sarcastically and then said slowly, bringing out each word forcefully:

"No. It's *our* affair. You must explain all the details to us. We don't want to have problems from the start."

Abul Khaizuran said in a decisive tone:

"I'll explain all the details to you when we've come to an agreement, not before."

Assad replied:

"We can't agree before we know the details. What do the others think?"

Nobody answered, so Assad repeated the question.

"What does Abu Qais think?"

Abu Qais replied:

"I think as you do."

"What's your opinion, Marwan?"

"I'm with you."

Assad spoke forcefully:

"Very well, let's be brief. It seems to me that old Abu Qais has no knowledge of this kind of thing, and as for Marwan, it's his first experience. I'm an old hand at this game. What is your opinion if I negotiate on your behalf?"

Abu Qais raised his hand in the air to show his agreement, and Marwan nodded. Assad turned to Abul Khaizuran:

"You see, they've made me responsible. Let me tell you something. We come from the same country. We want to earn money and so do you. Fine. But the whole thing must be quite fair. You must explain every step to us in detail, and tell us exactly how much you want. Of course, we'll give you the money after we arrive, not before."

Abu Qais remarked:

"Assad's quite right. We must be quite clear about things. If you start by making conditions, you end up satisfied, as the saying goes."

Abul Khaizuran took his hands out of his pockets and put them on his hips. He let his gaze wander slowly and coldly over all their faces, until it settled on Assad.

"First of all, you'll each pay ten dinars. Agreed?"

Abu Qais said:

"I agree."

Assad protested:

"Please. You have made me responsible, so let me speak. Ten dinars is a large sum. A professional smuggler takes fifteen. Then—"

Abul Khaizuran interrupted him.

"So we're disagreeing before we've started. That's what I was afraid of. Ten dinars, and not a penny less. Good-bye."

He turned his back and took two slow steps before Abu Qais caught up with him, shouting:

"Why have you lost your temper? It's a matter of question and answer, and agreement is the brother of patience."

"Very well. We'll give you ten dinars. But how will you take us?"

"Ah, now we're getting somewhere. Listen!" Abul Khaizuran sat on the concrete seat with the three standing round him. He explained to them, with the help of his long hands:

"I have a lorry that is licensed to cross the frontier. Now you must realize it's not mine. I'm a poor man, poorer than any of you, and I'm only connected with that lorry because I drive it. Its owner is rich and well known, and so it doesn't wait long at the frontier or get searched. The owner of the lorry is well known and respected, the lorry itself is well known and respected, and consequently the driver of the lorry is well known and respected."

Abul Khaizuran was an excellent driver. He had served in the British army for more than five years before 1948. When he left the army and joined the Freedom Fighters, he had the reputation of being the best lorry driver one could find. That was why the commandos in Al-Tira invited him to drive an old armored car that the village had captured after a Jewish attack. Although he had no experience of driving armored cars, he did not disappoint those who stood on both sides of the road, watching him as he climbed through the small armor-plated door and disappeared for a few minutes, after which the motor roared into action and the vehicle set off slowly down the narrow, sandy road. But it soon broke down, and none of Abul Khaizuran's efforts succeeded in putting it into running order again. If the villagers were greatly disappointed, Abul Khaizuran was still more so, but all the same he had increased the sum of his experiences in the world of mechanics. And who could say that this particular experience hadn't helped him when he joined the drivers working for Al-Haj Rida in Kuwait?

One day he had managed to drive a huge water tanker along a muddy salt road without its sinking into the earth and breaking down like all the other lorries in the convoy. Haj Rida had gone out into the desert with a number of his men for some days' hunting. But the spring was treacherous, and as they were returning, the road appeared firm and white, which encouraged the drivers to start along without hesitation. Then all the vehicles, big and small, began to sink into the mud one after the other. But Abul Khaizuran, who was driving his huge lorry behind them all, skillfully continued advancing, without stopping for a second. When he caught up with Haj Rida's car, whose wheels were three-quarters sunk in mud, he stopped his lorry. Getting out, he went up to Haj Rida, saying:

"How would Haj Rida like to get into my lorry? It'll take more than four hours to extricate these cars, and by then Haj Rida will have reached home."

Haj Rida replied:

"Splendid. The noise of your lorry's motor is kinder to the system than stopping here four hours."

Abul Khaizutan drove his huge lorry for six hours over that treacherous ground, which looked hard and white because of a fine film of salt that had dried on the surface. The whole of the way he was moving the steering wheel lightly and quickly to left and right so that the two front wheels could open a path slightly wider than necessary.

Haj Rida was delighted with Abul Khaizuran's skill, and mentioned it to all his friends for months. He was even more delighted when he learned that Abul Khaizuran had refused several offers of work elsewhere, made to him after the story became known. He asked to see him and congratulated him, and then he increased his wages a little. What was more important was that Haj Rida imposed a condition that Abul Khaizuran should be an obligatory companion on every hunting trip or long journey.

A week earlier Haj Rida had set off with a convoy of lorries on a hunting trip he had organized specially for some guests staying with him. He had asked Abul Khaizuran to drive the big water tanker, which would accompany the convoy the whole way to ensure a supply of water for the entire journey, lasting more than two days. The convoy had driven far into the desert, when suddenly Haj Rida decided to follow a different route on the return journey, which would bring him to Al-Zubair, and then from Al-Zubair he could take the main road to Kuwait. Abul Khaizuran could have been in Kuwait by now with the rest of the convoy if his lorry hadn't developed a small fault that had kept him in Basra two days longer to have it repaired, before catching up with those who had gone on ahead.

"So you want to put us inside the water tank on your lorry when you drive back?"

"Exactly. I said to myself: 'Why not seize the opportunity to earn an honest penny, while you're here, and as your lorry does not get searched?'"

Marwan looked at Abu Qais and then at Assad. They both looked at him in their turn, questioningly.

"Listen, Abul Khaizuran. I don't like the sound of this game. Can you imagine it? In heat like this, who could sit in a closed water tank?"

"Don't make a mountain out of a molehill. This isn't the first time. Do you know what will happen? You'll get into the tank five minutes from the frontier, and fifty meters beyond it you'll climb out. We'll repeat the performance for another five minutes at Murtlaa on the Kuwait border, and then suddenly you'll find yourselves in Kuwait!"

Assad shook his head and stared at the ground, grimacing with his lower lip. Marwan had begun to play with a dry twig, while Abu Qais went on staring at the tall driver. Suddenly Marwan asked:

"Is there any water in the tank?"

"Of course not. What are you thinking of? Am I a smuggler or a swimming teacher?" It seemed that Abul Khaizuran liked the idea, for he started to chuckle, hitting his thighs with his hands and turning round. "What are you thinking of? Am I a swimming teacher? Listen, my boy, the tank hasn't seen any water for six months."

"I thought you were carrying the water for a hunting expedition a week ago," said Assad quietly.

"Oh well . . . you know. You know what I mean."

"No. I don't know."

"I mean for six days. One exaggerates sometimes. Now, are we agreed? Let's bring this momentous meeting to an end."

Abu Qais stood up, preparing to say the decisive word. But before he spoke he let his eyes wander over them all and then waited a little, looking at Assad as though he were imploring his help. He went up to Abul Khaizuran.

"Listen, Abul Khaizuran, I'm a simple man and I don't understand all these complications. But that story of the hunting expedition . . . I didn't like it. You say you carried water for Haj Rida, and now you say that the tank of your lorry hasn't had sight or smell of water for six months. I'll tell you the truth, and I hope you won't be angry. I doubt whether you have a lorry at all." Abu Qais turned to the others and continued in a sad tone of voice: "I prefer to pay fifteen dinars and go with a smuggler by the desert road. I don't want any more problems."

Abul Khaizuran laughed, saying loudly:

"Go and see what it's like . . . do you think I don't know those smugglers? They leave you in the middle of the road and melt away like a lump of salt. And you, in turn, will melt away in the August heat without anyone knowing. Go on, go and see what it's like. Many have tried before you. Would you like me to show you the way? Why do you think they take the money from you first?"

"But I know many people who've arrived there by way of the smugglers."

"Ten percent at the most. Go and ask them, and they will tell you that they finished the journey without a smuggler or a guide, and that their luck helped them to survive."

Abu Qais froze in his place. For a moment it seemed he would fall. Marwan noticed that Abu Qais resembled his father closely, and he looked away from him, no longer able to concentrate his mind on a single subject. Abul Khaizuran went on, shouting:

"You must decide quickly! I've no time to waste. I swear to you on my honor—"

Assad quietly interrupted him:

"Leave the subject of honor for another time. Things go better when a man doesn't swear by his honor."

Abul Khaizuran turned to him:

"No, Mr. Assad. You are an intelligent, experienced man. What do you think?"

"About what?"

"About everything."

Assad smiled, noticing that Abu Qais and Marwan were waiting to hear his decision. He started speaking slowly and sarcastically:

"First, excuse us from believing the story of the hunting expedition. It seems to me that Haj Rida and you, sir, are involved in smuggling. I beg your pardon, let me finish. Haj Rida believes that smuggling people on the return journey is a trivial matter, so he leaves it to you—while you in turn leave him the smuggling of more important things, for a reasonable share of the profits. Or do you think he doesn't know you smuggle people on the return journey?"

Abul Khaizuran smiled broadly, showing his clean white teeth again. He seemed not to want to answer Assad. Marwan blurted out:

"And the story of the hunt?"

Assad replied:

"The story of the hunt is cooked up for the frontier guards, not for us. But Abul Khaizuran sees no harm in telling it. . . ."

Abul Khaizuran smiled more broadly than before and began to exchange glances with the men, without saying a word. For a moment he looked like an idiot. Abu Qais remarked:

"But what does Haj Rida smuggle? You said that he's rich."

They all looked at Abul Khaizuran, who suddenly stopped smiling, his face again taking on an expression of carelessness and authority. He spoke decisively:

"And now, that's enough chatter. You mustn't think, Mr. Assad, that you're so clever. What have you decided?"

Assad said quietly:

"Personally, I'm only interested in reaching Kuwait. I'm not concerned with anything else. That is why I shall travel with Abul Khaizuran."

Marwan said excitedly:

"I will go along with you both."

Abu Qais said:

"Do you think that I'm capable of accompanying you? I'm an old man."

Abul Khaizuran laughed violently, then linked his arm with Abu Qais's. "Aha! Ah, Abu Qais, who's given you the idea that you're so old? Umm Qais, perhaps? You must come with us."

They had walked a few steps forward and left Marwan and Assad standing by the big concrete seat. Abul Khaizuran looked back over his shoulder and shouted:

"Abu Qais will sleep in the lorry with me. I'll come and sound my horn in front of the hotel tomorrow morning, early."

The Road

It was not too uncomfortable riding on the back of the huge lorry. Although the sun was pouring its inferno down on them without any respite, the breeze that they felt because of the lorry's speed lessened the intensity of the heat. Abu Qais had climbed up on top with Marwan, and they sat side by side on the edge of the tank. They had drawn lots, and it was Assad's turn to sit beside the driver for the first part of the journey.

Assad said to himself: "The old man will be last to sit in the shade here. But it doesn't matter; in any case the sun is still bearable now. At midday the old man will be lucky."

Abul Khaizuran spoke suddenly, raising his voice so that Assad could hear over the roar of the motor:

"Just imagine! In my own mind I compare these hundred and fifty kilometers to the path that God in the Quran promised his creatures they must cross before being directed either to Paradise or to Hell. If anyone falls he goes to Hell, and if anyone crosses safely he reaches Paradise. Here the angels are the frontier guards."

Abul Khaizuran burst out laughing as though he were not the person who had made the remark, then he began to hit the steering wheel with both hands and shake his head. "You know, I'm afraid the goods will perish, up there. . . ."

He indicated by a movement of his neck where the old man was sitting with Marwan on the tank, and laughed violently.

Assad asked quietly:

"Tell me, Abul Khaizuran. Have you ever been married?"

"Me?" he asked in surprise, and his thin face became veiled in sadness as though he hadn't been laughing a moment before. Then he replied slowly: "Why do you ask?"

"For no particular reason. I was thinking that you have a splendid life. No one to drag you in any direction. You can fly off alone wherever you like . . . you can fly off alone."

Abul Khaizuran shook his head, then he narrowed his eyes to meet the sunlight that had suddenly struck the windscreen. The light was shining so brightly that at first he could see nothing. But he felt a terrible pain coiled between his thighs. After a few moments he could make out that his legs were tied to two supports that kept them suspended, and that there were several men surrounding him. He closed his eyes for a moment, and then opened them as wide as he could. The circular light above his head hid the ceiling from him and blinded him. As he lay there, tied firmly in that strange fashion, he could only remember one thing that had happened to him a moment before, and nothing else. He and a number of armed men were running along when all hell exploded in front of him and he fell forward on his face. That was all. And now, the terrible pain was still plunging between his thighs and the huge round light was hanging over his eyes and he was trying to see things and people, narrowing his eyes as much as he could. Suddenly a black thought occurred to him and he began to scream like a madman. He couldn't remember what he said then, but he felt a hand covered with a slippery glove placed over his mouth with a violent movement. The voice reached him as though it were coming through cotton:

"Be sensible. Be sensible. At least it's better than dying."

He didn't know if they could hear him as he shouted through his teeth, while the slippery hand covered his mouth. Or was his voice lost in his throat? At any rate, he could still hear the same voice as though someone else was shouting in his ear:

"No. It's better to be dead."

Now . . . ten years had passed since that horrible scene. Ten years had passed since they took his manhood from him, and he had lived that humiliation day after day and hour after hour. He had swallowed it with his pride, and examined it every moment of those ten years. And still he hadn't yet got used to it, he hadn't accepted it. For ten long years he had been trying to accept the situation? But what situation? To confess quite simply that he had lost his manhood while fighting for his country? And what good had it done? He had lost his manhood and his country, and damn everything in this bloody world.

No, he couldn't consent, even after ten years, to forget his tragedy and get used to it. He couldn't even accept it when he was under the knife and they were trying to convince him that it was better to lose one's manhood than one's life. O God of devils! They don't even know that, they don't know anything, and then take it on themselves to teach people everything. Hadn't he accepted it, or was he incapable of accepting? From the first few moments he had decided not to accept; yes, that was it. Moreover, he couldn't entirely picture what had happened, and so he had fled from the hospital instinctively and blindly, before he had completely recovered. It was as though his flight could bring things back to normal again. He had needed a long time merely to accustom himself just to being alive, but had he succeeded? No, not yet. Each time he was asked, casually, "Why haven't you got married?" the same feeling of pain plunging between his thighs came back to him, as though he were still lying under the bright round light with his legs suspended in the air.

The light blazed so piercingly that his eyes began to water. Assad stretched out his hand at that moment and brought down the long sun shield to shade Abul Khaizuran's face.

"Yes, that's better. Thanks. Do you know, Abu Qais is a lucky man."

Assad realized that Abul Khaizuran wanted to change the subject of marriage, which his question had raised, so he simply responded:

"Why?"

"If he'd been fated to go with the smugglers, it would have been nothing less than a miracle if he'd reached Kuwait." Hunching his arms around the steering wheel, Abul Khaizuran rested his chest on them: "You don't know how things are here. None of you know. It's me you should ask, me. I know as many stories as there are hairs on a cat."

"The fat man seems kindhearted. I liked him."

Abul Khaizuran bent his head and wiped the sweat from his forehead with his sleeve, which was lying on the wheel. Then he said:

"Ah! The fat man doesn't cross the frontier with you, and he doesn't know what happens."

"What does happen?"

"I have a cousin called Hasanain, who was smuggled across the border once. After more than seven hours' walking, darkness fell. Then the smuggler pointed to a cluster of far-off lights, saying: 'There's Kuwait. You'll reach it when you've walked for half an hour.' Do you know what happened? That wasn't Kuwait, it was a remote Iraqi village. I can tell you thousands of stories like that. Stories of men who became like dogs as they looked for one drop of water to moisten their cracked tongues with. What do you think happened when they saw bedouin encampments? They bought a mouthful of water in exchange for all the money or wedding rings or watches they owned. People say Hatim was a bedouin. But I think that's a complete lie. That time has passed, Abu Saad, it has passed. But you don't realize it. You think that the fat man has the power to do everything. I know someone who survived alone in the desert for four days; when a car picked him up on the road to Al-Jahra he was at his last gasp. Guess what he did! He wanted just one thing out of life; he wanted to go back to Basra as soon as he recovered, even if it meant going back through the desert. Do you know why? He told me he wanted to go back there to get his hands round the fat man's neck and throttle him, and then let all hell break loose. He'd started out with two friends of his youth, from Gaza, across Israel, across Jordan, across Iraq. Then the smuggler abandoned them in the desert, before they had crossed the Kuwaiti border. He had buried his two friends in that unknown region and was carrying their identity cards in the hope that he would reach Kuwait and send them to their families. He didn't want anyone to give him advice; he said he didn't want to forget or forgive. After less than a month had passed, he retraced his steps to Iraq, but he was arrested, and now he is spending his second year in a miserable prison. What are you thinking of? You come to us straight from school like babes, thinking that life is easy. Do you suppose that Abu Qais wasn't gambling with his life? And he would have been the loser. I'm as sure of that as I am of this damned sun. Tomorrow, when you get to Kuwait, you'll speak well of me and say: 'Abul Khaizuran was telling the truth,' and you'll thank God a thousand times because I rescued you from the claws of the fat man. Have you ever in your life seen a skeleton lying on the sand?"

"What did you say?"

"I asked you: have you ever in your life seen a skeleton lying on the sand?"

"No."

Abul Khaizuran gave a sharp turn to the steering wheel to avoid a wide rut in the sand, and then the lorry began to jog and jolt over a road like an extended flight of steps. Assad felt his entrails were almost leaping past his chattering teeth out of his mouth.

"You would have seen many if you'd gone with the smugglers. And in any case, it won't mean anything."

"Why?"

"Because you'll be too busy to think about it, or, as Hasanain said, you won't want to think about it."

Assad merely smiled stupidly, not knowing what he ought to do. Then, nudging Abul Khaizuran in the ribs, he asked:

"Then why do you smuggle?"

"Me? Smuggle?"

Assad laughed and hit Abul Khaizuran's thigh with his hand.

"Then what do you call this?"

"Shall I tell you the truth? I want more money, more money, much more. And I find it difficult to accumulate money honestly. Do you see this miserable being which is me? I have some money. In two years I'll leave everything and settle down. I want to relax, to stretch out, to rest in the shade, thinking or not thinking. I don't want to make a single movement. I've had more than enough exhaustion in my life. Yes indeed, more than enough."

Abul Khaizuran quickly switched off the motor, opened the door and jumped down. He started shouting: "Now the serious part is beginning. Come on! I'll open the cover of the tank for you. Ha! The climate will be like the next world inside there."

He climbed lightly up the small iron ladder and set to work on the round cover of the tank. Marwan thought slowly: "He has strong arms." They were dripping with sweat, while his shirt was completely soaked and his face appeared daubed in mud.

The cover opened with a sound like an explosion, and Abul Khaizuran lifted up the edge of the metal disk, till it was vertical over its hinge and its inside could be seen, red with rust. Abul Khaizuran sat beside the opening, with his legs hanging down wide apart, and began to mop his sweat with the red handkerchief with which he covered the back of his neck, under the collar of the blue shirt. He was panting.

"I advise you to take your shirts off. The heat's stifling, terrifying, and you'll sweat as though you were in an oven. But it's only for five or seven minutes, and I'll drive as fast as I can. Inside there are iron girders, one in each corner, and I would rather you

523

held on to them tightly, or else you'll roll around like balls. Of course you must take your shoes off."

They all remained standing on the ground, motionless. Abul Khaizuran got up and then jumped down, trying to laugh.

"One could sleep inside if the weather were a little kinder."

Abu Qais looked at Marwan and they both looked at Assad. Under the pressure of those glances, he took a couple of small steps forward, and then came back and stood still again, while Abul Khaizuran watched him.

"I advise you to hurry up a little. We're still in the early morning, but soon the inside of the tank will become a real oven. You can take a water bottle with you, but don't use it when you feel the lorry's standing still."

Marwan made up his mind and walked quickly up to the iron ladder. But Assad rushed to climb it before him, and then leaned over the uncovered opening. He put his head down into the tank for a few minutes, and brought it out again:

"This is hell. It's on fire."

Abul Khaizuran spread out his hands, saying:

"I told you that before."

Marwan too had climbed up and poked his head through the opening, taking it out again with a look of disgust and fear on his face. Abu Qais got up beside them, panting. Abul Khaizuran shouted up from below:

"Do you know what to do if any of you wants to sneeze?"

Assad smiled wanly, while Marwan looked down, and Abu Qais seemed not to understand the question.

"Hold your finger straight under your nostrils like this." Abul Khaizuran imitated the gesture, and his faced looked ridiculous.

Walking forward, Assad said:

"I don't think any of us will sneeze in this oven. Don't be worried on that score." Assad put his hands on his hips and stood beside the opening of the tank, with his head bowed, as though he wanted to see what was inside; meanwhile Abu Qais took off his shirt and carefully rolled it up, putting it under his arm. His chest appeared, covered with grizzled hair, and his protruding shoulder blades could be seen. He sat on the edge of the opening, dangling his legs inside. He threw his shirt in first, then slipped down, slow and straight, supporting himself on his arms, which were braced over the edge of the opening, until his feet touched the bottom and he let his arms go, sliding his body down carefully. His head was swallowed up and his arms disappeared.

Assad bent down and shouted:

"How do things look?"

A resounding voice echoed from inside, as though from a great depth.

"It's a cursed well. Come on!"

Assad looked at Marwan, who had taken off his shirt and stood waiting while Abul Khaizuran again climbed the ladder.

"Whose turn?"

"Mine." Marwan went up to the opening, and turned his back to it. He let his legs down first, leaning his stomach on the edge. His whole body slid skilfully down, and his two hands remained for a moment holding on to the frame of the opening before they disappeared.

Assad followed his companions without taking off his shirt, and when the opening hid him from sight, Abul Khaizuran bent down trying to see what it was like inside. But he couldn't make out anything, for each time he looked, his body blocked out the light from the opening and it was impossible to see. At last he shouted: "Well?"

A resonant voice replied:

"What are you waiting for? Hurry up! We're almost suffocating."

Abul Khaizuran quickly closed the cover and turned its curved handle twice. He jumped down and rushed to his seat. Before the cab door was shut the lorry had begun to eat up the road.

In those few minutes there was only one thought in Abul Khaizuran's mind. The rutted road, like an extended flight of steps, was shaking and jolting the lorry ceaselessly and mercilessly. This shaking was enough to turn eggs into omelettes more quickly than an electric whisk could. It didn't matter as far as Marwan was concerned: he was a boy. And it didn't matter to Assad, who was strongly built. But what about Abu Qais? No doubt his teeth were chattering like those of a man almost freezing to death, with the difference that here there was no frost.

Abul Khaizuran could eliminate some of the shaking if he increased his speed, if he made this infernal tank travel at one hundred and twenty instead of the ninety the speedometer was indicating now. But if he did so, who could guarantee that the lorry wouldn't overturn on a bloody road like this? It didn't matter if the lorry overturned, since it wasn't his, but what if it came to rest on its roof? And who knew if the engine would bear that kind of speed in weather like this, on this sort of terrain? They always put high numbers on the speedometer that it's not wise for a skillful driver to get up to.

He didn't slow down when he reached Safwan, nor, as he turned into the square, making for the police post on the left, did he raise his foot a hair's breadth from the accelerator. He swept around, sending up dust in a wide circle, and only lifted his foot when he sharply pressed the brake, in front of the entrance. He shot inside like an arrow.

The customs square at Safwan is broad and sandy, with one large, isolated tree in the middle whose long drooping leaves throw a wide shadow in the square. Round it stand rooms with low wooden doors, which are occupied by crowded offices and men who are always busy. As Abul Khaizuran's tall figure rushed across the square, he noticed nothing except some women sitting in the shade of the tree, wrapped in their veils. One or two children were standing by the water tap, and the watchman was sleeping on his old cane chair.

"Abul Khaizuran's in a hurry today."

"Yes. Haj Rida's waiting. If I'm late he'll sack me."

"Haj Rida won't sack you. Don't worry. He won't find another young man like you."

"Ah, the world's as full of young men as it is of mushrooms. If he made one gesture, they would be all over him like flies."

"What've you got with you?"

"Arms. Tanks. Armored cars. And six planes and two guns."

The man broke into a hearty laugh. Abul Khaizuran lightly slid the papers away from under his hands and darted outside. Entering another room he said to himself: "The most difficult part's over." After a minute he came out of the other room, and in less than the twinkling of an eye he was switching on the engine, rending the silence that had settled over Safwan, and setting off again.

While the lorry sped away like an arrow, leaving a trail of dust behind it, Abul Khaizuran streamed with sweat, which traced a network of channels over his face, meeting at his chin. The sun blazed brightly and the wind was hot, and carried a fine dust like flour. "Never in my life have I seen such awful weather." He undid the buttons of his shirt and his fingers touched the thick hair on his chest, which was soaked. The road had flattened out, and the lorry no longer jolted as before, so he accelerated. The speedometer leapt forward like a white dog tied to a tent peg.

He peered forward, his eyes drowned in sweat, and made out the edge of the little hill. Behind that hill Safwar would be hidden, and it was there that he must stop.

He pressed harder on the accelerator so that the lorry would climb the hill without slowing down. He felt his leg muscles were knotted into a ball and about to tear. The ground sped past and the lorry roared. The glass blazed and the sweat burned his eyes. But the top of the hill still seemed as far away as eternity. O almighty, omnipotent God! How could the top of a hill arouse all these feelings, which surged through his veins and poured their fire onto his dust-stained skin as salt sweat. O almighty God, you who have never been with me, who have never looked in my direction, whom I have never believed in, can you possibly be here this time? Just this time?

He blinked several times to clear the sweat from his eyelids, and when he opened his eyes the hilltop stood in front of him. He climbed to the top, stopped the engine, and let the lorry roll along a little before he stopped it and jumped from the door to the back of the tank.

Marwan emerged first. He raised his arms, and Abul Khaizuran roughly pulled him out and left him lying on top of the tank. Abu Qais pushed his head out and tried to climb up but it was beyond him. So he got his arms out and let Abul Khaizuran help him. Assad was able to climb through the opening. He had taken his shirt off.

Abul Khaizuran sat on top of the hot tank. He was panting, and he seemed to have aged. In the meantime Abu Qais had slipped slowly down over the wheels and lay in the shadow of the lorry face down. Assad stood for a moment, breathing deeply. He seemed to want to say something but couldn't. Finally he panted:

"Oh! It's so cold here."

His face had become red and damp. His trousers were soaked with sweat, and his chest, which had marks left by rust, looked as though it were spattered with blood. Marwan got up and came down the iron ladder, exhausted. His eyes were reddened, and his chest was dyed with rust. When he reached the ground, he rested his head on Abu Qais's thigh, slowly stretching out his body beside the wheel. Assad followed him a moment later, and then Abul Khaizuran. They sat resting their heads on their knees, their legs bent. Abu Khaizuran spoke after a while:

"Was it terrible?"

No one answered him. His gaze wandered over their faces, which seemed to him yellow and mummified. If Marwan's chest had not been rising and falling and Abu Qais's breathing an audible whistle, he would have thought they were dead.

"I told you seven minutes. And all the same, the whole thing didn't take more than six."

Assad glared at him, Marwan opened his eyes without focusing on anything in particular, and Abu Qais turned his face away.

"I swear to you on my honor! Six minutes exactly. Look! Why don't you want to look? I told you so, I said it from the beginning, and now you think I'm lying to you. Here's the watch. Look! Look!"

Marwan raised his head, propped himself up on his arms, and began looking in Abul Khaizuran's direction with his head slightly tilted back. He appeared not to see him clearly.

"Have you tried sitting there for six minutes?"

"I told you. . . ."

"It wasn't six minutes."

"Why don't you look at your watch? Why don't you? It's on your wrist. Come on, look! Look! And stop staring at me like an idiot." Abu Qais spoke:

"It was six minutes. I was counting the whole time. From one to sixty, a minute. That's how I reckoned. I counted six times. The last time I counted very slowly."

He was talking haltingly, in a low voice, and Assad asked:

"What's wrong with you, Abu Qais? Are you ill?"

"Me? Me? Ah . . . no. But I'm breathing my share of air."

Abu Khaizuran stood up and brushed the sand from his trousers. He set his hands on his hips and began to look from one to the other of the three men.

"Come on. We mustn't waste any more time. You have another Turkish bath in front of you in a few minutes' time."

Abu Qais stood up and went over to the driver's cab, and Assad climbed the iron ladder, but Marwan stayed sitting in the shade. Abu Khaizuran asked:

"Don't you want to get up?"

"Why can't we rest a little?"

Assad shouted down:

"We'll have a long rest when we arrive, not before. Come on."

Abul Khaizuran gave a loud laugh. He struck Marwan on the shoulder with his hand and said:

"Come and sit beside Abu Qais. You are thin and won't bother us much. And you look very tired."

Climbing up, Marwan sat beside Abu Qais. Abul Khaizuran shouted loudly before he closed the door:

"Put on your shirt, Assad, or you'll be roasted in the sun."

Marwan murmured in a weak voice to Abul Khaizuran:

"Tell him to leave the oven door open and perhaps it will cool down."

Abul Khaizuran cried cheerfully:

"And leave the tank door open."

The engine roared and the big lorry began to trace a misty line across the desert, which rose and then dissolved in the heat.

Sun and Shade

The lorry, a small world, black as night, made its way across the desert like a heavy drop of oil on a burning sheet of tin. The sun hung high above their heads, round, blazing, and blindingly bright. None of them bothered to dry their sweat any longer. Assad spread his shirt over his head, bent his legs, and let the sun roast him without resistance. Marwan leaned his head on Abu Qais's shoulder and closed his eyes. Abu Qais stared at the road, tightly closing his lips under his thick gray moustache.

None of the four wanted to talk anymore, not only because they were exhausted by their efforts, but because each one was swallowed up in his own thoughts. The huge lorry was carrying them along the road, together with their dreams, their families, their hopes and ambitions, their misery and despair, their strength and weakness, their past and future, as if it were pushing against the immense door to a new, unknown destiny, and all eyes were fixed on the door's surface as though bound to it by invisible threads.

We'll be able to send Qais to school and buy one or two olive shoots. Perhaps we'll build a cottage to live in, which will be ours. I'm an old man; I may arrive or I may not. And do you think that the life you lead here is better than death? Why don't you try, as we do? Why don't you get up off that cushion and set out through God's world in search of a living? Will you spend the whole of your life eating the flour ration for one kilo of which you sacrifice all your honor at the doors of officials?

The lorry traveled on over the burning earth, its engine roaring remorselessly.

Shafiqa is an innocent woman. She was an adolescent when a mortar bomb smashed her leg and the doctors amputated it from the top of the thigh. And his mother didn't like anyone to talk about his father. Zakaria has gone. There, in Kuwait, you'll find everything out. You'll learn everything. You're still a boy, and you know no more of life than a babe in arms knows of its house. School teaches nothing. It only teaches laziness. So leave it and plunge into the frying pan with the rest of humanity.

The lorry traveled on over the burning earth, its engine roaring with an intolerable noise.

Perhaps it was buried in the ground, the bomb he trod on as he was running; or maybe it was thrown in front of him by a man hidden in a nearby ditch. None of that is important now. His legs were suspended in the air and his shoulders were still on the comfortable white bed, and the terrible pain was still plunging between his thighs. There was a woman there, helping the doctors. Whenever he remembered it, his face was suffused with shame. And what good did patriotism do you? You spend your life in an adventure, and now you are incapable of sleeping with a woman! And what good did you do? Let the dead bury their dead. I only want more money now, more money.

The lorry traveled on over the burning earth, its engine roaring loudly.

The policeman pushed him in front of the officer, who said to him: "You think you're a hero when the donkeys carry you on their shoulders, demonstrating in the street." He spat in his face, but Assad didn't move as the saliva ran slowly down his forehead and gathered on the tip of his nose in a nasty viscous mess. They led him out, and when he was in the corridor he heard the policeman who was grasping his shoulder say in a low voice: "Damn this uniform!" Then he let him go, and Assad ran off. His uncle, wishing to marry him off to his daughter, wanted him to make a start in life. Otherwise he would never have collected fifty dinars in the whole of his life.

The lorry traveled on over the burning earth, its roaring engine a gigantic mouth devouring the road.

The sun in the middle of the sky traced a broad dome of white flame over the desert, and the trail of dust reflected an almost blinding glare. They used to be told that someone wasn't coming back from Kuwait because he'd died; he'd been killed by sunstroke. He'd been driving his shovel into the earth when he fell onto one knee and then on both. And then what? He was killed by sunstroke. Do you want him buried here or there? That was all, sunstroke. It was quite right. Who called it "sunstroke"? Wasn't he a genius? This desert was like a giant in hiding, flogging their heads with whips of fire and boiling pitch. But could the sun kill them and all the stench imprisoned in their breasts? The thoughts seemed to run from one head to another, laden with the same suspicions, for their eyes suddenly met. Abul Khaizuran looked at Marwan and then at Abu Qais, whom he found staring at him. He tried to smile, and failed, so he wiped the sweat from his forehead with his sleeve, murmuring:

"This is the Hell that I have heard of."

"God's Hell?"

"Yes."

Abul Khaizuran reached out his hand and turned off the engine; then he slowly got down, followed by Marwan and Abu Qais, while Assad remained perched above them.

Abul Khaizuran sat in the shade of the lorry and lit a cigarette. He said in a low voice:

"Let's rest a little before we begin the performance again."

Abu Qais asked:

"Why didn't you set out with us yesterday evening so that we would be saved by the cool of the night from all this trouble?"

Without raising his eyes from the ground, Abul Khaizuran replied:

"The road between Safwan and Mutlaa is full of patrols at night. During the day no patrol can run the risk of making a reconnaissance in heat like this."

Marwan remarked:

"If your lorry is sacrosanct and never searched, why can't we stay outside that terrible prison?"

Abul Khaizuran replied sharply:

"Don't be silly. Are you so afraid of spending five or six minutes inside? We've done more than half the journey, and only the easiest part is left." He stood up, went over to the water skin hanging outside the door, and opened it. "I'll put on a splendid lunch for you when we arrive. I'll have two chickens killed . . ." He raised the water skin and poured the water into his mouth until it began to trickle out at the corners onto his chin and his wet shirt. When he had quenched his thirst he poured the rest of the contents over his head, letting the water run down over his forehead, neck, and chest, which gave him an extraordinary appearance. He hung the water bottle outside the door again, spread his big hands and cried:

"Come on, you've learned the art well. What time is it now? Half past eleven. Think, in seven minutes at the outside I'll open the cover for you. Remember that, half past eleven."

Marwan looked at his watch and nodded. He tried to say something but it was beyond him, so he took a few steps over to the iron ladder and began to climb it.

Assad rolled up his shirt and plunged into the opening. Marwan hesitated a little and then followed him, leaning with his stomach on the edge and then skilfully sliding down with a sharp movement. Abu Qais shook his head, saying: "Seven minutes?"

"At the outside!"

Abul Khaizuran patted Abu Qais on the shoulder and looked straight into his eyes. They stood there together streaming with sweat, neither of them able to speak.

Abu Qais climbed the ladder with firm steps, and let his legs down through the opening. The two younger men helped him down.

Abul Khaizuran closed the cover and turned the curved metal handle twice before jumping quickly down and rushing to his seat.

Only a minute and a half later he had driven his lorry through the big open gate in the barbed-wire fence round the post of Mutlaa. He brought it to a stop in front of the wide steps leading to the tiled one-story building flanked on both sides by small rooms with low, closed windows. Opposite it were a few stalls selling food, and the noise of air conditioners filled the air.

There were only one or two cars parked waiting at the edge of the big square. The silence hung heavy and unbroken, except for the hum of the air conditioners attached to all the windows looking out onto the square. Only one soldier was standing in a small wooden hut beside the wide flight of steps.

Abul Khaizuran hurried up the steps and made for the third room on the right. Immediately he opened the door and went in, he felt, from the glances directed at him by the officials, that something was going to happen. But he didn't pause, pushing his papers in front of the fat official sitting in the center of the room.

"Aha! Abu Khaizurana!" shouted the official, as he slid the papers to one side with deliberate carelessness, and crossed his arms on the metal desk. "Where have you been all this time?"

Abul Khaizuran panted:

"In Basra."

"Haj Rida asked after you more than six times."

"The lorry had broken down."

The three officials in the room broke into loud laughter and Abul Khaizuran turned round, at a loss. Then he fixed his eyes on the fat man's face.

"What is it that amuses you this morning?"

The three officials exchanged glances and then burst out laughing again. Abul Khaizuran said tensely, shuffling from one foot to the other:

"Now, Abu Baqir, I've no time for jokes. Please. . . ."

Stretching out his hand he moved the papers closer in front of the official, but again Abu Baqir pushed them away to the edge of the desk, folded his arms and smiled wickedly.

"Haj Rida asked about you six times."

"I told you, the lorry was not working. And Haj Rida and I can come to an understanding when we meet. Please sign the papers. I'm in a hurry."

He slid the papers closer again, but once more Abu Baqir pushed them away.

"Your lorry wasn't working?"

"Yes. Please! I'm in a hurry."

The three officials looked at one another and quietly gave a knowing laugh. The desk of one of them was completely bare except for a small glass of tea; the other had stopped working to follow what was happening.

The fat man called Abu Baqir said, belching:

"Now, be sensible, Abu Khaizurana. Why do you hurry your journey in terrible weather like this? The room here's cool, and I'll order you a glass of tea. So enjoy the comfort."

Abul Khaizuran picked up the papers, took the pen lying in front of Abu Baqir and went round the table to stand beside him. He pushed the pen towards him, nudging his shoulder with his arm.

"I'll spend an hour sitting with you when I come back, but now let me leave, for Baqir's sake and Baqir's mother's sake. Here!"

Abu Baqir, however, did not move his hand but continued to stare stupidly at the driver, on the point of bursting out laughing again.

"Ali, you devil, Abu Khaizurana! Why don't you remember that you are in a hurry when you are in Basra? Eh?"

"I told you, the lorry was in the garage."

Again he pushed the pen towards Abu Baqir, but he didn't move.

"Don't lie, Abu Khaizurana, don't lie! Haj Rida has told us the story from A to Z."

"What story?"

They all exchanged glances, as Abul Khaizuran's face turned white with terror, and the pen began to tremble in his hand.

"The story of that dancer. What's her name, Ali?"

From the other side of the empty desk, Ali answered:

"Kawkab."

Abu Baqir hit his desk with his hand and gave a broad smile.

"Kawkab. Kawkab. Abu Khaizurana, you devil. Why don't you tell us what you get up to in Basra? You make out to us that you are a decent, well-behaved fellow, and then you go to Basra and commit mortal sins with that dancer, Kawkab. Yes, Kawkab, that's the name."

"What's all this rubbish about Kawkab? Let me go before Haj Rida gives me the sack."

Abu Baqir replied:

"Impossible. Tell us about this dancer. The Haj knows the whole story and he's told it to us. Come on."

"If Haj Rida's told it to you, why do you want me to tell it again?"

Abu Baqir stood up and gave a bull-like roar.

"Ah! So it's true. It's a true story." He walked round the desk and came to the middle of the room. The story of depravity had excited him. He had thought about it day and night, endowing it with all the obscenity created by his long, tormenting deprivation. The idea that a friend of his had slept with a prostitute was exciting, and worth all those dreams.

"You go to Basra and make out that the lorry isn't working, and then you spend the happiest nights of your life with Kawkab. Good heavens, Abu Khaizurana! Good heavens, you devil! But tell us how she has shown her love for you. Haj Rida says that she loves you so much that she spends her money on you and gives you checks. Ah, Abu Khaizurana, you devil!"

He came up to Abul Khaizuran, his face red. Obviously, he'd enjoyed himself thinking about the story as Haj Rida had told it to him over the telephone. He leaned over and whispered hoarsely in his ear:

"Is it your virility? Or aren't there many men about?"

Abul Khaizuran laughed hysterically and shoved the papers at Abu Baqir's chest. He picked up the pen and began signing them automatically, shaking with suppressed laughter. But when Abul Khaizuran stretched out his hand to take them, Abu Baqir hid them behind his back, warding off Abul Khaizuran with his other arm.

"Next time I'll go with you to Basra. Agreed? You'll introduce me to this Kawkab. Haj Rida says she's really beautiful."

Abul Khaizuran said in a trembling voice as he stretched out his arm, trying to reach the papers:

"I agree."

"On your honor?"

"On my honor."

Abu Baqir collapsed into renewed laughter, shaking his round head as he want back to his desk, while Abul Khaizuran rushed outside with his papers, pursued by Abu Baqir's voice:

"You devil, Abu Khaizurana! He's deceived us for two years, but now he's been shown up. Ah, you devil, Abu Khaizurana!"

Abul Khaizuran burst into the other room, looking at his watch. A quarter to twelve. The signing of the other papers didn't take more than a minute. When he shut the door after him the heat lashed him again, but he took no notice, jumping down the wide steps two at a time until he stood in front of his lorry. He looked at the tank for a moment and he had the impression that the metal was about to melt under that fearful sun. The engine responded to the first touch, and he instantly closed the door, not waving to the guard. The road now was completely level and he had a minute or a minute and a half before he could round the first bend, hiding him from the post. He was forced to slow down a little when he met a large lorry, but then he put his foot down till the vehicle was going at top speed. When he reached the bend the wheels set up a screech like a howl and almost touched the sand verge as they made their enormous turn. There was nothing in his mind but terror, and he thought he would collapse over his steering wheel in a faint. The wheel was hot and he felt it scorch his hard hands, but he didn't slacken his hold on it. The leather seat burned under him and the glass windscreen was dusty and blazed with the sun's glare.

A loud hiss came from the wheels as though they were flaying the asphalt. Did you have to talk so much rubbish, Abu Baqir? Did you have to spew up all your filth onto my face and theirs? The curse of almighty God be upon you. The curse of almighty God, who doesn't exist anywhere, be visited upon you, Abu Baqir! And on you, Haj Rida, you liar! A dancer! Kawkab? God damn you all!

He stopped the lorry sharply, and climbed over the wheel to the roof of the tank. When his hands touched the metal roof he felt them burn, and couldn't keep them there. He moved them away and leaned his elbows, in their sleeves, on the metal roof crawling to the angular lock. He took hold of it with a corner of his blue shirt and turned it, so that it burst open and the rusty metal disk stood vertical over its hinge.

As he let go of the disk he caught sight of the heads of the watch on his wrist. They pointed to nine minutes to twelve. The round glass had cracked into little pieces. The uncovered opening yawned empty for a moment. Abul Khaizuran's face, drawn to it, twitched compulsively, his lower lip trembling as he panted for breath, overcome with terror. A drop of sweat from his forehead fell onto the metal roof of the tank and immediately dried. He put his hands on his knees, bent his soaked back until his face was over the black hole, and shouted in a dry, grating voice:

"Assad!"

The sound reverberated in the tank and almost pierced his eardrums as it came back to him. Before the echo of the rumble that his first cry had set up had died away, he shouted again:

"Hey there!"

He put two firm hands on the edge of the opening and, supporting himself on his strong arms, slid down inside the tank. It was very dark there, and at first he couldn't make out anything, but when he moved his body away from the opening a circle of yellow light fell into the depths and showed a chest covered with thick gray hair that began to shine brightly as though coated with tin. Abul Khaizuran bent to put his ear to the damp gray hair. The body was cold and still. Stretching out his hand, he felt his way to the back of the tank. The other body was still holding on to the metal support. He tried to find the head but could only feel the wet shoulders; then he made out the head, bowed on the chest. When his hand touched the face, it fell into a mouth open as wide as it could go.

Abul Khaizuran had a choking sensation. His body had begun to run with sweat at such an amazing rate that he felt he was coated in thick oil, and he couldn't tell whether he was trembling because of this oil covering his chest and back or whether it was caused by fear. Bending down, he felt his way to the opening, and when he put his head through it, Marwan's face came into his mind for some reason, and wouldn't go away. He felt the face take possession of him from within, like a fresco shimmering on a wall, so he started to shake his head violently as he slipped down from the opening and the merciless sun burned it. He stood for a moment breathing in fresh air. He couldn't think of anything. Marwan's face had surged up to take complete possession of his mind, like a spring that bursts from the earth and sends its water high into the air. When he reached his seat he remembered Abu Qais, whose shirt was still lying on the seat beside him. He took it in his long fingers and threw it far away. He switched on the lorry's motor and it began to roar again, as the lorry made its slow, majestic way down the slope.

He turned round to look through the small, wire-netted window, and saw the round disk open, standing straight over its hinge, with its inside corroded with rust. Suddenly the metal disk disappeared behind drops of salt water, which filled his eyes. He had a headache and vertigo such as he had never felt before. Were those salty drops tears, or sweat running from his burning forehead?

The Grave

As darkness fell, Abul Khaizuran drove his lorry away from the sleeping city. Pale lights trembled along the side of the road, and he knew that those lampposts that were retreating in front of the window would come to an end shortly, when he had left the city far behind him. The darkness would be unbroken. The night was moonless, and the edge of the desert would be silent as the grave.

He turned his lorry off the asphalt road and drove along a sandy track that led into the desert. He had made up his mind at noon to bury them, one by one, in three graves. Now he felt consumed with exhaustion, as though a drug had been injected into his arms. He had no strength to work, and he wouldn't be capable of wielding a spade for long hours to dig three graves. Before he went to take his lorry out of Haj Rida's garage, he told himself that he wouldn't bury them. He would throw the three corpses into the desert and return home. But now he wasn't pleased with the idea. He didn't like to think that his companions' bodies should be lost in the desert, at the mercy of birds and beasts of prey, and that there would be nothing left of them after a few days except white bones lying on the sand.

The lorry moved over the sandy track with a muted noise, while he went on thinking. He wasn't thinking in the strict sense of the term, but a series of disconnected scenes was passing ceaselessly through his brain, incoherent and inexplicable. He could sense exhaustion creeping through his limbs like straight columns of ants.

A breeze sprang up and carried to his nostrils a smell of putrefaction. He said to himself: "The municipality piles up the rubbish here." Then he reflected: "If I dumped the bodies here they would be discovered in the morning and buried under official auspices." He turned his steering wheel and followed the tracks of many wheels that had dug their path through the sand before him, and then he switched off the headlamps, advancing slowly by the light of the side-lamps alone. When the black heaps of rubbish rose up in front of him, he switched off the side lamps. The air around him filled with the putrid stench, but he soon got used to it. Then he stopped his lorry and climbed down.

Abul Khaizuran stood beside his lorry for a few moments to make sure that no one was watching him, then he climbed up onto the back of the tank. It was cold and damp. He turned the curved metal handle slowly and pulled the iron disk up so that it burst open with a sharp explosion. Supporting himself on his arms, he slid lightly down inside. The first corpse was cold and firm, and he tossed it over his shoulder. He pushed the head out of the opening first and then, holding the corpse by its legs, he lifted it and threw it upwards, hearing the heavy sound it made as it slid over the edge of the tank, and the muffled bump as it struck the sand. He had great difficulty in prising the hands of the other corpse away from the iron support, but then he pulled it by its legs to the opening and threw it out over his shoulder, straight and stiff. He heard it strike the earth. The third corpse was easier than either of its companions.

He jumped down, slowly closed the opening, and climbed down the ladder to the ground. There was thick darkness everywhere, and he was relieved that he would be saved by it from seeing the faces. Holding them by their feet, he dragged the corpses one by one and threw them onto the end of the road, where the municipality's dustcarts usually stopped to dump their rubbish, so that the first driver arriving in the morning would easily have an opportunity to see them.

He climbed into his seat, turned on the engine and slowly reversed, trying his utmost to mingle the tracks of his lorry's wheels with those of others. He had decided to drive back to the main road in reverse, in order to confuse the traces completely. But a thought occurred to him when he had covered some distance, and he switched off the engine again, walked back to where he had left the bodies, and took the money from their pockets. He also removed Marwan's watch. Then he retraced his steps to the lorry, walking on the edge of his soles.

As he returned to the lorry and lifted one leg up, a sudden thought flashed into his mind. He stood rigid in his place, trying to do or say something. He thought of shouting, but immediately realized what a stupid idea that was. He tried to finish climbing into the lorry, but didn't feel strong enough. He thought that his head would explode. All the exhaustion which he felt suddenly rose to his head and began to hum in it, and so he put his head in his hands and began to pull his hair to expel the thought. But it was still there, huge and resounding, unshakeable and inescapable. He turned to look back to where he had left the corpses, but he could see nothing, and that glance simply set the thought ablaze so that it began to burn in his mind. All at once he could no longer keep it within his head, and he dropped his hands to his sides and stared into the darkness with his eyes wide open.

The thought slipped from his mind and ran onto his tongue: "Why didn't they knock on the sides of the tank?" He turned right round once, but he was afraid he would fall, so he climbed into his seat and leaned his head on the wheel.

"Why didn't you knock on the sides of the tank? Why didn't you say anything? Why?"

The desert suddenly began to send back the echo:

"Why didn't you knock on the sides of the tank? Why didn't you bang the sides of the tank? Why? Why? Why?"

A Temporary Matter
(1998)

The notice informed them that it was a temporary matter: for five days their electricity would be cut off for one hour, beginning at eight P.M. A line had gone down in the last snowstorm, and the repairmen were going to take advantage of the milder evenings to set it right. The work would affect only the houses on the quiet tree-lined street, within walking distance of a row of brick-faced stores and a trolley stop, where Shoba and Shukumar had lived for three years.

"It's good of them to warn us," Shoba conceded after reading the notice aloud, more for her own benefit than Shukumar's. She let the strap of her leather satchel, plump with files, slip from her shoulders, and left it in the hallway as she walked into the kitchen. She wore a navy blue poplin raincoat over gray sweatpants and white sneakers, looking, at thirty-three, like the type of woman she'd once claimed she would never resemble.

She'd come from the gym. Her cranberry lipstick was visible only on the outer reaches of her mouth, and her eyeliner had left charcoal patches beneath her lower lashes. She used to look this way sometimes, Shukumar thought, on mornings after a party or a night at a bar, when she'd been too lazy to wash her face, too eager to collapse into his arms. She dropped a sheaf of mail on the table without a glance. Her eyes were still fixed on the notice in her other hand. "But they should do this sort of thing during the day."

"When I'm here, you mean," Shukumar said. He put a glass lid on a pot of lamb, adjusting it so only the slightest bit of steam could escape. Since January he'd been working at home, trying to complete the final chapters of his dissertation on agrarian revolts in India. "When do the repairs start?"

"It says March nineteenth. Is today the nineteenth?" Shoba walked over to the framed corkboard that hung on the wall by the fridge, bare except for a calendar of William Morris wallpaper patterns. She looked at it as if for the first time, studying the wallpaper pattern carefully on the top half before allowing her eyes to fall to the numbered grid on the bottom. A friend had sent the calendar in the mail as a Christmas gift, even though Shoba and Shukumar hadn't celebrated Christmas that year.

"Today then," Shoba announced. "You have a dentist appointment next Friday, by the way."

He ran his tongue over the tops of his teeth; he'd forgotten to brush them that morning. It wasn't the first time. He hadn't left the house at all that day, or the day before. The more Shoba stayed out, the more she began putting in extra hours at work and taking on additional projects, the more he wanted to stay in, not even leaving to get the mail, or to buy fruit or wine at the stores by the trolley stop.

Six months ago, in September, Shukumar was at an academic conference in Baltimore when Shoba went into labor, three weeks before her due date. He hadn't wanted to go to the conference, but she had insisted; it was important to make contacts, and he would be entering the job market next year. She told him that she had his number at the hotel, and a copy of his schedule and flight numbers, and she had arranged with her friend Gillian for a ride to the hospital in the event of an emergency. When the cab pulled away that morning for the airport, Shoba stood waving good-bye in her robe, with one arm resting on the mound of her belly as if it were a perfectly natural part of her body.

Each time he thought of that moment, the last moment he saw Shoba pregnant, it was the cab he remembered most, a station wagon, painted red with blue lettering. It was cavernous compared to their own car. Although Shukumar was six feet tall, with hands too big ever to rest comfortably in the pockets of his jeans, he felt dwarfed in the back seat. As the cab sped down Beacon Street, he imagined a day when he and Shoba might need to buy a station wagon of their own, to cart their children back and forth from music lessons and dentist appointments. He imagined himself gripping the wheel, as Shoba turned around to hand the children juice boxes. Once, these images of parenthood had troubled Shukumar, adding to his anxiety that he was still a student at thirty-five. But that early autumn morning, the trees still heavy with bronze leaves, he welcomed the image for the first time.

A member of the staff had found him somehow among the identical convention rooms and handed him a stiff square of stationery. It was only a telephone number, but Shukumar knew it was the hospital. When he returned to Boston it was over. The baby had been born dead. Shoba was lying on a bed, asleep, in a private room so small there was barely enough space to stand beside her, in a wing of the hospital they hadn't been to on the tour for expectant parents. Her placenta had weakened and she'd had a cesarean, though not quickly enough. The doctor explained that these things happen. He smiled in the kindest way it was possible to smile at people known only professionally. Shoba would be back on her feet in a few weeks. There was nothing to indicate that she would not be able to have children in the future.

These days Shoba was always gone by the time Shukumar woke up. He would open his eyes and see the long black hairs she shed on her pillow and think of her, dressed, sipping her third cup of coffee already; in her office downtown, where she searched for typographical errors in textbooks and marked them, in a code she had once explained to him, with an assortment of colored pencils. She would do the same for his dissertation, she promised, when it was ready. He envied her the specificity of her task, so unlike the elusive nature of his. He was a mediocre student who had a facility for absorbing details without curiosity. Until September he had been diligent if not dedicated, summarizing chapters, outlining arguments on pads of yellow lined paper. But now he would lie in their bed until he grew bored, gazing at his side of the closet which Shoba always left partly open, at the row of the tweed jackets and corduroy trousers he would not have to choose from to teach his classes that semester. After the baby died it was too late to withdraw from his teaching duties. But his adviser had arranged things so that he had the spring semester to himself. Shukumar was in his sixth year of graduate school. "That and the summer should give you a good push," his adviser had said. "You should be able to wrap things up by next September."

But nothing was pushing Shukumar. Instead he thought of how he and Shoba had become experts at avoiding each other in their three-bedroom house, spending as much time on separate floors as possible. He thought of how he no longer looked forward to weekends, when she sat for hours on the sofa with her colored pencils and her files, so that he feared that putting on a record in his own house might be rude. He thought of how long it had been since she looked into his eyes and smiled, or whispered his name on those rare occasions they still reached for each other's bodies before sleeping.

In the beginning he had believed that it would pass, that he and Shoba would get through it all somehow. She was only thirty-three. She was strong, on her feet again. But it wasn't a consolation. It was often nearly lunchtime when Shukumar would finally pull himself out of bed and head downstairs to the coffeepot, pouring out the extra bit Shoba left for him, along with an empty mug, on the countertop.

Shukumar gathered onion skins in his hands and let them drop into the garbage pail, on top of the ribbons of fat he'd trimmed from the lamb. He ran the water in the sink, soaking the knife and the cutting board, and rubbed a lemon half along his fingertips to get rid of the garlic smell, a trick he'd learned from Shoba. It was seven-thirty. Through the window he saw the sky, like soft black pitch. Uneven banks of snow still lined the sidewalks, though it was warm enough for people to walk about without hats or gloves. Nearly three feet had fallen in the last storm, so that for a week people had to walk single file, in narrow trenches. For a week that was Shukumar's excuse for not leaving the house. But now the trenches were widening, and water drained steadily into grates in the pavement.

"The lamb won't be done by eight," Shukumar said. "We may have to eat in the dark."

"We can light candles," Shoba suggested. She unclipped her hair, coiled neatly at her nape during the days, and pried the sneakers from her feet without untying them. "I'm going to shower before the lights go," she said, heading for the staircase. "I'll be down."

Shukumar moved her satchel and her sneakers to the side of the fridge. She wasn't this way before. She used to put her coat on a hanger, her sneakers in the closet, and she paid bills as soon as they came. But now she treated the house as if it were a hotel. The fact that the yellow chintz armchair in the living room clashed with the blue-and-maroon Turkish carpet no longer bothered her. On the enclosed porch at the back of the house, a crisp white bag still sat on the wicker chaise, filled with lace she had once planned to turn into curtains.

While Shoba showered, Shukumar went into the downstairs bathroom and found a new toothbrush in its box beneath the sink. The cheap, stiff bristles hurt his gums, and he spit some blood into the basin. The spare brush was one of many stored in a metal basket. Shoba had bought them once when they were on sale, in the event that a visitor decided, at the last minute, to spend the night.

It was typical of her. She was the type to prepare for surprises, good and bad. If she found a skirt or a purse she liked she bought two. She kept the bonuses from her job in a separate bank account in her name. It hadn't bothered him. His own mother had fallen to pieces when his father died, abandoning the house he grew up in and moving back to Calcutta, leaving Shukumar to settle it all. He liked that Shoba was different. It astonished him, her capacity to think ahead. When she used to do the shopping, the pantry was always stocked with extra bottles of olive and corn oil, depending on whether they were cooking Italian or Indian. There were endless boxes of pasta in all shapes and colors, zippered sacks of basmati rice, whole sides of lambs and goats from the Muslim butchers at Haymarket, chopped up and frozen in endless plastic bags.

Every other Saturday they wound through the maze of stalls Shukumar eventually knew by heart. He watched in disbelief as she bought more food, trailing behind her with canvas bags as she pushed through the crowd, arguing under the morning sun with boys too young to shave but already missing teeth, who twisted up brown paper bags of artichokes, plums, gingerroot, and yams, and dropped them on their scales, and tossed them to Shoba one by one. She didn't mind being jostled, even when she was pregnant. She was tall, and broad-shouldered, with hips that her obstetrician assured her were made for childbearing. During the drive back home, as the car curved along the Charles, they invariably marveled at how much food they'd bought.

It never went to waste. When friends dropped by, Shoba would throw together meals that appeared to have taken half a day to prepare, from things she had frozen and bottled, not cheap things in tins but peppers she had marinated herself with rosemary, and chutneys that she cooked on Sundays, stirring boiling pots of tomatoes and prunes. Her labeled mason jars lined the shelves of the kitchen, in endless sealed pyramids, enough, they'd agreed, to last for their grandchildren to taste. They'd eaten it all by now. Shukumar had been going through their supplies steadily, preparing meals for the two of them, measuring out cupfuls of rice, defrosting bags of meat day after day. He combed through her cookbooks every afternoon, following her penciled instructions to use two teaspoons of ground coriander seeds instead of one, or red lentils instead of yellow. Each of the recipes was dated, telling the first time they had eaten the dish together. April 2, cauliflower with fennel. January 14, chicken with almonds and sultanas. He had no memory of eating those meals, and yet there they were, recorded in her neat proofreader's hand. Shukumar enjoyed cooking now. It was the one thing that made him feel productive. If it weren't for him, he knew, Shoba would eat a bowl of cereal for her dinner.

Tonight, with no lights, they would have to eat together. For months now they'd served themselves from the stove, and he'd taken his plate into his study, letting the meal grow cold on his desk before shoving it into his mouth without pause, while Shoba took her plate to the living room and watched game shows, or proofread files with her arsenal of colored pencils at hand.

At some point in the evening she visited him. When he heard her approach he would put away his novel and begin typing sentences. She would rest her hands on his shoulders and stare with him into the blue glow of the computer screen. "Don't work too hard," she would say after a minute or two, and head off to bed. It was the one time in the day she sought him out, and yet he'd come to dread it. He knew it was something she forced herself to do. She would look around the walls of the room, which they had decorated together last summer with a border of marching ducks and rabbits playing trumpets and drums. By the end of August there was a cherry crib under the window, a white changing table with mint-green knobs, and a rocking chair with checkered cushions. Shukumar had disassembled it all before bringing Shoba back from the hospital, scraping off the rabbits and ducks with a spatula. For some reason the room did not haunt him the way it haunted Shoba. In January, when he stopped working at his carrel in the library, he set up his desk there deliberately, partly because the room soothed him, and partly because it was a place Shoba avoided.

Shukumar returned to the kitchen and began to open drawers. He tried to locate a candle among the scissors, the eggbeaters and whisks, the mortar and pestle she'd bought in a bazaar in Calcutta, and used to pound garlic cloves and cardamom pods, back when she used to cook. He found a flashlight, but no batteries, and a half-empty box of birthday candles. Shoba had thrown him a surprise birthday party last May. One hundred and twenty people had crammed into the house—all the friends and the friends of friends they now systematically avoided. Bottles of vinho verde had nested in a bed of ice in the bathtub. Shoba was in her fifth month, drinking ginger ale from a martini glass. She had made a vanilla cream cake with custard and spun sugar. All night she kept Shukumar's long fingers linked with hers as they walked among the guests at the party.

Since September their only guest had been Shoba's mother. She came from Arizona and stayed with them for two months after Shoba returned from the hospital. She cooked dinner every night, drove herself to the supermarket, washed their clothes, put them away. She was a religious woman. She set up a small shrine, a framed picture of a lavender-faced goddess and a plate of marigold petals, on the bedside table in the guest room, and prayed twice a day for healthy grandchildren in the future. She was polite to Shukumar without being friendly. She folded his sweaters with an expertise she had learned from her job in a department store. She replaced a missing button on his winter coat and knit him a beige and brown scarf, presenting it to him without the least bit of ceremony, as if he had only dropped it and hadn't noticed. She never talked to him about Shoba; once, when he mentioned the baby's death, she looked up from her knitting, and said, "But you weren't even there."

It struck him as odd that there were no real candles in the house. That Shoba hadn't prepared for such an ordinary emergency. He looked now for something to put the birthday candles in and settled on the soil of a potted ivy that normally sat on the windowsill over the sink. Even though the plant was inches from the tap, the soil was so dry that he had to water it first before the candles would stand straight. He pushed aside the things on the kitchen table, the piles of mail, the unread library books. He remembered their first meals there, when they were so thrilled to be married, to be living together in the same house at last, that they would just reach for each other foolishly, more eager to make love than to eat. He put down two embroidered place mats, a wedding gift from an uncle in Lucknow, and set out the plates and wineglasses they usually saved for guests. He put the ivy in the middle, the white-edged, star-shaped leaves girded by ten little candles. He switched on the digital clock radio and tuned it to a jazz station.

"What's all this?" Shoba said when she came downstairs. Her hair was wrapped in a thick white towel. She undid the towel and draped it over a chair, allowing her hair, damp and dark, to fall across her back. As she walked absently toward the stove she took out a few tangles with her fingers. She wore a clean pair of sweatpants, a T-shirt, an old flannel robe. Her stomach was flat again, her waist narrow before the flare of her hips, the belt of the robe tied in a floppy knot.

It was nearly eight. Shukumar put the rice on the table and the lentils from the night before into the microwave oven, punching the numbers on the timer.

"You made *rogan josh*," Shoba observed, looking through the glass lid at the bright paprika stew.

Shukumar took out a piece of lamb, pinching it quickly between his fingers so as not to scald himself. He prodded a larger piece with a serving spoon to make sure the meat slipped easily from the bone. "It's ready," he announced.

The microwave had just beeped when the lights went out, and the music disappeared.

"Perfect timing," Shoba said.

"All I could find were birthday candles." He lit up the ivy, keeping the rest of the candles and a book of matches by his plate.

"It doesn't matter," she said, running a finger along the stem of her wineglass. "It looks lovely."

In the dimness, he knew how she sat, a bit forward in her chair, ankles crossed against the lowest rung, left elbow on the table. During his search for the candles, Shukumar had found a bottle of wine in a crate he had thought was empty. He clamped the bottle between his knees while he turned in the corkscrew. He worried about spilling, and so he picked up the glasses and held them close to his lap while he filled them. They served themselves, stirring the rice with their forks, squinting as they extracted bay leaves and cloves from the stew. Every few minutes Shukumar lit a few more birthday candles and drove them into the soil of the pot.

"It's like India," Shoba said, watching him tend his makeshift candelabra. "Sometimes the current disappears for hours at a stretch. I once had to attend an entire rice ceremony in the dark. The baby just cried and cried. It must have been so hot."

Their baby had never cried, Shukumar considered. Their baby would never have a rice ceremony, even though Shoba had already made the guest list, and decided on which of her three brothers she was going to ask to feed the child its first taste of solid food, at six months if it was a boy, seven if it was a girl.

"Are you hot?" he asked her. He pushed the blazing ivy pot to the other end of the table, closer to the piles of books and mail, making it even more difficult for them to see each other. He was suddenly irritated that he couldn't go upstairs and sit in front of the computer.

"No. It's delicious," she said, tapping her plate with her fork. "It really is."

He refilled the wine in her glass. She thanked him.

They weren't like this before. Now he had to struggle to say something that interested her, something that made her look up from her plate, or from her proofreading files. Eventually he gave up trying to amuse her. He learned not to mind the silences.

"I remember during power failures at my grandmother's house, we all had to say something," Shoba continued. He could barely see her face, but from her tone he knew her eyes were narrowed, as if trying to focus on a distant object. It was a habit of hers.

"Like what?"

"I don't know. A little poem. A joke. A fact about the world. For some reason my relatives always wanted me to tell them the names of my friends in America. I don't know why the information was so interesting to them. The last time I saw my aunt she asked after four girls I went to elementary school with in Tucson. I barely remember them now."

Shukumar hadn't spent as much time in India as Shoba had. His parents, who settled in New Hampshire, used to go back without him. The first time he'd gone as an infant he'd nearly died of amoebic dysentery. His father, a nervous type, was afraid to take him again, in case something were to happen, and left him with his aunt and uncle in Concord. As a teenager he preferred sailing camp or scooping ice cream during the summers to going to Calcutta. It wasn't until after his father died, in his last year of college, that the country began to interest him, and he studied its history from course books as if it were any other subject. He wished now that he had his own childhood story of India.

"Let's do that," she said suddenly.

"Do what?"

"Say something to each other in the dark."

"Like what? I don't know any jokes."

"No, no jokes." She thought for a minute. "How about telling each other something we've never told before."

"I used to play this game in high school," Shukumar recalled. "When I got drunk."

"You're thinking of truth or dare. This is different. Okay, I'll start." She took a sip of wine. "The first time I was alone in your apartment, I looked in your address book to see if you'd written me in. I think we'd known each other two weeks."

"Where was I?"

"You went to answer the telephone in the other room. It was your mother, and I figured it would be a long call. I wanted to know if you'd promoted me from the margins of your newspaper."

"Had I?"

"No. But I didn't give up on you. Now it's your turn."

He couldn't think of anything, but Shoba was waiting for him to speak. She hadn't appeared so determined in months. What was there left to say to her? He thought back to their first meeting, four years earlier at a lecture hall in Cambridge, where a group of Bengali poets were giving a recital. They'd ended up side by side, on folding wooden chairs. Shukumar was soon bored; he was unable to decipher the literary diction, and couldn't join the rest of the audience as they sighed and nodded solemnly after certain phrases. Peering at the newspaper folded in his lap, he studied the temperatures of cities around the world. Ninety-one degrees in Singapore yesterday, fifty-one in Stockholm. When he turned his head to the left, he saw a woman next to him making a grocery list on the back of a folder, and was startled to find that she was beautiful.

"Okay," he said, remembering. "The first time we went out to dinner, to the Portuguese place, I forgot to tip the waiter. I went back the next morning, found out his name, left money with the manager."

"You went all the way back to Somerville just to tip a waiter?"

"I took a cab."

"Why did you forget to tip the waiter?"

The birthday candles had burned out, but he pictured her face clearly in the dark, the wide tilting eyes, the full grape-toned lips, the fall at age two from her high chair still visible as a comma on her chin. Each day, Shukumar noticed, her beauty, which had once overwhelmed him, seemed to fade. The cosmetics that had seemed superfluous were necessary now, not to improve her but to define her somehow.

"By the end of the meal I had a funny feeling that I might marry you," he said, admitting it to himself as well as to her for the first time. "It must have distracted me."

The next night Shoba came home earlier than usual. There was lamb left over from the evening before, and Shukumar heated it up so that they were able to eat by seven. He'd gone out that day, through the melting snow, and bought a packet of taper candles from the corner store, and batteries to fit the flashlight. He had the candles ready on the countertop, standing in brass holders shaped like lotuses, but they ate under the glow of the copper-shaded ceiling lamp that hung over the table.

When they had finished eating, Shukumar was surprised to see that Shoba was stacking her plate on top of his, and then carrying them over to the sink. He had assumed she would retreat to the living room, behind her barricade of files.

"Don't worry about the dishes," he said, taking them from her hands.

"It seems silly not to," she replied, pouring a drop of detergent onto a sponge. "It's nearly eight o'clock."

His heart quickened. All day Shukumar had looked forward to the lights going out. He thought about what Shoba had said the night before, about looking in his address book. It felt good to remember her as she was then, how bold yet nervous she'd been when they first met, how hopeful. They stood side by side at the sink, their reflections fitting together in the frame of the window. It made him shy, the way he felt the first time they stood together in a mirror. He couldn't recall the last time they'd been photographed. They had stopped attending parties, went nowhere together. The film in his camera still contained pictures of Shoba, in the yard, when she was pregnant.

After finishing the dishes, they leaned against the counter, drying their hands on either end of a towel. At eight o'clock the house went black. Shukumar lit the wicks of the candles, impressed by their long, steady flames.

"Let's sit outside," Shoba said. "I think it's warm still."

They each took a candle and sat down on the steps. It seemed strange to be sitting outside with patches of snow still on the ground. But everyone was out of their houses tonight, the air fresh enough to make people restless. Screen doors opened and closed. A small parade of neighbors passed by with flashlights.

"We're going to the bookstore to browse," a silver-haired man called out. He was walking with his wife, a thin woman in a windbreaker, and holding a dog on a leash. They were the Bradfords, and they had tucked a sympathy card into Shoba and Shukumar's mailbox back in September. "I hear they've got their power."

"They'd better," Shukumar said. "Or you'll be browsing in the dark."

The woman laughed, slipping her arm through the crook of her husband's elbow. "Want to join us?"

"No thanks," Shoba and Shukumar called out together. It surprised Shukumar that his words matched hers.

He wondered what Shoba would tell him in the dark. The worst possibilities had already run through his head. That she'd had an affair. That she didn't respect him for being thirty-five and still a student. That she blamed him for being in Baltimore the way her mother did. But he knew those things weren't true. She'd been faithful, as had he. She believed in him. It was she who had insisted he go to Baltimore. What didn't they know about each other? He knew she curled her fingers tightly when she slept, that her body twitched during bad dreams. He knew it was honeydew she favored over cantaloupe. He knew that when they returned from the hospital the first thing she did when she walked into the house was pick out objects of theirs and toss them into a pile in the hallway: books from the shelves, plants from the windowsills, paintings from walls, photos from tables, pots and pans that hung from the hooks over the stove. Shukumar had stepped out of her way, watching as she moved methodically from room to room. When she was satisfied, she stood there staring at the pile she'd made, her lips drawn back in such distaste that Shukumar had thought she would spit. Then she'd started to cry.

He began to feel cold as he sat there on the steps. He felt that he needed her to talk first, in order to reciprocate.

"That time when your mother came to visit us," she said finally. "When I said one night that I had to stay late at work, I went out with Gillian and had a martini."

He looked at her profile, the slender nose, the slightly masculine set of her jaw. He remembered that night well; eating with his mother, tired from teaching two classes back to back, wishing Shoba were there to say more of the right things because he came up with only the wrong ones. It had been twelve years since his father had died, and his mother had come to spend two weeks with him and Shoba, so they could honor his father's memory together. Each night his mother cooked something his father had liked, but she was too upset to eat the dishes herself, and her eyes would well up as Shoba stroked her hand. "It's so touching," Shoba had said to him at the time. Now he pictured Shoba with Gillian, in a bar with striped velvet sofas, the one they used to go to after the movies, making sure she got her extra olive, asking Gillian for a cigarette. He imagined her complaining, and Gillian sympathizing about visits from in-laws. It was Gillian who had driven Shoba to the hospital.

"Your turn," she said, stopping his thoughts.

At the end of their street Shukumar heard sounds of a drill and the electricians shouting over it. He looked at the darkened facades of the houses lining the street. Candles glowed in the windows of one. In spite of the warmth, smoke rose from the chimney.

"I cheated on my Oriental Civilization exam in college," he said. "It was my last semester, my last set of exams. My father had died a few months before. I could see the blue book of the guy next to me. He was an American guy, a maniac. He knew Urdu and Sanskrit. I couldn't remember if the verse we had to identify was an example of a *ghazal* or not. I looked at his answer and copied it down."

It had happened over fifteen years ago. He felt relief now, having told her.

She turned to him, looking not at his face, but at his shoes—old moccasins he wore as if they were slippers, the leather at the back permanently flattened. He wondered if it bothered her, what he'd said. She took his hand and pressed it. "You didn't have to tell me why you did it," she said, moving closer to him.

They sat together until nine o'clock, when the lights came on. They heard some people across the street clapping from their porch, and televisions being turned on. The Bradfords walked back down the street, eating ice-cream cones and waving. Shoba and Shukumar waved back. Then they stood up, his hand still in hers, and went inside.

Somehow, without saying anything, it had turned into this. Into an exchange of confessions—the little ways they'd hurt or disappointed each other, and themselves. The following day Shukumar thought for hours about what to say to her. He was torn between admitting that he once ripped out a photo of a woman in one of the fashion magazines she used to subscribe to and carried it in his books for a week, or saying that he really hadn't lost the sweater-vest she bought him for their third wedding anniversary but had exchanged it for cash at Filene's, and that he had gotten drunk alone in the middle of the day at a hotel bar. For their first anniversary, Shoba had cooked a ten-course dinner just for him. The vest depressed him. "My wife gave me a sweater-vest for our anniversary," he complained to the bartender, his head heavy with cognac. "What do you expect?" the bartender had replied. "You're married."

As for the picture of the woman, he didn't know why he'd ripped it out. She wasn't as pretty as Shoba. She wore a white sequined dress, and had a sullen face and lean, mannish legs. Her bare arms were raised, her fists around her head, as if she were about to punch herself in the ears. It was an advertisement for stockings. Shoba had been pregnant at the time, her stomach suddenly immense, to the point where Shukumar no longer wanted to touch her. The first time he saw the picture he was lying in bed next to her, watching her as she read. When he noticed the magazine in the recycling pile he found the woman and tore out the page as carefully as he could. For about a week he allowed himself a glimpse each day. He felt an intense desire for the woman, but it was a desire that turned to disgust after a minute or two. It was the closest he'd come to infidelity.

He told Shoba about the sweater on the third night, the picture on the fourth. She said nothing as he spoke, expressed no protest or reproach. She simply listened, and then she took his hand, pressing it as she had before. On the third night, she told him that once after a lecture they'd attended, she let him speak to the chairman of his department without telling him that he had a dab of pâté on his chin. She'd been irritated with him for some reason, and so she'd let him go on and on, about securing his fellowship for the following semester, without putting a finger to her own chin as a signal. The fourth night, she said that she never liked the one poem he'd ever published in his life, in a literary magazine in Utah. He'd written the poem after meeting Shoba. She added that she found the poem sentimental.

Something happened when the house was dark. They were able to talk to each other again. The third night after supper they'd sat together on the sofa, and once it was dark he began kissing her awkwardly on her forehead and her face, and though it was dark he closed his eyes, and knew that she did, too. The fourth night they walked carefully upstairs, to bed, feeling together for the final step with their feet before the landing, and making love with a desperation they had forgotten. She wept without sound, and whispered his name, and traced his eyebrows with her finger in the dark. As he made love to her he wondered what he would say to her the next night, and what she would say, the thought of it exciting him. "Hold me," he said, "hold me in your arms." By the time the lights came back on downstairs, they'd fallen asleep.

The morning of the fifth night Shukumar found another notice from the electric company in the mailbox. The line had been repaired ahead of schedule, it said. He was disappointed. He had planned on making shrimp *malai* for Shoba, but when he arrived at the store he didn't feel like cooking anymore. It wasn't the same, he thought, knowing that the lights wouldn't go out. In the store the shrimp looked gray and thin. The coconut milk tin was dusty and overpriced. Still, he bought them, along with a beeswax candle and two bottles of wine.

She came home at seven-thirty. "I suppose this is the end of our game," he said when he saw her reading the notice.

She looked at him. "You can still light candles if you want." She hadn't been to the gym tonight. She wore a suit beneath the raincoat. Her makeup had been retouched recently.

When she went upstairs to change, Shukumar poured himself some wine and put on a record, a Thelonius Monk album he knew she liked.

When she came downstairs they ate together. She didn't thank him or compliment him. They simply ate in a darkened room, in the glow of a beeswax candle. They had survived a difficult time. They finished off the shrimp. They finished off the first bottle of wine and moved on to the second. They sat together until the candle had nearly burned away. She shifted in her chair, and Shukumar thought that she was about to say something. But instead she blew out the candle, stood up, turned on the light switch, and sat down again.

"Shouldn't we keep the lights off?" Shukumar asked.

She set her plate aside and clasped her hands on the table. "I want you to see my face when I tell you this," she said gently.

His heart began to pound. The day she told him she was pregnant, she had used the very same words, saying them in the same gentle way, turning off the basketball game he'd been watching on television. He hadn't been prepared then. Now he was.

Only he didn't want her to be pregnant again. He didn't want to have to pretend to be happy.

"I've been looking for an apartment and I've found one," she said, narrowing her eyes on something, it seemed, behind his left shoulder. It was nobody's fault, she continued. They'd been through enough. She needed some time alone. She had money saved up for a security deposit. The apartment was on Beacon Hill, so she could walk to work. She had signed the lease that night before coming home.

She wouldn't look at him, but he stared at her. It was obvious that she'd rehearsed the lines. All this time she'd been looking for an apartment, testing the water pressure, asking a Realtor if heat and hot water were included in the rent. It sickened Shukumar, knowing that she had spent these past evenings preparing for a life without him. He was relieved and yet he was sickened. This was what she'd been trying to tell him for the past four evenings. This was the point of her game.

Now it was his turn to speak. There was something he'd sworn he would never tell her, and for six months he had done his best to block it from his mind. Before the ultrasound she had asked the doctor not to tell her the sex of their child, and Shukumar had agreed. She had wanted it to be a surprise.

Later, those few times they talked about what had happened, she said at least they'd been spared that knowledge. In a way she almost took pride in her decision, for it enabled her to seek refuge in a mystery. He knew that she assumed it was a mystery for him, too. He'd arrived too late from Baltimore—when it was all over and she was lying on the hospital bed. But he hadn't. He'd arrived early enough to see their baby, and to hold him before they cremated him. At first he had recoiled at the suggestion, but the doctor said holding the baby might help him with the process of grieving. Shoba was asleep. The baby had been cleaned off, his bulbous lids shut tight to the world.

"Our baby was a boy," he said. "His skin was more red than brown. He had black hair on his head. He weighed almost five pounds. His fingers were curled shut, just like yours in the night."

Shoba looked at him now, her face contorted with sorrow. He had cheated on a college exam, ripped a picture of a woman out of a magazine. He had returned a sweater and got drunk in the middle of the day instead. These were the things he had told her. He had held his son, who had known life only within her, against his chest in a darkened room in an unknown wing of the hospital. He had held him until a nurse knocked and took him away, and he promised himself that day that he would never tell Shoba, because he still loved her then, and it was the one thing in her life that she had wanted to be a surprise.

Shukumar stood up and stacked his plate on top of hers. He carried the plates to the sink, but instead of running the tap he looked out the window. Outside the evening was still warm, and the Bradfords were walking arm in arm. As he watched the couple the room went dark, and he spun around. Shoba had turned the lights off. She came back to the table and sat down, and after a moment Shukumar joined her. They wept together, for the things they now knew.

The Ones Who Walk Away from Omelas
Variations on a Theme by William James[1]
(1973)

URSULA K LEGUIN

With a clamor of bells that set the swallows soaring, the Festival of Summer came to the city Omelas, bright-towered by the sea. The rigging of the boats in harbor sparkled with flags. In the streets between houses with red roofs and painted walls, between old moss-grown gardens and under avenues of trees, past great parks and public buildings, processions moved. Some were decorous: old people in long stiff robes of mauve and grey, grave master workmen, quiet, merry women carrying their babies and chatting as they walked. In other streets the music beat faster, a shimmering of gong and tambourine, and the people went dancing, the procession was a dance. Children dodged in and out, their high calls rising like the swallows' crossing flights over the music and the singing. All the processions wound towards the north side of the city, where on the great water-meadow called the Green Fields boys and girls, naked in the bright air, with mud-stained feet and ankles and long, lithe arms, exercised their restive horses before the race. The horses wore no gear at all but a halter without bit. Their manes were braided with streamers of silver, gold, and green. They flared their nostrils and pranced and boasted to one another; they were vastly excited, the horse being the only animal who has adopted our ceremonies as his own. Far off to the north and west the mountains stood up half encircling Omelas on her bay. The air of morning was so clear that the snow still crowning the Eighteen Peaks burned with white-gold fire across the miles of sunlit air, under the dark blue of the sky. There was just enough wind to make the banners that marked the racecourse snap and flutter now and then. In the silence of the broad green meadows one could hear the music winding through the city streets, farther and nearer and ever approaching, a cheerful faint sweetness of the air that from time to time trembled and gathered together and broke out into the great joyous clanging of the bells.

Joyous! How is one to tell about joy? How describe the citizens of Omelas?

They were not simple folk, you see, though they were happy. But we do not say the words of cheer much any more. All smiles have become archaic. Given a description such as this one tends to make certain assumptions. Given a description such as this one tends to look next for the King, mounted on a splendid stallion and surrounded by his noble knights, or perhaps in a golden litter borne by great-muscled slaves. But there was no king. They did not use swords, or keep slaves. They were not barbarians. I do not know the rules and laws of their

1. American philosopher and experimental psychologist (1842–1910).

society, but I suspect that they were singularly few. As they did without monarchy and slavery, so they also got on without the stock exchange, the advertisement, the secret police, and the bomb. Yet I repeat that these were not simple folk, not dulcet shepherds, noble savages, bland utopians. They were not less complex than us. The trouble is that we have a bad habit, encouraged by pedants and sophisticates, of considering happiness as something rather stupid. Only pain is intellectual, only evil interesting. This is the treason of the artist: a refusal to admit the banality of evil and the terrible boredom of pain. If you can't lick 'em, join 'em. If it hurts, repeat it. But to praise despair is to condemn delight, to embrace violence is to lose hold of everything else. We have almost lost hold, we can no longer describe a happy man, nor make any celebration of joy. How can I tell you about the people of Omelas? They were not naïve and happy children—though their children were, in fact, happy. They were mature, intelligent, passionate adults whose lives were not wretched. O miracle! but I wish I could describe it better. I wish I could convince you. Omelas sounds in my words like a city in a fairy tale, long ago and far away, once upon a time. Perhaps it would be best if you imagined it as your own fancy bids, assuming it will rise to the occasion, for certainly I cannot suit you all. For instance, how about technology? I think that there would be no cars or helicopters in and above the streets; this follows from the fact that the people of Omelas are happy people. Happiness is based on a just discrimination of what is necessary, what is neither necessary nor destructive, and what is destructive. In the middle category, however—that of the unnecessary but undestructive, that of comfort, luxury, exuberance, etc.—they could perfectly well have central heating, subway trains, washing machines, and all kinds of marvelous devices not yet invented here, floating light-sources, fuelless power, a cure for the common cold. Or they could have none of that: it doesn't matter. As you like it. I incline to think that people from towns up and down the coast have been coming in to Omelas during the last days before the Festival on very fast little trains and double-decked trams, and that the train station of Omelas is actually the handsomest building in town, though plainer than the magnificent Farmers' Market. But even granted trains, I fear that Omelas so far strikes some of you as goody-goody. Smiles, bells, parades, horses, bleh. If so, please add an orgy. If an orgy would help, don't hesitate. Let us not, however, have temples from which issue beautiful nude priests and priestesses already half in ecstasy and ready to copulate with any man or woman, lover or stranger, who desires union with the deep godhead of the blood, although that was my first idea. But really it would be better not to have any temples in Omelas—at least, not manned temples. Religion yes, clergy no. Surely the beautiful nudes can just wander about, offering themselves like divine soufflés to the hunger of the needy and the rapture of the flesh. Let them join the processions. Let tambourines be struck above the copulations, and the glory of desire be proclaimed upon the gongs, and (a not unimportant point) let the offspring of these delightful rituals be beloved and looked after by all. One thing I know there is none of in Omelas is guilt. But what else should there be? I thought at first there were no drugs, but that is puritanical. For those who like it, the faint insistent sweetness of *drooz* may perfume the ways of the city, *drooz* which first brings a great lightness and brilliance to the mind and limbs, and then after some hours a dreamy languor, and wonderful visions at last of the very arcana and inmost secrets of the Universe, as well as exciting the pleasure of sex beyond all belief; and it is not habit-forming. For more modest tastes I think there ought to be beer. What else, what else belongs in the joyous city? The sense of victory, surely, the celebration of courage. But as we did without clergy, let us do without soldiers. The joy built upon successful slaughter is not the right kind of joy; it will not do; it is fearful and it is trivial. A boundless and generous contentment, a magnanimous triumph felt not against some outer enemy but in communion with the finest and fairest in the souls of all men everywhere and the splendor of the world's summer: this is what swells the hearts of the people of Omelas, and the victory they celebrate is that of life. I really don't think many of them need to take *drooz*.

Most of the procession have reached the Green Fields by now. A marvelous smell of cooking goes forth from the red and blue tents of the provisioners. The faces of small children are amiably sticky; in the benign grey beard of a man a couple of crumbs of rich pastry are entangled. The youths and girls have mounted their horses and are beginning to group around the starting line of the course. An old woman, small, fat, and laughing, is passing out flowers from a basket, and tall young men wear her flowers in their shining hair. A child of nine or ten sits at the edge of the crowd, alone, playing on a wooden flute. People pause to listen, and they smile, but they do not speak to him, for he never ceases playing and never sees them, his dark eyes wholly rapt in the sweet, thin magic of the tune.

He finishes, and slowly lowers his hands holding the wooden flute.

As if that little private silence were the signal, all at once a trumpet sounds from the pavilion near the starting line: imperious, melancholy, piercing. The horses rear on their slender legs, and some of them neigh in answer. Sober-faced, the young riders stroke the horses' necks and soothe them, whispering, "Quiet, quiet, there my beauty, my hope. . . . " They begin to form in rank along the starting line. The crowds along the racecourse are like a field of grass and flowers in the wind. The Festival of Summer has begun.

Do you believe? Do you accept the festival, the city, the joy? No? Then let me describe one more thing.

In a basement under one of the beautiful public buildings of Omelas, or perhaps in the cellar of one of its more spacious private homes, there is a room. It has one locked door, and no window. A little light seeps in dustily between cracks in the boards, secondhand from a cobwebbed window somewhere across the cellar. In one corner of the little room a couple of mops, with stiff, clotted, foul-smelling heads, stand near a rusty bucket. The floor is dirt, a little damp to the touch, as cellar dirt usually is. The room is about three paces long and two wide: a mere broom closet or disused tool room. In the room a child is sitting. It could be a boy or a girl. It looks about six, but actually is nearly ten. It is feeble-minded. Perhaps it was born defective, or perhaps it has become imbecile through fear, malnutrition, and neglect. It picks its nose and occasionally fumbles vaguely with its toes or genitals, as it sits hunched in the corner farthest from the bucket and the two mops. It is afraid of the mops. It finds them horrible. It shuts its eyes, but it knows the mops are still standing there; and the door is locked; and nobody will come. The door is always locked; and nobody ever comes, except that sometimes—the child has no understanding of time or interval—sometimes the door rattles terribly and opens, and a person, or several people, are there. One of them may come in and kick the child to make it stand up. The others never come close, but peer in at it with frightened, disgusted eyes. The food bowl and the water jug are hastily filled, the door is locked, the eyes disappear. The people at the door never say anything, but the child, who has not always lived in the tool room, and can remember sunlight and its mother's voice, sometimes speaks. "I will be good," it says. "Please let me out. I will be good!" They never answer. The child used to scream for help at night, and cry a good deal; but now it only makes a kind of whining, "eh-haa, eh-haa," and it speaks less and less often. It is so thin there are no calves to its legs; its belly protrudes; it lives on a half-bowl of corn meal and grease a day. It is naked. Its buttocks and thighs are a mass of festered sores, as it sits in its own excrement continually.

They all know it is there, all the people of Omelas. Some of them have come to see it, others are content merely to know it is there. They all know that it has to be there. Some of them understand why, and some do not, but they all understand that their happiness, the beauty of their city, the tenderness of their friendships, the health of their children, the wisdom of their scholars, the skill of their makers, even the abundance of their harvest and the kindly weathers of their skies, depend wholly on this child's abominable misery.

This is usually explained to children when they are between eight and twelve, whenever they seem capable of understanding; and most of those who come to see the child are young people, though often enough an adult comes, or comes back, to see the child. No matter how well the matter has been explained to them, these young spectators are always shocked and sickened at the sight. They feel disgust, which they had thought themselves superior to. They feel anger, outrage, impotence, despite all the explanations. They would like to do something for the child. But there is nothing they can do. If the child were brought up into the sunlight out of the vile place, if it were cleaned and fed and comforted, that would be a good thing, indeed; but if it were done, in that day and hour all the prosperity and beauty and delight of Omelas would wither and be destroyed. Those are the terms. To exchange all the goodness and grace of every life in Omelas for that single, small improvement: to throw away the happiness of thousands for the chance of the happiness of one: that would be to let guilt within the walls indeed.

The terms are strict and absolute; there may not even be a kind word spoken to the child.

Often the young people go home in tears, or in a tearless rage, when they have seen the child and faced this terrible paradox. They may brood over it for weeks or years. But as time goes on they begin to realize that even if the child could be released, it would not get much good of its freedom: a little vague pleasure of warmth and food, no doubt, but little more. It is too degraded and imbecile to know any real joy. It has been afraid too long ever to be free of fear. Its habits are too uncouth for it to respond to humane treatment. Indeed, after so long it would probably be wretched without walls about it to protect it, and darkness for its eyes, and its own excrement to sit in. Their tears at the bitter injustice dry when they begin to perceive the terrible justice of reality, and to accept it. Yet it is their tears and anger, the trying of their generosity and the acceptance of their helplessness, which are perhaps the true source of the splendor of their lives. Theirs is no vapid, irresponsible happiness. They know that they, like the child, are not free. They know compassion. It is the existence of the child, and their knowledge of its existence, that makes possible the nobility of their architecture, the poignancy of their music, the profundity of their science. It is because of the child that they are so gentle with children. They know that if the wretched one were not there snivelling in the dark, the other one, the flute-player, could make no joyful music as the young riders line up in their beauty for the race in the sunlight of the first morning of summer.

Now do you believe in them? Are they not more credible? But there is one more thing to tell, and this is quite incredible.

At times one of the adolescent girls or boys who go to see the child does not go home to weep or rage, does not, in fact, go home at all. Sometimes also a man or woman much older falls silent for a day or two, and then leaves home. These people go out into the street, and walk down the street alone. They keep walking, and walk straight out of the city of Omelas, through the beautiful gates. They keep walking across the farmlands of Omelas. Each one goes alone, youth or girl, man or woman. Night falls; the traveler must pass down village streets, between the houses with yellow-lit windows, and on out into the darkness of the fields. Each alone, they go west or north, towards the mountains. They go on. They leave Omelas, they walk ahead into the darkness, and they do not come back. The place they go towards is a place even less imaginable to most of us than the city of happiness. I cannot describe it at all. It is possible that it does not exist. But they seem to know where they are going, the ones who walk away from Omelas.

1975

To Room Nineteen
(1963)

DORIS MAY LESSING

This is a story, I suppose, about a failure in intelligence: the Rawlings' marriage was grounded in intelligence.

They were older when they married than most of their married friends: in their well-seasoned late twenties. Both had had a number of affairs, sweet rather than bitter; and when they fell in love—for they did fall in love—had known each other for some time. They joked that they had saved each other "for the real thing." That they had waited so long (but not too long) for this real thing was to them a proof of their sensible discrimination. A good many of their friends had married young, and now (they felt) probably regretted lost opportunities; while others, still unmarried, seemed to them arid, self-doubting, and likely to make desperate or romantic marriages.

Not only they, but others, felt they were well matched: their friends' delight was an additional proof of their happiness. They had played the same roles, male and female, in this group or set, if such a wide, loosely connected, constantly changing constellation of people could be called a set. They had both become, by virtue of their moderation, their humour, and their abstinence from painful experience people to whom others came for advice. They could be, and were, relied on. It was one of those cases of a man and a woman linking themselves whom no one else had ever thought of linking, probably because of their similarities. But then everyone exclaimed: Of course! How right! How was it we never thought of it before!

And so they married amid general rejoicing, and because of their foresight and their sense for what was probable, nothing was a surprise to them.

Both had well-paid jobs. Matthew was a subeditor on a large London newspaper, and Susan worked in an advertising firm. He was not the stuff of which editors or publicised journalists are made, but he was much more than "a subeditor," being one of the essential background people who in fact steady, inspire and make possible the people in the limelight. He was content with this position. Susan had a talent for commercial drawing. She was humorous about the advertisements she was responsible for, but she did not feel strongly about them one way or the other.

Both, before they married, had had pleasant flats, but they felt it unwise to base a marriage on either flat, because it might seem like a submission of personality on the part of the one whose flat it was not. They moved into a new flat in South Kensington on the clear understanding that when their marriage had settled down (a process they knew would not take long, and was in fact more a humorous concession to popular wisdom than what was due to themselves) they would buy a house and start a family.

555

And this is what happened. They lived in their charming flat for two years, giving parties and going to them, being a popular young married couple, and then Susan became pregnant, she gave up her job, and they bought a house in Richmond. It was typical of this couple that they had a son first, then a daughter, then twins, son and daughter. Everything right, appropriate, and what everyone would wish for, if they could choose. But people did feel these two had chosen; this balanced and sensible family was no more than what was due to them because of their infallible sense for *choosing* right.

And so they lived with their four children in their gardened house in Richmond and were happy. They had everything they had wanted and had planned for.

And yet . . .

Well, even this was expected, that there must be a certain flatness. . . .

Yes, yes, of course, it was natural they sometimes felt like this. Like what?

Their life seemed to be like a snake biting its tail. Matthew's job for the sake of Susan, children, house, and garden—which caravanserai needed a well-paid job to maintain it. And Susan's practical intelligence for the sake of Matthew, the children, the house and the garden—which unit would have collapsed in a week without her.

But there was no point about which either could say: "For the sake of *this* is all the rest." Children? But children can't be a centre of life and a reason for being. They can be a thousand things that are delightful, interesting, satisfying, but they can't be a wellspring to live from. Or they shouldn't be. Susan and Matthew knew that well enough.

Matthew's job? Ridiculous. It was an interesting job, but scarcely a reason for living. Matthew took pride in doing it well; but he could hardly be expected to be proud of the newspaper: the newspaper he read, *his* newspaper, was not the one he worked for.

Their love for each other? Well, that was nearest it. If this wasn't a centre, what was? Yes, it was around this point, their love, that the whole extraordinary structure revolved. For extraordinary it certainly was. Both Susan and Matthew had moments of thinking so, of looking in secret disbelief at this thing they had created: marriage, four children, big house, garden, charwomen, friends, cars . . . and this *thing*, this entity, all of it had come into existence, been blown into being out of nowhere, because Susan loved Matthew and Matthew loved Susan. Extraordinary. So that was the central point, the wellspring.

And if one felt that it simply was not strong enough, important enough, to support it all, well whose fault was that? Certainly neither Susan's nor Matthew's. It was in the nature of things. And they sensibly blamed neither themselves nor each other.

On the contrary, they used their intelligence to preserve what they had created from a painful and explosive world: they looked around them, and took lessons. All around them, marriages collapsing, or breaking, or rubbing along (even worse, they felt). They must not make the same mistakes, they must not.

They had avoided the pitfall so many of their friends had fallen into—of buying a house in the country *for the sake of the children;* so that the husband became a weekend husband, a weekend father, and the wife always careful not to ask what went on in the town flat which they called (in joke) a bachelor flat. No Matthew was a full-time husband, a full-time father, and at nights, in the big married bed in the big married bedroom (which had an attractive view of the river) they lay beside each other talking and he told her about his day, and what he had done, and whom he had met; and she told him about her day (not as interesting, but that was not her fault) for both knew of the hidden resentments and deprivations of the woman who has lived her own life–and above all, has earned her own living–and is now dependent on a husband for outside interests and money.

Nor did Susan make the mistake of taking a job for the sake of her independence, which she might very well have done, since her old firm, missing her qualities of humour, balance, and sense, invited her often to go back. Children needed their mother to a certain age, that both parents knew and agreed on; and when these four healthy wisely brought-up children were of the right age, Susan would work again, because she knew, and so did he, what happened to women of fifty at the height of their energy and ability, with grown-up children who no longer needed their full devotion.

So here was this couple, testing their marriage, looking after it, treating it like a small boat full of helpless people in a very stormy sea. Well, of course, so it was. . . . The storms of the world were bad, but not too close–which is not to say they were selfishly felt: Susan and Matthew were both well-informed and responsible people. And the inner storms and quick-sands were understood and charted. So everything was all right. Everything was in order. Yes, things were under control.

So what did it matter if they felt dry, flat? People like themselves, fed on a hundred books (psychological, anthropological, sociological) could scarcely be unprepared for the dry, con-trolled wistfulness which is the distinguishing mark of the intelligent marriage. Two people, endowed with education, with discrimination, with judgement, linked together voluntarily from their will to be happy together and to be of use to others–one sees them everywhere, one knows them, one even is that thing oneself: sadness because so much is after all so little. These two, unsurprised, turned towards each other with even more courtesy and gentle love: this was life, that two people, no matter how carefully chosen, could not be everything to each other. In fact, even to say so, to think in such a way, was banal, they were ashamed to do it.

It was banal, too, when one night Matthew came home late and confessed he had been to a party, taken a girl home and slept with her. Susan forgave him, of course. Except that forgiveness is hardly the word. Understanding, yes. But if you understand something, you don't forgive it, you are the thing itself: forgiveness is for what you *don't* understand. Nor had he *confessed*–what sort of word is that?

The whole thing was not important. After all, years ago they had joked: Of course I'm not going to be faithful to you, no one can be faithful to one other person for a whole lifetime. (And there was the word *faithful*–stupid, all these words, stupid, belonging to a savage old world.) But the incident left both of them irritable. Strange, but they were both bad-tempered, annoyed. There was something unassimilable about it.

Making love splendidly after he had come home that night, both had felt that the idea that Myra Jenkins, a pretty girl met at a party, could be even relevant was ridiculous. They had loved each other for over a decade, would love each other for years more. Who, then, was Myra Jenkins?

Except, thought Susan, unaccountably bad-tempered, she was (is?) the first. In ten years. So either the ten years' fidelity was not important, or she isn't. (No, no, there is something wrong with this way of thinking, there must be.) But if she isn't important, presumably it wasn't important either when Matthew and I first went to bed with each other that afternoon whose delight even now (like a very long shadow at sundown) lays a long, wand-like finger over us. (Why did I say sundown?) Well, if what we felt that afternoon was not important, nothing is important, because if it hadn't been for what we felt, we wouldn't be Mr. and

Mrs. Rawlings with four children, etc., etc. The whole thing is *absurd*—for him to have come home and told me was absurd. For him not to have told me was absurd. For me to care, or for that matter not to care, is absurd . . . and who is Myra Jenkins? Why, no one at all.

There was only one thing to do, and of course these sensible people did it: they put the thing behind them, and consciously, knowing what they were doing, moved forward into a different phase of their marriage, giving thanks for past good fortune as they did so.

For it was inevitable that the handsome, blond, attractive, manly man, Matthew Rawlings, should be at times tempted (oh, what a word!) by the attractive girls at parties she could not attend because of the four children; and that sometimes he would succumb (a word even more repulsive, if possible) and that she, a good-looking woman in the big well-tended garden at Richmond, would sometimes be pierced as by an arrow from the sky with bitterness. Except that bitterness was not in order, it was out of court. Did the casual girls touch the marriage? They did not. Rather it was they who knew defeat because of the handsome Matthew Rawlings' marriage body and soul to Susan Rawlings.

In that case why did Susan feel (though luckily not for longer than a few seconds at a time) as if life had become a desert, and that nothing mattered, and that her children were not her own?

Meanwhile her intelligence continued to assert that all was well. What if her Matthew did have an occasional sweet afternoon, the odd affair? For she knew quite well, except in her moments of aridity, that they were very happy, that the affairs were not important.

Perhaps that was the trouble? It was in the nature of things that the adventures and delights could no longer be hers, because of the four children and the big house that needed so much attention. But perhaps she was secretly wishing, and even knowing that she did, that the wildness and the beauty could be his. But he was married to her. She was married to him. They were married inextricably. And therefore the gods could not strike him with the real magic, not really. Well, was it Susan's fault that after he came home from an adventure he looked harassed rather than fulfilled? (In fact, that was how she knew he had been *unfaithful*, because of his sullen air, and his glances at her, similar to hers at him: What is it that I share with this person that shields all delight from me?) But none of it by anybody's fault. (But what did they feel ought to be somebody's fault?) Nobody's fault, nothing to be at fault, no one to blame, no one to offer or to take it ... and nothing wrong, either, except that Matthew never was really struck, as he wanted to be, by joy; and that Susan was more and more often threatened by emptiness. (It was usually in the garden that she was invaded by this feeling: she was coming to avoid the garden, unless the children or Matthew were with her.) There was no need to use the dramatic words, unfaithful, forgive, and the rest: intelligence forbade them. Intelligence barred, too, quarrelling, sulking, anger, silences of withdrawal, accusations and tears. Above all, intelligence forbids tears.

A high price has to be paid for the happy marriage with the four healthy children in the large white gardened house.

And they were paying it, willingly, knowing what they were doing. When they lay side by side or breast to breast in the big civilised bedroom overlooking the wild sullied river, they laughed, often, for no particular reason; but they knew it was really because of these two small people, Susan and Matthew, supporting such an edifice on their intelligent love. The laugh comforted them; it saved them both, though from what, they did not know.

They were now both fortyish. The older children, boy and girl, were ten and eight, at school. The twins, six, were still at home. Susan did not have nurses or girls to help her: childhood is short; and she did not regret the hard work. Often enough she was bored, since small children can be boring; she was often very tired; but she regretted nothing. In another decade, she would turn herself back into being a woman with a life of her own.

Soon the twins would go to school, and they would be away from home from nine until four. These hours, so Susan saw it, would be the preparation for her own slow emancipation away from the role of hub-of-the-family into woman-with-her-own-life. She was already planning for the hours of freedom when all the children would be "off her hands." That was the phrase used by Matthew and by Susan and by their friends, for the moment when the youngest child went off to school. "They'll be off your hands, darling Susan, and you'll have time to yourself." So said Matthew, the intelligent husband, who had often enough commended and consoled Susan, standing by her in spirit during the years when her soul was not her own, as she said, but her children's.

What it amounted to was that Susan saw herself as she had been at twenty-eight, unmarried; and then again somewhere about fifty, blossoming from the root of what she had been twenty years before. As if the essential Susan were in abeyance, as if she were in cold storage. Matthew said something like this to Susan one night: and she agreed that it was true—she did feel something like that. What, then, was this essential Susan? She did not know. Put like that it sounded ridiculous, and she did not really feel it. Anyway, they had a long discussion about the whole thing before going off to sleep in each other's arms.

So the twins went off to their school, two bright affectionate children who had no problems about it, since their older brother and sister had trodden this path so successfully before them. And now Susan was going to be alone in the big house, every day of the school term, except for the daily woman who came in to clean.

It was now, for the first time in this marriage, that something happened which neither of them had foreseen.

This is what happened. She returned, at nine-thirty, from taking the twins to the school by car, looking forward to seven blissful hours of freedom. On the first morning she was simply restless, worrying about the twins "naturally enough" since this was their first day away at school. She was hardly able to contain herself until they came back. Which they did happily, excited by the world of school, looking forward to the next day. And the next day Susan took them, dropped them, came back, and found herself reluctant to enter her big and beautiful home because it was as if something was waiting for her there that she did not wish to confront. Sensibly, however, she parked the car in the garage, entered the house, spoke to Mrs. Parkes the daily woman about her duties, and went up to her bedroom. She was possessed by a fever which drove her out again , downstairs, into the kitchen, where Mrs. Parkes was making cake and did not need her, and into the garden. There she sat on a bench and tried to calm herself, looking at trees, at a brown glimpse of the river. But she was filled with tension, like a panic: as if an enemy was in the garden with her. She spoke to herself severely, thus: All this is quite natural. First, I spent twelve years of my adult life working, *living my own life*. Then I married, and from the moment I became pregnant for the first time I signed myself over, so to speak, to other people. To the children. Not for one moment in twelve years have I been alone, had time to myself. So now I have to learn to be myself again. That's all.

And she went indoors to help Mrs. Parkes cook and clean, and found some sewing to do for the children. She kept herself occupied every day. At the end of the first term she understood she felt two contrary emotions. First: secret astonishment and dismay that during those weeks when the house was empty of children she had in fact been more occupied (had been careful to keep herself occupied) than ever she had been when the children were around her needing her continual attention. Second: that now she knew the house would be full of them, and for five weeks, she resented the fact she would never be alone. She was already looking back at those hours of sewing, cooking (but by herself), as at a lost freedom which would not be hers for five long weeks. And the two months of term which would succeed the five weeks stretched alluringly open to her–freedom. But what freedom–when in fact she had been so careful *not* to be free of small duties during the last weeks? She looked at herself, Susan Rawlings, sitting in a big chair by the window in the bedroom, sewing shirts or dresses, which she might just as well have bought. She saw herself making cakes for hours at a time in the big family kitchen: yet usually she bought cakes. What she saw was a woman alone, that was true, but she had not felt alone. For instance, Mrs. Parkes was always somewhere in the house. And she did not like being in the garden at all, because of the closeness there of the enemy–irritation, restlessness, emptiness, whatever it was, which keeping her hands occupied made less dangerous for some reason.

Susan did not tell Matthew of these thoughts. They were not sensible. She did not recognize herself in them. What should she say to her dear friend and husband Matthew? "When I go into the garden, that is, if the children are not there, I feel as if there is an enemy there waiting to invade me." "What enemy, Susan darling?" "Well I don't know, really. . . ." "Perhaps you should see a doctor?"

No, clearly this conversation should not take place. The holidays began and Susan welcomed them. Four children, lively, energetic, intelligent, demanding: she was never, not for a moment of her day, alone. If she was in a room, they would be in the next room, or waiting for her to do something for them; or it would soon be time for lunch or tea, or to take one of them to the dentist. Something to do: five weeks of it, thank goodness.

On the fourth day of these so welcome holidays, she found she was storming with anger at the twins, two shrinking beautiful children who (and this is what checked her) stood hand in hand looking at her with sheer dismayed disbelief. This was their calm mother, shouting at them. And for what? They had come to her with some game, some bit of nonsense. They looked at each other, moved closer for support, and went off hand in hand, leaving Susan holding on to the windowsill of the living room, breathing deep, feeling sick. She went to lie down, telling the older children she had a headache. She heard the boy Harry telling the little ones: "It's all right, Mother's got a headache." She heard that *It's all right* with pain.

That night she said to her husband: "Today I shouted at the twins, quite unfairly." She sounded miserable, and he said gently: "Well, what of it?"

"It's more of an adjustment than I thought, their going to school."

"But Susie, Susie darling. . . ." For she was crouched weeping on the bed. He comforted her: "Susan, what is all this about? You shouted at them? What of it? If you shouted at them fifty times a day it wouldn't be more than the little devils deserve." But she wouldn't laugh. She wept. Soon he comforted her with his body. She became calm. Calm, she wondered what was wrong with her, and why she should mind so much that she might, just once, have behaved unjustly with the children. What did it matter? They had forgotten it all long ago: Mother had a headache and everything was all right.

It was a long time later that Susan understood that that night, when she had wept and Matthew had driven the misery out of her with his big solid body, was the last time, ever in their married life, that they had been—to use their mutual language—with each other. And even that was a lie, because she had not told him of her real fears at all.

The five weeks passed, and Susan was in control of herself, and good and kind, and she looked forward to the holidays with a mixture of fear and longing. She did not know what to expect. She took the twins off to school (the elder children took themselves to school) and she returned to the house determined to face the enemy wherever he was, in the house, or the garden or—where?

She was again restless, she was possessed by restlessness. She cooked and sewed and worked as before, day after day, while Mrs. Parkes remonstrated: "Mrs. Rawlings, what's the need for it? I can do that, it's what you pay me for."

And it was so irrational that she checked herself. She would put the car into the garage, go up to her bedroom, and sit, hands in her lap, forcing herself to be quiet. She listened to Mrs. Parkes moving around the house. She looked out into the garden and saw the branches shake the trees. She sat defeating the enemy, restlessness. Emptiness. She ought to be thinking about her life, about herself. But she did not. Or perhaps she could not. As soon as she forced her mind to think about Susan (for what else did she want to be alone for?) it skipped off to thoughts of butter or school clothes. Or it thought of Mrs. Parkes. She realised that she sat listening for the movements of the cleaning woman, following her every turn, bend, thought. She followed her in her mind from kitchen to bathroom, from table to oven, and it was as if the duster, the cleaning cloth, the saucepan, were in her own hand. She would hear herself saying: No, not like that, don't put that there. . . . Yet she did not give a damn what Mrs. Parkes did, or if she did it at all. Yet she could not prevent herself from being conscious of her, every minute. Yes, this was what was wrong with her: she needed, when she was alone, to be really alone, with no one near. She could not endure the knowledge that in ten minutes or in half an hour Mrs. Parkes would call up the stairs: "Mrs. Rawlings, there's no silver polish. Madam, we're out of flour."

So she left the house and went to sit in the garden where she was screened from the house by trees. She waited for the demon to appear and claim her, but he did not.

She was keeping him off, because she had not, after all, come to an end of arranging herself.

She was planning how to be somewhere where Mrs. Parkes would not come after her with a cup of tea, or a demand to be allowed to telephone (always irritating since Susan did not care who she telephoned or how often), or just a nice talk about something. Yes, she needed a place, or a state of affairs, where it would not be necessary to keep reminding herself: In ten minutes I must telephone Matthew about . . . and at half past three I must leave early for the children because the car needs cleaning. And at ten o'clock tomorrow I must remember. . . . She was possessed with resentment that the seven hours of freedom in every day (during weekdays in the school term) were not free, that never, not for one second, ever, was she free from the pressure of time, from having to remember this or that. She could never forget herself; never really let herself go into forgetfulness.

Resentment. It was poisoning her. (She looked at this emotion and thought it was absurd. Yet she felt it.) She was a prisoner. (She looked at this thought too, and it was no good telling herself it was a ridiculous one.) She must tell Matthew—but what? She was filled with emotions that were utterly ridiculous, that she despised, yet that nevertheless she was feeling so strongly she could not shake them off.

The school holidays came round, and this time they were for nearly two months, and she behaved with a conscious controlled decency that nearly drove her crazy. She would lock herself in the bathroom, and sit on the edge of the bath, breathing deep, trying to let go into some kind of calm. Or she went up into the spare room, usually empty, where no one would expect her to be. She heard the children calling "Mother, Mother," and kept silent, feeling guilty. Or she went to the very end of the garden, by herself, and looked at the slow-moving brown river; she looked at the river and closed her eyes and breathed slow and deep, taking it into her being, into her veins.

Then she returned to the family, wife and mother, smiling and responsible, feeling as if the pressure of these people–four lively children and her husband–were a painful pressure on the surface of her skin, a hand pressing on her brain. She did not once break down into irritation during these holidays, but it was like living out a prison sentence, and when the children went back to school, she sat on a white stone seat near the flowing river, and she thought: It is not even a year since the twins went to school, since *they were off my hands* (What on earth did I think I meant when I used that stupid phrase?) and yet I'm a different person. I'm simply not myself. I don't understand it.

Yet she had to understand it. For she knew that this structure–big white house, on which the mortgage still cost four hundred a year, a husband, so good and kind and insightful, four children, all doing so nicely, and the garden where she sat, and Mrs. Parkes the cleaning woman–all this depended on her, and yet she could not understand why, or even what it was she contributed to it.

She said to Matthew in their bedroom: "I think there must be something wrong with me."

And he said: "Surely not, Susan? You look marvellous–you're as lovely as ever."

She looked at the handsome blond man, with his clear, intelligent, blue-eyed face, and thought: Why is it I can't tell him? Why not? And she said: "I need to be alone more than I am."

At which he swung his slow blue gaze at her, and she saw what she had been dreading: Incredulity. Disbelief. And fear. An incredulous blue stare from a stranger who was her husband, as close to her as her own breath.

He said: "But the children are at school and off your hands."

She said to herself: I've got to force myself to say: Yes, but do you realize that I never feel free? There's never a moment I can say to myself: There's nothing I have to remind myself about, nothing I have to do in half an hour, or an hour, or two hours. . . .

But she said: "I don't feel well."

He said: "Perhaps you need a holiday."

She said, appalled: "But not without you, surely?" For she could not imagine herself going off without him. Yet that was what he meant. Seeing her face, he laughed, and opened his arms, and she went into them, thinking: Yes, yes, but why can't I say it? And what is it I have to say?

She tried to tell him, about never being free. And he listened and said: "But Susan, what sort of freedom can you possibly want–short of being dead! Am I ever free? I go to the office, and I have to be there at ten–all right, half past ten, sometimes. And I have to do this or that, don't I? Then I've got to come home at a certain time–I don't mean it, you know I don't–but if I'm not going to be back home at six I telephone you. When can I ever say to myself: I have nothing to be responsible for in the next six hours?"

Susan, hearing this, was remorseful. Because it was true. The good marriage, the house, the children, depended just as much on his voluntary bondage as it did on hers. But why did he not feel bound? Why didn't he chafe and become restless? No, there was something really wrong with her and this proved it.

And that word *bondage*–why had she used it? She had never felt marriage, or the children, as bondage. Neither had he, or surely they wouldn't be together lying in each other's arms content after twelve years of marriage.

No, her state (whatever it was) was irrelevant, nothing to do with her real good life with her family. She had to accept the fact that after all, she was an irrational person and to live with it. Some people had to live with crippled arms, or stammers, or being deaf. She would have to live knowing she was subject to a state of mind she could not own.

Nevertheless, as a result of this conversation with her husband, there was a new regime next holidays.

The spare room at the top of the house now had a cardboard sign saying: PRIVATE! DO NOT DISTURB! on it. (This sign had been drawn in coloured chalks by the children, after a discussion between the parents in which it was decided this was psychologically the right thing.) The family and Mrs. Parkes knew this was "Mother's Room" and that she was entitled to her privacy. Many serious conversations took place between Matthew and the children about not taking Mother for granted. Susan overheard the first, between father and Harry, the older boy, and was surprised at her irritation over it. Surely she could have a room somewhere in that big house and retire into it without such a fuss being made? Without it being so solemnly discussed? Why couldn't she simply have announced: "I'm going to fit out the little top room for myself, and when I'm in it I'm not to be disturbed for anything short of fire"? Just that, and finished; instead of long earnest discussions. When she heard Harry and Matthew explaining it to the twins with Mrs. Parkes coming in–"Yes, well, a family sometimes gets on top of a woman"–she had to go right away to the bottom of the garden until the devils of exasperation had finished their dance in her blood.

But now there was a room, and she could go there when she liked, she used it seldom: she felt even more caged there than in her bedroom. One day she had gone up there after a lunch for ten children she had cooked and served because Mrs. Parkes was not there, and had sat alone for a while looking into the garden. She saw the children stream out from the kitchen and stand looking up at the window where she sat behind the curtains. They were all–her children and their friends–discussing Mother's Room. A few minutes later, the chase of children in some game came pounding up the stairs, but ended as abruptly as if they had fallen over a ravine, so sudden was the silence. They had remembered she was there, and had gone silent in a great gale of "Hush! Shhhhhh! Quiet, you'll disturb her. . . ." And they went tiptoeing downstairs like criminal conspirators. When she came down to make tea for them, they all apologised. The twins put their arms around her, from front and back, making a human cage of loving limbs, and promised it would never occur again. "We forgot, Mummy, we forgot all about it!"

What it amounted to was that Mother's Room, and her need for privacy, had become a valuable lesson in respect for other people's rights. Quite soon Susan was going up to the room only because it was a lesson it was a pity to drop. Then she took sewing up there, and the children and Mrs. Parkes came in and out: it had become another family room.

She sighed, and smiled, and resigned herself–she made jokes at her own expense with Matthew over the room. That is, she did from the self she liked, she respected. But at the same time, something inside her howled with impatience, with rage. . . . And she was frightened.

One day she found herself kneeling by her bed and praying: "Dear God, keep it away from me, keep him away from me." She meant the devil, for she now thought of it, not caring if she were irrational, as some sort of demon. She imagined him, or it, as a youngish man, or perhaps a middle-aged man pretending to be young. Or a man young-looking from immaturity? At any rate, she saw the young-looking face which, when she drew closer, had dry lines about mouth and eyes. He was thinnish, meagre in build. And he had a reddish complexion, and ginger hair. That was he—a gingery, energetic man, and he wore a reddish hairy jacket, unpleasant to the touch.

Well, one day she saw him. She was standing at the bottom of the garden, watching the river ebb past, when she raised her eyes and saw this person, or being, sitting on the white stone bench. He was looking at her, and grinning. In his hand was a long crooked stick, which he had picked off the ground, or broken off the tree above him. He was absent-mindedly, out of an absent-minded or freakish impulse of spite, using the stick to stir around in the coils of a blindworm or a grass snake (or some kind of snakelike creature: it was whitish and unhealthy to look at, unpleasant). The snake was twisting about, flinging its coils from side to side in a kind of dance of protest against the teasing prodding stick.

Susan looked at him thinking: Who is the stranger? What is he doing in our garden? Then she recognised the man around whom her terrors had crystallised. As she did so, he vanished. She made herself walk over to the bench. A shadow from a branch lay across thin emerald grass, moving jerkily over its roughness, and she could see why she had taken it for a snake, lashing and twisting. She went back to the house thinking: Right, then, so I've seen him with my own eyes, so I'm not crazy after all—there *is* a danger because I've seen him. He is lurking in the garden and sometimes even in the house, and he wants *to get into me and to take me over.*

She dreamed of having a room or a place, anywhere, where she could go and sit, by herself, no one knowing where she was.

Once, near Victoria, she found herself outside a news agent that had Rooms to Let advertised. She decided to rent a room, telling no one. Sometimes she could take the train in to Richmond and sit alone in it for an hour or two. Yet how could she? A room would cost three or four pounds a week, and she earned no money, and how could she explain to Matthew that she needed such a sum? What for? It did not occur to her that she was taking it for granted she wasn't going to tell him about the room.

Well, it was out of the question, having a room; yet she knew she must.

One day, when a school term was well established, and none of the children had measles or other ailments, and everything seemed in order, she did the shopping early, explained to Mrs. Parkes she was meeting an old school friend, took the train to Victoria, searched until she found a small quiet hotel, and asked for a room for the day. They did not let rooms by the day, the manageress said, looking doubtful, since Susan so obviously was not the kind of woman who needed a room for unrespectable reasons. Susan made a long explanation about not being well, being unable to shop without frequent rests for lying down. At last she was allowed to rent the room provided she paid a full night's price for it. She was taken up by the manageress and a maid, both concerned over the state of her health . . . which must be pretty bad if, living at Richmond (she had signed her name and address in the register), she needed a shelter at Victoria.

The room was ordinary and anonymous, and was just what Susan needed. She put a shilling in the gas fire, and sat, eyes shut, in a dingy armchair with her back to a dingy window. She was alone. She was alone. She was alone. She could feel pressures lifting off her. First the sounds of traffic came very loud; then they seemed to vanish; she might even have slept a little. A knock on the door: it was Miss Townsend the manageress, bringing her a cup of tea with her own hands, so concerned was she over Susan's long silence and possible illness.

Miss Townsend was a lonely woman of fifty, running this hotel with all the rectitude expected of her, and she sensed in Susan the possibility of understanding companionship. She stayed to talk. Susan found herself in the middle of a fantastic story about her illness, which got more and more improbable as she tried to make it tally with the large house at Richmond, well-off husband, and four children. Suppose she said instead: Miss Townsend, I'm here in your hotel because I need to be alone for a few hours, above all *alone and with no one knowing where I am.* She said it mentally, and saw, mentally, the look that would inevitably come on Miss Townsend's elderly maiden's face.

"Miss Townsend, my four children and my husband are driving me insane, do you understand that? Yes, I can see from the gleam of hysteria in your eyes that comes from loneliness controlled but only just contained that I've got everything in the world you've ever longed for. Well, Miss Townsend, I don't want any of it. You can have it, Miss Townsend. I wish I was absolutely alone in the world, like you. Miss Townsend, I'm besieged by seven devils, Miss Townsend, Miss Townsend, let me stay here in your hotel where the devils can't get me. . . ." Instead of saying all this, she described her anaemia, agreed to try Miss Townsend's remedy for it, which was raw liver, minced, between whole-meal bread, and said yes, perhaps it would be better if she stayed at home and let a friend do shopping for her. She paid her bill and left the hotel, defeated.

At home Mrs. Parkes said she didn't really like it, no, not really, when Mrs. Rawlings was away from nine in the morning until five. The teacher had telephoned from school to say Joan's teeth were paining her, and she hadn't known what to say; and what was she to make for the children's tea, Mrs. Rawlings hadn't said.

All this was nonsense, of course. Mrs. Parkes's complaint was that Susan had withdrawn herself spiritually, leaving the burden of the big house on her.

Susan looked back at her day of "freedom" which had resulted in her becoming a friend to the lonely Miss Townsend, and in Mrs. Parkes's remonstrances. Yet she remembered the short blissful hour of being alone, really alone. She was determined to arrange her life, no matter what it cost, so that she could have that solitude more often. An absolute solitude, where no one knew her or cared about her.

But how? She thought of saying to her old employer: I want you to back me up in a story with Matthew that I am doing part-time work for you. The truth is that . . . but she would have to tell him a lie too, and which lie? She could not say: I want to sit by myself three or four times a week in a rented room. And besides, he knew Matthew, and she could not really ask him to tell lies on her behalf, apart from his being bound to think it meant a lover.

Suppose she really took a part-time job, which she could get through fast and efficiently, leaving time for herself. What job? Addressing envelopes? Canvassing?

And there was Mrs. Parkes, working widow, who knew exactly what she was prepared to give to the house, who knew by instinct when her mistress withdrew in spirit from her responsibilities. Mrs. Parkes was one of the servers of this world, but she needed someone to serve. She had to have Mrs. Rawlings, her madam, at the top of the house or in the garden, so that she could come and get support from her: "Yes, the bread's not what it was when I was a girl. . . . Yes, Harry's got a wonderful appetite, I wonder where he puts it all. . . . Yes, it's lucky the twins are so much of a size, they can wear each other's shoes, that's a saving in these hard times. . . . Yes, the cherry jam from Switzerland is not a patch on the jam from Poland, and three times the price. . . ." And so on. That sort of talk Mrs. Parkes must have, every day, or she would leave, not knowing herself why she left.

Susan Rawlings, thinking these thoughts, found that she was prowling through the great thicketed garden like a wild cat: she was walking up the stairs, down the stairs, through the rooms, into the garden, along the brown running river, back, up through the house, down again. . . . It was a wonder Mrs. Parkes did not think it strange. But on the contrary, Mrs. Rawlings could do what she liked, she could stand on her head if she wanted, provided she was *there*. Susan Rawlings prowled and muttered through her house, hating Mrs. Parkes, hating poor Miss Townsend, dreaming of her hour of solitude in the dingy respectability of Miss Townsend's hotel bedroom, and she knew quite well she was mad. Yes, she was mad.

She said to Matthew that she must have a holiday. Matthew agreed with her. This was not as things had been once-how they had talked in each other's arms in the marriage bed. He had, she knew, diagnosed her finally as *unreasonable*. She had become someone outside himself that he had to manage. They were living side by side in this house like two tolerably friendly strangers.

Having told Mrs. Parkes, or rather, asked for her permission, she went off on a walking holiday in Wales. She chose the remotest place she knew of. Every morning the children telephoned her before they went off to school, to encourage and support her, just as they had over Mother's Room. Every evening she telephoned them, spoke to each child in turn, and then to Matthew. Mrs. Parkes, given permission to telephone for instructions or advice, did so every day at lunchtime. When, as happened three times, Mrs. Rawlings was out on the mountainside, Mrs. Parkes asked that she should ring back at such and such a time, for she would not be happy in what she was doing without Mrs. Rawlings' blessing.

Susan prowled over wild country with the telephone wire holding her to her duty like a leash. The next time she must telephone, or wait to be telephoned, nailed her to her cross. The mountains themselves seemed trammelled by her unfreedom. Everywhere on the mountains, where she met no one at all, from breakfast time to dusk, excepting sheep, or a shepherd, she came face to face with her own craziness which might attack her in the broadest valleys, so that they seemed too small; or on a mountaintop from which she could see a hundred other mountains and valleys, so that they seemed too low, too small, with the sky pressing down too close. She would stand gazing at a hillside brilliant with ferns and bracken, jewelled with running water, and see nothing but her devil, who lifted inhuman eyes at her from where he leaned negligently on a rock, switching at his ugly yellow boots with a leafy twig.

She returned to her home and family, with the Welsh emptiness at the back of her mind like a promise of freedom.

She told her husband she wanted to have an *au pair* girl.

They were in their bedroom, it was late at night, the children slept. He sat, shirted and slippered, in a chair by the window, looking out. She sat brushing her hair and watching him in the mirror. A time-hallowed scene in the connubial bedroom. He said nothing, while she heard the arguments coming into his mind, only to be rejected because every one was *reasonable*.

566

"It seems strange to get one now, after all, the children are in school most of the day. Surely the time for you to have help was when you were stuck with them day and night. Why don't you ask Mrs. Parkes to cook for you? She's even offered to–I can understand if you are tired of cooking for six people. But you know that an *au pair* girl means all kinds of problems, it's not like having an ordinary char in during the day. . . ."

Finally he said carefully: "Are you thinking of going back to work?"

"No," she said, "no, not really." She made herself sound vague, rather stupid. She went on brushing her black hair and peering at herself so as to be oblivious of the short uneasy glances her Matthew kept giving her. "Do you think we can't afford it?" she went on vaguely, not at all the old efficient Susan who knew exactly what they could afford.

"It's not that," he said, looking out of the window at dark trees, so as not to look at her. Meanwhile she examined a round, candid, pleasant face with clear dark brows and clear grey eyes. A sensible face. She brushed thick healthy black hair and thought: Yet that's the reflection of a madwoman. How very strange! Much more to the point if what looked back at me was the gingery green-eyed demon with his dry meagre smile. . . . Why wasn't Matthew agreeing? After all, what else could he do? She was breaking her part of the bargain and there was no way of forcing her to keep it: that her spirit, her soul, should live in this house, so that the people in it could grow like plants in water, and Mrs. Parkes remain content in their service. In return for this, he would be a good loving husband and responsible towards the children. Well, nothing like this had been true of either of them for a long time. He did his duty, perfunctorily; she did not even pretend to do hers. And he had become like other husbands, with his real life in his work and the people he met there, and very likely a serious affair. All this was her fault.

At last he drew heavy curtains, blotting out the trees, and turned to force her attention: "Susan, are you really sure we need a girl?" But she would not meet his appeal at all: She was running the brush over her hair again and again, lifting fine black clouds in a small hiss of electricity. She was peering in and smiling as if she were amused at the clinging hissing hair that followed the brush.

"Yes, I think it would be a good idea on the whole," she said, with the cunning of a madwoman evading the real point.

In the mirror she could see her Matthew lying on his back, his hands behind his head, staring upwards, his face sad and hard. She felt her heart (the old heart of Susan Rawlings) soften and call out to him. But she set it to be indifferent.

He said: "Susan, the children?" It was an appeal that *almost* reached her. He opened his arms, lifting them from where they had lain by his sides, palms up, empty. She had only to run across and fling herself into them, onto his hard, warm chest, and melt into herself, into Susan. But she could not. She would not see his lifted arms. She said vaguely: "Well, surely it'll be even better for them? We'll get a French or a German girl and they'll learn the language."

In the dark she lay beside him, feeling frozen, a stranger. She felt as if Susan had been spirited away. She disliked very much this woman who lay here, cold and indifferent beside a suffering man, but she could not change her.

Next morning she set about getting a girl, and very soon came Sophie Traub from Hamburg, a girl of twenty, laughing, healthy, blue-eyed, intending to learn English. Indeed, she already spoke a good deal. In return for a room–"Mother's Room"–and her food, she undertook to do some light cooking, and to be with the children when Mrs. Rawlings asked. She was an intelligent girl and understood perfectly what was needed. Susan said: "I go off sometimes, for the morning or for the day—well, sometimes the children run home from school, or they ring up, or a teacher rings up. I should be here, really. And there's the daily woman. . . ." And Sophie laughed her deep fruity *Fräulein's* laugh, showed her fine white teeth and her dimples, and said: "You want some person to play mistress of the house sometimes, not so?"

"Yes, that is just so," said Susan, a bit dry, despite herself, thinking in secret fear how easy it was, how much nearer to the end she was than she thought. Healthy Fräulein Traub's instant understanding of their position proved this to be true.

The *au pair* girl, because of her own common sense, or (as Susan said to herself with her new inward shudder) because she had been *chosen* so well by Susan, was a success with everyone, the children liking her, Mrs. Parkes forgetting almost at once that she was German, and Matthew finding her "nice to have around the house." For he was now taking things as they came, from the surface of life, withdrawn both as a husband and a father from the household.

One day Susan saw how Sophie and Mrs. Parkes were talking and laughing in the kitchen, and she announced that she would be away until teatime. She knew exactly where to go and what she must look for. She took the District Line to South Kensington, changed to the Circle, got off at Paddington, and walked around looking at the smaller hotels until she was satisfied with one which had FRED'S HOTEL painted on windowpanes that needed cleaning. The façade was a faded shiny yellow, like unhealthy skin. A door at the end of a passage said she must knock; she did, and Fred appeared. He was not at all attractive, not in any way, being fattish, and run-down, and wearing a tasteless striped suit. He had small sharp eyes in a white creased face, and was quite prepared to let Mrs. Jones (she chose the farcical name deliberately, staring him out) have a room three days a week from ten until six. Provided of course that she paid in advance each time she came? Susan produced fifteen shillings (no price had been set by him) and held it out, still fixing him with a bold unblinking challenge she had not known until then she could use at will. Looking at her still, he took up a ten-shilling note from her palm between thumb and forefinger, fingered it; then shuffled up two half crowns, held out his own palm with these bits of money displayed thereon, and let his gaze lower broodingly at them. They were standing in the passage, a red-shaded light above, bare boards beneath, and a strong smell of floor polish rising about them. He shot his gaze up at her over the still-extended palm, and smiled as if to say: What do you take me for? "I shan't," said Susan, "be using this room for the purposes of making money." He still waited. She added another five shillings, at which he nodded and said: "You pay, and I ask no questions." "Good," said Susan. He now went past her to the stairs, and there waited a moment: the light from the street door being in her eyes, she lost sight of him momentarily. Then she saw a sober-suited, white-faced, white-balding little man trotting up the stairs like a waiter, and she went after him. They proceeded in utter silence up the stairs of this house where no questions were asked–Fred's Hotel, which could afford the freedom for its visitors that poor Miss Townsend's hotel could not. The room was hideous. It had a single window, with thin green brocade curtains, a three-quarter bed that had a cheap green satin bedspread on it, a fireplace with a gas fire and a shilling meter by it, a chest of drawers, and a green wicker armchair.

"Thank you," said Susan, knowing that Fred (if this was Fred, and not George, or Herbert or Charlie) was looking at her, not so much with curiosity, an emotion he would not own to,

568

for professional reasons, but with a philosophical sense of what was appropriate. Having taken her money and shown her up and agreed to everything, he was clearly disapproving of her for coming here. She did not belong here at all, so his look said. (But she knew, already, how very much she did belong: the room had been waiting for her to join it.) "Would you have me called at five o'clock, please?" and he nodded and went downstairs.

It was twelve in the morning. She was free. She sat in the armchair, she simply sat, she closed her eyes and sat and let herself be alone. She was alone and no one knew where she was. When a knock came on the door she was annoyed, and prepared to show it: but it was Fred himself, it was five o'clock and he was calling her as ordered. He flicked his sharp little eyes over the room–bed, first. It was undisturbed. She might never have been in the room at all. She thanked him, said she would be returning the day after tomorrow, and left. She was back home in time to cook supper, to put the children to bed, to cook a second supper for her husband and herself later. And to welcome Sophie back from the pictures where she had gone with a friend. All these things she did cheerfully, willingly. But she was thinking all the time of the hotel room, she was longing for it with her whole being.

Three times a week. She arrived promptly at ten, looked Fred in the eyes, gave him twenty shillings, followed him up the stairs, went into the room, and shut the door on him with gentle firmness. For Fred, disapproving of her being here at all, was quite ready to let friendship, or at least acquaintanceship, follow his disapproval, if only she would let him. But he was content to go off on her dismissing nod, with the twenty shillings in his hand.

She sat in the armchair and shut her eyes.

What did she *do* in the room? Why, nothing at all. From the chair, when it had rested her, she went to the window, stretching her arms, smiling, treasuring her anonymity, to look out. She was no longer Susan Rawlings, mother of four, wife of Matthew, employer of Mrs. Parkes and of Sophie Traub, with these and those relations with friends, schoolteachers, tradesmen. She no longer was mistress of the big white house and garden, owning clothes suitable for this and that activity or occasion. She was Mrs. Jones, and she was alone, and she had no past and no future. Here I am, she thought, after all these years of being married and having children and playing those roles of responsibility–and I'm just the same. Yet there have been times I thought that nothing existed of me except the roles that went with being Mrs. Matthew Rawlings. Yes, here I am, and if I never saw any of my family again, here I would still be . . . how very strange that is! And she leaned on the sill, and looked into the street, loving the men and women who passed, because she did not know them. She looked at the downtrodden buildings over the street, and at the sky, wet and dingy, or sometimes blue, and she felt she had never seen buildings or sky before. And then she went back to the chair, empty, her mind a blank. Sometimes she talked aloud, saying nothing–an exclamation, meaningless, followed by a comment about the floral pattern on the thin rug, or a stain on the green satin coverlet. For the most part, she woolgathered–what word is there for it?–brooded, wandered, simply went dark, feeling emptiness run deliciously through her veins like the movement of her blood.

This room had become more her own than the house she lived in. One morning she found Fred taking her a flight higher than usual. She stopped, refusing to go up, and demanded her usual room, Number 19. "Well, you'll have to wait half an hour then," he said. Willingly she descended to the dark disinfectant-smelling hall, and sat waiting until the two, man and woman, came down the stairs, giving her swift indifferent glances before they hurried out into the street, separating at the door. She went up to the room, *her* room, which they had just vacated. It was no less hers, though the windows were set wide open, and a maid was straightening the bed as she came in.

After these days of solitude, it was both easy to play her part as mother and wife, and difficult—because it was so easy: she felt an impostor. She felt as if her shell moved here, with her family, answering to Mummy, Mother, Susan, Mrs. Rawlings. She was surprised no one saw through her, that she wasn't turned out of doors, as a fake. On the contrary, it seemed the children loved her more; Matthew and she "got on" pleasantly, and Mrs. Parkes was happy in her work under (for the most part, it must be confessed) Sophie Traub. At night she lay beside her husband, and they made love again, apparently just as they used to, when they were really married. But she, Susan, or the being who answered so readily and improbably to the name of Susan, was not there: she was in Fred's Hotel, in Paddington, waiting for the easing hours of solitude to begin.

Soon she made a new arrangement with Fred and with Sophie. It was for five days a week. As for the money, five pounds, she simply asked Matthew for it. She saw that she was not even frightened he might ask what for: he would give it to her, she knew that, and yet it was terrifying it could be so, for this close couple, these partners, had once known the destination of every shilling they must spend. He agreed to give her five pounds a week. She asked for just so much, not a penny more. He sounded indifferent about it. It was as if he were paying her, she thought: *paying her off*—yes, that was it. Terror came back for a moment, when she understood this, but she stilled it: things had gone too far for that. Now, every week, on Sunday nights, he gave her five pounds, turning away from her before their eyes could meet on the transaction. As for Sophie Traub, she was to be somewhere in or near the house until six at night, after which she was free. She was not to cook, or to clean, she was simply to be there. So she gardened or sewed, and asked friends in, being a person who was bound to have a lot of friends. If the children were sick, she nursed them. If teachers telephoned, she answered them sensibly. For the five daytimes in the school week, she was altogether the mistress of the house.

One night in the bedroom, Matthew asked: "Susan, I don't want to interfere—don't think that, please—but are you sure you are well?"

She was brushing her hair at the mirror. She made two more strokes on either side of her head, before she replied: "Yes, dear, I am sure I am well."

He was again lying on his back, his big blond head on his hands, his elbows angled up and part-concealing his face. He said: "Then Susan, I have to ask you this question, though you must understand, I'm not putting any sort of pressure on you." (Susan heard the word pressure with dismay, because this was inevitable, of course she could not go on like this.) "Are things going to go on like this?"

"Well," she said, going vague and bright and idiotic again, so as to escape: "Well, I don't see why not."

He was jerking his elbows up and down, in annoyance or in pain, and, looking at him, she saw he had got thin, even gaunt; and restless angry movements were not what she remembered of him. He said: "Do you want a divorce, is that it?"

At this, Susan only with the greatest difficulty stopped herself from laughing: she could hear the bright bubbling laughter she *would* have emitted, had she let herself. He could only mean one thing: she had a lover, and that was why she spent her days in London, as lost to him as if she had vanished to another continent.

Then the small panic set in again: she understood that he hoped she did have a lover, he was begging her to say so, because otherwise it would be too terrifying.

She thought this out, as she brushed her hair, watching the fine black stuff fly up to make its little clouds of electricity, hiss, hiss, hiss. Behind her head, across the room, was a blue wall. She realised she was absorbed in watching the black hair making shapes against the blue. She should be answering him. "Do *you* want a divorce, Matthew?"

He said: "That surely isn't the point, is it?"

"You brought it up, I didn't," she said, brightly, suppressing meaningless tinkling laughter.

Next day she asked Fred: "Have enquiries been made for me?"

He hesitated, and she said: "I've been coming here a year now. I've made no trouble, and you've been paid every day. I have a right to be told."

"As a matter of fact, Mrs. Jones, a man did come asking."

"A man from a detective agency?"

"Well, he could have been, couldn't he?"

"I was asking you . . . well, what did you tell him?"

"I told him a Mrs. Jones came every weekday from ten until five or six and stayed in Number Nineteen by herself."

"Describing me?"

"Well Mrs. Jones, I had no alternative. Put yourself in my place."

"By rights I should deduct what that man gave you for the information."

He raised shocked eyes: she was not the sort of person to make jokes like this! Then he chose to laugh: a pinkish wet slit appeared across his white crinkled face: his eyes positively begged her to laugh, otherwise he might lose some money. She remained grave, looking at him.

He stopped laughing and said: "You want to go up now?"—returning to the familiarity, the comradeship, of the country where no questions are asked, on which (and he knew it) she depended completely.

She went up to sit in her wicker chair. But it was not the same. Her husband had searched her out. (The world had searched her out.) The pressures were on her. She was here with his connivance. He might walk in at any moment, here, into Room 19. She imagined the report from the detective agency: "A woman calling herself Mrs. Jones, fitting the description of your wife (etc., etc., etc.), stays alone all day in Room No. 19. She insists on this room, waits for it if it is engaged. As far as the proprietor knows, she receives no visitors there, male or female." A report something on these lines, Matthew must have received.

Well of course he was right: things couldn't go on like this. He had put an end to it all simply by sending the detective after her.

She tried to shrink herself back into the shelter of the room, a snail pecked out of its shell and trying to squirm back. But the peace of the room had gone. She was trying consciously to revive it, trying to let go into the dark creative trance (or whatever it was) that she had found there. It was no use, yet she craved for it, she was as ill as a suddenly deprived addict.

Several times she returned to the room, to look for herself there, but instead she found the unnamed spirit of restlessness, a prickling fevered hunger for movement, an irritable self-consciousness that made her brain feel as if it had coloured lights going on and off inside it. Instead of the soft dark that had been the room's air, were now waiting for her demons that made her dash blindly about, muttering words of hate; she was impelling herself from point to point like a moth dashing itself against a windowpane, sliding to the bottom, fluttering off on broken wings, then crashing into the invisible barrier again. And again and again. Soon she was exhausted, and she told Fred that for a while she would not be needing the room, she was going on holiday. Home she went, to the big white house by the river. The middle of a weekday, and she felt guilty at returning to her own home when not expected. She stood unseen, looking in at the kitchen window. Mrs. Parkes, wearing a discarded floral overall of Susan's, was stooping to slide something into the oven. Sophie, arms folded, was leaning her back against a cupboard and laughing at some joke made by a girl not seen before by Susan–a dark foreign girl, Sophie's visitor. In an armchair Molly, one of the twins, lay curled, sucking her thumb and watching the grownups. She must have some sickness, to be kept from school. The child's listless face, the dark circles under her eyes, hurt Susan: Molly was looking at the three grownups working and talking in exactly the same way Susan looked at the four through the kitchen window: she was remote, shut off from them.

But then, just as Susan imagined herself going in, picking up the little girl, and sitting in an armchair with her, stroking her probably heated forehead, Sophie did just that: she had been standing on one leg, the other knee flexed, its foot set against the wall. Now she let her foot in its ribbon-tied red shoe slide down the wall, stood solid on two feet, clapping her hands before and behind her, and sang a couple of lines in German, so that the child lifted her heavy eyes at her and began to smile. Then she walked, or rather skipped, over to the child, swung her up, and let her fall into her lap at the same moment she sat herself. She said "Hopla! Hopla! Molly . . ." and began stroking the dark untidy young head that Molly laid on her shoulder for comfort.

Well. . . . Susan blinked the tears of farewell out of her eyes, and went quietly up the house to her bedroom. There she sat looking at the river through the trees. She felt at peace, but in a way that was new to her. She had no desire to move, to talk, to do anything at all. The devils that had haunted the house, the garden, were not there; but she knew it was because her soul was in Room 19 in Fred's Hotel; she was not really here at all. It was a sensation that should have been frightening: to sit at her own bedroom window, listening to Sophie's rich young voice sing German nursery songs to her child, listening to Mrs. Parkes clatter and move below, and to know that all this had nothing to do with her: she was already out of it.

Later, she made herself go down and say she was home: it was unfair to be here unannounced. She took lunch with Mrs. Parkes, Sophie, Sophie's Italian friend Maria, and her daughter Molly, and felt like a visitor.

A few days later, at bedtime, Matthew said: "Here's your five pounds," and pushed them over at her. Yet he must have known she had not been leaving the house at all.

She shook her head, gave it back to him, and said, in explanation, not in accusation: "As soon as you knew where I was, there was no point."

He nodded, not looking at her. He was turned away from her: thinking, she knew, how best to handle this wife who terrified him.

He said: "I wasn't trying to . . . it's just that I was worried."

"Yes, I know."

"I must confess that I was beginning to wonder. . ."

"You thought I had a lover?"

"Yes, I am afraid I did."

She knew that he wished she had. She sat wondering how to say: "For a year now I've been spending all my days in a very sordid hotel room. It's the place where I'm happy. In fact, without it I don't exist." She heard herself saying this, and understood how terrified he was that she might. So instead she said: "Well, perhaps you're not far wrong."

Probably Matthew would think the hotel proprietor lied: he would want to think so.

"Well," he said, and she could hear his voice spring up, so to speak, with relief: "in that case I must confess I've got a bit of an affair on myself."

She said, detached and interested: "Really? Who is she?" and saw Matthew's startled look because of this reaction.

"It's Phil. Phil Hunt."

She had known Phil Hunt well in the old unmarried days. She was thinking: No, she won't do, she's too neurotic and difficult. She's never been happy yet. Sophie's much better: Well Matthew will see that himself, as sensible as he is.

This line of thought went on in silence, while she said aloud: "It's no point telling you about mine, because you don't know him."

Quick, quick, invent, she thought. Remember how you invented all that nonsense for Miss Townsend.

She began slowly, careful not to contradict herself: "His name is Michael"–(*Michael What?*)–"Michael Plant." (What a silly name!) "He's rather like you—in looks, I mean." And indeed, she could imagine herself being touched by no one but Matthew himself. "He's a publisher." (Really? Why?) "He's got a wife already and two children."

She brought out this fantasy, proud of herself.

Matthew said: "Are you two thinking of marrying?"

She said, before she could stop herself: "Good God, *no!*"

She realised, if Matthew wanted to marry Phil Hunt, that this was too emphatic, but apparently it was all right, for his voice sounded relieved as he said: "It is a bit impossible to imagine oneself married to anyone else, isn't it?" With which he pulled her to him, so that her head lay on his shoulder. She turned her face into the dark of his flesh, and listened to the blood pounding through her ears saying: I am alone, I am alone, I am alone.

In the morning Susan lay in bed while he dressed.

He had been thinking things out in the night, because now he said: "Susan, why don't we make a foursome?"

Of course, she said to herself, of course he would be bound to say that. If one is sensible, if one is reasonable, if one never allows oneself a base thought or an envious emotion, naturally one says: Let's make a foursome!

"Why not?" she said.

"We could all meet for lunch. I mean, it's ridiculous, you sneaking off to filthy hotels, and me staying late at the office, and all the lies everyone has to tell."

What on earth did I say his name was?–she panicked, then said: "I think it's a good idea, but Michael is away at the moment. When he comes back though–and I'm sure you two would like each other."

"He's away, is he? So that's why you've been . . ." Her husband put his hand to the knot of his tie in a gesture of male coquetry she would not before have associated with him; and he bent to kiss her cheek with the expression that goes with the words: Oh you naughty little puss! And she felt its answering look, naughty and coy, come onto her face.

Inside she was dissolving in horror at them both, at how far they had both sunk from honesty of emotion.

So now she was saddled with a lover, and he had a mistress! How ordinary, how reassuring, how jolly! And now they would make a foursome of it, and go about to theatres and restaurants. After all, the Rawlings could well afford that sort of thing, and presumably the publisher Michael Plant could afford to do himself and his mistress quite well. No, there was nothing to stop the four of them developing the most intricate relationship of civilised tolerance, all enveloped in a charming afterglow of autumnal passion. Perhaps they would all go off on holidays together? She had known people who did. Or perhaps Matthew would draw the line there? Why should he, though, if he was capable of talking about "foursomes" at all?

She lay in the empty bedroom, listening to the car drive off with Matthew in it, off to work. Then she heard the children clattering off to school to the accompaniment of Sophie's cheerfully ringing voice. She slid down into the hollow of the bed, for shelter against her own irrelevance. And she stretched out her hand to the hollow where her husband's body had lain, but found no comfort there: he was not her husband. She curled herself up in a small tight ball under the clothes: she could stay here all day, all week, indeed, all her life.

But in a few days she must produce Michael Plant, and—but how? She must presumably find some agreeable man prepared to impersonate a publisher called Michael Plant. And in return for which she would—what? Well, for one thing they would make love. The idea made her want to cry with sheer exhaustion. Oh no, she had finished with all that—the proof of it was that the words "make love," or even imagining it, trying hard to revive no more than the pleasures of sensuality, let alone affection, or love, made her want to run away and hide from the sheer effort of the thing. . . . Good Lord, why make love at all? Why make love with anyone? Or if you are going to make love, what does it matter who with? Why shouldn't she simply walk into the street, pick up a man and have a roaring sexual affair with him? Why not? Or even with Fred? What difference did it make?

But she had let herself in for it—an interminable stretch of time with a lover, called Michael, as part of a gallant civilised foursome. Well, she could not, and she would not.

She got up, dressed, went down to find Mrs. Parkes, and asked her for the loan of a pound, since Matthew, she said, had forgotten to leave her money. She exchanged with Mrs. Parkes variations on the theme that husbands are all the same, they don't think, and without saying a word to Sophie, whose voice could be heard upstairs from the telephone, walked to the underground, travelled to South Kensington, changed to the Inner Circle, got out at Paddington, and walked to Fred's Hotel. There she told Fred that she wasn't going on holiday after all, she needed the room. She would have to wait an hour, Fred said. She went to a busy tearoom-cum-restaurant around the corner, and sat watching the people flow in and out the door that kept swinging open and shut, watched them mingle and merge and separate, felt her being flow into them, into their movement. When the hour was up she left a half crown for her pot of tea, and left the place without looking back at it, just as she had left her house, the big, beautiful white house, without another look, but silently dedicating it to Sophie. She returned to Fred, received the key of No. 19, now free, and ascended the grimy stairs slowly, letting floor after floor fall away below her, keeping her eyes lifted, so that floor after floor descended jerkily to her level of vision, and fell away out of sight.

No. 19 was the same. She saw everything with an acute, narrow, checking glance: the cheap shine of the satin spread, which had been replaced carelessly after the two bodies had finished their convulsions under it; a trace of powder on the glass that topped the chest of drawers; an intense green shade in a fold of the curtain. She stood at the window, looking down, watching people pass and pass and pass until her mind went dark from the constant movement. Then she sat in the wicker chair, letting herself go slack. But she had to be careful, because she did not want, today, to be surprised by Fred's knock at five o'clock.

The demons were not here. They had gone forever, because she was buying her freedom from them. She was slipping already into the dark fructifying dream that seemed to caress her inwardly, like the movement of her blood . . . but she had to think about Matthew first. Should she write a letter for the coroner? But what should she say? She would like to leave him with the look on his face she had seen this morning—banal, admittedly, but at least confidently healthy. Well, that was impossible, one did not look like that with a wife dead from suicide. But how to leave him believing she was dying because of a man—because of the fascinating publisher Michael Plant? Oh, how ridiculous! How absurd! How humiliating! But she decided not to trouble about it, simply not to think about the living. If he wanted to believe she had a lover, he would believe it. And he *did* want to believe it. Even when he had found out that there was no publisher in London called Michael Plant, he would think: Oh poor Susan, she was afraid to give me his real name.

And what did it matter whether he married Phil Hunt or Sophie? Though it ought to be Sophie, who was already the mother of those children . . . and what hypocrisy to sit here worrying about the children, when she was going to leave them because she had not got the energy to stay.

She had about four hours. She spent them delightfully, darkly, sweetly, letting herself slide gently, gently, to the edge of the river. Then, with hardly a break in her consciousness, she got up, pushed the thin rug against the door, made sure the windows were tight shut, put two shillings in the meter, and turned on the gas. For the first time since she had been in the room she lay on the hard bed that smelled stale, that smelled of sweat and sex.

She lay on her back on the green satin cover, but her legs were chilly. She got up, found a blanket folded in the bottom of the chest of drawers, and carefully covered her legs with it. She was quite content lying there, listening to the faint soft hiss of the gas that poured into the room, into her lungs, into her brain, as she drifted off into the dark river.

The Faery Handbag
(2005)

KELLY LINK

I used to go to thrift stores with my friends. We'd take the train into Boston, and go to The Garment District, which is this huge vintage clothing warehouse. Everything is arranged by color, and somehow that makes all of the clothes beautiful. It's kind of like if you went through the wardrobe in the Narnia books, only instead of finding Aslan and the White Witch and horrible Eustace, you found this magic clothing world—instead of talking animals, there were feather boas and wedding dresses and bowling shoes, and paisley shirts and Doc Martens and everything hung up on racks so that first you have black dresses, all together, like the world's largest indoor funeral, and then blue dresses—all the blues you can imagine—and then red dresses and so on. Pink reds and orangey reds and purple reds and exit-light reds and candy reds. Sometimes I would close my eyes and Natasha and Natalie and Jake would drag me over to a rack, and rub a dress against my hand. "Guess what color this is."

We had this theory that you could learn how to tell, just by feeling, what color something was. For example, if you're sitting on a lawn, you can tell what color green the grass is, with your eyes closed, depending on how silky-rubbery it feels. With clothing, stretchy velvet stuff always feels red when your eyes are closed, even if it's not red. Natasha was always best at guessing colors, but Natasha is also best at cheating at games and not getting caught.

One time we were looking through kids' T-shirts and we found a Muppets T-shirt that had belonged to Natalie in third grade. We knew it belonged to her, because it still had her name inside, where her mother had written it in permanent marker when Natalie went to summer camp. Jake bought it back for her, because he was the only one who had money that weekend. He was the only one who had a job.

Maybe you're wondering what a guy like Jake is doing in The Garment District with a bunch of girls. The thing about Jake is that he always has a good time, no matter what he's doing. He likes everything, and he likes everyone, but he likes me best of all. Wherever he is now, I bet he's having a great time and wondering when I'm going to show up. I'm always running late. But he knows that.

We had this theory that things have life cycles, the way that people do. The life cycle of wedding dresses and feather boas and T-shirts and shoes and handbags involves The Garment District. If clothes are good, or even if they're bad in an interesting way, The Garment District is where they go when they die. You can tell that they're dead, because of the way that they smell. When you buy them, and wash them, and start wearing them again, and they

577

start to smell like you, that's when they reincarnate. But the point is, if you're looking for a particular thing, you just have to keep looking for it. You have to look hard.

Down in the basement at The Garment District they sell clothing and beat-up suitcases and teacups by the pound. You can get eight pounds' worth of prom dresses—a slinky black dress, a poufy lavender dress, a swirly pink dress, a silvery, starry lamé dress so fine you could pass it through a key ring—for eight dollars. I go there every week, hunting for Grandmother Zofia's faery handbag.

The faery handbag: It's huge and black and kind of hairy. Even when your eyes are closed, it feels black. As black as black ever gets, like if you touch it, your hand might get stuck in it, like tar or black quicksand or when you stretch out your hand at night, to turn on a light, but all you feel is darkness.

Fairies live inside it. I know what that sounds like, but it's true.

Grandmother Zofia said it was a family heirloom. She said that it was over two hundred years old. She said that when she died, I had to look after it. Be its guardian. She said that it would be my responsibility.

I said that it didn't look that old, and that they didn't have handbags two hundred years ago, but that just made her cross. She said, "So then tell me, Genevieve, darling, where do you think old ladies used to put their reading glasses and their heart medicine and their knitting needles?"

I know that no one is going to believe any of this. That's okay. If I thought you would, then I couldn't tell you. Promise me that you won't believe a word. That's what Zofia used to say to me when she told me stories. At the funeral, my mother said, half-laughing and half-crying, that her mother was the world's best liar. I think she thought maybe Zofia wasn't really dead. But I went up to Zofia's coffin, and I looked her right in the eyes. They were closed. The funeral parlor had made her up with blue eyeshadow, and blue eyeliner. She looked like she was going to be a news anchor on Fox television, instead of dead. It was creepy and it made me even sadder than I already was. But I didn't let that distract me.

"Okay, Zofia," I whispered. "I know you're dead, but this is important. You know exactly how important this is. Where's the handbag? What did you do with it? How do I find it? What am I supposed to do now?"

Of course, she didn't say a word. She just lay there, this little smile on her face, as if she thought the whole thing—death, blue eyeshadow, Jake, the handbag, faeries, Scrabble, Baldeziwurlekistan, all of it—was a joke. She always did have a weird sense of humor. That's why she and Jake got along so well.

I grew up in a house next door to the house where my mother lived when she was a little girl. Her mother, Zofia Swink, my grandmother, babysat me while my mother and father were at work.

Zofia never looked like a grandmother. She had long black hair, which she plaited up in spiky towers. She had large blue eyes. She was taller than my father. She looked like a spy or ballerina or a lady pirate or a rock star. She acted like one too. For example, she never drove anywhere. She rode a bike. It drove my mother crazy. "Why can't you act your age?" she'd say, and Zofia would just laugh.

Zofia and I played Scrabble all the time. Zofia always won, even though her English wasn't all that great, because we'd decided that she was allowed to use Baldeziwurleki vocabulary. Baldeziwurlekistan is where Zofia was born, over two hundred years ago. That's what Zofia said. (My grandmother claimed to be over two hundred years old. Or maybe even older. Sometimes she claimed that she'd even met Genghis Khan. He was much shorter than her. I probably don't have time to tell that story.) Baldeziwurlekistan is also an incredibly valuable word in Scrabble points, even though it doesn't exactly fit on the board. Zofia put it down the first time we played. I was feeling pretty good because I'd gotten forty-one points for *zippery* on my turn.

Zofia kept rearranging her letters on her tray. Then she looked over at me, as if daring me to stop her, and put down *eziwurlekistan*, after *bald*. She used *delicious, zippery, wishes, kismet,* and *needle,* and made *to* into *toe*. *Baldeziwurlekistan* went all the way across the board and then trailed off down the righthand side.

I started laughing.

"I used up all my letters," Zofia said. She licked her pencil and started adding up points.

"That's not a word," I said. "*Baldeziwurlekistan* is not a word. Besides, you can't do that. You can't put an eighteen-letter word on a board that's fifteen squares across."

"Why not? It's a country," Zofia said. "It's where I was born, little darling."

"Challenge," I said. I went and got the dictionary and looked it up. "There's no such place."

"Of course there isn't nowadays," Zofia said. "It wasn't a very big place, even when it was a place. But you've heard of Samarkand, and Uzbekistan and the Silk Road and Genghis Khan. Haven't I told you about meeting Genghis Khan?"

I looked up Samarkand. "Okay," I said. "Samarkand is a real place. A real word. But Baldeziwurlekistan isn't."

"They call it something else now," Zofia said. "But I think it's important to remember where we come from. I think it's only fair that I get to use Baldeziwurleki words. Your English is so much better than me. Promise me something, mouthful of dumpling, a small, small thing. You'll remember its real name. Baldeziwurlekistan. Now when I add it up, I get three hundred and sixty-eight points. Could that be right?"

If you called the faery handbag by its right name, it would be something like *orzipanikanikcz*, which means the "bag of skin where the world lives," only Zofia never spelled that word the same way twice. She said you had to spell it a little differently each time. You never wanted to spell it exactly the right way, because that would be dangerous.

I called it the faery handbag because I put *faery* down on the Scrabble board once. Zofia said that you spelled it with an *i*, not an e. She looked it up in the dictionary, and lost a turn.

Zofia said that in Baldeziwurlekistan they used a board and tiles for divination, prognostication, and sometimes even just for fun. She said it was a little like playing Scrabble. That's probably why she turned out to be so good at Scrabble. The Baldeziwurlekistanians used their tiles and board to communicate with the people who lived under the hill. The people who lived under the hill knew the future. The Baldeziwurlekistanians gave them fermented milk and honey, and the young women of the village used to go and lie out on the hill and sleep under the stars. Apparently the people under the hill were pretty cute. The important thing was that you never went down into the hill and spent the night there, no matter how cute the guy from under the hill was. If you did, even if you spent only a single night under the hill, when you came out again, a hundred years might have passed. 'Remember that," Zofia said to me. "It doesn't matter how cute a guy is. If he wants you to come back to his place, it isn't a good idea. It's okay to fool around, but don't spend the night."

Every once in a while, a woman from under the hill would marry a man from the village, even though it never ended well. The problem was that the women under the hill were terrible cooks. They couldn't get used to the way time worked in the village, which meant that supper always got burnt, or else it wasn't cooked long enough. But they couldn't stand to be criticized. It hurt their feelings. If their village husband complained, or even if he looked like he wanted to complain, that was it. The woman from under the hill went back to her home, and even if her husband went and begged and pleaded and apologized, it might be three years or thirty years or a few generations before she came back out.

Even the best, happiest marriages between the Baldeziwurlekistanians and the people under the hill fell apart when the children got old enough to complain about dinner. But everyone in the village had some hill blood in them.

"It's in you," Zofia said, and kissed me on the nose. "Passed down from my grandmother and her mother. It's why we're so beautiful."

When Zofia was nineteen, the shaman-priestess in her village threw the tiles and discovered that something bad was going to happen. A raiding party was coming. There was no point in fighting them. They would burn down everyone's houses and take the young men and women for slaves. And it was even worse than that. There was going to be an earthquake as well, which was bad news because usually, when raiders showed up, the village went down under the hill for a night and when they came out again, the raiders would have been gone for months or decades or even a hundred years. But this earthquake was going to split the hill right open.

The people under the hill were in trouble. Their home would be destroyed, and they would be doomed to roam the face of the earth, weeping and lamenting their fate until the sun blew out and the sky cracked and the seas boiled and the people dried up and turned to dust and blew away. So the shaman-priestess went and divined some more, and the people under the hill told her to kill a black dog and skin it and use the skin to make a purse big enough to hold a chicken, an egg, and a cooking pot. So she did, and then the people under the hill made the inside of the purse big enough to hold all of the village and all of the people under the hill and mountains and forests and seas and rivers and lakes and orchards and a sky and stars and spirits and fabulous monsters and sirens and dragons and dryads and mermaids and beasties and all the little gods that the Baldeziwurlekistanians and the people under the hill worshipped.

"Your purse is made out of dog skin?" I said. "That's disgusting!"

"Little dear pet," Zofia said, looking wistful, "Dog is delicious. To Baldeziwurlekistanians, dog is a delicacy."

Before the raiding party arrived, the village packed up all of their belongings and moved into the handbag. The clasp was made out of bone. If you opened it one way, then it was just a purse big enough to hold a chicken and an egg and a clay cooking pot, or else a pair of reading glasses and a library book and a pillbox. If you opened the clasp another way, then you found yourself in a little boat floating at the mouth of a river. On either side of you was forest, where the Baldeziwurlekistanian villagers and the people under the hill made their new settlement.

If you opened the handbag the wrong way, though, you found yourself in a dark land that smelled like blood. That's where the guardian of the purse (the dog whose skin had been been sewn into a purse) lived. The guardian had no skin. Its howl made blood come out of your ears and nose. It tore apart anyone who turned the clasp in the opposite direction and opened the purse in the wrong way.

"Here is the wrong way to open the handbag," Zofia said. She twisted the clasp, showing me how she did it. She opened the mouth of the purse, but not very wide, and held it up to me. "Go ahead, darling, and listen for a second."

I put my head near the handbag, but not too near. I didn't hear anything. "I don't hear anything," I said.

"The poor dog is probably asleep," Zofia said. "Even nightmares have to sleep now and then."

After he got expelled, everybody at school called Jake Houdini instead of Jake. Everybody except for me. I'll explain why, but you have to be patient. It's hard work telling everything in the right order.

Jake is smarter and also taller than most of our teachers. Not quite as tall as me. We've known each other since third grade. Jake has always been in love with me. He says he was in love with me even before third grade, even before we ever met. It took me a while to fall in love with Jake.

In third grade, Jake knew everything already, except how to make friends. He used to follow me around all day long. It made me so mad that I kicked him in the knee. When that didn't work, I threw his backpack out the window of the school bus. That didn't work either, but the next year Jake took some tests and the school decided that he could skip fourth and fifth grade. Even I felt sorry for Jake then. Sixth grade didn't work out. When the sixth graders wouldn't stop flushing his head down the toilet, he went out and caught a skunk and set it loose in the boys' locker room.

The school was going to suspend him for the rest of the year, but instead Jake took two years off while his mother homeschooled him. He learned Latin and Hebrew and Greek, how to write sestinas, how to make sushi, how to play bridge, and even how to knit. He learned fencing and ballroom dancing. He worked in a soup kitchen and made a Super 8 movie about Civil War reenactors who play extreme croquet in full costume instead of firing off cannons. He started learning how to play guitar. He even wrote a novel. I've never read it—he says it was awful.

When he came back two years later, because his mother had cancer for the first time, the school put him back with our year, in seventh grade. He was still way too smart, but he was finally smart enough to figure out how to fit in. Plus he was good at soccer and he was yummy. Did I mention that he played guitar? Every girl in school had a crush on Jake, but he used to come home after school with me and play Scrabble with Zofia and ask her about Baldeziwurlekistan.

Jake's mom was named Cynthia. She collected ceramic frogs and knock-knock jokes. When we were in ninth grade, she had cancer again. When she died, Jake smashed all of her frogs. That was the first funeral I ever went to. A few months later, Jake's father asked Jake's fencing teacher out on a date. They got married right after the school expelled Jake for his AP project on Houdini. That was the first wedding I ever went to. Jake and I stole a bottle of wine and drank it, and I threw up in the swimming pool at the country club. Jake threw up all over my shoes.

So, anyway, the village and the people under the hill lived happily ever after for a few weeks in the handbag, which they had tied around a rock in a dry well that the people under the hill had determined would survive the earthquake. But some of the Baldeziwurlekistanians wanted to come out again and see what was going on in the world. Zofia was one of them. It had been summer when they went into the bag, but when they came out again, and climbed out of the well, snow was falling and their village was ruins and crumbly old rubble. They walked through the snow, Zofia carrying the handbag, until they came to another village, one that they'd never seen before. Everyone in that village was packing up their belongings and leaving, which gave Zofia and her friends a bad feeling. It seemed to be just the same as when they went into the handbag.

They followed the refugees, who seemed to know where they were going, and finally everyone came to a city. Zofia had never seen such a place. There were trains and electric lights and movie theaters, and there were people shooting each other. Bombs were falling. A war going on. Most of the villagers decided to climb right back inside the handbag, but Zofia volunteered to stay in the world and look after the handbag. She had fallen in love with movies and silk stockings and with a young man, a Russian deserter.

Zofia and the Russian deserter married and had many adventures and finally came to America, where my mother was born. Now and then Zofia would consult the tiles and talk to the people who lived in the handbag and they would tell her how best to avoid trouble and how she and her husband could make some money. Every now and then one of the Baldeziwudekistanians or one of the people from under the hill came out of the handbag and wanted to go grocery shopping, or to a movie or an amusement park to ride on roller coasters, or to the library.

The more advice Zofia gave her husband, the more money they made. Her husband became curious about Zofia's handbag, because he could see that there was something odd about it, but Zofia told him to mind his own business. He began to spy on Zofia, and saw that strange men and women were coming in and out of the house. He became convinced that either Zofia was a spy for the Communists, or maybe that she was having affairs. They fought and he drank more and more, and finally he threw away her divination tiles. "Russians make bad husbands," Zofia told me. Finally, one night while Zofia was sleeping, her husband opened the bone clasp and climbed inside the handbag.

"I thought he'd left me," Zofia said. "For almost twenty years I thought he'd left me and your mother and taken off for California. Not that I minded. I was tired of being married and cooking dinners and cleaning house for someone else. It's better to cook what I want to eat, and clean up when I decide to clean up. It was harder on your mother, not having a father. That was the part that I minded most.

"Then it turned out that he hadn't run away after all. He spent one night in the handbag and came out again twenty years later, exactly as handsome as I remembered, and enough time had passed that I had forgiven him all the quarrels. We made up and it was all very romantic and then when we had another fight the next morning, he went and kissed your mother, who had slept right through his visit, on the cheek, and then he climbed right back inside the handbag. I didn't see him again for another twenty years. The last time he showed up, we went to see *Star Wars* and he liked it so much that he went back inside the handbag to tell everyone else about it. In a couple of years they'll all show up and want to see it on video and all of the sequels too."

"Tell them not to bother with the prequels," I said.

The thing about Zofia and libraries is that she's always losing library books. She says that she hasn't lost them, and in fact that they aren't even overdue, really. It's just that even one week inside the faery handbag is a lot longer in library-world time. So what is she supposed to do about it? The librarians all hate Zofia. She's banned from using any of the branches in our area. When I was eight, she got me to go to the library for her and check out biographies and science books and Georgette Heyer romance novels. My mother was livid when she found out, but it was too late. Zofia had already misplaced most of them.

It's really hard to write about somebody as if they're really dead. I still think Zofia must be sitting in her living room, in her house, watching some old horror movie, dropping popcorn into her handbag. She's waiting for me to come over and play Scrabble.

Nobody is ever going to return those library books now.

My mother used to come home from work and roll her eyes. "Have you been telling them your fairy stories?" she'd say. "Genevieve, your grandmother is a horrible liar."

Zofia would fold up the Scrabble board and shrug at me and Jake. "I'm a wonderful liar," she'd say. "I'm the best liar in the world. Promise me you won't believe a single word."

But she wouldn't tell the story of the faery handbag to Jake. Only the old Baldeziwurlek-istanian folktales and fairy tales about the people under the hill. She told him about how she and her husband made it all the way across Europe, hiding in haystacks and in barns. What she told me was how once, when her husband went off to find food, a farmer found her hiding in his chicken coop and tried to rape her. But she opened up the faery handbag in the way she showed me, and the dog came out and ate the farmer and all his chickens too.

She was teaching Jake and me how to curse in Baldeziwurleki. I also know how to say *I love you*, but I'm not going to ever say it to anyone again, except to Jake, when I find him.

When I was eight, I believed everything Zofia told me. By the time I was thirteen, I didn't believe a single word. When I was fifteen, I saw a man come out of her house and get on Zofia's three-speed bicycle and ride down the street. He wore funny clothes. He was a lot younger than my mother and father, and even though I'd never seen him before, he was familiar; I followed him on my bike, all the way to the grocery store. I waited just past the checkout lanes while he bought peanut butter, Jack Daniel's, half a dozen instant cameras, and at least sixty packs of Reese's peanut butter cups, three bags of Hershey's Kisses, a handful of Milky Way bars and other stuff from the rack of checkout candy. While the checkout clerk was helping him bag up all of that chocolate, he looked up and saw me.

"Genevieve?" he said. "That's your name, right?"

I turned and ran out of the store. He grabbed up the bags and ran after me. I don't even think he got his change back. I was still running away, and then one of the straps on my flip-flops popped out of the sole, the way they do, and that made me really angry so I just stopped. I turned around.

"Who are you?" I said.

But I already knew. He looked like he could have been my mom's younger brother. He was really cute. I could see why Zofia had fallen in love with him.

His name was Rustan. Zofia told my parents that he was an expert in Baldeziwurlekistanian folklore who would be staying with her for a few days. She brought him over for dinner. Jake was there too, and I could tell that Jake knew something was up. Everybody except my dad knew something was going on.

"You mean Baldeziwurlekistan is a real place?" my mother asked Rustan. "My mother is telling the truth?"

I could see that Rustan was having a hard time with that one. He obviously wanted to say that his wife was a horrible liar, but then where would he be? Then he couldn't be the person that he was supposed to be.

There were probably a lot of things that he wanted to say. What he said was, "This is really good pizza."

Rustan took a lot of pictures at dinner. The next day I went with him to get the pictures developed. He'd brought back some film with him, with pictures he'd taken inside the faery handbag, but those didn't come out well. Maybe the film was too old. We got doubles of the pictures from dinner so that I could have some too. There's a great picture of Jake, sitting outside on the porch. He's laughing, and he has his hand up to his mouth, like he's going to catch the laugh. I have that picture up on my computer, and also up on my wall over my bed.

I bought a Cadbury Creme Egg for Rustan. Then we shook hands and he kissed me once on each cheek. "Give one of those kisses to your mother," he said, and I thought about how the next time I saw him, I might be Zofia's age, and he would be only a few days older. The next time I saw him, Zofia would be dead. Jake and I might have kids. That was too weird.

I know Rustan tried to get Zofia to go back with him, to live in the handbag, but she wouldn't.

"It makes me dizzy in there," she used to tell me. "And they don't have movie theaters. And I have to look after your mother and you. Maybe when you're old enough to look after the handbag, I'll poke my head inside, just long enough for a little visit."

I didn't fall in love with Jake because he was smart. I'm pretty smart myself. I know that smart doesn't mean nice, or even mean that you have a lot of common sense. Look at all the trouble smart people get themselves into.

I didn't fall in love with Jake because he could make maki rolls and had a black belt in fencing, or whatever it is that you get if you're good in fencing. I didn't fall in love with Jake because he plays guitar. He's a better soccer player than he is a guitar player.

Those were the reasons why I went out on a date with Jake. That, and because he asked me. He asked if I wanted to go see a movie, and I asked if I could bring my grandmother and Natalie and Natasha. He said sure and so all five of us sat and watched *Bring It On* and every once in a while Zofia dropped a couple of Milk Duds or some popcorn into her purse. I don't know if she was feeding the dog, or if she'd opened the purse the right way, and was throwing food at her husband.

I fell in love with Jake because he told stupid knock-knock jokes to Natalie, and told Natasha that he liked her jeans. I fell in love with Jake when he took me and Zofia home. He walked her up to her front door and then he walked me up to mine. I fell in love with Jake when he didn't try to kiss me. The thing is, I was nervous about the whole kissing thing. Most guys think that they're better at it than they really are. Not that I think I'm a real genius at kissing either, but I don't think kissing should be a competitive sport. It isn't tennis.

Natalie and Natasha and I used to practice kissing with each other. Just for practice. We got pretty good at it. We could see why kissing was supposed to be fun.

But Jake didn't try to kiss me. Instead he just gave me this really big hug. He put his face in my hair and he sighed. We stood there like that, and then finally I said, "What are you doing?"

"I just wanted to smell your hair," he said.

"Oh," I said. That made me feel weird, but in a good way. I stuck my nose in his hair, which is brown and curly. I smelled it. We stood there and smelled each other's hair, and I felt so good. I felt so happy.

Jake said into my hair, "Do you know that actor John Cusack?"

I said, "Yeah. One of Zofia's favorite movies is *Better Off Dead*. We watch it all the time."

"So he likes to go up to women and smell their armpits."

"Gross!" I said. "That's such a lie! What are you doing now? That tickles."

"I'm smelling your ear," Jake said.

Jake's hair smelled like iced tea with honey in it, after all the ice has melted.

Kissing Jake is like kissing Natalie or Natasha, except that it isn't just for fun. It feels like something there isn't a word for in Scrabble.

The deal with Houdini is that Jake got interested in him during Advanced Placement American History. He and I were both put in tenth-grade history. We were doing biography projects. I was studying Joseph McCarthy. My grandmother had all sorts of stories about McCarthy. She hated him for what he did to Hollywood.

Jake didn't turn in his project—instead he told everyone in our AP class except for Mr. Streep (we call him Meryl) to meet him at the gym on Saturday. When we showed up, Jake reenacted one of Houdini's escapes with a laundry bag, handcuffs, a gym locker, bicycle chains, and the school's swimming pool. It took him three and a half minutes to get free, and this guy named Roger took a bunch of photos and then put the photos online. One of the photos ended up in the *Boston Globe,* and Jake got expelled. The really ironic thing was that while his mom was in the hospital, Jake had applied to M.I.T. He did it for his mom. He thought that way she'd have to stay alive. She was so excited about M.I.T. A couple of days after he'd been expelled, right after the wedding, while his dad and the fencing instructor were

585

in Bermuda, he got an acceptance letter in the mail and a phone call from this guy in the admissions office who explained why they had to withdraw the acceptance.

⁂

My mother wanted to know why I let Jake wrap himself up in bicycle chains and then watched while Peter and Michael pushed him into the deep end of the school pool. I said that Jake had a backup plan. Ten more seconds and we were all going to jump into the pool and open the locker and get him out of there. I was crying when I said that. Even before he got in the locker, I knew how stupid Jake was being. Afterwards, he promised me that he'd never do anything like that again.

That was when I told him about Zofia's husband, Rustan, and about Zofia's handbag. How stupid am I?

So I guess you can figure out what happened next. The problem is that Jake believed me about the handbag. We spent a lot of time over at Zofia's, playing Scrabble. Zofia never let the faery handbag out of her sight. She even took it with her when she went to the bathroom. I think she even slept with it under her pillow.

I didn't tell her that I'd said anything to Jake. I wouldn't ever have told anybody else about it. Not Natasha. Not even Natalie, who is the most responsible person in all of the world. Now, of course, if the handbag turns up and Jake still hasn't come back, I'll have to tell Natalie. Somebody has to keep an eye on the stupid thing while I go find Jake.

What worries me is that maybe one of the Baldeziwurlekistanians or one of the people under the hill or maybe even Rustan popped out of the handbag to run an errand and got worried when Zofia wasn't there. Maybe they'll come looking for her and bring it back. Maybe they know I'm supposed to look after it now. Or maybe they took it and hid it somewhere. Maybe someone turned it in at the lost-and-found at the library and that stupid librarian called the FBI. Maybe scientists at the Pentagon are examining the handbag right now. Testing it. If Jake comes out, they'll think he's a spy or a superweapon or an alien or something. They're not going to just let him go.

Everyone thinks Jake ran away, except for my mother, who is convinced that he was trying out another Houdini escape and is probably lying at the bottom of a lake somewhere. She hasn't said that to me, but I can see her thinking it. She keeps making cookies for me.

What happened is that Jake said, "Can I see that for just a second?"

He said it so casually that I think he caught Zofia off guard. She was reaching into the purse for her wallet. We were standing in the lobby of the movie theater on a Monday morning. Jake was behind the snack counter. He'd gotten a job there. He was wearing this stupid red paper hat and some kind of apron bib thing. He was supposed to ask us if we wanted to supersize our drinks.

He reached over the counter and took Zofia's handbag right out of her hand. He closed it and then he opened it again. I think he opened it the right way. I don't think he ended up in the dark place. He said to me and Zofia, "I'll be right back." And then be wasn't there anymore. It was just me and Zofia and the handbag, lying there on the counter where he'd dropped it.

If I'd been fast enough, I think I could have followed him. But Zofia had been guardian of the faery handbag for a lot longer. She snatched the bag back and glared at me. "He's a very bad boy," she said. She was absolutely furious. "You're better off without him, Genevieve, I think."

"Give me the handbag," I said. "I have to go get him."

"It isn't a toy, Genevieve," she said. "It isn't a game. This isn't Scrabble. He comes back when he comes back. If he comes back."

"Give me the handbag," I said. "Or I'll take it from you."

She held the handbag up high over her head, so that I couldn't reach it. I hate people who are taller than me. "What are you going to do now?" Zofia said. "Are you going to knock me down? Are you going to steal the handbag? Are you going to go away and leave me here to explain to your parents where you've gone? Are you going to say good-bye to your friends? When you come out again, they will have gone to college. They'll have jobs and babies and houses and they won't even recognize you. Your mother will be an old woman and I will be dead."

"I don't care," I said. I sat down on the sticky red carpet in the lobby and started to cry. Someone wearing a little metal name tag came over and asked if we were okay. His name was Missy. Or maybe he was wearing someone else's tag.

"We're fine," Zofia said. "My granddaughter has the flu."

She took my hand and pulled me up. She put her arm around me and we walked out of the theater. We never even got to see the stupid movie. We never even got to see another movie together. I don't ever want to go see another movie. The problem is, I don't want to see unhappy endings. And I don't know if I believe in the happy ones.

"I have a plan," Zofia said. "I will go find Jake. You will stay here and look after the handbag."

"You won't come back either," I said. I cried even harder. "Or if you do, I'll be like a hundred years old and Jake will still be sixteen."

"Everything will be okay," Zofia said. I wish I could tell you how beautiful she looked right then. It didn't matter if she was lying or if she actually knew that everything was going to be okay. The important thing was how she looked when she said it. She said, with absolute certainty, or maybe with all the skill of a very skillful liar, "My plan will work. First we go to the library, though. One of the people under the hill just brought back an Agatha Christie mystery, and I need to return it."

"We're going to the library?" I said. "Why don't we just go home and play Scrabble for a while." You probably think I was just being sarcastic here, and I was being sarcastic. But Zofia gave me a sharp look. She knew that if I was being sarcastic then my brain was working again. She knew that I knew she was stalling for time. She knew that I was coming up with my own plan, which was a lot like Zofia's plan, except that I was the one who went into the handbag. *How* was the part I was working on.

"We could do that," she said. "Remember, when you don't know what to do, it never hurts to play Scrabble. It's like reading the I Ching or tea leaves."

"Can we please just hurry?" I said.

Zofia just looked at me. "Genevieve, we have plenty of time. If you're going to look after the handbag, you have to remember that. You have to be patient. Can you be patient?"

"I can try," I told her. I'm trying, Zofia. I'm trying really hard. But it isn't fair. Jake is off having adventures and talking to talking animals, and who knows, learning how to fly and some beautiful three-thousand-year-old girl from under the hill is teaching him how to speak fluent Baldeziwurleki. I bet she lives in a house that runs around on chicken legs, and she tells Jake that she'd love to hear him play something on the guitar. Maybe you'll kiss her, Jake, because she's put a spell on you. But whatever you do, don't go up into her house. Don't fall asleep in her bed. Come back soon, Jake, and bring the handbag with you.

I hate those movies, those books, where some guy gets to go off and have adventures and meanwhile the girl has to stay home and wait. I'm a feminist. I subscribe to *Bust* magazine, and I watch *Buffy* reruns. I don't believe in that kind of shit.

We hadn't been in the library for five minutes before Zofia picked up a biography of Carl Sagan and dropped it in her purse. She was definitely stalling for time. She was trying to come up with a plan that would counteract the plan that she knew I was planning. I wondered what she thought I was planning. It was probably much better than anything I'd come up with.

"Don't do that!" I said.

"Don't worry," Zofia said. "Nobody was watching."

"I don't care if nobody saw! What if Jake's sitting there in the boat, or what if he was coming back and you just dropped it on his head!"

"It doesn't work that way," Zofia said. Then she said, "It would serve him right, anyway."

That was when the librarian came up to us. She had a name tag on as well. I was so sick of people and their stupid name tags. I'm not even going to tell you what her name was. "I saw that," the librarian said.

"Saw what?" Zofia said. She smiled down at the librarian, like she was Queen of the Library, and the librarian was a petitioner.

The librarian stared hard at her. "I know you," she said, almost sounding awed, like she was a weekend bird-watcher who had just seen Bigfoot. "We have your picture on the office wall. You're Ms. Swink. You aren't allowed to check out books here."

"That's ridiculous," Zofia said. She was at least two feet taller than the librarian. I felt a bit sorry for the librarian. After all, Zofia had just stolen a seven-day book. She probably wouldn't return it for a hundred years. My mother has always made it clear that it's my job to protect other people from Zofia. I guess I was Zofia's guardian before I became the guardian of the handbag.

The librarian reached up and grabbed Zofia's handbag. She was small but she was strong. She jerked the handbag and Zofia stumbled and fell back against a work desk. I couldn't believe it. Everyone except for me was getting a look at Zofia's handbag. What kind of guardian was I going to be?

"Genevieve," Zofia said. She held my hand very tightly, and I looked at her. She looked wobbly and pale. She said, "I feel very bad about all of this. Tell your mother I said so."

Then she said one last thing, but I think it was in Baldeziwurleki.

The librarian said, "I saw you put a book in here. Right here." She opened the handbag and peered inside. Out of the handbag came a long, lonely, ferocious, utterly hopeless scream of rage. I don't ever want to hear that noise again. Everyone in the library looked up. The librarian made a choking noise and threw Zofia's handbag away from her. A little trickle of blood came out of her nose and a drop fell on the floor. What I thought at first was that it was just plain luck that the handbag was closed when it landed. Later on I was trying to figure out what Zofia said. My Baldeziwurleki isn't very good, but I think she was saying something like "Figures. Stupid librarian. I have to go take care of that damn dog." So maybe that's what happened. Maybe Zofia sent part of herself in there with the skinless dog. Maybe she fought it and won and closed the handbag. Maybe she made friends with it. I mean, she used to feed it popcorn at the movies. Maybe she's still in there.

What happened in the library was Zofia sighed a little and closed her eyes. I helped her sit down in a chair, but I don't think she was really there anymore. I rode with her in the ambulance, when the ambulance finally showed up, and I swear I didn't even think about the handbag until my mother showed up. I didn't say a word. I just left her there in the hospital with Zofia, who was on a respirator, and I ran all the way back to the library. But it was closed. So I ran all the way back again, to the hospital, but you already know what happened, right? Zofia died. I hate writing that. My tall, funny, beautiful, book-stealing, Scrabble-playing, storytelling grandmother died.

But you never met her. You're probably wondering about the handbag. What happened to it. I put up signs all over town, like Zofia's handbag was some kind of lost dog, but nobody ever called.

So that's the story so far. Not that I expect you to believe any of it. Last night Natalie and Natasha came over and we played Scrabble. They don't really like Scrabble, but they feel like it's their job to cheer me up. I won. After they went home, I flipped all the tiles upside-down and then I started picking them up in groups of seven. I tried to ask a question, but it was hard to pick just one. The words I got weren't so great either, so I decided that they weren't English words. They were Baldeziwurleki words.

Once I decided that, everything became perfectly clear. First I put down *kirif*, which means "happy news", and then I got a *b*, an *o*, an *l*, an *e*, an *f*, another *i*, an *s*, and a *z*. So then I could make *kirif* into *bolekirifisz*, which could mean "the happy result of a combination of diligent effort and patience."

I would find the faery handbag. The tiles said so. I would work the clasp and go into the handbag and have my own adventures and would rescue Jake. Hardly any time would have gone by before we came back out of the handbag. Maybe I'd even make friends with that poor dog and get to say good-bye, for real, to Zofia. Rustan would show up again and be really sorry that he'd missed Zofia's funeral and this time he would be brave enough to tell my mother the whole story. He would tell her that he was her father. Not that she would believe him. Not that you should believe this story. Promise me that you won't believe a word.

The Departure of the Train
(1974)

CLARICE LISPECTOR

The departure was from Central Station, with its enormous clock, the largest in the world. It showed the time as six in the morning. Angela Pralini paid for her taxi and picked up her small suitcase. Dona Maria Rita Alvarenga Chagas Souza Melo emerged from her daughter's Opala and set off toward the tracks. A well-dressed elderly lady with jewels. From the wrinkles that masked her came the pure form of a nose lost in age and of a mouth that once must have been full and sensitive. But what does it matter. You reach a certain point—and what once was, no longer matters. A new race begins. An old woman cannot make herself understood. She received a cold kiss from her daughter, who left before the train departed. She had first helped her up into the car. Since no middle seats were free, she had taken a place to one side. When the locomotive began to move, it surprised her a bit: she hadn't expected the train to go in that direction and had seated herself facing backward.

Angela Pralini noticed her startled movement and asked: "Would you like to change places with me?"

Dona Maria Rita, delicately surprised, said no, thank you, for her it was all the same. But she seemed troubled. She passed her hand over her cameo, with its gold filigree, pinned to her breast, fumbled at her broach, took her hand away, lifted it to her felt hat with its cloth rose, and again took it away. Stiff. Offended? Finally she asked Angela Pralini:

"Could it be for my sake you're offering to change seats?"

Surprised, Angela Pralini said no, and the old woman was surprised for the same reason: one doesn't accept favors from an old lady. She smiled a little too much, and her stretched lips covered with talcum powder split into dry furrows: she was enchanted. And a bit excited:

"How very nice of you," she said, "how very kind."

There was a moment of confusion as Angela Pralini also laughed, and the old woman continued to laugh, showing her spotless dentures. She gave a discreet little pull downward on her belt, which was too tight.

"How kind of you," she repeated.

She then composed herself again, rather suddenly, crossing her hands over her purse, which held everything you could imagine. Her wrinkles, when she laughed, had taken on meaning, thought Angela. Now they were once again incomprehensible, superimposed once again on a face unmalleable. But Angela had already broken her tranquillity. She had already seen many nervous young ladies telling themselves: if I laugh anymore I will ruin everything, it will be ridiculous, I have to stop—and it had been impossible. The situation

591

was very sad. With great pity, Angela saw a cruel wart on her chin, a wart from which emerged a stiff black hair. But Angela had taken her peace away. You could see she was about to smile at any moment: Angela had the old woman on tenterhooks. Now she was one of those little old ladies who seem to think that they are always late, that the hour has passed. A moment later she couldn't contain herself and got up to look out the window, as if it were impossible to stay seated.

"Are you trying to close the window, ma'am," said a young fellow listening to Handel on a transistor radio.

"Ah," she exclaimed, terrified.

Oh, no, thought Angela, everything was getting spoiled, the young man shouldn't have said that, it was too much, no one should have touched her again. For the old woman, almost on the point of losing the attitude which had sustained her throughout life, almost about to lose a certain bitterness, quavered like harpsichord music between a smile and the deepest enchantment:

"No, no, no," she said with a false tone of authority, "not at all, thank you, I only wanted to look out."

She sat down immediately as if being observed by the politeness of the young man and the girl. The old woman, before getting into the train, had made the sign of the cross three times over her heart, discreetly kissing her fingertips. She was in a black dress with a genuine lace collar and a cameo of pure gold. On her dark left hand were a widow's two thick wedding rings, thick the way they don't make them anymore. From the next car you could hear a group of girl scouts singing their high-pitched praises of "Brazil." Luckily it was in the next car. The music on the young fellow's radio merged with the music of another fellow: he was listening to Edith Piaf singing "J'attendrai."

It was then that the train suddenly gave a jolt and the wheels began to move. The departure had begun. The old woman said softly: Ah, Jesus! She had soaked herself in sweet Jesus. Amen. A woman's transistor informed them that it was six-thirty in the morning, a chilly morning. The old woman thought: Brazil was improving its road signs. A certain Kissinger seemed to be running the world.

No one knows where I am, thought Angela Pralini, and this frightened her somewhat, she was a fugitive.

"My name is Maria Rita Alvarenga Chagas Souza Melo—Alvarenga Chagas was my father's surname," she added, as if begging pardon for having to say so many words just in telling her name. "Chagas," she added modestly, "were the Chagas, the 'stigmata,' of Christ. But you can call me Dona Maria Ritinha. And your name? What might one call you?"

"My name is Angela Pralini. I'm going to spend six months with my uncles on their farm. And you?"

"Ah, I'm going to my son's farm. I'm going to stay there for the rest of my life, my daughter took me to the train, and my son will pick me up with his cart at the station. I am like a package being passed from hand to hand."

Angela's uncles had no children and treated her like a daughter. Angela remembered the note she had left for Eduardo: "Don't look for me. I am vanishing from your life forever. I love you more than ever. Farewell. I would have been more yours had you wished it so."

They remained silent. Angela Pralini gave herself up to the rhythmic sound of the train. Dona Maria Rita looked again at that ring of diamonds and pearls on her finger and smoothed down her golden cameo: "I am old but I am rich, richer than anyone in this car. I am rich, I am rich." She glanced at her watch, but in order to see the thick gold plate rather than the time. "I am very rich, I am not just any old lady." But she knew, ah, how well she knew, that she was indeed any old lady, just a little old lady frightened of the littlest things. She remembered herself, the whole day all alone in the rocking chair, alone with the servants, while her "public relations" daughter spent the whole day out, only returning at eight in the evening, and not even giving her a kiss. She had gotten up this morning at five o'clock, everything still dark; and it had been cold.

After the kindness of the young man she had been extraordinarily excited, and all smiles. She looked drained. With her laugh she revealed herself as one of those little old ladies with a mouthful of teeth. The discordant cruelty of teeth. The young man had already moved off. She opened and shut her eyelids. Suddenly she tapped Angela on the thigh, quickly and gently:

"Today everyone is truly, but truly friendly. How really nice, how very nice!"

Angela smiled. The old woman continued to smile without taking her deep and empty eyes from those of the girl. "Come on, let's go, let's go," they snapped at her from all sides, and she looked here and there as if to choose. "Let's go, let's go." They jostled against her, laughing from all sides, and she fluttered, there, smiling, dainty, refined.

"How friendly everyone is on this train," she said.

Suddenly she tried to recompose herself, she cleared her throat unnecessarily, she drew herself in. It was going to be difficult. She feared that she had reached the point where she wouldn't be able to stop herself. She held herself severe and trembling, closing her lips over her innumerable teeth. But she couldn't fool anyone: her face had such hope in it that it disturbed the eyes of whoever looked at her. She no longer depended on anyone: now that they had touched her, she could go away—she, alone, tall, thin, radiant. She still would have liked to say something and in fact was preparing a sociable nod of the head, full of studied grace. Angela wondered if she would know how to express herself. She seemed to be thinking and thinking and then to find with tenderness a thought all ready-made in which somehow or other she could cradle her feelings. She said with the care and wisdom of the aged, as if it were necessary to put on such an air in order to speak like an elderly person:

"Youth! Gracious youth."

Her laughter was somewhat forced. "Was she going to have an attack of nerves?" thought Angela Pralini. For she was so marvelous. But now she cleared her throat again with austerity, tapping the seat with her fingertips as if urgently calling an orchestra to order for a new piece. She opened her purse, took out a small square of newspaper, unfolded it, unfolded it until it had become a large and normal newspaper from three days before—as Angela saw from the date. She began to read.

Angela had lost seven kilos. On the farm she would eat herself sick: bean stew and cabbage á la Mineira, to regain the precious lost kilos. She was this thin from having tried to keep up with Eduardo's brilliant, uninterrupted chain of thought: she had drunk coffee without sugar endlessly in order to stay awake. Angela Pralini had very pretty breasts, they were her strong point. She had pointed ears and a pretty, kissable, rounded mouth. Eyes with dark shadows. She took advantage of the scream of the train's whistle so that it might become her own scream. It was a sharp cry, hers, but turned inward. She was the woman who had drunk the most whiskey in Eduardo's group. She could take six or seven in a row, retaining a terrifying lucidity. At the farm she would drink thick cow's milk. One thing linked the old woman to

Angela: both were going to be received with open arms, but neither knew this of the other. Angela suddenly shivered: who would give the dog its last day of deworming pills. Ah, Ulysses, she thought, to the dog, I didn't abandon you because I wanted to, it's that I had to flee Eduardo, before he destroyed me completely with his lucidity: a lucidity that illumined too much and singed everything. Angela knew that her uncles had a medicine for snakebite: she intended to enter the heart of the thick, verdant forest, with high boots smeared with insect repellent. As if leaving the Transamazonico highway behind, she, the explorer. What beasts would she encounter? It would be better to take along a rifle, food, and water. And a compass. Since having discovered—but having *really* discovered, with a shock—that she would die one day, she had no longer feared life and, thanks to death, now had all her rights: she would risk everything. After having had two relationships that had ended in nothing, this third that had ended in love—adoration, cut short by the fated desire to survive. Eduardo had transformed her: he had given her eyes within. But now she was looking out. Through the window, she saw the mountains, the breasts of the earth. Little birds exist, Eduardo! Clouds exist, Eduardo! There is a world of stallions and mares, and cows, Eduardo, and when I was a girl I raced bareback on a horse, without a saddle! I am fleeing my suicide, Eduardo. I'm sorry, Eduardo, but I don't want to die. I want to be fresh and rare as a pomegranate.

The old woman pretended to be reading the newspaper. But she was thinking: her world was a sigh. She didn't want the others to suppose that she was abandoned. God gave me good health so that I could travel alone. Also my mind is sound, I don't talk to myself, and I bathe on my own every day. She smelled of rose water, of withered macerated roses, her aged and musty perfume. That rhythmic respiration, thought Angela of the old woman, was the most beautiful thing remaining to Dona Maria Rita from her birth. It was life.

Dona Maria Rita was thinking: after getting old, she had begun to disappear for others, had become a passing glimpse. Old age: the supreme moment. She was a stranger to the general strategy of the world and her own was negligible. She had lost the longest-range objectives. She was, in fact, already the future.

Angela thought: I think that if I were to find the truth, I wouldn't be able to think it. It would be mentally unpronounceable.

The old woman had always been a bit empty, a little bit, anyway. Death? It was strange, it wasn't part of the passing days. And even "not to exist" didn't exist, it was impossible not-to-exist. Not to exist didn't fit into our daily life. Her daughter wasn't loving. On the other hand, her son was very loving, good-natured, a bit chubby. The daughter was as bone dry as her rapid little kisses, "public relations." The old woman had a certain laziness about living. It was monotony, however, that sustained her.

Eduardo listened to music with his thoughts. And he understood the dissonance of modern music, he only knew how to understand. His intelligence smothered her. You are temperamental, Angela, he said to her once. And so? What's wrong with that? I am what I am and not what you think I am. The proof that I am is in the departure of this train. My proof is also Dona Maria Rita, there across from me. Proof of what? Yes. She had already had plenitude. When she and Eduardo had been so passionately in love that being beside each other in bed, holding hands, they had felt their lives complete. Few people have known plenitude. And since plenitude is also an explosion, she and Eduardo had, like cowards, begun to live "normally." For you cannot prolong the ecstasy without dying. They had separated for a frivolous, almost artificial reason: they didn't want to die of passion. Plenitude is one of the truths you encounter. But the necessary break was surgery for her, just as there are women whose uteruses and ovaries have been removed. Empty within.

Dona Maria Rita was so ancient that in her daughter's house they were accustomed to her as if to an old piece of furniture. She was news to no one. But it never entered her head that she was a solitary. Just that she had nothing to do. It was an enforced leisure that at times pierced her to the bone: she had nothing to do in the world. Just live like a cat or a dog. She wished she could be an attentive companion to some lady, but such things didn't exist anymore, and anyway no one would believe in her strength at seventy-seven. They would all think she was weak. She didn't do anything, she only did this: to be old. Sometimes she would get depressed: she would feel that she was of no use, no use even to God. Dona Maria Ritinha didn't have an inferno within. Why is it that the old, even those who don't tremble, suggest something delicately tremulous? Dona Maria Rita had a brittle trembling like the music from a hurdy-gurdy.

But when it's a question of life itself—who can shore us up? for each one is a one. And each life has to be supported by its own life, only that one. Each one of us: that's all we can count on. Since Dona Maria Rita had always been an ordinary person, she thought that to die was not a normal thing. To die was surprising. It was as if she wasn't up to the act of death, since until now nothing extraordinary in life had happened to her that could justify all of a sudden another extraordinary event. She spoke and even thought about death, but deep down she was skeptical and suspicious. She believed that you died when there was an accident or when someone killed someone. The old woman had little experience. Sometimes she had palpitations: the heart's bacchanal. But that's all, and it had been with her since girlhood. At her first kiss, for example, her heart had gone out of control. And it had been a good thing alongside the bad. It was something that recalled her past, not as events, but as life: a sensation of vegetation in shadows, ferns, maidenhair, green coolness. When she felt this anew, she smiled. One of the most erudite words she used was "picturesque." It was good. It was like hearing the bubbling of a spring and not knowing where it had its source.

A conversation she carried on with herself:

"Are you doing something?"

"Yes, I am: I'm being sad."

"Doesn't it disturb you to be alone?"

"No, I'm thinking."

Sometimes she didn't think. Sometimes a person just is. She didn't need to be doing. To be was already a doing. One could *be* slowly or somewhat quickly.

On the seat behind, two women talked and talked without end. Their continuous sound mingled with the noise of the train wheels on the tracks.

Indeed, Dona Maria Rita had hoped that her daughter would remain on the platform to give her a little farewell, but it hadn't happened. The train immobile. Until the first lurch came.

"Angela," she said, "a woman never tells her age, so I can only tell you that I am very old. But no, for you—may I speak this way?—I'll tell you a secret: I am seventy-seven years old."

"I'm thirty-seven," said Angela Pralini.

It was seven in the morning.

"When I was young I was quite a little liar. I would lie for nothing just like that."

Later, as if she had become disenchanted with the magic of lies, she had stopped lying.

Angela, looking at old Dona Maria Rita, was afraid of growing old and dying. Hold my hand, Eduardo, so that I won't fear death. But he never held anything. The only thing he did was: think, think, and think. Oh, Eduardo, I need the gentleness of Schumann! Her life was dissolving, an evanescent life. She lacked hard bone, rough and strong, against which no one could do a thing. Who would be that essential bone? To keep at bay her feeling of enormous need, she thought: how did they manage to live in the Middle Ages without telephone and airplane? A mystery. Middle Ages, I adore you, you and your black-laden clouds that streamed into the luminous and fresh Renaissance.

As for the old woman, she had retreated. She was staring at nothingness.

Angela gazed at herself in her little pocket mirror. I look like a swoon. Beware the abyss, I say to the one who looks like a swoon. When I die I will have such a longing for you, Eduardo! The sentence could not stand up to logic, though there was an improbable sense to it. It was as if she had wished to express one thing and had expressed another.

The old woman was already the future. She seemed ashamed. Ashamed of being old? At some point in her life there surely must have been a mistake, and the result was this strange state she was in. Which, however, had not carried her to death. Death was always such a surprise for the one who died. She was, however, proud that she didn't dribble or make weewee in her bed, as if this form of brute health had been the meritorious result of an act of her will. Only she wasn't a lady, an elderly lady, for she had no arrogance: she was a dignified little old creature who suddenly would take on a frightened look. She—well, then, she praised her very self, considering herself an old woman full of precocity like a precocious child. But the true purpose of her life, that she did not know.

Angela dreamed of the farm: there you heard cries, barks, and howling at night. Eduardo, she thought to him, I was tired of trying to be what you assumed I was. I have a bad side—it is the stronger, and it prevailed, although I tried to hide it because of you-on this strong side I'm a cow. I'm a mare running free who paws the ground, I'm a woman of the streets, I'm a slut—and not a "woman of letters." I know that I am intelligent and that sometimes I hide it in order not to offend others with my intelligence, I who am of the subconscious. I fled from you, Eduardo, because you were killing me with your genius—intellect that practically forced me to cover my ears with my hands and scream out in horror and exhaustion. And now I will remain six months on the farm, you don't know where I'll be, and every day I'll bathe in the river, mixing with its clay my own blessed mud. I am vulgar, Eduardo! I want you to know that I like to read true romance magazines, my love, oh my love! how I love you and how I love your terrifying spells, ah, how I adore you, your slave, slave that I am. But I am physical, my love, I am physical, and I had to hide from you the glory of being physical. And you, who are the very splendor of rational thought, though you don't know it, you were nourished by me. You, super-intellectual and brilliant, leaving everyone filled with wonder, mouths agape.

I believe, the old woman said to herself slowly, I believe that that pretty girl is not interested in talking to me. I don't know why, but no one speaks with me anymore. And even when I am right there with people, they seem not to remember me. And after all, it's not my fault I'm old. But it doesn't matter, I'll keep myself company. And I still have Nandinho, my dear son who adores me.

The long-suffering pleasure of scratching oneself! thought Angela. I, eh, I who don't go for this or for that, am free!!! I'm getting healthier, oh to swear out loud and startle everyone. Wouldn't the old lady understand? I don't know, she must have given birth a few times. Unhappiness is the only certainty—I'm not going to fall for that, Eduardo. I want to savor everything and then die and may I be damned! damned! damned! Though the old woman may in fact be unhappy without knowing it. Passivity. I'm not going to fall for that either, no passivity for me.

I want to bathe naked in the muddy river that looks like me, naked and free! Viva! Three vivas! I'm leaving everything behind! everything! and therefore I am not abandoned, I don't want to depend on anyone but some three people and as for the rest: Hello, how are you? O.K. Edu, you know? I'm leaving you. You, in the depths of your intellectualism, aren't worth the life of a dog. I'm leaving you, then. And I'm leaving the pseudo-intellectual group that demanded of me an unending vain and nervous exercise of a false and hurried intelligence. I needed for God to abandon me before I could feel his presence. I need to kill someone within me. You ruined my intelligence with yours, which is that of a genius. And you forced me to know, to know, to know. Ah, Eduardo, don't worry, I'm taking along the books you gave me in order "to do a home study course," as you wished. I will study philosophy beside the river, for the love I bear you.

Angela Pralini had such deep thoughts that there were no words to express them. It was a lie to say that one could only have one thought at a time: she had numerous thoughts that crossed each other, and they were all different. Not to mention the "subconscious" that explodes in me, whether I want it or you don't. I'm a fountain, thought Angela, thinking at the same time where she had put her kerchief, wondering whether the dog had drunk the milk she had left for him, thinking of Eduardo's shirts, and of his extreme physical and mental exhaustion. And of old Dona Maria Rita. I will never forget your face, Eduardo. It was a somewhat surprised face, surprised at its own intelligence. He was ingenuous. And he loved without knowing that he loved. He would be stunned when he discovered that she had gone off, leaving the dog and him. I'm leaving for lack of nourishment, she thought. At the same time she was thinking of the old lady seated across from her. It wasn't true that you thought only one thought at a time. She was able, for example, to write a perfect check, without an error, while thinking of her life. Which wasn't a good one but at least was hers. Hers once again. Coherence, I don't want it anymore. Coherence is mutilation. I want disorder. I only sense through a vehement incoherence. In order to meditate I draw myself before myself and feel the emptiness. It is in emptiness that time passes. She who loved a good beach, with sun, sand and sun. The man is abandoned, he has lost contact with the earth, with the sky. He no longer lives, he exists. The atmosphere between her and Eduardo Gomes was that of an emergency. He had transformed her into an urgent woman. And, one who, to keep the urgency awake, took drugs, stimulants that made her thinner and thinner and killed her appetite. I want to eat, Eduardo, I'm hungry, Eduardo, I'm hungry for lots of food! I'm organic!

"Meet tomorrow's supertrain today." *Reader's Digests* that she used to read behind Eduardo's back. It was like the *Digests* that said: Meet tomorrow's supertrain today. She was positively not meeting it today. But Eduardo was the supertrain. Super everything. She knew today the super of tomorrow. And she couldn't stand it. She couldn't stand the perpetual motion. You are the desert, and I'm going to Oceania, to the South Seas, to Tahiti. Even if it's ruined by tourism. You are no more than a tourist, Eduardo. I am going toward my own life, Edu. And I say, like Fellini: in darkness and ignorance I create more. The life she had with Eduardo smelled like a newly painted pharmacy. She preferred the living smell of manure no matter how nauseating it might be. He was as proper as a tennis court. In fact, he played tennis to keep in shape. When all was said and done, he was a bore, whom she used to love and almost loved no longer. She was recovering here in the train itself her mental health. She remained in love with Eduardo. And he, unknowingly, with her as well. I who can't manage to do anything right, except make omelettes. With one hand alone I would break eggs with incredible speed, and empty them into the bowl without spilling a drop.

Eduardo would die of envy before such elegance and efficiency. He sometimes gave lectures at universities, and they adored him. She, too, attended; she, too, adored him. How was it exactly that he began? "I feel ill at ease seeing people rise upon hearing that I am about to speak." Angela always was afraid that the others would withdraw, leaving them alone.

The old woman, as if she had received a thought transmission, thought: may they not leave me alone. How old am I really? Humph, I don't even remember.

Quickly, then, she emptied her mind. And she was peacefully nothing. Barely existing. It was good like that, really very good. Plunges into nothingness.

Angela Pralini, in order to calm herself, told herself a most calming, most tranquil story: once upon a time there was a man who loved the jaboticaba fruit. So he went to an orchard where there were trees covered with black protuberances, smooth and glistening, which fell with abandon into his hands and from his hands spilled down to his feet. The jaboticaba berries were so abundant that he gave himself the luxury of stepping on them. And they made a most delicious sound. They went: doc-doc-doc etc. Angela calmed down like the jaboticaba man. On the farm they had jaboticaba, and she would make a moist and soft cloc-cloc-cloc with her bare feet. She never knew whether or not you ought to swallow the pits. Who would answer that question? No one. Only perhaps a man who, like Ulysses the dog, and unlike Eduardo, would answer: "Mangia, bella, que te fa bene." She knew a bit of Italian but was never sure of being right. And, after the man spoke those words, she would swallow the pits. Another delicious tree was one whose scientific name she had forgotten but which, in childhood, everyone had known quite directly, without science, one which in the Botanical Garden in Rio made a dry little cloc-cloc. See? See how you are being reborn? A cat's seven breaths. The number seven always accompanied her, was her secret, her strength. She felt beautiful. She wasn't. But that's how she felt. She also felt generous. With tenderness for old Maria Ritinha, who had put on her glasses and was reading the paper. Everything was slow about old Maria Rita. Near her end? ah, how it hurts to die. In life one suffers, but you have something in your hand: ineffable life. But what about the question of death? You had to have no fear: to go forward, always.

Always.

Like the train.

Somewhere there is something written on a wall. And it is for me, thought Angela. From the flames of hell a fresh telegram will come for me. And never again will my hopes be deceived. Never. Never again.

The old woman was as anonymous as a hen, as a certain Clarice had said speaking of a shameless old woman, madly in love with Roberto Carlos. That Clarice made you uncomfortable. She made the old woman cry out: there must be a way out ! And there was, too. For example, the way out for that old lady was her husband, who would return the next day, her acquaintances, her housemaid, intense and fruitful prayer in the face of despair. Angela repeated to herself as if madly biting herself: there must be a way out. For me just as well as for Dona Maria Rita.

I could not stop time, thought Maria Rita Alvarenga Chagas Sousa Melo. I failed. I am old. And she pretended to read the newspaper just to give herself composure.

I need shadows, moaned Angela. I need shadows and anonymity.

The old woman thought: her son was so kind, so warm-hearted, so gentle! He called her "Mom." Yes, perhaps I'll spend the rest of my life on the farm, far from "public relations," who doesn't need me. And my life ought to be very long, to judge by my parents and grandparents. I could easily, easily, reach a hundred, she thought comfortably. And die suddenly in order not to have time to feel fear. She crossed herself discreetly and begged God for a good death.

Ulysses, if his face were seen from a human point of view, would be monstrous and ugly. He was lovely from a dog's point of view. He was filled with vigor like a horse, white and free, only he was a soft brown, orangeish, whiskey-color. But his coat was beautiful like that of an energetic, prancing horse. The muscles of his neck were vigorous, and you could hold those muscles in your hands with knowing fingers. Ulysses was a man. Without a dog's world. He was gentle like a man. A woman must treat a man well.

The train coming to the fields: the crickets cricketing, high pitched and shrill.

Eduardo, once in a while, awkwardly, like someone forced to fulfill a function—would present her with the gift of an icy, uncut, diamond stone. She who preferred them cut. Well, she sighed, things are as they are. At times, looking down from her apartment, she had felt like killing herself. Ah, not because of Eduardo, but because of a kind of fatal curiosity. She wouldn't tell this to anyone, for fear of influencing a latent suicide. She wanted life, life flat and full, really nice, reading *Reader's Digest* for all to see. She wanted to die at ninety, not before, in the middle of an act of life, without feeling a thing. The ghost of madness stalks us. What are you doing? I am awaiting the future.

When the train had finally set in motion, Angela Pralini had lit her cigarette in hallelujah: she had feared before the train had left that she wouldn't have the courage to go and would end up getting off. But after a bit they had become aware of the action of shock-absorbers and, despite this, the sudden jolts of the wheels. The train was moving. And old Maria Rita sighed: she was closer to her beloved son. With him she could be a mother, she who was castrated by her daughter.

Once when Angela had had menstrual cramps, Eduardo had tried, quite awkwardly, to comfort her. And he had said something horrid to her: It was enough to make you blush with shame. You've got a tummy ache, don't you?

The train rushed on as fast as it could. The engineer delighted: this is the good life, and he blew the whistle at every curve. It was the long, heavy whistle of a train underway, clicking off the miles. The morning was cool and full of high green grasses. Yes, that's the way, onward, onward, said the engineer to the engine. The engine responded joyfully.

The old woman was nothing. And gazed into the air as one looks at God. She was made of God. That is, of all or nothing. The old woman was vulnerable, Angela thought. Vulnerable to love, love of her son. The mother was Franciscan, the daughter pollution.

God, thought Angela, if you exist, reveal yourself! For the hour has come. It is this hour, this minute, and this second.

And the result was that she had to hide the tears that came to her eyes. God in some way had answered her. She was happy and swallowed a muffled sob. How painful life was. Living was an open wound. To live is to be like my dog. Ulysses has nothing in common with Joyce's Ulysses. I tried to read Joyce, but I stopped because he was boring, sorry, Eduardo. Only he's a boring genius. Angela was feeling love for the old woman who was nothing, the mother she lacked. A mother, gentle, ingenuous, long-suffering. Her mother who had died when she was nine years old. Even sick, just being alive was enough. Even paralyzed.

Between her and Eduardo the air tasted like Saturday. And suddenly the two of them were rare, a rarity in the air. They felt rare, apart from the thousand people walking in the streets.

At times the two were accomplices, they had a secret life because no one would have understood them. And also because rare ones are persecuted by the people who do not tolerate the insulting offence of those who are different. They hid their love in order not to wound the eyes of others with envy. In order not to wound them with a spark too luminous for eyes.

Bowwow wow, yapped my dog. My big puppy.

The old woman thought: I am an involuntary person. So much so that when she laughed—which was rare—you didn't know if she were laughing or crying. Yes. She was involuntary.

Meanwhile Angela Pralini, fizzling like the bubbles in Caxamba mineral water, was one too: all of a sudden. Just like that. All of a sudden what? Just all of a sudden. Zero. Nothing. She was thirty-seven years old and always intending to begin her life anew. Like the fizzling effervescent bubbles of Caxamba water. The seven letters of Pralini gave her strength. The six letters of Angela made her anonymous.

With a drawn-out wailing whistle, they arrived at the small station where Angela Pralini was going to jump out. She picked up her suitcase. In the space between the porter's cap and the nose of a young woman, there was the old lady sleeping, inflexible, her head priggishly erect beneath its felt hat, her fist closed over the newspaper.

Angela stepped down from the train.

Naturally this hadn't the slightest importance: there are people who always tend to regret, it's a trait of certain guilty natures. But the vision of the old woman waking up, the image of her face, surprised by Angela's empty seat, began to disturb her. In the end no one could know if she had fallen asleep thanks to her trust in Angela.

Trust in the world.

In a Far Country
(1899)

JACK LONDON

When a man journeys into a far country, he must be prepared to forget many of the things he has learned, and to acquire such customs as are inherent with existence in the new land; he must abandon the old ideals and the old gods, and oftentimes he must reverse the very codes by which his conduct has hitherto been shaped. To those who have the protean faculty of adaptability, the novelty of such change may even be a source of pleasure; but to those who happen to be hardened to the ruts in which they were created, the pressure of the altered environment is unbearable, and they chafe in body and in spirit under the new restrictions which they do not understand. This chafing is bound to act and react, producing divers evils and leading to various misfortunes. It were better for the man who cannot fit himself to the new groove, to return to his own country; if he delay too long, he will surely die.

The man who turns his back upon the comforts of an elder civilization, to face the savage youth, the primordial simplicity of the North, may estimate success at an inverse ratio to the quantity and quality of his hopelessly fixed habits. He will soon discover, if he be a fit candidate, that the material habits are the less important. The exchange of such things as a dainty menu for rough fare, of the stiff leather shoe for the soft, shapeless moccasin, of the feather bed for a couch in the snow, is after all a very easy matter. But his pinch will come in learning properly to shape his mind's attitude toward all things, and especially toward his fellowman. For the courtesies of ordinary life, he must substitute unselfishness, forbearance, and tolerance. Thus, and thus only, can he gain that pearl of great price,—true comradeship. He must not say "Thank you"; he must mean it without opening his mouth, and prove it by responding in kind. In short, he must substitute the deed for the word, the spirit for the letter.

When the world rang with the tale of Arctic gold, and the lure of the North gripped the heartstrings of men, Carter Weatherbee threw up his snug clerkship, turned the half of his savings over to his wife, and with the remainder bought an oufit. There was no romance in his nature,—the bondage of commerce had crushed all that; he was simply tired of the ceaseless grind, and wished to risk great hazards in view of corresponding returns. Like many another fool, disdaining the old trails used by the Northland pioneers for a score of years, he hurried to Edmonton in the spring of the year,—and there, unluckily for his soul's welfare, he allied himself with a party of men.

There was nothing unusual about this party, except its plans. Even its goal, like that of all other parties, was the Klondike. But the route it had mapped out to attain that goal, took away the breath of the hardiest native, born and bred to the vicissitudes of the Northwest. Even Jacques Baptiste, born of a Chippewa woman and a renegade *voyageur*, (having raised his first whimpers in a deerskin lodge north of the sixty-fifth parallel, and had the same hushed by blissful sucks of raw tallow,) was surprised. Though he sold his services to them and agreed to travel even to the never-opening ice, he shook his head ominously whenever his advice was asked.

Percy Cuthfert's evil star must have been in the ascendant, for he too joined this company of argonauts. He was an ordinary man, with a bank account as deep as his culture, which is saying a good deal. He had no reason to embark on such a venture,—no reason in the world, save that he suffered from an abnormal development of sentimentality. He mistook this for the true spirit of romance and adventure. Many another man has done the like, and made as fatal a mistake.

The first break-up of spring found the party following the ice-run of Elk River. It was an imposing fleet, for the outfit was large and they were accompanied by a disreputable contingent of half-breed *voyageurs* with their women and children. Day in and day out, they labored with the batteaus and canoes, fought mosquitoes and other kindred pests, or sweated and swore at the portages. Severe toil like this lays a man naked to the very roots of his soul, and ere Lake Athabasca was lost in the south, each member of the party had hoisted his true colors.

The two shirks and chronic grumblers were Carter Weatherbee and Percy Cuthfert. The whole party complained less of its aches and pains than did either of them. Not once did they volunteer for the thousand and one petty duties of the camp. A bucket of water to be brought, an extra armful of wood to be chopped, the dishes to be washed and wiped, a search to be made through the outfit for some suddenly indispensable article,—and these two effete scions of civilization discovered sprains or blisters requiring instant attention. They were the first to turn in at night, with a score of tasks yet undone; the last to turn out in the morning, when the start should be in readiness before the breakfast was begun. They were the first to fall to at meal-time, the last to have a hand in the cooking; the first to dive for a slim delicacy, the last to discover they had added to their own another man's share. If they toiled at the oars, they slyly cut the water at each stroke and allowed the boat's momentum to float up the blade. They thought nobody noticed; but their comrades swore under their breaths and grew to hate them, while Jacques Baptiste sneered openly and damned them from morning till night. But he was no gentleman.

At the Great Slave, Hudson Bay dogs were purchased, and the fleet sank to the guards with its added burden of dried fish and pemmican. Then canoe and batteau answered to the swift current of the Mackenzie, and they plunged into the Great Barren Ground. Every likely-looking "feeder" was prospected, but the elusive "pay-dirt" danced ever to the north. At the Great Bear, overcome by the common dread of the Unknown Lands, their *voyageurs* began to desert, and Fort of Good Hope saw the last and bravest bending to the tow-lines as they bucked the current down which they had so treacherously glided. Jacques Baptiste alone remained. Had he not sworn to travel even to the never-opening ice?

The lying charts, compiled in main from hearsay, were now constantly consulted. And they felt the need of hurry, for the sun had already passed its northern solstice and was leading the winter south again. Skirting the shores of the bay, where the Mackenzie disembogues into the Arctic Ocean, they entered the mouth of the Little Peel River. Then began the arduous up-stream toil, and the two Incapables fared worse than ever. Tow-line and pole, paddle and tump-line, rapids and portages,—such tortures served to give the one a deep disgust for great hazards, and printed for the other a fiery text on the true romance of adventure. One day they waxed mutinous, and being vilely cursed by Jacques Baptiste, turned, as worms sometimes will. But the half-breed thrashed the twain, and sent them, bruised and bleeding, about their work. It was the first time either had been manhandled.

Abandoning their river craft at the head-waters of the Little Peel, they consumed the rest of the summer in the great portage over the Mackenzie watershed to the West Rat. This little stream fed the Porcupine, which in turn joined the Yukon where that mighty highway of the North countermarches on the Arctic Circle. But they had lost in the race with winter, and one day they tied their rafts to the thick eddy-ice and hurried their goods ashore. That night the river jammed and broke several times; the following morning it had fallen asleep for good.

"We can't be more 'n four hundred miles from the Yukon," concluded Sloper, multiplying his thumb nails by the scale of the map. The council, in which the two Incapables had whined to excellent disadvantage, was drawing to a close.

"Hudson Bay Post, long time ago. No use um now." Jacques Baptiste's father had made the trip for the Fur Company in the old days, incidentally marking the trail with a couple of frozen toes.

"Sufferin' cracky!" cried another of the party. "No whites?"

"Nary white," Sloper sententiously affirmed; "but it's only five hundred more up the Yukon to Dawson. Call it a rough thousand from here."

Weatherbee and Cuthfert groaned in chorus.

"How long'll that take, Baptiste?"

The half-breed figured for a moment. "Workum like hell, no man play out, ten—twenty—forty—fifty days. Um babies come," (designating the Incapables,) "no can tell. Mebbe when hell freeze over; mebbe not then."

The manufacture of snow-shoes and moccasins ceased. Somebody called the name of an absent member, who came out of an ancient cabin at the edge of the camp-fire and joined them. The cabin was one of the many mysteries which lurk in the vast recesses of the North. Built when and by whom, no man could tell. Two graves in the open, piled high with stones, perhaps contained the secret of those early wanderers. But whose hand had piled the stones?

The moment had come. Jacques Baptiste paused in the fitting of a harness and pinned the struggling dog in the snow. The cook made mute protest for delay, threw a handful of bacon into a noisy pot of beans, then came to attention. Sloper rose to his feet. His body was a ludicrous contrast to the healthy physiques of the Incapables. Yellow and weak, fleeing from a South American fever-hole, he had not broken his flight across the zones, and was still able to toil with men. His weight was probably ninety pounds, with the heavy hunting-knife thrown in, and his grizzled hair told of a prime which had ceased to be. The fresh, young muscles of either Weatherbee or Cuthfert were equal to ten times the endeavor of his; yet he could walk them into the earth in a day's journey. And all this day he had whipped his stronger comrades into venturing a thousand miles of the stiffest hardship man can conceive. He was the incarnation of the unrest of his race, and the old Teutonic stubbornness, dashed with the quick grasp and action of the Yankee, held the flesh in the bondage of the spirit.

"All those in favor of going on with the dogs as soon as the ice sets, say aye."

"Aye!" rang out eight voices,—voices destined to string a trail of oaths along many a hundred miles of pain.

"Contrary minded?"

"No!" For the first time the Incapables were united without some compromise of personal interests.

"And what are you going to do about it?" Weatherbee added belligerently.

"Majority rule! Majority rule!" clamored the rest of the party.

"I know the expedition is liable to fall through if you don't come," Sloper replied sweetly; "but I guess, if we try real hard, we can manage to do without you. What do you say, boys?"

The sentiment was cheered to the echo.

"But I say, you know," Cuthfert ventured apprehensively; "what's a chap like me to do?"

"Ain't you coming with us?"

"No—o."

"Then do as you d—n well please. We won't have nothing to say."

"Kind o' calkilate yuh might settle it with that canoodlin' pardner of yourn," suggested a heavy-going Westerner from the Dakotas, at the same time pointing out Weatherbee. "He'll be shore to ask yuh what yur a-goin' to do when it comes to cookin' an' gatherin' the wood."

"Then we'll consider it all arranged," concluded Sloper. "We'll pull out tomorrow, if we camp within five miles,—just to get everything in running order and remember if we've forgotten anything."

The sleds groaned by on their steel-shod runners, and the dogs strained low in the harnesses in which they were born to die. Jacques Baptiste paused by the side of Sloper to get a last glimpse of the cabin. The smoke curled up pathetically from the Yukon stove-pipe. The two Incapables were watching them from the doorway.

Sloper laid his hand on the other's shoulder. "Jacques Baptiste, did you ever hear of the Kilkenny cats?"

The half-breed shook his head.

"Well, my friend and good comrade, the Kilkenny cats fought till neither hide, nor hair, nor yowl, was left. You understand?—till nothing was left. Very good. Now, these two men, don't like work. They won't work. We know that. They'll be all alone in that cabin all winter,—a mighty long, dark winter. Kilkenny cats,—well?"

The Frenchman in Baptiste shrugged his shoulders, but the Indian in him was silent. Nevertheless, it was an eloquent shrug, pregnant with prophecy.

Things prospered in the little cabin at first. The rough badinage of their comrades had made Weatherbee and Cuthfert conscious of the mutual responsibility which had devolved upon them; besides, there was not so much work after all for two healthy men. And the removal of the cruel whip-hand, or in other words, the bulldozing half-breed, had brought with it a joyous reaction. At first, each strove to outdo the other, and they performed petty tasks with an unction which would have opened the eyes of their comrades who were now wearing out bodies and souls on the Long Trail.

All care was banished. The forest, which shouldered in upon them from three sides, was an inexhaustible woodyard. A few yards from their door slept the Porcupine, and a hole through its winter robe formed a bubbling spring of water, crystal-clear and painfully cold.

But they soon grew to find fault with even that. The hole would persist in freezing up, and thus gave them many a miserable hour of ice-chopping. The unknown builders of the cabin had extended the side-logs so as to support a cache at the rear. In this was stored the bulk of the party's provisions. Food there was, without stint, for three times the men who were fated to live upon it. But the most of it was of the kind which built up brawn and sinew but did not tickle the palate. True, there was sugar in plenty for two ordinary men; but these two were little else than children. They early discovered the virtues of hot water judiciously saturated with sugar, and they prodigally swam their flapjacks and soaked their crusts in the rich, white syrup. Then coffee and tea, and especially the dried fruits, made disastrous inroads upon it. The first word they had was over the sugar question. And it is a really serious thing when two men, wholly dependent upon each other for company, begin to quarrel.

Weatherbee loved to discourse blatantly on politics, while Cuthfert, who had been prone to clip his coupons and let the commonwealth jog on as best it might, either ignored the subject or delivered himself of startling epigrams. But the clerk was too obtuse to appreciate the clever shaping of thought, and this waste of ammunition irritated Cuthfert. He had been used to blinding people by his brilliancy, and it worked him quite a hardship, this loss of an audience. He felt personally aggrieved and unconsciously held his mutton-head companion responsible for it.

Save existence, they had nothing in common,—came in touch on no single point. Weatherbee was a clerk who had known naught but clerking all his life; Cuthfert was a master of arts, a dabbler in oils, and had written not a little. The one was a lower-class man who considered himself a gentleman, and the other was a gentleman who knew himself to be such. From this it may he remarked that a man can be a gentleman without possessing the first instinct of true comradeship. The clerk was as sensuous as the other was aesthetic, and his love of adventures, told at great length and chiefly coined from his imagination, affected the supersensitive master of arts in the same way as so many whiffs of sewer-gas. He deemed the clerk a filthy, uncultured brute, whose place was in the muck with the swine, and told him so, and he was reciprocally informed that he was a milk-and-water sissy and a cad. Weatherbee could not have defined "cad" for his life; but it satisfied its purpose, which after all seems the main point in life.

Weatherbee flatted every third note and sang such songs as "The Boston Burglar" and "The Handsome Cabin Boy," for hours at a time, while Cuthfert wept with rage, till he could stand it no longer and fled into the outer cold. But there was no escape. The intense frost could not be endured for long at a time, and the little cabin crowded them—beds, stove, table, and all—into a space of ten by twelve. The very presence of either became a personal affront to the other, and they lapsed into sullen silences which increased in length and strength as the days went by. Occasionally, the flash of an eye or the curl of a lip got the better of them, though they strove to wholly ignore each other during these mute periods. And a great wonder sprang up in the breast of each, as to how God had ever come to create the other.

With little to do, time became an intolerable burden to them. This naturally made them still lazier. They sank into a physical lethargy which there was no escaping, and which made them rebel at the performance of the smallest chore. One morning when it was his turn to cook the common breakfast, Weatherbee rolled out of his blankets, and to the snoring of his companion, lighted first the slush-lamp and then the fire. The kettles were frozen hard, and there was no water in the cabin with which to wash. But he did not mind that. Waiting for it to thaw, he sliced the bacon and plunged into the hateful task of bread-making. Cuthfert had been slyly watching through his half-closed lids. Consequently there was a scene, in which they fervently blessed each other, and agreed, henceforth, that each do his own cooking. A week later, Cuthfert neglected his morning ablutions, but none the less complacently ate the meal which he had cooked. Weatherbee grinned. After that the foolish custom of washing passed out of their lives.

As the sugar-pile and other little luxuries dwindled, they began to be afraid they were not getting their proper shares, and in order that they might not be robbed, they fell to gorging themselves. The luxuries suffered in this gluttonous contest, as did also the men. In the absence of fresh vegetables and exercise, their blood became impoverished, and a loathsome, purplish rash crept over their bodies. Yet they refused to heed the warning. Next, their muscles and joints began to swell, the flesh turning black, while their mouths, gums, and lips, took on the color of rich cream. Instead of being drawn together by their misery, each gloated over the other's symptoms as the scurvy took its course.

They lost all regard for personal appearance, and for that matter, common decency. The cabin became a pig-pen, and never once were the beds made or fresh pine boughs laid underneath. Yet they could not keep to their blankets, as they would have wished; for the frost was inexorable and the fire-box consumed much fuel. The hair of their heads and faces grew long and shaggy, while their garments would have disgusted a rag-picker. But they did not care. They were sick, and there was no one to see; besides, it was very painful to move about.

To all this was added a new trouble,—the Fear of the North. This Fear was the joint child of the Great Cold and the Great Silence, and was born in the darkness of December, when the sun dipped below the southern horizon for good. It affected them according to their natures. Weatherbee fell prey to the grosser superstitions, and did his best to resurrect the spirits which slept in the forgotten graves. It was a fascinating thing, and in his dreams they came to him from out of the cold, and snuggled into his blankets, and told him of their toils and troubles ere they died. He shrank away from the clammy contact as they drew closer and twined their frozen limbs about him, and when they whispered in his ear of things to come, the cabin rang with his frightened shrieks. Cuthfert did not understand,—for they no longer spoke,—and when thus awakened he invariably grabbed for his revolver. Then he would sit up in bed, shivering nervously, with the weapon trained on the unconscious dreamer. Cuthfert deemed the man going mad, and so came to fear for his life.

His own malady assumed a less concrete form. The mysterious artisan who had laid the cabin, log by log, had pegged a wind-vane to the ridge-pole. Cuthfert noticed it always pointed south, and one day, irritated by its steadfastness of purpose, he turned it toward the east. He watched eagerly, but never a breath came by to disturb it. Then he turned the vane to the north, swearing never again to touch it till the wind did blow. But the air frightened him with its unearthly calm, and he often rose in the middle of the night to see if the vane had veered,—ten degrees would have satisfied him. But no, it poised above him as unchangeable as fate. His imagination ran riot, till it became to him a fetich, invested with all the attributes of a sphinx. Sometimes he followed the path it pointed across the dismal dominions, and allowed his soul to become saturated with the Fear. He dwelt upon the unseen and the unknown till the burden of eternity appeared to be crushing him. Everything in the Northland had that crushing effect,—the absence of life and motion; the darkness; the infinite peace of the brooding land; the ghastly silence, which made the echo of each heartbeat a sacrilege; the solemn forest which seemed to guard an awful, inexpressible something, which neither word nor thought could compass.

The world he had so recently left, with its busy nations and great enterprises, seemed very far away. Recollections occasionally obtruded,—recollections of marts and galleries and crowded thoroughfares, of evening dress and social functions, of good men and dear women he had known,—but they were dim memories of a life he had lived long centuries ago, on some other planet. This phantasm was the Reality. Standing beneath the wind-vane, his eyes fixed on the polar skies, he could not bring himself to realize that the Southland really existed, that at that very moment it was a-roar with life and action. There was no Southland, no men being born of women, no giving and taking marriage. Beyond his bleak sky-line there stretched vast solitudes, and beyond these still vaster solitudes. There were no lands of sunshine, heavy with the perfume of flowers. Such things were only old dreams of paradise. The sunlands of the West and the spicelands of the East, the smiling Arcadias and blissful Islands of the Blest,—ha! ha! His laughter split the void and shocked him with its unwonted sound. There was no sun. This was the Universe, dead and cold and dark, and he its only citizen. Weatherbee? At such moments Weatherbee did not count. He was a Caliban, a monstrous phantom, fettered to him for untold ages, the penalty of some forgotten crime.

He lived with Death among the dead, emasculated by the sense of his own insignificance, crushed by the passive mastery of the slumbering ages. The magnitude of all things appalled him. Every thing partook of the superlative save himself,—the perfect cessation of wind and motion, the immensity of the snow-covered wilderness, the height of the sky and the depth of the silence. That wind-vane,—if it would only move. If a thunderbolt would fall, or the forest flare up in flame. The rolling up of the heavens as a scroll, the crash of Doom—anything, anything. But no, nothing moved; the silence crowded in, and the Fear of the North laid icy fingers on his heart.

Once, like another Crusoe, by the edge of the river he came upon a track,—the faint tracery of a snow-shoe rabbit on the delicate snow-crust. It was a revelation. There was life in the Northland. He would follow it, look upon it, gloat over it. He forgot his swollen muscles, plunging through the deep snow in an ecstasy of anticipation. The forest swallowed him up, and the brief midday twilight vanished; but he pursued his quest till exhausted nature asserted itself and laid him helpless in the snow. There he groaned and cursed his folly, and knew the track to be the fancy of his brain; and late that night he dragged himself into the cabin on hands and knees, his cheeks frozen and a strange numbness about his feet. Weatherbee grinned malevolently, but made no offer to help him. He thrust needles into his toes and thawed them out by the stove. A week later mortification set in.

But the clerk had his own troubles. The dead men came out of their graves more frequently now, and rarely left him, waking or sleeping. He grew to wait and dread their coming, never passing the twin cairns without a shudder. One night they came to him in his sleep and led him forth to an appointed task. Frightened into inarticulate horror, he awoke between the heaps of stones and fled wildly to the cabin. But he had lain there for some time, for his feet and cheeks were also frozen.

Sometimes he became frantic at their insistent presence, and danced about the cabin, cutting the empty air with an ax and smashing everything within reach. During these ghostly encounters, Cuthfert huddled into his blankets and followed the madman about with a cocked revolver, ready to shoot him if he came too near. But, recovering from one of these spells, the clerk noticed the weapon trained upon him with deadly intent. His suspicions were aroused, and thenceforth he too lived in fear of his life. They watched each other closely after that, and faced about in startled fright whenever either passed behind the other's back. This apprehensiveness became a mania which controlled them even in their sleep. Through mutual fear they tacitly let the slush-lamp burn all night, and saw to a plentiful supply of bacon-grease before retiring. The slightest movement on the part of one was sufficient to arouse the other, and many a still watch their gazes countered as they shook beneath their blankets with fingers on the trigger-guards.

What with the Fear of the North, the mental strain, and the ravages of the disease, they lost all semblance of humanity, taking on the appearance of wild beasts, hunted and desperate. Their cheeks and noses, as an aftermath of the freezing, had turned black. Their frozen toes had begun to drop away at the first and second joints. Every movement brought pain, but the fire-box was insatiable, wringing a ransom of torture from their miserable bodies. Day in, day out, it demanded its food,—a veritable pound of flesh,—and they dragged themselves into the forest to chop wood on their knees. Once, crawling thus in search of dry sticks, unknown to each other they entered a thicket from opposite sides. Suddenly, without warning, two peering death's-heads confronted each other. Suffering had so transformed them that recognition was impossible. They sprang to their feet, shrieking with terror, and dashed away on their mangled stumps; and falling at the cabin door, they clawed and scratched like demons till they discovered their mistake.

Occasionally they lapsed normal, and during one of these sane intervals, the chief bone of contention, the sugar, had been divided equally between them. They guarded their separate sacks, stored up in the cache, with jealous eyes; for there were but a few cupfuls left, and they were totally devoid of faith in each other. But one day Cuthfert made a mistake. Hardly able to move, sick with pain, with his head swimming and eyes blinded, he crept into the cache, sugar canister in hand, and mistook Weatherbee's sack for his own.

January had been born but a few days when this occurred. The sun had some time since passed its lowest southern declination, and at meridian now threw flaunting streaks of yellow light upon the northern sky. On the day following his mistake with the sugar-bag, Cuthfert found himself feeling better, both in body and in spirit. As noontime drew near and the day brightened, he dragged himself outside to feast on the evanescent glow, which was to him an earnest of the sun's future intentions. Weatherbee was also feeling somewhat better, and crawled out beside him. They propped themselves in the snow beneath the moveless wind-vane and waited.

The stillness of death was about them. In other climes, when nature falls into such moods, there is a subdued air of expectancy, a waiting for some small voice to take up the broken strain. Not so in the North. The two men had lived seeming eons in this ghostly peace. They could remember no song of the past; they could conjure no song of the future. This unearthly calm had always been,—the tranquil silence of eternity.

Their eyes were fixed upon the north. Unseen, behind their backs, behind the towering mountains to the south, the sun swept toward the zenith of another sky than theirs. Sole spectators of the mighty canvas, they watched the false dawn slowly grow. A faint flame began to glow and smolder. It deepened in intensity, ringing the changes of reddish-yellow, purple, and saffron. So bright did it become that Cuthfert thought the sun must surely be behind it,—a miracle, the sun rising in the north. Suddenly, without warning and without fading, the canvas was swept clean. There was no color in the sky. The light had gone out of the day. They caught their breaths in half-sobs. But lo! the air was a-glint with particles of scintillating frost, and there, to the north, the wind-vane lay in vague outline on the snow. A shadow! A shadow! It was exactly midday. They jerked their heads hurriedly to the south. A golden rim peeped over the mountain's snowy shoulder, smiled upon them an instant, then dipped from sight again.

There were tears in their eyes as they sought each other. A strange softening came over them. They felt irresistibly drawn toward each other. The sun was coming back again. It would be with them to-morrow, and the next day, and the next. And it would stay longer every visit, and a time would come when it would ride their heaven day and night, never once dropping below the sky-line. There would be no night. The ice-locked winter would be broken; the winds would blow and the forests answer; the land would bathe in the blessed sunshine and renew life. Hand in hand, they would quit this horrid dream and journey back to the Southland. They lurched blindly forward, and their hands met,—their poor maimed hands, swollen and distorted beneath their mittens.

But the promise was destined to remain unfulfilled. The Northland is the Northland, and men work out their souls by strange rules, which other men, who have not journeyed into a far country, cannot come to understand.

An hour later, Cuthfert put a pan of bread into the oven, and fell to speculating on what the surgeons could do with his feet when he got back. Home did not seem so very far away now. Weatherbee was rummaging in the cache. Of a sudden, he raised a whirlwind of blasphemy, which in turn ceased with startling abruptness. The other man had robbed his sugar-sack. Still, things might have happened differently, had not the two dead men come out from under the stones and hushed the hot words in his throat. They led him quite gently from the cache, which he forgot to close. That consummation was reached; that something they had whispered to him in his dreams was about to happen. They guided him gently, very gently, to the wood-pile, where they put the ax in his hands. Then they helped him shove open the cabin door, and he felt sure they shut it after him,—at least he had heard it slam and the latch fall sharply into place. And he knew they were waiting just without, waiting for him to do his task.

"Carter! I say, Carter!"

Percy Cuthfert was frightened at the look on the clerk's face, and he made haste to put the table between them.

Carter Weatherbee followed, without haste and without enthusiasm. There was neither pity nor passion in his face, but rather the patient, stolid look of one who has certain work to do and goes about it methodically.

"I say, what's the matter?"

The clerk dodged back, cutting off his retreat to the door, but never opening his mouth.

"I say, Carter, I say; let's talk. There's a good chap."

The master of arts was thinking rapidly, now, shaping a skillful flank movement on the bed where his Smith & Wesson lay. Keeping his eyes on the madman, he rolled backward on the bunk, at the same time clutching the pistol.

"Carter!"

The powder flashed full in Weatherbee's face, but he swung his weapon and leaped forward. The ax bit deeply at the base of the spine, and Percy Cuthfert felt all consciousness of his lower limbs leave him. Then the clerk fell heavily upon him, clutching him by the throat with feeble fingers. The sharp bite of the ax had caused Cuthfert to drop the pistol, and as his lungs panted for release, he fumbled aimlessly for it among the blankets. Then he remembered. He slid a hand up the clerk's belt to the sheath-knife; and they drew very close to each other in that last clinch.

Percy Cuthfert felt his strength leave him. The lower portion of his body was useless. The inert weight of Weatherbee crushed him,—crushed him and pinned him there like a bear under a trap. The cabin became filled with a familiar odor, and he knew the bread to be burning. Yet what did it matter? He would never need it. And there were all of six cupfuls of sugar in the cache,—if he had foreseen this he would not have been so saving the last several days. Would the wind-vane ever move? It might even be veering now. Why not? Had he not seen the sun to-day? He would go and see. No; it was was impossible to move. He had not thought the clerk so heavy a man.

How quickly the cabin cooled! The fire must be out. The cold was forcing in. It must be below zero already, and the ice creeping up the inside of the door. He could not see it, but his past experience enabled him to gauge its progress by the cabin's temperature. The lower hinge must be white ere now. Would the tale of this ever reach the world? How would his friends take it? They would read it over their coffee, most likely, and talk it over at the clubs. He could see them very clearly. "Poor Old Cuthfert," they murmured; "not such a bad sort of a chap, after all." He smiled at their eulogies, and passed on in search of a Turkish bath. It was the same old crowd upon the streets. Strange, they did not notice his moosehide moccasins and tattered German socks! He would take a cab. And after the bath a shave would not be bad. No; he would eat first. Steak, and potatoes, and green things,—how fresh it all was! And what was that? Squares of honey, streaming liquid amber! But why did they bring so much? Ha! ha! he could never eat it all. Shine! Why certainly. He put his foot on the box. The bootblack looked curiously up at him, and he remembered his moosehide moccasins and went away hastily.

Hark! The wind-vane must be surely spinning. No; a mere singing in his ears. That was all,—a mere singing. The ice must have passed the latch by now. More likely the upper hinge was covered. Between the moss-chinked roof-poles, little points of frost began to appear. How slowly they grew! No; not so slowly. There was a new one, and there another. Two—three—four; they were coming too fast to count. There were two growing together. And there, a third had joined them. Why, there were no more spots. They had run together and formed a sheet.

Well, he would have company. If Gabriel ever broke the silence of the North, they would stand together, hand in hand, before the great White Throne. And God would judge them, God would judge them!

Then Percy Cuthfert closed his eyes and dropped off to sleep.

The Magic Barrel
(1954)

BERNARD MALAMUD

Not long ago there lived in uptown New York, in a small, almost meager room, though crowded with books, Leo Finkle, a rabbinical student in the Yeshivah University. Finkle, after six years of study, was to be ordained in June and had been advised by an acquaintance that he might find it easier to win himself a congregation if he were married. Since he had no present prospects of marriage, after two tormented days of turning it over in his mind, he called in Pinye Salzman, a marriage broker whose two-line advertisement he had read in the *Forward*.

The matchmaker appeared one night out of the dark fourth-floor hallway of the graystone rooming house where Finkle lived, grasping a black, strapped portfolio that had been worn thin with use. Salzman, who had been long in the business, was of slight but dignified build, wearing an old hat, and an overcoat too short and tight for him. He smelled frankly of fish, which he loved to eat, and although he was missing a few teeth, his presence was not displeasing, because of an amiable manner curiously contrasted with mournful eyes. His voice, his lips, his wisp of beard, his bony fingers were animated, but give him a moment of repose and his mild blue eyes revealed a depth of sadness, a characteristic that put Leo a little at ease although the situation, for him, was inherently tense.

He at once informed Salzman why he had asked him to come, explaining that his home was in Cleveland, and that but for his parents, who had married comparatively late in life, he was alone in the world. He had for six years devoted himself almost entirely to his studies, as a result of which, understandably, he had found himself without time for a social life and the company of young women. Therefore he thought it the better part of trial and error—of embarrassing fumbling—to call in an experienced person to advise him on these matters. He remarked in passing that the function of the marriage broker was ancient and honorable, highly approved in the Jewish community, because it made practical the necessary without hindering joy. Moreover, his own parents had been brought together by a matchmaker. They had made, if not a financially profitable marriage—since neither had possessed any worldly goods to speak of—at least a successful one in the sense of their everlasting devotion to each other. Salzman listened in embarrassed surprise, sensing a sort of apology. Later, however, he experienced a glow of pride in his work, an emotion that had left him years ago, and he heartily approved of Finkle.

The two went to their business. Leo had led Salzman to the only clear place in the room, a table near a window that overlooked the lamp-lit city. He seated himself at the matchmaker's side but facing him, attempting by an act of will to suppress the unpleasant tickle in his throat. Salzman eagerly unstrapped his portfolio and removed a loose rubber band from a thin packet of much-handled cards. As he flipped through them, a gesture and sound that physically hurt Leo, the student pretended not to see and gazed steadfastly out the window. Although it was still February, winter was on its last legs, signs of which he had for the first time in years begun to notice. He now observed the round white moon, moving high in the sky through a cloud menagerie, and watched with half-open mouth as it penetrated a huge hen, and dropped out of her like an egg laying itself. Salzman, though pretending through eyeglasses he had just slipped on, to be engaged in scanning the writing on the cards, stole occasional glances at the young man's distinguished face, noting with pleasure the long, severe scholar's nose, brown eyes heavy with learning, sensitive yet ascetic lips, and a certain, almost hollow quality of the dark cheeks. He gazed around at shelves upon shelves of books and let out a soft, contented sigh.

When Leo's eyes fell upon the cards, he counted six spread out in Salzman's hand.

"So few?" he asked in disappointment.

"You wouldn't believe me how much cards I got in my office," Salzman replied. "The drawers are already filled to the top, so I keep them now in a barrel, but is every girl good for a new rabbi?"

Leo blushed at this, regretting all he had revealed of himself in a curriculum vitae he had sent to Salzman. He had thought it best to acquaint him with his strict standards and specifications, but in having done so, felt he had told the marriage broker more than was absolutely necessary.

He hesitantly inquired, "Do you keep photographs of your clients on file?"

"First comes family, amount of dowry, also what kind promises," Salzman replied, unbuttoning his tight coat and settling himself in the chair. "After comes pictures, rabbi."

"Call me Mr. Finkle. I'm not yet a rabbi."

Salzman said he would, but instead called him doctor, which he changed to rabbi when Leo was not listening too attentively.

Salzman adjusted his horn-rimmed spectacles, gently cleared his throat and read in an eager voice the contents of the top card:

"Sophie P. Twenty four years. Widow one year. No children. Educated high school and two years college. Father promises eight thousand dollars. Has wonderful wholesale business. Also real estate. On the mother's side comes teachers, also one actor. Well known on Second Avenue."

Leo gazed up in surprise. "Did you say a widow?"

"A widow don't mean spoiled, rabbi. She lived with her husband maybe four months. He was a sick boy she made a mistake to marry him."

"Marrying a widow has never entered my mind."

"This is because you have no experience. A widow, especially if she is young and healthy like this girl, is a wonderful person to marry. She will be thankful to you the rest of her life. Believe me, if I was looking now for a bride, I would marry a widow."

Leo reflected, then shook his head.

Salzman hunched his shoulders in an almost imperceptible gesture of disappointment. He placed the card down on the wooden table and began to read another:

"Lily H. High school teacher. Regular. Not a substitute. Has savings and new Dodge car. Lived in Paris one year. Father is successful dentist thirty-five years. Interested in professional man. Well Americanized family. Wonderful opportunity."

"I knew her personally," said Salzman. "I wish you could see this girl. She is a doll. Also very intelligent. All day you could talk to her about books and theyater and what not. She also knows current events."

"I don't believe you mentioned her age?"

"Her age?" Salzman said, raising his brows. "Her age is thirty-two years."

Leo said after a while, "I'm afraid that seems a little too old."

Salzman let out a laugh. "So how old are you, rabbi?"

"Twenty-seven."

"So what is the difference, tell me, between twenty-seven and thirty-two? My own wife is seven years older than me. So what did I suffer?—Nothing. If Rothschild's a daughter wants to marry you, would you say on account her age, no?"

"Yes," Leo said dryly.

Salzman shook off the no in the yes. "Five years don't mean a thing. I give you my word that when you will live with her for one week you will forget her age. What does it mean five years—that she lived more and knows more than somebody who is younger? On this girl, God bless her, years are not wasted. Each one that it comes makes better the bargain."

"What subject does she teach in high school?"

"Languages. If you heard the way she speaks French, you will think it is music. I am in the business twenty-five years, and I recommend her with my whole heart. Believe me, I know what I'm talking, rabbi."

"What's on the next card?" Leo said abruptly.

Salzman reluctantly turned up the third card:

"Ruth K. Nineteen years. Honor student. Father offers thirteen thousand cash to the right bridegroom. He is a medical doctor. Stomach specialist with marvelous practice. Brother in law owns own garment business. Particular people."

Salzman looked as if he had read his trump card.

"Did you say nineteen?" Leo asked with interest.

"On the dot."

"Is she attractive?" He blushed. "Pretty?"

Salzman kissed his finger tips. "A little doll. On this I give you my word. Let me call the father tonight and you will see what means pretty."

But Leo was troubled. "You're sure she's that young?"

"This I am positive. The father will show you the birth certificate."

"Are you positive there isn't something wrong with her?" Leo insisted.

"Who says there is wrong?"

"I don't understand why an American girl her age should go to a marriage broker."

A smile spread over Salzman's face.

"So for the same reason you went, she comes."

Leo flushed. "I am pressed for time."

Salzman, realizing he had been tactless, quickly explained. "The father came, not her. He wants she should have the best, so he looks around himself. When we will locate the right boy he will introduce him and encourage. This makes a better marriage than if a young girl without experience takes for herself. I don't have to tell you this."

"But don't you think this young girl believes in love?" Leo spoke uneasily.

Salzman was about to guffaw but caught himself and said soberly, "Love comes with the right person, not before."

Leo parted dry lips but did not speak. Noticing that Salzman had snatched a glance at the next card, he cleverly asked, "How is her health?"

"Perfect," Salzman said, breathing with difficulty. "Of course, she is a little lame on her right foot from an auto accident that it happened to her when she was twelve years, but nobody notices on account she is so brilliant and also beautiful."

Leo got up heavily and went to the window. He felt curiously bitter and upbraided himself for having called in the marriage broker. Finally, he shook his head.

"Why not?" Salzman persisted, the pitch of his voice rising.

"Because I detest stomach specialists."

"So what do you care what is his business? After you marry her do you need him? Who says he must come every Friday night in your house?"

Ashamed of the way the talk was going, Leo dismissed Salzman, who went home with heavy, melancholy eyes.

Though he had felt only relief at the marriage broker's departure, Leo was in low spirits the next day. He explained it as arising from Salzman's failure to produce a suitable bride for him. He did not care for his type of clientele. But when Leo found himself hesitating whether to seek out another matchmaker, one more polished than Pinye, he wondered if it could be— his protestations to the contrary, and although he honored his father and mother—that he did not, in essence, care for the match-making institution? This thought he quickly put out of mind yet found himself still upset. All day he ran around in the woods—missed an important appointment, forgot to give out his laundry, walked out of a Broadway cafeteria without paying and had to run back with the ticket in his hand; had even not recognized his landlady in the street when she passed with a friend and courteously called out, "A good evening to you, Doctor Finkle." By nightfall, however, he had regained sufficient calm to sink his nose into a book and there found peace from his thoughts.

Almost at once there came a knock on the door. Before Leo could say enter, Salzman, commercial cupid, was standing in the room. His face was gray and meager, his expression hungry, and he looked as if he would expire on his feet. Yet the marriage broker managed, by some trick of the muscles, to display a broad smile.

"So good evening. I am invited?"

Leo nodded, disturbed to see him again, yet unwilling to ask the man to leave.

Beaming still, Salzman laid his portfolio on the table. "Rabbi, I got for you tonight good news."

"I've asked you not to call me rabbi. I'm still a student."

"Your worries are finished. I have for you a first-class bride."

"Leave me in peace concerning this subject." Leo pretended lack of interest.

"The world will dance at your wedding."

"Please, Mr. Salzman, no more."

"But first must come back my strength," Salzman said weakly. He fumbled with the portfolio straps and took out of the leather case an oily paper bag, from which he extracted a hard, seeded roll and a small, smoked white fish. With a quick motion of his hand he stripped the fish out of its skin and began ravenously to chew. "All day in a rush," he muttered.

Leo watched him eat.

"A sliced tomato you have maybe?" Salzman hesitantly inquired.

"No."

The marriage broker shut his eyes and ate. When he had finished he carefully cleaned up the crumbs and rolled up the remains of the fish, in the paper bag. His spectacled eyes roamed the room until he discovered, amid some piles of books, a one-burner gas stove. Lifting his hat he humbly asked, "A glass tea you got, rabbi?"

Conscience-stricken, Leo rose and brewed the tea. He served it with a chunk of lemon and two cubes of lump sugar, delighting Salzman.

After he had drunk his tea, Salzman's strength and good spirits were restored.

"So tell me, rabbi," he said amiably, "you considered some more the three clients I mentioned yesterday?"

"There was no need to consider."

"Why not?"

"None of them suits me."

"What then suits you?"

Leo let it pass because he could give only a confused answer.

Without waiting for a reply, Salzman asked, "You remember this girl I talked to you—the high school teacher?"

"Age thirty-two?"

But, surprisingly, Salzman's face lit in a smile. "Age twenty-nine."

Leo shot him a look. "Reduced from thirty-two?"

"A mistake," Salzman avowed. "I talked today with the dentist. He took me to his safety deposit box and showed me the birth certificate. She was twenty-nine years last August. They made her a party in the mountains where she went for her vacation. When her father spoke to me the first time I forgot to write the age and I told you thirty-two, but now I remember this was a different client, a widow."

"The same one you told me about? I thought she was twenty-four?"

"A different. Am I responsible that the world is filled with widows?"

"No, but I'm not interested in them, nor for that matter, in school teachers."

Salzman pulled his clasped hands to his breast. Looking at the ceiling he devoutly exclaimed, "Yiddishe kinder, what can I say to somebody that he is not interested in high school teachers? So what then you are interested?"

Leo flushed but controlled himself.

"In what else will you be interested," Salzman went on, "if you not interested in this fine girl that she speaks four languages and has personally in the bank ten thousand dollars? Also her father guarantees further twelve thousand. Also she has a new car, wonderful clothes, talks on all subjects, and she will give you a first-class home and children. How near do we come in our life to paradise?"

"If she's so wonderful, why wasn't she married ten years ago?"

"Why?" said Salzman with a heavy laugh. "—Why? Because she is *partikiler*. This is why. She wants the *best*."

Leo was silent, amused at how he had entangled himself. But Salzman had aroused his interest in Lily H., and he began seriously to consider calling on her. When the marriage broker observed how intently Leo's mind was at work on the facts he had supplied, he felt certain they would soon come to an agreement.

Late Saturday afternoon, conscious of Salzman, Leo Finkle walked with Lily Hirschorn along Riverside Drive. He walked briskly and erectly, wearing with distinction the black fedora he had that morning taken with trepidation out of the dusty hat box on his closet shelf, and the heavy black Saturday coat he had thoroughly whisked clean. Leo also owned a walking stick, a present from a distant relative, but quickly put temptation aside and did not use it. Lily, petite and not unpretty, had on something signifying the approach of spring. She was au courant, animatedly, with all sorts of subjects, and he weighed her words and found her surprisingly sound—score another for Salzman, whom he uneasily sensed to be somewhere around, hiding perhaps high in a tree along the street, flashing the lady signals with a pocket mirror; or perhaps a cloven-hoofed Pan, piping nuptial ditties as he danced his invisible way before them, strewing wild buds on the walk and purple grapes in their path, symbolizing fruit of a union, though there was of course still none.

Lily startled Leo by remarking, "I was thinking of Mr. Salzman, a curious figure, wouldn't you say?"

Not certain what to answer, he nodded.

She bravely went on, blushing, "I for one am grateful for his introducing us. Aren't you?"

He courteously replied, "I am."

"I mean," she said with a little laugh—and it was all in good taste, or at least gave the effect of being not in bad—"do you mind that we came together so?"

He was not displeased with her honesty, recognizing that she meant to set the relationship aright, and understanding that it took a certain amount of experience in life, and courage, to want to do it quite that way. One had to have some sort of past to make that kind of beginning.

He said that he did not mind. Salzman's function was traditional and honorable—valuable for what it might achieve, which, he pointed out, was frequently nothing.

Lily agreed with a sigh. They walked on for a while and she said after a long silence, again with a nervous laugh, "Would you mind if I asked you something a little bit personal? Frankly, I find the subject fascinating." Although Leo shrugged, she went on half embarrassedly, "How was it that you came to your calling? I mean was it a sudden passionate inspiration?"

Leo, after a time, slowly replied, "I was always interested in the Law."

"You saw revealed in it the presence of the Highest?"

He nodded and changed the subject. "I understand that you spent a little time in Paris, Miss Hirschorn?"

"Oh, did Mr. Salzman tell you, Rabbi Finkle?" Leo winced but she went on, "It was ages ago and almost forgotten. I remember I had to return for my sister's wedding."

And Lily would not be put off. "When," she asked in a trembly voice, "did you become enamored of God?"

He stared at her. Then it came to him that she was talking not about Leo Finkle, but of a total stranger, some mystical figure, perhaps even passionate prophet that Salzman had dreamed up for her—no relation to the living or dead. Leo trembled with rage and weakness. The trickster had obviously sold her a bill of goods, just as he had him, who'd expected to become acquainted with a young lady of twenty-nine, only to behold, the moment he laid eyes upon her strained and anxious face, a woman past thirty-five and aging rapidly. Only his self control had kept him this long in her presence.

"I am not," he said gravely, "a talented religious person," and in seeking words to go on, found himself possessed by shame and fear. "I think," he said in a strained manner, "that I came to God not because I loved Him, but because I did not."

This confession he spoke harshly because its unexpectedness shook him.

Lily wilted. Leo saw a profusion of loaves of bread go flying like ducks high over his head, not unlike the winged loaves by which he had counted himself to sleep last night. Mercifully, then, it snowed, which he would not put past Salzman's machinations.

He was infuriated with the marriage broker and swore he would throw him out of the room the minute he reappeared. But Salzman did not come that night, and when Leo's anger had subsided, an unaccountable despair grew in its place. At first he thought this was caused by his disappointment in Lily, but before long it became evident that he had involved himself with Salzman without a true knowledge of his own intent. He gradually realized—with an emptiness that seized him with six hands—that he had called in the broker to find him a bride because he was incapable of doing it himself. This terrifying insight he had derived as a result of his meeting and conversation with Lily Hirschorn. Her probing questions had somehow irritated him into revealing—to himself more than her—the true nature of his relationship to God, and from that it had come upon him, with shocking force, that apart from his parents, he had never loved anyone. Or perhaps it went the other way, that he did not love God so well as he might, because he had not loved man. It seemed to Leo that his whole life stood starkly revealed and he saw himself for the first time as he truly was—unloved and loveless. This bitter but somehow not fully unexpected revelation brought him to a point of panic, controlled only by extraordinary effort. He covered his face with his hands and cried.

The week that followed was the worst of his life. He did not eat and lost weight. His beard darkened and grew ragged. He stopped attending seminars and almost never opened a book. He seriously considered leaving the Yeshivah, although he was deeply troubled at the thought of the loss of all his years of study—saw them like pages torn from a book, strewn over the city—and at the devastating effect of this decision upon his parents. But he had lived without knowledge of himself, and never in the Five Books and all the Commentaries—mea culpa—had the truth been revealed to him. He did not know where to turn, and in all this desolating loneliness there was no *to whom*, although he often thought of Lily but not once could bring himself to go downstairs and make the call. He became touchy and irritable, especially with his landlady, who asked him all manner of personal questions; on the other hand, sensing his own disagreeableness, he waylaid her on the stairs and apologized abjectly, until mortified, she ran from him. Out of this, however, he drew the consolation that he was a Jew and that a Jew suffered. But gradually, as the long and terrible week drew to a close, he regained his composure and some idea of purpose in life: to go on as planned. Although he was imperfect, the ideal was not. As for his quest of a bride, the thought of continuing afflicted him with anxiety and heartburn, yet perhaps with this new knowledge of himself he would be more successful than in the past. Perhaps love would now come to him and a bride to that love. And for this sanctified seeking who needed a Salzman?

The marriage broker, a skeleton with haunted eyes, returned that very night. He looked, withal, the picture of frustrated expectancy—as if he had steadfastly waited the week at Miss Lily Hirschorn's side for a telephone call that never came.

Casually coughing, Salzman came immediately to the point: "So how did you like her?"

Leo's anger rose and he could not refrain from chiding the matchmaker: "Why did you lie to me, Salzman?"

Salzman's pale face went dead white, the world had snowed on him.

"Did you not state that she was twenty-nine?" Leo insisted.

"I give you my word—"

"She was thirty-five, if a day. *At least* thirty-five."

"Of this don't be too sure. Her father told me—"

"Never mind. The worst of it was that you lied to her."

"How did I lie to her, tell me?"

"You told her things about me that weren't true. You made me out to be more, consequently less than I am. She had in mind a totally different person, a sort of semi-mystical Wonder Rabbi."

"All I said, you was a religious man."

"I can imagine."

Salzman sighed. "This is my weakness that I have," he confessed. "My wife says to me I shouldn't be a salesman, but when I have two fine people that they would be wonderful to be married, I am so happy that I talk too much." He smiled wanly. "This is why Salzman is a poor man."

Leo's anger left him. "Well, Salzman, I'm afraid that's all."

The marriage broker fastened hungry eyes on him.

"You don't want any more a bride?"

"I do," said Leo, "but I have decided to seek her in a different way. I am no longer interested in an arranged marriage. To be frank, I now admit the necessity of premarital love. That is, I want to be in love with the one I marry."

"Love?" said Salzman, astounded. After a moment he remarked, "For us, our love is our life, not for the ladies. In the ghetto they—"

"I know, I know," said Leo. "I've thought of it often. Love, I have said to myself, should be a by-product of living and worship rather than its own end. Yet for myself I find it necessary to establish the level of my need and fulfill it."

Salzman shrugged but answered, "Listen, rabbi, if you want love, this I can find for you also. I have such beautiful clients that you will love them the minute your eyes will see them."

Leo smiled unhappily. "I'm afraid you don't understand."

But Salzman hastily unstrapped his portfolio and withdrew a manila packet from it.

"Pictures," he said, quickly laying the envelope on the table.

Leo called after him to take the pictures away, but as if on the wings of the wind, Salzman had disappeared.

March came. Leo had returned to his regular routine. Although he felt not quite himself yet—lacked energy—he was making plans for a more active social life. Of course it would cost something, but he was an expert in cutting corners; and when there were no corners left he would make circles rounder. All the while Salzman's pictures had lain on the table, gathering dust. Occasionally as Leo sat studying, or enjoying a cup of tea, his eyes fell on the manila envelope, but he never opened it.

The days went by and no social life to speak of developed with a member of the opposite sex—it was difficult, given the circumstances of his situation. One morning Leo toiled up the stairs to his room and stared out the window at the city. Although the day was bright his view of it was dark. For some time he watched the people in the street below hurrying along and then turned with a heavy heart to his little room. On the table was the packet. With a sudden relentless gesture he tore it open. For a half-hour he stood by the table in a state of excitement, examining the photographs of the ladies Salzman had included. Finally, with a deep sigh he put them down. There were six, of varying degrees of attractiveness, but look at them long enough and they all became Lily Hirschorn: all past their prime, all starved behind bright smiles, not a true personality in the lot. Life, despite their frantic yoohooings, had passed them by; they were pictures in a brief case that stank of fish. After a while, however, as Leo attempted to return the photographs into the envelope, he found in it another, a snapshot of the type taken by a machine for a quarter. He gazed at it a moment and let out a cry.

Her face deeply moved him. Why, he could at first not say. It gave him the impression of youth—spring flowers, yet age—a sense of having been used to the bone, wasted; this came from the eyes, which were hauntingly familiar, yet absolutely strange. He had a vivid impression that he had met her before, but try as he might he could not place her although he could almost recall her name, as if he had read it in her own handwriting. No, this couldn't be; he would have remembered her. It was not, he affirmed, that she had an extraordinary beauty—no, though her face was attractive enough; it was that *something* about her moved him. Feature for feature, even some of the ladies of the photographs could do better; but she leaped forth to his heart—had *lived*, or wanted to—more than just wanted, perhaps regretted how she had lived—had somehow deeply suffered: it could be seen in the depths of those reluctant eyes, and from the way the light enclosed and shone from her, and within her, opening realms of possibility: this was her own. Her he desired. His head ached and eyes narrowed with the intensity of his gazing, then as if an obscure fog had blown up in the mind, he experienced fear of her and was aware that he had received an impression, somehow, of evil. He shuddered, saying softly, it is thus with us all. Leo brewed some tea in a small pot and sat sipping it without sugar, to calm himself. But before he had finished drinking, again with excitement he examined the face and found it good: good for Leo Finkle. Only such a one could understand him and help him seek whatever he was seeking. She might, perhaps, love him. How she had happened to be among the discards in Salzman's barrel he could never guess, but he knew he must urgently go find her.

Leo rushed downstairs, grabbed up the Bronx telephone book and searched for Salzman's home address. He was not listed, nor was his office. Neither was he in the Manhattan book. But Leo remembered having written down the address on a slip of paper after he had read Salzman's advertisement in the "personals" column of the *Forward*. He ran up to his room and tore through his papers, without luck. It was exasperating. Just when he needed the matchmaker he was nowhere to be found. Fortunately Leo remembered to look in his wallet. There on a card he found his name written and a Bronx address. No phone number was listed, the reason—Leo now recalled—he had originally communicated with Salzman by letter. He got on his coat, put a hat on over his skull cap and hurried to the subway station. All the way to the far end of the Bronx he sat on the edge of his seat. He was more than once tempted to take out the picture and see if the girl's face was as he remembered it, but he refrained, allowing the snapshot to remain in his inside coat pocket, content to have her so close. When the train pulled into the station he was waiting at the door and bolted out. He quickly located the street Salzman had advertised.

The building he sought was less than a block from the subway, but it was not an office building, nor even a loft, nor a store in which one could rent office space. It was a very old tenement house. Leo found Salzman's name in pencil on a soiled tag under the bell and climbed three dark flights to his apartment. When he knocked, the door was opened by a thin, asthmatic, gray-haired woman, in felt slippers.

"Yes?" she said, expecting nothing. She listened without listening. He could have sworn he had seen her, too, before but knew it was an illusion.

"Salzman—does he live here? Pinye Salzman," he said, "the matchmaker?"

She stared at him a long minute. "Of course."

He felt embarrassed. "Is he in?"

"No." Her mouth, though left open, offered nothing more.

"The matter is urgent. Can you tell me where his office is?"

"In the air." She pointed upward.

"You mean he has no office?" Leo asked.

"In his socks."

He peered into the apartment. It was sunless and dingy, one large room divided by a half-open curtain, beyond which he could see a sagging metal bed. The near side of a room was crowded with rickety chairs, old bureaus, a three-legged table, racks of cooking utensils, and all the apparatus of a kitchen. But there was no sign of Salzman or his magic barrel, probably also a figment of the imagination. An odor of frying fish made Leo weak to the knees.

"Where is he?" he insisted. "I've got to see your husband."

At length she answered, "So who knows where he is? Every time he thinks a new thought he runs to a different place. Go home, he will find you."

"Tell him Leo Finkle."

She gave no sign she had heard.

He walked downstairs, depressed.

But Salzman, breathless, stood waiting at his door.

Leo was astounded and overjoyed. "How did you get here before me?"

"I rushed."

"Come inside."

They entered. Leo fixed tea, and a sardine sandwich for Salzman. As they were drinking he reached behind him for the packet of pictures and handed them to the marriage broker.

Salzman put down his glass and said expectantly, "You found somebody you like?"

"Not among these."

The marriage broker turned away.

"Here is the one I want." Leo held forth the snapshot.

Salzman slipped on his glasses and took the picture into his trembling hand. He turned ghastly and let out a groan.

"What's the matter?" cried Leo.

"Excuse me. Was an accident this picture. She isn't for you."

Salzman frantically shoved the manila packet into his portfolio. He thrust the snapshot into his pocket and fled down the stairs.

Leo, after momentary paralysis, gave chase and cornered the marriage broker in the vestibule. The landlady made hysterical outcries but neither of them listened.

"Give me back the picture, Salzman."

"No." The pain in his eyes was terrible.

"Tell me who she is then."

"This I can't tell you. Excuse me."

He made to depart, but Leo, forgetting himself, seized the matchmaker by his tight coat and shook him frenziedly.

"Please," sighed Salzman. *"Please."*

Leo ashamedly let him go. "Tell me who she is," he begged. "It's very important for me to know."

"She is not for you. She is a wild one—wild, without shame. This is not a bride for a rabbi."

"What do you mean wild?"

"Like an animal. Like a dog. For her to be poor was a sin. This is why to me she is dead now."

"In God's name, what do you mean?"

"Her I can't introduce to you," Salzman cried.

"Why are you so excited?"

"Why, he asks," Salzman said, bursting into tears. "This is my baby, my Stella, she should burn in hell."

Leo hurried up to bed and hid under the covers. Under the covers he thought his life through. Although he soon fell asleep he could not sleep her out of his mind. He woke, beating his breast. Though he prayed to be rid of her, his prayers went unanswered. Through days of torment he endlessly struggled not to love her; fearing success, he escaped it. He then concluded to convert her to goodness, himself to God. The idea alternately nauseated and exalted him.

He perhaps did not know that he had come to a final decision until he encountered Salzman in a Broadway cafeteria. He was sitting alone at a rear table, sucking the bony remains of a fish. The marriage broker appeared haggard, and transparent to the point of vanishing.

Salzman looked up at first without recognizing him. Leo had grown a pointed beard and his eyes were weighted with wisdom.

"Salzman," he said, "love has at last come to my heart."

"Who can love from a picture?" mocked the marriage broker.

"It is not impossible."

"If you can love her, then you can love anybody. Let me show you some new clients that they just sent me their photographs. One is a little doll."

"Just her I want," Leo murmured.

"Don't be a fool, doctor. Don't bother with her."

"Put me in touch with her, Salzman," Leo said humbly. "Perhaps I can be of service."

Salzman had stopped eating and Leo understood with emotion that it was now arranged.

Leaving the cafeteria, he was, however, afflicted by a tormenting suspicion that Salzman had planned it all to happen this way.

Leo was informed by letter that she would meet him on a certain corner, and she was there one spring night, waiting under a street lamp. He appeared, carrying a small bouquet of violets and rosebuds. Stella stood by the lamp post, smoking. She wore white with red shoes, which fitted his expectations, although in a troubled moment he had imagined the dress red, and only the shoes white. She waited uneasily and shyly. From afar he saw that her eyes—clearly her father's—were filled with desperate innocence. He pictured, in her, his own redemption. Violins and lit candles revolved in the sky. Leo ran forward with flowers outthrust.

Around the corner, Salzman, leaning against a wall, chanted prayers for the dead.

Bartleby, the Scrivener:
A Story of Wall-Street
(1853)

HERMAN MELVILLE

I am a rather elderly man. The nature of my avocations for the last thirty years has brought me into more than ordinary contact with what would seem an interesting and somewhat singular set of men, of whom as yet nothing that I know of has ever been written:—I mean the law-copyists or scriveners. I have known very many of them, professionally and privately, and if I pleased, could relate divers histories, at which good-natured gentlemen might smile, and sentimental souls might weep. But I waive the biographies of all other scriveners for a few passages in the life of Bartleby, who was a scrivener of the strangest I ever saw or heard of. While of other law-copyists I might write the complete life, of Bartleby nothing of that sort can be done. I believe that no materials exist for a full and satisfactory biography of this man. It is an irreparable loss to literature. Bartleby was one of those beings of whom nothing is ascertainable, except from the original sources, and in his case those are very small. What my own astonished eyes saw of Bartleby, *that* is all I know of him, except, indeed, one vague report which will appear in the sequel.

Ere introducing the scrivener, as he first appeared to me, it is fit I make some mention of myself, my *employees*, my business, my chambers, and general surroundings; because some such description is indispensable to an adequate understanding of the chief character about to be presented.

Imprimis: I am a man who, from his youth upwards, has been filled with a profound conviction that the easiest way of life is the best. Hence, though I belong to a profession proverbially energetic and nervous, even to turbulence, at times, yet nothing of that sort have I ever suffered to invade my peace. I am one of those unambitious lawyers who never addresses a jury, or in any way draws down public applause; but in the cool tranquility of a snug retreat, do a snug business among rich men's bonds and mortgages and title-deeds. All who know me, consider me an eminently *safe* man. The late John Jacob Astor, a personage little given to poetic enthusiasm, had no hesitation in pronouncing my first grand point to be prudence; my next, method. I do not speak it in vanity, but simply record the fact, that I was not unemployed in my profession by the late John Jacob Astor; a name which, I admit, I love to repeat, for it hath a rounded and orbicular sound to it, and rings like unto bullion. I will freely add, that I was not insensible to the late John Jacob Astor's good opinion.

Some time prior to the period at which this little history begins, my avocations had been largely increased. The good old office, now extinct in the State of New York, of a Master in Chancery, had been conferred upon me. It was not a very arduous office, but very pleasantly remunerative. I seldom lose my temper; much more seldom indulge in dangerous indignation at wrongs and outrages; but I must be permitted to be rash here and declare, that I consider the sudden and violent abrogation of the office of Master in Chancery, by the new Constitution, as a—premature act; inasmuch as I had counted upon a life-lease of the profits, whereas I only received those of a few short years. But this is by the way.

My chambers were up stairs at No.—Wall-street. At one end they looked upon the white wall of the interior of a spacious sky-light shaft, penetrating the building from top to bottom. This view might have been considered rather tame than otherwise, deficient in what landscape painters call "life." But if so, the view from the other end of my chambers offered, at least, a contrast, if nothing more. In that direction my windows commanded an unobstructed view of a lofty brick wall, black by age and everlasting shade; which wall required no spy-glass to bring out its lurking beauties, but for the benefit of all near-sighted spectators, was pushed up to within ten feet of my window panes. Owing to the great height of the surrounding buildings, and my chambers being on the second floor, the interval between this wall and mine not a little resembled a huge square cistern.

At the period just preceding the advent of Bartleby, I had two persons as copyists in my employment, and a promising lad as an office-boy. First, Turkey; second, Nippers; third, Ginger Nut. These may seem names, the like of which are not usually found in the Directory. In truth they were nicknames, mutually conferred upon each other by my three clerks, and were deemed expressive of their respective persons or characters. Turkey was a short, pursy Englishman of about my own age, that is, somewhere not far from sixty. In the morning, one might say, his face was of a fine florid hue, but after twelve o'clock, meridian—his dinner hour—it blazed like a grate full of Christmas coals; and continued blazing—but, as it were, with a gradual wane—till 6 o'clock, P.M. or thereabouts, after which I saw no more of the proprietor of the face, which gaining its meridian with the sun, seemed to set with it, to rise, culminate, and decline the following day, with the like regularity and undiminished glory. There are many singular coincidences I have known in the course of my life, not the least among which was the fact, that exactly when Turkey displayed his fullest beams from his red and radiant countenance, just then, too, at that critical moment, began the daily period when I considered his business capacities as seriously disturbed for the remainder of the twenty-four hours. Not that he was absolutely idle, or averse to business then; far from it. The difficulty was, he was apt to be altogether too energetic. There was a strange, inflamed, flurried, flighty recklessness of activity about him. He would be incautious in dipping his pen into his inkstand. All his blots upon my documents, were dropped there after twelve o'clock, meridian. Indeed, not only would he be reckless and sadly given to making blots in the afternoon, but some days he went further, and was rather noisy. At such times, too, his face flamed with augmented blazonry, as if cannel coal had been heaped on anthracite. He made an unpleasant racket with his chair; spilled his sand-box; in mending his pens, impatiently split them all to pieces, and threw them on the floor in a sudden passion; stood up and leaned over his table, boxing his papers about in a most indecorous manner, very sad to behold in an elderly man like him. Nevertheless, as he was in many ways a most valuable person to me, and all the time before twelve o'clock, meridian, was the quickest, steadiest creature too, accomplishing a great deal of work in a style not easy to be matched—for these reasons, I was willing to overlook his eccentricities, though indeed, occasionally, I remonstrated with him. I did this very gently, however, because, though the civilest, nay, the blandest and most reverential of men in the morning, yet in the afternoon he was disposed, upon provocation, to be slightly rash with his tongue, in fact, insolent. Now, valuing his morning services as I did, and resolved not to lose them; yet, at the same time made uncomfortable by his inflamed ways after twelve o'clock; and being a man of peace, unwilling by my admonitions to call forth unseemly retorts from him; I took upon me, one Saturday noon (he was always worse on Saturdays), to hint to him, very kindly, that perhaps now that he was growing old, it might be well to abridge his labors; in short, he need not come to my chambers after twelve o'clock, but, dinner over, had best go home to his lodgings and rest himself till teatime. But no; he insisted upon his afternoon devotions. His countenance became intolerably fervid, as he oratorically assured me—gesticulating with a long ruler at the other end of the room—that if his services in the morning were useful, how indispensable, then, in the afternoon?

"With submission, sir," said Turkey on this occasion, "I consider myself your right-hand man. In the morning I but marshal and deploy my columns; but in the afternoon I put myself at their head, and gallantly charge the foe, thus!"—and he made a violent thrust with the ruler.

"But the blots, Turkey," intimated I.

"True,—but, with submission, sir, behold these hairs! I am getting old. Surely, sir, a blot or two of a warm afternoon is not to be severely urged against gray hairs. Old age—even if it blot the page—is honorable. With submission, sir, we *both* are getting old."

This appeal to my fellow-feeling was hardly to be resisted. At all events, I saw that go he would not. So I made up my mind to let him stay, resolving, nevertheless, to see to it, that during the afternoon he had to do with my less important papers.

Nippers, the second on my list, was a whiskered, sallow, and, upon the whole, rather piratical-looking young man of about five and twenty. I always deemed him the victim of two evil powers—ambition and indigestion. The ambition was evinced by a certain impatience of the duties of a mere copyist, an unwarrantable usurpation of strictly professional affairs, such as the original drawing up of legal documents. The indigestion seemed betokened in an occasional nervous testiness and grinning irritability, causing the teeth to audibly grind together over mistakes committed in copying; unnecessary maledictions, hissed, rather than spoken, in the heat of business; and especially by a continual discontent with the height of the table where he worked. Though of a very ingenious mechanical turn, Nippers could never get this table to suit him. He put chips under it, blocks of various sorts, bits of pasteboard, and at last went so far as to attempt an exquisite adjustment by final pieces of folded blotting paper. But no invention would answer. If, for the sake of easing his back, he brought the table lid at a sharp angle well up towards his chin, and wrote there like a man using the steep roof of a Dutch house for his desk:—then he declared that it stopped the circulation in his arms. If now he lowered the table to his waistbands, and stooped over it in writing, then there was a sore aching in his back. In short, the truth of the matter was, Nippers knew not what he wanted. Or, if he wanted any thing, it was to be rid of a scrivener's table altogether. Among the manifestations of his diseased ambition was a fondness he had for receiving visits from certain ambiguous-looking fellows in seedy coats, whom he called his clients. Indeed I was aware that not only was he, at times, considerable of a ward-politician, but he occasionally did a little business at the Justices' courts, and was not unknown on the steps of the Tombs. I have good reason to believe, however, that one individual who called upon him at my chambers, and who, with a grand air, he insisted was his client, was no other than a dun, and the alleged title-deed, a bill. But with all his failings, and the annoyances he caused me, Nippers, like his compatriot Turkey, was a very useful man to me; wrote a neat, swift hand; and, when he chose, was not deficient in a gentlemanly sort of deportment. Added to this, he always dressed in a gentlemanly sort of way; and so, incidentally, reflected credit upon my chambers. Whereas with respect to Turkey, I had much ado to keep him from being a reproach to me. His clothes were apt to look oily and smell of eating-houses. He wore his pantaloons very loose and baggy in summer. His coats were execrable; his hat not to be handled. But while the hat was a thing of indifference to me, inasmuch as his natural civility and deference, as a dependent Englishman, always led him to doff it the moment he entered the room, yet his coat was another matter. Concerning his coats, I reasoned with him; but with no effect. The truth was, I suppose, that a man of so small an income, could not afford to sport such a lustrous face and a lustrous coat at one and the same time. As Nippers once observed, Turkey's money went chiefly for red ink. One winter day I presented Turkey with a highly-respectable looking coat of my own, a padded gray coat, of a most comfortable warmth, and which buttoned straight up from the knee to the neck. I thought Turkey would appreciate the favor, and abate his rashness and obstreperousness of afternoons. But no. I verily believe that buttoning himself up in so downy and blanket-like a coat had a pernicious effect upon him; upon the same principle that too much oats are bad for horses. In fact, precisely as a rash, restive horse is said to feel his oats, so Turkey felt his coat. It made him insolent. He was a man whom prosperity harmed.

Though concerning the self-indulgent habits of Turkey I had my own private surmises, yet touching Nippers I was well persuaded that whatever might be his faults in other respects, he was, at least, a temperate young man. But indeed, nature herself seemed to have been his vintner, and at his birth charged him so thoroughly with an irritable, brandy-like disposition, that all subsequent potations were needless. When I consider how, amid the stillness of my chambers, Nippers would sometimes impatiently rise from his seat, and stooping over his table, spread his arms wide apart, seize the whole desk, and move it, and jerk it, with a grim, grinding motion on the floor, as if the table were a perverse voluntary agent, intent on thwarting and vexing him; I plainly perceive that for Nippers, brandy and water were altogether superfluous.

It was fortunate for me that, owing to its peculiar cause—indigestion—the irritability and consequent nervousness of Nippers, were mainly observable in the morning, while in the afternoon he was comparatively mild. So that Turkey's paroxysms only coming on about twelve o'clock, I never had to do with their eccentricities at one time. Their fits relieved each other like guards. When Nippers' was on, Turkey's was off; and *vice versa*. This was a good natural arrangement under the circumstances.

Ginger Nut, the third on my list, was a lad some twelve years old. His father was a carman, ambitious of seeing his son on the bench instead of a cart, before he died. So he sent him to my office as student at law, errand boy, and cleaner and sweeper, at the rate of one dollar a week. He had a little desk to himself, but he did not use it much. Upon inspection, the drawer exhibited a great array of the shells of various sorts of nuts. Indeed, to this quick-witted youth the whole noble science of the law was contained in a nut-shell. Not the least among the employments of Ginger Nut, as well as one which he discharged with the most alacrity, was his duty as cake and apple purveyor for Turkey and Nippers. Copying law papers being proverbially dry, husky sort of business, my two scriveners were fain to moisten their mouths very often with Spitzenbergs to be had at the numerous stalls nigh the Custom House and Post Office. Also, they sent Ginger Nut very frequently for that peculiar cake—small, flat, round, and very spicy—after which he had been named by them. Of a cold morning when business was but dull, Turkey would gobble up scores of these cakes, as if they were mere wafers—indeed they sell them at the rate of six or eight for a penny—the scrape of his pen blending with the crunching of the crisp particles in his mouth. Of all the fiery afternoon blunders and flurried rashnesses of Turkey, was his once moistening a ginger-cake between his lips, and clapping it on to a mortgage for a seal. I came within an ace of dismissing him then. But he mollified me by making an oriental bow, and saying—"With submission, sir, it was generous of me to find you in stationery on my own account."

Now my original business—that of a conveyancer and title hunter, and drawer-up of recondite documents of all sorts—was considerably increased by receiving the master's office. There was now great work for scriveners. Not only must I push the clerks already with me, but I must have additional help. In answer to my advertisement, a motionless young man one morning, stood upon my office threshold, the door being open, for it was summer. I can see that figure now—pallidly neat, pitiably respectable, incurably forlorn! It was Bartleby.

After a few words touching his qualifications, I engaged him, glad to have among my corps of copyists a man of so singularly sedate an aspect, which I thought might operate beneficially upon the flighty temper of Turkey, and the fiery one of Nippers.

I should have stated before that ground glass folding-doors divided my premises into two parts, one of which was occupied by my scriveners, the other by myself. According to my humor I threw open these doors, or closed them. I resolved to assign Bartleby a corner by the folding-doors, but on my side of them, so as to have this quiet man within easy call, in case any trifling thing was to be done. I placed his desk close up to a small side-window in that part of the room, a window which originally had afforded a lateral view of certain grimy back-yards and bricks, but which, owing to subsequent erections, commanded at present no view at all, though it gave some light. Within three feet of the panes was a wall, and the light came down from far above, between two lofty buildings, as from a very small opening in a dome. Still further to a satisfactory arrangement, I procured a high green folding screen, which might entirely isolate Bartleby from my sight, though not remove him from my voice. And thus, in a manner, privacy and society were conjoined.

At first Bartleby did an extraordinary quantity of writing. As if long famishing for something to copy, he seemed to gorge himself on my documents. There was no pause for digestion. He ran a day and night line, copying by sun-light and by candle-light. I should have been quite delighted with his application, had he been cheerfully industrious. But he wrote on silently, palely, mechanically.

It is, of course, an indispensable part of a scrivener's business to verify the accuracy of his copy, word by word. Where there are two or more scriveners in an office, they assist each other in this examination, one reading from the copy, the other holding the original. It is a very dull, wearisome, and lethargic affair. I can readily imagine that to some sanguine temperaments it would be altogether intolerable. For example, I cannot credit that the mettlesome poet Byron would have contentedly sat down with Bartleby to examine a law document of, say five hundred pages, closely written in a crimpy hand.

Now and then, in the haste of business, it had been my habit to assist in comparing some brief document myself, calling Turkey or Nippers for this purpose. One object I had in placing Bartleby so handy to me behind the screen, was to avail myself of his services on such trivial occasions. It was on the third day, I think, of his being with me, and before any necessity had arisen for having his own writing examined, that, being much hurried to complete a small affair I had in hand, I abruptly called to Bartleby. In my haste and natural expectancy of instant compliance, I sat with my head bent over the original on my desk, and my right hand sideways, and somewhat nervously extended with the copy, so that immediately upon emerging from his retreat, Bartleby might snatch it and proceed to business without the least delay.

In this very attitude did I sit when I called to him, rapidly stating what it was I wanted him to do—namely, to examine a small paper with me. Imagine my surprise, nay, my consternation, when without moving from his privacy, Bartleby in a singularly mild, firm voice, replied, "I would prefer not to."

I sat awhile in perfect silence, rallying my stunned faculties. Immediately it occurred to me that my ears had deceived me, or Bartleby had entirely misunderstood my meaning. I repeated my request in the clearest tone I could assume. But in quite as clear a one came the previous reply, "I would prefer not to."

"Prefer not to," echoed I, rising in high excitement, and crossing the room with a stride. "What do you mean? Are you moon-struck? I want you to help me compare this sheet here—take it," and I thrust it towards him.

"I would prefer not to," said he.

I looked at him steadfastly. His face was leanly composed; his gray eye dimly calm. Not a wrinkle of agitation rippled him. Had there been the least uneasiness, anger, impatience or impertinence in his manner; in other words, had there been any thing ordinarily human about him, doubtless I should have violently dismissed him from the premises. But as it was, I should have as soon thought of turning my pale plaster-of-paris bust of Cicero out of doors. I stood gazing at him awhile, as he went on with his own writing, and then reseated myself at my desk. This is very strange, thought I. What had one best do? But my business hurried me. I concluded to forget the matter for the present, reserving it for my future leisure. So calling Nippers from the other room, the paper was speedily examined.

A few days after this, Bartleby concluded four lengthy documents, being quadruplicates of a week's testimony taken before me in my High Court of Chancery. It became necessary to examine them. It was an important suit, and great accuracy was imperative. Having all things arranged I called Turkey, Nippers and Ginger Nut from the next room, meaning to place the four copies in the hands of my four clerks, while I should read from the original. Accordingly Turkey, Nippers and Ginger Nut had taken their seats in a row, each with his document in hand, when I called to Bartleby to join this interesting group.

"Bartleby! quick, I am waiting."

I heard a slow scrape of his chair legs on the uncarpeted floor, and soon he appeared standing at the entrance of his hermitage.

"What is wanted?" said he mildly.

"The copies, the copies," said I hurriedly. "We are going to examine them. There"—and I held towards him the fourth quadruplicate.

"I would prefer not to," he said, and gently disappeared behind the screen.

For a few moments I was turned into a pillar of salt, standing at the head of my seated column of clerks. Recovering myself, I advanced towards the screen, and demanded the reason for such extraordinary conduct.

"*Why* do you refuse?"

"I would prefer not to."

With any other man I should have flown outright into a dreadful passion, scorned all further words, and thrust him ignominiously from my presence. But there was something about Bartleby that not only strangely disarmed me, but in a wonderful manner touched and disconcerted me. I began to reason with him.

"These are your own copies we are about to examine. It is labor saving to you, because one examination will answer for your four papers. It is common usage. Every copyist is bound to help examine his copy. Is it not so? Will you not speak? Answer!"

"I prefer not to," he replied in a flute-like tone. It seemed to me that while I had been addressing him, he carefully revolved every statement that I made; fully comprehended the meaning; could not gainsay the irresistible conclusions; but, at the same time, some paramount consideration prevailed with him to reply as he did.

"You are decided, then, not to comply with my request—a request made according to common usage and common sense?"

He briefly gave me to understand that on that point my judgment was sound. Yes: his decision was irreversible.

It is not seldom the case that when a man is browbeaten in some unprecedented and violently unreasonable way, he begins to stagger in his own plainest faith. He begins, as it were, vaguely to surmise that, wonderful as it may be, all the justice and all the reason is on the other side. Accordingly, if any disinterested persons are present, he turns to them for some reinforcement for his own faltering mind.

"Turkey," said I, "what do you think of this? Am I not right?"

"With submission, sir," said Turkey, with his blandest tone, "I think that you are."

"Nippers," said I, "what do *you* think of it?"

"I think I should kick him out of the office."

(The reader of nice perceptions will here perceive that, it being morning, Turkey's answer is couched in polite and tranquil terms, but Nippers replies in ill-tempered ones. Or, to repeat a previous sentence, Nippers' ugly mood was on duty and Turkey's off.)

"Ginger Nut," said I, willing to enlist the smallest suffrage in my behalf, "what do you think of it?"

"I think, sir, he's a little *luny*," replied Ginger Nut with a grin.

"You hear what they say," said I, turning towards the screen, "come forth and do your duty."

But he vouchsafed no reply. I pondered a moment in sore perplexity. But once more business hurried me. I determined again to postpone the consideration of this dilemma to my future leisure. With a little trouble we made out to examine the papers without Bartleby, though at every page or two, Turkey deferentially dropped his opinion that this proceeding was quite out of the common; while Nippers, twitching in his chair with a dyspeptic nervousness, ground out between his set teeth occasional hissing maledictions against the stubborn oaf behind the screen. And for his (Nippers') part, this was the first and the last time he would do another man's business without pay.

Meanwhile Bartleby sat in his hermitage, oblivious to every thing but his own peculiar business there.

Some days passed, the scrivener being employed upon another lengthy work. His late remarkable conduct led me to regard his ways narrowly. I observed that he never went to dinner; indeed that he never went any where. As yet I had never of my personal knowledge known him to be outside of my office. He was a perpetual sentry in the corner. At about eleven o'clock though, in the morning, I noticed that Ginger Nut would advance toward the opening in Bartleby's screen, as if silently beckoned thither by a gesture invisible to me where I sat. The boy would then leave the office jingling a few pence, and reappear with a handful of ginger-nuts which he delivered in the hermitage, receiving two of the cakes for his trouble.

He lives, then, on ginger-nuts, thought I; never eats a dinner, properly speaking; he must be a vegetarian then; but no; he never eats even vegetables, he eats nothing but ginger-nuts. My mind then ran on in reveries concerning the probable effects upon the human constitution of living entirely on ginger-nuts. Ginger-nuts are so called because they contain ginger as one of their peculiar constituents, and the final flavoring one. Now what was ginger? A hot, spicy thing. Was Bartleby hot and spicy? Not at all. Ginger, then, had no effect upon Bartleby. Probably he preferred it should have none.

Nothing so aggravates an earnest person as a passive resistance. If the individual so resisted be of a not inhumane temper, and the resisting one perfectly harmless in his passivity; then, in the better moods of the former, he will endeavor charitably to construe to his imagination what proves impossible to be solved by his judgment. Even so, for the most part, I regarded Bartleby and his ways. Poor fellow! thought I, he means no mischief; it is plain he intends no insolence; his aspect sufficiently evinces that his eccentricities are involuntary. He is useful to me. I can get along with him. If I turn him away, the chances are he will fall in with some less indulgent employer, and then he will be rudely treated, and perhaps driven forth miserably to starve. Yes. Here I can cheaply purchase a delicious self-approval. To befriend Bartleby; to humor him in his strange willfulness, will cost me little or nothing, while I lay up in my soul what will eventually prove a sweet morsel for my conscience. But this mood was not invariable with me. The passiveness of Bartleby sometimes irritated me. I felt strangely goaded on to encounter him in new opposition, to elicit some angry spark from him answerable to my own. But indeed I might as well have essayed to strike fire with my knuckles against a bit of Windsor soap. But one afternoon the evil impulse in me mastered me, and the following little scene ensued:

"Bartleby," said I, "when those papers are all copied, I will compare them with you."

"I would prefer not to."

"How? Surely you do not mean to persist in that mulish vagary?"

No answer.

I threw open the folding-doors near by, and turning upon Turkey and Nippers, exclaimed in an excited manner—

"He says, a second time, he won't examine his papers. What do you think of it, Turkey?"

It was afternoon, be it remembered. Turkey sat glowing like a brass boiler, his bald head steaming, his hands reeling among his blotted papers.

"Think of it?" roared Turkey; "I think I'll just step behind his screen, and black his eyes for him!"

So saying, Turkey rose to his feet and threw his arms into a pugilistic position. He was hurrying away to make good his promise, when I detained him, alarmed at the effect of incautiously rousing Turkey's combativeness after dinner.

"Sit down, Turkey," said I, "and hear what Nippers has to say. What do you think of it, Nippers? Would I not be justified in immediately dismissing Bartleby?"

"Excuse me, that is for you to decide, sir. I think his conduct quite unusual, and indeed unjust, as regards Turkey and myself. But it may only be a passing whim."

"Ah," exclaimed I, "you have strangely changed your mind then—you speak very gently of him now."

"All beer," cried Turkey; "gentleness is effects of beer—Nippers and I dined together to-day. You see how gentle *I* am, sir. Shall I go and black his eyes?"

"You refer to Bartleby, I suppose. No, not to-day, Turkey," I replied; "pray, put up your fists."

I closed the doors, and again advanced towards Bartleby. I felt additional incentives tempting me to my fate. I burned to be rebelled against again. I remembered that Bartleby never left the office.

"Bartleby," said I, "Ginger Nut is away; just step round to the Post Office, won't you? (it was but a three minute walk,) and see if there is any thing for me."

"I would prefer not to."

"You *will* not?"

"I *prefer* not."

I staggered to my desk, and sat there in a deep study. My blind inveteracy returned. Was there any other thing in which I could procure myself to be ignominiously repulsed by this lean, penniless wight?—my hired clerk? What added thing is there, perfectly reasonable, that he will be sure to refuse to do?

"Bartleby!"

No answer.

"Bartleby," in a louder tone.

No answer.

"Bartleby," I roared.

Like a very ghost, agreeably to the laws of magical invocation, at the third summons, he appeared at the entrance of his hermitage.

"Go to the next room, and tell Nippers to come to me."

"I prefer not to," he respectfully and slowly said, and mildly disappeared.

"Very good, Bartleby," said I, in a quiet sort of serenely severe self-possessed tone, intimating the unalterable purpose of some terrible retribution very close at hand. At the moment I half intended something of the kind. But upon the whole, as it was drawing towards my dinner-hour, I thought it best to put on my hat and walk home for the day, suffering much from perplexity and distress of mind.

Shall I acknowledge it? The conclusion of this whole business was, that it soon became a fixed fact of my chambers, that a pale young scrivener, by the name of Bartleby, and a desk there; that he copied for me at the usual rate of four cents a folio (one hundred words); but he was permanently exempt from examining the work done by him, that duty being transferred to Turkey and Nippers, one of compliment doubtless to their superior acuteness; moreover, said Bartleby was never on any account to be dispatched on the most trivial errand of any sort; and that even if entreated to take upon him such a matter, it was generally understood that he would prefer not to—in other words, that he would refuse pointblank.

As days passed on, I became considerably reconciled to Bartleby. His steadiness, his freedom from all dissipation, his incessant industry (except when he chose to throw himself into a standing revery behind his screen), his great, stillness, his unalterableness of demeanor under all circumstances, made him a valuable acquisition. One prime thing was this,—*he was always there;*—first in the morning, continually through the day, and the last at night. I had a singular confidence in his honesty. I felt my most precious papers perfectly safe in his hands. Sometimes to be sure I could not, for the very soul of me, avoid falling into sudden spasmodic passions with him. For it was exceeding difficult to bear in mind all the time those strange peculiarities, privileges, and unheard of exemptions, forming the tacit stipulations on Bartleby's part under which he remained in my office. Now and then, in the eagerness of dispatching pressing business, I would inadvertently summon Bartleby, in a short, rapid tone, to put his finger, say, on the incipient tie of a bit of red tape with which I was about compressing some papers. Of course, from behind the screen the usual answer, "I prefer not to," was sure to come; and then, how could a human creature with the common infirmities of our nature, refrain from bitterly exclaiming upon such perverseness—such unreasonableness. However, every added repulse of this sort which I received only tended to lessen the probability of my repeating the inadvertence.

Here it must be said, that according to the custom of most legal gentlemen occupying chambers in densely-populated law buildings, there were several keys to my door. One was kept by a woman residing in the attic, which person weekly scrubbed and daily swept and dusted my apartments. Another was kept by Turkey for convenience sake. The third I sometimes carried in my own pocket. The fourth I knew not who had.

Now, one Sunday morning I happened to go to Trinity Church, to hear a celebrated preacher, and finding myself rather early on the ground, I thought I would walk around to my chambers for a while. Luckily I had my key with me; but upon applying it to the lock, I found it resisted by something inserted from the inside. Quite surprised, I called out; when to my consternation a key was turned from within; and thrusting his lean visage at me, and holding the door ajar, the apparition of Bartleby appeared, in his shirt sleeves, and otherwise in a strangely tattered dishabille, saying quietly that he was sorry, but he was deeply engaged just then, and—preferred not admitting me at present. In a brief word or two, he moreover added, that perhaps I had better walk round the block two or three times, and by that time he would probably have concluded his affairs.

Now, the utterly unsurmised appearance of Bartleby, tenanting my law-chambers of a Sunday morning, with his cadaverously gentlemanly *nonchalance*, yet withal firm and self-possessed, had such a strange effect upon me, that incontinently I slunk away from my own door, and did as desired. But not without sundry twinges of impotent rebellion against the mild effrontery of this unaccountable scrivener. Indeed, it was his wonderful mildness chiefly, which not only disarmed me, but unmanned me, as it were. For I consider that one, for the time, is a sort of unmanned when he tranquilly permits his hired clerk to dictate to him, and order him away from his own premises. Furthermore, I was full of uneasiness as to what Bartleby could possibly be doing in my office in his shirt sleeves, and in an otherwise dismantled condition of a Sunday morning. Was any thing amiss going on? Nay, that was out of the question. It was not to be thought of for a moment that Bartleby was an immoral person. But what could he be doing there?—copying? Nay again, whatever might be his eccentricities, Bartleby was an eminently decorous person. He would be the last man to sit down to his desk in any state approaching to nudity. Besides, it was Sunday; and there was something about Bartleby that forbade the supposition that he would by any secular occupation violate the proprieties of the day.

Nevertheless, my mind was not pacified; and full of a restless curiosity, at last I returned to the door. Without hindrance I inserted my key, opened it, and entered. Bartleby was not to be seen. I looked round anxiously, peeped behind his screen; but it was very plain that he was gone. Upon more closely examining the place, I surmised that for an indefinite period Bartleby must have ate, dressed, and slept in my office, and that too without plate, mirror, or bed. The cushioned seat of a rickety old sofa in one corner bore the faint impress of a lean, reclining form. Rolled away under his desk, I found a blanket; under the empty grate, a blacking box and brush; on a chair, a tin basin, with soap and a ragged towel; in a newspaper a few crumbs of ginger-nuts and a morsel of cheese. Yes, thought I, it is evident enough that Bartleby has been making his home here, keeping bachelor's hall all by himself. Immediately then the thought came sweeping across me, What miserable friendlessness and loneliness are here revealed! His poverty is great; but his solitude, how horrible! Think of it. Of a Sunday, Wall-street is deserted as Petra; and every night of every day it is an emptiness. This building too, which of week-days hums with industry and life, at nightfall echoes with sheer vacancy, and all through Sunday is forlorn. And here Bartleby makes his home; sole spectator of a solitude which he has seen all populous—a sort of innocent and transformed Marius brooding among the ruins of Carthage!

For the first time in my life a feeling of overpowering stinging melancholy seized me. Before, I had never experienced aught but a not-unpleasing sadness. The bond of a common humanity now drew me irresistibly to gloom. A fraternal melancholy! For both I and Bartleby were sons of Adam. I remembered the bright silks and sparkling faces I had seen that day, in gala trim, swan-like sailing down the Mississippi of Broadway; and I contrasted them with the pallid copyist, and thought to myself, Ah, happiness courts the light, so we deem the world is gay; but misery hides aloof, so we deem that misery there is none. These sad fancyings—chimeras, doubtless, of a sick and silly brain—led on to other and more special thoughts, concerning the eccentricities of Bartleby. Presentiments of strange discoveries hovered round me. The scrivener's pale form appeared to me laid out, among uncaring strangers, in its shivering winding sheet.

Suddenly I was attracted by Bartleby's closed desk, the key in open sight left in the lock.

I mean no mischief, seek the gratification of no heartless curiosity, thought I; besides, the desk is mine, and its contents too, so I will make bold to look within. Every thing was methodically arranged, the papers smoothly placed. The pigeon holes were deep, and removing the files of documents, I groped into their recesses. Presently I felt something there, and dragged it out. It was an old bandanna handkerchief, heavy and knotted. I opened it, and saw it was a savings' bank.

I now recalled all the quiet mysteries which I had noted in the man. I remembered that he never spoke but to answer; that though at intervals he had considerable time to himself, yet I had never seen him reading—no, not even a newspaper; that for long periods he would stand looking out, at his pale window behind the screen, upon the dead brick wall; I was quite sure he never visited any refectory or eating house; while his pale face clearly indicated that he never drank beer like Turkey, or tea and coffee even, like other men; that he never went any where in particular that I could learn; never went out for a walk, unless indeed that was the case at present; that he had declined telling who he was, or whence he came, or whether he had any relatives in the world; that though so thin and pale, he never complained of ill health. And more than all, I remembered a certain unconscious air of pallid—how shall I call it?—of pallid haughtiness, say, or rather an austere reserve about him, which had positively awed me into my tame compliance with his eccentricities, when I had feared to ask him to do the slightest incidental thing for me, even though I might know, from his long-continued motion-lessness, that behind his screen he must be standing in one of those dead-wall reveries of his.

Revolving all these things, and coupling them with the recently discovered fact that he made my office his constant abiding place and home, and not forgetful of his morbid moodiness; revolving all these things, a prudential feeling began to steal over me. My first emotions had been those of pure melancholy and sincerest pity; but just in proportion as the forlornness of Bartleby grew and grew to my imagination, did that same melancholy merge into fear, that pity into repul-sion. So true it is, and so terrible too, that up to a certain point the thought or sight of misery enlists our best affections; but, in certain special cases, beyond that point it does not. They err who would assert that invariably this is owing to the inherent selfishness of the human heart. It rather proceeds from a certain hopelessness of remedying excessive and organic ill. To a sensitive being, pity is not seldom pain. And when at last it is perceived that such pity cannot lead to effec-tual succor, common sense bids the soul rid of it. What I saw that morning persuaded me that the scrivener was the victim of innate and incurable disorder. I might give alms to his body; but his body did not pain him; it was his soul that suffered, and his soul I could not reach.

I did not accomplish the purpose of going to Trinity Church that morning. Somehow, the things I had seen disqualified me for the time from church-going. I walked homeward, think-ing what I would do with Bartleby. Finally, I resolved upon this;—I would put certain calm questions to him the next morning, touching his history, etc., and if he declined to answer them openly and unreservedly (and I supposed he would prefer not), then to give him a twenty dollar bill over and above whatever I might owe him, and tell him his services were no longer required; but that if in any other way I could assist him, I would be happy to do so, especially if he desired to return to his native place, wherever that might be, I would willingly help to defray the expenses. Moreover, if, after reaching home, he found himself at any time in want of aid, a letter from him would be sure of a reply.

The next morning came.

"Bartleby," said I, gently calling to him behind his screen.

No reply.

"Bartleby," said I, in a still gentler tone, "come here; I am not going to ask you to do any thing you would prefer not to do—I simply wish to speak to you."

Upon this he noiselessly slid into view.

"Will you tell me, Bartleby, where you were born?"

"I would prefer not to."

"Will you tell me *any thing* about yourself?"

"I would prefer not to."

"But what reasonable objection can you have to speak to me? I feel friendly towards you."

He did not look at me while I spoke, but kept his glance fixed upon my bust of Cicero, which as I then sat, was directly behind me, some six inches above my head.

"What is your answer, Bartleby?" said I, after waiting a considerable time for a reply, during which his countenance remained immovable, only there was the faintest conceivable tremor of the white attenuated mouth.

"At present I prefer to give no answer," he said, and retired into his hermitage.

It was rather weak in me I confess, but his manner on this occasion nettled me. Not only did there seem to lurk in it a certain calm disdain, but his perverseness seemed ungrateful, considering the undeniable good usage and indulgence he had received from me.

Again I sat ruminating what I should do. Mortified as I was at his behavior, and resolved as I had been to dismiss him when I entered my offices, nevertheless I strangely felt something superstitious knocking at my heart, and forbidding me to carry out my purpose, and denouncing me for a villain if I dared to breathe one bitter word against this forlornest of mankind. At last, familiarly drawing my chair behind his screen, I sat down and said: "Bartleby, never mind then about revealing your history; but let me entreat you, as a friend, to comply as far as may be with the usages of this office. Say now you will help to examine papers to-morrow or next day: in short, say now that in a day or two you will begin to be a little reasonable:—say so, Bartleby."

"At present I would prefer not to be a little reasonable," was his mildly cadaverous reply.

Just then the folding-doors opened, and Nippers approached. He seemed suffering from an unusually bad night's rest, induced by severer indigestion then common. He overheard those final words of Bartleby.

"*Prefer not*, eh?" gritted Nippers—"I'd *prefer* him, if I were you, sir," addressing me—"I'd *prefer* him; I'd give him preferences, the stubborn mule! What is it, sir, pray, that he *prefers* not to do now?"

Bartleby moved not a limb.

"Mr. Nippers," said I, "I'd prefer that you would withdraw for the present."

Somehow, of late I had got into the way of involuntarily using this word "prefer" upon all sorts of not exactly suitable occasions. And I trembled to think that my contact with the scrivener had already and seriously affected me in a mental way. And what further and deeper aberration might it not yet produce? This apprehension had not been without efficacy in determining me to summary means.

As Nippers, looking very sour and sulky, was departing, Turkey blandly and deferentially approached.

"With submission, sir," said he, "yesterday I was thinking about Bartleby here, and I think that if he would but prefer to take a quart of good ale every day, it would do much towards mending him, and enabling him to assist in examining his papers."

"So you have got the word too," said I, slightly excited.

"With submission, what word, sir," asked Turkey, respectfully crowding himself into the contracted space behind the screen, and by so doing, making me jostle the scrivener. "What word, sir?"

"I would prefer to be left alone here," said Bartleby, as if offended at being mobbed in his privacy.

"*That's* the word, Turkey," said I—"that's it."

"Oh, *prefer*? oh yes—queer word. I never use it myself. But, sir, as I was saying, if he would but prefer—"

"Turkey," interrupted I, "you will please withdraw."

"Oh certainly, sir, if you prefer that I should."

As he opened the folding-door to retire, Nippers at his desk caught a glimpse of me, and asked whether I would prefer to have a certain paper copied on blue paper or white. He did not in the least roguishly accent the word prefer. It was plain that it involuntarily rolled form his tongue. I thought to myself, surely I must get rid of a demented man, who already has in some degree turned the tongues, if not the heads of myself and clerks. But I thought it prudent not to break the dismission at once.

The next day I noticed that Bartleby did nothing but stand at his window in his dead-wall revery. Upon asking him why he did not write, he said that he had decided upon doing no more writing.

"Why, how now? what next?" exclaimed I, "do no more writing?"

"No more."

"And what is the reason?"

"Do you not see the reason for yourself," he indifferently replied.

I looked steadfastly at him, and perceived that his eyes looked dull and glazed. Instantly it occurred to me, that his unexampled diligence in copying by his dim window for the first few weeks of his stay with me might have temporarily impaired his vision.

I was touched. I said something in condolence with him. I hinted that of course he did wisely in abstaining from writing for a while; and urged him to embrace that opportunity of taking wholesome exercise in the open air. This, however, he did not do. A few days after this, my other clerks being absent, and being in a great hurry to dispatch certain letters by the mail, I thought that, having nothing else earthly to do, Bartleby would surely be less inflexible than usual, and carry these letters to the post-office. But he blankly declined. So, much to my inconvenience, I went myself.

Still added days went by. Whether Bartleby's eyes improved or not, I could not say. To all appearance, I thought they did. But when I asked him if they did, he vouchsafed no answer. At all events, he would do no copying. At last, in reply to my urgings, he informed me that he had permanently given up copying.

"What!" exclaimed I; "suppose your eyes should get entirely well—better than ever before—would you not copy then?"

"I have given up copying," he answered, and slid aside.

He remained as ever, a fixture in my chamber. Nay—if that were possible—he became still more of a fixture than before. What was to be done? He would do nothing in the office: why should he stay there? In plain fact, he had now become a millstone to me, not only useless as a necklace, but afflictive to bear. Yet I was sorry for him. I speak less than truth when I say that, on his own account, he occasioned me uneasiness. If he would but have named a single relative or friend, I would instantly have written, and urged their taking the poor fellow away to some convenient retreat. But he seemed alone, absolutely alone in the universe. A bit of wreck in the mid Atlantic. At length, necessities connected with my business tyrannized over all other considerations. Decently as I could, I told Bartleby that in six days' time he must unconditionally leave the office. I warned him to take measures, in the interval, for procuring some other abode. I offered to assist him in this endeavor, if he himself would but take the first step towards a removal. "And when you finally quit me, Bartleby," added I, "I shall see that you go not away entirely unprovided. Six days from this hour, remember."

At the expiration of that period, I peeped behind the screen, and lo! Bartleby was there.

I buttoned up my coat, balanced myself; advanced slowly towards him, touched his shoulder, and said, "The time has come; you must quit this place; I am sorry for you; here is money; but you must go."

"I would prefer not," he replied, with his back still towards me.

"You *must*."

He remained silent.

Now I had an unbounded confidence in this man's common honesty. He had frequently restored to me sixpences and shillings carelessly dropped upon the floor, for I am apt to be very reckless in such shirt-button affairs. The proceeding then which followed will not be deemed extraordinary.

"Bartleby," said I, "I owe you twelve dollars on account; here are thirty-two; the odd twenty are yours.—Will you take it?" and I handed the bills towards him.

But he made no motion.

"I will leave them here then," putting them under a weight on the table. Then taking my hat and cane and going to the door I tranquilly turned and added—"After you have removed your things from these offices, Bartleby, you will of course lock the door—since every one is now gone for the day but you—and if you please, slip your key underneath the mat, so that I may have it in the morning. I shall not see you again; so good-bye to you. If hereafter in your new place of abode I can be of any service to you, do not fail to advise me by letter. Good-bye, Bartleby, and fare you well."

But he answered not a word; like the last column of some ruined temple, he remained standing mute and solitary in the middle of the otherwise deserted room.

As I walked home in a pensive mood, my vanity got the better of my pity. I could not but highly plume myself on my masterly management in getting rid of Bartleby. Masterly I call it, and such it must appear to any dispassionate thinker. The beauty of my procedure seemed to consist in its perfect quietness. There was no vulgar bullying, no bravado of any sort, no choleric hectoring, and striding to and fro across the apartment, jerking out vehement commands for Bartleby to bundle himself off with his beggarly traps. Nothing of the kind. Without loudly bidding Bartleby depart—as an inferior genius might have done—I *assumed* the ground that depart he must; and upon that assumption built all I had to say. The more I thought over my procedure, the more I was charmed with it. Nevertheless, next morning, upon awakening, I had my doubts,—I had somehow slept off the fumes of vanity. One of the coolest and wisest hours a man has, is just after he awakes in the morning. My procedure seemed as sagacious as ever.—But only in theory. How it would prove in practice—there was the rub. It was truly a beautiful thought to have assumed Bartleby's departure; but, after all, that assumption was simply my own, and none of Bartleby's. The great point was, not whether I had assumed that he would quit me, but whether he would prefer so to do. He was more a man of preferences than assumptions.

After breakfast, I walked down town, arguing the probabilities *pro* and *con*. One moment I thought it would prove a miserable failure, and Bartleby would be found all alive at my office as usual; the next moment it seemed certain that I should see his chair empty. And so I kept veering about. At the corner of Broadway and Canal-street, I saw quite an excited group of people standing in earnest conversation.

"I'll take odds he doesn't," said a voice as I passed.

"Doesn't go?—done!" said I, "put up your money."

I was instinctively putting my hand in my pocket to produce my own, when I remembered that this was an election day. The words I had overheard bore no reference to Bartleby, but to the success or non-success of some candidate for the mayoralty. In my intent frame of mind, I had, as it were, imagined that all Broadway shared in my excitement, and were debating the same question with me. I passed on, very thankful that the uproar of the street screened my momentary absent-mindedness.

As I had intended, I was earlier than usual at my office door. I stood listening for a moment. All was still. He must be gone. I tried the knob. The door was locked. Yes, my procedure had worked to a charm; he indeed must be vanished. Yet a certain melancholy mixed with this: I was almost sorry for my brilliant success. I was fumbling under the door mat for the key, which Bartleby was to have left there for me, when accidentally my knee knocked against a panel, producing a summoning sound, and in response a voice came to me from within—"Not yet; I am occupied."

It was Bartleby.

I was thunderstruck. For an instant I stood like the man who, pipe in mouth, was killed one cloudless afternoon long ago in Virginia, by a summer lightning; at his own warm open window he was killed, and remained leaning out there upon the dreamy afternoon, till some one touched him, when he fell.

"Not gone!" I murmured at last. But again obeying that wondrous ascendancy which the inscrutable scrivener had over me, and from which ascendancy, for all my chafing, I could not completely escape, I slowly went down stairs and out into the street, and while walking round the block, considered what I should next do in this unheard-of perplexity. Turn the man out by an actual thrusting I could not; to drive him away by calling him hard names would not do; calling in the police was an unpleasant idea; and yet, permit him to enjoy his cadaverous triumph over me,—this too I could not think of. What was to be done? or, if nothing could be done, was there any thing further that I could *assume* in the matter? Yes, as before I had prospectively assumed that Bartleby would depart, so now I might retrospectively assume that departed he was. In the legitimate carrying out of this assumption, I might enter my office in a great hurry, and pretending not to see Bartleby at all, walk straight against him as if he were air. Such a proceeding would in a singular degree have the appearance of a home-thrust. It was hardly possible that Bartleby could withstand such an application of the doctrine of assumptions. But upon second thoughts the success of the plan seemed rather dubious. I resolved to argue the matter over with him again.

"Bartleby," said I, entering the office, with a quietly severe expression, "I am seriously displeased. I am pained, Bartleby. I had thought better of you. I had imagined you of such a gentlemanly organization, that in any delicate dilemma a slight hint would have suffice—in short, an assumption. But it appears I am deceived. Why," I added, unaffectedly starting, "you have not even touched that money yet," pointing to it, just where I had left it the evening previous.

He answered nothing.

"Will you, or will you not, quit me?" I now demanded in a sudden passion, advancing close to him.

"I would prefer *not* to quit you," he replied, gently emphasizing the *not*.

"What earthly right have you to stay here? Do you pay any rent? Do you pay my taxes? Or is this property yours?"

He answered nothing.

"Are you ready to go on and write now? Are your eyes recovered? Could you copy a small paper for me this morning? or help examine a few lines? or step round to the post-office? In a word, will you do any thing at all, to give a coloring to your refusal to depart the premises?"

He silently retired into his hermitage.

I was now in such a state of nervous resentment that I thought it but prudent to check myself at present from further demonstrations. Bartleby and I were alone. I remembered the tragedy of the unfortunate Adams and the still more unfortunate Colt in the solitary office of the latter; and how poor Colt, being dreadfully incensed by Adams, and imprudently permitting himself to get wildly excited, was at unawares hurried into his fatal act—an act which certainly no man could possibly deplore more than the actor himself. Often it had occurred to me in my ponderings upon the subject, that had that altercation taken place in the public street, or at a private residence, it would not have terminated as it did. It was the circumstance of being alone in a solitary office, up stairs, of a building entirely unhallowed by humanizing domestic associations—an uncarpeted office, doubtless, of a dusty, haggard sort of appearance;—this it must have been, which greatly helped to enhance the irritable desperation of the hapless Colt.

But when this old Adam of resentment rose in me and tempted me concerning Bartleby, I grappled him and threw him. How? Why, simply by recalling the divine injunction: "A new commandment give I unto you, that ye love one another." Yes, this it was that saved me. Aside from higher considerations, charity often operates as a vastly wise and prudent principle—a great safeguard to its possessor. Men have committed murder for jealousy's sake, and anger's sake, and hatred's sake, and selfishness' sake, and spiritual pride's sake; but no man that ever I heard of, ever committed a diabolical murder for sweet charity's sake. Mere self-interest, then, if no better motive can be enlisted, should, especially with high-tempered men, prompt all beings to charity and philanthropy. At any rate, upon the occasion in question, I strove to drown my exasperated feelings towards the scrivener by benevolently construing his conduct. Poor fellow, poor fellow! thought I, he don't mean any thing; and besides, he has seen hard times, and ought to be indulged.

I endeavored also immediately to occupy myself, and at the same time to comfort my despondency. I tried to fancy that in the course of the morning, at such time as might prove agreeable to him, Bartleby, of his own free accord, would emerge from his hermitage, and take up some decided line of march in the direction of the door. But no. Half-past twelve o'clock came; Turkey began to glow in the face, overturn his inkstand, and become generally obstreperous; Nippers abated down into quietude and courtesy; Ginger Nut munched his noon apple; and Bartleby remained standing at his window in one of his profoundest dead-wall reveries. Will it be credited? Ought I to acknowledge it? That afternoon I left the office without saying one further word to him.

Some days now passed, during which, at leisure intervals I looked a little into "Edwards on the Will," and "Priestly on Necessity." Under the circumstances, those books induced a salutary feeling. Gradually I slid into the persuasion that these troubles of mine touching the scrivener, had been all predestinated from eternity, and Bartleby was billeted upon me for some mysterious purpose of an all-wise Providence, which it was not for a mere mortal like me to fathom. Yes, Bartleby, stay there behind your screen, thought I; I shall persecute you no more; you are harmless and noiseless as any of these old chairs; in short, I never feel so private as when I know you are here. At last I see it, I feel it; I penetrate to the predestinated purpose of my life. I am content. Others may have loftier parts to enact; but my mission in this world, Bartleby, is to furnish you with office-room for such period as you may see fit to remain.

I believe that this wise and blessed frame of mind would have continued with me, had it not been for the unsolicited and uncharitable remarks obtruded upon me by my professional friends who visited the rooms. But thus it often is, that the constant friction of illiberal minds wears out at last the best resolves of the more generous. Though to be sure, when I reflected upon it, it was not strange that people entering my office should be struck by the peculiar aspect of the unaccountable Bartleby, and so be tempted to throw out some sinister observations concerning him. Sometimes an attorney having business with me, and calling at my office and finding no one but the scrivener there, would undertake to obtain some sort of precise information from him touching my whereabouts; but without heeding his idle talk, Bartleby would remain standing immovable in the middle of the room. So after contemplating him in that position for a time, the attorney would depart, no wiser than he came.

Also, when a Reference was going on, and the room full of lawyers and witnesses and business was driving fast; some deeply occupied legal gentleman present, seeing Bartleby wholly unemployed, would request him to run round to his (the legal gentleman's) office and fetch some papers for him. Thereupon, Bartleby would tranquilly decline, and yet remain idle as before. Then the lawyer would give a great stare, and turn to me. And what could I say? At last I was made aware that all through the circle of my professional acquaintance, a whisper of wonder was running round, having reference to the strange creature I kept at my office. This worried me very much. And as the idea came upon me of his possibly turning out a long-lived man, and keep occupying my chambers, and denying my authority; and perplexing my visitors; and scandalizing my professional reputation; and casting a general gloom over the premises; keeping soul and body together to the last upon his savings (for doubtless he spent but half a dime a day), and in the end perhaps outlive me, and claim possession of my office by right of his perpetual occupancy: as all these dark anticipations crowded upon me more and more, and my friends continually intruded their relentless remarks upon the apparition in my room; a great change was wrought in me. I resolved to gather all my faculties together, and for ever rid me of this intolerable incubus.

Ere revolving any complicated project, however, adapted to this end, I first simply suggested to Bartleby the propriety of his permanent departure. In a calm and serious tone, I commended the idea to his careful and mature consideration. But having taken three days to meditate upon it, he apprised me that his original determination remained the same in short, that he still preferred to abide with me.

What shall I do? I now said to myself, buttoning up my coat to the last button. What shall I do? what ought I to do? what does conscience say I *should* do with this man, or rather ghost. Rid myself of him, I must; go, he shall. But how? You will not thrust him, the poor, pale, passive mortal,—you will not thrust such a helpless creature out of your door? you will not dishonor yourself by such cruelty? No, I will not, I cannot do that. Rather would I let him live and die here, and then mason up his remains in the wall. What then will you do? For all your coaxing, he will not budge. Bribes he leaves under your own paperweight on your table; in short, it is quite plain that he prefers to cling to you.

Then something severe, something unusual must be done. What! surely you will not have him collared by a constable, and commit his innocent pallor to the common jail? And upon what ground could you procure such a thing to be done?—a vagrant, is he? What! he a vagrant, a wanderer, who refuses to budge? It is because he will *not* be a vagrant, then, that you seek to count him *as* a vagrant. That is too absurd. No visible means of support: there I have him. Wrong again: for indubitably he *does* support himself, and that is the only unanswerable proof that any man can show of his possessing the means so to do. No more then. Since he will not quit me, I must quit him. I will change my offices; I will move elsewhere; and give him fair notice, that if I find him on my new premises I will then proceed against him as a common trespasser.

Acting accordingly, next day I thus addressed him: "I find these chambers too far from the City Hall; the air is unwholesome. In a word, I propose to remove my offices next week, and shall no longer require your services. I tell you this now, in order that you may seek another place."

He made no reply, and nothing more was said.

On the appointed day I engaged carts and men, proceeded to my chambers, and having but little furniture, every thing was removed in a few hours. Throughout, the scrivener remained standing behind the screen, which I directed to be removed the last thing. It was withdrawn; and being folded up like a huge folio, left him the motionless occupant of a naked room. I stood in the entry watching him a moment, while something from within me upbraided me.

I re-entered, with my hand in my pocket—and—and my heart in my mouth.

"Good-bye, Bartleby; I am going—good-bye, and God some way bless you; and take that," slipping something in his hand. But it dropped upon the floor, and then,—strange to say—I tore myself from him whom I had so longed to be rid of.

Established in my new quarters, for a day or two I kept the door locked, and started at every footfall in the passages. When I returned to my rooms after any little absence, I would pause at the threshold for an instant, and attentively listen, ere applying my key. But these fears were needless. Bartleby never came nigh me.

I thought all was going well, when a perturbed looking stranger visited me, inquiring whether I was the person who had recently occupied rooms at No.—Wall-street.

Full of forebodings, I replied that I was.

"Then sir," said the stranger, who proved a lawyer, "you are responsible for the man you left there. He refuses to do any copying; he refuses to do any thing; he says he prefers not to; and he refuses to quit the premises."

"I am very sorry, sir," said I, with assumed tranquility, but an inward tremor, "but, really, the man you allude to is nothing to me—he is no relation or apprentice of mine, that you should hold me responsible for him."

"In mercy's name, who is he?"

"I certainly cannot inform you. I know nothing about him. Formerly I employed him as a copyist; but he has done nothing for me now for some time past."

"I shall settle him then,—good morning, sir."

Several days passed, and I heard nothing more; and though I often felt a charitable prompting to call at the place and see poor Bartleby, yet a certain squeamishness of I know not what withheld me.

All is over with him, by this time, thought I at last, when through another week no further intelligence reached me. But coming to my room the day after, I found several persons waiting at my door in a high state of nervous excitement.

"That's the man—here he comes," cried the foremost one, whom I recognized as the lawyer who had previously called upon me alone.

"You must take him away, sir, at once," cried a portly person among them, advancing upon me, and whom I knew to be the landlord of No.—Wall-street. "These gentlemen, my tenants, cannot stand it any longer; Mr. B—" pointing to the lawyer, "has turned him out of his room, and he now persists in haunting the building generally, sitting upon the banisters of the stairs by day, and sleeping in the entry by night. Every body is concerned; clients are leaving the offices; some fears are entertained of a mob; something you must do, and that without delay."

Aghast at this torrent, I fell back before it, and would fain have locked myself in my new quarters. In vain I persisted that Bartleby was nothing to me—no more than to any one else. In vain:—I was the last person known to have any thing to do with him, and they held me to the terrible account. Fearful then of being exposed in the papers (as one person present obscurely threatened) I considered the matter, and at length said, that if the lawyer would give me a confidential interview with the scrivener, in his (the lawyer's) own room, I would that afternoon strive my best to rid them of the nuisance they complained of.

Going up stairs to my old haunt, there was Bartleby silently sitting upon the banister at the landing.

"What are you doing here, Bartleby?" said I.

"Sitting upon the banister," he mildly replied.

I motioned him into the lawyer's room, who then left us.

"Bartleby," said I, "are you aware that you are the cause of great tribulation to me, by persisting in occupying the entry after being dismissed from the office?"

No answer.

"Now one of two things must take place. Either you must do something, or something must be done to you. Now what sort of business would you like to engage in? Would you like to re-engage in copying for some one?"

"No; I would prefer not to make any change."

"Would you like a clerkship in a dry-goods store?"

"There is too much confinement about that. No, I would not like a clerkship; but I am not particular."

"Too much confinement," I cried, "why you keep yourself confined all the time!"

"I would prefer not to take a clerkship," he rejoined, as if to settle that little item at once.

"How would a bar-tender's business suit you? There is no trying of the eyesight in that."

"I would not like it at all; though, as I said before, I am not particular."

His unwonted wordiness inspirited me. I returned to the charge.

"Well then, would you like to travel through the country collecting bills for the merchants? That would improve your health."

"No, I would prefer to be doing something else."

"How then would going as a companion to Europe, to entertain some young gentleman with your conversation,—how would that suit you?"

"Not at all. It does not strike me that there is any thing definite about that. I like to be stationary. But I am not particular."

"Stationary you shall be then," I cried, now losing all patience, and for the first time in all my exasperating connection with him fairly flying into a passion. "If you do not go away from these premises before night, I shall feel bound—indeed I *am* bound—to—to—to quit the premises myself!" I rather absurdly concluded, knowing not with what possible threat to try to frighten his immobility into compliance. Despairing of all further efforts, I was precipitately leaving him, when a final thought occurred to me—one which had not been wholly unindulged before.

"Bartleby," said I, in the kindest tone I could assume under such exciting circumstances, "will you go home with me now—not to my office, but my dwelling—and remain there till we can conclude upon some convenient arrangement for you at our leisure? Come, let us start now, right away."

"No: at present I would prefer not to make any change at all."

I answered nothing; but effectually dodging every one by the suddenness and rapidity of my flight, rushed from the building, ran up Wall-street towards Broadway, and jumping into the first omnibus was soon removed from pursuit. As soon as tranquility returned I distinctly perceived that I had now done all that I possibly could, both in respect to the demands of the landlord and his tenants, and with regard to my own desire and sense of duty, to benefit Bartleby, and shield him from rude persecution. I now strove to be entirely care-free and quiescent; and my conscience justified me in the attempt; though indeed it was not so successful as I could have wished. So fearful was I of being again hunted out by the incensed landlord and his exasperated tenants, that, surrendering my business to Nippers, for a few days I drove about the upper part of the town and through the suburbs, in my rockaway; crossed over to Jersey City and Hoboken, and paid fugitive visits to Manhattanville and Astoria. In fact I almost lived in my rockaway for the time.

When again I entered my office, lo, a note from the landlord lay upon the desk. I opened it with trembling hands. It informed me that the writer had sent to the police, and had Bartleby removed to the Tombs as a vagrant. Moreover, since I knew more about him than any one else, he wished me to appear at that place, and make a suitable statement of the facts. These tidings had a conflicting effect upon me. At first I was indignant; but at last almost approved. The landlord's energetic, summary disposition had led him to adopt a procedure which I do not think I would have decided upon myself; and yet as a last resort, under such peculiar circumstances, it seemed the only plan.

As I afterwards learned, the poor scrivener, when told that he must be conducted to the Tombs, offered not the slightest obstacle, but in his pale unmoving way, silently acquiesced.

Some of the compassionate and curious bystanders joined the party; and headed by one of the constables arm in arm with Bartleby, the silent procession filed its way through all the noise, and heat, and joy of the roaring thoroughfares at noon.

The same day I received the note I went to the Tombs, or to speak more properly, the Halls of Justice. Seeking the right officer, I stated the purpose of my call, and was informed that the individual I described was indeed within. I then assured the functionary that Bartleby was a perfectly honest man, and greatly to be compassionated, however unaccountably eccentric. I narrated all I knew, and closed by suggesting the idea of letting him remain in as indulgent confinement as possible till something less harsh might be done—though indeed I hardly knew what. At all events, if nothing else could be decided upon, the alms-house must receive him. I then begged to have an interview.

Being under no disgraceful charge, and quite serene and harmless in all his ways, they had permitted him freely to wander about the prison, and especially in the inclosed grass-platted yard thereof. And so I found him there, standing all alone in the quietest of the yards, his face towards a high wall, while all around, from the narrow slits of the jail windows, I thought I saw peering out upon him the eyes of murderers and thieves.

"Bartleby!"

"I know you," he said, without looking round,—"and I want nothing to say to you."

"It was not I that brought you here, Bartleby," said I, keenly pained at his implied suspicion. "And to you, this should not be so vile a place. Nothing reproachful attaches to you by being here. And see, it is not so sad a place as one might think. Look, there is the sky, and here is the grass."

"I know where I am," he replied, but would say nothing more, and so I left him.

As I entered the corridor again, a broad meat-like man, in an apron, accosted me, and jerking his thumb over his shoulder said—"Is that your friend?"

"Yes."

"Does he want to starve? If he does, let him live on the prison fare, that's all."

"Who are you?" asked I, not knowing what to make of such an unofficially speaking person in such a place.

"I am the grub-man. Such gentlemen as have friends here, hire me to provide them with something good to eat."

"Is this so?" said I, turning to the turnkey.

He said it was.

"Well then," said I, slipping some silver into the grub-man's hands (for so they called him). "I want you to give particular attention to my friend there; let him have the best dinner you can get. And you must be as polite to him as possible."

"Introduce me, will you?" said the grub-man, looking at me with an expression which seem to say he was all impatience for an opportunity to give a specimen of his breeding.

Thinking it would prove of benefit to the scrivener, I acquiesced; and asking the grub-man his name, went up with him to Bartleby.

"Bartleby, this is Mr. Cutlets; you will find him very useful to you."

"Your sarvant, sir, your sarvant," said the grub-man, making a low salutation behind his apron. "Hope you find it pleasant here, sir;—spacious grounds—cool apartments, sir—hope you'll stay with us some time—try to make it agreeable. May Mrs. Cutlets and I have the pleasure of your company to dinner, sir, in Mrs. Cutlets' private room?"

"I prefer not to dine to-day," said Bartleby, turning away. "It would disagree with me; I am unused to dinners." So saying he slowly moved to the other side of the inclosure, and took up a position fronting the dead-wall.

"How's this?" said the grub-man, addressing me with a stare of astonishment. "He's odd, aint he?"

"I think he is a little deranged," said I, sadly.

"Deranged? deranged is it? Well now, upon my word, I thought that friend of yourn was a gentleman forger; they are always pale and genteel-like, them forgers. I can't pity 'em—can't help it, sir. Did you know Monroe Edwards?" he added touchingly, and paused. Then, laying his hand pityingly on my shoulder, sighed, "he died of consumption at Sing-Sing. So you weren't acquainted with Monroe?"

"No, I was never socially acquainted with any forgers. But I cannot stop longer. Look to my friend yonder. You will not lose by it. I will see you again."

Some few days after this, I again obtained admission to the Tombs, and went through the corridors in quest of Bartleby; but without finding him.

"I saw him coming from his cell not long ago," said a turnkey, "may be he's gone to loiter in the yards."

So I went in that direction.

"Are you looking for the silent man?" said another turnkey passing me. "Yonder he lies—sleeping in the yard there. 'Tis not twenty minutes since I saw him lie down."

The yard was entirely quiet. It was not accessible to the common prisoners. The surrounding walls, of amazing thickness, kept off all sounds behind them. The Egyptian character of the masonry weighed upon me with its gloom. But a soft imprisoned turf grew under foot. The heart of the eternal pyramids, it seemed, wherein, by some strange magic, through the clefts, grass-seed, dropped by birds, had sprung.

Strangely huddled at the base of the wall, his knees drawn up, and lying on his side, his head touching the cold stones, I saw the wasted Bartleby. But nothing stirred. I paused; then went close up to him; stooped over, and saw that his dim eyes were open; otherwise he seemed profoundly sleeping. Something prompted me to touch him. I felt his hand, when a tingling shiver ran up my arm and down my spine to my feet.

The round face of the grub-man peered upon me now. "His dinner is ready. Won't he dine to-day, either? Or does he live without dining?"

"Lives without dining," said I, and closed his eyes.

"Eh!—He's asleep, aint he?"

"With kings and counselors," murmured I.

There would seem little need for proceeding further in this history. Imagination will readily supply the meager recital of poor Bartleby's interment. But ere parting with the reader, let me say, that if this little narrative has sufficiently interested him, to awaken curiosity as to who Bartleby was, and what manner of life he led prior to the present narrator's making his acquaintance, I can only reply, that in such curiosity I fully share, but am wholly unable to gratify it. Yet here I hardly know whether I should divulge one little item of rumor, which came to my ear a few months after the scrivener's decease. Upon what basis it rested, I could never ascertain; and hence, how true it is I cannot now tell. But inasmuch as this vague report has not been without certain strange suggestive interest to me, however sad, it may prove the same with some others; and so I will briefly mention it. The report was this: that Bartleby had been a subordinate clerk in the Dead Letter Office at Washington, from which he had been suddenly removed by a change in the administration. When I think over this rumor, I cannot adequately express the emotions which seize me. Dead letters! does it not sound like dead men? Conceive a man by nature and misfortune prone to a pallid hopelessness, can any business seem more fitted to heighten it than that of continually handling these dead letters, and assorting them for the flames? For by the cart-load they are annually burned. Sometimes from out the folded paper the pale clerk takes a ring:—the finger it was meant for, perhaps, moulders in the grave; a bank-note sent in swiftest charity:—he whom it would relieve, nor eats nor hungers any more; pardon for those who died despairing; hope for those who died unhoping; good tidings for those who died stifled by unrelieved calamities. On errands of life, these letters speed to death.

Ah Bartleby! Ah humanity!

Recitatif
(1983)

TONI MORRISON

My mother danced all night and Roberta's was sick. That's why we were taken to St. Bonny's. People want to put their arms around you when you tell them you were in a shelter, but it really wasn't bad. No big long room with one hundred beds like Bellevue. There were four to a room, and when Roberta and me came, there was a shortage of state kids, so we were the only ones assigned to 406 and could go from bed to bed if we wanted to. And we wanted to, too. We changed beds every night and for the whole four months we were there we never picked one out as our own permanent bed.

It didn't start out that way. The minute I walked in and the Big Bozo introduced us, I got sick to my stomach. It was one thing to be taken out of your own bed early in the morning— it was something else to be stuck in a strange place with a girl from a whole other race. And Mary, that's my mother, she was right. Every now and then she would stop dancing long enough to tell me something important and one of the things she said was that they never washed their hair and they smelled funny. Roberta sure did. Smell funny, I mean. So when the Big Bozo (nobody ever called her Mrs. Itkin, just like nobody ever said St. Bonaventure)— when she said, "Twyla, this is Roberta. Roberta, this is Twyla. Make each other welcome." I said, "My mother won't like you putting me in here."

"Good," said Bozo. "Maybe then she'll come and take you home."

How's that for mean? If Roberta had laughed I would have killed her, but she didn't. She just walked over to the window and stood with her back to us.

"Turn around," said the Bozo. "Don't be rude. Now Twyla. Roberta. When you hear a loud buzzer, that's the call for dinner. Come down to the first floor. Any fights and no movie." And then, just to make sure we knew what we would be missing, "*The Wizard of Oz.*"

Roberta must have thought I meant that my mother would be mad about my being put in the shelter. Not about rooming with her, because as soon as Bozo left she came over to me and said, "Is your mother sick too?"

"No," I said. "She just likes to dance all night."

"Oh," she nodded her head and I liked the way she understood things so fast. So for the moment it didn't matter that we looked like salt and pepper standing there and that's what the other kids called us sometimes. We were eight years old and got F's all the time. Me because I couldn't remember what I read or what the teacher said. And Roberta because she couldn't read at all and didn't even listen to the teacher. She wasn't good at anything except jacks, at which she was a killer: pow scoop pow scoop pow scoop.

We didn't like each other all that much at first, but nobody else wanted to play with us because we weren't real orphans with beautiful dead parents in the sky. We were dumped. Even the New York City Puerto Ricans and the upstate Indians ignored us. All kinds of kids were in there, black ones, white ones, even two Koreans. The food was good, though. At least I thought so. Roberta hated it and left whole pieces of things on her plate: Spam, Salisbury steak—even jello with fruit cocktail in it, and she didn't care if I ate what she wouldn't. Mary's idea of supper was popcorn and a can of Yoo-Hoo. Hot mashed potatoes and two weenies was like Thanksgiving for me.

It really wasn't bad, St. Bonny's. The big girls on the second floor pushed us around now and then. But that was all. They wore lipstick and eyebrow pencil and wobbled their knees while they watched TV. Fifteen, sixteen, even, some of them were. They were put-out girls, scared runaways most of them. Poor little girls who fought their uncles off but looked tough to us, and mean. God did they look mean. The staff tried to keep them separate from the younger children, but sometimes they caught us watching them in the orchard where they played radios and danced with each other. They'd light out after us and pull our hair or twist our arms. We were scared of them, Roberta and me, but neither of us and wanted the other one to know it. So we got a good list of dirty names we could shout back when we ran from them through the orchard. I used to dream a lot and almost always the orchard was there. Two acres, four maybe, of these little apple trees. Hundreds of them. Empty and crooked like beggar women when I first came to St. Bonny's but fat with flowers when I left. I don't know why I dreamt about that orchard so much. Nothing really happened there. Nothing all that important, I mean. Just the big girls dancing and playing the radio. Roberta and me watching. Maggie fell down there once. The kitchen woman with legs like parentheses. And the big girls laughed at her. We should have helped her up, I know, but we were scared of those girls with lipstick and eyebrow pencil. Maggie couldn't talk. The kids said she had her tongue cut out, but I think she was just born that way: mute. She was old and sandy-colored and she worked in the kitchen. I don't know if she was nice or not. I just remember her legs like parentheses and how she rocked when she walked. She worked from early in the morning till two o'clock, and if she was late, if she had too much cleaning and didn't get out till two-fifteen or so, she'd cut through the orchard so she wouldn't miss her bus and have to wait another hour. She wore this really stupid little hat—a kid's hat with ear flaps—and she wasn't much taller than we were. A really awful little hat. Even for a mute, it was dumb—dressing like a kid and never saying anything at all.

"But what about if somebody tries to kill her?" I used to wonder about that. "Or what if she wants to cry? Can she cry?"

"Sure," Roberta said. "But just tears. No sounds come out."

"She can't scream?"

"Nope. Nothing."

"Can she hear?"

"I guess."

"Let's call her," I said. And we did.

"Dummy! Dummy!" She never turned her head.

"Bow legs! Bow legs!" Nothing. She just rocked on, the chin straps of her baby-boy hat swaying from side to side. I think we were wrong. I think she could hear and didn't let on.

And it shames me even now to think there was somebody in there after all who heard us call her those names and couldn't tell on us.

We got along all right, Roberta and me. Changed beds every night, got F's in civics and communication skills and gym. The Bozo was disappointed in us, she said. Out of 130 of us state cases, 90 were under twelve. Almost all were real orphans with beautiful dead parents in the sky. We were the only ones dumped and the only ones with F's in three classes including gym. So we got along—what with her leaving whole pieces of things on her plate and being nice about not asking questions.

I think it was the day before Maggie fell down that we found out our mothers were coming to visit us on the same Sunday. We had been at the shelter twenty-eight days (Roberta twenty-eight and a half) and this was their first visit with us. Our mothers would come at ten o'clock in time for chapel, then lunch with us in the teachers' lounge. I thought if my dancing mother met her sick mother it might be good for her. And Roberta thought her sick mother would get a big bang out of a dancing one. We got excited about it and curled each other's hair. After breakfast we sat on the bed watching the road from the window. Roberta's socks were still wet. She washed them the night before and put them on the radiator to dry. They hadn't, but she put them on anyway because their tops were so pretty—scalloped in pink. Each of us had a purple construction-paper basket that we had made in craft class. Mine had a yellow crayon rabbit on it. Roberta's had eggs with wiggly lines of color. Inside were cellophane grass and just the jelly beans because I'd eaten the two marshmallow eggs they gave us. The Big Bozo came herself to get us. Smiling she told us we looked very nice and to come downstairs. We were so surprised by the smile we'd never seen before, neither of us moved.

"Don't you want to see your mommies?"

I stood up first and spilled the jelly beans all over the floor. Bozo's smile disappeared while we scrambled to get the candy up off the floor and put it back in the grass.

She escorted us downstairs to the first floor, where the other girls were lining up to file into the chapel. A bunch of grown-ups stood to one side. Viewers mostly. The old biddies who wanted servants and the fags who wanted company looking for children they might want to adopt. Once in a while a grandmother. Almost never anybody young or anybody whose face wouldn't scare you in the night. Because if any of the real orphans had young relatives they wouldn't be real orphans. I saw Mary right away. She had on those green slacks I hated and hated even more now because didn't she know we were going to chapel? And that fur jacket with the pocket linings so ripped she had to pull to get her hands out of them. But her face was pretty—like always, and she smiled and waved like she was the little girl looking for her mother—not me.

I walked slowly, trying not to drop the jelly beans and hoping the paper handle would hold. I had to use my last Chiclet because by the time I finished cutting everything out, all the Elmer's was gone. I am left handed and the scissors never worked for me. It didn't matter, though; I might just as well have chewed the gum. Mary dropped to her knees and grabbed me, mashing the basket, the jelly beans, and the grass into her ratty fur jacket.

"Twyla, baby. Twyla, baby!"

I could have killed her. Already I heard the big girls in the orchard the next time saying, "Twyyyyyla, baby!" But I couldn't stay mad at Mary while she was smiling and hugging me and smelling of Lady Esther dusting powder. I wanted to stay buried in her fur all day.

To tell the truth I forgot about Roberta. Mary and I got in line for the traipse into chapel and I was feeling proud because she looked so beautiful even in those ugly green slacks that made her behind stick out. A pretty mother on earth is better than a beautiful dead one in the sky even if she did leave you all alone to go dancing.

I felt a tap on my shoulder, turned, and saw Roberta smiling. I smiled back, but not too much lest somebody think this visit was the biggest thing that ever happened in my life. Then Roberta said, "Mother, I want you to meet my roommate, Twyla. And that's Twyla's mother."

I looked up it seemed for miles. She was big. Bigger than any man and on her chest was the biggest cross I'd ever seen. I swear it was six inches long each way. And in the crook of her arm was the biggest Bible ever made.

Mary, simple-minded as ever, grinned and tried to yank her hand out of the pocket with the raggedy lining—to shake hands, I guess. Roberta's mother looked down at me and then looked down at Mary too. She didn't say anything, just grabbed Roberta with her Bible-free hand and stepped out of line, walking quickly to the rear of it. Mary was still grinning because she's not too swift when it comes to what's really going on. Then this light bulb goes off in her head and she says "That bitch!" really loud and us almost in the chapel now. Organ music whining; the Bonny Angels singing sweetly. Everybody in the world turned around to look. And Mary would have kept it up—kept calling names if I hadn't squeezed her hand as hard as I could. That helped a little, but she still twitched and crossed and uncrossed her legs all through service. Even groaned a couple of times. Why did I think she would come there and act right? Slacks. No hat like the grandmothers and viewers, and groaning all the while. When we stood for hymns she kept her mouth shut. Wouldn't even look at the words on the page. She actually reached in her purse for a mirror to check her lipstick. All I could think of was that she really needed to be killed. The sermon lasted a year, and I knew the real orphans were looking smug again.

We were supposed to have lunch in the teachers' lounge, but Mary didn't bring anything, so we picked fur and cellophane grass off the mashed jelly beans and ate them. I could have killed her. I sneaked a look at Roberta. Her mother had brought chicken legs and ham sandwiches and oranges and a whole box of chocolate-covered grahams. Roberta drank milk from a thermos while her mother read the Bible to her.

Things are not right. The wrong food is always with the wrong people. Maybe that's why I got into waitress work later—to match up the right people with the right food. Roberta just let those chicken legs sit there, but she did bring a stack of grahams up to me later when the visit was over. I think she was sorry that her mother would not shake my mother's hand. And I liked that and I liked the fact that she didn't say a word about Mary groaning all the way through the service and not bringing any lunch.

Roberta left in May when the apple trees were heavy and white. On her last day we went to the orchard to watch the big girls smoke and dance by the radio. It didn't matter that they said, "Twyyyyyla, baby." We sat on the ground and breathed. Lady Esther. Apple blossoms. I still go soft when I smell one or the other. Roberta was going home. The big cross and the big Bible was coming to get her and she seemed sort of glad and sort of not. I thought I would die in that room of four beds without her and I knew Bozo had plans to move some other dumped kid in there with me. Roberta promised to write every day, which was really sweet of her because she couldn't read a lick so how could she write anybody. I would have drawn pictures and sent them to her but she never gave me her address. Little by little she faded.

Her wet socks with the pink scalloped tops and her big serious-looking eyes—that's all I could catch when I tried to bring her to mind.

I was working behind the counter at the Howard Johnson's on the Thruway just before the Kingston exit. Not a bad job. Kind of a long ride from Newburgh, but okay once I got there. Mine was the second night shift—eleven to seven. Very light until a Greyhound checked in for breakfast around six-thirty. At that hour the sun was all the way clear of the hills behind the restaurant. The place looked better at night—more like shelter—but I loved it when the sun broke in, even if it did show all the cracks in the vinyl and the speckled floor looked dirty no matter what the mop boy did.

It was August and a bus crowd was just unloading. They would stand around a long while: going to the john, and looking at gifts and junk-for-sale machines, reluctant to sit down so soon. Even to eat. I was trying to fill the coffee pots and get them all situated on the electric burners when I saw her. She was sitting in a booth smoking a cigarette with two guys smothered in head and facial hair. Her own hair was so big and wild I could hardly see her face. But the eyes. I would know them anywhere. She had on a powder-blue halter and shorts outfit and earrings the size of bracelets. Talk about lipstick and eyebrow pencil. She made the big girls look like nuns. I couldn't get off the counter until seven o'clock, but I kept watching the booth in case they got up to leave before that. My replacement was on time for a change, so I counted and stacked my receipts as fast as I could and signed off. I walked over to the booth, smiling and wondering if she would remember me. Or even if she wanted to remember me. Maybe she didn't want to be reminded of St. Bonny's or to have anybody know she was ever there. I know I never talked about it to anybody.

I put my hands in my apron pockets and leaned against the back of the booth facing them.
"Roberta? Roberta Fisk?"
She looked up. "Yeah?"
"Twyla."
She squinted for a second and then said, "Wow."
"Remember me."
"Sure. Hey. Wow."
"It's been a while," I said, and gave a smile to the two hairy guys.
"Yeah. Wow. You work here?"
"Yeah," I said. "I live in Newburgh."
"Newburgh? No kidding?" She laughed then a private laugh that included the guys but only the guys, and they laughed with her. What could I do but laugh too and wonder why I was standing there with my knees showing out from under that uniform. Without looking I could see the blue and white triangle on my head, my hair shapeless in a net, my ankles thick in white oxfords. Nothing could have been less sheer than my stockings. There was this silence that came down right after I laughed. A silence it was her turn to fill up. With introductions, maybe, to her boyfriends or an invitation to sit down and have a Coke. Instead she lit a cigarette off the one she'd just finished and said, "We're on our way to the Coast. He's got an appointment with Hendrix." She gestured casually toward the boy next to her.
"Hendrix? Fantastic," I said. "Really fantastic. What's she doing now?"
Roberta coughed on her cigarette and the two guys rolled their eyes up at the ceiling.
"Hendrix. Jimi Hendrix, asshole. He's only the biggest—Oh, wow. Forget it."
I was dismissed without anyone saying goodbye, so I thought I would do it for her.

"How's your mother?" I asked. Her grin cracked her whole face. She swallowed. "Fine," she said. "How's yours?"

"Pretty as a picture," I said and turned away. The backs of my knees were damp. Howard Johnson's really was a dump in the sunlight.

James is as comfortable as a house slipper. He liked my cooking and I liked his big loud family. They have lived in Newburgh all of their lives and talk about it the way people do who have always known a home. His grandmother is a porch swing older than his father and when they talk about streets and avenues and buildings they call them names they no longer have. They still call the A & P Rico's because it stands on property once a mom and pop store owned by Mr. Rico. And they call the new community college Town Hall because it once was. My mother-in-law puts up jelly and cucumbers and buys butter wrapped in cloth from a dairy. James and his father talk about fishing and baseball and I can see them all together on the Hudson in a raggedy skiff. Half the population of Newburgh is on welfare now, but to my husband's family it was still some upstate paradise of a time long past. A time of ice houses and vegetable wagons, coal furnaces and children weeding gardens. When our son was born my mother-in-law gave the crib blanket that had been hers.

But the town they remembered had changed. Something quick was in the air. Magnificent old houses, so ruined they had become shelter for squatters and rent risks, were bought and renovated. Smart IBM people moved out of their suburbs back into the city and put shutters up and herb gardens in their backyards. A brochure came in the mail announcing the opening of a Food Emporium. Gourmet food it said—and listed items the rich IBM crowd would want. It was located in a new mall at the edge of town and I drove out to shop there one day—just to see. It was late in June. After the tulips were gone and the Queen Elizabeth roses were open everywhere. I trailed my cart along the aisle tossing in smoked oysters and Robert's sauce and things I knew would sit in my cupboard for years. Only when I found some Klondike ice cream bars did I feel less guilty about spending James's fireman's salary so foolishly. My father-in-law ate them with the same gusto little Joseph did.

Waiting in the check-out line I heard a voice say, "Twyla!"

The classical music piped over the aisles had affected me and the woman leaning toward me was dressed to kill. Diamonds on her hand, a smart white summer dress. "I'm Mrs. Benson," I said.

"Ho. Ho. The Big Bozo," she sang.

For a split second I didn't know what she was talking about. She had a bunch of asparagus and two cartons of fancy water.

"Roberta!"

"Right."

"For heaven's sake. Roberta."

"You look great," she said.

"So do you. Where are you? Here? In Newburgh?"

"Yes. Over in Annandale."

I was opening my mouth to say more when the cashier called my attention to her empty counter.

"Meet you outside." Roberta pointed her finger and went into the express line.

I placed the groceries and kept myself from glancing around to check Roberta's progress. I remembered Howard Johnson's and looking for a chance to speak only to be greeted with a stingy "wow." But she was waiting for me and her huge hair was sleek now, smooth around a small, nicely shaped head. Shoes, dress, everything lovely and summery and rich. I was dying to know what happened to her, how she got from Jimi Hendrix to Annandale, a neighborhood full of doctors and IBM executives. Easy, I thought. Everything is so easy for them, They think they own the world.

"How long," I asked her. "How long have you been here?"

"A year. I got married to a man who lives here. And you, you're married too, right? Benson, you said."

"Yeah. James Benson."

"And is he nice?"

"Oh, is he nice?"

"Well, is he?" Roberta's eyes were steady as though she really meant the question and wanted an answer.

"He's wonderful, Roberta. Wonderful."

"So you're happy."

"Very."

"That's good," she said and nodded her head. "I always hoped you'd be happy. Any kids? I know you have kids."

"One. A boy. How about you?"

"Four."

"Four?"

She laughed. "Step kids. He's a widower."

"Oh."

"Got a minute? Let's have a coffee."

I thought about the Klondikes melting and the inconvenience of going all the way to my car and putting the bags in the trunk. Served me right for buying all that stuff I didn't need. Roberta was ahead of me.

"Put them in my car. It's right here."

And then I saw the dark blue limousine.

"You married a Chinaman?"

"No," she laughed. "He's the driver."

"Oh, my. If the Big Bozo could see you now."

We both giggled. Really giggled. Suddenly, in just a pulse beat, twenty years disappeared and all of it came rushing back. The big girls (whom we called gar girls—Roberta's misheard word for the evil stone faces described in a civics class) there dancing in the orchard, the ploppy mashed potatoes, the double weenies, the Spam with pineapple. We went into the coffee shop holding on to one another and I tried to think why we were glad to see each other this time and not before. Once, twelve years ago, we passed like strangers. A black girl and a white girl meeting in a Howard Johnson's on the road and having nothing to say. One in a blue and white triangle waitress hat—the other on her way to see Hendrix. Now we were behaving like sisters separated for much too long. Those four short months were nothing in time. Maybe it was the thing itself. Just being there, together. Two little girls who knew what nobody else in the world knew—how not to ask questions. How to believe what had to be believed. There was politeness in that reluctance and generosity as well. Is your mother sick too? No, she dances all night. Oh—and an understanding nod.

We sat in a booth by the window and fell into recollection like veterans.

"Did you ever learn to read?"

"Watch." She picked up the menu. "Special of the day. Cream of corn soup. Entrées. Two dots and a wriggly line. Quiche. Chef salad, scallops. . ."

I was laughing and applauding when the waitress came up.

"Remember the Easter baskets?"

"And how we tried to *introduce* them?"

"Your mother with that cross like two telephone poles."

"And yours with those tight slacks."

We laughed so loudly heads turned and made the laughter harder to suppress.

"What happened to the Jimi Hendrix date?"

Roberta made a blow-out sound with her lips.

"When he died I thought about you."

"Oh, you heard about him finally?"

"Finally. Come on, I was a small-town country waitress."

"And I was a small-town country dropout. God, were we wild. I still don't know how I got out of there alive."

"But you did."

"I did. I really did. Now I'm Mrs. Kenneth Norton."

"Sounds like a mouthful."

"It is."

"Servants and all?"

Roberta held up two fingers.

"Ow! What does he do?"

"Computers and stuff. What do I know?"

"I don't remember a hell of a lot from those days, but Lord, St. Bonny's is as clear as daylight. Remember Maggie? The day she fell down and those gar girls laughed at her?"

Roberta looked up from her salad and stared at me. "Maggie didn't fall," she said.

"Yes, she did. You remember."

"No, Twyla. They knocked her down. Those girls pushed her down and tore her clothes. In the orchard."

"I don't—that's not what happened."

"Sure it is. In the orchard. Remember how scared we were?"

"Wait a minute. I don't remember any of that."

"And Bozo was fired."

"You're crazy. She was there when I left. You left before me."

"I went back. You weren't there when they fired Bozo."

"What?"

"Twice. Once for a year when I was about ten, another for two months when I was fourteen. That's when I ran away."

"You ran away from St. Bonny's?"

"I had to. What do you want? Me dancing in that orchard?"

"Are you sure about Maggie?"

"Of course I'm sure. You've blocked it, Twyla. It happened. Those girls had behavior problems, you know."

"Didn't they, though. But why can't I remember the Maggie thing?"

"Believe me. It happened. And we were there."

"Who did you room with when you went back?" I asked her as if I would know her. The Maggie thing was troubling me.

"Creeps. They tickled themselves in the night."

My ears were itching and I wanted to go home suddenly. This was all very well but she couldn't just comb her hair, wash her face and pretend everything was hunky-dory. After the Howard Johnson's snub. And no apology. Nothing.

"Were you on dope or what that time at Howard Johnson's?" I tried to make my voice sound friendlier than I felt.

"Maybe a little. I never did drugs much. Why?"

"I don't know; you acted sort of like you didn't want to know me then."

"Oh, Twyla, you know how it was in those days: black—white. You know how everything was."

But I didn't know. I thought it was just the opposite. Busloads of blacks and whites came into Howard Johnson's together. They roamed together then: students, musicians, lovers, protesters. You got to see everything at Howard Johnson's and blacks were very friendly with whites in those days. But sitting there with nothing on my plate but two hard tomato wedges wondering about the melting Klondikes it seemed childish remembering the slight. We went to her car, and with the help of the driver, got my stuff into my station wagon.

"We'll keep in touch this time," she said.

"Sure," I said. "Sure. Give me a call."

"I will," she said, and then just as I was sliding behind the wheel, she leaned into the window. "By the way. Your mother. Did she ever stop dancing?"

I shook my head. "No. Never."

Roberta nodded.

"And yours? Did she ever get well?"

She smiled a tiny sad smile. "No. She never did. Look, call me, okay?"

"Okay," I said, but I knew I wouldn't. Roberta had messed up my past somehow with that business about Maggie. I wouldn't forget a thing like that. Would I?

Strife came to us that fall. At least that's what the paper called it. Strife. Racial strife. The word made me think of a bird—a big shrieking bird out of 1,000,000,000 B.C. Flapping its wings and cawing. Its eye with no lid always bearing down on you. All day it screeched and at night it slept on the rooftops. It woke you in the morning and from the *Today* show to the eleven o'clock news it kept you an awful company.

I couldn't figure it out from one day to the next. I knew I was supposed to feel something strong, but I didn't know what, and James wasn't any help. Joseph was on the list of kids to be transferred from the junior high school to another one at some far-out-of-the-way place and I thought it was a good thing until I heard it was a bad thing. I mean I didn't know. All the schools seemed dumps to me, and the fact that one was nicer looking didn't hold much weight. But the papers were full of it and then the kids began to get jumpy. In August, mind you. Schools weren't even open yet. I thought Joseph might be frightened to go over there, but he didn't seem scared so I forgot about it, until I found myself driving along Hudson Street out there by the school they were trying to integrate and saw a line of women marching. And who do you suppose was in line, big as life, holding a sign in front of her bigger than her mother's cross? MOTHERS HAVE RIGHTS TOO! it said.

I drove on, and then changed my mind. I circled the block, slowed down, and honked my horn.

Roberta looked over and when she saw me she waved. I didn't wave back, but I didn't move either. She handed her sign to another woman and came over to where I was parked.

"Hi."

"What are you doing?"

"Picketing. What's it look like?"

"What for?"

"What do you mean, 'What for?' They want to take my kids and send them out of the neighborhood. They don't want to go."

"So what if they go to another school? My boy's being bussed too, and I don't mind. Why should you?"

"It's not about us, Twyla. Me and you. It's about our kids."

"What's more *us* than that?"

"Well, it is a free country."

"Not yet, but it will be."

"What the hell does that mean? I'm not doing anything to you."

"You really think that?"

"I know it."

"I wonder what made me think you were different."

"I wonder what made me think you were different."

"Look at them," I said. "Just look. Who do they think they are? Swarming all over the place like they own it. And now they think they can decide where my child goes to school. Look at them, Roberta. They're Bozos."

Roberta turned around and looked at the women. Almost all of them were standing still now, waiting. Some were even edging toward us. Roberta looked at me out of some refrigerator behind her eyes. "No, they're not. They're just mothers."

"And what am I? Swiss cheese?"

"I used to curl your hair."

"I hated your hands in my hair."

The women were moving. Our faces looked mean to them of course and they looked as though they could not wait to throw themselves in front of a police car, or better yet, into my car and drag me away by my ankles. Now they surrounded my car and gently, gently began to rock it. I swayed back and forth like a sideways yo-yo. Automatically I reached for Roberta, like the old days in the orchard when they saw us watching them and we had to get out of there, and if one of us fell the other pulled her up and if one of us was caught the other stayed to kick and scratch, and neither would leave the other behind. My arm shot out of the car window but no receiving hand was there. Roberta was looking at me sway from side to side in the car and her face was still. My purse slid from the car seat down under the dashboard. The four policemen who had been drinking Tab in their car finally got the message and strolled over, forcing their way through the women. Quietly, firmly they spoke. "Okay, ladies. Back in line or off the streets."

Some of them went away willingly; others had to be urged away from the car doors and the hood. Roberta didn't move. She was looking steadily at me. I was fumbling to turn on the ignition, which wouldn't catch because the gearshift was still in drive. The seats of the car were a mess because the swaying had thrown my grocery coupons all over it and my purse was sprawled on the floor.

"Maybe I am different now, Twyla. But you're not. You're the same little state kid who kicked a poor old black lady when she was down on the ground. You kicked a black lady and you have the nerve to call me a bigot."

The coupons were everywhere and the guts of my purse were bunched under the dashboard. What was she saying? Black? Maggie wasn't black.

"She wasn't black," I said.

"Like hell she wasn't, and you kicked her. We both did. You kicked a black lady who couldn't even scream."

"Liar!"

"You're the liar! Why don't you just go on home and leave us alone, huh?"

She turned away and I skidded away from the curb.

The next morning I went into the garage and cut the side out of the carton our portable TV had come in. It wasn't nearly big enough, but after a while I had a decent sign: red spray-painted letters on a white background—AND SO DO CHILDREN****. I meant just to go down to the school and tack it up somewhere so those cows on the picket line across the street could see it, but when I got there, some ten or so others had already assembled—protesting the cows across the street. Police permits and everything. I got in line and we strutted in time on our side while Roberta's group strutted on theirs. That first day we were all dignified, pretending the other side didn't exist. The second day there was name calling and finger gestures. But that was about all. People changed signs from time to time, but Roberta never did and neither did I. Actually my sign didn't make sense without Roberta's. "And so do children what?" one of the women on my side asked me. Have rights, I said, as though it was obvious.

Roberta didn't acknowledge my presence in any way and I got to thinking maybe she didn't know I was there. I began to pace myself in the line, jostling people one minute and lagging behind the next, so Roberta and I could reach the end of our respective lines at the same time and there would be a moment in our turn when we would face each other. Still, I couldn't tell whether she saw me and knew my sign was for her. The next day I went early before we were scheduled to assemble. I waited until she got there before I exposed my new creation. As soon as she hoisted her MOTHERS HAVE RIGHTS TOO I began to wave my new one, which said, HOW WOULD YOU KNOW? I know she saw that one, but I had gotten addicted now. My signs got crazier each day, and the women on my side decided that I was a kook. They couldn't make heads or tails out of my brilliant screaming posters.

I brought a painted sign in queenly red with huge black letters that said, IS YOUR MOTHER WELL? Roberta took her lunch break and didn't come back for the rest of the day or any day after. Two days later I stopped going too and couldn't have been missed because nobody understood my signs anyway.

It was a nasty six weeks. Classes were suspended and Joseph didn't go to anybody's school until October. The children—everybody's children—soon got bored with that extended vacation they thought was going to be so great. They looked at TV until their eyes flattened. I spent a couple of mornings tutoring my son, as the other mothers said we should. Twice I opened a text from last year that he had never turned in. Twice he yawned in my face. Other mothers organized living room sessions so the kids would keep up. None of the kids could concentrate so they drifted back to *The Price Is Right* and *The Brady Bunch*. When the school finally opened there were fights once or twice and some sirens roared through the streets every once in a while. There were a lot of photographers from Albany. And just when ABC was about to send up a news crew, the kids settled down like nothing in the world had happened. Joseph hung my HOW WOULD YOU KNOW? sign in his bedroom. I don't know what became of AND SO DO CHILDREN****. I think my father-in-law cleaned some fish on it. He was always puttering around in our garage. Each of his five children lived in Newburgh and he acted as though he had five extra homes.

I couldn't help looking for Roberta when Joseph graduated from high school, but I didn't see her. It didn't trouble me much what she had said to me in the car. I mean the kicking part. I know I didn't do that, I couldn't do that. But I was puzzled by her telling me Maggie was black. When I thought about it I actually couldn't be certain. She wasn't pitch-black. I knew, or I would have remembered that. What I remember was the kiddie hat, and the semicircle legs. I tried to reassure myself about the race thing for a long time until it dawned on me that the truth was already there, and Roberta knew it. I didn't kick her; I didn't join in with the gar girls and kick that lady, but I sure did want to. We watched and never tried to help her and never called for help. Maggie was my dancing mother. Deaf, I thought, and dumb. Nobody inside. Nobody who would hear you if you cried in the night. Nobody who could tell you anything important that you could use. Rocking, dancing, swaying as she walked. And when the gar girls pushed her down, and started roughhousing, I knew she wouldn't scream, couldn't—just like me—and I was glad about that.

We decided not to have a tree, because Christmas would be at my mother-in-law's house, so why have a tree at both places? Joseph was at SUNY New Paltz and we had to economize, we said. But at the last minute, I changed my mind. Nothing could be that bad. So I rushed around town looking for a tree, something small but wide. By the time I found a place, it was snowing and very late. I dawdled like it was the most important purchase in the world and the tree man was fed up with me. Finally I chose one and had it tied onto the trunk of the car. I drove away slowly because the sand trucks were not out yet and the streets could be murder at the beginning of a snowfall. Downtown the streets were wide and rather empty except for a cluster of people coming out of the Newburgh Hotel. The one hotel in town that wasn't built out of cardboard and Plexiglas. A party, probably. The men huddled in the snow were dressed in tails and the women had on furs. Shiny things glittered from underneath their coats. It made me tired to look at them. Tired, tired, tired. On the next corner was a small diner with loops and loops of paper bells in the window. I stopped the car and went in. Just for a cup of coffee and twenty minutes of peace before I went home and tried to finish everything before Christmas Eve.

"Twyla."

There she was. In a silvery evening gown and dark fur coat. A man and another woman were with her, the man fumbling for change to put in the cigarette machine. The woman was humming and tapping on the counter with her fingernails. They all looked a little bit drunk.

"Well. It's you."

"How are you?"

I shrugged. "Pretty good. Frazzled. Christmas and all."

"Regular?" called the woman from the counter.

"Fine," Roberta called back and then, "Wait for me in the car."

She slipped into the booth beside me. "I have to tell you something, Twyla. I made up my mind if I ever saw you again, I'd tell you."

"I'd just as soon not hear anything, Roberta. It doesn't matter now, anyway."

"No," she said "Not about that."

"Don't be long," said the woman. She carried two regulars to go and the man peeled his cigarette pack as they left.

"It's about St. Bonny's and Maggie."

"Oh, please."

"Listen to me. I really did think she was black. I didn't make that up. I really thought so. But now I can't be sure. I just remember her as old, so old. And because she couldn't talk—well, you know, I thought she was crazy. She'd been brought up in an institution like my mother was and like I thought I would be too. And you were right. We didn't kick her. It was the gar girls. Only them. But, well, I wanted to. I really wanted them to hurt her. I said we did it, too. You and me, but that's not true. And I don't want you to carry that around. It was just that I wanted to do it so bad that day—wanting to is doing it."

Her eyes were watery from the drinks she'd had, I guess. I know it's that way with me. One glass of wine and I start bawling over the littlest thing.

"We were kids, Roberta."

"Yeah. Yeah. I know, just kids."

"Eight."

"Eight."

"And lonely."

"Scared, too."

She wiped her cheeks with the heel of her hand and smiled. "Well, that's all I wanted to say."

I nodded and couldn't think of any way to fill the silence that went from the diner past the paper bells on out into the snow. It was heavy now. I thought I'd better wait for the sand trucks before starting home.

"Thanks, Roberta."

"Sure."

"Did I tell you? My mother, she never did stop dancing."

"Yes. You told me. And mine, she never got well." Roberta lifted her hands from the table-top and covered her face with her palms. When she took them away she really was crying. "Oh shit, Twyla. Shit, shit, shit. What the hell happened to Maggie?"

Forty-Five a Month
(1943)

R.K. NARAYAN

Shanta could not stay in her class any longer. She had done clay-modelling, music, drill, a bit of alphabets and numbers, and was now cutting coloured paper. She would have to cut till the bell rang and the teacher said, "Now, you may all go home," or "Put away the scissors and take up your alphabets———" Shanta was impatient to know the time. She asked her friend sitting next, " Is it five now?"

"Maybe," she replied.

"Or is it six?"

"I don't think so," her friend replied, "because night comes at six."

"Do you think it is five?"

"Yes."

"Oh, I must go. My father will be back at home now. He has asked me to be ready at five. He is taking me to the cinema this evening. I must go home." She threw down her scissors and ran up to the teacher. "Madam, I must go home."

"Why, Shanta Bai?"

"Because it is five o'clock now."

"Who told you it was five?"

"Kamala."

"It is not five now. It is—do you see the clock there? Tell me what the time is. I taught you to read the clock the other day." Shanta stood gazing at the clock in the hall, counted the figures laboriously and declared, " It is nine o'clock."

The teacher called the other girls and said, "Who will tell me the time from that clock?" Several of them concurred with Shanta and said it was nine o'clock, till the teacher said, "You are only seeing the long hand. See the short one, where is it?"

"Two and a half."

"So what is the time?"

"Two and a half."

"It is two forty-five, understand? Now you may all go to your seats——— " Shanta returned to the teacher in about ten minutes and asked, "Is it five, Madam, because I have to be ready at five ? Otherwise my father will be very angry with me. He asked me to return home early."

"At what time?"

"Now." The teacher gave her permission to leave, and Shanta picked up her books and dashed out of the class with a cry of joy. She ran home, threw her books on the floor, and shouted, "Mother, Mother," and Mother came running from the next house where she had gone to chat with her friends.

Mother asked, "Why are you back so early?"

"Has father come home?" Shanta asked. She would not take her coffee or tiffin, but insisted on being dressed first. She opened the trunk and insisted on wearing the thinnest frock and knickers, while her mother wanted to dress her in a long skirt and thick coat for the evening. Shanta picked out a gorgeous ribbon from a cardboard soap box in which she kept pencils, ribbons and chalk bits. There was a heated argument between mother and daughter over the dress, and finally mother had to give in. Shanta put on her favourite pink frock, braided her hair, and flaunted a green ribbon on her pigtail. She powdered her face and pressed a vermilion mark on her forehead. She said, "Now father will say what a nice girl I am because I'm ready. Aren't you also coming, mother?"

"Not today."

Shanta stood at the little gate looking down the street.

Mother said: "Father will come only after five; don't stand in the sun. It is only four o'clock."

The sun was disappearing behind the house on the opposite row, and Shanta knew that presently it would be dark. She ran in to her mother and asked, "Why hasn't father come home yet, mother?"

"How can I know? He is perhaps held up in the office."

Shanta made a wry face: "I don't like these people in the office. They are bad people——"

She went back to the gate and stood looking out. Her mother shouted from inside: "Come in, Shanta. It is getting dark, don't stand there." But Shanta would not go in. She stood at the gate and a wild idea came to her head. Why should she not go to the office and call out father and then go to the cinema? She wondered where his office might be. She had no notion. She had seen her father take the turn at the end of the street every day. If one went there, one perhaps went automatically to father's office. She threw a glance about to see if mother was anywhere and moved down the street.

It was twilight. Everyone going about looked gigantic, walls of houses appeared very high, and cycles and carriages looked as though they would bear down on her. She walked on the very edge of the road. Soon the lamps were twinkling: and the passers-by looked like shadows. She had taken two turns and did not know where she was. She sat down on the edge of the road biting her nails. She wondered how she was to reach home. A servant employed in the next house was passing along, and she picked herself up and stood before him.

"Oh, what are you doing here all alone?" he asked. She replied, "I don't know. I came here. Will you take me to our house?" She followed him and was soon back in her house.

❀

Venkat Rao, Shanta's father, was about to start for his office that morning when a jutka passed along the street distributing cinema handbills. Shanta dashed to the street and picked up a handbill. She held it up and asked: "Father, will you take me to the cinema today?" He felt unhappy at the question. Here was the child growing up without having any of the amenities and the simple pleasures of life. He had hardly taken her twice to the cinema. He had no time for the child. While children of her age in other houses had all the dolls, dresses, and outings that they wanted, this child was growing up all alone and like a barbarian more or less. He

662

felt furious with his office. For forty rupees a month they seemed to have purchased him out-right.

He reproached himself for neglecting his wife and child—even the wife could have her own circle of friends and so on: she was after all a grown-up, but what about the child? What a drab colourless existence was hers! Every day they kept him at the office till seven or eight in the evening and when he came home the child was asleep. Even on Sundays they wanted him at the office. Why did they think he had no personal life, a life of his own? They gave him hardly any time to take the child to the park or the pictures. He was going to show them that they weren't to toy with him. Yes, he was prepared even to quarrel with his manager if necessary.

He said with resolve: "I will take you to the cinema this evening. Be ready at five."

"Really! Mother!" Shanta shouted. Mother came out of the kitchen.

"Father is taking me to a cinema in the evening."

Shanta's mother smiled cynically. "Don't make false promises to the child——" Venkat Rao glared at her. "Don't talk nonsense. You think you are the only person who keeps promises——"

He told Shanta: "Be ready at five, and I will come and take you positively. If you are not ready, I will be very angry with you."

He walked to his office full of resolve. He would do his normal work and get out at five. If they started any old tricks of theirs, he was going to tell the boss: "Here is my resignation. My child's happiness is more important to me than these horrible papers of yours."

All day the usual stream of papers flowed on to his table and out of it. He scrutinized, signed, and drafted. He was corrected, admonished, and insulted. He had a break of only five minutes in the afternoon for his coffee.

When the office clock struck five and the other clerks were leaving, he went up to the manager and said: "May I go, sir?" The manager looked up from his paper: "You!" It was unthink-able that the cash and account section should be closing at five. "How can you go?"

"I have some urgent, private business, sir," he said, smothering the lines he had been rehearsing since the morning: "Herewith my resignation." He visualized Shanta standing at the door, dressed, and palpitating with eagerness.

"There shouldn't be anything more urgent than the office work; go back to your seat. You know how many hours I work?" asked the manager. The manager came to the office three hours before the opening time and stayed nearly three hours after closing, even on Sundays. The clerks commented among themselves: "His wife must be whipping him whenever he is seen at home; that is why the old owl seems so fond of his office."

"Did you trace the source of that Ten-Eight difference?" asked the manager.

"I shall have to examine two hundred vouchers. I thought we might do it tomorrow."

"No, no, this won't do. You must rectify it immediately." Venkat Rao mumbled, "Yes, sir," and slunk back to his seat.

The clock showed five-thirty. Now it meant two hours of excruciating search among vouchers. All the rest of the office had gone. Only he and another clerk in his section were working, and, of course, the manager was there. Venkat Rao was furious. His mind was made up. He wasn't a slave who had sold himself for forty rupees outright. He could make that money easily; and if he couldn't it would be more honourable to die of starvation.

He took a sheet of paper and wrote: "Herewith my resignation. If you people think you have bought me body and soul for forty rupees, you are mistaken. I think it would be far

663

better for me and my family to die of starvation than slave for this petty forty rupees on which you have kept me for years and years. I suppose you have not the slightest notion of giving me an increment. You give yourselves heavy slices frequently, and I don't see why you shouldn't think of us occasionally. In any case it doesn't interest me now, since this is my resignation. If I and my family perish of starvation, may our ghosts come and haunt you all your life——" He folded the letter, put it in an envelope, sealed the flap and addressed it to the manager. He left his seat and stood before the manager. The manager mechanically received the letter and put it on his pad.

"Venkat Rao," said the manager. "I'm sure you will be glad to hear this news. Our officer discussed the question of increments today, and I've recommended you for an increment of five rupees. Orders are not yet passed and so keep this to yourself for the present." Venkat Rao put out his hand, snatched the envelope from the pad and hastily slipped it in his pocket.

"What is that letter?"

"I have applied for a little casual leave, sir, but I think. . . ."

"You can't get any leave at least for a fortnight to come."

"Yes, sir. I realize that. That is why I am withdrawing my application, sir."

"Very well. Have you traced that mistake?"

"I'm scrutinizing the vouchers, sir. I will find it out within an hour. . . ."

It was nine o'clock when he went home. Shanta had already slept. Her mother said, "She wouldn't even change her frock, thinking that any moment you might be coming and taking her out. She hardly ate any food; and wouldn't lie down for fear of crumpling her dress. . . . ."

Venkat Rao's heart bled when he saw his child sleeping in her pink frock, hair combed, and face powdered, dressed and ready to be taken out. "Why should I not take her to the night show?" He shook her gently and called, "Shanta, Shanta." Shanta kicked her legs and cried, irritated at being disturbed. Mother whispered, "Don't wake her," and patted her back to sleep.

Venkat Rao watched the child for a moment. "I don't know if it is going to be possible for me to take her out at all—you see they are giving me an increment——" he wailed.

Minutes of Glory
(1975)

NGŨGĨ WA THIONG'O

Her name was Wanjiru. But she liked better her Christian one, Beatrice. It sounded more pure and more beautiful. Not that she was ugly; but she could not be called beautiful either. Her body, dark and full fleshed, had the form, yes, but it was as if it waited to be filled by the spirit. She worked in beer halls where sons of women came to drown their inner lives in beer cans and froth. Nobody seemed to notice her. Except, perhaps, when a proprietor or an impatient customer called out her name, Beatrice; then other customers would raise their heads briefly, a few seconds, as if to behold the bearer of such a beautiful name, but not finding anybody there, they would resume their drinking, their ribald jokes, their laughter and play with the other serving girls. She was like a wounded bird in flight: a forced landing now and then but nevertheless wobbling from place to place so that she would variously be found in Alaska, Paradise, The Modern, Thome and other beer-halls all over Limuru. Sometimes it was because an irate proprietor found she was not attracting enough customers; he would sack her without notice and without a salary. She would wobble to the next bar. But sometimes she was simply tired of nesting in one place, a daily witness of familiar scenes; girls even more decidedly ugly than she were fought over by numerous claimants at closing hours. What do they have that I don't have? She would ask herself, depressed. She longed for a bar-kingdom where she would be at least one of the rulers, where petitioners would bring their gifts of beer, frustrated smiles and often curses that hid more lust and love than hate.

She left Limuru town proper and tried the mushrooming townlets around. She worked at Ngarariga, Kamiritho, Rironi and even Tiekunu and everywhere the story was the same. Oh, yes, occasionally she would get a client; but none cared for her as she would have liked, none really wanted her enough to fight over her. She was always a hard-up customer's last resort. No make-believe even, not for her that sweet pretence that men indulged in after their fifth bottle of Tusker. The following night or during a pay-day, the same client would pretend not to know her; he would be trying his money-power over girls who already had more than a fair share of admirers.

She resented this. She saw in every girl a rival and adopted a sullen attitude. Nyagũthiĩ especially was the thorn that always pricked her wounded flesh. Nyagũthiĩ, arrogant and aloof, but men always in her courtyard; Nyagũthiĩ, fighting with men, and to her they would bring propitiating gifts which she accepted as of right. Nyagũthiĩ could look bored, impatient, or downright contemptuous and still men would cling to her as if they enjoyed being whipped with biting words, curled lips and the indifferent eyes of a free woman. Nyagũthiĩ was also a

665

bird in flight, never really able to settle in one place, but in her case it was because she hungered for change and excitement: new faces and new territories for her conquest. Beatrice resented her very shadow. She saw in her the girl she would have liked to be, a girl who was both totally immersed in and yet completely above the underworld of bar violence and sex. Wherever Beatrice went the long shadow of Nyagũthiĩ would sooner or later follow her.

She fled Limuru for Ilmorog in Chiri District. Ilmorog had once been a ghost village, but had been resurrected to life by that legendary woman, Nyang'endo, to whom every pop group had paid their tribute. It was of her that the young dancing Muthuu and Muchun g' wa sang:

When I left Nairobi for Ilmorog
Never did I know
I would bear this wonder-child mine
Nyang'endo.

As a result, Ilmorog was always seen as a town of hope where the weary and the down-trodden would find their rest and fresh water. But again Nyagũthiĩ followed her.

She found that Ilmorog, despite the legend, despite the songs and dances, was not different from Limuru. She tried various tricks. Clothes? But even here she never earned enough to buy herself glittering robes. What was seventy-five shillings a month without house allowance, *posho,* without salaried boy-friends? By that time Ambi had reached Ilmorog, and Beatrice thought that this would be the answer. Had she not, in Limuru, seen girls blacker than herself transformed overnight from ugly sins into white stars by a touch of skin-lightening creams? And men would ogle them, would even talk with exaggerated pride of their newborn girl friends. Men were strange creatures, Beatrice thought in moments of searching analysis. They talked heatedly against Ambi, Butone Firesnow, Moonsnow, wigs, straightened hair; but they always went for a girl with an Ambi-lightened skin and head covered with a wig made in imitation of European or Indian hair. Beatrice never tried to find the root cause of this black self-hatred, she simply accepted the contradiction and applied herself to Ambi with a vengeance. She had to rub out her black shame. But even Ambi she could not afford in abundance; she could only apply it to her face and to her arms so that her legs and her neck retained their blackness. Besides there were parts of her face she could not readily reach — behind the ears and above the eyelashes, for instance — and these were a constant source of shame and irritation to her Ambi-self.

She would always remember this Ambi period as one of her deepest humiliation before her later minutes of glory. She worked in Ilmorog Starlight Bar and Lodging. Nyagũthiĩ, with her bangled hands, her huge earrings, served behind the counter. The owner was a good Christian soul who regularly went to church and paid all his dues to *Harambee* projects. Potbelly. Grey hairs. Soft-spoken. A respectable family man, well known in Ilmorog. Hardworking even, for he would not leave the bar until the closing hours, or more precisely, until Nyagũthiĩ left. He had no eyes for any other girl; he hung around her, and surreptitiously brought her gifts of clothes without receiving gratitude in kind. Only the promise. Only the hope for tomorrow. Other girls he gave eighty shillings a month. Nyagũthiĩ had a room to herself. Nyagũthiĩ woke up whenever she liked to take the stock. But Beatrice and the other girls had to wake up at five or so, make tea for the lodgers, clean up the bar and wash dishes and glasses. Then they would hang around the bar in shifts until two o'clock when they would go for a small break. At five o'clock, they had to be in again, ready for customers whom they would now serve with frothy beers and smiles until twelve o'clock or for as long as there were customers thirsty for more Tuskers and Pilsners. What often galled Beatrice, although in her case it did not matter one way or another, was the owner's insistence that the girls should sleep in Starlight. They would otherwise be late for work, he said. But what he really wanted was for the girls to use their bodies to attract more lodgers in Starlight. Most of the girls, led by Nyagūthiī, defied the rule and bribed the watchman to let them out and in. They wanted to meet their regular or one-night boy-friends in places where they would be free and where they would be treated as not just barmaids. Beatrice always slept in. Her occasional one-night patrons wanted to spend the minimum. Came a night when the owner, refused by Nyagūthiī, approached her. He started by finding fault with her work; he called her names, then as suddenly he started praising her, although in a grudging almost contemptuous manner. He grabbed her, struggled with her, pot-belly, grey hairs, and everything. Beatrice felt an unusual revulsion for the man. She could not, she would not bring herself to accept that which had so recently been cast aside by Nyagūthiī. My God, she wept inside, what does Nyagūthiī have that I don't have? The man now humiliated himself before her. He implored. He promised her gifts. But she would not yield. That night she too defied the rule. She jumped through a window; she sought a bed in another bar and only came back at six. The proprietor called her in front of all the others and dismissed her. But Beatrice was rather surprised at herself.

She stayed a month without a job. She lived from room to room at the capricious mercy of the other girls. She did not have the heart to leave Ilmorog and start all over again in a new town. The wound hurt. She was tired of wandering. She stopped using Ambi. No money. She looked at herself in the mirror. She had so aged, hardly a year after she had fallen from grace. Why then was she scrupulous, she would ask herself. But somehow she had a horror of soliciting lovers or directly bartering her body for hard cash. What she wanted was decent work and a man or several men who cared for her. Perhaps she took that need for a man, for a home and for a child with her to bed. Perhaps it was this genuine need that scared off men who wanted other things from barmaids. She wept late at nights and remembered home. At such moments, her mother's village in Nyeri seemed the sweetest place on God's earth. She would invest the life of her peasant mother and father with romantic illusions of immeasurable peace and harmony. She longed to go back home to see them. But how could she go back with empty hands? In any case the place was now a distant landscape in the memory. Her life was here in the bar among this crowd of lost strangers. Fallen from grace, fallen from grace. She was part of a generation which would never again be one with the soil, the crops, the wind and the moon. Not for them that whispering in dark hedges, not for her that dance and love-making under the glare of the moon, with the hills of Tumu Tumu rising to touch the sky. She remembered that girl from her home village who despite a life of apparent glamour being the kept mistress of one rich man after another in Limuru, had gassed herself to death. This generation was not awed by the mystery of death, just as it was callous to the mystery of life; for how many unmarried mothers had thrown their babies into latrines rather than lose that glamour? The girl's death became the subject of jokes. She had gone metric — without pains, they said. Thereafter, for a week, Beatrice thought of going metric. But she could not bring herself to do it.

She wanted love; she wanted life.

A new bar was opened in Ilmorog. Treetop Bar, Lodging and Restaurant. Why Treetop, Beatrice could not understand unless because it was a storied building: tea-shop on the ground floor and beer-shop in a room at the top. The rest were rooms for five-minute or one-night lodgers. The owner was a retired civil servant but one who still played at politics. He was enormously wealthy with business sites and enterprises in every major town in Kenya. Big shots from all over the country came to his bar. Big men in Mercedes. Big men in their Bentleys. Big men in their Jaguars and Daimlers. Big men with uniformed chauffeurs drowsing with boredom in cars waiting outside. There were others not so big who came to pay respects to the great. They talked politics mostly. And about their work. Gossip was rife. Didn't you know? Indeed so and so has been promoted. Really? And so and so has been sacked. Embezzlement of public funds. So foolish you know. Not clever about it at all. They argued, they quarrelled, sometimes they fought it out with fists, especially during the elections campaign. The only point on which they were all agreed was that the Luo community was the root cause of all the trouble in Kenya; that intellectuals and University students were living in an ivory tower of privilege and arrogance; that Kiambu had more than a lion's share of developments; that men from Nyeri and Muranga had acquired all the big business in Nairobi and were even encroaching on Chiri District; that African workers, especially those on the farms, were lazy and jealous of 'us' who had sweated ourselves to sudden prosperity. Otherwise each would hymn his own praises or return compliments. Occasionally in moments of drunken ebullience and self-praise, one would order two rounds of beer for each man present in the bar. Even the poor from Ilmorog would come to Treetop to dine at the gates of the *nouveaux riches*.

Here Beatrice got a job as a sweeper and bedmaker. Here for a few weeks she felt closer to greatness. Now she made beds for men she had previously known as names. She watched how even the poor tried to drink and act big in front of the big. But soon fate caught up with her. Girls flocked to Treetop from other bars. Girls she had known at Limuru, girls she had known at Ilmorog. And most had attached themselves to one or several big men, often playing a hide-and-not-to-be-found game with their numerous lovers. And Nyagũthiĩ was there behind the counter, with the eyes of the rich and the poor fixed on her. And she, with her big eyes, bangled hands and earrings maintained the same air of bored indifference. Beatrice as a sweeper and bedmaker became even more invisible. Girls who had fallen into good fortune looked down upon her.

She fought life with dreams. In between putting clean sheets on beds that had just witnessed a five-minute struggle that ended in a half-strangled cry and a pool, she would stand by the window and watch the cars and the chauffeurs, so that soon she knew all the owners by the number plates of their cars and the uniforms of their chauffeurs. She dreamt of lovers who would come for her in sleek Mercedes sports cars made for two. She saw herself linking hands with such a lover, walking in the streets of Nairobi and Mombasa, tapping the ground with high heels, quick, quick short steps. And suddenly she would stop in front of a display glass window, exclaiming at the same time; Oh darling, won't you buy me those … ? Those what, he would ask, affecting anger. Those stockings, darling. It was as an owner of several stockings, ladderless and holeless, that she thought of her well-being. Never again would she mend torn things. Never, never, never. Do you understand? Never. She was next the proud owner of different coloured wigs, blonde wigs, brunette wigs, redhead wigs, Afro wigs, wigs, wigs, all the wigs in the world. Only then would the whole earth sing hallelujah to the one Beatrice. At such moments, she would feel exalted, lifted out of her murky self, no longer a floor sweeper and bedmaker for a five-minute instant love, but Beatrice, descendant of Wangu Makeri who made men tremble with desire at her naked body bathed in moonlight, daughter of Nyang'endo, the founder of modern Ilmorog, of whom they often sang that she had worked several lovers into impotence.

Then she noticed him and he was the opposite of the lover of her dreams. He came one Saturday afternoon driving a big five-ton lorry. He carefully parked it beside the Benzes, the Jaguars and the Daimlers, not as a lorry, but as one of those sleek cream-bodied frames, so proud of it he seemed to be. He dressed in a baggy grey suit over which he wore a heavy khaki military overcoat. He removed the overcoat, folded it with care, and put it in the front seat. He locked all the doors, dusted himself a little, then walked round the lorry as if inspecting it for damage. A few steps before he entered Treetop, he turned round for a final glance at his lorry dwarfing the other things. At Treetops he sat in a corner and, with a rather loud defiant voice, ordered a Kenya one. He drank it with relish, looking around at the same time for a face he might recognize. He indeed did recognize one of the big ones and he immediately ordered for him a quarter bottle of Vat 69. This was accepted with a bare nod of the head and a patronizing smile; but when he tried to follow his generosity with a conversation, he was firmly ignored. He froze, sank into his Muratina. But only for a time. He tried again: he was met with frowning faces. More pathetic were his attempts to join in jokes; he would laugh rather too loudly, which would make the big ones stop, leaving him in the air alone. Later in the evening he stood up, counted several crisp hundred shilling notes and handed them to Nyagūthiī behind the counter ostensibly for safekeeping. People whispered; murmured; a few laughed, rather derisively, though they were rather impressed. But this act did not win him immediate recognition. He staggered towards room no. 7 which he had hired. Beatrice brought him the keys. He glanced at her, briefly, then lost all interest.

Thereafter he came every Saturday. At five when most of the big shots were already seated. He repeated the same ritual, except the money act, and always met with defeat. He nearly always sat in the same corner and always rented room 7. Beatrice grew to anticipate his visits and, without being conscious of it, kept the room ready for him. Often after he had been badly humiliated by the big company, he would detain Beatrice and talk to her, or rather he talked to himself in her presence. For him, it had been a life of struggles. He had never been to school although getting an education had been his ambition. He never had a chance. His father was a squatter in the European settled area in the Rift Valley. That meant a lot in those colonial days. It meant among other things a man and his children were doomed to a future of sweat and toil for the white devils and their children. He had joined the freedom struggle and like the others had been sent to detention. He came from detention the same as his mother had brought him to this world. Nothing. With independence he found he did not possess the kind of education which would have placed him in one of the vacancies at the top. He started as a charcoal burner, then a butcher, gradually working his own way to become a big transporter of vegetables and potatoes from the Rift Valley and Chiri districts to Nairobi. He was proud of his achievement. But he resented that others, who had climbed to their present wealth through loans and a subsidized education, would not recognize his like. He would rumble on like this, dwelling on education he would never have, and talking of better chances for his children. Then he would carefully count the money, put it under the pillow, and then dismiss Beatrice. Occasionally he would buy her a beer, but he was clearly suspicious of women whom he saw as money-eaters of men. He had not yet married.

One night he slept with her. In the morning he scratched for a twenty shilling note and gave it to her. She accepted the money with an odd feeling of guilt. He did this for several weeks. She did not mind the money. It was useful. But he paid for her body as he would pay for a bag of potatoes or a sack of cabbages. With the one pound, he had paid for her services as a listener, a vessel of his complaints against those above, and as a one-night receptacle of his man's burden. She was becoming bored with his ego, with his stories that never varied in content, but somehow, in him, deep inside, she felt that something had been there, a fire, a seed, a flower which was being smothered. In him she saw a fellow victim and looked forward to his visits. She too longed to talk to someone. She too longed to confide in a human being who would understand.

And she did it one Saturday night, suddenly interrupting the story of his difficult climb to the top. She did not know why she did it. Maybe it was the rain outside. It was softly drumming the corrugated iron sheets, bringing with the drumming a warm and drowsy indifference. He would listen. He had to listen. She came from Karatina in Nyeri. Her two brothers had been gunned down by the British soldiers. Another one had died in detention. She was, so to speak, an only child. Her parents were poor. But they worked hard on their bare strip of land and managed to pay her fees in primary school. For the first six years she had worked hard. In the seventh year, she must have relaxed a little. She did not pass with a good grade. Of course she knew many with similar grades who had been called to good government secondary schools. She knew a few others with lesser grades who had gone to very top schools on the strength of their connections. But she was not called to any high school with reasonable fees. Her parents could not afford fees in a *Harambee* school. And she would not hear of repeating standard seven. She stayed at home with her parents. Occasionally she would help them in the shamba and with house chores. But imagine: for the past six years she had led a life with a different rhythm from that of her parents. Life in the village was dull. She would often go to Karatina and to Nyeri in search of work. In every office, they would ask her the same questions: what work do you want? What do you know? Can you type? Can you take shorthand? She was desperate. It was in Nyeri, drinking Fanta in a shop, tears in her eyes, that she met a young man in a dark suit and sun-glasses. He saw her plight and talked to her. He came from Nairobi. Looking for work? That's easy; in a big city there would be no difficulty with jobs. He would certainly help. Transport? He had a car—a cream-white Peugeot. Heaven. It was a beautiful ride, with the promise of dawn. Nairobi. He drove her to Terrace Bar. They drank beer and talked about Nairobi. Through the window she could see the neon-lit city and knew that here was hope. That night she gave herself to him, with the promise of dawn making her feel light and gay. She had a very deep sleep. When she woke in the morning, the man in the cream-white Peugeot was not there. She never saw him again. That's how she had started the life of a barmaid. And for one and half years now she had not been once to see her parents. Beatrice started weeping. Huge sobs of self-pity. Her humiliation and constant flight were fresh in her mind. She had never been able to take to bar culture, she always thought that something better would come her way. But she was trapped, it was the only life she now knew, although she had never really learnt all its laws and norms. Again she heaved out and in, tears tossing out with every sob. Then suddenly she froze. Her sobbing was arrested in the air. The man had long covered himself. His snores were huge and unmistakable.

She felt a strange hollowness. Then a bile of bitterness spilt inside her. She wanted to cry at her new failure. She had met several men who had treated her cruelly, who had laughed at her scruples, at what they thought was an ill-disguised attempt at innocence. She had accepted. But not this, Lord, not this. Was this man not a fellow victim? Had he not, Saturday after Saturday, unburdened himself to her? He had paid for her human services; he had paid away his responsibility with his bottle of Tuskers and hard cash in the morning. Her innermost turmoil had been his lullaby. And suddenly something in her snapped.

All the anger of a year and a half, all the bitterness against her humiliation were now directed at this man.

What she did later had the mechanical precision of an experienced hand.

She touched his eyes. He was sound asleep. She raised his head. She let it fall. Her tearless eyes were now cold and set. She removed the pillow from under him. She rummaged through it. She took out his money. She counted five crisp pink notes. She put the money inside her brassiere.

She went out of room no. 7. Outside it was still raining. She did not want to go to her usual place. She could not now stand the tiny cupboard room or the superior chatter of her roommate. She walked through mud and rain. She found herself walking towards Nyagūthiī 's room. She knocked at the door. At first she had no response. Then she heard Nyagūthiī 's sleepy voice above the drumming rain.

'Who is that?'

'It is me. Please open.'

'Who?'

'Beatrice.'

'At this hour of the night?'

'Please.'

Lights were put on. Bolts unfastened. The door opened. Beatrice stepped inside. She and Nyagūthiī stood there face to face. Nyagūthiī was in a see-through nightdress: on her shoulders she had a green pullover.

'Beatrice, is there anything wrong?' She at last asked, a note of concern in her voice.

'Can I rest here for a while? I am tired. And I want to talk to you.' Beatrice's voice carried assurance and power.

'But what has happened?'

'I only want to ask you a question, Nyagūthiī.'

They were still standing. Then, without a word, they both sat on the bed.

'Why did you leave home, Nyagūthiī?' Beatrice asked.

Another silent moment. Nyagūthiī seemed to be thinking about the question. Beatrice waited. Nyagūthiī 's voice when at last it came was slightly tremulous, unsteady.

'It is a long story, Beatrice. My father and mother were fairly wealthy. They were also good Christians. We lived under regulations. You must never walk with the heathen. You must not attend their pagan customs—dances and circumcision rites, for instance. There were rules about what, how and when to eat. You must even walk like a Christian lady. You must never be seen with boys. Rules, rules all the way. One day instead of returning home from school, I and another girl from a similar home ran away to Eastleigh. I have never been home once this last four years. That's all.'

Another silence. Then they looked at one another in mutual recognition.

671

'One more question, Nyagũthiĩ. You need not answer it. But I have always thought that you hated me, you despised me.'

'No, no, Beatrice, I have never hated you. I have never hated anybody. It is just that nothing interests me. Even men do not move me now. Yet I want, I need instant excitement. I need the attention of those false flattering eyes to make me feel myself, myself. But you, you seemed above all this — somehow you had something inside you that I did not have.'

Beatrice tried to hold her tears with difficulty.

Early the next day, she boarded a bus bound for Nairobi. She walked down Bazaar street looking at the shops. Then down Government Road, right into Kenyatta Avenue, and Kimathi Street. She went into a shop near Hussein Suleman's Street and bought several stockings. She put on a pair. She next bought herself a new dress. Again she changed into it. In a Bata Shoeshop, she bought high heeled shoes, put them on and discarded her old flat ones. On to an Akamba kiosk, and she fitted herself with earrings. She went to a mirror and looked at her new self. Suddenly she felt enormous hunger as if she had been hungry all her life. She hesitated in front of Moti Mahal. Then she walked on, eventually entering Fransae. There was a glint in her eyes that made men's eyes turn to her. This thrilled her. She chose a table in a corner and ordered Indian curry. A man left his table and joined her. She looked at him. Her eyes were merry. He was dressed in a dark suit and his eyes spoke of lust. He bought her a drink. He tried to engage her in conversation. But she ate in silence. He put his hand under the table and felt her knees. She let him do it. The hand went up and up her thigh. Then suddenly she left her unfinished food and her untouched drink and walked out. She felt good. He followed her. She knew this without once turning her eyes. He walked beside her for a few yards. She smiled at herself but did not look at him. He lost his confidence. She left him standing sheepishly looking at a glass window outside Gino's. In the bus back to Ilmorog, men gave her seats. She accepted this as of right. At Treetops bar she went straight to the counter. The usual crowd of big men was there. Their conversations stopped for a few seconds at her entry. Their lascivious eyes were turned to her. The girls stared at her. Even Nyagũthiĩ could not maintain her bored indifference. Beatrice bought them drinks. The manager came to her, rather unsure. He tried a conversation. Why had she left work? Where had she been? Would she like to work in the bar, helping Nyagũthiĩ behind the counter? Now and then? A barmaid brought her a note. A certain big shot wanted to know if she would join their table. More notes came from different big quarters with the one question; would she be free tonight? A trip to Nairobi even. She did not leave her place at the counter. But she accepted their drinks as of right. She felt a new power, confidence even.

She took out a shilling, put it in the slot and the juke box boomed with the voice of Robinson Mwangi singing *Hũnyũ wa Mashambani*. He sang of those despised girls who worked on farms and contrasted them with urban girls. Then she played a Kamaru and a D.K. Men wanted to dance with her. She ignored them, but enjoyed their flutter around her. She twisted her hips to the sound of yet another D.K. Her body was free. She was free. She sucked in the excitement and tension in the air.

Then suddenly at around six, the man with the five-ton Lorry stormed into the bar. This time he had on his military overcoat. Behind him was a policeman. He looked around. Everybody's eyes were raised to him. But Beatrice went on swaying her hips. At first he could not recognize Beatrice in the girl celebrating her few minutes of glory by the juke box. Then he shouted in triumph. 'That is the girl! Thief! Thief!'

People melted back to their seats. The policeman went and handcuffed her. She did not resist. Only at the door she turned her head and spat. Then she went out followed by the policeman.

In the bar the stunned silence broke into hilarious laughter when someone made a joke about sweetened robbery without violence. They discussed her. Some said she should have been beaten. Others talked contemptuously about 'these bar girls.' Yet others talked with a concern noticeable in unbelieving shakes of their heads about the rising rate of crime. Shouldn't the Hanging Bill be extended to all thefts of property? And without anybody being aware of it the man with the five-ton lorry had become a hero. They now surrounded him with questions and demanded the whole story. Some even bought him drinks. More remarkable, they listened, their attentive silence punctuated by appreciative laughter. The averted threat to property had temporarily knit them into one family. And the man, accepted for the first time, told the story with relish.

But behind the counter Nyagūthiī wept.

Good Country People
(1955)

FLANNERY O'CONNOR

Besides the neutral expression that she wore when she was alone, Mrs. Freeman had two others, forward and reverse, that she used for all her human dealings. Her forward expression was steady and driving like the advance of a heavy truck. Her eyes never swerved to left or right but turned as the story turned as if they followed a yellow line down the center of it. She seldom used the other expression because it was not often necessary for her to retract a statement, but when she did, her face came to a complete stop, there was an almost imperceptible movement of her black eyes, during which they seemed to be receding, and then the observer would see that Mrs. Freeman, though she might stand there as real as several grain sacks thrown on top of each other, was no longer there in spirit. As for getting anything across to her when this was the case, Mrs. Hopewell had given it up. She might talk her head off. Mrs. Freeman could never be brought to admit herself wrong on any point. She would stand there and if she could be brought to say anything, it was something like, "Well, I wouldn't of said it was and I wouldn't of said it wasn't," or letting her gaze range over the top kitchen shelf where there was an assortment of dusty bottles, she might remark, "I see you ain't ate many of them figs you put up last summer."

They carried on their most important business in the kitchen at breakfast. Every morning Mrs. Hopewell got up at seven o'clock and lit her gas heater and Joy's. Joy was her daughter, a large blonde girl who had an artificial leg. Mrs. Hopewell thought of her as a child though she was thirty-two years old and highly educated. Joy would get up while her mother was eating and lumber into the bathroom and slam the door, and before long, Mrs. Freeman would arrive at the back door. Joy would hear her mother call, "Come on in," and then they would talk for a while in low voices that were indistinguishable in the bathroom. By the time Joy came in, they had usually finished the weather report and were on one or the other of Mrs. Freeman's daughters, Glynese or Carramae. Joy called them Glycerin and Caramel. Glynese, a redhead, was eighteen and had many admirers; Carramae, a blonde, was only fifteen but already married and pregnant. She could not keep anything on her stomach. Every morning Mrs. Freeman told Mrs. Hopewell how many times she had vomited since the last report.

Mrs. Hopewell liked to tell people that Glynese and Carramae were two of the finest girls she knew and that Mrs. Freeman was a *lady* and that she was never ashamed to take her anywhere or introduce her to anybody they might meet. Then she would tell how she had happened to hire the Freemans in the first place and how they were a godsend to her and how she had had them four years. The reason for her keeping them so long was that they were not trash. They were good country people. She had telephoned the man whose name they had given as a reference and he had told her that Mr. Freeman was a good farmer but that his wife was the nosiest woman ever to walk the earth. "She's got to be into everything," the man said. "If she don't get there before the dust settles, you can bet she's dead, that's all. She'll want to know all your business. I can stand him real good," he had said, "but me nor my wife neither could have stood that woman one more minute on this place." That had put Mrs. Hopewell off for a few days.

She had hired them in the end because there were no other applicants but she had made up her mind before hand exactly how she would handle the woman. Since she was the type who had to be into everything, then, Mrs. Hopewell had decided, she would not only let her be into everything, she would *see to it* that she was into everything—she would give her the responsibility of everything, she would put her in charge. Mrs. Hopewell had no bad qualities of her own but she was able to use other people's in such a constructive way that she never felt the lack. She had hired the Freemans and she had kept them four years.

Nothing is perfect. This was one of Mrs. Hopewell's favorite sayings. Another was: that is life! And still another, the most important, was: well, other people have their opinions too. She would make these statements, usually at the table, in a tone of gentle insistence as if no one held them but her, and the large hulking Joy, whose constant outrage had obliterated every expression from her face, would stare just a little to the side of her, her eyes icy blue, with the look of someone who has achieved blindness by an act of will and means to keep it.

When Mrs. Hopewell said to Mrs. Freeman that life was like that, Mrs. Freeman would say, "I always said so myself." Nothing had been arrived at by anyone that had not first been arrived at by her. She was quicker than Mr. Freeman. When Mrs. Hopewell said to her after they had been on the place a while, "You know, you're the wheel behind the wheel," and winked, Mrs. Freeman had said, "I know it. I've always been quick. It's some that are quicker than others."

"Everybody is different," Mrs. Hopewell said.

"Yes, most people is," Mrs. Freeman said.

"It takes all kinds to make the world."

"I always said it did myself."

The girl was used to this kind of dialogue for breakfast and more of it for dinner; sometimes they had it for supper too. When they had no guest they ate in the kitchen because that was easier. Mrs. Freeman always managed to arrive at some point during the meal and to watch them finish it. She would stand in the doorway if it were summer but in the winter she would stand with one elbow on top of the refrigerator and look down on them, or she would stand by the gas heater, lifting the back of her skirt slightly. Occasionally she would stand against the wall and roll her head from side to side. At no time was she in any hurry to leave. All this was very trying on Mrs. Hopewell but she was a woman of great patience. She realized that nothing is perfect and that in the Freemans she had good country people and that if, in this day and age, you get good country people, you had better hang onto them.

She had had plenty of experience with trash. Before the Freemans she had averaged one tenant family a year. The wives of these farmers were not the kind you would want to be around you for very long. Mrs. Hopewell, who had divorced her husband long ago, needed someone to walk over the fields with her; and when Joy had to be impressed for these services, her remarks were usually so ugly and her face so glum that Mrs. Hopewell would say, "If you can't come pleasantly, I don't want you at all," to which the girl, standing square and rigid-shouldered with her neck thrust slightly forward, would reply, "If you want me, here I am—LIKE I AM."

Mrs. Hopewell excused this attitude because of the leg (which had been shot off in a hunting accident when Joy was ten). It was hard for Mrs. Hopewell to realize that her child was thirty-two now and that for more than twenty years she had had only one leg. She thought of her still as a child because it tore her heart to think instead of the poor stout girl in her thirties who had never danced a step or had any *normal* good times. Her name was really Joy but as soon as she was twenty-one and away from home, she had had it legally changed. Mrs. Hopewell was certain that she had thought and thought until she had hit upon the ugliest name in any language. Then she had gone and had the beautiful name, Joy, changed without telling her mother until after she had done it. Her legal name was Hulga.

When Mrs. Hopewell thought the name, Hulga, she thought of the broad blank hull of a battleship. She would not use it. She continued to call her Joy to which the girl responded but in a purely mechanical way.

Hulga had learned to tolerate Mrs. Freeman who saved her from taking walks with her mother. Even Glynese and Carramae were useful when they occupied attention that might otherwise have been directed at her. At first she had thought she could not stand Mrs. Freeman for she had found that it was not possible to be rude to her. Mrs. Freeman would take on strange resentments and for days together she would be sullen but the source of her displeasure was always obscure; a direct attack, a positive leer, blatant ugliness to her face—these never touched her. And without warning one day, she began calling her Hulga.

She did not call her that in front of Mrs. Hopewell who would have been incensed but when she and the girl happened to be out of the house together, she would say something and add the name Hulga to the end of it, and the big spectacled Joy-Hulga would scowl and redden as if her privacy had been intruded upon. She considered the name her personal affair. She had arrived at it first purely on the basis of its ugly sound and then the full genius of its fitness had struck her. She had a vision of the name working like the ugly sweating Vulcan who stayed in the furnace and to whom, presumably, the goddess had to come when called. She saw it as the name of her highest creative act. One of her major triumphs was that her mother had not been able to turn her dust into Joy, but the greater one was that she had been able to turn it herself into Hulga. However, Mrs. Freeman's relish for using the name only irritated her. It was as if Mrs. Freeman's beady steel-pointed eyes had penetrated far enough behind her face to reach some secret fact. Something about her seemed to fascinate Mrs. Freeman and then one day Hulga realized that it was the artificial leg. Mrs. Freeman had a special fondness for the details of secret infections, hidden deformities, assault upon children. Of diseases, she preferred the lingering or incurable. Hulga had heard Mrs. Hopewell give her the details of the hunting accident, how the leg had been literally blasted off, how she had never lost consciousness. Mrs. Freeman could listen to it any time as if it had happened an hour ago.

When Hulga stumped into the kitchen in the morning (she could walk without making the awful noise but she made it—Mrs. Hopewell was certain—because it was ugly-sounding), she glanced at them and did not speak. Mrs. Hopewell would be in her red kimono with her hair tied around her head in rags. She would be sitting at the table, finishing her breakfast and Mrs. Freeman would be hanging by her elbow outward from the refrigerator, looking down at the table. Hulga always put her eggs on the stove to boil and then stood over them with her arms folded, and Mrs. Hopewell would look at her—a kind of indirect gaze divided between her and Mrs. Freeman—and would think that if she would only keep herself up a little, she wouldn't be so bad looking. There was nothing wrong with her face that a pleasant expression wouldn't help. Mrs. Hopewell said that people who looked on the bright side of things would be beautiful even if they were not.

Whenever she looked at Joy this way, she could not help but feel that it would have been better if the child had not taken the Ph.D. It had certainly not brought her out any and now that she had it, there was no more excuse for her to go to school again. Mrs. Hopewell thought it was nice for girls to go to school to have a good time but Joy had "gone through." Anyhow, she would not have been strong enough to go again. The doctors had told Mrs. Hopewell that with the best of care, Joy might see forty-five. She had a weak heart. Joy had made it plain that if it had not been for this condition, she would be far from these red hills and good country people. She would be in a university lecturing to people who knew what she was talking about. And Mrs. Hopewell could very well picture her there, looking like a scarecrow and lecturing to more of the same. Here she went about all day in a six-year-old skirt and a yellow sweat shirt with a faded cowboy on a horse embossed on it. She thought this was funny; Mrs. Hopewell thought it was idiotic and showed simply that she was still a child. She was brilliant but she didn't have a grain of sense. It seemed to Mrs. Hopewell that every year she grew less like other people and more like herself—bloated, rude, and squint-eyed. And she said such strange things! To her own mother she had said—without warning, without excuse, standing up in the middle of a meal with her face purple and her mouth half full—"Woman! do you ever look inside? Do you ever look inside and see what you are *not*? God!" she had cried sinking down again and staring at her plate, "Malebranche was right: we are not our own light. We are not our own light!" Mrs Hopewell had no idea to this day what brought that on. She had only made the remark, hoping Joy would take it in, that a smile never hurt anyone.

The girl had taken the Ph.D. in philosophy and this left Mrs. Hopewell at a complete loss. You could say, "My daughter is a nurse," or "My daughter is a school teacher," or even, "My daughter is a chemical engineer." You could not say, "My daughter is a philosopher." That was something that had ended with the Greeks and Romans. All day Joy sat on her neck in a deep chair, reading. Sometimes she went for walks but she didn't like dogs or cats or birds or flowers or nature or nice young men. She looked at nice young men as if she could smell their stupidity.

One day Mrs. Hopewell had picked up one of the books the girl had just put down and opening it at random, she read, "Science, on the other hand, has to assert its soberness and seriousness afresh and declare that it is concerned solely with what-is. Nothing—how can it be for science anything but a horror and a phantasm? If science is right, then one thing stands firm: science wishes to know nothing of nothing. Such is after all the strictly scientific approach to Nothing. We know it by wishing to know nothing of Nothing." These words had been underlined with a blue pencil and they worked on Mrs. Hopewell like some evil incantation in gibberish. She shut the book quickly and went out of the room as if she were having a chill.

This morning when the girl came in, Mrs. Freeman was on Carramae. "She thrown up four times after supper," she said, "and was up twict in the night after three o'clock. Yesterday she didn't do nothing but ramble in the bureau drawer. All she did. Stand up there and see what she could run up on."

"She's got to eat," Mrs. Hopewell muttered, sipping her coffee, while she watched Joy's back at the stove. She was wondering what the child had said to the Bible salesman. She could not imagine what kind of a conversation she could possibly have had with him.

He was a tall gaunt hatless youth who had called yesterday to sell them a Bible. He had appeared at the door, carrying a large black suitcase that weighted him so heavily on one side that he had to brace himself against the door facing. He seemed on the point of collapse but he said in a cheerful voice, "Good morning, Mrs. Cedars!" and set the suitcase down on the mat. He was not a bad-looking young man though he had on a bright blue suit and yellow socks that were not pulled up far enough. He had prominent face bones and a streak of sticky-looking brown hair falling across his forehead.

"I'm Mrs. Hopewell," she said.

"Oh!" he said, pretending to look puzzled but with his eyes sparkling, "I saw it said 'The Cedars,' on the mailbox so I thought you was Mrs. Cedars!" and he burst out in a pleasant laugh. He picked up the satchel and under cover of a pant, he fell forward into her hall. It was rather as if the suitcase had moved first, jerking him after it. "Mrs. Hopewell!" he said and grabbed her hand. "I hope you are well!" and he laughed again and then all at once his face sobered completely. He paused and gave her a straight earnest look and said, "Lady, I've come to speak of serious things."

"Well, come in," she muttered, none too pleased because her dinner was almost ready. He came into the parlor and sat down on the edge of a straight chair and put the suitcase between his feet and glanced around the room as if he were sizing her up by it. Her silver gleamed on the two sideboards; she decided he had never been in a room as elegant as this.

"Mrs. Hopewell," he began, using her name in a way that sounded almost intimate, "I know you believe in Chrustian service."

"Well yes," she murmured.

"I know," he said and paused, looking very wise with his head cocked on one side, "that you're a good woman. Friends have told me."

Mrs. Hopewell never liked to be taken for a fool. "What are you selling?" she asked.

"Bibles," the young man said and his eye raced around the room before he added, "I see you have no family Bible in your parlor, I see that is the one lack you got!"

Mrs. Hopewell could not say, "My daughter is an atheist and won't let me keep the Bible in the parlor." She said, stiffening slightly, "I keep my Bible by my bedside." This was not the truth. It was in the attic somewhere.

"Lady," he said, "the word of God ought to be in the parlor."

"Well, I think that's a matter of taste," she began. "I think . . ."

"Lady," he said, "for a Chrustian, the word of God ought to be in every room in the house besides in his heart. I know you're a Chrustian because I can see it in every line of your face."

She stood up and said, "Well, young man, I don't want to buy a Bible and I smell my dinner burning."

He didn't get up. He began to twist his hands and looking down at them, he said softly, "Well lady, I'll tell you the truth—not many people want to buy one nowadays and besides, I know I'm real simple. I don't know how to say a thing but to say it. I'm just a country boy." He glanced up into her unfriendly face. "People like you don't like to fool with country people like me!"

"Why!" she cried, "good country people are the salt of the earth! Besides, we all have different ways of doing, it takes all kinds to make the world go 'round. That's life!"

"You said a mouthful," he said.

"Why, I think there aren't enough good country people in the world!" she said, stirred. "I think that's what's wrong with it!"

His face had brightened. "I didn't inraduce myself," he said. "I'm Manley Pointer from out in the country around Willohobie, not even from a place, just from near a place."

"You wait a minute," she said. "I have to see about my dinner." She went out to the kitchen and found Joy standing near the door where she had been listening.

"Get rid of the salt of the earth," she said, "and let's eat."

Mrs. Hopewell gave her a pained look and turned the heat down under the vegetables. "*I* can't be rude to anybody," she murmured and went back into the parlor.

He had opened the suitcase and was sitting with a Bible on each knee.

"You might as well put those up," she told him. "I don't want one."

"I appreciate your honesty," he said. "You don't see any more real honest people unless you go way out in the country."

"I know," she said, "real genuine folks!" Through the crack in the door she heard a groan.

"I guess a lot of boys come telling you they're working their way through college," he said, "but I'm not going to tell you that. Somehow," he said, "I don't want to go to college. I want to devote my life to Chrustian service. See," he said, lowering his voice, "I got this heart condition. I may not live long. When you know it's something wrong with you and you may not live long, well then, lady . . . " He paused, with his mouth open, and stared at her.

He and Joy had the same condition! She knew that her eyes were filling with tears but she collected herself quickly and murmured, "Won't you stay for dinner? We'd love to have you!" and was sorry the instant she heard herself say it.

"Yes mam," he said in an abashed voice, "I would sher love to do that!"

Joy had given him one look on being introduced to him and then throughout the meal had not glanced at him again. He had addressed several remarks to her, which she had pretended not to hear. Mrs. Hopewell could not understand deliberate rudeness, although she lived with it, and she felt she had always to overflow with hospitality to make up for Joy's lack of courtesy. She urged him to talk about himself and he did. He said he was the seventh child of twelve and that his father had been crushed under a tree when he himself was eight years old. He had been crushed very badly, in fact, almost cut in two and was practically not recognizable. His mother had got along the best she could by hard working and she had always seen that her children went to Sunday School and that they read the Bible every evening. He was now nineteen years old and he had been selling Bibles for four months. In that time he had sold seventy-seven Bibles and had the promise of two more sales. He wanted to become a missionary because he thought that was the way you could do most for people. "He who losest his life shall find it," he said simply and he was so sincere, so genuine and earnest that Mrs. Hopewell would not for the world have smiled. He prevented his peas from sliding onto the table by blocking them with a piece of bread which he later cleaned his plate with. She could see Joy observing sidewise how he handled his knife and fork and she saw too that every few minutes, the boy would dart a keen appraising glance at the girl as if he were trying to attract her attention.

After dinner Joy cleared the dishes off the table and disappeared and Mrs. Hopewell was left to talk with him. He told her again about his childhood and his father's accident and about various things that had happened to him. Every five minutes or so she would stifle a yawn. He sat for two hours until finally she told him she must go because she had an appointment in town. He packed his Bibles and thanked her and prepared to leave, but in the doorway he stopped and wrung her hand and said that not on any of his trips had he met a lady as nice as her and he asked if he could come again. She had said she would always be happy to see him.

Joy had been standing in the road, apparently looking at something in the distance, when he came down the steps toward her, bent to the side with his heavy valise. He stopped where she was standing and confronted her directly. Mrs. Hopewell could not hear what he said but she trembled to think what Joy would say to him. She could see that after a minute Joy said something and that then the boy began to speak again, making an excited gesture with his free hand. After a minute Joy said something else at which the boy began to speak once more. Then to her amazement, Mrs. Hopewell saw the two of them walk off together, toward the gate. Joy had walked all the way to the gate with him and Mrs. Hopewell could not imagine what they had said to each other, and she had not yet dared to ask.

Mrs. Freeman was insisting upon her attention. She had moved from the refrigerator to the heater so that Mrs. Hopewell had to turn and face her in order to seem to be listening. "Glynese gone out with Harvey Hill again last night," she said. "She had this sty."

"Hill," Mrs. Hopewell said absently, "is that the one who works in the garage?"

"Nome, he's the one that goes to chiropracter school," Mrs. Freeman said. "She had this sty. Been had it two days. So she says when he brought her in the other night he says, 'Lemme get rid of that sty for you,' and she says, 'How?' and he says, 'You just lay yourself down acrost the seat of that car and I'll show you.' So she done it and he popped her neck. Kept on a-popping it several times until she made him quit. This morning," Mrs. Freeman said, "she ain't got no sty. She ain't got no traces of a sty."

"I never heard of that before," Mrs. Hopewell said.

"He ast her to marry him before the Ordinary," Mrs. Freeman went on, "and she told him she wasn't going to be married in no *office*."

"Well, Glynese is a fine girl," Mrs. Hopewell said. "Glynese and Carramae are both fine girls."

"Carramae said when her and Lyman was married Lyman said it sure felt sacred to him. She said he said he wouldn't take five hundred dollars for being married by a preacher."

"How much would he take?" the girl asked from the stove.

"He said he wouldn't take five hundred dollars," Mrs. Freeman repeated.

"Well we all have work to do," Mrs. Hopewell said.

"Lyman said it just felt more sacred to him," Mrs. Freeman said. "The doctor wants Carramae to eat prunes. Says instead of medicine. Says them cramps is coming from pressure. You know where I think it is?"

"She'll be better in a few weeks," Mrs. Hopewell said.

"In the tube," Mrs. Freeman said. "Else she wouldn't be as sick as she is."

Hulga had cracked her two eggs into a saucer and was bringing them to the table along with a cup of coffee that she had filled too full. She sat down carefully and began to eat, meaning to keep Mrs. Freeman there by questions if for any reason she showed an inclination to leave. She could perceive her mother's eye on her. The first round about question would be about the Bible salesman and she did not wish to bring it on. "How did he pop her neck?" she asked.

Mrs. Freeman went into a description of how he had popped her neck. She said he owned a '55 Mercury but that Glynese said she would rather marry a man with only a '36 Plymouth who would be married by a preacher. The girl asked what if he had a '32 Plymouth and Mrs. Freeman said what Glynese had said was a '36 Plymouth.

Mrs. Hopewell said there were not many girls with Glynese's common sense. She said what she admired in those girls was their common sense. She said that reminded her that they had had a nice visitor yesterday, a young man selling Bibles. "Lord," she said, "he bored me to death but he was so sincere and genuine I couldn't be rude to him. He was just good country people, you know," she said, "— just the salt of the earth."

"I seen him walk up," Mrs. Freeman said, "and then later—I seen him walk off," and Hulga could feel the slight shift in her voice, the slight insinuation, that he had not walked off alone, had he? Her face remained expressionless but the color rose into her neck and she seemed to swallow it down with the next spoonful of egg. Mrs. Freeman was looking at her as if they had a secret together.

"Well, it takes all kinds of people to make the world go 'round," Mrs. Hopewell said. "It's very good we aren't all alike."

"Some people are more alike than others," Mrs. Freeman said.

Hulga got up and stumped, with about twice the noise that was necessary, into her room and locked the door. She was to meet the Bible salesman at ten o'clock at the gate. She had thought about it half the night. She had started thinking of it as a great joke and then she had begun to see profound implications in it. She had lain in bed imagining dialogues for them that were insane on the surface but that reached below to depths that no Bible salesman would be aware of. Their conversation yesterday had been of this kind.

He had stopped in front of her and had simply stood there. His face was bony and sweaty and bright, with a little pointed nose in the center of it, and his look was different from what it had been at the dinner table. He was gazing at her with open curiosity, with fascination, like a child watching a new fantastic animal at the zoo, and he was breathing as if he had run a great distance to reach her. His gaze seemed somehow familiar but she could not think where she had been regarded with it before. For almost a minute he didn't say anything. Then on what seemed an insuck of breath, he whispered, "You ever ate a chicken that was two days old?"

The girl looked at him stonily. He might have just put this question up for consideration at the meeting of a philosophical association. "Yes," she presently replied as if she had considered it from all angles.

"It must have been mighty small!" he said triumphantly and shook all over with little nervous giggles, getting very red in the face, and subsiding finally into his gaze of complete admiration, while the girl's expression remained exactly the same.

"How old are you?" he asked softly.

She waited some time before she answered. Then in a flat voice she said, "Seventeen."

His smiles came in succession like waves breaking on the surface of a little lake. "I see you got a wooden leg," he said. "I think you're real brave. I think you're real sweet."

The girl stood blank and solid and silent.

"Walk to the gate with me," he said. "You're a brave sweet little thing and I liked you the minute I seen you in the door."

Hulga began to move forward.

"What's your name?" he asked, smiling down on the top of her head.

"Hulga," she said.

"Hulga," he murmured, "Hulga. Hulga. I never heard of anybody name Hulga before. You're shy, aren't you, Hulga?" he asked.

She nodded, watching his large red hand on the handle of the giant valise.

"I like girls that wear glasses," he said. "I think a lot. I'm not like these people that a serious thought don't ever enter their heads. It's because I may die."

"I may die too," she said suddenly and looked up at him. His eyes were very small and brown, glittering feverishly.

"Listen," he said, "don't you think some people was meant to meet on account of what all they got in common and all? Like they both think serious thoughts and all?" He shifted the valise to his other hand so that the hand nearest her was free. He caught hold of her elbow and shook it a little. "I don't work on Saturday," he said. "I like to walk in the woods and see what Mother Nature is wearing. O'er the hills and far away. Pic-nics and things. Couldn't we go on a pic-nic tomorrow? Say yes, Hulga," he said and gave her a dying look as if he felt his insides about to drop out of him. He had even seemed to' sway slightly toward her.

During the night she had imagined that she seduced him. She imagined that the two of them walked on the place until they came to the storage barn beyond the two back fields and there, she imagined, that things came to such a pass that she very easily seduced him and that then, of course, she had to reckon with his remorse. True genius can get an idea across even to an inferior mind. She imagined that she took his remorse in hand and changed it into a deeper understanding of life. She took all his shame away and turned it into something useful.

She set off for the gate at exactly ten o'clock, escaping without drawing Mrs. Hopewell's attention. She didn't take anything to eat, forgetting that food is usually taken on a picnic. She wore a pair of slacks and a dirty white shirt, and as an afterthought, she had put some Vapex on the collar of it since she did not own any perfume. When she reached the gate no one was there.

She looked up and down the empty highway and had the furious feeling that she had been tricked, that he had only meant to make her walk to the gate after the idea of him. Then suddenly he stood up, very tall, from behind a bush on the opposite embankment. Smiling, he lifted his hat which was new and wide-brimmed. He had not worn it yesterday and she wondered if he had bought it for the occasion. It was toast-colored with a red and white band around it and was slightly too large for him. He stepped from behind the bush still carrying the black valise. He had on the same suit and the same yellow socks sucked down in his shoes from walking. He crossed the highway and said, "I knew you'd come!"

The girl wondered acidly how he had known this. She pointed to the valise and asked, "Why did you bring your Bibles!"

He took her elbow, smiling down on her as if he could not stop. "You can never tell when you'll need the word of God, Hulga," he said. She had a moment in which she doubted that this was actually happening and then they began to climb the embankment. They went down into the pasture toward the woods. The boy walked lightly by her side, bouncing on his toes. The valise did not seem to be heavy today; he even swung it. They crossed half the pasture without saying anything and then, putting his hand easily on the small of her back, he asked softly, "Where does your wooden leg join on?"

She turned an ugly red and glared at him and for an instant the boy looked abashed. "I didn't mean you no harm," he said. "I only meant you're so brave and all. I guess God takes care of you."

"No," she said, looking forward and walking fast, "I don't even believe in God."

"At this he stopped and whistled. "No!" he exclaimed as if he were too astonished to say anything else.

She walked on and in a second he was bouncing at her side, fanning with his hat. "That's very unusual for a girl," he remarked, watching her out of the corner of his eye. When they reached the edge of the wood, he put his hand on her back again and drew her against him without a word and kissed her heavily.

The kiss, which had more pressure than feeling behind it, produced that extra surge of adrenalin in the girl that enables one to carry a packed trunk out of a burning house, but in her, the power went at once to the brain. Even before he released her, her mind, clear and detached and ironic anyway, was regarding him from a great distance, with amusement but with pity. She had never been kissed before and she was pleased to discover that it was an unexceptional experience and all a matter of the mind's control. Some people might enjoy drain water if they were told it was vodka. When the boy, looking expectant but uncertain, pushed her gently away, she turned and walked on, saying nothing as if such business, for her, were common enough.

He came along panting at her side, trying to help her when he saw a root that she might trip over. He caught and held back the long swaying blades of thorn vine until she had passed beyond them. She led the way and he came breathing heavily behind her. Then they came out on a sunlit hillside, sloping softly into another one a little smaller. Beyond, they could see the rusted top of the old barn where the extra hay was stored.

The hill was sprinkled with small pink weeds. "Then you ain't saved?" he asked suddenly, stopping.

The girl smiled. It was the first time she had smiled at him at all. "In my economy," she said, "I'm saved and you are damned but I told you I didn't believe in God."

Nothing seemed to destroy the boy's look of admiration. He gazed at her now as if the fantastic animal at the zoo had put its paw through the bars and given him a loving poke. She thought he looked as if he wanted to kiss her again and she walked on before he had the chance.

"Ain't there somewheres we can sit down sometime?" he murmured, his voice softening toward the end of the sentence.

"In that barn," she said.

They made for it rapidly as if it might slide away like a train. It was a large two-story barn, cool and dark inside. The boy pointed up the ladder that led into the loft and said, "It's too bad we can't go up there."

"Why can't we?" she asked.

"Yer leg," he said reverently.

The girl gave him a contemptuous look and putting both hands on the ladder, she climbed it while he stood below, apparently awestruck. She pulled herself expertly through the opening and then looked down at him and said, "Well, come on if you're coming," and he began to climb the ladder, awkwardly bringing the suitcase with him.

"We won't need the Bible," she observed.

"You never can tell," he said, panting. After he had got into the loft, he was a few seconds catching his breath. She had sat down in a pile of straw. A wide sheath of sunlight, filled with dust particles, slanted over her. She lay back against a bale, her face turned away, looking out the front opening of the barn where hay was thrown from a wagon into the loft. The two pink-speckled hillsides lay back against a dark ridge of woods. The sky was cloudless and cold blue. The boy dropped down by her side and put one arm under her and the other over her and began methodically kissing her face, making little noises like a fish. He did not remove his hat but it was pushed far enough back not to interfere. When her glasses got in his way, he took them off of her and slipped them into his pocket.

The girl at first did not return any of the kisses but presently she began to and after she had put several on his cheek, she reached his lips and remained there, kissing him again and again as if she were trying to draw all the breath out of him. His breath was clear and sweet like a child's and the kisses were sticky like a child's. He mumbled about loving her and about knowing when he first seen her that he loved her, but the mumbling was like the sleepy fretting of a child being put to sleep by his mother. Her mind, throughout this, never stopped or lost itself for a second to her feelings. "You ain't said you loved me none," he whispered finally, pulling back from her. "You got to say that."

She looked away from him off into the hollow sky and then down at a black ridge and then down farther into what appeared to be two green swelling lakes. She didn't realize he had taken her glasses but this landscape could not seem exceptional to her for she seldom paid any close attention to her surroundings.

"You got to say it," he repeated. "You got to say you love me."

She was always careful how she committed herself. "In a sense," she began, "if you use the word loosely, you might say that. But it's not a word I use. I don't have illusions. I'm one of those people who see *through* to nothing."

The boy was frowning. "You got to say it. I said it and you got to say it," he said.

The girl looked at him almost tenderly. "You poor baby," she murmured. "It's just as well you don't understand," and she pulled him by the neck, face-down, against her. "We are all damned," she said, "but some of us have taken off our blindfolds and see that there's nothing to see. It's a kind of salvation."

The boy's astonished eyes looked blankly through the ends of her hair. "Okay," he almost whined, "but do you love me or don'tcher?"

"Yes," she said and added, "in a sense. But I must tell you something. There mustn't be anything dishonest between us." She lifted his head and looked him in the eye. "I am thirty years old," she said. "I have a number of degrees."

The boy's look was irritated but dogged. "I don't care," he said. "I don't care a thing about what all you done. I just want to know if you love me or don'tcher?" and he caught her to him and wildly planted her face with kisses until she said, "Yes, yes."

"Okay then," he said, letting her go. "Prove it."

She smiled, looking dreamily out on the shifty landscape. She had seduced him without even making up her mind to try. "How?" she asked, feeling that he should be delayed a little.

He leaned over and put his lips to her ear. "Show me where your wooden leg joins on," he whispered.

The girl uttered a sharp little cry and her face instantly drained of color. The obscenity of the suggestion was not what shocked her. As a child she had sometimes been subject to feelings of shame but education had removed the last traces of that as a good surgeon scrapes for cancer; she would no more have felt it over what he was asking than she would have believed in his Bible. But she was as sensitive about the artificial leg as a peacock about his tail. No one ever touched it but her. She took care of it as someone else would his soul, in private and almost with her own eyes turned away. "No," she said.

"I known it," he muttered, sitting up. "You're just playing me for a sucker."

"Oh no no!" she cried. "It joins on at the knee. Only at the knee. Why do you want to see it?"

The boy gave her a long penetrating look. "Because," he said, "it's what makes you different. You ain't like anybody else."

She sat staring at him. There was nothing about her face or her round freezing-blue eyes to indicate that this had moved her; but she felt as if her heart had stopped and left her mind to pump her blood. She decided that for the first time in her life she was face to face with real innocence. This boy, with an instinct that came from beyond wisdom, had touched the truth about her. When after a minute, she said in a hoarse high voice, "All right," it was like surrendering to him completely. It was like losing her own life and finding it again, miraculously, in his.

Very gently he began to roll the slack leg up. The artificial limb, in a white sock and brown flat shoe, was bound in a heavy material like canvas and ended in an ugly jointure where it was attached to the stump. The boy's face and his voice were entirely reverent as he uncovered it and said, "Now show me how to take it off and on."

She took it off for him and put it back on again and then he took it off himself, handling it as tenderly as if it were a real one. "See" he said with a delighted child's face. "Now I can do it myself!"

"Put it back on," she said. She was thinking that she would run away with him and that every night he would take the leg off and every morning put it back on again. "Put it back on," she said.

"Not yet," he murmured, setting it on its foot out of her reach. "Leave it off for a while. You got me instead."

She gave a little cry of alarm but he pushed her down and began to kiss her again. Without the leg she felt entirely dependent on him. Her brain seemed to have stopped thinking altogether and to be about some other function that it was not very good at. Different expressions raced back and forth over her face. Every now and then the boy, his eyes like two steel spikes, would glance behind him where the leg stood. Finally she pushed him off and said, "Put it back on me now."

"Wait," he said. He leaned the other way and pulled the valise toward him and opened it. It had a pale blue spotted lining and there were only two Bibles in it. He took one of these out and opened the cover of it. It was hollow and contained a pocket flask of whiskey, a pack of cards, and a small blue box with printing on it. He laid these out in front of her one at a time in an evenly-spaced row, like one presenting offerings at the shrine of a goddess. He put the blue box in her hand. THIS PRODUCT TO BE USED ONLY FOR THE PREVENTION OF DISEASE, she read, and dropped it. The boy was unscrewing the top of the flask. He stopped and pointed, with a smile, to the deck of cards. It was not an ordinary deck but one with an obscene picture on the back of each card. "Take a swig," he said, offering her the bottle first. He held it in front of her, but like one mesmerized, she did not move.

Her voice when she spoke had an almost pleading sound. "Aren't you," she murmured, "aren't you just good country people?"

The boy cocked his head. He looked as if he were just beginning to understand that she might be trying to insult him. "Yeah," he said, curling his lip slightly, "but it ain't held me back none. I'm as good as you any day in the week."

"Give me my leg," she said.

He pushed it farther away with his foot. "Come on now, let's begin to have us a good time," he said coaxingly. "We ain't got to know one another good yet."

"Give me my leg!" she screamed and tried to lunge for it but he pushed her down easily.

"What's the matter with you all of a sudden?" he asked, frowning as he screwed the top on the flask and put it quickly back inside the Bible. "You just a while ago said you didn't believe in nothing. I thought you was some girl!"

Her face was almost purple. "You're a Christian!" she hissed. "You're a fine Christian! You're just like them all—say one thing and do another. You're a perfect Christian, you're . . ."

The boy's mouth was set angrily. "I hope you don't think," he said in a lofty indignant tone, "that I believe in that crap! I may sell Bibles but I know which end is up and I wasn't born yesterday and I know where I'm going!"

"Give me my leg!" she screeched. He jumped up so quickly that she barely saw him sweep the cards and the blue box back into the Bible and throw the Bible into the valise. She saw him grab the leg and then she saw it for an instant slanted forlornly across the inside of the suitcase with a Bible at either side of its opposite ends. He slammed the lid shut and snatched up the valise and swung it down the hole and then stepped through himself.

When all of him had passed but his head, he turned and regarded her with a look that no longer had any admiration in it. "I've gotten a lot of interesting things," he said. "One time I got a woman's glass eye this way. And you needn't to think you'll catch me because Pointer ain't really my name. I use a different name at every house I call at and don't stay nowhere long. And I'll tell you another thing, Hulga," he said, using the name as if he didn't think much of it, "you ain't so smart. I been believing in nothing ever since I was born!" and then the toast-colored hat disappeared down the hole and the girl was left, sitting on the straw in the dusty sunlight. When she turned her churning face toward the opening, she saw his blue figure struggling successfully over the green speckled lake.

Mrs. Hopewell and Mrs. Freeman, who were in the back pasture, digging up onions, saw him emerge a little later from the woods and head across the meadow toward the highway. "Why, that looks like that nice dull young man that tried to sell me a Bible yesterday," Mrs. Hopewell said, squinting. "He must have been selling them to the Negroes back in there. He was so simple," she said, "but I guess the world would be better off if we were all that simple."

Mrs. Freeman's gaze drove forward and just touched him before he disappeared under the hill. Then she returned her attention to the evil-smelling onion shoot she was lifting from the ground. "Some can't be that simple," she said. "I know I never could."

First Confession
(1939)

FRANK O'CONNOR

All the trouble began when my grandfather died, and my grandmother—my father's mother—came to live with us. Relations in the one house are a trial at the best of times, but, to make it worse, my grandmother was a real old countrywoman, and quite unsuited to the life in town. She had a fat, wrinkled old face, and, to my mother's indignation, went round the house in bare feet—the boots had her crippled, she said. For dinner she had a jug of porter and a pot of potatoes, with, sometimes, a bit of salt fish, and she poured out the potatoes on the table and ate them slowly, with great enjoyment, using her fingers by way of a fork.

Now, girls are supposed to be fastidious, but I was the one who suffered from that. Nora, my sister, just sucked up to the old woman for the penny she got every Friday out of the old age pension, a thing I could not do. I was too honest; that was my trouble; and when I was playing with Bill Connell, the sergeant-major's son, and saw my grandmother steering up the path with the jug of porter sticking out from beneath her shawl, I was mortified. I made excuses not to let him come into the house, because I could never be sure what she would be up to when we went in.

When my mother was at work and my grandmother made the dinner I wouldn't even touch it. Nora tried to make me once, but I hid under the table from her, and took the bread-knife with me for safety. Nora let on to be very indignant (she wasn't, of course, but she knew that Mother saw through her and sided with Father and Gran) and came after me. I lashed out at her with the knife, and after that she left me alone. I stayed there till my mother came in from work, and she made dinner for me; but then my father came home and Nora said in a shocked voice: "Oh, Dadda, do you know what Jackie did at dinner-time?" Then, of course, it all came out, and he gave me a leathering and the mother interfered, and for days after he wouldn't even look at me. God knows, I was heart-scalded!

Then, to crown my misfortunes, I had to make my first confession and communion. It was an old woman called Ryan who prepared us for that. She was about the one age with Gran, only she was well-to-do, lived in a big house on Montenotte, wore a black cloak and bonnet, and came every day to the school at three o'clock when we should have been going home, to talk to us about hell. She may have mentioned the other place as well, but that could only have been by accident, for hell had the first place in her heart.

She lit a candle and took out a new half-crown and offered it to the first fellow who would hold one finger—only one finger!—in the flame for five minutes by the school clock. I was always very ambitious, and was tempted to volunteer, only as no one else did, I thought it might look greedy. Then she asked were we afraid of holding one finger—only one finger!—in a little bit of candle for five minutes, and not afraid of burning all over in roasting hot furnaces for all eternity. "All eternity! Just think of that! A whole lifetime goes by, and it's nothing; only a drop in the ocean of your sufferings." The woman was really interesting about hell, but I had very little attention to spare from the half-crown, which was still on the desk beside her. At the end of the lesson she put it back in her purse. It was a great disappointment in a religious woman like that.

Another day she said she knew a priest who woke one night to find a fellow he didn't recognize leaning over the end of his bed. The priest was a bit frightened—naturally enough—but he asked the fellow what he wanted, and the fellow said in a low, husky voice that he wanted to go to confession. The priest said it was an awkward time and wouldn't it do in the morning? But the other chap said the last time he went to confession there was one sin he kept back because he was ashamed to mention it, and now it was always on his mind. Then the priest knew it was a serious case, because the fellow was after making a bad confession and committing a mortal sin. He got up to dress, and just then the cock crew in the yard outside, and lo and behold! when the priest looked round there was no sign of the fellow at all, only an awful smell like burning timber, and when the priest looked at the bed didn't he see the print of two hands burned in it? That was because the fellow had made a bad confession. This story made a shocking impression on me.

But the worst of all was when she showed us how to examine our consciences. Did we take the name of God in vain? Did we honour our father and our mother? (I asked her did this include grandmothers and she said it did.) Did we love our neighbour as ourselves? Did we covet our neighbour's goods? They seemed to include every blooming thing down to the penny that Nora got on Fridays. I think, between one thing and another, I must have broken all the commandments, all on account of that old woman, and, as far as I could see as long as she was in the house I had no hope of ever doing anything else.

I was scared to death of confession. The day the whole class went I let on to have the toothache, hoping my absence from school wouldn't be noticed, but at three o'clock, just when I was feeling safe, along came a chap with a message from Mrs. Ryan to say I was to go to confession myself and be at the chapel for communion on Sunday morning. To make it worse, my mother couldn't come with me and sent Nora instead.

Now, that girl had ways of tormenting me that my mother never knew. She held my hand as we went down the hill, smiling and saying how sorry she was for me.

"Oh, God help us!" she said. "Isn't it a terrible pity you weren't a good boy? Oh, Jackie, my heart bleeds for you! How will you think of all your sins? Do you remember the time you kicked Gran on the shin?"

"Lemme go!" I wailed, trying to drag myself away from her. "I won't go to confession at all."

"Sure, you'll have to go, Jackie," she replied in the same regretful tone. "Sure, if you didn't the parish priest would be up to the house, looking for you. 'Tisn't, God knows, that I'm not sorry for you! Do you remember the time you tried to kill me with the bread-knife under the table? And the language you used to me? Oh, I don't know what'll he do to you at all. He might send you up to the Bishop."

I remember thinking that she didn't know the half of what I had to tell, if I did tell it. There is very little about that day that I don't remember—the steep hill down to the church, and the sunlit hillsides at the other side of the river valley seen between gaps in the houses, like Adam's last glimpse of Paradise.

Then, as she got me down the long flight of steps into the chapel yard and under the big limestone portico, Nora suddenly changed her tune.

"There you are!" she said with a yelp of triumph, hurling me from her through the church door. "And I hope he'll give you the penitential psalms, you dirty little caffler!"

I knew then I was lost. The door with the coloured glass panels swung shut behind me; the sunlight went out and gave place to deep shadow, and the wind whistled outside so that the silence seemed to be frozen and to crackle like ice under my feet as I tiptoed up the aisle. Nora sat in front of me beside the confession box. There were a couple of old women ahead of her, and then a miserable-looking poor devil came and wedged me in at the other side, so that I couldn't escape even if I wanted to. He joined his hands and rolled his eyes in the direction of the roof, muttering aspirations in an anguished tone, and I wondered had he a grandmother too. That, I felt, was the way you'd expect a fellow with a grandmother to behave, but I was worse off than he, for I knew that, just like the man in the story, I'd never have the nerve to tell all my sins; that I should make a bad confession and then die in the night and be continually coming back and burning people's furniture.

Nora's turn came, and I heard the sound of something slamming, and then I heard her voice as if butter wouldn't melt in her mouth, and the thing slammed again and it was all over. God, the hypocrisy of women! Her eyes were lowered, her hands were joined on her stomach, and she walked up the aisle to the side altar as if she were treading on eggshells. I remembered the devilish malice with which she had tormented me all the way from home, and I wondered if all religious people were like that. It was my turn now. I went in with the fear of damnation in my soul, and the confessional door closed of itself behind me.

It was pitch black inside. I couldn't see priest or anything else. Then I really began to be frightened. In the darkness it was a matter between God and me, and God had all the odds. He knew what my intentions were even before I started. I had no chance at all. All I had ever been told about confession got mixed up in my mind, and I knelt to one wall and said: "Bless me, father, for I have sinned; this is my first confession." I waited for a few minutes but nothing happened, so I tried it on the other wall. Nothing happened there either. He had me spotted all right.

It must have been then that I noticed the shelf at about the one height with my head. It struck me that it was probably the place you were supposed to kneel. Of course, it was on the high side, and not very deep, but by this time I was beyond all rational considerations. Mind you, it took some climbing, but I was always good at that, and I managed to get up all right. The trouble was to stay up. There was just room for my knees, but, apart from a sort of moulding in the outer wall, nothing you could get a grip on. I held on to the moulding and repeated the words a little louder, and this time something happened all right. A slide was slammed back and a man's voice asked after a moment: "Who's there?"

" 'Tis me, father," said I, for fear he mightn't see me and go away again. I couldn't see him at all. The place his voice came from was under the moulding, about level with my knees, so I took a good grip of the moulding and swung myself down till I saw the astonished face of a young priest looking up at me. He had to put his head on one side to see me, and I had to put mine on one side to see him, so we were more or less talking to one another upside down. It struck me as a very queer way to hear confessions, but I didn't feel it was my place to criticize.

"Bless me, father, for I have sinned; this is my first confession," I rattled off, all in one breath, and swung myself down the least shade more to make it easier for him.

"What are you doing up there?" he shouted in an angry voice, and the strain the politeness was putting on my hold of the moulding, and the shock of being addressed in that uncivil way were too much for me. Down I tumbled and hit the door an unmerciful wallop before I found myself on the flat of my back in the middle of the aisle. The priest opened the door of the middle box and came out, pushing the biretta back from his forehead. He looked something terrible. Then Nora came scampering down the aisle from the altar.

"Oh, you dirty little caffler!" she said. "I might have known you'd do it! I might have known you'd disgrace me! I can't leave you out of my sight for a minute."

Before I even got to my feet she bent down and gave me a smack across the ear. This reminded me that I was so stunned I had even forgotten to cry, so that people might think I wasn't hurt at all, when as a matter of fact I was probably crippled for life.

"What's all this about?" said the priest, getting angrier than ever, and pushing her off me. "How dare you hit the child like that, you little vixen?"

"But I can't do my penance with him, father," cried Nora, cocking an outraged eye up at him.

"Well, go on and do it," he said, giving me a hand up, "or I'll give you some more to do. . . . Was it coming to confession you were, my poor man?" he asked me.

" 'Twas, father," said I with a sob.

"Oh," he said in a respectful tone, "a big, hefty fellow like you must have terrible sins. Is this your first?"

" 'Tis, father," said I.

"Worse and worse," he said, shaking his head gloomily. "You have the crimes of a lifetime to tell. I don't know will I get rid of you at all today. You'd better sit down here and wait till I'm finished with these old ones. You can see by the looks of them they haven't much to tell."

"I will so, father," I said with something approaching joy.

The relief of it was enormous. Nora stuck out her tongue at me behind his back, but I couldn't even be bothered noticing it. I knew from the very moment that man opened his mouth that he was exceptionally intelligent. It only stood to reason that a fellow confessing his sins after seven years would have more to tell than people that went every week. That was what the priest expected, and the rest was only old women and girls and their talk about hell and the penitential psalms—people with no experience of life. I started to make my examination of conscience, and, barring the things about the grandmother, it didn't seem too bad.

The next time the priest steered me into the confession box himself and left the shutter back the way I'd see him sitting down at the other side with his biretta pulled well down over his eyes.

"Well now," he said, "what do they call you?"

"Jackie, father," said I.

"And what's a-trouble to you, Jackie?" he said.

"Father," I said, feeling I might as well get it over while I had him in good humour, "I had it all arranged to kill my grandmother!"

He seemed a bit shaken by that all right, because he didn't say anything for a while.

"My goodness," he said at last, "that'd be a shocking thing to do. What put that into your head?"

"Father," I said, feeling very sorry for myself, "she's an awful woman."

"Is she?" he asked. "What way is she awful?"

"She takes porter, father," said I, knowing well from the way the mother talked of porter that it must be a mortal sin, and hoping it might make the priest see my point of view.

"Oh, my!" he said.

"And snuff, father," said I.

"She's a bad case all right, Jackie," he said.

"And she goes round in her bare feet, father," said I. "And she knows I don't like her, and she gives pennies to Nora and none to me, and my da sides with her and beats me, so one night I was so heart-scalded I made up my mind I'd have to kill her."

"And what would you do with the body?" he asked with great interest.

"I was thinking I could cut it up and carry it away in a barrow I have," said I.

"Begor, Jackie," said he, "do you know, you're a terrible child?"

"I know, father," said I. (I was thinking the same thing myself.) "I tried to kill Nora too, with a bread-knife, under the table, only I missed her."

"Is that the little girl that was beating you just now?" he asked.

" 'Tis, father," said I.

"Someone will go for her with a bread-knife one day, and he won't miss her," he said. "But you must have great courage. There's lots of people I'd like to do the same to, between ourselves, but I'd never have the nerve. Hanging is an awful death."

"Is it, father?" said I with the deepest interest. (I was always very keen on hanging.) "Did you ever see a fellow hanged?"

"I saw dozens of them," he assured me solemnly, "and they all died roaring."

"Jay!" said I.

"Oh, 'tis a horrible death," he said with great satisfaction. "Lots of the fellows I saw killed their grandmothers too, but any of them I asked said 'twas never worth it."

He had me there for a full ten minutes, talking, and then walked out to the chapel yard with me. I was quite sorry to part with him because he was the most entertaining man I'd ever met in the religious line. Outside, the sunlight after the shadow of the church was like the roaring of waves on a beach; it dazzled me, and when the frozen silence melted and I heard the scream of trams on the road, the heart rose in me. But the best of all was to know I wouldn't die that night and come back leaving marks on my poor mother's furniture. I knew it would be a great worry to her and the poor soul had enough.

Nora was sitting on the railing, waiting for me, and she put on a very sour puss when she saw the priest along with me. She was mad jealous because a priest had never come out of the church with her.

"Well," she asked coldly after he parted me, "what did he give you?"

"Three Hail Marys," said I.

"Three Hail Marys?" she repeated incredulously. "You mustn't have told him anything."

"I told him everything," I said confidently.

"About Gran and all?"

"About Gran and all."

(All she wanted was to be able to go home and say I had made a bad confession.)

"Did you tell him you went for me with the bread-knife?" she asked with a frown.

"I did to be sure," said I.

"And he only gave you three Hail Marys?"

"That's all."

She got down off the railings slowly with a baffled air. Clearly, this was beyond her. As we mounted the steps to the main road she looked at me suspiciously.

"What are you sucking?" she asked.

"Bulls' eyes," I said.

"Was it the priest gave them to you?"

" 'Twas."

"Lord God!" she wailed bitterly. "Some people have all the luck! 'Tis no advantage to anybody trying to be good. I might just as well be a sinner like you."

How I Contemplated the World from the Detroit House of Correction and Began My Life Over Again
(1969)

JOYCE CAROL OATES

Notes for an essay for an english class at Baldwin country day school; poking around in debris; disgust and curiosity; a revelation of the meaning of life; a happy ending ...

I Events

1. The girl (myself) is walking through Branden's, that excellent store. Suburb of a large famous city that is a symbol for large famous American cities. The event sneaks up on the girl, who believes she is herding it along with a small fixed smile, a girl of fifteen, innocently experienced. She dawdles in a certain style by a counter of costume jewelry. Rings, earrings, necklaces. Prices from $5 to $50, all within reach. All ugly too. She eases over to the glove counter, where everything is ugly too. In her close-fitted coat with its black fur collar she contemplates the luxury of Branden's, which she has known for many years: its many mild pale lights, easy on the eye and the soul, its elaborate tinkly decorations, its women shoppers with their excellent shoes and coats and hairdos, all dawdling gracefully, in no hurry.

   Who was ever in a hurry here?

2. The girl seated at home. A small library, paneled walls of oak. Someone is talking to me. An earnest, husky, female voice drives itself against my ears, nervous, frightened, groping around my heart, saying, "If you wanted gloves, why didn't you say so? Why didn't you ask for them?" That store, Branden's, is owned by Raymond Forrest who lives on Du Maurier Drive. We live on Sioux Drive. Raymond Forrest. A handsome man? An ugly man? A man of fifty or sixty, with gray hair, or a man of forty with earnest, courteous eyes, a good golf game; who is Raymond Forrest, this man who is my salvation? Father has been talking to him. Father is not his physician; Dr. Berg is his physician.

Father and Dr. Berg refer patients to each other. There is a connection. Mother plays bridge with . . . On Mondays and Wednesdays our maid Billie works at . . . The strings draw together in a cat's cradle, making a net to save you when you fall . . . .

3. *Harriet Arnold's.* A small shop, better than Branden's. Mother in her black coat, I in my close-fitted blue coat. Shopping. Now look at this, isn't this cute, do you want this, why don't you want this, try this on, take this with you to the fitting room, take this also, what's wrong with you, what can I do for you, why are you so strange . . . ? "I wanted to steal but not to buy," I don't tell her. The girl droops along in her coat and gloves and leather boots, her eyes scan the horizon, which is pastel pink and decorated like Branden's, tasteful walls and modern ceilings with graceful glimmering lights.

4. Weeks later, the girl at a bus stop. Two o'clock in the afternoon, a Tuesday; obviously she has walked out of school.

5. The girl stepping down from a bus. Afternoon, weather changing to colder. Detroit. Pavement and closed-up stores; grillwork over the windows of a pawnshop. What is a pawnshop, exactly?

II Characters

1. The girl stands five feet five inches tall. An ordinary height. Baldwin Country Day School draws them up to that height. She dreams along the corridors and presses her face against the Thermoplex glass. No frost or steam can ever form on that glass. A smudge of grease from her forehead . . . could she be boiled down to grease? She wears her hair loose and long and straight in suburban teen-age style, 1968. Eyes smudged with pencil, dark brown. Brown hair. Vague green eyes. A pretty girl? An ugly girl? She sings to herself under her breath, idling in the corridor, thinking of her many secrets (the thirty dollars she once took from the purse of a friend's mother, just for fun, the basement window she smashed in her own house just for fun) and thinking of her brother who is at Susquehanna Boys' Academy, an excellent preparatory school in Maine, remembering him unclearly . . . he has long manic hair and a squeaking voice and he looks like one of the popular teen-age singers of 1968, one of those in a group, *The Certain Forces, The Way Out, The Maniacs Responsible.* The girl in her turn looks like one of those fieldsful of girls who listen to the boys' singing, dreaming and mooning restlessly, breaking into high sullen laughter, innocently experienced.

2. The mother. A Midwestern woman of Detroit and suburbs. Belongs to the Detroit Athletic Club. Also the Detroit Golf Club. Also the Bloomfield Hills Country Club. The Village Women's Club at which lectures are given each winter on Genet and Sartre and James Baldwin, by the Director of the Adult Education Program at Wayne State University. . . . The Bloomfield Art Association. Also the Founders Society of the Detroit Institute of Arts. Also . . . Oh, she is in perpetual motion, this lady, hair like blown-up gold and finer than gold, hair and fingers and body of inestimable grace. Heavy weighs the gold on the back of her hairbrush and hand mirror. Heavy heavy the candlesticks in the dining room. Very heavy is the big car, a Lincoln, long and black, that on one cool autumn day split a squirrel's body in two unequal parts.

3. The father. Dr.   . He belongs to the same clubs as #2. A player of squash and golf; he has a golfer's umbrella of stripes. Candy stripes. In his mouth nothing turns to sugar, however; saliva works no miracles here. His doctoring is of the slightly sick. The sick are sent elsewhere (to Dr. Berg?), the deathly sick are sent back for more tests and their bills are sent to their homes, the unsick are sent to Dr. Coronet (Isabel, a lady), an excellent psychiatrist for unsick people who angrily believe they are sick and want to do something about it. If they demand a male psychiatrist, the unsick are sent by Dr.   (my father) to Dr. Lowenstein, a male psychiatrist, excellent and expensive, with a limited practice.

4. Clarita. She is twenty, twenty-five, she is thirty or more? Pretty, ugly, what? She is a woman lounging by the side of a road, in jeans and a sweater, hitchhiking, or she is slouched on a stool at a counter in some roadside diner. A hard line of jaw. Curious eyes. Amused eyes. Behind her eyes processions move, funeral pageants, cartoons. She says, "I never can figure out why girls like you bum around down here. What are you looking for anyway?" An odor of tobacco about her. Unwashed underclothes, or no underclothes, unwashed skin, gritty toes, hair long and falling into strands, not recently washed.

5. Simon. In this city the weather changes abruptly, so Simon's weather changes abruptly. He sleeps through the afternoon. He sleeps through the morning. Rising, he gropes around for something to get him going, for a cigarette or a pill to drive him out to the street, where the temperature is hovering around 35°. Why doesn't it drop? Why, why doesn't the cold clean air come down from Canada; will he have to go up into Canada to get it? will he have to leave the Country of his Birth and sink into Canada's frosty fields . . . ? Will the F.B.I. (which he dreams about constantly) chase him over the Canadian border on foot, hounded out in a blizzard of broken glass and horns . . . ? "Once I was Huckleberry Finn," Simon says, "but now I am Roderick Usher." Beset by frenzies and fears, this man who makes my spine go cold, he takes green pills, yellow pills, pills of white and capsules of dark blue and green . . . he takes other things I may not mention, for what if Simon seeks me out and climbs into my girl's bedroom here in Bloomfield Hills and strangles me, what then . . . ? (As I write this I begin to shiver. Why do I shiver? I am now sixteen and sixteen is not an age for shivering.) It comes from Simon, who is always cold.

III World Events

Nothing.

IV People & Circumstances Contributing To This Delinquency

Nothing.

V Sioux Drive

George, Clyde G. 240 Sioux. A manufacturer's representative; children, a dog, a wife. Georgian with the usual columns. You think of the White House, then of Thomas Jefferson, then your mind goes blank on the white pillars and you think of nothing. Norris, Ralph W. 246 Sioux. Public relations. Colonial. Bay window, brick, stone, concrete, wood, green shutters, sidewalk, lantern, grass, trees, blacktop drive, two children, one of them my classmate Esther (Esther Norris) at

Baldwin. Wife, cars. Ramsey, Michael D. 250 Sioux. Colonial. Big living room, thirty by twenty-five, fireplaces in living room, library, recreation room, paneled walls wet bar five bathrooms five bedrooms two lavatories central air conditioning automatic sprinkler automatic garage door three children one wife two cars a breakfast room a patio a large fenced lot fourteen trees a front door with a brass knocker never knocked. Next is our house. Classic contemporary. Traditional modern. Attached garage, attached Florida room, attached patio, attached pool and cabana, attached roof. A front door mail slot through which pour *Time Magazine, Fortune, Life, Business Week,* the *Wall Street Journal,* the *New York Times,* the *New Yorker,* the *Saturday Review, MD., Modern Medicine, Disease of the Month* . . . and also . . . . And in addition to all this, a quiet sealed letter from Baldwin saying: *Your daughter is not doing work compatible with her performance on the Stanford-Binet.* . . . And your son is not doing well, not well at all, very sad. Where is your son anyway? Once he stole trick-and-treat candy from some six-year-old kids, he himself being a robust ten. The beginning. Now your daughter steals. In the Village Pharmacy she made off with, yes she did, don't deny it, she made off with a copy of *Pageant Magazine* for no reason, she swiped a roll of Life Savers in a green wrapper and was in no need of saving her life or even in need of sucking candy; when she was no more than eight years old she stole, don't blush, she stole a package of Turns only because it was out on the counter and available, and the nice lady behind the counter (now dead) said nothing. . . . Sioux Drive. Maples, oaks, elms. Diseased elms cut down. Sioux Drive runs into Roosevelt Drive. Slow, turning lanes, not streets, all drives and lanes and ways and passes. A private police force. Quiet private police, in unmarked cars. Cruising on Saturday evenings with paternal smiles for the residents who are streaming in and out of houses, going to and from parties, a thousand parties, slightly staggering, the women in their furs alighting from automobiles bought of Ford and General Motors and Chrysler, very heavy automobiles. No foreign cars. Detroit. In 275 Sioux, down the block in that magnificent French-Normandy mansion, lives   himself, who has the C   account itself, imagine that! Look at where he lives and look at the enormous trees and chimneys, imagine his many fireplaces, imagine his wife and children, imagine his wife's hair, imagine her fingernails, imagine her bathtub of smooth clean glowing pink, imagine their embraces, his trouser pockets filled with odd coins and keys and dust and peanuts, imagine their ecstasy on Sioux Drive, imagine their income tax returns, imagine their little boy's pride in his experimental car, a scaled-down C   , as he roars around the neighborhood on the sidewalks frightening dogs and Negro maids, oh imagine all these things, imagine everything, let your mind roar out all over Sioux Drive and Du Maurier Drive and Roosevelt Drive and Ticonderoga Pass and Burning Bush Way and Lincolnshire Pass and Lois Lane.

When spring comes, its winds blow nothing to Sioux Drive, no odors of hollyhocks or forsythia, nothing Sioux Drive doesn't already possess, everything is planted and performing. The weather vanes, had they weather vanes, don't have to turn with the wind, don't have to contend with the weather. There is no weather.

VI Detroit

There is always weather in Detroit. Detroit's temperature is always 32°. Fast-falling temperatures. Slow-rising temperatures. Wind from the north-northeast four to forty miles an hour, small-craft warnings, partly cloudy today and Wednesday changing to partly sunny through

Thursday . . . small warnings of frost, soot warnings, traffic warnings, hazardous lake conditions for small craft and swimmers, restless Negro gangs, restless cloud formations, restless temperatures aching to fall out the very bottom of the thermometer or shoot up over the top and boil everything over in red mercury.

Detroit's temperature is 32°. Fast-falling temperatures. Slow-rising temperatures. Wind from the north-northeast four to forty miles an hour. . . .

VII Events

1. The girl's heart is pounding. In her pocket is a pair of gloves! In a plastic bag! Airproof breathproof plastic bag, gloves selling for twenty-five dollars on Branden's counter! In her pocket! Shoplifted! . . . In her purse is a blue comb, not very clean. In her purse is a leather billfold (a birthday present from her grandmother in Philadelphia) with snapshots of the family in clean plastic windows, in the billfold are bills, she doesn't know how many bills. . . . In her purse is an ominous note from her friend Tykie *What's this about Joe H. and the kids hanging around at Louise's Sat. night? You heard anything?* . . . passed in French class. In her purse is a lot of dirty yellow Kleenex, her mother's heart would break to see such very dirty Kleenex, and at the bottom of her purse are brown hairpins and safety pins and a broken pencil and a ballpoint pen (blue) stolen from somewhere forgotten and a purse-size compact of Cover Girl Make-Up, Ivory Rose. . . . Her lipstick is Broken Heart, a corrupt pink; her fingers are trembling like crazy; her teeth are beginning to chatter; her insides are alive; her eyes glow in her head; she is saying to her mother's astonished face *I want to steal but not to buy.*

2. At Clarita's. Day or night? What room is this? A bed, a regular bed, and a mattress on the floor nearby. Wallpaper hanging in strips. Clarita says she tore it like that with her teeth. She was fighting a barbaric tribe that night, high from some pills; she was battling for her life with men wearing helmets of heavy iron and their faces no more than Christian crosses to breathe through, every one of those bastards looking like her lover Simon, who seems to breathe with great difficulty through the slits of mouth and nostrils in his face. Clarita has never heard of Sioux Drive. Raymond Forrest cuts no ice with her, nor does the C   account and its millions; Harvard Business School could be at the corner of Vernor and 12th Street for all she cares, and Vietnam might have sunk by now into the Dead Sea under its tons of debris, for all the amazement she could show . . . her face is overworked, overwrought, at the age of twenty (thirty?) it is already exhausted but fanciful and ready for a laugh. Clarita says mournfully to me *Honey somebody is going to turn you out let me give you warning.* In a movie shown on late television Clarita is not a mess like this but a nurse, with short neat hair and a dedicated look, in love with her doctor and her doctor's patients and their diseases, enamored of needles and sponges and rubbing alcohol. . . . Or no: she is a private secretary. Robert Cumming is her boss. She helps him with fantastic plots, the canned audience laughs, no, the audience doesn't laugh because nothing is funny, instead her boss is Robert Taylor and they are not boss and secretary but husband and wife, she is threatened by a young starlet, she is grim, handsome, wifely, a good companion for a good man . . . . She is Claudette Colbert. Her sister too is Claudette Colbert. They are twins, identical. Her husband Charles Boyer is a very rich handsome man and her sister, Claudette Colbert, is plotting her

death in order to take her place as the rich man's wife, no one will know because they are *twins*. . . . All these marvelous lives Clarita might have lived, but she fell out the bottom at the age of thirteen. At the age when I was packing my overnight case for a slumber party at Toni Deshield's she was tearing filthy sheets off a bed and scratching up a rash on her arms. . . . Thirteen is uncommonly young for a white girl in Detroit, Miss Brock of the Detroit House of Correction said in a sad newspaper interview for the *Detroit News;* fifteen and sixteen are more likely. Eleven, twelve, thirteen are not surprising in colored . . . they are more precocious. What can we do? Taxes are rising and the tax base is falling. The temperature rises slowly but falls rapidly. Everything is falling out the bottom, Woodward Avenue is filthy, Livernois Avenue is filthy! Scraps of paper flutter in the air like pigeons, dirt flies up and hits you right in the eye, oh Detroit is breaking up into dangerous bits of newspaper and dirt, watch out. . . .

Clarita's apartment is over a restaurant. Simon her lover emerges from the cracks at dark. Mrs. Olesko, a neighbor of Clarita's, an aged white wisp of a woman, doesn't complain but sniffs with contentment at Clarita's noisy life and doesn't tell the cops, hating cops, when the cops arrive. I should give more fake names, more blanks, instead of telling all these secrets. I myself am a secret; I am a minor.

3. My father reads a paper at a medical convention in Los Angeles. There he is, on the edge of the North American continent, when the unmarked detective put his hand so gently on my arm in the aisle of Branden's and said, "Miss, would you like to step over here for a minute?"

And where was he when Clarita put her hand on my arm, that wintry dark sulphurous aching day in Detroit, in the company of closed-down barber shops, closed-down diners, closed-down movie houses, homes, windows, basements, faces . . . she put her hand on my arm and said, "Honey, are you looking for somebody down here?"

And was he home worrying about me, gone for two weeks solid, when they carried me off . . . ? It took three of them to get me in the police cruiser, so they said, and they put more than their hands on my arm.

4. I work on this lesson. My English teacher is Mr. Forest, who is from Michigan State. Not handsome, Mr. Forest, and his name is plain, unlike Raymond Forrest's, but he is sweet and rodentlike, he has conferred with the principal and my parents, and everything is fixed . . . treat her as if nothing has happened, a new start, begin again, only sixteen years old, what a shame, how did it happen?—nothing happened, nothing could have happened, a slight physiological modification known only to a gynecologist or to Dr. Coronet. I work on my lesson. I sit in my pink room. I look around the room with my sad pink eyes. I sigh, I dawdle, I pause, I eat up time, I am limp and happy to be home, I am sixteen years old suddenly, my head hangs heavy as a pumpkin on my shoulders, and my hair has just been cut by Mr. Faye at the Crystal Salon and is said to be very becoming.

(Simon too put his hand on my arm and said, "Honey, you have got to come with me," and in his six-by-six room we got to know each other. Would I go back to Simon again? Would I lie down with him in all that filth and craziness? Over and over again

700

a Clarita is being
betrayed as in front of a Cunningham Drug Store she is nervously eying a colored
man who may or may not have money, or a nervous white boy of twenty with sideburns and an Appalachian look, who may or may not have a knife hidden in his
jacket pocket, or a husky red-faced man of friendly countenance who may or may
not be a member of the Vice Squad out for an early twilight walk.)

I work on my lesson for Mr. Forest. I have filled up eleven pages. Words
pour out of me and won't stop. I want to tell everything . . . what was the song
Simon was always humming, and who was Simon's friend in a very new trench
coat with an old high school graduation ring on his finger . . . ? Simon's bearded
friend? When I was down too low for him, Simon kicked me out and gave me to
him for three days, I think, on Fourteenth Street in Detroit, an airy room of cold
cruel drafts with newspapers on the floor. . . . Do I really remember that or am
I piecing it together from what they told me? Did they tell the truth? Did they
know much of the truth?

VIII Characters

1. Wednesdays after school, at four; Saturday mornings at ten. Mother drives me to
   Dr. Coronet. Ferns in the office, plastic or real, they look the same. Dr. Coronet is
   queenly, an elegant nicotine-stained lady who would have studied with Freud had
   circumstances not prevented it, a bit of a Catholic, ready to offer you some mystery
   if your teeth will ache too much without it. Highly recommended by Father! Forty
   dollars an hour, Father's forty dollars! Progress! Looking up! Looking better! That
   new haircut is so becoming, says Dr. Coronet herself, showing how
   normal she is for a woman with an I.Q. of 180 and many advanced degrees.

2. Mother. A lady in a brown suede coat. Boots of shiny black material, black gloves, a
   black fur hat. She would be humiliated could she know that of all the people in the
   world it is my ex-lover Simon who walks most like her . . . self-conscious and unreal,
   listening to distant music, a little bowlegged with craftiness. . . .

3. Father. Tying a necktie. In a hurry. On my first evening home he put his hand on my
   arm and said, "Honey, we're going to forget all about this."

4. Simon. Outside, a plane is crossing the sky, in here we're in a hurry. Morning. It
   must be morning. The girl is half out of her mind, whimpering and vague; Simon
   her dear friend is wretched this morning . . . he is wretched with morning itself . . .
   he forces her to give him an injection with that needle she knows is filthy, she has a
   dread of needles and surgical instruments and the odor of things that are to be sent
   into the blood, thinking somehow of her father. . . . This is a bad morning, Simon
   says that his mind is being twisted out of shape, and so he submits to the needle that
   he usually scorns and bites his lip with his yellowish teeth, his face going very pale.
   Ah baby! he says in his soft mocking voice, which with all women is a mockery of
   love, *do it like this—Slowly*—And the girl, terrified, almost drops the precious needle
   but manages to turn it up to the light from the window . . . is it an extension of herself then? She can give him this gift then? I *wish you wouldn't do this to me,* she says,
   wise in her terror, because it seems to her that Simon's danger—in a few minutes he
   may be dead—is a way of pressing her against him that is more powerful than any
   other embrace. She has to work over his arm, the knotted corded veins of his arm,

701

her forehead with perspiration as she pushes and releases the needle, starting at that mixture of liquid now stained with Simon's bright blood . . . When the drug hits him she can feel it herself, she feels that magic that is more than any woman can give him, striking back of his head and making his face stretch as if with the impact of a terrible sun. . . . She tries to embrace him but he pushes her aside and stumbles to his feet. *Jesus Christ,* he says. . . .

5. Princess; a Negro girl of eighteen. What is her charge? She is closed-mouthed about it, shrewd and silent, you know that no one had to wrestle her to the sidewalk to get her in here; she came with dignity. In the recreation room she sits reading *Nancy Drew and the Jewel Box Mystery,* which inspires in her face tiny wrinkles of alarm and interest: what a face! Light brown skin, heavy shaded eyes, heavy eyelashes, a serious sinister dark brow, graceful fingers, graceful wristbones, graceful legs, lips, tongue, a sugar-sweet voice, a leggy stride more masculine than Simon's and my mother's, decked out in a dirty white blouse and dirty white slacks; vaguely nautical is Princess' style. . . . At breakfast she is in charge of clearing the table and leans over me, saying, *Honey you sure you ate enough?*

6. The girl lies sleepless, wondering. Why here, why not there? Why Bloomfield Hills and not jail? Why jail and not her pink room? Why downtown Detroit and not Sioux Drive? What is the difference? Is Simon all the difference? The girl's head is a parade of wonders. She is nearly sixteen, her breath is marvelous with wonders, not long ago she was coloring with crayons and now she is smearing the landscape with paints that won't come off and won't come off her fingers either. She says to the matron *I am not talking about anything,* not because everyone has warned her not to talk but because, because she will not talk; because she won't say anything about Simon, who is her secret. And she says to the matron, *I won't go home,* up until that night in the lavatory when everything was changed. . . . "No, I won't go home I want to stay here," she says, listening to her own words with amazement, thinking that weeds might climb everywhere over that marvelous $180,000 house and dinosaurs might return to muddy the beige carpeting, but never never will she reconcile four o'clock in the morning in Detroit with eight o'clock breakfasts in Bloomfield Hills. . . . oh, she aches still for Simon's hands and his caressing breath, though he gave her little pleasure, he took everything from her (five-dollar bills, ten-dollar bills, passed into her numb hands by men and taken out of her hands by Simon) until she herself was passed into the hands of other men, police, when Simon evidently got tired of her and her hysteria. . . . *No, I won't* go home, *I don't want to be bailed out.* The girl thinks as a *Stubborn and Wayward Child* (one of several charges lodged against her), and the matron understands her crazy white-rimmed eyes that are seeking out some new violence that will keep her in jail, should someone threaten to let her out. Such children try to strangle the matrons, the attendants, or one another . . . they want the locks locked forever, the doors nailed shut . . . and this girl is no different up until that night her mind is changed for her. . . .

IX That Night

Princess and Dolly, a little white girl of maybe fifteen, hardy however as a sergeant and in the House of Correction for armed robbery, corner her in the lavatory at the farthest sink and the other girls look away and file out to bed, leaving her. God, how she is beaten up! Why is she beaten up? Why do they pound her, why such hatred? Princess vents all the hatred of a thousand silent Detroit winters on her body, this girl whose body belongs to me, fiercely she rides across the Midwestern plains on this girl's tender bruised body . . . revenge on the oppressed minorities of America! revenge on the slaughtered Indians! revenge on the female sex, on the male sex, revenge on Bloomfield Hills, revenge revenge. . . .

X Detroit

In Detroit, weather weighs heavily upon everyone. The sky looms large. The horizon shimmers in smoke. Downtown the buildings are imprecise in the haze. Perpetual haze. Perpetual motion inside the haze. Across the choppy river is the city of Windsor, in Canada. Part of the continent has bunched up here and is bulging outward, at the tip of Detroit; a cold hard rain is forever falling on the expressways. . . . Shoppers shop grimly, their cars are not parked in safe places, their windshields may be smashed and graceful ebony hands may drag them out through their shatterproof smashed windshields, crying, *Revenge for the Indians!* Ah, they all fear leaving Hudson's and being dragged to the very tip of the city and thrown off the parking roof of Cabo Hall, that expensive tomb, into the river. . . .

XI Characters We Are Forever Entwined With

1. Simon drew me into his tender rotting arms and breathed gravity into me. Then I came to earth, weighed down. He said, *You are such a little girl,* and he weighed me down with his delight. In the palms of his hands were teeth marks from his previous life experiences. He was thirty-five, they said. Imagine Simon in this room, in my pink room: he is about six feet tall and stoops slightly, in a feline cautious way, always thinking, always on guard, with his scuffed light suede shoes and his clothes that are anyone's clothes, slightly rumpled ordinary clothes that ordinary men might wear to not-bad jobs. Simon has fair long hair, curly hair, spent languid curls that are like . . . exactly like the curls of wood shavings to the touch, I am trying to be exact . . . and he smells of unheated mornings and coffee and too many pills coating his tongue with a faint green-white scum. . . . Dear Simon, who would be panicked in this room and in this house (right now Billie is vacuuming next door in my parents' room; a vacuum cleaner's roar is a sign of all good things), Simon who is said to have come from a home not much different from this, years ago, fleeing all the carpeting and the polished banisters . . . Simon has a deathly face, only desperate people fall in love with it. His face is bony and cautious, the bones of his cheeks prominent as if with the rigidity of his ceaseless thinking, plotting, for he has to make money out of girls to whom money means nothing, they're so far gone they can hardly count it, and in a sense money means nothing to him either except as a way of keeping on with his life. *Each Day's Proud Struggle,* the title of a novel we could read at jail. . . . Each day he needs a certain amount of money. He devours it. It wasn't love he uncoiled in me with his hollowed-out eyes and his courteous smile, that remnant of a prosperous past, but a dark terror that needed to press itself flat against him, or against another man . . . but he was the first, he came over to me

703

and took my arm, a claim. We struggled on the stairs and I said, *Let me loose, you're hurting my neck, my face*, it was such a surprise that my skin hurt where he rubbed it, and afterward we lay face to face and he breathed everything into me. In the end I think he turned me in.

2. Raymond Forrest. I just read this morning that Raymond Forrest's father, the chairman of the board at   , died of a heart attack on a plane bound for London. I would like to write Raymond Forrest a note of sympathy. I would like to thank him for not pressing charges against me one hundred years ago, saving me, being so generous . . . well, men like Raymond Forrest are generous men, not like Simon. I would like to write him a letter telling of my love, or of some other emotion that is positive and healthy. Not like Simon and his poetry, which he scrawled down when he was high and never changed a word . . . but when I try to think of something to say, it is Simon's language that comes back to me, caught in my head like a bad song, it is always Simon's language:

> *There is no reality only dreams*
> *Your neck may get snapped when you wake*
> *My love is drawn to some violent end*
> *She keeps wanting to get away*
> *My love is heading downward*
> *And I am heading upward*
> *She is going to crash on the sidewalk*
> *And I am going to dissolve into the clouds*

XII Events

1. Out of the hospital, bruised and saddened and converted, with Princess' grunts still tangled in my hair . . . and Father in his overcoat looking like a prince himself, come to carry me off. Up the expressway and out north to home. Jesus Christ, but the air is thinner and cleaner here. Monumental houses. Heartbreaking sidewalks, so clean.

2. Weeping in the living room. The ceiling is two stories high and two chandeliers hang from it. Weeping, weeping, though Billie the maid is *probably listening*. I will never leave home again. Never. Never leave home. Never leave this home again, never.

3. Sugar doughnuts for breakfast. The toaster is very shiny and my face is distorted in it. Is that my face?

4. The car is turning in the driveway. Father brings me home. Mother embraces me. Sunlight breaks in movieland patches on the roof of our traditional-contemporary home, which was designed for the famous automotive stylist whose identity, if I told you the name of the famous car he designed, you would all know, so I can't tell you because my teeth chatter at the thought of being sued . . . or having someone climb into my bedroom window with a rope to strangle me. . . . The car turns up the blacktop drive. The house opens to me like a doll's house, so lovely in the sunlight, the big living room beckons to me with its walls falling away in a delirium of joy at my return, Billie the maid is *no doubt* listening from the kitchen as I burst into tears

and the hysteria Simon got so sick of. Convulsed in Father's arms, I say I will never leave again, never, why did I leave, where did I go, what happened, my mind is gone wrong, my body is one big bruise, my backbone was sucked dry, it wasn't the men who hurt me and Simon never hurt me but only those girls . . . my God, how they hurt me I will never leave home again. . . . The car is perpetually turning up the drive and I am perpetually breaking down in the living room and we are perpetually taking the right exit from the expressway (Lahser Road) and the wall of the rest room is perpetually banging against my head and perpetually are Simon's hands moving across my body and adding everything up and so too are Father's hands on my shaking bruised back, far from the surface of my skin on the surface of my good blue cashmere coat (dry-cleaned for my release). . . . I weep for all the money here, for God in gold and beige carpeting, for the beauty of chandeliers and the miracle of a clean polished gleaming toaster and faucets that run both hot and cold water, and I tell them, *I will never leave home, this is my home, I love everything here, I am in love with everything here. . . .*

I am home.

I Stand Here Ironing
(1961)

TILLIE OLSEN

I stand here ironing, and what you asked me moves tormented back and forth with the iron.

"I wish you would manage the time to come in and talk with me about your daughter. I'm sure you can help me understand her. She's a youngster who needs help and whom I'm deeply interested in helping."

"Who needs help." . . . Even if I came, what good would it do? You think because I am her mother I have a key, or that in some way you could use me as a key? She has lived for nineteen years. There is all that life that has happened outside of me, beyond me.

And when is there time to remember, to sift, to weigh, to estimate, to total? I will start and there will be an interruption and I will have to gather it all together again. Or I will become engulfed with all I did or did not do, with what should have been and what cannot be helped.

She was a beautiful baby. The first and only one of our five that was beautiful at birth. You do not guess how new and uneasy her tenancy in her now-loveliness. You did not know her all those years she was thought homely, or see her poring over her baby pictures, making me tell her over and over how beautiful she had been—and would be, I would tell her—and was now, to the seeing eye. But the seeing eyes were few or non-existent. Including mine.

I nursed her. They feel that's important nowadays. I nursed all the children, but with her, with all the fierce rigidity of first motherhood, I did like the books then said. Though her cries battered me to trembling and my breasts ached with swollenness, I waited till the clock decreed.

Why do I put that first? I do not even know if it matters, or if it explains anything.

She was a beautiful baby. She blew shining bubbles of sound. She loved motion, loved light, loved color and music and textures. She would lie on the floor in her blue overalls patting the surface so hard in ecstasy her hands and feet would blur. She was a miracle to me, but when she was eight months old I had to leave her daytimes with the woman downstairs to whom she was no miracle at all, for I worked or looked for work and for Emily's father, who "could no longer endure" (he wrote in his good-bye note) "sharing want with us."

I was nineteen. It was the pre-relief, pre-WPA world of the depression. I would start running as soon as I got off the streetcar, running up the stairs, the place smelling sour, and awake or asleep to startle awake, when she saw me she would break into a clogged weeping that could not be comforted, a weeping I can hear yet.

After a while I found a job hashing at night so I could be with her days, and it was better. But it came to where I had to bring her to his family and leave her.

It took a long time to raise the money for her fare back. Then she got chicken pox and I had to wait longer. When she finally came, I hardly knew her, walking quick and nervous like her father, looking like her father, thin, and dressed in a shoddy red that yellowed her skin and glared at the pock marks. All the baby loveliness gone.

She was two. Old enough for nursery school they said, and I did not know then what I know now—the fatigue of the long day, and the lacerations of group life in the nurseries that are only parking places for children.

Except that it would have made no difference if I had known. It was the only place there was. It was the only way we could be together, the only way I could hold a job.

And even without knowing, I knew. I knew the teacher that was evil because all these years it has curdled into my memory, the little boy hunched in the corner, her rasp, "why aren't you outside, because Alvin hits you? that's no reason, go out, scaredy." I knew Emily hated it even if she did not clutch and implore "don't go Mommy" like the other children, mornings.

She always had a reason why we should stay home. Momma, you look sick. Momma, I feel sick. Momma, the teachers aren't there today, they're sick. Momma, we can't go, there was a fire there last night. Momma, it's a holiday today, no school, they told me.

But never a direct protest, never rebellion. I think of our others in their three-, four-year-oldness—the explosions, the tempers, the denunciations, the demands—and I feel suddenly ill. I put the iron down. What in me demanded that goodness in her? And what was the cost, the cost to her of such goodness?

The old man living in the back once said in his gentle way: "You should smile at Emily more when you look at her." What *was* in my face when I looked at her? I loved her. There were all the acts of love.

It was only with the others I remembered what he said, and it was the face of joy, and not of care or tightness or worry I turned to them—too late for Emily. She does not smile easily, let alone almost always as her brothers and sisters do. Her face is closed and sombre, but when she wants, how fluid. You must have seen it in her pantomimes, you spoke of her rare gift for comedy on the stage that rouses a laughter out of the audience so dear they applaud and applaud and do not want to let her go.

Where does it come from, that comedy? There was none of it in her when she came back to me that second time, after I had had to send her away again. She had a new daddy now to learn to love, and I think perhaps it was a better time. Except when we left her alone nights, telling ourselves she was old enough.

"Can't you go some other time, Mommy, like tomorrow?" she would ask. "Will it be just a little while you'll be gone? Do you promise?"

The time we came back, the front door open, the clock on the floor in the hall. She rigid awake. "It wasn't just a little while. I didn't cry. Three times I called you, just three times, and then I ran downstairs to open the door so you could come faster. The clock talked loud. I threw it away, it scared me what it talked."

She said the clock talked loud again that night I went to the hospital to have Susan. She was delirious with the fever that comes before red measles, but she was fully conscious all the week I was gone and the week after we were home when she could not come near the new baby or me.

She did not get well. She stayed skeleton thin, not wanting to eat, and night after night she had nightmares. She would call for me, and I would rouse from exhaustion to sleepily call back: "You're all right, darling, go to sleep, it's just a dream," and if she still called, in a sterner voice, "now go to sleep, Emily, there's nothing to hurt you." Twice, only twice, when I had to get up for Susan anyhow, I went in to sit with her.

Now when it is too late (as if she would let me hold and comfort her like I do the others) I get up and go to her at once at her moan or restless stirring. "Are you awake, Emily? Can I get you something, dear?" And the answer is always the same: "No, I'm all right, go back to sleep, Mother."

They persuaded me at the clinic to send her away to a convalescent home in the country where "she can have the kind of food and care you can't manage for her, and you'll be free to concentrate on the new baby." They still send children to that place. I see pictures on the society page of sleek young women planning affairs to raise money for it, or dancing at the affairs, or decorating Easter eggs or filling Christmas stockings for the children.

They never have a picture of the children so I do not know if the girls still wear those gigantic red bows and the ravaged looks on the every other Sunday when parents can come to visit "unless otherwise notified"—as we were notified the first six weeks.

Oh it is a handsome place, green lawns and tall trees and fluted flower beds. High up on the balconies of each cottage the children stand, the girls in their red bows and white dresses, the boys in white suits and giant red ties. The parents stand below shrieking up to be heard and the children shriek down to be heard, and between them the invisible wall "Not To Be Contaminated by Parental Germs or Physical Affection."

There was a tiny girl who always stood hand in hand with Emily. Her parents never came. One visit she was gone. "They moved her to Rose Cottage," Emily shouted in explanation. "They don't like you to love anybody here."

She wrote once a week, the labored writing of a seven-year-old. "I am fine. How is the baby. If I write my leter nicly I will have a star. Love." There never was a star. We wrote every other day, letters she could never hold or keep but only hear read—once. "We simply do not have room for children to keep any personal possessions," they patiently explained when we pieced one Sunday's shrieking together to plead how much it would mean to Emily, who loved so to keep things, to be allowed to keep her letters and cards.

Each visit she looked frailer. "She isn't eating," they told us.

(They had runny eggs for breakfast or mush with lumps, Emily said later, I'd hold it in my mouth and not swallow. Nothing ever tasted good, just when they had chicken.)

It took us eight months to get her released home, and only the fact that she gained back so little of her seven lost pounds convinced the social worker.

I used to try to hold and love her after she came back, but her body would stay stiff, and after a while she'd push away. She ate little. Food sickened her, and I think much of life too. Oh she had physical lightness and brightness, twinkling by on skates, bouncing like a ball up and down up and down over the jump rope, skimming over the hill; but these were momentary.

She fretted about her appearance, thin and dark and foreign-looking at a time when every little girl was supposed to look or thought she should look a chubby blonde replica of Shirley Temple. The door-bell sometimes rang for her, but no one seemed to come and play in the house or be a best friend. Maybe because we moved so much.

709

There was a boy she loved painfully through two school semesters. Months later she told me how she had taken pennies from my purse to buy him candy. "Licorice was his favourite and I brought him some every day, but he still liked Jennifer better'n me. Why, Mommy?" The kind of question for which there is no answer.

School was a worry to her. She was not glib or quick in a world where glibness and quickness were easily confused with ability to learn. To her overworked and exasperated teachers she was an overconscientious "slow learner" who kept trying to catch up and was absent entirely too often.

I let her be absent, though sometimes the illness was imaginary. How different from my now-strictness about attendance with the others. I wasn't working. We had a new baby, I was home anyhow. Sometimes, after Susan grew old enough, I would keep her home from school, too, to have them all together.

Mostly Emily had asthma, and her breathing, harsh and labored, would fill the house with a curiously tranquil sound. I would bring the two old dresser mirrors and her boxes of collections to her bed. She would select beads and single earrings, bottle tops and shells, dried flowers and pebbles, old postcards and scraps, all sorts of oddments; then she and Susan would play Kingdom, setting up landscapes and furniture, peopling them with action.

Those were the only times of peaceful companionship between her and Susan. I have edged away from it, that poisonous feeling between them, that terrible balancing of hurts and needs I had to do between the two, and did so badly, those earlier years.

Oh there are conflicts between the others too, each one human, needing, demanding, hurting, taking—but only between Emily and Susan, no, Emily toward Susan that corroding resentment. It seems so obvious on the surface, yet it is not obvious. Susan, the second child, Susan, golden- and curly-haired and chubby, quick and articulate and assured, everything in appearance and manner Emily was not; Susan, not able to resist Emily's precious things, losing or sometimes clumsily breaking them; Susan telling jokes and riddles to company for applause while Emily sat silent (to say to me later: that was *my* riddle, Mother, I told it to Susan); Susan, who for all the five years' difference in age was just a year behind Emily in developing physically.

I am glad for that slow physical development that widened the difference between her and her contemporaries, though she suffered over it. She was too vulnerable for that terrible world of youthful competition, of preening and parading, of constant measuring of yourself against every other, of envy, "If I had that copper hair," or "If I had that skin. . . ." She tormented herself enough about not looking like the others, there was enough of the unsureness, the having to be conscious of words before you speak, the constant caring—what are they thinking of me? What kind of an impression am I making?—there was enough without having it all magnified by the merciless physical drives.

Ronnie is calling. He is wet and I change him. It is rare there is such a cry now. That time of motherhood is almost behind me when the ear is not one's own but must always be racked and listening for the child cry, the child call. We sit for a while and I hold him, looking out over the city spread in charcoal with its soft aisles of light. "*Shoogily*," he breathes and curls closer. I carry him back to bed, asleep. *Shoogily*. A funny word, a family word, inherited from Emily, invented by her to say: *comfort*.

In this and other ways she leaves her seal, I say aloud. And startle at my saying it. What do I mean? What did I start to gather together, to try and make coherent? I was at the terrible, growing years. War years. I do not remember them well. I was working, there were four smaller ones now, there was not time for her. She had to help be a mother, and housekeeper, and shopper. She had to set her seal. Mornings of crisis and near hysteria trying to get lunches packed, hair combed, coats and shoes found, everyone to school or Child Care on time, the baby ready for transportation. And always the paper scribbled on by a smaller one, the book looked at by Susan then mislaid, the homework not done. Running out to that huge school where she was one, she was lost, she was a drop; suffering over the unpreparedness, stammering and unsure in her classes.

There was so little time left at night after the kids were bedded down. She would struggle over books, always eating (it was in those years she developed her enormous appetite that is legendary in our family) and I would be ironing, or preparing food for the next day, or writing V-mail to Bill, or tending the baby. Sometimes, to make me laugh, or out of her despair, she would imitate happenings or types at school.

I think I said once: "Why don't you do something like this in the school amateur show?" One morning she phoned me at work, hardly understandable through the weeping: "Mother, I did it. I won, I won; they gave me first prize; they clapped and clapped and wouldn't let me go."

Now suddenly she was Somebody, and as imprisoned in her difference as she had been in anonymity.

She began to be asked to perform at other high schools, even in colleges, then at city and statewide affairs. The first one we went to, I only recognized her that first moment when thin, shy, she almost drowned herself into the curtains. Then: Was this Emily? The control, the command, the convulsing and deadly clowning, the spell, then the roaring, stamping audience, unwilling to let this rare and precious laughter out of their lives.

Afterwards: You ought to do something about her with a gift like that—but without money or knowing how, what does one do? We have left it all to her, and the gift has as often eddied inside, clogged and clotted, as been used and growing.

She is coming. She runs up the stairs two at a time with her light graceful step, and I know she is happy tonight. Whatever it was that occasioned your call did not happen today.

"Aren't you ever going to finish the ironing, Mother? Whistler painted his mother in a rocker. I'd have to paint mine standing over an ironing board."

This is one of her communicative nights and she tells me everything and nothing as she fixes herself a plate of food out of the icebox.

She is so lovely. Why did you want me to come in at all? Why were you concerned? She will find her way.

She starts up the stairs to bed. "Don't get me up with the rest in the morning." "But I thought you were having midterms." "Oh, those," she comes back in, kisses me, and says quite lightly, "in a couple of years when we'll all be atom-dead they won't matter a bit."

She has said it before. She *believes it*. But because I have been dredging the past, and all that compounds a human being is so heavy and meaningful in me, I cannot endure it tonight.

I will never total it all. I will never come in to say: She was a child seldom smiled at. Her father left me before she was a year old. I had to work her first six years when there was work, or I sent her home and to his relatives. There were years she had care she hated. She was dark and thin and foreign-looking in a world where the prestige went to blondeness and curly hair and dimples, she was slow where glibness was prized. She was a child of anxious, not proud, love. We were poor and could not afford for her the soil of easy growth. I was a young mother, I was a distracted mother. There were the other children pushing up, demanding. Her younger sister seemed all that she was not. There were years she did not want me to touch her. She kept too much in herself, her life was such she had to keep too much in herself. My wisdom came too late. She has much to her and probably little will come of it. She is a child of her age, of depression, of war, of fear.

Let her be. So all that is in her will not bloom—but in how many does it? There is still enough left to live by. Only help her to know—help make it so there is cause for her to know—that she is more than this dress on the ironing board, helpless before the iron.

The Way of the Wind
(1962)

AMOS OZ

1

Gideon Shenhav's last day began with a brilliant sunrise.

The dawn was gentle, almost autumnal. Faint flashes of light flickered through the wall of cloud that sealed off the eastern horizon. Slyly the new day concealed its purpose, betraying no hint of the heat wave that lay enfolded in its bosom.

Purple glowed on the eastern heights, fanned by the morning breeze. Then the rays pierced through the wall of cloud. It was day. Dark loopholes blinked awake at daylight's touch. Finally the incandescent sphere rose, assaulted the mountains of cloud, and broke their ranks. The eastern horizon was adazzle. And the soft purple yielded and fled before the terrible crimson blaze.

The camp was shaken by reveille a few minutes before sunrise. Gideon rose, padded barefoot out of his hut, and, still asleep, looked at the gathering light. With one thin hand he shaded his eyes, still yearning for sleep, while the other automatically buttoned up his battle dress. He could already hear voices and metallic sounds; a few eager boys were cleaning their guns for morning inspection. But Gideon was slow. The sunrise had stirred a weary restlessness inside him, perhaps a vague longing. The sunrise was over, but still he stood there drowsily, until he was pushed from behind and told to get cracking.

He went back into the hut, straightened his camp bed, cleaned his submachine gun, and picked up his shaving kit. On his way, among whitewashed eucalyptus trees and clustering notices commending tidiness and discipline, he suddenly remembered that today was Independence Day, the Fifth of Iyar. And today the platoon was to mount a celebratory parachute display in the Valley of Jezreel. He entered the washroom and, while he waited for a free mirror, brushed his teeth and thought of pretty girls. In an hour and a half the preparations would be complete and the platoon would be airborne, on its way to its destination. Throngs of excited civilians would be waiting for them to jump, and the girls would be there, too. The drop would take place just outside Nof Harish, the kibbutz that was Gideon's home, where he had been born and brought up until the day he joined the army. The moment his feet touched the ground, the children of the kibbutz would close around him and jump all over him and shout, "Gideon, look, here's our Gideon!"

He pushed in between two much bigger soldiers and began to lather his face and try to shave. "Hot day," he said.

One of the soldiers answered, "Not yet. But it soon will be."

And another soldier behind him grumbled, "Hurry it up. Don't spend all day jawing."

713

Gideon did not take offense. On the contrary, the words filled him with a surge of joy for some reason. He dried his face and went out onto the parade ground. The blue light had changed meanwhile to gray-white, the grubby glare of a *khamsin*.

2

Shimshon Sheinbaum had confidently predicted the previous night that a *khamsin* was on its way. As soon as he got up he hurried over to the window and confirmed with calm satisfaction that he had been right yet again. He closed the shutters, to protect the room from the hot wind, then washed his face and his shaggy shoulders and chest, shaved, and prepared his breakfast, coffee with a roll brought last night from the dining hall. Shimshon Sheinbaum loathed wasting time, especially in the productive morning hours: you go out, walk to the dining hall, have a chat, read the paper, discuss the news, and that's half the morning gone. So he always made do with a cup of coffee and a roll, and by ten past six, after the early news summary, Gideon Shenhav's father was sitting at his desk. Summer and winter alike, with no concessions.

He sat at his desk and stared for a few minutes at the map of the country that hung on the opposite wall. He was straining to recapture a nagging dream which had taken hold of him in the early hours, just before he had awakened. But it eluded him. Shimshon decided to get on with his work and not waste another minute. True, today was a holiday, but the best way to celebrate was to work, not to slack off. Before it was time to go out and watch the parachutists—and Gideon, who might actually be among them and not drop out at the last minute—he still had several hours of working time. A man of seventy-five cannot afford to squander his hours, especially if there are many, painfully many, things he must set down in writing. So little time.

The name of Shimshon Sheinbaum needs no introduction. The Hebrew Labor Movement knows how to honor its founding fathers, and for decades now Shimshon Sheinbaum's name has been invested with a halo of enduring fame. For decades he has fought body and soul to realize the vision of his youth. Setbacks and disappointments have not shattered or weakened his faith but, rather, have enriched it with a vein of wise sadness. The better he has come to understand the weakness of others and their ideological deviations, the more ferociously he has fought against his own weaknesses. He has sternly eliminated them, and lived according to his principles, with a ruthless self-discipline and not without a certain secret joy.

At this moment, between six and seven o'clock on this Independence Day morning, Shimshon Sheinbaum is not yet a bereaved father. But his features are extraordinarily well suited to the role. A solemn, sagacious expression, of one who sees all but betrays no reaction, occupies his furrowed face. And his blue eyes express an ironic melancholy.

He sits erect at his desk, his head bent over the pages. His elbows are relaxed. The desk is made of plain wood, like the rest of the furniture, which is all functional and unembellished. More like a monastic cell than a bungalow in a long-established kibbutz.

This morning will not be particularly productive. Time and again his thoughts wander to the dream that flickered and died at the end of the night. He must recapture the dream, and then he will be able to forget it and concentrate on his work. There was a hose, yes, and some sort of goldfish or something. An argument with someone. No connection. Now to work. The Poalei Zion Movement appears to have been built from the start on an ideological contradiction that could never be bridged, and which it only succeeded in disguising by means of verbal acrobatics. But the contradiction is only apparent, and anyone who hopes to exploit it to undermine or attack the movement does not know what he is talking about. And here is the simple proof.

Shimshon Sheinbaum's rich experience of life has taught him how arbitrary, how senseless is the hand that guides the vagaries of our fate, that of the individual and that of the community alike. His sobriety has not robbed him of the straightforwardness which has animated him since his youth. His most remarkable and admirable characteristic is his stubborn innocence, like that of our pure, pious forebears, whose sagacity never injured their faith. Sheinbaum has never allowed his actions to be cut loose from his words. Even though some of the leaders of our movement have drifted into political careers and cut themselves off completely from manual labor, Sheinbaum has never abandoned the kibbutz. He has turned down all outside jobs and assignments, and it was only with extreme reluctance that he accepted nomination to the General Workers' Congress. Until a few years ago his days were divided equally between physical and intellectual work: three days gardening, three days theorizing. The beautiful gardens of Nof Harish are largely his handiwork. We can remember how he used to plant and prune and lop, water and hoe, manure, transplant, weed, and dig up. He did not permit his status as the leading thinker of the movement to exempt him from the duties to which every rank-and-file member is liable: he served as night watchman, took his turn in the kitchens, helped with the harvest. No shadow of a double standard has ever clouded the path of Shimshon Sheinbaum's life: he is a single complex of vision and execution, he has known no slackness or weakness of will—so the secretary of the movement wrote about him in a magazine a few years ago, on the occasion of his seventieth birthday.

True, there have been moments of stabbing despair. There have been moments of deep disgust. But Shimshon Sheinbaum knows how to transform such moments into secret sources of furious energy. Like the words of the marching song he loves, which always inspires him to a frenzy of action: *Up into the mountains we are climbing, Climbing up toward the dawning day; We have left all our yesterdays behind us, But tomorrow is a long long way away.* If only that stupid dream would emerge from the shadows and show itself clearly, he could kick it out of his mind and concentrate at last on his work. Time is slipping by. A rubber hose, a chess gambit, some goldfish, a great argument, but what is the connection?

For many years Shimshon Sheinbaum has lived alone. He has channeled all his vigor into his ideological productions. To this life's work he has sacrificed the warmth of a family home. He has managed, in exchange, to retain into old age a youthful clarity and cordiality. Only when he was fifty-six did he suddenly marry Raya Greenspan and father Gideon, and after that he left her and returned to his ideological work. It would be sanctimonious to pretend, however, that before his marriage Shimshon Sheinbaum maintained a monastic existence. His personality attracted women just as it attracted disciples. He was still young when his thick mop of hair turned white, and his sunbeaten face was etched with an appealing pattern of lines and wrinkles. His square back, his strong shoulders, the timbre of his voice—always warm, skeptical, and rather ruminative—and also his solitude, all attracted women to him like fluttering birds. Gossip attributes to his loins at least one of the urchins of the kibbutz, and elsewhere, too, stories are current. But we shall not dwell on this.

At the age of fifty-six Shimshon Sheinbaum decided that it befitted him to beget a son and heir to bear his stamp and his name into the coming generation. And so he conquered Raya Greenspan, a diminutive girl with a stammer who was thirty-three years his junior. Three months after the wedding, which was solemnized before a restricted company, Gideon was born. And before the kibbutz had recovered from its amazement, Shimshon sent Raya back to her former room and rededicated himself to his ideological work. This episode caused various ripples, and, indeed, it was preceded by painful heart-searchings in Shimshon Sheinbaum himself.

Now let's concentrate and think logically. Yes, it's coming back. She came to my room and called me to go there quickly to put a stop to that scandal. I didn't ask any questions, but hurried after her. Someone had had the nerve to dig a pond in the lawn in front of the dining hall, and I was seething because no one had authorized such an innovation an ornamental pond in front of the dining hall, like some Polish squire's chateau. I shouted. Who at, there is no clear picture. There were goldfish in the pond. And a boy was filling it with water from a black rubber hose. So I decided to put a stop to the whole performance there and then, but the boy wouldn't listen to me. I started walking along the hose to find the faucet and cut off the water before anybody managed to establish the pond as a *fait accompli*. I walked and walked until I suddenly discovered that I was walking in a circle, and the hose was not connected to a faucet but simply came back to the pond and sucked up water from it. Stuff and nonsense. That's the end of it. The original platform of the Poalei Zion Movement must be understood without any recourse to dialectics, it must be taken literally, word for word.

3

After his separation from Raya Greenspan, Shimshon Sheinbaum did not neglect his duties as his son's mentor, nor did he disclaim responsibility. He lavished on him, from the time the boy was six or seven, the full warmth of his personality. Gideon, however, turned out to be something of a disappointment, not the stuff of which dynasties are founded. As a child he was always sniveling. He was a slow, bewildered child, mopping up blows and insults without retaliating, a strange child, always playing with candy wrappers, dried leaves, silkworms. And from the age of twelve he was constantly having his heart broken by girls of all ages. He was always lovesick, and he published sad poems and cruel parodies in the children's newsletter. A dark, gentle youth, with an almost feminine beauty, who walked the paths of the kibbutz in obstinate silence. He did not shine at work; he did not shine in communal life. He was slow of speech and no doubt also of thought. His poems seemed to Shimshon incorrigibly sentimental, and his parodies venomous, without a trace of inspiration. The nickname Pinocchio suited him, there is no denying it. And the infuriating smiles he was perpetually spreading on his face seemed to Shimshon a depressingly exact replica of the smiles of Raya Greenspan.

And then, eighteen months before, Gideon had amazed his father. He suddenly appeared and asked for his written permission to enlist in the paratroopers—as an only son this required the written consent of both parents. Only when Shimshon Sheinbaum was convinced that this was not one of his son's outrageous jokes did he agree to give his consent. And then he gave it gladly: this was surely an encouraging turn in the boy's development. They'd make a man of him there. Let him go. Why not.

But Raya Greenspan's stubborn opposition raised an unexpected obstacle to Gideon's plan. No, she wouldn't sign the paper. On no account. Never.

Shimshon himself went to her room one evening, pleaded with her, reasoned with her, shouted at her. All in vain. She wouldn't sign. No reason, she just wouldn't. So Shimshon Sheinbaum had to resort to devious means to enable the boy to enlist. He wrote a private letter to Yolek himself, asking a personal favor. He wished his son to be allowed to volunteer. The mother was emotionally unstable. The boy would make a first-rate paratrooper. Shimshon himself accepted full responsibility. And incidentally, he had never before asked a personal favor. And he never would again. This was the one and only time in his whole life. He begged Yolek to see what he could do.

At the end of September, when the first signs of autumn were appearing in the orchards, Gideon Shenhav was enrolled in a parachute unit.

From that time on, Shimshon Sheinbaum immersed himself more deeply than ever in ideological work, which is the only real mark a man can leave on the world. Shimshon Sheinbaum has made a mark on the Hebrew Labor Movement that can never be erased. Old age is still far off. At seventy-five he still has hair as thick as ever, and his muscles are firm and powerful. His eyes are alert, his mind attentive. His strong, dry, slightly cracked voice still works wonders on women of all ages. His bearing is restrained, his manner modest. Needless to say, he is deeply rooted in the soil of Nof Harish. He loathes assemblies and formal ceremonies, not to mention commissions and official appointments. With his pen alone he has inscribed his name on the roll of honor of our movement and our nation.

4

Gideon Shenhav's last day began with a brilliant sunrise. He felt he could even see the beads of dew evaporating in the heat. Omens blazed on the mountain peaks far away to the east. This was a day of celebration, a celebration of independence and a celebration of parachuting over the familiar fields of home. All that night he had nestled in a half-dream of dark autumnal forests under northern skies, a rich smell of autumn, huge trees he could not name. All night long pale leaves had been dropping on the huts of the camp. Even after he had awakened in the morning, the northern forest with its nameless trees still continued to whisper in his ears.

Gideon adored the delicious moment of free fall between the jump from the aircraft and the unfolding of the parachute. The void rushes up toward you at lightning speed, fierce drafts of air lick at your body, making you dizzy with pleasure. The speed is drunken, reckless, it whistles and roars and your whole body trembles to it, red-hot needles work at your nerve ends, and your heart pounds. Suddenly, when you are lightning in the wind, the chute opens. The straps check your fall, like a firm, masculine arm bringing you calmly under control. You can feel its supporting strength under your armpits. The reckless thrill gives way to a more sedate pleasure. Slowly your body swings through the air, floats, hesitates, drifts a little way on the slight breeze, you can never guess precisely where your feet will touch ground, on the slope of that hill or next to the orange groves over there, and like an exhausted migrating bird you slowly descend, seeing roofs, roads, cows in the meadow, slowly as if you have a choice, as if the decision is entirely yours.

And then the ground is under your feet, and you launch into the practiced somersault which will soften the impact of landing. Within seconds you must sober up. The coursing blood slows down. Dimensions return to normal. Only a weary pride survives in your heart until you rejoin your commanding officer and your comrades and you're caught up in the rhythm of frenzied reorganization.

This time it is all going to happen over Nof Harish.

The older folk will raise their clammy hands, push back their caps, and try to spot Gideon among the gray dots dangling in the sky. The kids will rush around in the fields, also waiting excitedly for their hero to touch down. Mother will come out of the dining hall and stand peering upward, muttering to herself. Shimshon will leave his desk for a while, perhaps take a chair out onto his little porch and watch the whole performance with pensive pride.

Then the kibbutz will entertain the unit. Pitchers of lemonade glistening with chilly perspiration will be set out in the dining hall, there will be crates of apples, or perhaps cakes baked by the older women, iced with congratulatory phrases.

By six-thirty the sun had grown out of its colorful caprice and risen ruthlessly over the eastern mountain heights. A thick heat weighed heavily on the whole scene. The tin roofs of the camp huts reflected a dazzling glare. The walls began to radiate a dense, oppressive warmth into the huts. On the main road, which passed close to the perimeter fence, a lively procession of buses and trucks was already in motion: the residents of the villages and small towns were streaming to the big city to watch the military parade. Their white shirts could be discerned dimly through the clouds of dust, and snatches of exuberant song could be caught in the distance.

The paratroopers had completed their morning inspection. The orders of the day, signed by the Chief of Staff, had been read out and posted on the bulletin boards. A festive breakfast had been served, including a hard-boiled egg reposing on a lettuce leaf ringed with olives.

Gideon, his dark hair flopping forward onto his forehead, broke into a quiet song. The others joined him. Here and there someone altered the words, making them comical or even obscene. Soon the Hebrew songs gave way to a guttural, almost desperate Arabic wail. The platoon commander, a blond, good-looking officer whose exploits were feted around the campfires at night, stood up and said: That's enough. The paratroopers stopped singing, hastily downed the last of their greasy coffee, and moved toward the runways. Here there was another inspection; the commanding officer spoke a few words of endearment to his men, calling them "the salt of the earth," and then ordered them into the waiting aircraft.

The squadron commanders stood at the doors of the planes and checked each belt and harness. The CO himself circulated among the men, patting a shoulder, joking, predicting, enthusing, for all the world as though they were going into battle and facing real danger. Gideon responded to the pat on his shoulder with a hasty smile. He was lean, almost ascetic-looking, but very suntanned. A sharp eye, that of the legendary blond commander, could spot the blue vein throbbing in his neck.

Then the heat broke into the shady storage sheds, mercilessly flushing out the last strongholds of coolness, roasting everything with a gray glow. The sign was given. The engines gave a throaty roar. Birds fled from the runway. The planes shuddered, moved forward heavily, and began to gather the momentum without which takeoff cannot be achieved.

5

I must get out and be there to shake his hand.

Having made up his mind, Sheinbaum closed his note-book. The months of military training have certainly toughened the boy. It is hard to believe, but it certainly looks as though he is beginning to mature at last. He still has to learn how to handle women. He has to free himself once and for all from his shyness and his sentimentality: he should leave such traits to women and cultivate toughness in himself. And how he has improved at chess. Soon he'll be a serious challenge to his old father. May even beat me one of these days. Not just yet, though. As long as he doesn't up and marry the first girl who gives herself to him. He ought to break one or two of them in before he gets spliced. In a few years he'll have to give me some grandchildren. Lots of them. Gideon's children will have two fathers: my son can take care of them, and I'll take care of their ideas. The second generation grew up in the shadow of our achievements; that's why they're so confused. It's a matter of dialectics. But the third generation will be a wonderful synthesis, a successful outcome: they will inherit the spontaneity of their parents and the spirit of their grandparents. It will be a glorious heritage distilled from a twisted pedigree. I'd better jot that phrase down, it will come in handy one of these days. I feel so sad when I think of Gideon and his friends: they exude such an air of shallow despair, of nihilism, of cynical mockery. They can't love wholeheartedly, and they can't hate wholeheartedly, either. No enthusiasm, and no loathing. I'm not one to deprecate despair per se. Despair is the eternal twin of faith, but that's real despair. Virile and passionate, not this sentimental, poetic melancholy. Sit still, Gideon, stop scratching yourself, stop biting your nails. I want to read you a marvelous passage from Brenner. All right, make a face. So I won't read. Go outside and grow up to be a Bedouin, if that's what you want. But if you don't get to know Brenner, you'll never understand the first thing about despair or about faith. You won't find any soppy poems here about jackals caught in traps or flowers in the autumn. In Brenner, everything is on fire. Love, and hatred as well. Maybe you yourselves won't see light and darkness face to face, but your children will. A glorious heritage will be distilled from a twisted pedigree. And we won't let the third generation be pampered and corrupted by sentimental verses by decadent poetesses. Here come the planes now. We'll put Brenner back on the shelf and get ready to be proud of you for a change, Gideon Sheinbaum.

6

Sheinbaum strode purposefully across the lawn, stepped up onto the concrete path, and turned toward the plowed field in the southwest corner of the kibbutz, which had been selected for the landing. On his way he paused now and again at a flower bed to pull up a stray weed skulking furtively beneath a flowering shrub. His small blue eyes had always been amazingly skillful at detecting weeds. Admittedly, because of his age he had retired a few years previously from his work in the gardens, but until his dying day he would not cease to scan the flower beds mercilessly in search of undesirable intruders. At such moments he thought of the boy, forty years his junior, who had succeeded him as gardener and who fancied himself as the local water-colorist. He had inherited beautifully tended gardens, and now they were all going to seed before our very eyes.

A gang of excited children ran across his path. They were fiercely absorbed in a detailed argument about the types of aircraft that were circling above the valley. Because they were running, the argument was being carried out in loud shouts and gasps. Shimshon seized one of them by the shirttail, forcibly brought him to a halt, put his face close to the child's, and said:

"You are Zaki."

"Leave me alone," the child replied.

Sheinbaum said: "What's all this shouting? Airplanes, is that all you've got in your heads? And running across the flower beds like that where it says Keep Off, is that right? Do you think you can do whatever you like? Are there no rules any more? Look at me when I'm speaking to you. And give me a proper answer, or . . ."

But Zaki had taken advantage of the flood of words to wriggle out of the man's grasp and tear himself free. He slipped in among the bushes, made a monkey face, and stuck out his tongue.

Sheinbaum pursed his lips. He thought for an instant about old age, but instantly thrust it out of his mind and said to himself: All right. We'll see about that later. Zaki, otherwise Azariah. Rapid calculation showed that he must be at least eleven, perhaps twelve already. A hooligan. A wild beast.

Meanwhile the young trainees had occupied a vantage point high up on top of the water tower, from which they could survey the length and breadth of the valley. The whole scene reminded Sheinbaum of a Russian painting. For a moment he was tempted to climb up and join the youngsters on top of the tower, to watch the display comfortably from a distance. But the thought of the manly handshake to come kept him striding steadily on, till he reached the edge of the field. Here he stood, his legs planted well apart, his arms folded on his chest, his thick white hair falling impressively over his forehead. He craned his neck and followed the two transport planes with steady gray eyes. The mosaic of wrinkles on his face enriched his expression with a rare blend of pride, thoughtfulness, and a trace of well-controlled irony. And his bushy white eyebrows suggested a saint in a Russian icon. Meanwhile the planes had completed their first circuit, and the leading one was approaching the field again.

Shimshon Sheinbaum's lips parted and made way for a low hum. An old Russian tune was throbbing in his chest. The first batch of men emerged from the opening in the plane's side. Small dark shapes were dotted in space, like seeds scattered by a farmer in an old pioneering print.

Then Raya Greenspan stuck her head out of the window of the kitchen and gesticulated with the ladle she was holding as though admonishing the treetops. Her face was hot and flushed. Perspiration stuck her plain dress to her strong, hairy legs. She panted, scratched at her disheveled hair with the fingernails of her free hand, and suddenly turned and shouted to the other women working in the kitchens:

"Quick! Come to the window! It's Gidi up there! Gidi in the sky!"

And just as suddenly she was struck dumb.

While the first soldiers were still floating gently, like a handful of feathers, between heaven and earth, the second plane came in and dropped Gideon Shenhav's group. The men stood pressed close together inside the hatch, chest against back, their bodies fused into a single tense, sweating mass. When Gideon's turn came he gritted his teeth, braced his knees, and leapt out as though from the womb into the bright hot air. A long wild scream of joy burst from his throat as he fell. He could see his childhood haunts rushing up toward him as he fell he could see the roofs and treetops and he smiled a frantic smile of greeting as he fell toward the vineyards and concrete paths and sheds and gleaming pipes with joy in his heart as he fell. Never in his whole life had he known such overwhelming, spine-tingling love. All his muscles were tensed, and gushing thrills burst in his stomach and up his spine to the roots of his hair. He screamed for love like a madman, his fingernails almost drawing blood from his clenched palms. Then the straps drew taut and caught him under the armpits. His waist was clasped in a tight embrace. For a moment he felt as though an invisible hand were pulling him back up toward the plane into the heart of the sky. The delicious falling sensation was replaced by a slow, gentle swaying, like rocking in a cradle or floating in warm water. Suddenly a wild panic hit him. How will they recognize me down there. How will they manage to identify their only son in this forest of white parachutes. How will they be able to fix me and me alone with their anxious, loving gaze. Mother and Dad and the pretty girls and the little kids and everyone. I mustn't just get lost in the crowd. After all, this is me, and I'm the one they love.

That moment an idea flashed through Gideon's mind. He put his hand up to his shoulder and pulled the cord to release the spare chute, the one intended for emergencies. As the second canopy opened overhead he slowed down as though the force of gravity had lost its hold on him. He seemed to be floating alone in the void, like a gull or a lonely cloud. The last of his comrades had landed in the soft earth and were folding up their parachutes. Gideon Shenhav alone continued to hover as though under a spell with two large canopies spread out above him. Happy, intoxicated, he drank in the hundreds of eyes fixed on him. On him alone. In his glorious isolation.

As though to lend further splendor to the spectacle, a strong, almost cool breeze burst from the west, plowing through the hot air, playing with the spectators' hair, and carrying slightly eastward the last of the parachutists.

7

Far away in the big city, the massed crowds waiting for the military parade greeted the sudden sea breeze with a sigh of relief. Perhaps it marked the end of the heat wave. A cool, salty smell caressed the baking streets. The breeze freshened. It whistled fiercely in the treetops, bent the stiff spines of the cypresses, ruffled the hair of the pines, raised eddies of dust, and blurred the scene for the spectators at the parachute display. Regally, like a huge solitary bird, Gideon Shenhav was carried eastward toward the main road.

The terrified shout that broke simultaneously from a hundred throats could not reach the boy. Singing aloud in an ecstatic trance, he continued to sway slowly toward the main electric cables, stretched between their enormous pylons. The watchers stared in horror at the suspended soldier and the powerlines that crossed the valley with unfaltering straightness from west to east. The five parallel cables, sagging with their own weight between the pylons, hummed softly in the gusty breeze.

Gideon's two parachutes tangled in the upper cable. A moment later his feet landed on the lower one. His body hung backward in a slanting pose. The straps held his waist and shoulders fast, preventing him from falling into the soft plowland. Had he not been insulated by the thick soles of his boots, the boy would have been struck dead at the moment of impact. As it was, the cable was already protesting its unwonted burden by scorching his soles. Tiny sparks flashed and crackled under Gideon's feet. He held tight with both hands to the buckles on the straps. His eyes were open wide and his mouth was agape.

Immediately a short officer, perspiring heavily, leapt out of the petrified crowd and shouted:

"Don't touch the cables, Gidi. Stretch your body backward and keep as clear as you can!"

The whole tightly packed, panic-stricken crowd began to edge slowly in an easterly direction. There were shouts. There was a wail. Sheinbaum silenced them with his metallic voice and ordered everyone to keep calm. He broke into a fast run, his feet pounding on the soft earth, reached the spot, pushed aside the officers and curious bystanders and instructed his son:

"Quickly, Gideon, release the straps and drop. The ground is soft here. It's perfectly safe. Jump."

"I can't."

"Don't argue. Do as I tell you. Jump."

"I can't, Dad, I can't do it."

"No such thing as can't. Release the straps and jump before you electrocute yourself."

"I can't, the straps are tangled. Tell them to switch off the current quickly, Dad, my boots are burning."

Some of the soldiers were trying to hold back the crowd, discourage well-meaning suggestions, and make more room under the powerlines. They kept repeating, as if it were an incantation, "Don't panic please don't panic."

The youngsters of the kibbutz were rushing all around, adding to the confusion. Reprimands and warnings had no effect. Two angry paratroopers managed to catch Zaki, who was idiotically climbing the nearest pylon, snorting and whistling and making faces to attract the attention of the crowd.

The short officer suddenly shouted: "Your knife. You've got a knife in your belt. Get it out and cut the straps!"

But Gideon either could not or would not hear. He began to sob aloud.

"Get me down, Dad, I'll be electrocuted, tell them to get me down from here, I can't get down on my own."

"Stop sniveling," his father said curtly. "You've been told to use your knife to cut the straps. Now, do as you've been told. And stop sniveling."

The boy obeyed. He was still sobbing audibly, but he groped for the knife, located it, and cut the straps one by one. The silence was total. Only Gideon's sobbing, a strange, piercing sound, was to be heard intermittently. Finally one last strap was left holding him, which he did not dare to cut.

"Cut it," the children shrilled, "cut it and jump. Let's see you do it."

And Shimshon added in a level voice, "Now what are you waiting for?"

"I can't do it," Gideon pleaded.

"Of course you can," said his father.

"The current," the boy wept. "I can feel the current. Get me down quickly."

His father's eyes filled with blood as he roared:

"You coward! You ought to be ashamed of yourself!"

"But I can't do it, I'll break my neck, it's too high."

"You can do it and you must do it. You're a fool, that's what you are, a fool and a coward."

A group of jet planes passed overhead on their way to the aerial display over the city. They were flying in precise formation, thundering westward like a pack of wild dogs. As the planes disappeared, the silence seemed twice as intense. Even the boy had stopped crying. He let the knife fall to the ground. The blade pierced the earth at Shimshon Sheinbaum's feet.

"What did you do that for?" the short officer shouted.

"I didn't mean it," Gideon whined. "It just slipped out of my hand."

Shimshon Sheinbaum bent down, picked up a small stone, straightened up, and threw it furiously at his son's back.

"Pinocchio, you're a wet rag, you're a miserable coward!"

At this point the sea breeze also dropped.

The heat wave returned with renewed vigor to oppress both men and inanimate objects. A red-haired, freckled soldier muttered to himself, "He's scared to jump, the idiot, he'll kill himself if he stays up there." And a skinny, plain-faced girl, hearing this, rushed into the middle of the circle and spread her arms wide:

"Jump into my arms, Gidi, you'll be all right."

"It would be interesting," remarked a veteran pioneer in working clothes, "to know whether anyone has had the sense to phone the electric company to ask them to switch off the current." He turned and started off toward the kibbutz buildings. He was striding quickly, angrily, up the slight slope when he was suddenly alarmed by a prolonged burst of firing close at hand. For a moment he imagined he was being shot at from behind. But at once he realized what was happening: the squadron commander, the good-looking blond hero, was trying to sever the electric cables with his machine gun.

Without success.

Meanwhile, a beaten-up truck arrived from the farmyard. Ladders were unloaded from it, followed by the elderly doctor, and finally a stretcher.

At that moment it was evident that Gideon had been struck by a sudden decision. Kicking out strongly, he pushed himself off the lower cable, which was emitting blue sparks, turned a somersault, and remained suspended by the single strap with his head pointing downward and his scorched boots beating the air a foot or so from the cable.

It was hard to be certain, but it looked as though so far he had not sustained any serious injury. He swung limply upside down in space, like a dead lamb suspended from a butcher's hook.

This spectacle provoked hysterical glee in the watching children. They barked with laughter. Zaki slapped his knees, choking and heaving convulsively. He leapt up and down screeching like a mischievous monkey.

What had Gideon Shenhav seen that made him suddenly stretch his neck and join in the children's laughter? Perhaps his peculiar posture had unbalanced his mind. His face was blood-red, his tongue protruded, his thick hair hung down, and only his feet kicked up at the sky.

8

A second group of jets plowed through the sky overhead. A dozen metallic birds, sculpted with cruel beauty, flashing dazzlingly in the bright sunlight. They flew in a narrow spearhead formation. Their fury shook the earth. On they flew to the west, and a deep silence followed.

Meanwhile, the elderly doctor sat down on the stretcher, lit a cigarette, blinked vaguely at the people, the soldiers, the scampering children, and said to himself: We'll see how things turn out. Whatever has to happen will happen. How hot it is today.

Every now and again Gideon let out another senseless laugh. His legs were flailing, describing clumsy circles in the dusty air. The blood had drained from his inverted limbs and was gathering in his head. His eyes were beginning to bulge. The world was turning dark. Instead of the crimson glow, purple spots were dancing before his eyes. He stuck his tongue out. The children interpreted this as a gesture of derision. "Upside-down Pinocchio," Zaki shrilled, "why don't you stop squinting at us, and try walking on your hands instead?"

Sheinbaum moved to hit the brat, but the blow landed on thin air because the child had leapt aside. The old man beckoned to the blond commander, and they held a brief consultation. The boy was in no immediate danger, because he was not in direct contact with the cable, but he must be rescued soon. This comedy could not go on forever. A ladder would not help much: he was too high up. Perhaps the knife could be got up to him again somehow, and he could be persuaded to cut the last strap and jump into a sheet of canvas. After all, it was a perfectly routine exercise in parachute training. The main thing was to act quickly, because the situation was humiliating. Not to mention the children. So the short officer removed his shirt and wrapped a knife in it. Gideon stretched his hands downward and tried to catch the bundle. It slipped between his outstretched arms and plummeted uselessly to the ground. The children snickered. Only after two more unsuccessful attempts did Gideon manage to grasp the shirt and remove the knife. His fingers were numb and heavy with blood. Suddenly he pressed the blade to his burning cheek, enjoying the cool touch of the steel. It was a delicious moment. He opened his eyes and saw an inverted world. Everything looked comical: the truck, the field, his father, the army, the kids, and even the knife in his hand. He made a twisted face at the gang of children, gave a deep laugh, and waved at them with the knife. He tried to say something. If only they could see themselves from up here, upside down, rushing around like startled ants, they would surely laugh with him. But the laugh turned into a heavy cough; Gideon choked and his eyes filled.

9

Gideon's upside-down antics filled Zaki with demonic glee.

"He's crying," he shouted cruelly. "Gideon's crying, look, you can see the tears. Pinocchio the hero, he's sniveling with fear-o. We can see you, we can."

Once again Shimshon Sheinbaum's fist fell ineffectually on thin air.

"Zaki," Gideon managed to shout in a dull, pain-racked voice, "I'll kill you, I'll choke you, you little bastard." Suddenly he chuckled and stopped.

It was no good. He wouldn't cut the last strap by himself, and the doctor was afraid that if he stayed as he was much longer he was likely to lose consciousness. Some other solution would have to be found. This performance could not be allowed to go on all day.

And so the kibbutz truck rumbled across the plowland and braked at the point indicated by Shimshon Sheinbaum. Two ladders were hastily lashed together to reach the required height, and then supported on the back of the truck by five strong pairs of hands. The legendary blond officer started to climb. But when he reached the place where the two ladders overlapped, there was an ominous creak, and the wood began to bend with the weight and the height. The officer, a largish man, hesitated for a moment. He decided to retreat and fasten the ladders together more securely. He climbed down to the floor of the truck, wiped the sweat from his forehead, and said, "Wait, I'm thinking." Just then, in the twinkling of an eye, before he could be stopped, before he could even be spotted, the child Zaki had climbed high up the ladder, past the join, and leapt like a frantic monkey up onto the topmost rungs; suddenly he was clutching a knife—where on earth had he got it from? He wrestled with the taut strap. The spectators held their breath: he seemed to be defying gravity, not holding on, not caring, hopping on the top rung, nimble, lithe, amazingly efficient.

10

The heat beat down violently on the hanging youth. His eyes were growing dimmer. His breathing had almost stopped. With his last glimmer of lucidity he saw his ugly brother in front of him and felt his breath on his face. He could smell him. He could see the pointed teeth protruding from Zaki's mouth. A terrible fear closed in on him, as though he were looking in a mirror and seeing a monster. The nightmare roused Gideon's last reserves of strength. He kicked into space, flailed, managed to turn over, seized the strap, and pulled himself up. With outstretched arms he threw himself onto the cable and saw the flash. The hot wind continued to tyrannize the whole valley. And a third cluster of jets drowned the scene with its roaring.

11

The status of a bereaved father invests a man with a saintly aura of suffering. But Sheinbaum gave no thought to this aura. A stunned, silent company escorted him toward the dining hall. He knew, with utter certainty, that his place now was beside Raya.

On the way he saw the child Zaki, glowing, breathless, a hero. Surrounded by other youngsters: he had almost rescued Gideon. Shimshon laid a trembling hand on his child's head, and tried to tell him. His voice abandoned him and his lips quivered. Clumsily he stroked the tousled, dusty mop of hair. It was the first time he had ever stroked the child. A few steps later, everything went dark and the old man collapsed in a flower bed.

As Independence Day drew to a close the *khamsin* abated. A fresh sea breeze soothed the steaming walls. There was a heavy fall of dew on the lawns in the night.

What does the pale ring around the moon portend? Usually it heralds a *khamsin*. Tomorrow, no doubt, the heat will return. It is May, and June will follow. A wind drifts among the cypresses in the night, trying to comfort them between one heat wave and the next. It is the way of the wind to come and to go and to come again. There is nothing new.

The Shawl
(1980)

CYNTHIA OZICK

Stella, cold, cold, the coldness of hell. How they walked on the roads together, Rosa with Magda curled up between sore breasts, Magda wound up in the shawl. Sometimes Stella carried Magda. But she was jealous of Magda. A thin girl of fourteen, too small, with thin breasts of her own, Stella wanted to be wrapped in a shawl, hidden away, asleep, rocked by the march, a baby, a round infant in arms. Magda took Rosa's nipple, and Rosa never stopped walking, a walking cradle. There was not enough milk; sometimes Magda sucked air; then she screamed. Stella was ravenous. Her knees were tumors on sticks, her elbows chicken bones.

Rosa did not feel hunger; she felt light, not like someone walking but like someone in a faint, in trance, arrested in a fit, someone who is already a floating angel, alert and seeing everything, but in the air, not there, not touching the road. As if teetering on the tips of her fingernails. She looked into Magda's face through a gap in the shawl: a squirrel in a nest, safe, no one could reach her inside the little house of the shawl's windings. The face, very round, a pocket mirror of a face: but it was not Rosa's bleak complexion, dark like cholera, it was another kind of face altogether, eyes blue as air, smooth feathers of hair nearly as yellow as the Star sewn into Rosa's coat. You could think she was one of *their* babies.

Rosa, floating, dreamed of giving Magda away in one of the villages. She could leave the line for a minute and push Magda into the hands of any woman on the side of the road. But if she moved out of line they might shoot. And even if she fled the line for half a second and pushed the shawl-bundle at a stranger, would the woman take it? She might be surprised, or afraid; she might drop the shawl, and Magda would fall out and strike her head and die. The little round head. Such a good child, she gave up screaming, and sucked now only for the taste of the drying nipple itself. The neat grip of the tiny gums. One mite of a tooth tip sticking up in the bottom gum, how shining, an elfin tombstone of white marble gleaming there. Without complaining, Magda relinquished Rosa's teats, first the left, then the right; both were cracked, not a sniff of milk. The duct-crevice extinct, a dead volcano, blind eye, chill hole, so Magda took the corner of the shawl and milked it instead. She sucked and sucked, flooding the threads with wetness. The shawl's good flavor, milk of linen.

It was a magic shawl, it could nourish an infant for three days and three nights. Magda did not die, she stayed alive, although very quiet. A peculiar smell, of cinnamon and almonds, lifted out of her mouth. She held her eyes open every moment, forgetting how to blink or nap, and Rosa and sometimes Stella studied their blueness. On the road they raised one burden of a leg after another and studied Magda's face. "Aryan," Stella said, in a voice grown as thin as a string; and Rosa thought how Stella gazed at Magda like a young canni-bal. And the time that Stella said "Aryan," it sounded to Rosa as if Stella had really said "Let us devour her."

But Magda lived to walk. She lived that long, but she did not walk very well, partly because she was only fifteen months old, and partly because the spindles of her legs could not hold up her fat belly. It was fat with air, full and round. Rosa gave almost all her food to Magda, Stella gave nothing; Stella was ravenous, a growing child herself, but not growing much. Stella did not menstruate. Rosa did not menstruate. Rosa was ravenous, but also not; she learned from Magda how to drink the taste of a finger in one's mouth. They were in a place without pity, all pity was annihilated in Rosa, she looked at Stella's bones without pity. She was sure that Stella was waiting for Magda to die so she could put her teeth into the little thighs.

Rosa knew Magda was going to die very soon; she should have been dead already, but she had been buried away deep inside the magic shawl, mistaken there for the shivering mound of Rosa's breasts; Rosa clung to the shawl as if it covered only herself. No one took it away from her. Magda was mute. She never cried. Rosa hid her in the barracks, under the shawl, but she knew that one day someone would inform; or one day someone, not even Stella, would steal Magda to eat her. When Magda began to walk Rosa knew that Magda was going to die very soon, something would happen. She was afraid to fall asleep; she slept with the weight of her thigh on Magda's body; she was afraid she would smother Magda under her thigh. The weight of Rosa was becoming less and less; Rosa and Stella were slowly turning into air.

Magda was quiet, but her eyes were horribly alive, like blue tigers. She watched. Some-times she laughed—it seemed a laugh, but how could it be? Magda had never seen anyone laugh. Still, Magda laughed at her shawl when the wind blew its corners, the bad wind with pieces of black in it, that made Stella's and Rosa's eyes tear. Magda's eyes were always clear and tearless. She watched like a tiger. She guarded her shawl. No one could touch it; only Rosa could touch it. Stella was not allowed. The shawl was Magda's own baby, her pet, her little sister. She tangled herself up in it and sucked on one of the corners when she wanted to be very still.

Then Stella took the shawl away and made Magda die.

Afterward Stella said: "I was cold."

And afterward she was always cold, always. The cold went into her heart: Rosa saw that Stella's heart was cold. Magda flopped onward with her little pencil legs scribbling this way and that, in search of the shawl; the pencils faltered at the barracks opening, where the light began. Rosa saw and pursued. But already Magda was in the square outside the barracks, in the jolly light. It was the roll-call arena. Every morning Rosa had to conceal Magda under the shawl against a wall of the barracks and go out and stand in the arena with Stella and hundreds of others, sometimes for hours, and Magda, deserted, was quiet under the shawl, sucking on her corner. Every day Magda was silent, and so she did not die. Rosa saw that today Magda was going to die, and at the same time a fearful joy ran in Rosa's two palms, her fingers were on fire, she was astonished, febrile: Magda, in the sunlight, swaying on her pencil legs, was howling. Ever since the drying up of Rosa's nipples, ever since Magda's last scream on the road, Magda had been devoid of any syllable; Magda was a mute. Rosa believed that something had gone wrong with her vocal cords, with her windpipe, with the cave of her larynx; Magda was defective, without a voice; perhaps she was deaf; there might be something amiss with her intelligence; Magda was dumb. Even the laugh that came when the ash-stippled wind made a clown out of Magda's shawl was only the air-blown showing of her teeth. Even when the lice, head lice and body lice, crazed her so that she became as wild as one of the big rats that plundered the barracks at daybreak looking for carrion, she rubbed and scratched and kicked and bit and rolled without a whimper. But now Magda's mouth was spilling a long viscous rope of clamor.

"Maaaa—"

It was the first noise Magda had ever sent out from her throat since the drying up of Rosa's nipples.

"Maaaa . . . aaa!"

Again! Magda was wavering in the perilous sunlight of the arena, scribbling on such pitiful little bent shins. Rosa saw. She saw that Magda was grieving for the loss of her shawl, she saw that Magda was going to die. A tide of commands hammered in Rosa's nipples: Fetch, get, bring! But she did not know which to go after first, Magda or the shawl. If she jumped out into the arena to snatch Magda up, the howling would not stop, because Magda would still not have the shawl; but if she ran back into the barracks to find the shawl, and if she found it, and if she came after Magda holding it and shaking it, then she would get Magda back, Magda would put the shawl in her mouth and turn dumb again.

Rosa entered the dark. It was easy to discover the shawl. Stella was heaped under it, asleep in her thin bones. Rosa tore the shawl free and flew—she could fly, she was only air—into the arena. The sunheat murmured of another life, of butterflies in summer. The light was placid, mellow. On the other side of the steel fence, far away, there were green meadows speckled with dandelions and deep-colored violets; beyond them, even farther, innocent tiger lilies, tall, lifting their orange bonnets. In the barracks they spoke of "flowers," of "rain": excrement, thick turd-braids, and the slow stinking maroon waterfall that slunk down from the upper bunks, the stink mixed with a bitter fatty floating smoke that greased Rosa's skin. She stood for an instant at the margin of the arena. Sometimes the electricity inside the fence would seem to hum; even Stella said it was only an imagining, but Rosa heard real sounds in the wire: grainy sad voices. The farther she was from the fence, the more clearly the voices crowded at her. The lamenting voices strummed so convincingly, so passionately, it was impossible to suspect them of being phantoms. The voices told her to hold up the shawl, high; the voices told her to shake it, to whip with it, to unfurl it like a flag. Rosa lifted, shook, whipped, unfurled. Far off, very far, Magda leaned across her air-fed belly, reaching out with the rods of her arms. She was high up, elevated, riding someone's shoulder. But the shoulder that carried Magda was not coming toward Rosa and the shawl, it was drifting away, the speck of Magda was moving more and more into the smoky distance. Above the shoulder a helmet glinted. The light tapped the helmet and sparkled it into a goblet. Below the helmet a black body like a domino and a pair of black boots hurled themselves in the direction of the electrified fence. The electric voices began to chatter wildly. "Maamaa, maaamaaa," they all hummed together. How far Magda was from Rosa now, across the whole square, past a dozen barracks, all the way on the other side! She was no bigger than a moth.

All at once Magda was swimming through the air. The whole of Magda traveled through loftiness. She looked like a butterfly touching a silver vine. And the moment Magda's feathered round head and her pencil legs and balloonish belly and zigzag arms splashed against the fence, the steel voices went mad in their growling, urging Rosa to run and run to the spot where Magda had fallen from her flight against the electrified fence; but of course Rosa did not obey them. She only stood, because if she ran they would shoot, and if she tried to pick up the sticks of Magda's body they would shoot, and if she let the wolf's screech ascending now through the ladder of her skeleton break out, they would shoot; so she took Magda's shawl and filled her own mouth with it, stuffed it in and stuffed it in, until she was swallowing up the wolf's screech and tasting the cinnamon and almond depth of Magda's saliva; and Rosa drank Magda's shawl until it dried.

Big Blonde
(1929)

DOROTHY PARKER

Hazel Morse was a large, fair woman of the type that incites some men when they use the word "blonde" to click their tongues and wag their heads roguishly. She prided herself upon her small feet and suffered for her vanity, boxing them in snub-toed, high-heeled slippers of the shortest bearable size. The curious things about her were her hands, strange terminations to the flabby white arms splattered with pale tan spots—long, quivering hands with deep and convex nails. She should not have disfigured them with little jewels.

She was not a woman given to recollections. At her middle thirties, her old days were a blurred and flickering sequence, an imperfect film, dealing with the actions strangers.

In her twenties, after the deferred death of a hazy widowed mother, she had been employed as a model in a wholesale dress establishment—it was still the day of the big woman, and she was then prettily colored and erect and high-breasted. Her job was not onerous, and she met numbers of men and spent numbers of evenings with them, laughing at their jokes and telling them she loved their neckties. Men liked her, and she took it for granted that the liking of many men was a desirable thing. Popularity seemed to her to be worth all the work that had to be put into its achievement. Men liked you because you were fun, and when they liked you they took you out, and there you were. So, and successfully, she was fun. She was a good sport. Men like a good sport.

No other form of diversion, simpler or more complicated, drew her attention. She never pondered if she might not be better occupied doing something else. Her ideas, or, better, her acceptances, ran right along with those of the other substantially built blondes in whom she found her friends.

When she had been working in the dress establishment some years she met Herbie Morse. He was thin, quick, attractive, with shifting lines about his shiny, brown eyes and a habit of fiercely biting at the skin around his finger nails. He drank largely; she found that entertaining. Her habitual greeting to him was allusion to his state of the previous night.

"Oh, what a peach you had," she used to say, through her easy laugh. "I thought I'd die, the way you kept asking the waiter to dance with you."

She liked him immediately upon their meeting. She was enormously amused at his fast, slurred sentences, his interpolations of apt phrases from vaudeville acts and comic strips; she thrilled at the feel of his lean arm tucked firm beneath the sleeve of her coat; she wanted to touch the wet, flat surface of his hair. He was as promptly drawn to her. They were married six weeks after they had met.

She was delighted at the idea of being a bride; coquetted with it, played upon it. Other offers of marriage she had had, and not a few of them, but it happened that they were all from stout, serious men who had visited the dress establishment as buyers; men from Des Moines and Houston and Chicago and, in her phrase, even funnier places. There was always something immensely comic to her in the thought of living elsewhere than New York. She could not regard as serious proposals that she share a western residence.

She wanted to be married. She was nearing thirty now, and she did not take the years well. She spread and softened, and her darkening hair turned her to inexpert dabblings with peroxide. There were times when she had little flashes of fear about her job. And she had had a couple of thousand evenings of being a good sport among her male acquaintances. She had come to be more conscientious than spontaneous about it.

Herbie earned enough, and they took a little apartment far uptown. There was a Mission-furnished dining-room with a hanging central light globed in liver-colored glass; in the living-room were an "over-stuffed suite," a Boston fern, and a reproduction of the Henner "Magdalene" with the red hair and the blue draperies; the bedroom was in gray enamel and old rose, with Herbie's photograph on Hazel's dressing-table and Hazel's likeness on Herbie's chest of drawers.

She cooked—and she was a good cook—and marketed and chatted with the delivery boys and the colored laundress. She loved the flat, she loved her life, she loved Herbie. In the first months of their marriage, she gave him all the passion she was ever to know.

She had not realized how tired she was. It was a delight, a new game, a holiday, to give up being a good sport. If her head ached or her arches throbbed, she complained piteously, babyishly. If her mood was quiet, she did not talk. If tears came to her eyes, she let them fall.

She fell readily into the habit of tears during the first year of her marriage. Even in her good sport days, she had been known to weep lavishly and disinterestedly on occasion. Her behavior at the theater was a standing joke. She could weep at anything in a play—tiny garments, love both unrequited and mutual, seduction, purity, faithful servitors, wedlock, the triangle.

"There goes Haze," her friends would say, watching her. "She's off again."

Wedded and relaxed, she poured her tears freely. To her who had laughed so much, crying was delicious. All sorrows became her sorrows; she was Tenderness. She would cry long and softly over newspaper accounts of kidnaped babies, deserted wives, unemployed men, strayed cats, heroic dogs. Even when the paper was no longer before her, her mind revolved upon these things and the drops slipped rhythmically over her plump cheeks.

"Honestly," she would say to Herbie, "all the sadness there is in the world when you stop to think about it!"

"Yeah," Herbie would say.

She missed nobody. The old crowd, the people who had brought her and Herbie together, dropped from their lives, lingeringly at first. When she thought of this at all, it was only to consider it fitting. This was marriage. This was peace.

But the thing was that Herbie was not amused.

For a time, he had enjoyed being alone with her. He found the voluntary isolation novel and sweet. Then it palled with a ferocious suddenness. It was as if one night, sitting with her in the steam-heated living-room, he would ask no more; and the next night he was through and done with the whole thing.

He became annoyed by her misty melancholies. At first, when he came home to find her softly tired and moody, he kissed her neck and patted her shoulder and begged her to tell her Herbie what was wrong. She loved that. But time slid by, and he found that there was never anything really, personally, the matter.

"Ah, for God's sake," he would say. "Crabbing again. All right, sit here and crab your head off. I'm going out."

And he would slam out of the flat and come back late and drunk.

She was completely bewildered by what happened to their marriage. First they were lovers; and then, it seemed without transition, they were enemies. She never understood it.

There were longer and longer intervals between his leaving his office and his arrival at the apartment. She went through agonies of picturing him run over and bleeding, dead and covered with a sheet. Then she lost her fears for his safety and grew sullen and wounded. When a person wanted to be with a person, he came as soon as possible. She desperately wanted him to want to be with her; her own hours only marked the time till he would come. It was often nearly nine o'clock before he came home to dinner. Always he had had many drinks, and their effect would die in him, leaving him loud and querulous and bristling for affronts.

He was too nervous, he said, to sit and do nothing for an evening. He boasted, probably not in all truth, that he had never read a book in his life.

"What am I expected to do—sit around this dump on my tail all night?" he would ask, rhetorically. And again he would slam out.

She did not know what to do. She could not manage him. She could not meet him.

She fought him furiously. A terrific domesticity had come upon her, and she would bite and scratch to guard it. She wanted what she called "a nice home." She wanted a sober, tender husband, prompt at dinner, punctual at work. She wanted sweet, comforting evenings. The idea of intimacy with other men was terrible to her; the thought that Herbie might be seeking entertainment in other women set her frantic.

It seemed to her that almost everything she read—novels from the drug-store lending library, magazine stories, women's pages in the papers—dealt with wives who lost their husbands' love. She could bear those, at that, better than accounts of neat, companionable marriage and living happily ever after.

She was frightened. Several times when Herbie came home in the evening, he found her determinedly dressed—she had had to alter those of her clothes that were not new, to make them fasten—and rouged.

"Let's go wild tonight, what do you say?" she would hail him. "A person's got lots of time to hang around and do nothing when they're dead."

So they would go out, to chop houses and the less expensive cabarets. But it turned out badly. She could no longer find amusement in watching Herbie drink. She could not laugh at his whimsicalities, she was so tensely counting his indulgences. And she was unable to keep back her remonstrances—"Ah, come on, Herb, you've had enough, haven't you? You'll feel something terrible in the morning."

He would be immediately enraged. All right, crab; crab, crab, crab, crab, that was all she ever did. What a lousy sport *she* was! There would be scenes, and one or the other of them would rise and stalk out in fury.

She could not recall the definite day that she started drinking, herself. There was nothing separate about her days. Like drops upon a window-pane, they ran together and trickled away. She had been married six months; then a year; then three years.

She had never needed to drink, formerly. She could sit for most of a night at a table where the others were imbibing earnestly and never droop in looks or spirits, nor be bored by the doings of those about her. If she took a cocktail, it was so unusual as to cause twenty minutes or so of jocular comment. But now anguish was in her. Frequently, after a quarrel, Herbie would stay out for the night, and she could not learn from him where the time had been spent. Her heart felt tight and sore in her breast, and her mind turned like an electric fan.

She hated the taste of liquor. Gin, plain or in mixtures, made her promptly sick. After experiment, she found that Scotch whisky was best for her. She took it without water, because that was the quickest way to its effect.

Herbie pressed it on her. He was glad to see her drink. They both felt it might restore her high spirits, and their good times together might again be possible.

"'Atta girl," he would approve her. "Let's see you get boiled, baby."

But it brought them no nearer. When she drank with him, there would be a little while of gaiety and then, strangely without beginning, they would be in a wild quarrel. They would wake in the morning not sure what it had all been about, foggy as to what had been said and done, but each deeply injured and bitterly resentful. There would be days of vengeful silence.

There had been a time when they had made up their quarrels, usually in bed. There would be kisses and little names and assurances of fresh starts . . . . "Oh, it's going to be great now, Herb. We'll have swell times. I was a crab. I guess I must have been tired. But everything's going to be swell. You'll see."

Now there were no gentle reconciliations. They resumed friendly relations only in the brief magnanimity caused by liquor, before more liquor drew them into new battles. The scenes became more violent. There were shouted invectives and pushes, and sometimes sharp slaps. Once she had a black eye. Herbie was horrified next day at sight of it. He did not go to work; he followed her about, suggesting remedies and heaping dark blame on himself. But after they had had a few drinks—"to pull themselves together"—she made so many wistful references to her bruise that he shouted at her and rushed out and was gone for two days.

Each time he left the place in a rage, he threatened never to come back. She did not believe him, nor did she consider separation. Somewhere in her head or her heart was the lazy, nebulous hope that things would change and she and Herbie settle suddenly into soothing married life. Here were her home, her furniture, her husband, her station. She summoned no alternatives.

She could no longer bustle and potter. She had no more vicarious tears; the hot drops she shed were for herself. She walked ceaselessly about the rooms, her thoughts running mechanically round and round Herbie. In those days began the hatred of being alone that she was never to overcome. You could be by yourself when things were all right, but when you were blue you got the howling horrors.

She commenced drinking alone, little, short drinks all through the day. It was only with Herbie that alcohol made her nervous and quick in offense. Alone, it blurred sharp things for her. She lived in a haze of it. Her life took on a dream-like quality. Nothing was astonishing.

A Mrs. Martin moved into the flat across the hall. She was a great blonde woman of forty, a promise in looks of what Mrs. Morse was to be. They made acquaintance, quickly became inseparable. Mrs. Morse spent her days in the opposite apartment. They drank together, to brace themselves after the drinks of the nights before.

She never confided her troubles about Herbie to Mrs. Martin. The subject was too bewildering to her to find comfort in talk. She let it be assumed that her husband's business kept him much away. It was not regarded as important; husbands, as such, played but shadowy parts in Mrs. Martin's circle.

Mrs. Martin had no visible spouse; you were left to decide for yourself whether he was or was not dead. She had an admirer, Joe, who came to see her almost nightly. Often he brought several friends with him—"The Boys," they were called. The Boys were big, red, good-humored men, perhaps forty-five, perhaps fifty. Mrs. Morse was glad of invitations to join the parties—Herbie was scarcely ever at home at night now. If he did come home, she did not visit Mrs. Martin. An evening alone with Herbie meant inevitably a quarrel, yet she would stay with him. There was always her thin and wordless idea that, maybe, this night, things would begin to be all right.

The Boys brought plenty of liquor along with them whenever they came to Mrs. Martin's. Drinking with them, Mrs. Morse became lively and good-natured and audacious. She was quickly popular. When she had drunk enough to cloud her most recent battle with Herbie, she was excited by their approbation. Crab, was she? Rotten sport, was she? Well, there were some that thought different.

Ed was one of The Boys. He lived in Utica—had "his own business" there, was the awed report—but he came to New York almost every week. He was married. He showed Mrs. Morse the then current photographs of Junior and Sister, and she praised them abundantly and sincerely. Soon it was accepted by the others that Ed was her particular friend.

He staked her when they all played poker; sat next her and occasionally rubbed his knee against hers during the game. She was rather lucky. Frequently she went home with a twenty-dollar bill or a ten-dollar bill or a handful of crumpled dollars. She was glad of them. Herbie was getting, in her words, something awful about money. To ask him for it brought an instant row.

"What the hell do you do with it?" he would say. "Shoot it all on Scotch?"

"I try to run this house half-way decent," she would retort. "Never thought of that, did you? Oh, no, his lordship couldn't be bothered with that."

Again, she could not find a definite day, to fix the beginning of Ed's proprietorship. It became his custom to kiss her on the mouth when he came in, as well as for farewell, and he gave her little quick kisses of approval all through the evening. She liked this rather more than she disliked it. She never thought of his kisses when she was not with him.

He would run his hand lingeringly over her back and shoulders.

"Some dizzy blonde, eh?" he would say. "Some doll."

One afternoon she came home from Mrs. Martin's to find Herbie in the bedroom. He had been away for several nights, evidently on a prolonged drinking bout. His face was gray, his hands jerked as if they were on wires. On the bed were two old suitcases, packed high. Only her photograph remained on his bureau, and the wide doors of his closet disclosed nothing but coat-hangers.

"I'm blowing," he said. "I'm through with the whole works. I got a job in Detroit."

She sat down on the edge of the bed. She had drunk much the night before, and the four Scotches she had had with Mrs. Martin had only increased her fogginess.

"Good job?" she said.

"Oh, yeah," he said. "Looks all right."

He closed a suitcase with difficulty, swearing at it in whispers.

"There's some dough in the bank," he said. "The bank book's in your top drawer. You can have the furniture and stuff."

He looked at her, and his forehead twitched.

"God damn it, I'm through, I'm telling you," he cried. "I'm through."

"All right, all right," she said. "I heard you, didn't I?"

She saw him as if he were at one end of a cannon and she at the other. Her head was beginning to ache bumpingly, and her voice had a dreary, tiresome tone. She could not have raised it.

"Like a drink before you go?" she asked.

Again he looked at her, and a corner of his mouth jerked up.

"Cockeyed again for a change, aren't you?" he said. "That's nice. Sure, get a couple of shots, will you?"

She went to the pantry, mixed him a stiff highball, poured herself a couple of inches of whisky and drank it. Then she gave herself another portion and brought the glasses into the bedroom. He had strapped both suitcases and had put on his hat and overcoat.

He took his highball.

"Well," he said, and he gave a sudden, uncertain laugh. "Here's mud in your eye."

"Mud in your eye," she said.

They drank. He put down his glass and took up the heavy suitcases.

"Got to get a train around six," he said.

She followed him down the hall. There was a song, a song that Mrs. Martin played doggedly on the phonograph, running loudly through her mind. She had never liked the thing.

> *"Night and daytime,*
> *Always playtime.*
> *Ain't we got fun?"*

At the door he put down the bags and faced her.

"Well," he said. "Well, take care of yourself. You'll be all right, will you?"

"Oh, sure," she said.

He opened the door, then came back to her, holding out his hand.

"By, Haze," he said. "Good luck to you."

She took his hand and shook it.

"Pardon my wet glove," she said.

When the door had closed behind him, she went back to the pantry.

She was flushed and lively when she went in to Mrs. Martin's that evening. The Boys were there, Ed among them. He was glad to be in town, frisky and loud and full of jokes. But she spoke quietly to him for a minute.

"Herbie blew today," she said. "Going to live out west."

"That so?" he said. He looked at her and played with the fountain pen clipped to his waistcoat pocket.

"Think he's gone for good, do you?" he asked.

"Yeah," she said. "I know he is. I know. Yeah."

"You going to live on across the hall just the same?" he said. "Know what you're going to do?"

"Gee, I don't know," she said. "I don't give much of a damn."

"Oh, come on, that's no way to talk," he told her. "What you need—you need a little snifter. How about it?"

"Yeah," she said. "Just straight."

She won forty-three dollars at poker. When the game broke up, Ed took her back to her apartment.

"Got a little kiss for me?" he asked.

He wrapped her in his big arms and kissed her violently. She was entirely passive. He held her away and looked at her.

"Little tight, honey?" he asked, anxiously. "Not going to be sick, are you?"

"Me?" she said. "I'm swell."

II

When Ed left in the morning, he took her photograph with him. He said he wanted her picture to look at, up in Utica. "You can have that one on the bureau," she said.

She put Herbie's picture in a drawer, out of her sight. When she could look at it, she meant to tear it up. She was fairly successful in keeping her mind from racing around him. Whisky slowed it for her. She was almost peaceful, in her mist.

She accepted her relationship with Ed without question or enthusiasm. When he was away, she seldom thought definitely of him. He was good to her; he gave her frequent presents and a regular allowance. She was even able to save. She did not plan ahead of any day, but her wants were few, and you might as well put money in the bank as have it lying around.

When the lease of her apartment neared its end, it was Ed who suggested moving. His friendship with Mrs. Martin and Joe had become strained over a dispute at poker; a feud was impending.

"Let's get the hell out of here, " Ed said. "What I want you to have is a place near the Grand Central. Make it easier for me."

So she took a little flat in the Forties. A colored maid came in every day to clean and to make coffee for her—she was "through with that housekeeping stuff," she said, and Ed, twenty years married to a passionately domestic woman, admired this romantic uselessness and felt doubly a man of the world in abetting it.

The coffee was all she had until she went out to dinner, but alcohol kept her fat. Prohibition she regarded only as a basis for jokes. You could always get all you wanted. She was never noticeably drunk and seldom nearly sober. It required a larger daily allowance to keep her misty-minded. Too little, and she was achingly melancholy.

Ed brought her to Jimmy's. He was proud, with the pride of the transient who would be mistaken for a native, in his knowledge of small, recent restaurants occupying the lower floors of shabby brownstone houses; places where, upon mentioning the name of an habitué friend, might be obtained strange whisky and fresh gin in many of their ramifications. Jimmy's place was the favorite of his acquaintances.

There, through Ed, Mrs. Morse met many men and women, formed quick friendships. The men often took her out when Ed was in Utica. He was proud of her popularity.

She fell into the habit of going to Jimmy's alone when she had no engagement. She was certain to meet some people she knew, and join them. It was a club for her friends, both men and women.

The women at Jimmy's looked remarkably alike, and this was curious, for, through feuds, removals, and opportunities of more profitable contacts, the personnel of the group changed constantly. Yet always the newcomers resembled those whom they replaced. They were all big women and stout, broad of shoulder and abundantly breasted, with faces thickly clothed in soft, high-colored flesh. They laughed loud and often, showing opaque and lusterless teeth like squares of crockery. There was about them the health of the big, yet a slight, unwholesome suggestion of stubborn preservation. They might have been thirty-six or forty-five or anywhere between.

They composed their titles of their own first names with their husbands' surnames—Mrs. Florence Miller, Mrs. Vera Riley, Mrs. Lilian Block. This gave at the same time the solidity of marriage and the glamour of freedom. Yet only one or two were actually divorced. Most of them never referred to their dimmed spouses; some, a shorter time separated, described them in terms of great biological interest. Several were mothers, each of an only child—a boy at school somewhere, or a girl being cared for by a grandmother. Often, well on towards morning, there would be displays of kodak portraits and of tears.

They were comfortable women, cordial and friendly and irrepressibly matronly. Theirs was the quality of ease. Become fatalistic, especially about money matters, they were unworried. Whenever their funds dropped alarmingly, a new donor appeared; this had always happened. The aim of each was to have one man, permanently, to pay all her bills, in return for which she would have immediately given up other admirers and probably would have become exceedingly fond of him; for the affections of all of them were, by now, unexacting, tranquil, and easily arranged. This end, however, grew increasingly difficult yearly. Mrs. Morse was regarded as fortunate.

Ed had a good year, increased her allowance and gave her a sealskin coat. But she had to be careful of her moods with him. He insisted upon gaiety. He would not listen to admissions of aches or weariness.

"Hey, listen," he would say, "I got worries of my own, and plenty. Nobody wants to hear other people's troubles, sweetie. What you got to do, you got to be a sport and forget it. See? Well, slip us a little smile, then. That's my girl."

She never had enough interest to quarrel with him as she had with Herbie, but she wanted the privilege of occasional admitted sadness. It was strange. The other women she saw did not have to fight their moods. There was Mrs. Florence Miller who got regular crying jags, and the men sought only to cheer and comfort her. The others spent whole evenings in grieved recitals of worries and ills; their escorts paid them deep sympathy. But she was instantly undesirable when she was low in spirits. Once, at Jimmy's, when she could not make herself lively, Ed had walked out and left her.

"Why the hell don't you stay home and not go spoiling everybody's evening?" he had roared.

Even her slightest acquaintances seemed irritated if she were not conspicuously light-hearted.

"What's the matter with you, anyway?" they would say. "Be your age, why don't you? Have a little drink and snap out of it."

When her relationship with Ed had continued nearly three years, he moved to Florida to live. He hated leaving her; he gave her a large check and some shares of a sound stock, and his pale eyes were wet when he said good-by. She did not miss him. He came to New York infrequently, perhaps two or three times a year, and hurried directly from the train to see her. She was always pleased to have him come and never sorry to see him go.

Charley, an acquaintance of Ed's that she had met at Jimmy's, had long admired her. He had always made opportunities of touching her and leaning close to talk to her. He asked repeatedly of all their friends if they had ever heard such a fine laugh as she had. After Ed left, Charley became the main figure in her life. She classified him and spoke of him as "not so bad." There was nearly a year of Charley; then she divided her time between him and Sydney, another frequenter of Jimmy's; then Charley slipped away altogether.

Sydney was a little, brightly dressed, clever Jew. She was perhaps nearest contentment with him. He amused her always; her laughter was not forced.

He admired her completely. Her softness and size delighted him. And he thought she was great, he often told her, because she kept gay and lively when she was drunk.

"Once I had a gal," he said, "used to try and throw herself out of the window every time she got a can on. Jee-*zuss*," he added, feelingly.

Then Sydney married a rich and watchful bride, and then there was Billy. No—after Sydney came Ferd, then Billy. In her haze, she never recalled how men entered her life and left it. There were no surprises. She had no thrill at their advent, nor woe at their departure. She seemed to be always able to attract men. There was never another as rich as Ed, but they were all generous to her, in their means.

Once she had news of Herbie. She met Mrs. Martin dining at Jimmy's, and the old friendship was vigorously renewed. The still admiring Joe, while on a business trip, had seen Herbie. He had settled in Chicago, he looked fine, he was living with some woman—seemed to be crazy about her. Mrs. Morse had been drinking vastly that day. She took the news with mild interest, as one hearing of the sex peccadilloes of somebody whose name is, after a moment's groping, familiar.

"Must be damn near seven years since I saw him," she commented. "Gee. Seven years."

More and more, her days lost their individuality. She never knew dates, nor was sure of the day of the week.

"My God, was that a year ago!" she would exclaim, when an event was recalled in conversation.

She was tired so much of the time. Tired and blue. Almost everything could give her the blues. Those old horses she saw on Sixth Avenue—struggling and slipping along the car-tracks, or standing at the curb, their heads dropped level with their worn knees. The tightly stored tears would squeeze from her eyes as she teetered past on her aching feet in the stubby, champagne-colored slippers.

The thought of death came and stayed with her and lent her a sort of drowsy cheer. It would be nice, nice and restful, to be dead.

There was no settled, shocked moment when she first thought of killing herself; it seemed to her as if the idea had always been with her. She pounced upon all the accounts of suicides in the newspapers. There was an epidemic of self-killings—or maybe it was just that she searched for the stories of them so eagerly that she found many. To read of them roused reassurance in her; she felt a cozy solidarity with the big company of the voluntary dead.

She slept, aided by whisky, till deep into the afternoons, then lay abed, a bottle and glass at her hand, until it was time to dress to go out for dinner. She was beginning to feel towards alcohol a little puzzled distrust, as toward an old friend who has refused a simple favor. Whisky could still soothe her for most of the time, but there were sudden, inexplicable moments when the cloud fell treacherously away from her, and she was sawed by the sorrow and bewilderment and nuisance of all living. She played voluptuously with the thought of cool, sleepy retreat. She had never been troubled by religious belief and no vision of an after-life intimidated her. She dreamed by day of never again putting on tight shoes, of never having to laugh and listen and admire, of never more being a good sport. Never.

But how would you do it? It made her sick to think of jumping from heights. She could not stand a gun. At the theater, if one of the actors drew a revolver, she crammed her fingers into her ears and could not even look at the stage until after the shot had been fired. There was no gas in her flat. She looked long at the bright blue veins in her slim wrists—a cut with a razor blade, and there you'd be. But it would hurt, hurt like hell, and there would be blood to see. Poison—something tasteless and quick and painless—was the thing. But they wouldn't sell it to you in drugstores, because of the law.

She had few other thoughts.

There was a new man now—Art. He was short and fat and exacting and hard on her patience when he was drunk. But there had been only occasionals for some time before him, and she was glad of a little stability. Too, Art must be away for weeks at a stretch, selling silks, and that was restful. She was convincingly gay with him, though the effort shook her.

"The best sport in the world," he would murmur, deep in her neck. "The best sport in the world."

One night, when he had taken her to Jimmy's, she went into the dressing-room with Mrs. Florence Miller. There, while designing curly mouths on their faces with lip-rouge, they compared experiences of insomnia.

"Honestly," Mrs. Morse said, "I wouldn't close an eye if I didn't go to bed full of Scotch. I lie there and toss and turn and toss and turn. Blue! Does a person get blue lying awake that way!"

"Say, listen, Hazel," Mrs. Miller said, impressively, "I'm telling you I'd be awake for a year if I didn't take veronal. That stuff makes you sleep like a fool."

"Isn't it poison, or something?" Mrs. Morse asked.

"Oh, you take too much and you're out for the count," said Mrs. Miller. "I just take five grains—they come in tablets. I'd be scared to fool around with it. But five grains, and you cork off pretty."

"Can you get it anywhere?" Mrs. Morse felt superbly Machiavellian.

"Get all you want in Jersey," said Mrs. Miller. "They won't give it to you here without you have a doctor's prescription. Finished? We'd better go back and see what the boys are doing."

That night, Art left Mrs. Morse at the door of her apartment; his mother was in town. Mrs. Morse was still sober, and it happened that there was no whisky left in her cupboard. She lay in bed, looking up at the black ceiling.

She rose early, for her, and went to New Jersey. She had never taken the tube, and did not understand it. So she went to the Pennsylvania Station and bought a railroad ticket to

Newark. She thought of nothing in particular on the trip out. She looked at the uninspired hats of the women about her and gazed through the smeared window at the flat, gritty scene.

In Newark, in the first drug-store she came to, she asked for a tin of talcum powder, a nailbrush, and a box of veronal tablets. The powder and the brush were to make the hypnotic seem also a casual need. The clerk was entirely unconcerned. "We only keep them in bottles," he said, and wrapped up for her a little glass vial containing ten white tablets, stacked one on another.

She went to another drug-store and bought a face-cloth, an orange-wood stick, and a bottle of veronal tablets. The clerk was also uninterested.

"Well, I guess I got enough to kill an ox," she thought, and went back to the station.

At home, she put the little vials in the drawer of her dressing-table and stood looking at them with a dreamy tenderness.

"There they are, God bless them," she said, and she kissed her finger-tip and touched each bottle.

The colored maid was busy in the living-room.

"Hey, Nettie", Mrs. Morse called. "Be an angel, will you? Run around to Jimmy's and get me a quart of Scotch."

She hummed while she awaited the girl's return.

During the next few days, whisky ministered to her as tenderly as it had done when she first turned to its aid. Alone, she was soothed and vague, at Jimmy's she was the gayest of the groups. Art was delighted with her.

Then, one night, she had an appointment to meet Art at Jimmy's for an early dinner. He was to leave afterward on a business excursion, to be away for a week. Mrs. Morse had been drinking all the afternoon; while she dressed to go out, she felt herself rising pleasurably from drowsiness to high spirits. But as she came out into the street the effects of the whisky deserted her completely, and she was filled with a slow, grinding wretchedness so horrible that she stood swaying on the pavement, unable for a moment to move forward. It was a gray night with spurts of mean, thin snow, and the streets shone with dark ice. As she slowly crossed Sixth Avenue, consciously dragging one foot past the other, a big, scarred horse pulling a rickety express-wagon crashed to his knees before her. The driver swore and screamed and lashed the beast insanely, bringing the whip back over his shoulder for every blow, while the horse struggled to get a footing on the slippery asphalt. A group gathered and watched with interest.

Art was waiting, when Mrs. Morse reached Jimmy's.

"What's the matter with you, for God's sake?" was his greeting to her.

"I saw a horse," she said. "Gee, I—a person feels sorry for horses. I—it isn't just horses. Everything's kind of terrible, isn't it? I can't help getting sunk."

"Ah, sunk, me eye," he said. "What's the idea of all the bellyaching? What have you got to be sunk about?"

"I can't help it," she said.

"Ah, help it, me eye," he said. "Pull yourself together, will you? Come on and sit down, and take that face off you."

She drank industriously and she tried hard, but she could not overcome her melancholy. Others joined them and commented on her gloom, and she could do no more for them than smile weakly. She made little dabs at her eyes with her handkerchief, trying to time her movements so they would be unnoticed, but several times Art caught her and scowled and shifted impatiently in his chair.

When it was time for him to go to his train, she said she would leave, too, and go home.

"And not a bad idea, either," he said. "See if you can't sleep yourself out of it. I'll see you Thursday. For God's sake, try and cheer up by then, will you?"

"Yeah," she said. "I will."

In her bedroom, she undressed with a tense speed wholly unlike her usual slow uncertainty. She put on her nightgown, took off her hair-net and passed the comb quickly through her dry, vari-colored hair. Then she took the two little vials from the drawer and carried them into the bathroom. The splintering misery had gone from her, and she felt the quick excitement of one who is about to receive an anticipated gift.

She uncorked the vials, filled a glass with water and stood before the mirror, a tablet between her fingers. Suddenly she bowed graciously to her reflection, and raised the glass to it.

"Well, here's mud in your eye," she said.

The tablets were unpleasant to take, dry and powdery and sticking obstinately half-way down her throat. It took her a long time to swallow all twenty of them. She stood watching her reflection with deep, impersonal interest, studying the movements of the gulping throat. Once more she spoke aloud.

"For God's sake, try and cheer up by Thursday, will you?" she said. "Well, you know what he can do. He and the whole lot of them."

She had no idea how quickly to expect effect from the veronal. When she had taken the last tablet, she stood uncertainly, wondering, still with a courteous, vicarious interest, if death would strike her down then and there. She felt in no way strange, save for a slight stirring of sickness from the effort of swallowing the tablets, nor did her reflected face look at all different. It would not be immediate, then; it might even take an hour or so.

She stretched her arms high and gave a vast yawn.

"Guess I'll go to bed," she said. "Gee, I'm nearly dead."

That struck her as comic, and she turned out the bathroom light and went in and laid herself down in her bed, chuckling softly all the time.

"Gee, I'm nearly dead," she quoted. "That's a hot one!"

III

Nettie, the colored maid, came in late the next afternoon to clean the apartment, and found Mrs. Morse in her bed. But then, that was not unusual. Usually, though, the sounds of cleaning waked her, and she did not like to wake up. Nettie, an agreeable girl, had learned to move softly about her work.

But when she had done the living-room and stolen in to tidy the little square bedroom, she could not avoid a tiny clatter as she arranged the objects on the dressing-table. Instinctively, she glanced over her shoulder at the sleeper, and without warning a sickly uneasiness crept over her. She came to the bed and stared down at the woman lying there.

Mrs. Morse lay on her back, one flabby, white arm flung up, the wrist against her forehead. Her stiff hair hung untenderly along her face. The bed covers were pushed down, exposing a deep square of soft neck and a pink nightgown, its fabric worn uneven by many launderings;

her great breasts, freed from their tight confiner, sagged beneath her arm-pits. Now and then she made knotted, snoring sounds, and from the corner of her opened mouth to the blurred turn of her jaw ran a lane of crusted spittle.

"Mis' Morse," Nettie called. "Oh, Mis' Morse! It's terrible late."

Mrs. Morse made no move.

"Mis' Morse," said Nettie. "Look, Mis' Morse. How'm I goin' get this bed made?"

Panic sprang upon the girl. She shook the woman's hot shoulder.

"Ah, wake up, will yuh?" she whined. "Ah, please wake up."

Suddenly the girl turned and ran out in the hall to the elevator door, keeping her thumb firm on the black, shiny button until the elderly car and its Negro attendant stood before her. She poured a jumble of words over the boy, and led him back to the apartment. He tiptoed creakingly in to the bedside; first gingerly, then so lustily that he left marks in the soft flesh, he prodded the unconscious woman.

"Hey, there!" he cried, and listened intently, as for an echo.

"Jeez. Out like a light," he commented.

At his interest in the spectacle, Nettie's panic left her. Importance was big in both of them. They talked in quick, unfinished whispers, and it was the boy's suggestion that he fetch the young doctor who lived on the ground floor. Nettie hurried along with him. They looked forward to the limelit moment of breaking their news of something untoward, something pleasurably unpleasant. Mrs. Morse had become the medium of drama. With no ill wish to her, they hoped that her state was serious, that she would not let them down by being awake and normal on their return. A little fear of this determined them to make the most, to the doctor, of her present condition. "Matter of life and death," returned to Nettie from her thin store of reading. She considered startling the doctor with the phrase.

The doctor was in and none too pleased at interruption. He wore a yellow and blue striped dressing-gown, and he was lying on his sofa, laughing with a dark girl, her face scaly with inexpensive powder, who perched on the arm. Half-emptied highball glasses stood beside them, and her coat and hat were neatly hung up with the comfortable implication of a long stay.

Always something, the doctor grumbled. Couldn't let anybody alone after a hard day. But he put some bottles and instruments into a case, changed his dressing-gown for his coat and started out with the Negroes.

"Snap it up there, big boy," the girl called after him. "Don't be all night."

The doctor strode loudly into Mrs. Morse's flat and on to the bedroom, Nettie and the boy right behind him. Mrs. Morse had not moved; her sleep was as deep, but soundless, now. The doctor looked sharply at her, then plunged his thumbs into the lidded pits above her eyeballs and threw his weight upon them. A high, sickened cry broke from Nettie.

"Look like he tryin' to push her right on th'ough the bed," said the boy. He chuckled.

Mrs. Morse gave no sign under the pressure. Abruptly the doctor abandoned it, and with one quick movement swept the covers down to the foot of the bed. With another he flung her nightgown back and lifted the thick, white legs, cross-hatched with blocks of tiny, iris-colored veins. He pinched them repeatedly, with long, cruel nips, back of the knees. She did not awaken.

"What's she been drinking?" he asked Nettie, over his shoulder.

With the certain celerity of one who knows just where to lay hands on a thing, Nettie went into the bathroom, bound for the cupboard where Mrs. Morse kept her whisky. But she stopped at the sight of the two vials, with their red and white labels, lying before the mirror. She brought them to the doctor.

"Oh, for the Lord Almighty's sweet sake!" he said. He dropped Mrs. Morse's legs, and pushed them impatiently across the bed. "What did she want to go taking that tripe for? Rotten yellow trick, that's what a thing like that is. Now we'll have to pump her out, and all that stuff. Nuisance, a thing like that is; that's what it amounts to. Here, George, take me down in the elevator. You wait here, maid. She won't do anything."

"She won't die on me, will she?" cried Nettie.

"No," said the doctor. "God, no. You couldn't kill her with an ax."

IV

After two days, Mrs. Morse came back to consciousness, dazed at first, then with a comprehension that brought with it the slow, saturating wretchedness.

"Oh, Lord, oh, Lord," she moaned, and tears for herself and for life striped her cheeks.

Nettie came in at the sound. For two days she had done the ugly, incessant tasks in the nursing of the unconscious, for two nights she had caught broken bits of sleep on the living-room couch. She looked coldly at the big, blown woman in the bed.

"What you been tryin' to do, Mis' Morse?" she said. "What kine o' work is that, takin' all that stuff?"

"Oh, Lord," moaned Mrs. Morse, again, and she tried to cover her eyes with her arms. But the joints felt stiff and brittle, and she cried out at their ache.

"Tha's no way to ack, takin' them pills," said Nettie. "You can thank you' stars you heah at all. How you feel now?"

"Oh, I feel great," said Mrs. Morse. "Swell, I feel."

Her hot, painful tears fell as if they would never stop.

"Tha's no way to take on, cryin' like that," Nettie said. "After what you done. The doctor, he says he could have you arrested, doin' a thing like that. He was fit to be tied, here."

"Why couldn't he let me alone?" wailed Mrs. Morse. "Why the hell couldn't he have?"

"Tha's terr'ble, Mis' Morse, swearin' an' talkin' like that," said Nettie, "after what people done for you. Here I ain' had no sleep at all for two nights, an' had to give up goin' out to my other ladies!"

"Oh, I'm sorry, Nettie," she said. "You're a peach. I'm sorry I've given you so much trouble. I couldn't help it. I just got sunk. Didn't you ever feel like doing it? When everything looks just lousy to you?"

"I wouldn' think o' no such thing," declared Nettie. "You got to cheer up. Tha's what you got to do. Everybody's got their troubles."

"Yeah," said Mrs. Morse. "I know."

"Come a pretty picture card for you," Nettie said. "Maybe that will cheer you up."

She handed Mrs. Morse a post-card. Mrs. Morse had to cover one eye with her hand, in order to read the message; her eyes were not yet focusing correctly.

It was from Art. On the back of a view of the Detroit Athletic Club he had written: "Greeting and salutations. Hope you have lost that gloom. Cheer up and don't take any rubber nickles. See you on Thursday."

She dropped the card to the floor. Misery crushed her as if she were between great smooth stones. There passed before her a slow, slow pageant of days spent lying in her flat, of evenings at Jimmy's being a good sport, making herself laugh and coo at Art and other Arts; she saw a long parade of weary horses and shivering beggars and all beaten, driven, stumbling things. Her feet throbbed as if she had crammed them into the stubby champagne-colored slippers. Her heart seemed to swell and harden.

"Nettie," she cried, "for heaven's sake pour me a drink, will you?"

The maid looked doubtful.

"Now you know, Mis' Morse," she said, "you been near daid. I don' know if the doctor he let you drink nothin' yet."

"Oh, never mind him," she said. "You get me one, and bring in the bottle. Take one yourself."

"Well," said Nettie.

She poured them each a drink, deferentially leaving hers in the bathroom to be taken in solitude, and brought Mrs. Morse's glass in to her.

Mrs. Morse looked into the liquor and shuddered back from its odor. Maybe it would help. Maybe, when you had been knocked cold for a few days, your very first drink would give you a lift. Maybe whisky would be her friend again. She prayed without addressing a God, without knowing a God. Oh, please, please, let her be able to get drunk, please keep her always drunk.

She lifted the glass.

"Thanks, Nettie," she said. "Here's mud in your eye."

The maid giggled. "Tha's the way, Mis' Morse," she said. "You cheer up, now."

"Yeah," said Mrs. Morse. "Sure."

Blue Beard
(1697)

CHARLES PERRAULT

There was a man who had fine houses, both in town and country, a deal of silver and gold plate, embroidered furniture, and coaches gilded all over with gold. But this man had the misfortune to have a blue beard, which made him so frightfully ugly, that all the women and girls ran away from him.

One of his neighbours, a lady of quality, had two daughters who were perfect beauties. He desired of her one of them in marriage, leaving to her the choice which of the two she would bestow upon him. They would neither of them have him, and each made the other welcome of him, being not able to bear the thought of marrying a man who had a blue beard. And what besides gave them disgust and aversion, was his having already been married to several wives, and nobody ever knew what became of them.

Blue Beard, to engage their affection, took them, with the lady their mother, and three or four ladies of their acquaintance, with other young people of the neighbourhood, to one of his country seats, where they stayed a whole week. There was nothing then to be seen but parties of pleasure, hunting, fishing, dancing, mirth and feasting. Nobody went to bed, but all passed the night in playing tricks upon each other. In short, everything succeeded so well, that the youngest daughter began to think the master of the house not to have a beard so very blue, and that he was a mighty civil gentleman. As soon as they returned home, the marriage was concluded.

About a month afterwards Blue Beard told his wife that he was obliged to take a country journey for six weeks at least, about affairs of very great consequence, desiring her to divert herself in his absence, to send for her friends and acquaintances, to carry them into the country, if she pleased, and to make good cheer wherever she was.

"Here," said he, "are the keys of the two great wardrobes, wherein I have my best furniture; these are of my silver and gold plate, which is not every day in use; these open my strong boxes, which hold my money, both gold and silver; these my caskets of jewels; and this is the master-key to all my apartments. But for this little one here, it is the key of the closet at the end of the great gallery on the ground floor. Open them all; go into all and every one of them; except that little closet which I forbid you, and forbid it in such a manner that, if you happen to open it, there will be no bounds to my just anger and resentment."

She promised to observe, very exactly, whatever he had ordered; when he, after having embraced her, got into his coach and proceeded on his journey.

Her neighbours and good friends did not stay to be sent for by the newmarried lady, so great was their impatience to see all the rich furniture of her house, not daring to come while her husband was there, because of his blue beard which frightened them. They ran thro' all the rooms, closets, and wardrobes, which were all so rich and fine, that they seemed to surpass one another.

After that, they went up into the two great rooms, where were the best and richest furniture; they could not sufficiently admire the number and beauty of the tapestry, beds, couches, cabinets, stands, tables, and looking-glasses in which you might see yourself from head to foot; some of them were framed with glass, others with silver, plain and gilded, the finest and most magnificent which were ever seen. They ceased not to extol and envy the happiness of their friend, who in the mean time no way diverted herself in looking upon all these rich things, because of the impatience she had to go and open the closet of the ground floor. She was so much pressed by her curiosity, that, without considering that it was very uncivil to leave her company, she went down a little back-stair-case, and with such excessive haste, that she had twice or thrice like to have broken her neck.

Being come to the closet door, she made a stop for some time, thinking upon her husband's orders, and considering what unhappiness might attend her if she was disobedient; but the temptation was so strong she could not overcome it. She took then the little key, and opened it trembling; but could not at first see any thing plainly, because the windows were shut. After some moments she began to perceive that the floor was all covered over with clotted blood, in which were reflected the bodies of several dead women ranged against the walls: these were all the wives whom Blue Beard had married and murdered one after another. She was like to have died for fear, and the key, which she pulled out of the lock, fell out of her hand.

After having somewhat recovered her senses, she took up the key, locked the door, and went up stairs into her chamber to recover herself; but she could not, so much was she frightened. Having observed that the key of the closet was stained with blood, she tried two or three times to wipe it off, but the blood would not come off; in vain did she wash it, and even rub it with soap and sand, the blood still remained, for the key was a Fairy, and she could never make it quite clean; when the blood was gone off from one side, it came again on the other.

Blue Beard returned from his journey the same evening, and said, he had received letters upon the road, informing him that the affair he went about was ended to his advantage. His wife did all she could to convince him she was extremely glad of his speedy return. Next morning he asked her for the keys, which she gave him, but with such a trembling hand, that he easily guessed what had happened.

"What," said he, "is not the key of my closet among the rest?"

"I must certainly," answered she, "have left it above upon the table."

"Fail not," said Blue Beard, "to bring it me presently."

After putting him off several times, she was forced to bring him the key. Blue Beard, having very attentively considered it, said to his wife:

"How comes this blood upon the key?"

"I do not know," cried the poor woman, paler than death.

"You do not know," replied Blue Beard; "I very well know, you were resolved to go into the closet, were you not? Mighty well, Madam; you shall go in, and take your place among the ladies you saw there."

Upon this she threw herself at her husband's feet, and begged his pardon with all the signs of a true repentance for her disobedience. She would have melted a rock, so beautiful and sorrowful was she; but Blue Beard had a heart harder than any rock.

"You must die, Madam," said he, "and that presently."

"Since I must die," answered she, looking upon him with her eyes all bathed in tears, "give me some little time to say my prayers."

"I give you," replied Blue Beard, "half a quarter of an hour, but not one moment more."

When she was alone, she called out to her sister, and said to her:

"Sister Anne" (for that was her name), "go up I beg you, upon the top of the tower, and look if my brothers are not coming; they promised me that they would come to-day, and if you see them, give them a sign to make haste."

Her sister Anne went up upon the top of the tower, and the poor afflicted wife cried out from time to time, "Anne, sister Anne, do you see any one coming?"

And sister Anne said:

"I see nothing but the sun, which makes a dust, and the grass growing green."

In the mean while Blue Beard, holding a great scimitar in his hand, cried out as loud as he could bawl to his wife:

"Come down instantly, or I shall come up to you."

"One moment longer, if you please," said his wife, and then she cried out very softly:

"Anne, sister Anne, dost thou see any body coming?"

And sister Anne answered:

"I see nothing but the sun, which makes a dust, and the grass growing green."

"Come down quickly," cried Blue Beard, "or I will come up to you."

"I am coming," answered his wife; and then she cried:

"Anne, sister Anne, dost thou see any one coming?"

"I see," replied sister Anne, "a great dust that comes this way."

"Are they my brothers?"

"Alas! no, my dear sister, I see a flock of sheep."

"Will you not come down?" cried Blue Beard.

"One moment longer," said his wife, and then she cried out:

"Anne, sister Anne, dost thou see nobody coming?"

"I see," said she, "two horsemen coming, but they are yet a great way off."

"God be praised," she cried presently, "they are my brothers; I am beckoning to them, as well as I can, for them to make haste."

Then Blue Beard bawled out so loud, that he made the whole house tremble. The distressed wife came down, and threw herself at his feet, all in tears, with her hair about her shoulders.

"Nought will avail," said Blue Beard, "you must die"; then, taking hold of her hair with one hand, and lifting up his scimitar with the other, he was going to take off her head.

The poor lady turning about to him, and looking at him with dying eyes, desired him to afford her one little moment to recollect herself.

"No, no," said he, "recommend thyself to God," and was just ready to strike.

At this very instant there was such a loud knocking at the gate, that Blue Beard made a sudden stop. The gate was opened, and presently entered two horsemen, who drawing their swords, ran directly to Blue Beard. He knew them to be his wife's brothers, one a dragoon, the other a musqueteer; so that he ran away immediately to save himself; but the two brothers pursued so close, that they overtook him before he could get to the steps of the porch, when they ran their swords thro' his body and left him dead. The poor wife was almost as dead as her husband, and had not strength enough to rise and welcome her brothers.

Blue Beard had no heirs, and so his wife became mistress of all his estate. She made use of one part of it to marry her sister Anne to a young gentleman who had loved her a long while; another part to buy captains' commissions for her brothers; and the rest to marry herself to a very worthy gentleman, who made her forget the ill time she had passed with Blue Beard.

The Moral

O curiosity, thou mortal bane!
Spite of thy charms, thou causest often pain
And sore regret, of which we daily find
A thousand instances attend mankind:
For thou—O may it not displease the fair—
A fleeting pleasure art, but lasting care.
And always proves, alas! too dear the prize,
Which, in the moment of possession, dies.

Another

A very little share of common sense,
And knowledge of the world, will soon evince
That this a story is of time long pass'd;
No husbands now such panic terrors cast;
Nor weakly, with a vain despotic hand,
Imperious, what's impossible, command:
And be they discontented, or the fire
Of wicked jealousy their hearts inspire,
They softly sing; and of whatever hue
Their beards may chance to be, or black, or blue,
Grizeld, or russet, it is hard to say
Which of the two, the man or wife, bears sway.

The Murders in the Rue Morgue
(1841)

EDGAR ALLAN POE

What song the Syrens sang, or what name Achilles assumed when he hid himself among women, although puzzling questions, are not beyond all conjecture.

—Sir Thomas Browne.

The mental features discoursed of as the analytical, are, in themselves, but little susceptible of analysis. We appreciate them only in their effects. We know of them, among other things, that they are always to their possessor, when inordinately possessed, a source of the liveliest enjoyment. As the strong man exults in his physical ability, delighting in such exercises as call his muscles into action, so glories the analyst in that moral activity which *disentangles*. He derives pleasure from even the most trivial occupations bringing his talent into play. He is fond of enigmas, of conundrums, of hieroglyphics; exhibiting in his solutions of each a degree of *acumen* which appears to the ordinary apprehension præternatural. His results, brought about by the very soul and essence of method, have, in truth, the whole air of intuition. The faculty of re-solution is possibly much invigorated by mathematical study, and especially by that highest branch of it which, unjustly, and merely on account of its retrograde operations, has been called, as if *par excellence*, analysis. Yet to calculate is not in itself to analyse. A chess-player, for example, does the one without effort at the other. It follows that the game of chess, in its effects upon mental character, is greatly misunderstood. I am not now writing a treatise, but simply prefacing a somewhat peculiar narrative by observations very much at random; I will, therefore, take occasion to assert that the higher powers of the reflective intellect are more decidedly and more usefully tasked by the unostentatious game of draughts than by all the elaborate frivolity of chess. In this latter, where the pieces have different and *bizarre* motions, with various and variable values, what is only complex is mistaken (a not unusual error) for what is profound. The *attention* is here called powerfully into play. If it flag for an instant, an oversight is committed resulting in injury or defeat. The possible moves being not only manifold but involute, the chances of such oversights are multiplied; and in nine cases out of ten it is the more concentrative rather than the more acute player who conquers. In draughts, on the contrary, where the moves are *unique* and have but little variation, the probabilities of inadvertence are diminished, and the mere attention being left comparatively unemployed, what advantages are obtained by either party are obtained by superior *acumen*. To be less abstract—Let us suppose a game of draughts where the pieces are reduced to four kings, and where, of course, no oversight is to be expected. It is obvious that here the victory can be decided (the players being at all equal) only by some *recherché* movement, the result of some strong exertion of the intellect. Deprived of ordinary resources, the analyst throws himself into the spirit of his opponent, identifies himself therewith, and not unfrequently sees thus, at a glance, the sole methods (sometime indeed absurdly simple ones) by which he may seduce into error or hurry into miscalculation.

Whist has long been noted for its influence upon what is termed the calculating power; and men of the highest order of intellect have been known to take an apparently unaccountable delight in it, while eschewing chess as frivolous. Beyond doubt there is nothing of a similar nature so greatly tasking the faculty of analysis. The best chess-player in Christendom *may* be little more than the best player of chess; but proficiency in whist implies capacity for success in all those more important undertakings where mind struggles with mind. When I say proficiency, I mean that perfection in the game which includes a comprehension of *all* the sources whence legitimate advantage may be derived. These are not only manifold but multiform, and lie frequently among recesses of thought altogether inaccessible to the ordinary understanding. To observe attentively is to remember distinctly; and, so far, the concentrative chess-player will do very well at whist; while the rules of Hoyle (themselves based upon the mere mechanism of the game) are sufficiently and generally comprehensible. Thus to have a retentive memory, and to proceed by "the book," are points commonly regarded as the sum total of good playing. But it is in matters beyond the limits of mere rule that the skill of the analyst is evinced. He makes, in silence, a host of observations and inferences. So, perhaps, do his companions; and the difference in the extent of the information obtained, lies not so much in the validity of the inference as in the quality of the observation. The necessary knowledge is that of *what* to observe. Our player confines himself not at all; nor, because the game is the object, does he reject deductions from things external to the game. He examines the countenance of his partner, comparing it carefully with that of each of his opponents. He considers the mode of assorting the cards in each hand; often counting trump by trump, and honor by honor, through the glances bestowed by their holders upon each. He notes every variation of face as the play progresses, gathering a fund of thought from the differences in the expression of certainty, of surprise, of triumph, or of chagrin. From the manner of gathering up a trick he judges whether the person taking it can make another in the suit. He recognises what is played through feint, by the air with which it is thrown upon the table. A casual or inadvertent word; the accidental dropping or turning of a card, with the accompanying anxiety or carelessness in regard to its concealment; the counting of the tricks, with the order of their arrangement; embarrassment, hesitation, eagerness or trepidation—all afford, to his apparently intuitive perception, indications of the true state of affairs. The first two or three rounds having been played, he is in full possession of the contents of each hand, and thenceforward puts down his cards with as absolute a precision of purpose as if the rest of the party had turned outward the faces of their own.

The analytical power should not be confounded with ample ingenuity; for while the analyst is necessarily ingenious, the ingenious man is often remarkably incapable of analysis. The constructive or combining power, by which ingenuity is usually manifested, and to which the phrenologists (I believe erroneously) have assigned a separate organ, supposing it a primitive faculty, has been so frequently seen in those whose intellect bordered otherwise upon idiocy, as to have attracted general observation among writers on morals. Between ingenuity and the analytic ability there exists a difference far greater, indeed, than that between the fancy and the imagination, but of a character very strictly analogous. It will be found, in fact, that the ingenious are always fanciful, and the *truly* imaginative never otherwise than analytic.

The narrative which follows will appear to the reader somewhat in the light of a commentary upon the propositions just advanced.

Residing in Paris during the spring and part of the summer of 18—, I there became acquainted with a Monsieur C. Auguste Dupin. This young gentleman was of an excellent—indeed of an illustrious family, but, by a variety of untoward events, had been reduced to such poverty that the energy of his character succumbed beneath it, and he ceased to bestir himself in the world, or to care for the retrieval of his fortunes. By courtesy of his creditors, there still remained in his possession a small remnant of his patrimony; and, upon the income arising from this, he managed, by means of a rigorous economy, to procure the necessaries of life, without troubling himself about its superfluities. Books, indeed, were his sole luxuries, and in Paris these are easily obtained.

Our first meeting was at an obscure library in the Rue Montmartre, where the accident of our both being in search of the same very rare and very remarkable volume, brought us into closer communion. We saw each other again and again. I was deeply interested in the little family history which he detailed to me with all that candor which a Frenchman indulges whenever mere self is his theme. I was astonished, too, at the vast extent of his reading; and, above all, I felt my soul enkindled within me by the wild fervor, and the vivid freshness of his imagination. Seeking in Paris the objects I then sought, I felt that the society of such a man would be to me a treasure beyond price; and this feeling I frankly confided to him. It was at length arranged that we should live together during my stay in the city; and as my worldly circumstances were somewhat less embarrassed than his own, I was permitted to be at the expense of renting, and furnishing in a style which suited the rather fantastic gloom of our common temper, a time-eaten and grotesque mansion, long deserted through superstitions into which we did not inquire, and tottering to its fall in a retired and desolate portion of the Faubourg St. Germain.

Had the routine of our life at this place been known to the world, we should have been regarded as madmen—although, perhaps, as madmen of a harmless nature. Our seclusion was perfect. We admitted no visitors. Indeed the locality of our retirement had been carefully kept a secret from my own former associates; and it had been many years since Dupin had ceased to know or be known in Paris. We existed within ourselves alone.

It was a freak of fancy in my friend (for what else shall I call it?) to be enamored of the Night for her own sake; and into this *bizarrerie*, as into all his others, I quietly fell; giving myself up to his wild whims with a perfect *abandon*. The sable divinity would not herself dwell with us always; but we could counterfeit her presence. At the first dawn of the morning we closed all the messy shutters of our old building; lighting a couple of tapers which, strongly perfumed, threw out only the ghastliest and feeblest of rays. By the aid of these we then busied our souls in dreams—reading, writing, or conversing, until warned by the clock of the advent of the true Darkness. Then we sallied forth into the streets arm in arm, continuing the topics of the day, or roaming far and wide until a late hour, seeking, amid the wild lights and shadows of the populous city, that infinity of mental excitement which quiet observation can afford.

At such times I could not help remarking and admiring (although from his rich ideality I had been prepared to expect it) a peculiar analytic ability in Dupin. He seemed, too, to take an eager delight in its exercise—if not exactly in its display—and did not hesitate to confess the pleasure thus derived. He boasted to me, with a low chuckling laugh, that most men, in respect to himself, wore windows in their bosoms, and was wont to follow up such assertions by direct and very startling proofs of his intimate knowledge of my own. His manner at these moments was frigid and abstract; his eyes were vacant in expression; while his voice, usually a rich tenor, rose into a treble which would have sounded petulantly but for the deliberateness and entire distinctness of the enunciation. Observing him in these moods, I often dwelt meditatively upon the old philosophy of the Bi-Part Soul, and amused myself with the fancy of a double Dupin—the creative and the resolvent.

Let it not be supposed, from what I have just said, that I am detailing any mystery, or penning any romance. What I have described in the Frenchman, was merely the result of an excited, or perhaps of a diseased intelligence. But of the character of his remarks at the periods in question an example will best convey the idea.

We were strolling one night down a long dirty street in the vicinity of the Palais Royal. Being both, apparently, occupied with thought, neither of us had spoken a syllable for fifteen minutes at least. All at once Dupin broke forth with these words:

"He is a very little fellow, that's true, and would do better for the *Théâtre des Variétés*."

"There can be no doubt of that," I replied unwittingly, and not at first observing (so much had I been absorbed in reflection) the extraordinary manner in which the speaker had chimed in with my meditations. In an instant afterward I recollected myself, and my astonishment was profound.

"Dupin," said I, gravely, "this is beyond my comprehension. I do not hesitate to say that I am amazed, and can scarcely credit my senses. How was it possible you should know I was thinking of ——?" Here I paused, to ascertain beyond a doubt whether he really knew of whom I thought.

—"of Chantilly," said he, "why do you pause? You were remarking to yourself that his diminutive figure unfitted him for tragedy."

This was precisely what had formed the subject of my reflections. Chantilly was a *quondam* cobbler of the Rue St. Denis, who, becoming stage-mad, had attempted the *rôle* of Xerxes, in Crébillon's tragedy so called, and been notoriously Pasquinaded for his pains.

"Tell me, for Heaven's sake," I exclaimed, "the method—if method there is—by which you have been enabled to fathom my soul in this matter." In fact I was even more startled than I would have been willing to express.

"It was the fruiterer," replied my friend, "who brought you to the conclusion that the mender of soles was not of sufficient height for Xerxes *et id genus omne*."

"The fruiterer!—you astonish me—I know no fruiterer whomsoever."

"The man who ran up against you as we entered the street—it may have been fifteen minutes ago."

I now remembered that, in fact, a fruiterer, carrying upon his head a large basket of apples, had nearly thrown me down, by accident, as we passed from the Rue C —— into the thoroughfare where we stood; but what this had to do with Chantilly I could not possibly understand.

There was not a particle of *charlâtanerie* about Dupin. "I will explain," he said, "and that you may comprehend all clearly, we will first retrace the course of your meditations, from the moment in which I spoke to you until that of the *rencontre* with the fruiterer in question. The larger links of the chain run thus—Chantilly, Orion, Dr. Nichols, Epicurus, Stereotomy, the street stones, the fruiterer."

There are few persons who have not, at some period of their lives, amused themselves in retracing the steps by which particular conclusions of their own minds have been attained. The occupation is often full of interest and he who attempts it for the first time is astonished by the apparently illimitable distance and incoherence between the starting-point and the goal. What, then, must have been my amazement when I heard the Frenchman speak what he had just spoken, and when I could not help acknowledging that he had spoken the truth. He continued:

"We had been talking of horses, if I remember aright, just before leaving the Rue C ——. This was the last subject we discussed. As we crossed into this street, a fruiterer, with a large basket upon his head, brushing quickly past us, thrust you upon a pile of paving stones collected at a spot where the causeway is undergoing repair. You stepped upon one of the loose fragments, slipped, slightly strained your ankle, appeared vexed or sulky, muttered a few words, turned to look at the pile, and then proceeded in silence. I was not particularly attentive to what you did; but observation has become with me, of late, a species of necessity.

"You kept your eyes upon the ground—glancing, with a petulant expression, at the holes and ruts in the pavement, (so that I saw you were still thinking of the stones,) until we reached the little alley called Lamartine, which has been paved, by way of experiment, with the overlapping and riveted blocks. Here your countenance brightened up, and, perceiving your lips move, I could not doubt that you murmured the word 'stereotomy,' a term very affectedly applied to this species of pavement. I knew that you could not say to yourself 'stereotomy' without being brought to think of atomies, and thus of the theories of Epicurus; and since, when we discussed this subject not very long ago, I mentioned to you how singularly, yet with how little notice, the vague guesses of that noble Greek had met with confirmation in the late nebular cosmogony, I felt that you could not avoid casting your eyes upward to the great *nebula* in Orion, and I certainly expected that you would do so. You did look up; and I was now assured that I had correctly followed your steps. But in that bitter *tirade* upon Chantilly, which appeared in yesterday's '*Musée*,' the satirist, making some disgraceful allusions to the cobbler's change of name upon assuming the buskin, quoted a Latin line about which we have often conversed. I mean the line

Perdidit antiquum litera sonum.

"I had told you that this was in reference to Orion, formerly written Urion; and, from certain pungencies connected with this explanation, I was aware that you could not have forgotten it. It was clear, therefore, that you would not fail to combine the two ideas of Orion and Chantilly. That you did combine them I saw by the character of the smile which passed over your lips. You thought of the poor cobbler's immolation. So far, you had been stooping in your gait; but now I saw you draw yourself up to your full height. I was then sure that you reflected upon the diminutive figure of Chantilly. At this point I interrupted your meditations to remark that as, in fact, he was a very little fellow—that Chantilly—he would do better at the *Théâtre des Variétés*."

Not long after this, we were looking over an evening edition of the "Gazette des Tribunaux," when the following paragraphs arrested our attention.

"EXTRAORDINARY MURDERS.—This morning, about three o'clock, the inhabitants of the Quartier St. Roch were aroused from sleep by a succession of terrific shrieks, issuing, apparently, from the fourth story of a house in the Rue Morgue, known to be in the sole occupancy of one Madame L'Espanaye, and her daughter Mademoiselle Camille L'Espanaye. After some delay, occasioned by a fruitless attempt to procure admission in the usual manner, the gateway was broken in with a crowbar, and eight or ten of the neighbors entered accompanied by two gendarmes. By this time the cries had ceased; but, as the party rushed up the first flight of stairs, two or more rough voices in angry contention were distinguished and seemed to proceed from the upper part of the house. As the second landing was reached, these sounds, also, had ceased and everything remained perfectly quiet. The party spread themselves and hurried from room to room. Upon arriving at a large back chamber in the fourth story, (the door of which, being found locked, with the key inside, was forced open,) a spectacle presented itself which struck every one present not less with horror than with astonishment.

"The apartment was in the wildest disorder—the furniture broken and thrown about in all directions. There was only one bedstead; and from this the bed had been removed, and thrown into the middle of the floor. On a chair lay a razor, besmeared with blood. On the hearth were two or three long and thick tresses of grey human hair, also dabbled in blood, and seeming to have been pulled out by the roots. Upon the floor were found four Napoleons, an ear-ring of topaz, three large silver spoons, three smaller of *métal d'Alger*, and two bags, containing nearly four thousand francs in gold. The drawers of a *bureau*, which stood in one corner were open, and had been, apparently, rifled, although many articles still remained in them. A small iron safe was discovered under the *bed* (not under the bedstead). It was open, with the key still in the door. It had no contents beyond a few old letters, and other papers of little consequence.

"Of Madame L'Espanaye no traces were here seen; but an unusual quantity of soot being observed in the fire-place, a search was made in the chimney, and (horrible to relate!) the corpse of the daughter, head downward, was dragged therefrom; it having been thus forced up the narrow aperture for a considerable distance. The body was quite warm. Upon examining it, many excoriations were perceived, no doubt occasioned by the violence with which it had been thrust up and disengaged. Upon the face were many severe scratches, and, upon the throat, dark bruises, and deep indentations of finger nails, as if the deceased had been throttled to death.

"After a thorough investigation of every portion of the house, without farther discovery, the party made its way into a small paved yard in the rear of the building, where lay the corpse of the old lady, with her throat so entirely cut that, upon an attempt to raise her, the head fell off. The body, as well as the head, was fearfully mutilated—the former so much so as scarcely to retain any semblance of humanity.

"To this horrible mystery there is not as yet, we believe, the slightest clew."

The next day's paper had these additional particulars.

"*The Tragedy in the Rue Morgue.* Many individuals have been examined in relation to this most extraordinary and frightful affair. (The word 'affaire' has not yet, in France, that levity of import which it conveys with us,) "but nothing whatever has transpired to throw light upon it. We give below all the material testimony elicited.

"*Pauline Dubourg*, laundress, deposes that she has known both the deceased for three years, having washed for them during that period. The old lady and her daughter seemed on good terms—very affectionate towards each other. They were excellent pay. Could not speak in regard to their mode or means of living. Believed that Madame L. told fortunes for a living. Was reputed to have money put by. Never met any persons in the house when she called for the clothes or took them home. Was sure that they had no servant in employ. There appeared to be no furniture in any part of the building except in the fourth story.

"*Pierre Moreau*, tobacconist, deposes that he has been in the habit of selling small quantities of tobacco and snuff to Madame L'Espanaye for nearly four years. Was born in the neighborhood, and has always resided there. The deceased and her daughter had occupied the house in which the corpses were found, for more than six years. It was formerly occupied by a jeweller, who under-let the upper rooms to various persons. The house was the property of Madame L. She became dissatisfied with the abuse of the premises by her tenant, and moved into them herself, refusing to let any portion. The old lady was childish. Witness had seen the daughter some five or six times during the six years. The two lived an exceedingly retired life—were reputed to have money. Had heard it said among the neighbors that Madame L. told fortunes—did not believe it. Had never seen any person enter the door except the old lady and her daughter, a porter once or twice, and a physician some eight or ten times.

"Many other persons, neighbors, gave evidence to the same effect. No one was spoken of as frequenting the house. It was not known whether there were any living connexions of Madame L. and her daughter. The shutters of the front windows were seldom opened. Those in the rear were always closed, with the exception of the large back room, fourth story. The house was a good house—not very old.

"*Isidore Musèt, gendarme*, deposes that he was called to the house about three o'clock in the morning, and found some twenty or thirty persons at the gateway, endeavoring to gain admittance. Forced it open, at length, with a bayonet—not with a crowbar. Had but little difficulty in getting it open, on account of its being a double or folding gate, and bolted neither at bottom nor top. The shrieks were continued until the gate was forced—and then suddenly ceased. They seemed to be screams of some person (or persons) in great agony—were loud and drawn out, not short and quick. Witness led the way up stairs. Upon reaching the first landing, heard two voices in loud and angry contention—the one a gruff voice, the other much shriller—a very strange voice. Could distinguish some words of the former, which was that of a Frenchman. Was positive that it was not a woman's voice. Could distinguish the words 'sacré' and 'diable.' The shrill voice was that of a foreigner. Could not be sure whether it was the voice of a man or of a woman. Could not make out what was said, but believed the language to be Spanish. The state of the room and of the bodies was described by this witness as we described them yesterday.

"*Henri Duval*, a neighbor, and by trade a silver-smith, deposes that he was one of the party who first entered the house. Corroborates the testimony of Musèt in general. As soon as they forced an entrance, they reclosed the door, to keep out the crowd, which collected very fast, notwithstanding the lateness of the hour. The shrill voice, this witness thinks, was that of an Italian. Was certain it was not French. Could not be sure that it was a man's voice. It might have been a woman's. Was not acquainted with the Italian language. Could not distinguish the words, but was convinced by the intonation that the speaker was an Italian. Knew

Madame L. and her daughter. Had conversed with both frequently. Was sure that the shrill voice was not that of either of the deceased.

"—*Odenheimer, restaurateur.* This witness volunteered his testimony. Not speaking French, was examined through an interpreter. Is a native of Amsterdam. Was passing the house at the time of the shrieks. They lasted for several minutes—probably ten. They were long and loud—very awful and distressing. Was one of those who entered the building. Corroborated the previous evidence in every respect but one. Was sure that the shrill voice was that of a man—of a Frenchman. Could not distinguish the words uttered. They were loud and quick—unequal—spoken apparently in fear as well as in anger. The voice was harsh—not so much shrill as harsh. Could not call it a shrill voice. The gruff voice said repeatedly '*sacré,*' '*diable,*' and once '*mon Dieu.*'

"*Jules Mignaud,* banker, of the firm of Mignaud et Fils, Rue Deloraine. Is the elder Mignaud. Madame L'Espanaye had some property. Had opened an account with his banking house in the spring of the year—(eight years previously). Made frequent deposits in small sums. Had checked for nothing until the third day before her death, when she took out in person the sum of 4000 francs. This sum was paid in gold, and a clerk went home with the money.

"*Adolphe Le Bon,* clerk to Mignaud et Fils, deposes that on the day in question, about noon, he accompanied Madame L'Espanaye to her residence with the 4000 francs, put up in two bags. Upon the door being opened, Mademoiselle L. appeared and took from his hands one of the bags, while the old lady relieved him of the other. He then bowed and departed. Did not see any person in the street at the time. It is a bye-street—very lonely.

"*William Bird,* tailor deposes that he was one of the party who entered the house. Is an Englishman. Has lived in Paris two years. Was one of the first to ascend the stairs. Heard the voices in contention. The gruff voice was that of a Frenchman. Could make out several words, but cannot now remember all. Heard distinctly '*sacré*' and '*mon Dieu.*' There was a sound at the moment as if of several persons struggling—a scraping and scuffling sound. The shrill voice was very loud—louder than the gruff one. Is sure that it was not the voice of an Englishman. Appeared to be that of a German. Might have been a woman's voice. Does not understand German.

"Four of the above-named witnesses, being recalled, deposed that the door of the chamber in which was found the body of Mademoiselle L. was locked on the inside when the party reached it. Every thing was perfectly silent—no groans or noises of any kind. Upon forcing the door no person was seen. The windows, both of the back and front room, were down and firmly fastened from within. A door between the two rooms was closed, but not locked. The door leading from the front room into the passage was locked, with the key on the inside. A small room in the front of the house, on the fourth story, at the head of the passage was open, the door being ajar. This room was crowded with old beds, boxes, and so forth. These were carefully removed and searched. There was not an inch of any portion of the house which was not carefully searched. Sweeps were sent up and down the chimneys. The house was a four story one, with garrets (*mansardes.*) A trap-door on the roof was nailed down very securely—did not appear to have been opened for years. The time elapsing between the hearing of the voices in contention and the breaking open of the room door, was variously stated by the witnesses. Some made it as short as three minutes—some as long as five. The door was opened with difficulty.

"*Alfonzo Garcio,* undertaker, deposes that he resides in the Rue Morgue. Is a native of Spain. Was one of the party who entered the house. Did not proceed up stairs. Is nervous, and was apprehensive of the consequences of agitation. Heard the voices in contention. The gruff voice was that of a Frenchman. Could not distinguish what was said. The shrill voice was that of an Englishman—is sure of this. Does not understand the English language, but judges by the intonation.

"*Alberto Montani*, confectioner, deposes that he was among the first to ascend the stairs. Heard the voices in question. The gruff voice was that of a Frenchman. Distinguished several words. The speaker appeared to be expostulating. Could not make out the words of the shrill voice. Spoke quick and unevenly. Thinks it the voice of a Russian. Corroborates the general testimony. Is an Italian. Never conversed with a native of Russia.

"Several witnesses, recalled, here testified that the chimneys of all the rooms on the fourth story were too narrow to admit the passage of a human being. By 'sweeps' were meant cylindrical sweeping brushes, such as are employed by those who clean chimneys. These brushes were passed up and down every flue in the house. There is no back passage by which any one could have descended while the party proceeded up stairs. The body of Mademoiselle L'Espanaye was so firmly wedged in the chimney that it could not be got down until four or five of the party united their strength.

"*Paul Dumas*, physician, deposes that he was called to view the bodies about day-break. They were both then lying on the sacking of the bedstead in the chamber where Mademoiselle L. was found. The corpse of the young lady was much bruised and excoriated. The fact that it had been thrust up the chimney would sufficiently account for these appearances. The throat was greatly chafed. There were several deep scratches just below the chin, together with a series of livid spots which were evidently the impression of fingers. The face was fearfully discolored, and the eye-balls protruded. The tongue had been partially bitten through. A large bruise was discovered upon the pit of the stomach, produced, apparently, by the pressure of a knee. In the opinion of M. Dumas, Mademoiselle L'Espanaye had been throttled to death by some person or persons unknown. The corpse of the mother was horribly mutilated. All the bones of the right leg and arm were more or less shattered. The left *tibia* much splintered, as well as all the ribs of the left side. Whole body dreadfully bruised and discolored. It was not possible to say how the injuries had been inflicted. A heavy club of wood, or a broad bar of iron—a chair—any large, heavy, and obtuse weapon would have produced such results, if wielded by the hands of a very powerful man. No woman could have inflicted the blows with any weapon. The head of the deceased, when seen by witness, was entirely separated from the body, and was also greatly shattered. The throat had evidently been cut with some very sharp instrument—probably with a razor.

"*Alexandre Etienne*, surgeon, was called with M. Dumas to view the bodies. Corroborated the testimony, and the opinions of M. Dumas.

"Nothing farther of importance was elicited, although several other persons were examined. A murder so mysterious, and so perplexing in all its particulars, was never before committed in Paris—if indeed a murder has been committed at all. The police are entirely at fault—an unusual occurrence in affairs of this nature. There is not, however, the shadow of a clew apparent."

The evening edition of the paper stated that the greatest excitement still continued in the Quartier St. Roch—that the premises in question had been carefully re-searched, and fresh examinations of witnesses instituted, but all to no purpose. A postscript, however, mentioned that Adolphe Le Bon had been arrested and imprisoned—although nothing appeared to criminate him, beyond the facts already detailed.

Dupin seemed singularly interested in the progress of this affair—at least so I judged from his manner, for he made no comments. It was only after the announcement that Le Bon had been imprisoned, that he asked me my opinion respecting the murders.

I could merely agree with all Paris in considering them an insoluble mystery. I saw no means by which it would be possible to trace the murderer.

"We must not judge of the means," said Dupin, "by this shell of an examination. The Parisian police, so much extolled for *acumen*, are cunning, but no more. There is no method in their proceedings, beyond the method of the moment. They make a vast parade of measures; but, not unfrequently, these are so ill adapted to the objects proposed, as to put us in mind of Monsieur Jourdain's calling for his *robe-de-chambre—pour mieux entendre la musique.* The results attained by them are not unfrequently surprising, but, for the most part, are brought about by simple diligence and activity. When these qualities are unavailing, their schemes fail. Vidocq, for example, was a good guesser and a persevering man. But, without educated thought, he erred continually by the very intensity of his investigations. He impaired his vision by holding the object too close. He might see, perhaps, one or two points with unusual clearness, but in so doing he, necessarily, lost sight of the matter as a whole. Thus there is such a thing as being too profound. Truth is not always in a well. In fact, as regards the more important knowledge, I do believe that she is invariably superficial. The depth lies in the valleys where we seek her, and not upon the mountain-tops where she is found. The modes and sources of this kind of error are well typified in the contemplation of the heavenly bodies. To look at a star by glances—to view it in a side-long way, by turning toward it the exterior portions of the *retina* (more susceptible of feeble impressions of light than the interior), is to behold the star distinctly—is to have the best appreciation of its lustre—a lustre which grows dim just in proportion as we turn our vision *fully* upon it. A greater number of rays actually fall upon the eye in the latter case, but, in the former, there is the more refined capacity for comprehension. By undue profundity we perplex and enfeeble thought; and it is possible to make even Venus herself vanish from the firmament by a scrutiny too sustained, too concentrated, or too direct.

"As for these murders, let us enter into some examinations for ourselves, before we make up an opinion respecting them. An inquiry will afford us amusement," (I thought this an odd term, so applied, but said nothing) "and, besides, Le Bon once rendered me a service for which I am not ungrateful. We will go and see the premises with our own eyes. I know G—, the Prefect of Police, and shall have no difficulty in obtaining the necessary permission."

The permission was obtained, and we proceeded at once to the Rue Morgue. This is one of those miserable thoroughfares which intervene between the Rue Richelieu and the Rue St. Roch. It was late in the afternoon when we reached it; as this quarter is at a great distance from that in which we resided. The house was readily found; for there were still many persons gazing up at the closed shutters, with an objectless curiosity, from the opposite side of the way. It was an ordinary Parisian house, with a gateway, on one side of which was a glazed watch-box, with a sliding panel in the window, indicating a *loge de concierge.* Before going in we walked up the street, turned down an alley, and then, again turning, passed in the rear of the building—Dupin, meanwhile examining the whole neighborhood, as well as the house, with a minuteness of attention for which I could see no possible object.

Retracing our steps, we came again to the front of the dwelling, rang, and, having shown our credentials, were admitted by the agents in charge. We went up stairs—into the chamber where the body of Mademoiselle L'Espanaye had been found, and where both the deceased still lay. The disorders of the room had, as usual, been suffered to exist. I saw nothing beyond what had been stated in the "Gazette des Tribunaux." Dupin scrutinized every thing—not excepting the bodies of the victims. We then went into the other rooms, and into the yard; a *gendarme* accompanying us throughout. The examination occupied us until dark, when we took our departure. On our way home my companion stepped in for a moment at the office of one of the daily papers.

I have said that the whims of my friend were manifold, and that *Je les ménagais*:—for this phrase there is no English equivalent. It was his humor, now, to decline all conversation on the subject of the murder, until about noon the next day. He then asked me, suddenly, if I had observed any thing *peculiar* at the scene of the atrocity.

There was something in his manner of emphasizing the word "peculiar," which caused me to shudder, without knowing why.

"No, nothing *peculiar*," I said; "nothing more, at least, than we both saw stated in the paper."

"The 'Gazette,'" he replied, "has not entered, I fear, into the unusual horror of the thing. But dismiss the idle opinions of this print. It appears to me that this mystery is considered insoluble, for the very reason which should cause it to be regarded as easy of solution—I mean for the *outré* character of its features. The police are confounded by the seeming absence of motive—not for the murder itself—but for the atrocity of the murder. They are puzzled, too, by the seeming impossibility of reconciling the voices heard in contention, with the facts that no one was discovered up stairs but the assassinated Mademoiselle L'Espanaye, and that there were no means of egress without the notice of the party ascending. The wild disorder of the room; the corpse thrust, with the head downward, up the chimney; the frightful mutilation of the body of the old lady; these considerations, with those just mentioned, and others which I need not mention, have sufficed to paralyze the powers, by putting completely at fault the boasted *acumen*, of the government agents. They have fallen into the gross but common error of confounding the unusual with the abstruse. But it is by these deviations from the plane of the ordinary, that reason feels its way, if at all, in its search for the true. In investigations such as we are now pursuing, it should not be so much asked 'what has occurred,' as 'what has occurred that has never occurred before.' In fact, the facility with which I shall arrive, or have arrived, at the solution of this mystery, is in the direct ratio of its apparent insolubility in the eyes of the police."

I stared at the speaker in mute astonishment.

"I am now awaiting," continued he, looking toward the door of our apartment—"I am now awaiting a person who, although perhaps not the perpetrator of these butcheries, must have been in some measure implicated in their perpetration. Of the worst portion of the crimes committed, it is probable that he is innocent. I hope that I am right in this supposition; for upon it I build my expectation of reading the entire riddle. I look for the man here—in this room—every moment. It is true that he may not arrive; but the probability is that he will. Should he come, it will be necessary to detain him. Here are pistols; and we both know how to use them when occasion demands their use."

I took the pistols, scarcely knowing what I did, or believing what I heard, while Dupin went on, very much as if in a soliloquy. I have already spoken of his abstract manner at such times. His discourse was addressed to myself; but his voice, although by no means loud, had that intonation which is commonly employed in speaking to some one at a great distance. His eyes, vacant in expression, regarded only the wall.

"That the voices heard in contention," he said, "by the party upon the stairs, were not the voices of the women themselves, was fully proved by the evidence. This relieves us of all doubt upon the question whether the old lady could have first destroyed the daughter and afterward have committed suicide. I speak of this point chiefly for the sake of method; for the strength of Madame L'Espanaye would have been utterly unequal to the task of thrusting her daughter's corpse up the chimney as it was found; and the nature of the wounds upon her own person entirely preclude the idea of self-destruction. Murder, then, has been committed by some third party; and the voices of this third party were those heard in contention. Let me now advert—not to the whole testimony respecting these voices—but to what was *peculiar* in that testimony. Did you observe any thing peculiar about it?"

I remarked that, while all the witnesses agreed in supposing the gruff voice to be that of a Frenchman, there was much disagreement in regard to the shrill, or, as one individual termed it, the harsh voice.

"That was the evidence itself," said Dupin, "but it was not the peculiarity of the evidence. You have observed nothing distinctive. Yet there *was* something to be observed. The witnesses, as you remark, agreed about the gruff voice; they were here unanimous. But in regard to the shrill voice, the peculiarity is—not that they disagreed—but that, while an Italian, an Englishman, a Spaniard, a Hollander, and a Frenchman attempted to describe it, each one spoke of it as that *of a foreigner*. Each is sure that it was not the voice of one of his own countrymen. Each likens it—not to the voice of an individual of any nation with whose language he is conversant—but the converse. The Frenchman supposes it the voice of a Spaniard, and 'might have distinguished some words *had he been acquainted with the Spanish*.' The Dutchman maintains it to have been that of a Frenchman; but we find it stated that '*not understanding French this witness was examined through an interpreter*.' The Englishman thinks it the voice of a German, and '*does not understand German*.'

"The Spaniard 'is sure' that it was that of an Englishman, but 'judges by the intonation' altogether, '*as he has no knowledge of the English*.' The Italian believes it the voice of a Russian, but '*has never conversed with a native of Russia*.' A second Frenchman differs, moreover, with the first, and is positive that the voice was that of an Italian; but, *not being cognizant of that tongue*, is, like the Spaniard, 'convinced by the intonation.' Now, how strangely unusual must that voice have really been, about which such testimony as this *could* have been elicited!—in whose *tones*, even, denizens of the five great divisions of Europe could recognise nothing familiar! You will say that it might have been the voice of an Asiatic—of an African. Neither Asiatics nor Africans abound in Paris; but, without denying the inference, I will now merely call your attention to three points. The voice is termed by one witness 'harsh rather than shrill.' It is represented by two others to have been 'quick and *unequal*.' No words—no sounds resembling words—were by any witness mentioned as distinguishable.

"I know not," continued Dupin, "what impression I may have made, so far, upon your own understanding; but I do not hesitate to say that legitimate deductions even from this portion of the testimony—the portion respecting the gruff and shrill voices—are in themselves sufficient to engender a suspicion which should give direction to all farther progress in the investigation of the mystery. I said 'legitimate deductions;' but my meaning is not thus fully expressed. I designed to imply that the deductions are the *sole* proper ones, and that the suspicion arises *inevitably* from them as the single result. What the suspicion is, however, I will not say just yet. I merely wish you to bear in mind that, with myself, it was sufficiently forcible to give a definite form—a certain tendency—to my inquiries in the chamber.

"Let us now transport ourselves, in fancy, to this chamber. What shall we first seek here? The means of egress employed by the murderers. It is not too much to say that neither of us believe in præternatural events. Madame and Mademoiselle L'Espanaye were not destroyed by spirits. The doers of the deed were material, and escaped materially. Then how? Fortunately, there is but one mode of reasoning upon the point, and that mode *must* lead us to a definite decision.—Let us examine, each by each, the possible means of egress. It is clear that the assassins were in the room where Mademoiselle L'Espanaye was found, or at least in the room adjoining, when the party ascended the stairs. It is then only from these two apartments that we have to seek issues. The police have laid bare the floors, the ceilings, and the masonry of the walls, in every direction. No *secret* issues could have escaped their vigilance. But, not trusting to *their* eyes, I examined with my own. There were, then, no secret issues. Both doors leading from the rooms into the passage were securely locked, with the keys inside. Let us turn to the chimneys. These, although of ordinary width for some eight or ten feet above the hearths, will not admit, throughout their extent, the body of a large cat. The impossibility of egress, by means already stated, being thus absolute, we are reduced to the windows. Through those of the front room no one could have escaped without notice from the crowd in the street. The murderers *must* have passed, then, through those of the back room. Now, brought to this conclusion in so unequivocal a manner as we are, it is not our part, as reasoners, to reject it on account of apparent impossibilities. It is only left for us to prove that these apparent 'impossibilities' are, in reality, not such.

"There are two windows in the chamber. One of them is unobstructed by furniture, and is wholly visible. The lower portion of the other is hidden from view by the head of the unwieldy bedstead which is thrust close up against it. The former was found securely fastened from within. It resisted the utmost force of those who endeavored to raise it. A large gimlet-hole had been pierced in its frame to the left, and a very stout nail was found fitted therein, nearly to the head. Upon examining the other window, a similar nail was seen similarly fitted in it; and a vigorous attempt to raise this sash, failed also. The police were now entirely satisfied that egress had not been in these directions. And, *therefore*, it was thought a matter of supererogation to withdraw the nails and open the windows.

"My own examination was somewhat more particular, and was so for the reason I have just given—because here it was, I knew, that all apparent impossibilities *must* be proved to be not such in reality.

"I proceeded to think thus—*à posteriori*. The murderers did escape from one of these windows. This being so, they could not have refastened the sashes from the inside, as they were found fastened;—the consideration which put a stop, through its obviousness, to the scrutiny of the police in this quarter. Yet the sashes *were* fastened. They *must*, then, have the power of fastening themselves. There was no escape from this conclusion. I stepped to the unobstructed casement, withdrew the nail with some difficulty and attempted to raise the sash. It resisted all my efforts, as I had anticipated. A concealed spring must, I now know, exist; and this corroboration of my idea convinced me that my premises at least, were correct, however mysterious still appeared the circumstances attending the nails. A careful search soon brought to light the hidden spring. I pressed it, and, satisfied with the discovery, forbore to upraise the sash.

"I now replaced the nail and regarded it attentively. A person passing out through this window might have reclosed it, and the spring would have caught—but the nail could not have been replaced. The conclusion was plain, and again narrowed in the field of my investigations. The assassins *must* have escaped through the other window. Supposing, then, the springs upon each sash to be the same, as was probable, there *must* be found a difference between the nails, or at least between the modes of their fixture. Getting upon the sacking of the bedstead, I looked over the head-board minutely at the second casement. Passing my hand down behind the board, I readily discovered and pressed the spring, which was, as I had supposed, identical in character with its neighbor. I now looked at the nail. It was as stout as the other, and apparently fitted in the same manner—driven in nearly up to the head.

"You will say that I was puzzled; but, if you think so, you must have misunderstood the nature of the inductions. To use a sporting phrase, I had not been once 'at fault.' The scent had never for an instant been lost. There was no flaw in any link of the chain. I had traced the secret to its ultimate result,—and that result was *the nail*. It had, I say, in every respect, the appearance of its fellow in the other window; but this fact was an absolute nullity (conclusive as it might seem to be) when compared with the consideration that here, at this point, terminated the clew. 'There *must* be something wrong,' I said, 'about the nail.' I touched it; and the head, with about a quarter of an inch of the shank, came off in my fingers. The rest of the shank was in the gimlet-hole where it had been broken off. The fracture was an old one (for its edges were incrusted with rust), and had apparently been accomplished by the blow of a hammer, which had partially imbedded, in the top of the bottom sash, the head portion of the nail. I now carefully replaced this head portion in the indentation whence I had taken it, and the resemblance to a perfect nail was complete—the fissure was invisible. Pressing the spring, I gently raised the sash for a few inches; the head went up with it, remaining firm in its bed. I closed the window, and the semblance of the whole nail was again perfect.

"The riddle, so far, was now unriddled. The assassin had escaped through the window which looked upon the bed. Dropping of its own accord upon his exit (or perhaps purposely closed), it had become fastened by the spring; and it was the retention of this spring which had been mistaken by the police for that of the nail,—farther inquiry being thus considered unnecessary.

"The next question is that of the mode of descent. Upon this point I had been satisfied in my walk with you around the building. About five feet and a half from the casement in question there runs a lightning-rod. From this rod it would have been impossible for any one to reach the window itself, to say nothing of entering it. I observed, however, that the shutters of the fourth story were of the peculiar kind called by Parisian carpenters *ferrades*—a kind rarely employed at the present day, but frequently seen upon very old mansions at Lyons and Bourdeaux. They are in the form of an ordinary door, (a single, not a folding door) except that the lower half is latticed or worked in open trellis—thus affording an excellent hold for the hands. In the present instance these shutters are fully three feet and a half broad. When we saw them from the rear of the house, they were both about half open—that is to say, they stood off at right angles from the wall. It is probable that the police, as well as myself, examined the back of the tenement; but, if so, in looking at these *ferrades* in the line of their breadth (as they must have done), they did not perceive this great breadth itself, or, at all events, failed to take it into due consideration. In fact, having once satisfied themselves that no egress could have been made in this quarter, they would naturally bestow here a very cursory examination. It was clear to me, however, that the shutter belonging to the window at the head of the bed, would, if swung fully back to the wall, reach to within two feet of the lightning-rod. It was also evident that, by exertion of a very unusual degree of activity and courage, an entrance into the window, from the rod, might have been thus effected.—By reaching to the distance of two feet and a half (we now suppose the shutter open to its whole extent) a robber might have taken a firm grasp upon the trellis-work. Letting go, then, his hold upon the rod, placing his feet securely against the wall, and springing boldly from it, he might have swung the shutter so as to close it, and, if we imagine the window open at the time, might even have swung himself into the room.

"I wish you to bear especially in mind that I have spoken of a *very* unusual degree of activity as requisite to success in so hazardous and so difficult a feat. It is my design to show you, first, that the thing might possibly have been accomplished:—but, secondly and *chiefly*, I wish to impress upon your understanding the *very extraordinary*—the almost præternatural character of that agility which could have accomplished it.

"You will say, no doubt, using the language of the law, that 'to make out my case,' I should rather undervalue, than insist upon a full estimation of the activity required in this matter. This may be the practice in law, but it is not the usage of reason. My ultimate object is only the truth. My immediate purpose is to lead you to place in juxtaposition, that *very unusual* activity of which I have just spoken with that *very peculiar* shrill (or harsh) and *unequal* voice, about whose nationality no two persons could be found to agree, and in whose utterance no syllabification could be detected."

At these words a vague and half-formed conception of the meaning of Dupin flitted over my mind. I seemed to be upon the verge of comprehension without power to comprehend—men, at times, find themselves upon the brink of remembrance without being able, in the end, to remember. My friend went on with his discourse.

"You will see," he said, "that I have shifted the question from the mode of egress to that of ingress. It was my design to convey the idea that both were effected in the same manner, at the same point. Let us now revert to the interior of the room. Let us survey the appearances here. The drawers of the bureau, it is said, had been rifled, although many articles of apparel still remained within them. The conclusion here is absurd. It is a mere guess—a very silly one—and no more. How are we to know that the articles found in the drawers were not all these drawers had originally contained? Madame L'Espanaye and her daughter lived an exceedingly retired life—saw no company—seldom went out—had little use for numerous changes of habiliment. Those found were at least of as good quality as any likely to be possessed by these ladies. If a thief had taken any, why did he not take the best—why did he not take all? In a word, why did he abandon four thousand francs in gold to encumber himself with a bundle of linen? The gold *was* abandoned. Nearly the whole sum mentioned by Monsieur Mignaud, the banker, was discovered, in bags, upon the floor. I wish you, therefore, to discard from your thoughts the blundering idea of *motive*, engendered in the brains of the police by that portion of the evidence which speaks of money delivered at the door of the house. Coincidences ten times as remarkable as this (the delivery of the money, and murder committed within three days upon the party receiving it), happen to all of us every hour of our lives, without attracting even momentary notice. Coincidences, in general, are great stumbling-blocks in the way of that class of thinkers who have been educated to know nothing of the theory of probabilities—that theory to which the most glorious objects of human research are indebted for the most glorious of illustration. In the present instance, had the gold been gone, the fact of its delivery three days before would have formed something more than a coincidence. It would have been corroborative of this idea of motive. But, under the real circumstances of the case, if we are to suppose gold the motive of this outrage, we must also imagine the perpetrator so vacillating an idiot as to have abandoned his gold and his motive together.

"Keeping now steadily in mind the points to which I have drawn your attention—that peculiar voice, that unusual agility, and that startling absence of motive in a murder so singularly atrocious as this—let us glance at the butchery itself. Here is a woman strangled to death by manual strength, and thrust up a chimney, head downward. Ordinary assassins employ no such modes of murder as this. Least of all, do they thus dispose of the murdered. In the manner of thrusting the corpse up the chimney, you will admit that there was something *excessively outré*—something altogether irreconcilable with our common notions of human action, even when we suppose the actors the most depraved of men. Think, too, how great must have been that strength which could have thrust the body *up* such an aperture so forcibly that the united vigor of several persons was found barely sufficient to drag it *down!*

"Turn, now, to other indications of the employment of a vigor most marvellous. On the hearth were thick tresses—very thick tresses—of grey human hair. These had been torn out by the roots. You are aware of the great force necessary in tearing thus from the head even twenty or thirty hairs together. You saw the locks in question as well as myself. Their roots (a hideous sight!) were clotted with fragments of the flesh of the scalp—sure token of the prodigious power which had been exerted in uprooting perhaps half a million of hairs at a time. The throat of the old lady was not merely cut, but the head absolutely severed from the body: the instrument was a mere razor. I wish you also to look at the *brutal* ferocity of these deeds. Of the bruises upon the body of Madame L'Espanaye I do not speak. Monsieur Dumas, and his worthy coadjutor Monsieur Etienne, have pronounced that they were inflicted by some obtuse instrument; and so far these gentlemen are very correct. The obtuse instrument was clearly the stone pavement in the yard, upon which the victim had fallen from the window which looked in upon the bed. This idea, however simple it may now seem, escaped the police for the same reason that the breadth of the shutters escaped them—because, by the affair of the nails, their perceptions had been hermetically sealed against the possibility of the windows having ever been opened at all.

"If now, in addition to all these things, you have properly reflected upon the odd disorder of the chamber, we have gone so far as to combine the ideas of an agility astounding, a strength superhuman, a ferocity brutal, a butchery without motive, a *grotesquerie* in horror absolutely alien from humanity, and a voice foreign in tone to the ears of men of many nations, and devoid of all distinct or intelligible syllabification. What result, then, has ensued? What impression have I made upon your fancy?"

I felt a creeping of the flesh as Dupin asked me the question. "A madman," I said, "has done this deed—some raving maniac, escaped from a neighboring *Maison de Santé.*"

"In some respects," he replied, "your idea is not irrelevant. But the voices of madmen, even in their wildest paroxysms, are never found to tally with that peculiar voice heard upon the stairs. Madmen are of some nation, and their language, however incoherent in its words, has always the coherence of syllabification. Besides, the hair of a madman is not such as I now hold in my hand. I disentangled this little tuft from the rigidly clutched fingers of Madame L'Espanaye. Tell me what you can make of it."

"Dupin!" I said, completely unnerved; "this hair is most unusual—this is no *human* hair."

"I have not asserted that it is," said he; "but, before we decide this point, I wish you to glance at the little sketch I have here traced upon this paper. It is a *fac-simile* drawing of what has been described in one portion of the testimony as 'dark bruises, and deep indentations of finger nails,' upon the throat of Mademoiselle L'Espanaye, and in another, (by Messrs. Dumas and Etienne,) as a 'series of livid spots, evidently the impression of fingers.'

"You will perceive," continued my friend, spreading out the paper upon the table before us, "that this drawing gives the idea of a firm and fixed hold. There is no *slipping* apparent. Each finger has retained—possibly until the death of the victim—the fearful grasp by which it originally imbedded itself. Attempt, now, to place all your fingers, at the same time, in the respective impressions as you see them."

I made the attempt in vain.

"We are possibly not giving this matter a fair trial," he said. "The paper is spread out upon a plane surface; but the human throat is cylindrical. Here is a billet of wood, the circumference of which is about that of the throat. Wrap the drawing around it, and try the experiment again."

I did so; but the difficulty was even more obvious than before. "This," I said, "is the mark of no human hand."

"Read now," replied Dupin, "this passage from Cuvier."

It was a minute anatomical and generally descriptive account of the large fulvous Ourang-Outang of the East Indian Islands. The gigantic stature, the prodigious strength and activity, the wild ferocity, and the imitative propensities of these mammalia are sufficiently well known to all. I understood the full horrors of the murder at once.

"The description of the digits," said I, as I made an end of reading, "is in exact accordance with this drawing. I see that no animal but an Ourang-Outang, of the species here mentioned, could have impressed the indentations as you have traced them. This tuft of tawny hair, too, is identical in character with that of the beast of Cuvier. But I cannot possibly comprehend the particulars of this frightful mystery. Besides, there were *two* voices heard in contention, and one of them was unquestionably the voice of a Frenchman."

"True; and you will remember an expression attributed almost unanimously, by the evidence, to this voice,—the expression, '*mon Dieu!*' This, under the circumstances, has been justly characterized by one of the witnesses (Montani, the confectioner,) as an expression of remonstrance or expostulation. Upon these two words, therefore, I have mainly built my hopes of a full solution of the riddle. A Frenchman was cognizant of the murder. It is possible—indeed it is far more than probable—that he was innocent of all participation in the bloody transactions which took place. The Ourang-Outang may have escaped from him. He may have traced it to the chamber; but, under the agitating circumstances which ensued, he could never have re-captured it. It is still at large. I will not pursue these guesses—for I have no right to call them more—since the shades of reflection upon which they are based are scarcely of sufficient depth to be appreciable by my own intellect, and since I could not pretend to make them intelligible to the understanding of another. We will call them guesses then, and speak of them as such. If the Frenchman in question is indeed, as I suppose, innocent of this atrocity, this advertisement which I left last night, upon our return home, at the office of 'Le Monde,' (a paper devoted to the shipping interest, and much sought by sailors,) will bring him to our residence."

He handed me a paper, and I read thus:

CAUGHT—*In the Bois de Boulogne, early in the morning of the—inst., (the morning of the murder,) a very large, tawny Ourang-Outang of the Bornese species. The owner, (who is ascertained to be a sailor, belonging to a Maltese vessel,) may have the animal again, upon identifying it satisfactorily, and paying a few charges arising from its capture and keeping. Call at No. ——, Rue ——, Faubourg St. Germain—au troisiême.*

"How was it possible," I asked, "that you should know the man to be a sailor, and belonging to a Maltese vessel?"

"I do *not* know it," said Dupin. "I am not *sure* of it. Here, however, is a small piece of ribbon, which from its form, and from its greasy appearance, has evidently been used in tying the hair in one of those long *queues* of which sailors are so fond. Moreover, this knot is one which few besides sailors can tie, and is peculiar to the Maltese. I picked the ribbon up at the foot of the lightning-rod. It could not have belonged to either of the deceased. Now if, after all, I am wrong in my induction from this ribbon, that the Frenchman was a sailor belonging to a Maltese vessel, still I can have done no harm in saying what I did in the advertisement. If I am in error, he will merely suppose that I have been misled by some circumstance into which he will not take the trouble to inquire. But if I am right, a great point is gained. Cognizant although innocent of the murder, the Frenchman will naturally hesitate about replying to the advertisement—about demanding the Ourang-Outang. He will reason thus:—'I am innocent; I am poor; my Ourang-Outang is of great value—to one in my circumstances a fortune of itself—why should I lose it through idle apprehensions of danger? Here it is, within my grasp. It was found in the Bois de Boulogne—at a vast distance from the scene of that butchery. How can it ever be suspected that a brute beast should have done the deed? The police are at fault—they have failed to procure the slightest clew. Should they even trace the animal, it would be impossible to prove me cognizant of the murder, or to implicate me in guilt on account of that cognizance. Above all, *I am known.* The advertiser designates me as the possessor of the beast. I am not sure to what limit his knowledge may extend. Should I avoid claiming a property of so great value, which it is known that I possess, I will render the animal at least, liable to suspicion. It is not my policy to attract attention either to myself or to the beast. I will answer the advertisement, get the Ourang-Outang, and keep it close until this matter has blown over.'"

At this moment we heard a step upon the stairs.

"Be ready," said Dupin, "with your pistols, but neither use them nor show them until at a signal from myself."

The front door of the house had been left open, and the visiter had entered, without ringing, and advanced several steps upon the staircase. Now, however, he seemed to hesitate. Presently we heard him descending. Dupin was moving quickly to the door, when we again heard him coming up. He did not turn back a second time, but stepped up with decision, and rapped at the door of our chamber.

"Come in," said Dupin, in a cheerful and hearty tone.

A man entered. He was a sailor, evidently,—a tall, stout, and muscular-looking person, with a certain dare-devil expression of countenance, not altogether unprepossessing. His face, greatly sunburnt, was more than half hidden by whisker and *mustachio*. He had with him a huge oaken cudgel, but appeared to be otherwise unarmed. He bowed awkwardly, and bade us "good evening," in French accents, which, although somewhat Neufchatelish, were still sufficiently indicative of a Parisian origin.

"Sit down, my friend," said Dupin. "I suppose you have called about the Ourang-Outang. Upon my word, I almost envy you the possession of him; a remarkably fine, and no doubt a very valuable animal. How old do you suppose him to be?"

The sailor drew a long breath, with the air of a man relieved of some intolerable burden, and then replied, in an assured tone:

"I have no way of telling—but he can't be more than four or five years old. Have you got him here?"

"Oh no, we had no conveniences for keeping him here. He is at a livery stable in the Rue Dubourg, just by. You can get him in the morning. Of course you are prepared to identify the property?"

"To be sure I am, sir."

"I shall be sorry to part with him," said Dupin.

"I don't mean that you should be at all this trouble for nothing, sir," said the man. "Couldn't expect it. Am very willing to pay a reward for the finding of the animal—that is to say, any thing in reason."

"Well," replied my friend, "that is all very fair, to be sure. Let me think!—what should I have? Oh! I will tell you. My reward shall be this. You shall give me all the information in your power about these murders in the Rue Morgue."

Dupin said the last words in a very low tone, and very quietly. Just as quietly, too, he walked toward the door, locked it and put the key in his pocket. He then drew a pistol from his bosom and placed it, without the least flurry, upon the table.

The sailor's face flushed up as if he were struggling with suffocation. He started to his feet and grasped his cudgel, but the next moment he fell back into his seat, trembling violently, and with the countenance of death itself. He spoke not a word. I pitied him from the bottom of my heart.

"My friend," said Dupin, in a kind tone, "you are alarming yourself unnecessarily—you are indeed. We mean you no harm whatever. I pledge you the honor of a gentleman, and of a Frenchman, that we intend you no injury. I perfectly well know that you are innocent of the atrocities in the Rue Morgue. It will not do, however, to deny that you are in some measure implicated in them. From what I have already said, you must know that I have had means of information about this matter—means of which you could never have dreamed. Now the thing stands thus. You have done nothing which you could have avoided—nothing, certainly, which renders you culpable. You were not even guilty of robbery, when you might have robbed with impunity. You have nothing to conceal. You have no reason for concealment. On the other hand, you are bound by every principle of honor to confess all you know. An innocent man is now imprisoned, charged with that crime of which you can point out the perpetrator."

The sailor had recovered his presence of mind, in a great measure, while Dupin uttered these words; but his original boldness of bearing was all gone.

"So help me God," said he, after a brief pause, "I will tell you all I know about this affair;—but I do not expect you to believe one half I say—I would be a fool indeed if I did. Still, I am innocent, and I will make a clean breast if I die for it."

What he stated was, in substance, this. He had lately made a voyage to the Indian Archipelago. A party, of which he formed one, landed at Borneo, and passed into the interior on an excursion of pleasure. Himself and a companion had captured the Ourang-Outang. This companion dying, the animal fell into his own exclusive possession. After great trouble, occa-

sioned by the intractable ferocity of his captive during the home voyage, he at length succeeded in lodging it safely at his own residence in Paris, where, not to attract toward himself
the unpleasant curiosity of his neighbors, he kept it carefully secluded, until such time as it
should recover from a wound in the foot, received from a splinter on board ship. His ultimate
design was to sell it.

Returning home from some sailors' frolic the night, or rather in the morning of the murder,
he found the beast occupying his own bed-room, into which it had broken from a closet
adjoining, where it had been, as was thought, securely confined. Razor in hand, and fully
lathered, it was sitting before a looking-glass, attempting the operation of shaving, in which it
had no doubt previously watched its master through the key-hole of the closet. Terrified at the
sight of so dangerous a weapon in the possession of an animal so ferocious, and so well able to
use it, the man, for some moments, was at a loss what to do. He had been accustomed, however, to quiet the creature, even in its fiercest moods, by the use of a whip, and to this he now
resorted. Upon sight of it, the Ourang-Outang sprang at once through the door of the chamber, down the stairs, and thence, through a window, unfortunately open, into the street.

The Frenchman followed in despair; the ape, razor still in hand, occasionally stopping to
look back and gesticulate at its pursuer, until the latter had nearly come up with it. It then
again made off. In this manner the chase continued for a long time. The streets were profoundly quiet, as it was nearly three o'clock in the morning. In passing down an alley in the
rear of the Rue Morgue, the fugitive's attention was arrested by a light gleaming from the
open window of Madame L'Espanaye's chamber, in the fourth story of her house. Rushing to
the building, it perceived the lightning rod, clambered up with inconceivable agility, grasped
the shutter, which was thrown fully back against the wall, and, by its means, swung itself
directly upon the headboard of the bed. The whole feat did not occupy a minute. The shutter was kicked open again by the Ourang-Outang as it entered the room.

The sailor, in the meantime, was both rejoiced and perplexed. He had strong hopes of now
recapturing the brute, as it could scarcely escape from the trap into which it had ventured,
except by the rod, where it might be intercepted as it came down. On the other hand, there
was much cause for anxiety as to what it might do in the house. This latter reflection urged
the man still to follow the fugitive. A lightning rod is ascended without difficulty, especially
by a sailor; but, when he had arrived as high as the window, which lay far to his left, his career
was stopped; the most that he could accomplish was to reach over so as to obtain a glimpse
of the interior of the room. At this glimpse he nearly fell from his hold through excess of
horror. Now it was that those hideous shrieks arose upon the night, which had startled from
slumber the inmates of the Rue Morgue. Madame L'Espanaye and her daughter, habited in
their night clothes, had apparently been occupied in arranging some papers in the iron chest
already mentioned, which had been wheeled into the middle of the room. It was open, and
its contents lay beside it on the floor. The victims must have been sitting with their backs
toward the window; and, from the time elapsing between the ingress of the beast and the
screams, it seems probable that it was not immediately perceived. The flapping-to of the shutter would naturally have been attributed to the wind.

As the sailor looked in, the gigantic animal had seized Madame L'Espanaye by the hair,
(which was loose, as she had been combing it,) and was flourishing the razor about her face,
in imitation of the motions of a barber. The daughter lay prostrate and motionless; she had
swooned. The screams and struggles of the old lady (during which the hair was torn from her

head) had the effect of changing the probably pacific purposes of the Ourang-Outang into those of wrath. With one determined sweep of its muscular arm it nearly severed her head from her body. The sight of blood inflamed its anger into phrenzy. Gnashing its teeth, and flashing fire from its eyes, it flew upon the body of the girl, and imbedded its fearful talons in her throat, retaining its grasp until she expired. Its wandering and wild glances fell at this moment upon the head of the bed, over which the face of its master, rigid with horror, was just discernible. The fury of the beast, who no doubt bore still in mind the dreaded whip, was instantly converted into fear. Conscious of having deserved punishment, it seemed desirous of concealing its bloody deeds, and skipped about the chamber in an agony of nervous agitation; throwing down and breaking the furniture as it moved, and dragging the bed from the bedstead. In conclusion, it seized first the corpse of the daughter, and thrust it up the chimney, as it was found; then that of the old lady, which it immediately hurled through the window headlong.

As the ape approached the casement with its mutilated burden, the sailor shrank aghast to the rod, and, rather gliding than clambering down it, hurried at once home—dreading the consequences of the butchery, and gladly abandoning, in his terror, all solicitude about the fate of the Ourang-Outang. The words heard by the party upon the staircase were the Frenchman's exclamations of horror and affright, commingled with the fiendish jabberings of the brute.

I have scarcely anything to add. The Ourang-Outang must have escaped from the chamber, by the rod, just before the break of the door. It must have closed the window as it passed through it. It was subsequently caught by the owner himself, who obtained for it a very large sum at the *Jardin des Plantes*. Le Bon was instantly released, upon our narration of the circumstances (with some comments from Dupin) at the bureau of the Prefect of Police. This functionary, however well disposed to my friend, could not altogether conceal his chagrin at the turn which affairs had taken, and was fain to indulge in a sarcasm or two, about the propriety of every person minding his own business.

"Let him talk," said Dupin, who had not thought it necessary to reply. "Let him discourse; it will ease his conscience, I am satisfied with having defeated him in his own castle. Nevertheless, that he failed in the solution of this mystery, is by no means that matter for wonder which he supposes it; for, in truth, our friend the Prefect is somewhat too cunning to be profound. In his wisdom is no *stamen*. It is all head and no body, like the pictures of the Goddess Laverna,—or, at best, all head and shoulders, like a codfish. But he is a good creature after all. I like him especially for one master stroke of cant, by which he has attained his reputation for ingenuity. I mean the way he has '*de nier ce qui est, et d'expliquer ce qui n'est pas.*'" *

* Rousseau—Nouvelle Heloise.

The Day They Burned the Books
(1960)

JEAN RHYS

My friend Eddie was a small, thin boy. You could see the blue veins in his wrists and temples. People said that he had consumption and wasn't long for this world. I loved, but sometimes despised him.

His father, Mr Sawyer, was a strange man. Nobody could make out what he was doing in our part of the world at all. He was not a planter or a doctor or a lawyer or a banker. He didn't keep a store. He wasn't a schoolmaster or a government official. He wasn't – that was the point – a gentleman. We had several resident romantics who had fallen in love with the moon on the Caribees – they were all gentlemen and quite unlike Mr Sawyer who hadn't an 'h' in his composition. Besides, he detested the moon and everything else about the Caribbean and he didn't mind telling you so.

He was agent for a small steamship line which in those days linked up Venezuela and Trinidad with the smaller islands, but he couldn't make much out of that. He must have a private income, people decided, but they never decided why he had chosen to settle in a place he didn't like and to marry a coloured woman. Though a decent, respectable, nicely educated coloured woman, mind you.

Mrs Sawyer must have been very pretty once but, what with one thing and another, that was in days gone by.

When Mr Sawyer was drunk – this often happened – he used to be very rude to her. She never answered him.

'Look at the nigger showing off,' he would say; and she would smile as if she knew she ought to see the joke but couldn't. 'You damned, long-eyed gloomy half-caste, you don't smell right,' he would say; and she never answered, not even to whisper, 'You don't smell right to me, either.'

The story went that once they had ventured to give a dinner party and that when the servant, Mildred, was bringing in coffee, he had pulled Mrs Sawyer's hair. 'Not a wig, you see,' he bawled. Even then, if you can believe it, Mrs Sawyer had laughed and tried to pretend that it was all part of the joke, this mysterious, obscure, sacred English joke.

But Mildred told the other servants in the town that her eyes had gone wicked, like a soucriant's eyes, and that afterwards she had picked up some of the hair he pulled out and put it in an envelope, and that Mr Sawyer ought to look out (hair is obeah as well as hands).

Of course, Mrs Sawyer had her compensations. They lived in a very pleasant house in Hill Street. The garden was large and they had a fine mango tree, which bore prolifically. The fruit was small, round, very sweet and juicy – a lovely, red-and-yellow colour when it was ripe. Perhaps it was one of the compensations, I used to think.

Mr Sawyer built a room on to the back of this house. It was unpainted inside and the wood smelt very sweet. Bookshelves lined the walls. Every time the Royal Mail steamer came in it brought a package for him, and gradually the empty shelves filled.

Once I went there with Eddie to borrow *The Arabian Nights*. That was on a Saturday afternoon, one of those hot, still afternoons when you felt that everything had gone to sleep, even the water in the gutters. But Mrs Sawyer was not asleep. She put her head in at the door and looked at us, and I knew that she hated the room and hated the books.

It was Eddie with the pale blue eyes and straw-coloured hair – the living image of his father, though often as silent as his mother – who first infected me with doubts about 'home', meaning England. He would be so quiet when others who had never seen it – none of us had ever seen it – were talking about its delights, gesticulating freely as we talked – London, the beautiful, rosy-cheeked ladies, the theatres, the shops, the fog, the blazing coal fires in winter, the exotic food (whitebait eaten to the sound of violins), strawberries and cream – the word 'strawberries' always spoken with a guttural and throaty sound which we imagined to be the proper English pronunciation.

'I don't like strawberries,' Eddie said on one occasion.

'You *don't like* strawberries?'

'No, and I don't like daffodils either. Dad's always going on about them. He says they lick the flowers here into a cocked hat and I bet that's a lie.'

We were all too shocked to say, 'You don't know a thing about it.' We were so shocked that nobody spoke to him for the rest of the day. But I for one admired him. I also was tired of learning and reciting poems in praise of daffodils, and my relations with the few 'real' English boys and girls I had met were awkward. I had discovered that if I called myself English they would snub me haughtily: 'You're not English; you're a horrid colonial.' 'Well, I don't much want to be English,' I would say. 'It's much more fun to be French or Spanish or something like that – and, as a matter of fact, I am a bit.' Then I was too killingly funny, quite ridiculous. Not only a horrid colonial, but also ridiculous. Heads I win, tails you lose – that was the English. I had thought about all this, and thought hard, but I had never dared to tell anybody what I thought and I realized that Eddie had been very bold.

But he was bold, and stronger than you would think. For one thing, he never felt the heat; some coldness in his fair skin resisted it. He didn't burn red or brown, he didn't freckle much.

Hot days seemed to make him feel especially energetic. 'Now we'll run twice round the lawn and then you can pretend you're dying of thirst in the desert and that I'm an Arab chieftain bringing you water.'

'You must drink slowly,' he would say, 'for if you're very thirsty and you drink quickly you die.'

So I learnt the voluptuousness of drinking slowly when you are very thirsty – small mouthful by small mouthful, until the glass of pink, iced Coca-Cola was empty.

Just after my twelfth birthday Mr Sawyer died suddenly, and as Eddie's special friend I went to the funeral, wearing a new white dress. My straight hair was damped with sugar and water the night before and plaited into tight little plaits, so that it should be fluffy for the occasion.

When it was all over everybody said how nice Mrs Sawyer had looked, walking like a queen behind the coffin and crying her eyeballs out at the right moment, and wasn't Eddie a funny boy? He hadn't cried at all.

After this Eddie and I took possession of the room with the books. No one else ever entered it, except Mildred to sweep and dust in the mornings, and gradually the ghost of Mr Sawyer pulling Mrs Sawyer's hair faded though this took a little time. The blinds were always half-way down and going in out of the sun was like stepping into a pool of brown-green water. It was empty except for the bookshelves, a desk with a green baize top and a wicker rocking-chair.

'My room,' Eddie called it. 'My books,' he would say, 'my books.'

I don't know how long this lasted. I don't know whether it was weeks after Mr Sawyer's death or months after, that I see myself and Eddie in the room. But there we are and there, unexpectedly, are Mrs Sawyer and Mildred. Mrs Sawyer's mouth tight, her eyes pleased. She is pulling all the books out of the shelves and piling them into two heaps. The big, fat glossy ones – the good-looking ones, Mildred explains in a whisper – lie in one heap. The *Encyclopaedia Britannica, British Flowers, Birds and Beasts*, various histories, books with maps, Froude's *English in the West Indies* and so on – they are going to be sold. The unimportant books, with paper covers or damaged covers or torn pages, lie in another heap. They are going to be burnt – yes, burnt.

Mildred's expression was extraordinary as she said that – half hugely delighted, half-shocked, even frightened. And as for Mrs Sawyer-well, I knew bad temper (I had often seen it), I knew rage, but this was hate. I recognized the difference at once and stared at her curiously. I edged closer to her so that I could see the titles of the books she was handling.

It was the poetry shelf. *Poems*, Lord Byron, *Poetical Works*, Milton, and so on. Vlung, vlung, vlung – all thrown into the heap that were to be sold. But a book by Christina Rossetti, though also bound in leather, went into the heap that was to be burnt, and by a flicker in Mrs Sawyer's eyes I knew that worse than men who wrote books were women who wrote books – infinitely worse. Men could be mercifully shot; women must be tortured.

Mrs Sawyer did not seem to notice that we were there, but she was breathing free and easy and her hands had got the rhythm of tearing and pitching. She looked beautiful, too – beautiful as the sky outside which was a very dark blue, or the mango tree, long sprays of brown and gold.

When Eddie said 'No', she did not even glance at him.

'No,' he said again in a high voice. 'Not that one. I was reading that one.'

She laughed and he rushed at her, his eyes starting out of his head, shrieking, 'Now I've got to hate you too. Now I hate you too.'

He snatched the book out of her hand and gave her a violent push. She fell into the rocking-chair.

Well, I wasn't going to be left out of all this, so I grabbed a book from the condemned pile and dived under Mildred's outstretched arm.

Then we were both in the garden. We ran along the path, bordered with crotons. We pelted down the path, though they did not follow us and we could hear Mildred laughing – kyah, kyah, kyah, kyah. As I ran I put the book I had taken into the loose front of my brown holland dress. It felt warm and alive.

When we got into the street we walked sedately, for we feared the black children's ridicule. I felt very happy, because I had saved this book and it was my book and I would read it from the beginning to the triumphant words 'The End'. But I was uneasy when I thought of Mrs Sawyer.

'What will she do?' I said.

'Nothing,' Eddie said. 'Not to me.'

He was white as a ghost in his sailor suit, a blue-white even in the setting sun, and his father's sneer was clamped on his face.

'But she'll tell your mother all sorts of lies about you,' he said. 'She's an awful liar. She can't make up a story to save her life, but she makes up lies about people all right.'

'My mother won't take any notice of her.' I said. Though I was not at all sure.

'Why not? Because she's...because she isn't white?'

Well, I knew the answer to that one. Whenever the subject was brought up – people's relations and whether they had a drop of coloured blood or whether they hadn't – my father would grow impatient and interrupt. 'Who's white?' he would say. 'Damned few.'

So *I* said, 'Who's white? Damned few.'

'You can go to the devil,' Eddie said. 'She's prettier than your mother. When she's asleep her mouth smiles and she has curling eyelashes and quantities and quantities and *quantities* of hair.'

'Yes,' I said truthfully. 'She's prettier than my mother.'

It was a red sunset that evening, a huge, sad, frightening sunset.

'Look, let's go back,' I said. 'If you're sure she won't be vexed with you, let's go back. It'll be dark soon.'

At his gate he asked me not to go. 'Don't go yet, don't go yet.'

We sat under the mango tree and I was holding his hand when he began to cry. Drops fell on my hand like the water from the dripstone in the filter in our yard. Then I began to cry too and when I felt my own tears on my hand I thought, 'Now perhaps we're married.'

'Yes, certainly, now we're married,' I thought. But I didn't say anything. I didn't say a thing until I was sure he had stopped. Then I asked, 'What's your book?'

'It's *Kim*,' he said. 'But it got torn. It starts at page twenty now. What's the one you took?'

'I don't know; it's too dark to see,' I said.

When I got home I rushed into my bedroom and locked the door because I knew that this book was the most important thing that had ever happened to me and I did not want anybody to be there when I looked at it.

But I was very disappointed, because it was in French and seemed dull. *Fort Comme La Mort*, it was called . . . .

Defender of the Faith
(1959)

PHILIP ROTH

In May of 1945, only a few weeks after the fighting had ended in Europe, I was rotated back to the States, where I spent the remainder of the war with a training company at Camp Crowder, Missouri. Along with the rest of the Ninth Army, I had been racing across Germany so swiftly during the late winter and spring that when I boarded the plane, I couldn't believe its destination lay to the west. My mind might inform me otherwise, but there was an inertia of the spirit that told me we were flying to a new front, where we would disembark and continue our push eastward — eastward until we'd circled the globe, marching through villages along whose twisting, cobbled streets crowds of the enemy would watch us take possession of what, up till then, they'd considered their own. I had changed enough in two years not to mind the trembling of the old people, the crying of the very young, the uncertainty and fear in the eyes of the once arrogant. I had been fortunate enough to develop an infantryman's heart, which, like his feet, at first aches and swells but finally grows horny enough for him to travel the weirdest paths without feeling a thing.

Captain Paul Barrett was my C.O. in Camp Crowder. The day I reported for duty, he came out of his office to shake my hand. He was short, gruff, and fiery, and — indoors or out — he wore his polished helmet liner pulled down to his little eyes. In Europe, he had received a battlefield commission and a serious chest wound, and he'd been returned to the States only a few months before. He spoke easily to me, and at the evening formation he introduced me to the troops. "Gentlemen," he said, "Sergeant Thurston, as you know, is no longer with this company. Your new first sergeant is Sergeant Nathan Marx, here. He is a veteran of the European theater, and consequently will expect to find a company of soldiers here, and not a company of *boys*."

I sat up late in the orderly room that evening, trying half-heartedly to solve the riddle of duty rosters, personnel forms, and morning reports. The Charge of Quarters slept with his mouth open on a mattress on the floor. A trainee stood reading the next day's duty roster, which was posted on the bulletin board just inside the screen door. It was a warm evening, and I could hear radios playing dance music over in the barracks. The trainee, who had been staring at me whenever he thought I wouldn't notice, finally took a step in my direction.

"Hey, Sarge — we having a G.I. party tomorrow night?" he asked. A G.I. party is a barracks cleaning.

"You usually have them on Friday nights?" I asked him.

"Yes," he said, and then he added, mysteriously, "that's the whole thing."

"Then you'll have a G.I. party."

He turned away, and I heard him mumbling. His shoulders were moving, and I wondered if he was crying.

"What's your name, soldier?" I asked.

He turned, not crying at all. Instead, his green-speckled eyes, long and narrow, flashed like fish in the sun. He walked over to me and sat on the edge of my desk. He reached out a hand. "Sheldon," he said.

"Stand on your feet, Sheldon."

Getting off the desk, he said, "Sheldon Grossbart.' He smiled at the familiarity into which he'd led me.

"You against cleaning the barracks Friday night, Grossbart?" I said. "Maybe we shouldn't have G.I. parties. Maybe we should get a maid." My tone startled me. I felt I sounded like every top sergeant I had ever known.

"No, Sergeant." He grew serious, but with a seriousness that seemed to be only the stifling of a smile. "It's just — G.I. parties on Friday night, of all nights."

He slipped up onto the corner of the desk again — not quite sitting, but not quite standing, either. He looked at me with those speckled eyes flashing, and then made a gesture with his hand. It was very slight — no more than a movement back and forth of the wrist — and yet it managed to exclude from our affairs everything else in the orderly room, to make the two of us the center of the world. It seemed, in fact, to exclude everything even about the two of us except our hearts.

"Sergeant Thurston was one thing," he whispered, glancing at the sleeping C.Q., "but we thought that with you here things might be a little different."

"We?"

"The Jewish personnel."

"Why?" I asked, harshly. "What's on your mind?" Whether I was still angry at the "Sheldon" business, or now at something else, I hadn't time to tell, but clearly I was angry.

"We thought you — Marx, you know, like Karl Marx. The Marx Brothers. Those guys are all — M-a-r-x. Isn't that how *you* spell it, Sergeant?"

"M-a-r-x."

"Fishbein said —" He stopped. "What I mean to say, Sergeant —" His face and neck were red, and his mouth moved but no words came out. In a moment, he raised himself to attention, gazing down at me. It was as though he had suddenly decided he could expect no more sympathy from me than from Thurston, the reason being that I was of Thurston's faith, and not his. The young man had managed to confuse himself as to what my faith really was, but I felt no desire to straighten him out. Very simply, I didn't like him.

When I did nothing but return his gaze, he spoke, in an altered tone. "You see, Sergeant," he explained to me, "Friday nights, Jews are supposed to go to services."

"Did Sergeant Thurston tell you you couldn't go to them when there was a G.I. party?"

"No."

"Did he say you had to stay and scrub the floors?"

"No, Sergeant."

"Did the Captain say you had to stay and scrub the floors?"

"That isn't it, Sergeant. It's the other guys in the barracks." He leaned toward me. "They think we're goofing off. But we're not. That's when Jews go to services, Friday night. We have to."

"Then go."

"But the other guys make accusations. They have no right."

"That's not the Army's problem, Grossbart. It's a personal problem you'll have to work out yourself."

"But it's un*fair*."

I got up to leave. "There's nothing I can do about it," I said.

Grossbart stiffened and stood in front of me. "But this is a matter of *religion*, sir."

"Sergeant," I said.

"I mean 'Sergeant,'" he said, almost snarling.

"Look, go see the chaplain. You want to see Captain Barrett, I'll arrange an appointment."

"No, no. I don't want to make trouble, Sergeant. That's the first thing they throw up to you. I just want my rights!"

"Damn it, Grossbart, stop whining. You have your rights. You can stay and scrub floors or you can go to shul —"

The smile swam in again. Spittle gleamed at the corners of his mouth. "You mean church, Sergeant."

"I mean shul, Grossbart!"

I walked past him and went outside. Near me, I heard the scrunching of a guard's boots on gravel. Beyond the lighted windows of the barracks, young men in T shirts and fatigue pants were sitting on their bunks, polishing their rifles. Suddenly there was a light rustling behind me. I turned and saw Grossbart's dark frame fleeing back to the barracks, racing to tell his Jewish friends that they were right — that, like Karl and Harpo, I was one of them.

The next morning, while chatting with Captain Barrett, I recounted the incident of the previous evening. Somehow, in the telling, it must have seemed to the Captain that I was not so much explaining Grossbart's position as defending it. "Marx, I'd fight side by side with a nigger if the fella proved to me he was a man. I pride myself," he said, looking out the window, "that I've got an open mind. Consequently, Sergeant, nobody gets special treatment here, for the good *or* the bad. All a man's got to do is prove himself. A man fires well on the range, I give him a weekend pass. He scores high in P.T., he gets a weekend pass. He *earns* it." He turned from the window and pointed a finger at me. "You're a Jewish fella, am I right, Marx?"

"Yes, sir."

"And I admire you. I admire you because of the ribbons on your chest. I judge a man by what he shows me on the field of battle, Sergeant. It's what he's got *here*," he said, and then, though I expected he would point to his chest, he jerked a thumb toward the buttons straining to hold his blouse across his belly. "Guts," he said.

"O.K., sir. I only wanted to pass on to you how the men felt."

"Mr. Marx, you're going to be old before your time if you worry about how the men feel. Leave that stuff to the chaplain — that's his business, not yours. Let's us train these fellas to shoot straight. If the Jewish personnel feels the other men are accusing them of goldbricking — well, I just don't know. Seems awful funny that suddenly the Lord is calling so loud in Private Grossman's ear he's just got to run to church."

"Synagogue," I said.

"Synagogue is right, Sergeant. I'll write that down for handy reference. Thank you for stopping by."

That evening, a few minutes before the company gathered outside the orderly room for the chow formation, I called the C.Q., Corporal Robert LaHill, in to see me. LaHill was a dark, burly fellow whose hair curled out of his clothes wherever it could. He had a glaze in his eyes that made one think of caves and dinosaurs. "LaHill," I said "when you take the formation, remind the men that they're free to attend church services *whenever* they are held, provided they report to the orderly room before they leave the area."

La Hill scratched his wrist, but gave no indication that he'd heard or understood.

"LaHill," I said, "*church*. You remember? Church, priest, Mass, confession."

He curled one lip into a kind of smile; I took it for a signal that for a second he had flickered back up into the human race.

"Jewish personnel who want to attend services this evening are to fall out in front of the orderly room at 1900," I said. Then, as an afterthought, I added, "By order of Captain Barrett."

A little while later, as the day's last light — softer than any I had seen that year — began to drop over Camp Crowder, I heard LaHill's thick, inflectionless voice outside my window: "Give me your ears, troopers. Toppie says for me to tell you that at 1900 hours all Jewish personnel is to fall out in front, here, if they want to attend the Jewish Mass."

At seven o' clock, I looked out the orderly-room window and saw three soldiers in starched khakis standing on the dusty quadrangle. They looked at their watches and fidgeted while they whispered back and forth. It was getting dimmer, and, alone on the otherwise deserted field, they looked tiny. When I opened the door, I heard the noises of the G.I. party coming from the surrounding barracks — bunks being pushed to the walls, faucets pounding water into buckets, brooms whisking at the wooden floors, cleaning the dirt away for Saturday's inspection. Big puffs of cloth moved round and round on the windowpanes. I walked outside, and the moment my foot hit the ground I thought I heard Grossbart call to the others, " 'Ten-*hut!*" Or maybe, when they all three jumped to attention, I imagined I heard the command.

Grossbart stepped forward. "Thank you, sir," he said.

" 'Sergeant,' Grossbart," I reminded him. "You call officers 'sir.' I'm not an officer. You've been in the Army three weeks — you know that."

He turned his palms out at his sides to indicate that, in truth, he and I lived beyond convention. "Thank you, anyway," he said.

"Yes," a tall boy behind him said. "Thanks a lot."

And the third boy whispered, "Thank you," but his mouth barely fluttered, so that he did not alter by more than a lip's movement his posture of attention.

"For what?" I asked.

Grossbart snorted happily. "For the announcement. The Corporal's announcement. It helped. It made it — "

"Fancier." The tall boy finished Grossbart's sentence.

Grossbart smiled. "He means formal, sir. Public," he said to me. "Now it won't seem as though we're just taking off — goldbricking because the work has begun."

"It was by order of Captain Barrett," I said.

"Aaah, but you pull a little weight," Grossbart said. "So we thank you." Then he turned to his companions. "Sergeant Marx, I want you to meet Larry Fishbein."

The tall boy stepped forward and extended his hand. I shook it. "You from New York?" he asked.

"Yes."

"Me, too." He had a cadaverous face that collapsed inward from his cheekbone to his jaw, and when he smiled — as he did at the news of our communal attachment — revealed a mouthful of bad teeth. He was blinking his eyes a good deal, as though he were fighting back tears. "What borough?" he asked.

I turned to Grossbart. "It's five after seven. What time are services?"

"Shul," he said, smiling, "is in ten minutes. I want you to meet Mickey Halpern. This is Nathan Marx, our sergeant."

The third boy hopped forward. "Private Michael Halpern." He saluted.

"Salute officers, Halpern," I said. The boy dropped his hand, and, on its way down, in his nervousness, checked to see if his shirt pockets were buttoned.

"Shall I march them over, sir?" Grossbart asked. "Or are you coming along?"

From behind Grossbart, Fishbein piped up. "Afterward, they're having refreshments. A ladies' auxiliary from St. Louis, the rabbi told us last week."

"The chaplain," Halpern whispered.

"You're welcome to come along," Grossbart said.

To avoid his plea, I looked away, and saw, in the windows of the barracks, a cloud of faces staring out at the four of us. "Hurry along, Grossbart," I said.

"O.K., then," he said. He turned to the others. "Double time, *march!*"

They started off, but ten feet away Grossbart spun around and, running backward, called to me, "Good *shabbus*, sir!" And then the three of them were swallowed into the alien Missouri dusk.

Even after they had disappeared over the parade ground, whose green was now a deep blue, I could hear Grossbart singing the double-time cadence, and as it grew dimmer and dimmer, it suddenly touched a deep memory — as did the slant of the light — and I was remembering the shrill sounds of a Bronx playground where, years ago, beside the Grand Concourse, I had played on long spring evenings such as this. It was a pleasant memory for a young man so far from peace and home, and it brought so many recollections with it that I began to grow exceedingly tender about myself. In fact, I indulged myself in a reverie so strong that I felt as though a hand were reaching down inside me. It had to reach so very far to touch me! It had to reach past those days in the forests of Belgium, and past the dying I'd refused to weep over; past the nights in German farmhouses whose books we'd burned to warm us; past endless stretches when I had shut off all softness I might feel for my fellows, and had managed even to deny myself the posture of a conqueror — the swagger that I, as a Jew, might well have worn as my boots whacked against the rubble of Wesel, Münster, and Braunschweig.

But now one night noise, one rumor of home and time past, and memory plunged down through all I had anesthetized, and came to what I suddenly remembered was myself. So it was not altogether curious that, in search of more of me, I found myself following Grossbart's tracks to Chapel No. 3, where the Jewish services were being held.

I took a seat in the last row, which was empty. Two rows in front of me sat Grossbart, Fishbein, and Halpern, holding little white Dixie cups. Each row of seats was raised higher than the one in front of it, and I could see clearly what was going on. Fishbein was pouring the contents of his cup into Grossbart's, and Grossbart looked mirthful as the liquid made a purple arc between Fishbein's hand and his. In the glaring yellow light, I saw the chaplain standing on the platform at the front; he was chanting the first line of the responsive reading. Grossbart's prayer book remained closed on his lap; he was swishing the cup around. Only Halpern responded to the chant by praying. The fingers of his right hand were spread wide across the cover of his open book. His cap was pulled down low onto his brow, which made it round, like a yarmulke. From time to time, Grossbart wet his lips at the cup's edge; Fishbein, his long yellow face a dying light bulb, looked from here to there, craning forward to catch sight of the faces down the row, then of those in front of him, then behind. He saw me, and his eyelids beat a tattoo. His elbow slid into Grossbart's side, his neck inclined toward his friend, he whispered something, and then, when the congregation next responded to the chant, Grossbart's voice was among the others. Fishbein looked into his book now, too; his lips, however, didn't move.

Finally, it was time to drink the wine. The chaplain smiled down at them as Grossbart swigged his in one long gulp, Halpern sipped, meditating, and Fishbein faked devotion with an empty cup. "As I look down amongst the congregation" — the chaplain grinned at the word — "this night, I see many new faces, and I want to welcome you to Friday-night services here at Camp Crowder. I am Major Leo Ben Ezra, your chaplain." Though an American, the chaplain spoke deliberately — syllable by syllable, almost — as though to communicate, above all, with the lip readers in his audience. "I have only a few words to say before we adjourn to the refreshment room, where the kind ladies of the Temple Sinai, St. Louis, Missouri, have a nice setting for you."

Applause and whistling broke out. After another momentary grin, the chaplain raised his hands, palms out, his eyes flicking upward a moment, as if to remind the troops where they were and Who Else might be in attendance. In the sudden silence that followed, I thought I heard Grossbart cackle, "Let the goyim clean the floors!" Were those the words? I wasn't sure, but Fishbein, grinning, nudged Halpern. Halpern looked dumbly at him, then went back to his prayer book, which had been occupying him all through the rabbi's talk. One hand tugged at the black kinky hair that stuck out under his cap. His lips moved.

The rabbi continued. "It is about the food that I want to speak to you for a moment. I know, I know, I know," he intoned, wearily, "how in the mouths of most of you the *trafe* food tastes like ashes. I know how you gag, some of you, and how your parents suffer to think of their children eating foods unclean and offensive to the palate. What can I tell you? I can only say, close your eyes and swallow as best you can. Eat what you must to live, and throw away the rest. I wish I could help more. For those of you who find this impossible, may I ask that you try and try, but then come to see me in private. If your revulsion is so great, we will have to seek aid from those higher up."

A round of chatter rose and subsided. Then everyone sang "Ain Kelohainu"; after all those years, I discovered I still knew the words. Then, suddenly, the service over, Grossbart was upon me. "Higher up? He means the General?"

"Hey, Shelly," Fishbein said, "he means God." He smacked his face and looked at Halpern. "How high can you go!"

"Sh-h-h!" Grossbart said. "What do you think, Sergeant?"

"I don't know," I said. "You better ask the chaplain."

"I'm going to. I'm making an appointment to see him in private. So is Mickey."

Halpern shook his head. "No, no, Sheldon — "

"You have rights, Mickey," Grossbart said. "They can't push us around."

"It's O.K.," said Halpern. "It bothers my mother, not me."

Grossbart looked at me. "Yesterday he threw up. From the hash. It was all ham and God knows what else."

"I have a cold — that was why," Halpern said. He pushed his yarmulke back into a cap.

"What about you, Fishbein?" I asked. "You kosher, too?"

He flushed. "A little. But I'll let it ride. I have a very strong stomach, and I don't eat a lot anyway." I continued to look at him, and he held up his wrist to reinforce what he'd just said; his watch strap was tightened to the last hole, and he pointed that out to me.

"But services are important to you?" I asked him.

He looked at Grossbart. "Sure, sir."

" 'Sergeant.' "

"Not so much at home," said Grossbart, stepping between us, "but away from home it gives one a sense of his Jewishness."

"We have to stick together," Fishbein said.

I started to walk toward the door; Halpern stepped back to make way for me.

"That's what happened in Germany," Grossbart was saying, loud enough for me to hear. "They didn't stick together. They let themselves get pushed around."

I turned. "Look, Grossbart. This is the Army, not summer camp."

He smiled. "So?"

Halpern tried to sneak off, but Grossbart held his arm.

"Grossbart, how old are you?" I asked.

"Nineteen,"

"And you?" I said to Fishbein.

"The same. The same month, even."

"And what about him?" I pointed to Halpern, who had by now made it safely to the door.

"Eighteen," Grossbart whispered. "But like he can't tie his shoes or brush his teeth himself. I feel sorry for him."

"I feel sorry for all of us, Grossbart," I said, "but just act like a man. Just don't overdo it."

"Overdo what, sir?"

"The 'sir' business, for one thing. Don't overdo that," I said.

I left him standing there. I passed by Halpern, but he did not look at me. Then I was outside, but, behind, I heard Grossbart call, "Hey, Mickey, my *leben*, come on back. Refreshments!"

"Leben!" My grandmother's word for me!

One morning a week later, while I was working at my desk, Captain Barrett shouted for me to come into his office. When I entered, he had his helmet liner squashed down so far on his head that I couldn't even see his eyes. He was on the phone, and when he spoke to me, he cupped one hand over the mouthpiece. "Who the hell is Grossbart?"

"Third platoon, Captain," I said. "A trainee."

"What's all this stink about food? His mother called a goddam congressman about the food." He uncovered the mouthpiece and slid his helmet up until I could see his bottom eyelashes. "Yes, sir," he said into the phone. "Yes, sir. I'm still here, sir. I'm asking Marx, here, right now — "

He covered the mouthpiece again and turned his head back toward me. "Lightfoot Harry's on the phone," he said, between his teeth. "This congressman calls General Lyman, who calls Colonel Sousa, who calls the Major, who calls me. They're just dying to stick this thing on me. Whatsa matter?" He shook the phone at me. "I don't feed the troops? What is this?"

"Sir, Grossbart is strange —" Barrett greeted that with a mockingly indulgent smile. I altered my approach. "Captain, he's a very orthodox Jew, and so he's only allowed to eat certain foods."

"He throws up, the congressman said. Every time he eats something, his mother says, he throws up!"

"He's accustomed to observing the dietary laws, Captain."

"So why's his old lady have to call the White House?"

"Jewish parents, sir — they're apt to be more protective than you expect. I mean, Jews have a very close family life. A boy goes away from home, sometimes the mother is liable to get very upset. Probably the boy mentioned something in a letter, and his mother misinterpreted."

"I'd like to punch him one right in the mouth," the Captain said. "There's a war on, and he wants a silver platter!"

"I don't think the boy's to blame, sir. I'm sure we can straighten it out by just asking him. Jewish parents worry —"

"*All* parents worry, for Christ's sake. But they don't get on their high horse and start pulling strings —"

I interrupted, my voice higher, tighter than before. "The home life, Captain, is very important — but you're right, it may sometimes get out of hand. It's a very wonderful thing, Captain, but because it's so close, this kind of thing . . ."

He didn't listen any longer to my attempt to present both myself and Lightfoot Harry with an explanation for the letter. He turned back to the phone. "Sir?" he said. "Sir — Marx, here, tells me Jews have a tendency to be pushy. He says he thinks we can settle it right here in the company. ... Yes, sir. ... I *will* call back, sir, soon as I can." He hung up. "Where are the men, Sergeant?"

"On the range."

With a whack on the top of his helmet, he crushed it down over his eyes again, and charged out of his chair. "We're going for a ride," he said.

The Captain drove, and I sat beside him. It was a hot spring day, and under my newly starched fatigues I felt as though my armpits were melting down onto my sides and chest. The roads were dry, and by the time we reached the firing range, my teeth felt gritty with dust, though my mouth had been shut the whole trip. The Captain slammed the brakes on and told me to get the hell out and find Grossbart.

I found him on his belly, firing wildly at the five-hundred-feet target. Waiting their turns behind him were Halpern and Fishbein. Fishbein, wearing a pair of steel-rimmed G.I. glasses I hadn't seen on him before, had the appearance of an old peddler who would gladly have sold you his rifle and the cartridges that were slung all over him. I stood back by the ammo boxes, waiting for Grossbart to finish spraying the distant targets. Fishbein straggled back to stand near me.

"Hello, Sergeant Marx," he said.

"How are you?" I mumbled.

"Fine, thank you. Sheldon's really a good shot."

"I didn't notice."

"I'm not so good, but I think I'm getting the hang of it now. Sergeant, I don't mean to, you know, ask what I shouldn't — " The boy stopped. He was trying to speak intimately, but the noise of the shooting forced him to shout at me.

"What is it?" I asked. Down the range, I saw Captain Barrett standing up in the jeep, scanning the line for me and Grossbart.

"My parents keep asking and asking where we're going," Fishbein said. "Everybody says the Pacific. I don't care, but my parents — If I could relieve their minds, I think I could concentrate more on my shooting."

"I don't know where, Fishhein. Try to concentrate anyway."

"Sheldon says you might be able to find out."

"I don't know a thing, Fishbein. You just take it easy, and don't let Sheldon — "

"*I'm* taking it easy, Sergeant. It's at home — "

Grossbart had finished on the line, and was dusting his fatigues with one hand. I called to him. "Grossbart, the Captain wants to see you."

He came toward us. His eyes blazed and twinkled. "Hi!"

"Don't point that rifle!" I said.

"I wouldn't shoot you, Sarge." He gave me a smile as wide as a pumpkin, and turned the barrel aside.

"Damn you, Grossbart, this is no joke! Follow me,"

I walked ahead of him, and had the awful suspicion that, behind me, Grossbart was *marching*, his rifle on his shoulder, as though he were a one-man detachment. At the jeep, he gave the Captain a rifle salute. "Private Sheldon Grossbart, sir."

"At ease, Grossman." The Captain sat down, slid over into the empty seat, and, crooking a finger, invited Grossbart closer.

"Bart, sir. Sheldon *Grossbart*. It's a common error," Grossbart nodded at me; *I* understood, he indicated. I looked away just as the mess truck pulled up to the range, disgorging a half-dozen K.P.s with rolled-up sleeves. The mess sergeant screamed at them while they set up the chow-line equipment.

"Grossbart, your mama wrote some congressman that we don't feed you right. Do you know that?" the Captain said.

"It was my father, sir. He wrote to Representative Franconi that my religion forbids me to eat certain foods."

"What religion is that, Grossbart?"

"Jewish."

" 'Jewish, *sir*,' " I said to Grossbart.

"Excuse me, sir. Jewish, sir."

"What have you been living on?" the Captain asked. "You've been in the Army a month already. You don't look to me like you're falling to pieces."

"I eat because I have to, sir. But Sergeant Marx will testify to the fact that I don't eat one mouthful more than I need to in order to survive."

"Is that so, Marx?" Barrett asked.

"I've never seen Grossbart eat, sir," I said.

"But you heard the rabbi," Grossbart said. "He told us what to do, and I listened."

The Captain looked at me. "Well, Marx?"

"I still don't know what he eats and doesn't eat, sir."

Grossbart raised his arms to plead with me, and it looked for a moment as though he were going to hand me his weapon to hold. "But, Sergeant —"

"Look, Grossbart, just answer the Captain's questions," I said sharply.

Barrett smiled at me, and I resented it. "All right, Grossbart," he said. "What is it you want? The little piece of paper? You want out?"

"No, sir. Only to be allowed to live as a Jew. And for the others, too."

"What others?"

"Fishbein, sir, and Halpern."

"They don't like the way we serve, either?"

"Halpern throws up, sir. I've seen it."

"I thought you throw up."

"Just once, sir. I didn't know the sausage was sausage."

"We'll give menus, Grossbart. We'll show training films about the food, so you can identify when we're trying to poison you."

Grossbart did not answer. The men had been organized into two long chow lines. At the tail end of one, I spotted Fishbein — or, rather, his glasses spotted me. They winked sunlight back at me. Halpern stood next to him, patting the inside of his collar with a khaki handkerchief. They moved with the line as it began to edge up toward the food. The mess sergeant was still screaming at the K.P.s. For a moment, I was actually terrified by the thought that somehow the mess sergeant was going to become involved in Grossbart's problem.

"Marx," the Captain said, "you're a Jewish fella — am I right?"

I played straight man. "Yes, sir."

"How long you been in the Army? Tell this boy."

"Three years and two months."

"A year in combat, Grossbart. Twelve goddam months in combat all through Europe. I admire this man." The Captain snapped a wrist against my chest. "Do you hear him peeping about the food? Do you? I want an answer, Grossbart. Yes or no."

"No, sir."

"And why not? He's a Jewish fella."

"Some things are more important to some Jews than other things to other Jews."

Barrett blew up. "Look, Grossbart. Marx, here, is a good man — a goddam hero. When you were in high school, Sergeant Marx was killing Germans. Who does more for the Jews — you, by throwing up over a lousy piece of sausage, a piece of first-cut meat, or Marx, by killing those Nazi bastards? If I was a Jew, Grossbart, I'd kiss this man's feet. He's a goddam hero, and *he* eats what we give him. Why do you have to cause trouble is what I want to know! What is it you're buckin' for — a discharge?"

"No, sir."

"I'm talking to a wall! Sergeant, get him out of my way." Barrett swung himself back into the driver's seat. "I'm going to see the chaplain." The engine roared, the jeep spun around in a whirl of dust, and the Captain was headed back to camp.

For a moment, Grossbart and I stood side by side, watching the jeep. Then he looked at me and said, "I don't want to start trouble. That's the first thing they toss up to us."

When he spoke, I saw that his teeth were white and straight, and the sight of them suddenly made me understand that Grossbart actually did have parents — that once upon a time someone had taken little Sheldon to the dentist. He was their son. Despite all the talk about his parents, it was hard to believe in Grossbart as a child, an heir — as related by blood to anyone, mother, father, or, above all, to me. This realization led me to another.

"What does your father do, Grossbart?" I asked as we started to walk back toward the chow line.

"He's a tailor."

"An American?"

"Now, yes. A son in the Army," he said, jokingly.

"And your mother?" I asked.

He winked. "A *ballabusta*. She practically sleeps with a dustcloth in her hand."

"She's also an immigrant?"

"All she talks is Yiddish, still."

"And your father, too?"

"A little English. 'Clean,' 'Press,' 'Take the pants in.' That's the extent of it. But they're good to me."

"Then, Grossbart— " I reached out and stopped him. He turned toward me, and when our eyes met, his seemed to jump back, to shiver in their sockets. "Grossbart — you were the one who wrote that letter, weren't you?"

It took only a second or two for his eyes to flash happy again. "Yes." He walked on, and I kept pace. "It's what my father *would* have written if he had known how. It was his name, though. *He* signed it. He even mailed it. I sent it home. For the New York postmark."

I was astonished, and he saw it. With complete seriousness, he thrust his right arm in front of me. "Blood is blood, Sergeant," he said, pinching the blue vein in his wrist.

"What the hell *are* you trying to do, Grossbart?" I asked. "I've seen you eat. Do you know that? I told the Captain I don't know what you eat, but I've seen you eat like a hound at chow."

"We work hard, Sergeant. We're in training. For a furnace to work, you've got to feed it coal"

"Why did you say in the letter that you threw up all the time?"

"I was really talking about Mickey there. I was talking *for* him. He would never write, Sergeant, though I pleaded with him. He'll waste away to nothing if I don't help. Sergeant, I used my name — my father's name— but it's Mickey, and Fishbein, too, I'm watching out for."

"You're a regular Messiah, aren't you?"

We were at the chow line now.

"That's a good one, Sergeant," he said, smiling. "But who knows? Who can tell? Maybe you're the Messiah — a little bit. What Mickey says is the Messiah is a collective idea. He went to Yeshiva, Mickey, for a while. He says *together* we're the Messiah. Me a little bit, you a little bit. You should hear that kid talk, Sergeant, when he gets going."

"Me a little bit, you a little bit," I said. "You'd like to believe that, wouldn't you, Grossbart? That would make everything so clean for you."

"It doesn't seem too bad a thing to believe, Sergeant. It only means we should all *give* a little, is all."

I walked off to eat my rations with the other noncoms.

Two days later, a letter addressed to Captain Barrett passed over my desk. It had come through the chain of command — from the office of Congressman Franconi, where it had been received, to General Lyman, to Colonel Sousa, to Major Lamont, now to Captain Barrett. I read it over twice. It was dated May 14, the day Barrett had spoken with Grossbart on the rifle range.

Dear Congressman:

First let me thank you for your interest in behalf of my son, Private Sheldon Grossbart. Fortunately, I was able to speak with Sheldon on the phone the other night, and I think I've been able to solve our problem. He is, as I mentioned in my last letter, a very religious boy, and it was only with the greatest difficulty that I could persuade him that the religious thing to do — what God Himself would want Sheldon to do — would be to suffer the pangs of religious remorse for the good of his country and all mankind. It took some doing, Congressman, but finally he saw the light. In fact, what he said (and I wrote down the words on a scratch pad so as never to forget), what he said was "I guess you're right, Dad. So many millions of my fellow-Jews gave up their lives to the enemy, the least I can do is live for a while minus a bit of my heritage so as to help end this struggle and regain for all the children of God dignity and humanity." That, Congressman, would make any father proud.

By the way, Sheldon wanted me to know — and to pass on to you — the name of a soldier who helped him reach this decision: SERGEANT NATHAN MARX. Sergeant Marx is a combat veteran who is Sheldon's first sergeant. This man has helped Sheldon over some of the first hurdles he's had to face in the Army, and is in part responsible for Sheldon's changing his mind about the dietary laws. I know Sheldon would appreciate any recognition Marx could receive.

Thank you and good luck. I look forward to seeing your name on the next election ballot.

Respectfully,
Samuel E. Grossbart

Attached to the Grossbart communiqué was another, addressed to General Marshall Lyman, the post commander, and signed by Representative Charles E. Franconi, of the House of Representatives. The communiqué informed General Lyman that Sergeant Nathan Marx was a credit to the U.S. Army and the Jewish people.

What was Grossbart's motive in recanting? Did he feel he'd gone too far? Was the letter a strategic retreat — a crafty attempt to strengthen what he considered our alliance? Or had he actually changed his mind, via an imaginary dialogue between Grossbart *père* and Grossbart *fils?* I was puzzled, but only for a few days — that is, only until I realized that, whatever his reasons, he had actually decided to disappear from my life; he was going to allow himself to become just another trainee. I saw him at inspection, but he never winked; at chow formations, but he never flashed me a sign. On Sundays, with the other trainees, he would sit around watching the noncoms' softball team, for which I pitched, but not once did he speak an unnecessary word to me. Fishbein and Halpern retreated, too — at Grossbart's command, I was sure. Apparently he had seen that wisdom lay in turning back before he plunged over into the ugliness of privilege undeserved. Our separation allowed me to forgive him our past encounters, and, finally, to admire him for his good sense.

Meanwhile, free of Grossbart, I grew used to my job and my administrative tasks. I stepped on a scale one day, and discovered I had truly become a noncombatant; I had gained seven pounds. I found patience to get past the first three pages of a book. I thought about the future more and more, and wrote letters to girls I'd known before the war. I even got a few answers. I sent away to Columbia for a Law School catalogue. I continued to follow the war in the Pacific, but it was not my war. I thought I could see the end, and sometimes, at night, I dreamed that I was walking on the streets of Manhattan — Broadway, Third Avenue, 116th Street, where I had lived the three years I attended Columbia. I curled myself around these dreams and I began to be happy.

And then, one Sunday, when everybody was away and I was alone in the orderly room reading a month-old copy of the *Sporting News*, Grossbart reappeared.

"You a baseball fan, Sergeant?"

I looked up. "How are you?"

"Fine," Grossbart said. "They're making a soldier out of me."

"How are Fishbein and Halpern?"

"Coming along," he said. "We've got no training this afternoon. They're at the movies."

"How come you're not with them?"

"I wanted to come over and say hello."

He smiled — a shy, regular-guy smile, as though he and I well knew that our friendship drew its sustenance from unexpected visits, remembered birthdays, and borrowed lawnmowers. At first it offended me, and then the feeling was swallowed by the general uneasiness I felt at the thought that everyone on the post was locked away in a dark movie theater and I was here alone with Grossbart. I folded up my paper.

"Sergeant," he said, "I'd like to ask a favor. It is a favor, and I'm making no bones about it."

He stopped, allowing me to refuse him a hearing — which, of course, forced me into a courtesy I did not intend. "Go ahead."

"Well, actually it's two favors."

I said nothing.

"The first one's about these rumors. Everybody says we're going to the Pacific."

"As I told your friend Fishbein, I don't know," I said. "You'll just have to wait to find out. Like everybody else."

"You think there's a chance of any of us going East?"

"Germany?" I said. "Maybe."

"I meant New York."

"I don't think so, Grossbart. Offhand."

"Thanks for the information, Sergeant," he said.

"It's not information, Grossbart. Just what I surmise."

"It certainly would be good to be near home. My parents — you know." He took a step toward the door and then turned back. "Oh, the other thing. May I ask the other?"

"What is it?"

"The other thing is — I've got relatives in St. Louis, and they say they'll give me a whole Passover dinner if I can get down there. God, Sergeant, that'd mean an awful lot to me."

I stood up. "No passes during basic, Grossbart."

"But we're off from now till Monday morning, Sergeant. I could leave the post and no one would even know."

"I'd know. You'd know."

"But that's all. Just the two of us. Last night, I called my aunt, and you should have heard her. 'Come — come,' she said. 'I got gefilte fish, *chrain* — the works!' Just a day, Sergeant. I'd take the blame if anything happened."

"The Captain isn't here to sign a pass."

"You could sign."

"Look, Grossbart — "

"Sergeant, for two months, practically, I've been eating *trafe* till I want to die."

"I thought you'd made up your mind to live with it. To be minus a little bit of heritage."

He pointed a finger at me. "You!" he said. "That wasn't for you to read."

"I read it. So what?"

"That letter was addressed to a congressman."

"Grossbart, don't feed me any baloney. You *wanted* me to read it."

"Why are you persecuting me, Sergeant?"

"Are you kidding!"

"I've run into this before," he said, "but never from my own!"

"Get out of here, Grossbart! Get the hell out of my sight!"

He did not move. "Ashamed, that's what you are," he said. "So you take it out on the rest of us. They say Hitler himself was half a Jew. Hearing you, I wouldn't doubt it."

"What are you trying to do with me, Grossbart?" I asked him. "What are you after? You want me to give you special privileges, to change the food, to find out about your orders, to give you weekend passes."

"You even talk like a goy!" Grossbart shook his fist. "Is this just a weekend pass I'm asking for? Is a Seder sacred, or not?"

Seder! It suddenly occurred to me that Passover had been celebrated weeks before. I said so.

"That's right," he replied. "Who says no? A month ago — and I was in the field eating hash! And now all I ask is a simple favor. A Jewish boy I thought would understand. My aunt's willing to go out of her way — to make a Seder a month later. . . ." He turned to go, mumbling.

"Come back here!" I called. He stopped and looked at me. "Grossbart, why can't you be like the rest? Why do you have to stick out like a sore thumb?"

"Because I'm a Jew, Sergeant. I *am* different. Better, maybe not. But different."

"This is a war, Grossbart. For the time being *be* the same."

"I refuse."

"What?"

"I refuse. I can't stop being me, that's all there is to it." Tears came to his eyes. "It's a hard thing to be a Jew. But now I understand what Mickey says — it's a harder thing to stay one." He raised a hand sadly toward me. "Look at *you*."

"Stop crying!"

"Stop this, stop that, stop the other thing! *You* stop, Sergeant. Stop closing your heart to your own!" And, wiping his face with his sleeve, he ran out the door. "The least we can do for one another — the least . . . "

An hour later, looking out of the window, I saw Grossbart headed across the field. He wore a pair of starched khakis and carried a little leather ditty bag. I went out into the heat of the day. It was quiet; not a soul was in sight except, over by the mess hall, four K.P.s sitting around a pan, sloped forward from their waists, gabbing and peeling potatoes in the sun.

"Grossbart!" I called.

He looked toward me and continued walking.

"Grossbart, get over here!"

He turned and came across the field. Finally, he stood before me.

"Where are you going?" I asked.

"St. Louis. I don't care."

"You'll get caught without a pass."

"So I'll get caught without a pass."

"You'll go to the stockade."

"I'm *in* the stockade." He made an about-face and headed off.

I let him go only a step or two. "Come back here," I said, and he followed me into the office, where I typed out a pass and signed the Captain's name, and my own initials after it.

He took the pass and then, a moment later, reached out and grabbed my hand. "Sergeant, you don't know how much this means to me."

"O.K.," I said. "Don't get in any trouble."

"I wish I could show you how much this means to me."

"Don't do me any favors. Don't write any more congressmen for citations."

He smiled. "You're right. I won't. But let me do something."

"Bring me a piece of that gefilte fish. Just get out of here."

"I will!" he said. "With a slice of carrot and a little horseradish. I won't forget."

"All right. Just show your pass at the gate. And don't tell *anybody*."

"I won't. It's a month late, but a good Yom Tov to you."

"Good Yom Tov, Grossbart," I said.

"You're a good Jew, Sergeant. You like to think you have a hard heart, but underneath you're a fine, decent man. I mean that."

Those last three words touched me more than any words from Grossbart's mouth had the right to. "All right, Grossbart," I said. "Now call me 'sir,' and get the hell out of here."

He ran out the door and was gone. I felt very pleased with myself; it was a great relief to stop fighting Grossbart, and it had cost me nothing. Barrett would never find out, and if he did, I could manage to invent some excuse. For a while, I sat at my desk, comfortable in my decision. Then the screen door flew back and Grossbart burst in again. "Sergeant!" he said. Behind him I saw Fishbein and Halpern, both in starched khakis, both carrying ditty bags like Grossbart's.

"Sergeant, I caught Mickey and Larry coming out of the movies. I almost missed them."

"Grossbart — did I say tell no one?" I said.

"But my aunt said I could bring friends. That I should, in fact."

"*I'm* the Sergeant, Grossbart — not your aunt!"

Grossbart looked at me in disbelief. He pulled Halpern up by his sleeve. Mickey, tell the Sergeant what this would mean to you."

Halpern looked at me and, shrugging, said, "A lot."

Fishbein stepped forward without prompting. "This would mean a great deal to me and my parents, Sergeant Marx."

"No!" I shouted.

Grossbart was shaking his head. "Sergeant, I could see you denying me, but how you can deny Mickey, a Yeshiva boy — that's beyond me."

"I'm not denying Mickey anything," I said. "You just pushed a little too hard, Grossbart. *You* denied him."

"I'll give him my pass, then," Grossbart said. "I'll give him my aunt's address and a little note. At least let him go."

In a second, he had crammed the pass into Halpern's pants pocket. Halpern looked at me, and so did Fishbein. Grossbart was at the door, pushing it open. "Mickey, bring me a piece of gelfilte fish, at least," he said, and then he was outside again.

The three of us looked at one another, and then I said, "Halpern, hand that pass over."

He took it from his pocket and gave it to me. Fishbein had now moved to the doorway, where he lingered. He stood there for a moment with his mouth slightly open, and then he pointed to himself. "And me?" he asked.

His utter ridiculousness exhausted me. I slumped down in my seat and felt pulses knocking at the back of my eyes. "Fishbein," I said, "you understand I'm not trying to deny you anything, don't you? If it was my Army, I'd serve gefilte fish in the mess hall. I'd sell *kugel* in the PX, honest to God,"

Halpern smiled.

"You understand, don't you, Halpern?"

"Yes, Sergeant."

"And you, Fishbein? I don't want enemies. I'm just like you — I want to serve my time and go home. I miss the same things you miss."

"Then, Sergeant," Fishbein said, "why don't you come, too?"

"Where?"

"To St. Louis. To Shelly's aunt. We'll have a regular Seder. Play hide-the-matzoh." He gave me a broad, blacktoothed smile.

I saw Crossbart again, on the other side of the screen.

"Pst!" He waved a piece of paper. "Mickey, here's the address. Tell het I couldn't get away."

Halpern did not move. He looked at me, and I saw the shrug moving up his arms into his shoulders again. I took the cover off my typewriter and made out passes for him and Fishbein. "Go," I said. "The three of you."

I thought Halpern was going to kiss my hand.

That afternoon, in a bar in Joplin, I drank beer and listened with half an ear to the Cardinal game. I tried to look squarely at what I'd become involved in, and began to wonder if perhaps the struggle with Grossbart wasn't as much my fault as his. What was I that I had to *muster* generous feelings? Who was I to have been feeling so grudging, so tight-hearted? After all, I wasn't being asked to move the world. Had I a right, then, or a reason, to clamp down on Grossbart, when that meant clamping down on Halpern, too? And Fishbein — that ugly, agreeable soul? Out of the many recollections of my childhood that had tumbled over me these past few days I heard my grandmother's voice: "What are you making a *tsimmes?*" It was what she would ask my mother when, say, I had cut myself while doing something I shouldn't have done, and her daughter was busy bawling me out. I needed a hug and a kiss, and my mother would moralize. But my grandmother knew — mercy overrides justice. I should have known it, too. Who was Nathan Marx to be such a penny pincher with kindness? Surely, I thought, the Messiah himself — if He should ever come — won't niggle over nickels and dimes. God willing, he'll hug and kiss.

The next day, while I was playing softball over on the parade ground, I decided to ask Bob Wright, who was noncom in charge of Classification and Assignment, where he thought our trainees would be sent when their cycle ended, in two weeks. I asked casually, between innings, and he said, "They're pushing them all into the Pacific. Shulman cut the orders on your boys the other day."

The news shocked me, as though I were the father of Halpern, Fishbein, and Grossbart.

That night, I was just sliding into sleep when someone tapped on my door. "Who is it?" I asked.

"Sheldon."

He opened the door and came in. For a moment, I felt his presence without being able to see him. "How was it?" I asked.

He popped into sight in the near-darkness before me. "Great, Sergeant." Then he was sitting on the edge of the bed. I sat up.

"How about you?" he asked. "Have a nice weekend?"

"Yes,"

"The others went to sleep." He took a deep, paternal breath. We sat silent for a while, and a homey feeling invaded my ugly little cubicle; the door was locked, the cat was out, the children were safely in bed.

"Sergeant, can I tell you something? Personal?"

I did not answer, and he seemed to know why. "Not about me. About Mickey. Sergeant, I never felt for anybody like I feel for him. Last night I heard Mickey in the bed next to me. He was crying so, it could have broken your heart. Real sobs."

"I'm sorry to hear that."

"I had to talk to him to stop him. He held my hand, Sergeant — he wouldn't let it go. He was almost hysterical. He kept saying if he only knew where we were going. Even if he knew it *was* the Pacific, that would be better than nothing. Just to know."

Long ago, someone had taught Grossbart the sad rule that only lies can get the truth. Not that I couldn't believe in the fact of Halpern's crying; his eyes *always* seemed red-rimmed. But, fact or not, it became a lie when Grossbart uttered it. He was entirely strategic. But then — it came with the force of indictment — so was I! There are strategies of aggression, but there are strategies of retreat as well. And so, recognizing that I myself had not been without craft and guile, I told him what I knew. "It is the Pacific."

He let out a small gasp, which was not a lie. "I'll tell him. I wish it was otherwise."

"So do I."

He jumped on my words. "You mean you think you could do something? A change, maybe?"

"No, I couldn't do a thing."

"Don't you know anybody over at C. and A.?"

"Grossbart, there's nothing I can do," I said. "If your orders are for the Pacific, then it's the Pacific."

"But Mickey —"

"Mickey, you, me — everybody, Grossbart. There's nothing to be done. Maybe the war'll end before you go. Pray for a miracle."

"But —"

"Good night, Grossbart." I settled back, and was relieved to feel the springs unbend as Grossbart rose to leave. I could see him clearly now; his jaw had dropped, and he looked like a dazed prizefighter. I noticed for the first time a little paper bag in his hand.

"Grossbart." I smiled. "My gift?"

"Oh, yes, Sergeant. Here — from all of us." He handed me the bag. "It's egg roll."

"Egg roll?" I accepted the bag and felt a damp grease spot on the bottom. I opened it, sure that Grossbart was joking.

"We thought you'd probably like it. You know — Chinese egg roll. We thought you'd probably have a taste for —"

"Your aunt served egg roll?"

"She wasn't home."

"Grossbart, she invited you. You told me she invited you and your friends."

"I know," he said. "I just reread the letter. *Next* week."

I got out of bed and walked to the window. "Grossbart," I said. But I was not calling to him.

"What?"

"What are you, Grossbart? Honest to God, what are you?"

I think it was the first time I'd asked him a question for which he didn't have an immediate answer.

"How can you do this to people?" I went on.

"Sergeant, the day away did us all a world of good. Fishbein, you should see him, he *loves* Chinese food."

"But the Seder," I said.

"We took second best, Sergeant."

Rage came charging at me. I didn't sidestep. "Grossbart, you're a liar!" I said. "You're a schemer and a crook. You've got no respect for anything. Nothing at all. Not for me, for the truth — not even for poor Halpern! You use us all — "

"Sergeant, Sergeant, I feel for Mickey. Honest to God, I do. I *love* Mickey. I try — "

"You try! You feel!" I lurched toward him and grabbed his shirt front. I shook him furiously. "Grossbart, get out! Get out and stay the hell away from me. Because if I see you, I'll make your life miserable. *You understand that?*"

"Yes."

I let him free, and when he walked from the room, I wanted to spit on the floor where he had stood. I couldn't stop the fury. It engulfed me, owned me, till it seemed I could only rid myself of it with tears or an act of violence. I snatched from the bed the bag Grossbart had given me and, with all my strength, threw it out the window. And the next morning, as the men policed the area around the barracks, I heard a great cry go up from one of the trainees, who had been anticipating only his morning handful of cigarette butts and candy wrappers. "Egg roll!" he shouted. "Holy Christ, Chinese goddam egg roll!"

A week later, when I read the orders that had come down from C. and A., I couldn't believe my eyes. Every single trainee was to be shipped to Camp Stoneman, California, and from there to the Pacific — every trainee but one. Private Sheldon Grossbart. He was to be sent to Fort Monmouth, New Jersey. I read the mimeographed sheet several times. Dee, Farrell, Fishbein, Fuselli, Fylypowycz, Glinicki, Gromke, Gucwa, Halpern, Hardy, Helebrandt, right down to Anton Zygadlo — all were to be headed West before the month was out. All except Grossbart. He had pulled a string, and I wasn't it.

I lifted the phone and called C. and A.

The voice on the other end said smartly, "Corporal Shulman, sir."

"Let me speak to Sergeant Wright."

"Who is this calling, sir?"

"Sergeant Marx."

And, to my surprise, the voice said, *"Oh!"* Then, "Just a minute, Sergeant."

Shulman's *"Oh!"* stayed with me while I waited for Wright to come to the phone. Why *"Oh!"*? Who was Shulman? And then, so simply, I knew I'd discovered the string that Grossbart had pulled. In fact, I could hear Grossbart the day he'd discovered Shulman in the PX, or in the bowling alley, or maybe even at services. "Glad to meet you. Where you from? Bronx? Me, too. Do you know So-and-So? And So-and-So? Me, too! You work at C. and A.? Really? Hey, how's chances of getting East? Could you do something? Change something? Swindle, cheat, lie? We gotta help each other, you know. If the Jews in Germany . . ."

Bob Wright answered the phone. "How are you, Nate? How's the pitching arm?"

"Good. Bob, I wonder if you could do me a favor." I heard clearly my own words, and they so reminded me of Grossbart that I dropped more easily than I could have imagined into what I had planned. "This may sound crazy, Bob, but I got a kid here on orders to Monmouth who wants them changed. He had a brother killed in Europe, and he's hot to go to the Pacific. Says he'd feel like a coward if he wound up Stateside. I don't know, Bob — can anything be done? Put somebody else in the Monmouth slot?"

"Who?" he asked cagily.

"Anybody. First guy in the alphabet. I don't care. The kid just asked if something could be done."

"What's his name?"

"Grossbart, Sheldon."

Wright didn't answer.

"Yeah," I said. "He's a Jewish kid, so he thought I could help him out. You know."

"I guess I can do something," he finally said. "The Major hasn't been around here for weeks. Temporary duty to the golf course. I'll try, Nate, that's all I can say."

"I'd appreciate it, Bob. See you Sunday." And I hung up, perspiring.

The following day, the corrected orders appeared: Fishbein, Fuselli, Fylypowycz, Glinicki, Gromke, Grossbart, Gucwa, Halpern, Hardy … Lucky Private Harley Alton was to go to Fort Monmouth, New Jersey, where, for some reason or other, they wanted an enlisted man with infantry training.

After chow that night, I stopped back at the orderly room to straighten out the guard-duty roster. Grossbart was waiting for me. He spoke first.

"You son of a bitch!"

I sat down at my desk, and while he glared at me, I began to make the necessary alterations in the duty roster.

"What do you have against me?" he cried. "Against my family? Would it kill you for me to be near my father, God knows how many months he has left to him?"

"Why so?"

"His heart," Grossbart said. "He hasn't had enough troubles in a lifetime, you've got to add to them. I curse the day I ever met you, Marx! Shulman told me what happened over there. There's no limit to your anti-Semitism, is there? The damage you've done here isn't enough. You have to make a special phone call! You really want me dead!"

I made the last few notations in the duty roster and got up to leave. "Good night, Grossbart."

"You owe me an explanation!" He stood in my path.

"Sheldon, you're the one who owes explanations."

He scowled. "To *you?*"

"To me, I think so — yes. Mostly to Fishbein and Halpern."

"That's right, twist things around. I owe nobody nothing, I've done all I could do for them. Now I think I've got the right to watch out for myself."

"For each other we have to learn to watch out, Sheldon. You told me yourself."

"You call this watching out for me — what you did?"

"No. For all of us."

I pushed him aside and started for the door. I heard his furious breathing behind me, and it sounded like steam rushing from an engine of terrible strength.

"*You'll* be all right," I said from the door. And, I thought, so would Fishbein and Halpern be all right, even in the Pacific, if only Grossbart continued to see — in the obsequiousness of the one, the soft spirituality of the other — some profit for himself.

I stood outside the orderly room, and I heard Grossbart weeping behind me. Over in the barracks, in the lighted windows, I could see the boys in their T shirts sitting on their bunks talking about their orders, as they'd been doing for the past two days. With a kind of quiet nervousness, they polished shoes, shined belt buckles, squared away underwear, trying as best they could to accept their fate. Behind me, Grossbart swallowed hard, accepting his. And then, resisting with all my will an impulse to turn and seek pardon for my vindictiveness, I accepted my own.

The Prophet's Hair
(1981)

SALMAN RUSHDIE

Early in the year 19—, when Srinagar was under the spell of a winter so fierce it could crack men's bones as if they were glass, a young man upon whose cold-pinked skin there lay, like a frost, the unmistakable sheen of wealth was to be seen entering the most wretched and disreputable part of the city, where the houses of wood and corrugated iron seemed perpetually on the verge of losing their balance, and asking in low, grave tones where he might go to engage the services of a dependably professional burglar. The young man's name was Atta, and the rogues in that part of town directed him gleefully into ever darker and less public alleys, until in a yard wet with the blood of a slaughtered chicken he was set upon by two men whose faces he never saw, robbed of the substantial bank-roll which he had insanely brought on his solitary excursion, and beaten within an inch of his life.

Night fell. His body was carried by anonymous hands to the edge of the lake, whence it was transported by shikara across the water and deposited, torn and bleeding, on the deserted embankment of the canal which led to the gardens of Shalimar. At dawn the next morning a flower-vendor was rowing his boat through water to which the cold of the night had given the cloudy consistency of wild honey when he saw the prone form of young Atta, who was just beginning to stir and moan, and on whose now deathly pale skin the sheen of wealth could still be made out dimly beneath an actual layer of frost.

The flower-vendor moored his craft and by stooping over the mouth of the injured man was able to learn the poor fellow's address, which was mumbled through lips that could scarcely move; whereupon, hoping for a large tip, the hawker rowed Atta home to a large house on the shores of the lake, where a beautiful but inexplicably bruised young woman and her distraught, but equally handsome mother, neither of whom, it was clear from their eyes, had slept a wink from worrying, screamed at the sight of their Atta—who was the elder brother of the beautiful young woman—lying motionless amidst the funereally stunted winter blooms of the hopeful florist.

The flower-vendor was indeed paid off handsomely, not least to ensure his silence, and plays no further part in our story. Atta himself, suffering terribly from exposure as well as a broken skull, entered a coma which caused the city's finest doctors to shrug helplessly. It was therefore all the more remarkable that on the very next evening the most wretched and disreputable part of the city received a second unexpected visitor. This was Huma, the sister of the unfortunate young man, and her question was the same as her brother's, and asked in the same low, grave tones:

'Where may I hire a thief?'

The story of the rich idiot who had come looking for a burglar was already common knowledge in those insalubrious gullies, but this time the young woman added: 'I should say that I am carrying no money, nor am I wearing any jewellery items. My father has disowned me and will pay no ransom if I am kidnapped; and a letter has been lodged with the Deputy Commissioner of Police, my uncle, to be opened in the event of my not being safe at home by morning. In that letter he will find full details of my journey here, and he will move Heaven and Earth to punish my assailants.'

Her exceptional beauty, which was visible even through the enormous welts and bruises disfiguring her arms and forehead, coupled with the oddity of her inquiries, had attracted a sizable group of curious onlookers, and because her little speech seemed to them to cover just about everything, no one attempted to injure her in any way, although there were some raucous comments to the effect that it was pretty peculiar for someone who was trying to hire a crook to invoke the protection of a high-up policeman uncle.

She was directed into ever darker and less public alleys until finally in a gully as dark as ink an old woman with eyes which stared so piercingly that Huma instantly understood she was blind motioned her through a doorway from which darkness seemed to be pouring like smoke. Clenching her fists, angrily ordering her heart to behave normally, Huma followed the old woman into the gloom-wrapped house.

The faintest conceivable rivulet of candlelight trickled through the darkness; following this unreliable yellow thread (because she could no longer see the old lady), Huma received a sudden sharp blow to the shins and cried out involuntarily, after which she at once bit her lip, angry at having revealed her mounting terror to whoever or whatever waited before her, shrouded in blackness.

She had, in fact, collided with a low table on which a single candle burned and beyond which a mountainous figure could be made out, sitting cross-legged on the floor. 'Sit, sit,' said a man's calm, deep voice, and her legs, needing no more flowery invitation, buckled beneath her at the terse command. Clutching her left hand in her right, she forced her voice to respond evenly:

'And you, sir, will be the thief I have been requesting?'

Shifting its weight very slightly, the shadow-mountain informed Huma that all criminal activity originating in this zone was well organised and also centrally controlled, so that all requests for what might be termed freelance work had to be channelled through this room.

He demanded comprehensive details of the crime to be committed, including a precise inventory of items to be acquired, also a clear statement of all financial inducements being offered with no gratuities excluded, plus, for filing purposes only, a summary of the motives for the application.

At this, Huma, as though remembering something, stiffened both in body and resolve and replied loudly that her motives were entirely a matter for herself; that she would discuss details with no one but the thief himself; but that the rewards she proposed could only be described as 'lavish'.

'All I am willing to disclose to you, sir, since it appears that I am on the premises of some sort of employment agency, is that in return for such lavish rewards I must have the most desperate criminal at your disposal, a man for whom life holds no terrors, not even the fear of God.

'The worst of fellows, I tell you—nothing less will do!'

At this a paraffin storm-lantern was lighted, and Huma saw facing her a grey-haired giant down whose left cheek ran the most sinister of scars, a cicatrice in the shape of the letter *sín* in the Nastaliq script. She was gripped by the insupportably nostalgic notion that the bogeyman of her childhood nursery had risen up to confront her, because her ayah had always forestalled any incipient acts of disobedience by threatening Huma and Atta: 'You don't watch out and I'll send that one to steal you away – that Sheikh Sín, the Thief of Thieves!'

Here, grey-haired but unquestionably scarred, was the notorious criminal himself – and was she out of her mind, were her ears playing tricks, or had he truly just announced that, given the stated circumstances, he himself was the only man for the job?

Struggling hard against the newborn goblins of nostalgia, Huma warned the fearsome volunteer that only a matter of extreme urgency and peril would have brought her unescorted into these ferocious streets.

'Because we can afford no last-minute backings-out,' she continued, 'I am determined to tell you everything, keeping back no secrets whatsoever. If, after hearing me out, you are still prepared to proceed, then we shall do everything in our power to assist you, and to make you rich.'

The old thief shrugged, nodded, spat. Huma began her story.

Six days ago, everything in the household of her father, the wealthy moneylender Hashim, had been as it always was. At breakfast her mother had spooned khichri lovingly on to the moneylender's plate; the conversation had been filled with those expressions of courtesy and solicitude on which the family prided itself.

Hashim was fond of pointing out that while he was not a godly man he set great store by 'living honourably in the world'. In that spacious lakeside residence, all outsiders were greeted with the same formality and respect, even those unfortunates who came to negotiate for small fragments of Hashim's large fortune, and of whom he naturally asked an interest rate of over seventy per cent, partly, as he told his khichri-spooning wife, 'to teach these people the value of money; let them only learn that, and they will be cured of this fever of borrowing borrowing all the time—so you see that if my plans succeed, I shall put myself out of business!'

In their children, Atta and Huma, the moneylender and his wife had successfully sought to inculcate the virtues of thrift, plain dealing and a healthy independence of spirit. On this, too, Hashim was fond of congratulating himself.

Breakfast ended; the family members wished one another a fulfilling day. Within a few hours, however, the glassy contentment of that household, of that life of porcelain delicacy and alabaster sensibilities, was to be shattered beyond all hope of repair.

The moneylender summoned his personal shikara and was on the point of stepping into it when, attracted by a glint of silver, he noticed a small vial floating between the boat and his private quay. On an impulse, he scooped it out of the glutinous water.

It was a cylinder of tinted glass cased in exquisitely wrought silver, and Hashim saw within its walls a silver pendant bearing a single strand of human hair.

Closing his fist around this unique discovery, he muttered to the boatman that he'd changed his plans, and hurried to his sanctum, where, behind closed doors, he feasted his eyes on his find.

🌸

There can be no doubt that Hashim the moneylender knew from the first that he was in possession of the famous relic of the Prophet Muhammad, that revered hair whose theft from its shrine at Hazratbal mosque the previous morning had created an unprecedented hue and cry in the valley.

The thieves—no doubt alarmed by the pandemonium, by the procession through the streets of endless ululating crocodiles of lamentation, by the riots, the political ramifications and by the massive police search which was commanded and carried out by men whose entire careers now hung upon the finding of this lost hair—had evidently panicked and hurled the vial into the gelatine bosom of the lake.

Having found it by a stroke of great good fortune, Hashim's duty as a citizen was clear: the hair must be restored to its shrine, and the state to equanimity and peace.

But the moneylender had a different notion.

All around him in his study was the evidence of his collector's mania. There were enormous glass cases full of impaled butterflies from Gulmarg, three dozen scale models in various metals of the legendary cannon Zamzama, innumerable swords, a Naga spear, ninety-four terracotta camels of the sort sold on railway station platforms, many samovars, and a whole zoology of tiny sandalwood animals, which had originally been carved to serve as children's bathtime toys.

'And after all,' Hashim told himself, 'the Prophet would have disapproved mightily of this relic-worship. He abhorred the idea of being deified! So, by keeping this hair from its distracted devotees, I perform—do I not?—a finer service than I would by returning it! Naturally, I don't want it for its religious value . . . I'm a man of the world, of this world. I see it purely as a secular object of great rarity and blinding beauty. In short, it's the silver vial I desire, more than the hair.

'They say there are American millionaires who purchase stolen art masterpieces and hide them away—they would know how I feel. I must, must have it!'

Every collector must share his treasures with one other human being, and Hashim summoned—and told—his only son Atta, who was deeply perturbed but, having been sworn to secrecy, only spilled the beans when the troubles became too terrible to bear.

The youth excused himself and left his father alone in the crowded solitude of his collections. Hashim was sitting erect in a hard, straight-backed chair, gazing intently at the beautiful vial.

🌸

It was well known that the moneylender never ate lunch, so it was not until evening that a servant entered the sanctum to summon his master to the dining-table. He found Hashim as Atta had left him. The same, and not the same—for now the moneylender looked swollen, distended. His eyes bulged even more than they always had, they were red-rimmed, and his knuckles were white.

He seemed to be on the point of bursting! As though, under the influence of the misappropriated relic, he had filled up with some spectral fluid which might at any moment ooze uncontrollably from his every bodily opening.

He had to be helped to the table, and then the explosion did indeed take place.

Seemingly careless of the effect of his words on the carefully constructed and fragile constitution of the family's life, Hashim began to gush, to spume long streams of awful truths. In horrified silence, his children heard their father turn upon his wife, and reveal to her that for many years their marriage had been the worst of his afflictions. 'An end to politeness!' he thundered. 'An end to hypocrisy!'

Next, and in the same spirit, he revealed to his family the existence of a mistress; he informed them also of his regular visits to paid women. He told his wife that, far from being the principal beneficiary of his will, she would receive no more than the eighth portion which was her due under Islamic law. Then he turned upon his children, screaming at Atta for his lack of academic ability — 'A dope! I have been cursed with a dope!' — and accusing his daughter of lasciviousness, because she went around the city barefaced, which was unseemly for any good Muslim girl to do. She should, he commanded, enter purdah forthwith.

Hashim left the table without having eaten and fell into the deep sleep of a man who has got many things off his chest, leaving his children stunned, in tears, and the dinner going cold on the sideboard under the gaze of an anticipatory bearer.

At five o'clock the next morning the moneylender forced his family to rise, wash and say their prayers. From then on, he began to pray five times daily for the first time in his life, and his wife and children were obliged to do likewise.

Before breakfast, Huma saw the servants, under her father's direction, constructing a great heap of books in the garden and setting fire to it. The only volume left untouched was the Qur'an, which Hashim wrapped in a silken cloth and placed on a table in the hall. He ordered each member of his family to read passages from this book for at least two hours per day. Visits to the cinema were forbidden. And if Atta invited male friends to the house, Huma was to retire to her room.

By now, the family had entered a state of shock and dismay; but there was worse to come.

That afternoon, a trembling debtor arrived at the house to confess his inability to pay the latest instalment of interest owed, and made the mistake of reminding Hashim, in somewhat blustering fashion, of the Qur'an's strictures against usury. The moneylender flew into a rage and attacked the fellow with one of his large collection of bullwhips.

By mischance, later the same day a second defaulter came to plead for time, and was seen fleeing Hashim's study with a great gash in his arm, because Huma's father had called him a thief of other men's money and had tried to cut off the wretch's right hand with one of the thirty-eight kukri knives hanging on the study walls.

These breaches of the family's unwritten laws of decorum alarmed Atta and Huma, and when, that evening, their mother attempted to calm Hashim down, he struck her on the face with an open hand. Atta leapt to his mother's defence and he, too, was sent flying.

'From now on,' Hashim bellowed, 'there's going to be some discipline around here!'

The moneylender's wife began a fit of hysterics which continued throughout that night and the following day, and which so provoked her husband that he threatened her with divorce, at which she fled to her room, locked the door and subsided into a raga of sniffling. Huma now lost her composure, challenged her father openly, and announced (with that same independence of spirit which he had encouraged in her) that she would wear no cloth over her face; apart from anything else, it was bad for the eyes.

On hearing this, her father disowned her on the spot and gave her one week in which to pack her bags and go.

By the fourth day, the fear in the air of the house had become so thick that it was difficult to walk around. Atta told his shock-numbed sister: 'We are descending to gutter-level—but I know what must be done.'

That afternoon, Hashim left home accompanied by two hired thugs to extract the unpaid dues from his two insolvent clients. Atta went immediately to his father's study. Being the son and heir, he possessed his own key to the moneylender's safe. This he now used, and removing the little vial from its hiding-place, he slipped it into his trouser pocket and re-locked the safe door.

Now he told Huma the secret of what his father had fished out of Lake Dal, and exclaimed: 'Maybe I'm crazy—maybe the awful things that are happening have made me cracked – but I am convinced there will be no peace in our house until this hair is out of it.'

His sister at once agreed that the hair must be returned, and Atta set off in a hired shikara to Hazratbal mosque. Only when the boat had delivered him into the throng of the distraught faithful which was swirling around the desecrated shrine did Atta discover that the relic was no longer in his pocket. There was only a hole, which his mother, usually so attentive to household matters, must have overlooked under the stress of recent events.

Atta's initial surge of chagrin was quickly replaced by a feeling of profound relief.

'Suppose', he imagined, 'that I had already announced to the mullahs that the hair was on my person! They would never have believed me now—and this mob would have lynched me! At any rate, it has gone, and that's a load off my mind.' Feeling more contented than he had for days, the young man returned home.

Here he found his sister bruised and weeping in the hall; upstairs, in her bedroom, his mother wailed like a brand-new widow. He begged Huma to tell him what had happened, and when she replied that their father, returning from his brutal business trip, had once again noticed a glint of silver between boat and quay, had once again scooped up the errant relic, and was consequently in a rage to end all rages, having beaten the truth out of her—then Atta buried his face in his hands and sobbed out his opinion, which was that the hair was persecuting them, and had come back to finish the job.

It was Huma's turn to think of a way out of their troubles.

While her arms turned black and blue and great stains spread across her forehead, she hugged her brother and whispered to him that she was determined to get rid of the hair *at all costs*—she repeated this last phrase several times.

'The hair', she then declared, 'was stolen from the mosque; so it can be stolen from this house. But it must be a genuine robbery, carried out by a bona-fide thief, not by one of us who are under the hair's thrall—by a thief so desperate that he fears neither capture nor curses.'

Unfortunately, she added, the theft would be ten times harder to pull off now that their father, knowing that there had already been one attempt on the relic, was certainly on his guard.

'Can you do it?'

Huma, in a room lit by candle and storm-lantern, ended her account with one further question: 'What assurances can you give that the job holds no terrors for you still?'

The criminal, spitting, stated that he was not in the habit of providing references, as a cook might, or a gardener, but he was not alarmed so easily, certainly not by any children's djinni of a curse. Huma had to be content with this boast, and proceeded to describe the details of the proposed burglary.

'Since my brother's failure to return the hair to the mosque, my father has taken to sleeping with his precious treasure under his pillow. However, he sleeps alone, and very energetically; only enter his room without waking him, and he will certainly have tossed and turned quite enough to make the theft a simple matter. When you have the vial, come to my room,' and here she handed Sheikh Sín a plan of her home, 'and I will hand over all the jewellery owned by my mother and myself. You will find . . . it is worth . . . that is, you will be able to get a fortune for it . . .'

It was evident that her self-control was weakening and that she was on the point of physical collapse.

'Tonight,' she burst out finally. 'You must come tonight!'

No sooner had she left the room than the old criminal's body was convulsed by a fit of coughing: he spat blood into an old vanaspati can. The great Sheikh, the 'Thief of Thieves', had become a sick man, and every day the time drew nearer when some young pretender to his power would stick a dagger in his stomach. A lifelong addiction to gambling had left him almost as poor as he had been when, decades ago, he had started out in this line of work as a mere pickpocket's apprentice; so in the extraordinary commission he had accepted from the moneylender's daughter he saw his opportunity of amassing enough wealth at a stroke to leave the valley for ever, and acquire the luxury of a respectable death which would leave his stomach intact.

As for the Prophet's hair, well, neither he nor his blind wife had ever had much to say for prophets—that was one thing they had in common with the moneylender's thunderstruck clan.

It would not do, however, to reveal the nature of this, his last crime, to his four sons. To his consternation, they had all grown up to be hopelessly devout men, who even spoke of making the pilgrimage to Mecca some day. 'Absurd!' their father would laugh at them. 'Just tell me how you will go?' For, with a parent's absolutist love, he had made sure they were all provided with a lifelong source of high income by crippling them at birth, so that, as they dragged themselves around the city, they earned excellent money in the begging business.

The children, then, could look after themselves.

He and his wife would be off soon with the jewelboxes of the moneylender's women. It was a timely chance indeed that had brought the beautiful bruised girl into his corner of the town.

That night, the large house on the shore of the lake lay blindly waiting, with silence lapping at its walls. A burglar's night: clouds in the sky and mists on the winter water. Hashim the moneylender was asleep, the only member of his family to whom sleep had come that night. In another room, his son Atta lay deep in the coils of his coma with a blood-clot forming on his brain, watched over by a mother who had let down her long greying hair to show her grief, a mother who placed warm compresses on his head with gestures redolent of impotence. In a third bedroom Huma waited, fully dressed, amidst the jewel-heavy caskets of her desperation.

At last a bulbul sang softly from the garden below her window and, creeping downstairs, she opened a door to the bird, on whose face there was a scar in the shape of the Nastaliq letter *sín*.

Noiselessly, the bird flew up the stairs behind her. At the head of the staircase they parted, moving in opposite directions along the corridor of their conspiracy without a glance at one another.

Entering the moneylender's room with professional ease, the burglar, Sín, discovered that Huma's predictions had been wholly accurate. Hashim lay sprawled diagonally across his bed, the pillow untenanted by his head, the prize easily accessible. Step by padded step, Sín moved towards the goal.

It was at this point that, in the bedroom next door, young Atta sat bolt upright in his bed, giving his mother a great fright, and without any warning—prompted by goodness knows what pressure of the blood-clot upon his brain—began screaming at the top of his voice:

'*Thief! Thief! Thief!*'

⬡

It seems probable that his poor mind had been dwelling, in these last moments, upon his own father; but it is impossible to be certain, because having uttered these three emphatic words the young man fell back upon his pillow and died.

At once his mother set up a screeching and a wailing and a keening and a howling so earsplittingly intense that they completed the work which Atta's cry had begun—that is, her laments penetrated the walls of her husband's bedroom and brought Hashim wide awake.

Sheikh Sín was just deciding whether to dive beneath the bed or brain the moneylender good and proper when Hashim grabbed the tiger-striped swordstick which always stood propped up in a corner beside his bed, and rushed from the room without so much as noticing the burglar who stood on the opposite side of the bed in the darkness. Sín stooped quickly and removed the vial containing the Prophet's hair from its hiding-place.

Meanwhile Hashim had erupted into the corridor, having unsheathed the sword inside his cane. In his right hand he held the weapon and was waving it about dementedly. His left hand was shaking the stick. A shadow came rushing towards him through the midnight darkness of the passageway and, in his somnolent anger, the moneylender thrust his sword fatally through its heart. Turning up the light, he found that he had murdered his daughter, and under the dire influence of this accident he was so overwhelmed by remorse that he turned the sword upon himself, fell upon it and so extinguished his life. His wife, the sole surviving member of the family, was driven mad by the general carnage and had to be committed to an asylum for the insane by her brother, the city's Deputy Commissioner of Police.

Sheikh Sín had quickly understood that the plan had gone awry.

Abandoning the dream of the jewel-boxes when he was but a few yards from its fulfilment, he climbed out of Hashim's window and made his escape during the appalling events described above. Reaching home before dawn, he woke his wife and confessed his failure. It would be necessary, he whispered, for him to vanish for a while. Her blind eyes never opened until he had gone.

The noise in the Hashim household had roused their servants and even managed to awaken the night-watchman, who had been fast asleep as usual on his charpoy by the street-gate. They alerted the police, and the Deputy Commissioner himself was informed. When he heard of Huma's death, the mournful officer opened and read the sealed letter which his niece had given him, and instantly led a large detachment of armed men into the light-repellent gullies of the most wretched and disreputable part of the city.

The tongue of a malicious cat-burglar named Huma's fellow-conspirator; the finger of an ambitious bank-robber pointed at the house in which he lay concealed; and although Sín managed to crawl through a hatch in the attic and attempt a roof-top escape, a bullet from the Deputy Commissioner's own rifle penetrated his stomach and brought him crashing messily to the ground at the feet of Huma's enraged uncle.

From the dead thief's pocket rolled a vial of tinted glass, cased in filigree silver.

The recovery of the Prophet's hair was announced at once on All-India Radio. One month later, the valley's holiest men assembled at the Hazratbal mosque and formally authenticated the relic. It sits to this day in a closely guarded vault by the shores of the loveliest of lakes in the heart of the valley which was once closer than any other place on earth to Paradise.

But before our story can properly be concluded, it is necessary to record that when the four sons of the dead Sheikh awoke on the morning of his death, having unwittingly spent a few minutes under the same roof as the famous hair, they found that a miracle had occurred, that they were all sound of limb and strong of wind, as whole as they might have been if their father had not thought to smash their legs in the first hours of their lives. They were, all four of them, very properly furious, because the miracle had reduced their earning powers by 75 per cent, at the most conservative estimate; so they were ruined men.

Only the Sheikh's widow had some reason for feeling grateful, because although her husband was dead she had regained her sight, so that it was possible for her to spend her last days gazing once more upon the beauties of the valley of Kashmir.

Masculine Confession
(1969)

NAWĀL SA'DĀWĪ

Pour me another glass of wine, with a lot of ice. Let me talk and don't interrupt me. From time to time you can stroke my head or neck or chest or any part of my body you like, only don't stop me talking, because I came to you tonight to confess things I can't confess to anyone else, not even to God's agents on earth.

Actually, I don't believe in such agents, and I dislike any intermediaries between myself and God. That doesn't mean that I'm proud or arrogant or that I deal haughtily with people. Quite the opposite. I'm humble and compassionate, and I am concerned for all people and for myself as one of them.

My self-concern is limitless, because I love myself. Yes, I confess to you that my only true love is my love of myself. I fell in love with myself the moment my mother gave birth to me. Her eyes shone as she said to my father: It's a boy! I loved my masculinity and from the start I realized it was the reason for my being privileged. I always had to prove its existence, declare it, show it to people to make it clear and visible and so firm that it was not open to doubt.

One day, when I was young, I was standing in the street beside my father when suddenly a big fat foot trod on my toes. I screamed 'ow' in pain. My father looked at me angrily and said harshly: A man never says 'ow'. Since that day, I have never said 'ow'. I would hold back the pain and the tears when I was hurt or someone hit me and would brace the muscles of my back and neck and tell myself: I'm a man.

Once, when the doctor was digging his sharp scalpel into the sole of my foot to remove a splinter of glass, I felt my flesh tear and the blood flow. I was drowning in a sea of sweat from so much pain, but I didn't say 'ow'. That night, when everybody was asleep, I found myself crying in my sleep, softly murmuring 'ow, ow' until the morning.

When I awoke, I braced my back and neck muscles, put on my masculinity and wore it proudly, telling myself: I'm a man. What did you say, my dear? My feet and fingers are as soft as yours? That's true. I belong to the leisured class, the bourgeoisie, in other words. I only use my fingers to hold a glass of wine or to sign my name on some papers in the office or to wave to friends. My friends are many, as you know, and I love them all, just as I love all people. In other words, I love nobody. That doesn't mean that I hate them. It's just that I'm always self-concerned, always absorbed in loving myself. I'm ready at any time to defend myself, by any means, even by committing murder.

Don't look at me like that, as though I'm the only criminal on earth. Crime in the lives of us men is a matter of necessity. It's the only possible way for a man to prove he's a man. But since crime calls for bravery or authority, I'm unable to be a criminal. All I have are daydreams in which I imagine myself a bold hero, separating heads from bodies with a rapid blow of my sword. We men have great admiration for murderers. A man cannot admire another man without hating him. That's the reason I feel so ill at ease when I'm amongst important men in authority. And that's why I run away from the company of reputable men and why I feel at ease in the company of disreputable men. But in general, I prefer the company of women. For with a woman, no matter how important she is, one privilege remains mine—my masculinity. What did you say? Please don't interrupt me. Pour me another glass of wine, with a lot of ice, and let me unburden the crimes which weigh on my heart.

I'm not lying to you. All my crimes are human because they have one aim—to prove that I'm a man. No man can prove his masculinity except by beating other men. So I could not avoid entering into the eternal conflict, the conflict with all other men. In conference rooms or in bedrooms, the conflict is one and the same. Since in conference rooms I lack courage and authority, there's nothing left for me other than bedrooms. Don't call me a wolf or a womanizer. No, I'm a married man. I love my wife like I love my mother, with the same sort of spiritual, holy love. In other words, a love in which I take everything and to which I give nothing. That's ideal love. My wife is the only person (and before her it was my mother) with whom I can get angry and at whom I can rage freely. The reason's well known. She can't return my anger in the same way. We men can't show our anger with those who can be angry with us. I am never angry with my boss, but I get angry quickly with my mother. And with my wife I get angry and rage freely, as I do with my children. All of them I provide for and feed and if they got angry with me, they wouldn't find anyone to replace me.

That's what marriage is for. How else would it be possible for a man to give vent to his anger if it weren't for marriage? The poorest man from the lowest social class goes home to his wife, in the end, in order to be angry and to feel that he's a man. What did you say, my dear?

That's why you refused to get married? You're an intelligent woman. I don't think it's only your intelligence that draws me to your bed, you above all other women. So why is it to you especially that I confess, like a man does to his god? Why do I creep from my wife's bed every night to come to you? I'm not lying to you. It's not love, because as I said, I fell in love with myself from the start and that's the beginning and end of it.

The reason, my dear, is that you're the only person with whom I don't have to prove myself a man. That wasn't clear to me in the beginning. I used to ask myself: what ties me to this woman, why do I need her so much? I discovered the reason that night. Do you remember? It was the night I came to you after my shattering defeat to my rival in the election and the violent argument I had with my wife when I found her naked in my friend's arms. I came to you and cried in your arms, and as I cried I felt as though the tears had been bottled up inside me, like steam under pressure, ever since the time my father told me off when I was a child and had said: A man never says 'ow'. That night I saw my tears flow like a river and heard my voice shout 'ow' over and over again. When I came to, I found my head at your feet, kneeling at your altar like a person kneels in a house of worship. What did you say, my dear? You saw the first real smile on my face? I told you it was the happiest night of my life? It's true. For the first time in my life, I discovered how stupid I'd been. When I was a boy, I almost lost an eye in a fight to prove myself a man. In my teens, I nearly lost my life on a number of occasions because of my perpetual readiness to compete. As an adult, I almost lost my mental faculties because of my defeat and then my wife's betrayal. But everything changed that night. The false mask which we call masculinity fell away, and I began to see my real self. For the first time, I discovered that I did not have to prove to myself or to others that I was a man. What does 'man' mean, after all? This discovery was the happiest moment in my life. I was so happy, I began to smother you with kisses, to kiss your feet, and rub my nose in them and cry. I found that the taste of my tears and my lowly position at your feet was sweet. What did you say? I confessed my love to you that night? Yes, my dear, I told you that I loved you. But I admit that as soon as I left your place and went back home and then to my office, I felt ashamed of myself. I was ashamed when I realized how I'd revealed to you a hidden part of myself, the feminine part, the part which all men hide as an imperfection. I was so ashamed that I decided never to see you again. But I returned to you the following night and the next night and every night, without a break. I know that I am bound to you by the force of my desire not to be a man but to be myself, as I am. But I'm also bound to this false masculine world. I put on the mask and take my place in the ranks. I play my part. I deliver blows whenever the other cannot hit me, and I receive blows from those above me without responding. I suppress my anger until I get home to my wife, and I hold back the tears until I come to you. It's a fair division, my dear. Men like us need at least two women. A woman with whom he can get angry and a woman with whom he can cry. What did you say, my dear? Yes, my wife loves me. She betrayed me because she loves me so much. I wasn't sure of that, but now I'm convinced of it. I am devoted to my wife and desire her more and more. Yes, I desire her more, my dear, because through her I have discovered something new that I couldn't have discovered by myself. I discovered that I'm not the only man on earth. I confess to you that I feel very comforted by this discovery. It's the comfort of surrendering to a fact to which I was unable to surrender before. If men experienced such comfort just once, they'd encourage their wives to betray them as quickly as possible. How many years I lost without this comfort, my dear.

What did you say? I'm very late? Yes, yes. But I'm luckier than others. Some men die believing they're the only one on earth.

What did you say? Women know this from the start? Yes, my dear. Women are smarter than men. A woman always knows that she's not the only woman on earth. Pour me another glass, with a lot of ice. Let me die in your arms and don't interrupt me.

Moscow
(2000)

MARJANE SATRAPI

MOSCOW

SO MY FATHER WAS NOT A HERO.

IS EVERYTHING ALL RIGHT, MARJI?

YEAH, SURE...

IF ONLY HE HAD BEEN IN PRISON.

THEY CUT MY DAD'S LEG OFF, BUT HE STILL DIDN'T CONFESS!... SO THEY CUT OFF AN ARM AS WELL.

TOO MUCH!

LUCKILY, ONE DAY THEY TOLD ME ABOUT MY UNCLE ANOOSH.

THE ONLY ONE OF MY FATHER'S BROTHERS I HAD NEVER MET. BECAUSE HE HAD BEEN IN PRISON. AND NOW, FOR THE FIRST TIME IN 30 YEARS, MY GRANDMA WAS REUNITED WITH HER SIX CHILDREN.

AND I HAD A HERO IN MY FAMILY... NATURALLY I LOVED HIM IMMEDIATELY.

WHY DON'T YOU COME AND LIVE WITH US?

SUCH A SWEET CHILD! I'LL SLEEP HERE TONIGHT AND TELL YOU STORIES.

ARE YOU MARRIED? DO YOU HAVE CHILDREN? HOW OLD ARE YOU?

LATER MARJI, LATER.

DON'T BOTHER HIM TOO MUCH, HE'S TIRED.

GOOD NIGHT.

DON'T WORRY, WE'RE FINE.

OK, HERE GOES: I WAS 18 YEARS OLD WHEN MY UNCLE FEREYDOON AND HIS FRIENDS PROCLAIMED THE INDEPENDENCE OF THE IRANIAN PROVINCE OF AZERBAIJAN...

WOW!

FEREYDOON ELECTED HIMSELF MINISTER OF JUSTICE OF THIS NEW LITTLE REPUBLIC.

GENTLEMEN, JUSTICE IS THE BASIS OF DEMOCRACY. ALL MEN SHOULD BE EQUAL IN THE EYES OF THE LAW.

MY IDEAS WERE THE SAME AS HIS BUT YOUR GRANDFATHER REMAINED FAITHFUL TO THE SHAH.

MY SON, A TRAITOR! GO AWAY AND JOIN UP WITH MY IDIOTIC BROTHER!

YOU'LL BOTH END UP BEING EXECUTED! DO YOU HEAR ME? EXECUTED!

I BECAME FEREYDOON'S SECRETARY. IT WAS A TIME OF DREAMS AND ENTHUSIASM.

AZERBAIJAN IS ONLY THE BEGINNING. WE ARE GOING TO FREE IRAN PROVINCE BY PROVINCE!!!

I'M CERTAIN YOU'RE RIGHT, UNCLE.

ONE NIGHT I HAD A TERRIBLE NIGHTMARE: DEAD PEOPLE, BLOOD...

THE NEXT MORNING, I WAS SO TORMENTED. I HAD TO SEE FEREYDOON.

SHIT! THE SHAH'S SOLDIERS!

GOOD GOD! FEREYDOON!

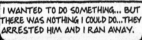

I WANTED TO DO SOMETHING... BUT THERE WAS NOTHING I COULD DO...THEY ARRESTED HIM AND I RAN AWAY.

WHAT A STORY!

FOR DAYS AND DAYS I WALKED THROUGH THE FALLING SNOW. I CROSSED THE ALBORZ MOUNTAINS TO FIND REFUGE AT MY PARENTS' HOUSE IN ASTARA.

I WAS HUNGRY, I WAS COLD, BUT I CONTINUED.

I WAS NEARLY DEAD WHEN I ARRIVED.

BANG! BANG! BANG!

MY GOD! ANOOSH!!!

WHAT'S GOING ON? WHO'S BOTHERING US AT THIS HOUR?

COME QUICKLY! IT'S OUR SON ANOOSH! HE HAS FAINTED!

WHAT IS HE DOING HERE? WHY DIDN'T HE STAY WITH HIS NICE UNCLE?

AFTER THE SEPARATION, I FELT VERY LONELY. I MISSED MY COUNTRY, MY PARENTS, MY BROTHERS. I DREAMT ABOUT THEM OFTEN.

I DECIDED TO GO HOME. I GOT A FALSE PASSPORT AND DISGUISED MYSELF.

I GUESS I WASN'T VERY CONVINCING. THEY SOON RECOGNIZED ME.

HEY! YOU WITH THE BEARD AND SUNGLASSES!

HALT!

THEY PUT ME IN PRISON FOR NINE YEARS.

NINE YEARS!

BETTER THAN LALY'S FATHER!

THEY SAY YOU WERE TORTURED TERRIBLY, LIKE SIAMAK, LALY'S FATHER.

YOUR FATHER TOLD YOU THAT?

NO, HE TOLD IT TO MOM AND I HEARD HIM.

WHAT MY WIFE MADE ME SUFFER WAS MUCH WORSE.

I TELL YOU ALL THIS BECAUSE IT'S IMPORTANT THAT YOU KNOW. OUR FAMILY MEMORY MUST NOT BE LOST. EVEN IF IT'S NOT EASY FOR YOU, EVEN IF YOU DON'T UNDERSTAND IT ALL.

DON'T WORRY, I'LL NEVER FORGET.

CivilWarLand in Bad Decline
(1992)

GEORGE SAUNDERS

Whenever a potential big investor comes for the tour the first thing I do is take him out to the transplanted Erie Canal Lock. We've got a good ninety feet of actual Canal out there and a well-researched dioramic of a coolie campsite. Were our faces ever red when we found out it was actually the Irish who built the Canal. We've got no budget to correct, so every fifteen minutes or so a device in the bunkhouse gives off the approximate aroma of an Oriental meal.

Today my possible Historical Reconstruction Associate is Mr. Haberstrom, founder of Burn'n'Learn. Burn'n'Learn is national. Their gimmick is a fully stocked library on the premises and as you tan you call out the name of any book you want to these high-school girls on roller skates. As we walk up the trail he's wearing a sweatsuit and smoking a cigar and I tell him I admire his acumen. I tell him some men are dreamers and others are doers. He asks which am I and I say let's face it, I'm basically the guy who leads the dreamers up the trail to view the Canal Segment. He likes that. He says I have a good head on my shoulders. He touches my arm and says he's hot to spend some reflective moments at the Canal because his great-grandfather was a barge guider way back when who got killed by a donkey. When we reach the clearing he gets all emotional and bolts off through the gambling plaster Chinese. Not to be crass but I sense an impending sizable contribution.

When I come up behind him however I see that once again the gangs have been at it with their spray cans, all over my Lock. Haberstrom takes a nice long look. Then he pokes me with the spitty end of his cigar and says not with his money I don't, and storms back down the trail.

I stand there alone a few minutes. The last thing I need is some fat guy's spit on my tie. I think about quitting. Then I think about my last degrading batch of résumés. Two hundred send-outs and no nibbles. My feeling is that prospective employers are put off by the fact that I was a lowly Verisimilitude Inspector for nine years with no promotions. I think of my car payment. I think of how much Marcus and Howie love the little playhouse I'm still paying off. Once again I decide to eat my pride and sit tight.

So I wipe off my tie with a leaf and start down to break the Haberstrom news to Mr. Alsuga.

Mr. A's another self-made man. He cashed in on his love of history by conceptualizing CivilWarLand in his spare time. He started out with just a settler's shack and one Union costume and now has considerable influence in Rotary.

His office is in City Hall. He agrees that the gangs are getting out of hand. Last month they wounded three Visitors and killed a dray horse. Several of them encircled and made fun of Mrs. Dugan in her settler outfit as she was taking her fresh-baked bread over to the simulated Towne Meeting. No way they're paying admission, so they're either tunneling in or coming in over the retaining wall.

Mr. Alsuga believes the solution to the gang problem is Teen Groups. I tell him that's basically what a gang is, a Teen Group. But he says how can it be a Teen Group without an adult mentor with a special skill, like whittling? Mr. Alsuga whittles. Once he gave an Old Tyme Skills Seminar on it in the Blacksmith Shoppe. It was poorly attended. All he got was two widowers and a chess-club type no gang would have wanted anyway. And myself. I attended. Evelyn called me a bootlicker, but I attended. She called me a bootlicker, and I told her she'd better bear in mind which side of the bread her butter was on. She said whichever side it was on it wasn't enough to shake a stick at. She's always denigrating my paystub. I came home from the Seminar with this kind of whittled duck. She threw it away the next day because she said she thought it was an acorn. It looked nothing like an acorn. As far as I'm concerned she threw it away out of spite. It made me livid and twice that night I had to step into a closet and perform my Hatred Abatement Breathing.

But that's neither here nor there.

Mr. Alsuga pulls out the summer stats. We're in the worst attendance decline in ten years. If it gets any worse, staff is going to be let go in droves. He gives me a meaningful look. I know full well I'm not one of his key players. Then he asks who we have that might be willing to fight fire with fire.

I say: I could research it.

He says: Why don't you research it?

So I go research it.

Sylvia Loomis IS the queen of info. It's in her personality. She enjoys digging up dirt on people. She calls herself an S&M buff in training. She's still too meek to go whole hog, so when she parties at the Make Me Club on Airport Road she limits herself to walking around talking mean while wearing kiddie handcuffs. But she's good at what she does, which is Security. It was Sylvia who identified the part-timer systematically crapping in the planters in the Gift Acquisition Center and Sylvia who figured out it was Phil in Grounds leaving obscene messages for the Teen Belles on MessageMinder. She has access to all records. I ask can she identify current employees with a history of violence. She says she can if I buy her lunch.

We decide to eat in-Park. We go over to Nate's Saloon. Sylvia says don't spread it around but two of the nine cancan girls are knocked up. Then she pulls out her folder and says that according to her review of the data, we have a pretty tame bunch on our hands. The best she can do is Ned Quinn. His records indicate that while in high school he once burned down a storage shed. I almost die laughing. Quinn's an Adjunct Thespian and a world-class worrywart. I can't count the times I've come upon him in Costuming, dwelling on the gory details of his Dread Disease Rider. He's a failed actor who won't stop trying. He says this is the only job he could find that would allow him to continue to develop his craft. Because he's ugly as sin he specializes in roles that require masks, such as Humpty-Dumpty during Mother Goose Days.

I report back to Mr. Alsuga and he says Quinn may not be much but he's all we've got. Quinn's dirt-poor with six kids and Mr. A says that's a plus, as we'll need someone between a rock and a hard place. What he suggests we do is equip the Desperate Patrol with live ammo and put Quinn in charge. The Desperate Patrol limps along under floodlights as the night's crowning event. We've costumed them to resemble troops who've been in the field too long. We used actual Gettysburg photos. The climax of the Patrol is a re-enacted partial rebellion, quelled by a rousing speech. After the speech the boys take off their hats and put their arms around each other and sing "I Was Born Under a Wandering Star." Then there's fireworks and the Parade of Old-Fashioned Conveyance. Then we clear the place out and go home.

"Why not confab with Quinn?" Mr. A says. "Get his input and feelings."

"I was going to say that," I say.

I look up the Thespian Center's SpeedDial extension and a few minutes later Quinn's bounding up the steps in the Wounded Grizzly suit.

"Desperate Patrol?" Mr. A says as Quinn sits down. "Any interest on your part?"

"Love it," Quinn says. "Excellent." He's been trying to get on Desperate Patrol for years. It's considered the pinnacle by the Thespians because of the wealth of speaking parts. He's so excited he's shifting around in his seat and getting some of his paw blood on Mr. A's nice cane chair.

"The gangs in our park are a damn blight," Mr. A says. "I'm talking about meeting force with force. Something in it for you? Oh yes."

"I'd like to see Quinn give the rousing speech myself," I say.

"Societal order," Mr. A says. "Sustaining the lifeblood of this goddamned park we've all put so much of our hearts into."

"He's not just free-associating," I say.

"I'm not sure I get it," Quinn says.

"What I'm suggesting is live ammo in your weapon only," Mr. A says. "Fire at your discretion. You see an unsavory intruder, you shoot at his feet. Just give him a scare. Nobody gets hurt. An additional two bills a week is what I'm talking."

"I'm an actor," Quinn says.

"Quinn's got kids," I say. "He knows the value of a buck."

"This is acting of the highest stripe," Mr. A says. "Act like a mercenary."

"Go for it on a trial basis," I say.

"I'm not sure I get it," Quinn says. "But jeez, that's good money."

"Superfantastic," says Mr. A.

Next evening Mr. A and I go over the Verisimilitude Irregularities List. We've been having some heated discussions about our bird-species percentages. Mr. Grayson, Staff Ornithologist, has recently recalculated and estimates that to accurately approximate the 1865 bird population we'll need to eliminate a couple hundred orioles or so. He suggests using air guns or poison. Mr. A says that, in his eyes, in fiscally troubled times, an ornithologist is a luxury, and this may be the perfect time to send Grayson packing. I like Grayson. He went way overboard on Howie's baseball candy. But I've got me and mine to think of. So I call Grayson in. Mr. A says did you botch the initial calculation or were you privy to new info. Mr. Grayson admits it was a botch. Mr. A sends him out into the hall and we confab.

"You'll do the telling," Mr. A says. "I'm getting too old for cruelty."

He takes his walking stick and beeper and says he'll be in the Great Forest if I need him.

I call Grayson back in and let him go, and hand him Kleenexes and fend off a few blows and almost before I know it he's reeling out the door and I go grab a pita.

Is this the life I envisioned for myself? My God no. I wanted to be a high jumper. But I have two of the sweetest children ever born. I go in at night and look at them in their fairly expensive sleepers and think: There are a couple of kids who don't need to worry about freezing to death or being cast out to the wolves. You should see their little eyes light up when I bring home a treat. They may not know the value of a dollar, but it's my intention to see that they never need to.

I'm filling out Grayson's Employee Retrospective when I hear gunshots from the perimeter. I run out and there's Quinn and a few of his men tied to the cannon. The gang guys took Quinn's pants and put some tiny notches in his penis with their knives. I free Quinn and tell him to get over to the Infirmary to guard against infection. He's absolutely shaking and can hardly walk, so I wrap him up in a Confederate flag and call over a hay cart and load him in.

When I tell Mr. A he says: Garbage in, garbage out, and that we were idiots for expecting a milquetoast to save our rears.

We decide to leave the police out of it because of the possible bad PR. So we give Quinn the rest of the week off and promise to let him play Grant now and then, and that's that.

When visitors first come in there's this cornball part where they sit in this kind of spaceship and supposedly get blasted into space and travel faster than the speed of light and end up in 1865. The unit's dated. The helmets we distribute look like bowls and all the paint's peeling off. I've argued and argued that we need to update. But in the midst of a budget crunch one can't necessarily hang the moon. When the tape of space sounds is over and the walls stop shaking, we pass out the period costumes. We try not to offend anyone, liability law being what it is. We distribute the slave and Native American roles equitably among racial groups. Anyone is free to request a different identity at any time. In spite of our precautions, there's a Herlicher in every crowd. He's the guy who sued us last fall for making him hangman. He claimed that for weeks afterwards he had nightmares and because he wasn't getting enough sleep botched a big contract by sending an important government buyer a load of torn pool liners. Big deal, is my feeling. But he's suing us for fifty grand for emotional stress because the buyer ridiculed him in front of his co-workers. Whenever he comes in we make him sheriff but he won't back down an inch.

Mr. A calls me into his office and says he's got bad news and bad news, and which do I want first. I say the bad news. First off, he says, the gangs have spraypainted a picture of Quinn's notched penis on the side of the Everly Mansion. Second, last Friday's simulated frontier hunt has got us in hot water, because apparently some of the beef we toughen up to resemble buffalo meat was tainted, and the story's going in the Sunday supplement. And finally, the verdict's come in on the Herlicher case and we owe that goofball a hundred grand instead of fifty because the pinko judge empathized.

I wait for him to say I'm fired but instead he breaks down in tears. I pat his back and mix him a drink. He says why don't I join him. So I join him.

"It doesn't look good," he says, "for men like you and I."

"No it doesn't," I say.

"All I wanted to do," he says, "was to give the public a meaningful perspective on a historical niche I've always found personally fascinating."

"I know what you mean," I say.

At eleven the phone rings. It's Maurer in Refuse Control calling to say that the gangs have set fire to the Anglican Church. That structure cost upwards of ninety thousand to transport from Clydesville and refurbish. We can see the flames from Mr. A's window.

"Oh Christ!" Mr. A says. "If I could kill those kids I would kill those kids. One shouldn't desecrate the dream of another individual in the fashion in which they have mine."

"I know it," I say.

We drink and drink and finally he falls asleep on his office couch.

On the way to my car I keep an eye out for the ghostly McKinnon family. Back in the actual 1860s all this land was theirs. Their homestead's long gone but our records indicate that it was located near present-day Information Hoedown. They probably never saw this many buildings in their entire lives. They don't realize we're chronically slumming, they just think the valley's prospering. Something bad must have happened to them because their spirits are always wandering around at night looking dismayed.

Tonight I find the Mrs. doing wash by the creek. She sees me coming and asks if she can buy my boots. Machine stitching amazes her. I ask how are the girls. She says Maribeth has been sad because no appropriate boy ever died in the valley so she's doomed to loneliness forever. Maribeth is a homely sincere girl who glides around mooning and pining and reading bad poetry chapbooks. Whenever we keep the Park open late for high-school parties, she's in her glory. There was one kid who was able to see her and even got a crush on her, but when he finally tried to kiss her near Hostelry and found out she was spectral it just about killed him. I slipped him a fifty and told him to keep it under wraps. As far as I know he's still in therapy. I realize I should have come forward but they probably would have nut-hutted me, and then where would my family be?

The Mrs. says what Maribeth needs is choir practice followed by a nice quilting bee. In better times I would have taken the quilting-bee idea and run with it. But now there's no budget. That's basically how I finally moved up from Verisimilitude Inspector to Special Assistant, by lifting ideas from the McKinnons. The Mrs. likes me because after she taught me a few obscure 1800s ballads and I parlayed them into Individual Achievement Awards, I bought her a Rubik's Cube. To her, colored plastic is like something from Venus. The Mr. has kind of warned me away from her a couple of times. He doesn't trust me. He thinks the Rubik's Cube is the devil's work. I've brought him lighters and *Playboys* and once I even dragged out Howie's little synth and the mobile battery pak. I set the synth for carillon and played it from behind a bush. I could tell he was tickled, but he stonewalled. It's too bad I can't make an inroad because he was at Antietam and could be a gold mine of war info. He came back from the war and a year later died in his cornfield, which is now Parking. So he spends most of his time out there calling the cars Beelzebubs and kicking their tires.

Tonight he's walking silently up and down the rows. I get out to my KCar and think oh jeez, I've locked the keys in. The Mr. sits down at the base of the A3 lightpole and asks did I see the fire and do I realize it was divine retribution for my slovenly moral state. I say thank you very much. No way I'm telling him about the gangs. He can barely handle the concept of women wearing trousers. Finally I give up on prying the window down and go call Evelyn for the spare set. While I wait for her I sit on the hood and watch the stars. The Mr. watches them too. He says there are fewer than when he was a boy. He says that even the heavens have fallen into disrepair. I think about explaining smog to him but then Evelyn pulls up.

She's wearing her bathrobe and as soon as she gets out starts with the lip. Howie and Marcus are asleep in the back. The Mr. says it's part and parcel of my fallen state that I allow a woman to speak to me in such a tone. He suggests I throttle her and lock her in the wood-shed. Meanwhile she's going on and on so much about my irresponsibility that the kids are waking up. I want to get out before the gangs come swooping down on us. The Parking Area's easy pickings. She calls me a thoughtless oaf and sticks me in the gut with the car keys.

Marcus wakes up all groggy and says: Hey, our daddy.

Evelyn says: Yes, unfortunately he is.

Just after lunch next day a guy shows up at Personnel looking so completely Civil War they immediately hire him and send him out to sit on the porch of the old Kriegal place with a butter churn. His name's Samuel and he doesn't say a word going through Costuming and at the end of the day leaves on a bike. I do the normal clandestine New Employee Observation from the O'Toole gazebo and I like what I see. He seems to have a passable knowledge of how to pretend to churn butter. At one point he makes the mistake of departing from the list of Then-Current Events to discuss the World Series with a Visitor, but my feeling is, we can work with that. All in all he presents a positive and convincing appearance, and I say so in my review.

Sylvia runs her routine check on him and calls me at home that night and says boy do we have a hot prospect on our hands if fucking with the gangs is still on our agenda. She talks like that. I've got her on speakerphone in the rec room and Marcus starts running around the room saying fuck. Evelyn stands there with her arms crossed, giving me a drop-dead look. I wave her off and she flips me the bird.

Sylvia's federal sources indicate that Samuel got kicked out of Vietnam for participating in a bloodbath. Sylvia claims this is oxymoronic. She sounds excited. She suggests I take a nice long look at his marksmanship scores. She says his special combat course listing goes on for pages.

I call Mr. A and he says it sounds like Sam's our man. I express reservations at arming an alleged war criminal and giving him free rein in a family-oriented facility. Mr. A says if we don't get our act together there won't be any family-oriented facility left in a month. Revenues have hit rock bottom and his investors are frothing at the mouth. There's talk of outright closure and liquidation of assets.

He says: Now get off your indefensible high horse and give me Sam's home phone.

So I get off my indefensible high horse and give him Sam's home phone.

Thursday after we've armed Samuel and sent him and the Patrol out, I stop by the Worship Center to check on the Foley baptism. Baptisms are an excellent revenue source. We charge three hundred dollars to rent the Center, which is the former lodge of the Siala utopian free-love community. We trucked it in from downstate, a redbrick building with a nice gold dome. In the old days if one of the Sialians was overeating to the exclusion of others or excessively masturbating, he or she would be publicly dressed down for hours on end in the lodge. Now we put up white draperies and pipe in Stephen Foster and provide at no charge a list of preachers of various denominations.

The Foleys are an overweight crew. The room's full of crying sincere large people wishing the best for a baby. It makes me remember our own sweet beaners in their little frocks. I sit down near the wood-burning heater in the Invalid area and see that Justin in Prep has forgotten to remove the mannequin elderly couple clutching rosaries. Hopefully the Foleys won't notice and withhold payment.

The priest dips the baby's head into the fake marble basin and the door flies open and in comes a racially mixed gang. They stroll up the aisle tousling hair and requisition a Foley niece, a cute redhead of about sixteen. Her dad stands up and gets a blackjack in the head. One of the gang guys pushes her down the aisle with his hands on her breasts. As she passes

828

she looks right at me. The gang guy spits on my shoe and I make my face neutral so he won't get hacked off and drag me into it.

The door slams and the Foleys sit there stunned. Then the baby starts crying and everyone runs shouting outside in time to see the gang dragging the niece into the woods. I panic. I try to think of where the nearest pay phone is. I'm weighing the efficiency of running to Administration and making the call from my cubicle when six fast shots come from the woods. Several of the oldest Foleys assume the worst and drop weeping to their knees in the churchyard.

I don't know the first thing about counseling survivors, so I run for Mr. A.

He's drinking and watching his bigscreen. I tell him what happened and he jumps up and calls the police. Then he says let's go do whatever little we can for these poor people who entrusted us with their sacred family occasion only to have us drop the ball by failing to adequately protect them.

When we get back to the churchyard the Foleys are kicking and upbraiding six gang corpses. Samuel's having a glass of punch with the niece. The niece's dad is hanging all over Sam trying to confirm his daughter's virginity. Sam says it wasn't even close and goes on and on about the precision of his scope.

Then we hear sirens.

Sam says: I'm going into the woods.

Mr. A says: We never saw you, big guy.

The niece's dad says: Bless you, sir.

Sam says: Adios.

Mr. A stands on the hitching post and makes a little speech, the gist of which is, let's blame another gang for killing these dirtbags so Sam can get on with his important work.

The Foleys agree.

The police arrive and we all lie like rugs.

The word spreads on Sam and the gangs leave us alone. For two months the Park is quiet and revenues start upscaling. Then some high-school kid pulls a butter knife on Fred Moore and steals a handful of penny candy from the General Store. As per specs, Fred alerts Mr. A of a Revenue-Impacting Event. Mr. A calls Security and we perform Exit Sealage. We look everywhere, but the kid's gone. Mr. A says what the hell, Unseal, it's just candy, profit loss is minimal. Sam hears the Unseal Tone on the PA and comes out of the woods all mad with his face painted and says that once the word gets out we've gone soft the gangs will be back in a heartbeat. I ask since when do gangs use butter knives. Sam says a properly trained individual can kill a wild boar with a butter knife. Mr. A gives me a look and says why don't we let Sam run this aspect of the operation since he possesses the necessary expertise. Then Mr. A offers to buy him lunch and Sam says no, he'll eat raw weeds and berries as usual.

I go back to my Verisimilitude Evaluation on the Cimarron Brothel. Everything looks super. As per my recommendations they've replaced the young attractive simulated whores with uglier women with a little less on the ball. We were able to move the ex-simulated whores over to the Sweete Shoppe, so everybody's happy, especially the new simulated whores, who were for the most part middle-aged women we lured away from fast-food places via superior wages.

When I've finished the Evaluation I go back to my office for lunch. I step inside and turn on the fake oil lamp and there's a damn human hand on my chair, holding a note. All around the hand there's penny candy. The note says: Sir, another pig disciplined who won't mess with us anymore and also I need more ammo. It's signed: Samuel the Rectifier.

I call Mr. A and he says Jesus. Then he tells me to bury the hand in the marsh behind Refreshments. I say shouldn't we call the police. He says we let it pass when it was six dead kids, why should we start getting moralistic now over one stinking hand?

I say: But sir, he killed a high-schooler for stealing candy.

He says: That so-called high-schooler threatened Fred Moore, a valued old friend of mine, with a knife.

A butter knife, I say.

He asks if I've seen the droves of unemployed huddled in front of Personnel every morning.

I ask if that's a threat and he says no, it's a reasonable future prognostication.

"What's done is done," he says. "We're in this together. If I take the fall on this, you'll eat the wienie as well. Let's just put this sordid ugliness behind us and get on with the business of providing an enjoyable living for those we love."

I hang up and sit looking at the hand. There's a class ring on it.

Finally I knock it into a garbage sack with my phone and go out to the marsh.

As I'm digging, Mr. McKinnon glides up. He gets down on his knees and starts sniffing the sack. He starts talking about bloody wagon wheels and a boy he once saw sitting in a creek slapping the water with his own severed arm. He tells how the dead looked with rain on their faces and of hearing lunatic singing from all corners of the field of battle and of king-sized rodents gorging themselves on the entrails of his friends.

It occurs to me that the Mr.'s a loon.

I dig down a couple feet and drop the hand in. Then I backfill and get out of there fast. I look over my shoulder and he's rocking back and forth over the hole mumbling to himself.

As I pass a sewer cover the Mrs. rises out of it. Seeing the Mr. enthralled by blood she starts shrieking and howling to beat the band. When she finally calms down she comes to rest in a tree branch. Tears run down her see-through cheeks. She says there's been a horrid violent seed in him since he came home from the war. She says she can see they're going to have to go away. Then she blasts over my head elongate and glowing and full of grief and my hat gets sucked off.

All night I have bad dreams about severed hands. In one I'm eating chili and a hand comes out of my bowl and gives me the thumbs-down. I wake up with a tingling wrist. Evelyn says if I insist on sleeping uneasily would I mind doing it on the couch, since she has a family to care for during the day and this requires a certain amount of rest. I think about confessing to her but then I realize if I do she'll nail me.

The nights when she'd fall asleep with her cheek on my thigh are certainly long past.

I lie there awhile watching her make angry faces in her sleep. Then I go for a walk. As usual Mr. Ebershom's practicing figure-skating moves in his foyer. I sit down by our subdivision's fake creek and think. First of all, burying a hand isn't murder. It doesn't say anywhere thou shalt not bury some guy's hand. By the time I got involved the kid was dead. Where his hand ended up is inconsequential.

Then I think: What am I saying? I did a horrible thing. Even as I sit here I'm an accomplice and an obstructor of justice.

But then I see myself in the penitentiary and the boys waking up scared in the night without me, and right then and there with my feet in the creek I decide to stay clammed up forever and take my lumps in the afterlife.

Halloween's special in the Park. Our brochure says: Lose Yourself in Eerie Autumnal Splendor. We spray cobwebs around the Structures and dress up Staff in ghoul costumes and hand out period-authentic treats. We hide holograph generators in the woods and project images of famous Americans as ghosts. It's always a confusing time for the McKinnons. Last year the Mr. got in a head-to-head with the image of Jefferson Davis. He stood there in the woods yelling at it for hours while the Mrs. and the girls begged him to come away. Finally I had to cut power to the unit.

I drive home at lunch and pick the boys up for trick-or-treating. Marcus is a rancher and Howie's an accountant. He's wearing thick fake lips and carrying a ledger. The Park's the only safe place to trick-or-treat anymore. Last year some wacko in a complex near our house laced his Snickers with a virus. I drove by the school and they were CPRing this little girl in a canary suit. So forget it.

I take them around to the various Structures and they pick up their share of saltwater taffy and hard tasteless frontier candy and wooden whistles and toy soldiers made of soap.

Then just as we start across the Timeless Green a mob of teens bursts out of the Feinstein Memorial Conifer Grove.

"Gangs!" I yell to the boys. "Get down!"

I hear a shot and look up and there's Samuel standing on a stump at tree line. Thank God, I think. He lets loose another round and one of the teens drops. Marcus is down beside me whimpering with his nose in my armpit. Howie's always been the slow one. He stands there with his mouth open, one hand in his plastic pumpkin. A second teen drops. Then Howie drops and his pumpkin goes flying.

I crawl over and beg him to be okay. He says there's no pain. I check him over and check him over and all that's wrong is his ledger's been shot. I'm so relieved I kiss him on the mouth and he yells at me to quit.

Samuel drops a third teen, then runs yipping into the woods.

The ambulance shows up and the paramedics load up the wounded teens. They're all still alive and one's saying a rosary. I take the boys to City Hall and confront Mr. A. I tell him I'm turning Sam in. He asks if I've gone daft and suggests I try putting food on the table from a jail cell while convicts stand in line waiting to have their way with my rear.

At this point I send the boys out to the foyer.

"He shot Howie," I say. "I want him put away."

"He shot Howie's ledger," Mr. A says. "He shot Howie's ledger in the process of saving Howie's life. But whatever. Let's not mince hairs. If Sam gets put away, we get put away. Does that sound to you like a desirable experience?"

"No," I say.

"What I'm primarily saying," he says, "is that this is a time for knowledge assimilation, not backstabbing. We learned a lesson, you and I. We personally grew. Gratitude for this growth is an appropriate response. Gratitude, and being careful never to make the same mistake twice."

He gets out a Bible and says let's swear on it that we'll never hire a crazed maniac to perform an important security function again. Then the phone rings. Sylvia's cross referenced today's Admissions data and found that the teens weren't a gang at all but a bird-watching group who made the mistake of being male and adolescent and wandering too far off the trail.

"Ouch," Mr. A says. "This could be a serious negative."

In the foyer the kids are trying to get the loaches in the corporate tank to eat bits of Styrofoam. I phone Evelyn and tell her what happened and she calls me a butcher. She wants to know how on earth I could bring the boys to the Park knowing what I knew. She says she doesn't see how I'm going to live with myself in light of how much they trusted and loved me and how badly I let them down by leaving their fates to chance.

I say I'm sorry and she seems to be thinking. Then she tells me just get them home without putting them in further jeopardy, assuming that's within the scope of my mental powers.

At home she puts them in the tub and sends me out for pizza. I opt for Melvin's Pasta Lair. Melvin's a religious zealot who during the Depression worked five jobs at once. Sometimes I tell him my troubles and he says I should stop whining and count my blessings. Tonight I tell him I feel I should take some responsibility for eliminating the Samuel problem but I'm hesitant because of the discrepancy in our relative experience in violence. He says you mean you're scared. I say not scared, just aware of the likelihood of the possibility of failure. He gives me a look. I say it must have been great to grow up when men were men. He says men have always been what they are now, namely incapable of coping with life without the intervention of God the Almighty. Then in the oven behind him my pizza starts smoking and he says case in point.

He makes me another and urges me to get in touch with my Lord personally. I tell him I will. I always tell him I will.

When I get home they're gone.

Evelyn's note says: I could never forgive you for putting our sons at risk. Goodbye forever, you passive flake. Don't try to find us. I've told the kids you sent us away in order to marry a floozy.

Like an idiot I run out to the street. Mrs. Schmidt is prodding her automatic sprinkler system with a rake, trying to detect leaks in advance. She asks how I am and I tell her not now. I sit on the lawn. The stars are very near. The phone rings. I run inside prepared to grovel, but it's only Mr. A. He says come down to the Park immediately because he's got big horrific news.

When I get there he's sitting in his office half-crocked. He tells me we're unemployed. The investors have gotten wind of the bird-watcher shootings and withdrawn all support. The Park is no more. I tell him about Evelyn and the kids. He says that's the least of his worries because he's got crushing debt. He asks if I have any savings he could have. I say no. He says that just for the record and my own personal development, he's always found me dull and has kept me around primarily for my yes-man capabilities and because sometimes I'm so cautious I'm a hoot.

Then he says: Look, get your ass out, I'm torching this shithole for insurance purposes.

I want to hit or at least insult him, but I need this week's pay to find my kids. So I jog off through the Park. In front of Information Hoedown I see the McKinnons cavorting. I get closer and see that they're not cavorting at all, they've inadvertently wandered too close to their actual death site and are being compelled to act out again and again the last minutes of their lives. The girls are lying side by side on the ground and the Mr. is whacking at them with an invisible scythe. The Mrs. is belly-up with one arm flailing in what must have been the parlor. The shrieking is mind-boggling. When he's killed everyone the Mr. walks out to his former field and mimes blowing out his brains. Then he gets up and starts over. It goes on and on, through five cycles. Finally he sits down in the dirt and starts weeping. The Mrs. and the girls backpedal away. He gets up and follows them, pitifully trying to explain.

Behind us the Visitor Center erupts in flames.

The McKinnons go off down the hill, passing through bushes and trees. He's shouting for forgiveness: He's shouting that he's just a man. He's shouting that hatred and war made him nuts. I start running down the hill agreeing with him. The Mrs. gives me a look and puts her hands over Maribeth's ears. We're all running. The Mrs. starts screaming about the feel of the scythe as it opened her up. The girls bemoan their unborn kids. We make quite a group. Since I'm still alive I keep clipping trees with my shoulders and falling down.

At the bottom of the hill they pass through the retaining wall and I run into it. I wake up on my back in the culvert. Blood's running out of my ears and a transparent boy's kneeling over me. I can tell he's no McKinnon because he's wearing sweatpants.

"Get up now," he says in a gentle voice. "Fire's coming."

"No," I say. "I'm through. I'm done living."

"I don't think so," he says. "You've got amends to make."

"I screwed up," I say. "I did bad things."

"No joke," he says, and holds up his stump.

I roll over into the culvert muck and he grabs me by the collar and sits me up.

"I steal four jawbreakers and a Slim Jim and your friend kills and mutilates me?" he says.

"He wasn't my friend," I say.

"He wasn't your enemy," the kid says.

Then he cocks his head. Through his clear skull I see Sam coming out of the woods. The kid cowers behind me. Even dead he's scared of Sam. He's so scared he blasts straight up in the air shrieking and vanishes over the retaining wall.

Sam comes for me with a hunting knife.

"Don't take this too personal," he says, "but you've got to go. You know a few things I don't want broadcast."

I'm madly framing calming words in my head as he drives the knife in. I can't believe it. Never again to see my kids? Never again to sleep and wake to their liquid high voices and sweet breaths?

Sweet Evelyn, I think, I should have loved you better.

Possessing perfect knowledge I hover above him as he hacks me to bits. I see his rough childhood. I see his mother doing something horrid to him with a broomstick. I see the hate in his heart and the people he has yet to kill before pneumonia gets him at eighty-three. I see the dead kid's mom unable to sleep, pounding her fists against her face in grief at the moment I was burying her son's hand. I see the pain I've caused. I see the man I could have been, and the man I was, and then everything is bright and new and keen with love and I sweep through Sam's body, trying to change him, trying so hard, and feeling only hate and hate, solid as stone.

Yellow Woman
(1974)

LESLIE MARMON SILKO

What Whirlwind Man Told Kochininako, Yellow Woman
    I myself belong to the wind
    and so it is we will travel swiftly
    this whole world
    with dust and with windstorms.

My thigh clung to his with dampness, and I watched the sun rising up through the tamaracks and willows. The small brown water birds came to the river and hopped across the mud, leaving brown scratches in the alkali-white crust. They bathed in the river silently. I could hear the water, almost at our feet where the narrow fast channel bubbled and washed green ragged moss and fern leaves. I looked at him beside me, rolled in the red blanket on the white river sand. I cleaned the sand out of the cracks between my toes, squinting because the sun was above the willow trees. I looked at him for the last time, sleeping on the white river sand.

I felt hungry and followed the river south the way we had come the afternoon before, following our footprints that were already blurred by lizard tracks and bug trails. The horses were still lying down, and the black one whinnied when he saw me but he did not get up—maybe it was because the corral was made out of thick cedar branches and the horses had not yet felt the sun like I had. I tried to look beyond the pale red mesas to the pueblo. I knew it was there, even if I could not see it, on the sandrock hill above the river, the same river that moved past me now and had reflected the moon last night.

The horse felt warm underneath me. He shook his head and pawed the sand. The bay whinnied and leaned against the gate trying to follow, and I remembered him asleep in the red blanket beside the river. I slid off the horse and tied him close to the other horse, I walked north with the river again, and the white sand broke loose in footprints over footprints.

"Wake up."

He moved in the blanket and turned his face to me with his eyes still closed. I knelt down to touch him.

"I'm leaving."

He smiled now, eyes still closed. "You are coming with me, remember?" He sat up now with his bare dark chest and belly in the sun.

835

"Where?"

"To my place."

"And will I come back?"

He pulled his pants on. I walked away from him, feeling him behind me and smelling the willows.

"Yellow Woman," he said.

I turned to face him. "Who are you?" I asked.

He laughed and knelt on the low, sandy bank, washing his face in the river. "Last night you guessed my name, and you knew why I had come."

I stared past him at the shallow moving water and tried to remember the night, but I could only see the moon in the water and remember his warmth around me.

"But I only said that you were him and that I was Yellow Woman—I'm not really her—I have my own name and I come from the pueblo on the other side of the mesa. Your name is Silva and you are a stranger I met by the river yesterday afternoon."

He laughed softly. "What happened yesterday has nothing to do with what you will do today, Yellow Woman."

"I know—that's what I'm saying—the old stories about the ka'tsina spirit and Yellow Woman can't mean us."

My old grandpa liked to tell those stories best. There is one about Badger and Coyote who went hunting and were gone all day, and when the sun was going down they found a house. There was a girl living there alone, and she had light hair and eyes and she told them that they could sleep with her. Coyote wanted to be with her all night so he sent Badger into a prairie-dog hole, telling him he thought he saw something in it. As soon as Badger crawled in, Coyote blocked up the entrance with rocks and hurried back to Yellow Woman.

"Come here," he said gently.

He touched my neck and I moved close to him to feel his breathing and to hear his heart. I was wondering if Yellow Woman had known who she was—if she knew that she would become part of the stories. Maybe she'd had another name that her husband and relatives called her so that only the ka'tsina from the north and the storytellers would know her as Yellow Woman. But I didn't go on; I felt him all around me, pushing me down into the white river sand.

Yellow Woman went away with the spirit from the north and lived with him and his relatives. She was gone for a long time, but then one day she came back and she brought twin boys.

"Do you know the story?"

"What story?" He smiled and pulled me close to him as he said this. I was afraid lying there on the red blanket. All I could know was the way he felt, warm, damp, his body beside me. This is the way it happens in the stories, I was thinking, with no thought beyond the moment she meets the ka'tsina spirit and they go.

"I don't have to go. What they tell in stories was real only then, back in time immemorial, like they say."

He stood up and pointed at my clothes tangled in the blanket. "Let's go," he said.

I walked beside him, breathing hard because he walked fast, his hand around my wrist. I had stopped trying to pull away from him, because his hand felt cool and the sun was high, drying the river bed into alkali. I will see someone, eventually I will see someone, and then

I will be certain that he is only a man—some man from nearby—and I will be sure that I am not Yellow Woman. Because she is from out of time past and I live now and I've been to school and there are highways and pickup trucks that Yellow Woman never saw.

It was an easy ride north on horseback. I watched the change from the cottonwood trees along the river to the junipers that brushed past us in the foothills, and finally there were only piñons, and when I looked up at the rim of the mountain plateau I could see pine trees growing on the edge. Once I stopped to look down, but the pale sandstone had disappeared and the river was gone and the dark lava hills were all around. He touched my hand, not speaking, but always singing softly a mountain song and looking into my eyes.

I felt hungry and wondered what they were doing at home now—my mother, my grandmother, my husband, and the baby. Cooking breakfast, saying, "Where did she go?—maybe kidnapped." And Al going to the tribal police with the details: "She went walking along the river."

The house was made with black lava rock and red mud. It was high above the spreading miles of arroyos and long mesas. I smelled a mountain smell of pitch and buck brush. I stood there beside the black horse, looking down on the small, dim country we had passed, and I shivered.

"Yellow Woman, come inside where it's warm."

He lit a fire in the stove. It was an old stove with a round belly and an enamel coffeepot on top. There was only the stove, some faded Navajo blankets, and a bedroll and cardboard box. The floor was made of smooth adobe plaster, and there was one small window facing east. He pointed at the box.

"There's some potatoes and the frying pan." He sat on the floor with his arms around his knees pulling them close to his chest and he watched me fry the potatoes. I didn't mind him watching me because he was always watching me—he had been watching me since I came upon him sitting on the river bank trimming leaves from a willow twig with his knife. We ate from the pan and he wiped the grease from his fingers on his Levi's.

"Have you brought women here before?" He smiled and kept chewing, so I said, "Do you always use the same tricks?"

"What tricks?" He looked at me like he didn't understand.

"The story about being a ka'tsina from the mountains. The story about Yellow Woman."

Silva was silent; his face was calm.

"I don't believe it. Those stories couldn't happen now," I said.

He shook his head and said softly, "But someday they will talk about us, and they will say, 'Those two lived long ago when things like that happened.'"

He stood up and went out. I ate the rest of the potatoes and thought about things—about the noise the stove was making and the sound of the mountain wind outside. I remembered yesterday and the day before, and then I went outside.

I walked past the corral to the edge where the narrow trail cut through the black rim rock. I was standing in the sky with nothing around me but the wind that came down from the blue mountain peak behind me. I could see faint mountain images in the distance miles across the vast spread of mesas and valleys and plains. I wondered who was over there to feel the mountain wind on those sheer blue edges—who walks on the pine needles in those blue mountains.

"Can you see the pueblo?" Silva was standing behind me.

I shook my head. "We're too far away."

"From here I can see the world." He stepped out on the edge. "The Navajo reservation begins over there." He pointed to the east. "The Pueblo boundaries are over here." He looked below us to the south, where the narrow trail seemed to come from. "The Texans have their ranches over there, starting with that valley, the Concho Valley. The Mexicans run some cattle over there too."

"Do you ever work for them?"

"I steal from them," Silva answered. The sun was dropping behind us and the shadows were filling the land below. I turned away from the edge that dropped forever into the valleys below.

"I'm cold," I said, "I'm going inside." I started wondering about this man who could speak the Pueblo language so well but who lived on a mountain and rustled cattle. I decided that this man Silva must be Navajo, because Pueblo men didn't do things like that.

"You must be a Navajo."

Silva shook his head gently. "Little Yellow Woman," he said, "you never give up, do you? I have told you who I am. The Navajo people know me, too." He knelt down and unrolled the bedroll and spread the extra blankets out on a piece of canvas. The sun was down, and the only light in the house came from outside—the dim orange light from sundown.

I stood there and waited for him to crawl under the blankets.

"What are you waiting for?" he said, and I lay down beside him. He undressed me slowly like the night before beside the river—kissing my face gently and running his hands up and down my belly and legs. He took off my pants and then he laughed.

"Why are you laughing?"

"You are breathing so hard."

I pulled away from him and turned my back to him.

He pulled me around and pinned me down with his arms and chest. "You don't understand, do you, little Yellow Woman? You will do what I want."

And again he was all around me with his skin slippery against mine, and I was afraid because I understood that his strength could hurt me. I lay underneath him and I knew that he could destroy me. But later, while he slept beside me, I touched his face and I had a feeling—the kind of feeling for him that overcame me that morning along the river. I kissed him on the forehead and he reached out for me.

When I woke up in the morning he was gone. It gave me a strange feeling because for a long time I sat there on the blankets and looked around the little house for some object of his—some proof that he had been there or maybe that he was coming back. Only the blankets and the cardboard box remained. The .30-30 that had been leaning in the corner was gone, and so was the knife I had used the night before. He was gone, and I had my chance to go now. But first I had to eat, because I knew it would be a long walk home.

I found some dried apricots in the cardboard box, and I sat down on a rock at the edge of the plateau rim. There was no wind and the sun warmed me. I was surrounded by silence. I drowsed with apricots in my mouth, and I didn't believe that there were highways or railroads or cattle to steal.

When I woke up, I stared down at my feet in the black mountain dirt. Little black ants were swarming over the pine needles around my foot. They must have smelled the apricots. I thought about my family far below me. They would be wondering about me, because this had never happened to me before. The tribal police would file a report. But if old Grandpa weren't dead he would tell them what happened—he would laugh and say, "Stolen by a ka'tsina, a mountain spirit. She'll come home—they usually do." There are enough of them to handle things. My mother and grandmother will raise the baby like they raised me. Al will find someone else, and they will go on like before, except that there will be a story about the day I disappeared while I was walking along the river. Silva had come for me; he said he had. I did not decide to go. I just went. Moonflowers blossom in the sand hills before dawn, just as I followed him. That's what I was thinking as I wandered along the trail through the pine trees.

It was noon when I got back. When I saw the stone house I remembered that I had meant to go home. But that didn't seem important any more, maybe because there were little blue flowers growing in the meadow behind the stone house and the gray squirrels were playing in the pines next to the house. The horses were standing in the corral, and there was a beef carcass hanging on the shady side of a big pine in front of the house. Flies buzzed around the clotted blood that hung from the carcass. Silva was washing his hands in a bucket full of water. He must have heard me coming because he spoke to me without turning to face me.

"I've been waiting for you."

"I went walking in the big pine trees."

I looked into the bucket full of bloody water with brown-and-white animal hairs floating in it. Silva stood there letting his hand drip, examining me intently.

"Are you coming with me?"

"Where?" I asked him.

"To sell the meat in Marquez."

"If you're sure it's O.K."

"I wouldn't ask you if it wasn't," he answered.

"He sloshed the water around in the bucket before he dumped it out and set the bucket upside down near the door. I followed him to the corral and watched him saddle the horses. Even beside the horses he looked tall, and I asked him again if he wasn't Navajo. He didn't say anything; he just shook his head and kept cinching up the saddle.

"But Navajos are tall."

"Get on the horse," he said, "and let's go."

The last thing he did before we started down the steep trail was to grab the .30-30 from the corner. He slid the rifle into the scabbard that hung from his saddle.

"Do they ever try to catch you?" I asked.

"They don't know who I am."

"Then why did you bring the rifle?"

"Because we are going to Marquez where the Mexicans live."

The trail leveled out on a narrow ridge that was steep on both sides like an animal spine. On one side I could see where the trail went around the rocky gray hills and disappeared into the southeast where the pale sandrock mesas stood in the distance near my home. On the other side was a trail that went west, and as I looked far into the distance I thought I saw the little town. But Silva said no, that I was looking in the wrong place, that I just thought I saw houses. After that I quit looking off into the distance; it was hot and the wildflowers were closing up their deep-yellow petals. Only the waxy cactus flowers bloomed in the bright sun, and I saw every color that a cactus blossom can be; the white ones and the red ones were still buds, but the purple and the yellow were blossoms, open full and the most beautiful of all.

Silva saw him before I did. The white man was riding a big gray horse, coming up the trail towards us. He was traveling fast and the gray horse's feet sent rocks rolling off the trail into the dry tumbleweeds. Silva motioned for me to stop and we watched the white man. He didn't see us right away, but finally his horse whinnied at our horses and he stopped. He looked at us briefly before he lapped the gray horse across the three hundred yards that separated us. He stopped his horse in front of Silva, and his young fat face was shadowed by the brim of his hat. He didn't look mad, but his small, pale eyes moved from the blood-soaked gunny sacks hanging from my saddle to Silva's face and then back to my face.

"Where did you get the fresh meat?" the white man asked.

"I've been hunting," Silva said, and when he shifted his weight in the saddle the leather creaked.

"The hell you have, Indian. You've been rustling cattle. We've been looking for the thief for a long time."

The rancher was fat, and sweat began to soak through his white cowboy shirt and the wet cloth stuck to the thick rolls of belly fat. He almost seemed to be panting from the exertion of talking, and he smelled rancid, maybe because Silva scared him.

Silva turned to me and smiled. "Go back up the mountain, Yellow Woman."

The white man got angry when he heard Silva speak in a language he couldn't understand. "Don't try anything, Indian. Just keep riding to Marquez. We'll call the state police from there."

The rancher must have been unarmed because he was very frightened and if he had a gun he would have pulled it out then. I turned my horse around and the rancher yelled, "Stop!" I looked at Silva for an instant and there was something ancient and dark—something I could feel in my stomach—in his eyes, and when I glanced at his hand I saw his finger on the trigger of the .30-30 that was still in the saddle scabbard. I slapped my horse across the flank and the sacks of raw meat swung against my knees as the horse leaped up the trail. It was hard to keep my balance, and once I thought I felt the saddle slipping backward; it was because of this that I could not look back.

I didn't stop until I reached the ridge where the trail forked. The horse was breathing deep gasps and there was a dark film of sweat on its neck. I looked down in the direction I had come from, but I couldn't see the place. I waited. The wind came up and pushed warm air past me. I looked up at the sky, pale blue and full of thin clouds and fading vapor trails left by jets.

I think four shots were fired—I remember hearing four hollow explosions that reminded me of deer hunting. There could have been more shots after that, but I couldn't have heard them because my horse was running again and the loose rocks were making too much noise as they scattered around his feet.

Horses have a hard time running downhill, but I went that way instead of uphill to the mountain because I thought it was safer. I felt better with the horse running southeast past the round gray hills that were covered with cedar trees and black lava rock. When I got to the plain in the distance I could see the dark green patches of tamaracks that grew along the river; and beyond the river I could see the beginning of the pale sandrock mesas. I stopped the horse and looked back to see if anyone was coming; then I got off the horse and turned the horse around, wondering if it would go back to its corral under the pines on the mountain. It looked back at me for a moment and then plucked a mouthful of green tumbleweeds before it trotted back up the trail with its ears pointed forward, carrying its head daintily to one side to avoid stepping on the dragging reins. When the horse disappeared over the last hill, the gunny sacks full of meat were still swinging and bouncing.

I walked toward the river on a wood-hauler's road that I knew would eventually lead to the paved road. I was thinking about waiting beside the road for someone to drive by, but by the time I got to the pavement I had decided it wasn't very far to walk if I followed the river back the way Silva and I had come.

The river water tasted good, and I sat in the shade under a cluster of silvery willows. I thought about Silva, and I felt sad at leaving him; still, there was something strange about him, and I tried to figure it out all the way back home.

I came back to the place on the river bank where he had been sitting the first time I saw him. The green willow leaves that he had trimmed from the branch were still lying there, wilted in the sand. I saw the leaves and I wanted to go back to him—to kiss him and to touch him—but the mountains were too far away now. And I told myself, because I believe it, he will come back sometime and be waiting again by the river.

I followed the path up from the river into the village. The sun was getting low, and I could smell supper cooking when I got to the screen door of my house. I could hear their voices inside—my mother was telling my grandmother how to fix the Jell-O and my husband, Al, was playing with the baby. I decided to tell them that some Navajo had kidnaped me, but I was sorry that old Grandpa wasn't alive to hear my story because it was the Yellow Woman stories he liked to tell best.

Breakfast
(1938)

JOHN STEINBECK

This thing fills me with pleasure. I don't know why, I can see it in the smallest detail. I find myself recalling it again and again, each time bringing more detail out of a sunken memory, remembering brings the curious warm pleasure.

It was very early in the morning. The eastern mountains were black-blue, but behind them the light stood up faintly colored at the mountain rims with a washed red, growing colder, greyer and darker as it went up and overhead until, at a place near the west, it merged with pure night.

And it was cold, not painfully so, but cold enough so that I rubbed my hands and shoved them deep into my pockets, and I hunched my shoulders up and scuffled my feet on the ground. Down in the valley where I was, the earth was that lavender grey of dawn. I walked along a country road and ahead of me I saw a tent that was only a little lighter grey than the ground. Beside the tent there was a flash of orange fire seeping out of the cracks of an old rusty iron stove. Grey smoke spurted up out of the stubby stovepipe, spurted up a long way before it spread out and dissipated.

I saw a young woman beside the stove, really a girl. She was dressed in a faded cotton skirt and waist. As I came close I saw that she carried a baby in a crooked arm and the baby was nursing, its head under her waist out of the cold. The mother moved about, poking the fire, shifting the rusty lids of the stove to make a greater draft, opening the oven door; and all the time the baby was nursing, but that didn't interfere with the mother's work, nor with the light quick gracefulness of her movements. There was something very precise and practiced in her movements. The orange fire flicked out of the cracks in the stove and threw dancing reflections on the tent.

I was close now and I could smell frying bacon and baking bread, the warmest, pleasantest odors I know. From the east the light grew swiftly. I came near to the stove and stretched my hands out to it and shivered all over when the warmth struck me. Then the tent flap jerked up and a young man came out and an older man followed him. They were dressed in new blue dungarees and in new dungaree coats with the brass buttons shining. They were sharp-faced men, and they looked much alike.

The younger had a dark stubble beard and the older had a grey stubble beard. Their heads and faces were wet, their hair dripped with water, and water stood out on their stiff beards and their cheeks shone with water. Together they stood looking quietly at the lightening east; they yawned together and looked at the light on the hill rims. They turned and saw me.

"Morning," said the older man. His face was neither friendly nor unfriendly.

"Morning, sir, " I said.

"Morning," said the young man.

The water was slowly drying on their faces. They came to the stove and warmed their hands at it.

The girl kept to her work, her face averted and her eyes on what she was doing. Her hair was tied back out of her eyes with a string and it hung down her back and swayed as she worked. She set tin cups on a big packing box, set tin plates and knives and forks out too. Then she scooped fried bacon out of the deep grease and laid it on a big tin platter, and the bacon cricked and rustled as it grew crisp. She opened the rusty oven door and took out a square pan full of high big biscuits.

When the smell of that hot bread came out, both of the men inhaled deeply. The young man said softly, "Keerist!"

The elder man turned to me, "Had you breakfast?"

"No."

"Well, sit down with us, then."

That was the signal. We went to the packing case and squatted on the ground about it. The young man asked, "Picking cotton?"

"No."

"We had twelve days' work so far," the young man said.

The girl spoke from the stove. "They even got new clothes."

The two men looked down at their new dungarees and they both smiled a little.

The girl set out the platter of bacon, the brown high biscuits, a bowl of bacon gravy and a pot of coffee, and then she squatted down by the box too. The baby was still nursing, its head up under her waist out of the cold. I could hear the sucking noises it made.

We filled our plates, poured bacon gravy over our biscuits and sugared our coffee. The older man filled his mouth full and he chewed and chewed and swallowed. Then he said, "God Almighty, it's good," and he filled his mouth again.

The young man said, "We been eating good for twelve days."

We all ate quickly, frantically, and refilled our plates and ate quickly again until we were full and warm. The hot bitter coffee scalded our throats. We threw the last little bit with the grounds in it on the earth and refilled our cups.

There was color in the light now, a reddish gleam that made the air seem colder. The two men faced the east and their faces were lighted by the dawn, and I looked up for a moment and saw the image of the mountain and the light coming over it reflected in the older man's eyes.

Then the two men threw the grounds from their cups on the earth and they stood up together. "Got to get going," the older man said.

The younger turned to me. " 'Fyou want to pick cotton, we could maybe get you on."

"No. I got to go along. Thanks for breakfast."

The older man waved his hand in a negative. "O. K. Glad to have you." They walked away together. The air was blazing with light at the eastern skyline. And I walked away down the country road.

That's all. I know, of course, some of the reasons why it was pleasant. But there was some element of great beauty there that makes the rush of warmth when I think of it.

The Body-Snatcher
(1884)

ROBERT LOUIS STEVENSON

Every night in the year, four of us sat in the small parlour of the George at Debenham - the undertaker, and the landlord, and Fettes, and myself. Sometimes there would be more; but blow high, blow low, come rain or snow or frost, we four would be each planted in his own particular arm-chair. Fettes was an old drunken Scotchman, a man of education obviously, and a man of some property, since he lived in idleness. He had come to Debenham years ago, while still young, and by a mere continuance of living had grown to be an adopted townsman. His blue camlet cloak was a local antiquity, like the church-spire. His place in the parlour at the George, his absence from church, his old, crapulous, disreputable vices, were all things of course in Debenham. He had some vague Radical opinions and some fleeting infidelities, which he would now and again set forth and emphasise with tottering slaps upon the table. He drank rum - five glasses regularly every evening; and for the greater portion of his nightly visit to the George sat, with his glass in his right hand, in a state of melancholy alcoholic saturation. We called him the Doctor, for he was supposed to have some special knowledge of medicine, and had been known, upon a pinch, to set a fracture or reduce a dislocation; but beyond these slight particulars, we had no knowledge of his character and antecedents.

One dark winter night - it had struck nine some time before the landlord joined us - there was a sick man in the George, a great neighbouring proprietor suddenly struck down with apoplexy on his way to Parliament; and the great man's still greater London doctor had been telegraphed to his bedside. It was the first time that such a thing had happened in Debenham, for the railway was but newly open, and we were all proportionately moved by the occurrence.

'He's come,' said the landlord, after he had filled and lighted his pipe.

'He?' said I. 'Who? - not the doctor?'

'Himself,' replied our host.

'What is his name?'

'Doctor Macfarlane,' said the landlord.

Fettes was far through his third tumbler, stupidly fuddled, now nodding over, now staring mazily around him; but at the last word he seemed to awaken, and repeated the name 'Macfarlane' twice, quietly enough the first time, but with sudden emotion at the second.

'Yes,' said the landlord, 'that's his name, Doctor Wolfe Macfarlane.'

Fettes became instantly sober; his eyes awoke, his voice became clear, loud, and steady, his language forcible and earnest. We were all startled by the transformation, as if a man had risen from the dead.

'I beg your pardon,' he said, 'I am afraid I have not been paying much attention to your talk. Who is this Wolfe Macfarlane?' And then, when he had heard the landlord out, 'It cannot be, it cannot be,' he added; 'and yet I would like well to see him face to face.'

'Do you know him, Doctor?' asked the undertaker, with a gasp.

'God forbid!' was the reply. 'And yet the name is a strange one; it were too much to fancy two. Tell me, landlord, is he old?'

'Well,' said the host, 'he's not a young man, to be sure, and his hair is white; but he looks younger than you.'

'He is older, though; years older. But,' with a slap upon the table, 'it's the rum you see in my face - rum and sin. This man, perhaps, may have an easy conscience and a good digestion. Conscience! Hear me speak. You would think I was some good, old, decent Christian, would you not? But no, not I; I never canted. Voltaire might have canted if he'd stood in my shoes; but the brains' - with a rattling fillip on his bald head - 'the brains were clear and active, and I saw and made no deductions.'

'If you know this doctor,' I ventured to remark, after a somewhat awful pause, 'I should gather that you do not share the landlord's good opinion.'

Fettes paid no regard to me.

'Yes,' he said, with sudden decision, 'I must see him face to face.'

There was another pause, and then a door was closed rather sharply on the first floor, and a step was heard upon the stair.

'That's the doctor,' cried the landlord. 'Look sharp, and you can catch him.'

It was but two steps from the small parlour to the door of the old George Inn; the wide oak staircase landed almost in the street; there was room for a Turkey rug and nothing more between the threshold and the last round of the descent; but this little space was every evening brilliantly lit up, not only by the light upon the stair and the great signal-lamp below the sign, but by the warm radiance of the bar-room window. The George thus brightly advertised itself to passers-by in the cold street. Fettes walked steadily to the spot, and we, who were hanging behind, beheld the two men meet, as one of them had phrased it, face to face. Dr. Macfarlane was alert and vigorous. His white hair set off his pale and placid, although energetic, countenance. He was richly dressed in the finest of broadcloth and the whitest of linen, with a great gold watch-chain, and studs and spectacles of the same precious material. He wore a broad-folded tie, white and speckled with lilac, and he carried on his arm a comfortable driving-coat of fur. There was no doubt but he became his years, breathing, as he did, of wealth and consideration; and it was a surprising contrast to see our parlour sot - bald, dirty, pimpled, and robed in his old camlet cloak - confront him at the bottom of the stairs.

'Macfarlane!' he said somewhat loudly, more like a herald than a friend.

The great doctor pulled up short on the fourth step, as though the familiarity of the address surprised and somewhat shocked his dignity.

'Toddy Macfarlane!' repeated Fettes.

The London man almost staggered. He stared for the swiftest of seconds at the man before him, glanced behind him with a sort of scare, and then in a startled whisper, 'Fettes!' he said, 'You!'

'Ay,' said the other, 'me! Did you think I was dead too? We are not so easy shut of our acquaintance.'

'Hush, hush!' exclaimed the doctor. 'Hush, hush! this meeting is so unexpected - I can see you are unmanned. I hardly knew you, I confess, at first; but I am overjoyed - overjoyed to have this opportunity. For the present it must be how-d'ye-do and good-bye in one, for my fly is waiting, and I must not fail the train; but you shall - let me see - yes - you shall give me your address, and you can count on early news of me. We must do something for you, Fettes. I fear you are out at elbows; but we must see to that for auld lang syne, as once we sang at suppers.'

'Money!' cried Fettes; 'money from you! The money that I had from you is lying where I cast it in the rain.'

Dr. Macfarlane had talked himself into some measure of superiority and confidence, but the uncommon energy of this refusal cast him back into his first confusion.

A horrible, ugly look came and went across his almost venerable countenance. 'My dear fellow,' he said, 'be it as you please; my last thought is to offend you. I would intrude on none. I will leave you my address, however - '

'I do not wish it - I do not wish to know the roof that shelters you,' interrupted the other. 'I heard your name; I feared it might be you; I wished to know if, after all, there were a God; I know now that there is none. Begone!'

He still stood in the middle of the rug, between the stair and doorway; and the great London physician, in order to escape, would be forced to step to one side. It was plain that he hesitated before the thought of this humiliation. White as he was, there was a dangerous glitter in his spectacles; but while he still paused uncertain, he became aware that the driver of his fly was peering in from the street at this unusual scene and caught a glimpse at the same time of our little body from the parlour, huddled by the corner of the bar. The presence of so many witnesses decided him at once to flee. He crouched together, brushing on the wainscot, and made a dart like a serpent, striking for the door. But his tribulation was not yet entirely at an end, for even as he was passing Fettes clutched him by the arm and these words came in a whisper, and yet painfully distinct, 'Have you seen it again?'

The great rich London doctor cried out aloud with a sharp, throttling cry; he dashed his questioner across the open space, and, with his hands over his head, fled out of the door like a detected thief. Before it had occurred to one of us to make a movement the fly was already rattling toward the station. The scene was over like a dream, but the dream had left proofs and traces of its passage. Next day the servant found the fine gold spectacles broken on the threshold, and that very night we were all standing breathless by the bar-room window, and Fettes at our side, sober, pale, and resolute in look.

'God protect us, Mr. Fettes!' said the landlord, coming first into possession of his customary senses. 'What in the universe is all this? These are strange things you have been saying.'

Fettes turned toward us; he looked us each in succession in the face. 'See if you can hold your tongues,' said he. 'That man Macfarlane is not safe to cross; those that have done so already have repented it too late.'

And then, without so much as finishing his third glass, far less waiting for the other two, he bade us good-bye and went forth, under the lamp of the hotel, into the black night.

We three turned to our places in the parlour, with the big red fire and four clear candles; and as we recapitulated what had passed, the first chill of our surprise soon changed into a glow of curiosity. We sat late; it was the latest session I have known in the old George. Each man, before we parted, had his theory that he was bound to prove; and none of us had any nearer business in this world than to track out the past of our condemned companion, and surprise the secret that he shared with the great London doctor. It is no great boast, but I believe I was a better hand at worming out a story than either of my fellows at the George;

and perhaps there is now no other man alive who could narrate to you the following foul and unnatural events.

In his young days Fettes studied medicine in the schools of Edinburgh. He had talent of a kind, the talent that picks up swiftly what it hears and readily retails it for its own. He worked little at home; but he was civil, attentive, and intelligent in the presence of his masters. They soon picked him out as a lad who listened closely and remembered well; nay, strange as it seemed to me when I first heard it, he was in those days well favoured, and pleased by his exterior. There was, at that period, a certain extramural teacher of anatomy, whom I shall here designate by the letter K. His name was subsequently too well known. The man who bore it skulked through the streets of Edinburgh in disguise, while the mob that applauded at the execution of Burke called loudly for the blood of his employer. But Mr. K- was then at the top of his vogue; he enjoyed a popularity due partly to his own talent and address, partly to the incapacity of his rival, the university professor. The students, at least, swore by his name, and Fettes believed himself, and was believed by others, to have laid the foundations of success when he had acquired the favour of this meteorically famous man. Mr. K- was a BON VIVANT as well as an accomplished teacher; he liked a sly illusion no less than a careful preparation. In both capacities Fettes enjoyed and deserved his notice, and by the second year of his attendance he held the half-regular position of second demonstrator or sub-assistant in his class.

In this capacity the charge of the theatre and lecture-room devolved in particular upon his shoulders. He had to answer for the cleanliness of the premises and the conduct of the other students, and it was a part of his duty to supply, receive, and divide the various subjects. It was with a view to this last - at that time very delicate - affair that he was lodged by Mr. K- in the same wynd, and at last in the same building, with the dissecting-rooms. Here, after a night of turbulent pleasures, his hand still tottering, his sight still misty and confused, he would be called out of bed in the black hours before the winter dawn by the unclean and desperate interlopers who supplied the table. He would open the door to these men, since infamous throughout the land. He would help them with their tragic burden, pay them their sordid price, and remain alone, when they were gone, with the unfriendly relics of humanity. From such a scene he would return to snatch another hour or two of slumber, to repair the abuses of the night, and refresh himself for the labours of the day.

Few lads could have been more insensible to the impressions of a life thus passed among the ensigns of mortality. His mind was closed against all general considerations. He was incapable of interest in the fate and fortunes of another, the slave of his own desires and low ambitions. Cold, light, and selfish in the last resort, he had that modicum of prudence, miscalled morality, which keeps a man from inconvenient drunkenness or punishable theft. He coveted, besides, a measure of consideration from his masters and his fellow-pupils, and he had no desire to fail conspicuously in the external parts of life. Thus he made it his pleasure to gain some distinction in his studies, and day after day rendered unimpeachable eye-service to his employer, Mr. K-. For his day of work he indemnified himself by nights of roaring, blackguardly enjoyment; and when that balance had been struck, the organ that he called his conscience declared itself content.

The supply of subjects was a continual trouble to him as well as to his master. In that large and busy class, the raw material of the anatomists kept perpetually running out; and the business thus rendered necessary was not only unpleasant in itself, but threatened dangerous consequences to all who were concerned. It was the policy of Mr. K- to ask no questions in his dealings with the trade. 'They bring the body, and we pay the price,' he used to say, dwelling on the alliteration - 'QUID PRO QUO.' And, again, and somewhat profanely, 'Ask no questions,' he would tell his assistants, 'for conscience' sake.' There was no understanding that the subjects were provided by the crime of murder. Had that idea been broached to him in words, he would have recoiled in horror; but the lightness of his speech upon so grave a matter was, in itself, an offence against good manners, and a temptation to the men with whom he dealt. Fettes, for instance, had often remarked to himself upon the singular freshness of the bodies. He had been struck again and again by the hang-dog, abominable looks of the ruffians who came to him before the dawn; and putting things together clearly in his private thoughts, he perhaps attributed a meaning too immoral and too categorical to the unguarded counsels of his master. He understood his duty, in short, to have three branches: to take what was brought, to pay the price, and to avert the eye from any evidence of crime.

One November morning this policy of silence was put sharply to the test. He had been awake all night with a racking toothache - pacing his room like a caged beast or throwing himself in fury on his bed - and had fallen at last into that profound, uneasy slumber that so often follows on a night of pain, when he was awakened by the third or fourth angry repetition of the concerted signal. There was a thin, bright moonshine; it was bitter cold, windy, and frosty; the town had not yet awakened, but an indefinable stir already preluded the noise and business of the day. The ghouls had come later than usual, and they seemed more than usually eager to be gone. Fettes, sick with sleep, lighted them upstairs. He heard their grumbling Irish voices through a dream; and as they stripped the sack from their sad merchandise he leaned dozing, with his shoulder propped against the wall; he had to shake himself to find the men their money. As he did so his eyes lighted on the dead face. He started; he took two steps nearer, with the candle raised.

'God Almighty!' he cried. 'That is Jane Galbraith!'

The men answered nothing, but they shuffled nearer the door.

'I know her, I tell you,' he continued. 'She was alive and hearty yesterday. It's impossible she can be dead; it's impossible you should have got this body fairly.'

'Sure, sir, you're mistaken entirely,' said one of the men.

But the other looked Fettes darkly in the eyes, and demanded the money on the spot.

It was impossible to misconceive the threat or to exaggerate the danger. The lad's heart failed him. He stammered some excuses, counted out the sum, and saw his hateful visitors depart. No sooner were they gone than he hastened to confirm his doubts. By a dozen unquestionable marks he identified the girl he had jested with the day before. He saw, with horror, marks upon her body that might well betoken violence. A panic seized him, and he took refuge in his room. There he reflected at length over the discovery that he had made; considered soberly the bearing of Mr. K-'s instructions and the danger to himself of interference in so serious a business, and at last, in sore perplexity, determined to wait for the advice of his immediate superior, the class assistant.

This was a young doctor, Wolfe Macfarlane, a high favourite among all the reckless students, clever, dissipated, and unscrupulous to the last degree. He had travelled and studied abroad. His manners were agreeable and a little forward. He was an authority on the stage, skilful on the ice or the links with skate or golf-club; he dressed with nice audacity, and, to put the finishing touch upon his glory, he kept a gig and a strong trotting-horse. With Fettes he was on terms of intimacy; indeed, their relative positions called for some community of life; and when subjects were scarce the pair would drive far into the country in Macfarlane's gig, visit and desecrate some lonely graveyard, and return before dawn with their booty to the door of the dissecting-room.

On that particular morning Macfarlane arrived somewhat earlier than his wont. Fettes heard him, and met him on the stairs, told him his story, and showed him the cause of his alarm. Macfarlane examined the marks on her body.

'Yes,' he said with a nod, 'it looks fishy.'

'Well, what should I do?' asked Fettes.

'Do?' repeated the other. 'Do you want to do anything? Least said soonest mended, I should say.'

'Some one else might recognise her,' objected Fettes. 'She was as well known as the Castle Rock.'

'We'll hope not,' said Macfarlane, 'and if anybody does - well, you didn't, don't you see, and there's an end. The fact is, this has been going on too long. Stir up the mud, and you'll get K- into the most unholy trouble; you'll be in a shocking box yourself. So will I, if you come to that. I should like to know how any one of us would look, or what the devil we should have to say for ourselves, in any Christian witness-box. For me, you know there's one thing certain - that, practically speaking, all our subjects have been murdered.'

'Macfarlane!' cried Fettes.

'Come now!' sneered the other. 'As if you hadn't suspected it yourself!'

'Suspecting is one thing - '

'And proof another. Yes, I know; and I'm as sorry as you are this should have come here,' tapping the body with his cane. 'The next best thing for me is not to recognise it; and,' he added coolly, 'I don't. You may, if you please. I don't dictate, but I think a man of the world would do as I do; and I may add, I fancy that is what K- would look for at our hands. The question is, Why did he choose us two for his assistants? And I answer, because he didn't want old wives.'

This was the tone of all others to affect the mind of a lad like Fettes. He agreed to imitate Macfarlane. The body of the unfortunate girl was duly dissected, and no one remarked or appeared to recognise her.

One afternoon, when his day's work was over, Fettes dropped into a popular tavern and found Macfarlane sitting with a stranger. This was a small man, very pale and dark, with coal-black eyes. The cut of his features gave a promise of intellect and refinement which was but feebly realised in his manners, for he proved, upon a nearer acquaintance, coarse, vulgar, and stupid. He exercised, however, a very remarkable control over Macfarlane; issued orders like the Great Bashaw; became inflamed at the least discussion or delay, and commented rudely on the servility with which he was obeyed. This most offensive person took a fancy to Fettes on the spot, plied him with drinks, and honoured him with unusual confidences on his past career. If a tenth part of what he confessed were true, he was a very loathsome rogue; and the lad's vanity was tickled by the attention of so experienced a man.

'I'm a pretty bad fellow myself,' the stranger remarked, 'but Macfarlane is the boy - Toddy Macfarlane I call him. Toddy, order your friend another glass.' Or it might be, 'Toddy, you jump up and shut the door.' 'Toddy hates me,' he said again. 'Oh yes, Toddy, you do!'

'Don't you call me that confounded name,' growled Macfarlane.

'Hear him! Did you ever see the lads play knife? He would like to do that all over my body,' remarked the stranger.

'We medicals have a better way than that,' said Fettes. 'When we dislike a dead friend of ours, we dissect him.'

Macfarlane looked up sharply, as though this jest were scarcely to his mind.

The afternoon passed. Gray, for that was the stranger's name, invited Fettes to join them at dinner, ordered a feast so sumptuous that the tavern was thrown into commotion, and when all was done commanded Macfarlane to settle the bill. It was late before they separated; the man Gray was incapably drunk. Macfarlane, sobered by his fury, chewed the cud of the money he had been forced to squander and the slights he had been obliged to swallow. Fettes, with various liquors singing in his head, returned home with devious footsteps and a mind entirely in abeyance. Next day Macfarlane was absent from the class, and Fettes smiled to himself as he imagined him still squiring the intolerable Gray from tavern to tavern. As soon as the hour of liberty had struck he posted from place to place in quest of his last night's companions. He could find them, however, nowhere; so returned early to his rooms, went early to bed, and slept the sleep of the just.

At four in the morning he was awakened by the well-known signal. Descending to the door, he was filled with astonishment to find Macfarlane with his gig, and in the gig one of those long and ghastly packages with which he was so well acquainted.

'What?' he cried. 'Have you been out alone? How did you manage?'

But Macfarlane silenced him roughly, bidding him turn to business. When they had got the body upstairs and laid it on the table, Macfarlane made at first as if he were going away. Then he paused and seemed to hesitate; and then, 'You had better look at the face,' said he, in tones of some constraint. 'You had better,' he repeated, as Fettes only stared at him in wonder.

'But where, and how, and when did you come by it?' cried the other.

'Look at the face,' was the only answer.

Fettes was staggered; strange doubts assailed him. He looked from the young doctor to the body, and then back again. At last, with a start, he did as he was bidden. He had almost expected the sight that met his eyes, and yet the shock was cruel. To see, fixed in the rigidity of death and naked on that coarse layer of sackcloth, the man whom he had left well clad and full of meat and sin upon the threshold of a tavern, awoke, even in the thoughtless Fettes, some of the terrors of the conscience. It was a CRAS TIBI which re-echoed in his soul, that two whom he had known should have come to lie upon these icy tables. Yet these were only secondary thoughts. His first concern regarded Wolfe. Unprepared for a challenge so momentous, he knew not how to look his comrade in the face. He durst not meet his eye, and he had neither words nor voice at his command.

It was Macfarlane himself who made the first advance. He came up quietly behind and laid his hand gently but firmly on the other's shoulder.

'Richardson,' said he, 'may have the head.'

Now Richardson was a student who had long been anxious for that portion of the human subject to dissect. There was no answer, and the murderer resumed: 'Talking of business, you must pay me; your accounts, you see, must tally.'

Fettes found a voice, the ghost of his own: 'Pay you!' he cried. 'Pay you for that?'

'Why, yes, of course you must. By all means and on every possible account, you must,' returned the other. 'I dare not give it for nothing, you dare not take it for nothing; it would compromise us both. This is another case like Jane Galbraith's. The more things are wrong the more we must act as if all were right. Where does old K- keep his money?'

'There,' answered Fettes hoarsely, pointing to a cupboard in the corner.

'Give me the key, then,' said the other, calmly, holding out his hand.

There was an instant's hesitation, and the die was cast. Macfarlane could not suppress a nervous twitch, the infinitesimal mark of an immense relief, as he felt the key between his fingers. He opened the cupboard, brought out pen and ink and a paper-book that stood in one compartment, and separated from the funds in a drawer a sum suitable to the occasion.

'Now, look here,' he said, 'there is the payment made - first proof of your good faith: first step to your security. You have now to clinch it by a second. Enter the payment in your book, and then you for your part may defy the devil.'

The next few seconds were for Fettes an agony of thought; but in balancing his terrors it was the most immediate that triumphed. Any future difficulty seemed almost welcome if he could avoid a present quarrel with Macfarlane. He set down the candle which he had been carrying all this time, and with a steady hand entered the date, the nature, and the amount of the transaction.

'And now,' said Macfarlane, 'it's only fair that you should pocket the lucre. I've had my share already. By the bye, when a man of the world falls into a bit of luck, has a few shillings extra in his pocket - I'm ashamed to speak of it, but there's a rule of conduct in the case. No treating, no purchase of expensive class-books, no squaring of old debts; borrow, don't lend.'

'Macfarlane,' began Fettes, still somewhat hoarsely, 'I have put my neck in a halter to oblige you.'

'To oblige me?' cried Wolfe. 'Oh, come! You did, as near as I can see the matter, what you downright had to do in self-defence. Suppose I got into trouble, where would you be? This second little matter flows clearly from the first. Mr. Gray is the continuation of Miss Galbraith. You can't begin and then stop. If you begin, you must keep on beginning; that's the truth. No rest for the wicked.'

A horrible sense of blackness and the treachery of fate seized hold upon the soul of the unhappy student.

'My God!' he cried, 'but what have I done? and when did I begin? To be made a class assistant - in the name of reason, where's the harm in that? Service wanted the position; Service might have got it. Would HE have been where I am now?'

'My dear fellow,' said Macfarlane, 'what a boy you are! What harm HAS come to you? What harm CAN come to you if you hold your tongue? Why, man, do you know what this life is? There are two squads of us - the lions and the lambs. If you're a lamb, you'll come to lie upon these tables like Gray or Jane Galbraith; if you're a lion, you'll live and drive a horse like me, like K-, like all the world with any wit or courage. You're staggered at the first. But look at K-! My dear fellow, you're clever, you have pluck. I like you, and K- likes you. You were born to lead the hunt; and I tell you, on my honour and my experience of life, three days from now you'll laugh at all these scarecrows like a High School boy at a farce.'

And with that Macfarlane took his departure and drove off up the wynd in his gig to get under cover before daylight. Fettes was thus left alone with his regrets. He saw the miserable peril in which he stood involved. He saw, with inexpressible dismay, that there was no limit to his weakness, and that, from concession to concession, he had fallen from the arbiter of Macfarlane's destiny to his paid and helpless accomplice. He would have given the world to have been a little braver at the time, but it did not occur to him that he might still be brave. The secret of Jane Galbraith and the cursed entry in the day-book closed his mouth.

Hours passed; the class began to arrive; the members of the unhappy Gray were dealt out to one and to another, and received without remark. Richardson was made happy with the head; and before the hour of freedom rang Fettes trembled with exultation to perceive how far they had already gone toward safety.

For two days he continued to watch, with increasing joy, the dreadful process of disguise.

On the third day Macfarlane made his appearance. He had been ill, he said; but he made up for lost time by the energy with which he directed the students. To Richardson in particular he extended the most valuable assistance and advice, and that student, encouraged by the praise of the demonstrator, burned high with ambitious hopes, and saw the medal already in his grasp.

Before the week was out Macfarlane's prophecy had been fulfilled. Fettes had outlived his terrors and had forgotten his baseness. He began to plume himself upon his courage, and had so arranged the story in his mind that he could look back on these events with an unhealthy pride. Of his accomplice he saw but little. They met, of course, in the business of the class; they received their orders together from Mr. K-. At times they had a word or two in private, and Macfarlane was from first to last particularly kind and jovial. But it was plain that he avoided any reference to their common secret; and even when Fettes whispered to him that he had cast in his lot with the lions and foresworn the lambs, he only signed to him smilingly to hold his peace.

At length an occasion arose which threw the pair once more into a closer union. Mr. K- was again short of subjects; pupils were eager, and it was a part of this teacher's pretensions to be always well supplied. At the same time there came the news of a burial in the rustic graveyard of Glencorse. Time has little changed the place in question. It stood then, as now, upon a cross road, out of call of human habitations, and buried fathom deep in the foliage of six cedar trees. The cries of the sheep upon the neighbouring hills, the streamlets upon either hand, one loudly singing among pebbles, the other dripping furtively from pond to pond, the stir of the wind in mountainous old flowering chestnuts, and once in seven days the voice of the bell and the old tunes of the precentor, were the only sounds that disturbed the silence around the rural church. The Resurrection Man - to use a byname of the period - was not to be deterred by any of the sanctities of customary piety. It was part of his trade to despise and desecrate the scrolls and trumpets of old tombs, the paths worn by the feet of worshippers and mourners, and the offerings and the inscriptions of bereaved affection. To rustic neighbourhoods, where love is more than commonly tenacious, and where some bonds of blood or fellowship unite the entire society of a parish, the body-snatcher, far from being repelled by natural respect, was attracted by the ease and safety of the task. To bodies that had been laid in earth, in joyful expectation of a far different awakening, there came that hasty, lamp-lit, terror-haunted resurrection of the spade and mattock. The coffin was forced, the cerements torn, and the melancholy relics, clad in sackcloth, after being rattled for hours on moonless byways, were at length exposed to uttermost indignities before a class of gaping boys.

Somewhat as two vultures may swoop upon a dying lamb, Fettes and Macfarlane were to be let loose upon a grave in that green and quiet resting-place. The wife of a farmer, a woman who had lived for sixty years, and been known for nothing but good butter and a godly conversation, was to be rooted from her grave at midnight and carried, dead and naked, to that far-away city that she had always honoured with her Sunday's best; the place beside her family was to be empty till the crack of doom; her innocent and almost venerable members to be exposed to that last curiosity of the anatomist.

Late one afternoon the pair set forth, well wrapped in cloaks and furnished with a formidable bottle. It rained without remission - a cold, dense, lashing rain. Now and again there blew a puff of wind, but these sheets of falling water kept it down. Bottle and all, it was a sad and silent drive as far as Penicuik, where they were to spend the evening. They stopped once, to hide their implements in a thick bush not far from the churchyard, and once again at the Fisher's Tryst, to have a toast before the kitchen fire and vary their nips of whisky with a glass of ale. When they reached their journey's end the gig was housed, the horse was fed and comforted, and the two young doctors in a private room sat down to the best dinner and the best wine the house afforded. The lights, the fire, the beating rain upon the window, the cold, incongruous work that lay before them, added zest to their enjoyment of the meal. With every glass their cordiality increased. Soon Macfarlane handed a little pile of gold to his companion.

'A compliment,' he said. 'Between friends these little d-d accommodations ought to fly like pipe-lights.'

Fettes pocketed the money, and applauded the sentiment to the echo. 'You are a philosopher,' he cried. 'I was an ass till I knew you. You and K- between you, by the Lord Harry! but you'll make a man of me.'

'Of course we shall,' applauded Macfarlane. 'A man? I tell you, it required a man to back me up the other morning. There are some big, brawling, forty-year-old cowards who would have turned sick at the look of the d-d thing; but not you - you kept your head. I watched you.'

'Well, and why not?' Fettes thus vaunted himself. 'It was no affair of mine. There was nothing to gain on the one side but disturbance, and on the other I could count on your gratitude, don't you see?' And he slapped his pocket till the gold pieces rang.

Macfarlane somehow felt a certain touch of alarm at these unpleasant words. He may have regretted that he had taught his young companion so successfully, but he had no time to interfere, for the other noisily continued in this boastful strain:

'The great thing is not to be afraid. Now, between you and me, I don't want to hang - that's practical; but for all cant, Macfarlane, I was born with a contempt. Hell, God, Devil, right, wrong, sin, crime, and all the old gallery of curiosities - they may frighten boys, but men of the world, like you and me, despise them. Here's to the memory of Gray!'

It was by this time growing somewhat late. The gig, according to order, was brought round to the door with both lamps brightly shining, and the young men had to pay their bill and take the road. They announced that they were bound for Peebles, and drove in that direction till they were clear of the last houses of the town; then, extinguishing the lamps, returned upon their course, and followed a by-road toward Glencorse. There was no sound but that of their own passage, and the incessant, strident pouring of the rain. It was pitch dark; here and there a white gate or a white stone in the wall guided them for a short space across the night; but for the most part it was at a foot pace, and almost groping, that they picked their way through that resonant blackness to their solemn and isolated destination. In the sunken woods that traverse the neighbourhood of the burying-ground the last glimmer failed them, and it became necessary to kindle a match and re-illumine one of the lanterns of the gig. Thus, under the dripping trees, and environed by huge and moving shadows, they reached the scene of their unhallowed labours.

They were both experienced in such affairs, and powerful with the spade; and they had scarce been twenty minutes at their task before they were rewarded by a dull rattle on the coffin lid. At the same moment Macfarlane, having hurt his hand upon a stone, flung it carelessly above his head. The grave, in which they now stood almost to the shoulders, was close to the edge of the plateau of the graveyard; and the gig lamp had been propped, the better to illuminate their labours, against a tree, and on the immediate verge of the steep bank descending to the stream. Chance had taken a sure aim with the stone. Then came a clang of broken glass; night fell upon them; sounds alternately dull and ringing announced the bounding of the lantern down the bank, and its occasional collision with the trees. A stone or two, which it had dislodged in its descent, rattled behind it into the profundities of the glen; and then silence, like night, resumed its sway; and they might bend their hearing to its utmost pitch, but naught was to be heard except the rain, now marching to the wind, now steadily falling over miles of open country.

They were so nearly at an end of their abhorred task that they judged it wisest to complete it in the dark. The coffin was exhumed and broken open; the body inserted in the dripping sack and carried between them to the gig; one mounted to keep it in its place, and the other, taking the horse by the mouth, groped along by wall and bush until they reached the wider road by the Fisher's Tryst. Here was a faint, diffused radiancy, which they hailed like daylight; by that they pushed the horse to a good pace and began to rattle along merrily in the direction of the town.

They had both been wetted to the skin during their operations, and now, as the gig jumped among the deep ruts, the thing that stood propped between them fell now upon one and now upon the other. At every repetition of the horrid contact each instinctively repelled it with the greater haste; and the process, natural although it was, began to tell upon the nerves of the companions. Macfarlane made some ill-favoured jest about the farmer's wife, but it came hollowly from his lips, and was allowed to drop in silence. Still their unnatural burden bumped from side to side; and now the head would be laid, as if in confidence, upon their shoulders, and now the drenching sack-cloth would flap icily about their faces. A creeping chill began to possess the soul of Fettes. He peered at the bundle, and it seemed somehow larger than at first. All over the country-side, and from every degree of distance, the farm dogs accompanied their passage with tragic ululations; and it grew and grew upon his mind that some unnatural miracle had been accomplished, that some nameless change had befallen the dead body, and that it was in fear of their unholy burden that the dogs were howling.

'For God's sake,' said he, making a great effort to arrive at speech, 'for God's sake, let's have a light!'

Seemingly Macfarlane was affected in the same direction; for, though he made no reply, he stopped the horse, passed the reins to his companion, got down, and proceeded to kindle the remaining lamp. They had by that time got no farther than the cross-road down to Auchenclinny. The rain still poured as though the deluge were returning, and it was no easy matter to make a light in such a world of wet and darkness. When at last the flickering blue flame had been transferred to the wick and began to expand and clarify, and shed a wide circle of misty brightness round the gig, it became possible for the two young men to see each other and the thing they had along with them. The rain had moulded the rough sacking to the outlines of the body underneath; the head was distinct from the trunk, the shoulders plainly modelled; something at once spectral and human riveted their eyes upon the ghastly comrade of their drive.

For some time Macfarlane stood motionless, holding up the lamp. A nameless dread was swathed, like a wet sheet, about the body, and tightened the white skin upon the face of Fettes; a fear that was meaningless, a horror of what could not be, kept mounting to his brain. Another beat of the watch, and he had spoken. But his comrade forestalled him.

'That is not a woman,' said Macfarlane, in a hushed voice.

'It was a woman when we put her in,' whispered Fettes.

'Hold that lamp,' said the other. 'I must see her face.'

And as Fettes took the lamp his companion untied the fastenings of the sack and drew down the cover from the head. The light fell very clear upon the dark, well-moulded features and smooth-shaven cheeks of a too familiar countenance, often beheld in dreams of both of these young men. A wild yell rang up into the night; each leaped from his own side into the roadway: the lamp fell, broke, and was extinguished; and the horse, terrified by this unusual commotion, bounded and went off toward Edinburgh at a gallop, bearing along with it, sole occupant of the gig, the body of the dead and long-dissected Gray.

The Girl Who Was Plugged In
(1973)

JAMES TIPTREE, JR.

Listen, zombie. Believe me. What I could tell you—you with your silly hands leaking sweat on your growth-stocks portfolio. One-ten lousy hacks of AT&T on twenty-point margin and you think you're Evel Knievel. AT&T? You doubleknit dummy, how I'd love to show you something.

Look, dead daddy, I'd say. See for instance that rotten girl?

In the crowd over there, that one gaping at her gods. One rotten girl in the city of the future (That's what I said.) Watch.

She's jammed among bodies, craning and peering with her soul yearning out of her eyeballs. Love! Oo-ooh, love them! Her gods are coming out of a store called Body East. Three young-bloods, larking along loverly. Dressed like simple street-people but . . . smashing. See their great eyes swivel above their nose-filters, their hands lift shyly, their inhumanly tender lips melt? The crowd moans. Love! This whole boiling megacity, this whole fun future world loves its gods.

You don't believe in gods, dad? Wait. Whatever turns you on, there's a god in the future for you, custom-made. Listen to this mob. "I touched his foot! Ow-oow, I TOUCHED Him!"

Even the people in the GTX tower up there love the gods—in their own way and for their own reasons.

The funky girl on the street, she just loves. Grooving on their beautiful lives, their mysterioso problems. No one ever told her about mortals who love a god and end up as a tree or a sighing sound. In a million years it'd never occur to her that her gods might love her back.

She's squashed against the wall now as the godlings come by. They move in a clear space. A holocam bobs above, but its shadow never falls on them. The store display-screens are magically clear of bodies as the gods glance in and a beggar underfoot is suddenly alone. They give him a token. "Aaaaah!" goes the crowd.

Now one of them flashes some wild new kind of timer and they all trot to catch a shuttle, just like people. The shuttle stops for them—more magic. The crowd sighs, closing back. The gods are gone.

(In a room far from—but not unconnected to—the GTX tower a molecular flipflop closes too, and three account tapes spin.)

Our girl is still stuck by the wall while guards and holocam equipment pull away. The adoration's fading from her face. That's good, because now you can see she's the ugly of the world. A tall monument to pituitary dystrophy. No surgeon would touch her. When she smiles, her jaw—it's half purple—almost bites her left eye out. She's also quite young, but who could care?

The crowd is pushing her along now, treating you to glimpses of her jumbled torso, her mismatched legs. At the corner she strains to send one last fond spasm after the godlings' shuttle. Then her face reverts to its usual expression of dim pain and she lurches onto the moving walkway, stumbling into people. The walkway junctions with another. She crosses, trips and collides with the casualty rail. Finally she comes out into a little bare place called a park. The sportshow is working, a basketball game in three-di is going on right overhead. But all she does is squeeze onto a bench and huddle there while a ghostly free-throw goes by her ear.

After that nothing at all happens except a few furtive hand-mouth gestures which don't even interest her bench mates.

But you're curious about the city? So ordinary after all, in the FUTURE?

Ah, there's plenty to swing with here—and it's not all that *far* in the future, dad. But pass up the sci-fi stuff for now, like for instance the holovision technology that's put TV and radio in museums. Or the worldwide carrier field bouncing down from satellites, controlling communication and transport systems all over the globe. That was a spin-off from asteroid mining, pass it by. We're watching that girl.

I'll give you just one goodie. Maybe you noticed on the sportshow or the streets? No commercials. No ads.

That's right. NO ADS. An eyeballer for you.

Look around. Not a billboard, sign, slogan, jingle, sky-write, blurb, sublimflash, in this whole fun world. Brand names? Only in those ticky little peep-screens on the stores, and you could hardly call that advertising. How does that finger you?

Think about it. That girl is still sitting there.

She's parked right under the base of the GTX tower, as a matter of fact. Look way up and you can see the sparkles from the bubble on top, up there among the domes of godland. Inside that bubble is a boardroom. Neat bronze shield on the door: Global Transmissions Corporation—not that that means anything.

I happen to know there are six people in that room. Five of them technically male, and the sixth isn't easily thought of as a mother. They are absolutely unremarkable. Those faces were seen once at their nuptials and will show again in their obituaries and impress nobody either time. If you're looking for the secret Big Blue Meanies of the world, forget it. I know. Zen, do I know! Flesh? Power? Glory? You'd horrify them.

What they do like up there is to have things orderly, especially their communications. You could say they've dedicated their lives to that, to freeing the world from garble. Their nightmares are about hemorrhages of information; channels screwed up, plans misimplemented, garble creeping in. Their gigantic wealth only worries them, it keeps opening new vistas of disorder. Luxury? They wear what their tailors put on them, eat what their cooks serve them. See that old boy there—his name is Isham—he's sipping water and frowning as he listens to a databall. The water was prescribed by his medistaff. It tastes awful. The databall also contains a disquieting message about his son, Paul.

But it's time to go back down, far below to our girl. Look!

She's toppled over sprawling on the ground.

A tepid commotion ensues among the bystanders. The consensus is she's dead, which she disproves by bubbling a little. And presently she's taken away by one of the superb ambulances of the future, which are a real improvement over ours when one happens to be around.

At the local bellevue the usual things are done by the usual team of clowns aided by a saintly mop-pusher. Our girl revives enough to answer the questionnaire without which you can't die, even in the future. Finally she's cast up, a pumped-out hulk on a cot in the long, dim ward.

Again nothing happens for a while except that her eyes leak a little from the understandable disappointment of finding herself still alive.

But somewhere one GTX computer has been tickling another, and toward midnight something does happen. First comes an attendant who pulls screens around her. Then a man in a business doublet comes daintily down the ward. He motions the attendant to strip off the sheet and go.

The groggy girl-brute heaves up, big hands clutching at bodyparts you'd pay not to see.

"Burke? P. Burke, is that your name?"

"Y-yes." Croak. "Are you . . . policeman?"

"No. They'll be along shortly, I expect. Public suicide's a felony."

". . . *I'm sorry.*"

He has a 'corder in his hand. "No family, right?"

"No."

"You're seventeen. One year city college. What did you study?

"La—languages."

"H'mm. Say something."

Unintelligible rasp.

He studies her. Seen close, he's not so elegant. Errand-boy type.

"Why did you try to kill yourself?"

She stares at him with dead-rat dignity, hauling up the gray sheet. Give him a point, he doesn't ask twice.

"Tell me, did you see Breath this afternoon?"

Dead as she nearly is, that ghastly love-look wells up. Breath is the three young gods, a loser's cult. Give the man another point, he interprets her expression.

"How would you like to meet them?"

The girl's eyes bug out grotesquely.

"I have a job for someone like you. It's hard work. If you did well you'd be meeting Breath and stars like that all the time."

Is he insane? She's deciding she really did die.

"But it means you never see anybody you know again. Never, *ever.* You will be legally dead. Even the police won't know. Do you want to try?"

It all has to be repeated while her great jaw slowly sets. *Show me the fire I walk through.* Finally P. Burke's prints are in his 'corder, the man holding up the big rancid girl-body without a sign of distaste. It makes you wonder what else he does.

And then—THE MAGIC. Sudden silent trot of litterbearers tucking P. Burke into something quite different from a bellevue stretcher, the oiled slide into the daddy of all luxury ambulances—real flowers in that holder!—and the long jarless rush to nowhere. Nowhere is warm and gleaming and kind with nurses. (Where did you hear that money can't buy genuine kindness?) And clean clouds folding P. Burke into bewildered sleep.

. . . Sleep which merges into feedings and washings and more sleeps, into drowsy moments of afternoon where midnight should be, and gentle businesslike voices and friendly (but very few) faces, and endless painless hyposprays and peculiar numbnesses. And later comes the steadying rhythm of days and nights, and a quickening which P. Burke doesn't identify as health, but only knows that the fungus place in her armpit is gone. And then she's up and following those few new faces with growing trust, first tottering, then walking strongly, all better now, clumping down the short hall to the tests, tests, tests, and the other things.

And here is our girl, looking—

If possible, worse than before. (You thought this was Cinderella transistorized?)

The disimprovement in her looks comes from the electrode jacks peeping out of her sparse hair, and there are other meldings of flesh and metal. On the other hand, that collar and spinal plate are really an asset; you won't miss seeing that neck.

P. Burke is ready for training in her new job.

The training takes place in her suite and is exactly what you'd call a charm course. How to walk, sit, eat, speak, blow her nose, how to stumble, to urinate, to hiccup—DELICIOUSLY. How to make each nose-blow or shrug delightfully, subtly, different from any ever spooled before. As the man said, it's hard work.

But P. Burke proves apt. Somewhere in that horrible body is a gazelle, a houri, who would have been buried forever without this crazy chance. See the ugly duckling go!

Only it isn't precisely P. Burke who's stepping, laughing, shaking out her shining hair. How could it be? P. Burke is doing it all right, but she's doing it through something. The something is to all appearances a live girl. (You were warned, this is the FUTURE.)

When they first open the big cryocase and show her her new body, she says just one word. Staring, gulping, "How?"

Simple, really. Watch P. Burke in her sack and scuffs stump down the hall beside Joe, the man who supervises the technical part of her training. Joe doesn't mind P. Burke's looks, he hasn't noticed them. To Joe, system matrices are beautiful.

They go into a dim room containing a huge cabinet like a one-man sauna and a console for Joe. The room has a glass wall that's all dark now. And just for your information, the whole shebang is five hundred feet underground near what used to be Carbondale, Pa.

Joe opens the sauna cabinet like a big clamshell standing on end with a lot of funny business inside. Our girl shucks her shift and walks into it bare, totally unembarrassed. *Eager.* She settles in face-forward, butting jacks into sockets. Joe closes it carefully onto her humpback. Clunk. She can't see in there or hear or move. She hates this minute. But how she loves what comes next!

Joe's at his console, and the lights on the other side of the glass wall come up. A room is on the other side, all fluff and kicky bits, a girly bedroom. In the bed is a small mound of silk with a rope of yellow hair hanging out.

The sheet stirs and gets whammed back flat.

Sitting up in the bed is the darlingest girl child you've EVER seen. She quivers—porno for angels. She sticks both her little arms straight up, flips her hair, looks around full of sleepy pazazz. Then she can't resist rubbing her hands down over her minibreasts and belly. Because, you see, it's the god-awful P. Burke who is sitting there hugging her perfect girl-body, looking at you out of delighted eyes.

Then the kitten hops out of bed and crashes flat on the floor.

From the sauna in the dim room comes a strangled noise. P. Burke, trying to rub her wired-up elbow, is suddenly smothered in *two* bodies, electrodes jerking in her flesh. Joe juggles inputs, crooning into his mike. The flurry passes; it's all right.

860

In the lighted room the elf gets up, casts a cute glare at the glass wall, and goes into a transparent cubicle. A bathroom, what else? She's a live girl, and live girls have to go to the bathroom after a night's sleep even if their brains are in a sauna cabinet in the next room. And P. Burke isn't in that cabinet, she's in the bathroom. Perfectly simple, if you have the glue for that closed training circuit that's letting her run her neural system by remote control.

Now let's get one thing clear. P. Burke does not *feel* her brain is in the sauna room, she feels she's in that sweet little body. When you wash your hands, do you feel the water is running on your brain? Of course not. You feel the water on your hand, although the "feeling" is actually a potential-pattern flickering over the electrochemical jelly between your ears. And it's delivered there via the long circuits from your hands. Just so, P. Burke's brain in the cabinet feels the water on her hands in the bathroom. The fact that the signals have jumped across space on the way in makes no difference at all. If you want the jargon, it's known as eccentric projection or sensory reference and you've done it all your life. Clear?

Time to leave the honeypot to her toilet training—she's made a booboo with the toothbrush, because P. Burke can't get used to what she sees in the mirror—

But wait, you say. Where did that girl-body come from?

P. Burke asks that too, dragging out the words.

"They grow 'em," Joe tells her. He couldn't care less about the flesh department. "PDs. Placental decanters. Modified embryos, see? Fit the control implants in later. Without a Remote Operator it's just a vegetable. Look at the feet—no callus at all." (He knows because they told him.)

"Oh . . . oh, she's incredible . . . ."

"Yeah, a neat job. Want to try walking-talking mode today? You're coming on fast."

And she is. Joe's reports and the reports from the nurse and the doctor and style man go to a bushy man upstairs who is some kind of medical cybertech but mostly a project administrator. His reports in turn go—to the GTX boardroom? Certainly not, did you think this is a *big* thing? His reports just go up. The point is, they're green, very green. P. Burke promises well.

So the bushy man—Dr. Tesla—has procedures to initiate. The little kitten's dossier in the Central Data Bank, for instance. Purely routine. And the phase-in schedule which will put her on the scene. This is simple: a small exposure in an off-network holoshow.

Next he has to line out the event which will fund and target her. That takes budget meetings, clearances, coordinations. The Burke project begins to recruit and grow. And there's the messy business of the name, which always gives Dr. Tesla an acute pain in the bush.

The name comes out weird, when it's suddenly discovered that Burke's "P." stands for "Philadelphia." Philadelphia? The astrologer grooves on it. Joe thinks it would help identification. The semantics girl references *brotherly love, Liberty Bell, main line, low teratogenesis,* blah-blah. Nicknames Philly? Pala? Pooty? Delphi? Is it good, bad? Finally "Delphi" is gingerly declared goodo. ("Burke" is replaced by something nobody remembers.)

Coming along now. We're at the official checkout down in the underground suite, which is as far as the training circuits reach. The bushy Dr. Tesla is there, braced by two budgetary types and a quiet fatherly man whom he handles like hot plasma.

Joe swings the door wide and she steps shyly in.

Their little Delphi, fifteen and flawless.

Tesla introduces her around. She's child-solemn, a beautiful baby to whom something so wonderful has happened you can feel the tingles. She doesn't smile, she . . . brims. That brimming joy is all that shows of P. Burke, the forgotten hulk in the sauna next door. But P. Burke doesn't know she's alive—it's Delphi who lives, every warm inch of her.

One of the budget types lets go a libidinous snuffle and freezes. The fatherly man, whose name is Mr. Cantle, clears his throat.

"Well, young lady, are you ready to go to work?"

"Yes, sir," gravely from the elf.

"We'll see. Has anybody told you what you're going to do for us?"

"No, sir." Joe and Tesla exhale quietly.

"Good." He eyes her, probing for the blind brain in the room next door.

"Do you know what *advertising* is?"

He's talking dirty, hitting to shock. Delphi's eyes widen and her little chin goes up. Joe is in ecstasy at the complex expressions P. Burke is getting through. Mr. Cantle waits.

"It's, well, it's when they used to tell people to buy things." She swallows. "It's not allowed."

"That's right." Mr. Cantle leans back, grave. "Advertising as it used to be is against the law. *A display other than the legitimate use of the product, intended to promote its sale.* In former times every manufacturer was free to tout his wares any way, place, or time he could afford. All the media and most of the landscape was taken up with extravagant competing displays. The thing became uneconomic. The public rebelled. Since the so-called Huckster Act sellers have been restrained to, I quote, displays in or on the product itself, visible during its legitimate use or in on-premise sales." Mr. Cantle leans forward. "Now tell me, Delphi, why do people buy one product rather than another?"

"Well . . . " Enchanting puzzlement from Delphi. "They, um, they see them and like them, or they hear about them from somebody?" (Touch of P. Burke there; she didn't say, from a friend.)

"Partly. Why did *you* buy your particular body-lift?"

"I never had a body-lift, sir."

Mr. Cantle frowns; what gutters do they drag for these Remotes?

"Well, what brand of water do you drink?"

"Just what was in the faucet, sir," says Delphi humbly. "I—I did try to boil it—"

"Good god." He scowls; Tesla stiffens. "Well, what did you boil it in? A cooker?" The shining yellow head nods.

"What *brand* of cooker did you buy?"

"I didn't buy it, sir," says frightened P. Burke through Delphi's lips. "But—I know the best kind! Ananga has a Burnbabi. I saw the name when she—"

"Exactly!" Cantle's fatherly beam comes back strong; the Burnbabi account is a strong one, too. "You saw Ananga using one so you thought it must be good, eh? And it is good, or a great human being like Ananga wouldn't be using it. Absolutely right. And now, Delphi, you know what you're going to be doing for us. You're going to show some products. Doesn't sound very hard, does it?"

"Oh, no, sir . . ." Baffled child's stare; Joe gloats.

"And you must never, *never* tell anyone what you're doing." Cantle's eyes bore for the brain behind this seductive child.

"You're wondering why we ask you to do this, naturally. There's a very serious reason. All those products people use, foods and healthaids and cookers and cleaners and clothes and cars—they're all made by *people*. Somebody put in years of hard work designing and making them. A man comes up with a fine new idea for a better product. He has to get a factory and machinery, and hire workmen. Now. What happens if people have no way of hearing about his product? Word of mouth is far too slow and unreliable. Nobody might ever stumble onto his new product or find out how good it was, right? And then he and all the people who worked for him—they'd go bankrupt, right? So, Delphi, there has to be *some way* that large numbers of people can get a look at a good new product, right? How? By letting people see you using it. You're giving that man a chance."

Delphi's little head is nodding in happy relief.

"Yes, sir, I do see now—but sir, it seems so sensible, why don't they let you—"

Cantle smiles sadly.

"It's an overreaction, my dear. History goes by swings. People overreact and pass harsh unrealistic laws which attempt to stamp out an essential social process. When this happens, the people who understand have to carry on as best they can until the pendulum swings back." He sighs. "The Huckster Laws are bad, inhuman laws, Delphi, despite their good intent. If they were strictly observed they would wreak havoc. Our economy, our society, would be cruelly destroyed. We'd be back in caves!" His inner fire is showing; if the Huckster Laws were strictly enforced he'd be back punching a databank.

"It's our duty, Delphi. Our solemn social duty. We are not breaking the law. You will be using the product. But people wouldn't understand, if they knew. They would become upset just as you did. So you must be very, very careful not to mention any of this to anybody."

(And somebody will be very, very carefully monitoring Delphi's speech circuits.)

"Now we're all straight, aren't we? Little Delphi here" —he is speaking to the invisible creature next door—"little Delphi is going to live a wonderful, exciting life. She's going to be a girl people watch. And she's going to be using fine products people will be glad to know about and helping the good people who make them. Yours will be a genuine social contribution." He keys up his pitch; the creature in there must be older.

Delphi digests this with ravishing gravity.

"But sir, how do I—?"

"Don't worry about a thing. You'll have people behind you whose job it is to select the most worthy products for you to use. Your job is just to do as they say. They'll show you what outfits to wear to parties, what suncars and viewers to buy, and so on. That's all you have to do."

Parties—clothes—suncars! Delphi's pink mouth opens. In P. Burke's starved seventeen-year-old head the ethics of product sponsorship float far away.

"Now tell me in your own words what your job is, Delphi."

"Yes, sir. I—I'm to go to parties and buy things and use them as they tell me, to help the people who work in factories."

"And what did I say was so important?"

"Oh—I shouldn't let anybody know, about the things."

"Right." Mr. Cantle has another paragraph he uses when the subject shows, well, immaturity. But he can sense only eagerness here. Good. He doesn't really enjoy the other speech.

"It's a lucky girl who can have all the fun she wants while doing good for others, isn't it?" He beams around. There's a prompt shuffling of chairs. Clearly this one is go.

Joe leads her out, grinning. The poor fool thinks they're admiring her coordination.

It's out into the world for Delphi now, and at this point the up-channels get used. On the administrative side account schedules are opened, subprojects activated. On the technical side the reserved bandwidth is cleared. (That carrier field, remember?) A new name is waiting for Delphi, a name she'll never hear. It's a long string of binaries which have been quietly cycling in a GTX tank ever since a certain Beautiful Person didn't wake up.

The name winks out of cycle, dances from pulses into modulations of modulations, whizzes through phasing, and shoots into a giga-band beam racing up to a synchronous satellite poised over Guatemala. From there the beam pours twenty thousand miles back to Earth again, forming an all-pervasive field of structured energies supplying tuned demand-points all over the CanAm quadrant.

With that field, if you have the right credit rating, you can sit at a GTX console and operate an ore-extractor in Brazil. Or—if you have some simple credentials like being able to walk on water—you could shoot a spool into the network holocam shows running day and night in every home and dorm and rec site. *Or* you could create a continentwide traffic jam. Is it any wonder GTX guards those inputs like a sacred trust?

Delphi's "name" appears as a tiny analyzable nonredundancy in the flux, and she'd be very proud if she knew about it. It would strike P. Burke as magic; P. Burke never even understood robotcars. But Delphi is in no sense a robot. Call her a waldo if you must. The fact is she's just a girl, a real-live girl with her brain in an unusual place. A simple real-time on-line system with plenty of bit-rate—even as you and you.

The point of all this hardware, which isn't very much hardware in this society, is so Delphi can walk out of that underground suite, a mobile demand-point draining an omnipresent field-form. And she does—eighty-nine pounds of tender girl flesh and blood with a few metallic components, stepping out into the sunlight to be taken to her new life. A girl with everything going for her including a meditech escort. Walking lovely, stopping to widen her eyes at the big antennae system overhead.

The mere fact that something called P. Burke is left behind down underground has no bearing at all. P. Burke is totally unselfaware and happy as a clam in its shell. (Her bed has been moved into the waldo cabinet room now.) And P. Burke isn't in the cabinet; P. Burke is climbing out of an airvan in a fabulous Colorado beef preserve, and her name is Delphi. Delphi is looking at live Charolais steers and live cottonwoods and aspens gold against the blue smog and stepping over live grass to be welcomed by the reserve super's wife.

The super's wife is looking forward to a visit from Delphi and her friends, and by a happy coincidence there's a holocam outfit here doing a piece for the nature nuts.

You could write the script yourself now, while Delphi learns a few rules about structural interferences and how to handle the tiny time lag which results from the new forty-thousand-mile parenthesis in her nervous system. That's right—the people with the leased holocam rig naturally find the gold aspen shadows look a lot better on Delphi's flank than they do on a steer. And Delphi's face improves the mountains too, when you can see them. But the nature freaks aren't quite as joyful as you'd expect.

"See you in Barcelona, kitten," the headman says sourly as they pack up.

"Barcelona?" echoes Delphi with that charming little subliminal lag. She sees where his hand is and steps back.

"Cool, it's not her fault," another man says wearily. He knocks back his grizzled hair. "Maybe they'll leave in some of the gut."

Delphi watches them go off to load the spools on the GTX transport for processing. Her hand roves over the breast the man had touched. Back under Carbondale, P. Burke has discovered something new about her Delphi-body.

About the difference between Delphi and her own grim carcass.

She's always known Delphi has almost no sense of taste or smell. They explained about that: only so much bandwidth. You don't have to taste a suncar, do you? And the slight overall dimness of Delphi's sense of touch—she's familiar with that, too. Fabrics that would prickle P. Burke's own hide feel like a cool plastic film to Delphi.

But the blank spots. It took her a while to notice them. Delphi doesn't have much privacy; investments of her size don't. So she's slow about discovering there's certain definite places where her beastly P. Burke body *feels* things that Delphi's dainty flesh does not. H'mm! Channel space again, she thinks—and forgets it in the pure bliss of being Delphi.

You ask how a girl could forget a thing like that? Look. P. Burke is about as far as you can get from the concept *girl*. She's a female, yes—but for her, sex is a four-letter word spelled P-A-I-N. She isn't quite a virgin. You don't want the details; she'd been about twelve and the freak lovers were bombed blind. When they came down, they threw her out with a small hole in her anatomy and a mortal one elsewhere. She dragged off to buy her first and last shot, and she can still hear the clerk's incredulous guffaws.

Do you see why Delphi grins, stretching her delicious little numb body in the sun she faintly feels? Beams, saying, "Please, I'm ready now."

Ready for what? For Barcelona like the sour man said, where his nature-thing is now making it strong in the amateur section of the Festival. A winner! Like he also said, a lot of strip mines and dead fish have been scrubbed, but who cares with Delphi's darling face so visible?

So it's time for Delphi's face and her other delectabilities to show on Barcelona's Playa Nueva. Which means switching her channel to the EurAf synchsat.

They ship her at night so the nanosecond transfer isn't even noticed by that insignificant part of Delphi that lives five hundred feet under Carbondale, so excited the nurse has to make sure she eats. The circuit switches while Delphi "sleeps," that is, while P. Burke is out of the waldo cabinet. The next time she plugs in to open Delphi's eyes it's no different—do you notice which relay boards your phone calls go through?

And now for the event that turns the sugarcube from Colorado into the PRINCESS.

Literally true, he's a prince, or rather an Infante of an old Spanish line that got shined up in the Neomonarchy. He's also eighty-one, with a passion for birds—the kind you see in zoos. Now it suddenly turns out that he isn't poor at all. Quite the reverse; his old sister laughs in their tax lawyer's face and starts restoring the family hacienda while the Infante totters out to court Delphi. And little Delphi begins to live the life of the gods.

What do gods do? Well, everything beautiful. But (remember Mr. Cantle?) the main point is Things. Ever see a god empty-handed? You can't be a god without at least a magic girdle or an eight-legged horse. But in the old days some stone tablets or winged sandals or a chariot drawn by virgins would do a god for life. No more! Gods make it on novelty now. By Delphi's time the hunt for new god-gear is turning the earth and seas inside-out and sending frantic fingers to the stars. And what gods have, mortals desire.

So Delphi starts on a Euromarket shopping spree squired by her old Infante, thereby doing her bit to stave off social collapse.

865

Social what? Didn't you get it, when Mr. Cantle talked about a world where advertising is banned and fifteen billion consumers are glued to their holocam shows? One capricious self-powered god can wreck you.

Take the nose-filter massacre. Years, the industry sweated years to achieve an almost invisible enzymatic filter. So one day a couple of pop-gods show up wearing nose-filters like *big purple bats.* By the end of the week the world market is screaming for purple bats. Then it switched to bird-heads and skulls, but by the time the industry retooled the crazies had dropped bird-heads and gone to injection globes. Blood!

Multiply that by a million consumer industries, and you can see why it's economic to have a few controllable gods. Especially with the beautiful hunk of space R&D the Peace Department laid out for and which the taxpayers are only too glad to have taken off their hands by an outfit like GTX, which everybody knows is almost a public trust.

And so you—or rather, GTX—find a creature like P. Burke and give her Delphi. And Delphi helps keep things *orderly,* she does what you tell her to. Why? That's right, Mr. Cantle never finished his speech.

But here come the tests of Delphi's button-nose twinkling in the torrent of news and entertainment. And she's noticed. The feedback shows a flock of viewers turning up the amps when this country baby gets tangled in her new colloidal body-jewels. She registers at a couple of major scenes, too, and when the Infante gives her a suncar, little Delphi trying out suncars is a tiger. There's a solid response in high-credit country. Mr. Cantle is humming his happy tune as he cancels a Benelux subnet option to guest her on a nude cook-show called Wok Venus.

And now for the superposh old-world wedding! The hacienda has Moorish baths and six-foot silver candelabra and real black horses, and the Spanish Vatican blesses them. The final event is a grand gaucho ball with the old prince and his little Infanta on a bowered balcony. She's a spectacular doll of silver lace, wildly launching toy doves at her new friends whirling by below.

The Infante beams, twitches his old nose to the scent of her sweet excitement. His doctor has been very helpful. Surely now, after he has been so patient with the suncars and all the nonsense—

The child looks up at him, saying something incomprehensible about "breath." He makes out that she's complaining about the three singers she had begged for.

"They've changed!" she marvels. "Haven't they changed? They're so dreary. I'm so happy now!"

And Delphi falls fainting against a gothic vargueno.

Her American duenna rushes up, calls help. Delphi's eyes are open, but Delphi isn't there. The duenna pokes among Delphi's hair, slaps her. The old prince grimaces. He has no idea what she is beyond an excellent solution to his tax problems, but he had been a falconer in his youth. There comes to his mind the small pinioned birds which were flung up to stimulate the hawks. He pockets the veined claw to which he had promised certain indulgences and departs to design his new aviary.

And Delphi also departs with her retinue to the Infante's newly discovered yacht. The trouble isn't serious. It's only that five thousand miles away and five hundred feet down P. Burke has been doing it too well.

They've always known she has terrific aptitude. Joe says he never saw a Remote take over so fast. No disorientations, no rejections. The psychomed talks about self-alienation. She's going into Delphi like a salmon to the sea.

She isn't eating or sleeping, they can't keep her out of the body-cabinet to get her blood moving, there are necroses under her grisly sit-down. Crisis!

So Delphi gets a long "sleep" on the yacht and P. Burke gets it pounded through her perforated head that she's endangering Delphi. (Nurse Fleming thinks of that, thus alienating the psychomed.)

They rig a pool down there (Nurse Fleming again) and chase P. Burke back and forth. And she loves it. So naturally when they let her plug in again Delphi loves it too. Every noon beside the yacht's hydrofoils darling Delphi clips along in the blue sea they've warned her not to drink. And every night around the shoulder of the world an ill-shaped thing in a dark burrow beats its way across a sterile pool.

So presently the yacht stands up on its foils and carries Delphi to the program Mr. Cantle has waiting. It's long-range; she's scheduled for at least two decades' product life. Phase One calls for her to connect with a flock of young ultrariches who are romping loose between Brioni and Djakarta where a competitor named PEV could pick them off.

A routine luxgear op, see; no politics, no policy angles, and the main budget items are the title and the yacht, which was idle anyway. The storyline is that Delphi goes to accept some rare birds for her prince—who cares? The *point* is that the Haiti area is no longer radioactive and look!—the gods are there. And so are several new Carib West Happy Isles which can afford GTX rates, in fact two of them are GTX subsids.

But you don't want to get the idea that all these newsworthy people are wired-up robbies, for pity's sake. You don't need many if they're placed right. Delphi asks Joe about that when he comes down to Barranquilla to check her over. (P. Burke's own mouth hasn't said much for a while.)

"Are there many like me?"

"Nobody's like you, buttons. Look, are you still getting Van Allen warble?"

"I mean, like Davy. Is he a Remote?"

(Davy is the lad who is helping her collect the birds. A sincere redhead who needs a little more exposure.)

"Davy? He's one of Matt's boys, some psychojob. They haven't any channel."

"What about the real ones? Djuma van O, or Ali, or Jim Ten?"

"Djuma was born with a pile of GTX basic where her brain should be, she's nothing but a pain. Jimsy does what his astrologer tells him. Look, peanut, where do you get the idea you aren't real? You're the realest. Aren't you having joy?"

"Oh, Joe!" Flinging her little arms around him and his analyzer grids. "Oh, *me gusto mucho, muchisimo!*"

"Hey, hey." He pets her yellow head, folding the analyzer. Three thousand miles north and five hundred feet down a forgotten hulk in a body-waldo glows.

And is she having joy. To waken out of the nightmare of being P. Burke and find herself a peri, a star-girl? On a yacht in paradise with no more to do than adorn herself and play with toys and attend revels and greet her friends—her, P. Burke, having friends!—and turn the right way for the holocams? Joy!

And it shows. One look at Delphi and the viewers know: DREAMS CAN COME TRUE.

Look at her riding pillion on Davy's sea-bike, carrying an apoplectic macaw in a silver hoop. Oh, *Morton, let's go there this winter!* Or learning the Japanese chinchona from that Kobe group, in a dress that looks like a blowtorch rising from one knee, and which should sell big in Texas. *Morton, is that real fire?* Happy, happy little girl!

And Davy. He's her pet and her baby, and she loves to help him fix his red-gold hair. (P. Burke marveling, running Delphi's fingers through the curls.) Of course Davy is one of Matt's boys—not impotent exactly, but very *very* low drive. (Nobody knows exactly what Matt does with his bitty budget, but the boys are useful and one or two have made names.) He's perfect for Delphi; in fact the psychomed lets her take him to bed, two kittens in a basket. Davy doesn't mind the fact that Delphi "sleeps" like the dead. That's when P. Burke is out of the body-waldo up at Carbondale, attending to her own depressing needs.

A funny thing about that. Most of her sleepy-time Delphi's just a gently ticking lush little vegetable waiting for P. Burke to get back on the controls. But now and again Delphi all by herself smiles a bit or stirs in her "sleep." Once she breathed a sound: "Yes."

Under Carbondale P. Burke knows nothing. She's asleep too, dreaming of Delphi, what else? But if the bushy Dr. Tesla had heard that single syllable, his bush would have turned snow-white. Because Delphi is TURNED OFF.

He doesn't. Davy is too dim to notice, and Delphi's staff boss, Hopkins, wasn't monitoring.

And they've all got something else to think about now, because the cold-fire dress sells half a million copies, and not only in Texas. The GTX computers already know it. When they correlate a minor demand for macaws in Alaska the problem comes to human attention: Delphi is something special.

It's a problem, see, because Delphi is targeted on a limited consumer bracket. Now it turns out she has mass-pop potential—those macaws in *Fairbanks*, man!—it's like trying to shoot mice with an ABM. A whole new ball game. Dr. Tesla and the fatherly Mr. Cantle start going around in headquarters circles and buddy-lunching together when they can get away from a seventh-level weasel boy who scares them both.

In the end it's decided to ship Delphi down to the GTX holocam enclave in Chile to try a spot on one of the mainstream shows. (Never mind why an Infanta takes up acting.) The holocam complex occupies a couple of mountains where an observatory once used the clean air. Holocam total-environment shells are very expensive and electronically superstable. Inside them actors can move freely without going off-register, and the whole scene or any selected part will show up in the viewer's home in complete three-di, so real you can look up their noses and much denser than you get from mobile rigs. You can blow a tit ten feet tall when there's no molecular skiffle around.

The enclave looks—well, take everything you know about Hollywood-Burbank and throw it away. What Delphi sees coming down is a neat giant mushroom-farm, domes of all sizes up to monsters for the big games and stuff. It's orderly. The idea that art thrives on creative flamboyance has long been torpedoed by proof that what art needs is computers. Because this showbiz has something TV and Hollywood never had—*automated inbuilt viewer feedback*. Samples, ratings, critics, polls? Forget it. With that carrier field you can get real-time response-sensor readouts from every receiver in the world, served up at your console. That started as a thingie to give the public more influence on content.

Yes.

Try it, man. You're at the console. Slice to the sex-age-educ-econ-ethno-cetera audience of your choice and start. You can't miss. Where the feedback warms up, give 'em more of that. Warm—warmer—*hot!* You've hit it—the secret itch under those hides, the dream in those hearts. You don't need to know its name. With your hand controlling all the input and your eye reading all the response, you can make them a god . . . and somebody'll do the same for you.

But Delphi just sees rainbows, when she gets through the degaussing ports and the field relay and takes her first look at the insides of those shells. The next thing she sees is a team of shapers and technicians descending on her, and millisecond timers everywhere. The tropical leisure is finished. She's in gigabuck mainstream now, at the funnel maw of the unceasing hose that's pumping the sight and sound and flesh and blood and sobs and laughs and dreams of *reality* into the world's happy head. Little Delphi is going plonk into a zillion homes in prime time and nothing is left to chance. Work!

And again Delphi proves apt. Of course it's really P. Burke down under Carbondale who's doing it, but who remembers that carcass? Certainly not P. Burke, she hasn't spoken through her own mouth for months. Delphi doesn't even recall dreaming of her when she wakes up.

As for the show itself, don't bother. It's gone on so long no living soul could unscramble the plotline. Delphi's trial spot has something to do with a widow and her dead husband's brother's amnesia.

The flap comes after Delphi's spots begin to flash out along the world-hose and the feedback appears. You've guessed it, of course. Sensational! As you'd say, they IDENTIFY.

The report actually says something like InskinEmp with a string of percentages, meaning that Delphi not only has it for anybody with a Y chromosome, but also for women and everything in between. It's the sweet supernatural jackpot, the million-to-one.

Remember your Harlow? A sexpot, sure. But why did bitter hausfraus in Gary and Memphis know that the vanilla-ice-cream goddess with the white hair and crazy eyebrows was *their baby girl?* And write loving letters to Jean warning her that their husbands weren't good enough for her? Why? The GTX analysts don't know either, but they know what to do with it when it happens.

(Back in his bird sanctuary the old Infante spots it without benefit of computers and gazes thoughtfully at his bride in widow's weeds. It might, he feels, be well to accelerate the completion of his studies.)

The excitement reaches down to the burrow under Carbondale where P. Burke gets two medical exams in a week and a chronically inflamed electrode is replaced. Nurse Fleming also gets an assistant who doesn't do much nursing but is very interested in access doors and identity tabs.

And in Chile, little Delphi is promoted to a new home up among the stars' residential spreads and a private jitney to carry her to work. For Hopkins there's a new computer terminal and a full-time schedule man. What is the schedule crowded with?

Things.

And here begins the trouble. You probably saw that coming too.

"What does she think she is, a goddamn *consumer rep?*" Mr. Cantle's fatherly face in Carbondale contorts.

"The girl's upset," Miss Fleming says stubbornly. "She *believes* that, what you told her about helping people and good new products."

"They are good products," Mr. Cantle snaps automatically, but his anger is under control. He hasn't got where he is by irrelevant reactions.

"She says the plastic gave her a rash and the glo-pills made her dizzy."

"Good god, she shouldn't swallow them," Dr. Tesla puts in agitatedly.

"You told her she'd use them," persists Miss Fleming.

Mr. Cantle is busy figuring how to ease this problem to the feral-faced young man. What, was it a goose that lays golden eggs?

Whatever he says to Level Seven, down in Chile the offending products vanish. And a symbol goes into Delphi's tank matrix, one that means roughly *Balance unit resistance against PR index.* This means that Delphi's complaints will be endured as long as her Pop Response stays above a certain level. (What happens when it sinks need not concern us.) And to compensate, the price of her exposure-time rises again. She's a regular on the show now and response is still climbing.

See her under the sizzling lasers, in a holocam shell set up as a walkway accident. (The show is guesting an acupuncture school shill.)

"I don't think this new body-lift is safe," Delphi's saying. "It's made a funny blue spot on me—look, Mr. Vere."

She wiggles to show where the mini-grav pak that imparts a delicious sense of weightlessness is attached.

"So don't leave it *on*, Dee. With your meat—watch that deckspot, it's starting to synch."

"But if I don't wear it it isn't honest. They should insulate it more or something, don't you see?"

The show's beloved old father, who is the casualty, gives a senile snigger.

"I'll tell them," Mr. Vere mutters. "Look now, as you step back bend like this so it just shows, see? And hold two beats."

Obediently Delphi turns, and through the dazzle her eyes connect with a pair of strange dark ones. She squints. A quite young man is lounging alone by the port, apparently waiting to use the chamber.

Delphi's used by now to young men looking at her with many peculiar expressions, but she isn't used to what she gets here. A jolt of something somber and knowing. *Secrets.*

"Eyes! Eyes, Dee!"

She moves through the routine, stealing peeks at the stranger. He stares back. He knows something.

When they let her go she comes shyly to him.

"Living wild, kitten." Cool voice, hot underneath.

"What do you mean?"

"Dumping on the product. You trying to get dead?"

"But it isn't right," she tells him. "They don't know, but I do, I've been wearing it."

His cool is jolted.

"You're out of your head."

"Oh, they'll see I'm right when they check it," she explains. "They're just so busy. When I tell them—"

He is staring down at little flower-face. His mouth opens, closes. "What are you doing in this sewer anyway? Who are you?"

Bewilderedly she says, "I'm Delphi."

"Holy Zen."

"What's wrong? Who are you, please?"

Her people are moving her out now, nodding at him.

"Sorry we ran over, Mr. Uhunh," the script girl says.

He mutters something, but it's lost as her convoy bustles her toward the flower-decked jitney. (Hear the click of an invisible ignition-train being armed?)

"Who was he?" Delphi asks her hairman.

The hairman is bending up and down from his knees as he works.

"Paul. Isham. Three," he says and puts a comb in his mouth.

"Who's that? I can't see."

He mumbles around the comb, meaning, "Are you jiving?" Because she has to be, in the middle of the GTX enclave.

Next day there's a darkly smoldering face under a turban-towel when Delphi and the show's paraplegic go to use the carbonated pool.

She looks.

He looks.

And the next day, too.

(Hear the automatic sequencer cutting in? The system couples, the fuels begin to travel.)

Poor old Isham senior. You have to feel sorry for a man who values order: when he begets young, genetic information is still transmitted in the old ape way. One minute it's a happy midget with a rubber duck—look around and here's this huge healthy stranger, opaquely emotional, running with god knows who. Questions are heard where there's nothing to question, and eruptions claiming to be moral outrage. When this is called to Papa's attention—it may take time, in that boardroom—Papa does what he can, but without immortality-juice the problem is worrisome.

And young Paul Isham is a bear. He's bright and articulate and tender-souled and incessantly active, and he and his friends are choking with appallment at the world their fathers made. And it hasn't taken Paul long to discover that *his* father's house has many mansions and even the GTX computers can't relate everything to everything else. He noses out a decaying project which adds up to something like, Sponsoring Marginal Creativity (the free-lance team that "discovered" Delphi was one such grantee). And from there it turns out that an agile lad named Isham can get his hands on a viable packet of GTX holocam facilities.

So here he is with his little band, way down the mushroom-farm mountain, busily spooling a show which has no relation to Delphi's. It's built on bizarre techniques and unsettling distortions pregnant with social protest. An *underground* expression to you.

All this isn't unknown to his father, of course, but so far it has done nothing more than deepen Isham senior's apprehensive frown.

Until Paul connects with Delphi.

And by the time Papa learns this, those invisible hypergolics have exploded, the energy-shells are rushing out. For Paul, you see, is the genuine article. He's serious. He dreams. He even reads—for example, *Green Mansions*—and he wept fiercely when those fiends burned Rima alive.

When he hears that some new GTX pussy is making it big, he sneers and forgets it. He's busy. He never connects the name with this little girl making her idiotic, doomed protest in the holocam chamber. This strangely simple little girl.

And she comes and looks up at him and he sees Rima, lost Rima the enchanted bird girl, and his unwired human heart goes twang.

And Rima turns out to be Delphi.

Do you need a map? The angry puzzlement. The rejection of the dissonance Rima-hustling-for-GTX-My-Father. Garbage, cannot be. The loitering around the pool to confirm the swindle . . . dark eyes hitting on blue wonder, jerky words exchanged in a peculiar stillness . . . the dreadful reorganization of the image into Rima-Delphi *in my Father's tentacles*—

You don't need a map.

Nor for Delphi either, the girl who loved her gods. She's seen their divine flesh close now, heard their unamplified voices call her name. She's played their god-games, worn their garlands. She's even become a goddess herself, though she doesn't believe it. She's not disenchanted, don't think that. She's still full of love. It's just that some crazy kind of *hope* hasn't—

Really you can skip all this, when the loving little girl on the yellow-brick road meets a Man. A real human male burning with angry compassion and grandly concerned with human justice, who reaches for her with real male arms and—boom! She loves him back with all her heart.

A happy trip, see?

Except.

Except that it's really P. Burke five thousand miles away who loves Paul. P. Burke the monster down in a dungeon smelling of electrode paste. A caricature of a woman burning, melting, obsessed with true love. Trying over twenty-double-thousand miles of hard vacuum to reach her beloved through girl-flesh numbed by an invisible film. Feeling his arms around the body he thinks is hers, fighting through shadows to give herself to him. Trying to taste and smell him through beautiful dead nostrils, to love him back with a body that goes dead in the heart of the fire.

Perhaps you get P. Burke's state of mind?

She has phases. The trying, first. And the shame. The SHAME. *I am not what thou lovest.* And the fiercer trying. And the realization that there is no, no way, none. Never. *Never* . . . A bit delayed, isn't it, her understanding that the bargain she made was forever? P. Burke should have noticed those stories about mortals who end up as grasshoppers.

You see the outcome—the funneling of all this agony into one dumb protoplasmic drive to fuse with Delphi. To leave, to close out the beast she is chained to. *To become Delphi.*

Of course it's impossible.

However, her torments have an effect on Paul. Delphi-as-Rima is a potent enough love object, and liberating Delphi's mind requires hours of deeply satisfying instruction in the rottenness of it all. Add in Delphi's body worshiping his flesh, burning in the fire of P. Burke's savage heart—do you wonder Paul is involved?

That's not all.

By now they're spending every spare moment together and some that aren't so spare.

"Mr. Isham, would you mind staying out of this sports sequence? The script calls for Davy here."

(Davy's still around, the exposure did him good.)

"What's the difference?" Paul yawns. "It's just an ad. I'm not blocking that thing."

Shocked silence at his two-letter word. The script girl swallows bravely.

"I'm sorry, sir, our directive is to do the *social sequence* exactly as scripted. We're having to respool the segments we did last week. Mr. Hopkins is very angry with me."

"Who the hell is Hopkins? Where is he?"

"Oh, please, Paul. *Please.*"

Paul unwraps himself, saunters back. The holocam crew nervously check their angles. The GTX boardroom has a foible about having things *pointed* at them and theirs. Cold shivers, when the image of an Isham nearly went onto the world beam beside that Dialadinner.

Worse yet, Paul has no respect for the sacred schedules which are now a full-time job for ferret boy up at headquarters. Paul keeps forgetting to bring her back on time, and poor Hopkins can't cope.

So pretty soon the boardroom data-ball has an urgent personal action-tab for Mr. Isham senior. They do it the gentle way, at first.

"I can't today, Paul."

"Why not?"

"They say I have to, it's *very* important."

He strokes the faint gold down on her narrow back. Under Carbondale, Pa., a blind mole-woman shivers.

"Important. Their importance. Making more gold. Can't you see? To them you're just a thing to get scratch with. A *huckster*. Are you going to let them screw you, Dee? Are you?"

"Oh Paul—"

He doesn't know it, but he's seeing a weirdie; Remotes aren't hooked up to flow tears.

"Just say no, Dee. No. Integrity. You have to."

"But they say, it's my job—"

"Will you believe I can take care of you, Dee? Baby, baby, you're letting them rip us. You have to choose. Tell them, no."

"Paul . . . I w-will. . . ."

And she does. Brave little Delphi (insane P. Burke). Saying, "No, please, I promised, Paul."

They try some more, still gently.

"Paul, Mr. Hopkins told me the reason they don't want us to be together so much. It's because of who you are, your father."

She thinks his father is like Mr. Cantle, maybe.

"Oh, great. Hopkins. I'll fix him. Listen, I can't think about Hopkins now. Ken came back today, he found out something."

They are lying on the high Andes meadow watching his friends dive their singing kites.

"Would you believe, on the coast the police have *electrodes in their heads?*"

She stiffens in his arms.

"Yeah, weird. I thought they only used PP on criminals and the army. Don't you see, Dee—something has to be going on. Some movement. Maybe somebody's organizing. How can we find out?" He pounds the ground behind her: "We should make *contact!* If we could only find out."

"The, the news?" she asks distractedly.

"The news." He laughs. "There's nothing in the news except what they want people to know. Half the country could burn up, and nobody would know it if they didn't want. Dee, can't you take what I'm explaining to you? They've got the whole world programmed! Total control of communication. They've got everybody's minds wired in to think what they show them and want what they give them and they give them what they're programmed to want—you can't break in or out of it, you can't get *hold* of it anywhere. I don't think they even have a plan except to keep things going round and round—and god knows what's happening to the people or the Earth or the other planets, maybe. One great big vortex of lies and garbage pouring round and round, getting bigger and bigger, and nothing can ever change. If people don't wake up soon we're through!"

He pounds her stomach softly.

"You have to break out, Dee."

"I'll try, Paul, I will—"

"You're mine. They can't have you."

And he goes to see Hopkins, who is indeed cowed.

But that night up under Carbondale the fatherly Mr. Cantle goes to see P. Burke.

P. Burke? On a cot in a utility robe like a dead camel in a tent, she cannot at first comprehend that he is telling her to break it off with Paul. P. Burke has never seen Paul. *Delphi* sees Paul. The fact is, P. Burke can no longer clearly recall that she exists apart from Delphi.

Mr. Cantle can scarcely believe it either, but he tries.

He points out the futility, the potential embarrassment, for Paul. That gets a dim stare from the bulk on the bed. Then he goes into her duty to GTX, her job, isn't she grateful for the opportunity, etcetera. He's very persuasive.

The cobwebby mouth of P. Burke opens and croaks.

"No."

Nothing more seems to be forthcoming.

Mr. Cantle isn't dense, he knows an immovable obstacle when he bumps one. He also knows an irresistible force: GTX. The simple solution is to lock the waldo-cabinet until Paul gets tired of waiting for Delphi to wake up. But the cost, the schedules! And there's something odd here . . . he eyes the corporate asset hulking on the bed and his hunch-sense prickles.

You see, Remotes don't love. They don't have real sex, the circuits designed that out from the start. So it's been assumed that it's *Paul* who is diverting himself or something with the pretty little body in Chile. P. Burke can only be doing what comes natural to any ambitious gutter-meat. It hasn't occurred to anyone that they're dealing with the real hairy thing whose shadow is blasting out of every holoshow on Earth.

Love?

Mr. Cantle frowns. The idea is grotesque. But his instinct for the fuzzy line is strong; he will recommend flexibility.

And so, in Chile:

"Darling, I don't have to work tonight! And Friday too—isn't that right, Mr. Hopkins?"

"Oh, great. When does she come up for parole?"

"Mr. Isham, please be reasonable. Our schedule—surely your own production people must be needing you?"

This happens to be true. Paul goes away. Hopkins stares after him, wondering distastefully why an Isham wants to ball a waldo. How sound are those boardroom belly-fears—garble creeps, creeps in! It never occurs to Hopkins that an Isham might not know what Delphi is.

Especially with Davy crying because Paul has kicked him out of Delphi's bed.

Delphi's bed is under a real window.

"Stars," Paul says sleepily. He rolls over, pulling Delphi on top. "Are you aware that this is one of the last places on Earth where people can see the stars? Tibet, too, maybe."

"Paul . . ."

"Go to sleep. I want to see you sleep."

"Paul, I . . . I sleep so *hard*, I mean, it's a joke how hard I am to wake up. Do you mind?"

"Yes."

But finally, fearfully, she must let go. So that five thousand miles north a crazy spent creature can crawl out to gulp concentrates and fall on her cot. But not for long. It's pink dawn when Delphi's eyes open to find Paul's arms around her, his voice saying rude, tender things. He's been kept awake. The nerveless little statue that was her Delphi-body nuzzled him in the night.

Insane hope rises, is fed a couple of nights later when he tells her she called his name in her sleep.

And that day Paul's arms keep her from work and Hopkins's wails go up to headquarters where the weasel-faced lad is working his sharp tailbone off packing Delphi's program. Mr. Cantle defuses that one. But next week it happens again, to a major client. And ferret-face has connections on the technical side.

Now you can see that when you have a field of complexly heterodyned energy modulations tuned to a demand-point like Delphi, there are many problems of standwaves and lashback and skiffle of all sorts which are normally balanced out with ease by the technology of the future. By the same token they can be delicately unbalanced too, in ways that feed back into the waldo operator with striking results.

"Darling—what the hell! What's wrong? DELPHI!"

Helpless shrieks, writhings. Then the Rima-bird is lying wet and limp in his arms, her eyes enormous.

"I . . . I wasn't supposed to . . ." she gasps faintly. "They told me not to. . . ."

"Oh, my god—*Delphi.*"

And his hard fingers are digging in her thick yellow hair. Electronically knowledgeable fingers. They freeze.

"You're a *doll!* You're one of those PP implants. They control you. I should have known. Oh, god, I should have known."

"No, Paul," she's sobbing. "No, no, no—"

"Damn them. Damn them, what they've done—you're not you—"

He's shaking her, crouching over her in the bed and jerking her back and forth, glaring at the pitiful beauty.

"No!" she pleads (it's not true, that dark bad dream back there). "I'm Delphi!"

"My father. Filth, pigs—damn them, damn them, damn them."

"No, no," she babbles. "They were good to me—" P. Burke underground mouthing, "They were good to me—AAH-AAAAH!"

Another agony skewers her. Up north the sharp young man wants to make sure this so-tiny interference works. Paul can scarcely hang on to her, he's crying too. "I'll kill them."

His Delphi, a wired-up slave! Spikes in her brain, electronic shackles in his bird's heart. Remember when those savages burned Rima alive?

"I'll *kill* the man that's doing this to you." He's still saying it afterward, but she doesn't hear. She's sure he hates her now, all she wants is to die. When she finally understands that the fierceness is tenderness, she thinks it's a miracle. *He knows—and he still loves!*

How can she guess that he's got it a little bit wrong?

You can't blame Paul. Give him credit that he's even heard about pleasure-pain implants and snoops, which by their nature aren't mentioned much by those who know them most intimately. That's what he thinks is being used on Delphi, something to *control* her. And to listen—he burns at the unknown ears in their bed.

Of waldo-bodies and objects like P. Burke he has heard nothing.

So it never crosses his mind as he looks down at his violated bird, sick with fury and love, that he isn't holding *all* of her. Do you need to be told the mad resolve jelling in him now?

To free Delphi.

How? Well, he is, after all, Paul Isham III. And he even has an idea where the GTX neurolab is. In Carbondale.

But first things have to be done for Delphi, and for his own stomach. So he gives her back to Hopkins and departs in a restrained and discreet way. And the Chile staff is grateful and do not understand that his teeth don't normally show so much.

And a week passes in which Delphi is a very good, docile little ghost. They let her have the load of wildflowers Paul sends and the bland loving notes. (He's playing it coony.) And up in headquarters weasel boy feels that *his* destiny has clicked a notch onward and floats the word up that he's handy with little problems.

And no one knows what P. Burke thinks in any way whatever, except that Miss Fleming catches her flushing her food down the can and next night she faints in the pool. They haul her out and stick her with IVs. Miss Fleming frets, she's seen expressions like that before. But she wasn't around when crazies who called themselves Followers of the Fish looked through flames to life everlasting. P. Burke is seeing Heaven on the far side of death, too. Heaven is spelled P-a-u-l, but the idea's the same. *I will die and be born again in Delphi.*

Garbage, electronically speaking. No way.

Another week and Paul's madness has become a plan. (Remember, he does have friends.) He smolders, watching his love paraded by her masters. He turns out a scorching sequence for his own show. And finally, politely, he requests from Hopkins a morsel of his bird's free time, which duly arrives.

"I thought you didn't want me anymore," she's repeating as they wing over mountain flanks in Paul's suncar. "Now you *know*—"

"Look at me!"

His hand covers her mouth, and he's showing her a lettered card.

DON'T TALK THEY CAN HEAR EVERYTHING WE SAY.

I'M TAKING YOU AWAY NOW.

She kisses his hand, He nods urgently, flipping the card.

DON'T BE AFRAID. I CAN STOP THE PAIN IF THEY TRY TO HURT YOU.

With his free hand he shakes out a silvery scrambler-mesh on a power pack. She is dumbfounded.

THIS WILL CUT THE SIGNALS AND PROTECT YOU DARLING.

She's staring at him, her head going vaguely from side to side, No.

"Yes!" He grins triumphantly, "Yes!"

For a moment she wonders. That powered mesh will cut off the field, all right. It will also cut off Delphi. But he is Paul. *Paul* is kissing her, she can only seek him hungrily as he sweeps the suncar through a pass.

Ahead is an old jet ramp with a shiny bullet waiting to go. (Paul also has credits and a Name.) The little GTX patrol courier is built for nothing but speed. Paul and Delphi wedge in behind the pilot's extra fuel tank, and there's no more talking when the torches start to scream.

They're screaming high over Quito before Hopkins starts to worry. He wastes another hour tracking the beeper on Paul's suncar. The suncar is sailing a pattern out to sea. By the time they're sure it's empty and Hopkins gets on the hot flue to headquarters, the fugitives are a sourceless howl above Carib West.

Up at headquarters weasel boy gets the squeal. His first impulse is to repeat his previous play, but then his brain snaps to. This one is too hot. Because, see, although in the long run they can make P. Burke do anything at all except maybe live, instant emergencies can be tricky. And—Paul Isham III.

"Can't you order her back?"

They're all in the GTX tower monitor station, Mr. Cantle and ferret-face and Joe and a very neat man who is Mr. Isham senior's personal eyes and ears.

"No, sir," Joe says doggedly. "We can read channels, particularly speech, but we can't interpolate organized pattern. It takes the waldo op to send one-to-one—"

"What are they saying?"

"Nothing at the moment, sir." The console jockey's eyes are closed. "I believe they are, ah, embracing."

"They're not answering," a traffic monitor says. "Still heading zero zero three zero—due north, sir."

"You're certain Kennedy is alerted not to fire on them?" the neat man asks anxiously.

"Yes, sir."

"Can't you just turn her off?" The sharp-faced lad is angry. "Pull that pig out of the controls!"

"If you cut the transmission cold you'll kill the Remote," Joe explains for the third time. "Withdrawal has to be phased right, you have to fade over to the Remote's own autonomics. Heart, breathing, cerebellum, would go blooey. If you pull Burke out you'll probably finish her too. It's a fantastic cybersystem, you don't want to do that."

"The investment." Mr. Cantle shudders.

Weasel boy puts his hand on the console jock's shoulder, it's the contact who arranged the no-no effect for him.

"We can at least give them a warning signal, sir." He licks his lips, gives the neat man his sweet ferret smile. "We know that does no damage."

Joe frowns, Mr. Cantle sighs. The neat man is murmuring into his wrist. He looks up. "I am authorized," he says reverently, "I am authorized to, ah, direct a signal. If this is the only course. But minimal, minimal."

Sharp-face squeezes his man's shoulder.

In the silver bullet shrieking over Charleston Paul feels Delphi arch in his arms. He reaches for the mesh, hot for action. She thrashes, pushing at his hands, her eyes roll. She's afraid of that mesh despite the agony. (And she's right.) Frantically Paul fights her in the cramped space, gets it over her head. As he turns the power up she burrows free under his arm and the spasm fades.

"They're calling you again, Mr. Isham!" the pilot yells.

"Don't answer. Darling, keep this over your head damn it how can I—"

An AX90 barrels over their nose, there's a flash.

"Mr. Isham! Those are Air Force jets!"

"Forget it," Paul shouts back. "They won't fire. Darling, don't be afraid."

Another AX90 rocks them.

"Would you mind pointing your pistol at my head where they can see it, sir?" the pilot howls.

Paul does so. The AX90s take up escort formation around them. The pilot goes back to figuring how he can collect from GTX too, and after Goldsboro AB the escort peels away.

"Holding the same course." Traffic is reporting to the group around the monitor. "Apparently they've taken on enough fuel to bring them to towerport here."

"In that case it's just a question of waiting for them to dock." Mr. Cantle's fatherly manner revives a bit.

"Why can't they cut off that damn freak's life-support," the sharp young man fumes. "It's ridiculous."

"They're working on it," Cantle assures him.

What they're doing, down under Carbondale, is arguing.

Miss Fleming's watchdog has summoned the bushy man to the waldo room.

"Miss Fleming, you will obey orders."

"You'll kill her if you try that, sir. I can't believe you meant it, that's why I didn't. We've already fed her enough sedative to affect heart action; if you cut any more oxygen she'll die in there."

The bushy man grimaces. "Get Dr. Quine here fast."

They wait, staring at the cabinet in which a drugged, ugly madwoman fights for consciousness, fights to hold Delphi's eyes open.

High over Richmond the silver pod starts a turn. Delphi is sagged into Paul's arm, her eyes swim up to him.

"Starting down now, baby. It'll be over soon, all you have to do is stay alive, Dee."

" . . . stay alive . . ."

The traffic monitor has caught them. "Sir! They've turned off for Carbondale—Control has contact—"

"Let's go."

But the headquarters posse is too late to intercept the courier wailing into Carbondale. And Paul's friends have come through again. The fugitives are out through the freight dock and into the neurolab admin port before the guard gets organized. At the elevator Paul's face plus his handgun gets them in.

"I want Doctor—what's his name, Dee? Dee!"

" . . . Tesla . . ." She's reeling on her feet.

"Dr. Tesla. Take me down to Tesla, fast."

Intercoms are squalling around them as they whoosh down, Paul's pistol in the guard's back. When the door slides open the bushy man is there.

"I'm Tesla."

"I'm Paul Isham. *Isham*. You're going to take your flaming implants out of this girl—now. Move!"

"What?"

"You heard me. Where's your operating room? Go!"

"But—"

"Move! Do I have to burn somebody?"

Paul waves the weapon at Dr. Quine, who has just appeared.

"No, no," says Tesla hurriedly. "But I can't, you know. It's impossible, there'll be nothing left."

"You screaming well can, right now. You mess up and I'll kill you," says Paul murderously. "Where is it, there? And wipe the feke that's on her circuits now."

He's backing them down the hall, Delphi heavy on his arm.

"Is this the place, baby? Where they did it to you?"

"Yes," she whispers, blinking at a door. "Yes . . ."

Because it is, see. Behind that door is the very suite where she was born.

Paul herds them through it into a gleaming hall. An inner door opens, and a nurse and a gray man rush out. And freeze.

Paul sees there's something special about that inner door. He crowds them past it and pushes it open and looks in.

Inside is a big mean-looking cabinet with its front door panels ajar.

And inside that cabinet is a poisoned carcass to whom something wonderful, unspeakable, is happening. Inside is P. Burke, the real living woman who knows that HE is there, coming closer—Paul whom she had fought to reach through forty thousand miles of ice—PAUL is here!—is yanking at the waldo doors—

The doors tear open and a monster rises up.

"Paul darling!" croaks the voice of love, and the arms of love reach for him.

And he responds.

Wouldn't you, if a gaunt she-golem flab-naked and spouting wires and blood came at you clawing with metal-studded paws—

"Get away!" He knocks wires.

It doesn't much matter which wires. P. Burke has, so to speak, her nervous system hanging out. Imagine somebody jerking a handful of your medulla—

She crashes onto the floor at his feet, flopping and roaring *PAUL-PAUL-PAUL* in rictus.

It's doubtful he recognizes his name or sees her life coming out of her eyes at him. And at the last it doesn't go to him. The eyes find Delphi, fainting by the doorway, and die.

Now of course Delphi is dead, too.

There's a total silence as Paul steps away from the thing by his foot.

"You killed her," Tesla says. "That was her."

"Your control." Paul is furious, the thought of that monster fastened into little Delphi's brain nauseates him. He sees her crumpling and holds out his arms. Not knowing she is dead. And Delphi comes to him.

One foot before the other, not moving very well—but moving. Her darling face turns up. Paul is distracted by the terrible quiet, and when he looks down he sees only her tender little neck.

"Now you get the implants out," he warns them. Nobody moves.

"But, but she's dead," Miss Fleming whispers wildly.

Paul feels Delphi's life under his hand, they're talking about their monster. He aims his pistol at the gray man.

"You. If we aren't in your surgery when I count three, I'm burning off this man's leg."

"Mr. Isham," Tesla says desperately, "you have just killed the person who animated the body you call Delphi. Delphi herself is dead. If you release your arm you'll see what I say is true."

The tone gets through. Slowly Paul opens his arm, looks down.

"Delphi?"

She totters, sways, stays upright. Her face comes slowly up.

"Paul . . ." Tiny voice.

"Your crotty tricks," Paul snarls at them. "Move!"

"Look at her eyes," Dr. Quine croaks.

They look. One of Delphi's pupils fills the iris, her lips writhe weirdly.

"Shock." Paul grabs her to him. "*Fix* her!" He yells at them, aiming at Tesla.

"For god's sake . . . bring it in the lab." Tesla quavers.

"Good-bye-bye," says Delphi clearly. They lurch down the hall, Paul carrying her, and meet a wave of people.

Headquarters has arrived.

Joe takes one look and dives for the waldo room, running into Paul's gun.

"Oh, no, you don't."

Everybody is yelling. The little thing in his arm stirs, says plaintively, "I'm Delphi."

And all through the ensuing jabber and ranting she hangs on, keeping it up, the ghost of P. Burke or whatever whispering crazily, "Paul . . . Paul . . . Please, I'm Delphi . . . Paul?"

"I'm here, darling, I'm here." He's holding her in the nursing bed. Tesla talks, talks, talks unheard.

"Paul . . . don't sleep . . ." The ghost-voice whispers. Paul is in agony, he will not accept, WILL NOT believe.

Tesla runs down.

And then near midnight Delphi says roughly, "Ag-ag-ag—" and slips onto the floor, making a rough noise like a seal.

Paul screams. There's more of the *ag-ag* business and more gruesome convulsive disintegrations, until by two in the morning Delphi is nothing but a warm little bundle of vegetative functions hitched to some expensive hardware—the same that sustained her before her life began. Joe has finally persuaded Paul to let him at the waldo-cabinet. Paul stays by her long enough to see her face change in a dreadfully alien and coldly convincing way, and then he stumbles out bleakly through the group in Tesla's office.

Behind him Joe is working wet-faced, sweating to reintegrate the fantastic complex of circulation, respiration, endocrines, midbrain homeostases, the patterned flux that was a human being—it's like saving an orchestra abandoned in midair. Joe is also crying a little; he alone had truly loved P. Burke. P. Burke, now a dead pile on a table, was the greatest cybersystem he has ever known, and he never forgets her.

The end, really.

You're curious?

Sure, Delphi lives again. Next year she's back on the yacht getting sympathy for her tragic breakdown. But there's a different chick in Chile, because while Delphi's new operator is competent, you don't get two P. Burkes in a row—for which GTX is duly grateful.

The real belly-bomb of course is Paul. He was *young*, see. Fighting abstract wrong. Now life has clawed into him and he goes through gut rage and grief and grows in human wisdom and resolve. So much so that you won't be surprised, sometime later, to find him—where?

In the GTX boardroom, dummy. Using the advantage of his birth to radicalize the system. You'd call it "boring from within."

That's how he put it, and his friends couldn't agree more. It gives them a warm, confident feeling to know that Paul is up there. Sometimes one of them who's still around runs into him and gets a big hello.

And the sharp-faced lad?

Oh, he matures too. He learns fast, believe it. For instance, he's the first to learn that an obscure GTX research unit is actually getting something with their loopy temporal anomalizer project. True, he doesn't have a physics background, and he's bugged quite a few people. But he doesn't really learn about that until the day he stands where somebody points him during a test run—

—and wakes up lying on a newspaper headlined NIXON UNVEILS PHASE TWO.

Lucky he's a fast learner.

Believe it, zombie. When I say growth, I mean *growth*. Capital appreciation. You can stop sweating. There's a great future there.

Blood-Burning Moon[1]
(1923)

JEAN TOOMER

1

Up from the skeleton stone walls, up from the rotting floor boards and the solid hand-hewn beams of oak of the pre-war cotton factory, dusk came. Up from the dusk the full moon came. Glowing like a fired pine-knot, it illumined the great door and soft showered the Negro shanties aligned along the single street of factory town. The full moon in the great door was an omen. Negro women improvised songs against its spell.

Louisa sang as she came over the crest of the hill from the white folks' kitchen. Her skin was the color of oak leaves on young trees in fall. Her breasts, firm and up-pointed like ripe acorns. And her singing had the low murmur of winds in fig trees. Bob Stone, younger son of the people she worked for, loved her. By the way the world reckons things, he had won her. By measure of that warm glow which came into her mind at thought of him, he had won her. Tom Burwell, whom the whole town called Big Boy, also loved her. But working in the fields all day, and far away from her gave him no chance to show it. Though often enough of evenings he had tried to. Somehow, he never got along. Strong as he was with hands upon the ax or plow, he found it difficult to hold her. Or so he thought. But the fact was that he held her to factory town more firmly than he thought for. His black balanced, and pulled against, the white of Stone, when she thought of them. And her mind was vaguely upon them as she came over the crest of the hill, coming from the white folks' kitchen. As she sang softly at the evil face of the full moon.

A strange stir was in her. Indolently, she tried to fix upon Bob or Tom as the cause of it. To meet Bob in the canebrake, as she was going to do an hour or so later, was nothing new. And Tom's proposal which she felt on its way to her could be indefinitely put off. Separately, there was no unusual significance to either one. But for some reason, they jumbled when her eyes gazed vacantly at the rising moon. And from the jumble came the stir that was strangely within her. Her lips trembled. The slow rhythm of her song grew agitant and restless. Rusty black and tan spotted hounds, lying in the dark corners of porches or prowling around back yards, put their noses in the air and caught its tremor. They began plaintively to yelp and

1. First published in *Prairie* (March—April 1923): 18.

howl. Chickens woke up and cackled. Intermittently, all over the countryside dogs barked and roosters crowed as if heralding a weird dawn or some ungodly awakening. The women sang lustily. Their songs were cotton-wads to stop their ears. Louisa came down into factory town and sank wearily upon the step before her home. The moon was rising towards a thick cloud-bank which soon would hide it.

> *Red nigger moon. Sinner!*
> *Blood-burning moon. Sinner!*
> *Come out that fact'ry door.*

2

Up from the deep dusk of a cleared spot on the edge of the forest a mellow glow arose and spread fan-wise into the low-hanging heavens. And all around the air was heavy with the scent of boiling cane. A large pile of cane-stalks lay like ribboned shadows upon the ground. A mule, harnessed to a pole, trudged lazily round and round the pivot of the grinder. Beneath a swaying oil lamp, a Negro alternately whipped out at the mule, and fed cane-stalks to the grinder. A fat boy waddled pails of fresh ground juice between the grinder and the boiling stove. Steam came from the copper boiling pan. The scent of cane came from the copper pan and drenched the forest and the hill that sloped to factory town, beneath its fragrance. It drenched the men in circle seated around the stove. Some of them chewed at the white pulp of stalks, but there was no need for them to, if all they wanted was to taste the cane. One tasted it in factory town. And from factory town one could see the soft haze thrown by the glowing stove upon the low-hanging heavens.

Old David Georgia stirred the thickening syrup with a long ladle, and ever so often drew it off. Old David Georgia tended his stove and told tales about the white folks, about moon-shining and cotton picking, and about sweet nigger gals, to the men who sat there about his stove to listen to him. Tom Burwell chewed cane-stalk and laughed with the others till some one mentioned Louisa. Till some one said something about Louisa and Bob Stone, about the silk stockings she must have gotten from him. Blood ran up Tom's neck hotter than the glow that flooded from the stove. He sprang up. Glared at the men and said, "She's my gal." Will Manning laughed. Tom strode over to him. Yanked him up and knocked him to the ground. Several of Manning's friends got up to fight for him. Tom whipped out a long knife and would have cut them to shreds if they hadnt ducked into the woods. Tom had had enough. He nodded to Old David Georgia and swung down the path to factory town. Just then, the dogs started barking and the roosters began to crow. Tom felt funny. Away from the fight, away from the stove, chill got to him. He shivered. He shuddered when he saw the full moon rising towards the cloud-bank. He who didnt give a godam for the fears of old women. He forced his mind to fasten on Louisa. Bob Stone. Better not be. He turned into the street and saw Louisa sitting before her home. He went towards her, ambling, touched the brim of a marvelously shaped, spotted, felt hat, said he wanted to say something to her, and then found that he didnt know what he had to say, or if he did, that he couldnt say it. He shoved his big fists in his overalls, grinned, and started to move off.

"Youall want me, Tom?"

"Thats what us wants, sho, Louisa."

"Well, here I am—"

"An here I is, but that aint ahelpin none, all th same."

"You wanted to say something? . . . "

"I did that, sho. But words is like th spots on dice: no matter how y fumbles em, there's times when they jes wont come. I dunno why. Seems like th love I feels fo yo done stole m tongue. I got it now. Whee! Louisa, honey, I oughtnt tell y, I feel I oughtnt cause yo is young an goes t church an I has had other gals, but Louisa I sho do love y. Lil gal, Ise watched y from them first days when youall sat right here befo yo door befo th well an sang sometimes in a way that like t broke m heart. Ise carried y with me into th fields, day after day, an after that, an I sho can plow when yo is there, an I can pick cotton. Yassur! Come near beatin Barlo yesterday. I sho did. Yassur! An next year if ole Stone'll trust me, I'll have a farm. My own. My bales will buy yo what y gets from white folks now. Silk stockings an purple dresses—course I dont believe what some folks been whisperin as t how y gets them things now. White folks always did do for niggers what they likes. An they jes cant help alikin yo, Louisa. Bob Stone likes y. Course he does. But not th way folks is awhisperin. Does he, hon?"

"I dont know what you mean, Tom."

"Course y dont. Ise already cut two niggers. Had t hon, t tell em so. Niggers always tryin t make somethin out a nothin. An then besides, white folks aint up t them tricks so much nowadays. Godam better not be. Leastawise not with yo. Cause I wouldnt stand f it. Nassur."

"What would you do, Tom?"

"Cut him jes like I cut a nigger."

"No, Tom—"

"I said I would an there aint no mo to it. But that aint th talk f now. Sing, honey Louisa, an while I'm listenin t y I'll be makin love."

Tom took her hand in his. Against the tough thickness of his own, hers felt soft and small. His huge body slipped down to the step beside her. The full moon sank upward into the deep purple of the cloud-bank. An old woman brought a lighted lamp and hung it on the common well whose bulky shadow squatted in the middle of the road, opposite Tom and Louisa. The old woman lifted the welllid, took hold the chain, and began drawing up the heavy bucket. As she did so, she sang. Figures shifted, restlesslike, between lamp and window in the front rooms of the shanties. Shadows of the figures fought each other on the gray dust of the road. Figures raised the windows and joined the old woman in song. Louisa and Tom, the whole street, singing:

> *Red nigger moon. Sinner!*
> *Blood-burning moon. Sinner!*
> *Come out that fact'ry door.*

3

Bob Stone sauntered from his veranda out into the gloom of fir trees and magnolias. The clear white of his skin paled, and the flush of his cheeks turned purple. As if to balance this outer change, his mind became consciously a white man's. He passed the house with its huge open hearth which, in the days of slavery, was the plantation cookery. He saw Louisa bent over that hearth. He went in as a master should and took her. Direct, honest, bold. None of this sneaking that he had to go through now. The contrast was repulsive to him. His family had lost ground. Hell no, his family still owned the niggers, practically. Damned if they did,

883

or he wouldnt have to duck around so. What would they think if they knew? His mother? His sister? He shouldnt mention them, shouldnt think of them in this connection. There in the dusk he blushed at doing so. Fellows about town were all right, but how about his friends up North? He could see them incredible, repulsed. They didnt know. The thought first made him laugh. Then, with their eyes still upon him, he began to feel embarrassed. He felt the need of explaining things to them. Explain hell. They wouldnt understand, and moreover, who ever heard of a Southerner getting on his knees to any Yankee, or anyone. No sir. He was going to see Louisa to-night, and love her. She was lovely—in her way. Nigger way. What way was that? Damned if he knew. Must know. He'd known her long enough to know. Was there something about niggers that you couldnt know? Listening to them at church didnt tell you anything. Looking at them didnt tell you anything. Talking to them didnt tell you anything—unless it was gossip, unless they wanted to talk. Of course, about farming, and licker, and craps—but those werent nigger. Nigger was something more. How much more? Something to be afraid of, more? Hell no. Who ever heard of being afraid of a nigger? Tom Burwell. Cartwell had told him that Tom went with Louisa after she reached home. No sir. No nigger had ever been with his girl. He'd like to see one try. Some position for him to be in. Him, Bob Stone, of the old Stone family, in a scrap with a nigger over a nigger girl. In the good old days ... Ha! Those were the days. His family had lost ground. Not so much, though. Enough for him to have to cut through old Lemon's canefield by way of the woods, that he might meet her. She was worth it. Beautiful nigger gal. Why nigger? Why not, just gal? No, it was because she was nigger that he went to her. Sweet ... The scent of boiling cane came to him. Then he saw the rich glow of the stove. He heard the voices of the men circled around it. He was about to skirt the clearing when he heard his own name mentioned. He stopped. Quivering. Leaning against a tree, he listened.

"Bad nigger. Yassur, he sho is one bad nigger when he gets started."

"Tom Burwell's been on th gang three times fo cuttin men."

"What y think he's agwine t do t Bob Stone?"

"Dunno yet. He aint found out. When he does—Baby!"

"Aint no tellin."

"Young Stone aint no quitter an I ken tell y that. Blood of th old uns in his veins."

"Thats right. He'll scrap, sho."

"Be gettin too hot f niggers round this away."

"Shut up, nigger. Y dont know what y talkin bout."

Bob Stone's ears burned as though he had been holding them over the stove. Sizzling heat welled up within him. His feet felt as if they rested on red-hot coals. They stung him to quick movement. He circled the fringe of the glowing. Not a twig cracked beneath his feet. He reached the path that led to factory town. Plunged furiously down it. Halfway along, a blindness within him veered him aside. He crashed into the bordering canebrake. Cane leaves cut his face and lips. He tasted blood. He threw himself down and dug his fingers in the ground. The earth was cool. Cane-roots took the fever from his hands. After a long while, or so it seemed to him, the thought came to him that it must be time to see Louisa. He got to his feet and walked calmly to their meeting place. No Louisa. Tom Burwell had her. Veins in his forehead bulged and distended. Saliva moistened the dried blood on his lips. He bit down on his lips. He tasted blood. Not his own blood; Tom Burwell's blood. Bob drove through the cane and out again upon the road. A hound swung down the path before him towards factory town. Bob couldnt see it. The dog loped aside to let him pass. Bob's blind rushing made him stumble over it. He fell with a thud that dazed him. The hound yelped. Answering yelps came from all over the countryside. Chickens cackled. Roosters crowed, heralding the blood-shot eyes of southern awakening. Singers in the town were silenced. They shut their windows down. Palpitant between the rooster crows, a chill hush settled upon the huddled forms of Tom and Louisa. A figure rushed from the shadow and stood before them. Tom popped to his feet.

"Whats y want?"

"I'm Bob Stone."

"Yassur—an I'm Tom Burwell. Whats y want?"

Bob lunged at him. Tom side-stepped, caught him by the shoulder, and flung him to the ground. Straddled him.

"Let me up."

"Yassur—but watch yo doins,[2] Bob Stone."

A few dark figures, drawn by the sound of scuffle, stood about them. Bob sprang to his feet.

"Fight like a man. Tom Burwell, an I'll lick y."

Again he lunged. Tom side-stepped and flung him to the ground. Straddled him.

"Get off me, you godam nigger you."

"Yo sho has started somethin now. Get up."

Tom yanked him up and began hammering at him. Each blow sounded as if it smashed into a precious, irreplaceable soft something. Beneath them, Bob staggered back. He reached in his pocket and whipped out a knife.

"Thats my game, sho."

Blue flash, a steel blade slashed across Bob Stone's throat. He had a sweetish sick feeling. Blood began to flow. Then he felt a sharp twitch of pain. He let his knife drop. He slapped one hand against his neck. He pressed the other on top of his head as if to hold it down. He groaned. He turned, and staggered towards the crest of the hill in the direction of white town. Negroes who had seen the fight slunk into their homes and blew the lamps out. Louisa, dazed, hysterical, refused to go indoors. She slipped, crumbled, her body loosely propped against the woodwork of the well. Tom Burwell leaned against it. He seemed rooted there.

Bob reached Broad Street. White men rushed up to him. He collapsed in their arms.

"Tom Burwell. . . ."

White men like ants upon a forage rushed about. Except for the taut hum of their moving, all was silent. Shotguns, revolvers, rope, kerosene, torches. Two high-powered cars with glaring searchlights. They came together. The taut hum rose to a low roar. Then nothing could be heard but the flop of their feet in the thick dust of the road. The moving body of their silence preceded them over the crest of the hill into factory town. It flattened the Negroes beneath it. It rolled to the wall of the factory, where it stopped. Tom knew that they were coming. He couldnt move. And then he saw the search-lights of the two cars glaring down on him. A quick shock went through him. He stiffened. He started to run. A yell went up from the mob. Tom wheeled about and faced them. They poured down on him. They swarmed. A large man with dead-white face and flabby cheeks came to him and almost jabbed a gun-barrel through his guts.

2. "Doings," actions.

"Hands behind y, nigger."

Tom's wrists were bound. The big man shoved him to the well. Burn him over it, and when the woodwork caved in, his body would drop to the bottom. Two deaths for a godam nigger. Louisa was driven back. The mob pushed in. Its pressure, its momentum was too great. Drag him to the factory. Wood and stakes already there. Tom moved in the direction indicated. But they had to drag him. They reached the great door. Too many to get in there. The mob divided and flowed around the walls to either side. The big man shoved him through the door. The mob pressed in from the sides. Taut humming. No words. A stake was sunk into the ground. Rotting floor boards piled around it. Kerosene poured on the rotting floor boards. Tom bound to the stake. His breast was bare. Nails' scratches let little lines of blood trickle down and mat into the hair. His face, his eyes were set and stony. Except for irregular breathing, one would have thought him already dead. Torches were flung onto the pile. A great flare muffled in black smoke shot upward. The mob yelled. The mob was silent. Now Tom could be seen within the flames. Only his head, erect, lean, like a blackened stone. Stench of burning flesh soaked the air. Tom's eyes popped. His head settled downward. The mob yelled. Its yell echoed against the skeleton stone walls and sounded like a hundred yells. Like a hundred mobs yelling. Its yell thudded against the thick front wall and fell back. Ghost of a yell slipped through the flames and out the great door of the factory. It fluttered like a dying thing down the single street of factory town. Louisa, upon the step before her home, did not hear it, but her eyes opened slowly. They saw the full moon glowing in the great door. The full moon, an evil thing, an omen, soft showering the homes of folks she knew. Where were they, these people? She'd sing, and perhaps they'd come out and join her. Perhaps Tom Burwell would come. At any rate, the full moon in the great door was an omen which she must sing to:

> *Red nigger moon. Sinner!*
> *Blood-burning moon. Sinner!*
> *Come out that fact'ry door.*

Cannibalism in the Cars
(1867)

MARK TWAIN

I visited St. Louis lately, and on my way West, after changing cars at Terre Haute, Indiana, a mild, benevolent-looking gentleman of about forty-five, or maybe fifty, came in at one of the way-stations and sat down beside me. We talked together pleasantly on various subjects for an hour, perhaps, and I found him exceedingly intelligent and entertaining. When he learned that I was from Washington, he immediately began to ask questions about various public men, and about Congressional affairs; and I saw very shortly that I was conversing with a man who was perfectly familiar with the ins and outs of political life at the Capital, even to the ways and manners, and customs of procedure of Senators and Representatives in the Chambers of the national Legislature. Presently two men halted near us for a single moment, and one said to the other:

"Harris, if you'll do that for me, I'll never forget you, my boy."

My new comrade's eye lighted pleasantly. The words had touched upon a happy memory, I thought. Then his face settled into thoughtfulness —almost into gloom. He turned to me and said,

"Let me tell you a story; let me give you a secret chapter of my life —a chapter that has never been referred to by me since its events transpired. Listen patiently, and promise that you will not interrupt me."

I said I would not, and he related the following strange adventure, speaking sometimes with animation, sometimes with melancholy, but always with feeling and earnestness.

The Stranger's Narrative

"On the 19th of December, 1853, I started from St. Louis on the evening train bound for Chicago. There were only twenty-four passengers, all told. There were no ladies and no children. We were in excellent spirits, and pleasant acquaintanceships were soon formed. The journey bade fair to be a happy one; and no individual in the party, I think, had even the vaguest presentiment of the horrors we were soon to undergo.

"At 11 P.M. it began to snow hard. Shortly after leaving the small village of Welden, we entered upon that tremendous prairie solitude that stretches its leagues on leagues of houseless dreariness far away toward the jubilee Settlements. The winds, unobstructed by trees or hills, or even vagrant rocks, whistled fiercely across the level desert, driving the falling snow before it like spray from the crested waves of a stormy sea. The snow was deepening fast; and we knew, by the diminished speed of the train, that the engine was plowing through it with steadily increasing difficulty. Indeed, it almost came to a dead halt sometimes, in the midst of great drifts that piled themselves like colossal graves across the track. Conversation began to flag. Cheerfulness gave place to grave concern. The possibility of being imprisoned in the snow, on the bleak prairie, fifty miles from any house, presented itself to every mind, and extended its depressing influence over every spirit.

"At two o'clock in the morning I was aroused out of an uneasy slumber by the ceasing of all motion about me. The appalling truth flashed upon me instantly—we were captives in a snow-drift! 'All hands to the rescue!' Every man sprang to obey. Out into the wild night, the pitchy darkness, the billowy snow, the driving storm, every soul leaped, with the consciousness that a moment lost now might bring destruction to us all. Shovels, hands, boards—anything, everything that could displace snow, was brought into instant requisition. It was a weird picture, that small company of frantic men fighting the banking snows, half in the blackest shadow and half in the angry light of the locomotive's reflector.

"One short hour sufficed to prove the utter uselessness of our efforts. The storm barricaded the track with a dozen drifts while we dug one away. And worse than this, it was discovered that the last grand charge the engine had made upon the enemy had broken the fore-and-aft shaft of the driving-wheel! With a free track before us we should still have been helpless. We entered the car wearied with labor, and very sorrowful. We gathered about the stoves, and gravely canvassed our situation. We had no provisions whatever—in this lay our chief distress. We could not freeze, for there was a good supply of wood in the tender. This was our only comfort. The discussion ended at last in accepting the disheartening decision of the conductor, viz., that it would be death for any man to attempt to travel fifty miles on foot through snow like that. We could not send for help, and even if we could it would not come. We must submit, and await, as patiently as we might, succor or starvation! I think the stoutest heart there felt a momentary chill when those words were uttered.

"Within the hour conversation subsided to a low murmur here and there about the car, caught fitfully between the rising and falling of the blast; the lamps grew dim; and the majority of the castaways settled themselves among the flickering shadows to think—to forget the present, if they could—to sleep, if they might.

"The eternal night—it surely seemed eternal to us—wore its lagging hours away at last, and the cold gray dawn broke in the east. As the light grew stronger the passengers began to stir and give signs of life, one after another, and each in turn pushed his slouched hat up from his forehead, stretched his stiffened limbs, and glanced out of the windows upon the cheerless prospect. It was cheer less, indeed!—not a living thing visible anywhere, not a human habitation; nothing but a vast white desert; uplifted sheets of snow drifting hither and thither before the wind—a world of eddying flakes shutting out the firmament above.

"All day we moped about the cars, saying little, thinking much. Another lingering dreary night—and hunger.

"Another dawning—another day of silence, sadness, wasting hunger, hopeless watching for succor that could not come. A night of restless slumber, filled with dreams of feasting—wakings distressed with the gnawings of hunger.

"The fourth day came and went—and the fifth! Five days of dreadful imprisonment! A savage hunger looked out at every eye. There was in it a sign of awful import—the foreshadowing of a something that was vaguely shaping itself in every heart—a something which no tongue dared yet to frame into words.

"The sixth day passed—the seventh dawned upon as gaunt and haggard and hopeless a company of men as ever stood in the shadow of death. It must out now! That thing which had been growing up in every heart was ready to leap from every lip at last! Nature had been taxed to the utmost—she must yield. RICHARD H. GASTON of Minnesota, tall, cadaverous, and pale, rose up. All knew what was coming. All prepared—every emotion, every semblance of excitement—was smothered—only a calm, thoughtful seriousness appeared in the eyes that were lately so wild.

"'Gentlemen: It cannot be delayed longer! The time is at hand! We must determine which of us shall die to furnish food for the rest!'

"MR. JOHN J. WILLIAMS of Illinois rose and said: 'Gentlemen—I nominate the Rev. James Sawyer of Tennessee.'

"MR. Wm. R. ADAMS of Indiana said: 'I nominate Mr. Daniel Slote of New York.'

"MR. CHARLES J. LANGDON: 'I nominate Mr. Samuel A. Bowen of St. Louis.'

"MR. SLOTE: 'Gentlemen—I desire to decline in favor of Mr. John A. Van Nostrand, Jun., of New Jersey.'

"MR. GASTON: 'If there be no objection, the gentleman's desire will be acceded to.'

"MR. VAN NOSTRAND objecting, the resignation of Mr. Slote was rejected. The resignations of Messrs. Sawyer and Bowen were also offered, and refused upon the same grounds.

"MR. A. L. BASCOM of Ohio: 'I move that the nominations now close, and that the House proceed to an election by ballot.'

"MR. SAWYER: 'Gentlemen—I protest earnestly against these proceedings. They are, in every way, irregular and unbecoming. I must beg to move that they be dropped at once, and that we elect a chairman of the meeting and proper officers to assist him, and then we can go on with the business before us understandingly.'

"MR. BELL of Iowa: 'Gentlemen—I object. This is no time to stand upon forms and ceremonious observances. For more than seven days we have been without food. Every moment we lose in idle discussion increases our distress. I am satisfied with the nominations that have been made—every gentleman present is, I believe—and I, for one, do not see why we should not proceed at once to elect one or more of them. I wish to offer a resolution—'

"MR. GASTON: 'It would be objected to, and have to lie over one day under the rules, thus bringing about the very delay you wish to avoid. The gentleman from New Jersey—'

"MR. VAN NOSTRAND: 'Gentlemen—I am a stranger among you; I have not sought the distinction that has been conferred upon me, and I feel a delicacy—'

"MR. MORGAN Of Alabama (interrupting): 'I move the previous question.'

"The motion was carried, and further debate shut off, of course. The motion to elect officers was passed, and under it Mr. Gaston was chosen chairman, Mr. Blake, secretary, Messrs. Holcomb, Dyer, and Baldwin a committee on nominations, and Mr. R. M. Howland, purveyor, to assist the committee in making selections.

"A recess of half an hour was then taken, and some little caucusing followed. At the sound of the gavel the meeting reassembled, and the committee reported in favor of Messrs. George Ferguson of Kentucky, Lucien Herrman of Louisiana, and W. Messick of Colorado as candidates. The report was accepted.

"MR. ROGERS of Missouri: 'Mr. President. The report being properly before the House now, I move to amend it by substituting for the name of Mr. Herrman that of Mr. Lucius Harris of St. Louis, who is well and honorably known to us all. I do not wish to be understood as casting the least reflection upon the high character and standing of the gentleman from Louisiana far from it. I respect and esteem him as much as any gentleman here present possibly can; but none of us can be blind to the fact that he has lost more flesh during the week that we have lain here than any among us—none of us can be blind to the fact that the committee has been derelict in its duty, either through negligence or a graver fault, in thus offering for our suffrages a gentleman who, however pure his own motives may be, has really less nutriment in him—'

"THE CHAIR: 'The gentleman from Missouri will take his seat. The Chair cannot allow the integrity of the committee to be questioned save by the regular course, under the rules. What action will the House take upon the gentleman's motion?'

"MR. HALLIDAY of Virginia: 'I move to further amend the report by substituting Mr. Harvey Davis of Oregon for Mr. Messick. It may be urged by gentlemen that the hardships and privations of a frontier life have rendered Mr. Davis tough; but, gentlemen, is this a time to cavil at toughness? Is this a time to be fastidious concerning trifles? Is this a time to dispute about matters of paltry significance? No, gentlemen, bulk is what we desire—substance, weight, bulk—these are the supreme requisites now—not talent, not genius, not education. I insist upon my motion.'

"MR. MORGAN (excitedly): 'Mr. Chairman—I do most strenuously object to this amendment. The gentleman from Oregon is old, and furthermore is bulky only in bone—not in flesh. I ask the gentleman from Virginia if it is soup we want instead of solid sustenance? if he would delude us with shadows? if he would mock our suffering with an Oregonian specter? I ask him if he can look upon the anxious faces around him, if he can gaze into our sad eyes, if he can listen to the beating of our expectant hearts, and still thrust this famine-stricken fraud upon us? I ask him if he can think of our desolate state, of our past sorrows, of our dark future, and still unpityingly foist upon us this wreck, this ruin, this tottering swindle, this gnarled and blighted and sapless vagabond from Oregon's hospitable shores? Never!' [Applause.]

"The amendment was put to vote, after a fiery debate, and lost. Mr. Harris was substituted on the first amendment. The balloting then began. Five ballots were held without a choice. On the sixth, Mr. Harris was elected, all voting for him but himself. It was then moved that his election should be ratified by acclamation, which was lost, in consequence of his again voting against himself.

"MR. RADWAY moved that the House now take up the remaining candidates, and go into an election for breakfast. This was carried.

"On the first ballot—there was a tie, half the members favoring one candidate on account of his youth, and half favoring the other on account of his superior size. The President gave the casting vote for the latter, Mr. Messick. This decision created considerable dissatisfaction among the friends of Mr. Ferguson, the defeated candidate, and there was some talk of demanding a new ballot; but in the midst of it a motion to adjourn was carried, and the meeting broke up at once.

"The preparations for supper diverted the attention of the Ferguson faction from the discussion of their grievance for a long time, and then, when they would have taken it up again, the happy announcement that Mr. Harris was ready drove all thought of it to the winds.

"We improvised tables by propping up the backs of car-seats, and sat down with hearts full of gratitude to the finest supper that had blessed our vision for seven torturing days. How changed we were from what we had been a few short hours before! Hopeless, sad-eyed misery, hunger, feverish anxiety, desperation, then; thankfulness, serenity, joy too deep for utterance now. That I know was the cheeriest hour of my eventful life. The winds howled, and blew the snow wildly about our prison house, but they were powerless to distress us any more. I liked Harris. He might have been better done, perhaps, but I am free to say that no man ever agreed with me better than Harris, or afforded me so large a degree of satisfaction. Messick was very well, though rather high-flavored, but for genuine nutritiousness and delicacy of fiber, give me Harris. Messick had his good points—I will not attempt to deny it, nor do I wish to do it but he was no more fitted for breakfast than a mummy would be, sir—not a bit. Lean?—why, bless me!—and tough? Ah, he was very tough! You could not imagine it—you could never imagine anything like it."

"Do you mean to tell me that—"

"Do not interrupt me, please. After breakfast we elected a man by the name of Walker, from Detroit, for supper. He was very good. I wrote his wife so afterward. He was worthy of all praise. I shall always remember Walker. He was a little rare, but very good. And then the next morning we had Morgan of Alabama for breakfast. He was one of the finest men I ever sat down to handsome, educated, refined, spoke several languages fluently a perfect gentleman he was a perfect gentleman, and singularly juicy. For supper we had that Oregon patriarch, and he was a fraud, there is no question about it—old, scraggy, tough, nobody can picture the reality. I finally said, gentlemen, you can do as you like, but I will wait for another election. And Grimes of Illinois said, 'Gentlemen, I will wait also. When you elect a man that has something to recommend him, I shall be glad to join you again.' It soon became evident that there was general dissatisfaction with Davis of Oregon, and so, to preserve the good will that had prevailed so pleasantly since we had had Harris, an election was called, and the result of it was that Baker of Georgia was chosen. He was splendid! Well, well—after that we had Doolittle, and Hawkins, and McElroy (there was some complaint about McElroy, because he was uncommonly short and thin), and Penrod, and two Smiths, and Bailey (Bailey had a wooden leg, which was clear loss, but he was otherwise good), and an Indian boy, and an organ-grinder, and a gentleman by the name of Buckminster—a poor stick of a vagabond that wasn't any good for company and no account for breakfast. We were glad we got him elected before relief came."

"And so the blessed relief did come at last?"

"Yes, it came one bright, sunny morning, just after election. John Murphy was the choice, and there never was a better, I am willing to testify; but John Murphy came home with us, in the train that came to succor us, and lived to marry the widow Harris—"

"Relict of—"

"Relict of our first choice. He married her, and is happy and respected and prosperous yet. Ah, it was like a novel, sir—it was like a romance. This is my stopping-place, sir; I must bid you goodby. Any time that you can make it convenient to tarry a day or two with me, I shall be glad to have you. I like you, sir; I have conceived an affection for you. I could like you as well as I liked Harris himself, sir. Good day, sir, and a pleasant journey."

He was gone. I never felt so stunned, so distressed, so bewildered in my life. But in my soul I was glad he was gone. With all his gentleness of manner and his soft voice, I shuddered whenever he turned his hungry eye upon me; and when I heard that I had achieved his perilous affection, and that I stood almost with the late Harris in his esteem, my heart fairly stood still!

I was bewildered beyond description. I did not doubt his word; I could not question a single item in a statement so stamped with the earnestness of truth as his; but its dreadful details overpowered me, and threw my thoughts into hopeless confusion. I saw the conductor looking at me. I said, "Who is that man?"

"He was a member of Congress once, and a good one. But he got caught in a snow-drift in the cars, and like to have been starved to death. He got so frost-bitten and frozen up generally, and used up for want of something to eat, that he was sick and out of his head two or three months afterward. He is all right now, only he is a monomaniac, and when he gets on that old subject he never stops till he has eat up that whole car-load of people he talks about. He would have finished the crowd by this time, only he had to get out here. He has got their names as pat as A B C. When he gets them all eat up but himself, he always says: 'Then the hour for the usual election for breakfast having arrived; and there being no opposition, I was duly elected, after which, there being no objections offered, I resigned. Thus I am here.'"

I felt inexpressibly relieved to know that I had only been listening to the harmless vagaries of a madman instead of the genuine experiences of a bloodthirsty cannibal.

Welcome to the Monkey House
(1968)

KURT VONNEGUT

So Pete Crocker, the sheriff of Barnstable County, which was the whole of Cape Cod, came into the Federal Ethical Suicide Parlor in Hyannis one May afternoon—and he told the two six-foot Hostesses there that they weren't to be alarmed, but that a notorious nothinghead named Billy the Poet was believed headed for the Cape.

A nothinghead was a person who refused to take his ethical birth-control pills three times a day. The penalty for that was $10,000 and ten years in jail.

This was at a time when the population of Earth was 17 billion human beings. That was far too many mammals that big for a planet that small. The people were virtually packed together like drupelets.

Drupelets are the pulpy little knobs that compose the outside of a raspberry.

So the World Government was making a two-pronged attack on overpopulation. One pronging was the encouragement of ethical suicide, which consisted of going to the nearest Suicide Parlor and asking a Hostess to kill you painlessly while you lay on a Barcalounger. The other pronging was compulsory ethical birth control.

The sheriff told the Hostesses, who were pretty, tough-minded, highly intelligent girls, that roadblocks were being set up and house-to-house searches were being conducted to catch Billy the Poet. The main difficulty was that the police didn't know what he looked like. The few people who had seen him and known him for what he was were women—and they disagreed fantastically as to his height, his hair color, his voice, his weight, the color of his skin.

"I don't need to remind you girls," the sheriff went on, "that a nothinghead is very sensitive from the waist down. If Billy the Poet somehow slips in here and starts making trouble, one good kick in the right place will do wonders."

He was referring to the fact that ethical birth-control pills, the only legal form of birth control, made people numb from the waist down.

Most men said their bottom halves felt like cold iron or balsawood. Most women said their bottom halves felt like wet cotton or stale ginger ale. The pills were so effective that you could blindfold a man who had taken one, tell him to recite the Gettysburg Address, kick him in the balls while he was doing it, and he wouldn't miss a syllable.

The pills were ethical because they didn't interfere with a person's ability to reproduce, which would have been unnatural and immoral. All the pills did was take every bit of pleasure out of sex.

893

Thus did science and morals go hand in hand.

The two Hostesses there in Hyannis were Nancy McLuhan and Mary Kraft. Nancy was a strawberry blonde. Mary was a glossy brunette. Their uniforms were white lipstick, heavy eye makeup, purple body stockings with nothing underneath, and black-leather boots. They ran a small operation—with only six suicide booths. In a really good week, say the one before Christmas, they might put sixty people to sleep. It was done with a hypodermic syringe.

"My main message to you girls," said Sheriff Crocker, "is that everything's well under control. You can just go about your business here."

"Didn't you leave out part of your main message?" Nancy asked him.

"I don't get you."

"I didn't hear you say he was probably headed straight for us."

He shrugged in clumsy innocence. "We don't know that for sure."

"I thought that was all anybody *did* know about Billy the Poet: that he specializes in deflowering Hostesses in Ethical Suicide Parlors." Nancy was a virgin. All Hostesses were virgins. They also had to hold advanced degrees in psychology and nursing. They also had to be plump and rosy, and at least six feet tall.

America had changed in many ways, but it had yet to adopt the metric system.

Nancy McLuhan was burned up that the sheriff would try to protect her and Mary from the full truth about Billy the Poet—as though they might panic if they heard it. She told the sheriff so.

"How long do you think a girl would last in the E. S. S.," she said, meaning the Ethical Suicide Service, "if she scared that easy?"

The sheriff took a step backward, pulled in his chin. "Not very long, I guess."

"That's very true," said Nancy, closing the distance between them and offering him a sniff of the edge of her hand, which was poised for a karate chop. All Hostesses were experts at judo and karate. "If you'd like to find out how helpless we are, just come toward me, pretending you're Billy the Poet."

The sheriff shook his head, gave her a glassy smile. "I'd rather not."

"That's the smartest thing you've said today," said Nancy, turning her back on him while Mary laughed. "We're not scared—we're *angry*, Or we're not even *that*. He isn't *worth* that. We're *bored*. How boring that he should come a great distance, should cause all this fuss, in order to—" She let the sentence die there. "It's just too absurd."

"I'm not as mad at *him* as I am at the women who let him do it to them without a struggle"—said Mary—"who let him do it and then couldn't tell the police what he looked like. Suicide Hostesses at that!"

"Somebody hasn't been keeping up with her karate," said Nancy.

It wasn't just Billy the Poet who was attracted to Hostesses in Ethical Suicide Parlors. All nothingheads were. Bombed out of their skulls with the sex madness that came from taking nothing, they thought the white lips and big eyes and body stocking and boots of a Hostess spelled *sex, sex, sex*.

The truth was, of course, that sex was the last thing any Hostess ever had in mind.

"If Billy follows his usual M. O.," said the sheriff, "he'll study your habits and the neighborhood. And then he'll pick one or the other of you and he'll send her a dirty poem in the mail."

"Charming," said Nancy.

"He has also been known to use the telephone."

"How brave," said Nancy. Over the sheriff's shoulder, she could see the mailman coming.

A blue light went on over the door of a booth for which Nancy was responsible. The person in there wanted something. It was the only booth in use at the time.

The sheriff asked her if there was a possibility that the person in there was Billy the Poet, and Nancy said, "Well, if it is, I can break his neck with my thumb and forefinger."

"Foxy Grandpa," said Mary, who'd seen him, too. A Foxy Grandpa was any old man, cute and senile, who quibbled and joked and reminisced for hours before he let a Hostess put him to sleep.

Nancy groaned. "We've spent the past two hours trying to decide on a last meal."

And then the mailman came in with just one letter. It was addressed to Nancy in smeary pencil. She was splendid with anger and disgust as she opened it, knowing it would be a piece of filth from Billy.

She was right. Inside the envelope was a poem. It wasn't an original poem. It was a song from olden days that had taken on new meanings since the numbness of ethical birth control had become universal. It went like this, in smeary pencil again:

> *We were walking through the park,*
> A-goosing statues in the dark.
> If Sherman's horse can take it,
> So can you.

When Nancy came into the suicide booth to see what he wanted, the Foxy Grandpa was lying on the mint-green Barcalounger, where hundreds had died so peacefully over the years. He was studying the menu from the Howard Johnson's next door and beating time to the Muzak coming from the loudspeaker on the lemon-yellow wall. The room was painted cinder block. There was one barred window with a Venetian blind.

There was a Howard Johnson's next door to every Ethical Suicide Parlor, and vice versa. The Howard Johnson's had an orange roof and the Suicide Parlor had a purple roof, but they were both the Government. Practically everything was the Government.

Practically everything was automated, too. Nancy and Mary and the sheriff were lucky to have jobs. Most people didn't. The average citizen moped around home and watched television, which was the Government. Every fifteen minutes his television would urge him to vote intelligently or consume intelligently, or worship in the church of his choice, or love his fellowmen, or obey the laws—or pay a call to the nearest Ethical Suicide Parlor and find out how friendly and understanding a Hostess could be.

The Foxy Grandpa was something of a rarity, since he was marked by old age, was bald, was shaky, had spots on his hands. Most people looked twenty-two, thanks to anti-aging shots they took twice a year. That the old man looked old was proof that the shots had been discovered after his sweet bird of youth had flown.

"Have we decided on a last supper yet?" Nancy asked him. She heard peevishness in her own voice, heard herself betray her exasperation with Billy the Poet, her boredom with the old man. She was ashamed, for this was unprofessional of her. "The breaded veal cutlet is very good."

The old man cocked his head. With the greedy cunning of second childhood, he had caught her being unprofessional, unkind, and he was going to punish her for it. "You don't sound very friendly. I thought you were all supposed to be friendly. I thought this was supposed to be a pleasant place to come."

"I beg your pardon," she said. "If I seem unfriendly, it has nothing to do with you."

"I thought maybe I bored you."

"No, no," she said gamely, "not at all. You certainly know some very interesting history." Among other things, the Foxy Grandpa claimed to have known J. Edgar Nation, the Grand Rapids druggist who was the father of ethical birth control.

"Then *look* like you're interested," he told her. He could get away with that sort of impudence. The thing was, he could leave any time he wanted to, right up to the moment he asked for the needle—and he had to *ask* for the needle. That was the law.

Nancy's art, and the art of every Hostess, was to see that volunteers didn't leave, to coax and wheedle and flatter them patiently, every step of the way.

So Nancy had to sit down there in the booth, to pretend to marvel at the freshness of the yarn the old man told, a story everybody knew, about how J. Edgar Nation happened to experiment with ethical birth control.

"He didn't have the slightest idea his pills would be taken by human beings someday," said the Foxy Grandpa. "His dream was to introduce morality into the monkey house at the Grand Rapids Zoo. Did you realize that?" he inquired severely.

"No. No, I didn't. That's very interesting."

"He and his eleven kids went to church one Easter. And the day was so nice and the Easter service had been so beautiful and pure that they decided to take a walk through the zoo, and they were just walking on clouds."

"Um." The scene described was lifted from a play that was performed on television every Easter.

The Foxy Grandpa shoehorned himself into the scene, had himself chat with the Nations just before they got to the monkey house. " 'Good morning, Mr. Nation,' I said to him. 'It certainly is a nice morning.' 'And a good morning to *you*, Mr. Howard,' he said to me. 'There is nothing like an Easter morning to make a man feel clean and reborn and at one with God's intentions.' "

"Um." Nancy could hear the telephone ringing faintly, naggingly, through the nearly soundproof door.

"So we went on to the monkey house together, and what do you think we saw?"

"I can't imagine." Somebody had answered the phone.

"We saw a monkey playing with his private parts!"

"No!"

"Yes! And J. Edgar Nation was so upset he went straight home and he started developing a pill that would make monkeys in the springtime fit things for a Christian family to see."

There was a knock on the door.

"Yes—?" said Nancy.

"Nancy," said Mary, "telephone for you."

When Nancy came out of the booth, she found the sheriff choking on little squeals of law-enforcement delight. The telephone was tapped by agents hidden in the Howard Johnson's. Billy the Poet was believed to be on the line. His call had been traced. Police were already on their way to grab him.

"Keep him on, keep him on," the sheriff whispered to Nancy, and he gave her the telephone as though it were solid gold.

"Yes—?" said Nancy.

"Nancy McLuhan?" said a man. His voice was disguised. He might have been speaking through a kazoo. "I'm calling for a mutual friend."

"Oh?"

"He asked me to deliver a message."

"I see."

"It's a poem."

"All right."

"Ready?"

"Ready." Nancy could hear sirens screaming in the background of the call.

The caller must have heard the sirens, too, but he recited the poem without any emotion. It went like this:

> *"Soak yourself in Jergen's Lotion.*
> *Here comes the one-man population*
> *explosion."*

They got him. Nancy heard it all—the thumping and clumping, the argle-bargle and cries.

The depression she felt as she hung up was glandular. Her brave body had prepared for a fight that was not to be.

The sheriff bounded out of the Suicide Parlor, in such a hurry to see the famous criminal he'd helped catch that a sheaf of papers fell from the pocket of his trench coat.

Mary picked them up, called after the sheriff. He halted for a moment, said the papers didn't matter any more, asked her if maybe she wouldn't like to come along. There was a flurry between the two girls, with Nancy persuading Mary to go, declaring that she had no curiosity about Billy. So Mary left, irrelevantly handing the sheaf to Nancy.

The sheaf proved to be photocopies of poems Billy had sent to Hostesses in other places. Nancy read the top one. It made much of a peculiar side effect of ethical birth-control pills: They not only made people numb—they also made people piss blue. The poem was called *What the Somethinghead Said to the Suicide Hostess*, and it went like this:

> *I did not sow, I did not spin,*
> *And thanks to pills I did not sin.*
> *I loved the crowds, the stink, the noise.*
> *And when I peed, I peed turquoise.*
>
> *I ate beneath a roof of orange;*
> *Swung with progress like a door hinge.*
> *'Neath purple roof I've come today*
> *To piss my azure life away.*
>
> *Virgin hostess, death's recruiter,*
> *Life is cute, but you are cuter.*
> *Mourn my pecker, purple daughter—*
> *All it passed was sky-blue water.*

"You never heard that story before—about how J. Edgar Nation came to invent ethical birth control?" the Foxy Grandpa wanted to know. His voice cracked.

"Never did," lied Nancy.

"I thought everybody knew that."

"It was news to me."

"When he got through with the monkey house, you couldn't tell it from the Michigan Supreme Court. Meanwhile, there was this crisis going on in the United Nations. The people who understood science said people had to quit reproducing so much, and the people who understood morals said society would collapse if people used sex for nothing but pleasure."

The Foxy Grandpa got off his Barcalounger, went over to the window, pried two slats of the blind apart. There wasn't much to see out there. The view was blocked by the backside of a mocked-up thermometer twenty feet high, which faced the street. It was calibrated in billions of people on Earth, from zero to twenty. The make-believe column of liquid was a strip of translucent red plastic. It showed how many people there were on Earth. Very close to the bottom was a black arrow that showed what the scientists thought the population ought to be.

The Foxy Grandpa was looking at the setting sun through that red plastic, and through the blind, too, so that his face was banded with shadows and red.

"Tell me—" he said, "when I die, how much will that thermometer go down? A foot?"

"No."

"An inch?"

"Not quite."

"You know what the answer is, don't you?" he said, and he faced her. The senility had vanished from his voice and eyes. "One inch on that thing equals 83,333 people. You knew that, didn't you?"

"That—that might be true," said Nancy, "but that isn't the right way to look at it, in my opinion."

He didn't ask her what the right way was, in her opinion. He completed a thought of his own, instead. "I'll tell you something else that's true: I'm Billy the Poet, and you're a very good-looking woman."

With one hand, he drew a snub-nosed revolver from his belt. With the other, he peeled off his bald dome and wrinkled forehead, which proved to be rubber. Now he looked twenty-two.

"The police will want to know exactly what I look like when this is all over," he told Nancy with a malicious grin. "In case you're not good at describing people, and it's surprising how many women aren't:

> I'm five foot two,
> With eyes of blue,
> With Brown hair to my shoulders—
> A manly elf
> So full of self
> The ladies say he smolders."

Billy was ten inches shorter than Nancy was. She had about forty pounds on him. She told him he didn't have a chance, but Nancy was much mistaken. He had unbolted the bars on the window the night before and he made her go out the window and then down a manhole that was hidden from the street by the big thermometer.

He took her down into the sewers of Hyannis. He knew where he was going. He had a flashlight and a map. Nancy had to go before him along the narrow catwalk, her own shadow dancing mockingly in the lead. She tried to guess where they were, relative to the real world above. She guessed correctly when they passed under the Howard Johnson's, guessed from noises she heard. The machinery that processed and served the food there was silent. But, so people wouldn't feel too lonesome when eating there, the designers had provided sound effects for the kitchen. It was these Nancy heard—a tape recording of the clashing of silverware and the laughter of Negroes and Puerto Ricans.

After that she was lost. Billy had very little to say to her other than "Right," or, "Left," or "Don't try anything funny, Juno, or I'll blow your great big fucking head off."

Only once did they have anything resembling a conversation. Billy began it, and ended it, too. "What in hell is a girl with hips like yours doing selling death?" he asked her from behind.

She dared to stop. "I can answer that," she told him. She was confident that she could give him an answer that would shrivel him like napalm.

But he gave her a shove, offered to blow her fucking head off again.

"You don't even want to hear my answer," she taunted him. "You're afraid to hear it."

"I never listen to a woman till the pills wear off," sneered Billy. That was his plan, then—to keep her a prisoner for at least eight hours. That was how long it took for the pills to wear off.

"That's a silly rule."

"A woman's not a woman till the pills wear off."

"You certainly manage to make a woman feel like an object rather than a person."

"Thank the pills for that," said Billy.

There were 80 miles of sewers under Greater Hyannis, which had a population of 400,000 drupelets, 400,000 souls. Nancy lost track of the time down there. When Billy announced that they had at last reached their destination, it was possible for Nancy to imagine that a year had passed.

She tested this spooky impression by pinching her own thigh, by feeling what the chemical clock of her body said. Her thigh was still numb.

Billy ordered her to climb iron rungs that were set in wet masonry. There was a circle of sickly light above. It proved to be moonlight filtered through the plastic polygons of an enormous geodesic dome. Nancy didn't have to ask the traditional victim's question, "Where am I?" There was only one dome like that on Cape Cod. It was in Hyannis Port and it sheltered the ancient Kennedy Compound.

It was a museum of how life had been lived in more expansive times. The museum was closed. It was open only in the summertime.

The manhole from which Nancy and then Billy emerged was set in an expanse of green cement, which showed where the Kennedy lawn had been. On the green cement, in front of the ancient frame houses, were statues representing the fourteen Kennedys who had been Presidents of the United States or the World. They were playing touch football.

The President of the World at the time of Nancy's abduction, incidentally, was an ex-Suicide Hostess named "Ma" Kennedy. Her statue would never join this particular touch-football game. Her name was Kennedy, all right, but she wasn't the real thing. People complained of her lack of style, found her vulgar. On the wall of her office was a sign that said, YOU DON'T HAVE TO BE CRAZY TO WORK HERE, BUT IT SURE HELPS, and another one that said THIMK!, and another one that said, SOMEDAY WE'RE GOING TO HAVE TO GET ORGANIZED AROUND HERE.

Her office was in the Taj Mahal.

Until she arrived in the Kennedy Museum, Nancy McLuhan was confident that she would sooner or later get a chance to break every bone in Billy's little body, maybe even shoot him with his own gun. She wouldn't have minded doing those things. She thought he was more disgusting than a blood-filled tick.

It wasn't compassion that changed her mind. It was the discovery that Billy had a gang. There were at least eight people around the manhole, men and women in equal numbers, with stockings pulled over their heads. It was the women who laid firm hands on Nancy, told her to keep calm. They were all at least as tall as Nancy and they held her in places where they could hurt her like hell if they had to.

Nancy closed her eyes, but this didn't protect her from the obvious conclusion: These perverted women were sisters from the Ethical Suicide Service. This upset her so much that she asked loudly and bitterly, "How can you violate your oaths like this?"

She was promptly hurt so badly that she doubled up and burst into tears.

When she straightened up again, there was plenty more she wanted to say, but she kept her mouth shut. She speculated silently as to what on Earth could make Suicide Hostesses turn against every concept of human decency. Nothingheadedness alone couldn't begin to explain it. They had to be drugged besides.

Nancy went over in her mind all the terrible drugs she'd learned about in school, persuaded herself that the women had taken the worst one of all. That drug was so powerful, Nancy's teachers had told her, that even a person numb from the waist down would copulate repeatedly and enthusiastically after just one glass. That had to be the answer: The women, and probably the men, too, had been drinking gin.

They hastened Nancy into the middle frame house, which was dark like all the rest, and Nancy heard the men giving Billy the news. It was in this news that Nancy perceived a glint of hope. Help might be on its way.

The gang member who had phoned Nancy obscenely had fooled the police into believing that they had captured Billy the Poet, which was bad for Nancy. The police didn't know yet that Nancy was missing, two men told Billy, and a telegram had been sent to Mary Kraft in Nancy's name, declaring that Nancy had been called to New York City on urgent family business.

That was where Nancy saw the glint of hope: Mary wouldn't believe that telegram. Mary knew Nancy had no family in New York. Not one of the 63,000,000 people living there was a relative of Nancy's.

The gang had deactivated the burglar-alarm system of the museum. They had also cut through a lot of the chains and ropes that were meant to keep visitors from touching anything of value. There was no mystery as to who and what had done the cutting. One of the men was armed with brutal lopping shears.

They marched Nancy into a servant's bedroom upstairs. The man with the shears cut the ropes that fenced off the narrow bed. They put Nancy into the bed and two men held Nancy while a woman gave her a knockout shot.

Billy the Poet had disappeared.

As Nancy was going under, the woman who had given her the shot asked her how old she was.

Nancy was determined not to answer, but discovered that the drug had made her power-less not to answer. "Sixty-three," she murmured.

"How does it feel to be a virgin at sixty-three?"

Nancy heard her own answer through a velvet fog. She was amazed by the answer, wanted to protest that it couldn't possibly be hers. "Pointless," she'd said.

Moments later, she asked the woman thickly, "What was in that needle?"

"What was in the needle, honey bunch? Why, honey bunch, they call that 'truth serum.'"

The moon was down when Nancy woke up—but the night was still out there. The shades were drawn and there was candlelight. Nancy had never seen a lit candle before.

What awakened Nancy was a dream of mosquitoes and bees. Mosquitoes and bees were extinct. So were birds. But Nancy dreamed that millions of insects were swarming about her from the waist down. They didn't sting. They fanned her. Nancy was a nothinghead.

She went to sleep again. When she awoke next time, she was being led into a bathroom by three women, still with stockings over their heads. The bathroom was already filled with the steam from somebody else's bath. There were somebody else's wet footprints crisscross-ing the floor and the air reeked of pine-needle perfume.

Her will and intelligence returned as she was bathed and perfumed and dressed in a white nightgown. When the women stepped back to admire her, she said to them quietly, "I may be a nothinghead now. But that doesn't mean I have to think like one or act like one."

Nobody argued with her.

Nancy was taken downstairs and out of the house. She fully expected to be sent down a manhole again. It would be the perfect setting for her violation by Billy, she was thinking—down in a sewer.

But they took her across the green cement, where the grass used to be, and then across the yellow cement, where the beach used to be, and then out onto the blue cement, where the harbor used to be. There were twenty-six yachts that had belonged to various Kennedys, sunk up to their water lines in blue cement. It was to the most ancient of these yachts, the Marlin, once the property of Joseph P. Kennedy, that they delivered Nancy.

It was dawn. Because of the high-rise apartments all around the Kennedy Museum, it would be an hour before any direct sunlight would reach the microcosm under the geodesic dome.

Nancy was escorted as far as the companionway to the forward cabin of the Marlin. The women pantomimed that she was expected to go down the five steps alone.

Nancy froze for the moment and so did the women. And there were two actual statues in the tableau on the bridge. Standing at the wheel was a statue of Frank Wirtanen, once skip-per of the Marlin. And next to him was his son and first mate, Carly. They weren't paying any attention to poor Nancy. They were staring out through the windshield at the blue cement.

901

Nancy, barefoot and wearing a thin white nightgown, descended bravely into the forward cabin, which was a pool of candlelight and pine-needle perfume. The companionway hatch was closed and locked behind her.

Nancy's emotions and the antique furnishings of the cabin were so complex that Nancy could not at first separate Billy the Poet from his surroundings, from all the mahogany and leaded glass. And then she saw him at the far end of the cabin, with his back against the door to the forward cockpit. He was wearing purple silk pajamas with a Russian collar. They were piped in red, and writhing across Billy's silken breast was a golden dragon. It was belching fire.

Anticlimactically, Billy was wearing glasses. He was holding a book.

Nancy poised herself on the next-to-the-bottom step, took a firm grip on the handholds in the companionway. She bared her teeth, calculated that it would take ten men Billy's size to dislodge her.

Between them was a great table. Nancy had expected the cabin to be dominated by a bed, possibly in the shape of a swan, but the Marlin was a day boat. The cabin was anything but a seraglio. It was about as voluptuous as a lower-middle-class dining room in Akron, Ohio, around 1910.

A candle was on the table. So were an ice bucket and two glasses and a quart of champagne. Champagne was as illegal as heroin.

Billy took off his glasses, gave her a shy, embarrassed smile, said, "Welcome."

"This is as far as I come."

He accepted that. "You're very beautiful there."

"And what am I supposed to say—that you're stunningly handsome? That I feel an overwhelming desire to throw myself into your manly arms?"

"If you wanted to make me happy, that would certainly be the way to do it." He said that humbly.

"And what about *my* happiness?"

The question seemed to puzzle him. "Nancy—that's what this is all about."

"What if my idea of happiness doesn't coincide with yours?"

"And what do you think my idea of happiness is?"

"I'm not going to throw myself into your arms, and I'm not going to drink that poison, and I'm not going to budge from here unless somebody makes me," said Nancy. "So I think your idea of happiness is going to turn out to be eight people holding me down on that table, while you bravely hold a cocked pistol to my head—and do what you want. That's the way it's going to have to be, so call your friends and get it over with!"

Which he did.

He didn't hurt her. He deflowered her with a clinical skill she found ghastly. When it was all over, he didn't seem cocky or proud. On the contrary, he was terribly depressed, and he said to Nancy, "Believe me, if there'd been any other way—"

Her reply to this was a face like stone—and silent tears of humiliation.

His helpers let down a folding bunk from the wall. It was scarcely wider than a bookshelf and hung on chains. Nancy allowed herself to be put to bed in it, and she was left alone with Billy the Poet again. Big as she was, like a double bass wedged onto that narrow shelf, she felt like a pitiful little thing. A scratchy, war-surplus blanket had been tucked in around her. It was her own idea to pull up a corner of the blanket to hide her face.

Nancy sensed from sounds what Billy was doing, which wasn't much. He was sitting at the table, sighing occasionally, sniffing occasionally, turning the pages of a book. He lit a cigar and the stink of it seeped under her blanket. Billy inhaled the cigar, then coughed and coughed and coughed.

When the coughing died down, Nancy said loathingly through the blanket, "You're so strong, so masterful, so healthy. It must be wonderful to be so manly."

Billy only sighed at this.

"I'm not a very typical nothinghead," she said. "I hated it—hated everything about it."

Billy sniffed, turned a page.

"I suppose all the other women just loved it—couldn't get enough of it."

"Nope."

She uncovered her face. "What do you mean, 'Nope'?"

"They've all been like you."

This was enough to make Nancy sit up and stare at him. "The women who helped you tonight—"

"What about them?"

"You've done to them what you did to me?"

He didn't look up from his book. "That's right."

"Then why don't they kill you instead of helping you?"

"Because they understand." And then he added mildly, "They're *grateful.*"

Nancy got out of bed, came to the table, gripped the edge of the table, leaned close to him. And she said to him tautly, "I am not grateful."

"You will be."

"And what could possibly bring about that miracle?"

"Time," said Billy.

Billy closed his book, stood up. Nancy was confused by his magnetism. Somehow he was very much in charge again.

"What you've been through, Nancy," he said, "is a typical wedding night for a strait-laced girl of a hundred years ago, when everybody was a nothinghead. The groom did without helpers, because the bride wasn't customarily ready to kill him. Otherwise, the spirit of the occasion was much the same. These are the pajamas my great-great-grandfather wore on his wedding night in Niagara Falls.

"According to his diary, his bride cried all that night, and threw up twice. But, with the passage of time, she became a sexual enthusiast."

It was Nancy's turn to reply by not replying. She understood the tale. It frightened her to understand so easily that, from gruesome beginnings, sexual enthusiasm could grow and grow.

"You're a very typical nothinghead," said Billy. "If you dare to think about it now, you'll realize that you're angry because I'm such a bad lover, and a funny-looking shrimp besides. And what you can't help dreaming about from now on is a really suitable mate for a Juno like yourself.

"You'll find him, too—tall and strong and gentle. The nothinghead movement is growing by leaps and bounds."

"But—" said Nancy, and she stopped there. She looked out a porthole at the rising sun.

"But what?"

"The world is in the mess it is today because of the nothingheadedness of olden times. Don't you see?" She was pleading weakly. "The world can't afford sex anymore."

"Of course it can afford sex," said Billy. "All it can't afford anymore is reproduction."

"Then why the laws?"

"They're bad laws," said Billy. "If you go back through history, you'll find that the people who have been most eager to rule, to make the laws, enforce the laws and to tell everybody exactly how God Almighty wants things here on Earth—those people have forgiven themselves and their friends for anything and everything. But they have been absolutely disgusted and terrified by the natural sexuality of common men and women.

"Why this is, I do not know. That is one of the many questions I wish somebody would ask the machines. I do know this: The triumph of that sort of disgust and terror is now complete. Almost every man and woman looks and feels like something the cat dragged in. The only sexual beauty that an ordinary human being can see today is in the woman who will kill him. Sex is death. There's a short and nasty equation for you: 'Sex is death. Q. E. D.'

"So you see, Nancy," said Billy, "I have spent this night, and many others like it, attempting to restore a certain amount of innocent pleasure to the world, which is poorer in pleasure than it needs to be."

Nancy sat down quietly and bowed her head.

"I'll tell you what my grandfather did on the dawn of his wedding night," said Billy.

"I don't think I want to hear it."

"It isn't violent. It's—it's meant to be tender."

"Maybe that's why I don't want to hear it."

"He read his bride a poem." Billy took the book from the table, opened it. "His diary tells which poem it was. While we aren't bride and groom, and while we may not meet again for many years, I'd like to read this poem to you, to have you know I've loved you."

"Please—no. I couldn't stand it."

"All right, I'll leave the book here, with the place marked, in case you want to read it later. It's the poem beginning:

> How do I love thee? Let me count the ways.
> I love thee to the depth and breadth and height
> My soul can reach, when feeling out of sight
> For the ends of Being and ideal Grace."

Billy put a small bottle on top of the book. "I am also leaving you these pills. If you take one a month, you will never have children. And still you'll be a nothinghead."

And he left. And they all left but Nancy.

When Nancy raised her eyes at last to the book and bottle, she saw that there was a label on the bottle. What the label said was this: WELCOME TO THE MONKEY HOUSE.

Roselily
(1973)

ALICE WALKER

Dearly Beloved

She dreams; dragging herself across the world. A small girl in her mother's white robe and veil, knee raised waist high through a bowl of quicksand soup feels like she is sinking. The man who stands beside her is against this standing on the front porch of her house, being married to the sound of cars whizzing by on highway 61.

we are gathered here

Like cotton to be weighed. Her fingers at the last minute busily removing dry leaves and twigs. Aware it is a superficial sweep. She knows he blames Mississippi for the respectful way the men turn their heads up in the yard, the women stand waiting and knowledgeable, their children held from mischief by teachings from the wrong God. He glares beyond them to the occupants of the cars, white faces glued to promises beyond a country wedding, noses thrust forward like dogs on a track. For him they usurp the wedding.

in the sight of God

Yes, open house. That is what country black folks like. She dreams she does not already have three children. A squeeze around the flowers in her hands chokes off three and four and five years of breath. Instantly she is ashamed and frightened in her superstition. She looks for the first time at the preacher, forces humility into her eyes, as if she believes he is, in fact, a man of God. She can imagine God, a small black boy, timidly pulling the preacher's coattail.

to join this man and this woman

She thinks of ropes, chains, handcuffs, his religion. His place of worship. Where she will be required to sit apart with covered head. In Chicago, a word she hears when thinking of smoke, from his description of what a cinder was, which they never had in Panther Burn. She sees hovering over the heads of the clean neighbors in her front yard black specks falling, clinging, from the sky. But in Chicago. Respect, a chance to build. Her children at last from underneath the detrimental wheel. A chance to be on top. What a relief, she thinks. What a vision, a view, from up so high.

in holy matrimony.

Her fourth child she gave away to the child's father who had some money. Certainly a good job. Had gone to Harvard. Was a good man but weak because good language meant so much to him he could not live with Roselily. Could not abide TV in the living room, five beds in three rooms, no Bach except from four to six on Sunday afternoons. No chess at all. She does not forget to worry about her son among his father's people. She wonders if the New England climate will agree with him. If he will ever come down to Mississippi, as his father did, to try to right the country's wrongs. She wonders if he will be stronger than his father. His father cried off and on throughout her pregnancy. Went to skin and bones. Suffered nightmares, retching and falling out of bed. Tried to kill himself. Later told his wife he found the right baby through friends. Vouched for, the sterling qualities that would make up his character.

It is not her nature to blame. Still, she is not entirely thankful. She supposes New England, the North, to be quite different from what she knows. It seems right somehow to her that people who move there to live return home completely changed. She thinks of the air, the smoke, the cinders. Imagines cinders big as hailstones; heavy, weighing on the people. Wonders how this pressure finds its way into the veins, roping the springs of laughter.

If there's anybody here that knows a reason why

But of course they know no reason why beyond what they daily have come to know. She thinks of the man who will be her husband, feels shut away from him because of the stiff severity of his plain black suit. His religion. A lifetime of black and white. Of veils. Covered head. It is as if her children are already gone from her. Not dead, but exalted on a pedestal, a stalk that has no roots. She wonders how to make new roots. It is beyond her. She wonders what one does with memories in a brand-new life. This had seemed easy, until she thought of it. "The reasons why . . . the people who" . . . she thinks, and does not wonder where the thought is from.

these two should not be joined

She thinks of her mother, who is dead. Dead, but still her mother. Joined. This is confusing. Of her father. A gray old man who sold wild mink, rabbit, fox skins to Sears, Roebuck. He stands in the yard, like a man waiting for a train. Her young sisters stand behind her in smooth green dresses, with flowers in their hands and hair. They giggle, she feels, at the absurdity of the wedding. They are ready for something new. She thinks the man beside her should marry one of them. She feels old. Yoked. An arm seems to reach out from behind her and snatch her backward. She thinks of cemeteries and the long sleep of grandparents mingling in the dirt. She believes that she believes in ghosts. In the soil giving back what it takes.

together,

In the city. He sees her in a new way. This she knows, and is grateful. But is it new enough? She cannot always be a bride and virgin, wearing robes and veil. Even now her body itches to be free of satin and voile, organdy and lily of the valley. Memories crash against her. Memories of being bare to the sun. She wonders what it will be like. Not to have to go to a job. Not to work in a sewing plant. Not to worry about learning to sew straight seams in workingmen's overalls, jeans, and dress pants. Her place will be in the home, he has said, repeatedly, promising her rest she had prayed for. But now she wonders. When she is rested, what will she do? They will make babies—she thinks practically about her fine brown body, his strong black one. They will be inevitable. Her hands will be full. Full of what? Babies. She is not comforted.

let him speak

She wishes she had asked him to explain more of what he meant. But she was impatient. Impatient to be done with sewing. With doing everything for three children, alone. Impatient to leave the girls she had known since childhood, their children growing up, their husbands hanging around her, already old, seedy. Nothing about them that she wanted, or needed. The fathers of her children driving by, waving, not waving; reminders of times she would just as soon forget. Impatient to see the South Side, where they would live and build and be respectable and respected and free. Her husband would free her. A romantic hush. Proposal. Promises. A new life! Respectable, reclaimed, renewed. Free! In robe and veil.

or forever hold

She does not even know if she loves him. She loves his sobriety. His refusal to sing just because he knows the tune. She loves his pride. His blackness and his gray car. She loves his understanding of her *condition*. She thinks she loves the effort he will make to redo her into what he truly wants. His love of her makes her completely conscious of how unloved she was before. This is something; though it makes her unbearably sad. Melancholy. She blinks her eyes. Remembers she is finally being married, like other girls. Like other girls, women? Something strains upward behind her eyes. She thinks of the something as a rat trapped, cornered, scurrying to and fro in her head, peering through the windows of her eyes. She wants to live for once. But doesn't know quite what that means. Wonders if she has ever done it. If she ever will. The preacher is odious to her. She wants to strike him out of the way, out of her light, with the back of her hand. It seems to her he has always been standing in front of her, barring her way.

his peace.

The rest she does not hear. She feels a kiss, passionate, rousing, within the general pandemonium. Cars drive up blowing their horns. Firecrackers go off. Dogs come from under the house and begin to yelp and bark. Her husband's hand is like the clasp of an iron gate. People congratulate. Her children press against her. They look with awe and distaste mixed with hope at their new father. He stands curiously apart, in spite of the people crowding about to grasp his free hand. He smiles at them all but his eyes are as if turned inward. He knows they cannot understand that he is not a Christian. He will not explain himself. He feels different, he looks it. The old women thought he was like one of their sons except that he had somehow got away from them. Still a son, not a son. Changed.

She thinks how it will be later in the night in the silvery gray car. How they will spin through the darkness of Mississippi and in the morning be in Chicago, Illinois. She thinks of Lincoln, the president. That is all she knows about the place. She feels ignorant, *wrong*, backward. She presses her worried fingers into his palm. He is standing in front of her. In the crush of well-wishing people, he does not look back.

The New Accelerator
(1901)

H.G. WELLS

Certainly, if ever a man found a guinea when he was looking for a pin it is my good friend Professor Gibberne. I have heard before of investigators overshooting the mark, but never quite to the extent that he has done. He has really, this time at any rate, without any touch of exaggeration in the phrase, found something to revolutionise human life. And that when he was simply seeking an all-round nervous stimulant to bring languid people up to the stresses of these pushful days. I have tasted the stuff now several times, and I cannot do better than describe the effect the thing had on me. That there are astonishing experiences in store for all in search of new sensations will become apparent enough.

Professor Gibberne, as many people know, is my neighbour in Folkestone. Unless my memory plays me a trick, his portrait at various ages has already appeared in The Strand Magazine—I think late in 1899; but I am unable to look it up because I have lent that volume to some one who has never sent it back. The reader may, perhaps, recall the high forehead and the singularly long black eyebrows that give such a Mephistophelian touch to his face. He occupies one of those pleasant little detached houses in the mixed style that make the western end of the Upper Sandgate Road so interesting. His is the one with the Flemish gables and the Moorish portico, and it is in the little room with the mullioned bay window that he works when he is down here, and in which of an evening we have so often smoked and talked together. He is a mighty jester, but, besides, he likes to talk to me about his work; he is one of those men who find a help and stimulus in talking, and so I have been able to follow the conception of the New Accelerator right up from a very early stage. Of course, the greater portion of his experimental work is not done in Folkestone, but in Gower Street, in the fine new laboratory next to the hospital that he has been the first to use.

As every one knows, or at least as all intelligent people know, the special department in which Gibberne has gained so great and deserved a reputation among physiologists is the action of drugs upon the nervous system. Upon soporifics, sedatives, and anaesthetics he is, I am told, unequalled. He is also a chemist of considerable eminence, and I suppose in the subtle and complex jungle of riddles that centres about the ganglion cell and the axis fibre there are little cleared places of his making, little glades of illumination, that, until he sees fit to publish his results, are still inaccessible to every other living man. And in the last few years he has been particularly assiduous upon this question of nervous stimulants, and already, before the discovery of the New Accelerator, very successful with them. Medical science has

909

to thank him for at least three distinct and absolutely safe invigorators of unrivalled value to practising men. In cases of exhaustion the preparation known as Gibberne's B Syrup has, I suppose, saved more lives already than any lifeboat round the coast.

"But none of these little things begin to satisfy me yet," he told me nearly a year ago. "Either they increase the central energy without affecting the nerves or they simply increase the available energy by lowering the nervous conductivity; and all of them are unequal and local in their operation. One wakes up the heart and viscera and leaves the brain stupefied, one gets at the brain champagne fashion and does nothing good for the solar plexus, and what I want—and what, if it's an earthly possibility, I mean to have—is a stimulant that stimulates all round, that wakes you up for a time from the crown of your head to the tip of your great toe, and makes you go two—or even three—to everybody else's one. Eh? That's the thing I'm after."

"It would tire a man," I said.

"Not a doubt of it. And you'd eat double or treble—and all that. But just think what the thing would mean. Imagine yourself with a little phial like this"—he held up a little bottle of green glass and marked his points with it—"and in this precious phial is the power to think twice as fast, move twice as quickly, do twice as much work in a given time as you could otherwise do."

"But is such a thing possible?"

"I believe so. If it isn't, I've wasted my time for a year. These various preparations of the hypophosphites, for example, seem to show that something of the sort. . . Even if it was only one and a half times as fast it would do."

"It *would* do," I said.

"If you were a statesman in a corner, for example, time rushing up against you, something urgent to be done, eh?"

"He could dose his private secretary," I said.

"And gain—double time. And think if YOU, for example, wanted to finish a book."

"Usually," I said, "I wish I'd never begun 'em."

"Or a doctor, driven to death, wants to sit down and think out a case. Or a barrister—or a man cramming for an examination."

"Worth a guinea a drop," said I, "and more to men like that."

"And in a duel, again," said Gibberne, "where it all depends on your quickness in pulling the trigger."

"Or in fencing," I echoed.

"You see," said Gibberne, "if I get it as an all-round thing it will really do you no harm at all—except perhaps to an infinitesimal degree it brings you nearer old age. You will just have lived twice to other people's once—"

"I suppose," I meditated, "in a duel—it would be fair?"

"That's a question for the seconds," said Gibberne.

I harked back further. "And you really think such a thing IS possible?" I said.

"As possible," said Gibberne, and glanced at something that went throbbing by the window, "as a motor-bus. As a matter of fact—"

He paused and smiled at me deeply, and tapped slowly on the edge of his desk with the green phial. "I think I know the stuff. . . Already I've got something coming." The nervous smile upon his face betrayed the gravity of his revelation. He rarely talked of his actual experimental work unless things were very near the end. "And it may be, it may be—I shouldn't be surprised—it may even do the thing at a greater rate than twice."

"It will be rather a big thing," I hazarded.

"It will be, I think, rather a big thing."

But I don't think he quite knew what a big thing it was to be, for all that.

I remember we had several talks about the stuff after that. "The New Accelerator" he called it, and his tone about it grew more confident on each occasion. Sometimes he talked nervously of unexpected physiological results its use might have, and then he would get a little unhappy; at others he was frankly mercenary, and we debated long and anxiously how the preparation might be turned to commercial account. "It's a good thing," said Gibberne, "a tremendous thing. I know I'm giving the world something, and I think it only reasonable we should expect the world to pay. The dignity of science is all very well, but I think somehow I must have the monopoly of the stuff for, say, ten years. I don't see why ALL the fun in life should go to the dealers in ham."

My own interest in the coming drug certainly did not wane in the time. I have always had a queer little twist towards metaphysics in my mind. I have always been given to paradoxes about space and time, and it seemed to me that Gibberne was really preparing no less than the absolute acceleration of life. Suppose a man repeatedly dosed with such a preparation: he would live an active and record life indeed, but he would be an adult at eleven, middle-aged at twenty-five, and by thirty well on the road to senile decay. It seemed to me that so far Gibberne was only going to do for any one who took his drug exactly what Nature has done for the Jews and Orientals, who are men in their teens and aged by fifty, and quicker in thought and act than we are all the time. The marvel of drugs has always been great to my mind; you can madden a man, calm a man, make him incredibly strong and alert or a helpless log, quicken this passion and allay that, all by means of drugs, and here was a new miracle to be added to this strange armoury of phials the doctors use! But Gibberne was far too eager upon his technical points to enter very keenly into my aspect of the question.

It was the 7th or 8th of August when he told me the distillation that would decide his failure or success for a time was going forward as we talked, and it was on the 10th that he told me the thing was done and the New Accelerator a tangible reality in the world. I met him as I was going up the Sandgate Hill towards Folkestone—I think I was going to get my hair cut, and he came hurrying down to meet me—I suppose he was coming to my house to tell me at once of his success. I remember that his eyes were unusually bright and his face flushed, and I noted even then the swift alacrity of his step.

"It's done," he cried, and gripped my hand, speaking very fast; "it's more than done. Come up to my house and see."

"Really?"

"Really!" he shouted. "Incredibly! Come up and see."

"And it does—twice?"

"It does more, much more. It scares me. Come up and see the stuff. Taste it! Try it! It's the most amazing stuff on earth." He gripped my arm and, walking at such a pace that he forced me into a trot, went shouting with me up the hill. A whole *chár-a-banc*-ful of people turned and stared at us in unison after the manner of people in *chárs-a-banc*. It was one of those hot, clear days that Folkestone sees so much of, every colour incredibly bright and every outline hard. There was a breeze, of course, but not so much breeze as sufficed under these conditions to keep me cool and dry. I panted for mercy.

"I'm not walking fast, am I?" cried Gibberne, and slackened his pace to a quick march.

"You've been taking some of this stuff," I puffed.

"No," he said. "At the utmost a drop of water that stood in a beaker from which I had washed out the last traces of the stuff. I took some last night, you know. But that is ancient history, now."

"And it goes twice?" I said, nearing his doorway in a grateful perspiration.

"It goes a thousand times, many thousand times!" cried Gibberne, with a dramatic gesture, flinging open his Early English carved oak gate.

"Phew!" said I, and followed him to the door.

"I don't know how many times it goes," he said, with his latch-key in his hand.

"And you—"

"It throws all sorts of light on nervous physiology, it kicks the theory of vision into a perfectly new shape! . . . Heaven knows how many thousand times. We'll try all that after—The thing is to try the stuff now."

"Try the stuff?" I said, as we went along the passage.

"Rather," said Gibberne, turning on me in his study. "There it is in that little green phial there! Unless you happen to be afraid?"

I am a careful man by nature, and only theoretically adventurous. I WAS afraid. But on the other hand there is pride.

"Well," I haggled. "You say you've tried it?"

"I've tried it," he said, "and I don't look hurt by it, do I? I don't even look livery and I FEEL—"

I sat down. "Give me the potion," I said. "If the worst comes to the worst it will save having my hair cut, and that I think is one of the most hateful duties of a civilised man. How do you take the mixture?"

"With water," said Gibberne, whacking down a carafe.

He stood up in front of his desk and regarded me in his easy chair; his manner was suddenly affected by a touch of the Harley Street specialist. "It's rum stuff, you know," he said.

I made a gesture with my hand.

"I must warn you in the first place as soon as you've got it down to shut your eyes, and open them very cautiously in a minute or so's time. One still sees. The sense of vision is a question of length of vibration, and not of multitude of impacts; but there's a kind of shock to the retina, a nasty giddy confusion just at the time, if the eyes are open. Keep 'em shut."

"Shut," I said. "Good!"

"And the next thing is, keep still. Don't begin to whack about. You may fetch something a nasty rap if you do. Remember you will be going several thousand times faster than you ever did before, heart, lungs, muscles, brain—everything—and you will hit hard without knowing it. You won't know it, you know. You'll feel just as you do now. Only everything in the world will seem to be going ever so many thousand times slower than it ever went before. That's what makes it so deuced queer."

"Lor'," I said. "And you mean—"

"You'll see," said he, and took up a little measure. He glanced at the material on his desk. "Glasses," he said, "water. All here. Mustn't take too much for the first attempt."

The little phial glucked out its precious contents.

"Don't forget what I told you," he said, turning the contents of the measure into a glass in the manner of an Italian waiter measuring whisky. "Sit with the eyes tightly shut and in absolute stillness for two minutes," he said. "Then you will hear me speak."

He added an inch or so of water to the little dose in each glass.

"By-the-by," he said, "don't put your glass down. Keep it in your hand and rest your hand on your knee. Yes—so. And now—"

He raised his glass.

"The New Accelerator," I said.

"The New Accelerator," he answered, and we touched glasses and drank, and instantly I closed my eyes.

You know that blank non-existence into which one drops when one has taken "gas." For an indefinite interval it was like that. Then I heard Gibberne telling me to wake up, and I stirred and opened my eyes. There he stood as he had been standing, glass still in hand. It was empty, that was all the difference.

"Well?" said I.

"Nothing out of the way?"

"Nothing. A slight feeling of exhilaration, perhaps. Nothing more."

"Sounds?"

"Things are still," I said. "By Jove! yes! They ARE still. Except the sort of faint pat, patter, like rain falling on different things. What is it?"

"Analysed sounds," I think he said, but I am not sure. He glanced at the window. "Have you ever seen a curtain before a window fixed in that way before?"

I followed his eyes, and there was the end of the curtain, frozen, as it were, corner high, in the act of flapping briskly in the breeze.

"No," said I; "that's odd."

"And here," he said, and opened the hand that held the glass. Naturally I winced, expecting the glass to smash. But so far from smashing it did not even seem to stir; it hung in midair—motionless.

"Roughly speaking," said Gibberne, "an object in these latitudes falls 16 feet in the first second. This glass is falling 16 feet in a second now. Only, you see, it hasn't been falling yet for the hundredth part of a second. That gives you some idea of the pace of my Accelerator." And he waved his hand round and round, over and under the slowly sinking glass. Finally, he took it by the bottom, pulled it down, and placed it very carefully on the table. "Eh?" he said to me, and laughed.

"That seems all right," I said, and began very gingerly to raise myself from my chair. I felt perfectly well, very light and comfortable, and quite confident in my mind. I was going fast all over. My heart, for example, was beating a thousand times a second, but that caused me no discomfort at all. I looked out of the window. An immovable cyclist, head down and with a frozen puff of dust behind his driving-wheel, scorched to overtake a galloping *chár-a-banc* that did not stir. I gaped in amazement at this incredible spectacle. "Gibberne," I cried, "how long will this confounded stuff last?"

"Heaven knows!" he answered. "Last time I took it I went to bed and slept it off. I tell you, I was frightened. It must have lasted some minutes, I think—it seemed like hours. But after a bit it slows down rather suddenly, I believe."

I was proud to observe that I did not feel frightened—I suppose because there were two of us. "Why shouldn't we go out?" I asked.

"Why not?"

"They'll see us."

"Not they. Goodness, no! Why, we shall be going a thousand times faster than the quickest conjuring trick that was ever done. Come along! Which way shall we go? Window, or door?"

And out by the window we went.

Assuredly of all the strange experiences that I have ever had, or imagined, or read of other people having or imagining, that little raid I made with Gibberne on the Folkestone Leas, under the influence of the New Accelerator, was the strangest and maddest of all. We went out by his gate into the road, and there we made a minute examination of the statuesque passing traffic. The tops of the wheels and some of the legs of the horses of this *chár-a-banc,* the end of the whip-lash and the lower jaw of the conductor—who was just beginning to yawn—were perceptibly in motion, but all the rest of the lumbering conveyance seemed still. And quite noiseless except for a faint rattling that came from one man's throat! And as parts of this frozen edifice there were a driver, you know, and a conductor, and eleven people! The effect as we walked about the thing began by being madly queer, and ended by being disagreeable. There they were, people like ourselves and yet not like ourselves, frozen in careless attitudes, caught in mid-gesture. A girl and a man smiled at one another, a leering smile that threatened to last for evermore; a woman in a floppy capelline rested her arm on the rail and stared at Gibberne's house with the unwinking stare of eternity; a man stroked his moustache like a figure of wax, and another stretched a tiresome stiff hand with extended fingers towards his loosened hat. We stared at them, we laughed at them, we made faces at them, and then a sort of disgust of them came upon us, and we turned away and walked round in front of the cyclist towards the Leas.

"Goodness!" cried Gibberne, suddenly; "look there!"

He pointed, and there at the tip of his finger and sliding down the air with wings flapping slowly and at the speed of an exceptionally languid snail—was a bee.

And so we came out upon the Leas. There the thing seemed madder than ever. The band was playing in the upper stand, though all the sound it made for us was a low-pitched, wheezy rattle, a sort of prolonged last sigh that passed at times into a sound like the slow, muffled ticking of some monstrous clock. Frozen people stood erect, strange, silent, self-conscious-looking dummies hung unstably in mid-stride, promenading upon the grass. I passed close to a little poodle dog suspended in the act of leaping, and watched the slow movement of his legs as he sank to earth. "Lord, look here!" cried Gibberne, and we halted for a moment before a magnificent person in white faint-striped flannels, white shoes, and a Panama hat, who turned back to wink at two gaily dressed ladies he had passed. A wink, studied with such leisurely deliberation as we could afford, is an unattractive thing. It loses any quality of alert gaiety, and one remarks that the winking eye does not completely close, that under its drooping lid appears the lower edge of an eyeball and a little line of white. "Heaven give me memory," said I, "and I will never wink again."

"Or smile," said Gibberne, with his eye on the lady's answering teeth.

"It's infernally hot, somehow," said I. "Let's go slower."

"Oh, come along!" said Gibberne.

We picked our way among the bath-chairs in the path. Many of the people sitting in the chairs seemed almost natural in their passive poses, but the contorted scarlet of the bandsmen was not a restful thing to see. A purple-faced little gentleman was frozen in the midst of a violent struggle to refold his newspaper against the wind; there were many evidences that all these people in their sluggish way were exposed to a considerable breeze, a breeze that had no existence so far as our sensations went. We came out and walked a little way from the crowd, and turned and regarded it. To see all that multitude changed, to a picture, smitten rigid, as it were, into the semblance of realistic wax, was impossibly wonderful. It was absurd, of course; but it filled me with an irrational, an exultant sense of superior advantage. Consider the wonder of it! All that I had said, and thought, and done since the stuff had begun to work in my veins had happened, so far as those people, so far as the world in general went, in the twinkling of an eye. "The New Accelerator—" I began, but Gibberne interrupted me.

"There's that infernal old woman!" he said.

"What old woman?"

"Lives next door to me," said Gibberne. "Has a lapdog that yaps. Gods! The temptation is strong!"

There is something very boyish and impulsive about Gibberne at times. Before I could expostulate with him he had dashed forward, snatched the unfortunate animal out of visible existence, and was running violently with it towards the cliff of the Leas. It was most extraordinary. The little brute, you know, didn't bark or wriggle or make the slightest sign of vitality. It kept quite stiffly in an attitude of somnolent repose, and Gibberne held it by the neck. It was like running about with a dog of wood. "Gibberne," I cried, "put it down!" Then I said something else. "If you run like that, Gibberne," I cried, "you'll set your clothes on fire. Your linen trousers are going brown as it is!"

He clapped his hand on his thigh and stood hesitating on the verge. "Gibberne," I cried, coming up, "put it down. This heat is too much! It's our running so! Two or three miles a second! Friction of the air!"

"What?" he said, glancing at the dog.

"Friction of the air," I shouted. "Friction of the air. Going too fast. Like meteorites and things. Too hot. And, Gibberne! Gibberne! I'm all over pricking and a sort of perspiration. You can see people stirring slightly. I believe the stuff's working off! Put that dog down."

"Eh?" he said.

"It's working off," I repeated. "We're too hot and the stuff's working off! I'm wet through."

He stared at me. Then at the band, the wheezy rattle of whose performance was certainly going faster. Then with a tremendous sweep of the arm he hurled the dog away from him and it went spinning upward, still inanimate, and hung at last over the grouped parasols of a knot of chattering people. Gibberne was gripping my elbow.

"By Jove!" he cried. "I believe—it is! A sort of hot pricking and—yes. That man's moving his pocket-handkerchief! Perceptibly. We must get out of this sharp."

But we could not get out of it sharply enough. Luckily, perhaps! For we might have run, and if we had run we should, I believe, have burst into flames. Almost certainly we should have burst into flames! You know we had neither of us thought of that. . . But before we could even begin to run the action of the drug had ceased. It was the business of a minute fraction of a second. The effect of the New Accelerator passed like the drawing of a curtain, vanished in the movement of a hand. I heard Gibberne's voice in infinite alarm. "Sit down," he said, and flop, down upon the turf at the edge of the Leas I sat—scorching as I sat. There is a patch of burnt grass there still where I sat down. The whole stagnation seemed to wake up as I did so, the disarticulated vibration of the band rushed together into a blast of music, the promenaders put their feet down and walked their ways, the papers and flags began flapping, smiles passed into words, the winker finished his wink and went on his way complacently, and all the seated people moved and spoke.

The whole world had come alive again, was going as fast as we were, or rather we were going no faster than the rest of the world. It was like slowing down as one comes into a railway station. Everything seemed to spin round for a second or two, I had the most transient feeling of nausea, and that was all. And the little dog which had seemed to hang for a moment when the force of Gibberne's arm was expended fell with a swift acceleration clean through a lady's parasol!

That was the saving of us. Unless it was for one corpulent old gentleman in a bath-chair, who certainly did start at the sight of us and afterwards regarded us at intervals with a darkly suspicious eye, and, finally, I believe, said something to his nurse about us, I doubt if a solitary person remarked our sudden appearance among them. Plop! We must have appeared abruptly. We ceased to smoulder almost at once, though the turf beneath me was uncomfortably hot. The attention of every one—including even the Amusements' Association band, which on this occasion, for the only time in its history, got out of tune—was arrested by the amazing fact, and the still more amazing yapping and uproar caused by the fact that a respectable, over-fed lap-dog sleeping quietly to the east of the bandstand should suddenly fall through the parasol of a lady on the west—in a slightly singed condition due to the extreme velocity of its movements through the air. In these absurd days, too, when we are all trying to be as psychic, and silly, and superstitious as possible! People got up and trod on other people, chairs were overturned, the Leas policeman ran. How the matter settled itself I do not know—we were much too anxious to disentangle ourselves from the affair and get out of range of the eye of the old gentleman in the bath-chair to make minute inquiries. As soon as we were sufficiently cool and sufficiently recovered from our giddiness and nausea and confusion of mind to do so we stood up and, skirting the crowd, directed our steps back along the road below the Metropole towards Gibberne's house. But amidst the din I heard very distinctly the gentleman who had been sitting beside the lady of the ruptured sunshade using quite unjustifiable threats and language to one of those chair-attendants who have "Inspector" written on their caps. "If you didn't throw the dog," he said, "who DID?"

The sudden return of movement and familiar noises, and our natural anxiety about ourselves (our clothes were still dreadfully hot, and the fronts of the thighs of Gibberne's white trousers were scorched a drabbish brown), prevented the minute observations I should have liked to make on all these things. Indeed, I really made no observations of any scientific value on that return. The bee, of course, had gone. I looked for that cyclist, but he was already out of sight as we came into the Upper Sandgate Road or hidden from us by traffic; the *chár-a-banc*, however, with its people now all alive and stirring, was clattering along at a spanking pace almost abreast of the nearer church.

We noted, however, that the window-sill on which we had stepped in getting out of the house was slightly singed, and that the impressions of our feet on the gravel of the path were unusually deep.

So it was I had my first experience of the New Accelerator. Practically we had been running about and saying and doing all sorts of things in the space of a second or so of time. We had lived half an hour while the band had played, perhaps, two bars. But the effect it had upon us was that the whole world had stopped for our convenient inspection. Considering all things, and particularly considering our rashness in venturing out of the house, the experience might certainly have been much more disagreeable than it was. It showed, no doubt, that Gibberne has still much to learn before his preparation is a manageable convenience, but its practicability it certainly demonstrated beyond all cavil.

Since that adventure he has been steadily bringing its use under control, and I have several times, and without the slightest bad result, taken measured doses under his direction; though I must confess I have not yet ventured abroad again while under its influence. I may mention, for example, that this story has been written at one sitting and without interruption, except for the nibbling of some chocolate, by its means. I began at 6.25, and my watch is now very nearly at the minute past the half-hour. The convenience of securing a long, uninterrupted spell of work in the midst of a day full of engagements cannot be exaggerated. Gibberne is now working at the quantitative handling of his preparation, with especial reference to its distinctive effects upon different types of constitution. He then hopes to find a Retarder with which to dilute its present rather excessive potency. The Retarder will, of course, have the reverse effect to the Accelerator; used alone it should enable the patient to spread a few seconds over many hours of ordinary time, and so to maintain an apathetic inaction, a glacier-like absence of alacrity, amidst the most animated or irritating surroundings. The two things together must necessarily work an entire revolution in civilised existence. It is the beginning of our escape from that Time Garment of which Carlyle speaks. While this Accelerator will enable us to concentrate ourselves with tremendous impact upon any moment or occasion that demands our utmost sense and vigour, the Retarder will enable us to pass in passive tranquillity through infinite hardship and tedium. Perhaps I am a little optimistic about the Retarder, which has indeed still to be discovered, but about the Accelerator there is no possible sort of doubt whatever. Its appearance upon the market in a convenient, controllable, and assimilable form is a matter of the next few months. It will be obtainable of all chemists and druggists, in small green bottles, at a high but, considering its extraordinary qualities, by no means excessive price. Gibberne's Nervous Accelerator it will be called, and he hopes to be able to supply it in three strengths: one in 200, one in 900, and one in 2000, distinguished by yellow, pink, and white labels respectively.

No doubt its use renders a great number of very extraordinary things possible; for, of course, the most remarkable and, possibly, even criminal proceedings may be effected with impunity by thus dodging, as it were, into the interstices of time. Like all potent preparations it will be liable to abuse. We have, however, discussed this aspect of the question very thoroughly, and we have decided that this is purely a matter of medical jurisprudence and altogether outside our province. We shall manufacture and sell the Accelerator, and, as for the consequences—we shall see.

The Hitch-Hikers
(1941)

EUDORA WELTY

Tom Harris, a thirty-year-old salesman traveling in office supplies, got out of Victory a little after noon and saw people in Midnight and Louise, but went on toward Memphis. It was a base, and he was thinking he would like to do something that night.

Toward evening, somewhere in the middle of the Delta, he slowed down to pick up two hitchhikers. One of them stood still by the side of the pavement, with his foot stuck out like an old root, but the other was playing a yellow guitar which caught the late sun as it came in a long straight bar across the fields.

Harris would get sleepy driving. On the road he did some things rather out of a dream. And the recurring sight of hitch-hikers waiting against the sky gave him the flash of a sensation he had known as a child: standing still, with nothing to touch him, feeling tall and having the world come all at once into its round shape underfoot and rush and turn through space and make his stand very precarious and lonely. He opened the car door.

"How you do?"

"How you do?"

Harris spoke to hitch-hikers almost formally. Now resuming his speed, he moved over a little in the seat. There was no room in the back for anybody. The man with the guitar was riding with it between his legs. Harris reached over and flicked on the radio.

"Well, music!" said the man with the guitar. Presently he began to smile. "Well, we been there a whole day in that one spot," he said softly. "Seen the sun go clear over. Course, part of the time we laid down under that one tree and taken our ease."

They rode without talking while the sun went down in red clouds and the radio program changed a few times. Harris switched on his lights. Once the man with the guitar started to sing "The One Rose That's Left in My Heart," which came over the air, played by the Aloha Boys. Then in shyness he stopped, but made a streak on the radio dial with his blackly calloused finger tip.

"I 'preciate them big 'lectric gittars some have," he said.

"Where are you going?"

"Looks like north."

"It's north," said Harris. "Smoke?"

The other man held out his hand.

"Well . . . rarely," said the man with the guitar.

At the use of the unexpected word, Harris's cheek twitched, and he handed over his pack of cigarettes. All three lighted up. The silent man held his cigarette in front of him like a piece of money, between his thumb and forefinger. Harris realized that he wasn't smoking it, but was watching it burn.

"My! gittin' night agin," said the man with the guitar in a voice that could assume any social surprise.

"Anything to eat?" asked Harris.

The man gave a pluck to a low string and glanced at him.

"Dewberries," said the other man. It was his only remark, and it was delivered in a slow and pondering voice.

"Some nice little rabbit come skinnin' by," said the man with the guitar, nudging Harris with a slight punch in his side, "but it run off the way it come."

The other man was so bogged in inarticulate anger that Harris could imagine him running down a cotton row after the rabbit. He smiled but did not look around.

"Now to look out for a place to sleep—is that it?" he remarked doggedly.

A pluck of the strings again, and the man yawned.

There was a little town coming up; the lights showed for twenty miles in the flat land.

"Is that Dulcie?" Harris yawned too.

"I bet you ain't got no idea where all I've slep'," the man said, turning around in his seat and speaking directly to Harris, with laughter in his face that in the light of a road sign appeared strangely teasing.

"I could eat a hamburger," said Harris, swinging out of the road under the sign in some automatic gesture of evasion. He looked out of the window, and a girl in red pants leaped onto the running board.

"Three and three beers?" she asked, smiling, with her head poked in. "Hi," she said to Harris.

"How are you?" said Harris. "That's right."

"My," said the man with the guitar. "Red sailor-boy britches." Harris listened for the guitar note, but it did not come. "But not purty," he said.

The screen door of the joint whined, and a man's voice called, "Come on in, boys, we got girls."

Harris cut off the radio, and they listened to the nickelodeon which was playing inside the joint and turning the window blue, red and green in turn.

"Hi," said the car-hop again as she came out with the tray. "Looks like rain."

They ate the hamburgers rapidly, without talking. A girl came and looked out of the window of the joint, leaning on her hand. The same couple kept dancing by behind her. There was something brassy playing, a swing record of "Love, Oh Love, Oh Careless Love."

"Same songs ever'where," said the man with the guitar softly. "I come down from the hills. . . . We had us owls for chickens and fox for yard dogs but we sung true."

Nearly every time the man spoke Harris's cheek twitched. He was easily amused. Also, he recognized at once any sort of attempt to confide, and then its certain and hasty retreat. And the more anyone said, the further he was drawn into a willingness to listen. I'll hear him play his guitar yet, he thought. It had got to be a pattern in his days and nights, it was almost automatic, his listening, like the way his hand went to his pocket for money.

"That'n's most the same as a ballat," said the man, licking mustard off his finger. "My ma, she was the one for ballats. Little in the waist as a dirt-dauber, but her voice carried. Had her a whole lot of tunes. Long ago dead an' gone. Pa 'd come home from the courthouse drunk as a wheel-barrow, and she'd just pick up an' go sit on the front step facin' the hill an' sing. Ever'thing she knowed, she'd sing. Dead an' gone, an' the house burned down." He gulped at his beer. His foot was patting.

"This," said Harris, touching one of the keys on the guitar. "Couldn't you stop somewhere along here and make money playing this?"

Of course it was by the guitar that he had known at once that they were not mere hitch-hikers. They were tramps. They were full blown, abandoned to this. Both of them were. But when he touched it he knew obscurely that it was the yellow guitar, that bold and gay burden in the tramp's arms, that had caused him to stop and pick them up.

The man hit it flat with the palm of his hand.

"This box? Just play it for myself."

Harris laughed delightedly, but somehow he had a desire to tease him, to make him swear to his freedom.

"You wouldn't stop and play somewhere like this? For them to dance? When you know all the songs?"

Now the fellow laughed out loud. He turned and spoke completely as if the other man could not hear him. "Well, but right now I got *him*."

"Him?" Harris stared ahead.

"He'd gripe. He don't like foolin' around. He wants to git on. You always git a partner got notions."

The other tramp belched. Harris laid his hand on the horn.

"Hurry back," said the car-hop, opening a heart-shaped pocket over her heart and dropping the tip courteously within.

"Aw river!" sang out the man with the guitar.

As they pulled out into the road again, the other man began to lift a beer bottle, and stared beseechingly, with his mouth full, at the man with the guitar.

"Drive back, mister. Sobby forgot to give her back her bottle. Drive back."

"Too late," said Harris rather firmly, speeding on into Dulcie, thinking, I was about to take directions from him.

Harris stopped the car in front of the Dulcie Hotel on the square.

" 'Preciated it," said the man, taking up his guitar.

"Wait here,"

They stood on the walk, one lighted by the street light, the other in the shadow of the statue of the Confederate soldier, both caved in and giving out an odor of dust, both sighing with obedience.

Harris went across the yard and up the one step into the hotel.

Mr. Gene, the proprietor, a white-haired man with little dark freckles all over his face and hands, looked up and shoved out his arm at the same time.

"If he ain't back." He grinned. "Been about a month to the day—I was just remarking."

"Mr. Gene, I ought to go on, but I got two fellows out front. O.K., but they've just got nowhere to sleep tonight, and you know that little back porch."

"Why, it's a beautiful night out!" bellowed Mr. Gene, and he laughed silently.

"They'd get fleas in your bed," said Harris, showing the back of his hand. "But you know that old porch. It's not so bad. I slept out there once, I forget how."

The proprietor let his laugh out like a flood. Then he sobered abruptly.

"Sure. O.K.," he said. "Wait a minute—Mike's sick. Come here, Mike, it's just old Harris passin' through."

Mike was an ancient collie dog. He rose from a quilt near the door and moved over the square brown rug, stiffly, like a table walking, and shoved himself between the men, swinging his long head from Mr. Gene's hand to Harris's and bearing down motionless with his jaw in Harris's palm.

"You sick, Mike?" asked Harris.

"Dyin' of old age, that's what he's doin'!" blurted the proprietor as if in anger.

Harris began to stroke the dog, but the familiarity in his hands changed to slowness and hesitancy. Mike looked up out of his eyes.

"His spirit's gone. You see?" said Mr. Gene pleadingly.

"Say, look," said a voice at the front door.

"Come in, Cato, and see poor old Mike," said Mr. Gene.

"I knew that was your car, Mr. Harris," said the boy. He was nervously trying to tuck a Bing Crosby cretonne shirt into his pants like a real shirt. Then he looked up and said, "They was tryin' to take your car, and down the street one of 'em like to bust the other one's head wide op'm with a bottle. Looks like you would 'a' heard the commotion. Everybody's out there. I said, 'That's Mr. Tom Harris's car, look at the out-of-town license and look at all the stuff he all time carries around with him, all bloody.'"

"He's not dead though," said Harris, kneeling on the seat of his car.

It was the man with the guitar. The little ceiling light had been turned on. With blood streaming from his broken head, he was slumped down upon the guitar, his legs bowed around it, his arms at either side, his whole body limp in the posture of a bareback rider. Harris was aware of the other face not a yard away: the man the guitar player had called Sobby was standing on the curb, with two men unnecessarily holding him. He looked more like a bystander than any of the rest, except that he still held the beer bottle in his right hand.

"Looks like if he was fixin' to hit him, *he* would of hit *him* with that gittar," said a voice. "That 'd be a real good thing to hit somebody with. Whang!"

"The way I figure this thing out is," said a penetrating voice, as if a woman were explaining it all to her husband, "the men was left to 'emselves. So—that 'n' yonder wanted to make off with the car—he's the bad one. So the good one says, 'Naw, that ain't right.'"

Or was it the other way around? thought Harris dreamily.

"So the other one says bam! bam! He whacked him over the head. And so dumb—right where the movie was letting out."

"Who's got my car keys!" Harris kept shouting. He had, without realizing it, kicked away the prop, the guitar; and he had stopped the blood with something.

Nobody had to tell him where the ramshackle little hospital was—he had been there once before, on a Delta trip. With the constable scuttling along after and then riding on the running board, glasses held tenderly in one fist, the handcuffed Sobby dragged alongside by the other, with a long line of little boys in flowered shirts accompanying him on bicycles, riding in and out of the headlight beam, with the rain falling in front of him and with Mr. Gene shouting in a sort of plea from the hotel behind and Mike beginning to echo the barking of the rest of the dogs, Harris drove in all carefulness down the long tree-dark street, with his wet hand pressed on the horn.

The old doctor came down the walk and, joining them in the car, slowly took the guitar player by the shoulders.

"I 'spec' he gonna die though," said a colored child's voice mournfully. "Wonder who goin' to git his box?"

In a room on the second floor of the two-story hotel Harris put on clean clothes, while Mr. Gene lay on the bed with Mike across his stomach.

"Ruined that Christmas tie you came in." The proprietor was talking in short breaths. "It took it out of Mike, I'm tellin' you." He sighed. "First time he's barked since Bud Milton shot up that Chinese." He lifted his head and took a long swallow of the hotel whisky, and tears appeared in his warm brown eyes. "Suppose they'd done it on the porch."

The phone rang.

"See, everybody knows you're here," said Mr. Gene.

"Ruth?" he said, lifting the receiver, his voice almost contrite.

But it was for the proprietor.

When he had hung up he said, "That little peanut—he ain't ever goin' to learn which end is up. The constable. Got a nigger already in the jail, so he's runnin' round to find a place to put this fella of yours with the bottle, and damned if all he can think of ain't the hotel!"

"Hell, is he going to spend the night with me?"

"Well, the same thing. Across the hall. The other fella may die. Only place in town with a key but the bank, he says."

"What time is it?" asked Harris all at once.

"Oh, it ain't *late*," said Mr. Gene.

He opened the door for Mike, and the two men followed the dog slowly down the stairs. The light was out on the landing. Harris looked out of the old half-open stained-glass window.

"Is that rain?"

"It's been rainin' since dark, but you don't ever know a thing like that—it's proverbial." At the desk he held up a brown package. "Here. I sent Cato after some Memphis whisky for you. He had to do something."

"Thanks."

"I'll see you. I don't guess you're goin' to get away very shortly in the mornin'. I'm real sorry they did it in your car if they were goin' to do it."

"That's all right," said Harris. "You'd better have a little of this."

"That? It'd kill me," said Mr. Gene.

In a drugstore Harris phoned Ruth, a woman he knew in town, and found her at home having a party.

"Tom Harris! Sent by heaven!" she cried. "I was wondering what I'd do about Carol—this *baby!*"

"What's the matter with her?"

"No date."

Some other people wanted to say hello from the party. He listened awhile and said he'd be out.

This had postponed the call to the hospital. He put in another nickel. . . . There was nothing new about the guitar player.

"Like I told you," the doctor said, "we don't have the facilities for giving transfusions, and he's been moved plenty without you taking him to Memphis."

Walking over to the party, so as not to use his car, making the only sounds in the dark wet street, and only partly aware of the indeterminate shapes of houses with their soft-shining fanlights marking them off, there with the rain falling mistlike through the trees, he almost forgot what town he was in and which house he was bound for.

Ruth, in a long dark dress, leaned against an open door, laughing. From inside came the sounds of at least two people playing a duet on the piano.

"He would come like this and get all wet!" she cried over her shoulder into the room. She was leaning back on her hands. "What's the matter with your little blue car? I hope you brought us a present."

He went in with her and began shaking hands, and set the bottle wrapped in the paper sack on a table.

"He never forgets!" cried Ruth.

"Drinkin' whisky!" Everybody was noisy again.

"So this is the famous 'he' that everybody talks about all the time," pouted a girl in a white dress. "Is he one of your cousins, Ruth?"

"No kin of mine, he's nothing but a vagabond," said Ruth, and led Harris off to the kitchen by the hand.

I wish they'd call me "you" when I've got here, he thought tiredly.

"More has gone on than a little bit," she said, and told him the news while he poured fresh drinks into the glasses. When she accused him of nothing, of no carelessness or disregard of her feelings, he was fairly sure she had not heard about the assault in his car.

She was looking at him closely. "Where did you get that sunburn?"

"Well, I had to go to the Coast last week," he said.

"What did you do?"

"Same old thing." He laughed; he had started to tell her about something funny in Bay St. Louis, where an eloping couple had flagged him down in the residential section and threatened to break up if he would not carry them to the next town. Then he remembered how Ruth looked when he mentioned other places where he stopped on trips.

Somewhere in the house the phone rang and rang, and he caught himself jumping. Nobody was answering it.

"I thought you'd quit drinking," she said, picking up the bottle.

"I start and quit," he said, taking it from her and pouring his drink. "Where's my date?"

"Oh, she's in Leland," said Ruth.

They all drove over in two cars to get her.

She was a slight little thing, with her nightgown in some sort of little bag. She came out when they blew the horn, before he could go in after her . . .

"Let's go holler off the bridge," said somebody in the car ahead.

They drove over a little gravel road, miles through the misty fields, and came to the bridge out in the middle of nowhere.

"Let's dance," said one of the boys. He grabbed Carol around the waist, and they began to tango over the boards.

"Did you miss me?" asked Ruth. She stayed by him, standing in the road.

"Woo-hoo!" they cried.

"I wish I knew what makes it holler back," said one girl. "There's nothing anywhere. Some of my kinfolks can't even hear it."

"Yes, it's funny," said Harris, with a cigarette in his mouth.

"Some people say it's an old steamboat got lost once,"

"Might be."

They drove around and waited to see if it would stop raining.

Back in the lighted rooms at Ruth's he saw Carol, his date, give him a strange little glance. At the moment he was serving her with a drink from the tray.

"Are you the one everybody's 'miratin' and gyratin' over?" she said, before she would put her hand out.

"Yes," he said. "I come from afar." He placed the strongest drink from the tray in her hand, with a little flourish.

"Hurry back!" called Ruth.

In the pantry Ruth came over and stood by him while he set more glasses on the tray and then followed him out to the kitchen. Was she at all curious about him? he wondered. For a moment, when they were simply close together, her lips parted, and she stared off at nothing; her jealousy seemed to let her go free. The rainy wind from the back porch stirred her hair.

As if under some illusion, he set the tray down and told her about the two hitch-hikers. Her eyes flashed.

"What a—stupid thing!" Furiously she seized the tray when he reached for it.

The phone was ringing again. Ruth glared at him.

It was as though he had made a previous engagement with the hitch-hikers.

Everybody was meeting them at the kitchen door.

"Aha!" cried one of the men, Jackson. "He tries to put one over on you, girls. Somebody just called up, Ruth, about the murder in Tom's car."

"Did he die?" asked Harris, without moving.

"I knew all about it!" cried Ruth, her cheeks flaming. "He told me all about it. It practically ruined his car. Didn't it!"

"Wouldn't he get into something crazy like that?"

"It's because he's an angel," said the girl named Carol, his date, speaking in a hollow voice from her highball glass.

"Who phoned?" asked Harris.

"Old Mrs. Daggett, that old lady about a million years old that's always calling up. She was right there."

Harris phoned the doctor's home and woke the doctor's wife. The guitar player was still the same.

"This is so exciting, tell us all," said a fat boy. Harris knew he lived fifty miles up the river and had driven down under the impression that there would be a bridge game.

"It was just a fight."

"Oh, he wouldn't tell you, he never talks. I'll tell you," said Ruth. "Get your drinks, for goodness' sake."

So the incident became a story. Harris grew very tired of it.

"It's marvelous the way he always gets in with somebody and then something happens," said Ruth, her eyes completely black.

"Oh, he's my hero," said Carol, and she went out and stood on the back porch.

"Maybe you'll still be here tomorrow," Ruth said to Harris, taking his arm. "Will you be detained, maybe?"

"If he dies," said Harris.

He told them all good-bye.

"Let's all go to Greenville and get a Coke," said Ruth.

"No," he said. "Good night."

" 'Aw river,' " said the girl in the white dress. "Isn't that what the little man said?"

"Yes," said Harris, the rain falling on him, and he refused to spend the night or to be taken in a car back to the hotel.

In the antlered lobby, Mr. Gene bent over asleep under a lamp by the desk phone. His freckles seemed to come out darker when he was asleep.

Harris woke him. "Go to bed," he said. "What was the idea? Anything happened?"

"I just wanted to tell you that little buzzard's up in 202. Locked and double-locked, handcuffed to the bed, but I wanted to tell you."

"Oh. Much obliged."

"All a gentleman could do," said Mr. Gene. He was drunk. "Warn you what's sleepin' under your roof."

"Thanks," said Harris. "It's almost morning. Look."

"Poor Mike can't sleep," said Mr. Gene. "He scrapes somethin' when he breathes. Did the other fella poop out?"

"Still unconscious. No change," said Harris. He took the bunch of keys which the proprietor was handing him.

"You keep 'em," said Mr. Gene.

In the next moment Harris saw his hand tremble and he took hold of it.

"A murderer!" whispered Mr. Gene. All his freckles stood out. "Here he came . . . with not a word to say . . ."

"Not a murderer yet," said Harris, starting to grin.

When he passed 202 and heard no sound, he remembered what old Sobby had said, standing handcuffed in front of the hospital, with nobody listening to him. "I was jist tired of him always uppin' an' makin' a noise about ever'thing."

In his room, Harris lay down on the bed without undressing or turning out the light. He was too tired to sleep. Half blinded by the unshaded bulb he stared at the bare plaster walls and the equally white surface of the mirror above the empty dresser. Presently he got up and turned on the ceiling fan, to create some motion and sound in the room. It was a defective fan which clicked with each revolution, on and on. He lay perfectly still beneath it, with his clothes on, unconsciously breathing in a rhythm related to the beat of the fan.

He shut his eyes suddenly. When they were closed, in the red darkness he felt all patience leave him. It was like the beginning of desire. He remembered the girl dropping money into her heart-shaped pocket, and remembered a disturbing possessiveness, which meant nothing, Ruth leaning on her hands. He knew he would not be held by any of it. It was for relief, almost, that his thoughts turned to pity, to wonder about the two tramps, their conflict, the sudden brutality when his back was turned. How would it turn out? It was in this suspense that it was more acceptable to him to feel the helplessness of his life.

He could forgive nothing in this evening. But it was too like other evenings, this town was too like other towns, for him to move out of this lying still clothed on the bed, even into comfort or despair. Even the rain—there was often rain, there was often a party, and there had been other violence not of his doing—other fights, not quite so pointless, but fights in his car; fights, unheralded confessions, sudden love-making—none of any of this his, not his to keep, but belonging to the people of these towns he passed through, coming out of their rooted pasts and their mock rambles, coming out of their time. He himself had no time. He was free; helpless. He wished he knew how the guitar player was, if he was still unconscious, if he felt pain.

He sat up on the bed and then got up and walked to the window.

"Tom!" said a voice outside in the dark.

Automatically he answered and listened. It was a girl. He could not see her, but she must have been standing on the little plot of grass that ran around the side of the hotel. Wet feet, pneumonia, he thought. And he was so tired he thought of a girl from the wrong town.

He went down and unlocked the door. She ran in as far as the middle of the lobby as though from impetus. It was Carol, from the party.

"You're wet," he said. He touched her.

"Always raining." She looked up at him, stepping back. "How are you?"

"O.K., fine," he said.

"I was wondering," she said nervously. "I knew the light would be you. I hope I didn't wake up anybody." Was old Sobby asleep? he wondered.

"Would you like a drink? Or do you want to go to the All-Nite and get a Coca-Cola?" he said.

"It's open," she said, making a gesture with her hand. "The All-Nite's open—I just passed it."

They went out into the mist, and she put his coat on with silent protest, in the dark street not drunken but womanly.

"You didn't remember me at the party," she said, and did not look up when he made his exclamation. "They say you never forget anybody, so I found out they were wrong about that anyway."

"They're often wrong," he said, and then hurriedly, "Who are you?"

"We used to stay at the Manning Hotel on the Coast every summer—I wasn't grown. Carol Thames. Just dances and all, but you had just started to travel then, it was on your trips, and you—you talked at intermission."

He laughed shortly, but she added:

"You talked about yourself."

They walked past the tall wet church, and their steps echoed.

"Oh, it wasn't so long ago—five years," she said. Under a magnolia tree she put her hand out and stopped him, looking up at him with her child's face. "But when I saw you again tonight I wanted to know how you were getting along."

He said nothing, and she went on.

"You used to play the piano."

They passed under a street light, and she glanced up as if to look for the little tic in his cheek.

"Out on the big porch where they danced," she said, walking on. "Paper lanterns . . . "

"I'd forgotten that, is one thing sure," he said. "Maybe you've got the wrong man. I've got cousins galore who all play the piano."

"You'd put your hands down on the keyboard like you'd say, 'Now this is how it really is!'" she cried, and turned her head away. "I guess I was crazy about you, though."

"Crazy about me then?" He struck a match and held a cigarette between his teeth.

"No—yes, and now too!" she cried sharply, as if driven to deny him.

927

They came to the little depot where a restless switch engine was hissing, and crossed the black street. The past and present joined like this, he thought, it never happened often to me, and it probably won't happen again. He took her arm and led her through the dirty screen door of the All-Nite.

He waited at the counter while she sat down by the wall table and wiped her face all over with her handkerchief. He carried the black coffees over to the table himself, smiling at her from a little distance. They sat under a calendar with some picture of giant trees being cut down.

They said little. A fly bothered her. When the coffee was all gone he put her into the old Cadillac taxi that always stood in front of the depot.

Before he shut the taxi door he said, frowning, "I appreciate it . . . . You're sweet."

Now she had torn her handkerchief. She held it up and began to cry. "What's sweet about me?" It was the look of bewilderment in her face that he would remember.

"To come out, like this—in the rain—to be here. . . ." He shut the door, partly from weariness.

She was holding her breath. "I hope your friend doesn't die," she said. "All I hope is your friend gets well."

But when he woke up the next morning and phoned the hospital, the guitar player was dead. He had been dying while Harris was sitting in the All-Nite.

"It *was* a murderer," said Mr. Gene, pulling Mike's ears. "That was just plain murder. No way anybody could call that an affair of honor."

The man called Sobby did not oppose an invitation to confess. He stood erect and turning his head about a little, and almost smiled at all the men who had come to see him. After one look at him Mr. Gene, who had come with Harris, went out and slammed the door behind him.

All the same, Sobby had found little in the night, asleep or awake, to say about it. "I done it, sure," he said. "Didn't ever'body see me, or was they blind?"

They asked him about the man he had killed.

"Name Sanford," he said, standing still, with his foot out, as if he were trying to recall something particular and minute. "But he didn't have nothing and he didn't have no folks. No more'n me. Him and me, we took up together two weeks back." He looked up at their faces as if for support. "He was uppity, though. He bragged. He carried a gittar around." He whimpered. "It was his notion to run off with the car."

Harris, fresh from the barbershop, was standing in the filling station where his car was being polished.

A ring of little boys in bright shirt-tails surrounded him and the car, with some colored boys waiting behind them.

"Could they git all the blood off the seat and the steerin' wheel, Mr. Harris?"

He nodded. They ran away.

"Mr. Harris," said a little colored boy who stayed. "Does you want the box?"

"The what?"

He pointed, to where it lay in the back seat with the sample cases. "The po' kilt man's gittar. Even the policemans didn't want it."

"No," said Harris, and handed it over.

The Mark on the Wall
(1921)

VIRGINIA WOOLF

Perhaps it was the middle of January in the present year that I first looked up and saw the mark on the wall. In order to fix a date it is necessary to remember what one saw. So now I think of the fire; the steady film of yellow light upon the page of my book; the three chrysanthemums in the round glass bowl on the mantelpiece. Yes, it must have been the winter time, and we had just finished our tea, for I remember that I was smoking a cigarette when I looked up and saw the mark on the wall for the first time. I looked up through the smoke of my cigarette and my eye lodged for a moment upon the burning coals, and that old fancy of the crimson flag flapping from the castle tower came into my mind, and I thought of the cavalcade of red knights riding up the side of the black rock. Rather to my relief the sight of the mark interrupted the fancy, for it is an old fancy, an automatic fancy, made as a child perhaps. The mark was a small round mark, black upon the white wall, about six or seven inches above the mantelpiece.

How readily our thoughts swarm upon a new object, lifting it a little way, as ants carry a blade of straw so feverishly, and then leave it. . . . If that mark was made by a nail, it can't have been for a picture, it must have been for a miniature—the miniature of a lady with white powdered curls, powder-dusted cheeks, and lips like red carnations. A fraud of course, for the people who had this house before us would have chosen pictures in that way—an old picture for an old room. That is the sort of people they were—very interesting people, and I think of them so often, in such queer places, because one will never see them again, never know what happened next. They wanted to leave this house because they wanted to change their style of furniture, so he said, and he was in process of saying that in his opinion art should have ideas behind it when we were torn asunder, as one is torn from the old lady about to pour out tea and the young man about to hit the tennis ball in the back garden of the suburban villa as one rushes past in the train.

But as for that mark, I'm not sure about it; I don't believe it was made by a nail after all; it's too big, too round, for that. I might get up, but if I got up and looked at it, ten to one I shouldn't be able to say for certain; because once a thing's done, no one ever knows how it happened. Oh! dear me, the mystery of life; The inaccuracy of thought! The ignorance of humanity! To show how very little control of our possessions we have—what an accidental affair this living is after all our civilization—let me just count over a few of the things lost in one lifetime, beginning, for that seems always the most mysterious of losses—what cat would gnaw, what rat would nibble—three pale blue canisters of book-binding tools? Then there

929

were the bird cages, the iron hoops, the steel skates, the Queen Anne coal-scuttle, the bagatelle board, the hand organ—all gone, and jewels, too. Opals and emeralds, they lie about the roots of turnips. What a scraping paring affair it is to be sure! The wonder is that I've any clothes on my back, that I sit surrounded by solid furniture at this moment. Why, if one wants to compare life to anything, one must liken it to being blown through the Tube at fifty miles an hour—landing at the other end without a single hairpin in one's hair! Shot out at the feet of God entirely naked! Tumbling head over heels in the asphodel meadows like brown paper parcels pitched down a shoot in the post office! With one's hair flying back like the tail of a race-horse. Yes, that seems to express the rapidity of life, the perpetual waste and repair; all so casual, all so haphazard. . . .

But after life. The slow pulling down of thick green stalks so that the cup of the flower, as it turns over, deluges one with purple and red light. Why, after all, should one not be born there as one is born here, helpless, speechless, unable to focus one's eyesight, groping at the roots of the grass, at the toes of the Giants? As for saying which are trees, and which are men and women, or whether there are such things, that one won't be in a condition to do for fifty years or so. There will be nothing but spaces of light and dark, intersected by thick stalks, and rather higher up perhaps, rose-shaped blots of an indistinct colour—dim pinks and blues—which will, as time goes on, become more definite, become—I don't know what. . . .

And yet that mark on the wall is not a hole at all. It may even be caused by some round black substance, such as a small rose leaf, left over from the summer, and I, not being a very vigilant housekeeper—look at the dust on the mantelpiece, for example, the dust which, so they say, buried Troy three times over, only fragments of pots utterly refusing annihilation, as one can believe.

The tree outside the window taps very gently on the pane. . . . I want to think quietly, calmly, spaciously, never to be interrupted, never to have to rise from my chair, to slip easily from one thing to another, without any sense of hostility, or obstacle. I want to sink deeper and deeper, away from the surface, with its hard separate facts. To steady myself, let me catch hold of the first idea that passes. . . . Shakespeare. . . . Well, he will do as well as another. A man who sat himself solidly in an arm-chair, and looked into the fire, so—A shower of ideas fell perpetually from some very high Heaven down through his mind. He leant his forehead on his hand, and people, looking in through the open door,—for this scene is supposed to take place on a summer's evening—But how dull this is, this historical fiction! It doesn't interest me at all. I wish I could hit upon a pleasant track of thought, a track indirectly reflecting credit upon myself, for those are the pleasantest thoughts, and very frequent even in the minds of modest mouse-coloured people, who believe genuinely that they dislike to hear their own praises. They are not thoughts directly praising oneself; that is the beauty of them; they are thoughts like this:

"And then I came into the room. They were discussing botany. I said how I'd seen a flower growing on a dust heap on the site of an old house in Kingsway. The seed, I said, must have been sown in the reign of Charles the First. What flowers grew in the reign of Charles the First?" I asked—(but I don't remember the answer). Tall flowers with purple tassels to them perhaps. And so it goes on. All the time I'm dressing up the figure of myself in my own mind, lovingly, stealthily, not openly adoring it, for if I did that, I should catch myself out, and stretch my hand at once for a book in self-protection. Indeed, it is curious how instinctively one protects the image of oneself from idolatry or any other handling that could make it ridiculous, or too unlike the original to be believed in any longer. Or is it not so very curious after all? It is a matter of great importance. Suppose the looking glass smashes, the image disappears, and the romantic figure with the green of forest depths all about it is there no longer, but only that shell of a person which is seen by other people—what an airless, shallow, bald, prominent world it becomes! A world not to be lived in. As we face each other in omnibuses and underground railways we are looking into the mirror; that accounts for the vagueness, the gleam of glassiness, in our eyes. And the novelists in future will realize more and more the importance of these reflections, for of course there is not one reflection but an almost infinite number; those are the depths they will explore, those the phantoms they will pursue, leaving the description of reality more and more out of their stories, taking a knowledge of it for granted, as the Greeks did and Shakespeare perhaps—but these generalizations are very worthless. The military sound of the word is enough. It recalls leading articles, cabinet ministers—a whole class of things indeed which as a child one thought the thing itself, the standard thing, the real thing, from which one could not depart save at the risk of nameless damnation. Generalizations bring back somehow Sunday in London, Sunday afternoon walks, Sunday luncheons, and also ways of speaking of the dead, clothes, and habits—like the habit of sitting all together in one room until a certain hour, although nobody liked it. There was a rule for everything. The rule for tablecloths at that particular period was that they should be made of tapestry with little yellow compartments marked upon them, such as you may see in photographs of the carpets in the corridors of the royal palaces. Tablecloths of a different kind were not real tablecloths. How shocking, and yet how wonderful it was to discover that these real things, Sunday luncheons, Sunday walks, country houses, and tablecloths were not entirely real, were indeed half phantoms, and the damnation which visited the disbeliever in them was only a sense of illegitimate freedom. What now takes the place of those things I wonder, those real standard things? Men perhaps, should you be a woman; the masculine point of view which governs our lives, which sets the standard, which establishes Whitaker's Table of Precedency, which has become, I suppose, since the war half a phantom to many men and women, which soon, one may hope, will be laughed into the dustbin where the phantoms go, the mahogany sideboards and the Landseer prints, Gods and Devils, Hell and so forth, leaving us all with an intoxicating sense of illegitimate freedom—if freedom exists. . . .

In certain lights that mark on the wall seems actually to project from the wall. Nor is it entirely circular. I cannot be sure, but it seems to cast a perceptible shadow, suggesting that if I ran my finger down that strip of the wall it would, at a certain point, mount and descend a small tumulus, a smooth tumulus like those barrows on the South Downs which are, they say, either tombs or camps. Of the two I should prefer them to be tombs, desiring melancholy like most English people, and finding it natural at the end of a walk to think of the bones stretched beneath the turf. . . . There must be some book about it. Some antiquary must have dug up those bones and given them a name. . . . What sort of a man is an antiquary, I wonder? Retired Colonels for the most part, I daresay, leading parties of aged labourers to the top here, examining clods of earth and stone, and getting into correspondence with the neighbouring clergy, which, being opened at breakfast time, gives them a feeling of importance, and the comparison of arrow-heads necessitates cross-country journeys to the county towns, an agreeable necessity both to them and to their elderly wives, who wish to make plum jam or to clean out the study, and have every reason for keeping that great question of the camp or the tomb in perpetual suspension, while the Colonel himself feels agreeably philosophic in accumulating evidence on both sides of the question. It is true that he does finally incline to believe in the camp; and, being opposed, indites a pamphlet which he is about to read at the quarterly meeting of the local society when a stroke lays him low, and his last conscious thoughts are not of wife or child, but of the camp and that arrowhead there, which is now in the case at the local museum, together with the foot of a Chinese murderess, a handful of Elizabethan nails, a great many Tudor clay pipes, a piece of Roman pottery, and the wine-glass that Nelson drank out of—proving I really don't know what.

No, no, nothing is proved, nothing is known. And if I were to get up at this very moment and ascertain that the mark on the wall is really—what shall we say?—the head of a gigantic old nail, driven in two hundred years ago, which has now, owing to the patient attrition of many generations of housemaids, revealed its head above the coat of paint, and is taking its first view of modern life in the sight of a white-walled fire-lit room, what should I gain?—Knowledge? Matter for further speculation? I can think sitting still as well as standing up. And what is knowledge? What are our learned men save the descendants of witches and hermits who crouched in caves and in woods brewing herbs, interrogating shrew-mice and writing down the language of the stars? And the less we honour them as our superstitions dwindle and our respect for beauty and health of mind increases. . . . Yes, one could imagine a very pleasant world. A quiet, spacious world, with the flowers so red and blue in the open fields. A world without professors or specialists or house-keepers with the profiles of policemen, a world which one could slice with one's thought as a fish slices the water with his fin, grazing the stems of the water-lilies, hanging suspended over nests of white sea eggs. . . . How peace-ful it is down here, rooted in the centre of the world and gazing up through the grey waters, with their sudden gleams of light, and their reflections—if it were not for Whitaker's Almanack—if it were not for the Table of Precedency!

I must jump up and see for myself what that mark on the wall really is—a nail, a rose-leaf, a crack in the wood?

Here is nature once more at her old game of self-preservation. This train of thought, she perceives, is threatening mere waste of energy, even some collision with reality, for who will ever be able to lift a finger against Whitaker's Table of Precedency? The Archbishop of Canterbury is followed by the Lord High Chancellor; the Lord High Chancellor is followed by the Archbishop of York. Everybody follows somebody, such is the philosophy of Whitaker; and the great thing is to know who follows whom. Whitaker knows, and let that, so Nature counsels, comfort you, instead of enraging you; and if you can't be comforted, if you must shatter this hour of peace, think of the mark on the wall.

I understand Nature's game—her prompting to take action as a way of ending any thought that threatens to excite or to pain. Hence, I suppose, comes our slight contempt for men of action—men, we assume, who don't think. Still, there's no harm in putting a full stop to one's disagreeable thoughts by looking at a mark on the wall.

Indeed, now that I have fixed my eyes upon it, I feel that I have grasped a plank in the sea; I feel a satisfying sense of reality which at once turns the two Archbishops and the Lord High Chancellor to the shadows of shades. Here is something definite, something real. Thus, waking from a midnight dream of horror, one hastily turns on the light and lies quiescent, worshipping the chest of drawers, worshipping solidity, worshipping reality, worshipping the impersonal world which is a proof of some existence other than ours. That is what one wants to be sure of. . . . Wood is a pleasant thing to think about. It comes from a tree; and trees grow, and we don't know how they grow. For years and years they grow, without paying any attention to us, in meadows, in forests, and by the side of rivers—all things one likes to think about. The cows swish their tails beneath them on hot afternoons; they paint rivers so green that when a moorhen dives one expects to see its feathers all green when it comes up again. I like to think of the fish balanced against the stream like flags blown out; and of water-beetles slowly raising domes of mud upon the bed of the river. I like to think of the tree itself: first the close dry sensation of being wood; then the grinding of the storm; then the slow, delicious ooze of sap. I like to think of it, too, on winter's nights standing in the empty field with all leaves close-furled, nothing tender exposed to the iron bullets of the moon, a naked mast upon an earth that goes tumbling, tumbling, all night long. The song of birds must sound very loud and strange in June; and how cold the feet of insects must feel upon it, as they make laborious progresses up the creases of the bark, or sun themselves upon the thin green awning of the leaves, and look straight in front of them with diamond-cut red eyes. . . . One by one the fibres snap beneath the immense cold pressure of the earth, then the last storm comes and, falling, the highest branches drive deep into the ground again. Even so, life isn't done with; there are a million patient, watchful lives still for a tree, all over the world, in bedrooms, in ships, on the pavement, lining rooms, where men and women sit after tea, smoking cigarettes. It is full of peaceful thoughts, happy thoughts, this tree. I should like to take each one separately—but something is getting in the way. . . . Where was I? What has it all been about? A tree? A river? The Downs? Whitaker's Almanack? The fields of asphodel? I can't remember a thing. Everything's moving, falling, slipping, vanishing. . . . There is a vast upheaval of matter. Someone is standing over me and saying—

"I'm going out to buy a newspaper."

"Yes?"

"Though it's no good buying newspapers. . . . Nothing ever happens. Curse this war; God damn this war!. . . All the same, I don't see why we should have a snail on our wall."

Ah, the mark on the wall! It was a snail.

Down by the Riverside
(1938)

RICHARD WRIGHT

I

Each step he took made the old house creak as though the earth beneath the foundations were soggy. He wondered how long the logs which supported the house could stand against the water. But what really worried him were the steps; they might wash away at any moment, and then they would be trapped. He had spent all that morning trying to make them secure with frayed rope, but he did not have much faith. He walked to the window and the half-rotten planks sagged under his feet. He had never realized they were that shaky. He pulled back a tattered curtain, wishing the dull ache would leave his head. Ah been feverish all day. Feels like Ah got the flu. Through a dingy pane he saw yellow water swirling around a corner of the barn. A steady drone filled his ears. In the morning the water was a deep brown. In the afternoon it was a clayey yellow. And at night it was black, like a restless tide of liquid tar. It was about six feet deep and still rising; it had risen two feet that day. He squinted at a tiny ridge of white foam where the yellow current struck a side of the barn and veered sharply. For three days he had been watching that tiny ridge of white foam. When it shortened he had hopes of seeing the ground soon; but when it lengthened he knew that the current was flowing strong again. All the seeds for spring planting were wet now. They gonna rot, he thought with despair. The morning before he had seen his only cow, Sally, lowing, wagging her head, rolling her eyes, and pushing through three feet of water for the hills. It was then that Sister Jeff had said that a man who would not follow a cow was a fool. Well, he had not figured it that way. This was his home. But now he would have to leave, for the water was rising and there was no telling when or where it would stop.

Two days ago he had told Bob to take the old mule to Bowman's plantation and sell it, or swap it for a boat, any kind of a boat. N Bob ain back here yit. Ef it ain one thing its ernother. When it rains it pos. But, Lawd, ef only tha ol levee don break. Ef only tha ol levee don break . . .

He turned away from the window, rubbing his forehead. A good dose of quinine would kill that fever. But he had no quinine. Lawd, have mercy!

And worst of all there was Lulu flat on her back these four days, sick with a child she could not deliver. His lips parted in silent agony. It just did not seem fair that one man should be hit so hard and on so many sides at once. He shifted the weight of his body from his right foot to his left, listening for sounds from the front room, wondering how Lulu was. Ef she don have the baby soon Ahma have t git her outta here, some way . . .

He leaned against a damp wall. Whut in the worls keepin Bob so long? Well, in a way all of this was his own fault. He had had a chance to get away and he had acted like a fool and had not taken it. He had figured that the water would soon go down. He had thought if he stayed he would be the first to get back to the fields and start spring plowing. But now even the mule was gone. Yes, he should have cleared-out when the Government offered him the boat. Now he had no money for a boat, and Bob had said that he could not even get near that Red Cross.

He took a gourd from the wall and dipped some muddy water out of a bucket. It tasted thick and bitter and he could not swallow it. He hung the gourd back and spat the water into a corner. He cocked his head, listening. It seemed he had heard the sound of a shot. There it was again. Something happenin in town, he thought. Over the yellow water he heard another shot, thin, dry, far away. Mus be trouble, mus be trouble somewhere. He had heard that the white folks were threatening to conscript all Negroes they could lay their hands on to pile sand- and cement-bags on the levee. And they were talking about bringing in soldiers, too. They were afraid of stores and homes being looted. Yes, it was hard to tell just what was happening in town. Shucks, in time like these they'll shoota nigger down jus lika dog n think nothin of it. Tha shootin might mean anything. But likely as not it, jus some po black man gone . . .

He faced the window again, thinking, Ahma git mah pistol outts the dresser drawer when Ah go inter Lulus room. He rolled the tattered curtain up as far as it would go; a brackish light seeped into the kitchen. He looked out; his house was about twelve feet above the water. And water was everywhere. Yellow water. Swirling water. Droning water. For four long days and nights it had been there, flowing past. For a moment he had the illusion that that water had always been there, and would always be there. Yes, it seemed that the water had always been there and this was just the first time he had noticed it. Mabbe somebody jus *dropped* them houses n tree down inter tha watah . . . He felt giddy and a nervous shudder went through him. He rubbed his eyes. Lawd, Ah got fever. His head ached and felt heavy; he wanted sleep and rest.

The view opposite his window was clear for half a mile. Most of the houses had already washed away. Nearby a few trees stood, casting black shadows into the yellow water. The sky was gray with the threat of rain. Suddenly every muscle in his body stretched taut as a low rumble of thunder rose and died away. He shook his head. Nothin could be worsen rain right now. A heavy rainll carry tha old levee erway sho as hell . . .

"Brother Mann!"

He turned and saw Sister Jeff standing in the hall door.

"How Lulu?" he asked.

The old woman shook her head.

"She poly."

"Yuh reckon she'll have it soon?"

"Cant say, Brother Mann. Mabbe she will n mabbe she wont. She havin the time of her life."

"Cant we do nothin fer her?"

"Naw. We jus have t wait, thas all. Lawd, Ahm scared she'll never have tha baby widout a doctah. Her hips is jus too little."

"There ain no way t git a doctah now."

"But yuh gotta do something, Brother Mann."

"Ah don know whut t do," he sighed. "Where Peewee?"

"He sleep, in Lulus room."

She came close to him and looked hard into his face.

"Brother Mann, there ain nothin t eat in the house. Yuh gotta do something."

He turned from her, back to the window.

"Ah sent Bob wid the mule t try t git a boat," he said.

She sighed. He swallowed with effort, hearing the whisper of her soft shoes die away down the hall. No boat. No money. No doctah. Nothin t eat. N Bob ain back here yit. Lulu could not last much longer this way. If Bob came with a boat he would pile Lulu in and row her over to that Red Cross Hospital, no matter *what*. The white folks would take her in. They would *have* to take her in. They would not let a woman die just because she was black; they would not let a baby kill a woman. They would *not*. He grew rigid, looking out of the window, straining to listen. He thought he had heard another shot. But the only sound was the drone of swirling water. The water was darkening. In the open stretches it was a muddy yellow; but near the houses and trees it was growing black. Its gittin night, he thought. Then came the sound of shots, thin, dry, distant. Wun ... Tuh . . . Three . . .

"Brother Mann! Its Bob!"

He hurried to the front door, walking heavily on the heels of his big shoes. He saw Bob standing far down on the long steps near the water, bending over and fumbling with a coil of rope. Behind him a white rowboat trembled in the current.

"How yuh come out, Bob?"

Bob looked up and flashed a while grin.

"See?" he said, pointing to the white boat.

Mann's whole body glowed. Thank Gawd, we gotta boat! Now we kin git erway . . .

"Who yuh git from?"

Bob did not answer. He drew the rope tight and came up the steps.

"Ahm one tired soul," Bob said.

They went into the hall. Mann watched Bob pull out a pocket handkerchief and mop his black face. Peewee came in, rubbing his eyes and looking at Bob.

"Yuh git a boat, Uncle Bob?"

"Keep quiet, Peewee," said Mann.

Sister Jeff and Grannie came and stood behind Peewee. They looked from Bob to Mann. Bob tucked his handkerchief away, taking his time to do it, laughing a little.

"Lawd, Ahm one tired soul," he said again.

"Who bought the mule?" asked Mann.

"Ol man Bowman bought the mule, but he didnt wanna pay me much." Bob paused and pulled out a crumpled wad of one-dollar bills. "He gimme fifteen dollars . . ."

"Is that *all* he give yuh?"

"Every penny, so hep me Gawd! N tha ol stingy white ape didnt wanna gimme tha, neither. Lawd, ol man Bowman had pila dough on im big ernuff t choka cow! Ah swear t Gawd Ah never wanted t rob a man so much in all mah life . . ."

"Don yuh go thinkin sin, Bob!" said Grannie. "Wes got ernuff trouble here now widout yuh thinkin sin!"

Bob looked at her.

"Its a boat!" cried Peewee, running from the front door.

Mann stood fingering the bills.

"But how yuh git tha boat, Bob?" he asked.

"Is it our boat?" Peewee asked.

"Hush, Peewee!" Grannie said.

"Don worry! Yuhll git a chance t ride in tha boat, Peewee," said Bob. He laughed and caught Peewee in his arms. He looked around, then dropped into a chair. "When Ah lef Bowmans place Ah caughta ride downtown in a motorboat wid Brother Hall. Ah went everwheres, lookin high n low fer a boat. Some wanted forty dollahs. Some fifty. Ah met one man whut wanted a hundred. Ah couldnt buy a boat nowheres, so Ah ups n steals a boat when nobody wuz lookin . . . "

"Yuh *stole* the boat?" asked Mann.

"There wouldnt be no boat out there now ef Ah hadnt."

"Son, yuh a fool t go stealin them white folks boats in times like these," said Grannie.

Bob slapped his thigh and laughed.

"Awright, Ma, Ahll take the boat back. Hows tha? Wan me t take it back?"

Grannie turned away.

"Ah ain gonna ride in it," she said.

"Awright. Stay here n drown in the watah," said Bob. Mann sighed.

"Bob, Ah sho wished yuh hadnt stole it."

"Aw," said Bob with an impatient wave of his hand. "Whut yuh so scared fer? Ain nobody gonna see yuh wid it. All yuh gotta do is git in n make fer the hills n make fer em quick. Ef Ah hadnt stole tha boat yuh all woulda had t stay here till the watah washed yuh erway . . ." He pushed Peewee off his knee and looked up seriously. "How Lulu?"

"She poly," said Sister Jeff.

Grannie came forward.

"Whutcha gonna do, Mann? Yuh gonna take Lulu in the boat Bob done stole? Yuh know them white folks is gonna be lookin fer tha boat. Sistah James boy got killed in a flood jus like this . . ."

"She cant stay here in the fix she in," said Mann.

"Is Ah goin, Pa?" asked Peewee.

"Shut up fo Ah slaps yuh!" said Grannie.

"Whutcha gonna do, Brother Mann?" asked Sister Jeff. Mann hesitated.

"Wrap her up," he said. "Ahma row her over t the Red Cross Hospital ... "

Bob stood up. "Red Cross Hospital? Ah thought yuh said yuh wuz gonna make fer the hills?"

"We gotta git Lulu t a doctah," said Mann.

"Yuh mean t take her in the boat Ah *stole?*"

"There ain nothin else t do."

Bob scratched his head.

"Mann, Ahm mighty scared yuhll git in trouble takin tha boat thu town. Ah stole tha boat from the Pos Office. Its old man Heartfields, n yuh know how he hates niggers. Everybody knows his boat when they see it; its white n yuh couldnt git erway wid it. N lissen, theres trouble a-startin in town, too. The levees still over-flowin in the Noth, n theys spectin the one by the cement plant t go any minute. They done put ever nigger they could fin on the levee by the railroad, pilin san n cement bags. They drivin em like slaves. Ah heard they done killed

938

two-three awready whut tried t run erway. N ef anything happened t yuh, yuh just couldn't git erway, cause two mo bridges done washed erway this mawnin n ain no trains runnin. Things awful bad there in town. A lotta them white folks done took down wid typhoid, n tha Red Cross is vaxinatin everybody, black n white. Everwhere Ah looked wuznt nothin but white men wid guns. They wuz a-waiting fer the soljers when Ah lef, n yuh know whut tha means . . ."

Bob's voice died away and they could hear Lulu groaning in the front room.

"Is yuh gonna take her, Brother Mann?" asked Sister Jeff.

"There ain nothin else t do," said Mann. "Ahll try t take tha boat back t the white folks aftah Ah git Lulu t the hospital. But Ah sho wish yuh hadnt stole tha boat, Bob. But we gotta use it now. Ah don like t rile them white folks . . ."

"Ah ain goin in tha boat!" said Grannie. "Ah ain goin outta here t meet mah death today!"

"Stay here n drown, then!" said Mann. "Ahm takin Lulu t the hospital!"

Grannie cried and went into the front room. Sister Jeff followed.

"Pa, is Ah goin?" asked Peewee.

"Yeah. Git yo cloes. N tell Grannie t git hers if she don wanna stay here, cause Ahm gittin ready t leave!"

Bob was restless. He pursed his lips and looked at the floor.

"Yuh gotta hard job, rowin tha boat from here t the hospital. Yuhll be rowin ergin the current ever inch n wid a boat full itll be the Devil t pay. The watahs twelve foot deep n flowin strong n tricky."

"There ain nothin else t do," sighed Mann.

"Yuh bettah take something wid yuh. Tha ain nobodys plaything there in town."

"Ahma take mah gun," said Mann. "But Ahm sho sorry yuh had t steal them white folks boat . . ."

Like a far away echo a voice floated over the water.

"Brother Mann! Yuh there, Brother Mann!"

"Thas Elder Murray," said Bob.

Mann opened the door. It was pitch black outside. A tall man was standing in a rowboat, his hand holding onto a rope by the steps.

"Tha yuh, Brother Mann?"

"How yuh, Elder?"

"Yuh all ain gone yit?"

"We jus fixin t go. Won't yuh come up?"

"Jes fer a minute."

Murray came up the steps and stood in the doorway, rubbing his hands.

"How Sistah Lulu?"

"We aimin t take her t the Red Cross . . ."

"Yuh mean t say she ain had tha baby *yit?*"

"She too little t have it widout a doctah, Elder."

"Lawd, have mercy! Kin Ah see her?"

Mann led the way into Lulu's room where a smoking pine-knot made shadows blink on the walls. Bob, Peewee, Sister Jeff, Grannie, Murray and Mann stood about the bed. Lulu lay on top of the bed-covers, wrapped in a heavy quilt. Her hair was disordered and her face was wet. Her breath came fast.

"How yuh feelin, Sistah Lulu?" asked Murray.

Lulu looked at him weakly. She was a small woman with large shining eyes. Her arms were stretched out at her sides and her hands clutched the quilt.

"How yuh feelin?" asked Murray again.

"She awful weak," said Grannie.

Murray turned to Mann.

"Lissen, yuh bettah be mighty careful takin tha boat thu town. Them white folks is makin trouble n that currents strong."

Mann turned from the bed to the dresser, eased his pistol out of the top drawer and slipped it into his pocket.

"Pa, whuts that?" asked Peewee.

"Hush!" said Mann.

"Brothers n Sistahs, les all kneel n pray," said Murray.

They all got to their knees. Lulu groaned. For a split second a blue sheet of lightning lit up the room, then a hard clap of thunder seemed to rock the earth. No one spoke until the last rumble had rolled away.

"Lawd Gawd Awmighty in Heaven, wes a-bowin befo Yuh once ergin, humble in Yo sight, a-pleadin fer fergiveness n mercy! Hear us today, Lawd! Hear us today ef Yuh ain never heard us befo! We needs Yuh now t hep us n guide us! N hep these po folks, Lawd! Deys Yo chillun! Yuh made em n Yuh made em in Yo own image! Open up their hearts n hep em t have faith in Yo word! N hep this po woman, Lawd! Ease her labor, fer Yuh said, Lawd, she has t bring foth her chillun in pain . . ."

Mann closed his eyes and rested his hands on his hips. That slow dull ache had come back to his head. He wished with all his heart that Elder Murray would hurry up and get through with the prayer, for he wanted to be in that boat. He would not feel safe until he was in that boat. It was too bad Bob had to steal it. But there was no help for that now. The quicker wes in tha boat the bettah, he thought. Ef them white folks come by here n take it back well all be jus where we wuz befo. Yeah, Ahma take tha boat back to the white folks aftah Ah git Lulu t the hospital. Oh, yeah! Mabbe the Elderll take *mah* boat n lemme have *his* since hes on his way t the hills? Lawd, yeah! Thall be a good way to dodge them white folks! Ahma ast im . . .

". . . Lawd, Yuh said call on Yo name n Yuhd answer! Yuh said seek n fin! Today wes callin on Yuh n wes seekin Yuh, Lawd! Yuh said believe in the blooda Yo son Jesus, n today wes believin n waitin fer Yuh t hep us! N soften the hard hearts of them white folks there in town, Lawd! Purify their hearts! Fer Yuh said, Lawd, only clean hearts kin come t Yuh fer mercy . . ."

Mann rubbed his eyes and cleared his throat. Naw, he thought, ain no use astin the Elder t take mah boat. Hell wanna know why n then Ahll have t tell im Bob stole it. N the Elder ain gonna hep nobody he thinks ain doin right. Mabee ef Ah tol ol man Hertfiel jus why Bob stole his boat mabbe he wont hol it ergin me? Yeah, he oughta be glad ef Ah brings im his boat back. N yeah, mabbe the Elder kin take Sistah Jeff n Bob t the hills in his boat? Thad hep a lots . . .

". . . n save our souls for Jesus sake! Ahmen!"

Murray stood up and began to sing. The others chimed in softly.

> *Ahm gonna lay down mah sword n shiel*
> *Down by the riverside*
> *Down by the riverside*

Down by the riverside
Ahm gonna lay down mah sword n shiel
Down by the riverside
Ah ain gonna study war no mo . . .

Ah ain gonna study war no mo
Ah ain gonna study war no mo
Ah ain gonna study war no mo
Ah ain gonna study war no mo
Ah ain gonna study war no mo
Ah ain gonna study war no mo . . .

Murray wiped his mouth with the back of his hand and fumbled with his hat.

"Waal, Brothers n Sistahs. Ahm gittin on t the hills. Mah folks is there awready. Ah gotta boatloada stuff outside, but theres room fer two-three mo ef anybody wanna go."

"Kin yuh take Sistah Jeff n Bob erlong?" asked Mann.

"Sho!"

Grannie was crying; she pulled on her coat and went into the hall. Bob came from the kitchen with a bundle. Mann lifted Lulu in his arms. Murray held the door for him. Peewee followed, holding a ragged teddy bear. Sister Jeff put out the pine-knot. They all paused in the front doorway.

"Bob, yuh bettah go down n steady tha boat," said Mann.

"Lemme go wid yuh!" said Peewee.

"Yuh c mere!" said Grannie, grabbing his arm.

Bob pulled the boat close to the steps. Mann went down sideways, slowly.

"Take it easy, Brother Mann!" called Murray.

Mann stepped into the boat and rested Lulu in the back seat. Bob held her by the shoulders. C mon, yuh all!" Mann called to Grannie and Peewee.

They came, stepping gingerly. Murray helped them down.

"Ahll see yuh all at the hills!" he said.

Bob and Sister Jeff got into Murray's boat. Murray was first to shove off.

"Ahm gone, folks! Good-bye n Gawd bless yuh!"

"Good-bye!"

Mann grasped the oars, wet the handles to prevent creaking, dipped, pulled, and the boat glided outward, over the darkening flood.

II

To all sides of Mann the flood rustled, gurgled, droned, glistening blackly like an ocean of bubbling oil. Above his head the sky was streaked with faint grey light. The air was warm, humid, blowing in fitful gusts. All around he was ringed in by walls of solid darkness. He knew that houses and trees were hidden by those walls and he knew he had to be careful. As he rowed he could feel the force of the current tugging at his left. With each sweep of the oars he weighed the bulk of the boat in his back, his neck, his shoulders. And fear flowed under everything. Lawd, ef only tha ol levee don break! An oak tree loomed ghostily, its leaves whispering. He remembered it had stood at the fork of a road. His mind weaved about the clue of the tree a quick image of cornfield in sunshine. He would have to turn here at a sharp angle and make for the railroad. With one oar resting, he turned by paddling with the other. The boat struck the current full, and spun. He bent to with the oars, straining, sweeping hard, feeling that now he must fight. He would have to keep the boat moving at a steady pace if he wanted to row in a straight line. And the strokes of the oars would have to be timed, not a second apart. He bent to, lifting the oars; he leaned back, dipping them; then he pulled with tight fingers, feeling the glide of the boat over the water in darkness. Lawd, ef only tha old levee don break!

He began to look for the cotton-seed mill that stood to the left of the railroad. He peered, longing to see black stack-pipes. They were along here somewhere. Mabbe Ah done passed it? He turned to the right, bending low, looking. Then he twisted about and squinted his eyes. He stopped the boat; the oars dangled. He felt a sudden swerve that tilted him.

"Peewee, keep still!" Grannie whispered.

Lulu groaned. Mann felt wild panic. Quickly he retraced in his mind the route over which he thought he had come, and wondered what could be on the ground, what landmarks the water hid. He looked again, to the right, to the left, and over his shoulder. Then he looked straight upward. Two tall, black stack-pipes loomed seemingly a foot from his eyes. Ah wuznt lookin high ernuff, he thought. Westward would be houses. And straight down would be Pikes' Road. That would be the shortest way.

"Pa, is we there?" asked Peewee.

"Hush!"

He rowed from the stack-pipes, rowed with the houses in his mind, yearning for something to come out of the darkness to match an inner vision. Every six or seven strokes he twisted around to look. The current became stiff and the darkness thickened. For awhile he had the feeling that the boat was not moving. He set his heels, bent to as far as he could go, and made his sweeps with the oars as long as his arms could reach. His back was getting tired. His fingers burned; he paused a second and dipped them into the cold black water. That helped some. But there was only darkness ahead of him each time he turned to look for the houses on Pikes' Road. He wondered if he were on the *wrong* side of the mill! Mabbe Ahm headin the wrong way? He could not tell. And with each yard forward the current grew stiffer. He thought of the levee. Suddenly the boat swerved and spun. He caught his breath and plied the oars, losing all sense of direction. Is tha ol levee done broke? He heard Grannie cry: "Mann!" The boat leaped: his head hit something: stars danced in the darkness: the boat crashed with a bang: he clung to the oars, one was loose: but the other was jammed and would not move. The boat was still save for a hollow banging against a wall he could not see. He dropped the oars and groped his hands ahead in the darkness. Wood. Ridged wood. Is these them houses? He sensed that he was drifting backwards and clutched with his fingers, wincing from the sharp entry of splinters. Then he grabbed something round, cold, smooth, wet . . . It was wood. He clung tightly and stopped the boat. He could feel the tugging and trembling of the current vibrating through his body as his heart gave soft, steady throbs. He breathed hard, trying to build in his mind something familiar around the cold, wet, smooth pieces of wood. A series of pictures flashed through his mind, but none fitted. He groped higher, thinking with his fingers. Then suddenly he saw the whole street: sunshine, wagons and buggies tied to a water trough. This is old man Toms sto. And these were the railings that went around the front porch he was holding in his hands. Pikes' Road was around the house, in front of him. He thought a moment before picking up the oars, wondering if he could make it in that wild current.

"Whuts the mattah, Mann?" Grannie asked.

"Its awright," he said.

He wanted to reassure them, but he did not know what to say. Instead he grabbed the oars and placed one of them against an invisible wall. He set himself, flexed his body, and gave a shove that sent the boat spinning into the middle of the current. He righted it, striving to keep away from the houses, seeking for the street. He strained his eyes till they ached; but all he could see were dark bulks threatening on either side. Yet, that was enough to steer him clear of them. And he rowed, giving his strength to the right oar and then to the left, trying to keep in the middle.

"Look, Pa!"

"Whut?"

"Hush, Peewee!" said Grannie.

"There's lights, see?"

"Where?"

"See? Right there, over yonder!"

Mann looked, his chin over his shoulder. There were two squares of dim, yellow light. For a moment Mann was puzzled. He plied the oars and steadied the boat. Those lights seemed *too* high up. He could not associate them. But they were on Pikes' Road and they seemed about a hundred yards away. Wondah whut kin tha be? Maybe he could get some help there. He rowed again, his back to the lights; but their soft, yellow glow was in his mind. They helped him, those lights. For awhile he rowed without effort. Where there were lights there were people, and where there were people there was help. Wondah whose house is tha? Is they white folks? Fear dimmed the lights for a moment; but he rowed on and they glowed again, their soft sheen helping him to sweep the oars.

"Pa, cant we go there?"

"Hush, Peewee!"

The closer the lights came the lower they were. His mind groped frantically in the past, sought for other times on Pikes' Road and for other nights to tell him who lived where those yellow lights gleamed. But the lights remained alone, and the past would tell him nothing. Mabbe they kin phone t town n git a boat t come n git Lulu? Mabbe she kin res some there. The lights were close now. Square yellow lights framed in darkness. They were windows. He steered for the lights, feeling hunger, fatigue, thirst. The dull ache came back to his head: the oars were heavy, almost too heavy to hold: the boat glided beneath the windows: he looked, sighing.

"Is this the hospital, Pa?" asked Peewee.

"We goin in there, Mann?" asked Grannie.

"Ahma call," said Mann.

He cupped his hands to his mouth.

"Hello!"

He waited and looked at the windows; he heard the droning water swallow his voice.

"Hello!" he hollered again.

A window went up with a rasping noise. A white face came into the light. Lawd! Its a white man . . .

"Whos there?"

"Mann!"

"Who?"

"Mann! Mah wifes sick! Shes in birth! Ahm takin her t the hospital! Yuh gotta phone in there?"

"Wait a minute!"

The window was empty. There was silence; he waited, his face turned upward. He plied the oars and steadied the boat in the swift current. Again a white face came through. A pencil of light shot out into the darkness; a spot of yellow caught the boat. He blinked, blinded.

"Yuh gotta phone there, Mistah?" he called again, dodging the glare of the flash-light. Silence.

"Mah wifes sick! Yuh gotta phone!"

A voice came, cold, angry.

"Nigger, where you steal that boat?"

The window became filled with white faces. Mann saw a white woman with red hair. He fumbled for the oars in fear. He blinked his eyes as the light jumped to and fro over his face.

"Where you steal that boat, nigger! Thats *my* boat!"

Then Mann heard softer voices.

"Thats our boat, Father! Its *white!*"

"Thats our boat, Henry! Thats *our* boat . . ."

"Don't you hear me, nigger! Bring that boat back here!"

There were two pistol shots. Grannie screamed. Mann swept the oars blindly; the boat spun. Lawd, thas Heartfiel! N hes gotta gun! Mann felt the water rocking him away.

"Nigger, dont you take that boat! Ill kill you!"

He heard two more shots: loudly the boat banged against wood: he was thrown flat on his back. He jerked up and tried to keep the yellow windows in sight. For a moment he thought the windows were dark, but only the flash-light had gone out. He held his breath and felt the boat skidding along a wall, shaking with the current. Then it was still: it seemed it had become wedged between two walls: he touched a solid bulk and tried to shove away: the boat lurched: a shower of cold water sprayed him: the boat became wedged again: he looked for the windows: a third square of light burst out: he watched a white man with a hard, red face come out onto a narrow second-story porch and stand framed in a light-flooded doorway. The man was wearing a white shirt and was playing the yellow flare over the black water. In his right hand a gun gleamed. The man walked slowly down an outside stairway and stopped, crouching, at the water's edge. A throaty voice bawled:

"Nigger, bring that boat here! You *nigger!*"

Mann held still, frozen. He stared at the gun in the white man's hand. A cold lump forced its way up out of his stomach into his throat. He saw the disc of yellow sweep over the side of a house. The white man stooped, aimed and shot. He thinks Ahm over there! Lawd! Mann's mouth hung open and his lips dried as he breathed.

"You sonofabitch! Bring my boat here!"

"Mann!" Grannie whispered.

Mann fumbled in his pocket for his gun and held it ready. His hand trembled. He watched the yellow disc jump fitfully over the black water some fifty feet from him. It zigzagged, pausing for instants only, searching every inch of the water. As it crept closer Mann raised his gun.

The flare flickered to and fro. His throat tightened and he aimed. Then the flare hovered some five feet from him. He fired, twice. The white man fell backwards on the steps and slipped with an abrupt splash into the water. The flashlight went with him, its one eye swooping downward, leaving a sudden darkness. There was a scream. Mann dropped the gun into the bottom of the boat, grabbed the oars, threw his weight desperately, shoved out from the wall and paddled against the current.

"Henry! Henry!"

Mann rowed: he heard Grannie crying: he felt weak from fear: he had a choking impulse to stop: he felt he was lost because he had shot a white man: he felt there was no use in his rowing any longer: but the current fought the boat and he fought back with the oars.

"Henry! Henry!"

It was a woman's voice, pleading; then a younger voice, shrill, adolescent, insistent.

"The nigger killed him! The nigger killed father!"

Mann rowed on into the darkness, over the black water. He could not see the lights now; he was on the other side of the building. But the screams came clearly.

"Stop, nigger! *Stop!* You killed my father! You bastard! You nigger!"

"Henry! Henry!"

Mann heard Grannie and Peewee crying. But their weeping came to him from a long way off, as though it were as far away as the voices that were screaming. It was difficult for him to get his breath as he bent on the left oar, then the right, keeping the boat in the middle of the bulks of darkness. Then all at once he was limp, nerveless; he felt that getting the boat to the hospital now meant nothing. Two voices twined themselves in his ears: Stop, nigger! Stop, nigger! Henry! Henry! They echoed and re-echoed even after he was long out of earshot.

Then suddenly the rowing became a little easier. He was in the clear again, away from the houses. He did not worry about directions now, for he knew exactly where he was. Only one-half mile across Barrett's Pasture, and he would strike streets and maybe lights. He rowed on, hearing Grannie's crying and seeing Heartfield coming down the narrow steps with the flashlight and the gun. But he shot at me fo Ah shot im . . . Another thought made him drop the oars. Spose Heartfields folks phone to town n tell em Ah shot im? He looked around hopelessly in the darkness. Lawd, Ah don wanna ride mah folks right inter death! The boat drifted sideways, shaking with the tug of the current.

"Lulu," Grannie was whispering.

"How Lulu?" Mann asked.

"She sleep, Ah reckon," sighed Grannie.

Naw, Ahm gain on, no mattah *whut!* He could not turn back now for the hills, not with Lulu in this boat. Not with Lulu in the fix she was in. He gritted his teeth, caught the oars, and rowed. High over his head a plane zoomed; he looked up and saw a triangle of red and green lights winging through the darkness. His fingers were hot and loose, as though all the feeling in his hands had turned into fire. But his body was cool; a listless wind was drying the sweat on him.

"There the lights o town, Mann!" Grannie spoke.

He twisted about. Sure enough, there they were. Shining, barely shining. Dim specks of yellow buried in a mass of blackness. Lawd only knows whut wes ridin inter ... If he could only get Lulu to the hospital, if he could only get Grannie and Peewee safely out of this water, then he would take a chance on getting away. He knew that that was what they would want him to do. He swept the oars, remembering hearing tales of whole families being killed because some relative had done something wrong.

A quick, blue fork of lightning lit up the waste of desolate and tumbling waters. Then thunder exploded, loud and long, like the sound of a mountain falling. It began to rain. A sudden, sharp rain. Water trickled down the back of his neck. He felt Grannie moving; she was covering Lulu with her coat. He rowed faster, peering into the rain, wanting to reach safety before the boat caught too much water. Another fifty yards or so and he would be among the houses. Yeah, ef they ast me erbout Heartfiel Ahms tell em the truth . . . But he knew he did not want to do that. He knew that that would not help him. But what else was there for him to do? Yes, he would have to tell the truth and trust God. Nobody but God could see him through this. Bob shouldna stole this boat . . . But here Ah am in it now . . . He sighed, rowing. N this rain! Tha ol levee might go wid this rain . . . Lawd, have mercy! He lowered his chin and determined not to think. He would have to trust God and keep on and go through with it, that was all. His feet and clothes were wet. The current stiffened and brought the boat almost to a standstill. Yeah, he thought, theres Rose Street. He headed the boat between two rows of houses.

"Halt! Who goes there?"

He pulled the oars. A glare of light shot from a second-story porch and made him blink. Two white soldiers in khaki uniforms leaned over the banisters. Their faces were like square blocks of red and he could see the dull glint of steel on the tips of their rifles. Well, he would know now. Mabbe they done foun out erbout Heartfiel?

"Where you going, nigger?"

"Ahm takin mah wife t the hospital, suh. Shes in birth, suh!"

"What?"

"Mah wifes in birth, suh! Ahm takin her t the Red Cross!"

"Pull up to the steps!"

"Yessuh!"

He turned the boat and paddled toward steps that led down to the water. The two soldiers loomed over him.

"Whats your name?"

"Mann, suh."

"You got a pass?"

"Nawsuh."

"Don't you know you're violating curfew?"

"Nawsuh."

"What was all that shooting back there a little while ago?"

"Ah don know, suh."

"Didnt you hear it?"

"Nawsuh."

"Frisk im, Mac," said one of the soldiers.

"O.K. Stand up, nigger!"

One of the soldiers patted Mann's hips. Lawd, Ah hope they don see tha gun in the boat . . .

"Hes awright."

"What you say your name was?"

"Mann, suh."

"Where you from?"

"The South En, suh."

"I mean where you bring that boat from?"

"The South En, suh."

"You *rowed* here?"

"Yessuh."

"In *that* boat?"

"Yessuh."

The soldiers looked at each other.

"You aint lying, are you, nigger?"

"Oh, nawsuh," said Mann.

"What wrong with your woman?"

"Shes in birth, suh."

One of the soldiers laughed.

"Well, Ill be Goddamned! Nigger, you take the prize! I always heard that a niggerd do anything, but I never thought anybody was fool enough to row a boat against that current. . ."

"But Mistah, mah wifes sick! She been sick fo days!"

"O.K. Stay here. Ill phone for a boat to take you in."

"Yessuh."

One of the soldiers ran up the steps and the other hooked Mann's boat to a rope.

"Nigger, you dont know how lucky you are," he said. "Six men were drowned today trying to make it to town in rowboats. And here you come, rowing *three* people . . .

The soldier who had gone to telephone came back.

"Mistah, please!" said Mann. "Kin Ah take mah wife in there, outta the rain?"

The soldier shook his head.

"I'm sorry, boy. Orders is that nobody but soldiers can be in these houses. Youll have to wait for the boat. Its just around the corner; it wont be long. But I dont see how in hell you rowed that boat between those houses without drowning! It mustve been tough hunh?"

"Yessuh."

Mann saw a motorboat swing around a curve, its head-light sweeping a wide arc, its motor yammering. It glided up swiftly in a churn of foam. It was manned by two soldiers whose slickers gleamed with rain.

"Whats the rush?"

"Boy," said one of the soldiers, "I got a nigger here who beat everybody. He rowed in from the South End, against the current. Can you beat that?"

The soldiers in the boat looked at Mann.

"Says you!" said one, with a scornful wave of his white palm.

"I'm telling the truth!" said the soldier. "Didnt you, boy?"

"Yessuh."

"Well, what you want us to do about it? Give im a medal?"

"Naw; his bitch is sick. Having a picaninny. Shoot em over to the Red Cross Hospital."

The soldiers in the boat looked at Mann again.

"They crowded out over there, boy . . ."

"Lawd, have mercy!" Grannie cried, holding Lulu's head on her lap.

"Mistah, please! Mah wife cant las much longer like this," said Maan.

"Awright! Hitch your boat, nigger, and lets ride!"

Mann grabbed the rope that was thrown at him and looped it to a hook on the end of his boat. He was standing when one of the soldiers yelled:

"Watch yourself, nigger!"

The motor roared and the boat shot forward; he fell back against Grannie, Lulu and Peewee. He straightened just as they made the turn. His boat leaned, scooping water, wetting him; then it righted itself. The rest of the drive was straight ahead, into darkness. He had hardly wiped the water out of his eyes before they slowed to a stop. His fingers groped nervously in the bottom of the boat for the gun; he found it and slipped it into his pocket.

"Awright, nigger, unload!"

He stood up and fronted a row of wide steps.

"Is this the hospital, suh?"

"Yeah; straight up!"

He lifted Lulu and stepped out. Grannie followed, leading Peewee by the hand. When he reached the top of the steps the door was opened by another white soldier.

"Where you going?"

"Ah got mah wife, suh. She sick . . ."

"Straight on to the back, till you see the sign."

"Yessuh."

He walked down a dim-lit hall. Grannie and Peewee shuffled behind. He smelled the warm scent of ether and disinfectant and it made him dizzy. Finally, he saw the sign:

FOR COLORED

He pushed open a door with his shoulder and stood blinking in a blaze of bright lights. A white nurse came.

"What you want?"

"Please, Mam . . . Mah wife . . . She sick!"

The nurse threw back the quilt and felt Lulu's pulse. She looked searchingly at Mann, then turned quickly, calling:

"Doctor Burrows!"

A white doctor came. He looked at Lulu's face. Her eyes were closed and her mouth was open.

"Bring her here, to the table," said the doctor.

Mann stretched Lulu out. Her face, her hair, and her clothes were soaking wet. Her left arm fell from the table and hung limp. The doctor bent over and pushed back the lids of her eyes.

"This your woman?"

"Yessuh."

"How long was she in birth?"

"Bout fo days, suh."

"Why didnt you bring her sooner?"

"Ah didnt hava boat n the watah had me trapped, suh."

The doctor lifted his eyes, rubbed his chin, and looked at Mann quizzically.

"Well, boy, shes dead."

"Suh?"

Grannie screamed and grabbed Peewee. The doctor straightened and laid the stethoscope on a white, marble-topped table. Lightning flicked through the room and thunder rolled rumblingly away, leaving a silence filled with the drone of hard, driving rain.

"*Suh!*" said Mann.

III

"Well, boy, it's all over," said the doctor. "Maybe if you could have gotten her here a little sooner we could have saved her. The baby, anyway. But it's all over now, and the best thing for you to do is get your folks to the hills."

Mann stared at the thin, black face; at the wet clothes; at the arm hanging still and limp. His lips moved, but he could not speak. Two more white nurses and another white doctor came and stood. Grannie ran to the table.

"Lulu!"

"Its awright, Aunty," said the doctor, pulling her away.

Grannie sank to the floor, her head on her knees.

"Lawd . . ."

Mann stood like stone now. Lulu dead? He seemed not to see the white doctors and nurses gathering around, looking at him. He sighed and the lids of his eyes drooped halfway down over the pupils.

"Poor nigger," said a white nurse.

Blankly, Mann stared at her. He wet his lips and swallowed. Something pressed against his knee and he looked down. Peewee was clinging to him, his little black face tense with fear. He caught Peewee by the hand, went over to the wall and stood above Grannie, hesitating. His fingers touched her shoulders.

"Awright," said the doctor. "Roll her out."

Mann turned and saw two white nurses rolling Lulu through a door. His throat tightened. Grannie struggled up and tried to follow the body. Mann pulled her back and she dropped to the floor again crying.

"It's awright, Grannie," said Mann.

"You got a boat, boy?" asked the doctor.

"Yessuh," said Mann.

"Youre lucky. You ought to start out right now for the hills, before that current gets stronger."

"Yessuh."

Again Mann looked at Grannie and twice his hands moved toward her and stopped. It seemed that he wanted ever so much to say something, to do something, but he did not know what.

"C mon, Grannie," he said.

She did not move. A white nurse giggled, nervously. Mann stood squeezing his blistered palms, taking out of the intense pain a sort of consolation, a sort of forgetfulness. A clock began to tick. He could hear Grannie's breath catching softly in her throat; he could hear the doctors and nurses breathing; and beyond the walls of the room was the beat of sweeping rain. Somewhere a bell tolled, faint and far off.

Crash!

Everybody jumped. One of the nurses gave a short scream.

"What's that?"

"Aw, just a chair fell over. Thats all . . ."

"Oh!"

The doctors looked at the nurses and the nurses looked at the doctors. Then all of them laughed, uneasily. There was another silence. The doctor spoke.

"Is that your mother there, boy?"

"Yessuh. Mah ma-in-law."

"Youll have to get her out of here."

"C mon, Grannie," he said again.

She did not move. He stooped and picked her up.

"C mon, Peewee."

He went through the door and down the hall with Peewee pulling at the tail of his coat.

"Hey, you!"

He stopped. A white soldier came up.

"Where you going?"

"Ahm gittin mah boat t take mah family t the hills . . ."

"Your boat was commandeered. Come over here and wait awhile."

"Comman . . ."

"We were short of boats and the boys had to take yours. But Ill get a motorboat to take you and your family to the hills. Wait right here a minute . . ."

He waited with Grannie in his arms. Lawd, they got me now! They knowed that was Heartfiel's boat! Mabbe they fixin t take me erway? What would they do to a black man who had killed a white man in a flood? He did not know. But whatever it was must be something far more terrible than at other times. He shifted his weight from foot to foot. He was more tired than he could ever remember having been. He saw Lulu lying on the table; he heard the doctor say: Well, boy, shes dead. His eyes burned. Lawd, Ah don care whut they do t me! Ah don care . . .

"Pa, where ma?"

"She gone, Peewee."

"Ain she comin wid us?"

"Naw, Peewee."

"How come, Pa?"

"She gonna stay wid Gawd now, Peewee."

"Awways?"

"Awways, Peewee."

Peewee cried.

"Hush, Peewee! Be a good boy, now! Don cry! Ahm here! N Grannies here . . ."

The white soldier came back with the colonel.

"Is this the nigger?"

"Thats him."

"Was that your rowboat outside?"

Mann hesitated.

"Yessuh, Capm."

"A white boat?"

"Yessuh."

"Are you sure it was yours?"

Mann swallowed and hesitated again.

"Yessuh."

"What was it worth?"

"Ah don know, Capm."

"What did you pay for it?"

"Bout f-fifty dollahs, Ah reckon."

"Here, sign this," said the colonel, extending a piece of paper and a pencil. "We can give you thirty-five dollars as soon as things are straightened out. We had to take your boat. We were short of boats. But I've phoned for a motorboat to take you and your family to the hills. Youll be safer in that anyway."

"Yessuh."

He sat Grannie on the floor and sighed.

"Is that your mother there?"

"Yessuh. Mah ma-in-law."

"What's wrong with her?"

"She jus ol, Capm. Her gal jus died n she takes it hard."

"When did she die?"

"Jus now, suh."

"Oh, I see . . . But whats wrong with you? Are you sick?"

"Nawsuh."

"Well, you dont have to go to the hills. Your folksll go on to the hills and you can stay here and help on the levee . . ."

"Capm, please! Ahm tired!"

"This is martial law," said the colonel, turning to the white soldier. "Put this woman and boy into a boat and ship them to the hills. Give this nigger some boots and a raincoat and ship him to the levee!"

The soldier saluted.

"Yessir, Colonel!"

"CAPM, PLEASE! HAVE MERCY ON ME, CAPM!"

The colonel turned on his heels and walked away.

"AHM TIRED! LEMME GO WID MAH FOLKS, PLEASE!"

The soldier glared at Mann.

"Aw, c mon, nigger! What in hells wrong with you? All the rest of the niggers are out there, how come you don't want to go?"

Mann watched the soldier go to the door, open it and look out into the rain.

"Mann!" Grannie whispered.

He leaned to her, his hands on his knees.

"Yuh go on t the levee! Mabbe them Heartfiel folks is out t the hills by now. Git over t where our folks is n mabbe yuh kin git erway . . ."

"C mon!" called the soldier. "Heres your boat!"

"*Here*, Grannie," whispered Mann. He slipped the fifteen dollars he had gotten from Bob into her hands.

951

"Naw," she said. "*Yuh* keep it!"

"Naw, *take* it!" said Mann. He pushed the money into the pocket of her coat.

"C MON, NIGGER! THIS BOAT CANT WAIT ALL NIGHT FOR YOU!"

He picked Grannie up again and carried her down the steps. Peewee followed, crying. It was raining hard. After he had helped them into the boat he stood on the steps. Lawd, Ah wished Ah could go!

"All set?"

"All set!"

The motor droned and the boat shot out over the water, its spotlight cutting ahead into the rain.

"Good-bye!" Peewee called.

"Good-bye!" Mann was not sure that Peewee had heard and he called again. "Good-bye!"

"C mon, boy! Lets get your boots and raincoat. Youre going to the levee."

"Yessuh."

He followed the soldier into the office.

"Jack, get some hip-boots and a raincoat for this nigger and call for a boat to take him to the levee," the soldier spoke to another soldier sitting behind a desk.

"O.K. Heres some boots. And heres a raincoat."

The first soldier went out. Mann hoisted the boots high on his legs and put on the raincoat.

"Tired, nigger?" asked the soldier.

"Yessuh."

"Well, youve got a hard night ahead of you, and thats no lie."

"Yessuh."

Mann sat down, rested his head against a wall, and closed his eyes. Lawd . . . He heard the soldier talking over the telephone.

"Yeah. Yeah."

" . . . "

"The Red Cross Hospital."

"The niggers here now, waiting."

" . . . "

"O.K."

Mann heard the receiver click.

"The boatll be along any minute," said the soldier. "And while youre resting, unpack those boxes and lay the stuff on the floor."

"Yessuh."

Mann stood up and shook his head. A sharp pain stabbed at the front of his eyes and would not leave. He went to the back of the room where a pile of wooden boxes was stacked and got a crowbar. He pried open the top of a box and began to pull out raincoats and rubber boots. He worked mechanically, slowly, leaning against boxes, smelling fresh rubber and stale tobacco smoke. He felt the pistol in his pocket and remembered Heartfield. Ah got t git outta here some way. Go where they cant fin me. Lawd, take care Grannie! Take care Peewee, Lawd! Take care Bob! N hep me. Lawd. He thought of Lulu lying stretched out on the marble table with her arm hanging limp. He dropped the bundle of raincoats he was holding and bent over, sobbing.

"Whats the matter, nigger?"

"Ahm tired, Capm! Gawd knows Ahm tired!"

He slipped to the floor.

"What you crying about?"

"Capm, mah wifes dead; *Dead!*"

"Shucks, nigger! You ought to be glad youre not dead in a flood like this," said the soldier.

Mann stared at the blurred boots and raincoats. Naw, Lawd! Ah cant break down now! Theyll know somethings wrong ef Ah keep acting like this . . . Ah cant cry, bout Lulu now . . . He wiped tears from his eyes with his fingers.

"Kin Ah have some watah, Capm?"

"Theres no water anywhere. You hungry?"

He was not hungry, but he wanted to reassure the soldier.

"Yessuh."

"Heres a sandwich you can have."

"Thank yuh, suh."

He took the sandwich and bit it. The dry bread balled in his mouth. He chewed and tried to wet it. Ef only that old soljerd quit lookin at me . . . He swallowed and the hard lump went down slowly, choking him.

"Thatll make you feel better," said the soldier.

"Yessuh."

The door swung in.

"Awright, boy! Here's your boat! Lets go!"

"Yessuh."

He put the sandwich in his pocket and followed the soldier to the steps.

"Is this the nigger?"

"Yeah"

"O.K. Pile in, boy!"

He got in; the boat turned; rain whipped his face. He bent low, holding onto the sides of the boat as it sped through water. He closed his eyes and again saw Heartfield come out on the narrow porch and down the steps. He heard again the two shots of his gun. But he shot at me fo Ah shot im! Then again he saw Lulu lying on the table with her arm hanging limp. Then he heard Peewee calling. Good-bye! Hate welled up in him; he saw the two soldiers in the front seat. Their heads were bent low. They might fin out any minute now . . . His gun nestled close to his thigh. Spose Ah shot em n took the boat? Naw! Naw! It would be better to wait till he got to the levee. He would know somebody there. And they would help him. He knew they would. N them white folks might be too busy botherin wid tha levee t think erbout jus one po black man . . . Mabbe Ah kin slip thu . . .

The boat slowed. Ahead loomed the dark stackpipe of the cement plant. Above his head a hundred spot-lights etched a wide fan of yellow against the rain. As the boat swerved through a gale entrance and pulled to a platform, he saw lights and soldiers, heard voices calling. Black men stood on the edges of the platforms and loaded bags of sand and cement into boats. Long lines of boats were running to and fro between the levee and the cement plant. He felt giddy; the boat rocked. Soldiers yelled commands. An officer stepped forward and bawled:

"You get im!"

"Yeah!"

"O.K.! We got another one here. C mon, boy, hop in!"

A black boy moved forward.

"Mistah, kin Ah hava drinka watah?" asked the boy.

"Hell, naw! There's no water anywhere! Get in the boat!"

"Yessuh."

Mann moved over to make room. He felt better already. He was with his people now. Maybe he could get away yet. He heard the officer talking to the soldiers.

"Hows things?"

"Pretty bad!"

"Hows it going?"

"Still overflowing from the North!"

"You think itll hold?"

"Im scared it wont!"

"Any cracks yet?"

"Shes cracking in two places!"

One of the soldiers whistled.

"Awright, let her go."

"O.K."

The boat started out, churning water.

"Yuh gotta cigarette, Mistah?"

Mann turned and looked at the boy sitting at his side.

"Naw; Ah don smoke."

"Shucks, Ah sho wish theyd lemme handle one of these boats," said the boy.

As they neared the levee Mann could see long, black lines of men weaving snake-fashion about the levee-top. In front of him he could feel the river as though it were a live, cold hand touching his face. The levee was a ridge of dry land between two stretches of black water. The men on the levee-top moved slowly, like dim shadows. They were carrying heavy bags on their shoulders and when they reached a certain point the bags were dumped down. Then they turned around slowly, with bent backs, going to get more bags. Yellow lanterns swung jerkily, blinking out and then coming back on when someone passed in front of them. At the water's edge men unloaded boats; behind them stood soldiers with rifles. Mann held still, looking; the boat stopped and waited for its turn to dock at the levee.

Suddenly a wild commotion broke out. A siren screamed. On the levee-top the long lines of men merged into one whirling black mass. Shouts rose in a mighty roar. There came a vague, sonorous drone, like the far away buzzing in a sea-shell. Each second it grew louder. Lawd! thought Mann. That levees gone! He saw boats filling with men. There was a thunder-like clatter as their motors started up. The soldiers in the front seat were yelling at each other.

"You better turn around, Jim!"

The boat turned and started back.

"Wait for that boat and see whats happened!"

They slowed and a boat caught up with them.

"What's happened?"

"The levees gone!"

"Step on it, Jim!"

Mann held his breath; behind him were shouts, and over the shouts was the siren's scream, and under the siren's scream was the loud roar of loosened waters.

IV

The boat shot back. The siren shrieked at needle-pitch, high, thin, shrill, quivering in his ears; and yellow flares turned restlessly in the sky. The boat slowed for the platform. There was a loud clamor and men rushed about. An officer bawled:

"Line up the boats for rescue work!"

"Its risin! Cant yuh *see* it risin?" The boy at Mann's side was nudging him. Mann looked at the water; a series of slow, heaving swells was rocking the boat. He remembered that the water had been some inches below the level of the platform when he had first come; now it was rising above it. As the men worked their boats splashed in the water.

"Who can handle a boat" the officer asked.

"Ah kin, Mistah!" yelled the boy.

"Get a partner and come on!"

The boy turned to Mann.

"Yuh wanna go?"

Mann hesitated.

"Yeah. Ahll go."

"C mon!"

He climbed out and followed the boy to the end of the platform.

"Where are we sending em, General?" the officer asked.

"Shoot the first twenty to the Red Cross Hospital!"

"O.K.!" said the officer. "Whos the driver here?"

"Ahm the driver!" said the boy.

"Can you really handle a boat?"

"Yessuh!"

"Is he all right?" asked the general.

"Ah works fer Mistah Bridges," said the boy.

"We dont want too many niggers handling these boats," said the general.

"We havent enough drivers," said the officer.

"All right; let him go! Whos next?"

"Yours is the Red Cross Hospital, boy! Get there as fast as you can and get as many people out as you can and take em to the hills, see?"

"Yessuh!"

"You know the way?"

"Yessuh!"

"Whats your name?"

"Brinkley, suh!"

"All right! Get going!"

They ran to a boat and scrambled in. Brinkley fussed over the motor a minute, then raced it.

"All set!"

"O.K.!"

The boat swung out of the wide gate entrance; they were the first to go. They went fast, against the current, fronting the rain. They were back among the houses before Mann realized it. As they neared the hospital Mann wondered about the boy at his side. Would he help him to get away? Could he trust him enough to tell? If he could only stay in the boat until they carried the first load to the hills, he could slip off. He tried to see Brinkley's face, but the rain and darkness would not let him. Behind him the siren still screamed and it seemed that a thousand bells were tolling. Then the boat stopped short; Mann looked around, tense, puzzled.

"This ain the hospital," he said.

"Yeah, tis," said Brinkley.

Then he understood. He had been watching for the steps up which he had carried Lulu. But the water had already covered the steps and was making for the first floor. He looked up. The same white soldier who had let him in before was standing guard.

"C mon in!"

They went in. The hospital was in an uproar. Down the hall a line of soldiers pushed the crowds back, using their rifles long-wise. The colonel came running out; he carried an axe in his hand.

"How many boats are coming?"

"Bout twenty, suh," said Brinkley.

"Are they on the way?"

"Yessuh."

"Theyll have to hurry. That water is rising at the rate of five feet an hour!"

The colonel turned to Mann.

"Come here, boy!"

"Yessuh!"

Mann followed the colonel up a flight of stairs. They stopped in a hall.

"Listen," began the colonel. "I want you . . ."

The lights went out, plunging them in darkness.

"Goddamn!"

Mann could hear the colonel breathing in heavy gasps. Then a circle of yellow light played over a wall. The colonel was standing in front of him with a flash-light.

"Get two of those tables from back there and pile one on top of the other, right here," said the colonel, indicating a spot just left of the stairway.

When the tables were up the colonel gave Mann the axe.

"Get up there and knock a hole through that ceiling!"

"Yessuh!"

He scampered up and fumbled for a hold on the rickety tables. When he was on top the colonel set the beam of the flash-light on the ceiling.

"Work fast, boy! You've got to cut a hole through there so we can take people out if that water beats the boats!"

"Yessuh!"

He whacked upward; with each blow the axe stuck in the wood; he set his feet wide apart on the tables and jerked downward to pull it out. He forgot everything but that he must cut a hole through this ceiling to save people. Even the memory of Lulu and Heartfield was gone from him. Then the lights came back just as suddenly as they had gone. He knew that that

956

meant that the electric plant at the South End was threatened by water. As he swung the axe he felt sweat breaking out all over his body. He heard the colonel below him, fidgeting. The lights dimmed and flared again.

"Keep that light on me, Capm!"

"Awright; but hurry!"

He had six planks out of the ceiling now. He used his hands and broke them off; his fingers caught splinters. He heard someone running up the steps. He looked down; a soldier was talking to the colonel.

"Its above the steps, Colonel! Its traveling for the first floor!"

"Any boats here yet?"

"Just three, sir!"

"Order everybody to this floor, and keep them quiet even if you have to shoot!"

"Yessir!"

Mann heard the soldier running down the steps.

"C mon, boy! Get that hole bigger than that! Youve got to cut a hole through that roof yet!"

"Yessuh!"

When the hole was big enough he pushed the axe through and pulled himself into the loft. It was dark and he could hear the rain pounding. Suddenly the siren stopped. He had been hearing it all along and had grown used to it; but now that he could hear it no longer the silence it left in his mind was terrifying.

"Ah need some light up here, Capm!"

"Keep cutting! Ill get somebody to bring the flash-light up!"

The roof was easier to cut than the ceiling. He heard someone climbing up behind him. It was a white soldier with a flash-light.

"Where you want it, boy?"

"Right here, suh!"

Quickly he tore a wide hole: he felt a rush of air: rain came into his face: droning water filled his ears: he climbed onto the roof and looked below. Opposite the hospital a bunch of motorboats danced in the current. He stiffened. There was a loud cracking noise, as of timber breaking. He stretched flat on the roof and clung to the wet shingles. Moving into one of the paths of yellow light was a small house, turning like a spool in the wild waters. Unblinkingly he watched it whirl out of sight. *Mabbe Ahll never git outta here* . . . More boats were roaring up, rocking. Then he stared at the water rising; he could *see* it rising. Across from him the roofs of one-story houses were barely visible.

"Here, give a lift!"

Mann caught hold of a white hand and helped to pull a soldier through. He heard the colonel hollering.

"All set?"

"Yessuh!"

"Send the boats to the side of the hospital! We are taking em from the roof!"

Boats roared and came slowly to the wall of the hospital.

"Awright! Coming through!"

On all fours Mann helped a white woman struggle through. She was wrapped in sheets and blankets. The soldier whipped the rope around the woman's body, high under her arms.

She whimpered. Lawd, Lulu down there somewhere, Mann thought. Dead! She gonna be lef here in the flood . . .

"C mon, nigger, n give me a hand!"

"Yessuh!"

Mann caught hold of the woman and they took her to the edge of the roof. She screamed and pulled back.

"Let her go!"

They shoved her over and eased her down with the rope. She screamed again and hung limp. They took another, tied the rope, and eased her over. One woman's face was bleeding; she had scratched herself climbing through the hole. Mann could hear the soldier's breath coming in short gasps as he worked. When six had been let down a motor roared. A boat, loaded to capacity, crawled slowly away. The water was full of floating things now. Objects swirled past, were sucked out of sight. The second boat was filled. The third. Then the fourth. The fifth. Sixth. When the women and children were gone they began to ease the men over. The work went easier and faster with the men. Mann heard them cursing grimly. Now and then he remembered Lulu and Heartfield and he felt dizzy; but he would urge himself and it would pass.

"How many more, Colonel?" asked a soldier.

"About twelve! You got enough boats?"

"Just enough!"

Mann knew they had gotten them all out safely when he saw the colonel climb through. Brinkley came through last.

"Heres one more boat, without a driver!" a soldier called.

"Thas mah boat!" said Brinkley.

"Then you go next!" said the colonel.

Mann looped one end of the rope around a chimney and tied it. Brinkley caught hold and slid down, monkey-like. The colonel crawled over to Mann and caught his shoulder.

"You did well! I wont forget you! If you get out of this, come and see me, hear?"

"Yessuh!"

"Here, take this!"

Mann felt a piece of wet paper in his fingers. He tried to read it, but it was dark.

"Thats the address of a woman with two children who called in for help," said the colonel. "If you and that boy think you can save 'em, then do what you can. If you cant, then try to make it to the hills . . ."

"Yessuh!"

The colonel went down. Mann was alone. For a moment a sense of what he would have to face if he was saved from the flood came to him. Would it not be better to stay here alone like this and go down into the flood with Lulu? Would not that be better than having to answer for killing a white man?

"Yuh comin?" Brinkley called.

Mann fumbled over the roof for the axe, found it, and stuck it in his belt. He put the piece of paper in his pocket, caught hold of the rope, and crawled to the edge. Rain peppered his face as he braced his feet against the walls of the house. He held still for a second and tried to see the boat.

"C mon!"

He slumped into the seat; the boat lurched. He sighed and shed a tension which had gripped him for hours. The boat was sailing against the current.

"Here's somebody callin fer hep," said Mann, holding the piece of paper in front of Brinkley.

"Take the flash-light! Switch it on n lemme see if Ah kin read it!"

Mann held the flash-light.

"Its Pikes' Road!" said Brinkley. "Its the Pos Office! Its Miz Heartfiel . . ."

Mann stared at Brinkley, open-mouthed; the flash-light dropped into the bottom of the boat. His fingers trembled and the wind blew the piece of paper away.

"Heartfiel?"

"Ahma try to make it!" said Brinkley.

The boat slowed, turned; they shot in the opposite direction, with the current. Mann watched the head-light cut a path through the rain. Heartfiel?

V

"Watch it!"

Mann threw his hands before his eyes as though to ward off a blow. Brinkley jerked the boat to the right and shut off the motor. The current swept them backwards. In front the head-light lit a yellow circle of wet wood, showing the side of a house. The house was floating down the middle of the street. The motor raced, the boat turned and sailed down the street, going back over the route they had come. Behind them the house followed, revolving slowly, looming large. They stopped at a telegraph pole and Mann stood up and held the boat steady by clinging to a strand of cable wire that stretched above his head in the dark. All about him the torrent tumbled, droned, surged. Then the spot of light caught the house full; it seemed like a living thing, spinning slowly with a long indrawn, sucking noise; its doors, its windows its porch turning to the light and then going into the darkness. It passed. Brinkley swung the boat around and they went back down the street, cautiously this time, keeping in the middle of the current. Something struck. They looked. A chair veered, spinning, and was sucked away. An uprooted tree loomed. They dodged it. They heard noises, but could not tell the direction from which they came. When they reached Barrett's Pasture they went slower. The rain had slackened and they could see better.

"Reckon we kin make it?" asked Brinkley.

"Ah don know," whispered Mann.

They swung a curve and headed for Pikes' Road. Mann thought of Heartfield. He saw the woman with red hair standing in the lighted window. He heard her scream. Thats our boat, Henry! Thats our boat! The boat slowed, swerving for Pikes' Road. Mann had the feeling that he was in a dream. Spose Ah tol the boy? The boat rushed on into the darkness. Ef we take that woman t the hills Ahm caught! Ahead he saw a box bob up out of water and shoot under again. But mabbe they didnt see me good? He could not be sure of that. The light had been on him a long time while he was under that window. And they knew his name; he had called it out to them, twice. He ought to tell Brinkley. Ahm black like he is. He oughta be willin t hep me fo he would them . . . He tried to look into Brinkley's face; the boy was bent forward, straining his eyes, searching the surface of the black water. Lawd, Ah *got* t tell im! The boat lurched and dodged something. Its mah life ergin theirs! The boat slid on over the water.

Mann swallowed; then he felt that there would not be any use in his telling; he had waited too long. Even if he spoke now Brinkley would not turn back; they had come too far. Wild-eyed, he gazed around in the watery darkness, hearing the white boy yell, You nigger! You bastard! Naw. Lawd! *Ah got t tell im!* He leaned forward to speak and touched Brinkley's arm. The boat veered again, dodging an object that spun away. Mann held tense, waiting, looking; the boat slid on over the black water. Then he sighed and wished with all his life that he had thrown that piece of paper away.

"Yuh know the place?" asked Brinkley.

"Ah reckon so," whispered Mann.

Mann looked at the houses, feeling that he did not want to look, but looking anyway. All he could see of the one-story houses were their roofs. There were wide gaps between them; some had washed away. But most of the two-story houses were still standing. Mann craned his neck, looking for Mrs. Heartfield's house, yet dreading to see it.

"Its erlong here somewhere," said Brinkley.

Brinkley turned the boat sideways and let the spot-light play over the fronts of the two-story houses. Mann wanted to tell him to turn around, to go back, to make for the hills. But he looked, his throat tight; he looked, gripping the sides of the boat; he looked for Mrs. Heartfield's house, seeing her hair framed in the lighted window.

"There it is!" yelled Brinkley.

At first Mann did not believe it was Mrs. Heartfield's house. It was dark. And he had been watching for two squares of yellow light, two lighted windows. And now, there it was, all dark. Mabbe they ain there? A hot wish rose in his blood a wish that they were gone. Just gone anywhere, as long as they were not there to see him. He wished that their white bodies were at the bottom of the black waters. They were now ten feet from the house; the boat slowed.

"Mabbe they ain there," whispered Mann.

"We bettah call," said Brinkley.

Brinkley cupped his hand to his mouth and hollered:

"Miz Heartfiel!"

They waited, listening, looking at the dark, shut windows. Brinkley must have thought that his voice had not carried, for he hollered again:

"Miz Heartfiel!"

"They ain there," whispered Mann.

"Look! Somebody's there! See?" breathed Brinkley. "Look!"

The window was opening; Brinkley centered the spot of light on it; a red head came through. Mann sat with parted lips, looking. He leaned over the side of the boat and waited for Mrs. Heartfield to call, Henry! Henry!

"Miz Heartfiel!" Brinkley called again.

"Can you get us? Can you get us?" she was calling.

"We comin! Wait, a . . ."

A deafening noise cut out his voice. It was long, vibrant, like the sound of trees falling in storm. A tide of water swept the boat backwards. Mann heard Mrs. Heartfield scream. He could not see the house now; the spot-light lit a path of swirling black water. Brinkley raced the motor and jerked the boat around, playing the light again on the window. It was empty. There was another scream, but it was muffled.

"The watahs got em!" said Brinkley.

Again the boat headed into the middle of the current. The light was on the empty window. The house was moving down the street. Mann held his breath, feeling himself suspended over a black void. The house reached the center of the street and turned violently. It floated away from them, amid a sucking rush of water and the sound of splitting timber. It floundered; it shook in a trembling grip; then it whirled sharply to the left and crashed, jamming itself between two smaller houses. Mann heard the motor race; he was gliding slowly over the water, going toward the house.

"Yuh reckon yuh kin make it? Reckon we can save em?" asked Brinkley.

Mann did not answer. Again they were ten feet from the house. The current speeding between the cracks emitted a thunderous roar. The outside walls tilted at an angle of thirty degrees. Brinkley carried the boat directly under the window and held it steady by clinging to a piece of jutting timber. Mann sat frozen, staring: in his mind he saw Mrs. Heartfield; something tickled his throat: he saw her red hair: he saw her white face: then he heard Brinkley speaking:

"Ahll hol the boat! Try t git in the windah!"

As though he were outside of himself watching himself, Mann felt himself stand up. He saw his hands reaching for the window ledge.

"Kin yuh make it? Here . . . Take the flash-light!"

Mann put the flash-light in his pocket and reached again. He could not make it. He tiptoed, standing on the top of the boat, hearing the rush of water below. His legs trembled; be stretched his arms higher.

"Kin yuh make it?"

"Naw . . ."

He rested a moment, looking at the window, wondering how he could reach it. Then he took the axe from his belt and thrust it into the window; he twisted the handle sideways and jerked. The blade caught. He leaned his weight against it. It held. He pulled up into the window and sat poised for a moment on his toes. He eased his feet to the floor. He stood a second in the droning darkness and something traveled over the entire surface of his body; it was cold, like the touch of wet feathers. He brought out the flash-light and focused it on the floor. He tried to call out Mrs. Heartfield's name but could not. He swept the light: he saw a broken chair: a crumpled rug: strewn clothing: a smashed dresser: a tumbled bed: then a circle of red hair and a white face. Mrs. Heartfield sat against a wall, her arms about her two children. Her eyes were closed. Her little girl's head lay on her lap. Her little boy sat at her side on the floor, blinking in the light.

"Take my mother!" he whimpered.

The voice startled Mann; he stiffened. It was the same voice that had yelled, You nigger! You bastard! The same wild fear he had known when he was in the boat rowing against the current caught him. He wanted to run from the room and tell Brinkley that he could find no one; he wanted to leave them here for the black waters to swallow.

"Take my mother! Take my mother!"

Mann saw the boy's fingers fumbling; a match flared. The boy's eyes grew big. His jaw moved up and down. The flame flickered out.

"Its the nigger! Its the nigger!" the boy screamed.

Mann gripped the axe. He crouched, staring at the boy, holding the axe stiffly in his right fist. Something hard began to press against the back of his head and he saw it all in a flash while staring at the white boy and hearing him scream, "Its the nigger!" Yes, now, if he could swing that axe they would never tell on him and the black waters of the flood would cover them forever and he could tell Brinkley he had not been able to find them and the whites would never know he had killed a white man . . . His body grew taut with indecision. Yes, now, he would swing that axe and they would never tell and he had his gun and if Brinkley found out he would point the gun at Brinkley's head. He saw himself in the boat with Brinkley; he saw himself pointing the gun at Brinkley's head; he saw himself in the boat going away; he saw himself in the boat, alone, going away . . . His muscles flexed and the axe was over his head and he heard the white boy screaming, "Its the nigger! Its the nigger!" Then he felt himself being lifted violently up and swung around as though by gravity of the earth itself and flung face downward into black space. A loud commotion filled his ears: his body rolled over and over and he saw the flash-light for an instant, its one eye whirling: then he lay flat, stunned; he turned over, pulled to his knees, dazed, surprised, shocked. He crawled to the flash-light and picked it up with numbed fingers. A voice whispered over and over in his ears, Ah gotta git outta here . . . He sensed he was at an incline. He swayed to his feet and held onto a wall. He heard the sound of rushing water. He swept the spot of yellow. Mrs. Heartfield was lying face downward in a V-trough to his right, where the floor joined the wall at a slant. The boy was crawling in the dark, whimpering "Mother! Mother!" Mann saw the axe, but seemed not to realize that he had been about to use it. He knew what had happened now; the house had tilted, had tilted in the rushing black water. He saw himself as he had stood a moment before, saw himself standing with the axe raised high over Mrs. Heartfield and her two children . . .

"Yuh fin em? Say, yuh fin em?"

Mann flinched, jerking his head around, trembling. Brinkley was calling. A chill went over Mann. He turned the spot on the window and saw a black face and beyond the face a path of light shooting out over the water. *Naw . . . Naw . . .* He could not kill now; he could not kill if someone were looking. He stood as though turned to steel. Then he sighed, heavily, as though giving up his last breath, as though giving up the world.

Brinkley was clinging to the window, still calling:

"C mon! Bring em out! The boats at the windah! C mon, Ah kin hep t take em out!"

Like a sleepwalker, Mann moved over to the white boy and grabbed his arm. The boy shrank and screamed:

"Leave me alone, you nigger!"

Mann stood over him, his shoulders slumped, his lips moving.

"Git in the boat," he mumbled.

The boy stared; then he seemed to understand.

"Get my mother . . ."

Like a child, Mann obeyed and dragged Mrs. Heartfield to the window. He saw white hands helping.

"Get my sister!"

He brought the little girl next. Then the boy went. Mann climbed through last.

He was again in the boat, beside Brinkley. Mrs. Heartfield and her two children were in the back. The little girl was crying, sleepily. The boat rocked. Mann looked at the house; it was slanting down to the water; the window through which he had just crawled was about a foot from the level of the rushing current. The motor raced, but the roar came to him from a long ways off, from out of a deep silence, from out of a time long gone by. The boat slid over the water and he was in it; but it was a far away boat, and it was someone else sitting in that boat; not he. He saw the light plunging ahead into the darkness and felt the lurch of the boat as it plowed through water. But none of it really touched him; he was beyond it all now; it simply passed in front of his eyes like silent, moving shadows; like dim figures in a sick dream. He felt nothing; he sat, looking and seeing nothing.

"Yuh hardly made it," said Brinkley.

He looked at Brinkley as though surprised to see someone at his side.

"Ah thought yuh wuz gone when tha ol house went over," said Brinkley.

The boat was in the clear now, speeding against the current. It had stopped raining.

"Its gittin daylight," said Brinkley.

The darkness was thinning to a light haze.

"Mother? Mother . . ."

"Hush!" whispered Mrs. Heartfield.

"Yes, Mann knew they were behind him. He felt them all over his body, and especially like something hard and cold weighing on top of his head; weighing so heavily that it seemed to blot out everything but one hard, tight thought: They got me now . . .

"Theres the hills!" said Brinkley.

Green slopes lay before him in the blurred dawn. The boat sped on and he saw jagged outlines of tents. Smoke drifted upward. Soldiers moved. Out of the depths of his tired body a prayer rose up in him, a silent prayer. Lawd, save me now! Save me now . . .

VI

It was broad daylight. The boat had stopped. The motor had stopped. And when Mann could no longer feel the lurch or hear the drone he grew hysterically tense.

"Waal, wes here," said Brinkley.

With fear Mann saw the soldiers running down the slopes. He felt the people in the seat behind him, felt their eyes on his back, his head. He knew that the white boy back there was hating him to death for having killed his father. He knew the white boy was waiting to scream, "You nigger! You bastard!" The soldiers closed in. Mann grabbed the side of the boat; Brinkley was climbing out.

"C mon," said Brinkley.

Mann stood up, swaying a little. They got me now, he thought. He stumbled on dry land. He took a step and a twig snapped. He looked around and tried to fight off a feeling of unreality. Mrs. Heartfield was crying.

"Here, take this blanket, Mrs. Heartfield," said one of the soldiers.

Mann walked right past them, waiting as he walked to hear the word that would make him stop. The landscape lay before his eyes with a surprising and fateful solidity. It was like a picture which might break. He walked on in blind faith. He reached level ground and went on past white people who stared sullenly. He wanted to look around, but could not turn his head. His body seemed encased in a tight vise, in a narrow black coffin that moved with him as he moved. He wondered if the white boy was telling the soldiers now. He was glad when he reached the tents. At least the tents would keep them from seeing him.

"Hey, you! Halt, there!"

He caught his breath, turning slowly. A white soldier walked toward him with a rifle. Lawd, this is it . . .

"Awright, you can take off that stuff now!"

"Suh?"

"You can take off that stuff, I say!"

"Suh? Suh?"

"Take off those boots and that raincoat, God-dammit!"

"Yessuh."

He pulled off the raincoat. He was trembling. He pushed the boots as far down his legs as they would go; then he stooped on his right knee while he pulled off the left boot, and on his left knee while he pulled off the right.

"Throw em over there in that tent!"

"Yessuh."

He walked on again, feeling the soldier's eyes on his back. Ahead, across a grassy square, were black people, his people. He quickened his pace. Mabbe Ah kin fin Bob. Er Elder Murray . . . Lawd, Ah wondah whuts become of Peewee? N Grannie? He thought of Lulu and his eyes blurred. He elbowed into a crowd of black men gathered around a kitchen tent. He sighed and a weight seemed to go from him. He looked into black faces, looked for hope. He had to get away from here before that white boy had the soldiers running him to the ground. He thought of the white boats he had seen tied down at the water's edge. Lawd, if Ah kin git inter one of them . . .

"Yuh had some cawfee?"

A small black woman stood in front of him holding a tin cup. He smelt steam curling up from it.

"Yuh had yo cawfee yit?" the woman asked again. "There ain nothin here but cawfee."

"Nom."

"Here."

He took the extended cup and stood watching the steam curl. The woman turned to walk away.

"Mam, yuh seen a man by the name of Bob Cobb?"

"Lawd knows, Mistah. We don know whos here n who ain. Why don yuh ast over t the Red Cross Station? Thas where everybodys signing in at."

No, he could not go to the Red Cross. They would catch him there surely. He walked a few steps, sipping the coffee, watching for white faces over the brim of his cup. Then suddenly he felt confused, as though all that had happened a few hours ago was but a dream. He had no need to be afraid now, had he? Just to imagine that it was all a dream made him feel better. Lawd. Ahm sho tired! He finished the cup and looked over to the tent. Heat was expanding in his stomach. He looked around again. There were no white faces. Black men stood, eating, talking, Ahma ast some of em t hep me . . . He went over and extended his cup for another helping. The black woman stared, her eyes looking beyond him, wide with fear. He heard her give a short, stifled scream. Then he was jerked violently from behind; he heard the soft clink of tin as the cup bounded from his fingers. The back of his head hit the mud.

"Is this the nigger?"

"Yeah; thats the one! Thats the nigger!"

He was on his back and he looked up into the faces of four white soldiers. Muzzles of rifles pointed at his chest. The white boy was standing, pointing into his face.

"Thats the nigger that killed father!"

They caught his arms and yanked him to his feet. Hunched, he looked up out of the corners of his eyes, his hands shielding his head.

"Get your hands up, nigger!"

He straightened.

"Move on!"

He walked slowly, vaguely, his hands high in the air. Two of the soldiers were in front of him, leading the way. He felt a hard prod on his backbone.

"Walk up, nigger, and dont turn rabbit!"

They led him among the tents. He marched, staring straight, hearing his shoes and the soldiers' shoes sucking in the mud. And he heard the quick steps of the white boy keeping pace. The black faces he passed were blurred and merged one into the other. And he heard tense talk, whispers. For a split second he was there among those blunt and hazy black faces looking silently and fearfully at the white folks take some poor black man away. Why don they help me? Yet he knew that they would not and could not help him, even as he in times past had not helped other black men being taken by the white folks to their death . . . Then he was back among the soldiers again, feeling the sharp prod of the muzzle on his backbone. He was led across the grassy square that separated the white tents from the black. There were only white faces now. He could hardly breathe.

"Look! They caughta coon!"

"C mon, they gotta nigger!"

He was between the soldiers, being pushed along, stumbling. Each step he took he felt his pistol jostling gently against his thigh. A thought circled round and round in his mind, circled so tightly he could hardly think it! They goin t kill me . . . They goin t kill me . . .

"This way!"

He turned. Behind him were voices; he knew a crowd was gathering. He saw Mrs. Heartfield looking at him; he saw her red hair. The soldiers stopped him in front of her. He looked at the ground.

"Is this the nigger, Mrs. Heartfield?"

"Yes, hes the one."

More white faces gathered around. The crowd blurred and wavered before his eyes. There was a rising mutter of talk. Then he could not move; they were pressing in.

"What did he do?"

"Did he bother a white woman?"

"She says he did something!"

He heard the soldiers protesting.

"Get back now and behave! Get back!"

The crowd closed in tightly; the soldiers stood next to him, between him and the yelling faces. He grabbed a soldier, clinging, surging with the crowd. They were screaming in his ears.

"Lynch im!"

"Kill the black bastard!"

The soldiers struggled.

"Get back! You cant do that!"

"Let us have im!"

He was lifted off his feet in a tight circle of livid faces. A blow came to his mouth. The crowd loosened a bit and he fell to all fours. He felt a dull pain in his thigh and he knew he had been kicked. Out of the corners of his eyes he saw a moving tangle of feet and legs.

"Kill the sonofabitch!"

"GET BACK! GET BACK OR WE WILL SHOOT!"

They were away from him now. Blood dripped from his mouth.

"The general says bring him in his tent!"

He was snatched up and pushed into a tent. Two soldiers held his arms. A red face behind a table looked at him. He saw Mrs. Heartfield, her boy, her little girl. He heard a clamor of voices.

"Keep those people back from this tent!"

"Yessir!"

It grew quiet. He felt faint and grabbed his knees to keep from falling. The soldiers were shaking him. He felt warm blood splashing on his hands.

"Cant you talk, you black bastard! Cant you talk!"

"Yessuh."

"Whats your name?"

"Mann, suh."

"Whats the charge against this nigger?"

"Looting and murder, General."

"Whom did he kill?"

"Heartfield, the Post Master, sir."

"*Heart*field?"

"Yessir."

"He stole our boat and killed father!" said the boy.

"Do you confess that, nigger?"

"Capm, he shot at me fo Ah shot im! He shot at me . . ."

"He stole our boat!" yelled the boy. "He stole our boat and killed father when he told him to bring it back!"

"Are you sure this is the man!"

"Hes the one, General! His name is Mann and I saw him under our window!"

"When was this?"

"Last night at the Post Office."

"Who saw this?"

"I did," said Mrs. Heartfield.

"I saw im!" said the boy.

"Ah didnt steal that boat. Capm! Ah swear fo Gawd, Ah didnt!"

"You did! You stole our boat and killed father and left us in the flood . . ."

The boy ran at Mann. The soldiers pulled him back.

"Ralph, come here!" called Mrs. Heartfield.

"Keep still, sonny," said a soldier. "We can handle this!"

"Did you have that boat, nigger?" asked the general.

"Yessuh, but . . ."

"Where did you get it?"

He did not answer.

"What did you do with the boat?"

"The man at the hospital took it. But Ah didnt steal it. Capm . . ."

"Get Colonel Davis!" the general ordered.

"Yessir!"

"Nigger, do you know the meaning of this?"

Mann opened his mouth, but no words came.

"Do you know this means your life?"

"Ah didn't mean t kill im! Ah wuz takin mah wife t the hospital . . ."

"What did you do with the gun?"

Again he did not answer. He had a wild impulse to pull it out and shoot, blindly; to shoot and be killed while shooting. But before he could act a voice stopped him.

"Search im!"

They found the gun and laid it on the table. There was an excited buzz of conversation. He saw white hands pick up the gun and break it. Four cartridges spilled out.

"He shot daddy twice! He shot im twice!" said the boy.

"Did he *bother* you, Mrs. Heartfield?"

"No; not *that* way."

"The little girl?"

"No; but he came back to the house and got us out. Ralph says he had an axe . . ."

"When was *this?*"

"Early this morning."

"What did you go back there for, nigger?"

He did not answer.

"Did he *bother* you *then,* Mrs. Heartfield?"

"He was going to kill us!" said the boy. "He was holding the axe over us and then the house went over in the flood . . ."

There was another buzz of conversation.

"Heres Colonel Davis. General!"

"You know this nigger, Colonel?"

Mann looked at the ground. A soldier knocked his head up.

"He was at the hospital."

"What did he do there?"

"He helped us on the roof."

"Did he have a boat?"

"Yes; but we took it and sent him to the levee. Here, he signed for it . . ."

"What kind of a boat was it?"

"A white rowboat."

"That was *our* boat!" said the boy.

The piece of paper Mann had signed in the hospital was shoved under his eyes.

"Did you sign this, nigger?"

He swallowed and did not answer.

A pen scratched on paper.

"Take im out!"

"White folks, have mercy! Ah didnt mean t kill im! Ah swear fo Awmighty Gawd, Ah didnt . . . He shot at me! Ah wuz takin mah wife t the hospital . . ."

"Take im out!"

He fell to the ground, crying.

"Ah didnt mean t kill im! Ah didn't . . ."

"When shall it be, General?"

"Take im out *now!* Whos next?"

They dragged him from the tent. He rolled in the mud. A soldier kicked him.

"Git up and walk, nigger! You aint dead yet!"

He walked blindly with bent back, his mouth dripping blood, his arms dangling loose. There were four of them and he was walking in between. Tears clogged his eyes. Down the slope to his right was a wobbly sea of brown water stretching away to a trembling sky. And there were boats, white boats, free boats, leaping and jumping like fish. There were boats and they were going to kill him. The sun was shining, pouring showers of yellow into his eyes. Two soldiers floated in front of him, and he heard two walking in back. He was between, walking, and the sun dropped spangles of yellow into his eyes. They goin t kill me! They goin . . . His knees buckled and he went forward on his face. For a moment he seemed not to breathe. Then with each heave of his chest he cried:

"Gawd, don let em kill me! Stop em from killin black folks!"

"Get up and walk, nigger!"

"Ah didnt mean t do it! Ah swear fo Gawd. Ah didnt!"

They jerked him up; he slipped limply to the mud again.

"What we going to do with this black bastard?"

"We will have to carry im."

"Ill be Goddam if *I* carry im."

One of them grabbed Mann's right arm and twisted it up the center of his back.

"Gawd!" he screamed. "Gawd, have mercy!"

"You reckon you can walk now, nigger?"

He pulled up and stumbled off, rigid with pain. They were among trees now, going up a slope. Through tears he saw the hazy tents of the soldiers' camp. Lawd, have mercy! Once there and he would be dead. There and then the end. Gawd Awmighty . . .

"Gotta cigarette, Charley?"

"Yeah."

A tiny flame glowed through spangles of yellow sunshine. A smoking match flicked past his eyes and hit waves of green, wet grass. His fear subsided into a cold numbness. Yes, now! Yes, through the trees? Right thu them trees! Gawd! They were going to kill him. Yes, now, he would die! He would die before he would let them kill him. Ahll die fo they kill me! Ahll *die* . . . He ran straight to the right, through the trees, in the direction of the water. He heard a shot.

"You sonofabitch!"

He ran among the trees, over the wet ground, listening as he ran for the crack of rifles. His shoes slipped over waves of green grass. Then came a shot. He heard it hit somewhere. Another sang by his head. He felt he was not running fast enough; he held his breath and ran, ran. He left the hazy trees and ran in the open over waves of green. He veered, hearing rifles cracking. His right knee folded; he fell, rolling over. He scrambled up, limping. His eyes caught a whirling glimpse of brown water and shouting white boats. Then he was hit again, in the shoulder. He was on all fours, crawling to the edge of the slope. Bullets hit his side, his back, his head. He fell, his face buried in the wet, blurred green. He heard the sound of pounding feet growing fainter and felt something hot bubbling in his throat; he coughed and then suddenly he could feel and hear no more.

The soldiers stood above him.

"You shouldntve run, nigger!" said one of the soldiers. "You shouldntve run, Goddammit! You shouldntve run . . ."

One of the soldiers stooped and pushed the butt of his rifle under the body and lifted it over. It rolled heavily down the wet slope and stopped about a foot from the water's edge; one black palm sprawled limply outward and upward, trailing in the brown current . . .

Copyright Acknowledgments

974